S0-AXV-799

The USERS

The USERS

by Brian Case

THE CITADEL PRESS, NEW YORK

First American Edition 1969

Copyright © 1968 by Brian Case

All rights reserved

Published by Citadel Press, Inc.

222 Park Avenue South

New York, N.Y. 10003

Originally published in Great Britain

by Peter Davies, London

Manufactured in the United States of America

Library of Congress Catalog Card Number 73-90395

To my wife, to Sandy
and to Nev

PART ONE

I

It was the first time they had used a tape-recorder in the morgue. Mr Reed was very excited. He polished all the instruments, pulled out the drawers of the refrigerator and combed everybody's hair. His eyes kept wandering over to the tape-recorder.

The pathologist would arrive at 4 p.m. to conduct his examination, this time recording his method and his findings, for the instruction of the medical students in the hospital. Mr Reed saw that he had twenty minutes in which to prepare for the session. The body lay naked and yellow under the bright, tented lights. A label tied to the left big toe read: SYDNEY JENKINS.

Mr Reed circled the porcelain table, scalpel poised like one mean spic bopper searching for an opening. Mr Reed made his own. He inserted the scalpel at the throat and drew a line down to the navel, then from there two lines to the groin to form an ultra-committed C.N.D. badge. With gloved fingers he pulled the wound open to expose the rib-cage. Experience told him that the saw would be unnecessary; the body was old and the bones would be fairly brittle. He selected a small knife from the range of instruments and applied it to the ribs, cutting out and removing a square of rib-cage like a trapdoor to reveal the lungs. Now Mr Reed again took up the scalpel and turned his attention to the head. He opened the mouth, pinched the tongue delicately between thumb and forefinger and severed the membrane securing it. He drew the tongue and trachea out through the new throat opening and onto the chest. And that was that. Mr Reed had few friends.

He stripped off the rubber gloves and leaned against the table. Normally he would have trepanned the corpse but the report had stated that the cause of death was drowning. Mr Reed was inclined to disagree. No signs of mucus foam around the nose and mouth; the hands, stiff of course, but not technically clutched. Anyway, if the doctor wanted to examine the cranium he would say so.

He padded on crêpe soles to the tape-recorder and lifted the lid. He looked inside; everything seemed in order to him though of course his forté lay elsewhere. Gingerly, his finger winkled the microphone out of its niche and uncoiled the lead; his fingertips seemed to respond to an habitual pattern—only the names were changed. He followed the instructions printed on the lid, and got the instrument ready for use. The doctor was due to arrive in a few minutes.

Crossing to the cupboard he removed two pairs of white wellingtons, two rubber aprons, two back-to-front overalls and a box of surgical gloves, dusted with talcum and rolled inside out.

'Funny thing,' he mused, unpacking the gloves, 'there's rolled-on rubbers at your beginning and rolled-on rubbers at your end. Ironic!' Thus Mr Reed bethought himself of man's estate, gliding effortlessly over schism and logic, as the outer door closed with a padded and pneumatic wheeze.

'Afternoon Mr Reed,' the doctor called breezily, divesting himself of hat and coat in the very act of entry.

'Good afternoon doctor,' said Mr Reed.

The doctor scooped up the report and read it, his sandy eyebrows twitching like riders over his eyes.

'Uh-huh,' he said at intervals, and 'Mmm', while Mr Reed ensnared his blind outstretched arms in an overall. The row of clothing diminished in direct proportion to his increasingly vestal appearance.

'Yep,' said the doctor, throwing the report onto the table. 'Conjecture, Mr Reed. All bloody conjecture. Presumed cause of death—estimated length of immersion—the rescuers alleged. Where would they be without us, Mr Reed? Buggered, Mr Reed.'

Mr Reed, a coathanger dependent from his fingers, in the act of hanging a jacket, judicially nodded.

'Did the machine come—the tape-recorder? Ah yes. Turn the thing on—and we'd better have the microphone thing—er' he glanced for the first time at the body on the table—'oh there you are—yes, put it between his knees.'

Mr Reed complied gravely, his heart singing within him, as he cleared his throat of extraneous mucus and incanted from one to ten. He played the result back; it was perfect. He seized the microphone again and began—'Ten, nine, eight. . . .'

'No, no, Mr Reed, I think we can assume that it's working satisfactorily from those initial soundings.' The doctor plunged his hands into the open body and interspersed fleshly squeakings with commentary in a You-are-there sort of technique.

'We know that the body is seventy years of age, male and reasonably healthy—er—up till the er—yes. *Presumed* cause of death—drowning. Condition of body *suggests* a duration of between one and two hours in the water. No signs of significant bruising or breaking etcetera. The lungs are free of water as indeed they would be if he had drowned. Asphyxia, of course. We'd better have a look at the cranium.'

'Shall I commence to trepan, doctor?' Mr Reed spoke in a strange nasal voice.

The doctor stared at his assistant. 'I didn't notice that his head was transparent, Mr Reed.'

The doctor switched off the tape-recorder and watched Mr Reed at work on the head; his face was arranged in a careful blank, his hands worked swiftly and surely. The doctor was sorry for his sarcasm; perhaps it was the presence of the noiseless third party; he had never transgressed the code of professional ethics before. 'You have educated fingers, Mr Reed,' he said.

Mr Reed looked up, his face flushed and smiling. 'We

can learn something from even the most ordinary lump of flesh, eh Doctor?' he said. 'It's all useful.'

'Do you want to see him sir?' asked Mr Reed when John had signed for the carrier bag. He indicated the sheet-covered trolley in the chapel.

Most of the time the chapel was used for teabreaks by Mr Reed and the technicians from the path. lab. The removal of ashtrays and the biscuit-buying roster from the wall made a big difference, no two ways about it, and setting up the plain wooden cross on the table was a visible staking out, no disrespect, of The Lord's claim. Nevertheless, he worried. It should be harder than that. And—he could see two ways about it.

John said, 'No thank you. Can I leave it for a while?'

Mr Reed discreetly withdrew and sat against the far wall to leave him to his grief. Oh yes—it was all right for the others to guzzle their tea in here and do their pools. They never saw the room when it was a chapel, but he did. He did, and it put him off his biscuits. Mr Reed had worried about the problem for ten years and had turned to his Bible for advice, combing in vain for an Eastern parallel. He had likened the path. lab. technicians to the moneylenders in the temple before the unfairness of this occurred to him. It just wasn't that simple. Bursting in the door and flailing about with plaited drainage tubes would solve nothing, besides being presumptuous. Simply it came to this: he did not know when the room stopped being a temple, chapel, and started being a place for teabreaks. How significant was the movement of furniture? He looked at his watch and saw that it would be teabreak in twenty minutes. More lugging about.

'Take your time sir,' he said, a foxy jostle. 'I know how it is to lose somebody. You just let me know when you're ready to view.'

'Thank you,' said John and continued to just stand.

Hospital sounds, the breezy confident sounds of people

halfway through the working day, colleagues in corridors, containers clanking, faintly reverberated against the double doors. John stood in the centre of the room facing the trolley, the cross on the table, the curtained window, and in that poor grey light there seemed to be no appreciable distance between them.

Mr Reed, sitting respectfully, small banjo-shaped shoes pressed together, knees touching, absented himself in his problem. A year ago at the union meeting he had suggested, all heads turning towards him, that they have the room sprinkled by a bishop. General laughter; ignorant laughter; that would put the mockers on the teabreaks. Render unto Caesar he had warned them and they had laughed loudly and called him Creeping Jesus among themselves. He frowned, remembering it.

The Egyptians removed the brains through the nose. Mr Reed admired the Egyptians for their diligence, patience and skill and he thought of them now to avoid thinking of his own bumbling ineptitude in settling the status of the room. It was easy for the Egyptians though. They had jam on it. No-one was likely to confuse a pyramid with a tearoom. Sprinkle three walls and then sit back for the next three thousand years: in his mind's eye he watched them file silently past silent bandaged upright corpses and out into the hot bustling day, straining black backs and CLUNK—the final stone. All sealed off. Nice. Proper. Not like this, he thought bitterly. Chopping and changing, never knowing where you were. No—wait a mo'. You knew where you were but you didn't know what it was where you were. . . . A very nice point. Bang it in the diary at teabreak.

He looked up at the mourner and saw that his eyes were dry and his face, profile, was completely still. Mr Reed had seen that before. They were the ones to watch, the awkward ones. All quiet at first, hypnotised as it were, then all of a sudden—Boom!—throw themselves on the body, screaming and laughing, spitty kisses all over, breaking the stitches, hell of a job. He shifted uneasily on his chair.

John was thinking about curtains, the curtains at the window. They were a completely unremarkable floral print, the stereotype of a million drawing-rooms, yet, strangely, they fascinated him. He wondered why. Was it perhaps that the windows they partly screened were frosted, needing none, redundant as water in a vase of plastic flowers? No, he didn't think it was that. It came to him then that it was their very unremarkableness that held him fixed. The curtains created a context that jarred hideously with the thing on the trolley and it seemed to him that it was here, in this room, as quiet and curtained against calamity as the drawing-room of his home, that his father had died. This was the very room of empty Sundays, of switch click and clock tick, where suddenly a monstrous hysteria had exploded, hatchet blade rising falling flinging black beads up the wallpaper, covering even the Radio Times with gore. The flashbulbs of police photographers, the note-takers, the doctors, the fingerprint men, chalklines on the floor like an amulet against evil, all raced through his mind before he found what he was groping for: that no-one need ever seek a motive in such a room.

All of which was, he reflected, a fairly typical excursion for his imagination, through landscape habitually hothouse and ornamental.

Mr Reed decided to take the initiative so he stood up and said: 'Are you ready to view sir?'

'All right,' said John and at once felt the inadequacy of the words. 'I am prepared,' he amended.

The attendant's shoes squeaked across the lino, wincing as it were with a sense of occasion. John fixed his eyes on the white contours of the sheet, a little nervous because he had never seen a dead body. The attendant swept the sheet aside in a perfect veronica so that the body was uncovered to the waist. John gasped, not because the face was frightening—it was, as in life, uncommunicative—but because he had expected to see it a good twelve inches higher. He had taken the lump of the pillow for the head under the sheet and now he had to re-adjust. In that moment the face had swum into the periphery of his tensed, directed gaze, ghostlike and in stealth.

'He looks just the same,' he said in an overloud voice but he knew that he didn't. His father looked fuller-faced, healthier, generally better; in fact, he thought, preferable.

'Oh yes, they do. This is only the earth suit,' replied Mr Reed, but experiencing nonetheless pride in his work. The toothless mouth padded out with cotton wool, the cochineal injection in the cheeks for rosiness, the small, neat, uniform stitches concealed by the hair; all the little things that came only with twenty years of experience. He smiled sadly at the corpse and felt a warm sympathy for the young man who had turned out to be, after all, just a quiet type paying his respects as a son.

'He wasn't drowned, sir. He fell and hit his head. It was mercifully quick. The police said he'd climbed under the jetty to cut his line free and then slipped and fallen.'

John stared at the body. 'The hair,' he said suddenly. 'You've got his hair all wrong. He never had a parting there.' With splayed fingers he reached out to take the hair back from the brow, but he could not bring himself to touch his father. He let his hand fall limply back to his side. After all, he told himself, his father had been a scruffy old bastard when he was alive, so let him go on with it.

'If I'd had a photo to go on . . .' Mr Reed murmured, watching him, expecting something now. John crackled the carrier bag, changing his grip, embarrassed.

'I'm sorry. I'm not criticizing . . .' he cleared his throat.

Mr Reed covered the body again and crossing, steered him by the elbow to the door, concealing the gentle pressure with assurances and platitudes. Life, he thought, as the doors closed behind the mourner, was so full of uncertainties. You never can tell. He opened his diary and licked the pencil stub, but before he could write, a horrible thought struck him. If he had the room done, consecrated, and they carried on borrowing it for a tearoom, would the digestives become The Body and the tea. . . ? He couldn't bear to think about it. It was so horrible that he stood up and went into the post-mortem room.

As the glass doors closed behind him John Jenkins took a deep breath, filling his lungs like people did in films to show they value life anew. Or have big tits, he thought. It was raining hard. He turned up the collar of his combat jacket, two pound ten U.S. surplus, supply your own combat, and ran through the hospital parking lot into the street. Bashing through the puddles it occurred to him that he ought to be photographed now, straight away while the ravages of grief were still hot on his features. Bang it in the old album with date and circumstance. He ran down the darkening street until he could see the dark bulk of the railway station and the unfortunate double steeple, a rudeness unto the Man, of St Christopher's; the automatic photo-booth was opposite the vestry, very handy for post-service, high-key, nimbus extra snapstrips.

Office workers poured out of offices into the street, wild-eyed and hell-bent for home, all elbows and umbrellas but a very regular army. Everybody peeled off from the paca-mass along dotted lines of departure, jostling no-one as they bought papers and boarded buses. John moved in mambo and foxtrot through them, demurely dipping his headlights for approaching dollies. He was in the habit of staring lustfully up to ten yards and then turning chicken, but he did pick up on the perfumed slip-stream as they passed, thinking of the little parachute of essence and its tale of dusted nooks and peppered crannies. Today, the rain made it extra nice: damp nooks, damp crannies: himself perhaps Terry Towelling, the fleecy frotteur.

He cursed the lights that kept him jigging at the kerb in the rain. Some of the office workers took a chance and ran to the island. John could see they were mad. Only a fool would trust a replica. Replicas of people were drawn on all three sides of the windscreen and windows as on children's toys but they didn't fool him. John played it close to the chest, waiting until he had solid bumpers of pedestrians, ranks of statistics (cars only killed statistics) on every side of him before conveying his quick kernel to the other side. He got as far as the island before the lights turned green. On either side of him cars roared into life, replicas frozen to the wheel. In a crowd, he crossed the final stretch.

At his approach the photo-booth bloomed into light. EXPOSURES DONE IN ONE MINUTE. FOUR SNAPS FOR TWO BOB. The light went off.

John waited in a shop doorway out of the wet. He pushed the water from his hair with a flat hand until it squeaked. His levis clung coldly to his shins. 'Hurry up,' he said. Would the little extra, the little 'ow you say, register on film? It never had. 'Hurry up in there,' he said again, *sotto voce*, scene hater, 'as I've just lost my father I was wondering if you could hurry up a bit see.'

The booth lit up for a fifth exposure, warranted, he deduced, by a further florin. More waiting. Shit. He thought of a hot drink and a sit down, won for bereavement. Carol would be the best and the nearest. Nice to have people making allowances—very pampering in an Eastern sort of way. He thought about the pampering in flamboyant fashion, revealing his lack of breeding and his early exposure to boys' comics. Wealth was to skate away the ragged boater with the poked up lid for a silky topper and astrakhan. Wealth was a dwarfing mound of banger and mash, bangers bounding like boomerangs from the waiter's tray; foaming regiments of pop and two cigars on a diamond pin. To this pre-pubertal picture he now added some sexual pampering, the mucky spoon lowered through the sprung lid of the boater and stirring in the brains.

The Richest Man in the World waddled into view heavy with pleasure, women's mouths glued to his erogenous zones like piglets. . . . He would have to wear a black armband.

It was cold and damp in the shop doorway and stamping about only brought new areas of leg into contact with his wet jeans. He tried to penetrate the green booth curtains with a laser gaze. What unspeakable rites were being enacted within before the unshockable eye? The Most Beautiful Woman in the World proffering nude buttocks to the emplacement, winds the mushroom stool, adjustable for babies and gnomes, and clambers up above the frontface collars and ties to a pinnacle of bad taste. Here, she bares breasts that turn her into a group. John was best in life at interior monologues.

When the celluloid strip poked slowly out of the slot and slid down the chute into the rain-filled delivery tray, he galloped to intercept it and scan its subject matter. Silver strokes, graves and acutes sprang from his boots as he ran and he had to stutter on one foot to avoid whamming into the booth. He stood in the doorway and looked down at the strip in his hand. It featured a small boy in a bowtie. His hair was brylcreemed flat to his head except for a pushed ridge in the front and a waterspout at the back. He looked like a ventriloquist's dummy. He wasn't even nude. John could see that lad was a unit in some grotesque family that held cheerfulness at a premium, and that saw the unit as being a universally likely lad. John's face ached merely looking at the grin and he replaced the photo in the delivery tray.

The wait and the wetting spoiled John's litmus: the little extra did not manifest.

2

'I am sorry, John—you know that,' said Carol from the alcove, cheek pressed against the windowpane, eyes glissading down the sad slate rooftops to sadder asphalt. 'There's nothing I can say.'

John nodded and kept his face grave and composed while behind it he watched her reactions to his tidings. These were disappointing in a way. The same beautiful Pre-Raphaelite tristesse took the field, face lengthening, eyes writ large, mien droopy; the same expression, in fact, that he had observed floating over Byron, over Shelley, amongst woods 'n fields. He had half-hoped for something special, kept under wraps perhaps and unfurled for the really big deals.

'We weren't very close,' he said. Cushioning fact.

'Would it help you to talk about it?'

He told her about the viewing in the morgue. He arranged it with facility into neat episodes, leaning heavily on literature and the movies for emotion, but limiting his palette to her range of empathy. He couldn't, however, resist the blade-straight exit into the rain from Hemingway; after all, he hadn't really stumbled away, eyes dazzled, in a cloak. The experience became a totality as he spoke until it ceased to exist except in these words, in this style, and his own unsounded feelings were buried alive. Still, he thought, her face warm now on his chest, inarticulate grief wouldn't do for her.

He held her away from him, held her hands and gave them a kindly chivvying little squeeze. 'Hey, come on kiddo. Ladies unmanned? You'll be lifting the seat next. Get me a nice cup of coffee.' And watched her obedient, rallying passage to the kitchen with a bidder's eye.

Sinking into her bed, he bore intact the image of her fashionable shoes retreating, plumply naked heels like bare, uncleft bottoms on pedestals. To stop this train of thought he forced his eyes to focus on his surroundings, the furnishings and fittings of Carol's familiar room. There was a lot of his history in the room. There were the shelves that he, cack-handed craftsman, had erected in two days of strain and congratulation, threatened now with a hundredweight of culture, some of which was his too. Really the room looked splendid, quite different from the rest of the house which was old, jaded and gloomy. He stared at the bright white walls, at the display of pressed, embossed ferns over the mantelpiece, anything to stop him thinking below the belt. Now he tried to midwife up a healthy remembrance posy for his father but drew only the Light programme and the little sticky sounds his schoolboy elbows made on the plastic tablecloth. Little enough for twenty years together. Anyway, the radio had gone off for poppa; light comedy, light music, soufflé serials; click—off. And the silence was balmy.

John sat up and reached for the carrier bag. He had already forgotten what he had signed for at the morgue. His hand shook a little as he plunged it into the neck and he wondered why people's things could upset when their death did not, gave that one up, and produced a silver watch on a long silver chain.

Carol, emerging from the kitchen with two pottery mugs saw him recumbent, Roman on one elbow, swinging the watch like a pendulum and gazing at it—she thought—like one facing the eternal questions. Tenderness flowed out from her to such beauty in bereavement.

'My father left me this,' he said. 'It doesn't work. His father gave it to him and he bequeathed it to me. My ancestors left me a stopped watch. Big symbol. It shouldn't have hands really but there you are.'

He gave a quick effacing grin but it was too late. Carol had been upset. She put down the coffee and took the watch from him. 'You mustn't let yourself get bitter John. They gave what they had.' She ran her slender fingers over the cracked glass, over the scrolled silver back like a blind person familiarizing, and suddenly John hated her, hated her for guessing wrong but more, an old hate for habitually touching things with her fingertips as if everything was meant to arch beneath them. It was all he could do to stop himself from snatching the watch from her, and then the feeling passed.

'You can have it if you want. It's no good to me. Get it mended and wear it round your neck.'

She was shocked. The watch had been handled and consulted by his family for a hundred years, therefore it was of value. Couldn't he appreciate that? It had marched through the night from the dresser and hung, beating, below the heart at countless weddings and innumerable christenings and it was theirs and their children's now as earth is, for they had mixed their sweat and their lives with it.

'Do you know Dylan's poem "Do Not Go Gentle Into That Good Night"?' She raised her lovely dark eyes to his, willing his reply.

'"Rage, Rage Against the Dying of the Light". He always did. I preferred the Third. That in a way could stand as an emblem of our mutual disinterest.' Then, forced into declaration, covering up the crude uncaring pun with more words, he began: 'Listen Carol. He's dead and I don't feel a damn thing. I would if I could. Those who cry are the lucky ones. My father wasn't remotely interested in me—in fact, he wasn't interested or involved in anything. I'm not making this up. There are millions of people like him, people that God uses for crowd scenes. He was dead from the neck up. He occupied a certain space in the dining-room, displaced so many cubic feet of air and sometimes he made noises at me and I made noises back. There was no purpose or meaning to it then and there's certainly none now because he's dead. For me he was never any other way.' John realized to his surprise that in a spontaneous sort of way he was waving good-bye to her. Carol would never sit still for this lot. Perversely, he went on.

'You never met him did you Carol? I get the feeling that you see him as a sort of D. H. Lawrence character—collar off, bony old calloused hands hanging between his knees as he sits at the fire. Sturdy old boots glowing red and then black again in the firelight. Believe me, I'd have settled for that too. I'm not a snob you know. In reality my father was a turd. In every respect turd-like, and you can't get life-affirming on a turd. For a start he never had an opinion on anything—he believed that opinions went before a fall. He lived as anonymously as possible, blended with the wallpaper, but, and here's the nasty little paradox, he prided himself on his looks. He spent pounds on his hair alone. He had his double crown returfed and a parting dug. . . .'

'Whatever he was, John, he was your father.' Carol sat on the edge of the bed and frowning, stroked the thick green pile of the blanket. The fading light from the street simplified her face into a pale, ethereal oval that seemed to hang in space, logical latitude eclipsed in the wash of black hair into the black mini-dress she had chosen for tragedy. None of it jelled, thought John, secretly gazing at the wistful girl with the sexy body, a fruity sundae with dream topping. Not that he could shout, Batman programmed to shrug, alike in a limbo of cancellation. A concealed zip snaked down the back of her dress, he noted.

'Labels and words,' he said irritably. 'Don't keep saying he was my father. I know he was my father. He was the cat's master too, and the factory's machine minder and the lavatory's most dramatic contributor. Why don't you pull some of them? He had a lot going for him. And now he's a stiff—his latest and greatest role. Sydney Jenkins, the Lord of the Flies.'

This was asking for trouble. He could see himself alone outside her door already, spurned zombie all washed up, but he could not stop sleepwalking towards that destination. The edges of his mind sniggered facetiously under the inflexible and liberating regime of this predestination. So why didn't she offer him the proverbial solace of her body? It would be very much Carol's style to balance father's end with hers, to get the old dam of pent-up feeling to break over her and then bathe in it for its spiritually cosmetic properties. But Carol spoke not a word.

'I suppose all the bloody diseased Jenkins line will turn out for the funeral,' he said, and sipped his coffee. She would not even look at him.

'He was lucky he wasn't run over,' he said provocatively but she wasn't biting. 'Because that would seem meaningless.'

Carol refused to enter into such a poltergeist spirit of things. 'Then again, it's a pity he wasn't murdered. That would have conferred importance on him, see. Sort of reassuring for the line.' He put out a hand to touch her but she shook him off with a movement like a shudder.

'You're a cold-hearted bastard,' she cried.

'Oh come on. I can't help it, can I? I've explained all that.'

Carol got up and stared out of the window into the darkening street. The roofs seemed to buckle silently into humps like some prehistoric armoured monster as she gazed through the streaming glass. Her world was reeling. As the tears ran down her cheeks, she traced the moving raindrops with her finger, and felt emotion and nature epiphanize into one.

'Just go away.'

Again the edges of his mind curled up like burning paper. 'I doubt if you'll put all this down to shock?' Inside, he was alive with laughter. His stomach fluttered and he thought he was going to be sick. He took out the strip of photos and laid them on the bed. Not much of a sacrifice really. The whole photo album idea had gone stale. He had nurtured the embryo idea through the waiting months of gestation to its brilliant birth; the strange longing to see a warp in life other than his nature, a woof other than Spot. One morning two years ago he had felt a tiny boot in his swollen lobes and before he could boil a kettle there it was, all shining and utterly absorbing. So he took the photos. None of them showed anything significant: the same unchanging face looked out of the album, coarsened by turkey, brutalized by pud, earthbound. Life had written nothing on those features. When he looked at the idea he was struck by its idiot, mongoloid aspect. John Jenkins, Columbus of the uterus. Old Carol could have them.

She heard the door quietly close behind him, a rush of air on her skin. Still crying she went instinctively to the typewriter as John had gone to the photo booth, and just as hopelessly tried to record her communion with sorrow. When she was happy the sun shone on her, when it rained she cried, herself a French reflexive verb. Carol was emotionally labile, balanced on a knife edge between tears and joy, though not as often as she could have wished. She was still a Luxemburg D.J. compared to Werther and Byron, but she was working at it. And she worked at it now, blanket-bombing the sheet, the room filled with the metallic clacking of artistic creation, the little typewriter bell tolling the knell of passing day.

3

John awoke in his bedroom at midday wondering what unprecendented and genial spirit had visited his father, staying his rudely poking finger at 7.30 a.m. Then he remembered that his father was dead. He lay there wondering if he cared today because today was a new day, and grief and loss might operate in the nature of a yeast. He tried all the corks. Firm as ever. He didn't care today either.

He tried Carol next. There was a faint and sluggish stirring which pleased him no end. He had actually felt a twinge, a real organic twinge, without shaking the bottle. He gave himself up to a contemplation of the silver lining; by next Saturday he might feel even worse. He lay flat on his back caring away, his eyes gliding easily over the familiarities of his room.

Should he write to her now on the strength of his expectation of grief? Would that be jumping the gun? The warmth of the bed sapped his resolve. He sneezed directly up into the air and felt the spray patter back deliciously on his face. It occurred to him suddenly that she may consider the affair off, and already be roistering around looking for a replacement. That almost flushed him from his thicket. John's better half remonstrated with him in the sensible didactic tone of a pipe-smoker; strike while the iron is hot, a stitch in time, stuff like that. This better half was essentially a knockabout figure, and John knew that one sidelong glance from him was enough to deflate the half down to a smirky accomplice. They had both been at it for a long time.

The conflict, to overstate this rubber sabre-rattling, was resolved by John's bladder. It needed emptying. He arose with a sigh, emptied it, and returning saw, incredibly, paper and pen in meaningful juxtaposition on his desk. He sat down and picked up the pen.

'Dear Carol,' he wrote, and then paused reflectively. He nibbled at the collar of his pyjamas. Had they drawn the ultimate curtain of intimacy, and there behind the arras pledged sacred vows as they commingled, gasping, clasping, to the very quick of their being? No, they hadn't. Still, that was hardly her fault.

'My dear Carol,' he wrote, and paused again. John Jenkins the last of the big pausers. He wondered if she would notice the new possessiveness and re-instate him. Should he underline it? He decided against; that would be as juvenile as writing S.W.A.L.K. on the back of the envelope. It was easy for him to write a moving letter, the naked soul dragging its poor lamed presence across the page. Too easy. Six four-foot stacks of novels stood against his bedroom wall; all the novelists that the sociologists predicted for him, as inexorably as 'A' follows 'O'. John had read them all and he could serve up a piping dollop of Kafka, Dostoievsky, Sartre and West that would have her crying on her loom for weeks. So what? What sort of relationship was he going to offer her? That was the problem.

John read it through. 'My dear Carol': all right so far. He took a new sheet, and resting his hand on the blotter wrote this out again for neatness. Really, he was becoming thoroughly disenchanted with his twinge of twenty minutes ago. If he had to go through this lot for a twinge, a flutter might scupper. Supposing he had loved his father, the no-mark, and mourned his passing? God, that would be rough. Holy smoke no joke. No wonder Mrs Next-Door—Mrs Plume—had belted hell out of the door at two a.m. last night to see if he was all right and to offer, could we have the cup back, her condolences. She should have offered herself with hubby Plume as afters. What Mrs Plume had said was:

'And so sudden—no warning at all.'

To which John in high spirits had replied:

'It would have been unreasonable to expect one as he fell into the estuary.'

This was hopeless. He stared at the paper in vexation for several seconds, rattling the pen against his teeth. Then hastily he bent again to the task and before he had quite gathered his thoughts the pen had written, as if possessed of some private and professional obligation of its own: 'I hope you are well.'

John jumped up and ran to the lavatory with the letter balled in his fist, hurled it into the pan and sent it speeding to some Lethe with a pull of the chain. Sod the letter. He went into the bathroom and ran the bath.

As it filled, his thoughts began to wander along the unsequestered path of sex. A myriad suspenders and brassières broke cover and scattered in panic at his passing. He thought of Carol's eager young thrusters and he thought of Carol's biteable buttocks. Vacantly, he unbuttoned his pyjama jacket and pulled the ripcord that sent his trousers bailing out over his feet. Steam rose from the bath. Why hadn't he leapt upon her? Had she not by woman's art, on bed and bower, hinted at the whirling vortex behind her underwear? A score of eager hands surged skywards: 'Please sir, me sir!' Indeed she had.

In a dream he bent to turn off the taps. Gazing at the plug, a wobbly blob, he tried to divine this whirling vortex behind her underwear. He boggled before the mysterious panel, through lack of information. The taps dripped musically into the bath. Perhaps scientific method was the answer; collect your information, assess it, draw a conclusion. Carol's eyebrows! On the hypothesis that the study of a single tree would indicate the nature of the forest, John tweezed an eyebrow from memory and examined it. He could rely on his specimen. Carol's face remained an outpost of truth, unplucked, unpruned; Diana of the Uplands. He concluded that Carol was splendidly endowed with maidenfern. This scientific method was a bugger, he mused, looking down at himself.

The Richest Man in the World sat in his director's chair in the boardroom, intermittently visible around the bobbing woman astride his lap. His commands were incoherent; his senses plethoric with tongues and tremors. His lowliest employee lived for the hour when the wingless bluebottle would sprint ticklingly around his helmet, a lighthouse in the bath.

John's bath was cold and accusing. Later, washed, shaved, combed and clad the idea took root that he must institute a new régime of early rising, constructive thought and hygienic movements, the latter perhaps in the park. Not that this idea was new; he had, in his head, an auto-change device for new leaves to eliminate wasted effort. Still, perhaps this time he would be able to stick to it. Perhaps his father's death would lend impetus to his resolve. There was no reason why the passing should go to waste when it could be useful as a calendar mark.

He flung open all the windows in his bedroom and took deep lungfuls of fresh air. He looked out at the street. Off-white net curtains as far as the eye could see, and in the next-door garden a few plastic soldiers sat in the dirt waiting for dinner to finish. A few gardens up, a To Let sign like a petrified flag.

John stripped down his bed, shook everything, put down clean sheets and remade it. Then he rounded up all the dirty socks, shirts and pants and stuffed them into a pink polythene bag for the laundry. All this was the flip-side of the leaf. Previously he had let his dirty stuff lie fallow for a while in the corner before wearing it again. Sitting on his bed extracting cuff-links, he devised a tariff of fines for his laundry: pants—skidmarked—one shilling: flare-pathed—one and three. As an added deterrent against recidivism he could send an accompanying letter:

Dear Laundry,

I enclose the following for your rhubarb. Use visor and tongs.

Yours, proud but ill-wiped, John Jenkins.

Like a coda came the memory of the manure races of his childhood. His father had pushed the coal shovel into his hand and he had raced, an Olympic relay-runner, out into the street to reach the pile of steaming manure left by Prince Philip, horse to F. P. Philip, Castoffs, before his panting neighbours. Success in this field really got through to his father. He would stand in the doorway laughing at the others as John ran home with his piping prize. Yes, the old man had loved the shitrace. Well, John sighed, recherchez-wise Proust hadn't got a lot to worry about.

He dabbed at a few dusty surfaces with a sock and then put that in with the rest of the washing. He emptied the ashtray out of the window. On the landing he remembered his father's room; his ex-father's ex-room.

He opened the door and went in. Naturally nothing had changed, nothing here was disturbed by the passing of the occupant. That was the way it went with inanimates, thought John, and that made it unanimous.

'You didn't make the bed,' he said into the pressing silence. He patted the foot of the bed to locate the hot-water bottle and found it sagging obscenely in a fold of sheet. It slid out and slapped onto the lino, cold and rubbery. He could hardly bear to touch it. When he pulled back the sheets he was suddenly aware of that same unveiling, the empty bed a more nauseating mansion for death, of his father's cold and tallow body in the morgue. It was an effort to go on, to strip the bed and roll back the mattress and impose a final order on the flotsam that remained of his father's life. He made himself see the job through, sorting out the clothes in the wardrobe, the shirts and socks and underwear in the chest of drawers, poking through the pockets and finding nothing. He had got the whole worthless bundle dragged out and into his own room when the bell went. Arthur stood on the porch.

'I just dropped round to say I heard about your dad.' He gave a crippling squeeze to John's shoulder and barged into the hall. John despondently followed him into the kitchen. Arthur bored him stiff; brute force personified. He was always disappointed that Arthur used doors, having simplified him down to Arthur-shaped egress holes in brickwork, a monolith avid over cow-pie. Arthur was sitting on a flimsy kitchen chair like a samurai. His fists rested loose on his knees and a hard bulge of belly and chest rose into the broad red warhead.

'Fooking sad,' he said.

'Here today and gone tomorrow,' replied John, feeding him a line he felt he could handle.

'Gone today,' said Arthur profoundly, reminding John that he had been hanging around with undergraduates. The university socialists had practically adopted him, and now he sat on every committee and on every platform, adding the weight and dignity of his wellies to their paleface dialectics. He had never been bashful; now he was unstoppable, talking and everything.

'Nice of you to come.' John always laid down a broad yellow stripe for the wellies to walk on and wished again that he wasn't taller than Arthur. Arthur had been known to resent height in others; clearly they were trying to make something of it. Still taller ten year old John Jenkins had hit C above C in the playground under the blows of the cub-capped crusher; neither had changed.

'I had the day off so I come.'

As he filled the kettle and placed it on the gas, John thought how Arthur's conversation tended towards the terminal. Perhaps because silence didn't bother him.

'Still got that sissy haircut then.'

'Hee hee,' laughed John at this fustian shaft.

'Haven't seen you at Bell's meetings then.'

A rallying visit like this could last all day, depending really on John's degree of supinity. Horrible when things were up to him.

"You go, do you Arthur?'

'Oh I go. I'm on the committee. I'm a big wheel.' His

deprecatory sniff downgraded the machine only. John was quick to take his cue.

'You're the only bloody worker there,' he said ardently and thought of Colin Bell's leather wrist-brace.

'Aye,' said Arthur. 'There's not one on them 'ud last five minutes down the dock. Any road—I don't need them but they do need me. So that's alreet.' He drank his tea boiling with great wet schlurps. John could see that Arthur was beginning to believe the politicians' picture of himself. He should get his arms tattooed: I LOVE SPLOSH: something like that.

'You don't want to keep it all bottled up you know,' said Arthur after a long noisy silence.

'The grief?' John was startled into an incautious reply.

'Aye. It must out somewhere. That's your trouble—' he leaned creakingly forward and jabbed an iron digit into John's side— 'you Intellectuals.'

John was sure something had come loose.

'What would you do if your old man died?' he painfully asked.

The huge red fist crashed onto the table. Shock waves caused a scurrying among the piled crockery on the draining board and one plate fell down and broke. John tried not to flick his eyes at the sink. When someone clears the way for a statement in that fashion, the audience is expected to pay attention; he'd read around.

'I'd run a-fooking-mok!'

There it was: clear: direct: stupid.

'Best thing,' said John.

'Only thing.'

Silence fell. It was Arthur's silence, put there for John to assimilate the message. He used it as respectfully as if it were his own, in which to think unconnected and irrelevant thoughts. 'The day our Binkie died I put four blokes away,' said Arthur.

This struck John as terrifically yielding of interpretation. Arthur put blokes away like a squirrel puts away nuts. Had Arthur put these blokes to death, tribal ritualistic, Golden Bough, to accompany Binkie on her journey to that bourne of shades, one to carry her cushion, one her saucer. . . ?

'You remember our Binkie.'

'Oh yes.' John started guiltily. 'Binkie was a helluva good——old Binks. Yes sir!'

'Used to watch you going to school with yer bloody great bag of books. Workin' lad getting on, I used to say.'

'I remember,' said John, blank on Binkie—what was the blasted thing?

'Had a crush on you, you know.'

He's taken leave, John thought. It had to be a female then, for Arthur would never admit to even an aberrant cat under his roof. An 'twere a blasted cat. Without thinking, John took a flier. 'We used to wave at each other in the mornings,' he blurted and then flushed crimson. Arthur was staring at him, lifting his great brows on their red cartilege like masonry on a stone face. Driven on in panic he said: 'I'd just wave—like this—Coo-oo, and she'd just wave her old—ha ha appendage.'

'You're trying to come it, shag.' The brows descended. Four had been put away already.

'I don't know what you mean, Arthur. Really.'

'You know fooking well what I mean. How could a fooking budgie wave at you, you daft twit.'

There it was. And there he was with egg on his face.

'Seemed to wave, Arthur. Trick of the light perhaps. Eyestrain ha ha—you know us Intellectuals. The eyes go first and then the pectorals.'

'You'd bloody well forgotten who Binkie was, hadn't you? Own up. I could see that a mile off.'

'Well, just for a moment. I hadn't thought of old——"

'And you thought I was going to thump you, you daft sod. D'you think I don't know as how you've more on your mind than our fooking Binkie?'

'I didn't want to hurt your feelings,' John offered.

'It was bloody years ago man.' Arthur yawned happily, stretching his arms and turning his wrists back and forth as if pumping the air out of his mouth. John felt obliged to watch so large a gesture. He hoped Arthur was off. He needed this solace like a hole in the head: but then Arthur ran a hole in the head business. Then suddenly, skittishly, John was off the ropes slugging.

'My father had a parrot,' he said with a sad expression.

Arthur made his mouth smaller.

'He was stationed in India in the war, miles from anywhere. All the men were yawning their heads off with nothing to do, my father said. There was a sort of craze for parrots on the camp—you know the kind of thing, Arthur.'

Arthur nodded, commanded by the serious manner. He fidgeted with the knife and fork on the table, moving them farther apart as if in anticipation of a larger meal.

'My father said it was a Green Hell in the barracks with all those parrots singing and swearing at once like underoiled machinery. There was a big Irish rifleman in my father's regiment who had a parrot called Tone—after Wolfe Tone the Hebrew cyclist. Tone could say anything. He was a genius. While all the other parrots were stumbling through beak-sullying epithets and pitiful drinking songs, Tone would be reciting Robert Emmet's epitaph. Everyone got very tensed up and competitive about it. You know how it is Arthur, you want the best for your parrot. My father said he used to blow into the neck feathers to check that his parrot's ears hadn't got bunged up with seed husks or a stray quill. No one could account for Tone's fantastic memory. They began to watch Tone and the Irishman to see if anything special passed between them but nothing ever did. It was weeks before they found out.

'One evening the Irishman and the parrot crossed the long hot room and disappeared through the door. My father watched them walking over the parade ground, one with long strides, one with short, side by side.'

At this point Arthur shifted uneasily on the kitchen chair and began to moon over his fists. He had to listen to this crap because it belonged to John's freshly corpsed father; respect demanded too that it was not funny. A heavy yoke.

John fixed blocky Arthur with a sombre eye and continued. He had enjoyed the story so far and he wondered interestedly what his father would discover.

'My father followed them, using available shadows and avoiding any twigs, until his quarries came to a halt just out of camp limits, by a well. As you know, Arthur, India abounded with wells at that time. From behind a convenient rock he saw the Irishman take a length of string and a book from his shirt pocket, tie the string around the parrot like a truss and hold the other end while the parrot jumped forward and down, disappearing from view. The Irishman began to read from his book, projecting his voice down the well.'

John was amazed that Arthur sat still for this lot. 'My father said it was very eerie. Picture it, Arthur. A deserted and parched wilderness at dusk—a lonely figure in shorts erect beside a well—silence swathing the world like a giant dhoti.'

'Pretty rum,' Arthur conceded, yawning with his mouth closed. 'Well, I'd better be. . . .' He slapped his knees and prised his mighty buttocks from the seat.

'It was one of the last stories my father told me before he . . .' said John. Arthur settled dourly back.

'My father said that parrots are shallow creatures and easily distracted. They lack, as a brood, concentration. Now you isolate your average parrot, Arthur; suspend him on a string down a well and drop your words down singly like pearls. Get my meaning? Anyway my father told the others what he'd seen and they all drifted out of the barracks in twos and threes and assembled at the well. They didn't really have a plan—it just happened. They sat swigging beer and laughing about the secret of Tone's wizardry. After a bit one of them went and pissed down the well and then they all followed, emptying their bladders in glittering and hilarious curves onto the moon's reflection. The water level rose a foot and a half and the next night Tone was DROWNED.

'When the Irishman hauled up his bird it was all sodden and stiff. That great beak was stilled, Arthur. Binkie all over again.'

John looked at Arthur, drawing his restless gaze into his own damp eyes.

'Fooking sad,' said Arthur and shook his head as if to clear it. He stood up. 'You want to take your mind off things man. Go down town. Get yourself fixed up with a bit of crumpet, eh?' He surged potently with his fist in the air, but his expression held a wilted quality. 'A bit of the other, eh?' And he blundered off.

4

John caught a bus, sat on it to the terminus and then got one going the other way. He jumped off where he had started from. All the way he had said to himself the names of the shops they were passing. Coming back he counted them. Then he went into the King's Head and drank six pints with six whiskies as chasers. He was depressed. Alcohol is a great panacea and soon he felt physically dislocated and depressed.

He recognized a face. 'Joseph,' he said. He was not reading; he just knew it was Joseph. He felt very warm and friendly towards Joseph although sometimes he bored him stiff. A big smile swilled around his face. Joseph smiled back because he liked to smile in public. They stood facing each other like heliograph experts.

'Hi Johnny,' said Joseph, reluctantly sheathing his smile. Joseph counted John as one of his friends and Joseph thought of his friends as family, cursing and cheating them as he did his kith, but never deserting them. He copied little bits of all his friends, their mannerisms, their opinions, and produced these before their eyes with a flourish like a team cup. Some people exchange comment about shared experiences, and this is the basis of their friendship: Joseph merely skipped the external stimulus and shared a common brain. His friends knew his sources and he knew that they knew and believed they would be flattered. They knew that he knew that they knew and wondered why he didn't feel a prick. John liked him.

They sat at one of the stone-topped tables. Every time John put his elbow on the table it rocked about and beer slopped out of the glasses because one of the legs was too short. He bent and stared under the table. A folded cigarette packet was wedged under the short leg, redressing about a quarter of an inch of the three inch gap. He sat up. His head felt like an egg-timer after this movement. Sound burst about his ears like a handful of flung coins. John put his elbow on the table and it rocked again, spilling the beer. He was behaving like a lobotomy case.

'Let's get out of here,' he said, and Joseph raised his glass, throat gulping and made little chops in the air to signify assent.

'I never liked this pubic house,' he said, re-issuing an old release—John's property. They barged through the crowd and out into the fresh air of the alley. They urinated in unison under the moon, backs arched back like two saxophone players, and the silvered notes plashed upon their shadows. Joseph felt very close to John and his breast ached with friendship and family feeling. He did not give voice to it because John hadn't buttoned up and he feared he might be misunderstood.

'Come on, I'll teach you snooker,' he said.

'I'm too pissed,' said John. 'How far is it?' He lurched against the wall.

'Just up the road. Not far.'

'Bags I Paul Newman.' John fell back against the wall screaming with laughter.

The pool hall was an old building, the air of a men's hostel clinging to it with the tenacity of a tramp's fart. The tables were threadbare and the rims were pocked with the burns of generations of unattended cigarettes. Little groups of men stood around watching the games from under cloth caps. Joseph always thought of the hall and the clientele as Fabian and this pleased him; the game itself he treated as a family craft, the wholesome fruit of class solidarity. He shouted greetings to various loungers—'great blokes'—and steered John to an empty table.

'Now this is the idea of the game,' he said, and explained.

John's head reeled. He couldn't seem to concentrate on what Joseph was saying but desperately stared at his opening and closing mouth. 'I'll watch you for a bit and pick it up,' he said.

'No no,' Joseph was insistent. 'You can't learn like that—you have to play. Come, on, you can start.'

Gripping the cue John bent over the table and sighted at the coloured balls prancing on the green like morris dancers. He missed everything except the cushions and his ball battered around for a while and slowly came to rest.

'Right, my go,' said Joseph and potted a ball. He strode around the table diminishing the balls in a series of sharp, efficient clicks. He had his jacket off, his hat over his eyes and he felt generally like the original hustler. 'Fifty,' he said 'red, six pocket.' Click—the red ball joined the bulging pocket with a clatter, the cigarette arced up, glowed, descended. 'You can't learn by watching, John. You have to get into the thick of it mate. Sixty. Green, four pocket.'

'Yes,' said John, and chalked his thumb.

The match lasted twenty-five minutes. Joseph scored one hundred and twenty and then declared. John idled against the wall and tried not to fall down.

'Let's go to my pad and hear some records,' said victor Joseph.

'I'd better go home now,' said John. 'Is it far?'

'Just up the road. Not far.'

Joseph's pad was very comfortable, Joseph thought. John thought so too tonight, but he was pissed. He slumped into an externally sprung armchair.

'I'll make you a black coffee,' said Joseph, making a chef's 'O' with finger and thumb. He had no milk. The machine outside had broken—he had hurt his foot kicking it and had retired in a flurry of spit and gristle with the toe of one boot bent up like a Turk's. Joseph always bought boots with Cuban heels to give height and two sizes too big to make his trousers look tighter. His trousers were sprayed on now but the mould beneath was short and stubby enough to resemble wheels.

John's rolling eyes slid over the familiar décor. The wall behind the gramophone was covered with record sleeves neatly spaced several inches apart. Where the wallpaper showed between it was laocoon and floral. It gave John the impression that the wall was bulging out toward him, each eruption represented by a straining negro face with a saxophone in it. Well, now there was nothing to stop him from altering his place to suit himself, except, of course, the unbearable responsibility involved in pleasing himself.

'Sorry to hear about your dad,' said Joseph, offering moist eyes like the grapes of a hospital visit, an enamel mug of black coffee in each hand.

'Don't worry about it. We never got on.'

Joseph would have envied that in the James Dean era, had he not been twelve at that time, but he was now in the blood and brotherhood grip of Marx and Ma Joad. So he said, coming right out with it, 'Still. . . .'

'Forget it.' John closed his eyes and leaned back to listen to the record, letting the cycles of tension and resolution fill his mind. He really listened in to it, anticipating the huge squalling sounds of Coltrane, vintage '65. He heard the drummer break out the cymbal under the soprano, splintering like ice under the shrill skater, ice flaring behind the skater no way out but ahead, moving always ahead of it. He heard the strain in it, tendons sticking through the sound, fibrous sounds of throat prolapsed into horn, strain in the hissing fragments that fell back like shavings, snapped and curled in the rush of passing. When it was over John saw that the skater drowning in spinning black swirls was an L.P. needle now clicking idiotically back and forth in the centre. You brought your own gerunds, he thought, and you left your ear at home. You took a great thing and you made it small enough to handle.

'That,' shouted Joseph, putting his hands on his head to keep it on, 'is one fat panic!'

'You've been at the sleeve notes again.'

A loud, hysterical knocking at the door presaged complaints. It was the girl from the next room. 'Turn that bloody racket down or I'll call. . . .'

'Racket! That's music—you wouldn't know music from a hole in the wall,' Joseph shouted.

'You turn it down!'

'You get stuffed.' As he slammed the door, Joseph licked his forefinger and drew a phantom score in the air. He felt very pleased with himself tonight. 'She fancies me, you know. Stupid gash.'

'Lay God's voice on her,' said John.

'Rollins.'

They played Rollins and Lester and Griffin and Bean and then switched to alto as a chaser and played Bird and Ornette. They became very hot.

"Will you get a gram now—you know?' Joseph made a vague gesture indicating the demise of Mr Jenkins, his planting elsewhere and the subsequent pastures of freedom: an inclusive gesture.

'I'd never go out,' John replied.

'Well, you can always hear mine. Oh yeah, thanks for the Emitex Anti-Magnetic Anti-Static Eeziwipe Record Cleaner.'

'Don't mention it.'

Comradeship hung in the air like cigar smoke. They got out the old jokes because the old jokes were the best; they kept the squares off the stand like the complex chord changes on the record player.

'You think Ayler is putting us on?'

'No.'

'Cecil Taylor?'

'No.'

'Brubeck?'

'He's gone too far.'

There was a lot of that, of thigh-slap and rib-tickle, before the drink wore off. It was Joseph who introduced a note of sobriety, returning, as if to ennoble the fun with brotherly feeling, to the subject of John's father. 'Don't you miss him at all?' he earnestly asked.

'Who?'

'Well, your father, of course. I thought you looked pretty low in the pub.'

'Not about that.'

'Something else?'

'It would be.'

Not put off, Joseph investigated further. 'Would it help you to talk about it? It helps to talk to a mate. You know, it sort of straightens things out—gives you perspective. You don't want to bottle it up inside you because that's dangerous for your personality—gives you——'

'You mean you want to know what's on my mind?' said John, remembering Arthur.

'Of course I don't! I don't personally give a shit what's on your mind. I was only thinking of you.' Joseph hoisted his eyebrows into his hat to show complete lack of interest in the matter. He went and lay on his bed under the shelf of sociology books with titles like *The Aged Poor in Action*. He couldn't afford to waste time on silly sods. He worked a cigarette out of his pocket without disclosing his source, an expertise he possessed in many fields, and stuck it into the corner of his mouth. He tried his pockets for a light, but in vain. By the time he had rolled off the bed and come back from the kitchen with a match he had forgotten that he was annoyed. His temperament and his movements were alike mercurial. A pinball machine, lighting up in all directions as the influences were fed into the slot.

'Johnnie?' he said.

'Yes?' John opened his eyes wearily.

'I've got a problem.'

'YOU'VE got a problem!'

Joseph surged over this and pulled up a chair. He sat on it, back to front, arms dangling over the back, as over a garden fence.

'This really bugs me, Johnnie. It gets so I can't sleep nights.'

He extended his packet of cigarettes to John.

'It must be worse than Hamlet's,' said John, eyes firing amazed tracers into the packet.

'Do you worry about, you know, sex? I mean, I've thought about it till its really hung me up the most. I can't sleep——'

'You said.'

'Man, I can't even hear my records sometimes!'

'When the gram's on?'

'Of course when the bleeding gram is on. You think I'm a bleeding idiot or something? I've got to talk to you about it—after all, that's what mates are for.'

'Sure I worry. We all worry. Everybody worries. In fact it's a load of worry all round. Everybody wants to be a stud: nobody is. Except me, of course.'

'Yes dad, but what do you worry about? You know, which bit?' Joseph hoped that John's worry was worse, more unmanning, than his, but he kept this from himself.

'I suppose I ought to worry because I don't want to do it. Not with either sex. It could be that I have a fear and hatred of children, that I carry over into the act—anyway that's what Carol says. Frequently. She says I'm an introvert. Worry all the time about the meaninglessness of life. Four generations of bobbing arses produced nothing but a line of mobile afterbirths, but its going to stop with me. Carol can tell you more about it, ask her.'

'Yes, that's a valid point of view.' Joseph was very intrigued by these disclosures, but nevertheless eager now to get on with his own. 'I worry about that all the time. Like what a bleeding washout the world is and how there's no hope and that. But of course you have to take the rough with the smooth.' John quietly boggled at the transition from Trotsky to Stalin. The lack of bloodshed never ceased to appal him. There was clearly a great chasm between them.

Joseph lobbed a pea into this chasm for John to cross. 'Well you know. No time, no time, dig everything.' He continued impatiently, 'I want kids, of course. I'm a great Admirer of my Father. He's—you dig—a Great Man and a Truly Warm Person. I want to be like him. I want my kids to look up to me, ask my advice.' He laid his stubby hand on his breast. 'My problem is really the flipside of yours, see. I worry that I won't be able to produce a family and worrying about that is putting the mockers on me performance. I got this trauma. Also, I don't get to test me performance in this crummy town. Worst of all is this frustration.' He stopped talking, and John understood that it was all up to him. He could see where he had gone wrong. He never should have let loose with Carol's diagnosis. Joseph had misunderstood, had assumed that John was giving him his all and had followed suit. Of course, he couldn't know that John was willing to throw in his father, his unremembered mother, a posy of used Kleenex, a child's garden of faeces, everything in fact that could be staked with words, add his marker, go home in a barrel with bracers and still be ahead. Because none of it was important.

'It's the mojo, Joseph. Chicken claws and effigies and pointing bones. That's why you can't get your leg over.'

A sudden and startling noise above cut him short.

'Christ!' John cried, half starting from his chair. 'What the hell is that?'

'It's all right,' shouted Joseph in an attempt to surf casually over the din. 'Go on about the mojo.'

'What the hell is that noise?'

'That rattling?' Joseph indicated the ceiling: useless farting against thunder.

'It's the only rattling we have.'

Joseph shrugged uncomfortably. 'Probably the bloke upstairs.'

'What's he doing, dying?'

'I don't know, do I? Ain't got X-ray eyes, have I?'

The noise rose to a crescendo and then stopped as abruptly as it had started, leaving Joseph bawling his rhetorical questions into a silent room.

'Anyway it's stopped,' he added, quieter. 'Go on about the mojo.' John stared at him. Between hat and button-down he was crimson. Joseph was blushing! John was so startled that he acquiesced but his mind was not on the story.

'The mojo,' he said flatly. 'Yes. The ladies are afraid.'

'Uh huh, uh huh, I gotcha,' urged Joseph, posed like the Boyhood of Raleigh.

'Feature a man, Joseph, who has all his wires crossed. He's been conditioned perhaps—or just come out of scarlet fever.'

'Or mumps.'

'Yes or mumps. Mumps can be a bugger in adulthood. A swan can break your arm with a single blow of its wing. Anyway. This man sees a woman. She sees him. They are attracted. They go back to her place and she changes into something more comfortable. They embrace. They fall to the couch——'

John saw the light fixture jerk back and forth and up and down in a grotesque dance.

'What happened then,' screamed Joseph, trying vainly to run a scream and a twinkle in harness.

John pointed to the jerking light. 'He'll be through the ceiling in a minute!'

Joseph cupped his hands to his mouth like a megaphone: 'Go on with the story.'

At that moment a huge golden 800 watt light bulb lit up in John's head: it had IDEA written in it and little lines radiated from the bulb. The noise was copulation. Or at least, and most important, Joseph thought it was. That was why he was blatting about like a blocked moth trying to keep him from the 800 watt light bulb. Obviously he was embarrassed by the speed and frequency of the performance above: more, he was afraid that it was normal: most, he was afraid that John would say it was.

The noise stopped.

'They fell to the couch?' said Joseph. Implored Joseph.

'O.K.' John shrugged. 'He begins to make love to her but his wires are crossed.'

'He's all hung up.'

'Yes. He listens to her neck, her breasts, her roseate halos. His ears begin to burn. He sniffs her parted lips. As his fever mounts a nasal hair protrudes. French sniffing now. He tastes her navel—quite nice—in passing, but his drive is all towards One Thing. He parts her thighs. Now he transfixes her with a long, virile, penetrating stare. He looks away. He stares again. Stares mount into glances, quicker and quicker, quiff tossing. Now he's glimpsing—glimpse, glimpse, glimpse—then the final agonizing, delicious blink. The man is satiated and he slumps on to the carpet. His nerveless fingers release the album of Eartha Kitt.'

'Does the woman like it? I mean, how can she pick up on this stuff?' As he waited tensely for the noise to recommence, Joseph tried to engage all of John's attention, scoop him up and enfeoff him, deaf to his environment until the final good night.

'No, she doesn't. That's the point. It's queers like that who stop men like you from getting their rights. They put a mojo on you. Now, that lady would think twice before she offered another bloke in.'

Joseph nodded vigorously. 'Could be, could be.'

'I thought I'd tell you straight rather than have you learn about it in some dirty furtive....'

The noise started again.

John put on his coat and prepared to leave, his host unquestioningly greasing his path.

'See ya tomorrow,' screamed Joseph into his ear, making him squeeze up his shoulder and bare his teeth.

John knocked quietly on the door upstairs. He felt his

visit justified, sanctified even by his kindly restraint below. A middle-aged man in pyjamas and socks appeared.

'What is that noise?' asked John.

'Dynamo,' said the man.

'Thank you,' said John, running down the stairs, tip-toeing past Joseph's door, laughing like a drain.

5

Dr Ostbahn put his head around the door. The waiting-room was almost empty. A plain-looking girl sat stiffly in the corner seat, flicking nervously through an ancient Punch magazine. By the empty fireplace a young man sat, doing nothing.

'Next please,' the doctor said in his heavy German accent. He went back into his surgery and sat in the padded swivel chair. It had been a long day. They were all long now. He was old and his fat white hands were blotched with brown marks. He pulled out his old-fashioned watch; eight-thirty. Soon he could turn off the lights and go home. He read the inscription on the watch for the umteenth time: 'Ein festes Burg ist unser Gott.' Heidelberg, 1920. Once he had replaced it in his waistcoat he could never remember if he had just read the inscription or merely seen it in his mind; time was fleeting, God was a rock. He yawned with his mouth shut. His nostrils bulged wide and tears came into his eyes.

There was a knock on his door.

'Come in,' he said.

The girl came into the surgery awkwardly clutching a big black handbag. Her shoes squeaked on the ancient lino. She sat very straight on the chair, feet together, the bag in her lap. It was easy to see what was on her mind; no wedding ring, last in the surgery. But the doctor knew instinctively, without studying behaviour patterns. 'Wichtig': important: pregnant. The word in German was very apt. She carried her importance about her like a nimbus and could no more elude it than Peter Pan his nailed-on shadow. She sat very upright on the chair like an exclamation mark.

Now the eternal pattern of question and answer must begin. Always the same, always the same. He suppressed another yawn.

'Well, Miss——?' he said.

'Miss Smith.' She didn't look up. Her fingers played nervously with the clasp of the handbag, and when it sprang open she rummaged around inside it.

'But of course. Miss Smith.' He smiled ironically. 'What seems to be the trouble?'

The girl placed the bag, half-open, on the floor beside her chair. She looked at him.

'I'm pregnant Dr Ostbahn.' The voice, like the gaze, was surprisingly direct—almost a challenge. Her lips came together tightly, with finality. She had passed the ball to him and now it was his turn.

'Ah. So you are going to have a baby.'

He knew that his reply was meaningless and he felt himself slip into the manner of a much older, much more ingenuous man. It was his habitual refuge, a putting on of spectacles before a fight.

'No. I said I was pregnant.' She ignored his infirmity.

Again he tried to guide the conversation into its proper channels, entrenching himself more firmly as the doddery, bespectacled alien for whom allowances have to be made.

'My dear, all women feel depression at some stage in pregnancy. It is natural. The back aches and the clothes do not fit. In the morning there is often sickness, nausea. Little things irritate. It is an irony that patience comes only with age.' The doctor leaned back and linked his fingers over his chest. 'When you are as old as me you will realize this. You cannot change nature. If you are pregnant you will have your baby. You can do nothing but wait.'

'I can get rid of it, can't I?' She smiled slightly.

'You are not married. Will the father stand by you?'

'I don't know who he is.'

'Ah, Youth, Youth.' He shook his head sadly. 'Never a thought for the morrow. But you must——'

'Will you help me get rid of it or not?' She sat tensely on the chair as if a refusal would send her instantly striding to the door.

Dr Ostbahn felt hustled, crowded into a corner. Protocol had been trampled underfoot and the consultation had not progressed along his lines at all. He always did the job in the end, but first he had to hear the desperation, the pleading and the gratitude to stifle the remains of his professional conscience. He looked around his surgery. Everything was second-rate and threadbare. One of the castors on the couch had broken off. Last year's copies of Lancet lay unopened on the windowsill. Thirty years ago he would have thrown her and her brazen demands out of his surgery. Thirty years ago. Before the compromises and evasions and the all-pervading tiredness had rotted the fibres of his life like a crawling malignant disease.

'How late are you?' he wearily asked.

'A month.'

'You are sure of that?'

'Yes.'

'I will not touch your case if you are more. You understand? I am a doctor not an abortionist.' His irritation was beginning to show. He wanted to get it over with and get rid of this patient. She stared at him, straight-backed and immobile.

'How much?' she said.

'First I must examine you. We will talk money afterwards.'

'No. First I must know how much you charge, Dr Ostbahn.'

A very business-like young woman. Precise. Flat shoes and buttoned-up overcoat. And very precise about names. He opened the drawer of his desk and took out a hypodermic syringe and a bottle of colourless fluid. Yes, her manner was almost German. And yet—it was not the manner of old Germany. Correct, but not courteous, the human being somehow eliminated.

'Very good,' he said. 'You will pay three guineas for each injection. I will give you one now after I have examined you, and one tomorrow.'

'That's very expensive.'

'It is what I charge. If it is too much,' he shrugged. 'This is not a charity after all. It is not a matter for your National Health.'

'Can I pay you in any other way?' The girl did not amplify her meaning by tone or gesture.

'In what other way?'

'You are not too old for sex.'

The veins in his temples stood out and his face went purple. 'God in Heaven!' he shouted. 'Have you no shame! I am a doctor not—not some filthy ponse!' He thrust his hands into his pockets, then took them out again. He thought of his wife and family. This filth, this disease, should not touch his home. He would confine his failure to the times on the brass plate outside. A dim memory of Dr Emmanuel Rat flickered on the edge of his mind like a warning. 'You will pay me money, do you understand? Now take off your clothes.'

The girl stood up and without taking her eyes from the doctor's face, she unbuttoned her coat. Her swollen belly showed all too clearly. She was at least three months pregnant. The doctor had to thrust his hands in his pockets again to keep from striking her.

'Get out!' he spat at her. 'Get out at once.'

She took a backward step, as if in fear, and picked up her handbag. The young man who had been waiting in the other room walked into the surgery without knocking.

'Hi, doc. Wie gehts?' he said, leaning against the door. Dr Ostbahn passed a weary hand over his eyes. 'Please go away. I can see nobody else tonight.'

'I'm not somebody else, doc. I'm like a riff on the same theme. We're the same abcess.'

'What do you want?'

'I want a part of the action, baby.' The young man smiled pleasantly.

'Get out of here!'

The young man took the handbag from the girl. He put his hand inside it. 'Bang bang! You're dead Fritz,' he said.

'Get out of here before I call the police.' The doctor seized the telephone and stood rigid, waiting for them to go.

'Nasty old kraut,' said the young man, and switched on the tape-recorder in the handbag.

'I am a doctor not an abortionist.'

'How much?'

'First I must examine you. We will talk money afterwards.'

'No. First I must know how much you charge, Dr Ostbahn.'

'Very good. You will pay three guineas for each injection——' The young man switched it off and then snapped his fingers.

'Swinging record, eh doc?' He gave the bag back to the girl. 'Split now baby. Take this home and keep it warm. The good doctor and I have business.'

She closed the door quietly behind her and neither of them spoke until the street door clicked shut. Then the young man sat in the swivel chair and swung his feet up onto the desk. He plaited his fingers together over his chest and smiled at Dr Ostbahn.

'Now what seems to be the trouble?' he said.

The doctor stood in the middle of the room, completely lost. It had all happened so quickly. He could not seem to assimilate what had happened, or indeed see quite how it applied to him. His mind was a blank. He waited for righteous wrath to take over and sweep this insolent young lout out of his chair and out of his life. But it didn't come; at least, not in any titanic proportions.

'Will you please remove your muddy feet from my desk,' he said stiffly.

'Not now,' smiled the young man.

The doctor's anger flickered and died. He needed time to think but his mind refused to focus. It skittered away like a tiddly-wink pressed by a big heavy thumb.

'What are you going to do?' he asked.

'Well now. . . .' The young man gazed at the ceiling. 'We could take 10 per cent of all the foreskins you collect. You see, I'm going to start a trend towards balaclavas for budgies. A kraut name in that line would be a big leg-up, you know, folks remember. Or then again we could lance that engrossed bank account of yours.'

'I don't understand.'

'Sit down, dad. Take the weight off.'

The doctor sat heavily in the patients' chair.

'Now what is it you don't understand?'

'What do you want—money?'

'Go on.' The young man leaned forward and rested his chin in his hand, very eager-beaver.

'You—you want money to destroy the recording?'

'Go on.'

'You will give it to the police if I refuse to pay you. You will——' the doctor swallowed hard—'you will destroy my reputation.'

'Well, I'm sorry, you haven't won the king-sized refrigerator, but you're still in the running for a crack at the one-week-just-reminiscin'-holiday in Israel. Do you want to go on?'

'I want you to tell me what you want from me.'

'Just when you were doing so well. You were bang on the nose about the threat. No flies on you, eh? Course I spotted the cerebrations behind those guesses and put two and two together. They weren't lucky guesses—not on your life. There was real teutonic thoroughness behind them. Method. You eliminated sex.' The young man held up his hand and folded down one finger. 'I probably wouldn't fancy you and anyway Luther was always a stickler for no feeling on a first date. Quite right. Don't let those decadent Rhinelanders tell you different—all that yodelling and leather shorts. It sullies the race. Next. I was just a head case. No, unless Miss Smith was too. Next. I was in it for the bread.' He folded down a third finger and watched it rise again. 'Sharp old dog. You guessed that I was motivated by an index finger.'

'Tell me how much you want, please,' said the doctor, who had barely understood a word. 'I will pay it if I can.'

'I want a piece of the action. You dig?'

'What is the action?'

'There you go again, dad. Look, it's no good trying to con me. I know all about you. You're king of the crochet hook scene baby. And I want to sit in.'

'Will you please talk English. I cannot understand what you are saying.' A fear grew in the doctor's mind. This madman must want narcotics. He recognized some of the vocabulary that he was using. He had seen it in his daughter's magazine, a terrible rag devoted to teenage music. He must be a rock and roll fanatic. He wanted purple hearts.

'You want purple hearts,' he said quickly.

'You know, I wonder about you,' said the young man, shaking his head. 'I think you should loosen your pickelhaube. It must be stewing your brains. Where do you get purple hearts from?'

Dr Ostbahn bit his thumbnail. Was the question rhetorical or did he want to know how to obtain them? He gave an equivocal answer.

'I don't know.'

'You're too hot-headed, you know that? Too mercurial by half.'

The doctor just sat staring bleakly at the door. The young man took his feet off the desk and stood up. He stood over the old man and placed his hands on the bowed shoulders. His face was an inch from Otto Ostbahn's.

'Now listen, you stupid squarehead. I'm spelling it out for you. You won't touch anything over a month. I will. Next time a female comes in here and she's fatter than a month, you don't say "ach Gott, I'm a doctor not an abortionist". You give her to me, got it? You say, "I haf zis, how you say, colleague—he vill help you".'

Protests welled to the doctor's lips; it was too horrible. He would have to work with this gangster until the police caught them both. And his wife—oh God, what if his wife should find out? The last remnants of his professional pride feebly stirred themselves.

'How do I know that you know what you are doing? How do I know that you won't kill some poor girl?'

'You don't.'

The doctor surfaced for the third time. 'I shall never be able to rest knowing that I have sent some poor young girl to—to——' His mouth quivered with emotion. 'And the risk——'

'I could only kill them. There's a choice of five ways.' Again, he held up his fingers and counted them off as he spoke. 'Septicaemia. Peritonitis and a gang of gassy bacilli. Right? The fastest way to go upstairs is by embolism. Zap—good-bye mummy. Then last, you got shock.'

Dr Ostbahn covered his face with his hands, rolls of fat protruding between like a fat man in a wicker chair. His face was sweating.

'And the fuzz. Oh man, the fuzz are hip. Towels, sheets and mattresses under the lights for stains. Obstetrical fluid stains, douche stains, soap stains, blood stains. Breakdown on the drugs in the bedside cabinet. Question the neighbours, question the husband, question the doctor. Fingerprints.' He grinned at the frightened old man.

'I'll tell you something doc. It doesn't scare me one little bit. I take care. I've taken care for eight years. I like what I do and I do it well. I like all of it—all the thrills and spills. I like catching gutless squares like you. See, I know all your tumblers. Old, seedy, running down, hot on excuses. All mouth, no action. You're the kick-start model.'

The young man got up and buttoned his coat. The doctor had begun to cry.

'In a day or so I'll let you know your contact. You needn't put me on the plate outside. I'm your silent partner. Also——' he pointed, very Method, at the baggy old heap on the straight-backed chair—'don't try telling me that business is slack. I want at least three a week even if you have to drum for work. Even if you have to screw them yourself. And I want Aryans too, you dig? You'll never know that the potbelly in the chair isn't another Miss Smith.'

He flung his arm up in a Nazi salute.

'Noch einmal eh, doc? Stay in the bleachers. I'll be hearing from you.' He closed the door quietly behind him.

PART TWO

I

God hovering might have seen the hurrying figure on the ground as a circle enclosing a smaller circle; a Mexican asleep in a child's puzzle; a mott and bailey castle on the hoof. Shop windows caught the hurrying figure for an instant amid pyramids of tins, released, lost, and overtaken in an ever-changing context.

Joseph wore his Frank Sinatra hat aslant, a turret; beneath, his cigarette menaced the empty street. Drops of rain pattered suddenly on the resonant straw of his hat[illegible] He swore, turned up the collar of his coat and hurried o[illegible] In his right-hand pocket he clutched a small bottle con[illegible]ing approx. one teaspoonful of his sperm. He had to kee[illegible] this warm. On the bottle was a label which read: THE DOSE. KEEP AWAY FROM CHILDREN. It was signed with a skull and crossbones motif.

He turned abruptly into a street of small mean houses. The upper windows streamed by in diagonal perspective each holding, immobile, a grey, oily, square of sky. The rain increased and he ran the last few yards to fling himself at the brass knocker of number 23. Sheltered by the porch the furious din on his hat ceased, and he leaned against the door, immediately stationary, as if all movement were motored by his hat and tumult a symptom of its working. Then he remembered his cigarettes and sprang to life. He removed all but one, secreting the naked remainder in his inside pocket, and returning the packet to the left-hand pocket. He always did this when he visited.

John was out. Turning, grievously offended, Joseph caught sight of the key projecting from under the mat.

Clearly, a trusted pal might enter. The hall was in darkness and the light wouldn't come on. He stood fiddling hopelessly with the switch, then he remembered the meter under the stairs and, by matchlight, rammed a grudged shilling piece into the slot.

'Like living in a fucking jukebox,' he said.

The lights came on and the radio in the kitchen, off station, hummed into life. 'It's all happening,' he said. He glared around the empty kitchen. 'Where is that bastard?'

Joseph stood in the centre of the room resting after delivering the three sentences, then emitted a series of little clicks in token of bitterness and disapproval. Next he opened the oven door and placed the small bottle inside, lit the gas, slammed the door and, after much deliberation, turned the dial to Regulo 9. He flung off his wet coat and jacket and bent to tug off his boots. A cascade of rain, hitherto dammed within the confines of his hat, fell from his bent head annointing his socks and his discarded jacket. His cigarettes emerged blotched and limp. Swearing, he placed them neatly spaced around the bottle in the oven. The scene in the oven now resembled some occult and anti-Christ ritual, the whole bathed in the unearthly light of the blue, flickering gas-jets.

'Where the hell is that bleeding git? What time does he call this?' Joseph's questions went unanswered. Ever-questing though man's spirit is, Joseph's pursuit of these truths quickly spavined to a halt. He took off his hat and shook the rain from it. He looked at himself in the cabinet mirror. He looked like a slick newborn stoat. Like the fabled unicorn glued to the glass by the singularity of its horn, Joseph was a pushover for a mirror. Much of his leisure was spent trying to increase the impact of his image. His best feature was his teeth. Rows of square white teeth set amid scenic bathos. He pondered. Teeth told in a snarl. He snarled. But snarls were infrequent things; M.G.M. rationed them to a few pre-credit outbursts; Lenin counselled the use of terror seldom, swiftly and all at once. He essayed the boyish grin, dabbing gauchely at a forelock as gamin and unruly as Hitler's bunker.

He sat on a kitchen chair, thought hard and came up with eating. The same old impasse had been reached. Oh that he could wear his teeth in his hat or perhaps as a crisp white fender under his nose.

The kitchen held nothing of interest. He began to sing to cheer himself up, holding the fork in the attitude of a microphone, and making extravagent movements on the chair.

> 'I gotta girl, name is Bony Moroni,
> She's as thin as a sticka macaroni.'

He hadn't thought of that song for years, last heard it fighting it out with the switchback on Blackheath fairground, an oldie but a goodie. Nostalgic.

If John didn't come back soon he'd have to go or the doctor's would be shut. He was worried about the sample in the bottle, about the whole business. He felt aggressive towards the medical profession for requiring such a sample even though they were, as yet, unacquainted with it. It had been his own idea and he suffered lapsed-Catholic pangs about the venal character of the culling. He thought of Onan. Onan had beaten his meat and the Lord had risen up and put the boot in. Blood and seed all over. Fucked confession for another week.

Catholicism had drooped when he came to university, bit the dust as he opened the E.U.P. Marx. He had grown instant proletarian parents toiling against a Lowry backdrop of scurrying ant-men and dark-satanic mills. There was injustice everywhere. A man could hardly stand upright, let alone sit tall in the saddle in a world where a wank was a sin and the capitalists rode chortling over the peasants' grain.

After a while his thoughts grew confused, an incredible scouse of fag-ends and half-digested concepts, the whole soused with the lemony flavour of bitterness. Twenty minutes passed. Then in came John.

'Hiya Joseph,' said John brightly, quite pleased to see him. 'What brings you here?'

'You bleeding asked me!' shouted Joseph and got off a snarl. 'What time do you call this?'

'I don't remember asking you to call—not that I'm not pleased to see you.'

'Well you did.' He let a huff aristocratize his pale features.

'O.K. then, I did.' John was easy.

A hurt whine now crept into Joseph's tone, his usual proposal for wooing. 'I suppose you've forgotten the rest of our conversation last night too.'

John sat down and considered. 'I seem to remember it was about reproduction. You were worried about your dynasty.'

'Yes. Well. I've taken steps.'

'Steps, eh.' Thinking, mucho mystery here.

'I'm getting the doctor to run a check on me. I have to know the Truth. I've got a sample for him.'

John cocked his head, advancing one ear to catch, as it were, every last rung of Joseph's steps. 'Sample?' he offered.

'Sperm.' Joseph took the hurdle with a small blush. 'A sample of my sperm. Well—I've got it, see, and I'm bringing it round.' Very defiant, expecting blockade.

'Bringing it round. How do you mean exactly "bringing it round"? Vinegar on the temples? Flapping at it with a towel? Sounds a pretty dozy sample.'

'Oh Christ, John! Give over dad. Look. Listen, I'm bringing it round to Dr Ostbahn for examination. See? I've got to keep it at body temperature.' His features now registered earnestness because it was his health, and expressed this by a knitting of the brows, a gathering in of the mouth. His hat moved slightly with the contractions.

'Good. Stout fellow. Where is IT?'

'I put it in the oven.'

'You WHAT!'

'I put it in the oven.'

'IN the oven?'

'Sure—you didn't come and I was afraid it—well Christ man, I had to keep it warm didn't I?'

'He put it in my oven,' John said tonelessly, as one bereaved. 'I cook in that oven. It's a sanitary area. It has gleaming white walls and a door to keep all the goodness IN and all the nasty dirt OUT! So you come along and stick your sperm in it to warm. Do you do that sort of thing in your own home? No, I bet you don't. Do you think I want your rotten old seed whipping about in my shepherds pie? For your information I don't! You're a dirty bugger.'

Joseph yelled at him. 'It's in a bastard BOTTLE you daft sod! It can't get OUT!'

'I suppose you've had a shit in my pillowcase while you were waiting. And put my——"

'I wish I had!'

'—put my toothbrush under your armpit.'

John stamped over to the oven and twisted open the door. He squatted down to see in. A choked cry escaped him and his jaw dropped. Thus: 'Aaaaaargh!' Then: 'No! No! Keep away—OH GOD! Horrible, horrible!' He clutched at his throat and fell back onto the carpet.

Joseph erupted from the chair with a great squeak of boots, agog, aghast. 'What is it? What's up?'

A wavering finger pointed into the oven: John seemed to be fighting for words. 'In there—in the baking tin. A little man—homunculus—in a hat—gas too high——'

Their cheeks almost touched as Joseph bent to peer into the depths: heat buffeted against his face; his forehead prickled. The little bottle stood in the centre of radiating columns of cigarettes like a little monarch. He burst out laughing.

'Oh come on mate. Pull the other one.' He went back to

his chair, annoyed to find it on its back. 'You've blown ya mind. Daft sod.'

'I saw him, I tell you. You don't believe I saw a little man?'

'Get off.'

'Inconceivable, you think?'

'You're darn tootin'. You must think I'm mental or something.'

'You think I'd entertain a figment in my oven?' John passed a weary hand over his face. 'Overwrought—working too hard—irregular diet and that. Bereaved too. But—the mind plays strange tricks, Joseph. Little high-heeled boots stamping on the baking tin. Spectral Zapateo. No, no, you're right. It cannot be; and yet——? We've only scratched the surface, Joseph, the surface of knowledge, for all our pride. The unknown....'

'Up you.'

'Das Unbekannt yawns beyond our ken, God wot.' John shook his head slowly as if returning from a queer reverie. 'Help me into a chair, old fellow. Nasty turn....'

His head bobbed on his neck with each great laboured breath. Joseph stared at him and gnawed his lip. He put his hands in his pockets and then he took them out. He whistled a soundless whistle. He was completely at a loss. It was an act and a bad one too. And Joseph had never—for a second perhaps?—never believed that there was someone in the oven. 'I may be Arts' he thought, 'and I know about the Twin Cultures and all that crap, but I'm not a bleeding half-wit. What does he take me for? It's insulting. He's twisted. Bent. Definitely. Strictly the surgical boot man.' But he did feel unnerved. He had an awful feeling that John, inert now in the chair, would have given this crazy act whether he, Joseph, had been there or not. After a while he spoke. 'Do you want to come along with us to the quack? We can have a coupla pints after.'

John was lured out of his grand wreck by trivia. ' "With US"?'

'Oh for chrissake!' He jabbed his preserved cigarette into his mouth and lit it, abrupting smoke at the stupid haperth in the chair.

John made his face apologetic. 'Old man,' he said, 'I don't know how to tell you this—but—the sample—it will be dead.'

'That's your fault then!'

'I can't help it. You should have gone straight round there in the first place instead of incinerating it in my oven. Why bring it to me? You want me to be your manager or something?'

'Because I wanted your advice. You're supposed to be my mate. Anyway, I won't ask you now.' Great dignity in the face of betrayal. Switch to pathos: 'I can't just go off and produce just like that. I'm not a bleeding rubber tree you know. And I was a Catholic.'

John made an effort to suppress hilarity. 'Look Joseph, rinse the bottle and get a fresh sample. Take the bottle to the lav.'

'Huh. I couldn't concentrate. It's impossible if I know you know.' He would not be persuaded and would not stop even for a cup of tea. He left the cigarettes too, which more than anything impressed John with the seriousness of the breach.

Joseph applied damp thumb to bell and squirted distant chimes out of the old house. Nobody came. He made the noise of tsk, substance of scratchy mood, nobody kept on not answering tonight, and squirted anew. On either side of him in the porch, laurel bushes dying of dogpiss dripped melodiously. Nothing was distinct in the front garden for the light from the street lamp petered out several doors away, but he could make out a broken hoe, gangs of dandelions, and some sodden newspaper. The brass plate was strictly, he thought, for braille readers. This was one palsied practice and Ostbahn would never pick up his bed and walk.

He furiously rang some more until lights—TILT—came on in the hall.

'You've left it a bit late,' said the man. Mid-twenties, white-coated, annoyed, in no special order. Joseph didn't really look at him because he never really looked at greengrocers, fishfryers, tobacconists, cops or conductors. They were what they did; you read their sign. Anyway, doctors were there to look at you.

He was in the consulting room and seated before the doctor could enter the room, brow ready furrowed with his problem.

'What's up with you then?' asked the doctor, leaning one fist on the desk and yawning at him.

Joseph found his manner very uncongenial. This doctor didn't seem to realize that his role was to be reassuring and sympathetic. Not bleeding rude. Probably saving it up for his private patients. Now Joseph's mother had instilled in him a sense of his rights before the panel, had swung the infant Romulus under the teat for codliver-oil and malt and milk and shots at metronome intervals; he was unlikely to take any wooden nipples tonight.

'I'm worried about personal potency,' he snapped.

The doctor laughed unfeelingly. 'Brewers' droop or the old war wound?' he asked.

'You can cut that out for a start. It ain't funny. What do you do when a mental patient comes in, catch your thumb? I want to know if I can give girls babies or. . . .' He waved his hands.

'Morally you mean?'

'No, I don't mean morally. Why would I ask your permission? Use your loaf. The priest is for that. I want to know if my stuff is the goods—if I'm capable of reproducing. You can check that on the National Health, can't you? Give a sample to frogs or rabbits or something?' Everybody was a wise guy tonight.

'I'd be glad to do that little thing for you,' said the doctor, 'only we ain't got frogs and we ain't got rabbits.

Also we ain't got a microscope. I can give you a note to the hospital if you like?' He sat at the desk, picked a pen from the blotter and wrote the date on Dr Ostbahn's headed notepaper. 'Name?'

'Joseph Clark no e. You'd better put c/o University, History Dept., because I move a lot.'

The doctor wrote away very awkwardly with his left hand for a few minutes and then put the note in an envelope and sealed it. 'I bet you're hell with those campus chicks?' he surprisingly said, squinting at the patient like a horse-player. A cigarette hung from the side of his mouth. Joseph thought he was pretty hip for a doctor.

'Some,' he said, very blasé, modestly exposing the tip of the iceberg.

'I'll bet you do. You do all right.' The doctor was grinning at him, a good guy after all.

'It helps coming from London. Sharp threads and like that. The competition is strictly hick up here—you know, fat pants and windsors. Very Dogpatch.'

'Yes, style seems very important to women,' said the doctor.

Joseph saw a caution in the verb and adroitly changed his tack. 'Of course style isn't everything, in fact it's pretty trivial. What is important is—well, naïve I guess—is old-time heart. Warmth. Feeling. Sincerity. Like that.'

'Feeling is important in a relationship.' The very faint emphasis was not lost on Joseph and he grinned. They were both men together, having a bit of a larf; they both knew the score. Joseph flashing the pearlies as a treat, said: 'You sure spilled a bibful babe.'

'O.K.' said the doctor.

'Doesn't hurt, does it?'

'That's right,' said the doctor.

Expansiveness and biography seemed in order. The desk lamp cast a very intimate glow over the homely old furniture and put a bucolic ruddiness into closed city faces.

'You're from the States?' Joseph asked, happy in his

flex-roll Oxford with the important extra collar button at the back.

'New York.'

'Man, you're lucky! The Promised Land. That's where I'm going after I graduate. I'm going to drain out my brains to the Village Vanguard, the Five Spot and 52nd Street.'

'It ain't all laughs,' the doctor said after a pause. 'Believe me, some of the kicks are in the groin. You want——' he pointed to Joseph's lapel—'to leave the buzzer at home.'

'Yeah, I know. They'll probably try and stop me getting in. I'm in the C.P. too. A plague bacillus.' No harm in letting the brains show a little: the Historian to the Doctor. 'Still, I don't have to tell Them that do I? You gotta use your loaf. Are you going back?'

'Let's just say that I can't.'

'C.I.A.?'

'It wasn't the Comanche.'

This doctor was a character. Joseph memorized the come-back, envied the uptake, deleted the quotes. It was great to be syncopating with an intelligent man after the baffling session at John's house. John was clever but he wasn't a NOW person; the delivery was wrong. He would be square enough to call this repartee.

'A buck on the side doesn't hurt, what do you say?' said the doctor.

'I'm not against it.'

'Take what you can when you can, eh?'

'As long as nobody's hurt.'

This brought a slight check to the fast, flat flow of things and Joseph sensed a squareness in his scruple. He stood up and put his foot on the chair. It seemed to him that this re-asserted his style.

The doctor continued. 'It seems to me they've really got the little guy nailed down over here. These—Tories? You can't get near the gravy for antecedents.'

Joseph nodded. 'Did you know that 90 per cent of the

wealth is owned by 10 per cent of the population and 80 per cent of the land by 5 per cent?'

'Is that a fact?'

'The Press won't print that. We reckon we're doing well to get a mention in the blats. We need a revolution to get those facts in balance.' His face set hard for action and he lifted one of the doctor's Luckies on the strength of their solidarity in the great share-out to come. The doctor lit it for him.

'I had you figured for a pacifist,' he said, indicating the badge again.

'Oh, the badge—yeah, that's for F.P. Foreign Policy.'

'Uh-huh. You have strong principles, don't you? Commitment. I like that in a man.'

'How do you get on with the old doctor?' asked Joseph, guessing further ground for empathy.

'Ostbahn is a real asshole. Professional etiquette forbids me to spill my guts about that asshole's activities. Him and his fifty guinea letters.'

'His letters?'

'Oh hell—I don't mind telling you. He works with a psychiatrist on the old abortion thing. For fifty guineas you get a letter saying you're too unstable to have the baby then the brain raper puts his cross on it and you're off to the private nursing home. That's private enterprise, professor.'

'Well, Christ, why don't you report the bastard? That's bleeding criminal!'

'That's a laugh. With my political record? They'd crucify me. Oh no, professor, I tread carefully. I don't go near the fuzz. I'm getting the figures in balance in my own way.' He gave a tight smile and stabbed out his cigarette on Dr Ostbahn's blotter. He seemed greatly preoccupied with dousing random sparks and did not look up. Joseph felt that the relationship was on the edge of slipping away from him.

'How?' he asked.

The young doctor put his hands behind his head and stared over Joseph's head at the plaster oak-cluster on the ceiling.

'Classified, professor.'

The brush-off cut Joseph to the quick. He saw himself suddenly as an outsider, a mouthy student not to be dealt in on the plans of pros. He made his play. 'Look, don't think I'm a stoolie or something. You're worried because it's not legal? What's legal to me? Legal schmegal. Capitalist legal is the big zero, right? Free thinking ain't legal here. Slums are. Poverty is. War is—it's all relative.'

The doctor was clearly impressed. He looked straight at Joseph and saw a man. And that was how Joseph got on the payroll of S.C. Second Chance, proprietor B. Herod. The plan was simple. Ostbahn, the psychiatrist, the whole Tory swindle, were to be undercut by a socialist co-operative. Second Chance gave just that to any woman poor or desperate enough to contact him.

The doctor, Ben Herod, spoke rapidly and directly, folding down his fingers as he made a point, tapping the blotter for emphasis. Joseph did the nodding. 'And it's free—absolutely free. We don't even charge expenses. Our group has been allocated a sum by the Party because they see our work as vital. If the state did it we wouldn't need to. There is a constant demand for S.C. The danger lies in the hustlers like Ostbahn on one side and the cut-price cracksmen on the other, not in the function. You dig so far?'

'I dig,' Joseph said, hung up completely by the glitter and splash of the principles the doctor was jettisoning in his explanation. Joseph worriedly tried to scurry ahead and sink his own so as to be free and fertile for the new ideas as they were unfolded. It was quite a regatta.

'We need a man on the campus and I think you could be that man. It's not important but you get five pounds for each applicant and if this bugs you you can plough it straight back into Party funds. You keep your lip buttoned and your ear to the ground and if that strikes you as too gymnastic we can call it off now.' He waited for Joseph's answer.

'When do I start?' said Joseph, like they do in movies.

'You just did.' They shook hands across the desk.

'I'll phone you every day at six p.m. to see what you've got. I realize it won't be much until after the Easter freak-out, but see what you can do. Also, another guy will be phoning you every so often with applicants to pass on to me. We thought it would be quite a joke if we got him to call himself Ostbahn and feature this German accent, so just play along.'

Joseph permitted himself a grin. 'Confusing for the fuzz too, if they're listening in.'

'That's right,' said the doctor, 'but if you stay in the bleachers the fuzz won't be listening in, O.K.?'

Joseph unleashed his high sign.

2

'Thank you for your trouble,' said John for the third time, following the receiver on its downward path to the cradle. What a waste of fourpence. Straightening, he noticed that his breath had conjured a small grinning Chad from the surface of the mirror.

'The General Public,' he thought, 'the fetid bloody general bloody public. My old man writ large. Only at home in the Public phone box and the Public Lavatory! They left the touch of their breath clinging round the receiver; they left tattered unnameable parcels of filth, foetus and catspee in the directory shelf; they drew Chad on the mirror and signed it, like they signed everything else, with a greasy, collective thumbprint. No wonder Caesar passed out.'

John barged out of the booth, his problem unsolved. He needed a dark suit for his father's funeral that very afternoon. He had phoned two outfitters but neither of them seemed able to understand what he meant by Mourning Dress. Obviously they were thick, and probably crooked too. They both wanted £3 a day for the hire.

'£3 a day!' cried John.

'Cleaning and pressing, sir,' said the outfitter.

'Oh come on.'

'And wear and tear.'

Shrunk lapels after funerals and torn flies after weddings, John supposed. He stood in the middle of the pavement undecided. Scraps of paper fluttered about his legs: a passing dog looked at him without interest; a member of the general public went into the phone box.

He'd have to borrow a suit from someone. Who did he know well enough to ask? Joseph had suits but Joseph was about a foot high. Most of the University had gone home for the Easter holiday. Except for the spades, of course. They shivered out a cold Passion in the Law Department Library, and he didn't know any.

'Colin Bell,' he said, snapping his fingers.

Of course Colin Bell—King of Recriminations. He was so tied up in local politics that he could never go home. And he was the right size. And he had a black suit.

John remembered that he had bought the suit on the occasion of the now famous demise of Reg Seeds. The demise had become so famous that John had difficulty in remembering exactly what had happened; what his eyes had seen had been so transformed by the lenses and persiflage of the Press that it had become two events, one on Ellis Street period and one on Ellis Street nerve-centre of a busy, warm-hearted fishing city. Mr Seeds had paused, on his way to work, canteen dishwashing—to buy a flag for Oxfam Day. He put a threepenny piece, distinctly remembered, into the tin and the vendor had pushed a flag into his lapel, pricking his chest and killing him. Mr Seeds, a lifelong haemophiliac and pigeon fancier, had collapsed at once, giving generously in a rush what he had hoarded for fifty years. Colin Bell was there before the civic swabs, getting the facts, poking his huge nose like a microphone into the faces of startled witnesses and generally rolling back the stone. A new, significant Seeds emerged from his articles—A *Local Schweitzer*; the faithless were vilified—*Townhall Silent on Seeds* and *Papal Indifference?* The flag vendor, an elderly widow, fled abroad in fear of a murder rap. The noise lasted a week and was interred with the remains of Mr Seeds, for which Colin Bell bought the suit and at which he circulated a petition.

John set off for City Square to find him.

'Hello there,' shouted Colin Bell, jigging his banner up and down at the head of a crocodile of marchers. 'Looking for me? Grapple on.'

John fell into step beside him. It was just the day for a

march, with a strong inspiriting wind in the air. To his left a guitarist in a forage cap strummed a plangent beef and all around him the banners flapped and slapped. John wondered what they were marching about for the banners offered a broad menu for redress.

'I wanted to see you about my father's funeral,' John said.

'Sorry about that. Dreadful business. I meant to call round but I've been up to my eyes in it.' Colin's banner wavered dangerously as he clapped at John's shoulder the clap of condolence.

The procession came to a ragged halt at the traffic lights and most of the bearers rested their banners on the ground.

'Bloody heavy these things,' said Colin, massaging his arms, and wiping a mucal caste mark onto his forehead with his handkerchief.

'You want one of those metal cups. You know, you wear it on a strap just over the navel.'

Colin turned eagerly—'Can you get hold of them?'

'You could try the scout shops.'

'No, that's out of the question, of course,' said Colin. 'We have imposed sanctions against the scouts.'

The marchers set off again flanked by cars and women with shopping bags who paused to watch them. A policeman looked at them and then set his watch. John remembered the feeling of being looked at. He had marched down this street ten years ago, an aching profile in the Boys' Brigade, and five years before that a blushing Cub. He looked at Colin marching. Bags of swank, narrow chest thrown out, hips shuddering like panniers on a mule. Around his mouth and chin sprang short, reddish hairs, a beard like a distraught magnetic field that exactly caught his public image. On some fairy morn the wind had changed and petrified for ever these bristles of his expostulation.

'Colin?' said John at last. The huge nose swung round to him.

'Colin? It's about that black suit. Could I borrow it for my father's funeral?'

'I don't see why not old chap. When is the funeral?'

'This afternoon.'

'Well. You could have it for a couple of hours or so, but I must have it back by six.'

'Yes that's O.K.,' said John.

Colin narrowed his eyes down from mere slits to blackheads and contemplated John.

'We could do a deal on this,' he said. 'You probably saw the news this morning. Twenty-two Vietcong shot down in cold blood. We're having a demonstration tonight—a march on the town hall. People just read about an atrocity like that and then turn to the racing results. That's why we're marching! Somebody's got to step in and stop it!'

A fine spray played over John throughout this discourse and he nodded repeatedly to avoid saturation of any one spot.

'Where do you stand?' sprayed Colin.

'I think someone should step in and stop it,' said John.

'Six o'clock, Queen's Park then. I've got a job for you. Oh yes—and wear the suit. I don't know how you can bear to be seen in that Fascist outfit. Something has got to be done about this Vietnam thing. People have got to be made to sit up. It's the numbing bloody apathy that's so shocking. So long as they've got their tellys and tigers in their bloody tanks they're as contented as castrated cats!' He continued in the same varicose vein for two intersections, dampening where he sought to inflame.

'Sit up and step in and stop it,' thought John, caught on the rhythmic hook. He wished he were somewhere else. He wished he could suddenly drop a big mirror in front of Colin Bell and watch an embarrassed red crawl over the yakking features, watch him fall onto his knees and plead for a lobotomy. They had never liked each other, had not in fact spoken since Colin had tried to veto the projected von Stroheim season as decadent and non-utilitarian. Of the many things that John hated about Colin one thing was uppermost: Colin had the comradely habit of repeating your last word with a nod, and then splashing into vociferous opposition, made all the more splenetic by his momentary lapse. John wondered how a habit like that got started. 'Hell's Bell,' he thought, arter Sartre.

'You know they've chucked me out of the L.P.? Oh yes, the S.O.Bs. The bloody broadcloth bastards! They called me a red for opposing the U.S. in Vietnam. Of course I was able to prove that dissent was a cardinal tenet of socialism and an inalienable human right. And of course the C.P. threw me out years ago over Hungary so that was eyewash. Eyewash!'

'Ho, ho, ho!' John entered the general merriment, but didn't slap his thighs. 'When can I pick up the suit then?'

'You want it now do you?'

'Well, I do really,' said John, loathing the apology in his tone.

3

Carol felt completely hung up. John had shaken her faith in humanity. She had always believed that everyone regardless of race or intelligence, reflected upon the great eternal triptych—Who are we—Why are we here—Where are we going? She in fact had the Gauguin painting of the same name over her bed, a return to the tonic (non-fizzy) after the secular improvisations of the day. Not everyone admitted their common humanity in public, she knew that. Marxists wouldn't speak personally and Zen Buddhists were hard to pin down, but they all surely knew that they walked the earth alone, and that they would return one day to dust. Now it seemed that there were those who never thought her questions. They ate, slept, made love and died but their motivation, soul and spirit were so alien that they formed a separate species. They were not conditioned into mutation: they were born so. John was one of these.

Carol threw on her tweed coat and covered her hair with a scarf. She never wore gloves. She put her notebook and pencil in her pocket in case of a pensée which was likely as she was going to the park. She always turned to the country for a spiritual fix, for a cosmic echo of her mood. The municipal park was not red in tooth and claw or unmarked by ruinous man, but it was the nearest bit of green.

The park was deserted and as she walked she felt a familiar peace. Hominids and mutants were leashed and no longer fouled the footpaths of her mind. The trees were still black and bare and uncomplicated. Everything was in its ordained place. The air was cold and clear and she filled her lungs with it and clenched her fists in her pockets. She walked around the perimeter of the park and then sat down on a bench. Across from where she was sitting a peacock suddenly materialized and glided over the fence, his tail, shabby now, was still a bright tremor on her retina.

She stared at the watery lemon sun and it seemed to her that it was pierced again and again by the sharp brittle branches until gobs of yellow fell upon the earth. This reminded her of Christ's blood on the robin's breast and she was off, scribbling it all down in her notebook. After a while she found it too cold sitting and so she set off for a final lap. Her feet rang on the earth, an iron collage, she noted, of stamped leaves and rimed mud. On the fence was a lost red glove waving for help; Carol ignored it; human flotsam was so artificial.

All this alchemy was arrested by a strange sight at the end of the rose walk. It was Joseph disporting himself like an ape. He must have seen her before she saw him because he was well into the part. His breath made fat cumulus clouds as he scuttled at random among the empty flower beds, scratching at his armpits, rounding out his jaw into apish curve with his tongue and shattering the silence with feral cries. Carol watched with interest. She didn't laugh until his Cuban heels caught in a root and he crashed, still flensing at his armpits, into a skeletal rosebush. She helped to dust him off, a maternal end to his primal display of plumage.

'Are you all right?'

He wouldn't look at her giggling face.

'I fell into that bloody thornbush.' Joseph snarled back at the gnarled snarl. 'The parkie wants to root that bugger up. What's it in aid of anyway, I want to know. Nasty lump of firewood.'

'Do you want to sit down, Joseph?' asked Carol.

He did, and spreading a *Melody Maker* on the bench, sat.

'I'm sure I've cut my leg to the bone,' he said, working

his trouser leg up to expose his stout white leg. 'Christ! Look at that!'

Carol squatted down and saw, through the goatish hair, an almost subliminal incision.

'Those thorns are poisonous you know,' he said, a little nettled by her equanimity. 'It's bound to go septic. Have you ever seen a tetanus case? Just your bloody heels and your bloody head touch the deck.'

'That would put the cinema off your list,' said Carol grinning at him but he was preoccupied. He cupped the dot with shaking hand and fished for a handkerchief.

'No, that's dirty,' said Carol and undid her scarf. 'Here, let me.'

'Is there a first aid post in this park?' asked Joseph enthroned while maiden knelt and tied a silken favour about his calf. She shook her head and tied a bow for a finalist Persian. 'You mean there's nothing?' He was incredulous. 'What is this—the Yukon? If you conked out in here you'd sodding die!'

He looked down on her sleek head bent over his wound. Oh God, why wasn't she his bird? Because he was short and ordinary? No, no—not that. Because his mate John had found her first. And John wouldn't lay her; he had to be crazy. It was wintry in the park but in Joseph's trousers it was perenially spring. Christ, if he didn't get it soon he'd need a wheelbarrow for his bollocks.

'I'll buy you a cuppa tea,' he said and got up. They walked over the frozen mud, Joseph leaning heavily on her arm, to the kiosk at the West Gate.

'Two splosh, luv.' Joseph clicked a florin on the counter. They sat on wrought-iron chairs at a wrought-iron table in the open.

'Don't you want your lumps, Carol?' He liked to use her name because it was good tactics. If she was dancing he was asking; if she wasn't he'd just take another turn around the animals. He had to find out if her affair with John was still current, of course. Meanwhile, there was no harm in laying down some grainy close ups. Their fingers brushed as he took her sugar lumps.

'Two treys,' he said shaking the lumps in cupped hands and then rattling them along the table. 'Bam! Tonight I gotta golden arm!'

'Now throw a single one,' said Carol.

'You saw the film,' cried Joseph, incredulous.

'John made me.'

'*Made you see it*,' he corrected. 'Great movie. You dug it?'

'No. I thought it was boring and gimmicky.'

'Yes—some of it was um——' Joseph drummed his fingers on the table—'trivial.'

Conversation lapsed. Carol drank her tea. She drank it in a series of little sips, moving the cup away from her mouth as she swallowed and then back again, never replacing it in the saucer. Joseph studied her over the rim of his steaming cup. He thought she looked like a slide trombonist on a ballad. Everything about this chick was a ballad. The white in her eyes was faintly blue like Christmas card snow.

'How's the work going?' he asked.

'So-so. I spend too much time on the poetry. I haven't looked at Anglo-Saxon.'

'I know what you mean. Those thegns are extra nothing. Me, I'm all the time at Marx you know. We do a paper on Roman Britain. Dragsvilla.'

Carol smiled and took another sip of tea. Somewhere nearby, a rodenty bunch of birds began chirruping, poetry to some but to Joseph bedsprings. Even a scrap of paper clicking over the frozen dirt did things to his sensitive skin. He couldn't stop thinking about getting his leg over.

'I was surprised to see you here,' she said after a while.

'In the park?'

'Uh huh. I don't know why. I just never pictured you in a park.' Joseph leaned his elbows on the table and his chin on his fists, a pyramid of great charm with a list to the lovely lodestar.

'Just where did you picture me, Carol?' he said.

'Oh, in the city—streets, cafés—you know.' She looked away from him at the line of gaunt trees. She turned up the collar of her coat and then turned it down. She was embarrassed. 'You've always seemed a very city sort of person.'

'People usually think I'm some sort of yob out of his nut with noise and kicks and——'

'No, I don't think that Joseph.'

Joseph. She'd used his name at last. He had scored, got through the ladylike pose and hit the button. She was on the run now and anything could happen. The elastic might break, please God.

'People used to talk through me all the time until I got to college. Then they had to rethink see. Hooraw for Joseph the educated ape, you know?' He had an ear like a seismograph for class; deep down in Carol Scott he heard the tiny rustle of a serviette unfolding—battle hymn of the drawing rooms. He could play on the inherited guilt of the bourgoeisie, earned by the Wobblies, the Communards, the Catalans, and played now on a hipster's barrel-organ.

'You know, Carol, people thought I was the Leap in the Dark.'

'Well, you know I'm not like——'

'No no. I don't mean you, Carol. People,' he nodded, remembering, 'just people.' He timed it perfectly, the pause, the hands gathering speed and pushing at air to make way for words. 'I have feelings. Not city boy feelings—just feelings, Carol. Period. I don't have many friends but they know me, they know what I care about. For one thing, I dig the country. So its corny. I dig——' he closed his eyes and tried to recall what was in the country, some corn for this free-range chick. He had last seen it at fifteen, a mistake, and had stood in a field staring at a cow for ten seconds before making—'O.K. I seen that. Now where's the action?'—for the railway. All that kept coming to him was the refrain, 'Beans could get no keener reception in a beanery.'

'I dig,' he said, 'mountains and greenery, beans——' Oh Christ, that slipped out. What had she said to Jane that time? At that no-mark party? 'Trees, cows, sticks and all like that.' As Joseph opened his eyes it came to him.

'I sometimes think that its only in the country you can really find your own rhythm. It's like a personal thing you know, Carol. I can't externalize it worth a damn.' He waved a wrist in self dismissal.

'I know what you mean, Joseph.' Carol was smiling at him.

'You know,' he flashed his teeth at her, 'I believe you do.'

'Joseph?' said Carol before he could follow up the teeth with the glims in one of his slow-burn features.

'Yes, Carol.'

'How would you feel if your father died?'

Joseph winced. He thought he was doing better than that. A cup of splosh and twenty minutes on him and Pan had bought him bugger all. John's old man! He said his piece though. What Is A Dad. As he spoke, a clutch of stay-out sparrows galloped home to make it all up with Poppa while he was still alive.

Carol nodded. 'John doesn't give a damn.' Her eyes filled with tears. Joseph's hand sped out to cover hers, his I.D. made a clang nothing like a brandy barrel on the wrought-iron table.

'No no no you don't believe that Carol. You know he cares about it.'

Carol was crying now. 'He joked about it—the same day.'

Joseph squirted solicitously at her hand. Resuscitation; next move, kiss of life, then perhaps his sticky solution for her knotty problem. But he knew this was the end of the line for him: terminus. Joseph would never steal a mate's bird, and John was still his mate. He sprang back from the mental clinch, arms high to show no foul intended.

'He's a very warm guy, Carol, I can tell you that. Personally I rate John one hundred per cent. He's like me—he doesn't flash his feelings around, you dig, but all the time he really cares a helluva lot. It's all locked up inside him. For instance take last night. I took him out and got him drunk and then, boy, the dam really burst. . . .'

'John cried?' Carol stared at him hard, starting a psychogalvanic response in his palms.

'Pretty near. He was really broken up about it.'

'What did he say then?'

'Or you know—how life wasn't worth living and so on.'

'What about his father?'

'Well I guess I'm to blame there. I tried to keep him off that. I figured that he oughtn't to dwell on that—too close to him, you dig.' Joseph was really sweating on this one; what he said could be checked. He tried pushing it over to Carol, keeping his face worried and boyish. 'Do you think I fouled up there, Carol? Is it better to make people face it or——'

'I don't know.'

He ground his fag out savagely. O.K. so he'd been trespassing, but this was getting to be The Biggest Rosary Ever Told.

'You want to hold onto him, Carol—you're good for him. You're a swell girl Carol,' he patted her hand, the Trappist's last feel, 'if you ever need a friend you know you can count on me.'

'Thank you, Joseph.'

'I mean it. One hundred per cent. Just call me.'

'Thank you.'

'Day or night.' He drove it all home with his candid gaze, and then brought the bouquet out from behind his back. 'Oh yes, if you're writing in your book there, put this in. Those dried leaves and that frost could be Smith's Crisps with salt. You dig, it's a metaphor.'

'So it is,' said Carol, very surprised. 'Thank you, Joseph.'

'That's O.K.' He got up, made a high-sign—'I'm gone'—and limped bravely towards the tall timbers.

Carol watched him until he was out of sight and then yawned enormously. A raffish dog made a three point landing on the crazy paving, dropped a stonehenge of turds, gave two little crouch steps to finish and then bounded off without a backward glance. She didn't put this down either.

4

They were all sitting round on their macs on a grassy bit of the park waiting for the funeral march to begin. John, sitting in the coffin, watched them with an uncommitted eye. Colin Bell was everywhere, now checking the banners, now conferring with a bespectacled girl holding a clipper board, waving his arms and shrilling down a gym-mistresses whistle that swung from his neck on a crimson sash. As he swept past the coffin, a firebrand in the gathering darkness, John was struck by the multitude of badges on his lapels. One in particular struck him. *God is alive and well in Argentina.* What could it mean? Musing thus, he now glimpsed Arthur somewhere in the middle distance doing difficult things to an oak tree, a crowd of admiring youths around him. Had Arthur seen the badge? Would a miracle-working goat lead them to the City Square amid the clangour of cymbals and the pibroch of prick-music?

A familiar voice sounded in his ear. It was Joseph, looking embarrassed either for dropping him after the Affair of the Oven or for being seen in this particular context.

'Cock-up innit?' he said, sneering at the assembly.

'Bell seems to know what he's doing.'

'Huh. Him?' retorted Joseph without cockcrow cue. 'He's roped you in at last then. What happened—get turned on?'

'Just a business deal. I borrowed his suit.'

They were a little formal with each other, gingerly putting weight on the fracture to test it. Joseph squatted on his heels beside the coffin and gazed over to the trees while John whistled a little tune. Both attitudes were meant to convey that they were ready to be nobody's fool at the drop of a hat.

Joseph too had an extra badge tonight. Its message was terse and handprinted and it glowed with a coating of luminous paint. It said: CLARK.

'Clark,' read John.

'Eh?' Joseph dangerously narrowed his eyes as he looked at him.

'Your name,' he pointed.

'I thought it would facilitate recognition. I don't wanna get lost in all this crowd.'

This struck John as a bit heretical but he diplomatically said nothing. There was another awkward silence and they both entrenched themselves in the observation of people. In the bushes stood the forbidding presence of the parkie, in his fist glinted an instrument for pinking litter. He licked his lips and waited, hoping.

'What do you think about abortion, John?'

Joseph was biting his thumb, a sure sign, not of worry, but of showing John that he was worried. And with the problem would come the frat pin; a package deal. Exit duo hoofing and waving boaters in unison. Them Two Funky Jays, back in the old I said back in the old routine.

'I think,' said John folding his hands across his chest very Elder Zossima in his box, 'it's very good.'

'What does that mean?'

'Well what do you mean, what do I think?'

'What do you think? Swiss clinics for the rich. The old fifty guinea letter. Cut-price backstreet cracksmen. The moral issue for chrissake. You must have read the papers man.'

'It's an old folk craft like thatching. I'd hate to see it go. There's too much uniformity. Haven't we room for a little insanitary fatality once in a while? Jenkins says we have. What do you say?'

'Crap.'

'O.K. I think they're the last heroes of the century, even the last possible heroes—I haven't worked that out though. I see them as essentially romantic in the sense that knights are romantic, tilting at the biggest dragon in the world with their bright lancets. Not an evil dragon because evil is a greater chimera than dragons. Overpopulation see. So they wipe the slate clean for thousands of unlucky fuckers.'

'A second chance,' Joseph offered.

'Exactly. And yet they're reviled, abused and hunted down by society. The last of the fast guns brought in from outa town to reduce the township of its troublemakers. They bring colour and drama into humdrum suburban lives—a whiff of cordite and mystery.'

'You don't think it's immoral then?' Joseph pursued.

John stared at him in amazement, pitching in lots of jaw-drop and orb-pop before he noticed that Joseph really was worried. He had stopped biting his thumb.

'You must be joking. Without God, that is, until He gets back from Argentina, morality means social expediency. When we're up to 500 million in England the cabinet will have to restore National Service. A new quiet deadly army of cap-fitters, queers, abortionists and interrupter instructors will spring up. Then it will stop being romantic.'

'That's sci-fi baby,' said Joseph doubtfully.

'The truth only.'

On the green the marchers were beginning to form up in ranks, Colin Bell on a tree-stump steed, palm upraised, badges glinting like chainmail.

'Who have you put up the spout then?'

Joseph was offended. He stood up and brushed at his knees and then checked that his levis hadn't got wedged in the back of his boots. 'I was talking about a social problem.'

'Oh I see,' said John, fed up with this on and off lark. What was up with the silly bugger—painters coming or what?

'It came up at Bell's meeting, that's all. I told them what I thought, pretty well your viewpoint actually, and they came on all square with me.'

'Didn't see it as an essential plank in the hustings next week?'

'It was just a discussion. No policy decision involved,' said Joseph very withdrawn now, eyebrows up in his hat with disdain as he gave John plenty of the old profile.

'Not much drawing power?'

'I'd better split—I don't want to get lumbered with carrying you and that bleeding great box down the road. See you around, dad.'

'There's ants and there's thinkers, eh baby?' John called after him but Joseph ignored these darts and strode off. Why did he do it—trample his friends' illusions to mash? Was it jealousy or was it his way of showing the leper's-bell round his neck? John decided it signified nothing. It was a meaningless improvisation like all the rest; wig-bubbles and collander farts.

Lying in the coffin, a cassock under his head, John stared at the moving rectangle of sky. The stars were out now but he lacked the ability to identify the Great Bear or the Southern Cross. He guessed that he was drifting down the middle of some wide avenue because no buildings broke on the horizontals of his craft. The jostling was regular and rhythmic. At times lights shone on his outstretched legs, and then again he was moving through darkness. Below, he was fitfully conscious of voices and heavy breathing humming through the wood like a sleeper's saw. His body fell away from him, and his mind, awash between sleeping and waking, recreated fragments of the day.

He saw bright white rows of tombs, yew trees, stone doors without knockers, black solitary people with watering cans, his father's grave at silly mid-off in the clipped green field.

'O.K. up there, Democracy?'

John started at the rap of knuckles on wood. Colin Bell's voice.

'Are you all right?'

'Yes, thanks,' he said.

'Not far now.'

John rubbed his eyes, scratched his belly and slowly raised himself on one elbow to see over the side. Stewart Street. Not far, the man sez. About two bloody miles is all. He could see shoulders and bent heads below him, and below that rows of boots; behind him was a forest of banners and beyond that—darkness.

Someone saw him and pointed. 'Oy look! The ghost walks!'

'Shut up!' shouted Colin Bell. 'You in the box—lie down!' John lay down and held up a wrist to see his watch, luminous numbers among stars. What a bastard Bell was. Fancy playing a trick like that. He felt his skin hot with embarrassment.

He had worn the suit to the funeral. Carol had been there and Mr Reed from the morgue, the vicar and the sexton. Thank God for small attendances. They had all stared at him. He felt as if he had just been caught pasting a note, three pints please, on the door of a family vault. He had just stood there blushing, gathering handfuls of slack suit into his pocketed fists. 'I know it's a bad fit——' he had said but Carol dropped her flowers onto the wet earth and ran, her hand clenched to her mouth. How could he have known about the suit? He had worried about the flapping trousers, the tiny shoulders, the hugely wading seat that hung vacantly from his hips; he had not seen the foot high letters on the back of the jacket:

THE CORPSE OF DEMOCRACY. VIETNAM 1967.

Mr Reed had lent him his mac but nobody seemed to believe him. Well, now it was all over, dust to dust, a dusting off of hands. His father was dead and buried; a useless life, a useless death, a farcical burying. There was a certain consistency in that. Of the blood, only he, John Jenkins, unaligned and uncaring, had attended his funeral, solely in his capacity as an object.

A banner slanted sail-like past the side of his coffin. STOP THIS USELESS—he couldn't see the rest. Roofs hove into view tilted at an angle, telegraph wires and lights and treetops. They were nearing the centre of town. A voice began singing 'We shall overcome' only to be instantly overcome by Colin Bell. 'Shut up you fool! This is a funeral march. Negro rights tomorrow.'

And Uncle Bert? Why hadn't he attended his brother's funeral? Uncle Bert, impresario of the packaged deal box, had been banging at the door, synchronizing watches, ordering wreaths and jotting down the time and place of the burial before Mr Reed had finished his embroidery. Then the silly old fool hadn't turned up. Silly old sod. And then it came to John, the penny clattering down the chute. He had told him two o'clock Monday, even watched him lick his pencil and write it into his battered diary without noticing the twenty-four hour discrepancy. Some earlier funeral had gained Uncle Bert, his glass eye, his open-shouldered acceptance of responsibility, his hairtrigger responses from the nave. John wondered when he had discovered his error. He saw Uncle Bert's confident back on the chief mourner's bench, ramrod straight among the ducking and bending of whisperers, the unknown kinsman with one weeping eye. Had he made it through to the ham supper on the crest of their reticence, Uncle Fitz-herbert, the blot on the escutcheon? Well, that was Uncle Bert off the Christmas list. He would have to re-orientate to a life without brylcreem and the Boys' Book of Sport.

'Keep well to the left. Let the traffic through!' shouted Colin Bell.

Bright faces gazed down at John in his coffin from the top of a bus, their mouths opening and shutting soundlessly like fish. John shut his eyes. Behind his lids he could see Mr Reed's mouth opening and shutting. A lot of it around. They were leaving the cemetery and Mr Reed was telling him something, something that seemed important but he couldn't focus on it because Carol was running again and again and everybody was staring at him. He picked a leaf from the hedge and dug little crescent scars in it with his thumbnail. Was it about his father? John reached back for the words, hearing the voice, the sound of their shoes on the flagstones. He furrowed his brow and squeezed his eyes shut to expel the splinter but nothing came. The coffin lurched suddenly from side to side losing height, and John grabbed at the sides in panic.

'Gently lads! Put it on the steps.'

They laid the coffin gently on the steps of the townhall and then retired to sit crosslegged on the pavement below. Those with hats doffed them. John stared up into the oratorically distended nostrils of the beloved leader. He saw the tiny chest fill with air like an elf's smalls, the bristles gather into some sort of order and then, in a roar, fall back in disarray.

'Comrades!' he bawled. 'We come here not to praise democracy but to bury it!' He waited instinctively for the sturdy throats and honest hands to fall silent again, which wasn't long. 'You all know why we're here tonight. To do honour to a brave concept that first flowered so many aeons ago at the knee of wise Plato the Greek. Yes, Friends. The Greeks were a race of Burkes.'

'Oh Gawd,' said John, prone under the fount of inspiration.

'Don't show your ignorance,' hissed Colin, 'lie still!'

Dere Colin Bell, i hope you are well. Most of us umans are esentialy figurs of fun and our postures ridiculus in the extrem especialy when we are ardent about things. You are the most ridiculus that has ever been seen on earth (by me). You do fulfil a roll but not the wun you think. You are *surposed* to be angry and cross and mone a lot. Yore words dont matter a fig or tittle jus so long as you keep them up. The Underdog is ment to be a massokisst like a lady is. If you reely wanted to be efective you wood do wot Oswald did exept that is a Rite Wing Thing. The Left wing Thing is to do it to yorself. Poor petrol on yore self and strik a lite. Do this in the Stranglers Galery in

Parlt. It wont do any good but at least you wont look ridiculus. A welwisher.

Colin Bell surveyed his audience. There were few students, so he switched into a lower gear. 'Today we see the death of democracy. Not a quiet death, friends. Not a natural death like you and me expect when our time comes. Not a quick death.'

He pushed his voice up an octave, adjusting the spray to needle-fine. 'It's being murdered! Bombed, riddled and gassed in Vietnam today and everyday!' He flung his arms up into the crucified position, held it, then let them fall limply down. 'A little country far away, you say? What has that got to do with us? We're doing nobody any harm—just minding our own business.'

Two policemen pushed through the sitting crowd and came up the steps to the speaker.

'Go home and mind your own business then,' said one of the policemen, quite off the cuff. The police had developed a special method for dealing with Colin Bell. They didn't want to pinch him because his feet smelled from all the marching and, worse, he was a Fabian Farter. (Fabian Farters let their wind run free in any company to establish common clay antecedents.) The smell of C. Bell made the cells hard on everybody and led to short tempers and rank-pulling on night-shift.

'That was a rhetorical question, officer. Not a statement of my beliefs.' Colin Bell drew himself up to his full height repeatedly. The crowd applauded. It was always the same. The police and the leader exchanged broadsides of wit and ridicule; if Colin lost he stormed off in a huff; if Colin won the police pinched him and lost.

'You know you're disturbing the peace,' said the less witty policeman.

'Peace!' said Colin. 'Peace!' he screamed. 'What peace? The peace of the deaf dumb and blind? The peace of the rabbit warren?'

'Peace off,' said the witty policeman, grinning.

The audience applauded. The less witty policeman leaned over to his colleague and said out of the corner of his mouth:

'Watch the language, George.'

'What peace can there be for us when our brothers are——'

'Hullo. What have you got in here?' The witty policeman shone his torch into the coffin. John squirmed in the light of those laughing eyes.

'While our brothers are——'

'Hop out. Come on, look sharp.'

John clambered awkwardly from the coffin and stood beside it, very diffident in his radical rockersuit. Fuzz frightened him. The glare of the torch hurt his eyes and made him think of footlights and turns, a thought clearly paramount in the policeman's mind.

'Your brothers are dying. As long as I am permitted to speak I shall continue to——' Colin Bell came to a halt. Horribly, no-one was stopping him. No-one was listening either.

'And what's your name, son?' said the witty policeman, upstaging any possible reply with Method twirdles of his torch.

'I am leather apron,' cried John notwithstanding, and turning, ran away amid great applause.

5

Joseph had a cold. He breathed heavily through his mouth and at intervals sniffed a dragging schlurppy sound like a soundtrack of the monster's end. He too felt as if he were drowning; it was all around him, all inside him and he could barely think for it. After a few hours he had learned to live with it, and looked forward to the good times like when one nostril broke free with a little pop and air rushed in, cold and clear as a peppermint. Somewhere in the centre of all this mucus was the real essential Joseph, damp but rational.

It was this Joseph, blundering about the room and honking into tissue paper who thought now, with the mulled radiance of a peat fire, of love. One day he would meet her, the one for him. Across the crowded room she would see him, love him, touch his hair as she passed his chair, notice his teeth. And the line would be secure: a quiverful of fletched and formidable Josephs to man the barricades. No fool, he saw that Spring would be a little late this year. And the next. Joseph had cased the scene and found only a dearth of Catholic, Marxist, hard-bopping chicks. The schismatic, the bourgeois, the cloth-eared in dull hegemony as far as the beshaded eye could see. But he could wait. He had one hundred per cent, straight up, no shit, litmus-tested proof of his potency from the hospital. Now he knew. He thought of yesterday's events, the mysterious doctor, the humiliation at John's, the loss of his rainsodden cigarettes. He trumpeted into a tissue and tried to suppress the lot.

The girl from next door thundered on his door.

'Wod id id now?' he shouted. 'Noise of Kleenex hiddig the floor too loud for you?'

'Phone,' she replied, curtly. 'And you'd have heard it if you hadn't ruined your ears.' She stood blocking the way, her hair piled up in curlers under a chiffon scarf.

'Balls,' said Joseph, elbowing past.

'Suck 'em,' the girl replied.

'Ib I had a mouth ad big ad yourd I could.'

'Keep sucking,' she said.

No response had ever been devised in this fugue of flighting, so Joseph lost. He blamed it on his run-down health and turning his back, picked up the receiver.

'Cidy desg,' he said urbanely.

'What? Is that Joseph Narodniki?' Thick German accent.

'No. Joseph Clarg no E. Id thad Ostbhad?'

'Yes, Ostbahn here—Is Herod there then?'

'Dough. Id alride. I cad tage a bessage.'

'But you're not Joseph Narodniki?'

'Alride—I cad be—I ab. I ged id, id alride. Joseph Narodnigi.'

'You are he?'

'Yeb. Shood bub.'

He took down the address and the appointment time and rang off. It didn't seem such a good idea now, this Second Chance, and he wished he hadn't joined. It was only in bed that night that he remembered all the questions he should have asked, would have asked if it hadn't seemed to impugn his uptake. For example, why should the C.P. care about abortion? It wasn't in Marx. That didn't prove it was all cock of course. It could be in Lenin. Part of the N.E.P. perhaps? That morning at the hospital, sniffing miserably and ejecting seed into a test tube, he had remembered the Kulaks. It was probably to do with them. 'Constrain the Kulaks.' That rang a bell. They voted with their feet, or was that someone else? Joseph kept the problem of the Kulaks and abortion suspended in his mind, uncorrelated but distinctly promising, for a later think-in.

The kettle broke into a whistle as he re-entered his room, and began to boil. He poured it into a bowl and mixed in the Friars Balsam, then burnoused in a municipal slipper-bath towel, he dangled his strangling features over the fumes. Moisture gathered on his skin and hung in minute droplets from his brows. A score of blackheads put forth their heads as both nostrils popped in vernal awakening. Joseph staggered back gasping. 'Man! That's nose candy like mother used to bake!' he thought, rubbing at his face with the limp towel, and returned for another fix which set the fumes coursing along his orifices. A ball of phlegm teetered at the back of his throat and with a giant hawk he sent it winging, fat plop, into the bowl. Joseph couldn't bear to look at it. He reeled to the cupboard and downed six Beechams, poking his tongue around the white residue in the glass. He was determined to beat this cold and he followed every rule like a West Pointer.

He settled back in the armchair and closed his eyes, exhausted for the moment by his own ministrations. He sat still for so long that he became afraid he would fall asleep. Asleep, he knew his mouth would gape, and worse, he would breathe through his mouth and awaken with a throat like a vulture's crutch. An effort of concentration was called for.

He dwelt on his newly established potency. Primitives may delve ditches and impale them with staffs, munch balls of their enemies and tap Calpurnia up in a fast passing; he, Joseph, needed no aids, no crutch for his crutch. Rattling poppy-like with seed, he arose to get the tissues, blew his nose and sat. Yes, he was dangerous to women; a man to be handled with care in the clinches, a left kicker with the aim of a Matthews.

A vast heat descended upon his skin like a sunburn. His eyes prickled. The mucus and the Beechams combined in an enveloping tumescence. Fears and inhibitions melted before his gathering lust. He could have flung himself on the cat or its whiskered cushion but he had neither. Joseph knew, brains descended, that he must have a woman this night or bust.

He flung on pullovers, jumpers, coats and scarves with antic, archive movie haste while his mind sped to a swifter removal. 'I'm rimshot tonight, baby' he thought, as he lanced through the door, bookgrant crackling in his pocket. On the first landing a door opened to reveal an aged eye and the floral spout of a lavatory-bound teapot. He said hullo and the door shut immediately, perhaps forever.

In the telephone box, red the colour of sex, he dialled the number and panted at his image in the mirror.

'Good evening,' said the black plastic receiver.

'Good evedig,' he replied in a pomaded voice.

'Can I help you?'

'I saw the Adverd. Dext to Strig Guverdess.' He had transferred this phone number from fag packet to fag packet for months.

'I'm sorry, our regular governess is on her sabbatical but we can probably——'

'Dough dough. You dode udderstad. I dode wad the guverdess.'

'Did you have one of our interviewers in mind then?'

Joseph felt as if he was shouting underwater. He shouted louder. 'I dode wad a blarded idderview. I wad a fuggig fug you twerb!'

'Sorry. I can't seem to understand you. Are you foreign—coloured?'

Joseph fumed. Discrimination! Chiffon-clad but hideous. Twice he had banned South African fruit. He prepared to terminate negotiations. 'Ibe greed!' he shouted rudely.

'Don't you worry about that dear. Lots of our clients have that trouble but it doesn't last long. Now, did you say you were British?'

Joseph gave up. 'Ibe Briddish,' he said with a germy sigh.

'You have a funny accent. I can't seem to place it for the moment.

'I hab a code.'

'Pardon?'

'CODE!' he screamed between coughs.

'I see. We have just the thing for you.'

'There'd a bug goig aboud.'

'Yes, I expect they do. Well, down to haha business. Our fee is two pounds for the interview, ancillary charges-depending on your placing of course. Will you want to see one of our specialists?'

'You are Rooby Toolbogs I presube?'

'Pardon?'

'ROOBY TOOLBOGS!'

'Roomy Toolbox? Yes, that's our professional advertisement.'

'Well thed, wad id all thid crab aboud idderviewd and spedialid? All I wad id a sibble bang.'

'We can talk about all that when you arrive.'

'Ibe norbal, you know. You dode hab do ged oud the Alsatiod for be, you dig?'

'Our address is 33 Princes Drive—you know how to get there?'

'Yed.'

'Bye-bye now.'

'Yed.' Joseph hung up and replaced the wet receiver in its cradle. He stuck a cigarette in his mouth and lit it. It tasted like a fog with pins in it and started him barking again. He pinched off the end with a practised parsimony and put it back in the packet. In the street he crammed a handful of cough lozenges into his mouth as he hastened, lust-ridden, to his tryst via the 27 red, no change. Joseph Clark, no E.

'We've got a funny one tonight,' the madam told her girls. 'I can't make out what he wants.'

'Kinky?' asked the redhead.

'Coo, I should say so. He kept rabbiting on about Alsatians and governesses and going round bugs. I gather he's green and frigid.'

'Frigid?'

'Cold, he said. So was Christie. You'd better keep an eye on him. We don't want any more trilbies in the lavatory.'

So when Joseph arrived, practically polevaulting in through the door, he found himself assigned to the biggest, fattest, most adaptable specialist in the house, a lady nominated in her absence and at present buying rock and chips twice at the corner shop.

The madam showed him up to her room to wait, rejoicing in his pigment—spades went on so—and went back to her telly, Panorama, with a lighter heart. Joseph had never been to a brothel before and going up the stairs, fuelled his fires with reflection like 'So this is a brothel' and 'I'm in this brothel then,' while outwardly he affected a jaunty ease. On the bus he had imagined their conversation—'You'd better use something because I can't—R.C. you dig. You don't want to take chances with me.' The danger was delicious and the thought of scattering seed, like fivers, into the wind, made him feel swashbuckling and affluent.

The bedroom door closed behind him and he stared with growing de-tumescence at the deployment of peculiar instruments on the coffee table. Some purposes he divined—whips, boots, handcuffs: some purposes were murky but just possible—bicycle tyres, oilskin hats: two things, purposeless and frightening, really hung him up and set the old frontals reeling. Nine jars of Vick and a stuffed cat. Not that Vick and stuffed cats turned his knees to water—some of his best friends and that—it was the context that harrowed. What the hell could you do with them—here? The possibilities made him cough. The stuffed cat glared at him from glass eyes. Its mouth was open wide and he could see into its red painted throat. It stood upright on the bedside table holding, in that clumsy way that cats have, and silently playing, a large gilt harp. Joseph went closer to inspect it by the intimate twilight of the brocade lamp. Close, it was worse. 'Chride! Ibe geddig oud. Fug thid for a gabe of skiddles,' moaned Joseph, with a twitch of the sphincter.

He started for the door, thinking feverishly for an excuse, finding none and meanwhile dabbing down the landing, boots in hand, leaving sweat marks on the lino. At the top of the stairs he heard a sound below and froze. The lavatory yawned vacantly, he flitted in, a muffled moth in his woollies, and hid behind the door. He held his breath as footsteps clacked by and a smell of chips wafted past this mute, inglorious Bisto Kid's smeller. Versatile, he breathed through his mouth, went hot and cold and listened. The steps slowly returned.

And then he coughed. Coughed with the clangour of playground cops and robbers.

The door was pushed with force enough to stamp 'wash your hands, please' on his seat.

'Come out from behind the door! Come on!' roared the biggest fattest specialist in the house. 'I'll have your guts for garters.'

'I card you twerb. Youb god be wedged!'

A large arm came into view, groping like a fun palace prize-picker and won Joseph, who felt himself roar into view, lacking only a cellophane bow.

'What were you doing in there might I ask?' she did ask.

'I wad taked shord,' replied Joseph.

'Oh yes? We've heard the one before. We know what you get up to in there. And where's your hat?'

'I didn't wear id. Sdraw wend soggy in the raid lard nide.'

'You sure it was in the rain?' She muscled him aside and peered into the lavatory bowl.

'Wod you lookig in the bog for? God barby hab you?'

'Kinky, that's what. My room is the place for that sort of filth, not the toilet.'

She herded him along the landing, he pulling on his boots as he went, hopping, graceful as a kick-start, and wiltingly into her boudoir. She closed the door and stared at him.

'I shall be very cross if I catch you skulking in my toilet again. It's no good for you. You know what happens to naughty boys.' She gave an arch look, licking vinegar from her thumb. Joseph sniffed powerfully to show he'd been around. Nobody panicked.

'Wod?' he asked petulantly.

'Naughty boys get smack bums.'

'Loog. I dode wad a smack bub. Ibe nod a poove, Bissis.'

'You asked for the governess on the phone so that's what you're getting. We haven't got any Alsatians so you'll have to make do.'

'I nebber asked for a fubbig gubberdess—I. . . .'

'Ooah! Listen to him. Wash your mouth out with soap.'

'Nebber.'

'Well, what do you want then. You want to browse through the menu or what?'

Haughtily Joseph sniffed an errant candle back up into its lair. 'Ibe norbal. I cabe here for a draightforward ride'—he noticed the tyre—'an ordinary fug. Nobody seebs to dough wad Ibe talkig aboud. Call thid a brothel—id a bloody wax-workd.'

'Oh is THAT it—she told me all wrong. You've never done it before luv and you were a bit nervy on the phone. You want me to coax you, I know all about it.'

She swarmed all over defiant Joseph—'Ibe changed by bind'—and elbowed him playfully into the armchair, stroking fingers depleting his studies of at least Das Kapital in the hardback.

'Eh ere!' he protested, grabbing abortively at his money.

'Removes embarrassment, luv,' she said. 'Now you can just relax and pretend I'm your little lady friend. Now take off your little coat.'

'Dough I hab a heaby code. I keep id od.'

'Come on, don't be shy.' She tugged at his mock mohair. Joseph twisted away and slapped at her hands.

'Off id!' he shouted. 'Greasy, fishy figgers off by obercoad. Cost boney, you dough.' She released him and stood up. 'I tage id off when Ibe ready. Dot before.'

'Don't be shy—look I'm taking off'—fingers unbuttoning—'ALL my clothes.' Huge breasts flopped red and white—'I don't know what's come'—ZIP, skirt falls—'over me'—big fat thighs lolled over stocking tops in a jungle of black suspenders slung low for a speedy draw. She advanced a pitted thigh, and slowly turned her hanging packet of buttocks towards him for his delectation. Her calves looked like boiled eggs in her cupping red bootees. Joseph looked hard and long at this mountain of lady, but he wouldn't pretend she was just his little girlfriend and his unease remained. He had never felt less lustful. He thought suddenly of representing his visit as an official C.P. feeler, but decided not to until he had unravelled the Kulak angle.

The cat glared at him from its harp, strung with a brother—a client?—as she moved, faith-powered, on her leather turntable. 'Oh dear,' she said, knickers descending, 'I seem to be losing my tight little scanties.'

She hid only her giggly face behind a pudgy fan of fingers, eyes darting fire and challenge at the sniffling swain. The whole works swished into view.

I'm not going in there, thought Joseph, and said 'Wod thad moggy for?'

'Naughty man. That's my little pussy'—she coyly buffed at her muff.

'Wod id for?'

'Don't you know? I should have thought a big boy like you would know.'

'Well, I dode.'

'Naughty tease—I know you only want to hear me say it.'

'Thad why Ibe askig, thicky. Wod you want with a mangy old thig like thad. I should thing id be full of flead.'

Scarlet, she flailed at him, a meaty whack hurled him into the slips. In shock, both nostrils popped and he smelt for the first time the heady brew of chips and talcum. 'Bastard!' she screamed, barging him into the bedside table. The cat fell onto the carpet and began to pluck the harp, a plangent Blue Danube, turning its head on every fourth bar to mew from frozen mouth at popeyed Joseph.

'Whiskers,' she sobbed, running. 'Mummy's coming.'

'Daddy's off!' Joseph cried, sprinting, scooping up money and Vick as pour-boire and pour-chest. 'Thangs for nothig.'

6

The laudable moral recovery of Dr Ostbahn owed its origin to fear, its termination to death, and it occupied the space of two weeks in his life. It formed a coda at the end of his life, a coda based on thematic material; encapsulated, recapitulant. All his life he had been tired and afraid; both now reached such a pitch in intensity that had he not been murdered he would have died of them.

His heart was weak due to a pneumonic condition dating from his boyhood when, tired as since and with an incredible lack of cran, he had fallen asleep during a snowball fight at scout camp in Austria. At this same date he had added fear to his characteristics, a fear that grew quieter as the years passed and he remained alive, but that never left him. Of late an equable relationship had grown between the enemy within and the tired doctor, like that between chess adversaries of long standing, so that when a sudden attack sent him reeling into the wall, he would pat his chest and smile and say wryly, 'Aha—mein old familiar.'

'Take it easy,' said the specialist, 'you've got to take it steady.' For Otto Ostbahn this was the wendepunkt, the big light on the Damascus road, and paradoxically his moral decline followed it. He took it easy throughout the World Wars, yawning through both and dicing with death only during the Great Pumpernickel Craze, when he overate. Moral attitudes were for the bell-sound; for him life was a dummy run. Only when taking it easy had brought him safely to sixty-five, with a faded wife, and an ebbing practice did Ben appear and apply the electrodes.

Sitting with his collar off before the television he mentally added the six five-pounds he had earned that week for phone calls to the proper channels, and deducted the frisson caused by the policeman with ingrowing toenails. The doctor felt he had come out of it on the profit side. Yes, it might turn out for the best after all. He yawned and turned his attention to the screen.

'Heildelberg,' he said.

'Heildelberg,' said the quizmaster.

'Very clever, dear,' said Mrs Ostbahn, looking up from her knitting. The programme ended and he rose and switched off the set. He remained standing for a while gazing off into space. Mrs Ostbahn knew that he would now ask her for the paper but she waited for him to say it, because she was a frugal wife and knew how to husband their relationship. Meanwhile she kept an eager, ready for anything expression on her face and unravelled a new ball of wool.

'Have you seen the paper?' he asked.

Her eyebrows rose. 'Why yes, dear. I'm sitting on it.' She gathered the knitting into one hand and heaving a buttock off the chair, scooped beneath her and produced it.

'Anything in it?'

Now she frowned and placed a finger on her cheek in token of thought. She always omitted international affairs, politics, opinion, sport, articles, reviews, astrology and the cartoons because her husband had no interest in any of them.

'Oh yes. There's a girl who miscarried on page three. The police seem to think there was something not quite nice about it. Column two, dear.'

Dr Ostbahn shook the paper open and started to read. Under the liner '*Police do not rule out quackery*' an account was given of a twenty-year-old unmarried girl who was admitted to St George's Hospital that morning with an internal haemorrhage from which she had since died. She had made no statement but the police believed she had been the victim of an illegal operation.

'Why do you always have to crumple the paper like

this?' he shouted at his wife, and thus began the laudable moral recovery of Dr Ostbahn. He could not rest until he had searched through his list of patients for the girl's name and he couldn't rest when he found it wasn't there. After a sleepless night he hammered downstairs at seven to see if the morning papers had arrived. From his surgery he phoned the number Ben had given him but there was no reply, and the words he had bravely prepared to terminate their partnership stayed with him, buzzing in his head. He was hooked but he couldn't find the man holding the line. 'A new leaf,' he muttered as he dusted at his desktop and bore a sea of tatty periodicals before him to the dustbin, past the amazed receptionist.

'Phone for a cleaner, miss,' he shouted, red with exertion, 'and I want her now. Today.' Then he put his head round the door again. 'And from now on I want you here every day. I pay you for every day. Monthlies arrive monthly, not twice a week on Mondays and Fridays. It is in their nature and conveyed in their name, monthlies. So we will have no more of it. And don't chew gum.'

The new Ostbahn didn't catch on. His wife cried in secret and the receptionist swore. 'He's gone on his drugs,' said Mrs Palmer, an elderly hypochondriac, smarting under his crisp demands for more coherent symptoms than 'funny'. The patients left to him after thirty years of inertia, had been pruned down to the hysterical—who leaned on his calm disinterest, the bored—who came to talk, and a shifting clientele of individuals who were actually sick enough to blunder in off the streets, win a note to a specialist and blunder out again. None of them were gassed by the new image, and high among the ungassed were the pregnant girls who were now informed that he knew no telephone numbers and definitely would not jab their buttocks with his hypodermic.

He spent a day reading his old university notes until the evening papers came, by which time he had realized that whatever else he had become in the years since graduation, he had not become a doctor of medicine. And now it was too late. He tried the phone again and heard the endless rise and fall of bells within walls he had never seen, did not need to see to know that they held his freedom and that the hook in his brain was held or had been held by the occupant of those walls. Joseph Narodniki. He paced his surgery and jangled the change in his pockets and then went out again. In the street the idea came to him that he could find his silent partner if he tapped the resources of the twentieth century. Of course. What a useless fool he had been! He would become a private detective.

Armed with the phone book for the city area and a ruler, he slid his eye down the number listings. The task could have taken weeks but Dr Ostbahn was lucky. Five pages in, he found what he wanted.

Joseph's door lolled open, his name printed on the card under the drawing pin, but Joseph was out. The doctor, wheezing from his climb, stared for a long time at the phone on the wall outside. It stood on a little shelf all by itself like a deity, an ikon. Was this what he had been looking for? On the wall in its immediate vicinity were cabalistic markings. He put on his reading glasses and read the list of cinemas, record shops and addresses in Joseph's fast flat fist. Among the aimless doodles of saxophones and quavers was his own phone number. He took out his pencil and with the eraser nub removed himself from the company; he copied down the other numbers into his diary and thus bequeathed a puzzle the equal of the *Marie Celeste* to his subsequent biographers at the police station.

The empty room diverted him for a full hour. Joseph had left a fascinating effluvium to the nosey, a rich skimming from the cream of his personality. The doctor pounced on the packing of a new shirt and read the trade name: BRUTE. Very appropriate! Under the shirts, the drawers were lined with old Melody Makers and Tribunes, a dead fly and a broken cufflink; in the fireplace he found a solid newspaper of fish and chips. And then he found it, Joseph's shameful secret, a little book concealed among his record covers, its title 'HIP WORDS'. The doctor recognized some of the hip words from Ben Herod; that made it a clue Joseph Clark was possibly Joseph Narodniki, henchman of Ben Herod. But he didn't find who held the hook.

'I wish to place an advertisement in the *Mail*.'

'Right ho, sir. Print the message on this form.' The pushed a biro into his hand. 'And it's six shillings a line.' The clerk read it aloud. 'That's it, is it?'

The doctor felt his heart swell until it touched the walls of his body. He stood very still, scarcely daring to breathe, waiting for the spasm to pass. Surely the message was too obvious? Everyone, this clerk, every *Mail* subscriber would know exactly who Mr Herod was. Why had he chosen such a stupidly obvious name? It was not too late to snatch it back and destroy it. He shot an agitated look at the clerk. The paper lay on the counter between his hands and the clerk was staring vacantly over the doctor's shoulder at the people passing in the street outside. He suspected nothing, the doctor was sure of that. He must go through with it because it was the only course of action that lay open to him. Only by finding the abortionist could he get off the hook. He would offer him a hundred pounds for the tape-recording and because the man was greedy he would take it. He would buy back his reputation, refuse to rent the honourable shelter of the medical profession to a quack who probably didn't even wash his hands before choking the baby in the womb.

'Yes. That is all,' he replied firmly.

Ben came out of the *Mail* offices at two o'clock the following day and Dr Ostbahn fell into step fifty yards behind him. The doctor had taken great care over his plan. He wore an overcoat that his wife had tried to throw out two winters ago and which even now bore the smell, bonfires, of a near miss. Only a fraction of his face was discernible between the pulled up collar and the pulled down hat, purchased yesterday. He wore Trotsky glasses and a khaki haversack. A great many people turned round to look at him as he passed. Every time Ben turned a corner and swung for an instant into profile, the doctor galvanized into a limp so complex and handicapping that had Ben lived any further from the *Mail* offices, he would have lost him.

He saw Ben disappear into a large, crumbling Victorian house, the first house off the main road. The doctor licked his lips. Now he had him—the man who held the hook. Radiant with malice, the private eye went home to wait for the evening edition.

The paperboy flexed new waxed biceps and handed the mighty order, two national evenings, a county, a weekly and a local, to Mrs Ostbahn who, strong on teamwork, handed to snatching spouse at her elbow. Under the legend 'Personal Ads' he found what he sought. There was eighteen shillings worth:

CATCH OSTBAHN'S LATEST HIT SINGLE
THE MOTHERS' LAMENT
ON THE FLIP—THE NEEDLEWORK SONG.

Sixteen teenagers drew a blank at their local disc centre and the tiny tremor registered on the national charts to be forgotten, along with the number one, in a week. The ad. ran for three nights and the coffee bars buzzed with the name of the old German doctor.

Dr Ostbahn was a square. He wished to God and back that he had never cut his single and prayed to Him that it never became a hit. Also, for the first time, he seriously entertained the idea of going to the police, telling all and taking his punishment like a fearless Queen's Evidence. He would be ruined but he would take his tormentor with him. The more he thought about that, the better he felt. If Ben had the hook in him, he had the hook in Ben, and now by facing up to his guilt he had gained a position of strength to bargain from; best of all, he didn't have to go to the police unless the proposed *détente* failed to take.

But Ben was out, had been out for several days and the newspaperman outside, who seemed to live there, did not know when or if he would be back. The doctor gave him a day, then two days, then three and at last played his penultimate counter. It took the form of two words in the *Mail*:

HEROD. POLICE.

This turned out to be his ultimate counter.

7

Jenny, feeling sick, fixed her mind on the richness of opportunity ahead. She lay half-propped amid pillows on the bed and carefully hiccoughed a vodka hiccough. So what was this 'ere richness of opportunity? To go on as they were? More parties, more clothes, more doing what they liked and when? And how! She couldn't see that Billy would alter his life or that she would alter it for him. What had happened after the last time? For a week he had saved money and devised the future; what people did when planning for a baby, he did after losing it; and then stopped. So they'd go on as they were. This, the here and now, was the price: here, now, why this man, this professional was methodically wiping each instrument on a white towel and replacing them in their box: why Billy was sitting a mile away in the Swan blotting up whisky and exuding sweaty fear. And she could afford it, both the fear and the pain, regretting only, despite logic, despite time, the child-shaped blank spreading its spatial memory through the guts.

Nausea spun the room around her and the man unravelled into a multiplication of outlines away from the black parent figure. When it passed she saw that he was at the sink coiling red rubber tube into the water and cleaning it. He did this with the utmost concentration and, watching, she knew she would feel nothing until he had finished, could feel no pain until he turned that incredible concentration to her.

Of course it took guts to get rid of it. Billy never stopped explaining this to people. You needed all those capitals—Courage, Decision, Strength of Purpose—to enjoy your life, qualities that people applauded in war, urged on sons of widowed mothers, and admired in careers. The pursuit of happiness took an iron man. Most people cracked under the responsibility of not holding down a job and a house, capitulated and threw up a palisade of babies to live for instead. And Billy was right.

'I can't bear to see you in pain,' he had said behind a Christ face, so she had given him a pound and a kiss and sent him off to the pub. So what? She didn't live with Billy for his strength or his reliability or even for his lovemaking. Jenny could make a list like Magna Carta of what she didn't live with Billy for. He wasn't even faithful, but that was all right: when he was with her he had her, and when he was away he had someone else. He always told her about it and he made her laugh until her head ached. That was what he had. Billy had words that changed your way of seeing until everything became funny as hell and quick and jerky like the Keystone Cops, and you could see all the mess and uncertainty disappear into whimsical little parcels. Billy was just a fact and she knew him better than she would ever know anyone. Even this would be funny. When he came back from the pub she would put his head on her breast and stroke his hair until he was himself again, because if he wasn't funny there wasn't anything else he was. Then she would hand him this afternoon of pain and fear and he would re-write it.

Jenny looked at the man, the professional, leaning against the wall, staring out of the window and smoking, completely contained, completely unassailable, and knew that soon he would become for her a sort of bungling, forelock-tugging plumber. But she wouldn't tell Billy everything because he couldn't use everything and if it broke him, it broke her. She would leave out the bit about the man demanding and taking her body when she was frantic with fear and drink and imposing a peace on her so that she felt good, wonderful, before the pain. Or for the pain? A nasty thought. Did he enjoy springing his seed before the avalanche: into the void, on to the eraser? She didn't know and she wouldn't ask. It had the Pill whacked all ends up. Then again, had it been done for her? To calm her? To establish an intimacy for their collaboration in the most basic way open to the species? If that was his aim he had achieved it, because here too he was a professional, unlike Billy, but unlike Billy he wasn't a person.

She moved her legs stiffly so as not to dislodge the folded wedge of towels at her groin. 'An elephant's jamdam,' Billy had said last time.

'How do you feel?' His hand gently rested on her brow.

'I feel—sort of waiting very hard. Leaning into it though it isn't there yet.'

'No pains?'

'No.'

He stroked her damp hair back from her forehead but she shook away.

'No, it's meant to be like that. It's supposed to be a carefree fringe. Billy cut it that way.' She removed a bare arm from the sheets and brushed her hair forward again.

'That's how he sees you?'

'That's how he sees me.'

'Does he know there's more?'

'More?'

'More to you.'

'He sees what he likes to see.'

'Uh huh.'

They smiled over absent gulping Billy.

'You're very good at your job.'

'I'm the best.'

'I've been done before you know. I'm qualified to pass an opinion.'

'You said.' He lit a cigarette from his and put it between her lips.

'He was hopeless. I had to go to hospital and of course they were very helpful and tried to save it. I told them I had fallen downstairs but I could see they didn't believe me. Not much they could do about it though. Anyway I was all right, I lost it and after a bit they sent me home. Anyway—oh yes—your colleague. He kept on bending over to look—you know, look up there. I don't know what he thought he could see. I mean I'm not illuminated. And he kept on saying "They could put me away for this, lady" and getting in a flap.'

Jenny assumed a throaty voice 'Gawd, I've left me hat inside,' but she knew that Billy did it better. When she tried to remember the first time, she couldn't. All she got was Billy's version and sometimes a picture of flesh staked back with pins that had also never happened, but came with the word abortion. How long would she remember this moment, these hands stroking her forehead as they had stroked her thighs before the greased red tube slid in and he had made his strike.

The man went over to the sink and put the enamel bucket she had dug out for the occasion under the tap, rinsed it and poured in a little disinfectant. She noticed the bottle of vodka on the glass shelf above the sink still half-full, he had not touched a drop, alien among the tooth brushes and talcums of everyday.

'You wouldn't let me off the money,' she said, just to probe his concentration. He finished the job without speaking or giving any indication that he had heard. Then he dried his hands.

'Nope,' he said.

'I didn't think you would.' He smiled and lit another cigarette.

'You smoke too much.'

'Too much for what?'

'For your health.'

'Smoking is good for you.'

'Would you give me a rebate for the free ride?' She felt bolder now, watching him from her impregnable invalid's bed.

'I don't charge for the ride. That was free. You got that for appearance.'

'Thanks a lot.' She felt her stomach heave and drew her legs up around the sudden pain. 'How did you learn this fine art?'

'I held the midwife's bike-clips.'

'You don't have to stay with me.'

'You want me to fade?'

'No,' she said, clutching his hand, 'not at that price.'

8

As they entered the almost deserted university Joseph turned his worried face to John and said: 'John, what do you know about the Kulaks?'

'Nothing. Sod all.'

'Where would I look then?'

John looked at him incredulously, so Joseph set off a smokescreen.

'Test me on History. Go on man—ask me anything.' Joseph sued his boon with a naïve little push at John's front.

'O.K.,' said John, 'what do you know about Henry VII?'

'Everything man,' said Joseph. 'Ask me something specific.'

He was bouncing around on his toes like a boxer in training and snapping his fingers.

'O.K.,' said John, starting to walk again, 'how did he make himself secure on the throne?'

'BAM! Two things bugged Henry when he got on the stand. 1485 man. One: he was strictly from the sticks—Mr Zero from Nilville. He had this chickencrud claim through the Clerk of the Wardrobe, Owen Chuder. Like he was only keeper of the royal threads but he managed to slip French Kate a length and that put the Chuder show on the road. Anyway, no-one had big eyes for Henry so he had to like bear down with his personality and make a big production of having God in his corner. And he made sure his court was where it was at, for, you know, for the Fifteenth Century. It featured all the noble cats of the time all in sharp threads man, and Henry sat at the top.

He made sure everybody could see he was King of Hip Castle.'

'What about the nobility?' John asked, squinting into the wind.

'Strictly defunct man. No scene any more. Do you mind stopping—I can't walk and coach man. All the real rockers got theirs in the Wars of the Roses and Henry really put the arm on the remains at Bosworth. Then he called a cool and to make sure it took he got the Fuzz—the Chuder Fuzz was called JPs see—he got the Fuzz to collect all their blades and pieces so they couldn't bop if they felt like it. Then he put a big tax on the liveried muscle to liquidate their gangs.'

'What was the second thing that bugged him?'

'I was coming to that. Henry was broke like he was really hurting for money. He even owed for out of town help in the Bosworth rumble. But now he's King see, so his worries are over. When you've made it it's easy to get some action—cash-wise, it's all there. All you've got to do is turn the handle like playing the fruit machines. He makes this royal decree they've all got to lay their bread on him and it starts rolling in. He makes a heap on sheep—sheep go like grease on the market—like the Dutch use them for threads. Then there's customs. Baby, whatever moves in or out he gets a slice of the action. He draws protection because he's Number One in the goddam realm. It's all his turf. Everybody has to shell out and I tell you, he ain't taking no wooden tally sticks. The groats start rolling in.'

Despite the discomfort of just standing there in the freezing wind, John was fascinated. The small animated figure in front of him exploded in all directions, arms waving to emphasize a point then hurled up to anchor the inevitable hat, feet chattering out a tempo for the words. He looked like a badly pegged tent in a hurricane.

'Why didn't all the previous kings get rich then? If it was all there?'

'Simple. The rockers took it. They was bent as hell, always cooking the books, stacking the pack. But Henry wasn't going to take that kind of crap. He lamps the books man and he sez—"This is a helluva note. You think I'm simple or something? From here on in I'm taking over accounts and you cats can go play with yourselves. Paste that in your visors".'

'Does the cool take?'

'It takes time. He hitches up with this Yorkist chick to show the cool is for real but the rockers start putting up pretenders. First there's this guy Lambert Simnel. He's just a dummy but the rockers put out this story he's one of the princes in the Tower. Natch Henry's hip to this angle—he knows these princes got turned off with a pillow by Hatchetman Tyrrel, so he figures it for a switch. Henry catches him—no strain at all. He doesn't even bother to kill him—this Simnel is just a fallguy see, just a dummy. Henry puts him in the royal kitchen throwing hash from sunup to sundown, so that's all right.'

Joseph seemed to have paused for breath. He frowned in irritation; for him, speed was merit and if you hungup you flopped. He had the greatest memory he had ever encountered and always cursed the faculty to hell for not giving oral exams, for not letting you smoke and for setting snide correlation questions. He lit a match in his hat and applied it to a fag. 'Ask me anything,' he said, putting his hat back into place.

John couldn't think of anything to ask. 'Did he like it there?' he said at last.

'What? Where?'

'In the royal kitchen?'

'How the hell should I know? I didn't write this stuff you know. Some old scribe did. You think he was going to say "I wunner if I should say he liked it there?" You think he was gonna worry himself about some Chuder counter-jerk?'

'You seem to know it pretty well,' said John placatingly.

'I've learnt it all up. Ask me anything.'

'No. I believe you. It's O.K.'

'I'll tell you about Canute and the Surfing Set?' Joseph offered, trotting along beside him again.

'No don't tell me any more Joseph—it confuses me.'

Joseph tightened his lips and raised his eyebrows. He was insulted. 'Sod you then. I thought I made it pretty clear.'

'Yes yes, you did but—I'm slower than you. I have to go over it.'

Joseph's sharp ears heard the note of appeasement and at once. Pity he didn't know about the Kulaks though.

They had reached the library by now, a huge box of concrete and tin emblazoned with an emblematic owl in left-over lumps of cement. Builders huts and a prefabricated bicycle shed flanked them and their boots slid over frozen mud.

'I'll see you at the pub at one. I've got to do some work first. Here, read this.' John gave him a brand new *Jazz Monthly* to get rid of him.

'O.K.,' said Joseph. 'I'll see you in the bar at one. Hang loose, dad.' He gave his Indian sign and bobbed off into the distance, one hand on his hat, the other holding the magazine in a convenient reading position.

John sighed and went in.

The enormous door closed behind him with a carpet-slipper farty sound—pfff—a sound to go with the hot canned air which now enveloped him. It was like, he thought, stepping into a tropical jungle. Only black students could bear it, work in it, rejoicing in the regular thumping pulse of the bookstamper. The bookstamper was thumping through a pile of books on the centre desk as if reading music. She produced three rhythmic timbres—the tap of bookcover on the wooden desk; the deep whump of the rubber datestamp; the pneumatic bump of cover descending on pages. Behind her flashing, bespectacled head he saw the dark grille of the taboo bookcase. At the desk he made a magic hand-painting in perspiration and laid down the books he was carrying.

'Can I check these in?' he asked, flipping them open at the datecard and intruding a double tap into her motif.

The stamper, a thirty-year-old lump in a forty-year-old Fair Isle cardigan with a bobbled zipper, flashed her glasses purposefully up at him and then down to the books. She set down her rubber stamp on an inked pad.

'You realize these are two months overdue?' she shrieked as if there were a bushfire in her drawers.

John fished out a crumpled ten shilling note and laid it beside the books. He thought it a pity that Carol could never see money as anything but filthy because it meant someone else had to stump up. The stamper ignored the money and continued to inspect the books, both volumes of Byron.

'Look at this! Disgraceful!' Her glasses wildly hurled prisms, neon splinters, aluminium at him. 'Damaged! The pages have been ripped loose of the binding! The frontispiece has gone too!'

The head librarian, who was apathetically piddling about with the filing cabinets, buttoned his leather-elbowed Harris and strode to the desk.

'What's the trouble?' he asked, hoping it was lots as business was slack, donning donnish frown that rattled back in corrugations over pink pate. The stamper's chair uttered a parakeet screech on the lino as she leaped up to thrust her defenceless femininity at the gaunt figure of her superior.

'Oh Mr Gorr! He's brought these books back two months overdue—not a word of apology of course—and this one has been torn away from its spine—it looks as if he's thrown it across the room and jumped on it. And this one has been rubbed in grass or something. Look at the state of the flyleaf! And to finish it off he's torn out Byron's frontispiece!'

The head librarian flung John an anchoring glare, the

mixture: foreboding and malice, equal parts. He presented his dome as he assessed the raped and overdue on the desk. The sward marks were undeniable.

John could appreciate the snapping tension. A dreadful hush fell on the library, a hush the worse for the sinister creak of Mr Gorr's spectacles as frowns buckled his averted features. Now and then, in the distance, John could hear the metallic thud of head slumping hopeless to desk. He looked away down the silent avenues of bookshelves and saw a sudden black visage break into a clearing, flash a crescent of white, duck away and reappear in duplicate.

The head librarian held the pages by their veriest tips, suggestive both of repugnance and of his own irreproachable reading method, and launched a ticking sound of little melodic interest. The stamper in the jumper was swift to add body to his ticking with deep heavy sighs, laden—she postulated—with cinnamon and with myrrh. His nearside pane fogged. Their fingers bumped.

'Could I possibly have your attention?' asked the librarian nastily. He held up a dry russet leaf and a feather. 'Can you explain these?'

'They're a leaf and a feather.' That was an easy one.

'That's patently obvious. One knows what they are. The question is, can you explain their presence in this volume? If you please.'

John smiled. He could see her pressing them into the book with love and reverence and of course forgetting them. He didn't mind all this fuss, he may as well be here as anywhere else, but he vaguely wished she were here to return her own books and turn the blade of the interrogation, with the tranquil gaze of the natural, into a consciousness for Mr Gorr of his rude and heinous materialism. Can any human being, Mr Gorr, read Byron without emotion? See how the crumpled page bore witness to her fury at man's inhumanity to man, this blotch, a tear drawn forth for the wandering outcast of his own dark mind. Joseph had nicked the frontispiece for Byron's shirt, a floppy flexroll number, reproducible, the tailor told him, for three quid.

'No,' said John.

'Give me your name,' said the librarian producing a pen filled with Zyklon B.

'Jenkins, J.,' said John, nothing loth.

'Faculty?'

'History finalist.'

'I see.' He wrote down all this biography, the titles of books, the extent of the damage, and then zoned in the stamper and her stamp with a pointing finger. 'You realize that as a member of this library you have been hitherto regarded as a civilized person, and that all books loaned to you were loaned in that belief. On trust, in short.'

'I do,' said John groomily.

'You fully appreciate that these works are on the English finals syllabus, and that by seeing fit to withhold them from circulation you have jeopardized the chances of some candidates in their examinations. Does this strike you as civilized behaviour?'

'Yes, No,' said John.

The head librarian's voice, hitherto in the style Deceptively Mild now rang forth roundly as he sprung his trap: 'Then why didn't you return them in January?'

John observed the unmistakable sense of drama in their demeanour; he, radiant with malice, his features cocked above irreproachable county check, waited; she, beside him, held the accused in tiny bondage on her glasses; neither knew that John loved above all things the waiting moment when activity congealed and time was immeasurable. This was his moment because he understood it, his alone because he could merge into it doing nothing, for once, with relevance and success. So he merely stood there and watched them realize their limbo. The jungle destroyed his moment, a black representative emerging from the law cubicles to present his complaint at the desk: 'Oh sir please could you be more quiet. It is arduous labour enough without the clangour of your voice. I am sitting for my Part Ones in three weeks.'

Safe in his pigment from sarcasm, rebuke or even the persiflage of friendship he retraced his path between the bookshelves.

'In January my father was ill with chickenpox,' said John. Thus, spotting his father's memory, he rejoined the fray. The librarian had lost heart. In a whisper he fell back on regulations. 'Did you have the books cleared by an M.O.?'

'No,' said John.

'I see,' seeing Byron aswarm and rubbing his fingers together.

'They weren't in the house, see.'

'Oh?'

'No. I had them in hospital with me.'

Behind thick lenses the librarian's eyes mutely begged to be left in ignorance.

'Unidentified skin disease.'

'Of course you handled the books as much as possible.'

'No. It was too noisy to concentrate in the ward. I like peace when I read.' John leaned forward confidentially. 'I like reading in the lav best.'

A nervous trill escaped the stamper. Both stared at her. She flushed and began riffling through the ticket file. Suddenly her fingers stopped, her mouth contracted into an O, as in whistling but poutless. 'Mr Gorr!' she breathed, 'a terrible thing. The books were loaned to Miss Carol Scott.'

There was a moment of heavy silence.

'Then these aren't your books?'

'No,' said John, with a puzzled frown.

'You're only returning them I take it?'

'Oh yes.'

'You didn't damage them?'

'Afraid not.'

'You've deliberately wasted my time then!'

'Nobody asked me if they were my books. I naturally assumed that you'd checked the tickets first. I was quite surprised in fact. Still, don't worry about wasting my time—I wouldn't have been doing anything else. A bit of last minute revision perhaps. I can tell Miss Scott about jeopardizing other students' chances and Byron's frontispiece and abusing the trust and so on, so you won't have to say it all again. Regard me as a sort of middleman.'

John got his money and walked softly away to the study cubicles. He felt curiously cheated of victory. His moment had been destroyed because he had been forced to initiate events, successfully it was true, but on their terms. Still, it made a funny story. He chose a History cubicle, choosing for lack of view and maximum neutrality. He had already lent out his magazine. He lowered himself into the chair. This was to be it. Work. He stared at the blank pad before him on the desk and then wrote: HENRY VII. He drew a line under this, utilizing the straight edge of his textbook and a red biro, and then, frowning added: TUDOR. He drew a line under that too.

Covering his face in sudden despair, he fought to see the warp and woof of it all. God what shit it all was! Couldn't they see how absurd the bloody subject was? Sixty-odd pages of Henry VII and no-one knew what he was like. Joseph's interpretation was the only one possible, to hoover the dust off the archive and use his own words to make it his. Among all those facts, councils, proclamations, institutions, conspiracies, marriages, not one of these proper students of mankind had touched the man. How did Henry's life seem to Henry?

John gazed at the small square of sky visible through the high window. What went through that antique Tudor bonse when he saw that same grey scudding sky? No-one knew because no-one could know. So what's it all about, Alfie?

John's life was eighty per cent incoherence; an itch in the crutch, half a thought rising, evaporating, a colour glimpsed, the etiolated scar of an old fear: indescribable. Old Henry's must have been the same. So must, he thought, his father's. The finalist historian had lived for twenty years with that old man, spoken with him every day, bore his mark. He knew nothing about him. He even made things up about him—like the hot cock he had sold Carol about his endless manicuring and barbering. Sydney Jenkins: the Man and the Thinker. He could sit down at this massive archive of letters, diaries, photos, relatives, workmates and memories and sift it, select it, correlate, vacuum the turn-ups, pursuing an overall pattern, a central strand. That way he would lose the eighty per cent. He might even find the strand, rosebud, but Sydney Jenkins hadn't.

John shook these thoughts from his mind. He found this serial form mourning very wearing and his musings derivative. He took up his biro and wrote:

THE STRAIGHT DOPE FROM THE INSIDER

Scuttlebutt has it that this year's examiners are description buffs. Insider tips the following:

1(a). An evocation of Nantes.

2. Who was the Great Seal?

2(a). A day in the life of a groat.

CAUTION! Do not read more than both sides of the paper.

Do not pass GO.
(This will clock up the marks for you!)

He left the paper on the desk as an inspiration to others and quietly left the hall of learning to a handful of Ghanaians, who worked on to the rhythmic pulse of the bookstamper.

9

Carol sat on the station bench and watched pale moths bump around the lamp. She had been gazing at them for the last half-hour; they were having lots of fun. Beyond the lamp the night sky was a thick purple, cracked and splintered by the shapes of the trees. In the perfect stillness she could hear her heart thumping. Suddenly the platform clock made a noise—clonk. She stared, her eyes jumped to the hands and her consciousness everted to receive her surroundings. It was the first definite movement she had made in an hour.

She had raced up the road from the beach and into the empty station to find, finger sliding down' the impossible runes of the timetable, that the next train would be tomorrow. And then, with the cold brass touch of the locked waiting-room door on her palm, she had stopped because there was nothing else she could do. All panic past, a strange mood of lethargy had settled upon her.

She got up now and started pacing about. 'Come to Scarborough' said a Bathing Belle with a peewee moustache and flowmaster nipples like stalks on berets: she spoke in Granby Condensed.

Carol fixed her eyes on the unblinking red light at the end of the platform and walked towards it. The roof stopped short of the end, its edge crenelated like the jaw of a whale; Carol stepped out into the open on the concrete tongue of the ramp. The wind stirred her hair at her neck and hummed gently in the telegraph wires, but she felt too strange to write any of it down. There were allotments to her left on the railway bank and she wondered in an alien gust of practicality whether she would find anything there to eat. She could dimly make out rows of knobbly cabbage stumps and on the skyline a palisade of bean poles hung with tinfoil and string. She remembered seeing lupins here last summer, pink and blue, and a scarecrow with silver railwayman's buttons that flashed in the sun. Pictures of still life for a hungry girl. Perhaps they kept iron rations in their sheds, hardtack and chocolate at least? She was afraid to go and look. Sheds frightened her ever since the little boy next door had shown all in the shed in return for the same, and had poked a button into hers so that she peed in four streams for a day, until her mother detected the change of note and visited his mother. Carol had never felt under any of her subsequent lovers a fraction of that guilt: it was her first and last scrutiny of the mechanics of sex before the romance of it all closed over her mind like the Index.

When she turned away she was startled to see a man standing under the light, his back to her, putting a coin into the cigarette machine. Even as she thought, let him go away without seeing me, he turned and stared straight at her.

'Hi,' he called and just stood there as if waiting for the echo. Carol felt stupidly, obviously supplicant, her hands clasped in front of her around a volume of poetry.

'Hi,' she said, walking towards him with a jauntiness she did not feel.

'Missed the last train?'

'I think so.' She knew so.

The young man tore off the cellophane wrapper and stuck a cigarette in his mouth. 'Where do you want to be?'

'Hull?' Carol heard it slip out in a request, the edges curled up like a begging letter. She looked at his tie.

'Then I say "Do you want a lift?" And you say. . . .'

She tried not to look as if she were assessing him, but her gaze lacked only a levelled pencil and a buckled eye. He wore a dark suit, a dark overcoat, looked expensive like the lack of publicity bought for financiers. His face was bony with deep shadows under the cheekbones; if he filed his teeth it didn't show.

'So who looks their best in gaslight?' he said. 'It's a loaded set-up.' His gaze was direct, completely self-contained; it offered nothing. Carol nervously cleared her throat.

'I had a barrel round my neck but it got lost,' he said.

Carol smiled and tried to think of something to say.

'You're afraid of me?'

'Well,' she replied, 'I don't know you.'

He shrugged. 'I don't know me either.'

They were silent for a minute, Carol scuffing a circle in the dust with her shoe, he levelly watching her, waiting, smoking his cigarette without touching his hand to it.

'Well, I don't know,' said Carol at last.

'How do you feel about the Germans?'

'How do you mean?'

'Leaving that aside for a bit—which bugs you worse, rape or death? Or is it nameless? You spy with your little eye something beginning with a lift.' He flicked his fag-end onto the line. 'What you're looking for baby is Brown Owl driving a mini. You'd really like me to be a eunuch, right? Square.' Carol blushed.

'Blusher,' he said and suddenly grinned. 'O.K. Credentials. The real warm well-documented me.' He undid his coat and reached into his pocket.

'Driving licence.' He slapped something down on the ticket counter and Carol saw that it was a folded handkerchief.

'Dog licence': a switch knife.

'Identity card': a pair of dark glasses.

He tried another pocket, his eyes never leaving her face.

'Birth certificate': a packet of Lucky Strike.

'Satisfied? Intellectually I mean.' His hand hovered over his overcoat pocket like a gunfighter's.

'What's your name?' asked Carol.

'Ben Down.'

'I don't believe that.'

'Ben anyway to save you pointing. Come on.' He took her arm and she went with him. Her decision lay literally in his hands now. Somehow, she felt that he had presented, in spite of his words, a real picture of himself. He had refused to compromise; she could feel his integrity in the strong grip of his hand on her arm. She walked with him to his car.

Carol never noticed cars but she noticed this one. It was a dark green American convertible with a chrome fender like a mandarin's molars. It was about twenty feet long and it was all car. She hated it for most reasons but she got in when he opened the door for her.

'Quite a car,' she said, resenting the marshmallow seat that sighed up to pamper her posterior. 'Does it wake you up with a cup of tea in the morning?' She was always acid on technology.

'Yes,' said Ben, opened the glove compartment, almost disappeared inside, and handed her a thermos flask. 'Only it's coffee. The ethnic bit, you dig.'

'Are you American?'

'Sometimes.'

Carol poured out a plastic cupful of steaming coffee and drank. When it was all gone she closed her eyes and said 'Ah.'

'Do you eat?' He produced a large bag of rolls and half a broiler chicken, and hefted them up and down in his hand.

'On your nose,' he said.

'Ben, I'm sorry I was rude,' said Carol, jettisoning about fifteen years in vocal development. 'But your car is a bit—overwhelming.'

'My one weakness. I could die of it.' Ben gave her the food, then watched her eat as if the process was somehow amazing. Not until she got to finger licking, without a net, did he turn away and start the car. The road unwound in the beam of the headlights, hedgerows and trees springing up ahead like stage flats.

'What do you do?' asked Carol, studying his profile.

'When?'

'Well, for a living.'

'Why's that?'

'Is it a mystery then?'

'Pardon?'

'A secret. Is what you do a secret?'

'Which do you want to know?'

'How, which?'

'Do you want to know if it's a mystery or a secret?'

'Um—is it—a mystery?'

'No, it isn't.'

'What do you do then?'

'Do you mean "how do you do"?'

'No I don't. I mean what do you do.'

'Don't you want to know if it's a secret?'

'All right.'

'Ask me then.'

'Is it a secret?'

'No it isn't.'

'What is it then?'

'Ask me if it's something else.'

'I can't seem to care any more. I've gone off it,' Carol said, laughing. Ben turned his head round and thrust his tongue into his cheek making a bulge like a tent pole and then returned to profile. Carol giggled into her hand like a bashful geisha.

'What do you want to talk about then?' she asked him.

'I don't know.'

'Talk about what you like doing. Things you're interested in.'

'Like people do?'

'Yes.'

'Best of all I like sexual intercourse with ladies. Then

second I dig thinking about it. Can you see your way clear to doing it with me?'

'I don't know you.'

'What do you have to know?'

'Well, a lot more than I know now.'

'Details?'

'What you do, what your name is, what you like doing....''

'You know all that.'

'What you believe in, what you were like as a boy, what sort of person you are....'

'You play all this back while the guys bounce up and down?'

'No, but knowing it gives me peace of mind afterwards. I have something of theirs.'

'Christ! Who have you been with?'

'That's a secret.' Carol suddenly saw herself as horribly set about with bourgeois rules of her own making; she had not been free at all. Prudent, cautious. The words were horrible. She couldn't face her own accusation so she made him the accuser and swung into her defence.

'Anyway, you haven't even asked my name.' She tilted her chin at him but he didn't look.

'I probably would have asked you but now I don't think I could bear the responsibility.' He didn't offer to explain or even indicate if this was a joke. 'I will ask you something though. Will anyone miss you if you don't get home?'

'What is that meant to mean?'

'You ain't got doll's ears.'

'I've got a big strong boy-friend. He'd miss me if I didn't get back tonight.'

'What was he like as a boy?'

'You're not very re-assuring,' said Carol, wasting one of her short-sighted feminine looks on his profile.

'You don't want to be re-assured.'

Carol saw the beach swing into view as they emerged

from the lane and the car jounced on its springs as they ran onto sand. It was as empty and desolate as a desert.

'Ben! This is the beach. Ben!' She heard her voice quaver in proferring the widow's mite of his name, all she had against his menace. 'You can't get onto the road this way. It goes nowhere.'

Ben turned the car in a wide curve until they were moving parallel to the sea and about a yard from the water's edge. In the headlights the wet sand was the bright artificial colour of builders sand.

'Push that,' he said, pointing at the glowing green button on the dashboard.

'What will it do?' Carol was scared now: talk was talk but this was the beach: she was scared to touch anything.

'Oh come on. Push it for Ben.'

She put her forefinger on the button and leaned, her eyes fixed anxiously on him as if expecting manacles to snatch at her arms and him to X-ray horribly into a monster of teeth and sockets. The canvas hood rose in the air and slowly concertina'd into a neat bundle over the boot; her relief was palpable.

The car sped shiningly between streams of sand and stars. She felt her body quieten now as the miles sped silently by, and she found herself smiling. Was he a romantic after all, a Sergeant Troy of the twentieth century paying his court with eye and wrist, with sinew and judgement, because that alone was true and clean? Ben, as if in answer to her thoughts, nudged the car into the shallows and zipped it through the flying spray like a lawnmower. The twin headlights flung a misty rainbow over the sea.

Distance, measurement sank without trace between those eternal streams: nothing existed beyond the grasp of the headlights, the drone of the engine. Carol closed her eyes and levitated out of her mind. Faster they went and she shouted her deeper deepest swoopingly fallingly stuff into the slipstream, or only thought it, or was it. What at last the car glided to a halt she did not want to open her eyes. From a long way off she heard her mind tell her that this was it, but she didn't care. She was free. If he touches me I shall. If he takes my face between his hands.

Her eyes blinked open on the empty sea, on a trembling star above the tilted horizon. The driver's seat was empty.

'Ben?' she called.

He was leaning on her door studying her face. Spray hung in her hair; and she knew it.

'Do you want to do it?'

Carol turned away and began twisting a fold in her coat.

'Ben, you mustn't ask me,' she said quietly.

He opened the door. 'Get out,' he said.

The door clunked shut behind her, seemed to bite a wedge out of the night air, out of her body. She could smell the wind off the sea and she filled her lungs like a sail.

Ben took her hand and led her around the front of the car to the driving seat. She looked at him. She learned nothing from his face.

'Get in,' he said.

'I can't drive Ben.'

'You're joking.'

'No, it's true. I can't. I'm afraid.'

'Get in.'

She got in. Ben squatted down in the sand, his hands dangling loosely over his knees, his overcoat curtsying around him. Carol said nervously, 'You look like Toulouse Lautrec.'

'On the extreme right you'll find a pedal. That's the gas pedal. If you bear down on that the car will go faster, you dig? Now you know it all.'

'But Ben'—he got into the passenger seat beside her—'I'm scared.'

He turned on the ignition and pulled the choke, and her foot, timidly resting on the accelerator, took off like a rocket as the engine roared into life.

'Don't go ape on the gas,' said Ben. 'You got another foot down there?'

Idiotically she nodded.

'O.K. Bring that other foot over towards me and push it down hard on the clutch pedal. Come on come on, squash it down. Like oppress the bastard. Now gimme your hand.'

Carol bumped her frightened hand at him without taking her eyes off the bonnet. She felt him grasp it and push the palm down onto the gear lever, his hand over hers, carrying the lever forward.

'Let this'—he tapped her left knee—'gorgeous gam—up, very gently.'

The car started moving.

'Cigarette?' said Ben.

'I don't smoke. Ben how do I stop it?'

'Wet your finger,' he replied sinking back down in the seat.

She licked her finger quickly. 'Like this?'

'Good. Now hold it in the air.'

She did. 'Like this?'

'A bit higher.'

'Like this then?'

'Yep. Now do you feel it getting drier?'

'In the wind. Yes it is—it feels dry.'

'Now. This is the hard bit. You mustn't move your finger at all or take your other hand off the wheel. This is the only drag about big American cars. O.K. Now you have to jump up and wet that finger again.'

'You're having me on.'

'Please yourself.'

'But Ben, I've never seen anyone going through all that to stop a car. It's ridiculous.'

'How many American cars have you been in?'

'What I can't understand is why you want me to do such a ridiculous thing.' Carol was staring rigidly ahead at the flying sands. 'It seems so primitive.'

'Anchors are primitive.'

'I meant you. Your tactics.'

'Forget it then,' he said, obviously not worried one way or the other. It was that that decided her, his disinterest in her decision; his disinterest in her. It was suddenly clear to her that her freedom lay in obeying his wishes; more, in discovering them and then obeying them. The bald man in the barber's.

'All right. I'll try,' she said. She clutched the wheel until the bones in her hand showed white, and tried to prepare herself for swift and sudden action. The wheel pulled her up inches short of her upheld finger, her tongue flicking out and in hopelessly before she plopped back into the seat. The car had altered course by about forty degrees and was now plunging straight towards the sea, headlights raking the creamy surf. Ben grabbed the wheel as the fender burst into the water and wrenched it right. The car slewed round in a great arc, a wall of water slapping against metal and mushrooming up like a depth-charge. They were gliding along the beach again before it fell.

Ben pulled the handbrake. They looked at each other. It was all right again. Carol started laughing.

'You are a bastard.' She was helpless with laughter. 'Why? Why?'

'I wanted to see your underwear,' he said flatly.

'You didn't?'

'No, your coat just covers it.'

'I meant, you didn't make me do all that jumping up and down just to see my underwear?'

'I wanted to see if you could lick your finger like that.'

'But why?'

'I guess I'm just interested in people.'

'You wanted to see if I was fool enough to try.'

'Please yourself baby.'

'Although you knew that I didn't believe you.'

'Talker.'

They looked at each other some more, then Ben reached

over and slid his hand under her hair onto the nape of her neck. His other hand flicked ash from his cigarette. Carol closed her eyes and her mouth parted for the kiss that didn't come. Ben caressed her neck languidly, almost inattentively, until she arched her throat like a purring cat. He watched her face in the light from the dashboard, her eyes trembling under the lids, her mouth silently murmuring as she leaned into his pressure.

'Get in the back seat.' His breath whispered hotly in her ear and she shuddered deliciously, pushing a shoulder up to protect herself.

'No Ben. The beach. I can't——'

'The back seat,' and he flicked his tongue into the depths of her ear.

'Eee,' she said, making a lemon face. 'All right.'

Carol took his hand in both of hers and rubbed it against her cheek and then kissed the palm. She didn't take her eyes off him.

'Ben. Be gentle with me.' And then she said, 'My name is Carol. It's important to me that you know.'

His face came too close for her to see, a shadow looming and she felt a stinging pain on her neck and at once his tongue on the pain, molluscine, soothing.

'Charlie,' he whispered.

When she stood up her legs trembled and she would have fallen but for his steadying arm. She stumbled awkwardly as in a boat between the seats and onto the wide seat at the back, sitting in the middle and drawing her long legs up sideways onto the leather so that they looked longer. She began to shiver. She was excited and afraid.

Ben clicked open the door and got out. She heard his feet crunch on the sand somewhere behind the car but she couldn't seem to turn her head to look. Could he be nervous too? It seemed impossible. What was he doing? 'Ben,' she called. Her voice came out in little bumping breaths.

'Take off your coat. Make with the silken rustlings.'

She unbuttoned her coat and folded it over the back of the

driver's seat. There was a briefcase beside her so she put that in the front too. Then she sat still again. Carol was wearing a brown and olive striped dress with a Victorian cameo at the neck: on her feet she wore brown flatties with a T-strap: her breath came in short pants despite the inclemency of the season. She looked like Alice waiting for the Rabbit.

As Ben got in he pushed the button and the hood rose over them, shutting out the sky.

'Oh Ben,' she said, as his arms closed around her. She felt her back suddenly naked under his hand: the band of her bra slackened and her breasts bore downwards in the lace; then the thick fabric of her dress fell in folds about her waist.

His hands brushed gently over her breasts, the nipples stiffening, following his slow palms, then springing back. Carol made little snorting noises with her nose: a row of jolting f's: then s's as his teeth closed on her nipple. She became oblivious of the cold leather at her back, did not hear the little tearing noises as she moved her body. His hand filled her senses, pulling and squeezing, like a drowsy milkmaid at her breasts.

Ben knelt on the floor in front of her and rolled up her skirt, pushing her hands away as she tried to undo the suspenders; he bit her thumb and her hand jerked away. He ran the back of his hand across her belly, then along her thighs, then—first left, first right, and round the corner—up to her loins. He slipped a finger under pantie elastic and moved it along the damp hair.

Carol said, 'Aaah,' like a straining constipate, the vocal range being small and a certain overlapping of designation unavoidable.

Then, 'Oh God!'

Then, 'Touch me there.'

Then, 'Ben, Ben.'

She thrust her bottom off the seat in an ungainly movement to help him roll off her panties, prancing her legs in a panicky drum-majorette fashion to kick free of them. Ben's head was bent over her, his overcoat, caught by a corner on the door handle, spread out like a bat. His hands softly pushed her knees apart, and then his mouth was on her. 'Oh do it,' she said, but he let her plunge around contacting nothing while he did some very supporting feature stuff on her thighs. And then she felt the shock of his touch on her again and desperately jerked herself up and down, like a gnat-bitten horse against a post. One of her arms was thrust out straight pushing her hand flat against the cold glass of the window.

When at last she could open her eyes he had gone. She did not immediately realize where she was. She felt as if she had been ill, sick perhaps with some fever that had left her depleted and unclean. He had not made love to her, not given himself at all. Her body shook uncontrollably.

After a while the beach became a seaside resort, bereft now of the gay wrappers and broken glass of summer, and Ben drove smoothly between the tarpaulined chalets onto the slipway and rejoined the road. She sat in the back seat in the shadows. Neither spoke. When they reached the outskirts of town Ben asked where she lived. Then he said, 'You feel humiliated don't you?'

She swallowed hard. 'Why did you—do that?'

'Suggest reasons.'

'No Ben. I don't want to play that game.'

'You loved it.'

In the back seat she covered her face with her hands.

'Didn't you?'

'Please—I don't want to talk about it.'

'Disgusting. Unnatural.'

'Don't!' She shouted the word in sudden violence. 'Don't speak about it!'

'Unspeakable,' he said.

He drew up outside her house and she lunged at the door handle and almost flung herself out of the car, but he had her firmly by the wrist. He stared up at her from the driver's seat. She made no attempt to pull free, just stood there, head bent, a hand shielding her face from his gaze; hopelessly off balance and near to tears.

'Now dig this. I'm giving you a reason and it's the last I'm ever giving you. When I've told you this you're going to push the gate and run into the house and scrub yourself all over in the bathroom. And all the time you'll be thinking about this and when you make it into your little bed you're going to think about it some more. Tonight the wind blew you over. I don't need that kind of help.'

He released her arm and she saw that he had strapped his own watch to her wrist, the face down against her pulse. She stared at it, uncomprehending.

'Now you know what time it is,' he said. 'So ruminate ruminant.'

As she pushed against the cold iron of the gate, the huge car made for him a Wellesian exit.

10

When Ben unlocked the door of his room and turned on the light he saw a folded square of paper on the lino. He bent and picked it up. The message was written on exercise book paper and the writing was large and childish—

YOU ARE BEEN WACHED.

He stared at it for the length of a minute, unblinking, unmoving. The draught from the open door sent the dust drifts silently tumbling across the lino. His image was caught in the mirror on the wall. Ben from the side, his near arm pulled straight down by the weight of the briefcase, a curve of wrist growing out of his profiled chest, the logical arm engorged; he closed his eyes—he seemed to be waiting as a tower besieged seals itself off and waits. Then his fingers began to move: slowly, lovingly gathered the paper into a ball and crushed it until the whole body shuddered in the convulsion. When he opened his hand the paper was spotted with blood. It fell to the floor. He leaned back against the wall his face wrung, sickly.

He switched the light off and padded surely between the vague shapes of furniture, twitched the curtain aside, and looked out. He looked straight down on the streetlamp and through the blue brightness he could see the empty street. If there had been anyone in the street he would have seen them. They would have stood out like fairground targets against the blank of hoardings opposite. There was nowhere to hide. The house stood at the corner of an intersection, thronged with dockworkers and fishbobbers at midnight and at dawn, a busy thoroughfare by day; now at one a.m. it was deserted. He could see the two empty crates below that the newspaper-seller sat on, and the old cigar box that held his change.

He stepped softly into the corridor. The whole house was asleep. Some pensioner refought Inkerman on the second floor with shrill, cracked oaths and then fell to mumbling. Ben stood outside the paperseller's door and listened. Not a sound. He turned the knob in that slow spooky way that people exhume for night. Doubtless it looked worse from the inside, causation invisible, but the occupant was pounding his ear in incurious sleep. It was quite light in the room. He had not drawn the curtains because, wrapped around his trousered legs, they would not have made much difference. Leg not legs. He had one personal leg and one wooden leg that lay apart from the parent on the table. Beside it, flanked by a sauce bottle and a crumpled newspaper containing fish skin and a pair of impossible chips lay the exercise book. Ben leafed through the book finding nothing but block capital headlines. Mr Wilks took his work seriously and practised headlines of pith and moment for his placard.

On the mantelpiece Mr Wilks kept his books, paperbacks stacked at one end, library books at the other, the yard between them asserting his honest intentions. All the books were about espionage except the library books: one of them was on counter-espionage and the other on ciphers. Ben leafed through the book of ciphers until he found a strip of newspaper marking Mr Wilks's place, then he turned back two pages.

ELEMENTARY CIPHER 'D': NUMBER SUBSTITUTION.

Ben read the directions, then replaced the book. He crossed to the table, picked up the biro and drew two blue and perfect circles on his wrist above where his watch had been. Then he sat on the end of the bed and gently shook the sleeper awake. Mr Wilks reluctantly surfaced, massaged his eyeballs and pushed a sentry's face at the figure on his bed.

'Who is it? Who's there?' he demanded.

'Ben Herod, Mr Wilks.'

'Hold on a mo—let's have some er——' but Ben stayed his waving arm. 'We don't need the light. It's about the note.'

Mr Wilks's voice became hoarse in token of secrecy. He sat up in the bed and prefaced his reply with a long, deliberate wink. 'You got my message? Communiqué?'

'Indeed I did, Mr Wilks,' said Ben. 'Now what's it all about?'

Ben offered his cigarettes, lit two and handed one to Mr Wilks.

'You're being watched, Mr Herod.'

'What did he look like?'

'Short. Fat. Sixty-fiveish. He had an assumed voice.'

'An assumed voice!'

'No two ways about it. It was assumed. Didn't fool me for a minute——'

'You're a pretty hard customer to fool, I'd say Mr Wilks.'

'He sounded like a Bosch but I could tell. It was assumed all right. I know Brother Bosch as well as I know you. I've heard them gabbling away over the sandbags more nights than I care to remember. Handy hock Fritz! That's what we said to the POWs—prisoners of war, you know.'

'That was in the Great War? A rough show that one.'

'Rough! Rough wasn't in it!' Thus the paperseller asserted seniority. 'I lost my leg in that one.'

'You gave your leg for your country? I'll warrant you'd have given your life too, eh old man, if the call had come?' His back to the light, Ben nodded. It was not in question.

Mr Wilks nodded back. 'Oh yes, not a lad in our battalion but wouldn't have given all his limbs if the call had come. Or laid down his life.'

'Gladly.'

'I think we knew where our duty lay.'

'When did the call come for your leg?' Ben asked, then quickly added, 'How did you lose it?'

'Mons. I was I/C Donkeys at the time. I was a bit back from the Front at this old farmhouse. The Frogs had skipped of course.'

'Huh!'

'Trust them! So I'd taken over the barn for the donkeys, until they were needed. I'd just got the mail from Blighty and I was sitting on this crate reading. I'd just got comfy, boots off, feet up, and I was reading away as if I was at home by my mother's hearth—except the paper was a week old, of course. Well, where was I?'

'Sitting in a barn. The war hardly existed for you.'

'VOOMM!' cried Mr Wilks, 'a ruddy great bang went off outside. I jumps up off the crate and has a peek and I sees that Jerry has dropped a 501 on the farmhouse. A direct hit. Only one wall left standing. The blast has blown the shutters off and all the shelves on the inside, but this is the funny part—one window was still in. Intact!'

Ben fingered his poll.

'Rum that,' he mused.

'Rum! You're telling me!' Mr Wilks cried, utilizing his jubilant National Unreadiness voice. 'It was uncanny. I leaned on the door, chin in hand, and tried to figure it out. I forgot where I was. The war hardly existed for me. You get like that after a bit—hardened to it. Don't care. Then I remembered the donkeys in the back. I had to get them before Jerry had another crack at us.'

'You set your own life at naught,' Ben asked.

'I'd got past that. I just never thought about it—you don't after——'

'Do you think Jerry knew about the donkeys?'

'Hard to say. He may have and then again he may not.'

'True.'

There was a long silence during which Mr Wilks remained with his mouth open in readiness should his thread become clear to him. Strain as he might he could not see beyond the black silhouette at the foot of the bed, the lamps beyond and the night sky.

'You feared the Bosch were zeroed on your manger?'

'That's only natural isn't it?' challenged Mr Wilks, irritated.

'Natural,' said Ben.

'I had to shift them right away before they had another go. They were all shoved in together—six of them, jammed—away in a manger. So I got their bridles and climbed over—it was a gate I'd tied to the front of the manger to keep them from scooting. They really had the jitters and that bang had set them off barging around against each other. Restive. Highly restive. So I started talking to them and stroking them to calm them down. I could hardly see them it was so dark. I was squashed up between them somehow and they kept on breathing hard—sort of "Huh Huh". I had this bridle in my hand and I was feeling for the right end when all of a sudden I got this terrible pain in my foot. Agonizing. Just for a split second I thought it was one of those shooting pains that everybody gets, you know, but it——'

'I never get shooting pains,' said Ben. 'I've never met anyone who has ever had a shooting pain like that.'

Mr Wilks was openly contemptuous; he snapped into his Outraged Opinion voice—'I've met thousands of people who are regular sufferers from shooting pains. Scores! You must be a bit peculiar. Search me why you're so special.'

'I hope you don't think I'm being rude, Mr Wilks, I certainly didn't mean to be. I just wasn't clear about the shooting pains and I thought it best to ask.' Ben extended his hand. Mr Wilks was magnanimous in victory, they shook hands heartily and Mr Wilks thought twice as much of his friend, legion of himself.

'It didn't pass off, though, it got worse and worse. Searing. I tried to bend down to have a look at it but I couldn't get room to move. I was jammed right up against those donkeys. I caught sight of the crate where I'd been reading and then I realized. My boots were still over there! One of those ruddy animals was standing on my foot!'

'You'd forgotten to put them on again. Seeing that window had put them clear out of your head,' cried Ben.

'Exactly. All I had on were my thick issue socks.'

'But you kept your head and tried to figure it out.'

'That's right! I tried to figure it out like you do when you're being driven mad with pain. Now, how can I distract this donkey's attention, I was thinking? So I started lashing out all round me. I pushed and I punched and I shoved and I barged. The thought of that shell lent strength to my arms. I thought I was a gonner. They wouldn't budge. Weighed a bally ton. I tried to figure out which one was on my foot. I suspected it was either Kaiser Bill or Wipers Willie.'

'What made you suspect them?'

'The Process of Elimination.'

'Phew,' said Ben, admiringly.

'Oh yes. I kept my head in spite of the searing agony. I remembered in some book I'd read—I was a great one for books, still am—about this camel driver who'd got out of a tight spot by twisting his mount's balls. Well, thinks I, if it works on camels, why not donkeys?'

'You had to be ruthless.'

'I'm not saying it was a thing to be proud of. You'd expect it of an Arab or a Dago or a Frog, of course, but it didn't feel natural to me. I suppose it was the pain. I've never felt pain like it—nothing to touch it.'

'They say pain like that can be unbearable.'

'Unbearable's putting it mildly! Pain like that can make a man do funny things.'

'You were at the end of your tether.'

'I felt along his belly but I couldn't find them. Either my arm was too short or I'd picked Nelly Dean in the dark. Anyway. . . .' The young Mr Wilks and the old Mr Wilks merged into the same impasse: the story went no further for either. The speaker fell silent again.

'What did you do next?'

'Eh?'

'What did you do next? You said you could hear the creak of harness and the canteens chiming together and you panting in the dark with the pain.'

'That's right,' said Mr Wilks. Perhaps, after all, it did go on. 'I remember I could hear the canteens bashing against each other—like bells they were—those cowbells they tie on cows in the Alps.'

'I've never been to the Alps, I'm afraid.'

'No, I haven't either come to think of it. That's what they sounded like though—perhaps I've heard them on the radio or somewhere.'

'That's right!' Ben snapped his fingers. 'They were on a request programme last Thursday. A most distinctive sound.'

'Ah, that would be it then. Of course.'

'And you were——?'

'At the end of my tether. Nearly passing out, blackness, a long black tunnel opened. Yawned.' Mr Wilks could not go on.

'You made a last despairing——'

'Flailed about, punching and pushing——'

'Set your teeth.'

'Despairingly I set my teeth into the nearest donkey's nose. I held on like grim death. Not a sound—just these distinctive bangings and creakings.'

'Shied away leaving your foot free.'

'I dunno,' said Mr Wilks morosely, exhausted now, just wanting to get the leg off and be done with it. 'I passed out then. When I came to the lads had got me out somehow. I never had time to ask because we attacked that same evening and took Jerry by surprise. They left me behind—my foot was a mess—the arch was broken. I couldn't walk. I wore this big white plimsoll to keep the wet out, but it was no good. When they got me to the field hospital it was too late. Gangrene. They took the leg off and shipped me home. And that was that.'

Reflection was at a premium for several minutes, then

Ben said: 'War is Hell, Mr Wilks. It takes our young men from us and sends them back crippled.'

'It's all wrong,' said Mr Wilks, bitterly brushing ash from his shirt-front.

Ben moved up the bed until he was a foot away from the paper-seller, stared at him levelly for several seconds and then at length nodded in satisfaction. 'You'll do, Mr Wilks. British, resourceful, discreet, plucky.' He rested a hand briefly on the Wilks shoulder and leaned forward. 'You know, Mr Wilks, today we're still fighting for the same values. The same cause in which you gave your lower leg. Now I don't have to tell you who we're fighting or why——'

'Communism. Democracy.' The tenderpad of the freedom-loving nations rang loudly in the sleeping house.

'Hush, man,' hushed Ben and rose to peer both ways up the corridor before rejoining his companion. 'Yes, I can see you've done your homework. I don't have to dot the i's or cross the t's for you about the cold war and espionage and all that. YOU know. That's why you've been chosen. I can't tell you who you'll be working for, but I can say that Her Majesty's Government will not be—shall we say—ungrateful.'

Mr Wilks brandished his winking eye, thrust his tongue into unshaven cheek and prodded his elbow into Ben's ribs: the point was fairly taken. And even as he sheathed these signals, Mr Wilks unfocused into an oak-panelled study of approximately ten foot by twelve. The speaker, tall, straight, still a fine figure, stood absently toasting his seat at the fire through parted tails. His clipped hair and moustache re-echoed the expensive gleam of cutlery, candelabra, crossed assegais on the wall. The only man for the job, almost a boy really, languidly lounged in the deep leather chair and swirled his firelit port in a crystal goblet. It was, of course, a pose. His red Saxon ears missed nothing, noted every nuance, inflexion in Intelligence's voice.

'I'm going under cover for a bit. They've got onto this

address. God knows where the leak is but we're working on that now. You see, in this game a word here, a nod there and the whole thing is shot to hell. Of course, I don't have to tell you that—you know how to keep your eyes open and your mouth shut. You are ideally placed to keep observation on this house, who comes to visit, who comes asking for me—anything at all that strikes you as suspicious. And remember! They may come disguised as policemen or vicars or even sporting assumed voices—whatever it is, I want to know. Which brings me to this.' Intelligence took a large, plain manila envelope out of an official-looking briefcase, and the young subaltern caught sight of the two blue circles on his wrist. His very blue eyes momentarily came to life with sardonic amusement.

'Lost your watch?'

Their eyes met, locked, British eye to British eye fairly matched in mutual divination, before Intelligence conceded the ghost of a twinkle.

'Now listen carefully—in here you'll find your story. Memorize it then destroy it—eat it, burn it, but get rid of it. Stick to that story through thick and thin if you're questioned. Understood? Good.' Intelligence rose and placed the envelope with deceptive casualness under a sculling trophy which often did duty as a rinsed shrimp-paste pot for collarstuds and barely franked stamps. 'If they do question you, show a bit of difficulty remembering. Let it come out bit by bit.'

'The old realism,' interjected the slim young subaltern, 'Blazer' Wilks to his cronies in the Ninth.

'Exactly.' Just the flicker of respect in that bronzed, leonine face and it was back to business. 'In this smaller envelope you'll find a locker key with a numbered disc attached to it. It opens locker 14 at the railway station. Not the lockers by the entrance but those over by the Loo. Now I want you to inspect that locker tomorrow afternoon. There may be nothing there and there may be a suitcase. If there is a suitcase, I want you to take it down to the old pier and sink it. Make sure it goes down. Go out to the end where it's deep. No one is to see you or follow you. Got it? Good man. If I want to contact you further I shall leave a note in the suitcase. Now we'd better use a code. Let me think. Do you know the Elementary Cipher "D": Number Substitution?'

'I do.' There was nothing languid in the crisp reply.

Intelligence vouchsafed a hint of amazement.

'The deuce you do! Good man. Now, number six: expenses. Here's a fiver for now—more if you need it. Don't look like that man—we don't expect you to risk your life for nothing! I know you don't expect reward for doing your duty but this is a little beyond that. You know the official joke—patriotism is not enough?'

'I've heard that somewhere,' frowned Mr Wilks.

'Can we count on you?'

'You can count on me sir.'

A great deal of manly feeling went tacitly into that handshake.

'Still favour the right pin I see,' said the voice that kept Mr Wilks from his sleep. The agent had gone but he couldn't seem to relax and he could feel his body trembling with excitement under the curtain.

'Silly thing really,' the drawling young voice said. 'Crocked it on a Bosch ranker's throat in the hand to hand at Mons.'

And the voices fell silent at last. Mr Wilks had one more thing to do. Pushing back the curtain, he worked himself painfully off the mattress and stood, one hand against the wall for balance. His flannel shirt hung to his knees and below, his single leg shone pallid in the moonlight. He looked like a banner. He seated himself at the table and inspected the wooden leg. It was the National Health model, the Speedlite Special with the hinged stride action. The rubber tip was worn thin. With a fishknife he prised it off, replacing it with a new instantfix tip from a box in the drawer. Then he oiled the hinge.

11

The door opened on John and her eager, nervous smile faded. 'Power cut?' said John, wryly according himself full Turd Status with clasp and ribbons. 'I'm sorry it's only me. I'm always sorry its only me.' He closed the door. 'Drab dependable John, tweedy poke agog with goodies for urchins and mangy dogs. Can I come in?'

'You are in,' said Carol and sat in her scarlet rocking chair in a despondent slouch. She was wearing her very big deal dress and gnawing a fingernail. John noticed that she was now wearing a man's wristwatch.

'Expecting someone?' A comment rather than a question.

'What makes you say that?' Her voice was formal, embattled; she didn't look at him.

'Manwise he opined the laird at least from the fluttering embonpoint of her....'

'Oh for God's sake shut up!' She flung a furious glance at him to establish his range and her voice rose to assault him.

'What business is it of yours? I don't want you making everything cheap with your stupid comments. If you've got something to say, say it and get out!'

In the silence that followed this outburst John grasped the doorknob and waited for hurt pride and dignity to sweep him headlong through the door. Nothing happened. Spontaneous reactions, he reflected, were what he notably lacked: if you were waiting for the quick to be stung or even a good bridle, it was best to bring a packed lunch. He held his breath and watched, as he had known he would watch, the gap between them silently widening, the congealing of possibilities. Every detail of the scene lay separately and graphically on his retina as in, already, memory;

dark hair falling, eyelids squeezed shut, the whitening tendons of the hand on the red wings of the chair; the chair held at the extremity of its backward flight. He could not close the door behind him on that arrested movement, tension pent unreleased, releasing like a joyful breath on his departure. A moment to stay the hand of the beadiest suicide.

Then he spoke: '"Oh Carrie, Carrie. In your rocking chair by your window dreaming, shall you long alone. In your rocking chair by the window shall you dream such happiness as you may never feel".'

Carol began to cry.

He knelt before her and she crumpled toward him. But the chair swooped forward at last and their heads clopped together in painful cerebro-cannon. John had to cork his ouch and dared not stop stroking and patting the heaving shoulders to touch the aching lump over his eye. She must have felt it! He felt a twinge of annoyance at her single-mindedness. Why couldn't he cry like this, drowning in it, sloshing about in it, undistractably distraught? How bloody lucky she was to have these special orifices to evacuate grief; he only got things in his.

'I'm so sorry, John,' she sobbed. 'Boohoo, I was being a bitch.'

'No no no—of course not—not at all,' and he used the conversation as a cover because the mechanics, the commonplace grunts and fulcrums of lifting her to her feet must not disturb her remorse. Over her head he scanned the bookshelves for the books he had lent her, but they were too far off and presented only a fence of penguin orange with a wobbly white band. She had probably left them in some bee-loud arbour. Carol lifted her face from his damp shirtfront, the second she had wet for him in a week. Her mascara, lonely cosmetic, had blotched around her eyes like a silent screen vamp's.

'John, why did you say that about dreaming by my window?'

'I just said it.'

'You must have meant something.'

'I suppose I intended it rather as a sort of compassionate revelation of the depths of ordinary men and women in all their frailty and humanity with the compassionate scalpel of the artist. That really.'

'It was very beautiful,' she said reverently. She patted his chest in a sort of attaboy gesture and went to clean up. John watched her walk into the kitchen. The line of her panties beneath her dress rose and fell rhythmically like seagull's wings against the cumulus of her buttocks. Thought John, this is the life, sitting in her chair, head nobly sculpted against the cold morning light.

'I like your dress,' he shouted above the splashing tap.

'Do you?'

'You look like a china Dresden doll. In your pretty skinny frock.'

Carol emerged looking shiny and scrubbed. She pinched the fabric of the skirt and held it away from her the better to appreciate it. She frowned: 'You don't think it's a bit too. . . ?'

'Emphatically not. If it were a fraction shorter the whole effect would be frankly frivolous. And of course you score heavily with the backs of your knees.'

Carol turned away from him to look down over her shoulder at her back view. She threw her weight on one hip, then the other.

'Yes, but John, don't you think perhaps it's a bit. . . ?'

'Daring? I should think not! It hints at contours beneath but that's all right. Hinting is O.K. And it doesn't hint more in one place than another—ideal for a first date, you know. Well, I'm keen on Ornette Coleman and Jean-Luc Godard and Axel Oxenstierna and I have a nice body in general. That sort of dress. Like selling you've got lots of interests. No-one could take umbrage at that—even Our Lord said This is my body, and nobody thought He was being over-salty. Now a heavily localized hint is a very different matter. If you drew those street signs—you know the pointing hand on a cuff—This Way, Up Here—on your dress all converging on your parts like a magnetic field and tried to pass it off as Pop or Op you'd get run in. Well, the point I'm making here is—Christ where did I put it—yes, that would be too daring.'

'You know I wonder about you, John. Sometimes I really think you're crackers.'

'Oh yes,' he said, remembering, 'I took your books back. The librarian was very stroppy with me.'

Carol came over to him and smiling felt his brow. Her fingers faintly smelled of some pampering soapbrand.

'Do you write that old tripe in exams?'

'Only the names are changed.'

'And do you pass?'

'You're joking! Of course I pass. I'm the only truly literate person I know.'

Carol went and got a hairbrush and began to reduce her hair to order. She stood in the mathematical centre of the room tilting her head this way and that as she brushed. John did not tie himself to the mast, but he watched enthralled. Then she stopped and folded her hands together in front of her. John noticed that there was no visual distractions within yards of her slim, solitary figure; it had to be confession time.

'John,' she said. 'I think I'm in love.'

John looked at the hairbrush in her still hands. He thought it resembled a dead centipede, back down, myriad legs aloft. 'And aren't you happy?' he asked.

'Frightened,' she said.

Sits, he thought. Squire closeted, snickers in dusty lust. Carol sat on the edge of the bed.

'Frightened that it won't work?' he asked.

'Frightened because I can't recognize myself in it. I didn't know that I was capable of this sort of feeling. It's. . . .' She broke off to stare into space. 'It's as if I were born anew—born with no outer skin so that——'

'Sloughed it off,' John suggested.

'Yes.' Her whole face implored his understanding. He did some nodding. 'Can you understand that John?'

'Intellectually.'

'But you've never had this feeling yourself?'

'No,' said the giant brain on a trolley, sci-fi hit of the '60s. She twiddled the brush. 'How can I explain it? It's like a new colour. One that no-one had ever imagined before—a colour as pure as red or blue but without a name.'

'And you can't relate to it?'

'It blinds me, John. I lose myself in it. There's no me left to relate.'

'Hmm,' said John. He was beginning to feel the strain. The whole conversation was like trying to sew a button on a fart. What had happened to the bloke in all this sloughing and colouring? John knew that she could wax post-coital over Grannie Smiths, so he probed for the catalyst.

'Does this colour come to you strongest with the lights out?' He retreated quickly. 'I mean with your eyes closed?'

Carol covered her face with her hands. 'You've got me all confused. Colours. No, not colours—that was just an example. I was trying to make you understand the feeling.

John's overloaded brain tipped into inhibition. 'Perhaps he's coloured? The man?' he said, then wildly, 'I mean—is he English, this chap. Does he love you... ?'

'You think it's funny!'

'No no! Does he love you is what I—it's not funny—I want you to be happy——' he jumped up to prove it—'I'm not making fun, taking the—I'm not jealous—I didn't hope—Oh I know I'm a failure——' he flurried on horribly conscious that he had introduced the fustian theme of *their* relationship which had obviously not occurred to her. He seized her hands and the hairbrush. 'Carol, I know I have no claim on you—we're still friends aren't we? Look, just say the word and I'll go—you say. I'll do whatever you want. I can't go smaller than that or I'll disappear.'

Carol clicked into place. She patted his head, changing it to a ruffle between equals as she realized her omission.

'Don't let's talk about it any more,' she said with a sad smile.

'Change the subject,' said John.

'Yes.'

'Can I have my books back?'

'Oh yes. They're on the shelf.'

Poor John, she thought. The very last person in the world to be telling about her love. How could she be so tactless? She looked at his familiar bulk, his large red hands slowly preoccupied among the bookshelves, the back of his neck shaggily intent and unmoving. Oh God, how much simpler it would all be if she could love him and not this strange frightening—Ben. Did she love Ben? Was it love? In the car, that. . . . No name. It was all confused. Did she feel what she felt for him or for herself, her own body awakening? Narcissus in thrall to the silvered fishlimbs spreading. . . . She might never see him again. The thought was pain to her.

'I want you to take me to the seaside,' she said suddenly.

John's hand retrieving stopped in the air, body turning in the slow series of amaze.

'It's winter,' he said, recalling his wideranging oaths of abnegation even as he spoke. 'Well, March.'

'Nevertheless,' she said in a final manner.

Eyebrows haughty, she drew chinky sticks at eyelids' end with a tiny paint brush.

So they went to the seaside. Laden with sixteen books in two carrier bags he ran heavily after her to the railway station, eyes intent as a lepidopterist's on the fluttering rim beneath the thin blue dress.

'But Carol,' he said in the empty compartment.

'Read your books,' was all that she would say. John gave up and began sorting through the books. He remembered lending her *Sister Carrie*; it wasn't among the pile in his lap. She certainly hadn't read that. He thought of all his lovely books, of all the ones she must have lost on buses, on trains, in cloakrooms, woods and beaches; all the wonderful lives he had lived now roaring up and down the country, set at naught by nosepickers, sold by the yard to dealers, freighted, thrust up bottoms in God knows what barbarian emergency: lost.

'Where's my *Sister Carrie* then?' His eyes were accusing.

Carol only smiled at the sliding grey landscape through the window, her face, as in her thoughts, imposed between her contemplation and its subject.

On the pier the wind was biting. John removed his U.S. issue combat jacket and put it around her shoulders. Then he flailed at himself in ostentatious martyrdom, but she refused to notice.

'Look at the waves!' she cried and tripped down the stone steps. Behind her back he stabbed the air viciously with two fingers but the gesture got snarled up amid the painful string of the carrier. He was glad to huddle in the shelter of a breakwater, the bags splayed out beside him like the udders of a floating cow. He presented a blank profile to the cold flinty pebbles and grey seas. She was off somewhere enjoying some attic bloody muse while he froze. What did she care if he did freeze, dropped dead, pined to death for his books? Rhetorical—strictly rhetorical. A robot was all she wanted, an obedient robot programmed to buzz encouragement to her hermaphroditic drivellings; to dissipate his voltage glowing empathetically at the mouldy waves. Right! He was a robot. He tried to get a tell-tale twitch going in his jaw, but it was sunk with all hands in the general chattering of his teeth.

'John. Help me down please.' Carol wobbled along the slimy edge of the breakwater, her shoes dangling from her hand, arms outflung. His khaki jacket was much too big for her, hung vacantly from her shoulders, the epaulets like handles on her upper arm. Her whole demeanour begged his protection, offered her frailty to him to cherish, him Tarzan, me Jane. He glared at the wet splash marks on his jacket and clanked towards her, arms whirring into position. Carol concentrated on his strong grip about her waist, the warm red hands making a delicious cocktail with the wet contact of the pebbles on her bare soles. Half a mile from this spot she knew the car had come to its momentous halt. She tilted her face up for his kiss.

'Got a pain?' said John, sitting down again between his bags. Carol opened her eyes again.

'How can you be so petty? What is the matter with you? You've done nothing but mope all afternoon—I don't know why you came.'

John was just ready for this.

'I'm being petty because I am petty. I thought you were ape about natural unaffected behaviour. Next, nothing's the matter with me except that I'm cold unto death because you have my nice warm jacket and my fingers are all strangled from the string handles of these bags. Should be more painful, ought to be painfuller still only you lost at least half my books including one hard-back. Next, I have not merely moped. I have shivered and I have reflected. To take a random example—why you should want me to kiss you when you can see I'm still the same humdrum pink I was before you met this psychedelic colour dispenser. Last, I don't know why I came either.'

'Good job you're such a masochist,' said Carol laughing down at him.

'Blessed is the lamb,' he replied, crosslegged and slowly bowing to indicate the lasting and worthwhile in a world of hectic kicks. Carol sat beside him and peered into his face.

'John—I want to hear the truth. Do you really worry about all those things—your books and so on?'

'Yes I do. I gnaw my mind down to the cuticle about all those trivial little things. Ashtrays was the worst. Now it's traffic.'

'Go on then.'

'Ashtrays?'

'Yes.' Carol rested her chin on her fists in the standard listening position and thought about something else. The beach was so different by day. Sad. Like the shards and embers after bonfire night? Not very good. The exact place must be under the sea. It was on sand and this was pebbles.

'Ashtrays caused me to give up smoking,' John arrestingly began. 'I was a twenty-a-day man and a feared Boss Recidivist. Air was too thin for fulfilling breathing—I could take it or leave it alone. Have you read *The Confessions of Zeno?*'

Carol nodded, wheels and flesh squealing in her head.

'I hadn't got what it took to be a real smoker. I lacked the hell-raising quality of the real smoker. I worried all the time. I used about 100 I.Q. units worrying about the ashtray. You see, it takes vast organizational skill to deploy an ashtray in a drawing-room so that you can flick without fear and read without distraction. You know your rocking chair? The hardest spot on earth to smoke in. You have to estimate motion, wind, slipstream and trajectory every time you tap your ash. It's like taking lighthousemen off in bad weather. Joseph's got it. He's the one real natural I know. He just never thinks about it. He scribbled one out on my knee in the pictures once....'

'I never knew you were so neurotic John. I couldn't be like that. It seems like such a waste of time.' Thus Carol doused the monologue.

'What else would I be doing?' said John.

It started to rain, the wind sloshing it down on them in squalls. John sprang up and stared wildly about him for shelter. Behind him ran low lumpy cliffs, homely as Flanders in the dissolving rain. A hundred yards away he saw a changing-hut.'

'Come on!' he shouted, clattering over the pebbles, a bag in each hand. A string handle pulled out of its limp wet socket and he scooped the splitting bag to his chest and ran on. When he reached the chained and padlocked door he jittered up and down in panic.

'You'll have to break the window,' said Carol.

John thought that was just typical. Didn't she realize that action submerged the self? Attracted the police, too.

'How do I do that then?'

'Punch it in or something—we've got to get in!'

He skipped up to the window and pushed at it with the sound bag. 'Blast. They're only paperbacks. See—if you'd only returned my hardb. . . .'

He stood at attention, eyes accusing under streaming fringe.

'Use a stone you fool—be quick!'

'Too much noise.'

'Oh God.'

'Burglars put treacle and brown paper over the pane and then it pushes out quietly in a lump,' John said.

'Really?' said Carol sarcastically. 'Now if you get out of the way and let me do it.'

'Oh,' said John. 'Right.' He thrust the two sodden bags into her arms and took a headlong running dive at the door. There was a rending crash as John and the door disappeared inside, the padlock and chain whirling after them like a bolas.

'Are you all right?' Carol tumbled books onto his heaving chest as she bent over his prostrate form.

'Did it make much noise?'

In the gloom she was laughing, her mirth disproportionate, wide mouth rushing at him noisily as if he were a meal. He lay still, watching her almost in fear of such excess. When she had finished she helped him into a sitting posture and began weakly butting his shoulder with her head, and laughing over-tired laughs as he had seen putty-necked three-year-olds do.

'Finished?' he asked icily.

'Oh John, don't be cross.' Another butt awarded. 'It was just so—so spectacular. No-one heard you—there's no-one around for miles.' She pushed herself up using his multiple bruising as a launching pad and stood looking at the rain through the splintered door-frame. She could smell the damp and the dust in the hut and felt somehow reassured. It was all so familiar, so right. The dim light from the shuttered window fluttered softly on her eyelids as she moved. Like a stick clattering along the railings of childhood, she thought, and remembered her notebook. She felt happier than she had done for a long time; then she remembered Ben. And all of her happiness, the clean cold wind, the rain outside their refuge, John himself, suddenly felt stale and confined. She would never write from a life of such contentments when the life itself was already pale nostalgia. And oh God, must Ben be the answer?

As she turned away from the window to John, John said, 'A sea-monster!'

Carol saw that he was holding up a large baggy rubber object. It had been lying in the corner.

'Let me see it.' She stretched out her hands.

'Wait till I blow it up for you.'

John sat crosslegged on the floor and inserted the nozzle in his mouth and started to blow. Knobs and carbuncles began to erupt from the flabby rubber, lines and circles of colour stretching into place until she saw that he had conjured up a silly seaside dragon. 'I feel like,' he panted, fingers pinching the valve, 'one of those fat cherubs at the top of maps.'

'Blow some more!' Carol cried.

He blew some more features into the monster. His temples throbbed with this act of creation, and he barely heard Carol announce that she and it were going for a swim. Opening his eyes at last, he found himself frankly facing a dark pubic forest. His face burned. He fumbled for light words to cover his perturbation, but the swollen monster, finding its valve unguarded, rushed windily out of its rubber prison and his urbanities were swept aside by racking coughs. By the time the fit had passed the startlingly mature emblem, the quarry of his Vilest Thoughts, had disappeared from view. His moist eyes darted about over the top of the diminished monster; his mouth by association or by chance, sought the nipple.

'Hurry up, John. Haven't you finished yet?' Standing on one foot with her back toward him, Carol glanced at the cowering shape behind the swelling dorsals. She was pleasantly aware of his scrutiny: she hugged herself appreciatively and smiled at him. 'You come in too—you're wet anyway.' She snatched the squeaking monster from him and was gone, bottom beautifully jouncing, quick-footed over the pebbles to the sea.

He could see her larking around in the shallows. The sea-monster bobbed up and down and made blundering rushes against her legs. He could appreciate its motivation, thinking, oh to feel the grip of those strong thighs along one's flanks, that brisk haircrackle on rubber back. He stole a glance at her scattered underwear on the floor. There was the lace border that made the ridge, a brief moment ago cloaking the mysterious forest. She had hidden nothing from him because she was only a woman and now he knew everything and everything was spoiled. In a little while he got up and started to undress.

'You look like the Bile Beans Girl,' he said, shivering at the water's edge and rummaging fluff from his navel.

'Get in! Get in!' Carol shouted. She slid off the monster's broad back to dissolve in pink fragments against the breakers. He stood watching the heaving seas and brooded upon his nudity as rain pelted on his head and shoulders. He wished he could be innocent. A buoyant bubbling Carol threw water into his face, seized his hands and dragged him into the waves. The cold made him frantic and his stumbling feet caught on a subterranean rock; sinking, he flailed at the waves and his flung hands struck her breasts, the sea-monster, a flotsam fish—he never knew which. When he surfaced he saw Carol riding the bucking steed against the crazily tilting horizon, one arm raised above her ragged hair. He swam towards her. The water was thick with seaweed that had torn away from the rocks, and he wriggled in revulsion as the cold fat rinds caught in his fingers. Plunging on through the waves with his powerful crawl he reduced the distance between them to a yard, but strain as he would the yard remained. He raised his head and stared across the rain-pocked surface at the laughing, gleeful rider.

'I can't—can't catch you!' he shouted.

Carol paddled the monster round in a circle towards him.

'Now try,' she said, and as his fingers touched the squealing wet sides of the sea-monster, he knew that he too had been caught.

Running blindly along the pier in the rain Carol cried because of what she had done. She would have given anything to undo her crime, to have the last ten minutes back again in which not to do it. His frightened face crumbled into a terrible anguish and her fingers had jerked away from his flesh. She had used him as she would an object, lugging him onto her with the sympathy of an irascible removals man, chafing boy scout-wise at his cold limp sex to kindle a performance that was over before she knew it had begun. She had proved to him that he was, as he had always said, admitting anything, really quite dead.

The wind plastered her wet dress against her running body. The station jerked up before her, offered nothing but flight. Let him forget her, forget her. She saw him curled into a whimpering ball on the floor of the hut, his arms hiding his face from her shocked pity. If he ever found out that it was on this beach she had. . . . The garden shed of her childhood swam nauseously before her eyes. Only at the station did she remember that her panties lay among the ruins of his pride in the beach hut, but purity of association spared her the significance of their juxtaposition amid the rubber and chains.

Ben waited for her in her room. Ben had it made.

PART THREE

I

On Thursday Dr Ostbahn knew suddenly, in the act of forking a strip of bacon into his mouth, that his obsession had entered a new phase. He had no tangible proof of this, yet he knew that somehow, though his relationship with Ben had returned to its outer form of silence, overnight, even as he fitfully slept, the gears had been slipped and the serrated edges of his fear locked in the new position.

As the knowledge struck him he dropped the fork onto the tablecloth and experienced a minor heart spasm. Mrs Ostbahn fumbled the cotton wool from the bottle and fed him two of his little white pills. 'You can't go in today dear. You must go and lie down and take it easy.' She stroked his hand, skin against skin, for solace: the Ostbahn beneath was untouchable, adamant. He donned the disreputable overcoat, the breadline hat and, groping for the spectacles in the pocket, breasted the icy winds of the city. Mrs Ostbahn watched him through the net curtains and when he was out of sight she cried because only a man in love with a young, passionate mistress acted as he had been acting.

The doctor did not go to his surgery, had not been there for two days, since his declaration—syndicated—of independence. Instead he walked to Ben's residence and took up his customary position opposite, standing foresquare to the house with a giant hoarding at the back of him like a mount. He wanted to be seen by his tormentor, seen as he saw himself—Nemesis—a daily and punctual rebuke; Ben would be forced to come crawling out of the house and negotiate before he, Ostbahn, told all. He had forgotten to remove his disguise. He stared fixedly at the windows, willing the curtains to twitch.

A few people walked past him on their way to a late clock-in, or an early shopping, who knows. Going somewhere. The newspaper man opposite watched him watching Ben's window. Time passed. A man poked threepence at the doctor and asked for the *Mail*. He stared at him wildly and the man went away: nothing made sense.

Two youths bounced past. 'Heard that Ostbahn yet?'

'That's bleedin' old stuff now. Course I have.'

'You're all mouth.'

'Who's all mouth?'

'You. Mouthy.'

The doctor's name hung in the air long after they had disappeared. The doctor no longer knew if his name had been spoken or, never absent, hung in the air of the city for pointing fingers: everything was possible. Violins rose in his chest and tears pricked his eyes behind his glasses. Couldn't Herod see that he was an old man? He was no use to him—he was finished. He pushed the glasses up off his nose, failed to notice the thick bundle of delivered papers under his arm, and wiped his eyes on blunt glove ends.

He slumped, frozen, into his leather surgery chair, and between his gloved hands emitted a harsh, shuddering breath. Yes, he would go to the police. He would give himself up. No more chances, no more waiting. At once. Now. He lifted his head. His troubled eye fell on the telephone. Surely it had been moved. For twenty years he had kept his phone at a precise and oblique angle to the desk pad so that he could jot his messages without moving his body. It had been moved an inch or more out of true. It couldn't have been the receptionist because....

Madness suddenly tilted at him as he saw it. In each concavity of the receiver, upsidedown and secured in place by strips of adhesive tape, hung an egg. The egg in the earpiece said, in licked indelible pencil: LADIES. BRING YOUR EGGS TO OSTBAHN. The egg in the mouthpiece, similarly wrought, said: OSTBAHN GOES TO WORK ON AN EGG.

The doctor's hand shot out and seized the receiver from the hook, releasing an empty, insect droning as he held it like an overturned jar of wasps. He stood up abruptly. He panted. He licked his lips.

He smiled. 'Now!' he said.

'Now,' he said.

'Now,' he said.

'Now,' he said. He laughed. He pulled open the drawer and felt for a knife. He cut the flex an inch from the receiver. He held it aloft and twisted it this way and that. He laughed at it. It was evidence.

He snatched up his briefcase and undid the straps. He laid the receiver very carefully on top of his instruments. He put the newspapers inside and he smoothed them. He closed the briefcase. He wrote in big letters on his pad: NOT OSTBAHN. He wrote it again on his desk. He wrote it again on the wall. It was biggest on the wall.

He knew it was behind him in the street but he just went faster. Nothing could stop him now. His coat spread out behind him. Once he stumbled and nearly fell. His glasses were shaken free from his nose and fell onto the pavement, but he didn't stop. It was close behind him now. At the corner he flung his head to the side to look. The street was a narrowing tube between walls; he could see right down it. Framed by the shoulders of two women and projecting above them like the sight on a rifle he could see him. He lifted the briefcase and shook it. 'Now!' he shouted. The figure didn't move.

The market place in front of the police station was filling up again and he plunged into waves of advancing and receding sound. People were everywhere in his path and he had to push. Bubbles of sound burst in his face with a bang and a rush of air. Soon he was treading the bubbles under his feet; they squeaked and tickled him and that made him giggle. His legs were bubbles now, now his arms. He let go of the briefcase. He could feel the air hissing into his chest, getting fuller, growing bigger, lighter, no weight at all; he WAS a balloon. He laughed as he felt his feet leave the ground, falling, falling upward, above them all, in the sky, above the noise. Two faint moons came towards him and the nearer they came the more indistinct they became. Bigger and bigger and he was swallowed up in them.

Ben pushed through the crowd around the fallen man. 'Stand back please. I'm a doctor,' he shouted, doctorlike behind Ostbahn's glasses. He knelt beside him among the split fruit and curly woodshavings on the concrete, undid the collar and slipped the tie down to get at his heart.

'My briefcase.' He lifted his head from the trembling chest to jerk a direction at a policeman. 'Over there.'

'Funny,' thought the policeman, hoarding a rich jest for the canteen. 'It's got nought nought on it. Licensed to kill. Very reassuring. Ho ho ho.' His finger rapped against his helmet. 'Here you are sir.' He forced a wider circle around the pair. Heads waved like anemones to get a better view; most of the stallholders, realizing they could not undercut this, brought their sandwiches over and made a lunchbreak of it. Ben opened the briefcase and peered in. It was hard to see what was inside through Ostbahn's glasses but he saw enough to flop the lid over his rummaging hand.

'It's all right constable. This man is a patient of mine. He's had a heart attack.'

'I'll phone for an ambulance, sir.'

'If you would.'

His hand came out of the briefcase holding a hypodermic syringe. He held it up to the light and saw that it was half full of some yellowish liquid. The crowd held its breath. He pushed the plunger, shooting a yellow stripe onto the concrete and then wiped the needle on his handkerchief. Ooh-Aah said the crowd as at fireworks, and watched the needle dimple then puncture the flesh at the neck, and deposit its killing air bubble into Dr Ostbahn's carotid artery.

When the evening edition hit the pavements Otto Ostbahn finally made it to the number one spot, not for his disc, or even for his laudable moral recovery; typically, he made it on his passivity; he had lain still under a hundred eyes while a killer slid two inches of hollow steel into him and let the daylight through.

The city police snapped into action. They were always thorough and this time maniacally thorough; the newspaper had given the jesting policeman celebrity coverage—after all, he had handed the killer his weapon. Within the hour they had Ben's description to a T. Height—average; build—average; eyes—blue; brown; black; glittery cat green; hair—yes; clothing—dark, average. Better, they had the killer's glasses—unusual and distinctive glasses, thick lenses in steel frames. By systematic investigation they were able to trace them to Dr Ostbahn. They did not find the briefcase and they did not find Ben. Both had disappeared long before the ambulance drove into the square to carry the dying, banderilla'd old balloon to the irrelevance of modern medicine.

2

At seven o'clock sharp Mr Wilks was at his pitch clad in his usual overcoat and beret, a thick khaki scarf wound about his neck against the cold. He felt ready for anything, despite a sleepless night. He had chosen his fastest shoe, a light construction of canvas and rubber and his wooden leg moved more easily for the oiling. If the action came thick and fast—well, he was the boyo.

Meanwhile, his mind on cut and thrust, he sorted his papers into handy ranks and made caches of various combinations of change. He spent a long time on his bulletins, worried for the first time that they did not look sufficiently genuine, sufficiently the work of a pukka paper-seller. Because today he wasn't. Today the whole set-up was a front. No good if passers-by rumbled him at once. He rubbed his fingertips in newsprint and smeared a bit of black around his mouth; newspapermen did lick their thumbs for riffling, he remembered. It would all be a sight more convincing if he had a kiosk, perhaps a big yellow one like the Frogs had.

He felt better after he had sold the first paper of the day. A bloke on a bike had bought the *Mirror* and cycled away without penetrating the disguise. Mr Wilks did a big turnover in *Mirrors* up to nine and then *Times* and *Telegraphs* after that. That was the pattern of things. No good getting aerated about it like that canvasser last week. Tall studenty geezer with a tatty beard had bought the *Morning Star* at midday, right out of phase of course. An argument had developed about the pattern of things in the paper-seller business but Mr Wilks had argued him flat: workers till nine, then the uppers. Natural Law.

Throughout the morning no-one penetrated Mr Wilks's

ensemble. By midday he'd sold most of the national dailies, had a cup of tea and was waiting for the early edition of the local paper. The street was flowing as usual, bits of conversation, averted accidents, the flash of traffic; all there for anyone with a taste for fragments. There was even a bonus today in the shape of rival electioneering vans, both equipped with loudspeakers, each discharging broadsides of raspberries and slogans as they passed on the road. A procession marched down the road, banners flying, everybody out of step but nevertheless calling out the time: Left! Left! Left! Sloppy bunch. Mr Wilks shook his head contemptuously and spat on the pavement when he saw that self-same scruffarse student at the head of the marchers shouting the odds and blowing on a whistle.

He watched the passing show with half an eye. Foremost in his mind was the Mission: he was thinking ahead. To the locker. To the wharf. Bombs like bowls fizzed in his thoughts. He cut the string on the evening bundle, waving absently to the van driver, placed the papers on his box beside a careful handful of change, and set off for the station.

He hadn't seen, had not had occasion to see, the inside of the railway station in fifty years, so that he stood in the entrance arch almost like a released lifer, conscious of eyes on him too, incredulously eyeing this incredibly altered prospect. The smoke had all gone and with it the memory of a foundry from which he had been flung, remade, passed over, hobbling on crutches on a raw, new, dead leg. Well, that was all a long time ago and leaves had grown on that leg. Fate, he reflected, was bringing him full circle. His country had called again and here he was, ready to embark.

He walked warily across the station parallel to the platforms, past the porters, past W. H. Smith's kiosk, the vendomat complex, up to the stack of key lockers. All right so far. No-one was watching him. Pretty muzak, released by aerosol into the atmosphere, was distinctly reassuring. Whistling along with the tune, he braced himself against the wall of tinlockers and felt for the key that Ben had given him.

Number 14 held, as promised, one small cheap fibre suitcase. He took it out. What he did next was capable of swelling his chest a year later, though his motive was no clearer. What he did was to spread the morning paper on the floor of the locker, lock the door and poke the key through the slot grille in the door. The key fell with a muffled sound onto the newspaper inside. He had executed it perfectly: it could be, perhaps, a sort of trademark—sang-froid with a flick-of-the-wrist. That would show 'em!

He bought a pennyworth of privacy in the subterranean Gents to satisfy his curiosity about the contents of the suitcase. Inside, he found a tape-recording and a Chalimeff set—moustache, goatee, eyebrows and a little tube of glue, all attached to the display card. On the card was written in Elementary Cipher 'D' the words 'Well Done'.

After reading the walls and door he left the closet and marched, canned Souza at his back, out of the station to complete Stage Two of his Mission.

The open car cruised slowly along keeping pace with Mr Wilks as he dot and carried breathlessly down the road. A fresh-faced young man in a sheepskin coat with a pretty rosette, prize bloodstock, stood up and, leaning his elbows on the wind-shield, looked carefully in every direction. It was all clear. The street, an unpopulated line of warehouses and scrapmetal yards, Mr Wilks the sole potwalloper in view. A bit of ragging would be quite in order. He lifted the megaphone to his curly lips: 'Sir, would you sin against Nature? No, of course you wouldn't. Would you repudiate the aristocratic principle of Nature, the eternal principle of force and energy, for mere numerical mass and its dead, dreary weight? No, of course you wouldn't.'

The driver and the girl with leaflets began to laugh. Nigel had a bloody good sense of humour. Bloody funny.

'Sir, would you deny the individual worth of the human personality? Raze—with a Z, sir—the very foundations of human existence and human civilization? You don't look like that sort of a chap to me, sir. Monstrous do you say? Indeed it is. But that is what the Socialists are asking you to do.'

Mr Wilks hurried faster, looking rigidly to the front. The last thing he wanted was to be followed, picked out in a spotlight of noise and attention. Not today, thank you. His ancient heart thumped painfully against his ribs.

'We've all heard them. Smash your Monarchy—smash your Church—smash your Public Schools. There's nothing they wouldn't drag in the mud. Are they worthy to belong to a great people? What do you say, sir? They call themselves Intellectuals. I don't know what that means. You don't know what that means. But we both know that Intellectuals make a Bish of things.' The candidate shifted his position to include the occupants of the car more fully in the joke. He stood up very straight and held one finger horizontally under his nose. His voice became raucous and bawling. 'We healthy people instinctively close our ranks against these Intellectuals and they run this way and that like hens in a poultry yard. That's Instinct not Argument. We are a Great People—God-willed and Blood conditioned. Our collective egoism is sacred. Are we going to tolerate these polluters of Blood, these deniers of Race?'

'No!' and 'Certainly not!' chorused from the car. The girl sang out: 'Hurrah for Smithy!' and then gave a nervous laugh.

'The socialist is the ferment of decomposition in a People! He is a pygmy who imagines he can stop with a few phrases the gigantic renewal of our People's Life. Shopkeepers and pacifists—they are insignificant little people, submissive as dogs and they sweat with embarrassment when you talk to them!'

He raised his clenched fist in the air like a hammer. His voice grated metallically through the megaphone. 'The long-haired socialist youth lies in wait for hours on end satanically glaring at our clean white Womanhood. He plans to adulterate her Blood with repulsive crooked legged black bastards! Who brought the blacks here? The ruck—spawn—scum, swarm of the jungles brought here to bastardise our Race? The socialists! They are paralyzing our Will to fight!' Flecks of spittle hung from his chin but he made no move to wipe them away.

'Don't overdo it, Nigel,' said the driver, exchanging anxious glances with the girl. The candidate was overdoing it a bit. One had to be a bit more circumspect about things nowadays. Of course, it had been a long hard grind and the candidate had not stinted himself, sleeping in hotels, eating at cafes, talking with anyone. No doubt that awful Bell type had taken his toll on the candidate's patience. They were rather relieved when Mr Wilks turned off into a sidestreet leading to the wharves, the way blocked to traffic by erect sunken cannons.

'Set your souls aflame!' screamed the candidate to blank walls. Frightened, the girl stood up and tugged at his coat. Above his upheld fist the sky streamed black with wheeling gulls. He would not be moved. 'A torrent of fire bursts forth as from a furnace and a Will of Steel is forged! A people hard as iron! When they cast in our teeth our intolerance we proudly acknowledge it. Ours is the Standard that dispenses with all others. One Will must dominate! One Discipline must weld Us together! As the magnet attracts steel splinters, so does Our Party attract the Strong, the Pure, the Unpolluted! It is my unalterable Will. . . .'

The car disappeared from view bearing the upright candidate into oblivion.

Mr Wilks looked down into the dirty water at the rising bubbles of Dr Ostbahn's vocal remains. He heaved a great sigh of relief.

3

She started off with love but it became something indefinable. She could see that his was a tortured flame and that attracted her. She could always feel his eyes on her wherever she moved in the flat; he needed her. Not a courtier's eyes but the eyes almost of a guard. In those first days, hers reflected only the racing sky and the clouds. His need fleshed her slim legs and added pounds to her breasts and buttocks so that she saw herself as hills, as an oak tree, as the earth, about which his lightning played and spent itself, her sward his sheath. She remained at eight stone two, but she thought big. This was the love as therapy stage and it lasted two days.

In the mornings he searched the newspapers and she cooked his food. She didn't trouble him at all, initiated nothing, accepted everything and let the remaining bubbles of her independence surface and dissolve. Whatever trouble he was in she felt loomingly as something of blood and honour like a Theban tragedy, but she never asked him about it.

Ben finished eating his breakfast, wiped his mouth and said: 'Why do you always speak between commas?'

She smiled at him, ready to play.

'I don't understand—I quote too much?'

'Think about it.' He just sat and waited.

'You mean that I always speak second-hand sentences from books?' Carol put her elbows on the table and searched his face for encouragement, showing with her smile her readiness to admit other viewpoints and any stones he cared to throw. 'Well, it seems to me that books are relevant to me, to my situation. The truly great writers will always be relevant in every age. Human—um—human nature is unchanging and this is what the novelist portrays. The novel is a distillation of wisdom and observation. . . .' She found it hard to go on. It was difficult to know how much he knew; whether this wasn't insultingly basic.

'Or perhaps you mean—yes, like John, that one is restricted by physical confines. Your commas of course. That one's Self is trapped within the confines of one's body. Kafka and so on. I'll quote for you—"Love has pitched his palace in the place of excrement"—something like that. I don't think that. That sort of thing seems to me a sickness. It's very sterile you know, books where the hero is always squeezing boils and glaring at his hands. Well, did you mean that sort of thing?'

'I'm just putting the coin in,' he said and laughed when she jumped up.

She wanted to slap his silly triumphant face but instead she began clattering the dirty plates together.

'Playing God are you?' she acidly said and scraped a shrill knife at the rinds and tomato skins. She had turned half away from him and didn't know he had moved until she felt his body suddenly up tight against her back. She tried to push him away but he had her wrists imprisoned, her palms flat on the greasy plates, her body pushed forward over the table. It began as a rape; she would never have chosen the moment or the position. It initiated the end of the love as therapy phase and the beginning of the more complicated phase. The real change occurred as he forced his way, slick now from the proper channels, past the prissy knot of the sphincter and into irredeemable impropriety.

From now on it seemed to her that he stopped the sun in its tracks and ruptured the full-bellied moon, her motor, enthroning in their place the gravitational tyranny of the bed. Her room became a prison and her body kept her there, hooked by a tab of thin cartilege like a hung garment, to the edge of some mortal, vertiginous free-fall. She burned with shame and she continued to feed the flames.

'Ben?' she said timidly, conscious of repetition, 'could we go out—just for a walk?'

'What's with you?' he said.

'I feel so stale stuck indoors all day. I need some fresh air.'

'Me, I like trusty old air best.' He looked away from her and yawned, stretching his arms above his head like a broken catapult. The morning editions lay around his chair in a disorderly heap. He wore only his socks and a new wristwatch, identical in every chromium detail to the one he had given Carol. 'So open a window,' he said at last.

Carol stared listlessly out of the window. She scratched at the back of her hand and then examined the marks.

Ben looked at his watch. 'Bedtime already!' he said in a surprised tone. 'Get your clothes off.' He got up and switched on the light. It was midday.

Carol could never get him to set foot outside the house while it was light, but he didn't actually prevent her from going out. One afternoon she set off for a walk in the park but she had to return within half an hour because she was exhausted and frightened. Everybody she passed had seemed unreal, alien; not alien as John had seemed, but actually physically alien as if they were made of something else. Then it occurred to her that it was she who had become alien, cutting herself off from them by her depravity. Only her room behind drawn curtains offered her sanctuary. Only there, with Ben, was her secret safe.

'Visual agnosia baby,' said Ben. 'Very sterile, like squeezing boils or glaring at your hands.'

After that she confined her journeys to the supermarket up the road which stayed open till late, filling her undyed hessian bag with polythene wrapped from the refrigerated interior. At eleven p.m. Ben turned his attention to the night and took that apart.

'Go get the car,' he said, tossing her the keys.

He had taught her to drive the huge convertible, not well but well enough to drive it from the all-night parking lot to the house, stopping to get the tank filled on the way. Outside the house she had to toot once on the horn and then move over quickly for the swift silent shadow that hit the driver's seat and wrenched the car from the kerb in one blurred movement. He always drove very fast and very carelessly and it seemed to her that he was indestructible. There was never much conversation. Going out for Ben meant swapping a stationary box for a moving one.

'This do you?' he would ask, jerking his head at barely discernible fields.

'No, let's go on a bit.' She could say that and he would drive on patiently until she saw what she wanted. He was not so much considerate as interested in the ritual. Apart from her freedom to choose, her choice meant nothing in itself because the entire countryside looked the same in the dark. They both knew that. This was her hour of exercise. When she had chosen, he would pull the car back off the road and turn off the lights.

'O.K. See you soon. Be good.'

The door would open and she would feel his kiss chill on her cheek in the night air as her feet moved over frosted unseen furrows. Carol loved this hour of silence and solitude and she hoarded it throughout the day, his day that fed on hers, as abjection hoards the promise of sleep. This was her hour. In this hour she could call the shots as capriciously as she wanted because it was the sole exercise of her franchise, the last of herself. The world was simplified into two equal bands of darkness, the lower one on which she walked black and invisible, and above it, separated by a horizontal line that was really the curve of a circle too vast to imagine, stretched the faintly paler vault of the sky. Sometimes she walked towards an objective, the black pole of a tree, a steeple, and sometimes she just walked until her watch told her she had come half-way. In this hour she tried to make her mind a blank, to purge her mind of him and just exist. She never obtained relief however, because Ben, the Ben that she loved, presented no separate identity.

The heaviest burden of him was in her senses: he was her.

At exactly the half-hour, turning back, she would see a tiny red light explode silently in the darkness, a point without depth or context, illuminating nothing yet drawing her in faith ever nearer to it like a sleepwalker. When she reached the car Ben would stare at her for a long moment and then as completely return to the obsession of endlessly unrolling tarmac. Carol, at this furthest point from her freedom, knew that without this hour she would leave him. And he must have known it. He never mocked at it or turned it into a game. It was his only defeat.

Every night they would cover three hundred miles, returning always before dawn when she would drop him at the house and return the car to the parking lot. As she walked back to the house, her blood seemed to drone in her veins and her eyes had the rigid, neutral quality of headlights. It became an unvarying routine each night, every road, merging in memory into one. Only once did he stop the car, abruptly, shockingly, and she felt his hands seize her shoulders.

'Shall we stay here?' His eyes bored into hers.

She was stunned. She didn't know if this was one of his painful jokes and she didn't know how to reply. The windscreen wipers hissed over the wet stone-coloured glass. They were a mile from some anonymous market town, three counties from where they had begun.

'I don't know what you want me to say.'

He didn't reply. She could feel a terrifying rigid tension in him, willing her to speak but she could not understand what he wanted from her.

'You know I'll do whatever you want Ben.'

When he spoke she knew that she had failed him, his voice hard and casual because of her equivocation.

'I wanted you to make your choice. It was up for grabs.'

He turned away.

'But why here?'

'Because it's elsewhere is why.'

'Yes but so is everywhere—everywhere we aren't living now.' She tried to make a game of it and then in desperation made to touch his shoulder.

'Ha ha laughs aplenty,' he said swinging the car round in the road and keeping the needle at eighty all the way home.

And all the next day he drowned her every word with a furious static of crude and unfunny jokes, introducing each one with a nudge in the ribs and a yelped 'Have you heard this one then?' Carol bore his revenge stoically, ironed his shirts, cooked his dinner and tried to initiate burgeoning and bright topics of conversation. By mid-afternoon she was exhausted. She felt as if she had just spent a week trying to direct a very colour-conscious Nigerian through labyrinthine suburbs to an impossibly pronounced destination. She went into the bathroom to escape the grinding fun.

She leaned over the communal sink and stared at her face in the mirror. She looked terrible. In just a few days her wistful melancholy, the asset that had set the boys waving their hats, had become a poverty of all expression, leaden, inanimate. Love didn't agree with her. In the webbed glass her face looked yellow, shining faintly with the greasy patina of sleeplessness. The area around her eyes appeared bruised. Resting the heels of her hands on the cold porcelain sink, she leaned forward until her nose touched the glass, and watched herself cry. But not depraved? Surely she didn't look depraved? Could she have experienced all this, the sore, wracking obscenities that her body forced her to, and yet not show it on her face?

And yet look no more damned than an insomniac.

John's words came into her head, a handful among so many empty, amusing torrents, spoken she remembered, in her room, now hers no longer and scoured of all former association as one scours an instrument of surgery. 'Snapping green eyes are your portion.' But now she cried.

Ben stood beside the open drawer of her writing desk, a sheaf of paper in his hand.

'Did you write this?' he demanded, tapping it with the back of his hand. 'This cleave and yearn jazz?'

She nodded, incapable of defending herself.

Without haste or anger he tore the paper across, tearing it again and again until it lay in a random mosaic on the floor. Then he stood still to watch what she would do. Carol felt nothing. It seemed inevitable, right, the action suited to the hands. She was him: she said nothing.

'Nobody sucks me like an orange. That crap sells me short, baby. Short by a million miles. I'm bigger than you know. So don't try to trap me with your shit scribblings.'

Carol stood very quietly and looked at him. He was cracking up. It was suddenly very clear to her that Ben was a man falling from a great height, conscious only of his damnation and resolved that his death should shatter the earth. She knew too that her silence had won her a great victory.

'Get on the bed,' he shouted. 'And leave the door open.'

'No Ben. You can do what you like to me but not with the door open.'

They stared at each other across the length of the room. It was the first time she had opposed him in anything.

Carol lying on the unmade bed, a blanket loose over her legs. Pushing back her hair because it irritated on her hot skin. 'I can't sleep. I can't just go to sleep like you do. Perhaps it's the light.' She lifted a flaccid arm to shield her eyes from the five p.m. light bulb.

'Poor little baby,' he said. He placed his thumbs very gently on her eyelids and gently stroked the quivering skin.

'My eyes have been hurting me,' she said in a little girl voice.

'Poor eyes,' Ben said, 'so tired, so sore. Ben stroke them.' He increased the pressure of his thumbs, denting her darkness until a spectrum of dazzling colours burst into splinters behind her eyes.

'Make me a new colour, Ben,' she murmured, lying there still and acquiescent for his magic.

'I will if you tell me a secret.'

'I don't know any secrets. I can make one up if you like.'

'I don't want you to make one up. I want you to tell me the secret about you and John.'

'That's a sad secret. You don't want to hear that.'

'What happened that day when I moved in with you baby. That's what I want to hear.'

'There's a bee under my eyelid. Did you know that? It's a bit of a quote.' Carol was very near to sleep now. 'The bee is a secret.'

'Colours baby—do you see them? Pretty colours, beautiful colours for my baby's eyes. All the jewels and rainbows and catherine wheels in the world for my baby to play with. I'm making a new colour for you baby—it's coming true. I can turn the world for you. I can revolve galaxies under your eyelids.' He buried his mouth in her hair. Carol drowsily took his hand in hers and kissed it. He sat up carefully so as not to disturb her.

'Ben will give you something to help you.' He took a key from his suit in the wardrobe and unlocked his briefcase. He took out a syringe and held it up to the light. It was still empty from the last patient, an emergency job in the market place. In the kitchen he collected a glass of water and a spoon, then he carefully tipped a little white powder out of a bottle in the briefcase.

'I'm nearly asleep now darling,' Carol murmured, her voice already blurred.

Ben sat beside her on the bed and placed his hand on the curve of her hip. He had hidden the key to the briefcase where even frantic fingers would not find it. He held the loaded spike in his free hand.

'This stuff is the greatest for dreams,' he said, smiling kindly. 'Strong on new colours too they tell me. Now that little secret bee may give you a little sting, but that won't worry my baby.'

'How much will you do for it?' he asked, his eyes on the streaming road.

Carol clutched his arm and said: 'Anything you want. You say.' It wasn't really bad yet but she could feel something blindly stirring in her dark.

'You know something baby? You've really come out of your shell since I've known you. You're a really switched on Sixties Romantic now.'

'I want it!' Her voice came out loud, surprising the little bit of her that was still capable of a mild thing like surprise.

'I don't think you should be too reliant on it,' he said and pursed up his mouth in a considering gesture. He slowed the car. 'This looks like a nice spot for a walk. What do you say?'

'Yes, all right. I don't care—anywhere.'

'No no.' He pushed his solicitude at her like a curled whip. 'I want you to get the best out of it. Suck it dry baby. Don't want to waste it. I keep you in all day so you just take your time about choosing.'

'This will do!' Carol was already opening the door. 'I don't care I tell you!'

She was gone only ten minutes, stumbling over the sharp mounds in the dark and cutting her knees and hands. She could not find the car again. She became hysterical when she couldn't see the bright red parking light and she started screaming. When at last she found it the doors were locked. Ben was invisible behind the steamy windows and she couldn't make him hear. Perhaps he had left her! Sobbing she fell to her knees in the road, her splayed fingers rushing shrilly down the cold wet glass.

'I'll do anything. I'll tell you the secret. I'll tell you!'

'You know best, dad,' Ben said into the receiver. 'You know the market—it's your turf.' He leaned back, craning his neck to look up the spiralling staircase. All the doors were shut. 'You name it—she'll do it. Yep, take my word.' He listened again and then said, 'I need the bread.'

A long pause. He frowned and began to wind the flex around his wrist. Under his jacket he held a gun gripped between his arm and his side.

'I said so, didn't I? And bring the money, see. Yes, she can cope—she's got great big eyes for it. Yeah, she's wearing me out. Yeah, beatnik number—skinny—long hair—very cute. She could be crazy.'

Finally, Ben repeated the address and rang off.

Later, Carol moaned as he moved inside her, levering her senses free. Sweat stood along her hairline and in the creases of her throat.

'I'm going to make you a big star,' he whispered.

4

John stood on deep carpeting and watched a horny Ruritanian princeling tear his ticket across, then hold the door open unceremoniously with mauve and gold-piped buttocks. Gorgeous stars looked down from gilt frames. Their breasts bore signatures artistic and personal like dropped string.

The usherette carved a bright path down the incline for his squeaking boots; he excused himself along the knees and sat down. His posture, because of his height, was that of a cellist. Knees splayed to each side and wedged under the ashtrays, perforce annexing sixpenn'orth of Lebensraum to east and to west. He tussled bonily for the armrests. The western neighbour appeased an inch at a time before John's inexorable advance and finally gave up, blotting a false cough to save face. The eastern neighbour dug in and held. Elbow waggled against elbow in the strain of deadlock. John switched his tactics to an attack on the eastern satellites. He fired a strategic toe up the arse of the man in front, coaxing him from grave to acute: east slumped more easterly to see: John captured the armrest.

Master, he retracted the back of his neck and tilted his face up to the warmth of the screen. In the cinema, and only there, he was a lion for his rights. Of the countless backdrops presented to him at birth only the cinema delighted; only there did he, veteran spectator, feel at home.

His fingers idly began peeling tiny torpedo rolls from his ticket. It was the adverts. He knew them by heart, anticipating each, yearning slightly ahead of the scheduled hunger, thirst and acquisitiveness. He bought nothing when the lights went up for intermission. He hated the lights. The audience sat revealed, horrible, pasty, screwing their faces backwards to stare at each other. Yobs bobbed down to the saleslady, whistling. John sat still and faced forward, correct and orthodox, and waited for the main feature.

It was from this screen just three weeks ago that he had learned of his father's death. It had appeared in fizzly writing on the film itself, a completely unbilled guest appearance.

WILL MR JENKINS PLEASE CALL AT THE MANAGERS OFFICE IMMEDIATELY.

He wondered now if the message had been erased, or was it perhaps even now travelling world circuits in 'The Left-Handed Gun', plucking a thousand Pakistani Jenkinses from their seats in converted nissen huts to dip pressed palms in the manager's office and break out their whites. Blenching black Kwame Jenkinses storm the Exit pushbar to munch deceased parts for strength and virility, sadly overriding owners protests. Cahier critics hail subtitle as pure alienation, a triumph of style. 'Ah, the common humanity of it all' he mused.

Bowelly architecture tastefully faded into a push-button twilight. The main feature began.

It was a British film with lots of heart, cautious French wobbles, and stolen freeze shots. John had hardly been out of the house for days so he tried to enjoy it. He concentrated like mad on the story, the acting, and the camera-work, but the Exit sign, the clock and the black cut-out bonse of the satellite in front offered strong competition. He tried spotting sources, his lips curling in the faintest sfumato of a sneer. It was hopeless. It was crap. He was not taken out of himself, but thrown back on his own thoughts. They were crap too.

Was he a pervert? Running nude into carwash tunnels to be flipped with chamois, prinked pink by rotating brushes, arm-pits gargled with needlespray? Not like that perhaps.

Worse.

People around and behind sighed at him as he vacated his seat, stooped in consideration for the Less Fortunate, wending a simian way to the Exit.

It had been raining. He remembered how Carol had once been depressed at missing a manifestation of the elements. Well, not quite that. They had emerged, he, Carol and Joseph, from the cinema into bright sunlight to find the pavements drying.

'So what,' said Joseph. 'Rain ain't much to watch.'

'When you've seen one raindrop you've seen them all,' he said, amplifying Joseph, gee-ing them both up.

'That's not what I meant,' she said. 'It makes me think of time lost—really lost—not assimilated into life. All this has happened and we didn't know.'

'We've made it irrelevant,' he had offered but there were no takers.

'You don't understand,' said Carol, and walked ahead.

Now John walked aimlessly down this same street listening to the voices from summer and laughter from the past and he wondered why he didn't give a damn. He had lost her at the seaside. Fat man sez I have lost my little willie. He stands in the sea. The wind is blowing up the channel today. It's great when you're in! Hairtrigger showdown: watch it sister or I'll drench ya knees!

He had come home from the seaside, self-destruction on his mind. Naturally not a new departure; rather, a new emphasis. He had always favoured a passive death, a spontaneous incombustion under the wet green sticks of his empty existence. Now he saw sharp edges and violent concussions. Walking, he saw himself stretched like a starfish on the window-ledge, a watery sun refracting his pyjamas into a striped numbus. The wind toyed with his ripcord. He nerved himself to jump. Off! In the air remembering that he had not left a note. Then changing it, kicking out, legs churning a bedroom slipper from his foot, employing the running-in-the-air method vindicated by Jesse Owens, the Black Auxilliary of the 1936 Berlin

Olympics, which won him the gold medal and set the Führer gnashing among the axminsters. And it carried him safely over the paving stones and into the rhubarb, his father's pride, tooth-roughening weed, jolting ankle-deep in stiff manure. Feeling how? Probably silly. Mr Plume weeding, straightening, not wanting to pry, great excitement on his face. Larf it off somehow. How? Morning. Reading Hedda Gabler. Overbalanced.

Have to go through his house—no front door key—to complete deadly purpose. Striped suicide ponders note in bedroom.

'IMBALANCE OF MIND DISTURBED'. Very good. Ho-Ho. Puts it. Pleased and proud. Not dead though.

John had taken to his bed for three days on a protracted blush-bat. That was at first, when death had seemed a serious proposition for a pervert. Then he had got up and dressed, putting on an old overcoat of his father's from the heap in his bedroom. His father had been some inches smaller but the coat went on. The cap, on the other hand, was enormous, like a great check table on his head. That was when he got the idea to try life at five foot five. Seen from his father's height, the house was a palace of material comforts; everything was to hand, spacious. And to five foot five six foot two was an affront, a haughty malcontent presenting nostril linings to every remark.

He had taken seventy pounds out of the insurance windfall and put it in his inside pocket, and as a final disguise before leaving the house he slipped on his sunglasses. He was lucky to get a taxi and he kept it waiting while he went into the gram. shop and bought, cash down, a gramophone and ten L.Ps. At the grocers he passed 20 pound notes over the counter with the request to keep food coming to number 23. He was safely home within thirty minutes.

He kept the disguise on, threatening the stitches in the overcoat with his exertions. Out went the T.V. and the radio, the chairs and the sideboard, splintering the door jamb and scratching the wallpaper. They made an impossible bottleneck in the hall. He did not dare go into the backyard because Mrs Plume was dawdling about with her washing, obviously crazy for chat. His impetus had slackened and he sat panting in the only chair, the one chair necessary for his new life, that was left in the front room. The sounds of a revolution shook the windows. The new gramophone was turned up beyond the numbers, playing the new music of Cecil Taylor. He had listened and the tears had rolled out from the sunglasses and down his cheeks.

The street lamps came on, blinking at first and then steady. John started whistling 'Round Midnight' but his timing was way off and his timbre monotonous. His crooked shadow jerked ahead, a metronome. The really depressing thing was that he no longer cared about any of it. Everything passes, happens outside, is like everything else. And that's a cliché.

He saw the gates of the railway sidings ahead of him. There was no-one in the watchman's hut because there was no reason to watch the few dozen empty goods-wagons quietly rusting into their rails. The real depôt had been moved in the war and the railings melted down for shells. Not that that would have stopped them from hiring a man to watch the hut.

He crossed the tracks. The unnoticed downpour had washed oil and rust whorls into the puddles for some Carol to find and frame. He walked on and came to the jetty. It was nearly too dark to see the water but he could hear it slapping about like obese lovers. He walked past the dim upright of the flagmast and out along the wooden catwalk. He knew now that his feet had been carrying him to this precise spot for the past half-hour, two miles on magnetism.

He rested his hands on the cold damp railing.

This was the last thing that his father had seen, image caught, water, sky, frozen flat final and unremarked on the retina as the hood descended. Had it spun, water rearing over sky, uncorrectable for ever as he fell to his death?

What a meaningless album these snatched photos would make, wrenched in spasm, eyes break, on sections of darkening wall, on cupboard doors, on gravel. And yet meaningful in that his last picture was perfectly meaningless like his life. Lives are lived out of context. What epitaph could he offer his father?

On an impulse he climbed over the rail and hung, feeling for the iron scaffolding below. His foot hit a strut and he carefully lowered himself until he was standing underneath the jetty on a wet, encrusted horizontal. The wind or the current must have drawn the fishing line backwards under the jetty until it had snagged on a cluster of mussels. It was too dark to see anything and he grew afraid of the immense presence of the sea. His body had sunk in this sea, his head filling with water like a cave.

What epitaph?

He swung back up onto the jetty and turned his back on the sea. The goods-trucks stood black and heavy against the skyline. A noise to his left caught his attention. The halyard had blown loose and swung in the wind, slapping against the mast like a whip. John walked quickly along the rickety catwalk and, seizing the line, tied it in a series of figure of eights to the cleat.

'Very moving,' he said aloud, and then, feeling in his breast pocket for a handkerchief, discovered Carol's panties.

5

Joseph went straight round to the alley at the back of John's house in assertion of their special relationship. When John's father, that miserable old sod, had been alive he had had to knock on the front door like any tradesman. Joseph's friendly visits carried his unique stamp; ideally, friends never knew he was in the house until the bedroom door opened to reveal the hatted figure bearing a tray of tea, which he would share as he sat on the end of the bed. This was a very friendly visit. He had just read about Ostbahn.

It was difficult to identify John's house from the back because each house was alike, the same sale curtains, the same tamped earth gardens. A small reflex of protest at standardization flicked through his mind, but it wasn't really his thing. The alley was full of cinder heaps, derelict prams, tin cans and wedges of lino. Joseph crunched to the end of the alley and then, more slowly, back again. He looked over the wire fences for clues. Then he found it. The slob hadn't put his dustbin out. The lid sat above the bin on a two foot dais of rubbish.

Joseph pushed open the gate, doing the usual with his cigarettes and tugging the brim of his hat down over one eye. He peered in through the kitchen window and gasped.

John was walking to and fro in the kitchen, stark naked save for a huge check cap, and staring at the contents of the shelves. His behind was thrust out like a mandrill's and his knees were bent. He looked as if he were carrying the white man's burden, perhaps in his cap. Joseph's gasps clouded the window and he wilted slowly down the pane, seeking clarity beneath each puff, until he too stood unconsciously crouched, the counterpart of a pederast's bookends. John waddled to the door and looked up at the hanging coats, then he stretched up slowly to touch the hook. There was wonderment on John's face. Joseph's nose was on the sill, eyes transfixed by the happenings before him.

John disappeared into the dining-room. No longer afraid to make a movement, Joseph rubbed the window clear and studied the kitchen. It was a normal kitchen, the selfsame kitchen of former visits. Dishes filled the sink and overflowed uphill onto the draining-board. Reassuring household names stood foursquare on the cardboard packets lining the shelves. So what was so fascinating? Why such big eyes for this scene all of a sudden? Joseph shook his head and tutted.

There was a wooden coalbox against the wall under the dining-room window so, as before, he had to present buttocks to watch the show. The same craziness obtained. John, gouty sleepwalker, peering up at pictures, china ducks and pelmets as if looking up an angel's skirt; his lips moved in secret wonderment. The room had been stripped of all its furniture except for one chair. A new gramophone stood in the centre of the room.

'What is it? What is it?' panted Joseph, as beside himself as a doppelgänger. His jaw had dropped into the nest of his rolling buttondown. His hatbrim was pushed up flat against the glass and his nose was slightly on the Kildare side. He looked like a fool.

John looked up at the light.

'You're having a vision! Taking a trip!'

John again raised his arm.

'It's a wasp! You're tracking a wasp!'

But the arm came down, touched nothing.

Joseph took a flyer. 'Neo-Nazi freak-out!'

John sat down in the one chair, crossed his hairy legs and picked up the *Radio Times*. Joseph couldn't see what his eyes were doing, reading or rolling, because of the wide peak of the cap.

'God,' said Joseph, his hand itching to cross himself, his principles keeping it in his pocket. Everybody was crazy! That fat pro in the knocking shop, the entire Ostbahn deal, John and the oven and now this. Another paid-up, card-carrying nutcase! He couldn't just go in and visit him now as if nothing had happened. He might turn violent like they did and he didn't fancy trying to hold his tongue and get a clothes-line round him. What a helluva note! It must have been his father's death that did it. What was it he'd heard about cerebral balance? Yes, when you'd over-loaded the brain, it just gave up and you started doing the exact opposite. That was it of course. He'd always walked tall and looked down his snoot at people; now it had struck—ZOCKO!—and there he was playing the flipside, creeping around all balled up.

Joseph took a last look at the sad ruin of his friend. There he sat, unnaturally quiet really, not a stitch on, reading the *Radio Times*. Good-bye old buddy. He thought he ought to go and tell Carol rather than blow the whistle on him, so he set off for her place at a trot.

In Carol's hall-mirror he shot his cuffs, put lick on his eyebrows and shot his trouser-bottoms from the niche in the back of his boots. His teeth arced like a verey light across the dingy mirror. Then he galloped up the stairs. He didn't knock on her door, paying her the compliment of assuming her round-the-clock chastity. At her kinkiest, she would be sniffing some flower. He opened the door on a Colt .45. It was aimed at him.

'Hey hey,' he squeaked, 'don't point that thing at me—Ben! It's me—Joseph.'

The gun remained trained on his head and he saw with horror that the hammer was already back.

'You should of knocked, professor,' said Ben. He released the hammer, holding it against the spring with his thumb, slowly letting the firing pin snick to rest on the cartridge. Only then did he lower the gun to his side.

Joseph fell into the nearest chair. He tried to get his

cigarettes out but his hands were shaking too much. Ben took them from him, lit four, kept one himself and put three between Joseph's unprotesting lips.

'Grandma, what big eyes you've got,' said Ben. The small sweaty figure moiled about in the chair and finally managed to stand up. The small sweaty face was very pale and very angry, so it shouted. 'That's a stupid bastard trick! What if that fucking gun had gone off! Eh! You'd have felt bleeding silly then wouldn't you! Pointing guns at people——'

When Joseph had finished emitting these cries and put the roses back in his cheeks, Ben extended a finger and tapped his chest. 'Why did you run out on me, fink,' he said.

Joseph went cold.

'What do you mean ran out on you? I've been out a lot is all. Can't I even go out without asking your permission?' His tone had a whining edge to it, but an edge nonetheless. 'I left you my number didn't I—you could have left a message. You never gave me your address. I don't like my room.'

'You chickened,' said Ben.

'I never,' said Joseph. He was scared to take his eyes off Ben because he was suddenly sure that he had been the mystery man who killed Ostbahn. If he'd killed once he could easily do it again. He had a gun to prove it too. Joseph thought that his only chance lay in posing as the rube he had been so effortlessly in the surgery. One bad hand.

'How's the old—er—second chance. Swell idea that,' he said. Ben sat on the end of the table and idly dangled his legs. He didn't look much like a killer in his square's drip-dry shirt and waistcoat. He wasn't even growing a moustache. Joseph wondered how he had ever found Ben's style so infectious. Maybe he helped out when the psychos were busy. He'd got the room right though—stacks of tinned food, ashtrays full of criminally wasted fags, the curtains drawn. He'd certainly made her room look like a hole-up.

'My heart went out of it when the doctor got rubbed out,' said Ben. Again Joseph drained of colour. He was like an egg-timer that needed upending every three minutes. He couldn't seem to speak even rube's words.

'You must have read about it, baby. Don't snow me. Your contact, old Dr Ostbahn, the old kraut who phoned you. Someone stuck a hypodermic through his neck.'

Joseph gulped. 'In the—market place.'

'Right.'

'But the one who phoned me wasn't Ostbahn. He only pretended to be—you remember—it was your idea. I never even knew his real name.' Joseph tried to look guileless. Better a rube than a stiff hipster. It hurt though.

'Yeah but did he know your real name? That's the big question professor. That's what you want to worry about. Because if he did and if he wrote it down, the cops are going to start filing your teeth So where were you when the doctor got outside the needle?'

'You're joking! I didn't kill him—I never even saw him. Why should I want to kill him?'

'Ostbahn was a well-known anti-semite, anti-spade, anti-socialist bastard. He wrote articles in *The Lancet* about the benevolent effect of fall-out. It's only time gone before some hot cop gets the big flash on that and starts checking on firebrands like you. He's only got to look at you man——' Ben pointed to his badges—'you've got motives pasted all over your lapels. My old man's A-dust man.'

This was an insult to Joseph's intelligence. He'd been played for a sucker once and the memory of that stung him to make a dangerous assertion. 'What about you then—where were you cleversticks?' He was more upset about the 'cleversticks' than any possible bullet.

'I was right here with old Carol. I never saw the doctor that day at all. You were the contact baby—me, I was only a sleeping partner.' Ben obviously didn't give a damn if he believed him or not. He had the gun.

'They'll soon find out what you've been doing,' said Joseph stoutly.

'From you?'

'What do you think I am—you think I'd go to the police?' No sense in going too far.

Ben leaned forward and thrust his face up close to Joseph's. His hot breath clouded Joseph's eyeballs. 'I don't know what you are but I'll tell you this for free. I know what you're going to be.' Joseph averted his eyes from this menacing sirocco and was suddenly, horribly aware of an inert form under the blankets of Carol's bed. Involuntarily, he gave a little quavery moan. Had he killed her too?

'You're going to be so mousy quiet that they think you're dead. You dig? Because if you finger me professor, the shit is going to hit the fan and everybody is going to catch a faceful. A contact man like you—if that's the most they can lay on you—will get five years.'

'He did know my christian name,' said Joseph, not knowing which bit to worry about first.

'Looks black, uh?' said Ben in mock sympathy. 'Well, you keep your trap shut and everything will be jake. After all, I know I didn't do it and you tell me you didn't do it so that makes it someone else, right? Once they catch him, they'll stop looking.'

It was no good. Even if it was his last bulletin Joseph had to know. Wincing at the word 'bulletin' he nevertheless tottered over to the bed and drew the sheets back from her face. Her hair was all over her face, and in the gloom it was impossible to tell whether she was dead or alive. Hardly daring to breathe he grasped her shoulder—warm! two candles—and shook her awake. But she was different. She was alive but she could sure keep a secret. She hardly looked like Carol at all. She stank of bed and stale sweat and she was a mess.

'What—what's the matter with her?' automatically turning from her to ask Ben, but Ben only pushed him aside and sat beside her. 'Where was I last Saturday, honey?'

His hand regularly smoothed back her hair.

One of the straps of her slip had broken and the filigreed top hung down exposing one breast. Joseph couldn't take his eyes off the breast. His stare had the quality of drinking; he stood transfixed while a cocktail of fear and lust and pity ran thickly up the straw.

'You were with me.' Carol's voice had the strange resonance of the deaf.

'All day,' said Ben.

'All day.'

'So that leaves just you, professor,' said Ben smiling at Joseph and then turning his attention back to Carol. 'Carol and I are going out together. She's my girlfriend—right, baby? She got fed up with John because he couldn't do it. She says he's a cripple—got a cripple's appetites too. She gave him back his frat pin because she wouldn't give houseroom to no pervert's pin. Just as well she found out in time—they were practically engaged you know.' Looking up suddenly Ben intercepted Joseph's communication with the breast. 'Tell him about the foul practices in the hut.'

'I don't want to hear!'

Carol covered her eyes with her bare arm as if dazzled by light. Joseph saw that her fingernails were torn and bleedy looking. Ben placed his hand on her naked breast, his eyes fixed on Joseph as he began stroking the soft flesh. His fingers caught at the nipple and he smiled. The nipple, pinched and drawn into stiffness, stood out between his fingers, a hard purple point that seemed to be staring straight at Joseph. He knew he had to get out of here, out of this insane set-up yet he didn't move. For the first time since Joseph had woken her, she lifted her eyes, not seeing him, passing over him and up to the bare white ceiling. She began to move, arching her body up towards the imprisoned flesh and panting.

'Tell him about John, baby. Tell him about that very traumatic beach hut—he wants to know. You'll never get well unless you talk about it.'

Ben wasn't laughing now. His face was a livid white. He seemed to have forgotten that Joseph was there. He tore back the blankets from her squirming body. Joseph thought he was going to be sick. He pushed blindly for the door. On the last flight of stairs he tripped and fell heavily into the hall, his outstretched hand toppling a bicycle onto his back. He grappled with it, sobbing aloud, his hat jammed over his eyes. Ludicrously, his thumb caught on the bell and sent a small metallic ping vibrating through the house.

When he got home he locked his door and tilted a chair against it. His hands were jumping so much that he had to sit on them. Familiar record covers stared down at this crumpled little hipster. He had lost all his cool.

Forgetting everybody else's problems, how could he prove where he was on Saturday? Nobody could have seen him because he'd been in bed with a cold. He searched his mind for corroborators, square, tory or rube. Sane was all.

Then he remembered the girl next door. She would have heard the gramophone, feed a cold, not evidence but something towards establishing his whereabouts. And then his face fell. She knew about the phone calls, had even called him to answer Ostbahn that time. Perhaps she'd forgotten. More candles.

He removed the flimsy barrier against fate and stepped out into the hall. She came to the door in a candlewick dressing gown and fluffy yellow slippers like chicks. Her head came at him like a knuckleduster, encrusted with tin curlers.

'What do you want, bumsquirt?'

Incredibly his manner became indolent, voice dripping innuendo. He couldn't afford to make a balls of this. Inside, he was a drowning man.

'Just felt like seeing you.' He offered her a cigarette.

She leaned, curlers coquettishly clanking, towards his light and shot him an up and under look that set his sphincter racing.

'You're shitting yourself about those phone calls aren't you?'

He almost fell.

'The coppers were here this morning while you were out, checking the phone number. You don't have to worry though. That's all they've got—no names. They're looking for a woman patient, see. He was an abortionist—as you know.'

He couldn't speak.

'Lucky I can be bought,' she said, helping him into her room and unbuckling his belt with a terrible mastery. There were lipstick stripes on the back of her hand.

6

Ben had been up and dressed and waiting for half an hour when the bell rang at 10 a.m. precisely. He shook Carol awake—'Get up!'—and ran downstairs to the front door. A black man and a white man stood on the step.

'Mr Ben Herod?' asked the white man. He wore heavy Buddy Holly glasses that transcended his features, and his hair, now at 35 down to a drooped aliceband, stood out wildly curling.

'Come in,' said Ben, keeping well back from the open door.

Outside were morning sounds of milk bottles and jobbing whistlers. They came into the dark hallway, the negro delicately wiping his shoes as if they were nibs, on the mat. He was very short and thin, fastidiously dressed in a black button-to-the-neck raglan and a near brimless hat. Both men carried bulky holdalls.

'Before we go up,' said Ben, 'she's never posed before. She doesn't know what you do or why you're here. She'll do what I tell her, but I don't want you interfering.'

The white man looked annoyed. He thought it was all fixed up.

'How long is all this going to take then?' He looked at his watch.

'Look, dad,' Ben made buffers of his hands, 'just don't crowd the pace, that's all. Be patient. When I've set it up you can film all day. Shoot Exodus if you like.'

'I won't do no kike movie,' said the negro.

They went upstairs. At the door Ben asked for the money.

'After,' said the white man, and they went in.

'Hey!' said the white man excitedly, dropping the holdall, shrugging out of his coat to reveal more wild black tendrils at the collar of his open neck shirt. 'White walls, lots of light and a black and white lady. I got that feeling Carlyle.' He put on his director's cap, a flipper cap with pouches for his clip-on sunglasses and, light meter in hand, advanced on Carol like a diviner. Carol sat on the edge of the rumpled bed and rhythmically scratched her shin. She did not look up when he held the light meter to her face and her eyes stared straight ahead when he gently lifted her chin on his fingers.

'Beautiful,' he said. 'The new Louise Brooks no less. Black hair, white body. Black and white.' He straightened up. 'That's the motif. Do you have any black sheets for a a sandwich shot?'

Ben took her hand away from her shin and held it. 'You'll make yourself sore, baby.'

They all stared at the silent girl in the grimy slip but nobody asked the obvious question. The negro leaned in dapper pose against the wall, legs crossed and hat tilted down over his eyes.

'There'll be no black and white motif if she ain't bathed. I'm telling you. I'm particular.'

'You'd make yourself more money if you got another star,' said Ben to the director, his face tight with hate, averted from the negro, and already speaking through a second.

'You should see my profile, white boy.' The negro made an airy and unseen wave of the hand that set his rings glittering.

'Leave it alone,' leaving who and what unspecified, the director had to get the show on the road. 'Stand her up,' he told Ben and then seized a handful of slip at the back to outline her body. 'She's tall but she's worth it. You'll have to use the crate, Carlyle.'

The negro peeled down to a sharp silk suit and a shaven head and signed off by shooting his cuffs. 'I don't wanna work with her. She's dirty and she's daft. Why can't we use a model?'

'Look, Carlyle. I'm the director so I cast this movie. I need a girl like this. She looks right. She's an original. Look at that face——' he gripped her jaw and swung her head to the critic—'vulnerable! Sensitive! I don't need to use the leg irons or the nun's outfit because they can see she's helpless. I can get millions of flyblown models with talented yodelling snatches, so who's involved in their fight for virtue? I'll tell you—no-one. And if they're not involved we don't make money.'

'Okay, okay,' said Carlyle and went into the kitchen.

'Get her washed,' said the director. 'Comb her hair.' Wire hangers rattled down the rail as he shoved through her dresses in the curtained alcove. He tried two of them, thrusting them up against her throat for comparison with an impersonal movement like a painter's thumb and choosing at last a black and white check gingham smock with yokel x's under the bust. He dropped the reject and checked the smock for easy access through the zipped back, then he gave it to Ben. 'Black shoes,' he said—'low heels and sling backs.' Increasingly his movements went with his hat, eyes slitting to gauge, hands chopping the air into frames, all movements abrupt as jump cuts. Now he jabbed a shop-wrapped parcel at Ben and flicked the twisted pink bow. 'Don't forget the rendables.' He stood back to admire his work—Ben, one arm holding Carol on her feet, the other laden for the purification, a livid Xmas tree for some season of hatred. 'Good,' said the director. 'Stay out of here for twenty minutes because I want to get the feel of the place. And don't come barging in. Knock.' He tried to take the edge off this with a boyish bevelled grin and then waved his eyebrows rapidly like a ventriloquist's doll, but he could see that his TAM rating stayed where it was.

'Plenty of soap!' shouted the negro from the kitchen, making cutlery sounds, but Ben had gone. As he heard the door close he added—'That man wants gutting.'

'Yes, yes, we know.' The director was getting the feel of it, the act of creation for the film of the same name. He sat on the bed, sat in the rocking chair, sat on the sofa, checked each location for light. 'Now what I want,' he spoke excitedly, 'is footage of this room. I can really,' he paced the floor, 'get something going here.'

'What a waste.' The negro emerged from the kitchen eating poached egg on toast. His little finger presided politely crooked over this activity.

The director had now unpacked his camera. 'Look Carlyle. I'm the director. You're the star. Let's keep it like that. I want thirty seconds of this room at the start of my movie, right? That establishes the context, then I build from there. I don't want to open with you stropping your pud, see? I'm not making movies for the jerkoff market. I make high-class coffee-table eroticism and that's where the money is.'

Camera in hand, he stood on the bed, crepe shoes nearly buried in pouting eiderdown, and moved it in a practise swathe from window to wall. Then he began to shoot film, and the glass eye whirred slowly and smoothly, housed on its pelvic hinge: smooth round apples rolled onto the spool and inflated slowly into close-up in his head. 'Carlyle!' he shouted suddenly, bouncing on the mattress. 'I've got an idea. Come here! Take a bite out of this apple.'

'Man I'm eating egg.'

'Come on come on come on,' he levered at the munching negro with his lens.

'I don't like apples.'

'You can spit it out. I only want the bite out of it.'

The negro shifted the plate to his left hand, anchored the toast with a thumb and took a bite of apple. 'I dunno why you couldn't of bit it yourself,' he complained and spat it onto his palm and threw the chunk in the fireplace.

'Because it would have felt wrong, that's why. Because I'm the director see. I get the erotic ideas and you act them out. It would be like masturbation for me to do it.' He placed the apple back in the bowl and arranged it so that the bite touched the apple next to it and both were in a pool of light. 'Mammarian emblems,' he breathed. 'I'll tell you Carlyle, I'm going to use these as a motif. Just the shape, round, luscious, quiescent see—a woman alone. I show the apples see then I zoom in fast and reveal the bite. The Marks of the Predator. It will sort of presage your arrival. And there's the Fall and so on if they want to see that in it.'

'I done this too runny,' said the negro eating.

The director flipped his peak up to prevent shadow and zoomed in on the bite, brightening as he saw the bonus of froth anointed on the peel. 'A film starring apples,' the negro sneered a yokey sneer. 'I'd better go and oil the muscle.'

'You wait. Eat your egg.' Having drained the apples, the camera moved among the net curtains in pursuit of an entoiled and iridescent bluebottle. The director bobbed and weaved, hoovering for eroticism, regretting the fretful buzz. 'Listen to him. Buzz buzz buzz and me without sound. Taps, raindrops, clocks, pigeons' wings, boots—all crashing away in their suggestive way and I can't do a thing about it.'

He sighed and switched off the camera.

'You want me to oil up?'

'Okay. Oil the prop. And get into the overalls. You're the gasman.'

Mutiny placed pink palms on narrow hips and drew Carlyle up to his full proud-backed five foot two. 'Oh come on, man. Have a heart. I played the gasman in the last three movies. I'm not going to be typecast like this.'

'You were a windowcleaner last time.'

'It's the same thing—the same drag. Bloody boilersuit. Can't I be a salesman, man?'

'Look, Carlyle. Listen. I've told you, this is for the English market. There's no outrage in the white collar bracket. Even vicars are dead. If we make you manual we've got all the fringe benefits of the class theme. Mucky, brutal gas-man rapes pale fragile girl—that's outrageous.'

'Why don't you use a ape?' Carlyle unpacked the boiler-suit and glared at it. It looked lacklustre despite his alterations, the padded shoulders, the buttondown collar, tapered ruler pocket.

'I haven't got an ape,' replied the director and regretted it at once. Carlyle let the implications lie fallow however, not choosing to quarrel with his bread and butter. He took the boilersuit and his make-up case, moroccan leather, the name in gold, and retired to the kitchen. In this green room's unsuitable clutter the black luminary dusted off a humble stool and sat down to transform his profile.

There was a large mirror over the sink and he unhooked it from its nail and placed it on the breadboard, propped against a loaf. From his make-up case he took a chamois leather cloth and, with almost reverent care, he huffed and buffed the impurities away. On the breadboard he laid his clean white initialled handtowel, and on that he arranged tubes and jars of his cosmetics. He sat and waited for the elevation with that blind faith of man in the mechanistic.

Soon the spirit descended upon him. He arose and dropped his trousers. It was awe inspiring, man and member in arbitrary combination like the centaur. Even he could not bring himself to look upon the sight, but with averted eyes he beheld in the mirror the gothic majesty of Real Presence.

He began to limber up. Pilgrim-shuffling in his anklet trousers, he presented himself to the mirror in a cinemascopic range of portrayals. To unheard Debussy he gently drifted his image across the glass in a series of limpid passes; every movement was perfect. Off screen his mood brightened and, turning, his legs began to pizzicato in their silken confines. He spun past the mirror like a cossack and finished the revel by springing the chuckling member up onto the screen in a limbless star-jump. Then irised out, very pleased, plopped bare buttocks onto the cold wood of the stool, and began his usual inspection.

'I gotta spot!'

The director spun about to see the star on the profane side of the kitchen doorway. His shirt was caught up and held under his chin and his trousers were cloth pools. He was quite beside himself.

Whenever the director entered the Presence he experienced cringing humility. His fingers itched up to the brim of his flippercap; only his annoyance with himself over this prevented scenes of abasement. Now he bent and looked.

'What do you think it is?' A very worried star.

'Nothing. Let's see. Just a spot.'

'JUST a spot the man says! It's symptomatic!'

'Of?'

'Of this whole crummy set-up is of what. Of you hiring that grubby ofay chick, that loony, to be in my movie. Of me having to unrobe in that loony's grubby kitchen. Of you wasting money and time—my time—snapping flies and apples in that loony's room. I'm very sensitive, you know that. I'm an artist. That's why I've got this psychosomatic spot.'

The director sighed. 'You're very unfair,' he said. 'Everybody is off-colour sometimes. It's not my fault.'

'I regard off-colour as very cheap.' He turned huffy buttocks on his colleague and shuffled away.

The director's face, arranged on mollifying lines, came round the kitchen door.

'You can use the light meter,' he said, thinking the burgers of Calais. The black neck did not move, brain brooding on blemish. He put the meter down on the initialled towel and had started to withdraw when the star sullenly spoke.

'You keep me in long shot, you hear.'

'Yes, Carlyle.' Thinking, like hell, also kiss my arse. He sat on the table and began thinking out the structure of his film in terms of chalk marks and angles. He wished his star was taller so that he needn't lie down to get menace footage.

Carlyle picked up the light meter and checked it against his Presence. The light meter made him feel like a realer star than the real star he knew he was. He wished he could read it. Figuring, he decided that a light make-up on the Presence would be a good idea, turning his natural body-colour to emphatic mascara. He uncapped the No. 9 and uncowled the Presence, but before they met, thoughts of the spot returned, and the spirit left him.

'This spot,' he said, his voice so crushed that the director hardly heard him.

'I said,' he said, 'this spot.'

'Make-up,' shouted the director, engrossed.

'Huh.' Carlyle doodled aimlessly. 'I can't raise one.'

Panic seized the director's voice. 'What's that!'

'I said I can't raise one. I'm not in the mood.'

'Carlyle. You're a professional. Try again now for God's sake.'

Very depressed star: 'It's no good.'

'Concentrate!'

'I am doing.'

'Maybe it's too close in there. Is it too close in there? You want a window open? His shoes are too tight. Carlyle—are you wearing those tight shoes again?'

'It's none of that. All that's O.K. I'm just depressed.'

'Oh God.'

'Do you ever get to thinking maybe there's no point in this? What's it all for? After all.'

The alarmed director looked down on the bowed black neck. 'Most people think that every so often, Carlyle, but it's different for you. I can't see how you can ever, ever doubt. Because it's not just you anymore. You have your public. Now me—I get depressed sometimes but that doesn't matter. I'm replaceable. I know that. Without you I'd be just one more lousy commercial cameraman. Clapperboy even. You can't ever let yourself get depressed because of your public. They pay to see you, Carlyle, and you know why? Star quality. Every guy in the audience is up there with you, letting them have it, doing the old thing with Carlyle. And the women! Carlyle, I'll tell you. I've sat in the audience and I've watched them in your movies. They can't sit still—they really eat up your profile I kid you not. Have you ever seen an audience watching anyone else's movies? You owe it to yourself to do that. It's a farce. It's an uproar. "Gertcha, we can see the buckles!" "He musta dozed off." Stuff like that—the big horse laugh. But your movies! Reverent. That's the word. You dominate. You know what I got yesterday? Slipped my mind, a letter from the Civil Rights people. They've sent a cheque to keep you off the screen.'

'How's that,' cried the star turning round, proudly smiling.

'About time,' said the spent director, a crystal row of sweatbeads along his cap-brim, his fingers itching up to touch the place.

In the bathroom Ben stood staring in revulsion at the bloodied palms of his hands. This time it had come over him without warning. He felt sick, strained in the guts.

Carol's head lay on the rim of the bath and her body seemed to melt in pink wavy lines through the steaming water. When he spoke to her she opened her eyes but she didn't look at him. She looked like a five-year-old: hair in a topknot, face flushed and sullen, she would ride through the adult night in a piggyback bound for a sheet-saving pee. As he watched, her eyes began to melt big fat silent tears.

'Shut up,' he said and bent over the bath to wash the blood from his hands. Underwater, his hand felt for her thighs and gently squeezed. She just went on crying with that some mindless five-year-old incontinence.

'Look,' said Ben, holding up the shopwrapped parcel. 'Pretties. A present for you.'

It was packed in gold paper, sellotaped along the edge with a superfluous twist of pink ribbon around it. Carol made no move to take it but she oozed a few more tears. Ben gave up and sat on the bathroom chair. Being in the bathroom made it the bathroom chair. Nothing in the bathroom was special except the bath. The mirror had come to the rooming house from a foreclosed barbershop and advertised a brand of hair grease; the rubber bath-mat was palette-shaped to fit a lavatory. Some genius had papered the walls and the steam had, as steam will, demoralized the fit so that it hung in loose floral bulges like a portrait of O. Wilde by D. Gray. Sodden pieces of wallpaper always clogged the plughole. Hot water cost a shilling.

'Today is the last day baby,' said Ben. 'And then I'm going away. I might even miss you, you never know. Boy, the kicks we've had together. I nearly dislocated my jaw yawning. Now if I had a photo I'd give it to you so's you'd remember me right. You know how I am, all mush inside.' He gingerly felt the little half-moon cuts on his palm. They were stinging from the water. 'No, on second thoughts I think we'll skip the photo bit. Not a good idea at all. I have to be so careful about my fool heart ruling my head, especially now with the fuzz breaking out their drop-handlebars and all.' He smiled and leaned across to unstrap the watch from her limp wrist.

'You still don't know what time it is do you baby. You stay that way. Stupid.' He kissed her softly on the forehead.

'When I'm gone you'll forget all about me. After all, you've got some of your own things going now. There's the addiction for one thing, and photography. You'll wake up and find the two mice and the pumkin outside your door again. It'll all seem like a dream.' Ben was gazing off into the distance like a medium. He seemed to be talking to himself and his American accent had disappeared.

'I'll fix you up with John again baby. I can get him back.

Good old John eh. You can sew leather patches on his elbows for him. Get a new elastic band for your pony-tail. Get married. It'll be hard on your finger baby but he is steady. You'll be very liberal—go round telling people that hanging is wrong. Yeah, you keep that bit up honey. That's noble work.'

Beyond knowing, Carol floating achieved immortal longings. In the porcelain womb of the bath she had reversed creation to become, unforming, her limits dissolving, lymph. Not happy lymph, not wistful lymph but just plain old lymph lymph. A lymph nymph. Carol wasn't Ben any more. Carol was bathwater. Out and into, went her body, and regret and anticipation sank without a trace in the busy mixture. There were needle marks in her upper arm.

'I can make all this disappear for you, baby. I can rub it all out. I can do it too. It's my job. The Great Eraser.'

Ben held up his hand as if in benediction and closed his eyes. 'You never sat on the platform that night so we never met. You got on the last train and went home and wrote that the sea had been grey and the sky full of candy floss. You never walked in the fields at night because nobody you knew had a car. You slept all night and stayed up all day like people do.'

Carol was conscious only of the drone of his voice. There was no place for him in the new order of things. Then he seized her hands and pulled her upright onto her feet. Her dreaming flesh streamed back through his fingers, outraged, cords and strings of water breaking from her, but he held her fast. He towelled her roughly and her head wobbled on its limp stalk. Fluid welled up in her eyes and rolled down her cheeks. Her arms hurt her, hurt someone, she didn't know; hurt. Now suddenly she could see him, grotesquely jolted against wedges of paper flowers, he was a flat white cut-out in a kaleidoscope. His mouth flew open, shook open into red and she heard, understanding nothing, the raw inhuman sound of his screaming.

'He did it! I'll kill him I'll——' His arm was a shuddering crescent above her head. 'Touched you! Touched you with his shit-filth hands and you let him!' He thrust the harsh scrubbing brush into her hands and crushed her fingers around it.

'Scrub! Scrub it off! Quick—use the brush! Do it all over all—EVERYWHERE! Harder. HARDER THAN THAT—BLEED! BLEED IT OUT! He touched you there. Filth! Black shit filth I'll kill him, I'LL KILL HIM!'

7

The jangling of the bell through the empty house brought John from his sleep, sliding down the shiny pole into the reality of his rumpled bed. He groped for the alarm and then remembered that he had not wound it for a week. That made it the front door bell. He half-fell out of bed onto the cold lino, and pressing his face to the window, looked down on the empty porch.

A six o'clock sun shone on the dry concrete, freezing the dull pools in the gutter to mercury, the rinsed milk bottles to clubs of ice. Diamonds of grit sparkled seductively on the pavement below, but John was not tempted. Only a fool would venture abroad in this mineral world, at this un-human hour. There was no sign of his caller. He hopped back into bed.

But he couldn't get back to sleep. He lay there thinking about things as they occurred to him, following nothing, unselective. He felt very strange. Sick almost. His father, Carol, Joseph passed through his mind like figures in a striking clock. He watched them without emotion. His head felt as if it were stolen goods, hot, snatched and urgent on the pillow. Now he recalled a nursery tale from his childhood. A thief steals some merchandise—a ring perhaps or a goose—and as he runs through the windy town the thing (the goose?) screams for help from between the guilty hands. There was a picture in the book which had terrified him. The thief was blue and red; his hands were red. There were no citizens in the windy town. A cat crouched on a brimming dustbin wolfing at lumps of rag. The lid had fallen off, was still falling, to the cobbles. Thief! Thief! Master!

It was no better in the bathroom. Surfaces, chrome, plastic, porcelain rang against his eyes. He was nauseously aware of being flesh amid mineral, all rosy and vulnerable for their sharp edges. He moved with exaggerated care. The tumbler perhaps to tumble—in its nature—burst in the bath, wound the cringing foot, wound opening under water, a dream of nausea. Call me a semantic fool. He washed and dried selected orifices with babycare, shivering in the pearly light.

He opened the door of his father's room and released an eddy of stale, closeted air. What he expected to find there he didn't know. Nothing had changed. On the floor lay the cold hotwater bottle where he had left it a week ago. It struck him forcefully that it would remain there, beached bladder, high and dry in linoleum latitudes, two feet from the bed and three from the wall for ever, unless he chose to move it. Everything in the house would stay where he left it now, for no good reason, forgotten reason, a little Pompeii in the suburbs. He felt like having the room sealed up. The double bed shone faintly with sunlight along its iron shank, unflocked skeleton, its unlapped sleepers re-united at last in a bony embrace.

The view from this window was over the back-yards. A neighbour crunched over the cinders in overalls, yawning immensely, blind to the familiar route to work. A handful of sparrows, dusty as old carpet, fled before his unhinged jaws. Plump sachets of yolk had popped in that mouth behind the discreet screen of the *Daily Mirror*. John let the curtain fall back into place and left the room.

On the hall mat his eyes fell on a plain unaddressed envelope. He slit it with his thumbnail and took out six photos. There was no other message.

Now the six photos were spread before him on the kitchen table. He thought he was going mad. They were his dreams. They had come to life, hideously alive and independent of him, jerking out the convulsions that he had willed for her in the hot dark of his bed. It was as if his jerking hand had pierced her limbs with wires. He covered his eyes with a shaking hand and it seemed for a moment as if he were going to faint. He was the thief. He had been caught in the bright white magic flashlight of day with a snowy goose clutched in his fingers, and his face was fixed in a ghastly corded glaring grimace. He could see her face looking up at him—Carol staring mindlessly at him and not seeing, held there at the neck by thin black fingers.

He was guilty. He felt it everywhere; in the pressure of the chair along his thighs, in the ache of his elbows on the table. His eyes opened on objects. He alone was guilty; he alone was flesh and that flesh had willed degradation on another. He burned with shame and in the general movement of blood along his veins a specific tumescence occurred which confirmed to him his diseased sexuality. He wanted to turn all the keys, close the curtains and nail them in place, bury his head under pillows and die, throttling on his guilt like a dog in his vomit.

Someone knew him more intimately than he had believed possible. Someone who had pointed his lens directly into the most secret chambers of his mind. He had delivered the photos to him like meat thrown to a leper. No message was necessary. The caller had run. John tried to think rationally. She had told this person about him, about the beach, and he had known exactly how to use it to hurt him. What was he after? He had calculated his reaction to the last spasm of shame but to what purpose, for what motive? Was he, John, meant to do something more? Come gunning, stamp lens and photographer to pulp under righteous heels; slash his own wrists?

John seized the photos and ran upstairs. He no longer knew if he was acting from pity or from vengeance or from a burning need for confrontation. He was acting. Even allowing for the double meaning that was miraculous. He was going to Carol. But he was not sure whether he had chosen or whether, unimaginably, he had been programmed by his tormentor as he had programmed her.

Fifty miles out of the city Ben pulled the big car off the

road onto a carpet of leaves. He sat holding the wheel and staring at the traffic slamming past. A continuous flash of metal hurtled past his elbow a few feet away. Bright lines pulled out of speed on the peripheries of his vision. Objects became their function; cars abstracted into movement, became a horizontal morse on the road. It seemed very beautiful to him.

Six-forty-five. On the seat beside him lay the briefcase, lid unbuckled, the opening towards him where the gun was. He turned on the radio and listened to the weather forecast. 'Snow,' said Ben smiling.

After a while he decided. At six-fifty the one car that really stuck out in a crowd was heading back to the city.

She was sitting in the rocking chair. She didn't look up when he closed the door. She didn't know that he had run out on her or why he had come back. She saw only the briefcase. That was all that existed.

Gently, Ben took the scissors from her cold bluish fingers. He examined the punctures she had made in her arms. Most of them were slight but a couple went deeper and were torn probably as the points jerked out. Carol started crying like a grizzly kid, on and on, flatly, without vehemence. She was still wearing the thick film make-up, a sad/funny clown's face, now blotched and red under the white. Streaks of black ran down her cheeks.

'Yoohoo honey. It's me—back from the office. Did you have a good day?' He bit his thumb, studying her.

'You don't seem to have much on the ball today. You're not yourself. You've been very distant with me since last Thursday. Wednesday, I tell a lie. It's getting me down. What's up? Huffy? Consty? Preggie? Junkie?' Ben paused between each question and cocked his head as if stepping back between brush-strokes.

'You could be civil. Just because you're a pregnant junkie. We've all got troubles. Self-centred is what.'

He turned away and went into the kitchen, still talking quietly against the unbroken sound of Carol's crying. He ran hot water into a basin and tore a handful of cotton wool from the roll. There was a tin of elastoplast in the cutlery drawer.

'I bet you wonder why I came back.' He started for the door laden with articles and saw her on her knees frantically pawing through the contents of his briefcase. His instruments fell in a heap, bottles, needles and coil strewn all over the floor. The briefcase had been dumped upside down.

He grabbed her hair and pulled her off balance away from the syringe before her out-thrust hands could connect. As she toppled weakly onto her side, he bent to retrieve it. Out of the corner of his eye he saw the big gun in her two hands.

The coldness of the brass doorknob stuck to his sweating palm like a burn. John could not seem to find the will to turn it and enter the room, the lists, the trying place appointed. It was very dark and damp-smelling on the landing and the sound of his own breathing reminded him farcically of Tone in the well.

Then he heard the explosion. Felt, rather, the huge impact of the brass on his flesh as the first bullet struck the door. He flung himself back against the wall and saw the door suddenly splinter, bristling up white daggers of wood from its varnished surface. The noise—he couldn't tell if it was one single reverberating explosion or a chain of clangour—ran through his jerking body like voltage. Even when it was over he could not recall where he was or what he had come to do. For a moment it seemed to him that he was in some forge, foundry, cavern of the Industrial Revolution, was flickering small and barefoot through steam and hurtling pistons.

The door would not come open and he had to lean his full weight against the panel before he felt the obstacle slowly give way. Ben had fallen at the door and, dying, slid a bloody swathe across the lino before the opening door.

John knelt beside him and saw dumbly the great ragged

exit-holes in Ben's chest before he raised his head and saw her. Carol sitting as if before a movie. A revolver loosely held in her hands. He spoke to her, saying her name in a voice that sounded too weak to reach her now. She looked at him without any expression, her eyes flat and blackly animal under her ragged cowl of hair. Everywhere that pearly unreal light turned the room white as a spun spectrum of colours is white.

It was difficult to take the gun from her for the fingers of both hands were laced around the trigger, and he had to apply strong pressure to each hand in turn. There were two live bullets left in the chamber; he was tucking the gun into his belt before he realized. Not the broken syringe on the floor; not the stab wounds on her soft, blue-bruised arms; not even his tormentor dead. The gun was a Colt .45. John stared at it. It was beautiful, the most beautiful thing he had ever seen, an object of glory. The myth of courage and virility lay cold and true in his hand, weighed his hand down with power. This was what he had come for. He had found his rôle.

He took out the photos of Carol and let them flutter down onto the corpse. Ben stared up sightlessly, his face a mask of agony and horror, Ben who had used everybody, buried beneath a mask, all used up. John realized that it was all settled now; better, settled in a convention cleaner and truer than life. He had shot him down like a dog for the prostitution of his lover.

He knew instinctively that feet would come running now, voices shouting, sucked by natural force into the vacuum left by the explosion. People would flood back and destroy the pattern. Oh yes. He knew himself, his weakness. He would help to spoil it, revoke, rescind, recant. But he mustn't! He gripped the gun, his gun, tightly in his fist.

He had one more thing to do here. He trailed the backs of his fingers absently down Carol's cheek, not feeling its smooth warmth, feeling no pity, no love. Observance of gesture was enough for him now, enough for this. 'Temple Drake,' he said and smiled. Squatting in front of her chair, he sighted on her eyes and released a short hard punch to her jaw, lifting her and the chair over backwards, unblocking with a flash—POW ! BLAM !—the dazzling new sun. She lay on the rug with her dirty slip wrinkled up over tight belly like a partly sloughed skin. Her attitude had the random, flung obscenity of a police photograph and it struck him that he had posed her again.

Checking her pulse, he heard them.

Voices raised in the hall. Feet on the stairs. No time for guilt now. He came through the doorway like a bull, bellowing. He had a blurred impression of red holes opening at him and then receding in confusion at the sight of his gun slashing through air at them, then he was past, hammering down the stairs head over heels almost and into the street.

People were running towards him as in a dream, completely absorbed in that action, were the action in inseparable plurality. And he was running. He threw up his arm and took aim and the mass parted. Some dropped to the ground, others dived into doorways. But he couldn't shoot into them, that famous freest act, instead, swinging the barrel round to a parked car bearing jokey transfer bullet-holes, he fired two jokey bullets into the windscreen.

Running now down the street, lungs bursting, laughing like a madman. Beside him ran the great ones. Bogart running, gun in hand to his deathfalling witness. Belmondo down that final boulevard, dying, a fag burning in his mouth. Cybulski sniffing his own blood among the washing and running to his death on the crapheap. And Billy going for an empty holster. They ran with John. He held on hard to them, to his movie ending.

He swerved out, tiring now, onto the flyover and ran up the gradient treading cats-eyes. Ahead jogged Technicolor notices. SLOW DOWN. NO LEARNERS. Behind him horns began to sound and he staggered to the left of the road. The great ones wouldn't come! Red flames leaped behind his eyes. 'Yes go on burn it all!' he shouted as the urchins pronged furniture and tree-boughs and petrol onto the bonfire. 'Burn it all up!' They circled and whooped behind protective dustbin lids. The flames shimmered up, leaping higher, hotter, creating a vacuum that sucked at property, that tore possessions from their places with the suction plop of departing eyeballs. His father's knuckles whitened around sideboard handles and from his screaming mouth ran hanging gobs of plastic, pink cysts containing teeth, a biteful of tiles from the roof....

Ten ton of steel hit him as he reached the top of the ramp. It broke upon him like a gigantic wave and it broke him. His eyes did not see the spire of the church below, the double spire, nor the kite trapped in the branches that were clearly visible from the top of the flyover.

The lorry driver flung on his air-brakes and the huge eight-wheel lorry jarred to a halt. The driver, a Korean War veteran in greasy overalls and an open-neck check shirt knelt down beside the body and vomited. The radiator had impressed the pattern of its metal grill on John's face, breaking his skull and stopping his heart. A motor-cycle cop pulled off his gauntlet and inserted a hand under the bloody combat jacket, just a formality, and then held back the traffic on the ramp until the body could be cleared.

Drivers craned through their windscreens for a look and then sat back ashen faced, staring bleakly down at their dashboards. Further back, not knowing the cause of the hold up, drivers beat their gloved hands impatiently on their steering wheels, lit up angry cigarettes. The fringes of the expanding blockage parted to let the ambulance through.

That Easter there were 23 road deaths in the county. John was number 19. In the morgue Mr Reed failed at first to recognize him. He had a hell of a job cutting through the finger tendons to free the empty gun for the police laboratory.

8

'Well, I blame him. It's all very well to say that he was highly strung, but it seems to me that he was the author of all your misfortunes. Your mother and I read some of his letters in your drawer when you were in hospital. Now don't look at me like that—we felt we ought to know everything. You're our only child after all.'

They sat on the park bench, fingers loosely entwined, a middle-aged man in a business suit and a very pregnant young woman. 'I don't think that was very nice.' But she didn't seem annoyed, just quietly sat there smiling at the children playing on the grass.

'I think we're out of the realms of nice, Carol.'

'Are we?' she said. She didn't know. She had a great sense of well-being, of everything in its ordered place. It was ludicrous to worry about whose baby she was carrying, John's, Ben's, or perhaps the negro's—it was part of her now, the centre where she most perfectly WAS. Everything else was trivial.

'He had a diseased imagination. Filthy. Sick. I wonder that you didn't see that. If you hadn't got mixed up with him, you would never have—done what you did with the Other.'

Carol wondered vaguely what she had done with the Other. Of course she'd read the newspaper accounts of the sordid business but none of it seemed to apply to her. They had fitted it all together like a—why not?—she'd finished with writing—like a jigsaw. Ben killed Ostbahn. John killed Ben and was killed in the road. Ben was an abortionist. He had taken dirty photos of her; that was why John killed him.

The weight of the sun on her closed eyelids stirred something, a faint orange fluttering beyond memory. It lasted only a moment, as brief as the blank after-image of the children and the geraniums that she had carried on her retina when her eyelids closed. That sensation was all that was left of Ben, sensation merchant, and it too was subsumed in the slow smiling warmth of her happiness. It was all erased as he had promised.

Her father studied her uptilted face and worried again about her sanity. One didn't smile like that after a nightmare. He cleared his throat.

'What bothers me is why that one came back after he'd got away. The police say that he'd been seen in that flashy car fifty miles away that very morning.'

He was asking her really, and his motives were unclear even to himself. Perhaps to jolt her out of this vacancy onto normal paths of expiation and catharsis; very much a pre-occupation of his generation. He was a good father and had shut the door on the reporters, set his back against the neighbours, only to find, painfully, that she didn't need him and didn't notice. Carol said: 'The papers said that John was in love with me.'

'No no. I'm talking about the other one.'

'Ben? The papers said that he was mad. He might have returned to abort me or because he loved me too, they weren't sure. Or perhaps even to see what John was going to do about the photos.'

'What do you think?' He looked very directly at her, trying to elicit a personal response.

'I don't know,' she said with a puzzled frown, puzzled at his asking her. 'Let me straighten this for you.' She extended her hand towards the knot of his tie, but was sidetracked by a tiny ladybird badge in his lapel. The tie stayed crooked.

'Why do you wear this?'

'It's for charity. You've seen it before.' So had the speaker, yet he nevertheless creased up his neck to squint down at it. His face looked very old and dried up and lined in the bright sunlight. That aspect always made her love him.

'Bearing witness, sort of thing?' she asked him slyly, and he remembered the family quarrels when she accused him of being all appearances and he told her that she was a beatnik. That all seemed a long time ago.

'It impresses the Joneses,' he laughed.

They sat together very comfortably and watched the children playing. Red buses could be seen over the tops of the bushes. A yob in a polka dot shirt and clip-on braces was playing his transistor. Carol thought that if she had a boy she would call him Heathcliff.

REFERENCE DEPARTMENT
WEYERHAEUSER LIBRARY
Macalester College
St. Paul, Minn. 55105

DO NOT CIRCULATE

WITHDRAWN FROM
MACALESTER COLLEGE
LIBRARY

REFERENCE DEPARTMENT
WEYERHAEUSER LIBRARY
Macalester College
St. Paul, Minn. 55105

TEST CRITIQUES: VOLUME IV

REFERENCE DEPARTMENT
WEYERHAEUSER LIBRARY
Macalester College
St. Paul, Minn. 55105

Daniel J. Keyser, Ph.D.
Richard C. Sweetland, Ph.D.
General Editors

TEST CRITIQUES

Volume IV

©1985

TEST CORPORATION OF AMERICA

© 1985 Test Corporation of America, a subsidiary of Westport Publishers, Inc., 330 W. 47th Street, Kansas City, Missouri, 64112. All rights reserved. No part of this publication may be reproduced, stored in a retrieval system, or transmitted in any form or by any means, electronic, mechanical, photocopying, recording, or otherwise, without the prior written permission of Test Corporation of America.

Library of Congress Cataloging in Publication Data
(Revised for vol. 4)
Main entry under title:

Test critiques.

Includes bibliographies.
1. Psychological tests—Evaluation. 2. Educational tests and measurements—Evaluation. 3. Business—Examinations—Evaluation. I. Keyser, Daniel J., 1935- . II. Sweetland, Richard C., 1931- .
BF176.T419 1984 150'.28'7 84-26895
ISBN 0-9611286-6-6 (v. 1)
ISBN 0-9611286-7-4 (v. 2)
ISBN 0-9611286-8-2 (v. 3)
ISBN 0-933701-02-0 (v. 4)

Printed in the United States of America

CONTENTS

ACKNOWLEDGEMENTS

The editors wish to acknowledge the special contributions of our test reviewers. They have done an outstanding job. Our thanks extend from our deep pleasure and gratitude over their participation and the quality of their work. We know many of the contributing reviewers were as "caught up" in this project as we, and are now writing additional reviews for subsequent volumes. And, thanks also go to the test publishers themselves who released information to the reviewers in an expeditious manner.

We also wish to express thanks to the staff members at Test Corporation of America who are involved in this project: Jane Doyle Guthrie, Jo Riley, Kelly Scanlon, and Barbara St. George. And our special thanks go to our colleague, Barry Hughes, Ph.D., who served as our manuscript editor. Eugene Strauss and Leonard Strauss, directors of Westport Publishers, Inc., have given freely and generously their support, encouragement, and business advice. Our indebtedness to both gentlemen is legion.

Finally, we want to express our warmest thanks to our readers. It is their use of *Test Critiques* that gives a final validity to this project. It is our sincerest desire that *Test Critiques* will have a true application for them.

INTRODUCTION

Test Critiques is a fulfillment of a goal of the editors and a continuation of a task begun with the publication of *Tests: A Comprehensive Reference for Assessments in Psychology, Education and Business* (1983) and its *Supplement* (1984). With this series, we believe we have moved into the final phase of our project—to include those vital parts that were not appropriate for our directory. With *Tests* and its supplements and the *Test Critiques* series, the reader will have a full spectrum of current test information.

When *Tests* was published, a decision was made to leave out important psychometric information relating to reliability, validity, and normative development. Normative data and questions of reliability and validity were considered simply too complex to be reduced to the "quick-scanning" desk reference format desired. It was also apparent to the editors that a fair treatment of these topics would unnecessarily burden less sophisticated readers. More learned readers were familiar with other source books where such information could be obtained. The editors were aware, however, that a fuller treatment of each test was needed. These complex issues, along with other equally important aspects of tests, deserved scholarly treatment compatible with our full range of readers.

The selections for each volume were in no way arbitrarily made by the editors. The editorial staff researched what were considered to be the most frequently used psychological, educational, and business tests. In addition, questionnaires were sent to members of various professional organizations and their views were solicited as to which tests should be critiqued. After careful study of the survey results, the staff selected what was felt to be a good balance for each of the several volumes of critiques and selection lists were prepared for invited reviewers. Each reviewer chose the area and test to be critiqued and as can be noted in each volume's table of contents, some reviewers suggested new tests that had not been treated to extensive reviews. As test specialists, some reviewers chose to review tests that they had extensively researched or were familiar with as users; some chose to review instruments that they were interested in but had never had the opportunity to explore. Needless to say, the availability of writers, their timetables, and the matching of tests and writers were significant variables.

Though the reviewers were on their own in making their judgments, we felt that their work should be straightforward and readable as well as comprehensive. Each test critique would follow a simple plan or outline. Technical terms when used would be explained, so that each critique would be meaningful to all readers—professors, clinicians, and students alike. Furthermore, not only would the questions of reliability and validity along with other aspects of test construction be handled in depth, but each critique would be written to provide practical, helpful information not contained in other reference works. *Test Critiques* would be useful both as a library reference tool containing the best of scholarship but also useful as a practical, field-oriented book, valued as a reference for the desks of all professionals involved in human assessments.

It might be helpful to review for the reader the outline design for each critique contained in this series. However, it must be stressed that we communicated with each critique writer and urged that scholarship and professional creativity not be sacrificed through total compliance to the proposed structure. To each reviewer we wrote, ". . . the test(s) which you are reviewing may in fact require small to major modifications of the outline. The important point for you to bear in mind is that your critique will appear in what may well become a standard reference book on human assessment; therefore, your judgment regarding the quality of your critique always supercedes the outline. Be mindful of the spirit of the project, which is to make the critique practical, straightforward, and of value to all users—graduate students, undergraduates, teachers, attorneys, professional psychologists, educators, and others."

The editors' outline for the critiques consisted of three major divisions and numerous subdivisions. The major divisions were Introduction, Practical Applications/Uses, and Technical Aspects, followed by the Critique section. In the Introduction the test is described in detail with relevant developmental background, to place the instrument in an historical context as well as to provide student users the opportunity to absorb the patterns and standards of test development. Practical Applications/Uses gives the reader information from a "user" standpoint—setting(s) in which the test is used, appropriate as well as inappropriate subjects, and administration, scoring, and interpretation guidelines. The section on Technical Aspects cites validity and reliability studies, test and retest situations, as well as what other experts have said about the test. Each review closes with an overall critique.

The reader may note in studying the various critiques in each volume that some authors departed from the suggested outline rather freely. In so doing they complied with their need for congruence and creativity—as was the editors' desire. Some tests, particularly brief and/or highly specialized instruments, simply did not lend themselves easily to our outline.

Instituted in Volume III, an updated cumulative subject index has been included in this volume. Each test has been given a primary classification within the focused assessment area under the main sections of psychology, education, and business. The subject index has been keyed to correspond with *Test* and its *Supplement*.

It is the editors' hope that this series will prove to be a vital component within the available array of test review resources—*The Mental Measurements Yearbooks,* the online computer services for the Buros Institute database, *Psychological Abstracts,* professional measurement journals, etc. To summarize the goals of the current volume, the editors had in mind the production of a comprehensive, scholarly reference volume that would have varied but practical uses. *Test Critiques* in content and scholarship represents the best of efforts of the reviewers, the editors, and the Test Corporation of America staff.

TEST CRITIQUES

individual items were field tested and were not rough drafts of tests. Norming (fall, winter, and spring) was accomplished during the 1983 school year on a national sample of 150,000 students in 49 states with the participation of over 100 school districts. Available within-grade norms include percentile ranks, stanines, normal curve equivalents, and grade equivalents. In addition, an algorithm was developed for the tests in order that results from various subtests (or subsets of items) could be transformed into an overall, common scale (CRTM Development Team, 1984). This common scale was developed with the use of the Rasch model (Wright & Stone, 1979) and is another innovative feature of AIMS.

Practical Applications/Uses

As a result of the many options within AIMS, a local school administrator could make meaningful performance comparisons at several levels: individual/group to national performance on a total test; individual/group mastery to national mastery by objective and/or subject; and individual to local group performance and mastery by test, objective, and subject. It could also be used to assess overall progress (e.g., in reading, from one point to another without reference to grade equivalents).

Clearly, the Academic Instruction Measurement System is *not* just another achievement test. AIMS is a measurement system that includes unique features. One of these is having the item bank on a microcomputer diskette with objectives, items, item statistics, student and teacher directions, and camera-ready artwork. This AIMS option requires an IBM-XT microcomputer with printer. Although this reviewer did not have a copy of this diskette, the program purports to be menu-driven for ease of use and includes a word-processing function for text editing and test building. The AIMS test-building capability should allow local districts to construct assessment instruments by objective, item content, item statistic, or random selection of items by objective within each grade level. In addition, locally developed or commercially purchased items can be added to the AIMS item bank as desired by the user.

AIMS is a practical, powerful assessment tool for school administrators. It enables districts to build tests based on their specific curricula or evaluation needs, rather than purchasing a test package that may be only tangentially related to district needs. Thus, AIMS returns control over testing to local leadership.

Technical Aspects

Technically, AIMS represents a major departure from the educational testing paradigm that has prevailed in this country since World War II. As Buros (1977) points out, testing in American education has moved away from assessing achievement or mastery of content and shifted to assessing aptitude or ability. Test developers and psychometricians have contributed to that movement by emphasizing test reliability over validity based on two major criteria: 1) grade-to-grade progression of item difficulties and 2) item contribution to the internal consistency reliability of the overall test. The result has been standardized tests in various subjects that are all relatively insensitive to the effects of instruction but highly related to each other and to general ability tests such as IQ and aptitude. AIMS reverses that movement while retaining the best features of standardized tests.

The validation strategy used by the AIMS development team reflects the emerging concerns in education with criterion-referenced testing and program evaluation that point to the need for student mastery information on specific educational topics in specific instructional contexts. The developers of AIMS initially focused on the content validity of items through the careful, detailed definition of the instructional domains to be tested and derivation of item specifications to tap those domains. By this approach, they clearly recognize the critical importance of content validity in achievement testing. Consistent with their intent to design a measurement system that would be sensitive to the effects of instruction, pre- and post-testing were included as part of the item tryout procedures. Developing and incorporating items that display change across instruction is a critical issue in the evaluation of the effectiveness of instructional programs.

However, traditional norm-referenced item characteristics were not ignored by the AIMS development team. The AIMS item bank was developed so that homogeneity across an entire test was not a major issue. Instead, high discrimination indices and some degree of inter-item homogeneity within objectives and content categories were sought. Thus, the expectation was that higher inter-item correlations would be found within objectives, and lower correlations would be found between objectives. Strict adherence to having high item intercorrelations was not desired, as is often the case in traditional standardized test development. At a higher level, objective scores rather than items were evaluated as part of the development process. They showed the expected pattern of higher inter-objective correlations within content categories (e.g., .2 or greater) and lower correlations (less than .10) for items between content categories. All of these evaluations, undertaken in 1983 (N = 5,465 first-graders) provided an interesting form of empirical evidence for the content validity of the test system by item, objective, and content category. Additionally, a factor analysis (N = 4,011 seventh-graders) was carried out, resulting in interpretable factors corresponding to the overall subjects of reading/language arts and mathematics as originally envisioned by the development staff.

The reliability of the AIMS item bank was evaluated by computing Cronbach's coefficient alpha (K-R 20) for each set of six to eight items within each objective at several grade levels and again across objectives at each grade level. For each grade level across objectives, the reliabilities ranged from .85 to .95, well within acceptable limits. The stability of AIMS scores was investigated by testing groups of students in the late spring of 1983 and again in the fall. The percentage of students demonstrating mastery over an objective remained relatively stable over the summer, providing evidence of the test-retest reliability of the measurement system when there is no intervening instruction.

Critique

In summary, the Academic Instructional Measurement System represents a major breakthrough in educational testing in terms of its conceptual base, development, validation, and execution. It refocuses measurement on actual student achievement and mastery of specified skills and content areas rather than the prediction of some nebulous (and often contaminated) criterion of "success" based on traditional latent-trait notions of ability. Additionally, AIMS returns control of testing to the local level based on school curricula as taught.

There are several final comments concerning the quality and availability of the materials supporting the development and validation of the AIMS and the acceptance and use of the tests by school districts. The textual documentation of AIMS is excellent. Available documentation includes a rather short AIMS manual/brochure (27 pages), the CRTM objectives catalog, and a thorough technical report (CRTM Development Staff, 1984). The latter is an outstanding example of how a technical manual should be developed. Nearly 100 pages (8½" x 11"), it is crammed with details and, most importantly, a good explanation of the rationale for the test development and validation. Reading the technical report is useful and informative even if one chooses not to use AIMS.

Finally, although these reviewers would endorse the use of AIMS for a wide variety of educational achievement-testing functions in schools, it is unclear whether school districts will choose to do so. Schools tend to be conservative organizations and usually have limited resources and expertise in testing. Thus, it may prove easier and "safer" to continue in the old testing ways. Under these circumstances, despite the hue and cry for raising educational standards and developing meaningful tests, AIMS may not receive the welcome that it should in the marketplace. This reviewer hopes that this is not the case and recommends that districts, even if they feel that AIMS is too innovative or complex to implement district-wide, use the system for special projects such as program evaluations. In this way, they will be introduced to a new form of achievement testing that better suits the demands of today's schools.

References

Buros, O. K. (1977). Fifty years in testing: Some reminiscences, criticisms, and suggestions. *Educational Researcher, 6*(7), 9-15.

CRTM Development Team. (1984). *Curriculum Referenced Tests of Mastery technical report I.* Columbus, OH: Charles E. Merrill Publishing Company.

Wright, B. D., & Stone, M. H. (1979). *Best test design.* Chicago: Mesa Press.

Donald W. Zimmerman, Ph.D.
Professor of Psychology, Carleton University, Ottawa, Canada.

AH5 GROUP TEST OF HIGH GRADE INTELLIGENCE

A. W. Heim. Windsor, England: NFER-Nelson Publishing Company, Ltd.

Introduction

The AH5 Group Test of High Grade Intelligence is a British test designed to discriminate among selected, highly intelligent adults and students from the age of 13 years to college level. To this end, the difficulty of the test items has been contrived so that scores will have extensive variability in selected groups. This effort seems to have been successful because the test norms exhibit a great deal of variability in scores among reference groups, such as university students, postgraduate students in education, science students, and engineering applicants. The items successfully attain a high level of difficulty and apparently sample a considerable range of conceptual skills without demanding specialized knowledge acquired in formal education.

The AH5 was developed by A. W. Heim who has pursued research and development of tests of high grade intelligence for four decades. It is one of a series of tests that have been used in England, Australia, and the United States, as well as in non-English-speaking countries such as Iran (see Mehryar & Shapurian, 1970). Other tests in the AH series are AH1, which measures perceptual or nonverbal reasoning of children aged 7-11 years; AH2/AH3 Group Test of General Ability (see Heim, 1947; Heim & Watts, 1960; Watts, 1953), which provides an appraisal of general reasoning and ability of children aged ten years and older and adults; AH4 Group Test of General Intelligence (see Nisbet, J., 1972 for a review), which measures general intelligence of children ten years and older and adults, including those of below average intelligence; and AH6 Group Test of High Level Intelligence (see Huck & Matuszek, 1984 for a review), an extension of AH5 for individuals aged 16 years to college level who have a slightly higher ability range than those who are appropriate subjects for the AH5. The AH5 was first published in 1956, a year after the publication of AH4. The AH1, AH2/AH3, and AH6, which were coauthored by K. P. Watts and V. Simmonds, appeared in the 1970s.

The 72-item AH5 consists of two parts (36 items each), with the first part comprised of verbal and numerical problems, and the second comprised of problems in diagrammatic form. The majority of the items are multiple-choice, having five choices per item. Interspersed among these are some completion items, as well as multiple-choice items with more than five, and as many as nine, choices per item. The first part is predominantly verbal and quantitative in nature—the type that are widely familiar in many group tests of general intelligence in North America. The last part is somewhat more esoteric and demands facility in visualizing forms, including geometric figures and spatial relations. There are more items of this type than are included in most group intelligence tests.

An example of a typical cleverly contrived item (not an actual test item) that recurs throughout the first section of the test would be as follows:

Which of the five words on the right bears a similar relation to each of the two words on the left?

Dark. Dull. (1) Hard (2) Bright (3) Soft (4) Glowing (5) Serene

Items of this sort can be made quite difficult and are well suited to the purpose of the test. They can be constructed from ordinary English vocabulary and do not call for information acquired in educational settings.

Practical Applications/Uses

The AH5 is appropriate for use with groups of highly intelligent high-school students; potential college, university, and graduate-school entrants; research workers; and entrants to the professions, all of whom shuld be 13 years of age or older.

The test is not suitable for those who are younger than 13 years or below average intelligence. Administration of the test is difficult. This difficulty arises from the fact that an extensive series of practice questions is part of the testing procedure. The manual gives specific instructions as to the manner in which examinees' questions are to be answered during this practice period. Although these preliminary exercises are beneficial, the reliability and validity of the instrument probably could be improved if half of the practice exercises were included in the test itself. The manual states that a competent examiner can administer the AH5 to groups of 20 to 25 examinees and that there should be an assistant for every additional 5 to 20 examinees.

A separate and somewhat confusing answer sheet is employed; for example, in some cases, answers have to be written in numerical form by examinees. Scoring, however, is by hand and quite easy. Although some of the questions are completion type, the correct answers are specific, so that scoring can be accomplished with a minimum of decision making.

The time limit for each part of the test is 20 minutes, but subjects are informed only about the total time required for completing the test. The extra time needed for preliminary instructions and practice exercises makes the total testing time between 60 and 70 minutes, which is manageable for most purposes. Although the test is not primarily a speed test, a time limit is probably essential due to the fact that many of the items could be solved by highly intelligent subjects given unlimited testing time. Subjects are also instructed to answer the questions in the order that they prefer because, according to the manual, the test's goal is to encourage subjects to work at their own tempo and first answer the questions that most appeal to them, for discovering which problems can be solved successfully is considered more important than ascertaining those that defeat them in the allotted time. There are no analyses of either scoring or interpretation, except for the consideration of total number right on each of the two subtests.

The test norms presented in the manual are a specialized and abbreviated form of percentiles. For each reference group (e.g., university students) raw scores corresponding to five grades—A, B, C, D, and E—are given. In all cases, "A" represents the upper 10% of examinees in the group, "B" the next 20%, "C" the next 40%, "D" the next 20%, and "E" the lowest 10%. Unfortunately, norms of this type omit information that is provided by the more complete tables of percentiles or standard scores commonly used with group tests. Furthermore, these letter "grades" invite confusion with traditional school marks.

Technical Aspects

Reliability data given in the test manual is totally inadequate. The manual provides a number of test-retest reliability coefficients, but they are generally uninformative. For example, 94 Cambridge University students, retested after a five-month interval, yielded a reliability coefficient of .84. However, several items were different on the second testing because the instrument was still being developed during this period. Although repeated retestings of small groups comprised of persons of heterogeneous intellectual levels yielded reliability coefficients ranging from .80 to higher than .90, exact figures were not given.

Correlations of this order would be expected from the strong dependence of the classical test-theory reliability coefficient on the homogeneity of the group tested, but they do not provide much information about the stability of the instrument. A high reliability coefficient may reflect variation in "true" scores in a heterogeneous group, rather than an absence of error. One further shortcoming is that no standard errors of measurement are given in the AH5 test manual. For many purposes the standard error of measurement is a more useful statistic than a reliability coefficient.

The relatively small number of items on the test (72) and the multiple-choice format of most of the items (63 of the 72 items have five choices) engenders considerable chance variability due to guessing, which would be expected to depress the reliability of the test. In addition, because of the nature of the test, considerable guessing might be expected by highly intelligent subjects. For example, if an examinee responds to 30 (about half) of these items purely on a chance basis, one can expect, from binomial probabilities, roughly $30(1/5) = $ six items correct by chance, on the average, as well as a *variance* of $30(1/5)(4/5) = 4.8$ for the number of items obtained correct by chance. In a 72-item test chance variability due to guessing is far from negligible. Thus, a substantial component of the standard error of measurement (whatever it is) is probably accounted for by the multiple-choice format.

In contrast to the sparsity of reliability data, extensive validity data are given in the manual, but, again, it is not possible to conclude much from this data. The manual provides two types of validity coefficients, neither of which—when considered alone—is wholly satisfactory, according to the author, but when considered jointly may yield a general idea of the test's value and limitations as a predictive tool in appropriate situations. These two validity coefficients are 1) correlations with scores on generally accepted intelligence tests (mainly British), test and general instructions and preparation for testing. Together, they provide a very readable introduction in layman's language to the test.

The fourth section is the largest and is devoted to directions for administering the test, with specific directions for administering each item given in English in one column and in Spanish on the other half of the page.

Following the administration directions are three shorter sections: the interpretation of test results, use of test results, and development of the test. The interpretation of test results section provides two tables that can be used to evaluate the children's scores. One of these provides percentile ranks based on total scores that have separate columns and entries for Spanish- and English-speaking students. These clearly show the differences in performance on this test for the two groups. For example, a raw score of 25 corresponds to the 44th percentile for English-speaking children and the 83rd percentile for Spanish-speaking children. The second table is for English-speaking students only and presents a breakdown of subtest scores and total score into three categories: high, middle, and low. These score boundaries correspond respectively to the upper 37½%, middle 37½%, and lowest 25% of the scores. In terms of the various subtests, these results show that Test 1, Visual Perception of Letters, is the least difficult. On this test, a child scoring seven or less right out of ten items (70% correct) is considered to be in the lowest score category. This compares to three of ten correct for the same designation on all three of the other subtests.

The two-page use of test results section provides both general and specific guidelines. For example, general guidelines pertaining to low scoring students would state that "low scores may indicate a lack of readiness or maturity, or the presence of personal problems which might interfere with the growth and learning process—but not failure" (Rodrigues, Vogler, & Wilson, 1972a, p. 14). An example of a more specific guideline is that given for interpreting total scores: "Children with total raw scores of 31 or better may be started immediately in appropriate programs" (p. 15). All of these guidelines are cleary directed toward the kindergarten teacher who is assumed to be the primary user of the test and test information.

The final three-page section, development of the test, provides three tables: the first describes the communities and regions of the country that took part in the standardization, the second gives reliability data, and the third provides discrimination information and a list of the names of the school districts that took part in the standardization of the test in 1970.

Several additional items at the back of the guide include a short list of references, the scoring key, and a two-page record sheet with places to accommodate the scores of 30 students.

Practical Applications/Uses

In considering the practical uses of the Analysis of Readiness Skills, one is hard-pressed to imagine much beyond that of a basic screening and placement device for children in the four-to-six-year age bracket. Indeed, one might argue that it may be of use for these age groups in only limited contexts because many changes have occurred in the area of early childhood education in a relatively short period (15 years) since this test was field-tested and standardized. Among these changes are the acceptance of television shows such as "Sesame Street" and "Mr. Rogers"; the wide availability of flashcards, books, and other educational materials for use with preschoolers; the increasing opportunity for participation in formal preschool programs (ranging from Headstart to corporate day-care); and the continuing decline in the size of families. All of these changes can alter the timing of the acquisition of basic skills, such as letter and number recognition, which are the only skills being measured on this test. Thus, it brings into question the appropriateness of this test as a screening or placement device for kindergarten children. The appropriateness and relevance of a test is always an issue, but it is particularly so when the test measures quite narrow, age-specific skills such as those presented here.

A related development in the area of early childhood education that may impact this test is the general concern about the concept of "readiness." Many educators now consider it to be an inappropriate concept. One reason is that a lack of "readiness" has often been used as an excuse for doing very little instructionally with young children. Although this may be simply another passing fancy in education, the fact that this test attempts to formalize the concept of readiness may make it less appealing to today's kindergarten teachers than it was in previous years.

A possible new use of this measure might be with younger children, such as four-year-olds. Currently, there are many existing and emerging preschool programs for four-year-olds, and the content of this test might be more appropriate for them than five-year-olds. A possible problem with this age group, however, is the group administration procedures and the lack of norm information. The former could be overcome simply by administering the test individually. The lack of norms is a problem, given the standard interpretation of "ready" or "not ready." However, the test might be used simply as a guide to understanding how many children in a class of four-year-olds are familiar with the letters and numbers.

Technical Aspects

When considering the technical aspects of this test, one is struck by the limited amount of information provided about the test's validity. Virtually no information is given in the manual about any further evaluations, follow-up studies, or other empirical studies of the test's validity as a measure of readiness. Further, as the earlier comments sought to convey, there is considerable question as to whether the test is content valid for five-year-olds. The fact that there is no evidence of any empirical validity studies carried out at any time raises further questions about the confidence that can be placed in the results.

A second aspect of a good test is more reliability. In the case of this test, reasonable reliability estimates are given for the overall measure based on testing in 1971. The overall score for reliability is reported as .90 for English-speaking samples and .81 for the Spanish-speaking sample. However, the reliabilities for the subtests are all lower than this level and in several instances below .60 (Rodrigues et al., 1972a). Although reliability must be interpreted relative to the score categories and decisions to be made based on the results, it is clear that the latter values are a bit below what would typically be considered acceptable. Accordingly, it seems that any decisions made should be made on the basis of the full test score. However, given that no empirical validity evidence has been presented for the utility and appropriateness of any cut scores, those given as guidelines for placement using the total scores would be difficult to recommend, that is, of course, unless users choose to validate their utility in the context in which they are using them.

Critique

The Analysis of Readiness Skills is a short, easy-to-use test with a clearly defined function: to provide kindergarten teachers with basic guidelines for the placement of children entering kindergarten. Although the format, the cost, and directions are clear and straightforward, serious issues are raised regarding its validity and utility. Part of the problem stems from the long interval since the test was developed and standardized, which raises the question as to whether the data provided still hold that today. Another more serious issue concerns its value—no empirical studies of the guidelines and utility of the test have ever been reported. It should be noted that this is not a new criticism; several earlier reviews noted the same shortcomings (e.g., Guthrie, 1978). Perhaps more importantly, times have changed and these changes are reflected in both the population for whom this test is designed and the standards of the consumers of such tests. The readiness concept is less relevant, as is the test's content. Finally, the technical documentation fails to establish the test's validity and the test is probably limited for other uses (i.e., could not be used for any purpose other than as a readiness test). Thus, this reviewer does not highly recommend its use.

References

Guthrie, J. T. (1978). Review of Analysis of Readiness Skills: Reading and Mathematics. In O. K. Buros (Ed.), *The eighth mental measurements yearbook* (p. 796). Highland Park, NJ: The Gryphon Press.

Rodrigues, M. C., Vogler, W. H., and Wilson, J. F. (1972a). *Teacher's manual: Analysis of Readiness Skills.* Chicago: The Riverside Publishing Company.

Rodrigues, M. C., Vogler, W. H. and Wilson, J. F. (1972b). *Analysis of Readiness Skills: Reading and Mathematics.* Chicago: The Riverside Publishing Company.

Donald E. Mowrer, Ph.D.

Professor of Speech Pathology, Department of Speech and Hearing Science, Arizona State University, Tempe, Arizona.

ARIZONA ARTICULATION PROFICIENCY SCALE: REVISED

Janet Barker Fudala. Los Angeles, California: Western Psychological Services.

Introduction

The Arizona Articulation Proficiency Scale: Revised (AAPS; Fudala, 1974) was designed to assess the articulation ability primarily of children aged 3:0 to 11:11 years, but also can be used to test the articulation of adolescents and adults. Based on the assumption that severity of an articulation problem is a result of how frequently a misarticulated sound occurs, a weighted score that provides an indication of the severity of the problem can be derived. This hand-scored test requires the subject to name individual black-and-white sketches of familiar objects or read sentences (third-grade reading level) that sample the production of 27 consonants in the initial and final positions of words and 20 vowels in either the medial or final position. Considerable knowledge about phonetics and the ability to make accurate discrimination between sounds is required to administer the test; consequently, a speech pathologist should administer this test. Administration time is typically from ten to 15 minutes. A numeric score representing the subject's articulation ability is derived, yielding one of six interpretations from unintelligible speech to occasional sound error. Age level norms, based on normative studies reporting ages at which 90% of the children tested in these studies mastered the sound, are presented.

This test, first published in 1963, was revised in 1974 when a few items were changed, some pictures updated, new data added to revise the average AAPS Score, and some cosmetic changes added to make the test easier to score. Another revision is currently taking place but is not available at the time of this review. Although the first edition issued in 1963 was not reviewed, at least three reviews exist for the 1970 revised edition (Falck, 1979; Hunter et al., 1977; Proger, 1972). According to the publisher, the new revised edition in progress will include normative data on approximately 4,000 subjects and will extend the scale to include a nonsense-imitation test and language screening.

The author has published at least two articles that this reviewer could find. Fudala was the senior author of one study about utilizing parents in a speech correction program (Fudala, England, & Ganoung, 1972) and coauthor of another article concerning determining severity of articulation disorders (Fudala & Ross, 1973). However, this reviewer could find no publication listing for Fudala in any of the journals published by the American Speech & Hearing Association. Fudala authored one other test (Quickscreen) designed to screen for speech, language, and learning problems (Fudala, 1982).

The test comes in an easy-to-carry, 9″ x 12″ cardboard box and contains a 12-page manual (Fudala, 1984), a spiral-bound set of stimulus material printed on heavy card stock to evoke responses, 25 survey test forms, and 25 four-page protocol booklets. The manual, which contains a sample of the survey form and protocol booklet, describes the rationale for giving weighted scores to different types of errors; describes the materials contained in the kit; identifies the uses of this test; reports reliability and validity statistics and determination of age norms; and gives a detailed description of how to administer and score the test, an example of how to score the picture test, an illustration on how to interpret the total score, and a brief description regarding use of this test as a language-screening device.

The stimulus material booklet contains 50 black-and-white sketches, two yellow and green pictures to evoke responses, and 25 sentences printed on six pages. The sketches are clearly drawn, and children should have no difficulty identifying the key words that the drawings were designed to evoke. On the card opposite each picture is printed the key word and sound to be tested. The survey form of this test, designed to keep a record of up to ten children who have been tested, allows one to rapidly identify the sound errors and would be useful as a form from which to choose children for therapy. The first page of the protocol booklet provides space for summary and routine information about the person tested (e.g., parent's name, teacher, room, birthdate). The second page is a worksheet on which the examiner can identify the tested sound and record the type of error produced. Each test sound contains a value from .05 to 7.0, which must be circled if an error is made on that sound. These values represent the number of times the sound probably would occur in 100 consecutive speech sounds, according to research results the author extracted from a study by French, Carter, and Koenig (1930). Large blocks of blacked out spaces represent sections of consonants or vowels that are not to be evaluated. At first, these black spaces appear to be somewhat confusing to someone not familiar with the test. The last page helps the examiner to determine the total score, compare this score with age norms, and make one of the six interpretations presented to evaluate the total score. Finally, a formula is presented to determine the percentage of speech improvement made between pre- and post-total scores. Two of the sketches are designed to evoke conversational speech in order that the examiner can get some idea about articulation ability in spontaneous speech.

Practical Applications/Uses

The examiner's role in presenting the test items is straightforward. Instructions for administering the test are fail-proof and "user-friendly," as are the scoring directions. This reviewer asked a student majoring in special education to administer this test to two children, and he had no difficulty with either the administration or scoring.

The examiner is required to present the stimulus item, evaluate it as being correct or incorrect, circle the appropriate value if the response is incorrect, add all of the values circled, and subtract this number from 100. The resulting total score is then compared with age norms from 3-12 years and evaluated as severe, moderate, or normal. For example, if the child were five-years-old and obtained a score of 83, the child would be rated as having a moderate articulation problem, and speech would be considered intelligible although errors would be noted. This interpretation is simple to compute and provides useful information. The only difficulty concerning this process is that accurate judgments about sound productions depend on the examiner's ability. This reviewer has accompanied students to schools and asked them to evaluate the articulation skills of young children, only to find that many students were inaccurate in identifying sound errors. The validity of this test depends soley on the speech-sound discrimination skills of the examiner. The test was designed for use by trained speech pathologists. This reviewer anticipates that such a person would have little difficulty evaluating speech responses. This reviewer would be cautious of test results administered by individuals in other professions (e.g., classroom teachers, psychologists, parents, counselors) because the test was not designed to be administered by those without speech training. Nevertheless, the untrained person should be able to identify the more glaring errors and produce a total score not too distant from one obtained by a speech pathologist.

The AAPS is usually used in clinical settings such as schools, rehabilitation centers, hospitals, and universities. It could be adapted to a blind population merely by asking the subject to repeat the examiner's speech response. Certainly those who speak dialects (such as black or Spanish-American) would be penalized for "misarticulating" certain sounds that are considered "correct" in their dialect form. Therefore, the examiner must take dialect into consideration when evaluating the test results. The author provides no information about racial or ethnic group performance on this test.

There will be some (e.g., Proger, 1972; Winitz, 1969) who would disagree with the author on her decision to evaluate severity based on frequency of occurrence of speech sounds. The type of substitution plays an important role in determining severity, and this factor is completely overlooked. For example, a rare *SH* (/ʃ/) substitution for *S* renders speech far more unintelligible than the more frequent *TH* (/θ/) for *S* substitution. Yet, devising a severity scale taking into account the type of substitution may be so complex that the effort would not be worth the result. The age at which sounds are mastered is also a matter of dispute among authorities (e.g., Prather, Hedrick, & Kern, 1975). The author uses data from a large number of normative studies that have suggested ages when children usually master consonant sounds. These data may provide useful guidelines for making judgments about when children can be expected to master certain sounds, but these data do not take into account individual differences among children in mastery of sounds. For example, many children master *R* and *S* at a much earlier age than would be expected based on large sample norms. The fact that most children master sounds at a later age, according to many surveys (Prather et al., 1975; Sander, 1972), does not mean that some children should master *R* and *S* at a later age. The author ignores "early" sound acquisition.

One cosmetic feature of the test booklet is somewhat annoying, and this criticism is aimed at the publishing company. A close inspection of the phonetic symbols indicates that the publisher had difficulty finding the proper fonts for various

Howard Tennen, Ph.D.
Associate Professor of Psychiatry, University of Connecticut School of Medicine, Farmington, Connecticut.

Sharon Herzberger, Ph.D.
Associate Professor of Psychology, Trinity College, Hartford, Connecticut.

ATTRIBUTIONAL STYLE QUESTIONNAIRE

Christopher Peterson, Amy Semmel, Carl von Baeyer, Lyn Y. Abramson, Gerald I. Metalsky, and Martin E. P. Seligman. New York, New York: Plenum Press.

Introduction

The Attributional Style Questionnaire (ASQ; Peterson, Semmel, von Baeyer, Abramson, Metalsky, & Seligman, 1982) is a self-report measure of patterns of "explanatory style" (Peterson & Seligman, 1984), which is the tendency to select certain causal explanations for good and bad events. The development of the ASQ has generated a spate of sophisticated investigations on the costs and benefits of certain attributional styles, particularly in the area of depression. Many of these studies will not be reviewed here, but representative studies that offer a sense of the current uses of the ASQ will be described. Peterson and Seligman (1984) offer a comprehensive review of the role of causal explanations in depression, including studies using the ASQ.

Attribution theory has a long history within social psychology. Drawing on the seminal work of Heider (1958) and later contributions by Kelley (1965), Weiner (1972, 1974) derived an attributional theory of achievement motivation that continues to guide most studies of attributions in the achievement realm. According to the theory, the causes of success and failure can be subsumed within a two-dimensional taxonomy: an internal-external (locus) dimension, which locates the cause within the actor or in the environment, and a stable-unstable (stability) dimension, which identifies the cause as one that is chronic or transient. Ickes and Layden (1976) subsequently described "attributional styles" or consistent ways of ascribing the causes of positive and negative events.

The immediate impetus for the development of the ASQ was Abramson, Seligman, and Teasdale's (1978) reformulation of the learned helplessness model of depression (Seligman, 1975). A brief overview of the model is critical to a full appreciation of the ASQ. The revised model states that when faced with an uncontrollable bad event, a person will wonder why it occurred. Many naturalistic studies of people experiencing misfortune (e.g., Wong & Weiner, 1981; Tennen, Affleck, &

These reviewers wish to thank Martin E. P. Seligman for his helpful comments and suggestions on an earlier version of this review.

Gershman, in press) support this basic contention. The model goes on to suggest that how people answer the question "why?" will help determine their adaptation to the event. Abramson et al. (1978) contend that there are three dimensions relevant to a person's causal attributions and that each dimension is associated with a particular aspect of adaptation to an uncontrollable event.

The first dimension is the *locus* of one's causal explanation: Did this event occur because of something about me (an internal attribution) or something about the situation (an external attribution)? The reformulation predicts that internal attributions, not external attributions, for bad events are associated with a subsequent loss of self-esteem. The second dimension is the *stability* of the causal explanation: Did this event occur because of something that will persist (a stable attribution) or something that is transient (an unstable attribution)? The reformulation predicts that stable attributions lead to more *chronic adaptational deficits* following exposure to an uncontrollable bad event. Finally, the model considers the *globality* of the causal explanation: Will the cause of this event influence many aspects of life (a global explanation) or influence only the currently experienced event? The globality of a person's causal explanation is thought to predict the generality of adaptational deficits across situations. Attributing the bad event to a global factor will lead to pervasive adaptational deficits, whereas attributing the event to a more specific cause will lead to less pervasive deficits.

It was with this conceptual framework in mind that Seligman and his colleagues developed the ASQ. To measure attributional *style* rather than an explanation for a particular event, the scale describes 12 hypothetical events. Half of the events described are good events and half are bad events. These events are presented in booklet form and can be administered individually or to groups.

The instructions are brief and clear. They ask respondents to imagine that they are in the situations described and that for each situation they write one cause of the outcome in the space provided. After writing a cause for the event, respondents are asked to rate on three seven-point scales 1) whether the outcome was due to something about them or something about other people or circumstances (Locus), 2) will this cause again be present? (Stability), and 3) does the cause influence just this situation or other areas of their life (Globality). Respondents circle one number from one to seven corresponding to their causal beliefs. The scales are anchored so that external, unstable, and specific attributions receive lower scores, whereas internal, stable, and global attributions receive higher scores.

The ASQ has been employed successfully with college students (Peterson, Semmel, von Baeyer, Abramson, Metalsky, & Seligman, 1982), clinically depressed individuals (Raps, Peterson, Reinhard, Abramson, & Seligman, 1982), and people undergoing various stressful events (O'Hara, Rehm, & Campbell, 1982; Manly, McMahon, Bradley, & Davidson, 1982). There have been no reports of respondents having problems completing the scale. These reviewers have found that severely disturbed psychiatric inpatients have some difficulty completing the ASQ.

For investigators interested in studying children's attributional style, Seligman, Peterson, Kaslow, Tanenbaum, Alloy, and Abramson (1984) devised the Children's Attributional Style Questionnaire (CASQ). The CASQ uses a forced-choice format in which, like the ASQ, the respondent is presented with a series of good and bad hypothetical events. Each event is followed by two possible causes. These reviewers have found that children as young as eight years can complete the CASQ, particularly when someone reads the items aloud as the child reads along. The CASQ has been employed with elementary-school children (Seligman et al., 1984) and with children requiring psychiatric hospitalization (Rae & Tennen, 1985). An in-depth description of the CASQ is beyond the scope of this review. Interested readers should consult the Seligman et al. (1984) article.

Practical Applications/Uses

The ASQ has been used thus far as a research instrument. Although it has been employed predominantly in studies of depression, available evidence summarized in this review indicates that the scale can be applied to research on achievement motivation, self-esteem, responses to aversive life events, life change, gender and sex role differences in causal attributions, and parental behavior. The children's version of the scale (CASQ) has also been limited to studies of depression, but may be applicable to understanding the cognitive underpinnings of certain conduct disorders. The ASQ was not designed as a clinical tool.

Technical Aspects

Internal consistency: Several studies have explored the ASQ's internal consistency. In their journal article, Peterson et al. (1982) report the internal consistencies of the Locus, Stability, and Globality Scales in a sample of 100 undergraduates. They found that these scales had but modest reliabilities, with Cronbach's (1951) alpha ranging from .44 to .69.

Tennen and Herzberger (in press) also report modest internal consistency for ASQ scales, with lower reliability for Locus scores. Cronbach's alpha was .56 for Stability ratings, α = .66 for Globality ratings, but α = .21 for Locus ratings. These findings of moderate internal consistency (with the exception of the Locus Scale) are consistent with the reports of several investigators (Seligman et al., 1979; Golin, Sweeney, & Shaeffer, 1981; Cutrona, Russell, & Jones, 1984). The modest levels of internal consistency found on the ASQ scales are uncommon in scales that have few items. In addition, the Locus Scale tends to produce ratings in the middle of the scale (Seligman et al., 1979; Tennen & Herzberger, in press), which may further adversely affect its reliability. Tennen and Herzberger (in press) found that separating scales into ratings for positive events and negative events produced similar levels of internal consistency.

Peterson and Seligman (1984) report that a revised version of the ASQ with 18 bad events produced coefficient alphas ranging from .66 to .88. The revised ASQ described by Peterson and Seligman (1984) appears to overcome this reliability problem. Two caveats should be mentioned. First, the revised ASQ, unlike the original, has not been employed extensively, so that evidence of its validity awaits further research. Furthermore, the revised ASQ does not present respondents with hypothetical positive events. This limitation may not encumber investigators interested in testing the reformulated learned helplessness model of depression because the model makes most of its predictions for bad events. However, for those interested in other aspects of attributional style, such as attributional evenhandedness (Abramson & Alloy, 1981; Raps et al., 1982) or the relation between attributional style and achievement-related behaviors (Weiner, 1974), the measurement of attributions for good events may be critical.

Seligman and associates offer a solution. Because the scales show considerable intercorrelation within good events and within bad events, these investigators recommend combining them into overall composites for good events and bad events. According to Peterson et al.'s journal article (1982), the composite scores have higher levels of internal consistency (.75 for good events and .72 for bad events). However, the psychological meaning of the composite score may require further clarification (Cochran & Hammen, 1985). Nonetheless, Seligman (personal communication, November 27, 1985) makes a cogent argument for the a priori validity of composite scores. He notes that reactions to stress and failure involve situationally and temporally global judgments. There is thus good reason to employ the composite scores.

Test-retest reliability: Learned helplessness theory, which provides the conceptual base from which the ASQ derives, posits that people have somewhat *enduring* attributional styles. Abramson et al. (1978) describe attributional style as a precursor of depression proneness. Similarly, Peterson and Seligman (1984, p. 355) note that according to the reformulation, "individuals have a *characteristic* [italics added] way of explaining events." The theory does not explicitly state that when depressed individuals recover, they maintain a "depressogenic" attributional style (i.e., a style that leads one to make internal, stable, and global attributions for bad events). Nonetheless, the model does generally suggest that ASQ scores should be relatively stable over time. The available literature indicates that in nonclinical samples, ASQ scores are temporally consistent.

Studies by Golin, Sweeney, and Schaeffer (1981) and Peterson, Semmel, von Baeyer, Abramson, Metalsky, & Seligman (1982) demonstrate that in undergraduate samples, attributional style is a stable aspect of personality functioning over a period of four to five weeks. It is possible, but fairly unlikely, that participants in these studies were consistent in their attribution ratings because they recalled their initial ratings.

Most recently, Persons and Rao (1985) followed depressed patients during their hospitalization and found statistically significant changes in ASQ scores for negative events as the patients approached discharge. Attributions for positive events did not change from admission to discharge. These investigators conclude that attributions are not stable aspects of personality. Rather, they change with changes in emotional state. In the Persons and Rao (1985) study, when depression scores shifted in the nondepressed direction, individuals showed less of a depressive attributional style. Hamilton and Abramson (1983) report similar findings. In fact, they found that by the time depressed subjects were preparing for hospital discharge there were no significant ASQ differences between depressed subjects and their control-group counterparts. Whether the reformulated learned helplessness model predicts stability or allows for changes in attributions is a conceptual matter that does not detract from the contributions of the ASQ to attribution theory research.

Validity: There is now a large literature supporting the criterion and construct validity of the ASQ. Here, the findings of a number of representative investigations will be summarized. Because the ASQ derives from a theory of depression, most validation studies have been concerned with aspects of a "depressive attributional style." Recently, however, there have been several studies that explore other constructs related to attributional processes.

Seligman and his associates (Peterson, Semmel, von Baeyer, Abramson, Metalsky, & Seligman, 1982) followed a correlational approach and devised several methods of demonstrating the criterion validity of the ASQ. Two studies examined the extent to which the ASQ predicts causal explanations that occur spontaneously. In the first study (Peterson, Bettes, & Seligman, 1982), college students were asked to write about the two worst events that had happened to them within the last year and then to complete the ASQ. Although in their open-ended descriptions of events the students were not prompted to discuss causes, they did so readily and provided explanations that could be coded along the dimensions represented in the ASQ. Correlations between the spontaneous explanations and the relevant scales on the ASQ ranged from .19 ($p<.10$) to .41 ($p<.001$), with the Locus and composite scores demonstrating the strongest association. A second study replicated these findings with a patient population. Depressed individuals' explanations for seeking treatment and for experiencing symptoms correlated with a composite score for negative events on the ASQ, and both attribution measures correlated with depressive symptoms measured by the Beck Depression Inventory (Beck, 1967). These results demonstrate construct validity for the ASQ in that it both taps spontaneously generated attributions and relates to theoretically relevant symptomatology.

Other investigators have used a criterion groups approach to validate the ASQ. Eaves and Rush (1984), for example, found that depressed female psychiatric patients provided more internal, stable, and global explanations for bad events than did controls. Seligman, Abramson, Semmel, and von Baeyer (1979) obtained the same results comparing depressed and nondepressed college students.

Other studies demonstrate that attributional style can predict response to a future task. Weinberger and Cash (1982) asked undergraduate females to complete the ASQ and then a month or two later asked them to interact with (ostensibly) a potential dating partner. After the subjects were rejected by the partner, they provided explanations for their rejection and described the likelihood of success with a different partner. Several ASQ indices predicted these responses, thus demonstrating the relative stability of attributional style.

Alloy, Peterson, Abramson, and Seligman (1984) employed the ASQ to test a fundamental premise of the reformulated learned helplessness model. The model predicts that people who habitually attribute negative outcomes to global causes will demonstrate behavioral deficits across a broad range of situations after being exposed to uncontrollable aversive outcomes. Those who tend to attribute negative outcomes to specific factors should show less pervasive deficits. Participants completed the ASQ and were then exposed to a series of uncontrollable noise bursts that have been employed in studies of learned helplessness. As predicted, subjects who on the ASQ had attributed negative events to global factors showed more generalized deficits on subsequent tasks. As Alloy et al. (1984) note, these findings add to the construct validity of the ASQ.

As one of the most creative investigations of the ASQ's validity, a study by Metal-

sky, Abramson, Seligman, Semmel, and Peterson (1982) deserves special note. These investigators tested the reformulated learned helplessness model's prediction that people who usually ascribe bad events to internal, stable, global causes are more likely to experience depression in the face of an aversive event. Undergraduates completed the ASQ several weeks before taking their midterm exams. Just before the exam, depressed mood state was assessed. Mood state was also measured just after participants received their midterm grades. Attributional style (locus and globality) for bad events predicted increases in depressed mood for students whose grades were lower than they had hoped for but not for students whose grades were at least as high as they had hoped. These findings provide elegant support for the model and the construct validity of the ASQ. Moreover, this study of helplessness in the classroom is an example of a prospective design that provides the most meaningful application of the ASQ as a measure of cognitive diathesis.

Three recent studies by Seligman and associates further support the construct validity of the ASQ. Zullow and Seligman (1985) hypothesized that ruminating about bad events and attributing those events to internal, stable, global factors (as measured by the ASQ) predicts later depression. In their study, people who were dispositionally inclined to ruminate and who manifested a depressive attributional style were at high risk for later depression. In two recent studies, Kamen and Seligman (1985) found that explanatory style, as measured by the ASQ, predicted later college grade-point average, even after controlling for other predictors, such as SAT scores, high school rank in class, and scores on achievement tests. In one of these studies, explanatory (attributional) style accounted for nearly as much variance in grade-point average as all other predictors combined. In another study, Seligman and Schulman (in press) found that insurance agents' attributional style predicted the *amount* of insurance they sold in their first two years of service. In a separate prospective study, ASQ scores also predicted which salespeople remained at their job and also predicted the amount of insurance they sold.

Other studies have attempted to examine the *causal* relation between attributional style and depression. Golin, Sweeney, and Shaeffer (1981) used a cross-lagged panel approach to examine the association between attributions and depression and supported the notion that attributional style may lead to depressed affect a month later. This study and others like it (e.g., O'Hara, Rehm, & Campbell, 1982) have been criticized, however, for failing to obtain a record of ongoing life events during the course of the study to enable the investigator to predict which subjects are more likely to develop depressive reactions. Because the reformulated learned helplessness model is best characterized as a diathesis-stress model (Metalsky et al., 1982) in which the depressive style is the diathesis and life events serve as the stress, it seems that to provide adequate tests of the model and make conceptually meaningful use of the ASQ investigators should include a measure of life stress. Childbirth represents one such potential stressor. Cutrona (1983) found that ASQ scores obtained approximately two months before delivery predicted a significant proportion of variance in "post-partum blues," even when initial levels of depression were statistically controlled. Prior ASQ scores also predicted post-partum depression.

Some investigators (e.g., Cochran & Hammen, 1985) recommend causal model-

ing rather than cross-lagged panel approaches when the investigator is interested in causal relations among attributional style, life stress, and depression.

Most studies using the ASQ examine the scales separately for positive and negative events and separately for internal, stable, and global attributions. Results have varied across studies. As noted above, Eaves and Rush (1984) and Seligman et al. (1979) found significant relations between internal, stable, and global attributions for negative events and depression. Metalsky et al. (1982), however, were unable to find a significant relation between stability ratings of negative events and depression over receipt of a low grade. Peterson and Seligman (1984) report no significant relation between stability and depression among lower SES women, and Persons and Rao (1985) obtained the same results in a patient population.

Consistent with the theory proposed by Abramson, Seligman, and Teasdale (1978), the ASQ scales pertaining to negative events are more likely to show significant relations to depression than the positive scales (Peterson & Seligman, 1984). The negative scales have been more likely to relate significantly to other constructs as well (see below). However, these results may be due to the nature of the constructs that have been investigated, which to a large extent are negative in tone (e.g., depression, anxiety, stuttering). Investigators interested in positive life events or situations that people might experience ambivalently should retain the positive scales.

Not all studies successfully relate the ASQ to other measures. Zimmerman, Coryell, and Corenthal (1984) found no relation between ASQ scores and a biological marker of melancholia (the Dexamethasone Suppression Test). This finding, however, is not particularly relevant to the validity of the ASQ in the prediction of depression, but rather for separating subclasses of depression. Burger (1985) found only marginally significant correlations between stable and global attributions and ratings of one's desire for control over positive events, with no other correlations approaching significance. The existence of a number of disconfirming studies led Peterson, Villanova, and Raps (1985) to compare studies that confirmed hypotheses by employing the ASQ and those that did not. They concluded that a composite score and the globality rating are most likely to demonstrate significant relations with other measures and that the stability rating is least likely to correlate significantly with other measures.

Coyne and Gotlib (1983), Peterson and Seligman (1984), and Peterson, Villanova, and Raps (1985) all agree that in the existing literature there is an inconsistent association between attributional style and depression. Coyne and Gotlib (1983) contend that studies that require participants to make attributions for hypothetical events (including studies that employ the ASQ) are more likely to yield findings supporting the notion of a depressive attributional style. Peterson et al. (1985) tested this hypothesis by reviewing 61 published tests of the reformulated learned helplessness model. They conclude that Coyne and Gotlib were correct, but because studies employing hypothetical events also had larger samples and presented participants with more events to rate, the independent effect of presenting hypothetical events could not be determined.

Since the publication of the reviews by Coyne and Gotlib (1983) and Peterson et al. (1985), Cochran and Hammen (1985) employed rating scales adapted from the ASQ and asked a geriatric sample and a group of college students to apply these

scales to two bad events that they experienced in the past year. Using a structural modeling approach, these investigators conclude that contrary to the theory that guided the construction of the ASQ, there was little evidence for a "cross-situational style in interpreting the causes of stressful life events" (p. 1569).

It appears that the ASQ allows the investigator to present a relatively large number of hypothetical events to many research participants. This approach is most likely to reveal a depressive attributional style. Yet the findings of Cochran and Hammen (1985) and others (as reviewed by Peterson & Seligman, 1984, and Peterson et al., 1985) imply that ASQ-derived findings may have limited ecological validity. Are these nonconfirming findings damaging to the learned helplessness reformulation, which predicts that people's attributions for real-life events should be associated with depressive symptoms (Peterson et al., 1985)? Do they suggest that findings reported in studies using the ASQ will not generalize to situations outside the testing session? The question is complex and turns, these reviewers believe, on the degree of ambiguity in real aversive events and the amount of time that has elapsed between the occurrence of the aversive event and the time the investigator asks for attributions.

When the causes of an aversive event—real or hypothetical—are ambiguous because certain information is unavailable (as is the case with ASQ items), these reviewers believe that people's attributional style will predict their responses to the event. This prediction is founded in a rich tradition of social learning theory (Rotter, 1954; Lefcourt, von Baeyer, Ware, & Cox, 1979). In fact, the ASQ strives to have participants "impose internal biases rather than report the reality of causes that happened to have occurred for real events" (M.E.P. Seligman, personal communication, November 27, 1985). When the circumstance is less ambiguous, ASQ scores will have less predictive value. The nature of the event aside, these reviewers believe that just after the occurrence of an aversive event, people have immediate tasks to attend to and are less concerned with causal search (Tennen, Affleck, & Gershman, in press). During this initial period, ASQ scores will predict aspects of a person's stress reaction. Indirect support for this hypothesis is provided by Metalsky et al. (1982). However, when people are asked to reflect on an event that occurred as long ago as a year (Cochran & Hammen, 1985), they have had an opportunity to test causal hypotheses, search for causes, and use consensus information to assess initial impressions. In these situations, attributional style is less likely to predict a person's response to aversive events. This limitation should not detract from the value of the ASQ or its theoretical underpinnings.

Several studies demonstrate convergent or discriminant validity of the ASQ. Blaney, Behar, and Head (1980) examined the relation between a measure of depressive cognition and ASQ scores. A moderate correlation was found, suggesting that the measures are tapping related, but not identical phenomena. Raps et al. (1982) compared the responses to the ASQ of depressed patients, nondepressed schizophrenics, and nondepressed medical students. The depressed sample was more likely to attribute bad outcomes to internal, stable, and global causes than were the other samples. Because the two psychiatric samples differed in terms of "depressive attributional style," the ASQ appears to measure content distinguishable from a general psychopathological style of thought.

Although the majority of studies have pertained to depression and the term

"depressive attributional style" has become associated with a set of responses to the ASQ, it is important to note that the ASQ has been used successfully with a range of constructs other than depression. For example, Tennen and Herzberger (in press) found strong relations between some ASQ scales and self-esteem. The ASQ has also been used successfully to differentiate between a group of child abusers and a group of parental controls (Belavic, 1982). Child abusers possessed a more internal, stable, and global attributional style for negative events than the control group. Thus, the ASQ should be regarded as a useful instrument with potentially broad applications.

Alternative Measures: Several other measures of attributional style have been reported in the social psychology literature. Ickes and Layden (1976) describe a measure devised by them that consists of 12 items. Like the ASQ, each item contains a brief description of the outcome of a hypothetical event. Four possible causes are then provided. Participants are asked to imagine that they had experienced the event and to choose what they believe to be the most likely cause. The four possible causes reflect the taxonomy of Weiner (1974): an internal-stable cause, an internal-unstable cause, an external-stable cause, and an external-unstable cause. This measure differs from the ASQ in two important ways: It does not tap the globality dimension and does not allow the *respondent* to rate the locus and stability of a given outcome.

Lefcourt, von Baeyer, Ware, and Cox (1979) developed the Multidimensional-Multiattributional Causality Scale (MMCS), which they describe as a "goal specific locus of control scale" (p. 286). Respondents complete 48 items on Likert scales. Half of these items are in the achievement realm and half reflect affiliation issues. Within each area, there are 12 items that concern success and 12 that concern failure. In addition, the items are divided so as to reflect attributions to stable, internal factors, unstable, internal factors, stable, external characteristics, and unstable, external events. Lefcourt et al. (1979) report moderate estimates of internal consistency and split-half correlations, and modest to moderate test-retest coefficients for periods ranging from one week to several months. A number of validation studies have been reported by Lefcourt and colleagues (Lefcourt, Martin, & Ware, 1984), and by Lewinsohn, Steinmetz, Larson, and Franklin (1981). Like the measure developed by Ickes and Layden (1976), the MMCS does not assess globality, nor does it allow respondents to rate the locus and stability of their attributions.

Anderson, Horowitz, and French (1983) developed the Attributional Style Assessment Test (ASAT). The ASAT consists of 20 hypothetical situations that include success and failure outcomes in interpersonal and noninterpersonal realms. As in the ASQ, respondents imagine themselves in the situation and choose one of six causes that reflect strategy, ability, effort, personality trait, mood, and external circumstances. Several indices of attributional style can be calculated, and Anderson and associates (Anderson, 1983; Anderson et al., 1983) present evidence from several studies supporting construct validity of the ASAT.

Finally, Russell (1982) describes the Causal Dimension Scale (CDS), which measures locus, stability, and controllability dimensions of attributional style. Respondents imagine themselves in eight hypothetical achievement situations. They then complete a series of semantic differential scales. Russell (1982) reports high levels

of internal consistency and several tests of the validity of the CDS. He also describes a factor analysis that confirms the three-dimensional structure of the scale. An important strength of the CDS is that, like the ASQ, it allows the respondent to make locus and stability ratings.

In sum, there are several alternative measures of attributional style. Aside from the ASQ, only the CDS allows respondents to rate relevant causal dimensions. None of the alternative measures share the ASQ's extensive validation across domains.

Critique

As evidenced by the many recent laboratory investigations and naturalistic studies employing the ASQ, this measure and the reformulated learned helplessness model that guided its construction have generated a good deal of enthusiasm in the academic community. With some exceptions, studies using the ASQ have generally produced findings consistent with the reformulated model. There remains, nonetheless, a number of psychometric and conceptual issues that should be the focus of future research.

As these reviewers have noted in this review, the internal consistency of the ASQ scales is modest. Several explanations for this reliability problem have emerged. Peterson and Seligman (1984) suggest that because each scale has only six items, one might expect lower reliability coefficients. Indeed, the revised ASQ, which these authors describe and which consists of 18 negative outcomes, does yield higher estimates of internal consistency. Cutrona (1983) suggests that the ASQ's low internal consistency might also reflect some problems in test construction or that people simply lack cross-situational consistency in their causal attributions. Whatever the reason, the low internal consistency of ASQ scales may reduce correlations with other theory-relevant measures, which in turn may explain some of the inconsistencies that have emerged in the literature.

Some of the scenarios described in the ASQ are irrelevant to certain groups of people, and this may further reduce its power to predict depression, demoralization, or other adaptational deficits. Items describing dating situations or those where one imagines receiving a poor grade seem to have little relevance for most women preparing for the birth of their first child (Cutrona, 1983; Manly et al., 1982), elderly people (Cochran & Hammen, 1985), or spouses of people who are chronically ill (Pagel, Becker, & Coppel, 1985). Future revisions of the ASQ might consider including only those scenarios that have more universal relevance.

Finally, it is important for investigators planning to use the ASQ to appreciate that adequate tests of the reformulated learned helplessness model require that research participants have encountered negative situations. This is important because the reformulated model predicts that people with a pre-existing depressive attributional style are more likely to become depressed than their counterparts *following a bad outcome* (Cutrona, 1983; Pagel et al., 1985). One promising approach is to select a group of people who are at risk for having an aversive experience (e.g., students preparing for an exam, Metalsky et al., 1982; expectant mothers, Manly et al., 1982) and administer the ASQ prior to the event. After the event, an assessment of whether the outcome was experienced as negative and adaptational indices could be administered. This prospective design promises to provide the most precise tests of the learned helplessness model and the most enlightening application of the ASQ.

References

Abramson, L. Y., & Alloy, L. B. (1981). Depression, nondepression, and cognitive illusion: Reply to Schwartz. *Journal of Experimental Psychology: General, 110,* 436-447.

Abramson, L. Y., Seligman, M. E. P., & Teasdale, J. D. (1978). Learned helplessness in humans: Critique and reformulation. *Journal of Abnormal Psychology, 87,* 49-74.

Alloy, L. B., Peterson, C., Abramson, L. Y., & Seligman, M. E. P. (1984). Attributional style and the generality of learned helplessness. *Journal of Personality and Social Psychology, 46,* 681-687.

Anderson, C. A. (1983). Motivational performance deficits in interpersonal settings: The effect of attributional style. *Journal of Personality and Social Psychology, 45,* 1136-1141.

Anderson, C. A., Horowitz, L. M., & French, R. deS. (1983). Attributional style of lonely and depressed people. *Journal of Personality and Social Psychology, 45,* 127-136.

Beck, A. T. (1967). *Depression: Clinical, experimental, and theoretical aspects.* New York: Hoeber.

Belavic, S. C. (1982). An investigation of the child abuser from the perspective of attribution theory. *Dissertation Abstracts International, 43,* 1981-B.

Blaney, P. H., Behar, V., & Head, R. (1980). Two measures of depressive cognition: Their association with depression and with each other. *Journal of Abnormal Psychology, 89,* 678-682.

Burger, J. M. (1985). Desire for control and achievement-related behaviors. *Journal of Personality and Social Psychology, 48,* 1520-1533.

Cochran, S. D., & Hammen, C. L. (1985). Perceptions of stressful life events and depression: A test of attributional models. *Journal of Personality and Social Psychology, 48,* 1562-1571.

Coyne, J. C., & Gotlib, I. H. (1983). The role of cognition in depression: A critical appraisal. *Psychological Bulletin, 94,* 472-505.

Cronbach, L. J. (1951). Coefficient alpha and the internal structure of tests. *Psychometrika, 16,* 297-334.

Cutrona, C. E. (1983). Causal attributions and perinatal depression. *Journal of Abnormal Psychology, 92,* 161-172.

Cutrona, C. E., Russell, D., & Jones, R. D. (1984). Cross-situational consistency in causal attributions: Does attributional style exist? *Journal of Personality and Social Psychology, 47,* 1043-1058.

Eaves, G., & Rush, A. J. (1984). Cognitive patterns in symptomatic and remitted unipolar major depression. *Journal of Abnormal Psychology, 93,* 31-40.

Golin, S., Sweeney, P. D., & Shaeffer, D. E. (1981). The causality of causal attributions in depression: A cross-lagged panel correlational analysis. *Journal of Abnormal Psychology, 90,* 14-22.

Hamilton, E. W., & Abramson, L. Y. (1983). Cognitive patterns and major depressive disorder: A longitudinal study in a hospital setting. *Journal of Abnormal Psychology, 92,* 173-184.

Heider, F. (1958). The psychology of interpersonal relations. New York: Wiley & Sons.

Ickes, W., & Layden, M. A. (1976). Attributional styles. In J. Harvey (Ed.), *New directions in attribution research* (Vol. 2, pp. 119-152), Hillsdale, NJ: Earlbaum.

Kamen, L. P., & Seligman, M. E. P. (1985). *Explanatory style predicts college grade point average.* Unpublished manuscript.

Kelley, H. H. (1967). Attribution theory in social psychology. In D. Levine (Ed.), *Nebraska symposium on motivation* (pp. 192-241). Lincoln, NE: University of Nebraska Press.

Lefcourt, H. M., Martin, R. A., & Ware, E. E. (1984). Locus of control, causal attributions, and effects in achievement-related contexts. *Canadian Journal of Behavioral Science, 16,* 57-64.

Lefcourt, H. M., von Baeyer, C. L., Ware, E. E., & Cox, D. J. (1979). The Multidimensional-Multiattributional Causality Scale: The development of a goal specific locus of control scale. *Canadian Journal of Behavioral Science, 11,* 286-304.

Lewinsohn, P. M., Steinmetz, J. L., Larson, D. W., & Franklin, J. (1981). Depression-related cognitions: Antecedent or consequence? *Journal of Abnormal Psychology, 90,* 213-219.

Manly, P. C., McMahon, R. J., Bradley, C. F., & Davidson, P. O. (1982). Depressive attributional style and depression following childbirth. *Journal of Abnormal Psychology, 91,* 245-254.

Metalsky, G. I., Abramson, L. Y., Seligman, M. E. P., Semmel, A., & Peterson, C. (1982). Attributional styles and life events in the classroom: Vulnerability and invulnerability to depressive mood reactions. *Journal of Personality and Social Psychology, 43,* 612-617.

O'Hara, M. W., Rehm, L. P., & Campbell, S. B. (1982). Predicting depressive symptomatology: Cognitive-behavioral models and postpartum depression. *Journal of Abnormal Psychology, 91,* 457-461.

Pagel, M. D., Becker, J., & Coppel, D. B. (1985). Loss of control, self-blame, and depression: An investigation of spouse caregivers of Alzheimer's disease patients. *Journal of Abnormal Psychology, 94,* 169-182.

Persons, J. B., & Rao, P. A. (1985). Longitudinal study of cognitions, life events, and depression in psychiatric inpatients. *Journal of Abnormal Psychology, 94,* 51-63.

Peterson, C., Bettes, B. A., & Seligman, M. E. P. (1982). *Spontaneous attributions and depressive symptoms.* Unpublished manuscript, Virginia Polytechnic Institute and State University, Blacksburg.

Peterson, C., & Seligman, M. E. P. (1984). Causal expectations as a risk factor for depression: Theory and evidence. *Psychological Review, 91,* 347-374.

Peterson, C., Semmel, A., von Baeyer, C., Abramson, L. Y., Metalsky, G. I., & Seligman, M. E. P. (1982). The Attributional Style Questionnaire. *Cognitive Therapy and Research, 6,* 287-299.

Peterson, C., Villanova, P., & Raps, C. (1985). Depression and attributions: Factors responsible for inconsistent results in the published literature. *Journal of Abnormal Psychology, 94,* 165-168.

Rae, M., & Tennen, H. (1985, April). *Children's depressive symptoms and attributional style in a clinical population.* Paper presented at the meetings of the Eastern Psychological Association, Boston.

Raps, C. S., Peterson, C., Reinhard, K. E., Abramson, L. Y., & Seligman, M. E. P. (1982). Attributional style among depressed patients. *Journal of Abnormal Psychology, 91,* 102-108.

Rotter, J. B. (1954). Social learning and clinical psychology. Englewood Cliffs, NJ: Prentice-Hall.

Russell, D. (1982). The Causal Dimension Scale: A measure of how individuals perceive causes. *Journal of Personality and Social Psychology, 42,* 1137-1145.

Seligman, M. E. P. (1975). *Helplessness: On depression, development, and death.* San Francisco: Freeman.

Seligman, M. E. P., Abramson, L. Y., Semmel, A., & von Baeyer, C. (1979). Depressive attributional style. *Journal of Abnormal Psychology, 88,* 242-247.

Seligman, M. E. P., Peterson, C., Kaslow, N. J., Tanenbaum, R. L., Alloy, L. B., & Abramson, L. Y. (1984). Explanatory style and depressive symptoms among children. *Journal of Abnormal Psychology, 93,* 235-238.

Seligman, M. E. P., & Shulman, P. (in press). Explanatory style as a predictor of productivity and quitting among life insurance agents. *Journal of Personality and Social Psychology.*

Tennen, H., Affleck, G., & Gershman, K. (in press). Self-blame among parents of infants with perinatal complications: The role of self-protective motives. *Journal of Personality and Social Psychology.*

Tennen, H., & Herzberger, S. (in press). Depression, self-esteem and the absence of self-protective attributional biases. *Journal of Personality and Social Psychology.*

Weinberger, H. L., & Cash, T. F. (1982). The relationship of attributional style to learned helplessness in the interpersonal context. *Basic and Applied Social Psychology, 3*, 141-154.

Weiner, B. (1972). *Theories of motivation: From mechanism to cognition.* Chicago: Rand-McNally.

Weiner, B. (1974). *Achievement motivation and attribution theory.* Morristown, NJ: General Learning Press.

Wong, P. T. P., & Weiner, B. (1981). When people ask "why" questions, and the heuristics of attributional search. *Journal of Personality and Social Psychology, 40*, 650-663.

Zimmerman, M., Coryell, W., & Corenthal, C. (1984). Attributional style, The Dexamethasone Suppression Test, and the diagnosis of melancholia in depressed inpatients. *Journal of Abnormal Psychology, 93*, 373-377.

Zullow, H. M., & Seligman, M. E. P. (1985). *Rumination and explanatory style interact to increase depression: A process model.* Unpublished manuscript.

Colleen B. Jamison, Ed.D.

Professor of Education, California State University, Los Angeles, California.

AUDITORY DISCRIMINATION TEST

Joseph M. Wepman. Los Angeles, California: Western Psychological Services.

Introduction

The Auditory Discrimination Test is used for determining auditory discrimination ability of children aged five to eight years. The test is designed to assess the ability of a child to recognize (hear) differences between phonemes used in English speech. It is commonly used with primary-age children who are experiencing difficulty in speech or in learning to read. "A phoneme is the smallest distinctive group or class of sounds in a language" (Eisenson & Ogilvie, 1983, p. 118). A phoneme may be described as a distinctive phonetic element in a word, a speech sound, or an utterance. On the Auditory Discrimination Test, the most common phonemic pattern presented takes the form of single-syllable words formed with consonant-vowel-consonant sounds. The test is designed so the child need only identify a pair of spoken words as same or different; no visual, speech, or reading ability is required. There are two forms of the test, with each consisting of 40 pairs of words. Thirty word pairs differ in a single phoneme: 13 differ in final consonants, 13 in initial consonants, and four in medial vowels. Ten word pairs are false choices. The test is administered individually within five to ten minutes once the task is understood. Cutoff scores indicate the level of auditory discrimination (Very good development, Above-average ability, Average ability, Below-average ability, Below level of threshold of adequacy) for age levels of five, six, seven, and eight years.

The Auditory Discrimination Test was originally developed by Joseph M. Wepman, following observations of many children in clinical speech situations. Wepman (1960) presented the order and time of acquisition of consonant sounds as reported by Poole (1934), which was generally accepted by students of speech development. According to Wepman, the motor component of speech might be the result of the developing process of auditory discrimination, which would make more and more speech sounds available to the speaker; the discrimination and retention of sounds allow an individual to make accurate comparisons of speech sounds and thereby monitor speech. Discrimination and retention develop later than auditory acuity and understanding, both of which are relatively easy to assess. Wepman believed that approximately 80% of all articulatory defects in childhood are accounted for by faulty auditory discrimination, thus he recognized a need to develop a test of auditory discrimination for primary-age children.

It was Wepman's contention that children should be assessed as they reach school age "to determine whether their auditory abilities have reached the level of maturation where they can benefit from phonic instruction in reading or from auditory training in speech" (1960, p. 332). He suggested using sight reading for children with poor discrimination until auditory discrimination skills were developed, which he maintains would occur before age eight if they were going to develop. Ability to discriminate sounds has not been shown to improve with training.

Both the 1958 version and the 1973 revision of the test present 40 word pairs on each of two forms. The word pairs were selected to meet three criteria. First, the word members of the pair had to appear with the same frequency in the language of childhood. Frequency was estimated using the Thorndike-Lorge *Teacher's Word Book of 30,000 Words* (1944). Second, the comparison sound was to be in the same position and within the same phonetic category. Third, the word pairs were to be of the same length. On the 1958 version, scoring and assessment were based on an error score for the 30 contrast word pairs. All tests with error scores of greater than 15 (or greater than three on the ten identical word pairs) were to be considered invalid, the assumption being that children with these scores probably would have a hearing loss or had not followed directions. Cutoff points are suggested as the criteria for late development of auditory discrimination. The cutoff points (age 5 = >6, age 6 = >5, age 7 = >4, age 8 = >3) were based on the results of testing 533 children from urban and nonurban communities.

The 1973 revision of the test is essentially the same as the 1958 version. The scoring standards and word pairs are identical. Directions for converting scores obtained on the 1958 version, which are included in the manual (Wepman, 1975), made longitudinal studies possible. The scoring form has been clarified in that the columns labeled "X" and "Y" have been labeled "Different" and "Same." The earlier version relied on an error score; scoring for the 1973 revision is based on the number of correct responses. Interpretation of the 1973 revision takes the form of rating scale ranges from +2 (Very good development) to –2 (Below level of threshold of adequacy) for ages five to eight. The scale appears to be based on percentile ranks. The manual reports that approximately 15% of the children tested scored +2, approximately 20% scored +1, approximately 30% scored 0, approximately 20% scored –1, and approximately 15% scored –2. No information, including characteristics, is given regarding the children in the normative sample.

Having two forms of the test allows for retesting or for using one form with the child for practice in understanding the concept of same/different before testing the child.

The test has not been modified for special groups; however, because the test requires that one be able only to understand same/different, hear speech sounds, and indicate same/different to the examiner in some way, the test is appropriate for individuals who are visually or physically handicapped. The test is primarily used for screening of auditory discrimination. Poor auditory discrimination is associated with general language delay; hence, it is of limited use when a language problem has already been identified.

Because some of the contrasts presented in the test are generally not made in nonstandard English (e.g., *e/i* and *v/th*, voiced), interpretation of the results should be made with caution. The test "is not suitable for bilingual or nonstandard-English-speaking children" (Lambert, 1981, p. 34).

Wepman described his interest in the pattern of acquisition of speech sounds

(Wepman, 1960). He referred to the work of Poole (1934); however, the work cited is limited to the acquisition of consonants. The Test of Auditory Discrimination includes contrasts in three of the five consonant sounds acquired at age 3½, five of the seven consonant sounds acquired at 4½, the one consonant sound acquired at age 5½, three of the five consonant sounds acquired at 6½, and two of the seven consonant sounds acquired at age 7½.

The materials for the test include a nine-page manual and forms for recording individual responses. The response form for the revised (1973) version is complete on two sides of one page and is offered in parallel forms, Form 1A and Form 2A. Abbreviated instructions are presented on one side of the test, with more complete information presented in a nine-page manual (Wepman, 1975). In addition to the 40 word pairs, two sample word pairs are included to be sure that the test directions are understood. It is suggested that in situations where the format may be unfamiliar, one form of the test be used as a training task, with the second form being used as the actual test. Administration procedures are clearly described in the manual, with information regarding scoring and interpretation easy to follow.

The child should be facing the examiner for the instructions and sample items. The sample pairs are presented (e.g., man-man, hat-pat), and the child is to say "Yes" or "Same," or "No" or "Different," or otherwise indicate the discrimination. Practice items are to be given until the examiner is confident that the child understands the procedures. At this point, the child is turned so his or her back is toward the examiner, precluding the child's seeing the words on the test or the examiner's mouth. The word pairs are read with a one-second pause between the words. The response is recorded on the test form by circling "D" (for different) or "S" (for same). If a child asks for a word pair to be repeated, the item is skipped and repeated after completing the test.

The test is intended for children from ages five to eight. The rationale is presented in the manual and described in more detail in an article by Wepman (1960). As described, five- and six-year-old children whose scores are low may be slow in developing auditory discrimination skills and may yet develop adequate ability. Children aged seven or eight are less likely to show improvement, and children above the age of eight show almost no improvement in auditory discrimination ability.

The test is considered invalid if fewer than ten of the 30 contrast items are correct or if less than seven of the ten identical items are correct. The range of possible scores (considering only contrast word pairs), therefore, is 10 to 30. The rating scale is as follows: +2 = Very good development (29-30), +1 = Above-average ability (27-29), 0 = Average ability (24-28), –1 = Below-average ability (19-26), and –2 = Below level of threshold of adequacy (10-25). The test has a low ceiling, with little discriminative information being provided about the better auditory discriminators at ages five through eight. Nevertheless, the rating scale does allow one to compare the score of an individual with others the same age.

Practical Applications/Uses

The Auditory Discrimination Test is a relatively simple yet accurate tool for assessing auditory discrimination ability among children from five to eight years of age. For younger children, the test may be used to identify children who are likely to have difficulty learning to read using a phonics approach. The test has also been used to account for children who seem delayed in developing speech accuracy. For older children, the test is used as part of a battery to assist in diagnosing reading and speech difficulties. "When poor discrimination has been found, it has proved useful to develop special techniques for increasing auditory perception or for increasing the visual modality of learning while the auditory modality is developing" (Wepman, 1975, p. 1).

The test is used in schools and clinics by psychologists, speech and language specialists, and diagnostic teachers. Special educators and diagnosticians should be aware of older children who do poorly on the test because psychometric or achievement test results may be affected, especially if oral test procedures are used. The test is a useful research tool for studying speakers of nonstandard English and limited English, children younger than five years, children older than eight years, and children in special education programs.

The test is appropriately used for normally developing children from ages five to eight. Because of the nature of the test it is not uncommon for it to be used as part of a battery for older children who are experiencing difficulty in school. Because of the low ceiling, the test is more appropriately used to identify below-average discrimination ability than to assess above-average ability. Perhaps the test is most appropriately used clinically to suggest approaches to teaching, as well as indicating the need for special attention. The manual suggests that the test be used in conjunction with tests of auditory memory and sequential ability in order to assess the auditory mode more completely. Because of the simplicity of the test it can be used with many groups and interpreted item by item.

The test is to be administered individually by an examiner who is familiar with standardized testing procedures. The manual directs the user to affirm that the child understands the task, using examples until this is certain. An inexperienced or insensitive examiner might begin the test proper too hastily, leading to faulty interpretation of the results. The instructions presented in the manual for administration and scoring are clear, and the conscientious examiner will not have difficulty in the proper administration of the test. If the task is understood by the child, administration takes but a few minutes, and scoring is accomplished quickly. "The Total Score is determined by counting the number of circled responses in the unshaded boxes in the 'Different' column" (Wepman, 1975, pp. 2-3). Table 1 in the manual, which gives the score and chronological age in years, immediately provides the user with the rating (+2, +1, 0, –1, or –2). Interpretation is based on the rating obtained and to some extent on the age of the child, assuming that younger children are still developing discriminatory ability.

Because many examiners look at individual word pairs when interpreting the test, it is important to consider the phonemes that are and are not assessed by this test. Particular attention should be paid to the evaluation of medial vowel sounds for students with learning disabilities who do not attend well to internal detail. Care should be taken not to assume that the results reflect discrimination ability for words in context, in conversational speech, or discrimination against a background of noise.

Technical Aspects

According to the manual, test-retest reliability of the test is high. A correlation of .91 was calculated using a sample of 109 children, and a correlation of .95 was calculated with a sample of 279 children. Alternate forms reliability has been estimated to be .92. Neither the characteristics of the children in the sample nor the time interval are discussed.

The validity of the test has not been well-established. Criterion validity is not mentioned, and predictive validity has not been established. The test has face validity and continues to be used as part of the test battery for children with reading and/or speech problems. Studies of validity presented in the manual provide information regarding construct validity. In a study of 1,000 children, the median total score at each age level was age 5 = 23.8, age 6 = 24.6, age 7 = 26.3, and age 8 = 27.3. When the scores are rounded off to become consistent with the precision of the original data, the scores are 24, 25, 26, and 27, respectively. Thus, auditory discrimination scores increase with age, at least between the ages of five and eight. Studies comparing first-graders with adequate and inadequate auditory discrimination scores showed that adequate scorers had higher reading scores, but both groups were reading well above average. Another study correlated Test of Auditory Discrimination scores of first-graders with Metropolitan Achievement Test scores. The correlations were .235 and .348, which were statistically significant but not practically significant.

Perhaps the most direct study of validity was reported by Wepman (1960). First-graders were divided into those with known speech articulatory inaccuracies and those without such inaccuracies. Significant differences between the groups were found for auditory discrimination and articulation; however, no differences were found for intelligence or reading achievement. Most diagnosticians would agree that children with poor discrimination tend to have very poor articulation and/or very poor phonic ability in reading. A cause and effect relationship, however, has not been established.

Content validity seems quite poor. Eisenson and Ogilvie (1983, pp. 119-120) list the common phonemes of American English: 25 consonants, 16 vowels, and seven diphthongs. The Test of Auditory Discrimination includes 14 consonants and six vowel sounds. According to Salvia and Ysseldyke, "There is no pair that tests discrimination of (1) acoustic characteristics [such as a stop-burst sound (*t*) versus an affricate (*ch*)], or (2) voicing of the sound versus nonvoicing (*s* versus *z*, for example). Also, some of the more frequently misarticulated sounds (*r, l, w, y*) are not even included in the test" (1981, pp. 404-405).

Critique

The Auditory Discrimination Test is a very usable tool for anyone working with children aged five through eight years in an educational or clinical setting. It is also appropriately used as part of a battery with older children who are not progressing well in school. The test is brief, inexpensive, and reasonably well-developed. Because the word pairs are identical on the 1958 and 1973 versions, longitudinal studies have been possible. Directions for administration and scoring are clearly presented in the manual. The test lends itself to clinical interpretation in the related areas of reading and speech; however, diagnosticians find it desirable to assess the discrimination of additional speech sounds for a comprehensive study. Because the normative group was not identified in the manual, the rating scale should not be used for the interpretation of individual cases. Test reliability is adequate; however, validity is not well-established. The manual suggests that children who score below a cutoff might be retested at a later time on the alternate form. It would be helpful if the manual included additional guidelines for further study or case studies to illustrate the clinical interpretation of such cases. Because of the simplicity of the response mode, the test is appropriate for many individuals in special education programs. The test may be used in conjunction with tests of auditory memory to further assess the auditory mode.

References

Eisenson, J., & Ogilvie, M. (1983). *Communication disorders in children* (5th ed.). New York: Macmillan.

Lambert, N. (Ed.). (1981). *Special education assessment matrix.* Monterey, CA: CTB/McGraw-Hill.

Poole, I. (1934). Genetic development of articulation of consonant sounds in speech. *Elementary English Review, 2,* 159-161.

Salvia, J., & Ysseldyke, J. (1981). *Assessment in special and remedial education* (2nd ed.). Boston: Houghton-Mifflin.

Thorndike, E. L., & Lorge, I. (1944). *The teacher's word book of 30,000 words.* New York: Bureau of Publications, Teacher's College, Columbia University.

Wepman, J. M. (1960). Auditory discrimination, speech, and reading. *Elementary School Journal, 60,* 325-333.

Wepman, J. M. (1975). *Auditory Discrimination Test manual* (rev. 1973). Los Angeles: Western Psychological Services.

Zoli Zlotogorski, Ph.D.

Professor of Psychology, The Hebrew University of Jerusalem, Mount Scopus, and Chief Neuropsychologist, Department of Psychiatry, Shaare Zedek Medical Center, Jerusalem, Israel.

AUDITORY MEMORY SPAN TEST/AUDITORY SEQUENTIAL MEMORY TEST

Joseph M. Wepman and Anne Morency. Los Angeles, California: Western Psychological Services.

Introduction

Auditory imperception appears to be a significant factor in many learning disabilities. The triad of auditory imperception includes discrimination, memory, and sequential memory. The Auditory Sequential Memory Test (ASMT) and the Auditory Memory Span Test (AMST) were developed in order to assess sequencing ability and auditory memory span in young children. Both of these tests are products of a series of studies (Wepman, 1951, 1960, 1964, 1972; Wepman & Haas, 1969; Wepman, Morency, & Haas, 1970) that investigated the role of audio-visual perception as the basis of learning.

Wepman (1972) has described three auditory developmental stages that are critical in the course of normal maturation. First, the child develops and refines the ability to receive, evaluate, and process auditory stimuli. Then, auditory memory, or the ability to encode discrete units (phoneme span), is developed. Finally, the child develops auditory memory for sequential units. This schema of development has been borne out in that normative digit span is two digits at 30 months, three digits at 36 months, four digits at 54 months, and five to seven digits thereafter. However, a note of caution is warranted lest the reader assume that the changes in mean utterance length are identical to a simple memory-span limit. This admonition is noted by Wepman and Morency (1975a), who observe that there is a connection between auditory sequential memory, auditory memory span, and language development. Thus, the child acquiring speech must be able to discriminate the sounds, retain learned material, and encode the material in a correct order to achieve intelligibility. In this manner the development of auditory perceptual processes are less related to utterance length than to accuracy of production.

Practical Applications/Uses

The Auditory Memory Span Test assesses the ability to recall the exact order of a string of nonredundant stimuli. Here, the task is to recall spoken single-syllable

---

This reviewer wishes to thank Galia Arzi, M.A., for assistance in preparing this review.

words in a progressively increasing series. The authors argue that the use of words rather than numbers or nonsense syllables tends to maintain and enhance attention. Words were randomly selected from frequency lists compiled by the authors by analysis of spontaneous storytelling of children aged five, six, and seven years. Clear and concise scoring forms provide comprehensive information on administration and scoring of the test. The virtual simplicity of administration and economies of time, cost, and coding clarity are obvious advantages. In addition, three trials are given at each level in order to reduce the chance factor that a single repetition at each level might produce an artificial span.

The Auditory Sequential Memory Test contains seven series of digits that vary in length from two to eight digits. Each series has two nonredundant trials. Once again, clear and concise scoring forms provide information on administration and scoring of the test. Essentially, this straightforward, simple digit-span memory test is identical in form to those familiar subscales commonly used in the Stanford-Binet, Kaufman, and Wechsler tests of children's intelligence.

Technical Aspects

A reliability coefficient of .92 is reported in the Auditory Memory Span Test manual for the AMST Form I versus Form II. However, the manual provides no reference to determine the number of subjects, ages, sex, or times between administrations. Other aspects of reliability, such as intraexaminer and interexaminer reliability, are also absent. Of the six references noted in the manual (Wepman & Morency, 1975a) three are unpublished dissertations, which at this time can shed little light on the issues of reliability and validity. Two studies (Morency, 1968; Morency & Wepman, 1973) explore the criterion validity of the AMST by correlating the test with subscales of the Metropolitan Achievement Test. The reported correlations are low and range between .20 to .30 for the third grade and .24 to .32 for the fourth to sixth grades. These low correlations suggest that auditory memory span is not a good predictor of academic achievement in elementary school. Because the positive relationship between mastery of language and elementary-school achievement is a well-documented finding, these low correlations raise doubt as to the utility of the AMST as a predictor of learning ability.

Reliability for the Auditory Sequential Memory Test is reported at .82 (Form I vs. Form II), which falls in the normal range for tests of digit memory span (Wepman & Morency, 1975b). However, the issue of validity is once again troubling. Three of the four references specifically relating to the issue of validity are unpublished and cannot be found in the literature.

Turaids, Wepman, and Morency (1972) examined a perceptual test battery that included the ASMT, AMST, and four other auditory and visual tests. This standardization study examined normal subjects divided into four age groups. Results indicate that all but two of the differences between age groups were statistically significant ($p < .05$). Yet, the authors fail to mention the number of tests performed or why this procedure was preferred to a one-way analysis of variance followed by post-hoc contrasts.

Although there were a number of statistically significant differences between age groups, the standard deviations were more than twice the difference between the mean scores. This finding raises doubts as to the diagnostic capability of the tests beyond obvious instances of dysfunction. In addition, Turaids, Wepman, and Morency (1972) provide data on the intercorrelations of scores on the perceptual test battery. The correlation between the ASMT and AMST weighted scores is reported as .638. The ASMT manual cites this correlation as supporting evidence for the validity of the test. However, given this reviewer's concern with regard to the validity of the AMST (cited above), one would prefer a more solid criterion.

Critique

The high correlation between the ASMT and AMST might indicate that they tap similar abilities and may thus, in fact, overlap. If this is the case, then use of either test would provide sufficient data for diagnostic purposes. It is regrettable that studies employing the rating and interpretation tables based on the standardization sample are as yet unpublished. Such studies may add some light as to the power of these tests to diagnose learning difficulties or developmental lags in auditory perception. However, given the paucity of corroborative research with these instruments, this reviewer advises the user to regard interpretation of the generated data with great caution.

References

Morency, A. (1968). Auditory modality and reading: Research and practice. In H. K. Smith (Ed.), *Perception and reading: Vol. 12* (pp. 17-21). Proceedings of the Twelfth Annual Convention of the International Reading Association.

Morency, A., & Wepman, J. M. (1973). Early perceptual ability and later school achievement. *Elementary School Journal, 73,* 323-324.

Turaids, O., Wepman, J. M., & Morency, A. (1972). A perceptual test battery: Development and standardization. *Elementary School Journal, 72,* 351-361.

Wepman, J. M. (1951). *Recovery from aphasia.* New York: The Roland Press Company.

Wepman, J. M. (1960). Auditory discrimination, speech and reading. *Elementary School Journal, 60,* 325-333.

Wepman, J. M. (1964). The perceptual basis for learning. In A. Robinson (Ed.), *Meeting individual differences in reading* (Supplementary Educational Monograph, No. 94, chap. 4). Chicago: University of Chicago Press.

Wepman, J. M. (1972). Auditory imperception: A perceptual-conceptual developmental construct. In B. Wolman (Ed.), *Manual of child psychopathology* (chap. 20). New York: McGraw-Hill.

Wepman, J. M., & Haas, W. (1969). *A spoken word count: Children 5, 6 and 7.* Chicago: Language Research Association Inc.

Wepman, J. M., & Morency, A. (1975a). *Manual for Auditory Memory Span Test.* Los Angeles: Western Psychological Services.

Wepman, J. M., & Morency, A. (1975b). *Manual for the Auditory Sequential Memory Test.* Los Angeles: Western Psychological Services.

Wepman, J. M., Morency, A., & Haas, S. K. (1970). Developmental speech inaccuracy and speech therapy in the early school years. *Elementary School Journal, 70,* 219-244.

James A. Sprunger, Ph.D.
Research Analyst, Department of Mental Health, Riverside County, Riverside, California.

BALTHAZAR SCALES OF ADAPTIVE BEHAVIOR I: SCALES OF FUNCTIONAL INDEPENDENCE

Earl E. Balthazar. Palo Alto, California: Consulting Psychologists Press, Inc.

Introduction

The Balthazar Scales of Adaptive Behavior I: Scales of Functional Independence (BSAB-I) were developed to measure very small differences in the self-care experiences of profoundly and severely mentally retarded children and adults. One use of the scales is to assess individual behavior in self-care skills and compare these scores with scores in normative groups. These scale measurements are also used to identify weaknesses in eating, dressing, and toileting skills in order to give appropriate training or treatment, after which they can be applied again to determine the amount of improvement in the skills where inadequacies were identified.

Earl E. Balthazar, who created and refined the BSAB-I, received his Ph.D. from the University of Illinois in developmental psychology. From 1960 to 1980 (when he retired), he was chief psychologist, research psychologist, and staff psychologist at the Central Wisconsin Center for the Developmentally Disabled. He was also a research scientist and chief of behavioral research at the Waisman Center, University of Wisconsin and in the 1960s, director of psychological services at the Wisconsin State Department of Health and Social Sciences. In addition, Balthazar was a lecturer at the University of Wisconsin between 1964 and 1969.

Observational studies in developing the BSAB-I began in 1964 and continued through 1968. The normative sample consisted of institutionalized residents at Central Wisconsin Center for the Developmentally Disabled in Madison, Wisconsin. Additional samples were obtained from Dixon State School, Northern Wisconsin Center for the Developmentally Disabled, and from institutions in England, Holland, and Belgium. A great majority of the normative sample were ambulant residents, although some were semi-ambulant. The age range of the normative sample was 5-57 years, with a median age of 17.3. Data obtained from observing behaviors of the more severely retarded group constituted an item pool, from which items were selected and transformed into subscales. For standardization, 122 subjects were tested on the Eating Scale, 200 on the Dressing Scale, and 129 on the Toileting Scale.

On the basis of the AAMD (American Association on Mental Deficiency) behavioral classification, the standardization sample ranged from Level IV to Level V in measured intelligence and in adaptive behavior. On global tests of intelligence, the range in IQ was less than 20-35. All normative subjects demonstrated severe to profound levels of deficiency on the basis of the AAMD classification. The behavioral observations embodied in the BSAB-I Scales were the criteria. There were no external criteria, such as observations or measurements from other instruments, such as the Slosson Intelligence Test. However, a comparison was made of the Balthazar Scales of Adaptive Behavior II: Scales of Social Adaptation (BSAB-II; Balthazar, 1973; for a review see Malgady, 1985) with the BSAB-I during pilot studies of both tests. It was concluded that functional skill performance (BSAB-I) was related significantly to indicators of general social coping behavior and language proficiency (BSAB-II).

The BSAB-I items are arranged conveniently in a four-page booklet, with a night-time supplementary toileting sheet as an insert. Recording and scoring are completed manually in spaces provided in the booklet. Identifying information is entered on the first page, except for information such as medication(s) administered or subject's code number. There are also spaces to the left or right of each item to record ratings and at the bottom of each scale to record the total score. Users may find the target behavior(s), pretest target behavior score(s), the brief description of program, and the posttest target behavior scores particularly useful. For those who are interested in complete score profiles, there are spaces for pre- and post-percentiles.

The Toileting Scale, presented on the second page of the booklet, contains three day-time toileting sections: Bladder (containing three items pertaining to bladder control and bladder independence), Bowel (containing two items pertaining to bowel control and wiping self), and General (containing three items pertaining to clothing adjustment and reporting "accidents"). A night-time supplementary section, containing four items relating to bowel and bladder control, is also included. Scores on these items are taken from entries on the night-time supplementary toileting sheet.

The Eating Scale, presented on the third sheet of the booklet, contains six sections: Class I—Dependent Feeding consisting of nine items, Class II—Finger Foods containing 13 items, Class III—Spoon Usage containing 13 items, Class IV—Fork Usage containing 13 items, Class V—Drinking containing 13 items, and an eating checklist containing 32 items in seven categories (self service, assistive devices, type of food, positioning, rate of eating, advanced utensil usage, and supervision).

The Dressing Scale, presented on the fourth page, includes both a male and a female section to accommodate differences in clothing. The section for males contains 32 items pertaining to shoes, socks, pants, briefs, shirts, and t-shirts/undershirts. The female section contains 30 items pertaining to shoes, socks, pants or skirts, briefs, t-shirts/undershirts, blouses, dresses, and brassieres. Generally, items deal with putting on and taking off the various clothing articles.

For the Toileting Scale, the examiner is asked to interview an aid who has had an opportunity to observe toileting skills of the subject at least five times during the past month. The method of administration for the other two scales (Eating and Dressing) is that of direct observation of the subject by the examiner.

Difficulty level of the scale items and instructions for administering and scoring appear to be at a level suitable for a nonprofessional rater technician, whom the manual (Balthazar, 1983a) recommends be the administrator. Conversion of scale scores to graphic profiles are described in the manual. The profiles can be applied to complete scores for all scales, to targeted scale items, or to group scale items. The targeted scale item profiles are particularly useful in demonstrating program progress for pretest vs. posttest situations.

Practical Applications/Uses

The BASB-I was designed to measure achievement in basic skills (eating, dressing, toileting) for severely and profoundly mentally retarded persons. The variables are skills observed and recorded by a rater technician. The manual suggests four uses in which the BSAB-I is appropriate: 1) as baseline measures of specific skills or groups of skills in which the subject is weak in order to focus on training and treatment, with posttraining measures used to indicate the degree of progress in weak skill areas; 2) use of the entire scale to compare profiles with normative groups, which may be in association with global intelligence scales for mentally retarded subjects (e.g., the Slosson Intelligence Test), or with social intelligence scales (e.g., the Vineland Social Maturity Scales); 3) in developing programs for the retarded in residential centers and in community referral systems; and 4) in research programs in institutions, with the BSAB-I as the key measuring instrument. (The BSAB-I has been used in research programs at Columbia University and the University of Wisconsin.)

Balthazar (personal communication, October, 1985) claims that the BSAB-I has been used in a variety of settings, such as the Madison (Wisconsin) Opportunity Center, in connection with a job training program. The BSAB-I has also had applications in homes, schools, and institutions in Texas, Alabama, California, New York, and Illinois. In addition, there have been a number of introductions of the BSAB-I in Sweden, Switzerland, France, and Poland, using the English version because there is no translated version.

The BSAB-I is appropriate for only profoundly or severely mentally retarded children and adults, who have IQs ranging from 20 to 35 on global intelligence tests. Because the age range for the standardization sample was 5-57 years, it is not advisable to deviate too far from this range. The use of the BSAB-I for persons with higher IQs or for those who are blind or are otherwise physically handicapped is not recommended.

The BSAB-I is administered individually. The Eating Scale requires unobtrusive observations of a subject by a rater technician during one or more mealtime periods, preferably lunch or dinner. The Dressing Scale is administered in a manner to elicit optimal performance (i.e., the rater technician should encourage the subject by verbal or other reinforcement to perform all stages of dressing and undressing as well as possible within a reasonable time limit).

Unlike the Eating and Dressing Scales, the Toileting Scale requires interviewing of aids on the day and night shifts in a residential setting. This scale could be administered in a family home environment, although the test author does not make specific reference to such application. An outpatient or other nonresidential setting is not appropriate, particularly for the Eating and Dressing Scales.

According to the manual (p. 5), the examiner can be "any reasonably articulate person who is conscientious, alert, and accurate." However, supervision of the rater by professional or managerial personnel during the examination and scoring is recommended. Instructions for administration are clear and cover material from general background information to specific instructions for each scale and scale item. Options for obtaining a complete BSAB-I profile for each scale or for selection of targeted scales and scale items in baseline and posttreatment measurement are available.

Instructions for scoring are also detailed and explicit. Scores for typical cases are included and helpful. The most complicated to score is the Eating Scale, due to indentation of scale items and the accompanying requirement that a scale item score cannot be higher than the item from which it was indented. Instructions for the Dressing and Toileting Scales are not as complicated.

At least two to three hours of intensive study would be required to become thoroughly familiar with the scoring procedures. Once these are mastered, entering scores in the boxes and checking off the checklist items are simple. The total time required for completing all items on all three scales—preliminary preparation, observation, and scoring—is judged to be about 60 minutes. If only some of the scale items are targeted, total administration and scoring time will be lessened.

In the manual, considerable space is given to suggestions for preparing profiles. Examples of graphs are presented, with suggestions for presenting baseline and retest scores for complete scales and for highlighting targeted scale items. Preparing these profiles graphically does not require a great deal of sophistication if an appropriate professional is available for guidance. The manual supplement (Balthazar, 1983b) recommends that the BSAB-I scores and graphic profiles be interpreted by a psychologist, a behavioral scientist, or someone with similar training.

Technical Aspects

The author's conception of validity for the BSAB-I is construct validity (i.e., the observed behavior is the criterion measure itself). There are no reported external validity studies. However, statistical relationships of the BSAB-I and indicators of general social coping behavior and language proficiency (BSAB-II) were established. Kendall's tau, a nonparametric technique, was used in establishing this association between BSAB-I and BSAB-II. Kendall's tau was appropriately selected because these were two sets of ordinal data where the ranks of the ordinal categories were not treated as interval scales, such as in Spearman's rho (rank-order correlation). The relationships of BSAB-I and BSAB-II were statistically significant, but this is by no means external validation; it is an association between the BSAB-I and social/language scales on the BSAB-II.

Reliabilities reported in the manual supplement were of two kinds: proportion agreements (i.e., the ratio of one rater's score on a scale item to a second rater's score on the same item) and correlation coefficients (presumably Pearson's *r*) across all scale items of the paired rater scores. The reliability coefficient was .873 for the Eating Scale, .965 for the Dressing Scale, and .939 for the Toileting Scale, resulting in respectable interrater reliability. Balthazar (1983b) states that intrarater reliabilities (same rater's observations over time) were also quite high; however, he does not give exact coefficients. The samples used for determining rater reliability were not clearly identified. It may be assumed that the normative samples were involved in at least some of the reliability estimates.

Critique

The BSAB-I represents Balthazar's successful attempt to identify some basic self-help skills and to measure the level of attainment pertaining to profoundly or severely mentally retarded individuals. Some of the customary psychometric requirements, however, are missing in accounts of the early development and standardization of the instrument. For instance, there are no establishing patterns of relationships with well-known reference instruments, such as the Slosson Intelligence Test. Although early versions of the BSAB-I (which included language/social ingredients) were correlated with the Vineland Social Maturity Scale (+.63), the present version was correlated with another Balthazar instrument only—the BSAB II (Balthazar Scales of Social Adaptation).

Another deficiency is that of seemingly ignoring a rich rating methodology literature. The importance of appropriate training and orientation of raters is stressed by Balthazar in his manual; however, both general and specific rater errors involving the rater, subject, and rating instrument still occur, even after extensive rater training.

The lack of external criteria in the validation process is not particularly disturbing, especially with a self-help skill instrument. However, the establishment of norms beyond the original standardization in Wisconsin would be helpful to the BSAB-I user. Perhaps some of the local studies that Balthazar recommends in his manual have been completed but not yet published. It is rather presumptuous to pass judgment on the BSAB-I with the same array of requirements and standards that one uses for evaluating instruments designed to cut across the complete range of human ability. Balthazar has spent a lifetime in working with profoundly and severely mentally retarded individuals. This reviewer is convinced, without any hard evidence to support this conviction, that the BSAB-I has played a major role in improving the life of many individuals who are profoundly or severely mentally retarded.

References

This list contains text citations as well as suggested additional reading.

Balthazar, E. E. (1973). *Balthazar Scales of Adaptive Behavior II: Scales of Social Adaptation*. Palo Alto, CA: Consulting Psychologists Press, Inc.

Balthazar, E. E. (1983a). *Balthazar Scales of Adaptive Behavior I: The Scales of Functional Independence manual*. Palo Alto, CA: Consulting Psychologists Press, Inc.

Balthazar, E. E. (1983b). *Balthazar Scales of Adaptive Behavior I: The Scales of Functional Independence*. BSAB-I Suggestions for the Professional Supervisor. Palo Alto, CA: Consulting Psychologists Press, Inc.

Balthazar, E. E., & Stevens, H. A. (1969). Scalar techniques for program evaluation with the severely mentally retarded. *Mental Retardation*, 7(3), 25-28.

Malgady, R. G. (1985). Review of the Balthazar Scales of Adaptive Behavior II: Scales of Social Adaptation. In D. J. Keyser & R. C. Sweetland (Eds.), *Test critiques* (Vol. II, pp. 56-62). Kansas City, MO: Test Corporation of America.

Naor, E. M., & Balthazar, E. E. (1973). The program planning paradigm: Application to the area of functional independence. *Mental Retardation, 11*(1), 22-26.

Naor, E. M., & Balthazar, E. E. (1975). Provision of a language index for severely and profoundly retarded individuals. *American Journal of Mental Deficiency, 79*(6), 717-725.

Robert B. Bartos, Ed.D.

Assistant Dean, School of Education, Georgia College, Milledgeville, Georgia.

Edward M. Wolpert, Ed.D.

Dean, School of Education, Georgia College, Milledgeville, Georgia.

BARBER SCALES OF SELF-REGARD FOR PRESCHOOL CHILDREN

Lucie W. Barber. Schenectady, New York: Union College Character Research Project.

Introduction

The Barber Scales of Self-Regard for Preschool Children were developed to rate personality in preschool children. Because, according to the scales' author, personality is so complex, it is better understood and easier to deal with when broken down into smaller components. The concept of self-regard, key to these scales, is broken down into seven scales (Barber, 1974). The scales, each of which describes five progressive steps through which small children pass sequentially in normal development toward maturity, may be studied separately or in dynamic relationship with one another. The scales are 1) *Purposeful Learning of Skills* (learning skills to increase potential), 2) *Completing Tasks* (learning to persist in activities), 3) *Coping with Fears* (learning to put fears into perspective), 4) *Children's Responses to Requests* (learning to cooperate willingly with parental requests), 5) *Dealing with Frustrations* (learning roles for channeling emotions positively), 6) *Socially Acceptable Behavior* (learning to evaluate behavior and to adjust socially), and 7) *Developing Imagination in Play* (learning to broaden world perspective by using imagination).

Generally speaking, the scales have two distinct uses: as assessment devices used by parents or parent surrogates (i.e., adults who know a child well through extensive exposure to and interaction with that child) and as essentially educational materials. These scales not only measure, they also teach by displaying normal developmental sequences in young children.

The decision to make self-regard the central theme came out of studies conducted by the Union College Character Research Project. (Barber & staff, 1973; Barber, Cernik, & Barton, 1973). These studies provided evidence that parents of young children were concerned for the development of positive self-regard.

The scales as presented are related to a theoretical model of an integrated human personality. The first published description of the model appeared in 1970 in an

---

The tables contained in this review are reproduced by permission of the test author, Lucie W. Barber, Ed.D.

article by Dr. Ernest M. Ligon (Ligon, 1970). Later references (Peatling & Tiedeman, 1977) have systematized a form of this model of an integrated human personality.

The Peatling-Tiedeman model of human personality is a hierarchical structure in which the elements of each of its various levels follow the principle of a mathematical group. The global concept of "self-image" (or "self-regard"), one of the elements of personality at the model's most differentiated level, consists of eight components: one involves the mathematical principle of identity; the other seven involve specific interactions of 14 personality elements that, because of the nature of a mathematical group, result in the fifteenth element, Self-Image. Each of these seven interactive components are measured by one of the seven preschool scales of self-regard.

This approach to the study of self-regard offers significant advantages. First, the model identifies that self-regard is a global concept that has several distinct, yet measurable, components, which may be studied separately or in a dynamic relation to one another. Second, the model specifies the nature of a limited number of such dynamic interactions and provides a road map for the study of a complex concept, the self-regard of a human being (Barber & Peatling, 1977).

Although the Peatling-Tiedeman model contains a basic symbolic equation for each specific interaction, in actual use parents and/or educators receive only the title of the scale and a set of descriptive phrases. The basic symbolic equations are theoretical, mathematically elegant ways of specifying something that can be recognized better in the concrete behavior descriptions. The theory underlies, informs, and directs these scales. However, a parent or educator does not need to be a theoretician, mathematician, or a developmental psychologist to use the scales to assess a child's level of normal development toward a positive self-regard (Barber & Peatling, 1977). A five-point rating scale is used to chart that development.

The developmental history of the Barber Scales centers around the time frame of 1974-76. In 1974, the Dealing with Frustrations Scale was first field tested. It involved 150 participants, and the results indicated that all scale points were descriptive of some child. These findings also indicated that the scale was adequate for the whole preschool period. Older children tended to be rated higher than younger ones. There also seemed to be a firm relationship between the age of the child and scale point as measured by parents, which suggested that the scale was measuring a developmental phenomenon.

This led to a full field test of all seven scales in 1974 with 125 parents, plus a few day-care-center teachers. The total number of ratings in this field test was 448. The boys and girls in the sample ranged in age from two to five years and were enrolled in suburban nursery schools, inner city day-care centers, and a church school class. The family income ranged from $10,000 to more than $20,000, the age of parents was generally between 20-40 years, and parental education ranged from high school through professional school.

In 1975, 175 children were rated on all seven scales. The demographic variables of the 1975 rating approximated the 1974 sample. These two major field testings involved a total of 351 parents of children aged two to five years. Family incomes and educational levels varied widely. Both sexes were assessed. In addition to par- assessments, the 1975 study provided 140 assessments by teachers in preschool programs. Altogether, during the 1974-75 field testings, 2,940 respondents were used (Barber & Peatling, 1977). There have been no revisions of the Barber Scales since their initial phase of development, nor are there any other forms of the scale.

In administering the Barber Scales the raters (parents or educators) are given a guide for parents, a 15-page booklet that briefly explains each of the scales and includes worksheets to be used by raters for each of the seven scales. For example, on the worksheet parents are asked 1) at what scale point did they place their child; 2) to list some of the tasks their child likes to do; 3) as they look at the next higher scale point, what progress do they feel their child can make; and 4) to list some ways they can reinforce their child to complete a task and thus progress to the next scale.

In addition, each rater is given seven individual sheets that explain the scale, describe characteristics at each scale point, and give examples at each scale point (e.g., for the Completing Tasks Scale, 5 = Children stick with even very complex tasks until they finish what they have set out to; 4 = Children are attempting more complex tasks; 3 = Children will complete a simple task, even by themselves; 2 = Children are beginning to stay with a simple task until it is completed, particularly if the task is done with a parent/educator; and 1 = Children will not stick with any task, no matter how simple). Parents are asked to indicate which of the five scale points *best* describes their child most of the time.

The examiner is there only to pass out and generally explain the materials. Subsequent involvement by the examiner should only come on the request of raters after ratings and worksheets have been completed. From the ratings a profile is developed for each child (see Figure 1), and subsequent profiles with overlays will indicate developmental growth.

Figure 1.
Example of a Profile for a Two-Year-Old Child

Scale Points	*Purposeful Learning of Skills*	*Completing Tasks*	*Coping with Fears*	*Responses to Requests*	*Dealing with Frustrations*	*Socially Acceptable Behavior*	*Developing Imagination in Play*
Five	5	5	5	5	5	5	5
Four	4	4	4	4	4	4	4
Three	**(3)**	3	3	3	3	3	3
Two	2	**(2)**	**(2)**	2	**(2)**	**(2)**	2
One	1	1	1	**(1)**	1	1	**(1)**

Practical Applications/Uses

There are two relatively distinct applications of the Barber Scales. First, they may be used as assessment devices with an individual child. For example, parents can use the scales with their own child. Second, they can be used as educational devices with interested adults. For example, they can be used in a class to exhibit a set of normal developmental sequences. It is possible to combine these two uses in a variety of ways as either educational or assessment devices. Three uses of the scales as educational devices are as follows:

1) Teachers at either the secondary or undergraduate level can use the seven scales in a course on early childhood development. Used in this way, the scales become a teaching device describing normal developmental sequences in building self-regard that can be seen between two and six years of age.

2) In the general community, persons engaged in adult education can also use the scales as an educational device. For example, counselors, mental-health personnel, parish coordinators of religious education, and other adult educators can use the scales to teach adults, who are or will be dealing with young children, about normal developmental sequences. Such professionals can also use the scales with any group of adults who are interested in learning more about human development during the formative preschool period.

3) A special category of adults in any community consists of those who are voluntarily involved in prebirth education. The scales can be used with such a group, especially if the group or the sponsoring agency is interested in postbirth parent education. These students can learn something about normal developmental sequences that, given a little time, they may expect to encounter as they become parents (Barber & Peatling, 1977).

Three uses of the scales as assessment devices are as follows:

1) Parents who do not have access to (or choose not to make use of) a program of parent education can make use of the scales. A guide for parents is available from the Character Research Press, and a variety of educational and assessment possibilities are described therein. In addition, this guide contains a set of worksheets that are designed to help parents help their own child to develop step by step through the sequences specified in each of the seven scales.

2) In all likelihood, one of the better ways to use the scales involves their use with a group of parents in a program of ongoing parent education. The guide for parents can become a structured part of such a program, and using the various scales to assess individual children can initiate group discussions. In addition, using the worksheets for each scale will help parents to set realistic, achievable goals for themselves and their children. It seems likely that only one of the seven scales should be used in any one session of such a parent-education group, with parents using the selected scale either before or during the session to assess their own child, and thereby generating realistic data for discussion and for learning.

Positive self-regard is important to both general and religious educators, as well as to the parents of preschoolers. However, such leaders of a parent education group must integrate the scales with whatever other educational goals they regard as important. Reference to the guide for parents and to the manual may be a help in achieving such an integration of goals. However, that integration is inescapably a local problem and can be answered best by the parents and leaders involved.

3) Programs for preschool children can use parental assessments of participating children as a means of evaluating the effectiveness of their attempts to achieve their own program goals. Such a use of the scales would inevitably involve a close cooperation between the parents (who assess their own children) and the professionals involved in the program (those who use the parental assessments to evaluate the program goals). For example, the scales could be used to ascertain what

percentage of the children in a program are reaching the more mature levels on *which one* of the seven scales or whether or not some components of positive self-regard were being ignored (i.e., the children in the program evidence less mature levels on some of the scales). The professionals could also use assessment results to create individual profiles or calculate average scores for each scale and compare the assessed children with the age-level means. In these ways a program of preschool education could use assessments based on the seven scales to evaluate program results through a comparison with the children involved in the 1974 and 1975 field tests (Barber & Peatling, 1977).

Technical Aspects

The number of separate studies completed are too great to report in any detail. In trying to summarize the results from these studies, a number of legitimate questions may be asked about the assessment instrument. For instance, do the Barber Scales measure separable components of self-regard, are the scales readily usable, and do the scales reflect sex differences?

Do the Barber Scales measure separable components of self-regard? The Peatling-Tiedeman model of human personality indicates that the global construct of self-regard should be constituted of seven specific interactions, which the Barber Scales presumedly assess. In Table 1, one approach to the question of separability is displayed. These product moment correlation coefficients indicate that the seven scales are, as one would expect, related one to another. This suggests that each may well be an assessment of a portion of a larger, underlying construct.

An inspection of Table 1 reveals that even the largest of the correlation coefficients ($r = .5974$ for the association between the Dealing with Frustrations Scale and the Socially Acceptable Behavior Scale) can "explain" only a little more than 36% of the observed variance. Each of the other correlation coefficients, therefore, accounts for less of the observed variance. Moreover, the overall average correlation coefficient is a modest .4152. These results suggest that the scales are separable components of a larger, more complex and global construct, such as self-regard (Barber-Peatling, 1977).

Are the scales readily usable? Evidence of the usability of the scales comes from the open-ended comments from all 448 administrations in the 1974 field test. These comments were placed into evaluative categories by two independent judges. In addition, a tally was kept of those scales that were returned without any comment. Table 2 displays the results of this study of the open-ended comments.

The results of this study of open-ended comments from the second (1974) field test of the scales indicate that 73.4% were returned with no open-ended comments. Approximately 86% of the returned scales carried either no comment or a positive comment. In no case did any one of the seven scales elicit more than 8% mixed and negative comments. Overall, approximately 7% of the comments on the returned scales fell into either the mixed or the negative categories. Thus, there seems to be clear evidence that across all 448 administrations in this second (1974) field test the scales were accepted readily by a majority of the users. Negativity toward any one of the seven scales seems to have been minimal.

In the second (1974) field test there was a subsample of some 26 parents (20.8% of

Table 1

Product Moment Correlation Coefficients between Scales of Self-Regard as Rated by Mothers in the 1975 Sample

	Purposeful Learning of Skills	Completing Tasks	Coping with Fears	Children's Responses to Requests	Dealing with Frustrations	Socially Acceptable Behavior	Developing Imagination in Play
Purposeful Learning of Skills		.34208 n = 172	.40731 n = 171	.33674 n = 172	.48477 n = 172	.52216 n = 172	.40611 n = 172
Completing Tasks			.40836 n = 171	.46133 n = 172	.34925 n = 172	.36010 n = 172	.51415 n = 172
Coping with Fears				.40238 n = 171	.32575 n = 171	.34224 n = 171	.35548 n = 171
Children's Responses to Requests					.45533 n = 172	.47525 n = 173	.40285 n = 172
Dealing with Frustrations						.59738 n = 172	.34645 n = 172
Socially Acceptable Behavior							.42209 n = 172

125 parents) whose children were enrolled in an inner-city day-care center where 61.7% of the mothers had only a high-school and/or vocational-school education. The average level of parental education in this second field test (N = 125), however, fell approximately at the college level.

The field-test edition of the scales provided a place where a parent could make comments in response to the question, "Was this project easy or difficult to do?" Out of a total of 76 administrations from the inner-city day-care center, only one comment stated that it was "difficult," nine that it was "easy," and two that it was "interesting." On all of the remaining 64 returned scales there was no comment at all, yet all of the 76 scales were filled out with a usable rating. Thus, it is apparent that the scales are usable by a subsample with this educational level and, by implication, that the reading level was suitable for them.

Out of the 351 parents involved in both the 1974 and the 1975 field tests, only five

Table 2

User Comments, Classified by Evaluative Categories
Second (1974) Field Test Data

	Evaluative Categories of Comments					*Scale by*
Scale Title	*None*	*Positive*	*Neutral*	*Mixed**	*Negative*	*Scale Sums*
Purposeful Learning of Skills	40 60.6%	14 21.2%	07 10.6%	05 07.6%	00 00.0%	66 100.0%
Completing Tasks	45 86.5%	06 11.5%	00 00.0%	00 00.0%	01 01.9%	52 100.0%
Coping with Fears	50 73.5%	09 13.2%	04 05.9%	05 07.4%	00 00.0%	68 100.0%
Children's Responses to Requests	38 73.1%	08 15.4%	02 03.8%	04 07.7%	00 00.0%	52 100.0%
Dealing with Frustrations	49 72.1%	07 10.3%	07 10.3%	00 00.0%	05 07.4%	68 100.0%
Socially Acceptable Behavior	57 78.1%	07 09.6%	03 04.1%	03 04.1%	03 04.1%	73 100.0%
Developing Imagination in Play	50 72.5%	07 10.1%	08 11.6%	01 01.4%	03 04.3%	69 100.0%
Category by Category Totals	329 73.4%	058 12.9%	031 06.9%	018 04.0%	012 02.7%	448 100.0%

*The Mixed Category consisted of comments that included some positive and some negative comments about a particular scale.

were unable to rate their child as predominantly at one and only one scale point. This was true for only one scale; these five parents were able to rate their child on each of the remaining six scales at one scale point. Thus, only 1.42% of all parents found that they could not identify their child with just one scale point on just one of the seven Scales.

Another way to address the same question is to note that out of the 2,940 scales returned from parents and teachers there were only eight that had a multiple rating entered on them. This is a mere 0.27% of the returned scales and suggests that most adults (parents or teachers) can, in fact, readily use the seven scales as they were intended to be used (Barber & Peatling, 1977).

Do the scales reflect sex differences? Mean scores based on mothers' ratings on each of the scales for male and female children are graphed in Figure 2. The data come from the 1975 sample. The product moment correlations between sex and scale point were zero order for all seven scales in the 1974 and the 1975 data.

The analysis proceeded a further step with the 1975 data. Male and female means were subjected to *t*-tests. Three-year-olds, four-year-olds, and five-year-olds were compared. Out of a possible 21 significant differences, none were found at the .05 level of probability. Only two were found at the .10 level. Five-year-old females rated higher than five-year-old males on the Completing Tasks Scale. Four-year-old males rated higher than four-year-old females on the Dealing with Frustrations Scale. The *t* statistics were closer to the .10 probability level than the .05 level. There may, indeed, be a clue here. However, these results give no strong indication of sex

Figure 2.
Mean Scores on Seven Scales of Self-Regard for Total Males and Total Females in 1975 Field Test Data

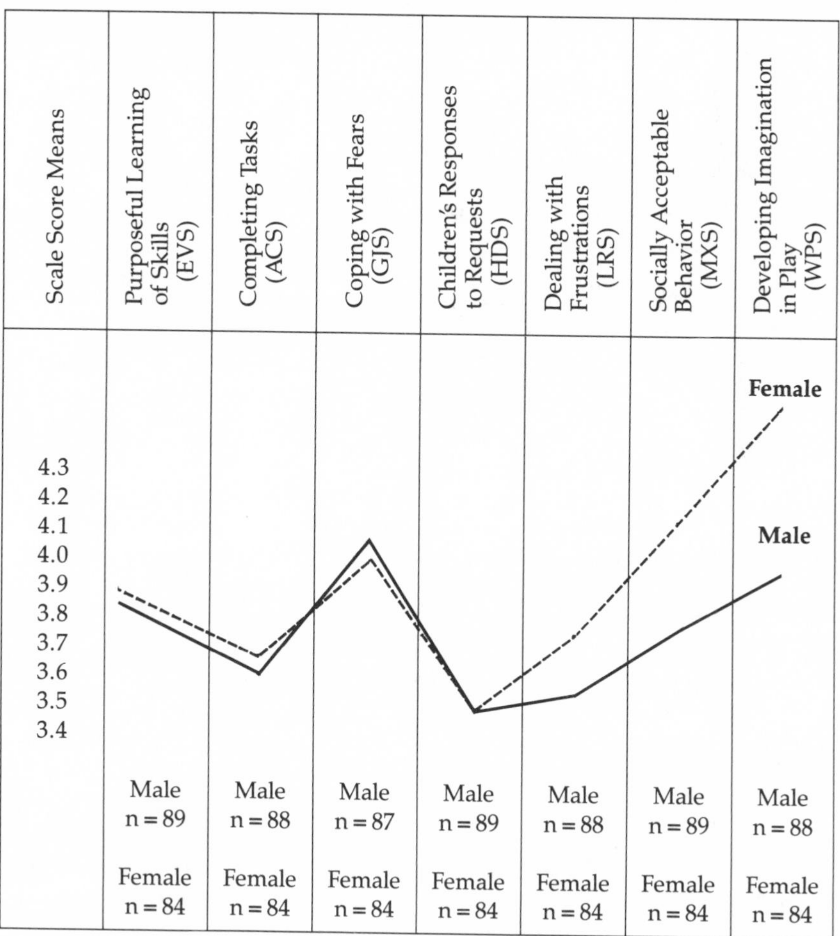

differences. The evidence for sex differences on the seven scales is so sparse that it would indicate that it is not a major problem in using the scales, at least with middle-class samples.

In 1977 and 1978 a test-retest opportunity existed to determine the reliability of the instrument. A parenting program was field-tested in Ohio. That program had as its core the seven Barber Scales of Self-Regard, on which parents rated their children (see Table 3 for test-retest correlations). Criterion-related validity was not examined.

Table 3

Product Moment Correlation Coefficients Between First Ratings and Second Ratings on the Barber Scales of Self-Regard: Preschool for a Sample of Mothers (N = 30) and Fathers (N = 30).*

Titles of the Barber Scales	*Mothers*	*Fathers*	*Time Span for Ratings*
Purposeful Learning of Skills	r_{12m} = .92	r_{12f} = .94	2-3 months
Completing Tasks	r_{12m} = .84	r_{12f} = .95	5 weeks-2½ months
Coping with Fears	r_{12m} = .90	r_{12f} = .85	4 weeks-2½ months
Children's Responses to Requests	r_{12m} = .93	r_{12f} = .84	3 weeks-2½ months
Dealing with Frustrations	r_{12m} = .96	r_{12f} = .96	2 weeks-2½ months
Socially Acceptable Behavior	r_{12m} = .96	r_{12f} = .89	1 week-1 month
Developing Imagination in Play	r_{12m} = 1.00	r_{12f} = 1.00	1 week-1 month

*All coefficients are statistically significant below the .01 level of probability.

Critique

The Barber Scales of Self-Regard for Preschool Children are basically regarded as assessment devices and educational resources. The scales' major purpose seems to be that if adults (parents and teachers) use these scales consistently in observing growth and development of preschoolers, these adults can become trained raters of development. This may be advantageous for the parenting process as well as day-care and nursery care. Although simplistic in application, the validity studies for the scales are well established, and test-retest correlations are quite high. The establishment of this process and its application to parents, teachers, and students studying growth and development is positive and is an important step in truly positive, preventive education for preschool children.

References

This list includes text citations as well as suggested additional reading.

Barber, L. W. (1974). *Self-concept of seven separable components of self-concept in preschool children* (Study No. 74-01-01s). Schenectady, NY: Union College Character Research Project.

Barber, L. W. (1975a). *Additional evidence for the objectivity of mother's ratings on their preschool child's self-regard* (Study No. 75-01-01p). Schenectady, NY: Union College Character Research Project.

Barber, L. W. (1975b). *Geographical area and the Barber Scales of Self-Regard for Preschool Children* (Study No. 75-01-01q). Schenectady, NY: Union College Character Research Project.

Barber, L. W. (1975c). *Does sex of child make a difference in mothers' ratings of the Barber Scales of Self-Regard for Preschoolers?* (Study No. 75-01-01o). Schenectady, NY: Union College Character Research Project.

Barber, L. W., & Barton K. (1975). *Usability by raters of the Barber Scales of Self-Regard for Preschool Children* (Study No. 75-01-01i). Schenectady, NY: Union College Character Research Project.

Barber, L. W., & Cernik, H. C. (1975a). *Normative data for the Barber Scales of Self-Regard for Preschool Children* (Study No. 75-01-01j). Schenectady, NY: Union College Character Research Project.

Barber, L. W., & Cernik, H. C. (1975b). *Additional evidence of separability of components assessed by the Barber Scales of Self-Regard* (Study No. 75-01-01o). Schenectady, NY: Union College Character Research Project.

Barber, L. W., & Cernik, H. C. (1975c). *Developmental scales of self-regard for preschool children* (Study No. 75-01-01l). Schenectady, NY: Union College Character Research Project.

Barber, L. W., & Cernik, H. C. (1976a). Patterns of uniqueness: Seven component profiles of self-regard in preschool children. *Character Potential, 7*(1), 8.

Barber, L. W., & Cernik, H. C. (1976b). *Do mothers and fathers agree on ratings of their preschool child on the Barber Scales of Self-Regard?* (Study No. 76-01-10). Schenectady, NY: Union College Character Research Project.

Barber, L. W., Cernik, H., & Barton, K. (1973). *Five areas of attitude development for the two-year-old* (Study No. 73-01-01e). Schenectady, NY: Union College Character Research Project.

Barber, L. W., Cernik, H. C., & Barton, K. (1975). *Description of the design and sample for the 1975 field-test of the Barber Scales of Self-Regard for Preschool Children* (Study No. 75-01-01g). Schenectady, NY: Union College Character Research Project.

Barber, L. W., & Peatling, J. H. (1975). *A profile of the child's self-regard*. Schenectady, NY: Character Research Press.

Barber, L. W., & Peatling, J. H. (1977). *A manual for the Barber Scales of Self-Regard, Preschool Form*. Schenectady, NY: Character Research Press.

Barber, L. W., & staff. (1973). *What is most important for a two-year-old to learn?* (Study No. 73-01-01d). Schenectady, NY: Union College Character Research Project.

Ligon, E. M. (1970). Map for character development: Mathematical group theory. *Character Potential, 5*, (1-2), 71-98.

Peatling, J. H., & Tiedeman, D. V. (1977). *Career development: Designing self.* Muncie, IN: Accelerated Development, Inc.

G. Cynthia Fekken, Ph.D.
Assistant Professor of Psychology, Queen's University, Kingston, Canada.

BARRON-WELSH ART SCALE

Frank Barron and George Welsh. Palo Alto, California: Consulting Psychologists Press, Inc.

Introduction

The Barron-Welsh Art Scale (BWAS) is an empirically derived measure originally designed to identify individuals whose preferences for abstract figures are similar to those of artists. The BWAS and its revision, the Revised Art Scale (RAS), have been interpreted as indices of creativity. Further, these measures have been integrated into a theoretical, two-dimensional framework derived from extensive research on the relationship of creativity, intelligence, and personality.

As a part of his Ph.D. thesis project at the University of Minnesota in the late 1940s, George Welsh began development of a test of psychiatric disorders comprising 200 stimuli in the form of freehand and ruled figures drawn on 3"x5" index cards. Respondents were asked to sort the figures into "like" versus "dislike" categories. Initially, the responses of 64 psychiatric patients (including three artists) were compared to those of 79 normal controls (also including three artists). Data were combined and factor analyzed, yielding a two-factor solution. The first factor appeared to be an acceptance-rejection factor but the second factor appeared to be an acceptance-rejection faction but the second factor reflected preferences for simple, symmetrical versus complex, asymmetrical figures. Interest in relating personality to esthetic preference led Welsh to examine various personality characteristics in the context of this second factor. Indeed, high scorers could be described as conservative and conventional, whereas low scorers could be described as antisocial and pessimistic. Of note was the finding that all six artists tended to score low on the second factor, prompting the suggestion that this factor pole might also tap "good taste." Such an informal hypothesis provided the impetus for explicitly comparing the figure preferences of artists and nonartists with an eye to developing a measure of artistic discrimination.

Construction of the Art Scale was conducted in collaboration with Frank Barron of the Institute of Personality Assessment and Research at the University of California at Berkeley. The initial pool of items, now known as the Welsh Figure Preference Test (WFPT), was increased to 400. A sample of 37 artists and art students was requested to indicate which figures were "liked" and which were "disliked." These figure preferences were compared to the responses of 75 men and 75 women, all nonselected with regard to artistic ability. The artists liked 40 figures significantly less and 25 figures significantly more than the control group, resulting in the 65-item version of the Barron-Welsh Art Scale described in the literature in 1952 (Barron & Welsh, 1952). Subsequently, three items (one "like," two "dislike") were eliminated, resulting in the current 62-item version of the BWAS (Welsh, 1959, 1980).

By having a scale composed of an unequal number of "like" and "dislike" items, the authors quickly recognized that stylistic responding (i.e., disliking all items) would yield a total BWAS score similar to the normative mean for artistic groups. Thus, the Revised Art Scale was constructed (Welsh, 1959). The empirical item analysis, based on the same 400 items that make up the Welsh Figure Preference Test was conducted anew. From a pool of 250 respondents, 12 individuals who scored high and 12 who scored low on the original BWAS had their responses re-examined. Altogether 30 items more liked and 30 items less liked by the high scorers were selected for the RAS. The RAS is not subject to the necessary correlation between the number of items disliked and total "artistic" score. Note, however, that the correlations between BWAS and the RAS tend to be very high, reported to range from .85 to .96 (Welsh, 1975). Such data led Welsh to conclude in the 1980 manual that the two scales may be considered equivalent, alternative versions of the same construct.

The Barron-Welsh Art Scale and the Revised Art Scale are available in two contexts. The scales' items are all contained in the Welsh Figure Preference Test (Welsh, 1959, 1980), which long ago evolved from a cardsorting procedure to a booklet format. The 62-item BWAS and the 60-item RAS are also available in a separate reusable booklet, which, due to item overlap, needs to contain only 86 items. Each of the items are black and/or gray line drawings on a 3½" x 2" white background. The figures differ on such dimensions as complexity, symmetry, angularity, and shading, ranging from circles or triangles to stimuli containing many lines of varying thicknesses and gray-black shades.

Although it seems most sensible to have culled the BWAS and RAS items out of the WFPT for user convenience, this tactic in fact proves to be rather confusing in the long run. Only the actual item set comprising the Art Scales is independently available—the answer sheet and manual are meant to be shared with the WFPT. For example, the answer sheet bears the dual label, "Welsh Figure Preference Test or Barron-Welsh Art Scale"; general directions plus a sample response appropriate to both measures are printed at the top of the form; and the main portion of the answer sheet consists of 400 spaces or boxes where "like" or "dislike" responses are to be indicated. Welsh (1980) quite reasonably notes that for the Art Scales the respondent is simply asked to use 86 response positions and to leave the rest blank. Such a makeshift strategy has the potential to be distracting and reduce the probability of detecting the common respondent mistake of being out by one response position as items are answered. The bottom of the answer sheet has codes for over 30 WFPT scale scores (including the BWAS and RAS), which contributes to an overall crowded appearance. The area reserved for name, age, sex, and date is especially cramped.

The joint manual, entitled, "Manual: Welsh Figure Preference Test," is equally frustrating. A footnote underneath the Table of Contents eventually clarifies that this manual includes discussion of the BWAS and the RAS. But, when reading through the manual, it becomes further evident that the overview of the Art Scales is quite limited because an extensive and, arguably, excellent literature review may be found in another source (i.e., Welsh, 1975). Provision of a separate answer sheet and collation of relevant empirical information into a distinct and complete manual would significantly contribute to the uncomplicated use of the BWAS and RAS. As it stands, the complaint George Helmstadter voiced in the *The Seventh Mental Measurements Yearbook* (1972) is still a valid one: on ordering the Barron-Welsh Art Scale, one may experience difficulty deciding whether the correct package has arrived.

The aforesaid reservations notwithstanding, the administration of the BWAS and RAS is ordinarily straightforward. Typically, the role of the examiner is minimal. The Art Scales are meant to be self-administering and clear directions to the respondent are provided. The 86-item version requires approximately 15 minutes to complete. Because an individual need not necessarily read English or, for that matter, be literate in any language, the examiner may be called on to translate or to read the instructions for responding. Further, if certain individuals (e.g., mentally retarded persons) are incapable of recording their own responses, it would be permissible for the examiner to do so, having ascertained that meaningful responses are being made. Alternatively, the test might be adapted back to its original card-sort format to simplify responding.

Practical Applications/Uses

Because the overall difficulty level of the tests is very low and because neither a verbal response nor sustained attention is required, the BWAS and RAS are appropriate for adults and children as young as three years, individuals of any educational level from preschool to graduate school, persons of normal or retarded intellectual development, non-English-speaking or illiterate persons, individuals from a wide variety of cultures, deaf or mute individuals, and psychiatrically disordered persons.

As a function of the simplicity of the required responses and of the nature of the stimuli comprising the BWAS and RAS, some interesting applications emerge. Few restrictions exist with regard to the type of population to which the Art Scales may be applied. This permits innovative use of the test, in addition to the more obvious educational, vocational counseling, and research applications. In schools, for example, the BWAS and RAS may guide selection of students for special training in art or in creativity, either because they demonstrate talent or a marked lacked of it. More generally, the BWAS and RAS may be useful for evaluating the success of such special education programs. Note again that suitable school assignments may vary across ages, grade levels, intellectual promise (e.g., gifted vs. "normal" vs. developmentally handicapped), cultures, and so on.

Given the Art Scales' potential for classifying creative versus noncreative persons within various occupations, the BWAS and RAS may have a role in vocational counseling. Success in particular vocations, such as artist, architect, musician, writer, may depend to a certain extent on creativity. As part of an assessment package, the BWAS and RAS may contribute one additional piece of information about the suitability of a particular individual for an occupation. Counseling settings need not be limited to the traditional high-school or university guidance centers. Welsh (1975) reports that the BWAS and RAS perform as expected with juvenile delinquent and criminal populations, in rural and urban centers, and in military settings.

To date, the BWAS and RAS have been primarily used as research instruments. Such research applications are only limited by the imagination. To the extent that the Art Scales are valid measures of creativity, they have potential for studying the relationships between creativity and intelligence, normal and abnormal personality dimensions, and vocational interests. Further, when evaluated in the context of other measures of creativity, the BWAS and RAS may bear on the nature of creativity within and across cultures. The stimulus figures on the Art Scales (indeed, on the entire WFPT) are amenable to studies of perception, cognition, and memory, largely due to their nonverbal quality. Research on general response strategies, operationalized in terms of Berg's deviation hypothesis (Sechrest & Jackson, 1962) and of role playing (Kroger & Turnbull, 1970), has also employed these stimuli.

Originally, the purpose of the BWAS was to discriminate artists from nonartists and further to yield information on artistic discrimination. The 1980 manual indicates that the initial conceptualization of the scale was too narrow and that, actually, "art" scale now constitutes something of a misnomer. The BWAS and RAW are believed better interpreted as indices of creativity, formally integrated into a personality typology based on origence and intellectence dimensions (Welsh, 1975). Welsh proposed this typology to summarize substantial empirical data on the interrelationship of intelligence and creativity. Intellectence describes a dimension anchored by abstract, symbolic, and theoretical approaches to life versus practical, literal, and concrete approaches. Orthogonal to intellectence is the origence dimension that reflects unstructured, nonconventional, and creative approaches versus structured, regular, and noncreative approaches to life. These two dimensions yield a fourfold taxonomy of personality, namely, High Intellectence-Low Origence, High Intellectence-High Origence, Low Intellectence-Low Origence, and Low Intellectence-High Origence. The BWAS and RAS tap creativity as related to origence. Thus, figure preferences reflect not only aspects of esthetic judgment, but also aspects of personality or approach to life.

Professionals who might use the Art Scales include research psychologists, vocational counselors, program evaluators, educators, and art school instructors. The BWAS and RAS are easily used in group settings, such as classrooms or large research sessions. However, individual administration is equally acceptable and sometimes necessary. These tests do not require professional training to administer—research assistants, proctors, and secretaries, in addition to psychologists, counselors, and educators, could all readily give the Art Scales.

The manual instructions for administering the Art Scales are clear, even providing advice on how to answer common questions, such as how many figures are to be placed in the "like" and "dislike" categories. The scoring instructions are slightly more difficult to follow. One source of mild confusion is that the BWAS and RAS can be scored in two ways: as a part of the 400-item WFPT and as a separate 86-item test. Use of a single answer sheet contributes to the problem because the same item numbers on the answer sheet are used in conjunction with one set of keyed responses for the entire WFPT and with another set for the 86-item booklet. A second minor problem concerns the lack of templates for hand-scoring. A recommendation is offered that templates be made from unused answer sheets. For someone unfamiliar with psychological tests, the instructions for constructing templates seem too vague to be useful. Although machine scoring and computer scoring are suggested, they do not appear to be available from the author or from another source. To learn the handscoring might require up to two hours. Once mastered, scoring a single protocol should not require more than ten minutes and may readily be performed by a nonprofessional.

Although obtaining BWAS and RAS scores is an objective procedure, interpreting the scores is more complicated. Some training in testing techniques would appear to be a prerequisite for score interpretation and familiarity with the literature on the empirically derived Art Scales would be a definite asset. Consider the following demands on the test interpreter: For the BWAS and the RAS, respectively, 46 and 52 sets of means and standards deviations are supplied along with the size of the sample and a two- or three-word description. There are no guidelines in the manual to direct selection of the appropriate comparison group. For example, should the RAS score of a 13-year-old girl be compared to norms for "writing girls, control," "artistic girls, control," "gifted adolescents, arts, female," "gifted adolescents, academic, female," or "8th-grade, regular pupils"? This latter example illustrates a concommitant problem, namely, not all groups are designated by sex. Where there are sex differences, females virtually always score higher than the corresponding male sample (see Welsh, 1975). There are no exceptions to this rule for the normative data listed in the manual. Admittedly, empirical studies report few sex differences in correlational patterns, for example, of Art Scale scores and personality variables. Although explicit evaluation of the sex differences issue may be ideal, it would seem imperative for the manual to provide relevant directions.

Once the test interpreter has selected the proper comparison group, the Art Scale scores of an individual or group must be contrasted to the norms. Calculating percentiles or T-Scores is suggested. A T-Score conversion table exists for ten of the most commonly used WFPT scales, but includes neither the BWAS nor the RAS. Some examples in the manual exemplifying the formulae for computing T-Scores would assist many test users.

The final interpretive issue concerns the theoretical context in which BWAS and RAS are correctly evaluated. For such empirically derived measures, the underlying construct becomes explicated mainly through intercorrelations with other indices. Thus, part of the rationale for viewing the BWAS and RAS as measures of origence comes from their extremely high (over .90) correlations with a WFPT scale specifically constructed to measure origence. Welsh (1980) states the conceptualization underlying the WFPT Origence Scale is appropriately generalized to the Art Scales. However, the WFPT Origence Scale is expressly intended for use in connection with the WFPT Intellectence Scale. The logical extension of this argument is that the BWAS and RAS are best employed and understood in conjunction with an intellectence measure. Clarification of this possibly inadvertent interpretive difficulty would seem mandatory.

Technical Aspects

Assessment of the reliability of the BWAS and RAS involves examining their test-retest stability, alternate forms reliability, and internal consistency. The six-month test-retest stability of the BWAS has been estimated at .91 for a group of 26 patients in psychotherapy and at .80 for a sample of 75 college students (Barron, 1965; Wrightsman, Wrightsman & Cook, 1964, cited in Welsh, 1975). The one year test-retest correlation for the RAS was estimated at .70 based on the responses of 32 gifted adolescents (Welsh, 1975). These data indicate that the Art Scale scores show adequate stability.

Alternate forms reliability has been addressed by comparing different response formats of the scales and by comparing the two scales to one another and to the WFPT Origence Scale. RAS scores derived from a 400-item card form of the entire WFPT and from an abbreviated 144-item booklet were found to correlate over .90 for two small student samples receiving the formats in counterbalanced order. Similarly, comparing a forced-choice version of the RAS to a booklet version yielded a .75 estimate of alternate forms reliability for each of two samples (Welsh, 1975).

The intercorrelations among the BWAS, the RAS, and WFPT Origence Scale range from .85 to .96, suggesting that they may reasonably be considered alternate forms. Welsh (1980) goes one step further, arguing that these high correlations may reflect a psychometric property like internal consistency. Such a hypothesis would seem overstated in light of the substantial item overlap among scales. On scales comprising 62, 60, and 93 items, 32 items are common to all three. Only one coefficient of internal consistency is readily available in the literature. Odd-even split-half reliability was estimated at .96 for 80 nonartists (Barron & Welsh, 1952). Somewhat related to the issue of internal consistency is a .96 estimate of consistency across the 400 WFPT items for the tendency to like or to dislike items (Welsh, 1980). Internal consistency, Welsh (1980) argues, is largely an irrelevant aspect of the design of measures empirically constructed to predict criteria. However, even empiricists are rarely content merely to categorize individuals. And once elucidation of the construct underlying a scale is started, scale homogeneity becomes relevant for meaningfully interpreting individual differences.

Integrating validity data for an empirically derived test involves attempts both to evaluate the test's predictive utility and to understand the test's underlying construct. The original purpose of the BWAS was to discriminate between criterion groups; hence, the concern for predictive validity. However, a second purpose has evolved, namely, the meaningful interpretation of individual differences in scores; hence, the concern for construct validity. For didactic purposes, studies on the validity of the BWAS and the RAS will be classified as follows: 1) replication of the artist/nonartist distinction; 2) examination of an empirical link to esthetic judgment; 3) extension of the tests' discrimination to more general indices of creativity or originality; 4) evaluation of discriminant and concurrent validity; 5) investigation of the Art Scales' relationship to personality; and, 6) assessment of stimulus-item properties and structure.

The BWAS and RAS have demonstrated potential for distinguishing between artists and nonartists (Welsh, 1975, 1980) in various studies that span across the original cross-replication (Barron & Welsh, 1952) to a study with children that compared eighth-grade art prizewinners and regular pupils to a cross-cultural setting where Indian fine and commercial artists were compared to nonartist controls (Golenn, 1962, & Raychaudhuri, 1963, cited in Welsh, 1975). Further, moderate correlations between the BWAS and art students' academic grades, as well as faculty ratings of their artwork, have been reported (Rosen, 1955) as have small, but significant correlations, of BWAS scores with formal education in art (Rump, 1977). However, the BWAS has shown no correlation with interest in art or with artistic achievement (Rump, 1977). In addition, scores on esthetic sensitivity as expressed in painting preferences have shown generally small and sometimes nonsignificant correlations with Art Scale scores (Child, 1965). Welsh (1975) argues that the figures comprising the test were not drawn to have esthetic value themselves, but that art scores and esthetic judgment may be mediated by another variable, such as a personality dimension. For example, Barron (1952) has interpreted differences in painting preferences associated with the BWAS in terms of an original, creative versus conventional, conforming dimension of perceptual decision making.

In keeping with such a broad definition of the underlying construct, a substantial number of studies has used the Art Scales to discriminate between members of a group designated as creative/original and members not so designated. This research has evaluated the BWAS and RAS across diverse occupational and educational categories, including artists, writers, musicians, graduate and undergraduate students, mathematicians, scientists, medical students, and business managers, to name a few. The specific "creative" and "noncreative" labels have been variously operationalized in terms of peer or faculty nominations, ratings of an artistic product, composite scores on other creativity measures or assignment to special education classes. Generally, significant mean-score differences have been obtained, supporting the hypothesis that the BWAS and RAS are able to distinguish between criterion groups. The predictive utility of the BWAS and RAS for individuals has received more modest support. An overview of the correlational evidence compiled by Welsh (1975) indicates that the Art Scales only account for a small proportion of the variance. For example, four small, independent samples of graduate students and medical students produced correlations ranging from .19 to .45 between BWAS scores and an index of originality. The correlations are in the expected direction, but the accuracy of individual prediction is not necessarily high.

Accepting that the Art Scales measure some aspect or aspects of creativity, the underlying construct may be partly elucidated by examining discriminant and concurrent validity. Apparently, the BWAS and RAS are not confounded with individual differences in intelligence test scores (Johnson, & Bradley, 1970;

Sechrest & Jackson, 1962; Welsh, 1966). This finding holds even when intelligence is subdivided into verbal and nonverbal components (Welsh, 1966). Two studies have reported modest correlations of the Art Scales with school achievement (Johnson & Bradley, 1970; Welsh, 1975). These results, however, may have limited generalizability because one involved a deaf population and the other permitted self-selection of instructional format.

Concurrent validity data for the BWAS and the RAS relative to other tests of creativity support the hypothesis and the Art Scales measure some unique facet of creativity. Nonsignificant correlations have been obtained with Torrance's three nonverbal indices (McWhinnie, 1967; Parsons, Tittler, & Cook, 1984), with the Remote Associates Test (Mendelsohn & Griswold, 1966), with the Meier Art Judgment Test (Millman & Chang, 1966), with an attitudinal measure of creativity (Eisenman, Borod, & Grossman, 1972), and with a creative independence scale (Rump, 1977). Welsh (1975) reviews studies in which small, but significant, correlations were found with a test of curiosity and with indices of fluency and originality associated with developing creative uses for a common object. Similarly, modest correlations have been recorded between the RAS and self- or peer-rated global creativity (Welsh, 1975), although the RAS has shown a .46 correlation with the Maitland-Graves Design Judgment Test, a nonverbal, abstract measure of design preferences (Millman & Chang, 1966).

The above findings might imply that the Art Scales do not tap dimensions of creative behavior substantially overlapping with those dimensions reflected in other commonly employed creativity tests. Yet, the BWAS and RAS are able, across professions and age groups, to predict original/creative group membership versus conforming/noncreative. What, then, is the nature of the construct mediating Art Scale scores? One empirical approach to this theoretical question has been to examine the personality characteristics of high and low scorers (e.g., Barron, 1952, 1953; Barron & Welsh, 1952; Cashdan & Welsh, 1966; Welsh, 1959, 1975). These studies have used diverse samples and diverse sets of personality traits and, hence, may be somewhat noncomparable. However, if one is willing to simplify, low scorers may be described as conforming, controlled, conservative, rigid, and socially-oriented, whereas high scorers tend to be more nonconforming, impulsive, radical, expressive, and self-directed. This conceptualization is derived primarily from self-report studies of personality but has also received support from experimental studies that have shown, for example, that low scorers on the BWAS are more likely than high scorers to conform in the Asch paradigm (Barron, 1953).

From the outset, researchers, dissatisfied solely to catalogue the Art Scales' correlates, sought to clarify what might mediate the creativity-personality relationships. Barron (1952) hypothesized that the critical third variable linking figure preferences and personality traits may be perceptual decision. Low scores on the BWAS and RAS are associated with preferences for simple, symmetrical figures, whereas high scores indicate preferences for complex, asymmetrical figures. Thus, Barron argues that both the personality characteristics outlined above and Art Scale scores connote a predisposition to favor a simple, noncomplex versus an elaborate, complicated orientation to life. However, objections to the simplicity—

complexity distinction as a moderator of the creativity—personality link have some empirical basis. Eysenck and Castle (1970) reason that the latent structure of the 86 unique items comprising the BWAS and RAS was inadequately described by a single simplicity-complexity dimension. Furthr, stimulus properties, such as symmetry-asymmetry and communicability of the figure, have been disentangled from simplicity-complexity and related to individuals' patterns of item responses (Moyles, Tuddenham, & Block, 1965; Ridley, 1979).

Critique

Clearly, explicit understanding of precisely which facet of creativity the Art Scales reflect and exactly how Art Scale scores and personality variables are mediated is still lacking. The original purpose of the Art Scales, in terms of discriminating between artists and nonartists, does appear to be met. In addition, the Art Scales can distinguish between subgroups of persons within an occupation who have been more generally defined as creative, original versus noncreative, and conforming. Other reviewers remark as well that such studies on predictive validity are based on small samples and have rarely been crossvalidated. Furthermore, the weak correlations of the BWAS and RAS with indices of artistic ability and with other measures of creativity would indicate that accuracy of prediction for individuals is limited. Minimal coefficients of convergent validity again raise questions about the nature of the construct underlying the Art Scales. Perhaps the Art Scales measure an aspect of creativity not yet well articulated. Formal sets of organizational characteristics have been proposed to explain both the preference for certain abstract figures and the relationship of that preference to personality. In particular, the simplicity-complexity dimension has been studied, but at the time of this review, the research findings are equivocal. Integrating the BWAS and RAS into an origence/intellectence framework is an interesting theoretical development, but much of Welsh's (1975) work is exploratory, requiring replication and extension. The BWAS and RAS may have legitimate roles as one part of a comprehensive assessment battery in applied settings. However, the conservative decision would be to restrict the Art Scales primarily to research investigations.

References

Barron, F. (1952). Personality style and perceptual choice. *Journal of Personality, 20,* 385-401.

Barron, F. (1953). Complexity-simplicity as a personality dimension. *Journal of Abnormal and Social Psychology, 48,* 162-172.

Barron, F., & Welsh, G. S. (1952). Artistic perception as a factor in personality style: Its measurement by a figure—preference test. *Journal of Psychology, 33,* 199-203.

Cashdan, S., & Welsh, G. S.(1966). Personality correlates of creative potential in talented high school students. *Journal of Personality, 34,* 445-455.

Child, J. L. (1965). Personality correlates of esthetic judgment in college students. *Journal of Personality, 33,* 476-511.

Eisenman, R., Borod, J., & Grossman, J. C. (1972). Sex differences in the interrelationships of authoritarianism, anxiety, creative attitudes, preference for complex polygons, and the Barron-Welsh Art Scale. *Journal of Clinical Psychology, 28,* 549-550.

Eysenck, H. J., & Castle, M. (1970). A factor-analytic study of the Barron-Welsh Art Scale. *Psychological Record, 20,* 523-526.

Helmstadter, G. C. (1972). The Barron-Welsh Art Scale. In O. K. Buros (Ed.), *The seventh mental measurements yearbook* (pp. 83-85). Highland Park, NJ: The Gryphon Press.

Johnson, G., & Bradley, W. (1970). Some correlational aspects of performance on the Art Scale of the WFPT among certain variables in a deaf population. *Journal of Experimental Education, 39,* 59-62.

Kroger, R. O., & Turnbull, W. (1970). Effects of role demands and test-cue properties on personality test performance: Replication and extension. *Journal of Consulting and Clinical Psychology, 35,* 381-387.

McWhinnie, H. J. (1967). A study of the relationship between creativity and perception in sixth-grade children. *Perceptual and Motor Skills, 25,* 979-980.

Mendelsohn, G. A., & Griswold, B. B. (1966). Assessed creative potential, vocabulary level, and sex as predictors of the use of incidental cues in verbal problem solving. *Journal of Personality and Social Psychology, 4,* 423-431.

Millman, M., & Chang, T. (1966). Inter-correlations among three widely used art tests. *Perceptual and Motor Skills, 23,* 1002.

Moyles, E. W., Tuddenham, R. D., & Block, J. (1965). Simplicity/Complexity or Symmetry/ Asymmetry? A re-analysis of the Barron-Welsh Art Scales. *Perceptual and Motor Skills, 20,* 685-690.

Parsons, R. J., Tittler, B. I., & Cook, V. J. (1984). A multi-trait multimethod evaluation of creativity and openness. *Psychological Reports, 54,* 403-410.

Ridley, D. R. (1979). Barron-Welsh scores and creativity: A second look. *Perceptual and Motor Skills, 49,* 756-758.

Rosen, J. C. (1955). The Barron-Welsh Art Scale as a predictor of originality and level of ability among artists. *Journal of Applied Psychology, 39,* 366-367.

Rump, E. E. (1977). Study of Graves Design Art Judgment Test and Barron-Welsh Revised Art Scale. *Perceptual and Motor Skills, 45,* 843-847.

Sechrest, L., & Jackson, D. N. (1962). The generality of deviant response tendencies. *Journal of Consulting Psychology, 26,* 395-401.

Welsh, G. S. (1959). *Preliminary manual, the Welsh Figure Preference Test,* (research ed.). Palo Alto, CA: Consulting Psychologists Press, Inc.

Welsh, G. S. (1966). Comparison of D-48, Terman CMT and Art Scale scores of gifted adolescents. *Journal of Consulting Psychology, 30,* 88.

Welsh, G. S. (1975). *Creativity and intelligence: A personality approach.* Chapel Hill, NC: Institute for Research in Social Science.

Welsh, G. S. (1980). *Manual: Welsh Figure Preference Test.* Palo Alto, CA: Consulting Psychologists Press, Inc.

Ellen Hedrick Bacon, Ph.D.
Assistant Professor of Special Education, Western Carolina University, Cullowhee, North Carolina.

Dale Carpenter, Ed.D.
Associate Professor of Special Education, Western Carolina University, Cullowhee, North Carolina.

BASIC SCHOOL SKILLS INVENTORY—DIAGNOSTIC

Donald D. Hammill and James E. Leigh. Austin, Texas: PRO-ED.

Introduction

The Basic School Skills Inventory-Diagnostic (BSSI-D) is an individually administered readiness test for children aged four-six years. It determines if they are functioning below age expectations and specifies strengths and weaknesses. The authors, Donald D. Hammill and James E. Leigh, consider this both a norm-referenced and a criterion-referenced instrument. The BSSI-D provides observational and performance measures in six areas: daily living skills, spoken language, reading, writing, mathematics, and classroom behavior. According to the manual (Hammill & Leigh, 1983, p. 1) the test has four primary uses: 1) to identify children who are significantly below their peers in early abilities related to these six areas, 2) to reveal specific strengths and deficits in the assessed areas for instructional purposes, 3) to document progress resulting from intervention in the respective areas, and 4) to function as a measurement instrument in research studies involving young children.

The BSSI-D was designed to be used by teachers to assess the skills and abilities needed by young children as they enter school. The authors constructed the test to meet a perceived need for a readiness test that directly measures the specific content and behaviors needed by young children in the school setting. Tasks and activities on the BSSI-D are intended to provide educationally relevant information on skills related to actual classroom demands. The test reflects the authors' belief in the critical role of the classroom teacher—a classroom teacher who has daily interaction with the child is the only one who can complete the test form. This belief is evidenced also in the authors' use of kindergarten teachers' statements of expected behaviors in the classroom as the basis of the test's content.

The BSSI-D is a revision of a 1976 test, the Basic School Skills Inventory (BSSI). Items for the BSSI were developed from a survey of 50 first-grade and kindergarten teachers in the Philadelphia area. Each teacher was asked to describe the educational and behavioral characteristics of two children who were "ready" for school and two who were "not ready." These children included an equal number of boys and girls and the same percentage of nonwhites as was representative of the community. The sample represented a variety of urban, suburban, and rural neighborhoods from both economically enriched and depressed areas of the city. The characteristics named most frequently by the teachers became the 67 initial items on the first experimental form of the BSSI. Items that were not considered teachable or were not related to classroom performance were excluded. The criterion for this decision was not explained in the manual.

This first experimental form was field tested on kindergarten and first-grade pupils in the Philadelphia area in 1971. Item analysis, reliability data, and teachers' suggestions were used to revise the inventory and add new items. The second experimental form was given to a new group of 105 kindergarten and first-grade pupils. Following revisions and additions of five new items, the authors submitted the third revision to national standardization and published it as the 1976 edition of the BSSI.

The BSSI-D contains a new subtest, Daily Living Skills, which was constructed to replace the Basic Information and Self-Help subtests of the BSSI. Specific information on the development of the 1983 test is not provided in the manual. It states that field testing was done on a sample of Missouri children and a sample of Texas children but does not give either the overall number in the sample or the number of children in each age group. Similarly, information is not provided on how or why the BSSI was revised as a new test, the BSSI-D.

One apparent addition to the BSSI-D is that of a stratified norming sample. The BSSI has been criticized for failure to stratify the norming sample on the basis of parental occupation and geographical location (Egeland, 1978). The new norms in the BSSI-D provide that information on the characteristics of the sample.

The standardization sample for the BSSI-D includes 813 children between the ages of 4-0 and 7-5 from 18 states. Characteristics of the sample compare favorably with characteristics of the U.S. population with regard to sex, race, and urban/rural residence. Comparisons of parent occupations show that the BSSI-D sample has a disproportionate number of blue-collar workers (66% in the sample as compared to 36% in the U.S. population) and underrepresentation of white-collar workers. In addition, the sample does not adequately represent the western states and draws heavily on children from southern states.

Another modification from the BSSI is the provision of percentile scores as well as standard scores. Subtests have standard scores with a mean of 10 and a standard deviation of 3. The skill quotient, based on combined raw scores, has a mean of 100 and a standard deviation of 15. Normative information is provided for six-month age intervals from ages 4-0 through 7-5.

The materials for the BSSI-D are packaged in a convenient book-sized box that contains the manual, a picture book, and the record forms. The picture book contains items used for direct testing on the Spoken Language, Reading, and Mathematics subtests. The manual contains the inventory, directions for administering and scoring, and the normative data tables. Pupil record forms provide a concise format of recording scores on one side and standard scores and profile data on the other side. In addition to the provided materials, examiners must use a variety of their own classroom supplies, such as number and letter flash cards, scissors, a clock, coins, chalk, a primary pencil, and paper.

Practical Applications/Uses

The BSSI-D could be used by teachers to determine general readiness skills for kindergarten or first grade. The test would be primarily useful for assessing children entering preschool, day-care, and kindergarten settings. The test should be administered by the child's teacher, class aide, or educational personnel familiar with the child's daily performance in school. The manual suggests that it is unlikely that parents, school psychologists, or counselors will have sufficient first-hand information to answer questions on the child's classroom functioning. Teachers should also be the primary interpreters and users of the scores in determining instructional objectives from the test results. Administration of the BSSI-D is primarily a judgment by the child's teacher as to whether or not the child has mastered the skill in question. Teachers-examiners are encouraged to take the time necessary to observe the children and collect sufficient information to make a judgment, then administer the specific items provided in the inventory for those items that they are unable to score by observation. That is, direct testing is done only when teachers cannot score an item from prior knowledge. Test questions are not provided for all items in the inventory.

The six subtests of the BSSI-D are Daily Living Skills, Spoken Language, Reading, Writing, Mathematics, and Classroom Behavior. Daily Living Skills primarily measures self-care behaviors (e.g., buttoning and zipping), motor behaviors (e.g., cutting with scissors), and independent behaviors (e.g., arriving and leaving without excessive assistance). Other items cover general information, such as naming days of the week and telling time. The manual states that the 20 items in this subtest measure the basic knowledge and skills typically required for participating in day-to-day activities in school.

In the Spoken Language subtest, which consists of 20 items covering linguistic abilities in phonology (articulating speech sounds), morphology (using plurals), syntax (asking questions), and semantics (using appropriate vocabulary), the teacher answers general questions about the child's language in combination with testing the child directly on some items. On the Reading subtest, the teacher answers a series of questions related to the child's letter knowledge, sight-word recognition, sound-symbol relationships, and reading comprehension. The manual states that the items on this subtest are not a sequence of skills related to reading but a list of abilities needed for reading comprehension. According to the manual, this is the only subtest in which skills are not necessarily sequential. Because the description of the BSSI-D refers to it as a criterion-related test, these reviewers assume that other subtests approximate a sequential skill development.

Writing, which has 15 items, requires the teacher to assess writing skills such as copying words, writing dictated words and sentences, and composing a story. In the Mathematics subtest, which measures knowledge of numerical concepts and arithmetic operations, teachers evaluate the child on skills such as numeration, equivalence, seriation, and simple computations. This subtest combines direct testing and general questioning of the child's mathematical abilities.

The Classroom Behavior subtest requires the teacher to make subjective judgments regarding the child's conformity to the classroom environment. Questions cover the child's attentiveness, cooperation, attitude, socialization, and work habits. There is no direct testing on this subtest, only questions relating to the child's behavior.

Answers are credited with a 1 or 0 on the answer form. Appropriate starting points for each age level are conveniently indicated on the score sheet. Basal and ceiling levels are also clearly indicated. On the reverse side, the examiner can show raw scores, percentiles, standard scores, and category of performance. The manual provides the following rating to accompany standard scores on the subtests, which have a mean of 10: 17-20 = superior, 14-16 = above average, 7-13 = average, 4-6 = below average, and 0-3 = poor. Subtest scores and skills quotient scores are charted on the profile, with scores falling above or below average shown on a shaded area and average scores shown on a white area.

There are no time limits on the administration of any item or subtest of the BSSI-D. According to the manual, 20 minutes should be adequate even if extensive direct testing is required. It encourages examiners to finish the inventory as soon as possible, but no limits for completion are stated (i.e., number of days or weeks). Obtaining a rating of the child's optimal performance is most important.

A basal of five correct items in a row is required for each subtest. Testing continues until a child reaches the ceiling of three successive failures. Indicators showing where the examiner should begin for each age level are shown for each subtest. From this starting point, the examiner tests downward until a basal is reached and then returns to the starting point and tests upward to obtain the ceiling. This procedure may be confusing to some examiners because it is more common to give a starting point as the lowest item expected and to test upward from that point.

The difficult aspect of administering the BSSI-D is making a judgment as to whether a child passes or fails an item where no direct questioning is provided. Many items request the teacher to rate whether the child requires "excessive assistance" or has "inappropriate behaviors." In some cases, clarification statements in the manual merely provide a justification for inclusion of the item on the test, with no behavioral criteria for rating it.

Scoring the BSSI-D involves adding up the correct answers, using the child's age to find the normative table, then recording the standard score and percentile. A standard score and percentile score is determined for each of the six subtests and for the sum of the raw scores, which gives the skills quotient. The skills quotient provides an overall indication of the child's readiness level based on a mean of 100 and a standard deviation of 15.

Interpretation of the standard scores and percentiles is more difficult than the scoring process. The manual states that the test may be used as both a norm-referenced and a criterion-referenced instrument, but interpretation from either perspective requires acumen on the part of the examiner.

The norm-referenced standard scores should indicate a child's areas of strengths and weaknesses. However, in the age range of 6-0 and above, a child cannot score above a standard score of 12 on three of the six subtests. Between the ages of six years, six months and six years, 11 months, a child cannot score above a standard score of 12 or percentile of 75 on five of the six subtests. For ages seven years, 0 months through seven years, five months this is true for all subtests. Although this is less of a problem at the younger ages, a standard score of 14 is the highest possible score a child between four years, 0 months and five years, 11 months can obtain on two of the six subtests. Unless an examiner is aware of the artificially low ceiling levels on this test, interpretation of strengths and weaknesses can be misleading. A child may have areas of strength that cannot be shown on this test. Profiles may indicate average performance in spite of a perfect score. For low-achieving, learning-disabled, and mentally handicapped students, masking their areas of strengths may lead to further lowering expections based on the test's artificial ceiling.

Use of the test as a criterion-referenced instrument may also prove to be unsatisfactory. Skills are broadly stated and are not clearly delineated by specific subskills. Teachers might reasonably expect to find from a CRT detailed information on subskills from major objectives. Instead, the BSSI-D provides the teacher with information on general readiness deficits only. The general nature of the items is apparent in the use of 15-20 items that cover major skill areas over a three-year span.

Technical Aspects

The primary measures of a test's technical adequacy are its validity and reliability. Reliability refers to the consistency or stability of a test. According to Salvia and Ysseldyke (1983, p. 77), "if a test is reliable and the tested trait or behavior is stable, a person will receive the same score on repeated testing." Hammill and Leigh (1983) report two types of reliability: internal consistency and alternate-form reliability.

Internal consistency was evaluated using coefficient alpha, and these coefficients were reported by age and subtest. For this type of reliability the manual reports acceptable to good reliability, with 16 of the 28 coefficients reaching .90 and 11 other coefficients reaching the .80 level. In general, these results indicate a high level of internal consistency or homogeneity, demonstrating that the items on the BSSI-D measure the same trait or behavior.

The manual also reports on the reliability coefficient obtained by correlating the total score of the BSSI-D with the total score of the Basic School Skills Inventory-Screen (BSSI-S), a 20-item observational screening measure that is similar to the BSSI-D (see succeeding review). Coefficients of .91, .92 and .88 were obtained for ages four, five, and six years, respectively. The BSSI-S was created by the same authors apparently at the same time as the BSSI-D, but it is not clear whether the items for the two forms were field tested at the same time. Information is needed as to whether the same teacher supplied the ratings on both tests at the same time. Additionally, it is not stated whether there is an overlap of items on the two tests. Means and standard deviations for the BSSI-S or the BSSI-D are not given. Until further data on the alternate-form reliability are made available, this measure of reliability should be questioned.

Although these measures are important, these reported measures of reliability do not demonstrate the stability of the test or that the child would be rated the same by a different examiner or by the same examiner at a later time. What the user of the test needs to know before relying on the normative data is whether the inventory would be scored similarly by different raters. To have confidence in this measure, information on interobserver reliability is necessary. The 1985 edition of *Standards for Educational and Psychological Testing* (American Educational Research Association, 1985, p. 22) lists the following as a primary or essential standard for a published test:

> Where judgmental processes enter into the scoring of a test, evidence on the degree of agreement between independent scoring should be provided. If such evidence has not yet been provided, attention should be drawn to scoring variations as a possible source of errors of measurements.

Validity, the extent to which a test measures what it claims to measure, is not measured directly but is judged on the appropriateness of the inferences that can be made on the basis of the test (Salvia & Ysseldyke, 1983). The BSSI-D claims to enable a teacher to identify whether a child has the skills that teachers consider important to school success. Judgment about the validity of the test should be based on demonstrations of the test's ability to identify accurately children who will be successful in school and those who will be delayed on school-related tasks. The manual addresses this issue in terms of content, criterion-related, and construct validity.

Content validity assesses the extent to which the items on a test represent the universe of the content to be measured. Content validity for this test was determined by a judgment on the part of experts as to the completeness and appropriateness of the items. The BSSI-D was developed from information on readiness behaviors provided by teachers, and items were field tested to eliminate those not considered important to teachers. Because of this heavy reliance on professional judgment in developing, generating, and revising items, the BSSI-D has strong content validity.

Criterion-related validity refers to evidence that the test score is related to some outcome criteria, or in the instance of the BSSI-D, to a valid measure of readiness. The BSSI-D is a measure of readiness skills based on teachers' perceptions. It purports to identify children who are significantly delayed in early abilities. The criterion measure chosen by the authors was another teacher ranking of individual readiness using a three-point scale. Correlations between the BSSI-D and the rankings were .35 for Daily Living Skills, .38 for Spoken language, .27 for Reading, .22 for Writing, .31 for Math, .37 for Classroom Behavior, and .43 for the total score. These coefficients are significant at the .001 level, but three of the subtests do not meet the .35 minimum level set by the authors. These three subtests, Reading, Writing, and Mathematics, did not correlate well with teachers' ratings. The authors state: "In part, this can be explained by the fact that the teachers were rating the children on 'general readiness' and in the 4-6 year period reading, writing and math may not be considered to be particularly relevant by the teachers doing the ratings" (Hammill & Leigh, 1983, p. 15). It is troublesome that the only measure of criterion-related validity does not support half of the subtests. The measure one would like to see is evidence that the BSSI-D identified children who later had difficulty in the first and second grades on achievement and social adjustment measures (Webster, 1985).

Construct validity refers to evidence that demonstrates that the test acts in a predictable way on a variety of related measures. The BSSI-D manual presents four types of construct validity:

Age differentiation: Age was found to correlate with test scores, supporting the assumption that the inventory is developmental.

Subtest interrelationships: Significant correlation coefficients were found for interrelationships among all subtests. The 14 coefficients ranged in size from .37 to .86, supporting the premise that the readiness areas are highly interrelated.

Group differentiation: Twelve learning-disabled children between four years, eight months and six years, six months were compared with 12 nondisabled children of the same ages. Differences between the subtests were all significant except for Classroom Behavior.

Item validity: The correlation of performance of the test items with the total score is presented as one type of evidence of construct validity. The BSSI-D manual reports acceptable levels of correlations between .15-.85 at the four age levels for all subtests except three.

In summary, the construct validity of the measure as a readiness diagnostic inventory is argued on the basis of the correlation of scores with age, the high interrelationships between subtests, the high interrelationships between items and subtest scores, and that the test differentiated 12 learning-disabled children from nondisabled children. On this last measure of group differentiation, more information is needed on the comparison groups in order to evaluate its relevance. No information is provided on IQ, language, SES, or sex for either group. No subtest means, standard deviations, or statistical levels of significance are reported.

Critique

The concepts behind the construction of the Basic School Skills Inventory-Diagnostic are sound. Development of a readiness test that uses teacher judgments as a foundation and requires little formal testing should be applauded. There is obvious merit in avoiding the errors in measurement and frustrations of testing young children in unfamiliar surroundings. Additionally, there is a need for a test that can differentiate strengths and weaknesses of preacademic skills of children aged four-six years with normative data.

However, some major problems with the test need to be resolved before it can be recommended without reservation. The norms at some ages have a restricted range providing percentiles and standard scores on children based on such low ceilings that students at certain ages cannot perform above average on certain subtests. These skewed profiles may provide false pictures of children's true abilities unless interpreted by teachers who are knowledgeable about the test's inherent ceilings.

The authors have presented considerable information on the reliability and validity of the test, but they have not answered two fundamental issues related to the test's reliability and validity: First, evidence of the degree of agreement between independent scorings is required because of the judgmental nature of the inventory. Without this evidence, the applicability of the norms for any child can be questioned. Second, the authors present evidence of content and construct validity. However, the study investigating criterion-related validity fails to demonstrate a strong case on the basic question of whether the test can identify children who will be unsuccessful in school.

The BSSI-D does not provide an acceptable norm-referenced measure of readiness skills. Nor does it provide adequate information or analyses of subskills in order to be a good criterion-referenced test. Nevertheless, it may provide a useful informal guide to teachers in structuring their observations of a child's readiness if the normative and profile information is not used in evaluation and placement decisions.

References

This list includes test citations as well as suggested additional reading.

American Education Research Association. (1985). *Standards for educational and psychological testing*. Washington, DC: American Psychological Association.

Egeland, B. R. (1978). Review of the Basic School Skills Inventory-Diagnostic. In O. K. Buros (Ed.), *The eighth mental measurements yearbook* (pp. 561-562). Highland Park, NJ: The Gryphon Press.

Gacka, R. C. (1978). The Basic School Skills Inventory as a preschool screening instrument. *Journal of Learning Disabilities, 11,* 66-68.

Hammill, D. D., & Leigh, J. E. (1983). *Basic School Skills Inventory: Diagnostic manual*. Austin, TX: PRO-ED.

Hawthorne, L. W., & Larsen, S. C. (1977). The predictive validity and reliability of the Basic School Skills Inventory. *Journal of Learning Disabilities, 10,* 50-56.

Salvia, J. D., & Ysseldyke, J. E. (1983). *Assessment in special and remedial education* (2nd ed.). Boston: Houghton Mifflin.

Webster, W. J. (1985). Review of the Basic School Skills Inventory-Diagnostic. In J. V. Mitchell, Jr. (Ed.), *The ninth mental measurements yearbook* (pp. 144-145). Lincoln, NE: Buros Institute of Mental Measurements.

Robert H. Bauernfeind, Ph.D.
Professor of Education, Northern Illinois University, DeKalb, Illinois.

BASIC SCHOOL SKILLS INVENTORY—SCREEN

Donald D. Hammill and James E. Leigh. Austin, Texas: PRO-ED.

Introduction

The Basic School Skills Inventory—Screen (BSSI-S) is a 20 item checklist of skills that will be needed for success in school. It is a measure of "school readiness." The authors developed the BSSI-S by using conventional item-analysis techniques to extract 20 highly discriminating items from the 110 skills items of the Basic School Skills Inventory—Diagnostic (Hammill & Leigh, 1983, see preceding review).

The BSSI-S package consists of a six-page manual, called a "Fact Sheet," and a four-page record sheet for each pupil. The pupil's record sheet shows the skills checklist on pages two and three, visual materials for three of the 20 items on page four, and norms with suggested "high risk" zones on the front cover. The 20-item checklist covers a variety of skills. Some, such as requiring subjects to name the number that comes after three and give the month of their birthday, are test items for pupils. Other items call for highly complicated summaries of the child's behavior in school (e.g., whether the student shows recognition of the rights and property of others; whether the student finds something acceptable to do after completing his or her work). Because these latter items require the administrator to have ample opportunities to observe the child's behaviors in school, the BSSI-S is best administered by classroom teachers and/or teacher aides.

Practical Applications/Uses

The BSSI-S was designed to identify children who may need remedial work, a more comprehensive examination, or referral for possible special services. The scores could also be used in setting up ability groups in kindergarten or first-grade classes.

The instrument was designed for use with children aged four, five, and six years, and general norms are provided for these three age groups. The BSSI-S is administered individually and can be completed in five-ten minutes, depending on how well the examiner knows the child.

Each item is scored as one or zero, with test items for the child marked right or wrong and each complex question for the teacher answered either "Yes" or "No." The total possible raw score is 20 points.

The front page of the BSSI-S record sheet shows three tables of general norms: one for four-year-olds, one for five-year-olds, and one for six-year-olds. For each raw score, each table shows a standard score conversion (M = 100, SD = 15) and the corresponding percentile-rank score, as well as gray shaded areas for percentiles 1-16. According to the manual (p. 4), percentile scores 1-16 represent a "high risk" group—children who are likely to have major difficulties in school.

Cognitive growth is so rapid during these ages (i.e., 4-6) that this reviewer questions having only yearly norms. It would be entirely possible to have nine four-month age groups with high-risk raw scores as follows:

Age Group	*"High Risk" Raw Scores*
4.0-4.3	0- 8
4.4-4.7	0- 9
4.8-4.11	0-10
5.0-5.3	0-11
5.4-5.7	0-12
5.8-5.11	0-13
6.0-6.3	0-14
6.4-6.7	0-15
6.8-6.11	0-16

Technical Aspects

General norms for the BSSI-S are inadequate, with, according to the manual, children who have white-collar parents, black children, and children in the western states underrepresented. This same criticism is noted by Doebler, (1985). However, normative adequacy is *not* a major consideration in the case of BSSI-S because the purpose of this instrument is to identify "high risk" pupils, which can be done simply with raw scores. General norms are irrelevant to that task.

The reliability of this instrument appears to be adequate. The authors report Kuder-Richardson Formula 21 reliabilities for the three age groups: .80 in Grade 4, .83 in Grade 5, and .83 in Grade 6. This reviewer checked these figures against the distributions of raw scores shown on the cover of the record sheet, and the resulting K-R 21 estimates are very close to those reported by the authors. (The alternate-forms data in Table 3 in the manual represent correlations between BSSI-S and the 110-item Basic School Skills Inventory—Diagnostic. As such, they are more properly viewed as concurrent validity studies.)

Several validity studies are reported in the manual (pp. 5-6), and all were encouraging. For the entire norming population of 376 children, the BSSI-S raw scores correlated in the .60s, .70s, and .80s with BSSI-D part scores and .92 with the BSSI-D total score. The BSSI-S raw scores correlated .43 with teachers' ratings of their children's "school readiness" and .57 with the children's chronological age. In a separate study, the BSSI-S raw scores sharply differentiated a "learning disabled" group from a "normal" group of children. In short, children with high raw scores tend to have higher scores on other cognitive measures than do those with low raw scores.

The least encouraging validity study showed a correlation of only .43 between BSSI-S raw scores and teacher' ratings of their children's "readiness" abilities. The authors may have *under*estimated the correlation with teachers' ratings of their children's "readiness" abilities (r = .43). Apparently, in this study all data from the three age groups were pooled. However, the teacher of four-year-olds would probably be more tolerant of these children's failure to recall their birth months than the teacher of six-year-olds. Though children in both age groups fail the same BSSI-S tasks, the four-year-olds may well receive a higher "readiness" rating than the six-year-olds. Thus, correlations calculated *within grades* will probably run higher than the single correlation from pooled data—perhaps more on the order of .60 than .43. Therefore, in future studies in single grades, test correlations with teacher ratings should run higher than .43, even as the underlying test reliabilities run lower.

Critique

The BSSI-S items seem to have been developed with professional skill. It seems clear that all 20 skills *are* relevant to "readiness for school." This reviewer believes that this instrument will show useful predictive validities in most schools. The schools will need to check their own validities (preferably with scattergrams) and will need to check their own data for "high risk" pupils. These "high risk" scores are almost certain to vary from one school system or neighborhood to another.

References

Doebler, L. K. (1985). Review of the Basic School Skills Inventory—Screen. In J. V. Mitchell, Jr. (Ed.), *The ninth mental measurements yearbook* (p. 145). Lincoln, NE: Buros Institute of Mental Measurements.

Hammill, D., & Leigh, J. E. (1983a). *The Basic School Skills Inventory—Diagnostic.* Austin, TX: PRO-ED.

Hammill, D., & Leigh, J. E. (1983b). *The Basic School Skills Inventory—Screen.* Austin, TX: PRO-ED.

Theodore R. Cromack, E.D.
Director, Commodity Donation Demonstration Study, Virginia Polytechnic Institute and State University, Washington, D.C.

Jim C. Fortune, Ed.D.
Professor of Educational Research and Evaluation, Virginia Polytechnic Institute and State University, Blacksburg, Virginia.

BASIC SKILLS ASSESSMENT PROGRAM, 1978 EDITION

Educational Testing Service. Monterey, California: CTB/ McGraw-Hill.

Introduction

The Basic Skills Assessment Program (BSA) was published as a national secondary-level testing program providing tests in the areas of reading, writing, and mathematics. Designed primarily for use with students in Grades 8-12, these tests emphasize everyday applications of practical and academic skills. The program has both secure and nonsecure testing components. The secure testing program is designed for schools to use as part of their graduation requirements, with test booklets shipped to authorized school personnel who agree to share the responsibility for maintaining test security. Schools use the nonsecure program for an early warning signal to identify students who are deficient in basic skills. Test security is maintained as warranted by the needs of school districts.

Three multiple-choice tests, which assess reading, writing skill, and mathematics for a general high school population and are scored by the Educational Testing Service (ETS), are described as follows:

Reading (65 items): Assesses literal comprehension (33 items) and inference/evaluation (32 items). Content deals with topics such as reading telephone directory, loan agreement, advertisement, newspaper, magazine, school catalog, book and periodical titles, driver's application form, political propaganda, community resources, medicine label directions, nutritional information, road map, job application, bus schedule, and work-related information.

Writer's Skills (75 items): Assesses skills in spelling, capitalization, punctuation, filling out forms, use of standard written English, and evaluation (organization). Content deals with skills including writing a letter to explain a problem, announcements, messages, request for information, business correspondence, narrative writing, and descriptive writing. Manual includes instructions for collecting and scoring a writing sample, a direct measure of writing ability that is scored by the school district. Five minutes are allowed for suggestions, five minutes for completing a form, 20 minutes for writing a business letter, ten minutes for conveying information, and 20 minutes for writing creatively.

Mathematics (70 items): Assesses skills in areas such as straightforward computation, consumer buying, banking, wages and salaries, mileage, statistical inference, and health and nutrition. In addition to computational items, it includes 41 application items.

The Basic Skills Assessment Program was a cooperative effort by ETS and a national consortium of school districts, with the copyright (1978) held by ETS. The acknowledgements section of the technical manual (Educational Testing Service, 1978, p. iii) states that the "manual represents the combined efforts of the Basics Skills Assessment staff members John Fremer (Chapters 1 and 2), Frances Swineford (Chapters 3 and 5), and Michael Zieky (Chapter 4). Cheryl Winer provided an extensive technical editing and Nathaniel Hartshorne turned the entire document into readable English."

In the fall of 1976 a nationwide consortium of school districts joined with ETS in the development of the BSA. The test content was based in part on a national test specification survey to which 800 school districts responded. Setting specifications was done in successive stages with various groups participating in the process. Initial broad decisions about the tests were made with the help of two complementary groups of educators: the preliminary advisory group and the basic skills assessment steering group. The preliminary advisory group was selected from the professional educational community that included such representatives as those from school districts and professional organizations. The steering committee was selected from within the nationwide consortium members of the school districts in the consortium. (Names of participants are given in Appendix A and Appendix B of the technical manual.) Test construction was based on the framework set by these two groups, who also reviewed other testing programs and studied research projects at ETS and elsewhere to look for related precedents for establishing appropriate test specifications. Building on this data base, BSA's staff members put together lists of possible skills in content areas that might measure basic skills. From these lists a survey questionnaire was developed and sent to school districts around the United States. Respondents were asked to rate each of the entries on the questionnaire in terms of relevance and importance for inclusion in a test of basic skills. The results were tabulated and a rank ordering of specifications by perceived importance was created. The consortium steering committee reviewed the results, which were then passed on to two nationally represented committees, one for reading and writing and one for mathematics. Members of these committees were selected from nominations of school district personnel by the consortium steering committee. At the end of this process a set of detailed specifications was designated as representative of the skills basic to meeting the demands of everyday life that were being taught in schools throughout the United States.

National norms are available for the BSA multiple-choice tests as a result of the norming study carried out in May of 1977. The instruments were administered to students in Grades 8, 9, and 12, making it possible to derive norms for high-school "entrants" (Grades 8 and 9 combined) and high-school "exits" (Grade 12).

Local school districts are encouraged to use the program as a method of identifying students who need additional help in basic skills. In such cases separate performance standards for each of the areas tested should be established locally. Instructions are provided to assist districts in setting up these local performance standards. It is suggested that districts identify students as masters and nonmasters of a subject area at the time of testing. ETS then applies statistical procedures to the distribution of students' scores in order to derive an appropriate local cutting or passing score. This local standard then appears on the school district standards roster, one of the four basic score reports provided by ETS. A manual, entitled "Passing Scores" (formerly called "Manual for Setting Standards on the Basic Skills"), is also available from the publisher.

Originally, norms were discussed with the steering committee with the idea that there might not be a need for national norms because the program should focus on helping schools find and assist students with basic skill deficiencies. However, there was a strong appeal for the development of national norms. The issue of credibility was frequently identified (Educational Testing Service, 1978, p. 19): "In the absence of good national norming data the basic skills assessment might not be accepted by parents or other community members as a legitimate basis for identifying students needing help."

If students are expected to have mastered certain basic skills by the time they graduate, it is necessary that the first testing take place at the beginning of secondary school. Tests administered to Grades 8 and 9 allow time to identify those who have not mastered these basic skills and provide the necessary remediation. Grade 12 norms are based on spring testing and are denoted as "exit" norms, the exit level from high school.

In determining the norming sample, the country was divided into five regions, each of which consisted of six to 17 states. In addition to equal representation of geographical regions, socioeconomic status was designed into the sample. Using the 1970 census data, an SES index was computed for each school district within the region. School districts within a region were then listed in order of their SES index and their public secondary-school population. The list was divided into nine SES strata, with approximately the same number of students in each. A random selection of two school districts from each subgroup was then made. These schools were asked to test 25 pupils in each of Grades 8, 9, and 12. Nonpublic schools were also invited to participate: four in region one and two in each of the other regions at random. Replacements were selected in the same manner. The ultimate norming group was drawn from 203 schools in 126 districts representing the national population with respect to SES. A total of 7,731 pupils were tested, 2,494 of whom were in eighth grade, 2,831 in ninth grade, and 2,406 in twelfth grade.

The scale selected for the reporting of the basic-skills scores has a mean of 150 and a standard deviation of 25 for the base group. Conversions to the scale are linear. Scale scores were established for the experimental form (Form ZBX4), and a procedure of score equating is intended to permit comparison of performances on all forms of a particular test. Score conversions and grade norms are provided for the test. These show the scale score corresponding to each raw score and grade group and the percent of scores lower than each scale score listed.

In addition to subscores for the tests, clusters in which items are summed to provide cluster scores are provided. For example, in the Reading Tests the two subscores are literal comprehension and inference (evaluation). The Reading clusters describe the type of item that is used, and although they may overlap, items are clustered into seven clusters: forms, charts and maps, prose, protector, producer, consumer, learner, and citizen. A Writer's Skills has nine clusters and four subscores: spelling, capitalization and punctuation, usage, and logic (evaluation). Mathematics has two subscores and ten clusters within the subscores. The first five clusters make up the computation subscore and the last five clusters make up the applications subscore.

To these reviewers' knowledge, there are no revisions of these tests. The test was developed in 1978 with the expectation that there would be considerable need for basic skills assessment. However, the expectation has not been fully realized because determination of basic skills has clearly been a local issue. Despite the fact that this was designed to allow local norms, it appears that local input is far more important to school districts than standardization of test items and comparison across school districts.

The test materials consist of a technical manual, directions for administering the multiple choice tests, and the three different forms of the tests (Reading, A Writer's Skills, and Mathematics). Each form consists of a single booklet containing the multiple-choice items and a basic skills assessment answer sheet for mark sense answering. A basic skills writing sample, which contains the writing tests, is also included. There were no instructions for administering the basic skills assessment writing sample included in the materials received by these reviewers, but they are available from the publisher.

The printing of the tests is excellent. The print is larger than standard with ample space so that it is quite easy to read. The test items seem appropriate. The Reading Test contains examples of job descriptions and questions about job descriptions, ads, cartoons and interpreting the cartoon, and editorials in which the examinee determines the position that the editorial writer has taken. In A Writer's Skills Test, there are questions that deal with whether one has filled out a check correctly, employment applications, and completion of sentences. In the Mathematics Test, there are computational items, questions about mileage, weight, and graph interpretation, and an item on reading a Form 1040 to determine the amount of tax to be paid.

Administration directions are clear for all three forms. The part to be read aloud to the examinees is clearly marked and, to the extent possible, all contingencies appear to have been considered. Because the tests are expected to be given in Grades 8, 9, and 12, the difficulty level is subject to some change over that period of time. The technical manual indicates that the difficulty level of Reading and A Writer's Skills is relatively low (i.e., easy), whereas that of Mathematics is moderate. The statistics of the experimental form bear out this claim; however, there is a definite increase in p values for Grade 12 over Grades 8 and 9. Nevertheless, the technical manual indicates that the tests are unspeeded and additional time can be provided if necessary and that the program norms can still be used as a reference.

Practical Applications/Uses

As mentioned earlier, the test was designed to meet the needs of school districts wishing to go into a basics-skills mastery program. There is both a secure and a nonsecure testing program because it was expected that school districts would purchase this test for two reasons: 1) to provide an early warning signal for students deficient in basic skills (nonsecure), and 2) to establish the graduation eligibility of twelfth graders (secure). As mentioned earlier, basic skills have become a strong local control issue, and generally, school districts have decided that they would prefer to establish their own basic-skills definition. Although some school boards and superintendents are concerned about comparing their students with other districts, such comparisons would probably be made on the basis of the SAT for the college-bound students.

These tests should be useful for making comparisons across districts for non-college-bound subjects. That they are not extensively used limits comparisons, and it is relatively clear that the limited usage has not warranted revision of the tests. The test editor, Carol Dwyer (personal communication, August 12, 1985), indicates that the BSA was a response to a perceived need in the late 1970s for a national basic-skills diagnostic instrument. Today it is clear that states or, in some instances, local school districts prefer locally developed basic skills tests.

Each of the forms requires approximately 45 minutes to administer. They are scored by ETS, which provides the school district with four types of score reports: alphabetical student score rosters, school standards rosters, cluster reports, and statistical summary reports.

The alphabetical student score roster provides two indications for each student: the percent who scored below the student's score in the norming sample and the standard score for comparing the student's performance on two forms of the same test. This is useful if the test is given in eighth or ninth grades and again in twelfth grade. The school standards roster lists students in rank order from highest to lowest and will indicate a local performance standard if the school district has requested such.

For each cluster of items the cluster report provides 1) the number of items in the cluster, 2) the school average percent correct raw score, 3) the school average percent equated score, and 4) the national percent correct. The school average percent correct equated shows the average percent of items that would have been answered correctly by the students in a grade if the norming form of the test had been given. This uses the delta to equate that form with the norming form (ZBX4). The national percent correct is the norm representing the average percent of items in this cluster that were answered correctly by the representative nationwide norming sample.

The statistical summary report consists of score intervals (standard scores), frequency, percent, cumulative frequency, the percentage of students in this grade in this district who had this score or below, and statistical data (the standard summary statistic including information such as range, means, and standard deviation).

Two optional reports, the individual item response report and the individual student adhesive label, are also available. The individual item response report provides student-by-student information on whether the student omitted an item, answered it correctly, or answered it incorrectly. As a diagnostic tool, this report provides information concerning specific difficulties on the basic skills to the school personnel, parents, and the student.

Interpretation of the scores is relatively straightforward. A standard score is easily converted on the tables from a raw score, and the percent below is also easily identifiable. There are no grade equivalent scores or IQ conversions. Such scores would be inappropriate, and it appears that, because this is a diagnostic test and a mastery test, the most appropriate scores are provided.

Technical Aspects

The technical aspects of the BSA include validity, reliability, items statistics, intercorrelation of tests, and speededness. The technical manual, which discusses both content and concurrent validity, states that "while no process can be said to guarantee the existence of content validity the steps carried out in developing the specifications for the BSA certainly resulted in a high probability of measures with content validity." There is certainly evidence that care was taken to provide test specifications, given the review of the research, other relevant testing programs, local school districts, and professional organizations. It might be noted, however, that the content specifications do not appear to be anchored in specific objectives.

Concurrent validity requires an outside criterion. In the case of the BSA the outside criterion was teachers' judgments of students' need for remediation. As part of the norming process teachers were asked to classify students taking the test into three groups: 1) definitely does not need help, 2) not certain whether help is required or not, and 3) definitely requires remedial help in mastering the skills. ETS prepared separate score reports for these groups and compared group 1 with group 3. A table is provided indicating the difference in these means. Because the sample size in most instances was quite large it would not be appropriate to provide *t*-tests of these differences. The differences certainly are of sufficient magnitude to indicate that the groups were different. However, the most compelling evidence of validation is predictive validity, and, as the manual indicates, predictive validity is to be examined at some future time.

A table of the reliabilities of the three tests' total scores and subscores is provided in the technical manual. Kuder-Richardson Formula 20 was used to estimate the reliabilities, which range for total scores on each test from 0.927 to 0.946. Subscores for Reading and Mathematics yield reliability coefficients between 0.85 and 0.89. A Writer's Skills has considerably more variability. Subtests for usage and logic (evaluation) range from 0.82 to 0.89; however, for spelling, capitalization, and punctuation, which have only 14 items each, reliability coefficients range between 0.73 and 0.77. The standard errors of measurement generally become smaller in a set pattern as grade level increases, and all are 10% of the number of items or less.

The difficulty for each item in the ZBX4 experimental form is shown. The tests are not of equal difficulty. The *p*-values (percent passing) are classified, according to these reviewers' arbitrary distinction, as difficult, moderate, and easy in Table 1 of this review merely to demonstrate the difference between the Grade 8, 9, and 12 difficulties and the differences across the three tests.

Biserial correlations were computed between item scores and the total score for all tests. A very low biserial correlation means that the items are quite different from the rest, and a high correlation means relatively homogeneous items that

Table 1

Difficulty Level (*p*-values)

Items	*Difficult* (.50 or below)		*Moderate* (.51 to .80)		*Easy* (.81 to .90)		*Total*
Grades	*8,9*	*12*	*8,9*	*12*	*8,9*	*12*	
Reading	2 3%	0 0%	26 40%	9 14%	37 57%	56 86%	65
A Writer's Skills	5 7%	3 4%	44 59%	20 27%	26 35%	52 69%	75
Mathematics	24 34%	11 16%	39 56%	35 50%	7 10%	24 34%	70

test the same thing. Evidence is that the test is quite homogeneous. In fact, intercorrelations among the subscores range from 0.569 to 0.730. The Reading Test, which has subtests of literal comprehension and inference (evaluation), shows intercorrelations of 0.849, 0.851, and 0.852 for Grades 8, 9, and 12, respectively. This would indicate that these two subtests measure essentially the same thing. Additionally, intercorrelation among the tests provides evidence that there is relatively little independence among the three tests. The lowest intercorrelation is a .651 (Mathematics and Reading) and a 0.669 (Mathematics and A Writer's Skills). All others are 0.70 and above.

An additional test characteristic resulting from item analysis is an indication of items that were not answered. Any items not answered within the test are assumed to be difficult and, therefore, were skipped only because the examinee did not know the answer. There were very few of these, and, in fact, the technical manual reports that the main number of skipped items per pupil is less than half an item. The manual provides a table that indicates the number of items not reached at the end of the test. The mean number of items not reached on all tests for all grades is less than 2.

Critique

In terms of the Basic Skills Assessment Program itself, reasonable validity and reliabilities for the total test are acceptable. The reliability for subtests is also reasonable. The idea of the clusters, however, is not well presented. How they were identified and how they are intended to be used is unclear.

The major concern that these reviewers have regarding this test is that no one is using it. We feel that there may be two reasons for this. First, if the tests were buttressed with objectives to which items could be tied, convenience of using the tests would be enhanced. By having the objectives from which the items were developed available for school system review, local districts could determine whether the tests are appropriate for their minimal competency program. Second, these reviewers suggest that many school districts may be unaware that these tests exist and that their quality makes them potentially useful for program evaluation as well as for pupil assessment.

References

Educational Testing Service. (1978). *Basic Skills Assessment Program technical manual.* Monterey, CA: CTB/McGraw-Hill.

Jerry B. Hutton, Ph.D.

Professor of Special Education, East Texas State University, Commerce, Texas.

BEHAVIOR EVALUATION SCALE

Stephen B. McCarney, James E. Leigh, and Jane A. Cornbleet. Austin, Texas: PRO-ED.

Introduction

The Behavior Evaluation Scale (BES) is a 52-item behavior rating scale to be completed by school personnel by recording the estimated frequency of specified behaviors of individual students. Each statement of behavior is rated as occurring 1) never or not observed, 2) less than once a month, 3) approximately once a month, 4) approximately once a week, 5) more than once a week, 6) daily at various times, or 7) continuously throughout the day. The items are organized into five subscales, each corresponding to one of the characteristics of emotional disturbance/behavior disorders described by Bower (1959). The authors use Bower's headings for the subscales as follows: 1) an inability to learn that cannot be explained by intellectual, sensory, or health factors; 2) an inability to build or maintain satisfactory interpersonal relationships with peers and teachers; 3) inappropriate types of behavior or feelings under normal circumstances; 4) a general pervasive mood of unhappiness or depression; and 5) a tendency to develop physical symptoms or fears associated with personal or school problems.

The BES was standardized on a sample of 1,018 students from ten states. The behavior of the students, who ranged from kindergarten through twelfth grade, was rated by 311 teachers. Demographic characteristics closely matched the percentages reported in the 1980 census.

The uses of the BES include screening for behavior problems, assessing the behavior for any referred student, assisting in the diagnosis of behavior disorders, developing individual education programs for special education students, documenting progress, and collecting data for research purposes. Raw scores are converted to standard scores for each subscale, and scores from 7 to 13 indicate behavior similar to the majority of the students included in the normative sample. A standard score of less than 6 indicates behaviors negative enough to cause concern; if a score is less than 4, the behaviors are considered extreme. The total score is expressed as a behavior quotient, with a mean of 100 and a standard deviation of 15. Behavior quotients less than 85 indicate negative behavior, and less than 70 suggests extreme "statistical deviance."

The work on the BES started in 1981 with original items generated by teachers of behaviorally disordered students in Missouri where the first author, Stephen B. McCarney, is a professor at the University of Missouri, Columbia. The final list of items underwent three reviews by different groups of teachers and related professionals before being completed and refined. The 52 items were then ranked according to their perceived severity and assigned weights of 1, 2, or 3 (e.g., 3 = top 20% of severity; 1 = bottom 20% of severity). The authors assigned each item to one of the five subscales according to the face value of the item. The items are distributed as follows: Learning Problems, seven items; Interpersonal Difficulties, ten items; Inappropriate Behaviors, 19 items; Unhappiness/Depression, seven items; and Physical Symptoms/Fears, nine items.

The BES consists of a student record form, a data collection form, and a manual (McCarney, Leigh, & Cornbleet, 1983). The student record form is completed by the student's teacher and a data summary sheet and profile are included on the six-page fold-out form. The student record form can be completed in ten to 20 minutes. The data collection form lists the 52 items and provides space for the teacher to record daily observations of each behavior, a feature that makes it possible to use continuous recording procedures if desired.

Practical Applications/Uses

The BES may be used in screening students referred as behavior problems and in assisting in the diagnosis of behavior disorders. Teacher observations are recognized as valuable in assessing problems in the classroom, and the BES organizes the observations according to the Bower characteristics of emotional disturbance. Because these characteristics are incorporated into the P.L. 94-142 regulations defining emotional disturbance, students in public schools and other educational facilities may be eligible for special education services if emotional disturbance is determined. As cautioned by the authors, no single test or formula exists to determine emotional disturbance. However, the BES can provide information to assist the professionals charged with the task of differential diagnosis.

Though not designed specifically for multiple observations, the BES could be completed by all teachers who have continued contact with the target student. These multiple observations could be compared in order to identify classrooms where the most deviant problems are being perceived. This information may assist in determining where direct observations are likely to be most helpful in obtaining more information, as well as settings where intervention is most likely needed.

Other uses include pre- and post-testing for students entering and exiting specialized programs. Additionally, teachers can select items that are scored as frequently occurring and incorporate the most critical behaviors into objectives in the Individual Education Plan (IEP). Thus, teachers, assessment personnel, and researchers may find the BES useful for a variety of purposes.

Technical Aspects

The technical aspects of the BES are presented in the manual and in an ERIC Education Document (McCarney, 1984). Due to the recency of the BES publication, no other research studies were located in the literature. Item selection procedures and analysis of items are satisfactory, with considerable attention given to field testing. The characteristics of the normative sample closely approximate national demographics.

Internal consistency and test-retest reliability are excellent. The authors report coefficient alphas for each of the subscales ranging from .76 on Unhappiness/Depression to .93 on Learning Problems. The coefficient alpha for the total scale was .96. Generally, coefficient alphas of approximately .80 are considered satisfactory. The test-retest reliability coefficients for the total and each of the five subscales were all over .97, indicating considerable consistency in ratings when ratings are made by the same teachers with a test-retest interval of ten days. The authors acknowledge the need for additional studies in test-retest reliability using observations earlier in the school year. The study reported in the manual involved 15 regular classroom teachers who rated the behavior of 57 students during the last part of the school year. Additional test-retest studies should vary the length of time between ratings.

A shortcoming of the BES is the oversight regarding interrater reliability. Data are not presently available regarding the reliability of ratings when different raters are rating the individual student in the same setting or when different raters are rating in different settings. Because multiple ratings can be very informative, it is important to consider interrater reliability.

Information regarding the content, criterion-related, and construct validity is reported in the manual. With regard to content validity, the BES is certainly adequate. As previously mentioned, considerable attention was given to item selection and item analysis. The items are stated in descriptive rather than inferential terms. The items represent behaviors considered by various types of teachers and assessment personnel as crucial in determining if behavior disorders exist. The response scaling may be a bit too differentiated, however, with seven response choices per item. As noted by Edelbrock (1983), differentiated response formats may appear more precise, but it is difficult to make fine distinctions in frequencies of behavior, particularly when informants are not trained specifically to make these types of discriminations.

Criterion-related validity was determined by correlating the BES total and subscale scores with the Teacher Rating Scale of the Behavior Rating Profile (BRP; Brown & Hammill, 1978; see this volume for a review). The coefficients were significant for all subscales except for Unhappiness/Depression. The *r* for the BES total score and the BRP was .64, significant at the .001 level. The authors note that the low correlation between Unhappiness/Depression and BRP was expected because the BRP Teacher Rating Scale contains few, if any, items that appear to be directly related to depression. The BES would be strengthened by additional studies that use multiple criteria.

The argument for construct validity is made by examining diagnostic validity, subscale interrelationships, and item validity. The BES scores for students with behavior disorders are significantly different from those completed on students randomly selected from the standardization sample. The 49 students with behavior disorders had a mean behavior quotient of 68, and the mean behavior quotient for the regular students was 98. The subscale interrelationships for 943 students were significant, with subscale intercorrelations ranging from .50 for Learning Problems and Physical Symptoms/Fears to .85 for Interpersonal Difficulties and Inappropriate Behavior. The authors consider the magnitude of the subscale correlations to support the contention that the subscales all measure the general construct of "behavior" and that the moderate coefficients, because they are all below .90, suggest that the subscales are not measuring essentially identical domains.

The BES is based on a rational description of emotional handicaps as reported by Bower (1959) and as adopted in P.L. 94-142. Because few behavior rating scales begin with the P.L. 94-142 definition of emotional disturbance, the BES is of considerable interest to assessment personnel and researchers. However, the items were assigned to the subscales based on their apparent membership and not by applying systematic statistical procedures, such as factor analysis. Thus, the construct validity of the BES may be suspect.

Critique

The BES is a new addition to the behavior rating scales available to assessment personnel who are concerned about the evaluation of students referred because of behavior problems. It is unique because it is based on the criteria used in P.L. 94-142 to define emotional disturbance. It is easy for teachers to use, although it may be difficult for them to make the fine discriminations necessary for determining the frequency of a behavior occurring in the classroom setting. The BES behavior quotient is helpful in comparing the total behavior rating with the standardization sample, and statistical deviance is easy to understand.

The items were substantially field tested and pertain directly to the behavior of the child or student rather than inferences about the cause of the behavior. The items are neither too global nor too specific to be useful. Another strength is that the BES was tailored specifically for teachers as the informants.

Reviewers of the BES vary regarding their endorsements. Konopasek (1983, p. 281) notes that the BES "appears to be a valuable tool to assist school personnel in making diagnostic, placement, and programming decisions for behaviorally disordered/emotionally disturbed children and adolescents." Strengths indicated by Konopasek (1983) include the basis of the BES, the most commonly used definition of emotional disturbance, and the potential benefit of the BES data collection form for continuous observations. Also noted is the measurability of the items of the BES.

Kavale (1984) reports that the BES appears adequate in many respects. However, Kavale notes that although the BES represents an attempt to furnish a scale providing educationally relevant information about student behavior, it should be used with caution primarily due to two serious deficiencies. More study of the BES is recommended with regard to interrater reliability and on the construct validity related to the structure of the BES.

This reviewer considers the Kavale (1984) criticisms of the BES to be important cautions for practitioners. When additional research answers the criticisms, the BES may indeed prove to be one of the most valuable instruments available for assessing behavior disorders in school children and adolescents.

References

Bower, E. (1959). The emotionally handicapped child and the school. *Exceptional Children, 26*, 6-11.

Brown, L. L., & Hammill, D. D. (1978). *Behavior Rating Profile.* Austin, TX: PRO-ED.

Edelbrock, C. (1983). Problems and issues in using rating scales to assess child personality and psychopathology. *School Psychology Review, 12,* 293-299.

Kavale, K. A. (1984). The Behavior Evaluation Scale. *Education and Training of the Mentally Retarded, 18,* 326-328.

Konopasek, D. E. (1983). Behavior Evaluation Scale. *Behavioral Disorders, 8,* 280-281.

McCarney, S. B. (1984). *The Behavior Evaluation Scale.* Columbia: University of Missouri. (ERIC Document Reproduction Service No. ED 244 460)

McCarney, S. B., Leigh, J. E., & Cornbleet, J. A. (1983). *The Behavior Evaluation Scale.* Columbia, MO: Educational Services.

Sam F. Broughton, Ph.D.
Director of Psychological Services, South Carolina Department of Mental Retardation, Pee Dee Region, Florence, South Carolina.

BEHAVIOR RATING PROFILE

Linda L. Brown and Donald D. Hammill. Austin, Texas: PRO-ED.

Introduction

The Behavior Rating Profile (BRP) is an ecological-behavioral assessment device consisting of six independent components. It assesses children's behavior in two settings (home and school) from the perspectives of four classes of informants (teachers, parents, target child, and peers). Five of the components are behavior rating scales: the Student Rating Scales (Home, School, and Peer), the Teacher Rating Scale, and the Parent Rating Scale. The sixth component, the Sociogram, solicits peer perceptions and attitudes toward the child being assessed. Because each of the six components represents an independent measure, each one may be used individually or in combination with any one or more of the other components. The specific part or parts of the BRP employed in a given evaluation is determined by the examiner on the basis of the nature of the referral problem, the setting or settings in which the problem behaviors occur, the perspective(s) sought, and the nature of data required to best answer assessment questions and plan additional assessment procedures or potential interventions.

The BRP was developed by Linda L. Brown and Donald D. Hammill in order to operationalize within a single battery of scales an ecological assessment philosophy most clearly espoused by Wallace and Larsen (1978) and to overcome weaknesses observed in existing child behavior rating scales and checklists. Although teacher checklists are available in what Carlson and Lahey (1983) refer to as "a confusing array," and parent rating scales are available to some degree, few self-rating scales exist for children. Furthermore, none of the available instruments was designed to examine behavior across the multiple settings in which children must function (Brown & Hammill, 1983). Additionally, Brown and Hammill (1983) assert that few rating scales meet the basic standards required of sound assessment devices, including adequate reliability, evidence of validity, and nationally representative norms.

The BRP was first published in 1978 by PRO-ED. At that time it consisted of the same six components currently available and was intended for use with children in

This reviewer would like to acknowledge the help of David V. Vandergriff and John Hester in conducting the literature search. The help of Susan Shapero in assisting with determination of the readability levels of the scales is appreciated as well. The Fry procedure was employed to determine readability levels with 100% agreement obtained between two raters for each scale. Specific items are cited with permission of the publisher.

Grades 1 through 7. The set of scales was based on a normative sample of 1,326 students, 645 teachers, and 847 parents (Brown & Hammill, 1978; Helton, Workman, & Matuszek, 1982). By 1981 the norms had been extended, and the current edition of the scales was published in 1983. No changes were made in the items or procedures. The primary purpose of the new edition was to increase the age/grade range for which the scales would be applicable and increase the size of the normative sample. The current edition of the BRP is standardized for students aged six through 18 years and Grades 1-12. A large unselected normative sample consisting of 1,966 students, 955 teachers, and 1,232 parents from 15 states was employed in the restandardization of the scales. Adequate description of the normative sample is provided in the 1983 manual to determine whether the scales are applicable for a given case.

In addition to the 1983 edition of the BRP for English-speaking students, parents, and teachers, a Spanish version is available, the *Pefil de Evaluación del Comportamiento* (PEC; Brown & Hammill, 1982). The PEC was standardized on 1,207 students, 253 teachers, and 83 parents from Mexico. Examiners may administer the PEC only as a translation and apply the United States norms or employ the Mexican norms, depending on the nature of the case.

The examiner's manual, included in the BRP kit, discusses the rationale for the scales, describes the format of the scales, outlines the construction and statistical characteristics of the scales, gives instructions for administration and scoring/interpretation, and discusses ethical considerations for the use of the scales. References and norms tables are also included in the manual.

The BRP kit contains the following four sets of forms:

Teacher Rating Scale: This scale consists of 30 items describing inappropriate classroom behaviors. Each item is rated by the teacher on a four-point descriptive scale, each of which is provided with a numerical weighting: "Very Much Like the Student" = zero, "Like the Student" = one, "Not Much Like the Student" = two, and "Not At All Like the Student" = three. The outcome of this weighting system is that children rated as exhibiting the listed *inappropriate* behaviors receive low scores, whereas students described as "not like" the listed behavior receive high scores. Users familiar with other child behavior checklists and rating scales should note that *high* scores on the BRP indicate the *absence* of maladaptive behavior. This scale is provided on a single sheet. The front of the sheet provides space for student and rater identifying information; scores from other relevant tests; comments and observations; and a conversion table of raw scores, standard scores, and percentile ranks. The reverse side of the sheet contains instructions for completing the rating scale, the 30 actual items with spaces for ratings, and space at the bottom for summing ratings and applying the appropriate weights.

Parent Rating Scale: This scale, similar in form to the Teacher Rating Scale, is contained on a single sheet, with space for parent and child identification, comments, and administration instructions on the front. The reverse side contains the 30 items to be rated according to the same four descriptive ratings as the Teacher Rating Scale. Space is provided at the bottom of the page for summing and weighting items. Again, high scores on this scale indicate the absence of the listed maladaptive behaviors. A score conversion table is not provided, so the examiner must refer to the manual to obtain standard scores and percentile ranks.

Student Rating Scales: These scales are contained within a four-page booklet. The cover page contains space for identifying information and instructions to aid the child in completing the scales. The second and third pages contain the actual items to be scored. The 60 items presented actually represent three scales: Home, School, and Peer, each of which is composed of 20 items. The items for each of three scales are randomly intermixed (but identified for the examiner) among the 60 total items and are scored on a two-point, true-false scale, rather than the four-point scale employed with the Parent and Teacher Scales. The raw score for each scale is the sum of the items scored as false, indicating that the listed maladaptive behaviors do not describe the child. Therefore, as with the Parent and Teacher Scales, high scores indicate the absence of maladaptive behaviors. The fourth page provides space for recording the raw score for each of the three scales and a conversion table for obtaining standard scores and percentiles.

The Sociogram is not provided as a preconstructed form; forms for it are constructed by the examiner from a set of eight pairs of questions listed in the manual. The questions are designed to solicit peer perceptions of the target child in the areas of friendship, academic ability, leadership skills, and athletic competence. The questions are constructed to be administered to the target child's entire class as a peer-nominating procedure in which the first question of each pair asks for the names of children regarded positively in regard to the attribute being sampled, and the second question requests the names of students valued negatively on the same attribute. The examiner decides which one or more pairs of questions should be employed, types each question on a single sheet with room for three names to be written underneath, and duplicates the question sheet to be given to each member of the class. Instructions to be read to the students are provided in the manual. The raw score is the child's rank in the class based on the number of times the child was nominated in response to positive questions (acceptances), minus the number of times the child was nominated in response to negative questions (rejections). The child's rank can then be converted to a standard score or percentile using a conversion table provided in the manual. In keeping with the scoring system for the checklists, the higher the child is ranked in the class, the more positively that child is valued by peers.

The final form provided in the BRP kit is the Behavior Rating Profile Sheet, a summary form for all scores obtained from the rating scales and sociogram. Space is provided on the front of the form for identifying information; evaluation date; birth date; the child's age; and raw scores, standard scores, and percentiles for each of the instruments employed. Also included on the front of the form is a profile for graphing the standard scores for the three Student Rating Scales, the Teacher Rating Scale for up to three different teachers, the Parent Rating Scale for both mother and father (or other in special cases), and three questions from the Sociogram. The reverse side of the profile sheet provides spaces for answering questions regarding how and why the student was referred, how and to whom instruments were administered, and which questions were employed on the sociogram. On completion of administration and scoring, the entire package of instruments can be stapled together with the profile sheet as a cover page.

Practical Applications/Uses

The most appropriate use of the BRP is for screening to identify children who may be behaviorally deviant (behavior disordered, emotionally disturbed, socially maladjusted or immature, or possibly learning disabled). It may also be used to identify the settings in which the child is viewed as deviant or in whose perception the child is disordered. It serves well as an initial assessment to determine whether a given child merits further study, to identify the areas to which additional assessment should be directed, and to generate hypotheses and questions to guide the selection of appropriate techniques and procedures for more in-depth analysis when indicated.

One potential use of the BRP, which is not mentioned in the manual and for which there is as yet no research support, is as a repeated measure during intervention programs. Because the BRP has been shown to discriminate normal children from children who are learning disabled, public-school emotionally disturbed, and institutionalized emotionally disturbed (Brown & Hammill, 1983), it is reasonable to assume that scores for a given child would increase as intervention resulted in approximations to more normal behavior. Additionally, because the BRP is a measure of informant perceptions of a child, interventions designed to modify a given individual's attitudes toward the child should produce improved ratings of the child by the target individual. It makes good behavioral sense from an intervention standpoint to employ the same measures during and after intervention as before. It should be emphasized, however, that the BRP has not been demonstrated to be reactive to treatment effects, and multiple measures should be employed in treatment evaluation.

The BRP should *not* be employed alone in making placement decisions. Neither should it be used for differential diagnosis. The lack of factor-analytic data in the manual precludes even preliminary classification of the target child's maladaptive behaviors by diagnostic or behavioral categories. Limited research (Slate, 1983) also indicates that the BRP should not be employed as an adaptive behavior measure to differentiate mentally retarded students from nonretarded students. Examiners should adhere to the uses recommended in the manual, screening of children exhibiting behavioral difficulties.

Ease of administration and scoring and the multiple settings to which the BRP applies make it a useful screening device for virtually any professional working in the education or mental-health fields with school-aged children. Each scale is brief and can be administered quickly, making the BRP economical of professional time and generally avoiding fatigue effects in respondents. The Student Scales can be administered in 15 to 30 minutes; the Teacher Rating Scale in ten to 15 minutes; the Parent Rating Scale in 15 to 20 minutes; and the Sociogram in five to ten minutes, not including time to prepare the sociogram form (Brown & Hammill, 1983). The BRP may be employed by teachers, psychologists, counselors, and educational diagnosticians who have familiarized themselves with the administration and scoring procedures outlined in the manual and have access to respondents who are thoroughly familiar with the referred child.

As noted earlier, each of the BRP components may be employed singly or in any combination. Brown and Hammill (1983) suggest a number of useful combinations:

1) the School Form of the Student Rating Scale and the Teacher Rating Scale when the school is the focus of assessment; 2) the Home Form of the Student Rating Scale and the Parent Rating Scale for behavior problems at home, with the Home Form administered to siblings and the Parent Rating Scale to both parents for each child in the family when a more complete assessment is desired; and 3) the Peer Form of the Student Rating Scales and the Sociogram for peer or socialization problems. Of course, for a comprehensive screening, the entire BRP may be administered.

Although the Sociogram is usually group administered, both it and the Student Rating Scales are suitable for either group or individual administration as long as care is taken to insure the confidentiality of responses in the group setting. The Parent and Teacher Rating Scales should be administered individually. When responses are obtained from more than one teacher or parent, the scales should be completed independently without respondents having knowledge of how others have responded. On all of the instruments, items may be read by the respondent or to the respondent by the examiner in an interview format, though oral administration of the Student Rating Scales is discouraged in the group setting. Reading levels required of respondents for self-administration are approximately eighth-grade level for the Parent Rating Scale, seventh-grade level for the Teacher Rating Scale, and second- to third-grade level for the Student Rating Scales. The Sociogram should not be administered to classes with fewer than 20 students or in special education classes (which are likely to be small) because the norms require 20 or more students in order to convert ranks to standard scores and percentiles.

Scoring the BRP, like administration, requires no special training and can be accomplished easily by following the procedures outlined in the manual. The format of the rating scales facilitates scoring, and the instructions in the manual are clear and straightforward. Scoring the Parent and Teacher Rating Scales requires the examiner to count or sum the number of items marked in each rating category (e.g., "Very Much Like . . ."), multiply each sum by the appropriate weight, and add the weight scores to obtain a total point score. The total point score is then located in the appropriate norms table for conversion to a standard score (mean of 10, standard deviation of 3) or percentile rank. Raw scores for each of the Student Rating Scales consist simply of the number of items in each scale rated as false (obtained by counting). Conversion of raw scores to standard scores and percentiles proceeds as for the Parent and Teacher Scales. The Sociogram presents the most complex scoring procedure, requiring the examiner to score each pair of questions separately by counting the number of times each child in the class was nominated by class members to the positive question of each set (acceptances) and the number of times each child was nominated for the negative question (rejections). The number of rejections is subtracted from the number of acceptances for each child on each question to yield a difference score. The difference scores for each child in the class are then ranked. The rank of the target child is then converted to a standard score or percentile using the appropriate conversion table.

Scoring of the Teacher and Student Rating Scales is facilitated by inclusion of the conversion tables on the rating forms and can be accomplished within two to four minutes. The Parent Rating Scale requires reference to the manual for scoring because the conversion table is not provided on the form but is easily scored in three to five minutes. Scoring of the sociogram can take upwards from 20 minutes.

depending on the number of question pairs presented and the size of the class. To this reviewer's knowledge, computer administration or scoring is not available for the BRP, but it is not really needed with the brief administration and scoring times required.

Interpretation of the BRP is facilitated by a standard score system for all six components familiar to most individuals employing educational or psychological tests (mean equals 10, standard deviation equals 3). As noted earlier, the standard scores from each BRP component can be plotted on the Behavior Rating Profile Sheet. The portion of the profile from one standard deviation above to one standard deviation below the mean (i.e., from 13 to 7) is unshaded. Scores falling within this range are considered by Brown and Hammill (1983) to be normal, whereas scores falling above or below this range (shaded areas) are considered to be "statistically deviant." The authors caution users to employ confidence bands, and they provide a table containing standard errors of measurement in the section on reliability in the manual.

Although interpretation of the BRP is based on norms and a standard score system, interpretation will be enhanced by clinical experience, insight, and problem-solving ability. The authors provide a number of helpful suggestions in the manual in the form of questions to be answered by the examiner. These include questions (with follow-up suggestions) such as "Does the Student score low (or high) only on measures relating to school, peers, or home?" and "Is there a discrepancy among raters?" This section of the manual deserves close reading by users. Additionally, interpretation of the BRP should be undertaken only within the context of the chapter in the manual on ethical considerations, which provides several important cautions in the use and interpretation of the instrument. In general, a basic interpretation of results may be undertaken by any of the disciplines (noted earlier) qualified to administer and score the BRP, provided the above cautions are observed. Diagnostic or intervention decisions should be made only with reference to considerable additional assessment information by qualified and experienced diagnosticians. The ease of administration, scoring, and basic interpretation of the BRP could lure the unqualified into unjustified decisions or interventions.

Technical Aspects

Two item selection procedures were employed in developing the BRP: 1) Existing checklists and rating scales were reviewed (especially the Behavior Problem Checklist, Devereux Scales, and Walker Problem Behavior Identification Checklist) and 2) parents of emotionally disturbed and learning disabled children and teachers of emotionally disturbed children were surveyed concerning characteristic behaviors. From these procedures 306 items were developed. These items were arranged into an experimental Parent Scale (77 items), Teacher Scale (81 items), and a Student Scale (140 items). Development of questions for the Sociogram is not described.

Brown and Hammill (1983) regarded each of the experimental rating scales to be too lengthy for practical use, and pilot testing indicated certain items to be duplicative, unclear, or poor discriminators. To reduce the number of items in each scale while keeping the best items, an item validity/internal consistency procedure employing the point biserial correlation method was used. Guilford's (1956) criterion for acceptable item validity (point biserial correlations between .30 and .80) was employed to insure that each item contributed significantly, yet relatively uniquely to the total score of each rating scale. After the final items for each scale had been selected, a sample of 150 protocols for each of the rating scales was drawn from the standardization group (whether this was 1978 or 1983 was not specified) and examined by the Guilford procedure. Correlations ranged from .43 to .83. Thus, the scales appear to possess items that, in fact, sample a single broad dimension of "behavioral deviance."

Actual items contained in the BRP are similar to other rating scales and range from behaviorally specific to quite subjective. Representative items from the Teacher Rating Scale include "Does not do homework assignments" and "Is self-centered." The Parent Rating Scale is composed of items such as "Complains about doing assigned chores" and "Is self-centered, egocentric." The three scales of the Student Rating Scales are constructed from such items as "I often break rules set by my parents" (Home), "I can't seem to stay in my desk at school" (School), and "Other kids are always picking on me" (Peer).

Demographic characteristics of the normative sample are provided briefly and primarily in tabular form in the manual. Relevant characteristics for participant students, parents, and teachers are presented. Data are presented as the percentage of the sample rather than number falling into each category, and no effort is made to relate sample characteristics to census data in any formal fashion. Although sufficient data are provided to allow the examiner to determine whether the BRP is appropriate in a given case, and the size of the sample is notably large for a set of rating scales, a nationally representative sample probably was not obtained. No students known to be receiving special education services were included in the norm group, though validation studies employed exceptional children. Thus, deviant scores are likely to represent actual as well as statistical deviance from normal, though the interpretive cautions mentioned earlier should be remembered.

The BRP is adequately reliable for its intended purposes. Brown and Hammill (1983) report internal consistency data (based on coefficient alpha) derived from protocols sampled from five grade levels in the standardization group (1978 or 1983 not specified). The Parent Rating Scale achieved coefficients from .82 to .91; the Teacher Rating Scale coefficients ranged from .87 to .98; and the Student Rating Scales produced the following ranges: .77 to .85 for Home, .74 to .87 for School, and .78 to .85 for Peer. Given the item-analysis procedure, fairly high internal consistency would be expected for the scales. No reliability data are reported in the manual for the Sociogram.

Test-retest reliability for normal children reported by Brown and Hammill (1983) is based on one small study of 36 normal high school students with a two-week retest interval. Although coefficients indicate adequate reliability for the high-school group (Parent Rating Scale = .94; Teacher Rating Scale = .91; and Student Rating Scales = .78 for Home, .83 for School, and .86 for Peer), the temporal consistency of the scales for elementary-aged students is not reported, and stability for any group over intervals greater than two weeks is not known.

Internal consistency and test-retest reliability are also adequate for disordered groups, with coefficients across the five scales ranging from .76 to .95 for institutionalized emotionally disturbed (ED) children, .78 to .97 for public-school elementary ED children, .76 to .92 for public-school secondary ED children, and .76 to .97 for public-school elementary learning-disabled children (Brown, Hammill, & Sherbenou, 1981).

Brown and Hammill (1983) discuss three types of validity for the scales: content, criterion-related, and construct. To demonstrate content validity they refer the reader to the item-selection and analysis procedures discussed earlier. Criterion-related validity was demonstrated by presenting correlations between the five BRP rating scales and the Walker Problem Behavior Identification Checklist, the Quay-Peterson Behavior Problem Checklist, and the Vineland Social Maturity Scale for normal and behaviorally disordered groups. Seventy-two correlations were produced, with 60 being significant at the .05 level or better. Four additional coefficients attained significance after correction for attenuation. The bulk of the nonsignificant correlations was associated with the Walker Problem Identification Checklist (six). Forty-six of the coefficients exceeded a magnitude of .70, and 62 exceeded Brown and Hammill's criterion for adequate validity (.35). It appears from these data that the BRP possesses sufficient relationship to other similar instruments to consider it valid. Because the Walker Checklist also provides cutoff scores for identifying potentially deviant children (Walker, 1983), a hit/miss comparison between the Walker and BRP would have been interesting but was not provided. Additionally, the substantial correlations obtained by Brown and Hammill (1983) between the BRP and Vineland are interesting in light of other research (Slate, 1983), which indicates that the BRP should not be employed as an adaptive behavior scale.

Construct validity was examined in three ways. First, because all of the scales were designed to measure the same construct (child behavior), the intercorrelations among the various BRP components were examined for normal, institutionalized ED, public-school ED, and public-school LD children. The 40 correlations produced ranged from .49 to .96 and were all significant beyond the .01 level. Secondly, a subset of these correlations was analyzed: the correlations between the ecologically paired components of the BRP (e.g., Student Rating Scales, School and the Teacher Rating Scale). Ten of the 11 resulting correlations exceeded the .35 criterion selected by the authors. Finally, scale-score differences between normal and disordered groups of children were studied. Although the appropriateness of Brown and Hammill's choice of the *t*-test to analyze the data could be questioned, results indicate that 1) normal children were rated as exhibiting fewer behavior problems than disordered children across all BRP components; 2) institutionalized children were rated as showing more behavior problems than public-school behavior problem children across all components; and 3) children rated themselves highest, parents rated their children lowest, and teachers produced intermediate ratings. The final result was replicated independently by Reisburg, Fudell, and Hudson (1982), with the additional finding that regular class teachers tended to rate students more positively than special class teachers. These results deserve to be remembered when BRP data are included in diagnostic assessments. On the whole, however, the BRP has been shown to discriminate adequately between normals and the diagnostic groups that it is intended to identify.

One final form of construct validity is *not* reported. Because Brown and Hammill

(1983) indicate that the contruct being validated is "behavior," one wonders why BRP scores have not been related to direct behavioral observation data in the home, school, and peer settings. Validity data for the Sociogram are not discussed except for the presentation of one correlation between the Sociogram and the Student Rating Scales: Peer derived from a group of 122 parochial school children.

Critique

The BRP is unique among informant-based measures of deviant child behavior in its use of multiple respondents across multiple ecologies. In fact, three views of the child's behavior are obtained for each setting (i.e., parent-child, teacher-child, peer-child). The normative sample, though not nationally representative, is large, diverse, and better than those available for the majority of child-rating scales and checklists. Reliability and validity data provided in the manual indicate that these characteristics are adequate for general use of the scales for their intended purposes (screening/identification of children with behavioral difficulties). The manual is written clearly and provides sufficient information to allow appropriate and ethical use by the intended professionals. Administration, scoring, and interpretation instructions are straightforward. The scales are economical of professional time, yet yield a wealth of information for the time invested. The scales prompt users to investigate setting variables of potential importance to deviant child behavior that might otherwise go unconsidered. The BRP deserves to be a part of most child psychological or educational diagnostician's assessment repertoire. It is, however, only a single assessment battery; its primary purpose is screening; it is an indirect measure of behavior and cannot substitute for a comprehensive assessment, including direct observation of behavior, antecedents, and consequences, or other diagnostic procedures. The BRP has not been researched widely by investigators other than the authors, though its assessment qualities occasionally have been investigated by others (Reisberg et al., 1982; Slate, 1983), and it has been used as a dependent or criterion variable in research designed to answer other questions (Nunn, Parish, & Worthing, 1983a, 1983b). The Sociogram, in particular, can be faulted for a lack of even basic reliability and validity research, even by the authors (who have concentrated on the rating scales).

With over 200 rating scales or checklists from which to choose, any set of rating scales should be carefully evaluated by the best currently available standards (Edelbrock, 1983; Evans & Nelson, 1977; McMahon, 1984; Sodac, Nichols, & Gallagher, 1985; Spivack & Swift, 1973; Wells, 1981). Using these standards, the BRP has much to recommend it: reliability, validity, utility, and use in multiple settings. However, the BRP also falls short in a number of ways.

The items on a good behavioral rating scale should represent overt child behaviors that require little or no inference on the part of raters. The BRP is constructed from a considerable number of high inference items. Some, in fact, relate more to the attitudes or actions of others than to the behavior of the child being assessed (e.g., "Is sent to the principal for discipline" and "Is kept after school" from the Teacher Rating Scale or "Has no regular, special activities with parents" from the Parent Rating Scale).

Rating scales should provide prescriptive utility, that is, they should provide information useful in planning interventions. Although the BRP can be helpful in identifying the settings in which intervention may be necessary, the items are too subjective and limited to suggest initial target behaviors without resorting to additional assessment procedures.

Factor-analytic data for the BRP are unavailable. Although this can be justified on the grounds that the BRP is a screening instrument and should not be used for differential diagnosis, initial indications of the *type* of behavior problem exhibited by a child could facilitate selection of subsequent, narrower-band assessment procedures. The Parent and Teacher Scales might be too short to yield robust factor structures, but the BRP as a whole could be fruitful ground for factor-analytic research. Furthermore, the Student Rating Scales are logically divided into the Home, School, and Peer Scales. Factor-analytic data could serve to validate (or refute) this logical classification system. The number of items is sufficient to accomplish this.

The Sociogram is designed to assess peer reactions to a child in regard to specified areas such as friendship, leadership, or academic ability. Questions are not labeled according to which area they are assumed to assess. Though most examiners will be able to determine the area purportedly assessed by simply reading each pair of questions, labels for the questions and validation of them would be most helpful.

Finally, the response format of rating scales should allow respondents multiple responses along a dimension rather than forcing them into arbitrary yes/no (true-false) decisions. The Parent and Teacher Scales accomplish this, whereas the Student Rating Scales do not. The dimension for rating should be objectively anchored, employing variables such as *frequency* of behavior rather than subjective dimensions such as *degree* of likeness. Here the BRP falls short.

Despite its shortcomings, the BRP is a very versatile and usable instrument. Users who employ it appropriately and within the proper contexts will be rewarded with useful assessment information. No rating scale can serve all assessment purposes. The BRP can be used to obtain information not available through most other checklists or rating scales.

References

Brown, L. L., & Hammill, D. D. (1978). *Behavior Rating Profile: An ecological approach.* Austin, TX: PRO-ED.

Brown, L. L., & Hammill, D. D. (1982). *Perfil de Evaluación del Comportamiento.* Austin, TX: PRO-ED.

Brown, L. L., & Hammill, D. D. (1983). *Behavior Rating Profile: An ecological approach.* Austin, TX: PRO-ED.

Brown, L. L., Hammill, D. D., & Sherbenou, R. S. (1981). The reliability of four measures of children's behavior with deviant populations. *Behavior Disorders, 6,* 180-182.

Carlson, C. L., & Lahey, B. B. (1983). Factor structure of teacher rating scales for children. *School Psychology Review, 12,* 285-292.

Edelbrock, C. (1983). Problems and issues in using rating scales to assess child personality and psychopathology. *School Psychology Review, 12,* 293-299.

Evans, I. M., & Nelson, R. O. (1977). Assessment of child behavior problems. In A. R. Ciminero, K. S. Calhoun, & H. E. Adams (Eds.), *Handbook of behavioral assessment* (pp. 603-681). New York: John Wiley & Sons.

Guilford, J. P. (1956). *Fundamental statistics in psychology and education* (3rd ed.). New York: McGraw-Hill.

Helton, G. B., Workman, E. A., & Matuszek, P. A. (1982). *Psychoeducational assessment: Integrating concepts and techniques.* New York: Grune & Stratton, Inc.

McMahon, R. J. (1984). Behavioral checklists and rating scales. In T. H. Ollendick & M. Hersen (Eds.), *Child behavioral assessment* (pp. 80-105). Elmsford, NY: Pergamon Press, Inc.

Nunn, G. D., Parish, T. S., & Worthing, R. J. (1983a). Concurrent validity of the Personal Attribute Inventory for Children with the State-Trait Anxiety Inventory for Children and the Behavior Rating Profile-Student Scales. *Educational and Psychological Measurement, 43,* 639-643.

Nunn, G. D., Parish, T. S., & Worthing, R. J. (1983b). Perceptions of personal and familial adjustment by children from intact, single-parent, and reconstituted families. *Psychology in the Schools, 20,* 166-174.

Reisberg, L. E., Fudell, I., & Hudson, F. (1982). Comparison of responses to the Behavior Rating Profile for mild to moderately behaviorally disordered subjects. *Psychological Reports, 50,* 136-138.

Slate, N. M. (1983). Nonbiased assessment of adaptive behavior: Comparison of three instruments. *Exceptional Children, 50,* 67-70.

Sodac, D., Nichols, P., & Gallagher, B. (1985). Pupil behavioral data. In F. H. Wood, C. R. Smith, & J. Grimes (Eds.), *The Iowa assessment model in behavioral disorders: A training manual* (pp. 151-219). Des Moines: State Department of Public Instruction.

Spivack, G., & Swift, M. (1973). The classroom behavior of children: A critical review of teacher administered rating scales. *Journal of Special Education, 7,* 55-89.

Walker, H. M. (1983). *Walker Problem Behavior Identification Checklist, Revised.* Los Angeles: Western Psychological Services.

Wallace, G., & Larsen, S. C. (1978). *Educational assessment of learning problems: Testing for teaching.* Boston: Allyn & Bacon, Inc.

Wells, K. C. (1981). Assessment of children in outpatient settings. In M. Hersen & A. S. Bellack (Eds.), *Behavioral assessment* (pp. 484-533). Elmsford, NY: Pergamon Press, Inc.

Maryann Santos de Barona, Ph.D.
Visiting Assistant Professor, Department of Educational Psychology, Texas A&M University, College Station, Texas.

BEHAVIORAL DEVIANCY PROFILE

Betty Ball and Rita Weinberg. Chicago, Illinois: Stoelting Company.

Introduction

The Behavioral Deviancy Profile is designed to determine the degree of deviancy or disturbance of children who are experiencing moderate to severe social and emotional problems. Intended for children ranging in age from preschool through adolescence, the instrument looks at total functioning by including ratings of deviance in four major areas: physical and motor development, cognitive development, speech and language, and social and emotional development. In addition, it purports to provide a means of training and upgrading the observational competencies of professionals by offering an objective method by which assessment, treatment, and intervention plans might be developed.

The test authors are Betty Ball, a private social-work consultant, and Rita Weinberg of the National College of Education. Both Ball and Weinberg have extensive clinical experience working with emotionally disturbed children and have been involved in the direct treatment of disturbed children, as well as in the development and coordination of mental-health services for children and adolescents.

The Behavioral Deviancy Profile was developed to its present copyright status over a ten-year period, during which time it was used in the diagnosis and treatment of emotionally disturbed children in preschool, latency-age, and adolescent day-treatment programs. Based on a statistical analysis and other assessments conducted in collaboration with Indiana University, revisions of the profile were undertaken (B. Ball, personal communication, October 17, 1985). A Glossary was developed during this process and the Behavioral Deviancy Profile was published in July 1981.

The Behavioral Deviancy Profile consists of a nine-page record booklet for rating items in 18 categories that are subsumed under the four major areas. The child is not present when the ratings are determined. Instead, it is recommended that a group of professionals who have close contact with the individual child in a variety of situations (e.g., nurses, teachers, physical therapists, and psychologists) evaluate the relevant sections prior to a general staff meeting where a final rating is determined.

Practical Applications/Uses

The Behavioral Deviancy Profile can be used by a group of professionals from a variety of disciplines who are involved in the planning and treatment of a socially or emotionally disturbed child. The authors report that the instrument is helpful for mental-health staff and educators working with disturbed populations because of its emphasis on an empirically based or observational approach in evaluating the many strengths and weaknesses in the child's total functioning. Additionally, it is viewed as a useful training tool for personnel and as an accountability strategy by which treatment can be effectively planned and monitored. Although the profile has a psychoanalytic flavor by its inclusion of items related to projection, reaction formation, displacement, and sublimation, observational and diagnostic skills are stressed. In addition, professionals are expected to make use of standardized instruments, such as intelligence tests, achievement tests, and medical growth charts, to assist in the determination of deviancy.

Use of the Behavioral Deviancy Profile requires familiarity with the rating scale and the categories to be assessed. A description of the seven-point scale used in rating all items is provided in the manual (Ball & Weinberg, 1981). This scale ranges from minus three to plus three, with the midpoint, zero, indicating no deviance. Ratings other than whole numbers (e.g., tenths) are permitted at the raters' discretion. Items that cannot be rated or are not applicable to a particular child are omitted. The authors recommend that a consensual approach be used in determining final ratings so that staff members can deal with disagreements in the evaluation of particular items. If the procedure of having all of the staff rate their sections prior to a general staff meeting is followed, final ratings and completion of the profile requires approximately one and a half to two hours. The manual recommends that one record booklet be used for each child, although this may prove to be difficult if independent raters are to evaluate their sections prior to a meeting.

Although plus items are noted on the rating scale, they are not considered deviant unless they adversely affect functioning. All rated items for a particular category are averaged to obtain a mean score for that category, and this mean score is then plotted on a graph in the record booklet to obtain a visual representation of the total deviance demonstrated by the child. This graph only represents the *degree* of deviancy from the norm; it is not possible to ascertain from examination of the graph if the deviance is in a positive or negative direction.

A glossary defining terminology is provided in the manual to facilitate an understanding of the profile items, although its use is not mandatory and other definitions are acceptable if used consistently. The definitions that are provided, however, lack behavioral detail, and items that involve psychoanalytic concepts are not well operationalized. In addition, it is not unusual to have a term defined merely as "self-explanatory." As a result, use of the profile either as a training tool or by psychologists with little background in psychoanalysis may be limited.

Technical Aspects

Technical information concerning the reliability and validity of the Behavioral Deviancy Profile is not provided in the manual. However, the manual does report that ratings by an undefined group on an unspecified number of individuals yielded a reliability of .90 and above for all items except two, which were not specified. No information is given regarding either the amount of time that the group(s) used the profile prior to participating in the reported rating or the amount of time it would take an average group of raters to become proficient in its use. Furthermore, although a review of the literature conducted by this reviewer did not identify any studies involving either the use of this instrument or its statistical properties, there are indications that recent work has been carried out in this area (e.g., Ball & Weinberg, 1983; Hrdina, 1984; Leeper, 1985).

Critique

There are several problems associated with scoring and interpreting the Behavioral Deviancy Profile. First, because use of the glossary definitions is optional, using alternative definitions may restrict the usefulness of the information gathered from the profile to the rating group because other professionals who use a different set of definitions might interpret the child's profile differently. Thus, the profile of a child transferred to a different therapeutic or educational setting should not be communicated to the receiving professionals without the accompaniment of the precise definitions used in evaluating that child.

Second, many of the categories require both professional expertise and access to other professional materials such as standardized tests and medical-growth charts. For each of the areas in which other materials are accessed, an individual must know what constitutes deviance. For example, nurses must have access to information concerning height, weight, head circumference, and sensory abilities. Additionally, they must know how much of a defect in each of these areas is considered mildly, moderately, or severely deviant. This information must then be translated into an appropriate rating-scale point.

Third, the authors frequently state in the manual that various items should be rated according to quality and age appropriateness. However, no norms or guidelines in these areas are provided and, therefore, it is necessary for raters to make their own determination regarding deviancy. As a result, a group of raters who work primarily with deviant or special populations may not recognize the true range of possible behaviors and, therefore, may tend to rate individuals in a skewed direction.

The instrument's greatest strength appears to lie in the opportunity provided for a multidisciplinary team of professionals to develop an internally consistent approach to the evaluation of a particular child. Its critical flaw, however, appears to be its disregard for psychometric properties normally associated with evaluation instruments. This flaw is most evident in the wide latitude allowed the user in all aspects of the evaluation: raters choose the external instruments to assess deviancy in a variety of areas and may elect to expand the point system to be used in the rating scale. In addition, they determine the quality and age-appropriateness of behavior in the absence of norms and decide how items will be interpreted. Because of these many options allowed the raters, the Behavioral Deviancy Profile, at best, should be considered a structured guide that serves as a reminder of the many aspects to be considered when evaluating a child's deviance, rather than an instrument that will consistently determine the degree of deviancy and allow uniform interpretation of findings.

References

Ball, B., & Weinberg, R. (1981). *Behavioral Deviancy Profile instruction manual.* Chicago: Stoelting Company.

Ball, B., & Weinberg, R. (1983). The Behavioral Deviancy Profile. *School Social Work Journal, 8*(1), 28-34.

Hrdina, C. (1984). *Inter-rater reliability of the Behavioral Deviancy Profile.* Unpublished master's thesis, National College of Education, Evanston, IL.

Leeper, D. (1985). *Reliability of the Behavioral Deviancy Profile.* Unpublished master's thesis, National College of Education, Evanston, IL.

Harvey N. Switzky, Ph.D.
Professor of Learning, Development, and Special Education, Northern Illinois University, DeKalb, Illinois.

BEHAVIOUR ASSESSMENT BATTERY, 2ND EDITION

Chris Kiernan and Malcolm Jones. Windsor, England: NFER-Nelson Publishing Company Ltd.

Introduction

The Behaviour Assessment Battery was designed to assess the cognitive, communicative, and self-help skills of the severely mentally handicapped and the profoundly mentally retarded (Grossman, 1983), including both the relative and absolute profoundly mentally retarded (Haywood, Meyers, & Switzky, 1982; Switzky & Haywood, 1985; Switzky, Haywood, & Rotatori, 1982). The Behaviour Assessment Battery was constructed to develop a set of criterion-referenced test items and an assessment procedure in order to produce a set of curriculum objectives to guide teaching and provide a fuller picture of the individual than is usually provided by developmental tests such as the Cattell Infant Intelligence Scale (Cattell, 1960) and the Bayley Scales of Infant Development (Bayley, 1969).

Kiernan and Jones (1980, 1982) devised the Behaviour Assessment Battery to provide a basis for the macroassessment of the behavioral repertoire of persons with profound mental retardation to achieve the following objectives: 1) to provide a broad coverage of behavior, including self-help skills and cognitive and emotional aspects of behavior, and to develop a comprehensive program of educational intervention; 2) to provide a standardized testing procedure in a flexible framework so as to optimize the motivation of the individual in the testing situation and in the unique testing procedures used; and 3) to provide a testing battery coordinated with existing procedures and macroassessment batteries of developmental and functional behavior by extending their coverage downward to the individual with profound mental retardation.

The Behaviour Assessment Battery was developed by two experimental psychologists, Chris C. Kiernan, Ph.D., and Malcolm Jones, MSc. Since 1969, Kiernan has been one of the leading psychologists in England in the field of mental handicap. Kiernan was a member of the Thomas Coram Research Unit of the University of London Institute of Education and is presently the director of the Hester Adrian Research Center for the Study of Learning Processes in the Mentally Handicapped at the University of Manchester. Jones' master's thesis (1971) was a source for some of the procedures used in the Behaviour Assessment Battery (C. Kiernan, personal communication, August 30, 1985; Kiernan & Jones, 1980, 1982).

The Behaviour Assessment Battery was initially created in response to an expressed need by the English Department of Health and Social Security to develop suitable testing procedures to be used by pediatricians to diagnose children who were likely to be profoundly mentally retarded. An intense interest soon evolved in educating all children no matter how handicapped because of the passage of England's Education (Handicapped Children) Act in 1970, and the focus of the Behaviour Assessment Battery was shifted to provide more of an educational framework and aid in the formation of a curriculum that practitioners could use in teaching profoundly mentally retarded, multiply handicapped students. The first edition of the Behaviour Assessment Battery was published in 1977 after six years of extensive work (1971-1977) with severely and profoundly mentally retarded, multiply handicapped children and youths aged two to 17 years. Revisions were made from 1980 to 1981, a chapter on the interpretation of test results was added, and an extensive revision of the sections on communication was made. A new procedure, the Sign Imitation Test, was devised to investigate the ability of children and adults to imitate hand postures, positions, and movements used in sign languages (Kiernan, Jordan, & Saunders, 1978; Kiernan, 1983). The second edition of the Behaviour Assessment Battery was published in 1982. An Italian version was translated with a more explicit teaching framework than the original Behaviour Assessment Battery.

The Behaviour Assessment Battery contains two general types of items: 1) interview schedule items, which are administered to the nurse, parent, guardian, caregiver, or others who are familiar with the individual, and 2) behavioral items, which consist of observational items, behavioral test items, and behavioral pretraining and testing components.

In regard to the behavioral pretesting and formal testing components, items, and procedures, the Behaviour Assessment Battery is uniquely innovative. It is often found that individuals with severe or profound mental retardation are at first unable to demonstrate the abilities to be examined because of their lack of understanding of test instructions and requirements or because of poor motivation. A pretraining phase of assessment may be necessary to prompt and reward the individual. The purpose of this pretraining phase is to teach individuals to be tested the requirements of the test setting and increase their motivation to "play the game." Then a phase of more structured behavioral testing may be initiated to assess the capabilities of the individual in a more valid manner. Formal pretraining is part of the assessment strategy of many of the subcomponents of the communication content area of the Behaviour Assessment Battery. In addition, Kiernan and Jones recommend that generally, before any assessment is attempted, the child be prompted and rewarded to look at the examiner on request and to sit quietly.

A major shift in emphasis in the Behaviour Assessment Battery from usual developmental assessment procedures lies in the explicit use of adequate incentives for ccorrect responding on all test items throughout testing. The majority of testing procedures assumes that the child will be adequately motivated either by the reward of task completion or by the minimal social reward allowed in the testing situation. Such subtle rewards are aften inadequate for mentally handicapped children who may score well below their actual abilities if standardized testing conditions are maintained. The Behaviour Assessment Battery standardization was conducted with the built-in assumption that adequate incentives are identified either by observation or by interview with parents, nurses, caregivers, or teachers before testing is attempted. These incentives are then used as objects on test items or as rewards for correct performance. It is essential that good incentives are isolated and used appropriately to elicit and reward behavior if the severely handicapped are to be tested fairly.

The Behaviour Assessment Battery is appropriate for all age groups of severely handicapped individuals. Extensive field testing was performed with severely and profoundly mentally retarded, multiply handicapped children and youth aged two to 17 years.

The Behaviour Assessment Battery consists of 13 content areas, which may be evaluated through interview, more formal behavioral testing, or by both interview and behavioral testing. A brief description of the 13 content areas are as follows:

Reinforcement and Experience: Obtains information on potential reinforcers and the reinforcement schedules used by parents, caregivers, and teachers, and on the child's experience and preferred activities in a free setting. Information is obtained by interview.

Visual Inspection: Obtains information regarding visual, sensory, and perceptual functioning, including effective visual fixation, examination of two- and three-dimensional visual displays, visual exploration of the environment, and visual defensive reactions. Includes behavioral test items and behavioral observational items. Necessary equipment includes a small flashlight, ten 2-cm red cubes in box, six 12-cm toys, three squeaky toys, white object, three toy cars, picture book, selection of candies (including small red ones), ten sheets of plain paper, nylon- or felt-tipped pens or crayons, and colored discs.

Visual Tracking: Obtains information regarding tracking of objects with the eyes, eyes and head, visual prediction of movement of test objects, visual prediction of movement in play, and object permanence. Contains behavioral test items. Necessary equipment includes a small flashlight, six 12-cm toys, three squeaky toys, white object, three toy cars, silent pull-along toy, ball (about 5 cm), two opaque screens (20 cm x 30 cm), and a soft pad.

Visuo-Motor Coordination: Obtains information regarding finger play, grasping and reaching for objects in space, gross and fine visual-motor integration. Consists of behavioral test items. Necessary materials include ten 2-cm red cubes in box, six 12-cm toys, three squeaky toys, white object, three toy cars, silent pull-along toy, ball (about 5 cm), and stand (40 cm x 40 cm x 6 cm).

Auditory Responsiveness: Obtains information regarding basic responsiveness to sound, audio-visual integration, responsiveness to the human voice, and sound-related play with a squeaky toy. Both behavioral test items and interviews are used. Necessary materials include six 12-cm toys, three squeaky toys, white object, small hand bell, rattle, and ten wooden cubes (4 cm x 5 cm).

Postural Control: Obtains information regarding head control, sitting, and standing performance by interviewing parents, teachers, and caregivers.

Exploratory Play: Obtains information regarding oral investigation of objects, visual examination of objects, visual-motor exploration of objects, rolling and pulling exploratory investigation of objects, auditory-visual exploration of objects, and the dropping-throwing schemata. Consists of behavioral test items. Necessary equipment includes six 12-cm toys, three squeaky toys, white object, three toy cars, silent pull-along toy, ball (about 5 cm), chime bars, small hand bell, rattle, large plastic nut and bolt, six dowels (1 cm x 5 cm) in pegboard, tambourine, ten wooden cubes (4 cm x 5 cm), tin foil, newspaper, two sandpaper boards (12 cm x 12 cm), and a ring or toy attached to a 60-cm string.

Constructive Play: Obtains information on constructive play behavior: playing with a ball, drawing with a crayon, building with cubes. Consists of behavioral test items. Necessary equipment includes ten sheets of plain paper, nylon- or felt-tipped pens or crayons, ball (about 5 cm), chime bars, screw barrels, eye glass case, ten wooden cubes (4 cm x 5 cm), wastepaper basket, stacking toy with blind ring, and three small boxes (about 10 cm x 10 cm) with easily opened lids.

Search Strategies: Obtains information regarding Piagetian object permanence concepts and their elaboration in search strategies: Following, Prediction of Movement, Simple and Complex Search, and Search in Play. Consists of behavioral test items. Necessary equipment includes six 12-cm toys, three squeaky toys, white object, three toy cars, selection of candies (including small red candies), two opaque screens (20 cm x 30 cm), soft pad, three half ball covers, orange cloth (300 cm x 300 cm), and search and perceptual problem-solving apparatus.

Perceptual Problem Solving: Obtains information regarding Piagetian tasks: Negotiation of Screens, Cause and Effect, Complex Strategies for Understanding Means-Ends Relationships for Handling Objects, and Complex Strategies for Understanding Means-Ends Relationships Concerning Other Human Beings. Consists of behavioral test items. Necessary equipment includes ten 2-cm red cubes in a box, six 12-cm toys, three squeaky toys, white object, three toy cars, selection of candies (including small red candies), two opaque screens (20 cm x 30 cm), transparent screen (20 cm x 20 cm), three half ball covers, orange cloth (300 cm x 300 cm), 600-cm cord, toy rake, suction cup with perspex platform, rattling stick, string of beads, narrow-necked container, and search and perceptual problem-solving apparatus.

Social (Behavior): Obtains information regarding general aspects of social responsiveness, such as cooperative play with other children and cooperation with adults, by interview. Other indices, such as watching and attending to adult's voice, awareness of adult restraint, simple cooperation, and responses to own images in a mirror, are obtained by more formal behavioral test item assessment. Necessary equipment includes six 12-cm toys, three squeaky toys, white object, three toy cars, picture book, ball (about 5 cm), and mirror.

Self-Help Skills: Obtains information regarding self-help skills in the domains of eating, washing, dressing, toileting, social responsibility, and sleeping. Information is obtained by interview.

Communication: Obtains information concerning the understanding and use of a variety of forms of communication skills and assesses the ability to imitate gross- and fine-motor responses and vocalizations. This section, the most elaborate one of the battery, is divided into eight components: three interviews and five tests. The interviews assess 1) receptive abilities regarding hearing and listening skills, and understanding need-related gestures, need-related words, need-related symbols (e.g., pictures and objects), the idea of naming, descriptive words, and simple phrases; 2) the development of oral sound production and imitative motor and oral responses regarding development of sounds, simple motor imitations, and imitation of speech sounds, and 3) the development of expressive abilities regarding the expression of basic needs through facial expressions and communicating with adults (asking) through motor manipulations (touching), pointing, gestures, sounds, a single spoken word or sign or symbol, and the use of phrases (including spoken words, signs, or symbols).

The next four components, Expressive Vocabulary Test, Receptive Vocabulary Test, Motor Imitation Test, and Verbal Imitation Test, were designed for use with the difficult-to-test child who, nonetheless, has some abilities. Each section comprises a pretraining phase and a test phase with behavioral items. The argument underlying the use of both procedures is that these children may not be able to demonstrate their abilities because they are not familiar with formal test settings. The first phase, pretraining, is designed to teach the children to "play the game," attend, and not be disruptive. In this phase they are first tested over eight trials on an easy problem to see if they play the game spontaneously. If they do, pretraining is terminated and the test phase follows. If they do not perform adequately on five out of the first eight tasks, they are prompted and reinforced for a block of trials until they have shown correct behavior on five consecutive trials or until they complete 32 trials. Trials 33 to 40, the final trials, are again unprompted. Evidence of improvement during the pretraining phase may be taken as some indication of educability in this area.

After a child performs adequately in pretraining and moves on to the test phase, correct responding is again rewarded. In each of these four test components a range of responses is tested on up to three occasions. Specific criteria vary from test to test, but in all cases two lists are provided. Although the second list represents more difficult items than the first, all lists should take approximately 20 minutes to administer. In addition, the Expressive Vocabulary and Receptive Vocabulary Tests may be tailored to the individual tested in order to cover material that may have been included in a particular training program. Both of these vocabulary tests can be used to check initial knowledge of words, signs, or symbols for a teaching program; assess progress in such programs; or identify the aspects of a complex stimulus to which the child may be responding. Procedures for isolating the particular components of a complex stimulus being responded to by a child are provided.

The Expressive Vocabulary Test obtains information regarding the child's performance in labeling 15 objects, color photographs of objects, or line-drawings of objects. The child's communicative response may include spoken words, manual signs, or symbols. A tape recorder is needed for both the pretraining and actual test. In addition, pretraining requires a bottle and a flower; the first list requires a wooden block, toy truck, toy car, ball, baby doll, toy hammer, cup, hat, watch, toy train, clock, toy boat, toy saucepan, toy cat, and apple; and the second list requires a toy bus, spoon, toy chair, hairbrush, book, toy telephone, plate, toy table, box, shoe, glass, sock, toy fish, nail, and toy bird.

The Receptive Vocabulary Test obtains information regarding the child's appropriate selection responses: pointing at, reaching for, or other responses indicating a choice in regard to a request from the examiner to select one of two objects, color photographs of objects, or line-drawings of objects. The examiner may communicate to the child by spoken word, manual sign, or by symbols. Pretraining requires a hat and baby doll. For the actual test, the first list requires a cup, clock, plate, spoon, watch, scissors, apple, ball, toy car, and pencil, and the second list requires a shoe, toy chair, book, glass, sock, toy telephone, toy table, knife, hat, and box.

The Motor Imitation Test obtains information regarding the imitation of object- or body- oriented fine- and gross-motor responses. Examples of object-oriented motor responses include ringing bells, stacking blocks, and rolling a ball. Examples of body-oriented motor responses include pulling comb through hair, placing hands on top of head, and rubbing hands together. Pretraining requires two squeaky toys, two cups, and two wooden beads. Necessary equipment for the actual test includes one sheet plain paper; felt- or nylon-tipped pen; four 4.5-cm square blocks; and two each of small bells, balls, sets of graduated cups, hats, spoons, toy cars, tambourines, drumsticks, pull-along cars, bracelets, combs, crayons, whistles, and boxes (10 cm square).

The Verbal Imitation Test obtains information regarding the imitation of speech sounds and words. All responses are tape recorded. Pretest and test require a tape recorder.

The eighth communication component, the Sign Imitation Test, is designed to obtain information from children without speech who may be in sign-language programs or who are being considered for placement in these programs. It is comprised of five subsections: 1) hand preference to assess which hand the student prefers, 2) hand postures, 3) combinations to assess the ability to imitate hand positions used in sign-language, 4) palm directions to assess the ability to imitate palm directions used in sign-language, and 5) movement to assess the ability to imitate hand and arm movements used in sign-language.

Items are scored onto lattices of the type first used by system analysts interested in behavioral analysis since the 1970s. Each lattice consists of a series of related items arranged vertically on stems. Each stem may have up to ten items. In general, a stem represents a particular type of task, function, or setting that can be related to a particular set of teaching situations. Each lattice represents a visual representation of the sequence of items and may consist of up to six stems.

Within each lattice, items are scaled in such a way that the easier items are at the base of the lattice with progressively more difficult ones placed toward the top of the lattice. Difficulty was assessed by frequency of occurrences of items in the standardization sample of severely and profoundly mentally retarded, multiply handicapped children. The more frequently occurring items were assumed to be the easiest, with the least frequently occurring items assumed to be the most difficult or advanced. There are 125 items organized into 15 lattices. Reinforcement and Experience is not summarized on a lattice. Each of the other content areas has one lattice, with the exception of Communication, which is broken down into lattices on Receptive Abilities, Sounds and Imitation, and Expressive Abilities; an overall program lattice is also included.

Test items are well-defined in terms of equipment needed, presentation strategy, and criterion behaviors. When the child achieves criterion on an item, it is crossed out on the lattice. If the child needed demonstration, prompting by pointing, or physical guidance preceding correct performance, it is noted on the lattice. Failed items are also noted on the lattice. Interview items are laid out in formal interview format, and responses are also noted on the lattice.

It is not possible to use the Behaviour Assessment Battery adequately by simply scoring the lattice without reference to the text. The purpose of the assessment is to set up training programs, i.e., target behaviors for teaching once the basic objectives have been derived (Kiernan, 1980). The manual provides many suggestions about the significance of results as they bear on program planning and most extensively on communications programs including those using sign and symbols.

Practical Applications/Uses

The Behaviour Assessment Battery originated to provide a framework that reflects a curriculum that practitioners could use in working with profoundly mentally retarded, multiply handicapped individuals. Teachers, who are the primary users of the battery, can select aspects of the domains of cognition, communication, self-help skills, sensation, and perception to probe in depth. The battery was not designed to be used as a single test procedure, but rather to allow practitioners to select aspects of the assessment battery that they felt would be valuable for individual children about whom they were puzzled. The Behaviour Assessment Battery employs a much larger number of items than do many other procedures and, therefore, can serve to fill in the picture sketched when using other formal and informal assessment measures, such as the Cattell Infant Intelligence Scale (Cattell, 1960), Bayley Scales of Infant Development (Bayley, 1969), Balthazar Scales of Adaptive Behavior (Balthazar, 1976), and The Uniform Performance Assessment System (Bendersky, Edgar, & White, 1976). See also Switzky (1979) and Owen (1985). Sections of the Behaviour Assessment Battery also cover more fundamental levels of development than do most other tests and probe aspects of behavior that are below the "floor" of other procedures. Though teachers are the usual users, mental-handicap nurses and other professionals who work with severely and profoundly handicapped populations (e.g., occupational and physical therapists) can also use this battery. However, the Behaviour Assessment Battery needs to be used in a context where practitioners are familiar with the use of behavioral objectives and structured teaching techniques. The Behaviour Assessment Battery is not a tool for beginners. Though there is a fairly thorough chapter on the use and interpretation of the Behaviour Assessment Battery in the second edition, there are not reams of teaching suggestions, and potential users need to be fairly imaginative in the construction of newer programs that go beyond the suggestions offered.

Although the Behaviour Assessment Battery was designed to be used with severely and profoundly mentally retarded, multiply handicapped persons who function at very low levels of development, components of the Communication section, which probe the development of nonverbal communication and the use of augmentative communication systems involving sign language or graphic symbols, may be useful for slightly higher functioning persons.

The Behaviour Assessment Battery assumes that the examiner will be willing to spend a fair amount of time administering the test. The full battery may require up to six or seven 20-minute sessions with the child, plus an interview with parents, teachers, caregivers, and other professionals, with each interview lasting up to an hour. There is nothing to prevent the examiner from using only one or two sections in isolation or interviewing respondents together. The child should be tested in the natural environment of the home or care-giving residence, as well as in the environment of the classroom. It is important to know how children function in all of the ecological environments that they inhabit (Switzky, 1979; Switzky & Haywood, 1984, 1985). Most importantly, one wants to determine the optimal performance of the child and so the examiner needs to motivate the child consistently throughout the assessment procedure. The manual provides detailed and clear instructions concerning assessment items and procedures. If the examiner has some experience with severely and profoundly mentally retarded, multiply handicapped individuals, techniques of criterion-referenced testing, and some familiarity with developmental and Piagetian theory and items, then reading the manual will be enough to use the battery. Nevertheless, the battery will probably have to be used by naive examiners under the direction of more experienced practitioners.

Directions for scoring are clear, and all behavioral lattices and interview forms are part of the manual. In this reviewer's opinion, it will take considerable time for a naive examiner to learn how to use and score the subsections of the battery because of the thoroughness of the assessment tasks. It is useful to copy all scoring sheets and then to strike the item through with a red felt pen when the child has achieved criterion on an item. If the child has needed a demonstration, this is indicated by "D" next to the item, prompting by pointing is indicated by "P," and physical guidance preceding correct performance is indicated by "PG." To indicate failed items, "F" is placed next to the relevant lattice items.

The interpretation of the Behaviour Assessment Battery depends on the practioner's level of clinical experience with severely and profoundly handicapped persons and the practitioner's familiarity with developmental, Piagetian, and operant theories. Practitioners also need to be familiar with the use of behavioral objectives and structured teaching techniques to convert the information supplied by the battery into practical teaching goals. Interpretation of the battery is based on the profiles of behavior scored by the examiner on the behavioral lattices and reading the chapter on use and interpretation that provides suggestions for programming. The more sophisticated that practitioner is initially, the more valuable will be the information supplied by the battery.

Technical Aspects

There were three phases in the development of the Behaviour Assessment Battery: 1) surveying existing tests and interview batteries for mentally handicapped persons, nonretarded infants, and preschool children; 2) organizing these items in ways that appeared to make theoretical sense into manageable groups to form a battery of items that could be assessed in a single testing session; and 3) administering the preliminary battery to 174 severely and profoundly mentally retarded children and youths varying in age from 2 to 17 years. Interobserver, interinterviewer, and test-retest reliabilities on the various sections were determined with three months between test administrations. Orderings of items within sections were explored using Guttman Scalogram Techniques (Edwards, 1957; Goodenough, 1944; Green, 1956; Guttman, 1944). This technique allows one to test whether the order of items within a group, judged by the relative ease with which items are passed, could have occurred by chance. If there is a sequence of difficulty in a group of items, it should emerge using this technique. The Guttman technique was used by Kiernan and Jones in an attempt to establish sequences that could be followed in teaching. All other factors being equal, the closer the Guttman coefficient of reproducibility approaches 1.00, the closer the set is to showing a perfect progression. Unfortunately, the coefficient of reproducibility is affected by the overall distribution of scores in the sample of individuals. If many subjects score highly on items in the section, then the coefficients will be inflated by this alone. The extent to which the coefficient of reproducibility is affected is assessed by the statistic, minimal marginal reproducibility. A comparison of minimal marginal reproducibility and the coefficient of reproducibility gives an indication of the extent to which scaling affects scores. High coefficients of reproducibility coupled with low minimal marginal reproducibility statistics indicate that behaviors scale in such a way that the developmental sequences involved are fairly clear-cut and invariant as reflected in the sample concerned. Table 1 presents the summary statistics.

A coefficient of reproducibility greater than .9 is viewed as the ideal criterion of scalability. Examination of Table 1 suggests that scaling within sections is adequate. The lower scores on the Exploratory Play and Auditory Responsiveness sections probably indicate the mixed nature of items in these content areas. Interobserver, interinterviewer, and test-retest reliabilities are adequate except for the Auditory Responsiveness and Social Behavior sections.

The 1982 edition of the Behaviour Assessment Battery included a new procedure, The Sign Imitation Test, devised specifically to investigate the ability of children and adults to imitate hand postures, positions, and movements used in sign language. The test was administered to 36 children between the ages of five to 13 years who were severely educationally subnormal. The test was administered a second time after a four-five month wait to assess test-retest reliability. Hand Preference showed some instability on retest. Hand Postures gave a reliability coefficient of +.71 and showed good scalability. Combinations showed good test-retest reliability and good scalability. Palm Direction gave very low test-retest reliability. Data reported in the 1982 edition of the Behaviour Assessment Battery are sketchy and preliminary as regards the Sign Imitation Test. Technical information regarding other sections of the Communication content areas is not reported.

Kiernan (1983; personal communication, August 30, 1985) is actively involved in exploring the communication systems and behaviors of severely handicapped persons. He and his colleagues have recently developed some newer assessment techniques (Kiernan & Reid, 1985a, 1985b), including an extensive validation study that overlaps with the Communication areas of the Behaviour Assessment Battery.

The Behaviour Assessment Battery represents a serious attempt to make some order out of the chaos usually associated with the assessment of the abilities and skills of children and youths who are severely and profoundly mentally retarded. Technically, the test is without equal in its concern for the psychometrical issues of test development, psychometric reliability, psychometric internal validity, and for procedures of optimizing test performance. The item domains and content areas sampled by the test are quite extensive and provide good face validity. The criterion-referenced nature of the item domains have contributed substantially to the

Table 1

Summary Statistics for the Behaviour Assessment Battery

Section	*Coefficient of Reproducibility*	*Minimal Marginal Reproducibility*	*Test-Retest Reliability*	*Percent Agreement of Scores*	*Interobserver Reliability*	*Interinterviewer Reliability*
Visual Inspection	0.89	0.61	0.95	83.96		
Visual Tracking	0.93	0.65	0.82	83.56		
Visuo-Motor Coordination	0.91	0.74	0.87	85.24		
Auditory Responsiveness	0.78	0.54	0.68	72.00		
Postural Control					0.99	
Exploratory Play	0.76	0.46	0.90	81.19		
Constructive Play	0.95	0.47	0.82	92.38		
Search Strategies	0.91	0.63	0.96	88.70		
Perceptual Problem Solving	0.86	0.68	0.94	92.86		
Social Behavior	0.81	0.56	0.67	79.64		
Self-Help Skills						
Feeding						0.98
Dressing						0.95
Washing						0.90
Toileting						0.96

overall good reliability and ease of use of this test. This battery is the finest assessment measure of its type. (See Switzky 1979; Switzky & Haywood, 1985).

Critique

The Behaviour Assessment Battery represents the most extensive, standardized, yet flexible set of assessment procedures for determining educational goals for severely and profoundly mentally retarded, multiply handicapped persons that is commercially available for practitioners. The battery provides a broad coverage of adaptive behavior domains and a comprehensive downward extension of tests of development. The criterion-referenced items that make up the battery are suitable to assess the behavioral functioning of even the most impaired, absolute profoundly mentally retarded student. The battery was carefully developed and had extensive field testing.

The Behaviour Assessment Battery, by using identified incentives and pretraining procedures before formal testing to generate optimal performance from well-motivated students, represents a variant of the current learning potential approach to assessment applied to profoundly mentally retarded learners (Haywood & Switzky, in press; Switzky & Haywood, 1985; Switzky & Rotatori, 1981). This represents a very innovative contribution to the assessment of extremely low-functioning students. Other innovations found in the Behaviour Assessment Battery include the extensive analysis of the communication abilities of low-functioning students and the sophisticated psychometrics of test construction.

The battery has a few problems that limit its effectiveness. First, the test requires a fairly sophisticated user. Second, the test lacks an explicit theory and cohesiveness, and, therefore, the programs of instruction and teaching that are generated also lack coherence. The Behaviour Assessment Battery could use more training materials, such as films and videotapes, to facilitate its use by practitioners. The test could also use a more extensive and integrated set of suggestions on how to organize the information it provides into programs of teaching. Yet, the Behaviour Assessment Battery represents one of the best and most sophisticated assessment batteries for the severely mentally handicapped. It is this reviewer's hope that Kiernan and the work of his colleagues will become better known in North America and that practitioners will be aided in solving some of the problems of educating the severely and profoundly mentally retarded.

References

Balthazar, E. E. (1976). *Training the retarded at home or in school.* Palo Alto, CA: Consulting Psychologists Press, Inc.

Bayley, N. (1969). *Infant Scales of Psychomotor and Mental Development.* Cleveland: The Psychological Corporation.

Bendersky, M., Edgar, E., & White, O. (1976). *Uniform Performance Assessment Systems (UPAS)* (Working Paper No. 65). Seattle: University of Washington, Experimental Education Unit, Child Development and Mental Retardation Center.

Cattell, P. (1960). *Cattell Infant Intelligence Scale.* Cleveland: The Psychological Corporation.

Edwards, A. L. (1957). *Techniques of attitude scale construction.* New York: Appleton-Century-Crofts.

Goodenough, W. H. (1944). A technique for scale analysis. *Educational and Psychological Measurement, 4,* 179-190.

Green, B. F. (1956). A method of scalogram analysis using summary statistics. *Psychometrika, 21,* 79-88.

Grossman, H. J. (Ed.). (1983). *Classification in mental retardation.* Washington, DC: American Association on Mental Deficiency.

Guttman, L. L. (1944). A basis for scaling qualitative data. *American Sociological Review, 9,* 139-150.

Haywood, H. C., Meyers, C. E., & Switzky, H. N. (1982). Mental retardation. In M. Rosenzweig (Ed.), *Annual review of psychology, 1982* (pp. 309-342). Palo Alto, CA: Annual Review Inc.

Haywood, H. C., & Switzky, H. N. (in press). The malleability of intelligence: Cognitive processes as a function of polygenic experiential interaction. *School Psychology Review.*

Jones, M. C. (1971). *A developmental schedule based on Piaget's sensori-motor writings: An examination of the schedule's potential value as an instrument for assessing severely and profoundly subnormal children.* Unpublished master's thesis, University of London Institute of Education, London, England.

Kiernan, C. C. (1980). General principles of curricular planning. In N. Crawford (Ed.), *Curriculum planning for ESN(S) child.* Kidderminster, England: BIMH.

Kiernan, C. C. (1983). The exploration of sign and symbol effects. In J. Hogg & P. J. Mittler (Eds.), *Advances in mental handicap research* (Vol. 2, pp. 27-68). New York: Wiley & Sons.

Kiernan, C. C., & Jones, M. C. (1980). The Behaviour Assessment Battery for use with the profoundly retarded. In J. Hogg & P. J. Mittler (Eds.), *Advances in mental handicap research* (Vol. 1, pp. 27-52). New York: Wiley & Sons.

Kiernan, C. C., & Jones, M. C. (1982). *Behaviour Assessment Battery, 2nd edition.* Windsor, England: NFER-Nelson Publishing Company Ltd.

Kiernan, C. C., Jordan, R., & Saunders, C. (1978). *Starting off.* London: Souvenir Press.

Kiernan, C. C., & Reid, B. (1985a). *Pre-verbal Communication (PVC) manual, third edition.* London: Thomas Coram Research Unit, University of London Institute of Education.

Kiernan, C. C., & Reid, B. (1985b). *Pre-verbal Communication Schedule (PVC), seventh edition.* London: Thomas Coram Research Unit, University of London Institute of Education.

Owen, R. (1985). Assessment of the severely mentally retarded population. In D. Bricker & J. Filler (Eds.), *Severe mental retardation* (pp. 161-184). Reston, VA: Council for Exceptional Children.

Switzky, H. N. (1979). Assessment of the severely and profoundly handicapped. In D. A. Sabatino & T. L. Miller (Eds.), *Describing learner characteristics of handicapped children and youth* (pp. 415-478). New York: Grune & Stratton.

Switzky, H. N., & Haywood, H. C. (1984). Bio-social ecological perspectives on mental retardation. In N. S. Endler & J. McV. Hunt (Eds.), *Personality and the behavior disorders, Vol. II* (2nd ed., pp. 851-896). New York: Wiley & Sons.

Switzky, H. N., & Haywood, H. C. (1985). Perspectives on methodological and research issues concerning severely retarded persons. In D. Bricker & J. Filler (Eds.), *Severe mental retardation* (pp. 264-284). Reston, VA: Council for Exceptional Children.

Switzky, H. N., & Rotatori, A. (1981). Assessment of perceptual cognitive functioning in nonverbal severely/profoundly handicapped children. *Early Child Development and Care, 7,* 29-44.

Switzky, H. N., Haywood, H. C., & Rotatori, A. (1982). Who are the severely and profoundly mentally retarded? *Education and Training of the Mentally Retarded, 17*(4), 268-272.

Les Sternberg, Ph.D.

Professor, Department of Exceptional Student Education, Florida Atlantic University, Boca Raton, Florida.

Ronald L. Taylor, Ed.D.

Professor, Department of Exceptional Student Education, Florida Atlantic University, Boca Raton, Florida.

CALLIER-AZUSA SCALE:G EDITION

Robert Stillman (Editor). Dallas, Texas: Callier Center for Communication Disorders, University of Texas at Dallas.

Introduction

The Callier-Azusa Scale is an individually administered instrument designed to assess the developmental functioning level in various critical skill areas of deaf-blind and severely or profoundly handicapped children. Information obtained from the test can be used to describe the general functioning level of a child and to assist practitioners in identifying specific objectives for instruction. The editor of the Callier-Azusa is Robert Stillman, Ph.D., Associate Professor and program head in communication disorders at the University of Texas at Dallas. He is also director of classroom programs for preverbal children at the Callier Center for Communication Disorders and currently serves as the project director of a program funded by the U. S. Office of Special Education. This project involves an investigation of procedures for assessing communicative interactions between deaf-blind persons and others.

The development of the Callier-Azusa Scale was initiated in 1972 as a cooperative endeavor between classroom personnel serving deaf-blind children and related services professionals representing the areas of child development, physical therapy, and occupational therapy. The goal of this venture was to compile a comprehensive developmental assessment scale for use with deaf-blind children so that information obtained from the scale could be used effectively for educational planning. Through field-testing efforts, an increased understanding of the abilities and behavior of deaf-blind children was obtained. This led to a series of revisions and expansions of the scale, which culminated in the G Edition, published in 1978. The overall longitudinal development of the scale from 1972 to 1978 was supported by grants from the U. S. Office of Special Education to the South-central Regional Center for Services to Deaf-Blind Children and Youth.

The Callier-Azusa Scale provides assessment items in five major areas: 1) Motor Development; 2) Perceptual Development; 3) Daily Living Skills; 4) Cognition, Communication, and Language; and 5) Social Development. Each area is divided into various subscales, with each subscale represented by a specific number of major developmental items. Each of these items represents a certain developmental milestone or developmental age attainment and is represented by one to five actual subitems.

The five areas contain the following subscales: Motor Development—Postural Control (18 items), Locomotion (17 items), Fine Motor Skills (20 items), and Visual Motor (21 items); Perceptual Development—Visual Development (15 items), Auditory Development (6 items), and Tactile Development (13 items); Daily Living Skills—Undressing and Dressing (16 items), Personal Hygiene (13 items), Feeding Skills (16 items), and Toileting (13 items); Cognition, Communication, and Language—Cognitive Development (21 items), Receptive Communication (18 items), Expressive Communication (20 items), and Development of Speech (10 items); and Social Development—Interactions with Adults (16 items), Interactions with Peers (17 items), and Interactions with Environment (10 items).

Although the overall developmental age range of items in the scale is from zero months to nine years, all subscales do not have items that represent this full range. For example, items in the Auditory Development subscale range from zero to 28 months, and items in the Undressing and Dressing subscale range from zero to 108 months. The general age range of items on the Callier-Azusa define the target population of deaf-blind children. However, with severely or profoundly handicapped children, the appropriate age range for administration can be elevated.

The following are examples of the lowest and highest level item (or subitem) per subscale (Stillman, 1978).

Postural Control: "Turns head from side to side while on stomach" to "advanced overhand throw."

Locomotion: "When suspended under arms with feet touching flat surface, child makes no attempt to move legs, or when top of foot touches surface leg will lift and step onto surface" to "kicks ball through the air from a running start."

Fine Motor Skills: "Does not grasp object or withdraws from object" to "ties shoelaces independently."

Visual Motor: "Does not respond to any visual stimulus" to "cuts out circles on line."

Visual Development: "Does not respond to visual stimulus" to "matches some short written words."

Auditory Development: "No response to sounds" to "anticipates a routine activity from sound cues."

Tactile Development: "Resists rough-textured or cold surfaces" to "points to exact spot on body part that has been touched."

Undressing and Dressing: "Lies passively during dressing; does not respond to dressing or undressing" to "in complete charge of dressing; selects appropriate clothing, hangs up, puts clothes in drawer."

Personal Hygiene: "Resists bathing, makes task difficult" to "complete independence in bathing, draws own water."

Feeding Skills: "Only takes bottle, resists being fed from spoon" to "prepares simple foods not requiring measurements; recognizes sequences of food preparation."

Toileting: "Urinates frequently, exhibits little or no bladder control" to "carries out all toileting functions independently."

Cognitive Development: "Unresponsive to the environment; movements are not in response to stimulation and appear to have no goal or purpose'' to ''demonstrates a systematic approach to ordering a group of items according to their size; after series is in order, child can insert new objects in the appropriate space.''

Receptive Communication: ''Unresponsive to the environment; movements are not in response to stimulation and appear to have no goal or purpose'' to ''responds appropriately to 'when' questions by answering with reference to time.''

Expressive Communication: ''Undifferentiated cry'' to ''asks for detailed explanations, using 'how' and 'why.'''

Development of Speech: ''No vocalizations other than crying'' to ''has 800 or more spoken words which are comprehensible to outsiders.''

Interactions with Adults: ''Shows no awareness of presence of adult'' to ''able to engage in symbolic or pretend play with an adult—must be child directed and not simply responding to an adult's directions.''

Interactions with Peers: "Shows no awareness of presence of peer" to "wants to win in games."

Interactions with Environment: ''Does not respond to environmental stimuli'' to ''is able to regulate his/her own social behavior even in the absence of an authority figure.''

The physical layout of the Callier-Azusa Scale includes a convenient feature; each major area of the scale is identified by different colored test item sheets, each of which is organized into three columns: item column (listing test items and subitems themselves), example column (providing written exemplars of those items or subitems that may present some interpretation problems), and comments column (providing space for any written comments that the test administrator may want to make).

Practical Applications/Uses

The Callier-Azusa Scale is designed to be administered individually to deaf-blind and severely or profoundly handicapped children by teachers or other individuals (e.g., related services personnel) who are thoroughly familiar with the children being assessed. Preferably, in this case, administration requires that the child be observed in natural classroom settings. The test editor (Stillman, 1978) states that this observation should be carried out for a period of at least two weeks. Once the observation has been completed, the test administrator completes the test profile sheet while referring to the items and subitems in the scale itself. This requires that the test administrator be completely familiar with the scale, in that the scale is completed *after* the period of observation.

The test profile sheet (see Figure 1) is comprised of five major vertical cells, with each cell representing one of the five major assessment areas. At the bottom of each cell (and representing one column each) are the names of each of the subscales. Proceeding upward from these designations are columns of numbers, each of which represents one item of each subscale. To the far left-hand side of the profile is an additional column that specifies developmental ages in months. By horizontally reading across the profile one can determine the approximate developmental level (age) that is represented by each item of each subscale.

The test profile is completed by evaluating the performance of the child on each

Figure 1.
Test Profile Sheet from the Callier-Azusa Scale*

Domain	Subscale		Items (in order along the months axis)
	MONTHS		0 6 12 18 24 36 48 60 72 84 96 108
MOTOR DEVELOPMENT	POST. CONT.	A	0 1 2 3 4 5 6 7 8 9 10 11 12 13 14 15 16 17
	LOCOMOTION	B	0 1 2 3 4 5 6 7 8 9 10 11 12 13 14 15 16
	FINE MOTOR	C	0 1 2 3 4 5 6 7 8 9 10 11 12 13 14 15 16 17 18 19
	VIS-MOTOR	D	0 1 2 3 4 5 6 7 8 9 10 11 12 13 14 15 16 17 18 19 20
PERCEPTUAL DEVELOPMENT	VISION	A	0 1 2 3 4 5 6 7 8 9 10 11 12 13 14
	AUDITORY	B	0 1 2 3 4 5
	TACTILE	C	0 1 2 3 4 5 6 7 8 9 10 11 12
DAILY LIVING SKILLS	DRESS.	A	0 1 2 3 4 5 6 7 8 9 10 11 12 13 14 15
	PERS. HYG.	B	0 1 2 3 4 5 6 7 8 9 10 11 12
	FEEDING	C	0 1 2 3 4 5 6 7 8 9 10 11 12 13 14 15
	TOILET	D	0 1 2 3 4 5 6 7 8 9 10 11 12
COGNITION, COMMUNICATION AND LANGUAGE	COGNITION	A	0 1 2 3 4 5 6 7 8 9 10 11 12 13 14 15 16 17 18 19 20
	RECEPTIVE	B	0 1 2 3 4 5 6 7 8 9 10 11 12 13 14 15 16 17
	EXPRESS.	C	0 1 2 3 4 5 6 7 8 9 10 11 12 13 14 15 16 17 18 19
	SPEECH	D	0 1 2 3 4 5 6 7 8 9
SOCIAL DEVELOPMENT	ADULTS	A	0 1 2 3 4 5 6 7 8 9 10 11 12 13 14 15
	PEERS	B	0 1 2 3 4 5 6 7 8 9 10 11 12 13 14 15 16
	ENVIRON.	C	0 1 2 3 4 5 6 7 8 9

NAME ______________________ DOB __________ PROGRAM ______________

OBSERVERS (pre) ______________________ DATE ______________

OBSERVERS (post) ______________________ DATE ______________

CHILD'S HANDICAPS:

*Reprinted by permission of R. Stillman from the Callier-Azusa Scale (1978) by R. Stillman (Ed.).

item (and corresponding subitems) of each subscale. In order to give a child credit for a particular item, the child must attain all subitems within that item. An item or subitem is considered correct or successfully exhibited only if the behavior described by that item or subitem is both spontaneous (i.e., behavior occurs without the use of any artificial prompts or cues) and integrated (i.e., behavior occurs across appropriate people and across appropriate situations). If a behavior is emerging or occurs only infrequently, only after prompting, or in specific situations, credit is not given. Some items and subitems in the scale are starred (*). These items or subitems can be omitted if "a child cannot be expected to exhibit the behavior because of a specific sensory or motor deficit" (Stillman, 1978, p. 4). This is another convenient feature; few tests have specific exclusion coding systems to use with children with sensory or motor impairments.

Two levels of performance can be analyzed using the scoring system that is advocated. The first is termed *base step performance,* which is defined as the highest item within each subscale that the child successfully performs before beginning to fail items. For example, if the child successfully performs items 1, 2, and 3 of the Postural Control subscale and begins to experience failure on item 4, the child's base step performance would be considered item 3. All base step items are circled on the test profile sheet, after which the test administrator evaluates performance on all remaining items and subitems of each subscale. If the child shows correct performance of any subitems of any item above the base step, the letters corresponding to these subitems should be written beside that item number. In the event that the child exhibits all of the subitems of any item above the base step, that item number is underlined on the test profile sheet.

Although the test editor does not give a specific term for the second level—the highest item or subitem that the child acquires above the base step—it could be referred to as the *ceiling level performance.*

Each subscale base and ceiling level step can be converted to "rough" age equivalencies by referring to the far left-hand column of the test profile sheet. The range between the base and ceiling level steps can also provide some pertinent information. Although a child's performance might best be described by referring to base step performance (e.g., the child's performance on the Auditory Development subtest is typical of a four-month-old child), one can get a more precise picture of the child by describing any performance above the base step (e.g., the child also exhibits some auditory behaviors that might be typical of an 18-month-old child).

The test editor provides a word of caution, however, about the interpretation of the scores from the instrument. Stillman (1978) states that any age equivalencies for behaviors are, at best, approximate and that age equivalencies are only given for comparisons *between* subscales. He concludes by stating that behavior sequences for a child, not the age norms, provide the most important information.

Although one might assume that the results from the Callier-Azusa can be used to directly specify instructional objectives for a child, this is not recommended by the test editor. Instead, results from the scale are to be used to help the practitioner to identify more general developmentally appropriate activities for a child. The scale can also be used in pretest-posttest fashion to evaluate progress. Given the many revisions of the Callier-Azusa, the test editor recommends that if progress is being measured, the practitioner either 1) use the same edition of the Callier-Azusa during both pretest/posttest or 2) transfer the pretest *behaviors* (not item numbers) to the different posttest scale (Stillman, 1978).

Although not stated or recommended by the test editor, other interpretations are also possible from the results, especially in regard to the test profile sheet. Stephens, Sternberg, and Jenkins (1980) have indicated that by connecting all base steps by a solid line and all ceiling steps by another solid line, one can obtain a graph-like version of the child's performance. This method can be used to earmark those areas that are most affected by the child's handicap and the basic strengths and weaknesses of the child. If group instruction is being considered, profiles of different children can be compared to determine similarities and differences in overall performance.

Sternberg, Battle, and Hill (1980) suggest that certain subscales of the Callier-Azusa can be used for program placement decisions. They state that certain behaviors sampled within the Cognitive Development, Receptive Communication, and Expressive Communication subscales can be used as determinants of appropriate prelanguage communication program interventions for severely and profoundly handicapped students.

Technical Aspects

Data pertaining to the reliability of an earlier version of the Callier-Azusa Scale (E Edition) were obtained in a study conducted by Day and Stillman (1975). Three basic questions were addressed: 1) Were data obtained from the Callier-Azusa Scale reliable when the scale was used by observer teams? 2) Were these data more reliable when compared to data obtained by individual observers? and 3) Were there significant differences in reliability measures between those that were obtained in day-school versus residential programs? For all three questions, reliability coefficients were obtained using interobserver reliability checks. Four observers independently completed item profiles on 80 children, all of whom were functioning at developmental levels appropriate for scale administration. The average of individual interobserver reliability coefficients was considered as the individual reliability coefficient. The four observers then formed two pairs and filled out, on a consensus basis, an additional item profile sheet. A correlation coefficient was then calculated to determine the degree of relationship between the pairs. All correlations for both individual and paired rating of subscales were significant ($p < .001$), regardless of whether the rating was based on raw score performance or age equivalency of each subscale. The range of correlations for subscales was between .66 and .97. On an overall basis, there tended to be higher correlations for motor scales than for scales of social abilities.

In reponse to the second research question, there were no significant differences between observations that were made by pairs of observers and those that were made by individuals. However, as the researchers pointed out, the individual interobserver reliability checks were averaged. Therefore, these coefficients do not reflect any noteworthy variance between individual observers, resulting in the recommendation that more than one person should complete item profiles on a single child.

In relation to the third question, no significant differences were found in interobserver reliability data when comparing observations of subjects from day-school and residential settings.

A study investigating the validity of the Callier-Azusa Scale, E Edition was conducted by Day (1975). The purpose of the study was to determine whether the items in certain subscales represent an ordinal scale. The subscales of Fine Motor Skills, Postural Control, Expressive Language, and Receptive Language were investigated. Three separate assessments were obtained on 58 children enrolled in a deaf-blind school over a period of several months. However, no analysis of subject data change over time was conducted due to the rather slow development of the children. Two analyses were completed. The first was the percentage of subjects who passed each item of the targeted subscales. An item was considered passed only if all subitems for an item were displayed by the subject. Percentage-passing data were calculated for each of the three assessments. Also, percentage-passing data were obtained for all three assessments combined. Comparing the data from individual assessments to the combined assessments, no difference in order of difficulty of items was discovered. However, as Day points out, certain discrepancies were noted in the relative position of specific subscale items in comparison to the percentage-passing data. This eventually resulted in changing the ordinal position of these subscale items.

The second database involved the use of a Guttman scaleogram analysis, a statistical procedure used to determine ordinality. Data from the three assessments were combined and coefficients of scalability were determined. In all cases, all subscale items were determined to be unidimensional and ordinal. (All obtained coefficients above .76.)

Although data are available supporting the reliability and ordinal validity of the Callier-Azusa Scale, these data pertain to an older version of the scale. Therefore, one should be cautious in generalizing these data to the current version, the G Edition.

Critique

In two reviews and analyses of the Callier-Azusa Scale, G Edition, Taylor (1982, 1984) states that the Callier-Azusa is one of few scales that is specifically designed for use with individuals with sensory and/or motor deficits. He stresses the point that the scale contains a representative number of items designed for lower functioning individuals. In terms of the scale's appropriate usage, he concurs with the scale's editor that the test should be used for the determination of strengths and weaknesses and as an assistive device in generating educational objectives rather than as an instrument to determine an individual's developmental level. Taylor's remarks certainly seem justified and summarize the uses and limitations of the Callier-Azusa Scale.

References

Day, P. (1975). *Validity of the ordinality of items in four subscales of the Callier-Azusa Scale—E Edition.* Unpublished manuscript, University of Texas at Dallas, Callier Center for Communication Disorders, Dallas.

Day, P., & Stillman, R. (1975). *Inter-observer reliability of the Callier-Azusa Scale.* Unpublished manuscript, University of Texas at Dallas, Callier Center for Communication Disorders, Dallas.

Stephens, B., Sternberg, L., & Jenkins, S. (1980). *Final report for programs for severely/profoundly mentally retarded children and youth* (Contract #300-77-0254). Washington, DC: U. S. Department of Education, Office of Special Education.

Sternberg, L., Battle, C., & Hill, J. (1980). Prelanguage communication programming for the severely and profoundly handicapped. *Journal of the Association for the Severely Handicapped, 5*(3), 224-233.

Stillman, R. (1978). *The Callier-Azusa Scale—G Edition.* Dallas, TX: Callier Center for Communication Disorders, The University of Texas at Dallas.

Taylor, R. L. (1982). Assessment. In L. Sternberg & G. L. Adams (Eds.), *Educating severely and profoundly handicapped students* (pp. 47-93). Rockville, MD: Aspen Systems.

Taylor, R. L. (1984). *Assessment of exceptional students: Educational and psychological procedures.* Englewood Cliffs, NJ: Prentice-Hall.

Joanne Gallivan, Ph.D.
Assistant Professor of Psychology, University College of Cape Breton, Sydney, Nova Scotia, Canada.

CANADIAN TESTS OF BASIC SKILLS

M. King, A. N. Hieronymus, E. F. Lindquist, H. D. Hoover, and Dale P. Scannell. Scarborough, Ontario: Nelson Canada.

Introduction

The Canadian Tests of Basic Skills (CTBS) consist of a battery of tests with Canadian content and standardization. They are designed to measure development of basic skills in the areas of vocabulary, reading, language, work-study skills, and mathematics, and, as such, are meant to assess generalized educational achievement, not content achievement.

Development of the tests began in the 1960s under the general editorship of Dr. Ethel King, Professor in the Faculty of Education at the University of Calgary. The Primary and Elementary Batteries are adapted from the Iowa Tests of Basic Skills (Hieronymus, Hoover, & Lindquist, 1982), which were first published in 1955 (for reviews see Herrick, 1959; Morgan, 1959; Remmers, 1959). The developers of those tests also participated in the design of the Canadian version. The high-school edition is an adaptation of the Tests of Achievement and Proficiency (Scannell, Haugh, Schild, & Umber, 1982), which were designed by staff of the School of Education at the University of Kansas and first published in 1978. One of the authors, Scannell, also participated in the design of the Canadian version. In addition, a number of Canadian curriculum consultants aided in the selection of test items for all batteries.

The Elementary Battery was first published in 1966; revised editions, incorporating changes in content and standardization, were produced in 1974 and 1982. In addition, a metric version was made available in 1976 in response to the introduction of the metric system as the official standard of measurement in Canada. The Primary Battery was added in 1972, reflecting the added emphasis on readiness skills in our educational systems. A metric version was introduced in 1976, and a revised edition was published in 1981. The High School Battery, which is fully metric, became available in 1981.

For all batteries, a single reusable test booklet contains all subtests. All questions use a multiple-choice format, and answers are marked by students on machine- or hand-scorable response sheets. The tests are divided into Levels 5-18, roughly corresponding to chronological age, with Levels 5-8 included in the Primary Battery, Levels 9-14 included in the Elementary Battery, and Levels 15-18 included in the High School Battery.

The 1981 edition of the Primary Battery is available in one form only. There are 13 subtests, suitable for use in the primary grades up to the beginning of third grade. The Listening subtest measures skills that contribute to comprehension of orally presented material (e.g., following directions, predicting outcomes, and attention span); Vocabulary assesses comprehension of words in isolation and in context; Word Analysis tests knowledge of sound-letter associations, phonetic analysis, and word structure; and Reading Comprehension assesses picture interpretation, sentence comprehension, and story comprehension skills. There are four separate components in the Language Skills Test, each of which yields a separate score in addition to the total score: Spelling, Capitalization, Punctuation, and Usage (requiring recognition of grammatical errors in sentences). Two subtests, which yield a total Work-study score in addition to individual scores, measure Work-study Skills: W-1, assessing the ability to correctly interpret maps, graphs, and tables, and W-2, assessing skills involved in the utilization of reference materials, such as alphabetization, classification, and use of tables of contents. There are three subtests, which yield a Mathematics total score as well as individual scores: M-1, measuring knowledge of the number system and basic arithmetical terms and operations; M-2, measuring the ability to solve addition and subtraction problems, which are presented in the form of verbal descriptions; and M-3, measuring the ability to solve similar problems that are presented out of context.

The Elementary (or Multilevel) Battery is available in two alternate forms, suitable for use in Grades 3-8. It consists of 11 subtests, which are essentially the same in format as those in the Primary Battery except the Listening and Word Analysis subtests are excluded. Each subtest is a single wide-range test. Pupils start and stop at various locations, depending on the grade being tested. Although this introduces economy because the same set of materials may be reused by many groups, it may create difficulties for the administrator, particularly in testing younger children.

The High School Battery is also a multilevel instrument, intended for use in Grades 10-12. It is available in one form only. The battery is divided into four subtests: Reading Comprehension, consisting of short reading selections followed by questions that assess comprehension of facts and ability to recognize inferences and generalizations that may be drawn from the material; Mathematics, measuring knowledge of basic mathematical concepts and operations, computation, and problem-solving, including algebra, geometry, and statistics; Written Expression, assessing skills of spelling, capitalization, punctuation, grammar and usage, organization (e.g., paragraphing), and forms (e.g., letters); and Using Sources of Information, measuring the ability to gain information from a wide variety of sources, including maps, graphs, tables, dictionaries, tables of contents, and indices. In addition to the subtest and total scores, an Applied Proficiency Skills score is also provided. This measure is derived from performance on a number of specific items within each subtest. These items are thought to measure ability to perform tasks that are frequently encountered in everyday life, such as communicating ideas to others in writing and using applied mathematics and reference materials. The test developers suggest that students who receive low Applied Proficiency Skills scores may have difficulty in responding effectively to many tasks that they will face in day-to-day situations outside of the academic setting.

Practical Applications/Uses

The Canadian Tests of Basic Skills are intended to measure educational growth and development in the general areas of vocabulary, reading, language, work-study skills, and mathematics. They may be used as either group indicators or individual assessment devices. The developers (Nelson Canada, 1984a) suggest that information from the tests can be used to identify strengths and weaknesses of instructional programs as a guide to curriculum change. As individual assessment tools, the tests allow the identification of pupil capabilities on which individualized adaptations in materials and methods can be made. The authors also suggest that the tests may be used to assess readiness of groups or individuals for progress to the next level or unit of instruction, as a method of reporting progress in basic skills to parents, and for grouping students for special programs. An example of the last-mentioned is the use of the tests by the Durham, Ontario, Board of Education as part of a battery to identify gifted students for program placement (Nelson Canada, 1984b).

The tests are specifically designed for classroom administration by teachers. Selected subtests, rather than the entire battery, may be given because norms are available for each subtest. In addition, adjustments in instructions or time limits may be introduced for students in special education settings, but these must be taken into account in interpretation of the results. Instructions for administration are clear and thorough. The total Primary Battery requires about five hours administration time, which should be spread over four or five days. Rest breaks should be given between sessions, which should be limited to a maximum of 35 minutes. Administration of the Primary Battery is most demanding because instructions for most of the subtests are given entirely orally. The Elementary Battery requires a total administration time of about five hours, which should be scheduled over at least four days and given in four to eight sessions. The High School Battery takes about three hours to complete and should be given in two half-day sessions, preferably on consecutive days.

Scoring the tests is relatively easy because all items are multiple-choice, clear instructions are given in the teacher's guides (King, Hieronymus, Lindquist, & Hoover, 1982a, 1982b; King & Scannell, 1982), and scoring masks are available. Machine scoring, the preferred method for large-scale administration, is available for the Elementary and High School Batteries. Tables in the teacher's guides allow ready conversion of raw scores to grade equivalents, percentile ranks, standard scores, and within-grade stanines. Norms are provided for fall, winter, and spring sessions.

Interpretation of scores is based on norms derived from a nationally representative standardization sample selected from over 100 schools in every province and territory of Canada. Score interpretation is explained in clear, jargon-free language in the teacher's guide accompanying each battery. This enables the information to be utilized even by individuals who are not expert in test interpretation. For the more technically minded, additional information on the scores and their derivations is available in the administrator's manual (Nelson Canada, 1984a).

Technical Aspects

The preparation of the Canadian Tests of Basic Skills was based on extensive research conducted over a period of decades at the University of Iowa and the University of Kansas in conjunction with the development of the tests from which the

Canadian battery is derived. Consequently, the authors rely mainly on the established technical merit of these prior instruments to support the view that the Canadian versions are technically sound. However, some information on the reliability and validity of the Canadian tests is available. Reliability coefficients for each subtest in all three batteries are given in the administrator's manual. These measures reflect internal consistency, that is, the consistency with which students in the norm group tended to respond on the items within each subtest. The values ranged from .64 to .93. These figures represent moderate to high levels of internal reliability for the subtests. Certainly, these are acceptable values for this type of test. The alternate forms for the Elementary Battery are essentially equivalent (i.e., will produce similar scores for the same individual in most cases). This was accomplished through a special equating study involving a large number of students. The information obtained was used to make statistical adjustments to the scoring system so that raw scores on the two forms are similar.

As the authors point out in the manuals, the validity of the tests for particular groups and purposes must, in large part, be determined by informed judgment. Administrators must decide on the basis of curriculum goals and other pertinent considerations to ascertain whether the tests provide valid and useful information for their purposes. Nonetheless, some evidence that suggests that the tests have a reasonable level of predictive validity is provided. Data made available to the publishers by the Cardston, Alberta, school district (Nelson Canada, 1984a) show moderate to high correlations (.53 to .76) between CTBS subtest scores and year-end course grades of ninth-grade students.

Critique

The Canadian Tests of Basic Skills constitute a unique instrument—a general abilities battery with Canadian content and Canadian norms based on a truly national sample. Like any similar instrument, this one has its shortcomings. The time involved in administration of the tests, particularly the Primary and Elementary Batteries, creates problems when materials are being shared widely. Teachers may find that only part of the testing has been completed when demands for the materials start coming in from others. These others, in turn, may be trying to schedule testing so that it takes place over the recommended four- or five-day period, but is completed before some deadline. The other problem with the tests is that all scores are grade-referenced and age norms are not provided. This limits the usefulness of the scores to some extent because there is considerable variation across the country in grade assignment and, indeed, many situations exist in which traditional grade placement is not used. However, in producing the tests, the publishers have not made the error of trying to start from scratch. They have adapted two existing batteries with sound reputations based on decades of research and revisions and reflecting advancements in test construction. Additionally, the test has constantly been updated, including metric versions and other revisions that were introduced to reflect curriculum changes as they occurred and norms that have been updated periodically to ensure their applicability to current student populations. (In fact, another standardization is currently in progress.) Overall, the strengths of the tests outweigh the deficiencies and make the Canadian Tests of Basic Skills a welcome contribution to educational assessment for Canadians.

References

Herrick, V. E. (1959). Canadian Tests of Basic Skills. In O. K. Buros (Ed.), *The fifth mental measurements yearbook* (pp. 30-34). Highland Park, NJ: The Gryphon Press.

Hieronymus, A. N., Hoover, H. D., & Lindquist, E. F. (1982). *Iowa Tests of Basic Skills.* Chicago: The Riverside Publishing Company.

King, E. M., Hieronymus, A. N., Lindquist, E. F., & Hoover, H. D. (1982a). *Canadian Tests of Basic Skills: Multilevel Edition teacher's guide.* Scarborough, Ontario: Nelson Canada.

King, E. M., Hieronymus, A. N., Lindquist, E. F., & Hoover, H. D. (1982b). *Canadian Tests of Basic Skills: Primary Battery teacher's guide.* Scarborough, Ontario: Nelson Canada.

King, E. M., & Scannell, D. P. (1982). *Canadian Tests of Basic Skills: High School Edition teacher's guide.* Scarborough, Ontario: Nelson Canada.

Morgan, G. A. V. (1959). Canadian Tests of Basic Skills. In O. K. Buros (Ed.), *The fifth mental measurements yearbook* (pp. 34-36). Highland Park, NJ: The Gryphon Press.

Nelson Canada. (1984a). *Canadian Tests of Basic Skills: Manual for administrators, supervisors, and counselors.* Scarborough, Ontario: Author.

Nelson Canada. (1984b). Identifying the gifted. *Measurement and Guidance News, 1,* 2-3.

Remmers, H. H. (1959). Canadian Tests of Basic Skills. In O. K. Buros (Ed.), *The fifth mental measurements yearbook* (pp. 36-37). Highland Park, NJ: The Gryphon Press.

Scannell, D. P., Haugh, O. M., Schild, A. H., & Ulmer, G. (1982). *Tests of Achievement and Proficiency.* Chicago: The Riverside Publishing Company.

Samuel D. Johnson, Jr., Ph.D.
Assistant Professor of Psychology and Education, Department of Social, Organizational and Counseling Psychology, Teachers College, Columbia University, New York, New York.

CAREER DEVELOPMENT INVENTORY

Donald E. Super, Albert S. Thompson, Richard H. Lindeman, Jean P. Jordaan, and Roger A. Myers. Palo Alto, California: Consulting Psychologists Press, Inc.

Introduction

The Career Development Inventory (CDI) is a psychometrically sound instrument designed to assess career development and vocational or career maturity. Career development, maturity, or adaptability has been defined as a multidimensional trait that is part emotional (affective) and part awareness and judgment (cognitive) and increases irregularly with age and experience. Each of the five CDI individual scales and three composite scales measures aspects of these components of career maturity.

The CDI has two standardized forms—a High School (S) Form (Grades 8-12) and a College and University (CU) Form, which are designed to help students make educational and vocational plans in terms appropriate to their educational developmental level. Each form contains 120 items and requires about 60 minutes to administer. Both result in five dimensions of career development scores, one affective factor, one cognitive factor, and one total career orientation score. In essence, the CDI provides clear indices of the qualities of students' readiness for vocational planning as an aid to counselors, teachers, and researchers of career or vocational development.

The current version of the CDI is the end product of over 30 years of vocational development research on the part of its authors, four of the most prominent counseling psychologists in the United States. In fact, its senior author, Donald Super, offered a revision of the operating definition of vocational guidance in 1951 that still represents the central foci of career guidance and counseling (Super, 1951). More than any other career psychologist, Super has been responsible for placing the study of career behavior in the context of human development (Crites, 1981). The CDI is primarily a core product of the career of Donald Super as a researcher and theorist of vocational development, which began with his first book, *The Dynamics of Vocational Adjustment* (Super, 1942) and culminated with the publication of the CDI in 1981.

Perhaps the most central endeavor to the development of the CDI has been the career pattern study (Super, Crites, Hummel, Moser, Overstreet, & Warnath, 1957), a longitudinal study of the ninth-grade males of Middletown, New York. The researchers involved in that study set the stage for the CDI by identifying and refining 20 possible indices of career maturity that were refined in a continuing research seminar between 1957 and 1960 when Super and Overstreet published *Vocational Maturity of Ninth Grade Boys,* which presented the results of the team's efforts in determining the construct validity of their indices. This research resulted in six measures that comprised the early model of vocational maturity derived from the career pattern study.

The career pattern study and several related efforts effectively framed the construct of career maturity or adaptability, demonstrated its multidimensional character, and explored ways of assessing it. The next move was to devise practical instruments for measuring these dimensions. In 1969, Myers, Minor, and Super decided to develop a multidimensional measure of vocational maturity as part of an effort to assess the impact of a computer-assisted educational and vocational exploration system for high-school students.

In the first of three studies of the Educational and Career Exploration System (ECES; Super, 1970), Thompson, Lindeman, Clack, and Bohn (1971) reported the development and implementation of a student questionnaire that offered five measures of "vocational developmental characteristics." All of these scales were based on the career pattern study and devised by Super and Jordaan, who were assisted by Forrest, Clark, Bohn, Myers, Lindeman, and Thompson. Their preliminary analysis yielded six vocational development scales: Planning Maturity, Decision-Making Principles, Amount of Decision-Making Information 1, Decision Making 2, Quality of Decision-Making Information, and Acceptance of Responsibility for Decisions (Thompson et al. cited in Super, 1970).

These scales demonstrated their psychometric and practical value in a series of field studies involving a 236-item Career Questionnaire based on the earlier work (Myers et al., 1972; Myers et al., 1975). Subsequently, an evaluation team of Teachers College professors, Bohn, Jordaan, Lindeman, Super, and Thompson, in collaboration with research assistants, Forrest and Heiner, produced the CDI Form I, a 193-item, multiple-choice instrument comprised of three scales or dimensions: Planning Orientation (Scale A), Resources for Exploration (Scale B), and Decision-Making and Information (Scale C). Super and Forrest (1972) report test-retest coefficients ranging from .71 to .85 over a time frame of two to four weeks (N = 48-65). The stability coefficients over six months ranged from .63 to .71, with no significant differences between the male and female tenth-graders who comprised the sample.

In response to large numbers of requests from evaluators of career education programs, the CDI High School Form I was made available, but because the developers were not satisfied with the instrument, it was not published. The authors clearly felt that they needed more complex measures of occupational information—one that would assess broad knowledge of the world of work and one that would measure knowledge of preferred occupation or occupation of greatest interest. Super, Thompson, and Jordaan had developed an occupational classification scheme for the DAT Career Planning Program (Super, 1973), an effort that eventually afforded a solution to this dilemma. They adapted that program's Career Planning Questionnaire to construct the Occupational Group Preference Form of the CDI.

Super (1974) proposed a developmental model that represented the first attempt at such a model for adolescence and went further with his efforts (Super, 1977; Super & Kidd, 1979; Super & Knasel, 1979) to suggest a model for adulthood. This work resulted in several additions to the career pattern study model. They were work values, work salience, autonomy, and reflection on experience.

Jordaan and Heyde (1979) recognized that measures that lacked conceptual and construct validity in the ninth grade might be valid in the twelfth grade and subsequently factor-analyzed them orthogonally and obliquely. They examined the students' similarities and differences in the ninth and twelfth grades, noting which measures showed increases as the Middletown boys progressed through school and determining correlates of those increases. At that state of the career pattern study they offered the following conclusion:

> Several important aspects of vocational maturity have emerged in a number of studies: awareness of and concern with present, impending and future decisions; awareness of factors to consider in making decisions, possession of various kinds of occupational information; and planning an approach to life. Less clear, either because their construct validity has not been satisfactorily demonstrated or because the data are sparse or contradictory, is the significance of acceptance of responsibility for choice, knowledge and use of resources for exploration, work experience, and wisdom of preference. (Jordaan & Heyde, 1979, pp. 170-171)

By 1979 several things seemed clear about the development of vocational maturity in adolescence and young adulthood. First, as age and experience increase, some traits that do not reflect maturity in the ninth grade appear to do so in the high-school and college years. Second, those traits that do reflect maturity in high school and college increase in their significance for aspects of career and occupational behavior in adulthood.

The CDI Form III emerged finally as an instrument with six scales derived from Form II, which existed only as an experimental version of the test. These six scales were named by Thompson, Lindeman, and Super (1978) and described by Super and Thompson (1979) as follows:

> Scale A: Extent of Planning (30 items)
> Scale B: Use and Evaluation of Resources (30 items)
> Scale C: Career Decision-Making (30 items)
> Scale D: Career Development Information (30 items)
> Scale E: World of Work Information (30 items)
> Scale F: Information about Preferred Occupation (41 items)

Scales A and B were virtually identical to those used in Form I. A great number of the items in Scales C and E came from the Career Decision-Making and Occupational Information Scale of Form I, but many more items were written, tested, and included. Scales D and F were predominantly new.

Form III was revised for college and university use. The principles for this adaptation consisted of content changes in identical items to make them apply to the college and university setting and to the types of occupations frequently entered by college graduates.

At this point in its development the CDI Form III was felt to be conceptually and psychometrically adequate but on a more practical basis was felt to be too long.

Field trials with the 191 multiple-choice item version indicated that Form III required two 40-minute periods for administration and with some populations of slower readers took part of a third school period. The CDI Form III was item-factor analyzed as part of refining and reducing it prior to standardization. This analysis clearly indicated that there was one cognitive factor (Scales C, D, and E) and one attitudinal factor (Scales A and B); because scale F had a lower correlation with the other scales, it was analyzed by itself as a cognitive factor. For an in-depth discussion of this process and other technical aspects of the CDI's development the reader is referred to Volume Two of the CDI manual (Thompson, Lindeman, Super, Jordaan, & Meyers, 1984).

In response to the factor structure and the high correlation between the Form III Career Development Information and World of Work Information Scales it was decided that the best way to shorten the CDI was to combine the best items from these two scales into a 20-item scale while also reducing the first three scales to 20-items each. Thus Part 1 of the final CDI form could be completed in one 40-minute period. Scale F (Scale PO in the final forms) was reduced by one item to retain broad coverage of occupational information and requires 20 minutes in the final form.

The CDI scale scores are standardized on a group that includes over 5,000 high-school students in the norming sample. The sample is not a representative national sample but does comprise groups that differ in relative characteristics, such as urban-suburban-rural, inner city, regional, gender, and grade. Eastern schools are more heavily represented in the standardization group than schools in the west, south, and midwest.

The CDI test materials are available in two forms: S (High School) and CU (College and University). Both forms consist of a test booklet and a color-coded answer sheet. The answer sheets are of the typical machine-scored type and should require no special instructions to complete either the identifying information or the test sections themselves. The Occupational Group Preference Section on the reverse side of the answer sheet might be confusing to some students and may require some explicit reminders to blacken only one preferred occupational group.

The CID may be administered in groups or to individuals and may be given in one or two sessions. The test is not timed and requires the examiner to be available only to clarify instructions and maintain a reasonable environment in the testing session. The CDI is intended for use with populations reading at the eighth-grade level and above. Its use with junior-high-school students might be hampered by the length of time required for some students to complete it or read it easily.

The CDI is administered in two parts, both of which are contained in the same reusable test booklet, and individual responses are recorded on a separate answer sheet.

Part One includes four subtests and requires about 40 minutes. They are as follows:

Career Planning (CP): Contains 20 items that ask examinees to indicate how much career planning they have engaged in, their degree of engagement in planning, and knowledge of the kind of work they would like to do.

Career Exploration (CE): Contains 20 items that ask examinees to indicate what sources they would consider obtaining career information from (10 items) and to rate usefulness of sources they may have already contacted for career information (10 items).

Decision Making (DM): Contains 20 brief sketches of individuals (identified only by initials to prevent sex-typing) who are confronting typical instances of career decisions. The scale contains a range of traditionally male and female careers and measures the ability to apply knowledge and insight to career planning.

World of Work Information (WW): Contains 20 items, ten of which assess knowledge of career development tasks and ten that test knowledge of the occupational structure of sample occupations in a range from semiskilled to professional.

Part Two consists of one subtest, Knowledge of the Preferred Occupational Group (PO), which requires 20 minutes to administer. It contains 40 items that pertain to all occupations categorized into 20 groups. Examinees are required to select a preferred occupational group on the back of the answer sheet and then answer the PO section with that group in mind. This section measures the results of in-depth exploration that should take place prior to choice of a training program or occupation.

The CDI profile is reported using eight scales, five based on each of the subtests (CP, CE, DM, WW, and PO) and three composite scales based on various combinations of the subtests. The composite scales are described as follows:

Career Development Attitudes (CDA): Combines CP and CE scales to create a more reliable but less specific index of attitude by collapsing planning with exploration.

Career Development Knowledge and Skills (CDK): Combines DM and WW scales to create a more reliable cognitive scale assessing knowledge of the world of work and career decision-making.

Career Orientation Total (COT): Combines CP, CE, DM, and WW. COT *approaches* a measure of career or vocational maturity but is not labeled so because it only measures four of the five aspects of career maturity.

CDI profiles are provided on each of the scales in the form of percentile ranks. Correctly completed answer sheets also allow the examiner to compile groups and receive local and group profiles for the CDI scales to be used in program development/planning. CDI reports also include frequency distributions for occupational group preferences for analysis of local needs. All data are returned in forms intended to facilitate the recommended uses of the CDI.

Practical Applictions/Uses

The CDI is clearly designed to be of primary use to counselors working with individual students or planning guidance programs for groups of students in a school population as well as counseling researchers interested in career development generally or within the context of counseling or psychoeducational interventions designed to have impact on the career maturity of its participants. Given this focus, it seems most likely that the CDI would find its widest use in educational settings where there is an extensive investment in vocational or career development. The CDI should have broad utility in high-school counseling and career education, college counseling centers, community counseling centers that conduct career counseling, some rehabilitation settings, and some funded career development programs. Its use in junior high schools will require careful attention to student reading abilities.

The test should be of benefit to most high-school counselors and useful to counselors working with junior-high-school students reading at or above eighth-grade level. Career counselors in private, college, and agency settings should also find the CDI a valuable resource in their individual counseling with young adults.

The authors (Thompson & Lindeman, 1981) recommend three main uses of the CDI: in counseling individuals to provide diagnostic data and predictors, in planning guidance programs as a survey instrument, and in evaluating programs and research to measure criteria or outcomes. In counseling individuals the CDI is more useful as a tool for assessing students' readiness for choice. Each of the CDI scales and profiles offers a basis of comparison and analysis of the career-related behavior and attitudes of individuals and local groups. Group profiles facilitate understanding and preparing for the career development needs of entire school classes and designated counseling groups.

The CDI is appropriate for subjects ranging from junior-high-school students reading at eighth-grade level and above (Form S) to college-aged adults (Form CU). Due to the relative recency of the test, there are no recommended clinical adaptations of the CDI.

Specific adaptations for research purposes include the use of specific item clusters as indices for growth in career maturity. Because the test is not timed, it seems appropriate for use with students who are blind and must be read the items. No information is available on braille or other forms of the test.

The CDI is administered individually or in groups. Testing should require no more than an appropriate test environment and oral review of the instructions. Experienced teachers, school counselors, school psychologists, and counseling psychologists should have no difficulty administering this test. The CDI can be administered in two sections over several periods or in one 65-minute period. The manuals accompanying the tests are clear and easily read. All instructions are comprehensive and easy to follow. The CDI is scored only by machine due to its measurement characteristics.

Interpretation of the CDI results is best conducted by trained counselors, school psychologists, or counseling psychologists because some comparison of statistical variables is required to determine significance in the interpretation. CDI interpretation is not especially difficult but should pose no problem for adequately school-trained personnel. As noted above, this task should be completed by counselors and psychologists with adequate background in testing, measurement, and statistics.

Interpretation of CDI results is based on comparison of the performance of the subjects tested with the percentile norms derived from the norming sample of over 5,000 students. Percentile norms have been constructed for Grades 9-12 and for male and female subgroups within each grade. A profile description of each subject's performance can be made from the percentile equivalents of the appropriate comparison group.

Any meaningful interpretation of the CDI results will require that it take place within the context of a counseling relationship that will afford the counselor the opportunity to clarify and expand on the test results. A trained counselor should be able to combine the CDI results with supplemental data from other sources and a knowledge of career development theory to provide a useful interpretation of any subject's performance as well as make recommendations for appropriate follow-up activities.

Technical Aspects

The CDI has been subjected to extensive studies of its reliability and validity. Data are reported on its internal consistency, standard error of measurement, stability, test-retest and item reliability, content validity, construct validity, and factor structure.

According to the CDI user's manual, measures of the internal consistency of the five CDI scales (Cronbach's alpha coefficients) and reliability estimates of the combined scales (alpha coefficients) suggest that the combined scales have clearly adequate reliability (range, .79-.88; median, .86) for use in counseling and analysis of group differences. The individual scales have a more mixed pattern. Scales CP, CE, and WW have median scale reliabilities of .89, .78, and .84, respectively, but the DM and PO Scales have median reliability estimates of .67 and .60. These coefficients suggest a degree of caution in making judgments about individuals based on DM and PO scores. The values are high enough to suggest their use for analyzing group differences. In both instances, scale reliability medians were lowered by subgroup values. For example, DM female median values are lower than those for males (.59 vs. .70). In the case of the PO Scale, values are much lower for Grade 9 than for Grade 12.

An alternative index of an instrument's reliability is its standard error of measurement (SE_M). A SE_M value may be understood as the approximate average error made when an instrument is used to measure an individual characteristic. The range of values for the SE_M of the CDI (from 6.5 to 13.3 across all measures, Grades 9-12) closely parallels the reliability estimates derived for the instrument (Thompson & Lindeman, 1981).

Additional support for the CDI's reliability has derived from short-term test-retest analyses conducted in two suburban high schools (Thompson et al., 1984). Test-retest correlations for Form S are consistently in the .70s and .80s for the combined scales CDA, CDK, and COT and for scale CP. The other scales had somewhat lower but still satisfactory correlations (.60s to .70s). Test-retest correlations were also analyzed for individual items in the five primary CDI scales (CP, CE, DM, WW, and PO). Means for items in scales CP and CE were in the low to middle .50s, whereas those for scales DM, WW, and PO were generally in the .30s. None of the items on any of the five scales evidenced a negative test-retest correlation, though in a few cases the minimum value in the range was below .10.

Form CU of the CDI has been subjected to similar test-retest reliability studies, with results roughly equivalent to those obtained with Form S. An additional index of the CDI's reliability as a comprehensive measure of vocational maturity is provided via a canonical correlation analysis of the data from the two high schools that were used in the test-retest analyses. This analysis was conducted to test the assumption that a linear combination of the five separate scales would provide a composite measure of vocational maturity that would also exhibit a high correlation between test administrations. This analysis resulted in statistical confirmation of such a correlation. The five canonical correlations were significant beyond the .001 level and ranged from .28 to .84. Form CU was subjected to a similar analysis that resulted in correlations ranging from .24 to .82. In the canonical correlation analyses of both CDI forms canonical coefficients suggested a stronger correlation among the affective variates than that among the cognitive variates (Thompson et al., 1984).

The content validity of the CDI would ideally rest on the judgment of experts that it is comprised of items that deal with those variables that comprise vocational maturity. The items that comprise the CDI are drawn from basic work conducted by Super and Jordaan (Super & Overstreet, 1960; Jordaan & Heyde, 1979) as part of the career pattern study. The CDI is based on a theoretical model that was derived from and tested in the career pattern study and several other independent investigations (Gribbons & Lohnes, 1968, 1982; Asis, 1971; Vriend, 1968; Wilstach, 1966). This model was tested by Crites (1973) and refined by Super (1974). An examination of the CDI items ought to confirm that they are consistent with the specifications of the model in order to establish their content validity. As noted earlier in this review, the model postulates five basic dimensions of vocational maturity (planfulness, exploration, decision making, information, and reality orientation). Each of the CDI scales addresses one of these dimensions, with the exception of reality orientation, which is based on a comparison of internal and external factors. The CDI does provide data that can create an opportunity to make some of the comparisons implicit in the notion of reality orientation. Given the history of its development and the close correspondence of the CDI items and scales with the components of the theoretical model of vocational maturity, it can be said to have content validity.

Construct validity is the degree to which an instrument measures a well-defined construct. Evidence of the CDI's construct validity is derived from the factor structure of the instrument and the subgroup differences exhibited among the population on which it was standardized. Because of the size of this sample (N = 5,039), tests of statistical significance offer little useful information pertaining to construct validity because small differences between means between males and females in a particular grade would be statistically significant beyond the .05 level. In this context a meaningful difference must exceed one-half of a standard deviation. Meaningful differences among subgroups in the CDI standardization sample did occur within grade, gender, and curricular subgroups.

Based on the developmental assumptions underlying the CDI, variation in performance on the CDI scales would be expected among groups in different grades. The scores of the students in the CDI standardization sample reflect a consistent pattern of grade-related differences that indicates an increase in vocational maturity as students progress from Grades 9 through 12. Even though all the differences among the means do not approach significance statistically, the pattern and consistency of the differences reported offer strong evidence of the construct validity of the CDI scales.

Career development theory would also predict a limited degree of gender difference in performance on the CDI based on the pattern of gender differences that exists among males and females in academic achievement. The performance of the female students in the CDI standardization sample was consistent with this prediction in that they did perform better on the cognitive scales of the CDI than did their male counterparts. This finding adds further support to the construct validity of the CDI.

Differences in academic program for the students in the standardization sample were examined as part of the construct validity study of the CDI. Even though career development theory would not predict specific differences in vocational maturity among students in varying academic programs, such differences should clearly occur based on the differential experiences afforded by preparation in one program versus another. As was anticipated, students in business and college preparatory programs tended to have higher scores than those in general and vocational programs, particularly on the cognitive scales. On the attitudinal scales, students in vocational technical programs tended to score higher, perhaps because they would be entering the work force sooner and had thus made more plans and conducted more exploration.

The CDI scales were also subjected to additional analyses focused on their construct validity. Discriminant analyses of scales CP, CE, DM, WW, and PO were conducted along with canonical correlation analyses of CP and CE versus DM, WW, and PO. According to the technical manual, the scales have also been correlated with other measures of career development and academic achievement, yielding findings supportive of the instrument's validity.

In summary, the CDI appears to be essentially sound psychometrically and seems to measure what it purports to measure. At issue in a larger sense is the notion of vocational maturity as a construct. The criteria used to operationalize maturity in this context seem to be well-reasoned, but at the same time several findings raise questions about the hypothetical construct itself. The authors acknowledge and this reviewer concurs that this construct might be more accurately labeled "career adaptability" or "readiness for vocational planning" due to the apparent impact of certain kinds of experiences that may or may not be equally available to developing adolescents and young adults. It is conceivable that judgments of vocational immaturity may still represent limited experience with the kinds of activities that impel individuals toward vocational choice.

The CDI has been used in several research efforts but still has a limited base of published research application. Several dissertation studies have included the instrument (or parts of it) among an array of career development measures. In general, there is continued support for its validity, stability, and reliability (Hilton, 1982; Jepsen & Prediger, 1981). On the issue of its validity Hilton (1982) notes: "Despite the efforts of many career theorists . . . , the relevant terms defy precise operational definition. Unlike needs and drives, we cannot experimentally arouse vocational maturity. We are left then with expert judgment, and piecing together evidence from a variety of studies" (p. 120).

Critique

The CDI is a well-researched instrument that measures the hypothetical construct of vocational maturity. It has the most thorough research base of any career development instrument. Tests of its reliability and validity continue to support its soundness psychometrically. Given the nature of the construct, the CDI shows great promise as a device for assessing the readiness for vocational planning among groups of students in educational settings. Using the instrument with individuals in counseling will require bringing other information to bear on the assessment of a student client's readiness for planning.

The authors' recommendations for using the test include diagnostic use with individuals, as a survey in program planning, and as a criterion measure in program evaluation and research. The instrument appears appropriate for this range of applications.

Scoring the CDI requires money, a factor that may restrict its use to college counseling centers and school districts that are well-funded or at least heavily committed to vocational assessment and career development. Researchers interested in these scales will also have to allow sufficient resources for scoring and reporting fees. On the other hand, the test reports are comprehensive and contain a wide range of useful information, including the capacity to generate locally relevant norms and occupational group preferences.

Several cautions seem appropriate in using the CDI. The first, mentioned above, relates to its use with individuals. Because the construct vocational maturity seems to rely so heavily on experience, individual assessment will have to include the examination of an array of situational factors. This seems evident in the capacity of some ethnic minority students to generate falsely immature ratings on the CDI. However, many of these shortcomings have less to do with the CDI itself than they do with the field of vocational/career development and our reliance on standardized methods of assessment. Given the status of this area of applied psychology, the CDI can be considered one of its premier products.

References

This list includes text citations as well as suggested additional reading.

Asis, E. G. (1971). *Vocational maturity of eighth grade Filipino boys: A comparative study.* Unpublished doctoral dissertation, University of California, Berkeley.

Crites, J. O. (1973). *Career Maturity Inventory.* Monterey, CA: CTB/McGraw-Hill.

Crites, J. O. (1981). *Career counseling.* New York: McGraw-Hill.

Gribbons, W. D., & Lohnes, P. R. (1968). *Emerging careers.* New York: Teachers College Press.

Gribbons, W. D., & Lohnes, P. R. (1982). *Careers in theory and experience.* Albany, NY: State University of New York Press.

Hilton, T. L. (1982). The Career Development Inventory. In J. T. Kapes & M. M. Mastie (Eds.), *A counselor's guide to vocational guidance instruments* (pp. 119-121). Washington, DC: National Vocational Guidance Association.

instrument analysis. *Journal of Vocational Behavior, 19,* 350-368.

Jordaan, J. P., & Heyde, M. B. (1979). *Vocational maturity in the high school years.* New York: Teachers College Press.

Kapes, J. T., & Mastie, M. M. (Eds.). (1982). *A counselor's guide to vocational guidance instruments.* Washington, DC: National Vocational Guidance Association.

Kuhlman-Harrison, J., & Neely, M. A. (1980). Discriminant validity of Career Development Inventory scales in grade 10 students. *Educational and Psychological Measurement, 40,* 475-478.

LoCasio, R. (1974). The vocational maturity of diverse groups. In D. E. Super (Ed.), *Measuring vocational maturity for counseling and evaluation* (pp. 151-163). Washington, DC: National Vocational Guidance Association.

Myers, R. A., Lindeman, R. H., Thompson, A. S., & Patrick, T. A. (1975). Effects of Educational and Career Exploration System on vocational maturity. *Journal of Vocational Behavior, 6,* 245-254.

Myers, R. A., Thompson, A. S., Lindeman, R. H., Super, D. E., Patrick, T. A., & Friel, T. A. (1972). *Educational and Career Exploration System: Report of a two-year trial.* New York: Teachers College, Columbia University.

Super, D. E. (1942). *The dynamics of vocational adjustment.* New York: Harper.

Super, D. E. (1951). Vocational adjustment: Implementing a self-concept. *Occupations, 30,* 88-92.

Super, D. E. (1953). A theory of vocational development. *American Psychologist, 8,* 185-190.

Super, D. E. (1955). The dimensions and measurement of vocational maturity. *Teachers College Record, 57,* 151-163.

Super, D. E. (Ed.). (1970). *Computer-assisted counseling.* New York: Teachers College Press.

Super, D. E. (1973). *Counselor's manual for Career Planning Program of the Differential Aptitude Tests.* Cleveland: The Psychological Corporation.

Super, D. E. (Ed.). (1974). *Measuring vocational maturity for counseling and evaluation.* Washington, DC: National Vocational Guidance Association.

Super, D. E. (1977). Vocational maturity in mid-career. *Vocational Guidance Quarterly, 25,* 294-302.

Super, D. E., (1980). A life-span, life-space approach to career development. *Journal of Vocational Behavior, 16,* 282-298.

Super, D. E., (1983). Assessment in career guidance: Toward truly developmental counseling. *Personnel and Guidance Journal, 61,* 555-561.

Super, D. E., Crites, J. O., Hummel, R. C., Moser, H. P., Overstreet, P. L., & Warnath, C. F. (1957). *Vocational development: A framework for research.* New York: Teachers College Press.

Super, D. E., & Forrest, D. J., (1972). *Career Development Inventory, Form I: Preliminary manual.* New York: Teachers College, Columbia University.

Super, D. E., & Kidd, J. M. (1979). Vocational maturity in adulthood: Toward turning a model into a measure. *Journal of Vocational Behavior, 14,* 255-270.

Super, D. E., & Knasel, E. G. (1979). *Development of a model, specifications, and sample items for measuring career adaptability (vocational maturity) in young blue-collar workers.* Cambridge, England: National Institute for Careers, Education, and Counselling.

Super, D. E., & Overstreet, P. L. (1960). *Vocational maturity of ninth-grade boys.* New York: Teachers College Press.

Super, D. E., & Thompson, A. S. (1979). A six-scale, two-factor measure of adolescent career or vocational maturity. *Vocational Guidance Quarterly, 28,* 6-15.

Thompson, A. S., & Lindeman, R. H. (1981). *Career Development Inventory, Volume 1: User's manual.* Palo Alto, CA: Consulting Psychologists Press, Inc.

Thompson, A. S., Lindeman, R. H., Clack, S., & Bohn, M. J., Jr. (1971). *Educational and Career Exploration System: Field trial and evaluation in Mont Clair High School.* New York: Teachers College, Columbia University.

Thompson, A. S., Lindeman, R. H., & Super, D. E. (1978). *Analysis of a six-scale measure of adolescent vocational maturity and comparison of its psychometric characteristics with those of a three-scale measurement* (A report for Occupational Career Analysis and Development Branch of the Canada Manpower Division). New York: Teachers College, Columbia University.

Thompson, A. S., Lindeman, R. H., Super, D. E., Jordaan, J. P., & Myers, R. A. (1984). *Career Development Inventory, Volume 2: Technical manual.* Palo Alto, CA: Consulting Psychologists Press, Inc.

Vriend, J. (1968). *Vocational maturity of seniors in two inner-city high schools.* Unpublished doctoral dissertation, Wayne State University, Detroit, Michigan.

Wilstach, I. M. (1966). *Vocational maturity of Mexican-American youth.* Unpublished doctoral dissertation, University of Southern California, Los Angeles.

Ronald R. Holden, Ph.D.
Assistant Professor of Psychology, Queen's University, Kingston, Canada.

CARLSON PSYCHOLOGICAL SURVEY

Kenneth A. Carlson. Port Huron, Michigan: Research Psychologists Press, Inc.

Introduction

The Carlson Psychological Survey (CPS; Carlson, 1982) is a structured self-report, 50-item, psychological test designed for the assessment and classification of criminal offenders, persons accused of crimes, and individuals who have been referred to the criminal justice or social welfare system. The CPS provides expedient, objective data that permit individual evaluation both in terms of specific content dimensions relevent to incarcerated persons and with reference to a multivariate typology of offenders.

Dr. Kenneth A. Carlson of the Minnesota Department of Corrections first published the CPS in 1981. The origins of the CPS, however, may be traced back to Carlson's earlier work and experiences at the University of Western Ontario (Carlson, 1972) and at the Guelph (Ontario) Correctional Centre (Carlson, 1981). The CPS was developed to fulfill a noticeable lack of appropriate, sensitive tests for criminal offenders. Futhermore, the CPS represents an inventory formulated explicitly to surmount difficulties associated with previous tests for offender populations.

Initially, the development of the CPS was based on the analysis of psychiatric, psychological, and social-work histories from case files in a correctional setting. From this survey, Carlson designated four primary content areas as being particularly relevant: Chemical Abuse, Thought Disturbance, Antisocial Tendencies, and Self-Depreciation. These constructs then served as the principal foci underlying the scales of the CPS. One additional scale, a validity index, was also deemed appropriate for use with offenders.

Following Carlson's identification of dimensions pertinent for a forensic population, actual test-item development began. This stage emphasized the production and revision of stimuli resulting in items that have five response options, require minimal reading ability, can be logically answered differently at different times, allow respondents to add additional comments, and permit each answer to be written on the same page beside its corresponding question. Based on administration of the CPS to 412 adult male first-incarcerates, convergent and discriminant item validity was fostered by revising and selecting items so that they correlated maximally with their own keyed scales and minimally with inappropriate nonkeyed scales.

Thus, the CPS assesses four content areas and has one validity check. In addition to these five scales, the CPS also allows test respondents to be classified, according to test profiles, into one of 18 different inmate classification types that have been empirically derived through a multivariate cluster analysis of a sample of first-time incarcerates. For normative data, the 1982 manual focuses on 412 Ontario, Canada, adult male first-incarcerates whose minimum sentence was 30 days and whose maximum sentence was two years definite and two years indefinite. Although analyses tend to suggest that national and racial differences are minimal, the CPS manual also supplies separate norms for 99 white males at a U.S. state prison, 43 black males at a U.S. state prison, 48 male inmates at a U.S. minimum-security federal facility, 311 Canadian female incarcerates, 25 probationers, 55 nonincarcerated psychiatric patients, and 27 inmate psychiatric patients.

The CPS is a 13-page, nonreusable booklet composed of 50 questions. Respondents' answers and comments are to be written in the actual question booklet. The test is appropriate for both adolescents and adults and requires only a fourth-grade level of reading ability. Testing may involve either group or individual assessment. Test responses are transferred to a scoring sheet on which scale scores may be calculated. Results may then be plotted on a normative profile sheet; however, only a profile sheet based on male norms (Carlson's 412 male first-incarcerates) is supplied in the test package.

Practical Applications/Uses

The CPS was designed to provide relevant, standardized, objective measures of deviant behavior in incarcerates. Professionals (e.g., psychiatrists, psychologists) may find the CPS useful as a screening device indicative of psychological status on psychopathological dimensions relevant to criminal offenders. Because of the explicit avoidance of many historical items, the CPS scales appear responsive to changes as a result of treatment, time, or other factors. Consequently, for rehabilitation specialists (e.g., social workers, therapists), the CPS may be beneficial for detecting therapeutic effects. Additionally, with the sensitivity of the CPS to change, researchers (e.g., program evaluators) may find the CPS scales to be useful outcome measures.

The CPS requires approximately 15 minutes to be completed. Test administration requires minimal instruction and any responsible individual should be capable of adequately supervising the testing procedure. Handscoring of the CPS is straightforward and readily learned, with an answer key provided on an accompanying scoring sheet. Ten minutes would seem to be the approximate amount of time needed for scoring the test. Because of the simplicity of the basic scoring system, no computerized scoring is offered.

Test interpretation is best carried out by a professional with training in testing and a knowledge of psychometrics. The CPS manual suggests that a master's degree in psychology or its equivalent should be the minimum qualification for supervising use of this instrument. Interpretation of the CPS is based on objective scores. Placing raw CPS scores on their profile sheet results in their immediate conversion to percentile ranks. These percentile ranks may then be interpreted on a scale-by-scale basis, using the content definitions supplied in the CPS manual. In addition to basic scale interpretation, the CPS provides an objective method of respondent classification based on profile configuration. That is, using the reference guide provided in the manual's appendix, individuals may be classified as belonging to one of 18 mutually exclusive offender types on the basis of their scale scores' combination. For each type, the manual then offers a detailed interpretation that includes a verifying profile figure, a descriptive summary, an index of probable institutional adjustment, predictions regarding outcome, and a case history example.

Technical Aspects

The reliability of the CPS scale scores has been examined with a variety of samples. The manual reports indices of reliability that include internal-consistency estimates (e.g., coefficient alphas) and measures of stability (e.g., test-retest reliability). Given that no alternate version of the test exists, no parallel-forms reliability is reported. For the content scales of the CPS, coefficient alphas range from .70 for the Chemical Abuse Scale to .82 for the Antisocial Tendencies Scale. Although the manual is somewhat unclear about this, these measures of internal consistency seem to have been based on the same data (i.e., 412 male first-incarcerates) that were used during test-item selection for the CPS. Consequently, these data may not represent cross-validated indices. Test-retest reliabilities are reported for two separate samples. Using a two-week interval with 32 inmates, content scale reliabilities range from .87 for Self Depreciation to .92 for Thought Disturbance. Using an eight-year interval with 20 recidivists, test-retest reliabilities of the content scales tend to be low, ranging from .10 for Antisocial Tendencies to .43 for Thought Disturbance. In fairness to the test, however, it must be noted that an eight-year interval introduces spurious influences attributable to confounds such as individual development and alterations in the law. Furthermore, this sample of recidivists is both small and nonrandom.

In general, this discussion has focused on the reliabilities of the CPS content scales. Carlson also reports reliabilities for the Validity Scale of the test. These are generally low; however, this fact is inconsequential for the test. This particular scale is not necessarily meant to be internally consistent or stable but rather to include heterogeneous content that is *very infrequently* endorsed (55% of inmates obtain the minimum score possible on this scale). Thus, with this intended restrictions of range of scores, reliabilities tend to be mathematically attenuated.

The validities of the CPS content scales, as described in the manual, have not been studied thoroughly. Two intepretable validity studies are outlined by Carlson (1982). One study demonstrates that the CPS is capable of discriminating among inmates charged with different types of offenses (i.e., personal offenses, property offenses, offenses against morals and decency, offenses against order and peace, or armed robbery). In this regard, the Antisocial Tendencies and Self Depreciation Scales are of particular significance. The other investigation of validity examines CPS scale changes as a result of eight weeks of transactional analysis therapy with inmates at a medium-security prison. Using a control-group design, results indicated the sensitivity of the Self Depreciation Scale to therapeutic intervention. The CPS manual cites two other "validity" studies; however, these appear to be flawed in their conceptualizations as validity studies (e.g., one treatment study has no control group).

Although sparse, other research is beginning to emerge concerning the psychometric properties of the CPS. These results appear to be most promising. Wright and Friesen (in press; Friesen, 1983) examined norms and reliabilities of the CPS scales. Using male adolescent offenders, data supported the appropriateness of the CPS manual norms. Furthermore, scale reliability estimates were also quite comparable to those cited in the manual. Wright and Friesen (in press) report content scale coefficient alphas ranging from .73 for the Self Depreciation Scale to .84 for the Chemical Abuse Scale. One-week test-retest reliabilities vary from .62 for the Self Depreciation Scale to .95 for the Chemical Abuse Scale. Friesen (1983) and Friesen and Wright (1984) have examined the factorial and predictive validity of the CPS with 350 male adolescent offenders. In general, results indicated support for the five-scale structure of the CPS. In particular, the items of the Chemical Abuse and Antisocial Tendencies Scale, demonstrated strong convergent and discriminant validity. From a predictive perspective, data attested to the utility of the Antisocial Tendencies Scale as an indicator of subsequent institutional adjustment measured by staff ratings and by officially recorded critical incidents (e.g., nonassaultive altercations with staff).

Critique

The development of a brief psychological status indicator appropriate for criminal offenders would serve to fill a noticeable void in forensic assessment. As a solution, the Carlson Psychological Survey represents a promising response, but is yet to be fully evaluated. On the negative side, some problems with the CPS exist. For example, the scope and choice of constructs would seem to be somewhat limited. Although Carlson's selection of scales is certainly clinically relevant, other constructs (e.g., impulsivity, locus of control) are also of theoretical importance. The assessment of additional areas of functioning, of course, would entail using a lengthier test instrument. An additional difficulty with the CPS concerns the manual. There are a number of annoying typographical errors, in places tabular data are excessively redundant, and very little explicit information exists on item-selection procedures for scale development (Lanyon, 1984). On the positive side, the CPS demonstrates a great deal of potential. Despite the obscurity of the manual, test-item development and selection seem to have cogently combined clinical considerations and statistial rigor. Psychometrically, the internal structure of the test appears sound. Practically, the instrument has been formatted to the requirements of a forensic population. In terms of validity, although preliminary results are encouraging, scant research exists. Thus, the CPS represents a hopeful inventory of relatively unknown clinical utility. As a research tool, it would appear to have a greal deal of merit; however, as a clinical instrument, additional applied studies are required to confirm the usefulness of the CPS.

References

Carlson, K. A. (1972). Classes of adult offenders: A multivariate approach. *Journal of Abnormal Psychology, 79,* 84-93.

Carlson, K. A. (1981). A modern personality test for offenders: The Carlson Psychological Survey. *Criminal Justice and Behavior, 8,* 185-200.

Carlson, K. A. (1982). *Carlson Psychological Survey Manual.* Port Huron, MI: Research Psychologists Press.

Friesen, W. J. (1983). *Use of the Carlson Psychological Survey with adolescents: Basic descriptive properties and validity of the Antisocial Tendencies Scale.* Unpublished master's thesis, Simon Fraser University, Burnaby, British Columbia, Canada.

Friesen, W. J., & Wright, P. G. (1984). *The validity of the Carlson Psychological Survey with adolescents.* Unpublished manuscript.

Lanyon, R. I. (1984). Personality assessment. *Annual Review of Psychology, 35,* 667-701.

Wright, P. G., & Friesen, W. J. (in press). The Carlson Psychological Survey with adolescents: Norms and scale reliabilities. *Canadian Journal of Behavioural Science.*

Judith L. Whatley, Ph.D.
Post-Doctoral Fellow, Counseling Service and Department of Psychiatry, University of Texas Health Science Center at San Antonio, San Antonio, Texas.

CATTELL INFANT INTELLIGENCE SCALE

Psyche Cattell. Cleveland, Ohio: The Psychological Corporation.

Introduction

The Cattell Infant Intelligence Scale (Cattell, 1960) was developed with the intention of being a standardized assessment of mental ability for children aged 2-30 months. Underlying the test is a view of intelligence as being maturationally and genetically controlled. The Cattell proposes to focus on mental development and *not* on motor development, to be standardized, be objective in scoring, appeal to young children, and provide numerical rather than simply descriptive assessments of mental ability.

The Infant Intelligence Scale was developed by Psyche Cattell in the United States beginning in the 1930s and was first published in 1940. The 1960 revision is essentially a reprinting with corrections for typographical errors, but with no substantive changes. The test was developed with the Gesell tests (Gesell, 1925) as a starting point, but items were converted, omitted, added, and arranged in an age scale, with the goal being to create a test compatible with the Stanford-Binet, Form L. This was done to provide a downward extension of that test of mental ability and to consequently extend the age range covered by an assessment instrument or set of compatible instruments. Goals that Cattell attempted to achieve with the development of this new test included 1) objective procedures in administration and scoring of test items, 2) exclusion of items markedly influenced by training, 3) exclusion of items that appear related more to motor control than mental development, 4) inclusion of scaling techniques to go beyond mere descriptive ratings of mental ability, 5) extension of age range beyond that covered by tests being used in the 1930s and distribution of test items more evenly across that age range, and 6) achievement of standardized procedures. These goals reflect an appreciation of the psychometric contribution to test development, as well as Cattell's assumptions about factors thought to control "intelligence," that is, genetic or maturational rather than experiential influences.

The Cattell was developed and tested on a standardization sample of 1,346 examinations made on 274 children enrolled in the Normal Child Series study at the Center for Research in Child Health and Development at the Harvard School of Public Health. Data were collected at ages 3, 6, 9, 12, 18, 24, 30, and 36 months. Items added during the later phases of the test's development were administered to fewer, although an unspecified number, children than were items included at the beginning of the research. Subjects for the Normal Child Series were selected during the prenatal period from pregnant women attending the Boston Lying-in Hospital clinics on the basis of evidence indicating the likelihood of a normal delivery of a normal child. Other criteria for inclusion in the study were that the child's father have permanent employment and be likely to remain in residence in the area throughout the course of the study; that at least three grandparents be of Northern European stock, thus excluding minority participation; and that the mother show ability and willingness to cooperate with the study. Use of this population resulted in the majority of the participants coming from the lower-middle class, with upper-most and lower-most economic-level participants being largely excluded from the study. Socially and mentally inadequate parents' children were also excluded. As of 1937, 37 cases were lost due to unsatisfactory cooperation and 34 were dropped from the data base due to moving, death, or some other apparently nonstudy-related reason. Thus, the study was subject to an attrition rate of approximately 25%.

The sample, clearly not representative of the United States population geographically, socioeconomically, or ethnically, is one of the weakest aspects of the Cattell's development. Moreover, that original sample is by now significantly dated. Caution is consequently warranted concerning the confidence with which one can generally employ its use, even with a "normal" group of children. No known standardized versions of the Cattell exist for use with groups of children with significant visual, auditory, or major physical handicaps, or with children from other language or cultural groups. It has also been used with what are described as minor modifications with children with multiple handicaps, such as blindness and deafness (DuBose, 1977); with children with cerebral palsy (Banham, 1972); and in the diagnosis of developmental delays (Erikson, 1968).

Test materials for the Cattell consist of a set of standardized, simple, manipular objects, visual and auditory stimuli that appeal to young children (ring, teaspoons, ball, rattle, mirror, key, sugar pellets, formboard, paper, bell, pencil, jointed doll, beads, toy dog, pegboard with pegs, cubes, picture cards, bottle), the Stanford-Binet Picture Vocabulary, and the Stanford-Binet formboard. These standardized materials are available through The Psychological Corporation.

The test consists of 95 items: five for each month period from 2-12 months, five for each two-month period during the second year of life, and five for each of the two quartiles of the first half of the third year of life. At each of these age periods, one or two alternate items, which are described as acceptable but somewhat less satisfactory than the standard items, are also included for use as needed. All 95 items are not administered to a given child at a given test administration or age level; only the items necessary to establish basal and ceiling levels are presented in order to obtain a child's mental age score.

Infants aged 2-30 months are the age group for whom this test is designed. Cattell suggests that, although the test was developed and standardized for use with children at particular age points within the above range (e.g., 3, 6, 9, 12, 18, 24, and 30 months), it can be used with only slightly less accuracy with children between those age ranges. Placement of test items for the ages between the designated intervals was done less rigorously and consequently may involve greater measurement error and lower reliability.

Similar to the Stanford-Binet, items on the Cattell are grouped by age level rather than by content, and no individual subtest scores are computed. The resultant score is a single score in the form of a mental age. A ratio IQ is also obtainable.

Practical Applications/Uses

The Cattell serves as one of several test instruments that might be employed to assess infants and young children's mental development. It requires a trained examiner, time (minimally a half hour), and space for administration. Due to these requirements for administration, it is not apt to be of frequent use as a general or quick screening tool. It is more apt to be used when a more detailed assessment of mental development is required (e.g., when there is some question about a child's development or an "at risk" group is being evaluated). Compared to the psychometrically more sophisticated Bayley Scales of Infant Development (Bayley, 1969), it is somewhat quicker to administer and may serve successfully as an alternate to that examination under some conditions. In a study of young handicapped children, Erikson, Johnson, and Campbell (1970) report a high positive correlation ($r = 0.97$) between scores on the Cattell and scores on the Bayley. Scores on the Cattell tended to be slightly higher than on the Bayley, but these authors felt that the two tests might be considered interchangeable for use with young children referred for diagnosis of developmental problems.

One of Cattell's interests was to develop an instrument compatible with the Stanford-Binet that could be used to extend the testable age range downward. Longitudinal studies would clearly benefit from the availability of such an instrument. The Cattell achieves that aim in format and scoring procedure. The extent to which it fulfills that goal conceptually is less clear, given the low correlations obtained when comparing longitudinally obtained data on the two tests. Scores obtained after the second year of life and close in time to one another compare more favorably.

The Cattell is limited to individual administration. Examiners should be individuals who are sensitive to and comfortable with young children, as well as experienced in psychometric procedures. Their role is an active one and is an integral part of test procedure. Consequently, administration is most likely to be carried out by a psychologist or other child development specialist.

The examiner's role is to present test materials to the child and to score the child's response to each test item and the spontaneous responses related to test criteria. The examiner, therefore, must be alert to the child's behavior and note performances by the child that are relevant to items not necessarily being administered at the moment. Such ad lib performances are scorable. Test items can be administered in any order, and a good examiner will be attuned to the child's energy and interest level and will administer items in an order taking these factors into account. It is especially important that the individual who administers the Cattell be sensitive to and comfortable with young children, as it is also the task of the examiner to motivate children and elicit their cooperation and participation. Specific other tasks that the examiner must carry out include recording verbatim the verbal responses of the child on particular items, judging that items are not passed by chance but reflect intentional or purposive behavior on the part of the child, and differentiating refusal to perform from lack of ability.

The test is administered with the child either lying on or seated at a table. Some items up to and including five-month items are administered with the child lying down, whereas all items from six months onward are presented with the child seated, either in a caregiver's lap or on a chair. The presence of a mother or another attendant is also part of the general administration procedure, although that adult may not directly help the child perform items. Cattell points out that it is often helpful to inform the mother or caregiver that some things will be presented to the child that are expected to be beyond the child's current developmental level.

Cattell cautions against testing young children when they are tired, sick, or in a negative mood. Such features can easily affect the child's willingness or motivation to perform, resulting in an invalid assessment.

The setting in which the testing is administered should be free from distracting noises and sights, and materials not being used at a given time should be kept out of the child's sight. On the other hand, the setting should not be so ''nondistracting'' as to be sterile and uncomfortable.

Testing generally begins with items thought to be within a child's ability. A basal level is established by testing downward until all five items of a given age level have been passed. Testing continues upward, although not necessarily in order, until all five items of a level are failed.

A specific aim of Cattell's in developing this test was to provide objective scoring criteria for each test item. The test manual (Cattell, 1940) specifies in objective terms the procedure for administering each item and objective criteria for scoring on a pass/fail basis. Illustrative photographs also appear in the manual. Each item's score is recorded on a standardized record form that briefly lists a short descriptor and a space for noting whether the item was passed or not. The last part of the record form provides space for continuation of a child's score on Stanford-Binet items when the two tests are used together. This extension is provided through the fourth year of life.

The test form also contains four five-point scales on which the examiner can rate the child's test behavior in terms of willingness, self-confidence, social confidence, and attention. These ratings do not figure directly into the scoring, but provide clinical information that may be helpful in interpreting test performance.

The time required to learn scoring of the examination will vary considerably, depending on the examiner's psychometric experience and experience and knowledge regarding young children's behavior. Although the objective, behavioral criteria for a pass are generally clearly specified in the test manual, the establishment of reliable administration and scoring by comparison with an experienced examiner would be an advantage. Generally, once the scoring is mastered, it should be possible to score the examination as it is administered, with only occasional reference to the scoring manual. This is also necessary because the items to be administered will be determined by efficiently establishing basal and ceiling levels. Administering unnecessary items may occupy time that could affect the ability to complete satisfactory administration of the test.

Interpreting the obtained score requires use of both the objective score and clinical judgment. The objective score in the form of a mental age indicates the age level at which the child is performing as determined by norms established by the standardization sample. Other statistical properties of the test, such as means and standard deviations, provide other important information for test interpretation. One of the main tasks of the interpreter is to explain the extent to which the test score indicates that mental development is delayed, advanced, or consistent with expected rates. Other questions of interpretation focus on the predictability of future intellectual functioning and consideration of possible intervention. The interpreter's clinical judgment is called into play in making such decisions, as well as decisions about the extent to which the test reflects a representative sample of the child's ability (i.e., are individual item scores due to refusal, lack of ability, lack of motivation, attentional problems, or even luck). As the Cattell produces only an overall score, analysis or comment on subcomponent abilities must rely on clinical judgment and should be offered cautiously. Furthermore, interpreting scores for children at the youngest end of the scale must rely heavily on clinical judgment given the low levels of test reliability for that portion of the test. As with administration and scoring, interpretation requires training in child development, as well as psychometrics, and is most likely carried out by a psychologist or other child development expert.

Technical Aspects

Reliability studies were conducted on the standardization sample, and data are reported in the manual. Predictive validity data, comparing the Cattell scores with Stanford-Binet, Form L, scores, are also reported for that same sample. At three months, the reliability estimate obtained by the split-half method and corrected by the Spearman-Brown formula was 0.56. Correlating those scores obtained at three months with scores at 36 months on Form L of the Stanford-Binet resulted in a value of only 0.10. Thus, the scores at age three months show neither statistical reliability or predictive validity. For 6, 9, and 12 months the split-half reliability coefficients were .88, .86, and .89, respectively, and correlations with the Stanford-Binet at 36 months were .34, .18, and .56, respectively. Although reliability estimates reach acceptable levels, the predictive validity scores do not. At ages 18, 24, and 30 months the reliability coefficients were .90, .85, and .71, respectively, with correlations with the Stanford-Binet for 36 months falling at .67, .71, and .83, respectively. Again, acceptable reliability estimates are achieved with the exception of the 30-month score. The predictive validity score at 24, and possibly at 18 months, appears acceptable, but the score at 30 months must be interpreted cautiously, given the low level of reliability at that age.

Some additional reliability and validity studies have been reported, usually conducted with selected samples, and generally the results have been similar to those presented by Cattell. Escalona (1950) and Gallagher (1953) each report research demonstrating the effects of nontest factors detracting from a child's optimal performance that can measurably decrease test-retest reliability. Escalona reports such data for a sample of adoptive children for whom she had judges' subjective appraisals concerning maximal performance on the Cattell; Gallagher also studied adopted infants on whom similar ratings had been made.

Use of the Cattell as a downward extension of the Stanford-Binet is not strongly supported, given the obtained correlations between the two instruments.

Although the two tests appear compatible in format and scoring, they cannot be empirically defended as being conceptually the same. Research has fairly consistently failed to find that tests of infant mental performance during the first year and one-half of life predict subsequent IQ (McCall, Hogarty, & Hurlburt, 1972; Escalona & Moriarity, 1961). This failure to predict may be due to differences in what is "intelligence" or is measurable as "intelligence" in infancy compared to later in life, due to the changeable nature of intelligence or to the unreliability of test instruments. Nonetheless, despite one's particular position in this debate, it cannot be concluded that the Cattell and the Stanford-Binet serve as extensions of one another, due to the low correlations between the two in most comparisons.

Escalona and Moriarity (1961) report results from a longitudinal study comparing the Cattell and Gesell scales with the Weschler Intelligence Scale for Children (WISC). Infants were assessed at ages one to eight months on both infant scales, whereas the WISC was employed between seven and eight and one-half years. Of interest here is the resulting correlation between the Cattell and the WISC, which was 0.05, showing virtually no predictability. Clinical appraisal data collected during infancy were considered of greater predictive ability than performance on either infant scale.

Finally, Erickson (1968) evaluated the predictive validity of the Cattell for young mentally retarded children in an effort to explore the possibility that greater predictability might be found in the case of children with subnormal ability. Her results were based on a study of children referred for diagnosis of developmental problems. IQs were measured as early as three months of age and were repeated annually through approximately age 72 months. Longitudinal comparisons of the children's IQ scores resulted in correlations ranging from .63 to .94. As with findings from other research, correlations were greater with increasing age of children at the time of initial examination, and IQs obtained during the first two years of life were less stable than those obtained later. Erikson argues that the Cattell can be used to predict subsequent performance when used with children below average in intellect, but most usefully only after the first two years of life.

Critique

The Cattell Infant Intelligence Scale is a standardized assessment instrument for the measurement of mental ability for children aged 2-30 months. It is based on the assumption that intelligence is largely maturationally and genetically controlled. Cattell developed this test with certain goals in mind, some of which were achieved, whereas others were not fully realized. Procedures for administration and scoring test items are reasonably objective and clearly specified. Cattell's goal of going beyond descriptive ratings of mental ability to the use of scaling techniques has been implemented with the use of objectively scored items with point values. However, the absence of item analyses beyond percentages passed by age, especially for items falling between major age points, somewhat reduces the reliability of the test, as well as its discrimination function. In general, test-retest reliability was found to be at acceptable levels, with the exception of the youngest ages where the examiner must rely more heavily on clinical judgment in interpreting the meaning of the individual's performance.

Cattell's attempt to provide a downward extension of the Stanford-Binet may be considered to have met some success in terms of format and scoring. There seems to be adequate predictive ability for children beyond the second year of life; for children younger than this, the predictive validity of the Cattell, based on correlations with the Stanford-Binet at later ages, fails to obtain empirical support for conceptual compatibility between the two tests. Use of the Cattell as a downward extension in these cases does not appear to be warranted and should be done cautiously.

Cattell's assumptions about intelligence as being maturationally or genetically controlled led to the exclusion of a motor development scale and to the removal of items thought to be strongly related to motor control and/or home training. However, some items that remain cannot be said to be completely free of these factors. For example, a number of items early in the scale, such as ''lifts head'' and ''head erect and steady,'' clearly involve motor ability. The absence of a separate motor scale may in some cases be a shortcoming of this test.

The greatest shortcoming of the Cattell, however, is its unrepresentative and, by now, dated standardization sample. The restricted sample, which is neither socioeconomically, ethnically, nor geographically representative of the United States population, severely restricts the confidence with which one can usefully apply the scale and interpret obtained results.

Cattell's ambitious effort in developing this test has contributed and will probably continue to contribute to our understanding of intellectual development in young children, as well as our efforts to improve our ability to measure intellectual functioning. The Cattell serves as an objective, standardized instrument that allows more objective testing of young children's functioning and facilitates clinical judgments in this area.

References

Banham, K. M. (1972). Progress in mental development of retarded cerebral palsied infants. *Exceptional Children, 39,* 240.

Bayley, N. (1969). *Bayley Scales of Infant Development.* Cleveland: The Psychological Corporation.

Cattell, P. (1940). *The measurement of intelligence of infants and young children.* Cleveland: The Psychological Corporation.

Cattell, P. (1960). *Cattell Infant Intelligence Scale.* Cleveland: The Psychological Corporation.

DuBose, R. F. (1977). Predictive value of infant intelligence scales with multiply handicapped children. *American Journal of Mental Deficiency, 81,* 388-390.

Erickson, M. T. (1968). The predictive validity of the Cattell Infant Intelligence Scale for young mentally retarded children. *American Journal of Mental Deficiency. 72,* 728-733.

Erickson, M. T., Johnson, N. M., & Campbell, F. A. (1970). Relationships among scores on infant tests for children with developmental problems. *American Journal of Mental Deficiency, 75,* 102-104.

Escalona, S. (1950). The use of infant tests for predictive purposes. *Bulletin of the Menninger Clinic, 14,* 117-128.

Escalona, S., & Moriarity, A. (1961). Prediction of schoolage intelligence from infant tests. *Child Development, 32,* 497-605.

Gallagher, J. J. (1953). Clinical judgment and the Cattell Infant Intelligence Scale. *Journal of Consulting Psychology, 17,* 303-305.

Gesell, A. (1925). *The mental growth of the preschool child.* New York: Macmillan.

McCall, R. B., Hogarty, P. S., & Hurlburt, N. (1972). Transitions in infant sensorimotor development and the prediction of childhood I.Q. *American Psychologist, 27,* 728-748.

Thomas S. Serwatka, Ph.D.
Associate Professor and Director of Special Education, College of Education and Human Services, University of North Florida, Jacksonville, Florida.

CENTRAL INSTITUTE FOR THE DEAF PRESCHOOL PERFORMANCE SCALE

Ann E. Geers and Helen S. Lane. Chicago, Illinois: Stoelting Company.

Introduction

The Central Institute for the Deaf (CID) Preschool Performance Scale is an intelligence test designed to be used with populations including hearing- and language-impaired children. The scale is an individually administered nonverbal battery that consists of six subtests. It has been normed on children ranging in age from two years to five years, five months. The scale is a revision of the Randall's Island Performance Series (Poull, 1931).

The authors of this version of the test, Dr. Ann Geers and Dr. Helen Lane, have a variety of experiences in the areas of assessing language- and hearing-impaired students. Geers, who received her doctorate from Washington University, is director of clinical services at Central Institute for the Deaf (CID). She has coauthored the Grammatical Analysis of Elicited Language test series (Moog, Kozak, & Geers, 1983, 1985a, 1985b), developed at CID. Lane, principal emeritus at CID, has been publishing in the field of assessing hearing- and language-impaired students for over 50 years. Her doctorate was awarded by Ohio State University.

The original version of this scale, Randall's Island Performance Series, was designed to be used as an intelligence test for mentally retarded children at Randall's Island, an institution run by New York City. Because of its nonverbal nature the series was adopted for use at CID in 1932. At CID the series was modified slightly, including the substitution of nonverbal instructions for the verbal instructions given in the original series. With these modifications, the test was used at CID in assessing both hearing- and language-impaired children.

In 1965, a computer record-keeping system was initiated at CID, thus allowing all test results from the series to be stored for later access. The individuals whose scores were accumulated from 1965-1980 using this system became the standardization population used in developing the CID Preschool Performance Scale in its present form.

In revising the Randall's Island Performance Series to develop the CID Preschool Performance Scale, most of the original test items were retained and regrouped into the present six subtests. Scoring procedures were also changed, allowing for scaled scores and a deviation IQ, and the test was published in its present form in 1984.

Standardization of the CID Preschool Performance Scale was based on the scores derived from 978 hearing-impaired and normal-hearing children aged 2-5½ years who were seen at CID in its clinics over a 15-year period and were tested using this instrument. The children are reported to "represent a fairly normal distribution of developmentally delayed, average and gifted children" (Geers & Lane, 1984, pp. 1-2). Most of the children are also reported to have exhibited some language delay. Because comparisons of scores for hearing-impaired and non-hearing-impaired children and for male and female children yielded no evidence of significant differences between and among groups, all of the children were combined in the normative data.

The six subtests included in the CID Preschool Performance Scale are described as follows:

Manual Planning: requires the child to perform tasks such as building a block tower, building block pyramids, and assembling a square and cross when given a template and masonite shapes that fit the template;

Manual Dexterity: requires the child to button different numbers of buttons and buttonholes and to place pegs correctly in wooden boards;

Form Perception: requires the child to match cards based on the shapes of the figures pictured on the cards and to correctly place ten cutout shapes into a form board;

Perceptual/Motor Skills: in the first part the child is required to tap four blocks in the pattern just demonstrated by the examiner (increasingly difficult patterns are used), in the second part the child is shown drawings of shapes and required to copy them, and in the third part the child folds paper into different shapes as demonstrated by the examiner.

Preschool Skills: requires the child to sort colors and count sticks.

Part/Whole Relations: requires the child to first assemble a wooden manikin into the shape of a man, then put together a series of increasingly more difficult wooden puzzles.

The instruction manual, a number of summary sheets for scoring an individual child's performance, and all of the equipment needed for each item in the test (with the exception of the time clock) are provided in the test kit. The pieces of equipment provided in the kit are well-constructed and durable, which becomes a major consideration when repeated use with large numbers of preschoolers is anticipated.

The summary sheet has a place for scoring the child's profile on each of the subtests, using scales scores provided in the manual.

Practical Applications/Uses

The CID Preschool Performance Scale is designed to be used by a skilled examiner to determine a preschool child's IQ score and provide a clinical picture of the child's performance. The nonverbal directions and responses make the scale usable with children who have difficulty with verbal tests by reason of language or hearing impairments. The scale is administered best by psychologists or educational diagnosticians familiar with working with preschool children who are either language- or hearing-impaired.

The manual stresses the need for administering this scale in a relaxed play-like atmosphere, but this, of course, is true of almost all test situations where preschool children are involved. Use of this scale requires that the examiner either has established rapport with the child earlier or is able to do so relatively quickly.

In administering the test the examiner presents the instructions for all of the items by using nonverbal behaviors. Typically, modeling or demonstration of the required performance is used in giving these instructions. Optional verbal instructions are given in the manual; however, these are to accompany, not replace, the nonverbal instructions. The manual contains clearly written descriptions of how each item is to be presented to the child and the sequence of presentation.

In administering many of the items the examiner is required to time the child's performance because the child's score on these items is based on the length of time that it takes the child to complete the task. Other test items are scored by determining the level of complexity at which the child was able to complete the task correctly.

The examiner records the child's level of performance on each item on the summary sheet as the test is being administered. Use of this sheet requires minimal orientation and practice.

On completion of the test, the examiner converts the raw scores received on each subtest into a scaled score. These scaled scores are then totaled, and this number is used to derive the child's IQ. Easily used charts for conversion of raw scores into scaled scores and then conversion of the total of these scaled scores into IQ scores are given in the manual. Using the scaled scores, the examiner plots the child's performance on each of the subtests on the summary sheet. This profile is meant to give the examiner a clinical picture of the child's performance, but no guidance is given in the manual on how to interpret this profile.

Technical Aspects

According to the manual, the test-retest reliability coefficient for the CID Preschool Performance Scale is .71. This coefficient is based on test-retest scores for 92 children whose retest intervals ranged from four months to three years, five months. In comparison to other similar scales this test-retest reliability should be considered good (Weiner, 1971). No other measures of reliability are reported by the authors or appear in the literature at this time.

Validity data reported by the authors in the manual include a correlation between scores for 112 children on both the CID Preschool Performance Scale and on the Wechsler Intelligence Scale for Children-Revised (WISC-R). This correlation is given as .485. The time intervals between administration of the CID Preschool Performance Scale and the WISC-R ranged from one year, five months to ten years, eight months. Thus, this correlation can be viewed as one demonstrating predictive validity. Recognizing the low predictive validity of most preschool intelligence scales, this scale seems to fair well in comparison to others (Aiken, 1985).

No data are given on concurrent validity between the performance of children on the CID Preschool Performance Scale and their performance on similar instruments. Data are given showing the correlations between chronological age and scores on each of the six subtests. These correlations range from .52 and .64, which seems reasonable for the standardization population.

Studies by other researchers using the CID Preschool Performance Scale have not been found in the literature, but the recent publication of the scale makes this understandable.

Critique

The recentness of publication and availability at the time of this review precludes the CID Preschool Performance Scale from having become an established scale for use with language- and hearing-impaired preschool children. However, the reported successful use of this instrument at CID since 1932 and the improvements made in the instrument in its present published form make this a test that psychologists and diagnosticians will want to consider when working with preschool children who are language or hearing impaired.

Although the procedures used for initial standardization and determination of validity and reliability are certainly adequate for initial publication, further study in these areas would help professionals who are considering adoption of the scale. Future studies in these areas, including concurrent validity, ought to incorporate the use of the scale with nonclinical populations. Checking the normative data against the data collected on a nonclinical population would also prove helpful.

The authors of the CID Preschool Performance Scale state that it can be used "to obtain a broad clinical picture of the child's ability as well as a numerical rating" (Geers & Lane, 1984, p. 1). It is assumed that this means that this broad clinical picture can be found by examining the child's performance profile showing his or her standard scores on the six subtests of the scale. However, examiners using this scale need to be cautioned against using this profile in any diagnostic fashion because of the limited number of items per subtest and their limited scope. Although the total sampling of behaviors on the entire scale appears sufficient to make some judgments concerning the child's overall performance level, judgments concerning particular types of performance need to be based on larger samplings of behavior in each particular area than are provided by this instrument.

The materials provided in the CID Preschool Performance Scale kit are generally durable and, with the exception of the puzzles used in the sixth subtest, attractive. In addition to not being particularly attractive, the pictures in these puzzles are dated and represent stereotypic white, middle-class scenes. In future editions of the scale, changes in these pictures need to be made by the authors or publisher.

Overall, the CID Preschool Performance Scale is a promising addition to tests now available for use with language- and hearing-impaired preschool children, for whom this scale may prove to be a benchmark in assessment. This instrument could be a valuable tool for professionals who work with either or both of these populations.

References

Aiken, L. R. (1985). *Psychological testing and assessment* (5th ed.). Boston: Allyn and Bacon, Inc.

Geers, A. E., & Lane, H. S. (1984). *Central Institute for the Deaf Preschool Performance Scale.* Chicago: Stoelting Company.

Moog, J. S., Kozak, V. J., & Geers, A. E. (1983). *Grammatical Analysis of Elicited Language:P.* St. Louis: Central Institute for the Deaf.

Moog, J. S., Kozak, V. J., & Geers, A. E. (1985a). *Grammatical Analysis of Elicited Language:S.* St. Louis: Central Institute for the Deaf.

Moog, J. S., Kozak, V. J., & Geers, A. E. (1985b). *Grammatical Analysis of Elicited Language:C.* St. Louis: Central Institute for the Deaf.

Poull, L. E. (1931). *Randall's Island Performance Series.* New York: Columbia University Press.

Weiner, P. A. (1971). Stability and validity of two measures of intelligence used with children whose language development is delayed. *Journal of Speech and Hearing Research, 14,* 252-261.

Leonard S. Milling, Ph.D.
Assistant Professor of Psychology, Department of Psychiatry, The Medical College of Ohio, Toledo, Ohio.

C. Eugene Walker, Ph.D.
Professor and Director of Pediatric Psychology, The University of Oklahoma Health Sciences Center, Oklahoma City, Oklahoma.

CHILDREN'S HYPNOTIC SUSCEPTIBILITY SCALE

Perry London. Palo Alto, California: Consulting Psychologists Press, Inc.

Introduction

The Children's Hypnotic Susceptibility Scale (CHSS) is a standardized measure of children's responsiveness to hypnotic suggestions (London, 1963). Hypnotic susceptibility or hypnotic responsiveness has been operationally defined as the frequency with which a subject acts like a hypnotized person when the behavioral responses are elicited by a standard hypnotic induction procedure (Cooper & London, 1978/1979). The CHSS is an individual behavioral measure of hypnotic responsiveness designed for children five to 17 years of age. The test includes a standardized induction procedure and a quantitative system for recording and scoring responses, as well as age-graded norms.

The CHSS was developed by Perry London, Ph.D., at the University of Illinois in 1962. London received his Ph.D. from Columbia University in 1956. Among his many professional affiliations and activities, London was Professor of Psychology at the University of Southern California and Professor of Psychiatry at its College of Medicine. Currently, he is director of the program in counseling and consulting psychology at Harvard University. He has published extensively on psychology and hypnosis.

The CHSS consists of 22 items providing a behavioral sample of hypnotic responsiveness. The test is divided into two sections. Part I, utilizing the same items as the Stanford Hypnotic Susceptibility Scale, Forms A and B, consists of the following 12 items: postural sway, eye closure, hand lowering, arm immobilization, finger lock, arm rigidity, hands together, verbal inhibition (name), auditory hallucination (fly), eye catalepsy, post-hypnotic suggestions (standing up), and amnesia. Part II, drawn from the unpublished Stanford Depth Scale (Hilgard, 1965), which served as the basis for the Stanford Hypnotic Susceptibility Scale, Form C (Weitzenhoffer & Hilgard, 1962) and the Stanford Profile Scales of

Hypnotic Susceptibility, Forms I and II (Weitzenhoffer & Hilgard, 1963), consists of ten items: post-hypnotic suggestion (reinduction), visual and auditory hallucination (television), cold hallucination, anesthesia, taste hallucination, smell hallucination (perfume), visual hallucination (rabbit), age regression, dream, and awakening and post-hypnotic suggestion (rabbit). These items were apparently selected for inclusion in the CHSS because they are said to represent generally acknowledged indices of hypnotic susceptibility (Cooper & London, 1978/1979). The scale was constructed as a power test in that scale items vary in difficulty and are assigned scores based on level of performance.

A test manual describes the procedure for administering the CHSS (London, 1963). Because the scale is intended for a wide age range, two forms of the CHSS are available. The younger form is designed for children aged five years, 0 months to 12 years, 11 months, and the older form is constructed for youth aged 13 years, 0 months to 16 years, 11 months. The test manual prescribes verbatim induction procedures and suggestions for each form. Because the CHSS is a test of typical hypnotic susceptibility, the manual cautions against attempts to induce maximum responsiveness that violate the standard administration. On the other hand, overly rigid adherence to the procedure that ignores individual differences in children's behavior is also discouraged. The test manual assumes that the examiner is skilled in psychological testing, hypnosis, and working with children.

Necessary test materials include a stopwatch, a chevreul pendulum, a sharp stylus, tongue depressors, a small bottle containing a mildly offensive liquid (e.g., dilute household ammonia), writing pencils, and a pad of 8½" X 11" unlined paper. Prior to administering the scale, the examiner asks the child to draw a picture of a man (for evaluating the age-regression item) and then prepares the child for induction by presenting some general information about hypnosis. It is recommended that the subject be seated in an armchair during the actual administration of the induction and suggestions. The entire 22-item scale can be completed in about 60 minutes. Alternatively, the test can be discontinued at the end of Part I (items 1-12), which takes about 30 minutes, if the child has failed more than seven of the first twelve items or because of time constraints.

Each item on the CHSS receives three scores. First, the Overt Behavior (OB) score indicates the degree to which the child's behavioral response matches the hypnotic suggestion along a four-point continuum (0-1-2-3), or according to a pass-fail dichotomy. The dichotomous scoring procedure is intended to be comparable to the Stanford Hypnotic Susceptibility Scale scoring system, whereas the four-point continuum is said to provide a more refined index of responsiveness. A scoring and observation form provides behavioral referents for the four-point continuum and these scores can be collapsed into the pass-fail dichotomy in which values of 0 or 1 correspond to fail scores and values of 2 or 3 correspond to pass scores. Because the normative data is based on the four-point scoring system, most users will want to employ this scoring procedure.

Second, the Subjective Involvement (SI) score reflects the examiner's impression of the genuineness of the behavior elicited by the hypnotic suggestions. Thus, if a passing OB score (a score of 2 or 3) is obtained, that item is then classified as "faking or role playing" (score of 1), "partially involved" (score of 2), or "deeply involved" (score of 3) (Cooper & London, 1978/1979). Unfortunately, behavioral referents are not provided for these three categories.

Finally, a Total (T) score may be calculated by multiplying the OB and SI scores obtained for a given item. This is a total for the *item,* not the category. Overall scores for Part I, Part II, or both parts of the test combined, may also be calculated for each of the three scoring categories (i.e., OB, SI, T). These are calculated by summing the relevant obtained values for a given scoring category.

The CHSS was first introduced in a journal article (London, 1962), and the test manual commercially published in 1963 (London, 1963). The initial version of the scale presented in the article and test manual utilized only the OB scoring system, and the normative data were not included. Information about normative data and scoring revisions (SI and T scores) must be obtained from other journal articles (London, 1965; London & Cooper, 1969). As a result, although instructions for scoring OB are clearly presented in the test manual and on the recording form, the method for arriving at SI and T scores is not presented in the manual or on the recording form; for these, as well as age-graded norms, the user must resort to the journal articles, which are not furnished by the publisher.

The age-graded norms are available for use with the CHSS in articles by London (1965), London and Cooper (1969), and Cooper and London (1978/1979). These norms are organized according to age grouping, sex, and type of susceptibility score (i.e., OB, SI, and T). The standardization sample on which the norms are based consisted of ten boys and ten girls at each age level between five and 16 years, yielding a total of 240 children. All subjects were randomly identified from the public school population of Urbana, Illinois and were volunteered for participation by their parents. Cooper and London (1978/1979) indicate that the selection procedure yielded a standardization sample that was similar to the Urbana population and noteworthy for its relatively high socioeconomic status.

Practical Applications/Uses

The CHSS has useful research and clinical applications in settings where information about children's hypnotic responsiveness is desired. For example, mental health and medical practitioners can employ the CHSS to identify children who may favorably respond to hypnotherapy. Because hypnosis with children is reported to be useful in treating psychological problems, habit disorders, problems in learning or performance, acute and chronic pain, and pediatric medical problems (Gardner & Olness, 1981), a broad range of situations exists where the CHSS could be employed to assist in determining the potential utility of hypnosis relative to other interventions. However, it should be noted that clinicians often choose to rely on their subjective judgments of responsiveness rather than expend the time and effort required to utilize this standardized instrument.

As a research tool, the CHSS is one of very few published measures of hypnotic responsiveness designed specifically for children (for another, see Morgan & Hilgard, 1978/79). Consequently, the CHSS may be of considerable value for studies of hypnotic processes in children where individual differences in responsiveness are of interest. Part I of the CHSS, which utilizes OB scores only, directly parallels the Stanford Hypnotic Susceptibility Scale, Forms A & B (Weitzenhoffer & Hilgard, 1959), thus providing the only available children's equivalent for an important and popular measure of adult hypnotic responsiveness.

Technical Aspects

Empirical research has documented the reliability of the CHSS and provided promising evidence of the scale's validity. A number of studies have investigated the interexaminer reliability of the CHSS scoring system. For example, London (1962) administered the CHSS to 36 children, three at each age level from 5-16 years, in which the examiner and an observer simultaneously scored the test. Correlations between raters' scores for OB, SI, and T on Part I and Part II of the CHSS ranged from .90 to .94.

In a similar study of interexaminer reliability, the CHSS was administered to 51 children and scored simultaneously by the examiner and an observer (London, 1965; London & Cooper, 1969). Correlations between the two sets of ratings yielded coefficients ranging from .86 to .97 for Part I, Part II, and full-scale OB, SI, and T scores.

There are several studies that provide evidence of the test-retest reliability of the CHSS. London (1962) administered the CHSS to 39 children twice (across an unspecified time period). A correlation of .92 between the two administrations was obtained utilizing the full-scale OB scores. Additionally, 69% of the children obtained scores on the second testing within two points of their scores on the first assessment.

In another study of test-retest reliability, the CHSS was administered twice to 50 children over a one-week period by different examiners (London, 1965). Correlations between the two administrations ranged from .65 to .84 for T scores on Part I, Part II, and full-scale CHSS. Furthermore, test-retest coefficients of .81 for full-scale OB and .75 for full-scale SI were obtained.

In a third study of test stability, a sample of 303 children aged five to 16 years was administered the CHSS, and then subsamples of children were retested at one-week, one-year, and two-year intervals (London & Cooper, 1969; Cooper & London, 1971). For the 201 children retested after one week, test-retest reliability coefficients of .79 for OB, .75 for SI, and .78 for T on the full-scale CHSS were obtained. After one year, 228 children achieved full-scale retest coefficients of .56 for OB, .56 for SI, and .59 for T. Finally, after the two-year interval, a subsample of 134 retested children yielded coefficients of .45 for OB, .45 for SI, and .46 for T on the full-scale CHSS. Collectively, these studies not only support the test-retest reliability of the CHSS, but also suggest that hypnotic responsiveness in children is somewhat stable over time.

The internal consistency and dimensionality of the CHSS has been the focus of a single study in which the scale was administered to 240 children aged five to 16 years (London, 1965; London & Cooper, 1969; Cooper & London, 1978/1979). Three kinds of internal consistency and dimensionality information were reported. First, with regard to internal consistency, reliability coefficients (Kuder-Richardson Formula 20) were .90 for OB, .94 for SI, and .94 for T on the full-scale CHSS. An item analysis was performed in which each scale item was correlated with the full-scale score (corrected for contribution of the item) for OB, SI, and T. On each of these three indices, item-total correlations ranged from .32 to .68, with a mean coefficient of .55.

A second component of this study examined scale dimensionality. Three principal-components factor analyses, with a varimax rotation performed on full-scale OB, SI, and T data, each produced eight factors accounting for most of the scale variance. Almost half of this variance was contributed by two factors. The "Challenge" factor, accounting for an average of 23% of the variance across the three scoring categories, was composed of five items: arm immobilization, finger lock, arm rigidity, verbal inhibition and eye catalepsy. The "Positive Hallucination" factor, accounting for an average of 26% of the variance across the three scoring categories, also consisted of five items: auditory hallucination, auditory and visual hallucination (television), cold hallucination, taste hallucination, and visual hallucination (rabbit).

The third component of this study explored correlations among the three scoring indices for Part I, Part II, and full-scale CHSS. Obtained coefficients were uniformly high. For example, correlations among OB, SI, and T for full-scale CHSS ranged from .85 to .98.

Overall, the findings of this study indicate that the CHSS possesses satisfactory internal consistency. Moreover, the results suggest that hypnotic responsiveness as measured by the CHSS is a relatively narrow construct operationalized by a highly interrelated set of construct referents. However, there is some evidence that within this narrow construct, certain subsets of referents tend to cluster together.

To establish the construct validity of a scale, it is generally accepted that a series of experiments varying persons, situations, and construct referents must be conducted. Research on the construct validity of the CHSS has investigated relationships between children's hypnotic responsiveness (as measured by the CHSS) and age, ability to simulate hypnosis, intelligence, sex, EEG patterns, and the outcome of hypnotic interventions in therapy.

Perhaps the most thoroughly researched correlate of children's hypnotic responsiveness as measured by the CHSS is age. It has been conjectured often that children are more hypnotically responsive than adults and that the peak of hypnotic responsiveness occurs between the ages of nine and 12 years (Tromater; 1961; London, 1962; Gardner & Olness, 1981). To investigate this hypothesis, London (1962) administered the CHSS tn 57 children aged 5-16 years and compared the results with adults' performance on the Stanford Hypnotic Susceptibility Scale (SHSS, A). He found that across items on Part I of the CHSS, an average of 74% of the childen received passing scores, whereas across the same items on the SHSS, A, an average of only 47% of the adults received passing scores. London concluded that children as a group are more responsive than adults. However, he was unable to demonstrate a curvilinear relationship between children's age and level of responsiveness.

In a similar study of 240 children aged 5-16 years, it was found that adults scored significantly lower on the SHSS, A than did children on Part I of the CHSS for OB scores (London, 1965; London & Cooper, 1969). Once again, a curvilinear relationship between children's age and responsiveness could not be demonstrated. However, a statistically significant complex nonlinear relationship that could not be easily interpreted was obtained. Significantly more children than adults passed ten of the 12 items. Furthermore, adults did significantly better than children on only one item—eye closure.

In a third study, Moore and Lauer (1963) compared the hypnotic responsiveness of 48 children aged six to 12 on Part I of the CHSS with the earlier findings reported by London (1962) and with two samples of adults on the SHSS, A. Overall differences between the child and adult samples were not observed. However, significant variations between adults and children in the patterns of passed items were found. More specifically, compared to adults, children were significantly more successful on auditory hallucination, amnesia, and post-hypnotic suggestion, but they were less successful on eye closure and eye catalepsy.

Overall, these findings tend to confirm the clinical observation that children are more hypnotically responsive than adults. Moreover, the sensitivity of the CHSS to detect this difference lends support to its validity as a measure of hypnotic responsiveness. However, studies employing the CHSS have failed to support the assertion that the peak of hypnotic responsiveness occurs between the ages of nine and 12.

A second area subjected to systematic investigation with the CHSS is the relationship between children's hypnotic responsiveness and role playing ability. Hypnotic behavior has been conceptualized by some to be a role assumed by the hypnotic subject (Sarbin, 1950) and preliminary research with the CHSS was said to support this hypothesis (London, 1962). Confirmation of a relationship between role-playing ability and hypnotic responsiveness as measured by the CHSS would not only provide evidence for the role-playing explanation of hypnosis, but would also offer support for the validity of the CHSS.

Madsen and London (1966) tested this hypothesis by administering measures of hypnotic responsiveness, dramatic-acting ability, and hypnotic simulation ability to 42 children aged eight to 12. During the first experimental session, subjects were administered the CHSS. Seven days later, subjects were given a structured dramatic acting test (Bowers & London, 1965) in which they assumed a series of familiar roles (e.g., mother, father) and the adequacy of their performance was rated on a series of four-point scales. Subjects were also given a hypnotic-simulation test in which they were told to act as if they were hypnotized on nine items from Part II of the CHSS, and their performances were rated using the CHSS scoring system. Hypnotic responsiveness was correlated with hypnotic-simulation ability, but it was not significantly related to dramatic-acting ability. (Somewhat surprisingly hypnotic-simulation ability and dramatic-acting ability were uncorrelated, possibly suggesting the lack of validity of one or both of these measures.)

In a similar study conducted to assess the impact of the order of tests, 34 children aged eight to 12 were administered the dramatic-acting and hypnotic-simulation tests during the initial assessment and the CHSS seven days later (London & Madsen, 1968; London & Madsen, 1969). Unlike the findings of the previous study, no significant relationships were observed among the three variables. Furthermore, SI scores on the CHSS were significantly lower in this experiment compared with the results of Madsen and London (1966) in which the CHSS was administered first, rather than last. This finding led the authors to speculate that genuineness of involvement in hypnosis is inhibited when preceded by role-playing hypnosis.

These two studies offer little support for a role-playing explanation of hypnosis. Furthermore, the lack of relationship between measures of general role-playing ability (i.e., dramatic-acting) and hypnotic role-playing ability is puzzling. Finally, it is difficult to assess the contribution of item overlap between the CHSS and the hypnotic simulation test (i.e., method variance) to the observed relationships between hypnotic responsiveness and hypnotic role-playing ability. However, the CHSS does appear to be sensitive to differences in instructional set and demand characteristics contained in the two studies. Consequently, they offer limited confirmation of the validity of the CHSS.

The relationship between children's hypnotic responsiveness, child-rearing practices, and EEG patterns was studied by Cooper and London (1976). This investigation was intended to duplicate the observed correlation between responsiveness and duration of EEG alpha waves in adults, as well as to examine a hypothesized relationship between responsiveness, brain-wave patterns, and child-rearing practices. Consequently, these authors measured hypnotic responsiveness on the CHSS, as well as EEG patterns, under two conditions—eyes open and eyes closed. About one week later, children and their parents engaged in a series of problem-solving tasks while their interactions were rated. Hypnotic responsiveness tended to be correlated with the duration of EEG alpha waves (thought to be associated with an alert state of consciousness) during the eyes-open condition only. Furthermore, during problem solving, more highly responsive children delayed longer in asking their parents for help, and their parents rated themselves as more demanding and strict than the parents of low-responsive children. The findings suggest that the CHSS is sensitive to differences in these neurological, cognitive, and interpersonal variables, although the meaning of such relationships remains somewhat unclear. The results provide, at best, limited support for the validity of the CHSS.

Surprisingly, only one study has employed the CHSS in evaluating the differential effectiveness of hypnotic interventions in treating behavioral or medical problems. Johnson, Johnson, Olson, and Newman (1981) utilized group and autohypnosis to promote the academic performance and self-esteem of learning-disabled children. Fifteen LD children aged seven to 13, as well as their parents and teachers, received a hypnotic therapy program that included three group-hypnosis training sessions and six weeks of autohypnosis. A group of 18 LD children aged eight to 12 served as controls. Both groups received pre- and post-assessments of academic performance and self-esteem. Also, the experimental group, but not the control group, was administered the CHSS prior to receiving therapy. Pre- to post-gains in academic performance and self-esteem were observed for the entire sample, although differences in improvement between experimentals and controls did not reach statistical significance. Hypnotic responsiveness as measured by the

CHSS appeared to be consistently related to changes in self-reported and observed self-esteem in children assigned to the experimental group. The ability of the CHSS to predict responsiveness to a hypnotic intervention designed to improve self-esteem provides good support for its construct validity. Moreover, the findings suggest the value of using measures such as the CHSS to identify children who are most appropriate for hypnosis. More research of this kind would help to demonstrate that the CHSS truly measures what it purports to measure.

Secondary foci of many of the preceding studies have been sex and IQ differences in children's hypnotic responsiveness as measured by the CHSS. There has been a consistent lack of differences between boys and girls in hypnotic responsiveness (London, 1965; London & Cooper, 1969; Moore & Lauer, 1963). However, greater hypnotic responsiveness as measured by the CHSS does appear to be related to higher IQ (London, 1965; Madsen & London, 1966; London & Madsen, 1969).

Overall, there have been surprisingly few studies of children's hypnotic responsiveness utilizing the CHSS. This lack of research is probably the greatest obstacle to definitive confirmation of the scale's construct validity. Thus far, the most useful area of research for this purpose has examined the relationship between responsiveness and age. The lack of empirical research employing the CHSS to predict hypnotherapeutic outcomes is particularly noteworthy. Certainly, children's hypnotic responsiveness is a fruitful area for more research.

Critique

The Children's Hypnotic Susceptibility Scale is a well-constructed measure of children's hypnotic responsiveness that evidences many strengths and relatively few weaknesses. Perhaps the scale's most notable deficiency is the test manual, which lacks normative data and information necessary to calculate Subjective Involvement (SI) and Total (T) scores. Consequently, the test manual should be revised to reflect this information. Also, some might question the content validity of the scale, criticizing the selection of items on the basis of their historical prominence rather than because of their psychometric properties or their fit with a well-developed definition of hypnotic responsiveness. However, because the CHSS samples a large number of referents of hypnotic responsiveness, item selection does not seem to be a serious flaw, with the possible exception that administering all 22 items may make the CHSS unwieldly for certain clinical and research situations. (The use of Part I or Part II alone shortens the time involved.)

As for its psychometric strengths, the scale is easily administered according to detailed instructions in the test manual and related articles. Also, the scale has been designed so it can be used with a wide age range of children. The CHSS is the only measure of children's hypnotic responsiveness for which age-graded norms are available. The scale possesses satisfactory empirical evidence of its inter-examiner and test-retest reliability, as well as its internal consistency. Support for the scale's construct validity is growing, but has been hampered by the absence of research into children's hypnotic responsiveness and by the apparent lack of correlates of hypnotic responsiveness. Finally, the scale has been constructed so that it can be used to parallel the Stanford Hypnotic Susceptibility Scale, Forms A and B, and is thus the only available children's equivalent for an important adult measure of hypnotic responsiveness.

Overall, the CHSS is a well-developed, reliable measure of children's hypnotic responsiveness that can serve many useful research and clinical purposes.

References

This list includes text citations as well as suggested additional reading.

Bowers, P., & London, P. (1965). Developmental correlates of dramatic role-playing ability. *Child Development, 36,* 499-508.

Cooper, L. M., & London, P. (1966). Sex and hypnotic susceptibility in children. *International Journal of Clinical and Experimental Hypnosis, 14,* 55-60.

Cooper, L. M., & London, P. (1971). The development of hypnotic susceptibility: A longitudinal (convergence) study. *Child Development, 42,* 487-503.

Cooper, L. M., & London, P. (1976). Children's hypnotic susceptibility, personality and EEG patterns. *The International Journal of Clinical and Experimental Hypnosis, 24,* 140-148.

Cooper, L. M., & London, P. M. (1978/1979). The Children's Hypnotic Susceptibility Scale. *The American Journal of Clinical Hypnosis, 21,* 170-184.

Curran, J. D., & Gibson, H. B. (1974). Critique of the Stanford Hypnotic Susceptibility Scale: British usage and factorial structure. *Perceptual Motor Skills, 39,* 695-704.

Dumas, R. A. (1977). EEG alpha-hypnotizability correlations: A review. *Psychophysiology, 14,* 431-438.

Gardner, G. G., & Olness, K. (1981). *Hypnosis and hypnotherapy with children.* Orlando, FL: Grune and Stratton.

Hilgard, E. R. (1965). *Hypnotic susceptibility.* New York: Harcourt Brace.

Johnson, L. S., Johnson, D. L., Olson, M. R., & Newman, J. P. (1981). The uses of hypnotherapy with learning disabled children. *Journal of Clinical Psychology, 37,* 291-299.

London, P. (1962). Hypnosis in children: An experimental approach. *The International Journal of Clinical and Experimental Hypnosis, 10,* 79-91.

London, P. (1963). *The Children's Hypnotic Susceptibility Scale.* Palo Alto, CA: Consulting Psychologists Press, Inc.

London, P. (1965). Developmental experiments in hypnosis. *Journal of Projective Techniques and Personality Assessment, 29,* 189-199.

London, P. (1966). Child hypnosis and personality. *American Journal of Clinical Hypnosis, 8,* 161-168.

London, P. (1976). Kidding around with hypnosis. *The International Journal of Clinical and Experimental Hypnosis, 24,* 105-121.

London, P., Cooper, L. M. (1969). Norms of hypnotic susceptibility in children. *Developmental Psychology, 1,* 113-124.

London, P., & Madsen, C. H. (1968). Effect of role playing on hypnotic susceptibility in children. *Journal of Personality and Social Psychology, 10,* 66-68.

London, P., & Madsen, C. H. (1969). Role playing and hypnotic susceptibility in children: II. An extension and partial replication. *The International Journal of Clinical and Experimental Hypnosis, 17,* 37-49.

Madsen, C. H., & London, P. (1966). Role playing and hypnotic susceptibility in children. *Journal of Personality and Social Psychology, 3,* 13-19.

Morgan, A. H., & Hilgard, J. R. (1978/1979). The Stanford Hypnotic Clinical Scale for Children. *American Journal of Clinical Hypnosis, 21,* 148-169.

Moore, R. K., & Cooper, L. M. (1966). Item difficulty in childhood hypnotic susceptibility scales as a function of item wording, repetition and age. *International Journal of Clinical and Experimental Hypnosis, 14,* 316-323.

Moore, R. K., & Lauer, L. W. (1963). Hypnotic susceptibility in middle childhood. *Journal of Clinical and Experimental Hypnosis, 11,* 167-174.

Moss, C. S. (1970). Review of the Children's Hypnotic Susceptibility Scale. In O. K. Buros (Ed.), *Personality tests and reviews* (pp. 982-983). Highland Park, NJ: The Gryphon Press.

O'Grady, D. J., & Hoffman, C. (1984). Hypnosis with children and adolescents in the medical setting. In W. C. Webster, II, & A. H. Smith, Jr. (Eds.), *Clinical hypnosis: A multi-disciplinary approach* (pp. 181-209). Philadelphia: J.B. Lippincott Co.

Sarbin, T. R. (1950). Contributions to role taking theory: I. Hypnotic behavior. *Psychological Reviews, 57,* 255-270.

Tromater, F. L. (1961). *Some developmental correlates of hypnotic susceptibility.* Unpublished master's thesis, University of Illinois, Urbana.

Watkins, J. G. (1970). Review of the Children's Hypnotic Susceptibility Scale. In O. K. Buros (Ed.), *Personality tests and reviews* (pp. 983-984). Highland Park, NJ: Gryphon Press.

Weitzenhoffer, A. M. (1963). Review of the Children's Hypnotic Susceptibility Scale. *American Journal of Clinical Hypnosis, 5,* 336-337.

Weitzenhoffer, A. M., and Hilgard, E. R. (1959). *Stanford Hypnotic Susceptibility Scale, Forms A and B.* Palo Alto, CA: Consulting Psychologists Press.

Weitzenhoffer, A. M., and Hilgard E. R. (1962). *Stanford Hypnotic Susceptibility Scale, Form C.* Palo Alto, CA: Consulting Psychologists Press.

Weitzenhoffer, A. M., and Hilgard, E. R. (1963). *Stanford Profile Scales of Hypnotic Susceptibility, Forms I and II.* Palo Alto, CA: Consulting Psychologists Press.

Susan D. Huard, Ph.D.
Professor of Reading, Developmental Studies Division, Community College of the Finger Lakes, Canandaiqua, New York.

CLARKE READING SELF-ASSESSMENT SURVEY

John H. Clarke and Simon Wittes. Novato, California: Academic Therapy Publications.

Introduction

The Clarke Reading Self-Assessment Survey (SAS) is a self-report, self-scored screening device that evaluates a student's need for possible academic assistance at the beginning of college coursework in the areas of reading comprehension, conceptualization, and writing. The SAS consists of three divisions: Part I—Reading Speed, Comprehension, and Interpretation; Part II—Organizing Facts and Ideas; and Part III—Word Usage, Sentence Structure, and Writing Mechanics. With the exception of Reading Speed, the SAS is untimed. The estimated time involved, including completing and scoring, is approximately one hour. Parts I and III employ a multiple-choice format; Part II requires the insertion of a list of words into a diagram that denotes their coordination and subordination. Scores achieved on the SAS are broken into three categories indicating that students require 1) additional self-directed examination of study skills, 2) tutorials, or 3) remedial/developmental coursework. The test authors recommend that colleges establish local cut scores and that students' results on the SAS be discussed with an academic advisor for purposes of course selection at registration.

John H. Clarke, Ed.D., and Simon Wittes, Ph.D., developed the SAS in response to the needs of the entering student population at the University of Massachusetts, Boston campus. The age and academic background of the entering freshmen varied considerably, and the SAS was originally designed to aid student placement in noncredit courses, mini-courses connected to particular courses, and tutorials or programmed-learning assistance packages (J. H. Clarke, personal communication, October 23, 1985). At present, there are no revisions or alternate forms.

Practical Applications/Uses

The SAS is a self-administered and self-scored instrument intended for use by entering college freshmen, high-school seniors, or anyone who is planning to take an initial college course. It can be administered individually or to groups. All of the exercises and answers are contained within a single booklet. In addition, a watch is needed to time the Reading Speed passage in Part I. The SAS is a gross screening device and, as such, asks for information of a rudimentary college nature. Typical questions assess knowledge of a main idea, details, punctuation, and contents of an essay.

In the first two sections of Part I (Reading Speed and Comprehension), the student first reads, under timing, a passage of approximately 750 words and then answers five multiple-choice questions that refer to the timed passage. The last section (Reading Interpretation) consists of a poem and five multiple-choice questions that probe the student's understanding of central ideas and poetic devices. Part II (Organizing Facts and Ideas) is also composed of a series of short exercises. The first, word lists, is comprised of seven four-item lists for which the examinee supplies a category chosen from an additional group of four. The second, concept diagrams, offers a collection of six diagrams that require the student to insert a list of words into the diagram to denote coordination and subordination of the individual words. The final exercise, paragraph parts, consists of five paragraphs with an omitted embedded sentence that require students to supply the missing sentence by choosing from four alternatives. In Part III, the student is tested on word usage (11 items), recognition of good sentence structure (five sentences and their variations), punctuation (a short exercise), writing forms (six multiple-choice questions), and locating information in a library (two multiple-choice questions).

After completing the tasks required in the SAS, the student scores responses by comparison to the answer key. Each correct response is given one point. Points are tallied and multiplied for each subtest, then totaled and averaged. Results are plotted by exercise and subtest on a chart. Finally, scores are interpreted by matching results to a skill development table, which provides three ranges for each subtest. These ranges indicate the need for individual independent skill review; coursework in reading, writing, or conceptualizing; or individual tutorials.

The SAS is designed primarily for use by a counselor or advisor who is assisting entering college students with their course selection. The SAS gives a broad sense of whether a student may need study-skills assistance in order to be successful; it does not specify weaknesses. For example, further diagnostic testing in reading comprehension would be necessary if Part I of the SAS indicated a low score. The SAS has also been employed by high-school counselors to anticipate a student's need for academic assistance in college. In this case, services available at the high school are provided in order to remedy deficiencies prior to the beginning of college coursework. Because the SAS is self-scored and contains clear step-by-step directions, anyone can administer it. The results also can be scored and interpreted by an untrained test proctor who is able to follow the process of scoring correct responses, tallying and multiplying points, and matching numerical results to a simple three-category range. Application of the information gained from the test results, however, would be most useful to an educator, advisor, or counselor who is guiding a student's course selection process.

One of the major strengths of the SAS is the level of language it employs. Clarke and Wittes (1978) carefully explain the purpose of the test and how it has been used previously by other incoming college freshmen. The tone—straightforward and conversational—is set in the introduction and carried through in many of the directions for subsequent activities within the survey. Except for the exercise, paragraph parts, a brief rationale precedes each exercise.

Another positive feature of the SAS is the choice of topics in Part I of the survey. The authors seem to be cognizant of their readers and their interests. Paragraphs and passages appear to deal with topics that are of interest to college students of all ages. The three sections in Part I build logically on one another. The comprehension questions, which follow the Reading Speed section, also examine reading skills in a logical sequence by first considering the main idea, then progressing to the author's implications. Moreover, poetry follows prose with a mixture of questions to evaluate literal understanding of the poem and basic knowledge of poetic devices.

Whereas Part I of the SAS is conventional in format and question-type, Part II is the unique section of this survey. The authors have created a series of tasks to evaluate a student's ability to organize information. Again, as in Part I, the SAS tasks follow a pattern of increasing difficulty. In both of the initial exercises, examinees employ terms that have been provided: in the first, they select a general term that encompasses the others, and, in the second, they insert the terms into a prearranged diagram. The first three diagrams seem to utilize common concepts and terms. Subsequent items (#4, 5, 6) require the student to have some understanding of the structure of subject matter in a college. Because of this additional knowledge prerequisite, some students may not be able to demonstrate their ability to organize concepts. However, the inability to fill in the last three diagrams would provide an advisor with important information about the student's familiarity with course offerings at the college level. The last exercise in Part II, paragraph parts, is a synthesis of the skills analyzed in the first two exercises, with the addition of the paragraph structure. This particular exercise, a modified cloze procedure, involves a combination of careful reading skills, such as the use of syntactic and semantic clues and reasoning. A marked difference in the scores achieved in each of these three exercises would provide a learning skills specialist with a useful, initial informal diagnosis.

Part III of the SAS, which explores usage and mechanics, is also conventional in its consideration of effective writing skills. Knowledge of verb tenses, homonyms, sentence structure, and punctuation is examined. This part of the test differs from the other parts in that it depends on knowledge of definitions in order to assess familiarity with a skill. Still, knowing the definition of a sentence, paragraph, and essay does not constitute the ability to construct any of these. Also the lack of test-item sophistication is apparent in the last exercise. The authors have included "all of the above" as a choice in the response sets only when it is the correct response. Finally, this part, more than the other two, points out the difficulties entailed in constructing a survey of this sort. Only two questions check familiarity with library sources. Due to the number of skills areas that are included in the SAS and the need for a reasonable time factor and easily interpretable data, all skills are treated in a superficial manner.

Technical Aspects

The SAS was administered to more than 3,000 entering college freshmen prior to publication, but no data are available regarding validity or reliability.

Critique

Although there is no available reliability or validity information concerning the SAS, the authors do note that several thousand entering students at one institution have taken the SAS. Part of the reason for the missing data probably has to do with the development of this survey. It was conceived as an in-house instrument to meet the advisement and retention problems of one particular school and later adopted by a commercial publisher. Despite its parochial beginnings, the SAS has definite value as long as it is employed merely as a screening device and an advisement tool. Its greatest strength lies in its ability to identify students who might experience failure due to study skills deficiencies. It is, however, not a replacement for the extensive diagnostic testing that may be warranted to facilitate academic success for the student.

References

Clarke, J. H., & Wittes, S. (1978). *The Clarke Reading Self-Assessment Survey.* Novato, CA: Academic Therapy Publications.

Thomas L. Layton, Ph.D.
Associate Professor of Speech and Hearing Sciences, University of North Carolina, Chapel Hill, North Carolina.

CLINICAL EVALUATION OF LANGUAGE FUNCTIONS: DIAGNOSTIC BATTERY

Eleanor Semel and Elisabeth Wiig. Columbus, Ohio: Charles E. Merrill Publishing Company.

Introduction

The Clinical Evaluation of Language Functions (CELF): Diagnostic Battery is an individually administered test designed to identify language functions in the areas of phonology, syntax, semantics, memory, word finding, and retrieval. There are 13 subtests in the instrument designed for children in Grades K-12. The instrument can be administered totally, or individual subtests can be given as selected language probes. In addition to the battery, there are two 20-minute CELF screening instruments available: Elementary (Grades K-5) and Advanced (Grades 5-12).

The test is divided between processing and production of language: six of the subtests and one supplementary subtest (processing) require recognition, interpretation, and/or recall, and ask for pointing, yes/no responses, or wh-questions/answers. The other five subtests and one supplemental subtest (production) require naming, word or sentence recall, or sentence formulation and production. The 11 subtests and two supplementary subtests are described as follows:

Processing Word and Sentence Structure (26 items): Assesses ability to process and interpret selected word and sentence structures (syntax). Requires the child to select the appropriate picture from an array of four (e.g., from a stimulus item showing boys pointing to themselves, the child must choose whether A) boys are pointing to themselves, B) pointing to them, C) pointing to it, or D) girls are pointing to themselves). Measures concepts such as prepositional phrases, pronouns, verb tenses, irregular plural nouns, noun possessives, negation, passives, wh-interrogatives, indirect objects, and relative clauses. Approximate administration time: six minutes.

Processing Word Classes (22 items): Evaluates ability to perceive relationships between verbal concepts and identify word pairs associated by class membership, antonymy, agent-action, or superordinate-subordinate relationships. Requires the child, who is presented with a string of three to four words (e.g., shoes, socks, bread), to name the two words that are related. Approximate administration time: five minutes.

Processing Linguistic Concepts (22 items): Assesses logical operations such as exclusion (e.g., not, all . . . except, no . . . instead), coordination (and), instrumental (with, without), temporal (e.g., often, before, when), conditional (e.g., if, don't . . . till), inclusion-exclusion (either . . . or), and inclusion (e.g., anyone, any . . .

all, some). Requires the child to process oral directions containing logical operations, such as "and," "either . . . or," and "if . . . then," with vocabulary limited to "point to," "line," and "red, blue, and yellow." Oral directions range from seven to 21 words (e.g., after examiner points to a yellow line and before pointing to a blue line, the child is instructed to point to a red line). Approximate administration time: five minutes.

Processing Relationships and Ambiguities (32 items): Evaluates ability to process logico-grammatical and ambiguous sentences containing relationships such as ones that are comparative, passive, temporal-sequential, familial, analogous, idiomatic, metaphoric, and proverbial (e.g., whether books are heavier than feathers; if big is to little as night is to day.) This is a revised version of the authors' experimental research instrument. Approximate administration time: eight minutes.

Processing Oral Directions (25 items): Evaluates ability to interpret, recall, and execute oral commands of increasing length and complexity (five to 18 words), with each noun having one, two, or three modifiers, and two- and three-word commands including either repetition of the action (point to) or coordination (and). Requires child to point to appropriate choice on a visual display that includes an array of black and white circles, squares, and/or triangles in two or three different sizes (e.g., pointing to the last small black circle to the left of the big black square when instructed to do so). Approximate administration time: six minutes.

Processing Spoken Paragraphs (35 items): Assesses ability to process spoken paragraphs and recall salient information such as proper names and numerical data (e.g., stating the color of a cat and who gave the cat to Jack after examiner has read a paragraph containing that information). Consists of four paragraphs containing 1) active declarative sentences, 2) the pronoun "this" and a relative clause, 3) two relative clauses and one embedded sentence, and 4) data in different locations that are tested by seven wh-interrogative sentences. Approximate administration time: ten minutes.

Producing Word Series (two items): Assesses accuracy, fluency, and speed in recalling and producing selected automatic-sequential word series. Requires accurate and rapid recall and retrieval for names of the days of the week or months of the year. Approximate administration time: two minutes.

Producing Names on Confrontation (108 items): Evaluates the accuracy, fluency, and speed in naming colors, forms, and color-form combinations. Consists of three cards that are displayed to child to elicit color naming (Card I), naming of geometric forms (Card II), or color and geometric forms (Card III). Responses are scored as 1) word finding problems associated with substitutions, omissions, additions, and perseverations, and 2) speed and fluency. Approximate administration time: five minutes.

Producing Word Associations (two items): Evaluates the quantity and quality of the retrieval of semantically related word series (food and animals) from long-term memory. The probes are 1) fluency in identifying and retrieving members of a semantic class, 2) speed of retrieval of semantic classes, and 3) use of associative grouping strategies. Requires the child to think of things that go together (e.g., shoes, socks, and jacket in response to things to wear). Scoring is both quantitative and qualitative. Approximate administration time: four minutes.

Producing Model Sentences (30 items): Assesses productive control of sentence structure in a repetition task. Sentences, ranging from six to 20 syllables or five to 17 words in length, probe for 1) active-affirmative-declarative sentences, 2) negatives, 3) passives, 4) interrogatives, 5) compound coordination, 6) conjunction deletions, 7) "if" conjunction, 8) relative clauses, and 9) syntactic and semantic variations. Each repetition is scored correct unless it contains a substitution, omission, addition, reversal, or transposition. Approximate administration time: five minutes.

Producing Formulated Sentences (12 items): Assesses ability to formulate sentences when presented with a single word such as "after." Words (e.g., car, yellow, because, tell, if) were selected based on the syntactic constraints they placed on sentence formulation (e.g., passives, negatives). Responses are scored by level of complexity. Approximate administration time: six minutes.

Processing Speech Sounds (supplemental; 60 items): Assesses auditory discrimination using minimally different word pairs. Requests the child, who is presented two words, to judge whether they are the same or different words (e.g., "pie-pie"; "rope-robe"). An error analysis grid is provided for analyzing the error patterns. Approximate administration time: six minutes.

Producing Speech Sounds (supplemental; 60 items): Assesses articulation by using aspects of language related to motor encoding and habitual patterns of speech. Requests the child to fill in the missing word after hearing part of a story, such as "Once upon a time there was a king and a _____ (queen)." The speech sounds being tested include 26 consonant blends, nine final consonants, and ten initial consonants. Approximate administration time: eight minutes.

Practical Applications/Uses

No specific theoretical model was presented by the authors for the development of the CELF or for the selection of individual subtests. The test appears to be based mainly on research of the authors (e.g., Wiig & Semel, 1975; Wiig, Semel, & Crouse, 1973) and others (e.g., Johnson & Myklebust, 1967; McGrady & Olson, 1970; Meier, 1971; Rosenthal, 1970) with language/learning disabled children. Although there is some historical and theoretical justification for designing the CELF, based on Guilford's (1967) structure-of-intellect model, the test authors do not mention Guilford's model in the CELF manual and materials (Semel & Wiig, 1980). One critical review of the CELF (Muma, 1984) questions whether any theoretical model actually underlies the CELF.

Semel and Wiig (1980) suggest that the 13 subtests measure language based on four concepts: 1) word and concept meaning (semantics), 2) sentence structure (syntax), 3) recall and retrieval (memory), and 4) speech sounds (phonology). However, only six of the subtests actually test for an isolated concept; the remainder measure concepts in two areas, with one (Processing Relationships and Ambiguities) measuring concepts in three areas. With this overlapping of areas, it is difficult to determine how many separate subtests actually exist. Consequently, an individual child might manifest a specific deficit (e.g., vocabulary), yet on the CELF the child's performance could be generally impaired across the various subtests.

The CELF manual contains only raw score criteria by grade level for each of the 13 subtests. In addition, it provides an error analysis grid, which can aid the clinician in planning for therapy. A series of four updates (Charles E. Merrill Publishing Co., 1981, 1982, 1983, 1984), which can be obtained from the publisher, details additional scoring and tables for the raw scores. Because these updates are not readily available and are crucial to interpreting the CELF, they are discussed as follows:

Update 1: Provides additional examples (not included in the manual) of how to score the diagnostic battery—many of which are helpful for obtaining accurate scores on each subtest—and includes a more thorough explanation for scoring the Producing Formulated Sentences subtest than the manual dces. Without this information it is nearly impossible to obtain an accurate score. It also contains tables for the screening version of the CELF.

Update 2: Discusses the selection of subjects for the diagnostic battery and details changes in scoring for three specific subtests: Producing Word Series, Producing Names on Confrontation, and Producing Formulated Sentences. It is clear in this update that only card III (i.e., naming colored shapes) is used for scoring the Producing Names on Confrontation subtest—a statement that was never made in the CELF manual. Test users should be aware of this for it makes a tremendous difference on the results for this subtest. It also provides new norms for the diagnostic battery, which include language age scores and percentile ranks by grade for Total Processing (i.e., a combination of subtests one through five) and Total Production (i.e., combining subtests six through 12).

Update 3: Contains some of the same information included in Update 2, plus the raw-score to percentile ranks for each subtest by grade level and Total Processing and Total Production raw-score to percentile ranks. It also contains a table for the minimal pass-fail criteria (set at the 20th percentile) for raw scores by grade for each subtest.

Update 4: Presents standard scores (mean = 100; standard deviation = 15) for Total Processing and Total Production by ages, beginning at five years, three months and ending at 15 years, ten months. It also contains a table that allows the standard scores to be converted to percentile ranks and provides means and standard deviations for each subtest by age level.

The original standardized sample for the CELF consisted of 139 children, but in Update 2 a new sample of 1,378 children was reported. Thus, it is important to use the larger normative data provided in the update for scoring purposes.

Subjects were representative of normal developing children between Grades K-12. Each child had to be free of any visual or physical handicap, speech or language disorders, learning disabilities, mental retardation, or emotional disorders. The final sample contained 52% males and 48% females; 75% whites, 19% blacks, 6% others; 19% from the northeast, 19% from the north central, 33% from the south, 29% from the west; and 5% with high SES, 63% with middle SES, and 32% with low SES. However, Semel and Wiig (1980) do not report how many subjects were present at each grade level. They do suggest that the diagnostic and screening populations were the same individuals, with the sample size for each grade being targeted at a minimum of 100. If this is true, then the sample size for the CELF can be considered adequate. However, this should not be assumed to be true based solely on the authors' vague statement. In fact, the selection procedure in general was vague. For one thing, no mention was made as to how subjects were selected (e.g., random selection or other?), who administered the test (e.g., trained professionals?), or where the test was administered (e.g., in the child's classroom, home, a quiet area?). Also, no subjects who had language handicaps—and this, after all, was why the test was designed—were included. Therefore, despite the size of the test sample being adequate, the uncertainty of the population sample makes it difficult to determine if one's own client is represented by the CELF sample.

Technical Aspects

The reliability data are presented in the manual, with no new information being reported in the updates. Stability measures were completed on 30 randomly selected academically achieving second-graders who were not language impaired and not part of the standardized population. The 30 children were tested twice during a six-week interval. The range of reliability for each subtest fell between .56 and .98, with the majority of scores being above the .80 level (Semel & Wiig, 1980). These results suggest good stability; however, the test user should be careful because the sample was so limited. More information is still needed on children of various ages and those with language disorders before the CELF can be considered a reliable instrument.

There were no reports of internal reliability. This increases the concern for the instrument's overall reliability. Also, no standard errors of measurement were reported. The authors did report means and standard deviations by age in Update 4 but did not provide subsequent standard errors.

This leads to the conclusion that the CELF has not been proven to be a reliable instrument. Therefore, its accuracy or usefulness as a diagnostic instrument has to be questioned.

Measures of validity for the CELF were not extensive. Semel and Wiig (1980) report on concurrent criterion-related validity but only on a limited sample of 30 learning-disabled children in fifth and sixth grades. Each of the children had been administerd the WISC-R and a "reading achievement" test and had exhibited academic deficits of two or more grade levels. Criterion measures used for measuring concurrent validity were 1) the verbal sections of the Illinois Test of Psycholinguistic Abilities (ITPA), 2) selected verbal sections of the Detroit Tests of Learning Aptitude, 3) Wepman's Test of Auditory Discrimination, 4) Fisher-Logemann Test of Articulation, 5) Northwestern Syntax Screening Test, and 6) part V of the Token Test.

All resulting pairwise correlations were positive and significant at the .01 level. The range of correlations were from .40 to .94. It is of interest to note, however, that out of the 35 positive correlations reported, 29 were only at the .40 and .50 levels and only six correlations were above the .60 level. Thus, despite positive correlations being reported, the correlations were only moderately strong; that is, only 16 to 36% of the total variance between the CELF subtests and their criterion measures were in common, whereas 64 to 84% of the total variance was due to some other variable. These relationships are too weak, according to Salvia and Ysseldyke (1978), to make any sound educational strategies. Pairwise correlations should approximate the .90 level, and in these instances few were.

Construct validity was reported in the manual. Intertest correlations were computed on the 13 subtests, with most being positive. However, the correlations ranged from a low of .02 to a high of .68. The main 11 subtests intercorrelated sufficiently low enough (at least partially) to suggest that the CELF subtests are not measuring the same concept. The two supplemental subtests also did not correlate with any of the other subtests; consequently, they also seem to be measuring concepts that differ from the other subtests.

The raw scores on the 11 main subtests were reported in Update 4. The raw scores did increase by each succeeding age level, but ceiling out around age 12 years; that is, for three of the processing subtests (Sentence Structure, Word Classes, and Linguistic Concepts) scores did not increase after age 12 years. For the remainder of the subtests the ceiling occurred at a later age level, but there were several ages (i.e, 11-6 to 14-6) where minimal changes occurred in mean scores (e.g., .3 differences). In fact, there were only two subtests that continually increased up to the last age level without establishing a ceiling. These were Processing Paragraphs and Production of Confrontation Naming. Still, even at those age levels below 12 years where scores increased, no statistical evidence was reported as to whether the differences were actually different. Consequently, construct validity has not been substantiated.

Besides the above, there was no evidence provided for content validity. Therefore, in general, validity of the CELF is lacking. Until such time that validity is demonstrated, test users should question the effectiveness of the CELF to measure the areas for which the test has been designed.

Critique

Considering the various shortcomings of the CELF—vagueness in sampling selection, inadequate measures of reliability, and absence of several validity measures—the instrument should be considered exploratory in nature and not a definitive diagnostic tool. Test users expect to know the make-up of the population sample and whether the instrument is valid and reliable in order to judge whether their examinees are being tested accurately. The CELF, in its current form, does not allow test users to do this. The users do not know how children with specific language problems will look. They might appear normal or they might demonstrate a global problem. The test does not provide any guarantees of how they will do.

On the other hand, in support of the CELF, the authors have an excellent research record (e.g., Semel & Wiig, 1975; Wiig & Semel, 1973, 1974, 1975; Wiig, Semel, & Abele, 1981; Wiig, Semel, & Crouse, 1973) in evaluating the language behavior of disordered children, and it was this experience from which they drew when designing the CELF. It is possible, given their professional expertise, that future updates with additional validity and reliability data could show the CELF to be a dependable, valid, and useful diagnostic instrument.

References

Guilford, J. P. (1967). *The nature of human intelligence.* New York: McGraw-Hill.

Johnson, D., & Myklebust, H. R. (1967). *Learning disabilities: Educational principles and practices.* New York: Grune & Stratton.

McGrady, H. J., & Olson, D. A. (1970). Visual and auditory learning processes in normal children and children with learning disabilities. *Exceptional Children, 36,* 581-589.

Meier, J. H. (1971). Prevalence and characteristics of learning disabilities found in second grade children. *Journal of Learning Disabilities, 4,* 1-16.

Muma, J. R. (1984). Semel and Wiig's CELF: Construct validity? *ASHA, 49,* 101-103.

Rosenthal, J. H. (1970). A preliminary psycholinguistic study of children with learning disabilities. *Journal of Learning Disabilities, 3,* 391-95.

Salvia, J., & Ysseldyke, J. E. (1978). *Assessment in special and remedial education.* Boston: Houghton Mifflin Company.

Semel, E. M., & Wiig, E. H. (1975). Comprehension of syntactic structures and critical verbal elements by children with learning disabilities. *Journal of Learning Disabilities, 8,* 53-58.

Semel, E. M., & Wiig, E. H. (1980). *Clinical Evaluation of Language Functions: Diagnostic battery.* Columbus, OH: Charles E. Merrill Publishing Company.

Charles E. Merrill Publishing Company. (1981). *Update 1: Clinical Evaluation of Language Functions.* Columbus, OH: Author.

Charles E. Merrill Publishing Company. (1982). *Update 2: Clinical Evaluation of Language Functions.* Columbus, OH: Author.

Charles E. Merrill Publishing Company. (1983). *Update 3: Clinical Evaluation of Language Functions.* Colubus, OH: Author.

Charles E. Merrill Publishing Company. (1984). *Update 4: Clinical Evaluation of Language Functions.* Columbus, OH: Author.

Wiig, E. H., & Semel, E. M. (1973). Comprehension of linguistic concepts requiring logical operations by learning disabled children. *Journal of Speech and Hearing Research, 16,* 627-636.

Wiig, E. H., & Semel, E. M. (1974). Development of comprehension of logico-grammatical sentences by grade school children. *Perceptual and Motor Skills, 38,* 171-176.

Wiig, E. H., & Semel, E. M. (1975). Productive language abilities in learning disabled adolescents. *Journal of Learning Disabilities, 8,* 578-586.

Wiig, E. H., Semel, E. M., & Abele, E. (1981). Perception and interpretation of ambiguous sentences by learning disabled twelve-year-olds. *Learning Disability Quarterly, 4,* 3-12.

Wiig, E. H., Semel, E. M., & Crouse, M.A.B. (1973). The use of morphology by high-risk and learning disabled children. *Journal of Learning Disabilities, 6,* 457-465.

Edward M. Wolpert, Ed.D.
Dean, School of Education, Georgia College, Milledgeville, Georgia.

Robert B. Bartos, Ed.D.
Assistant Dean, School of Education, Georgia College, Milledgeville, Georgia.

CLYMER-BARRETT READINESS TEST

Theodore Clymer and Thomas C. Barrett. Santa Barbara, California: Chapman, Brook & Kent.

Introduction

The Clymer-Barrett Readiness Test (CBRT) seeks to measure the readiness of a kindergarten or first-grade child to engage successfully in systematic reading instruction. The test's authors claim that the results of the test offer a diagnostic profile of a class of children that may be used for screening and grouping for instruction.

The authors of the test are Theodore Clymer and Thomas Barrett. Clymer is director of the Institute for Reading Research in Santa Barbara. He was formerly Professor of Education at the University of Minnesota and is a past president of the International Reading Association. He is also the senior author of the Ginn Reading 360, Ginn Reading 720, and Ginn Reading Program. Barrett is Professor of Education and head of the department of elementary education at the University of Wisconsin in Madison. He, too, is a past president of the International Reading Association and coauthor for the Ginn Reading 360 and the Ginn Reading 720 series. The CBRT bears a 1983 copyright and is published in a revised edition.

The test consists of a 16-page booklet, on which students mark their answers directly after receiving oral directions from their teacher. Subsequently, the pupils' marks are scored and interpreted. A manual (Clymer & Barrett, 1983a, 1983b) provides the teacher with specific instructions on the test's administration, including direct quotations of instructions to give the pupils. In addition, the teacher is directed to complete a readiness survey, which is included in the test. The survey rates children on certain other readiness skills that go beyond the CBRT's six subtests. The CBRT is available in two forms (A and B), as well as in a full form and a short form. Forms A and B are virtually identical, differing only in item content. The full form of either Form A or B consists of all six subtests; the short form consists of Subtest 1 (Recognizing Letters) and Subtest 3 (Beginning Sounds). The manuals (p. 1) state that the short form can be used to provide "a quick survey of readiness for instruction."

This test is designed to measure six elements of reading readiness that, according to the authors, are important in predicting future success in learning to read. Each of these elements is a subtest, with visual discrimination measured by the first two, auditory discrimination by the next two, and visual-motor coordination by the last two. On all of the first five subtests, pupils are given an opportunity to demonstrate understanding of the instructions and practice using the response format. Two unscored practice items are provided for Subtests 1-5; no practice item is given for Subtest 6. The six subtests are described as follows:

Recognizing Letters (35 items): Students are directed to observe a line of five letters and to draw a line with a pencil through a given letter (e.g., through the letter "G"). The first 25 items use lowercase letters, and the last ten use capitals.

Matching Words (20 items): Pupils are directed to look at a word in the lefthand column (the "little box") and the four words in the "big box" to the right of it. They are then instructed to draw a line through the one word out of the four that looks like the one in the little box.

Beginning Sounds (20 items): Pupils are directed to observe a picture in the lefthand column and are told what it is. From the three pictures that are presented to the right of it, they are directed to draw a line through the one that begins with the same sound as the picture on the left.

Ending Sounds (20 items): Pupils are told that a picture in a lefthand column has a certain sound and are asked to determine which of three pictures to the right of it has the same ending sound.

Completing Shapes (14 items): Students are directed to observe a geometric shape and duplicate it by completing a series of lines or curves representing a portion of that shape.

Copy-A-Sentence (one item): Pupils are directed to a seven-word sentence containing all letters of the alphabet and are told to copy that sentence in the space provided.

The Clymer-Barrett readiness survey consists of eight characteristics: Oral Language, Vocabulary and Concepts, Listening Skills, Thinking Abilities, Social Skills, Emotional Development, Attitudes Toward Learning, and Work Habits. Each characteristic is comprised of three descriptors to which a rating of low, average, or high is assigned. For example, Oral Language contains the three descriptors "Takes part in classroom discussions," "Expresses needs effectively," and "Relates a story clearly." According to the manuals, teachers are directed to rate the pupils on each descriptor of each characteristic and summarize these ratings in an overall rating of low, average, or high. Each child should score low, average, or high, depending on that child's rank in the classroom, not to all children.

On the back of the test booklet is a summary page with descriptive information on the child: name, sex, age, teacher, grade, school, city, state, testing date. There are also spaces to record the scores and stanines of each of the subtests, the full form, and the short form.

Practical Applications/Uses

This test is designed to be administered to a group of kindergarten or first-grade children by the classroom teacher. However, it might be administered to an individual if such information would be valuable to a teacher. The manuals recommend that the test be administered at the end of the kindergarten year or at the beginning of first grade. They also recommend that the test be given in several sittings and estimate that 30 minutes is required for the administration of each subtest. Subtest 6, Copy-A-Sentence, has a strict time limit of five minutes of pupil working time; Subtest 5, Completing Shapes, allows a limit of 15 seconds for each of the 20 items; and in Subtests 1-4, the examiner is directed to allow eight or ten seconds between the introduction of each item.

Scoring is done by the teacher directly from the pupil booklets. On Subtests 1-4, students mark a picture or letter indicating their response. The score on each of these subtests is the total number of items correctly marked. For Subtest 5, Completing Shapes, the teacher judges whether the correct shape has been drawn by the pupil. The manuals give standards for judging correct or incorrect shapes. The score on this subtest is the total number of correct shapes formed by the child. For Subtest 6, Copy-A-Sentence, the total possible score is 7. Examples are given for scores of 7, 6, 3, and 2, from which teachers may judge the scores pupils should be awarded according to the accuracy with which they copied the sentence. Scoring of the six subtests should be accomplished in seven or eight minutes per pupil booklet. Machine scoring is not available.

Subtests 1-4 yield data that merely need to be counted. Subtests 5 and 6 require some judgment on the part of the examiner; however, the standards presented should make these judgments fairly easy to accomplish.

A norm chart, which allows for conversion of total scores on the test to percentile ranks and stanines, is provided. Other norm charts, which allow conversion of visual discrimination, auditory discrimination, and visual-motor coordination into stanines only, are also provided.

Technical Aspects

The manuals report data in narrative and tabular formats that support the authors' claims that the test is reliable and valid. No bibliographic references are provided on the research studies that generated these data. The manuals report a study done with a norming population of 5,565 first-grade pupils. A random sample of 188 pupils, one from each of 188 classrooms in the norming group, was used to compute reliability coefficients yielding measures of internal consistency. In this analysis, the six subtests were combined, and reliability coefficients were computed (see Table 1). These coefficients indicate that the full test and the various combinations of subtests do indeed have a high degree of internal consistency, an index of the test's reliability. This means that in this test the various items "hang together" well (i.e., they all contribute more or less equally to the total score).

A further study of reliability was done on the use of the test with five "atypical groups" that "might present special testing problems" (Clymer & Barrett, 1983, p. 27). These atypical groups included regional, ethnic, and ability differences. The manual reports coefficients ranging from .89 to .98 on these groups.

Items for the published Forms A and B were drawn from a pool of items originally included in three forms. The items with the highest validity were selected for inclusion in Forms A and B and were alternately assigned to these forms on the basis of their difficulty and validity ratings. On a study of 2,468 pupils, an analysis of means and standard deviations of each subtest and the full form on each of Form A and B shows that the two forms are quite similar and may be used interchange-

Table 1

Reliability Coefficients for the Six CBRT Subtests

Subtest	*Combined Skill*	*Reliability Coefficient*
(1) Recognizing Letters (2) Matching Words	Visual Discrimination	.97
(3) Beginning Sounds (4) Ending Sounds	Auditory Discrimination	.90
(5) Completing Shapes (6) Copy-A-Sentence	Visual-Motor Coordination	.94
(1) Recognizing Letters (3) Beginning Sounds	Short Form	.96
All subtests	Full Form	.97

ably. Another analysis on the same group of 2,468 pupils shows that the two forms correlate highly; coefficients on the subtests range from .57 to .92. The coefficient for the full form is reported at .89. This, too, indicates that Form A and B are indeed equivalent (Clymer & Barrett, 1983a, 1983b).

The manuals claim that the test possesses content validity because the skills it measures are similar to those skills carried out in elementary classrooms during reading instruction. Similarly, construct validity is claimed on the basis of the subtests being "similar to the activities undertaken in reading instruction and in other areas of the primary curriculum" (p. 28). The manuals further discuss the correlation of the test with other readiness tests and intelligence tests, claiming that the correlations are high enough to show some concurrent validity (the two tests are measuring the same thing), yet not so high as to indicate that one test could replace the other. For example, correlations were .42 for the Stanford-Binet Form L-M, .55 for Pintner-Cunningham, .55 for California Test of Mental Maturity, and .55 for Kuhlman-Anderson.

According to the manuals, the predictive validity of the test, its ability to predict success in reading instruction, is claimed on the basis of several studies that correlate scores of the test taken in the fall with reading achievement scores taken in the spring. Using the test as the predictor variable and the subtests of each of four different reading achievement tests as the criterion variables, correlation coefficients ranging from .40 to .69 are reported. The studies used reasonably large numbers of pupils (87, 89, 98, 143, and 816). These coefficients indicate that the test is a fair predictor of reading achievement as measured by the four criterion measures (Stanford Achievement, Gates Primary Reading, Gates-MacGinitie Reading, and Metropolitan Achievement Test).

Critique

The CBRT appears to be a useful device for predicting the reading achievement in first grade for a group given reading instruction with typical basal-reader methodology. The test is fairly short, easy to administer, score, and interpret. There are, however, some issues and problems that need to be considered in deciding the usefulness and appropriateness of this test in an instructional program. One problem is with the test's reliability. The test purports to be reliable based on measures of its internal consistency. Although this is a measure of a test's reliability, an additional measure is needed: its stability. Unfortunately, no data from a test-retest study are provided. An indication of the test's stability over time would be reassuring—an examiner would be more confident that the score obtained on an individual or group is an accurate measure.

The other problem is with the test's validity. The predictive validity data present correlation coefficients derived from an analysis using the test as the predictor and reading achievement scores as a criterion. This is an analysis using *group data,* with coefficients ranging from .40 to .69. Although these coefficients are high enough to make predictions for a group of children, they are not high enough to be useful in predicting the success of an individual child in learning to read. However, the major problem with the test's validity is that the content validity of the test is questionable. The manuals (p. 28) state: "Major support for the content validity of the CBRT is found in its similarity in skill focus to the activities carried out in elementary classrooms during reading instruction." This is not a surprising statement from these test authors, both of whom authored basal-reader series and whose view of reading and reading instruction is no doubt influenced by their background and experience with basal readers. Although it is true that the large majority of reading instruction in elementary schools is delivered through the medium of basal readers, reading instruction cannot be viewed as a monolithic entity. Different methods of teaching reading stress different activities and approaches to word recognition and comprehension. The attributes of visual discrimination, auditory discrimination, and visual-motor coordination may or may not be important for some children and/or some instructional methods.

The attributes that do indeed influence reading readiness are many and varied. Although these attributes include those measured by the CBRT's six subtests, they include many more as well. From all possible attributes for testing and analysis, the authors have chosen six attributes represented by the six subtests that may be easily measured and interpreted. To the extent that these six attributes are more important or more representative than the many others, the test may be said to have a high degree of content validity. But this is not necessarily the case.

The authors recognize the multifaceted nature of reading readiness by providing the readiness survey as a part of the test, yet it is separate and distinct from the six subtests. This survey deals with some extremely important variables known to influence reading achievement (e.g., oral language development, motivation; thinking abilities) that do not lend themselves to the same ease and precision of measurement that the six subtests do. Some would argue that these characteristics rated in the readiness survey are more important than those measured by the subtests. However, the authors, in referring to the analysis and use of the total test, state that the readiness survey is "informal" and thus "detailed procedures for the analysis of results cannot be given" (Clymer & Barrett, 1983a, 1983b, p. 26). They direct the teacher to look for strengths and weaknesses for individuals and for the whole class and to plan classroom activities accordingly.

The readiness survey is not given much attention in the instructions for analysis and use of the test's results. Rather, it is presented as an adjunct to the six subtests even though the characteristics it rates may be more important. The variables that are easy to quantify, measure, and interpret, and are represented by the six subtests are the bulk of this test. Ease of measurement translates to importance; qualitative judgments are dismissed relatively lightly. This is the major fault of this (and many other such) readiness tests. However, with recognition of the limitations of the test, if administered and interpreted by a competent professional who is cognizant and appreciative of the many qualitative factors involved in judging reading readiness, the test can provide useful information to a teacher planning an instructional program in beginning reading.

References

Clymer, T., & Barrett, T. C. (1983a). *Clymer-Barrett Readiness Test, Form A manual.* Santa Barbara, CA: Chapman, Brook & Kent.

Clymer, T., & Barrett, T. C. (1983b). *Clymer-Barrett Readiness Test, Form B manual.* Santa Barbara, CA: Chapman, Brook & Kent.

Nancy E. Monroe, Ph.D.
Associate Professor of Speech-Language Pathology, Oklahoma State University, Stillwater, Oklahoma.

COMMUNICATIVE ABILITIES IN DAILY LIVING

Audrey L. Holland. Austin, Texas: PRO-ED.

Introduction

The Communicative Abilities in Daily Living (CADL) was designed to assess an aphasic individual's ability to communicate in everyday encounters using both language forms and nonverbal communication. In addition, this test assesses an aphasic's communicative strengths and weaknesses and provides direction for work on functional activities in therapy.

The CADL was developed by Audrey L. Holland, a professor in the department of speech and theatre arts at the University of Pittsburgh. Holland received her Ph.D. from the University of Pittsburgh and has been involved in research, teaching, and clinical work with aphasics for a number of years. She began work on developing this test in 1975 with support from the National Institute of Neurological, Communicative Disorders and Stroke because she perceived a need for a test that observed speech and communication acts in natural environments. Her work was influenced by writings in the areas of communicative competence, a holistic view of communication, and language functions or speech acts. These works prompted Holland to develop a test that would sample all of the ways in which aphasics communicate rather than focus on language alone. Up to this time the only other test for aphasics that measured functional communication was Sarno's (1969) Functional Communication Profile.

During the initial stages of test development, Holland and her colleagues sought input on the types of communicative activities in which people engage every day. This information formed a basis for developing 73 test items. The test developers attempted to design items that would not be influenced by life-style, age, socioeconomic status, or physical mobility. They also tried to control the linguistic complexity by using high frequency words and short, simple utterances. This initial version of the test was presented to 15 aphasics and 15 normal adults to determine the ease of presentation and the examiner's ability to discriminate and score responses. Scoring was done on a three-point scale. Test results were compared with actual observations of the communication of aphasic and normal subjects in daily life situations and with observations of family members gathered from interviews. Results were also compared with scores on the Porch Index of Communicative Ability (PICA), the Functional Communication Profile (FCP), and the Boston Diagnostic Aphasia Examination (BDAE).

After the initial testing, five CADL items were eliminated, and other items were rewritten for clarity. The published version of the test contains 68 items.

The pilot study was followed by two additional studies, which were designed to provide normative data, assess reliability and validity, and field test the CADL. The first study involved 80 aphasics who were given the CADL, the PICA, FCP, and BDAE. A behavioral observation and an interview with a family or a staff member were also included for comparative purposes. In order to participate in the study, aphasics had to be at least three months post onset, and there could be no indications of dementia or bilateral brain damage. Information was gathered concerning the age, sex, education, type of aphasia, severity of aphasia, time post onset, handedness, and presence of hemiplegia or hemiparesis for each subject in order to determine the possible effect of these variables on test performance.

The second study included 130 aphasics, with age, sex, and institutionalization controlled. The aphasic group, as well as a group of normally aging adults, was tested on the CADL. The effects of age, sex, and institutionalization on test performance were assessed for both groups.

Although special versions of the CADL have not been developed, the test has been used experimentally with groups other than aphasics, such as mentally retarded adults and hearing-aid users.

The published version of the CADL includes a manual and a loose-leaf notebook, which contains stimulus materials such as pictures, a training tape, and a supply of 16-page score booklets. It is necessary for the examiner to provide some additional materials, including shoelaces, soup packages, watches, a stethoscope, a white physician's jacket, coins, calendar pages, and signs. Paper and pencil are also provided by the examiner so that the client can respond by writing or drawing if desired.

The test is comprised of 68 items. Nine of these are individual items, and the remainder are presented in the context of four communicative situations (clinician-client interaction in the therapy setting, going to the doctor's office and driving home, going shopping, and using the telephone). Each item is scored on a three-point scale, with 0 indicating wrong, 1 indicating adequate or related, and 2 indicating correct.

The CADL yields a single score that can be compared to a cutoff score that demarcates the presence of a functional communication disorder. The CADL is not divided into subtests, but the results can be analyzed according to ten categories if the clinician desires more detailed information regarding areas of strength and weakness. The categories are 1) reading, writing, and calculating; 2) speech acts or pragmatic intents; 3) utilization of contextual information; 4) role playing; 5) performance of sequenced behavior and recognition of cause-effect relationships; 6) well-rehearsed social conventions; 7) divergences (formulating logical responses when presented with a situation); 8) nonverbal symbolic communication; 9) deixis (movement-related communicative behavior); and 10) humor, absurdity, and metaphor.

The 16-page score booklet gives complete test instructions and provides space to enter biographical information and to record and score the client's responses.

Practical Applications/Uses

The CADL was designed to assess communicative competence of aphasics. It can be used in a variety of settings, such as nursing homes, hospitals, clinics, and schools, but will probably be used most frequently in clinical settings that treat brain-damaged individuals. The speech-language pathologist would be the person most qualified to administer and score the test and interpret the results. Although other professionals could learn to administer the test, interpreting the test results is primarily a function of the speech-language pathologist.

This test was intended for use with adults, and normative data are provided for this population. However, it could be adapted for use with younger age groups. It can be used with aphasics of all severity levels. It will probably prove most informative with aphasics with moderate levels of impairment. However, with the severely nonverbal aphasic, it will provide some insight regarding alternative modes of communication. Although this test is used most commonly with aphasics, some application has been found with adults who have impaired language ability due to other reasons such as hearing loss or mental retardation. Holland tested both of these populations with the CADL. The retarded population performed much like the aphasic one, but less variability in scores was noted. The hearing-impaired population, consisting of people whose losses occurred after the acquisition of language, performed within the low normal range.

This test should be administered on an individual basis by a speech-language pathologist. Instructions to be used in administration are specified on the score sheet, and alternative instructions are provided for each item when no response is obtained. Examiners have an active role in the administration of this test and are called on to play several different roles with the client. It is suggested by the test developer that the examiner use a friendly, informal manner. Feedback from the examiner, as well as use of humor and acting ability, is encouraged. An audio training tape also provides an example of both test administration and scoring, and the potential user can learn how to administer the test from these materials. The authors report that it takes approximately 45 minutes to give the entire test; however, it can take 60 to 90 minutes with some clients. Although selected portions of the test might be administered for purposes of describing certain behaviors, the results can be used most effectively if the test is given in its entirety in the order specified.

A training tape and several additional example tests are provided in the manual in order to teach accurate scoring, which is based on a three-point scale. Reliable judgments can be made following approximately two hours of training. A "2" response appears the easiest to judge, with the distinction between "0" and "1" somewhat ambiguous at times. Once scoring is mastered, it can generally be done during the course of the test. However, in some situations, scoring might require an additional 30 minutes following the test. Due to the relative ease of scoring, it is not time consuming to do by hand.

Once testing is completed, the examiner totals the scores (0, 1, or 2) on the 68 test items to determine the overall score. Cutoff scores, distinguishing between normal and aphasic communication, are provided according to age, sex, and institutionalization. In addition, mean scores and standard deviations are provided for subjects according to age, sex, institutionalization, and type of aphasia. If the examiner would like to obtain additional descriptive information for planning therapy, an item analysis can be done. Correct responses in the ten subcategories mentioned previously can be determined.

After completing the recommended training provided in the manual, an examiner should be able to compute test results accurately. However, if the examiner wishes to go beyond test scores and describe communicative behavior in depth, this would require one to two years of working with aphasic clients.

Technical Aspects

The validity of the CADL was tested with a group of 80 aphasics who were also given the Boston Diagnostic Aphasia Examination (BDAE), the Porch Index of Communicative Ability (PICA), and the Functional Communication Profile (FCP). In addition, a four-hour behavioral observation and an interview with a family member or living staff member were conducted. Criterion validity was assessed by comparing CADL scores with observations. Comparisons were made of appropriate verbal and nonverbal communication behavior as a proportion of total communication attempts; total verbal communication attempts; and appropriate verbal behavior in the categories of social convention, requesting, answering, and volunteering. Correlations ranged from .60 to .71 (Holland, 1980).

According to the manual, performance on the CADL was compared to performance on the PICA (.93), the BDAE (.84), and the FCP (.87) in order to determine concurrent validity. Comparisons were also made between CADL scores and family-living staff ratings. Twenty-three behaviors were rated, and ratings and CADL scores concurred on 18 of 23 items. The overall correlation was .67.

In addition, construct validity was examined by comparing mean scores on the CADL among aphasics classified by type. Aphasic subgroups ranked as expected with the global aphasics most impaired, followed by transcortical, Wernicke's, mixed, Broca's, and anomic aphasics. These combined measures provide evidence that the CADL is a valid measure of language. The CADL's ability to reflect communicative competence adequately, as evidenced by observations, is not as strong.

In order to determine reliability, 20 subjects were tested by two examiners at different times with an intervening time interval of one to three weeks. This resulted in a correlation of .99 for interjudge reliability.

Reliability was tested further by assessing internal consistency across all items for all subjects (.97) and by comparing item scores and total scores. These item analyses indicated that three items were in need of revision or elimination because they failed to discriminate performance adequately.

Age, sex, and institutionalization were controlled during subject selection, and CADL scores were analyzed to determine the effects of these factors for both aphasics and nonaphasics. It was found that nonaphasics perform better than aphasics, noninstitutionalized aphasics perform better than institutionalized, scores drop as a function of age, and noninstitutionalized females perform better than noninstitutionalized males. This sex difference was not observed in institutionalized subjects.

Subject selection was not controlled for occupation, education, or social contacts. However, using various scaling devices, the effect of these factors was also assessed. Occupation and education did not have a significant effect on performance on the CADL. However, there was a significant correlation between social contacts and CADL scores for noninstitutionalized subjects but not for institutionalized subjects. Holland (1980) attributes this, in part, to the inadequacy of the measure used to determine social contacts.

As might be expected, there was a strong relationship (.729) between CADL scores and severity of aphasia. Differences were also found between subjects with different types of aphasia, as stated earlier. However, it should be noted that this comparison was confounded by the effects of age and institutionalization.

Performance on specific test items indicated that three categories (social conventions; divergences; and humor, absurdity, and metaphor) were most prominent in distinguishing between types of aphasics. Holland (1980) provides comprehensive statistical analyses for the initial publication of this test.

In addition to assessing aphasics, Holland tested 30 mentally retarded individuals (20 females and ten males), using the CADL. These subjects ranged in age from 29 to 50, ranged in IQ from 50-80, lived at home or in group living arrangements but were not institutionalized, had no visual or hearing difficulties, and were employed in sheltered workshops or more formal work settings. CADL scores were compared with work supervisors' ratings of work habits and ratings on a seven-point functional adaptability scale. Analysis of the results indicated that the mean score of this mentally retarded sample was similar to that of the aphasics tested. However, there was less variability in the scores for the retarded group. Comparisons yielded a correlation of .716 between CADL scores and IQ, $r = .435$ between CADL and functional adaptability, and $r = .355$ between CADL and work habits rating.

Holland also administered the CADL to a group of 30 adult, hearing-impaired subjects in order to determine if this test would also be useful in assessing communication skills secondary to a hearing loss. In order to meet the selection criteria, subjects had to have a Speech Reception Threshold (SRT) of 50 db or less, had to have acquired language before the onset of the hearing loss, and had to be experienced hearing-aid users. Test results indicated that these subjects' scores were slightly depressed in comparison to the normal hearing group. However, for the most part, they did function in the normal communicative range. This group was also asked questions regarding satisfaction with hearing-aid use, and responses were rated on a 16-point scale. There was not a significant relationship between CADL scores and the hearing-aid-use scale or SRT scores or speech discrimination scores. Holland concludes that the CADL might prove useful with a more inclusive sample of the hearing impaired.

Critique

The purpose of the CADL is to assess overall communication skills in practical situations. The CADL does provide some useful information regarding a client's pragmatic skills, ways a client attempts to respond, and modes of communication. However, this should be regarded as screening information. With one to two years of experience with aphasic clients, the clinician can gain additional descriptive information regarding a client's communication skills based on clinical judgment.

This test appears to be most useful with aphasic clients or high-level mentally retarded individuals. Its usefulness is more limited with clients who demonstrate moderate to severe verbal apraxia or emotional problems of clinical significance.

However, Wertz, LaPointe, and Rosenbek (1984) report that the CADL can be used with apraxics to determine how apraxic errors influence functional communication. They found with a limited sample of three subjects that the CADL scores accurately reflected functional communication skills.

The ability to assess functional communication is hampered by some of the stimulus materials. Some situations appear unrealistic, and some responses are too dependent on the use of stimulus pictures.

Overall, this test can provide screening information regarding a client's social and communicative skills. Linebaugh, Kryzer, Oden, and Myers (1982) report a significant correlation between percentage of communicative exchanges initiated by aphasic speakers and CADL scores. In addition, the CADL does represent a contribution to an area that needs the attention of aphasiologists—the discrepancy in communication performance between test situations and social situations. The test can also provide useful information regarding the direction and effects of long-term treatment. With some additional refinements, this test will probably achieve its purpose better.

References

This list includes text citations as well as suggested additional reading.

Chapey, R. (1981). *Language intervention strategies in adult aphasia.* Boston: Williams and Wilkins.

Holland, A. L. (1980). *The Communicative Abilities in Daily Living manual.* Austin, TX: PRO-ED.

Holland, A. L. (1984). *Language disorders in adults: Recent advances.* San Diego: College-Hill Press.

Linebaugh, C. W., Kryzer, K. M., Oden, S. E., & Myers, P. S. (1982). Reapportionment of communicative burden in aphasia. In R. H. Brookshire (Ed.), *Clinical aphasiology: Conference proceedings.* Minneapolis: BRK Publishers.

Sarno, M. T. (1969). *Functional Communication Profile.* New York: Institute of Rehabilitation Medicine.

Sarno, M. T. (1981). *Acquired aphasia.* New York: Academic Press.

Wertz, R., LaPointe, L., & Rosenbek, J. (1984). *Apraxia of speech in adults.* Orlando, FL: Grune & Stratton, Inc.

John L. Florell, Ph.D.
Executive Director, The Health Center, Bloomington, Illinois.

COMMUNICATIVE EVALUATION CHART FROM INFANCY TO FIVE YEARS

Ruth M. Anderson, Madeline Miles, and Patricia A. Matheny. Cambridge, Massachusetts: Educators Publishing Service, Inc.

Introduction

The Communicative Evaluation Chart From Infancy to Five Years (CEC) is designed to give a quick impression of a child's over-all abilities or disabilities in language and performance to see if a child needs to be referred for further assessment. It contains four printed pages of language and performance levels for the child aged three months, six months, nine months, 12 months, 18 months, 24 months, 36 months, four years, and five years.

Two speech pathologists, Ruth Anderson and Madeline Miles, and an audiologist, Patricia Matheny, developed the CEC while they were working at Children's Hospital in Denver, Colorado, in the early 1960s. The test took four years to develop, using the developmental concepts of Gesell (Gesell, Thompson, & Amatruda, 1934), Binet (Binet & Henir, 1896), Cattell (1960), and other developmentalists (e.g., Peck & Havighurst, 1960; Boyd & Mandler, 1951; Maurer, 1953; Illingworth, 1960). The authors wanted an instrument that audiologists, speech pathologists, and psychologists could use quickly to access age-appropriate language and performance and pick up potential deficiencies. Both Anderson and Miles had M.A. degrees in speech pathology. Anderson was director of the speech clinic at Children's Hospital in Denver from 1948 to 1963 and Assistant Professor in the Speech and Hearing Department at the University of Denver from 1963 to 1965. In 1965, she became Associate Professor in the Speech and Hearing Sciences Department of the University of Arizona in Tucson. Miles, a colleague of Anderson in the speech clinic at Children's Hospital, left Children's Hospital in 1963 to become clinical coordinator and later acting director of the Center for Disorders of Communication at the Medical Center Hospital of Vermont in Burlington. She served as a special education consultant for the state department of education, a visiting professor at the University of Vermont, and a speech consultant at Trinity College in Burlington. No biographical information is available on Matheny, the audiologist. All three authors are retired from professional service.

The CEC was developed using the patients of the speech clinic at Children's Hospital in Denver. The authors wanted to create a quick screening device for preschool children. It was intended to demonstrate whether a child should be referred for a complete diagnostic work-up. Children from six months to five years of age were the primary population. The speech clinic served a cross section of socioeconomic groups from the Denver metropolitan area (M. Mile, personal communication, February, 1985).

No revision has been done. A manual was developed but never approved by the authors. Puzzles, form board, and a pegman were briefly marketed but are no longer available.

The test is available only in English, and no other forms have been developed.

Items on the left side of each test page are based on the average child's capacity to gain and use language as a tool. They deal with coordination of speech musculature, development of hearing acuity and auditory perception, acquisition of the vowels and consonants, and growth of receptive and expressive language. Items on the right side of the page evaluate physical well-being, normal growth and development, motor coordination, and beginning visual-motor-perceptual skills.

The examiner marks the protocol " + " for present, "–" for not present, and " ± " for fluctuating while observing the child or getting some history of infants from parents. The examiner must observe physical behavior, simple speech patterns, and behavioral activity of the subject. The tests for each age group are short (15 to 30 items) and easy to administer. Each age group has its own set of items, and the test is not cumulative. All items and answers are on the same test sheet.

Practical Applications/Uses

The CEC is a screening device for preschool children who may be suspected of having language or performance difficulties. Although the CEC is most appropriately used by speech pathologists and audiologists, public health nurses, child psychologists, social workers, early childhood educators, and day-care specialists would find the CEC a potential instrument to use with middle-class, English-speaking preschool children whom they feel may have language or performance problems. The chart also seems to be effective in discovering children who need further evaluation.

Lack of a manual to guide the examiner and the absences of testing tools, such as puzzles and pegman figures, make the CEC difficult to administer. It is a gross screening test, is not meant to be substituted for a full developmental evaluation, and seems to have been used exclusively in speech clinics.

Although the test is designed to screen preschoolers for language and performance difficulties and measure speech mechanisms, hearing, auditory perception, growth motor coordination, and visual-motor-perceptual skills, if expanded to a broader population base, it could be used for preschool screening at the nursery-school and day-care level. However, to accomplish this it would need to be updated.

This chart would be good for most white, English-speaking preschoolers. It does not seem appropriate for non-English-speaking, lower socioeconomic, or nonwhite populations. There seems to be no adaptations for non-preschool or handicapped groups.

The CEC can be administered in clinical settings, such as physicians' offices, speech clinics, private offices, or any setting where the child can be free of distraction and directly in contact with the examiner. For older children (four and five years), a larger play area is needed to observe gross movement and play.

The CEC is simple to administer at lower age levels (up to two years), but the lack of a manual makes it difficult to administer to higher levels. Standardized testing tools, such as puzzles, form board and pegman, are no longer available commercially and must be improvised to use the CEC. The sequence of the test can be altered if deemed necessary; administration takes 8-15 minutes with subjects under 18 months and 15-30 minutes with subjects over 18 months.

Scoring, which is clearly presented and restricted to gross measures, can be learned in two or three hours. It is accomplished simultaneously with the administration. The main difficulty in scoring is that some subjective judgments must be made about the children's responses. The CEC is marked " + " (present), "−" (not present), and " ± " (fluctuating) for both language and performance areas. In evaluating children under three years, numerous minus marks or fluctuation marks serve as a warning that extensive examinations may be necessary. If the minus and fluctuating marks persist in the evaluation of three to five year olds, immediate help should be obtained. The chart can only be hand scored, but because measurement is simple, there are few problems in scoring.

Interpretation is based on clinical judgment, and test results are easy to interpret. The examiner must have basic knowledge of early childhood development and be able to interpret children's behaviors, as well as have some knowledge of age-appropriate behavior and speech development. Professionals in speech and hearing appear to be better suited to use the CEC because of the clinical judgment necessary.

Technical Aspects

The CEC is constructed on the basis of face validity. Norms of language and performance are predetermined and used as a checklist of development. There are no validity or reliability studies of the CEC. The population that was used to develop the CEC were children from the speech clinic of Children's Hospital in Denver, but reliability studies have not been performed with various groups. Additionally, a computer search of *Psychological Abstracts* back to 1967 and *Dissertation Abstracts* back to 1970 shows no reference to the CEC.

Critique

This reviewer used the CEC with ten preschoolers aged 18 months to five years and has conducted an extensive investigation of the CEC with the help of a public-school speech pathologist, a private speech pathologist, an audiologist, a public service nurse, a special education teacher, and a child psychologist. All were hampered by not having a manual to help in administration and had to improvise equipment as the CEC was administered to different age groups. Some areas, especially the assessment of vocabulary, consonant use, and self-correction in pronouncing new words, were too difficult for those not involved in regular diagnosis of speech or speech disorders. In addition, conducting observation was difficult due to the lack of instructions. The speech pathologist and audiologist felt that their professional experiences helped to interpret over-all speech performance but that some assessments were not possible without extensive observation.

There have been many developments in screening tests for preschool children since 1963 when the CEC was developed. School systems often provide similar screening for preschoolers as a regular part of their services and use a wide variety of better-packaged screening devices. Because the CEC has not been revised or standardized for different populations and has no reliability studies, statistical analysis, or manual to direct administration and standardize testing materials, the CEC is not as effective for screening children for language and performance disabilities as other available tests, such as the Mann-Suiter Primary Developmental Screening, Santa Clara Inventory of Developmental Tasks, and the ABC Inventory.

References

Anderson, R. M., Miles, M., & Matheny, P. A. (1963). *Communicative Evaluation Chart From Infancy to Five Years.* Cambridge, MA: Educators Publishing Service, Inc.

Binet, A., & Henir, V. (1896). Psychologie individuelle. *Annei Psychologie, 3,* 296-332.

Boyd, N., & Mandler, G. (1951). Children's responses to human stories and pictures. *Journal of Consulting Psychology, 19,* 367-371.

Cattell, P. (1960). *The measurement of intelligence in infants and young children.* Cleveland: The Psychological Corporation.

Gesell, A., Thompson, H., & Amatruda, C. S. (1934). *An atlas of infant behavior: A systematic delineation of the forms and early growth of human behavior patterns* (Vol. I). New Haven: Yale University Press.

Illingworth, R. S. (1960). *An introduction to developmental assessment in the first years.* London: The National Spastics Society.

Maurer, K. M. (1953). *Intellectual status at maturity as a criterion for selecting items in preschool tests* (Monograph Series No. 21). Minneapolis: University of Minnesota Press, University of Minnesota Institute of Child Welfare.

Peck, R. F., & Havighurst, R. J. (1960). *Psychology of character development.* New York: Wiley & Sons.

Peter F. Merenda, Ph.D.

Professor Emeritus of Psychology and Statistics, University of Rhode Island, and Vice Chairman and Senior Psychologist, Walter V. Clarke Associates, Inc., Providence, Rhode Island.

COMREY PERSONALITY SCALES

Andrew L. Comrey. San Diego, California: Educational and Industrial Testing Service.

Introduction

The Comrey Personality Scales (CPS) can best be defined on the basis of the Glossary definitions that appear in the current edition of the *Standards for Educational and Psychological Testing* (American Psychological Association, 1985). In general, it is an "inventory" which is defined as:

> A questionnaire or checklist, usually in the form of a self-report, that elicits information about an individual. Inventories are not tests in the strict sense; they are most often concerned with personality characteristics, interests, attitudes, preferences, personal problems, motivation, and so forth. (p. 92)

More specifically, it is a "personality inventory" which is defined as:

> An inventory that measures one or more characteristics that are regarded generally as psychological attributes or interpersonal skills. (p. 92)

The author is Andrew L. Comrey, who is Professor of Psychology at the University of California, Los Angeles. Professor Comrey received his Ph.D. degree in psychology in 1949 from the University of Southern California where he studied under the direction and supervision of J. P. Guilford. Undoubtedly, it was this doctoral-level preparation under an outstanding mentor that provided the author with an excellent background to pursue the extensive and productive developmental research that led to the publication of the scales in 1970. In his own words "The history of the *Comrey Personality Scales* extends back over fifteen years when the writer gradually shifted his interest to the psychometric investigation of personality following earlier work with the measurement of human abilities" (Comrey, 1970, p. 11). Comrey goes on to say that he became intrigued with the realization that the prominent factor analytic theorists of that period "revealed a surprising lack of agreement" in their respective descriptions of personality. This fact was in sharp contrast to the more general consensus shared by those working in the field of human abilities. At the same time Comrey's own early studies of items in personality inventories which were popular in the 1950s and 1960s began to convince him that the developmental methods used to construct these instruments were quite poor from a psychometric point of view. This was especially true of the persistently popular MMPI—an opinion which is shared by this reviewer.

Comrey reports in the manual that the scales were standardized and the norms established on the initial sample of "365 male and 362 female university students, their friends and family members, and some other university-connected individuals" (p. 10). Presumably this sample of volunteers from a university community was obtained just prior to 1970, the copyright date indicated on the Profile Sheet. No revisions of these norms have been attempted during the 15-year period since they were first published in spite of the fact that the author posits an appropriate caveat that the norms that underlie the personality profiles yielded by the scales may be inappropriate for other than university-connected groups.

No other forms have been developed to date for the scales. This fact renders misleading the indication that the only available form is "Form A."

The CPS is a personality inventory of the paper-and-pencil type. The materials used are a booklet presenting 180 statements to the respondent, a choice of one of two separate answer sheets—one for handscoring and one for optical scanning, and a profile sheet upon which the respondent's profile is plotted. The profile is plotted by connecting the standard scores on each of 8 subscales. If the respondent is a female, the 8-factor profile is constructed on the basis of the female norms; otherwise, on the male norms.

Twenty items (statements) comprise each of the eight scales. For each scale ten of the items are positively worded and ten are negatively worded. The statements are similar to those found on common personality inventories such as the MMPI and California Psychological Inventory. There are two "validity" scales. One of these is the Validity Check (V) Scale which consists of 8 items (4 positive and 4 negative). The other is the Response Bias (R) Scale which is designed to measure social desirability in responses and which consists of 12 items (6 positive and 6 negative).

The eight scales which form the interpretable profile are: T (Trust vs. Defensiveness); O (Orderliness vs. Lack of Compulsion); C (Social Conformity vs. Rebelliousness); A (Activity vs. Lack of Energy); S (Emotional Stability vs. Neuroticism); E (Extraversion vs. Introversion); M (Masculinity vs. Femininity); P (Empathy vs. Egocentrism).

In the administration of the scales, the examiner primarily assumes responsibility for reading aloud the instructions which are printed on the front page of the booklet and for answering any question examinees may have in understanding what is expected of them in taking the inventory. The scales may be administered by any responsible person who is adequately trained to do so. However, examiners who are not sufficiently trained in the basics of psychological measurement or assessment and are not thoroughly knowledgeable of the concepts underlying the CPS should not attempt to interpret the profiles yielded by the scales.

It is not directly evident from the main body of the manual itself what age levels are best suited for having their personality structures assessed by the scales. However, implications from a variety of construct and criterion-related (concurrent) validity studies summarized in the last part of the manual suggest that the CPS is mainly adaptable to college students.

The test booklets are accompanied by separate answer sheets. There are two types of answer sheets available. On one type the respondent writes down in the appropriate space the response for scale "X" items (ranging from 1 = "never" to 7

= "always") and for scale "Y" items (ranging from 1 = "definitely not" to 7 = "definitely"). The other type is an optical scanning answer sheet. It should be noted here that the *Directions* to the respondent on the face page of the test booklet have not been updated to reflect this later development. Obviously, at an earlier time the traditional answer sheet for use with the IBM 108 machine (marked-sensed) was employed. The instructions for mark-sensing with a high graphite-content pencil is still printed on the booklet!

As mentioned previously, there is a separate profile sheet for plotting the scores on the scales. The first two scores, V and R, are used by the interpreter to determine the validity of the test-taker's responses; i.e., freedom from susceptibility of faking or exceptionally high social desirability in responses given to the statements. If the interpreter decides to proceed with the interpretation, the profile based on either the female or male norms, as appropriate, is analyzed according to the author's instructions in the manual and an accompanying *Handbook of Interpretations for the Comrey Personality Scales* (Comrey, 1980).

Briefly, these instructions inform the user of the scales to interpret scores on the full ten-scale profile thusly:

(V) *Validity Check.* A score of 8 is the expected raw score. Any score on the V scale which gives a T-score equivalent below 70 is still within the normal range, however. Higher scores are suggestive of an invalid record.

(R) *Response Bias.* High scores indicate a tendency to answer questions in a socially desirable way, making the respondent look like a "nice" person.

(T) *Trust vs. Defensiveness.* High scores indicate a belief in the basic honesty, trustworthiness, and good intentions of other people.

(O) *Orderliness vs. Lack of Compulsion.* High scores are characteristic of careful, meticulous, orderly, and highly organized individuals.

(C) *Social Conformity vs. Rebelliousness.* Individuals with high scores accept the society as it is, resent non-conformity in others, seek the approval of society, and respect the law.

(A) *Activity vs. Lack of Energy.* High-scoring individuals have a great deal of energy and endurance, work hard, and strive to excel.

(S) *Emotional Stability vs. Neuroticism.* High-scoring persons are free from depression, optimistic, relaxed, stable in mood, and confident.

(E) *Extraversion vs. Introversion.* High-scoring individuals meet people easily, seek new friends, feel comfortable with strangers, and do not suffer from stage fright.

(M) *Masculinity vs. Femininity.* High-scoring individuals tend to be rather tough-minded people who are not bothered by blood, crawling creatures, vulgarity, and who do not cry easily or show much interest in love stories.

(P) *Empathy vs. Egocentrism.* High-scoring individuals describe themselves as helpful, generous, sympathetic people who are interested in devoting their lives to the service of others.

Practical Applications/Uses

The claims made by both the author and publisher strongly suggest that the CPS has significant application value in *research* where personality variables are investigated as to their relationship to other human attributes and behaviors; in *school settings* where personality organizations and structures of individuals are matters of interest; in *counseling situations* where possibilities of adjustment difficulties are suspected; in *clinical settings* where the possibility of serious personality difficulties may arise; and in *business and industry* for selection and classification purposes. However, of 90 references cited in the manual for the CPS, this reviewer could find no more than nine that have any relevance or lend support to these claims. Such statements in the manual (pp. 27-28) as "Experience has shown," "It is the writer's conviction," "More explicit suggestions for clinical use of the scales, however, must await the accumulation of research findings concerning their value as tools in this area," and "Use of the CPS for selection and classification should be is the writer's conviction", "More explicit suggestions for clinical use of the scales, however, must await the accumulation of research findings concerning their value as tools in this area" and "Use of the CPS for selection and classification should be based on local norms collected under conditions in which the inventory is to be used and should involve appropriate follow-up validation studies" serve to reinforce this reservation. In this light, the following caveat is offered to potential users of the CPS regarding its application value: accompany its use with research involving local norming and criterion-related validation. For its application in American business and industry, such research is likely to be mandated under the *Uniform Guidelines* (Federal Register, 1978) when CPS scores enter into employment decisions.

From what is presented in the manual and other technical materials regarding the establishment of norms for the CPS and its standardization, there is reason to believe that it is primarily and, possibly exclusively, applicable to college students. Comrey himself is quoted as saying that it ". . . has been used most extensively with college students so far, but past experience has shown that subjects from 16 to 60, or more, enjoy taking the test and find the profile feedback information interesting" (Comrey, 1970, p. 27). There are no further comments by him in this manual that would convince this reviewer of the practical application value of the CPS to other more specialized populations. However, in the more up-to-date handbook published in 1980, Comrey presents a table of means and standard deviations of CPS scores (pp. 69-70) for six non-student samples. These are: state penitentiary inmates; psychiatric inpatients; applicants for police patrolman positions; psychiatric outpatients; hospital nurses; incumbent and applicant female police and parking control officers; and unspecified non-student volunteers. Potential users are advised to refer to these data in spite of the fact that they are still quite restrictive in light of the rather general claims made in the manual regarding the application value of the CPS. A further piece of information and advice is that the handbook is listed on the order form for the CPS and must be ordered as a separate item from the publisher.

The CPS is a group paper-and-pencil test that can reasonably be administered in group settings that are conducive to the examinees having the opportunity to understand and properly follow the directions for responding to the 180 statements in the test booklet. However, there is a further consideration that Comrey properly calls attention to this in the section on CPS users in the manual (p. 27). This consideration deals with the issue of the motivational circumstances surrounding the test-taking situation for individual examinees. The author alerts the administrator to the fact that the norms and other data presented in the manual are all based on volunteer subjects who were motivated to respond both accurately and truthfully. Variations of this high motivational level could serve to severely distort the CPS profiles for individuals. Hence, administrators are cautioned to establish the necessary rapport with takers of the CPS to maximize the degree of accuracy and truthfulness in their responses that leads to producing valid profiles.

Scoring the responses to the 10 CPS separate scales is rather complex. However, the author's directions for scoring are quite explicit and straightforward. One factor contributing to the efficiency of scoring is the author's test development approach in constructing bipolar scales that avoids the necessity of algebraic addition. This reviewer took the CPS and scored it without any difficulty simply by following the steps which are clearly described in the manual.

While administration and scoring of the CPS are both rather simple and can be successfully performed by any reasonable and conscientious adult who has received adequate basic training in administration and scoring of an inventory, interpretation of the profile is another matter. According to the original qualifications of test users published by the American Psychological Association (1953), the CPS would be classified as a level B test at least, or even level C. This means that the interpretation of the test protocols must be limited to persons with some basic technical knowledge, at a minimum, of test construction and use as well as supporting psychological knowledge and skills. That this is still true to some extent with the CPS is evidenced by the fact that the order form to the publisher must be signed by a presumably responsible psychologist and, for graduate students and nonmembers of APA, by a sponsor who is a member of the American Psychological Association. Further, in the handbook, Comrey states, "As with most standard psychological measuring instruments, test materials should be available only to qualified professionals and should be interpreted only by such individuals" (p. 11).

Technical Aspects

Much of the foregoing review of the CPS has been descriptive of the inventory and has dealt with issues involving the description of the scales, the author's intent, matters relating to administration, scoring and interpretation, and the norming and standardization of the scales. More important, however, in the formal critique of a psychological test, broadly defined, are issues relating to its psychometric properties and its adherence to the *standards* on psychological tests and testing promulgated by the American Psychological Association. These latter sections of the critique are considered by this reviewer (and likely by the readers of this critique as well) to be of utmost importance. The comments, criticisms, and recommendations that follow are made mainly in consideration of the two most recent publications of the American Psychological Association's test standards (1974, 1985).

Before a psychological test is deemed ready for operational use, it must be accompanied by a comprehensive test manual and/or other technical publications that present evidences to support any and all claims for its use (see standard A1, APA, 1974). Comrey has essentially complied with this requirement, although as will be presented in further discussions of the issues, he has either failed in some specific areas to comply with certain requirements or fulfill the obligation of test authors to update psychometric properties of their instruments and to keep their norms, manuals, and other materials current. For sake of clarity, issues involved with specific psychometric properties and test development methodologies will be discussed in separate and specific contexts.

Manual: The CPS was published in 1970, after 15 years of developmental research as claimed by its author, Andrew Comrey. The manual that accompanies the CPS is still the original one, copyrighted in 1970. In order to be in compliance with standard A3 (APA, 1974) and standards 5.5 and 5.6 (APA, 1985), the author and publisher must realize that a revision and amendment of the original 1970 manual is not only due, but has been long overdue for sometime now.

Norms: The original and only norms on which the CPS profiles are based were established more than 15 years ago. These separate male and female norms are based on samples that are of reasonable size: N(males) = 365; N(females) = 362. However, there are several problems inherent in these two samples, or they at least involve qualities—or lack of them—that make them susceptible to negative criticism. Among these are the facts that they can only be assumed to be representative of university students, their friends and family members, and *some university-connected people*—presumably mainly or even exclusively from the UCLA campus; there are no age or SES data reported on them, and there is no adequate description of a sampling procedure (see standards D2, D2.1.2, D2.2.2, and D.2.2.2; [APA, 1974]). Moreover, these norms are now more than 15 years old—perhaps even much older. This fact raises the serious question of possible, if not likely, obsolescence of the norms. Further, in light of the claims presented in the manual relative to the different types of persons from many walks of life to whom the CPS is applicable, this reviewer would have expected that during the 15 years that the inventory has been operational that some attempt(s) would have been made to restandardize the scales on much more extensive mixed samples. It is to the author's credit that a caveat statement is included in the manual: "Such norms may not be suitable for other groups. . . . Hence, norms for other groups . . . should be applied as appropriate (p. 10)." However, inserting such a cautionary statement in the manual—no matter how appropriate it may be—does not, in the opinion of this reviewer, obviate the responsibility of the author to provide the user either with more relevant basic norms or norms for different groups. At this point it must be kept in mind that in interpreting personality profiles, other than in a purely ipsative way, there are three salient profile characteristics to be analyzed. These are elevation, shape, and scatter. All three may be substantially affected by differences in the normative distributions for varying groups.

Internal Consistency: Internal consistency of the items that comprise any given scale on a psychological measurement instrument is an important and fundamental psychometric property because it is basic to scale reliability, i.e., stability of the scale scores over time (an even more important psychometric property). Therefore, a well-prepared manual and one that adheres to the APA *Standards* would be expected to present separate sections, one on *internal consistency* of items comprising the scales and one on the *reliability* of the scale scores. The manual for the CPS presents only the internal consistency coefficients (split-half coefficients stepped-up by the Spearman-Brown formula) and labels them "reliability coefficients." This is certainly a misleading and unwarranted practice! The new 1985 APA *Standards* addresses once more this serious issue in standard 2.6 which reads:

> Coefficients based on internal analysis should not be interpreted as substitutes for alternate-form reliability or estimates of stability over time unless other evidence supports that interpretation in a particular context (Primary). (p. 21)

Issues regarding the linkage between the properties of internal consistency and reliability of test items and scores were also covered quite extensively in the third edition of the APA *Standards* (see APA, 1974, pp. 48-55).

Reliability: Reliability is one of the two most critical properties that a test must possess—the other is validity. This psychometric property presents evidence of the estimated degree to which the "observed" (reported) scores on individual scales are measures of the "true" scores of individuals being measured by the individual scales. There are basically two ways in which to determine test reliability. One is through the test-retest method; the other is through the alternate forms method. The manual for the CPS presents absolutely no reliability data as required by APA *Standards* and good test construction methodology as well. Incidentally, with regard to alternate forms, both the author and publisher must assume some responsibility in misleading the potential user that more than one form of the CPS exists. The one and only form that to this reviewer's knowledge has been developed by Comrey is indicated as "Form A." This evident fact is confirmed by the EdITS' order form which lists only a single CPS that can be ordered.

Granted that the so-called "reliability coefficients" (in reality, the internal consistency coefficients) are quite high for the eight scales. They range from .91 to .96. Nevertheless, high internal consistency coefficients are merely prerequisites, not guarantees, of high reliability coefficients. Furthermore, both the 1974 and 1985 APA *Standards* stress the importance of standard errors of measurement that are derived for each observed score from the reliability coefficient of that score. For example, standards F1 and F1.2 of the 1974 *Standards* read in part:

> *F.1*
> The test manual or research report should present evidence of reliability, including estimates of the standard error of measurement, that permits the reader to judge whether scores are sufficiently dependable for the intended uses of the text . . . [Essential]. (p. 50)
> *F1.2*
> Standard errors of measurement and reliability coefficients should be provided for every score, subscore, or combination of scores . . . that is recommended by the test manual . . . [Essential]. (p. 50)

The CPS manual provides none of this very important and required information.

Validity: For an inventory such as the CPS, the two important types of validity are construct and criterion-related. Evidence of positive validity results in validation research studies is properly evaluated in terms of *practical* significance (i.e., proportion of shared variance between the test scores and external measures). Mere statistical significance is a necessary, but not sufficient, condition for establishing test validity. The validities reported for the CPS are being evaluated in accordance with these standards.

A number of validity studies are summarized in the manual. Most are either studies of construct validity or criterion-related validity limited primarily to *concurrent* validity. A number of studies (N = 12) are incorrectly presented as reporting evidence of "factorial" validity. No such type of validity exists formally (see APA, 1985; "Glossary," pp. 89-95). Comrey's listing of these studies in which the CPS scales were factor analyzed is misleading at best. Factor analytic methods applied to items and scales can only reveal structures and/or patterns of the measures. The results of these studies might be useful as the first step in demonstrating the *construct* validity of the scales. However, further analyses of external data in relation to the factor structure would be necessary.

Since this critique includes the evaluation of certain studies reported by Comrey as presenting evidences of the CPS's construct validity, this important validity type for a personality inventory is discussed here. In the current APA *Standards* (APA, 1985, p. 90), construct validity is defined as "evidence that supports a proposed construct or theoretical implications associated with the construct label" and a construct is defined as "a psychological characteristic . . . that is not directly observable . . . [and] has been constructed to *explain* observable behavioral patterns." Hence, construct validity must be demonstrated by presenting *evidence* in terms of *observable behavior* that serves to demonstrate independently of the test itself that the factor structure of the test is meaningful in *explaining* behavior in terms of some underlying psychological model. Two of these studies are critiqued herein, primarily on the basis of the tabled data presented in the manual. They are the Cozier Study (manual, p. 23) and the Backer Study (Comrey & Backer, 1970).

The Cozier Study involved an "earlier" version of the CPS administered to 247 UCLA student volunteers. The validity coefficients reported in Table 7 are product-moment correlations between the six scales (E), (P), (S), (O), (T), and (A) and a host of biographical variables. Twenty-four statistically significant coefficients are reported. They range from a low or r = .13 to a high of r = .29. These are hardly any evidence of *practical* significance since $(.13)^2$ = .02 and (.29) = .09. R square equals the proportion of avariance shared by the X and Y variables.

The Backer Study involved 209 UCLA student volunteers who were administered the CPS and a biographical data inventory simultaneously. Validity coefficients for all eight scales correlated with 141 biographical variables, excluding the discrete sex dichotomy, range from a low of r = .14 to a high of r = −.54. The median absolute value of the 141 coefficients was r = .17. Again, such results do not present any convincing evidence of the construct validity of the CPS. A total of 100 of the 141 validity coefficients produced correlations (.14 to .18) that explained no more than 3% of shared variance!

A number of studies are reported in the manual that have investigated the relationships between the separate scales of the CPS and the factors underlying similar instruments developed by Guilford, Cattell, and Eysenck. Not surprisingly, many strong relationships were found between pairs of corresponding factors, thereby yielding evidence of the concurrent validity of the CPS. However, what is missing from the manual is any evidence of the predictive validity of the inventory. This omission is especially serious or even critical in light of the fact that the manual recommends the use of the CPS for selection and classification purposes in business and industry. While the *Uniform Guidelines* do provide for the submission of evidence of construct validity in cases of adverse impact, the courts expect, in the main, supportive evidence from criterion-related validity studies, particularly evidence of predictive validity (Psychological Corporation, 1978). Furthermore, the construct validity studies conducted by Comrey and his associates were all performed on college students, and none on general business and industrial employees. Hence, users of the CPS for purposes of employment decisions are likely to be vulnerable to unfair discrimination claims and charges, even though the *Uniform Guidelines* do permit the admission of evidence of construct validity from studies conducted by author of a psychological assessment instrument.

During the period of the preparation of this critique, this reviewer has received a number of reprints from the author of articles on the CPS published by Comrey and his associates. Most of these articles appeared in the professional refereed literature after the publication of the now outdated manual for the CPS. Some of them do present supportive evidences of validity of the CPS, especially for purposes of psychiatric screening in clinics. These are Comrey, Soufi, and Backer (1978), Comrey, Wong, & Backer (1978), Comrey (1980), Comrey and Schiebel (1983), Comrey and Schiebel (1985a), and Comrey and Schiebel (in press).

Factor Analysis Methodology in the Development of Scales: Personality inventories began to be developed more than a half century ago with the appearance of the Woodworth Scale and they continue to appear on the scene of psychological assessment. Only a few of these instruments have been developed by well-known statisticians and factor analysts. Comrey is one of these latter psychologists. It is this reviewer's opinion that some method of factor analysis is the proper method of data analysis for an author to employ in developing personality inventories. This holds whether the author seeks to develop an instrument to fit an underlying personality theoretical model or to develop a theoretical model from empirical data yielded by the factor analysis. Comrey, in a sense, attempted both approaches. When he began his work, he was quite knowledgeable of the work and productions of Cattell, Eysenck, and Guilford. Evidently, he used some of this knowledge as a starter in the development of test items and logical-intuitive scoring keys. However, to his credit, much of what proceeded beyond that point was original with Comrey. At least, some of his methods were uncommon.

To begin with, most early and even current personality assessment instruments use response categories in items that are dichotomous, as is the case in the MMPI, or even worse, trichotomous (when a "Can't Decide" option is added to the traditional Yes/No categories). As a factor analyst Comrey realized that before the R-matrix can properly be analyzed either by a method of component analysis or a method of common factor analysis, it must possess certain properties. Otherwise, the results become distorted or erroneous. He knew that the appropriate entries in an R- matrix are Pearson product-moment correlation coefficients. Since these statistics are influenced in a favorable direction by increasing the variance measured by the two variables, Comrey chose to use a 7-point response scale for each item rather than even using a 5-point Likert-type scale which would have been more common in the 1960s and 1970s.

Another unique feature of the CPS due to Comrey was his development of sub-variables which he labeled Factored Homogeneous Item Dimensions (FHIDs). Each FHID is composed of four items that are reasonably homogeneous with respect to content and item analysis statistics. It is a matrix of FHIDs as the off-diagonal elements that Comrey factor analyzed.

Still another unique feature is Comrey's own method of factor analysis known commonly among factor analysts as "Minires" (Comrey, 1973). This minimum residuals method of common-factor analysis attempts to overcome the effects of two serious problems in common factor analysis. These are 1) the determination of how many "real" factors emerge in the analysis, and 2) how to estimate as accurately as possible the communality values to insert in the diagonal element of the R- matrix to be factored. Comrey's method has received general acceptance by psychologists who understand factor analysis methodology.

In factor analysis, the F- matrix that emerges must then be "rotated" in order to obtain a clearer factor structure. At the time that Comrey was developing the CPS, the most commonly-used method of rotation (and one that continues to be most popular to this day) was Kaiser's (1958) Varimax Method. However, again to Comrey's credit, he found some fault with it so he developed his own method of orthogonal factor rotation which he called the "Tandem Criteria" (Comrey, 1967).

Factor Structure: Comrey performed the factor analysis of the FHIDs using the procedures briefly described above on the response data yielded by his original male sample (N = 362) and female sample (N = 384). The factor structure is presented in the manual in Table 1. Loadings of the FHIDs are reported separately for males, females, and for the combined sample. At first glance, the factor structure composed of the 8 CPS factors appears to be quite good. However, upon close examination, several problems become evident. Most of these problems are discussed by Comrey on pp. 16-17 of the manual, including the fact that an oblique solution by the author failed to produce a closer fit to "simple" structure criteria than did the orthogonal solution.

The major problem according to this reviewer is that the data of Table 1 raise serious questions as to whether some FHIDs should have been retained in the scoring keys. Certainly, even though they obviously were retained, such results would have called for continuous research, reanalysis, and revision of the factor structure and, therefore, of the CPS itself. The FHIDs in question are summarized below. The reader of this critique and/or potential user of the CPS can render his/her own judgment. (Note: this reviewer strongly disagrees with Comrey that a factor loading as low as .30, or lower, deserves to be included in a factor; $[.30]^2 = .09$).

Items/FHID	*Males*	*Females*	*Both*
24. Lack of Pessimism (T)	.36	.16	.22
9. Cautiousness (O)	.33	.38	.35
13. Intolerance of Non-Conformity (O)	.27	.28	.31
15. Need of Approval (O)	.16	.32	.26
18. Need to Excel (O)	.31	.24	.31
19. Liking for work (O)	.33	.30	.34
40. Unselfishness (C)	.17	.31	.23

22. Lack of Depression (A)	.36	.14	.19
24. Lack of Pessimism (A)	.32	.24	.22
37. Helpfulness (A)	.09	.32	.20
17. Energy (S)	.20	.32	.30
32. No Crying (S)	.32	.23	.21
17. Energy (M)	.27	.36	.31
35. Tolerance of Vulgarity (M)	.04	.22	.34
20. Stamina (M)	.15	.32	.17

Another problem, perhaps not so serious, is the fact that some of the factors that are involved in the CPS profile that yields the personality description are substantially intercorrelated. This is especially true of factors 0 and C (r = .48) and factors A and S (r = .42).

Personality Model: One of the disappointments to this reviewer was the failure of Comrey to provide the user of the CPS with an underlying integrative personality model upon which to base interpretations of the resulting CPS profiles. As mentioned previously in this critique, factor analysts who develop personality assessment instruments are likely to fall into one of two categories: those who develop inventories or other devices to measure some theoretical personality model, or those who build a model based on the results of the factor analysis of personality measurement statements or behaviorally descriptive adjectives. The Edwards, Gough, Eysenck, and Clarke instruments are examples of the first category. The Cattell, Guilford, and Thurstone scales are examples of the second category. To this reviewer, Comrey seems to have attempted to straddle the dividing line of this dichotomy. However, in doing so, it is felt that he could have postulated a model of personality organization that would have been integrative in nature. In the final analysis, it really doesn't matter whether the model is an a priori one or a post-priori one. What does matter is that given an underlying integrative personality model, an interpreter who understands and accepts the model is placed in a position to produce more meaningful personality descriptions. As a consequence of Comrey's failure to postulate an 8-dimensional integrative personality model that underlies his great—and in the main—successful factor analytic effort, the interpretations of CPS are based on analyses that emphasize only single scale scores. This criticism is made evident by reviewing the sample interpretations comprising the major portion of the *Handbook*. Moreover, the interpretative examples presented in this publication are replete with references to high and low scores on individual factors. Take for example, Profile 13 on pp. 96-97. Excerpts from the interpretation given by Comrey will serve to illustrate what I mean:

> The pattern of very *low* Emotional Stability (S), *low* Trust (T), *low* Empathy (P) and *high* Response Bias suggests emotional disturbance with considerable anger that is partially surpressed. All scores except Masculinity (M) are on the introverted side indicating a pattern of withdrawal.

Compare such an interpretation with one by this reviewer based on Activity Vector Analysis which is a multidimensional personality model. It describes a male personality on the basis of integration of four mutually independent factors comprising the underlying personality model.

> This person is highly dependent on others for guidance, assurance, and direction. He finds it difficult to make independent decisions, and works best when instructions are laid down. He is an anxious person and is likely to be a worrier, especially concerning actions which he has taken. Normally, he is the "yes" type of person who is more comfortable in doing the bidding of others rather than assuming a leadership role. . . . (Gelineau & Merenda, 1980)

Critique

There is much in the development and production of the CPS for which to commend Comrey and his associates. The early meditative years on the part of the author leading to the release of the CPS in 1970, and the untiring efforts of Comrey and his associates to continue substantive research with the scales to the present day is especially worthy of commendation. So too are his contributions to the field of factor analysis, all of which at some point were incorporated in the development of the CPS. Unfortunately, however, there is much fault to find with the scales and their use.

The manual is out-of-date; there have been several additional studies conducted with the CPS since its publications in 1970. These should be incorporated in a revised manual.

The norms upon which the CPS profiles are determined are based on samples that are somewhat ambiguous and, at best, quite restricted. The scales should be re-standardized on samples that are representative of more general adult populations.

The factor structure of the CPS, based on data yielded by the restricted student samples is, at best, adequate and is in need of improvement. There are too many FHIDs with rather low factor loadings that are included in the scales comprising the CPS profiles. These tend to lower the communality values for individual FHIDs, and low factor loadings contribute to low proportions of total variance accounted for by the factors that are retained. (Incidentally, no mention is made in the manual of the proportion of variance, total and common, that is accounted for by the 8 scales. However, an astute reader can determine this from Table 14 on page 40 of the manual. For the 40 basic FHIDs, 50.4% of the total variance is accounted for; for all 44 variables, 46.7% of the variance is accounted for.)

There are no reliabilities reported for the scales. Rather, internal consistency coefficients alone are presented in a way that misrepresents them as reliability coefficients. Since there exists only one form of the CPS, the only real reliability coefficients that are possible are test-retest ones. These should be calculated by the author and reported in a revised manual; a potential user of the scales deserves to have some idea of how stable the scores yielded by the instrument are likely to be over time. Since the CPS is a multifactor test, the stability of the profile scores should be determined through canonical correlation analysis (see Merenda, Bonaventura, & Novack, 1977).

There are no predictive validities reported for the scales; only concurrent validities are reported in terms of correlations between scores on the separate CPS scales and separate scales on similar personality inventories. Evidences of a higher level of criterion-related validity are required especially in view of the fact that the manual claims that the CPS has practical application value in a variety of operational settings and the handbook of interpretations cites 29 examples of such applications.

The construct validity results reported in the manual are disappointingly low. This is so even in terms of statistical significance alone as Comrey has chosen to interpret these construct validity coefficients. In terms of the more important and meaningful practical significance, the results of the studies reported in the manual, as well as in other publications, fail to support any claims for construct validity of the scales. Further, the construct validity studies that have been conducted by the author and his associates do not meet the requirements of the 1985 APA *Standards.* For an instrument like the CPS construct validity is of utmost importance. Hence, more comprehensive studies of the construct validity of the scales should be undertaken and reported in a revised manual and/or the professional refereed literature.

In light of the foregoing, it is this reviewer's considered judgment that the CPS in its present form fails to adequately meet the joint standards promulgated by the American Psychological Association, the American Educational Research Association, and the National Council of Measurement in Education. Further, it is not likely to qualify as a "professionally developed test" as required by the Federal Regulations, i.e., the *Uniform Guidelines.* The scales, however, do appear to have promise to meet these standards and requirements upon reanalyses and revisions. Certainly, the author, Andrew Comrey, is well qualified to do so, and considering his great investment in the CPS to date, in terms of time and effort expended, it is this reviewer's opinion that he should also have the motivation to follow the recommendations presented in this critique.

Finally, it would be unfair for this reviewer to suggest that the faults both implied and made explicit in this critique are responsibilities of the author alone; they apply to the publisher as well. It is hereby recommended that EdITS heed these comments and cooperate with the author in seeking to improve and republish a psychological assessment instrument in which both have made considerable investments to date and which possesses the foundation to become an outstanding personality inventory.

References

This list includes text citations as well as suggested additional reading.

American Psychological Association. (1953). *Ethical standards of psychologists.* Washington, DC: Author.

American Psychological Association. (1974). *Standards for educational and psychological tests* (3rd ed.). Washington, DC: Author.

American Psychological Association. (1985). *Standards for educational and psychological testing* (4th ed.). Washington, DC: Author.

Comrey, A. L. (1967). Tandem criteria for analytical rotation in factor analysis. *Psychometrika, 32,* 143-154.

Comrey, A. L. (1970). *Manual for the Comrey Personality Scales.* San Diego: Educational and Industrial Testing Service.

Comrey, A. L. (1973). *A first course in factor analysis.* New York: Academic Press, Inc.

Comrey, A. L. (1980). *Handbook of interpretations for the Comrey Personality Scales.* San Diego: Educational and Industrial Testing Service.

Comrey, A. L. (1981). Detecting emotional disturbance with the Comrey Personality Scales. *Psychological Reports, 48,* 703-710.

Comrey, A. L., & Backer, T. E. (1970). Construct validation of the Comrey Personality Scales. *Multivariate Behavior Research, 5,* 469-477.

Comrey, A. L., & Schiebel, D. (1983). Personality test correlates of psychiatric outpatient status. *Journal of Consulting and Clinical Psychology, 51,* 756-762.

Comrey, A. L., & Schiebel, D. (1985a). Personality test correlates of psychiatric case history data. *Journal of Consulting and Clinical Psychology, 53,* 470-479.

Comrey, A. L., & Schiebel, D. (in press). Personality factor structure in psychiatric outpatients and normals. *Multivariate Behavior Research.*

Comrey, A. L., Soufi, A., & Backer, T. E. (1978). Psychiatric screening with the Comrey Personality Scales. *Psychological Reports, 42,* 1127-1130.

Comrey, A. L., Wong, C., & Backer, T. E. (1978). Further validation of the Social Conformity Scale of the Comrey Personality Scales. *Psychological Reports, 43,* 165-166.

Gelineau, E. P., & Merenda, P. F. (1980). Students' perceptions of Jimmy Carter, Ted Kennedy, and the ideal president. *Perceptual and Motor Skills, 51,* 147-155.

Kaiser, H. F. (1958). The varimax criterion for analytic rotation in factor analysis. *Psychometrika, 23,* 187-200.

Merenda, P. F., Bonaventura, L., & Novack, H. S. (1977). An intensive study of the reliability of the Rhode Island Pupil Identification Scale. *Psychology in the Schools, 14,* 282-289.

The Psychological Corporation. (1978). *Summaries of court decisions on employment testing.* New York: Author.

Uniform Guidelines on Employee Selection Procedures. (1978). Washington, DC: *Federal Register, 43,* Friday, August 25, 1978, pp. 38296-28309.

Dale Carpenter, Ed.D.
Associate Professor of Special Education, Western Carolina University, Cullowhee, North Carolina.

CRITERION TEST OF BASIC SKILLS

Kerth Lundell, William Brown, and James Evans. Novato, California: Academic Therapy Publications.

Introduction

The Criterion Test of Basic Skills (CTBS) is an individually administered, criterion-referenced measure of basic elemental skills in reading and arithmetic. It is designed to measure skills that are usually learned in kindergarten through the third grade. The CTBS is actually a series of criterion-referenced subtests assessing 44 separate objectives, with the reading section consisting of 19 objectives (two of which are optional) and the arithmetic section consisting of 25 objectives (11 of which are optional).

The reading subtests measure six skill areas: Letter Recognition, Letter Sounding, Blending and Sequencing, Special Sounds, Sight Words, and Letter Writing. Letter Recognition assesses three objectives involving the identification of correctly formed letters and names of lowercase and capital letters. Letter Sounding assesses four ojectives involving names and sounds of vowels and consonants. Blending and Sequencing requires blending two- and three-letter sounds together and identifying correctly sequenced words. Special Sounds is an area of six tests in which examinees must read words containing consonant blends, consonant digraphs, vowel digraphs, controlling Rs, final Es, and dipthongs. Sight Words requires reading 220 sight words. Letter Writing consists of two optional assessments requiring writing lower-case and upper-case letters.

The arithmetic subtests measure 11 skill areas, the last five of which are optional: Correspondence, Numbers and Numerals, Addition, Subtraction, Multiplication, Division, Money Measurement, Telling Time, Symbols, Fractions, and Decimals and Percents. Correspondence assesses the single objective of counting. Numbers and Numerals assesses four objectives requiring the examinee to sequence numbers and sequence, read, and print numerals. Addition measures three objectives requiring addition of one- to three-digit numbers with and without regrouping. Subtraction measures three objectives involving subtraction of one- to three-digit numbers with and without regrouping. Multiplication assesses two objectives checking multiplication of one- and two-digit numbers. Division measures two objectives concerned with dividing one- to four-digit numbers with one- and two-digit divisors. Money Measurement consists of two objectives that involve recognizing currency up to a dollar and stating its value in cents. Telling Time assesses two objectives concerned with the ability to tell time to the nearest five-minute interval. Symbols assesses one objective involving the use of seven common math symbols correctly. Fractions consists of three objectives that require identifying fractional parts, transforming improper fractions and mixed numbers, and adding and subtracting fractions. Decimals and Percents measures three objectives concerned with converting fractions, decimals, and percents and reading numbers containing decimals.

The authors developed this test as part of tutoring programs in which they were involved. According to the manual (Lundell, Brown, & Evans, 1976), objectives measured by the CTBS are representative of popular reading and arithmetic programs. The final form was developed from revisions based on field testing of children aged six through ten years by school psychologists, teachers, learning disabilities tutors, and aids. Although field testing included children mainly between the ages of six through ten, the authors claim that the CTBS is appropriate for any students lacking the skills measured. No other information is provided concerning the development of the CTBS, such as how extensive field testing was, how particular items were selected, or why this format was chosen over others.

Materials for the CTBS include a paperback manual, stimulus cards, a separate assessment record for reading and arithmetic, and a reproducible math-problem sheet. In order to complete the assessment materials, some cutting and pasting is necessary to assemble the stimulus cards. The only materials not included are 220 basic sight-word cards. Examiners are instructed to use their own sight-word cards or list. Approximately ten pages of the manual describe the test, administration, scoring, and interpretation, and 73 pages suggest teaching strategies. Duplication masters are also included in the manual. Most of the items require the use of the stimulus cards, which are spiral-bound in a small booklet. The reading assessment and arithmetic records contain directions for each subtest.

To administer a typical subtest, the examiner needs pencils, the appropriate assessment record, and the stimulus cards. For example, the Vowels (visual-vocal) subtest directs the examiner to present a stimulus card showing letters for the five common vowels and to read from the assessment record, "Say the sounds of these letters." As the student responds orally, the examiner circles the corresponding letter on the assessment record if the response is correct. Circling correct responses in the assessment record is consistent for most of the subtests. Incorrect responses are marked and noted for diagnostic purposes. The examiner circles a number depicting the number of correct items, which determines whether the student has achieved frustration level, instructional level, or mastery level. Levels are based on percentage of correct responses for each subtest, and ranges are 0-49% for frustration, 50-89% for instructional, and 90-100% for mastery. Levels for each subtest are plotted on the front of the assessment record. The back of the assessment record provides space to list skill deficit areas and instructional materials and suggests learning activities to remedy deficit areas.

The examiner's manual includes a duplication master for skill grouping charts for reading and arithmetic, on which the teacher can list the names of over 30 pupils and indicate which objectives each student has mastered or not mastered, thus allowing students to be grouped by skills for instructional purposes. The CTBS is intended to be administered individually and is not adaptable for group administration, although it does aid in grouping students for specific skill instruction.

Practical Applications/Uses

The CTBS is intended to be used in instructional planning for individual students. The format was designed to allow educators to measure basic reading and arithmetic skills and to identify specific skills mastered or not mastered. It is important to note that the skills measured are very basic. Most of the reading skills measured are phonetic word-attack skills. Neither reading comprehension nor vocabulary knowledge is addressed. The arithmetic skills assessed are also basic, with application skills, such as word problems or linear measurement, omitted. The manual suggests that administration should be discontinued when a student has scored at a frustration level on two consecutive subtests, indicating that the CTBS is not intended to be a survey of skills. Rather, it is intended to identify skills for instructional purposes. When a student has scored at a frustration level on two consecutive subtests, the examiner has identified skill deficits for instruction. The authors (Lundell, Brown, & Evans, 1976) claim that skills are arranged on the CTBS in order of difficulty proceeding from least to most difficult. However, there is no claim that items within subtests are arranged in order of difficulty. According to the manual, the test is appropriate for any students lacking the skills on the test.

The CTBS is appropriate to administer to pupils with primary-level skills in reading and arithmetic. The reading skills assessed on the CTBS correspond with skills assessed by the Brigance Diagnostic Inventory of Basic Skills (Brigance, 1976) and are identified as skills usually included in the reading curriculum at below the third-grade level, with a few skills on or above the third-grade level. Similarly, the same reading skills are identified by Stephens, Hartman, and Lucas (1982) as Level-1 and Level-2 skills. The arithmetic skills measured on the CTBS are also measured on the Brigance Diagnostic Inventory of Basic Skills and have been identified at primary levels, with more on higher levels including a few at the sixth-grade level (e.g., those dealing with decimals and percents). The arithmetic skills measured on the CTBS are identified by Stephens, Hartman, and Lucas (1982) as mainly primary-level skills. Educators who teach pupils with primary-level skills and who are concerned with reading and arithmetic skills might use the CTBS to identify those basic skills needed by individual pupils. The authors suggest that the CTBS can also be used in a pretest and posttest fashion to determine growth in the skill areas. Because it is a criterion-referenced measure and the skills assessed are basic and specific, the CTBS would be of limited use to others, such as psychologists, who might be interested in the relative skill levels of students in reading or arithmetic.

The CTBS is a highly verbal test, particularly in reading, and is appropriate for students who hear well, see well, and can respond orally. It also requires that students be able to handle paper-and-pencil tasks. There are no instructions for adapting this test for handicapped pupils, and it appears that some adaptations would be difficult for many subtests. The test materials are clear, and letters and numerals are dark, bold, and large enough to see without difficulty. The materials do not appear juvenile and should not be offensive to older pupils to whom this test might be administered. Like some other tests of arithmetic computation, the math-problem sheet does not allocate enough space for many students to figure and to write answers.

Administration, scoring, and interpretation of the CTBS is simple and straightforward. No training is required to be able to administer the test, which requires no special setting or equipment. The manual suggests beginning at a point where the student will achieve at a mastery level on two consecutive subtests and ending at a point where the student achieves at a frustration level on two consecutive subtests. There is little help in deciding where to begin beyond those instructions, and examiners might fail to note these instructions unless they read the manual, which is not required as part of the materials for administering the test. The manual states that flexibility is necessary in selecting which subtests should be administered initially.

Scoring requires the examiner to count the number of items on each subtest circled and then circle the number indicating correct responses. There are no tables to consult or operations to perform. When the number of correct responses is circled, its placement on the form automatically indicates whether that performance is at the frustration, instructional, or mastery level. Plotting these levels on the front of the assessment records requires only that the examiner circle the correct level for each subtest and draw lines connecting performance levels on each subtest.

Interpretation consists of noting the performance levels of each subtest for a particular student. Item performance is available because the examiner circles correct responses on the assessment record and makes no mark for incorrect responses. Using the example of the Vowels (visual-vocal) subtest again, the examiner could note that the student responded correctly to three of five items. This would correspond to the instructional level. Further, the examiner might note that the student did not give the correct sound for the vowels *o* and *u*. (According to the manual, skills that are performed at the mastery level need little or no instructional planning, instructional level objectives need extensive instructional planning, and frustration level objectives are those for which the student may not be ready for instruction.) Therefore, in this example, the student needs to be instructed concerning vowel sounds (e.g., the vowel sounds *o* and *u*).

Administration, scoring, and interpretation require few skills and little time. Time of administration depends on the number of subtests administered and varies from student to student. A few subtests on both the reading and arithmetic components require two minutes or less, whereas others require five minutes or more. The manual states that most reading or arithmetic assessments will take only 10-15 minutes.

Technical Aspects

The publisher provides no information regarding validity and reliability. Carpenter and Carpenter (1980) conducted a study of the reliability and validity of the CTBS using 77 fourth-grade pupils. They investigated nine of the reading subtests: Two-letter Blending, Three-letter Blending, Letter Sequencing, Consonant Blends, Consonant Digraphs, Vowel Digraphs, Controling R, Final E, and Dipthongs. Reliability was investigated using four methods to estimate reliability of criterion-referenced instruments and two classical estimates of reliability. The experimental methods for estimating reliability confirmed the reliability of the subtests investigated. They revealed mastery decision agreements that were similar. If few students mastered a test on one administration, a like number mastered it a second time, and if one group had a high number of masters on a certain subtest, it was probable that a high number of students in an equivalent group would also master the subtest. Classical reliability estimates demonstrated internal consistency and test-retest stability. Alpha, an estimate of internal consistency, ranged from .34 for Letter Sequencing to .91 for Consonant Blends. Test-retest reliability coefficients were .49 to .92 except for Letter Sequencing, which had a nonsignificant correlation coefficient. Experimental and classical estimates of reliability presented different interpretations. For example, Letter Sequencing, consisting of six items, appeared to yield very comparable agreement in determining masters according to the four experimental methods, but the internal consistency estimate was relatively low, and the test-retest coefficient was low and insignificant. Although classical reliability estimates were different for some subtests than were experimental estimates, experimental estimates were designed for criterion-referenced measures and are more appropriate when determining mastery of skills such as the CTBS purports to do. Reliability as estimated by appropriate methods for the CTBS appears to be satisfactory for the nine subtests investigated in this study. No information is available on the reliability of the other 35 subtests.

Concurrent validity was computed by correlating the scores on the nine CTBS subtests with the 77 fourth-grade pupils' scores on the California Achievement Test (CAT) Reading subtest. Significant correlations were revealed for all subtests except Letter Sequencing. Significant correlations ranged from .39 to .57. Correlation for all nine subtests with the CAT Reading was .61 (Carpenter & Carpenter, 1980).

Content validity may be determined by examining test items to determine adequacy of three factors: the appropriateness of the types of items included, the completeness of the item sample, and the way in which the items assess the content (Salvia & Ysseldyke, 1985). Certainly the subtests measure reading and arithmetic skills, and the items on a particular subtest measure the subtest objective. The authors have been careful to state an objective for each subtest that accurately portrays the skills being measured. Subtest names dependably state what is being measured. Subtests sometimes have very few items. Many have only five items and may not have enough items to measure a particular objective adequately. The way in which subtests measure skills appears to be appropriate. Given the skills measured, the CTBS assesses them like classroom teachers would using curriculum materials or other tests.

Critique

The Criterion Test of Basic Skills provides educators with a quick measure of 44 very basic skills in reading and arithmetic for individual students. Materials are convenient, and directions are simple and easy to follow. The manual provides several activities to teach and reinforce the skills measured. The CTBS purports to measure mastery of basic skills. Unfortunately, the authors provide no evidence that it actually does. The 90% criterion for mastery and 50-89% criterion for instructional level are arbitrary and without support. Although the skills are supposed to be sequential, no support is available to show that they are. Mastery as an instructional concept in this context is without meaning. The authors need to demonstrate that mastery as defined by the CTBS is necessary on one subtest before a student should move on to the next subtest objective. They fail to provide such support. Furthermore, five items may not adequately or reliably indicate whether a pupil is master of a particular skill (Eaves, McLaughlin, & Foster, 1979). On the other hand, if each subtest had many more items, it would lose the characteristic of a quick measure. However, if the CTBS is to be used for instructional planning, one would want to be able to place confidence in test results. Having a quick measure seems less important than having results about which one can feel confident. Unless the results on a short subtest seem clear, the examiner may want to administer additional items measuring the same skill to determine if instruction is actually warranted. In that instance, the CTBS would be used as a quick beginning assessment and not as the sole determinant of instructional needs for the objectives measured.

Two other problems involve the skills being measured. For Sight Word Reading, the student is required to read the basic 220 sight words, and examiners are to use their own sight-word cards or list. Because sight-word lists differ, what is measured by one examiner may differ from words measured by another examiner. There may be an advantage for educators to use a sight-word list based on the specific curriculum program being used, but such a list may or may not have 220 words. If the authors refer to a specific list of 220 basic sight words, they should include them on the test.

Finally, the skills measured are elementary, specific, and atomistic. The skills measured on the reading component may or may not be basic to reading ability. For example, a student may be able to read and understand passages without being able to make the sound that two letters such as *re* represent (Smith, 1973). Likewise, the arithmetic subtests lack in application measures. There is some question as to how important the skills measured on the CTBS are. The authors should provide more information to substantiate content validity instead of simply stating that the CTBS assesses skills in popular curriculum programs. If the CTBS is to be taken seriously as an instructional planning assessment instrument, it must bear the burden of demonstrating reliability and validity. There is some evidence that it may be able to demonstrate reliability and validity (Carpenter & Carpenter, 1980), but much more information is needed. Without such information, the CTBS may be useful as a beginning point for skills measured. Without such information, Krichev (1978, p.145) suggests "devising your own test as based on local curriculum programs. Such a test would probably be more valid and equally reliable." Educators may feel just as comfortable with tests that they devise or may even find that they want to base their tests on the CTBS or use the CTBS in conjunction with teacher-made tests.

References

Brigance, A. H. (1976). *Brigance Diagnostic Inventory of Basic Skills.* North Billerica, MA: Curriculum Associates, Inc.

Carpenter, D., & Carpenter, S. (1980). The reliability and validity of the Criterion Test of Basic Skills. *Diagnostique, 6,* 16-23.

Eaves, R. C., McLaughlin, P. J., & Foster, G. G. (1979). Some simple statistical procedures for classroom use. *Diagnostique, 4,* 3-12.

Krichev, A. (1978). Criterion Test of Basic Skills. *Psychology in the Schools, 15,* 145.

Lundell, K., Brown, W., & Evans, J. (1976). *Criterion Test of Basic Skills: Manual of instruction and teaching strategies.* Novato, CA: Academic Therapy Publications.

Salvia, J., & Ysseldyke, J. E. (1985). *Assessment in special and remedial education* (3rd ed.). Boston: Houghton Mifflin.

Smith, F. (1973). *Psycholinguistics and reading.* New York: Holt, Rinehart and Winston.

Stephens, T. S., Hartman, A. C., & Lucas, V. H. (1982). *Teaching children basic skills: A curriculum handbook* (2nd ed.). Columbus, OH: Charles E. Merrill.

Toni Linder, Ed.D.
Associate Professor and Coordinator, Early Childhood Education, University of Denver, Denver, Colorado.

DEVELOPMENTAL INDICATORS FOR THE ASSESSMENT OF LEARNING—REVISED

Carol D. Mardell-Czudnowski and Dorothea S. Goldenberg. Edison, New Jersey: Childcraft Education Corporation.

Introduction

The Developmental Indicators for the Assessment of Learning—Revised (DIAL-R) is an untimed, team-administered, individual screening instrument that assesses motoric, conceptual, and language skills for children aged two to six years. The DIAL-R is a revised version of the DIAL (Mardell & Goldenberg, 1975). The DIAL was revised in order to 1) broaden the population sampling, which was originally only children from Illinois; 2) extend the testing age span from 2½-5½ years to 2-6 years; and 3) combine gross- and fine-motor items into one area. In addition, efforts were made to improve content, materials, and procedures based on scoring questions, administrator comments, and general recommendations from users of DIAL. A literature search and evaluation recommendations at the termination of the federally funded DIAL project also influenced DIAL-R revisions (Mardell-Czudnowski & Goldenberg, 1984).

The DIAL-R manual (Mardell-Czudnowski & Goldenberg, 1983) states that the criteria for acceptability for the DIAL-R included 1) technical adequacy in terms of norming, validity, and reliability for screening purposes; 2) a four-year age range; 3) individual administration; 4) short administration time; 5) multidimensional content; 6) objective scoring; 7) process and product orientation; 8) sensitivity to cultural differences; and 9) tasks of interest to young children.

The 315 behaviors originally developed from teachers' input were reduced to 155 tasks for standardization purposes, based on the criteria that the behavior 1) could be demonstrated, observed, and scored in a short time; 2) appeared to be developmental; and 3) could be elicited in an appealing manner. These 155 behaviors were clustered into 32 items from pilot study data. Between 1981 and 1983, 2,447 children were tested from four regions of the country in thirteen cities (which were grouped and identified by the authors as eight sites). The sample was stratified on the basis of age, sex, ethnicity, geographic region, and size of community. In addition, data were collected on the educational level of the parents and whether or not a second language was spoken in the home. Data on the 2,447 children were analyzed using the latent-trait method, a Rasch-Wright procedure (Wright & Stone, 1979) that determined whether each item in the battery "fit the model" and calibrated items independent of a particular norming sample. In addition, descriptive statistics were employed to determine means and standard deviations.

Items were discarded if they did not discriminate between age levels or if they duplicated previously known information. From the initial items, four (throwing, standing still, balancing, and clapping hands) were deleted from the Motor area; two (sorting and following directions) from the Concepts area; and two (telling a story and parts of speech) from the Language area. Of the final 24 items (see Table 1), three new items (writing name, naming letters, and sorting chips) were added, three items (touching fingers, classifying foods, and sentence length) were retained from the DIAL, and four items (catching, matching, copying, and articulating) were revised. The remaining 14 items were revised only for the new age range. As indicated on Table 1, items assess skills of perception, memory, previous learning association, kinesthetic awareness and coordination, and language.

Table 1

DIAL-R Items and Skills Assessed

		Skills				
	Items	Perception	Memory	Previous Learning Association	Kinesthetic Awareness & Coordination	Language
LANGUAGE	Catching	X			X	
	Jumping, etc.				X	
	Building	X	X		X	
	Touching fingers	X	X		X	
	Cutting	X			X	
	Matching	X			X	
	Copying	X			X	
	Writing name	X	X	X	X	X
	Naming colors		X	X		X
	Identifying body parts		X	X		X

CONCEPTS	Counting (rote)		X	X		X
	Counting (meaningful)		X	X		X
	Positioning		X	X		X
	Identifying concepts		X	X		X
	Naming letters		X	X		X
	Sorting chips	X	X			
MOTOR	Articulating		X			X
	Giving personal data		X	X		X
	Remembering	X	X		X	X
	Naming nouns		X	X		X
	Naming verbs		X	X		X
	Classifying foods		X	X		X
	Problem solving		X	X		X
	Sentence length					X

A five-point scale, which converts scores into developmental levels of under two years (0), between two and three years (1), between three and four years (2), between four and five years (3), and between five and six years (4) was also developed. Although a projection of DIAL-R total score was done to extrapolate cutoff points for ages 6-0 to 6-11, Mardell-Czudnowski and Goldenberg (personal communication, October, 1985) state that future manuals will delete the reference to extrapolation because the accuracy of the extrapolated score is questionable.

A factor analysis of all 24 items on the test revealed only two factors: 1) motor and concepts and 2) language. Because the Motor and Language areas did not appear to identify separate components, the total DIAL-R score was determined to be the most valid measure. However, in the manual the authors note that subsequent research indicates that the total DIAL-R score may overidentify "potentially advanced" children and may mask a potential problem. Thus, area cutoffs were statistically developed from the original norming sample. The manual provides recommendations for the use of these area scores.

Analysis was also done on the observational behavior data, which is scored after the child has completed an area. From these data, cutoff points were determined for referral of children for further social-emotional evaluation.

The largest norming sample (N = 2,447) consisted of boys (51.4%) and girls (48.6%) in eight six-month age groups (from two to six years) who were white (55.5%) and nonwhite (44.5%) and from cities of 50,000 population (52.8%) and under 50,000 populations (47.2%) in four regions: northwest (22.8%), north central (24.8%), south (28.2%), and west (24.2%).

Because the original sample did not resemble the 1980 census in terms of ethnicity, a subsample (N = 1,861) was identified by computer to match the 1980 census ratio of 73% white and 27% nonwhite. Cutoff scores were determined from this subsample, as well as supplementary cutoff points for the white standardization (N = 1,358) and the nonwhite standardization (N = 1,089). In addition, cutoff points are provided for the 5th and 95th percentiles and 10th and 90th percentiles.

Practical Applications/Uses

The DIAL-R is a 20-30 minute developmental test that reports the ability to screen the range of abilities from "severe dysfunction" to "potentially advanced" of children aged two to six years. Sixteen of the 24 test items evaluate cognitive and language areas, and eight evaluate gross- and fine-motor areas. The test is well standardized and easy to administer and score.

The DIAL-R is one of the few screening tests available that purports to be able to identify potentially advanced preschool- and kindergarten-aged children. Although further research is needed to substantiate its usefulness in this area, the preliminary study comparing DIAL-R results to Stanford-Binet results holds some promise (although all tests of mental abilities for young children are subject to predictive validity problems).

Another advantage of the DIAL-R is the potential for utilizing separate sets of norms for different populations. School districts are often advised to develop their own norms to meet their individual population, but with small numbers of children this is difficult, unreliable, and of questionable validity. The DIAL-R allows flexibility in that school districts may choose the norms that approximate their population or choose different cutoffs for lower or higher percentile identification.

The DIAL-R manual clearly denotes responsibilities for the DIAL-R screening, specifically outlining responsibilities for the coordinator, "operators," and volunteers. A suggested floor plan and recommendations are provided for orienting the child at a play table, registration, photographing the child, and filling out the parent-information form.

The child then moves from area to area, with each operator marking the child's score sheet with a different color-coded marker. Each task is observed and recorded on the score sheet by circling or underlining the child's response. All circles placed on the DIAL-R score sheet indicate oral responses, whereas underlines indicate motor responses. (There is a variation for the item, articulating.) Raw scores for each area are converted immediately to scaled scores in the appropriate corresponding area on the score sheet. A maximum of 31 points is possible for each area. The individual area scores are recorded and added to obtain a total score.

During the presentation of tasks in each area, eight additional behaviors are observed: 1) unable to separate from adult; 2) cries/whines; 3) unwilling to answer questions; 4) perseverative, repeats what says and does; 5) distractible, does not pay attention; 6) hyperactive, restless, fidgety, or "antsy"; 7) resistive, unwilling to try tasks; and 8) disruptive, interrupts testing procedure. The operator's subjective impressions are recorded by circling the behaviors observed. The total (of a possible 24) is added up at the end of the testing session. This score is used with a table in the manual to make referrals for further assessment of the child's social-emotional development.

Results from the DIAL-R can be reported using a variety of cutoff points. Cutoffs can be obtained for total score or area scores for all white or nonwhite populations, or for different percentile scores. The total-score cutoff points are charted by three-month and six-month intervals, indicating whether scores are 1) within 1.5 standard deviations in either direction of the mean of the norming sample, indicating average development; 2) 1.5 or more standard deviations above the mean, indicating "potentially advanced" development; or 3) 1.5 or more standard deviations below the mean, indicating a potential problem.

The authors recommend that area cutoff scores also be examined, as a total score may mask a weakness in a particular problem. "The use of area cutoffs significantly reduces the number of children who would have fallen into the highest category when total score cutoffs were used without reducing the number of children falling into the lowest category" (Mardell-Czudnowski & Goldenberg, 1983, p.58).

Technical Aspects

Test-retest reliabilities conducted at each of the eight sites within two weeks (N = 65) revealed reliabilities of .76 on Motor, .90 on Concepts, .77 on Language, and .87 for the total score. Internal consistency using the Cronbach alpha was established resulting in an overall coefficient of .96. The coefficients for each subtest were .91 for Motor, .92 for Concepts, and .86 for Language. The standard error of measurement for the total score fluctuates from three to four scaled points, depending on the age of the child (Mardell-Czudnowski & Goldenberg, 1983).

Construct validity was determined by evaluating whether the items demonstrated consistent developmental trends. Aggregate correlations of DIAL-R total score and age yielded a correlation of .98, demonstrating developmental trends with age. Content validity was based on the work on the original DIAL, where experts in the field reviewed all items. Because 21 of the 24 items in the DIAL-R are unchanged or revisions of DIAL items, the authors are using results from the DIAL study to substantiate content validity in the DIAL-R (Mardell-Czudnowski & Goldenberg, 1983).

Concurrent validity was established using a comparison with Stanford-Binet results (N = 125). A moderate, but significant, relationship was found between the DIAL-R and the Stanford-Binet (r = .40). A further analysis of sensitivity and specificity with these two instruments showed complete agreement on 82.4% of the children who were identified as 1.5 standard deviations above or below the mean. However, 10.4% were identified as false positives or overreferrals. Seven percent who were identified as potentially advanced on DIAL-R were not identified on the Stanford-Binet, and 3% who were selected by the DIAL-R as "potential problem" were not so identified on the Stanford-Binet. In addition, 7% were identified as false negatives or underreferrals. Five percent had scores of 124 or more on the Stanford-Binet but were missed on the DIAL-R, whereas 2% had scores of 76 or less on the Stanford-Binet but were missed on the DIAL-R. The majority of these children fell into the lowest or highest age range of the DIAL. This may indicate the lesser degree of validity of the DIAL-R at its extremes, but as Mardell-Czudnowski and Goldenberg (1984) note, it may also reflect problems with the lower extremes of the Stanford-Binet.

The authors report no predictive validity studies, citing that "it is not possible to collect such data currently because it is unethical, as well as illegal, to withhold services from children who appear to require them in order to establish that the same children who fall ±1.58 standard deviations from the mean now will fall in the same relative position one or more years from now" (Mardell-Czudnowski & Goldenberg, 1982, pp. 83-84). The one study reported in the manual does not provide sufficient evidence of the test's ability to actually predict which children will have difficulty in school. Future studies are also needed in relation to the validity of the cutoff scores for the subgroup populations. Results of a follow-up study with DIAL are reported in the manual, but further research is needed on the DIAL-R's predictive ability.

The authors also report face validity based on the "inclusion of tasks, novel materials, colorful pictures, age-appropriate manipulatives, and carefully controlled entry and exit requirements" (Mardell-Czudnowski & Goldenberg, 1983, p. 84). Ecological validity is found in the environment in which the test is performed, which the authors state is "real-life educational environments."

Critique

Objective criteria for comparison of norm-referenced tests is set forth in the American Psychological Associations's *Standard for Educational and Psychological Tests* (1974). McCauley and Swisher (1984) condensed this list to ten criteria: description of the normative sample, adequate sample size, item analysis, the reporting of measures of central tendency and variability, concurrent validity, predictive validity, test-retest reliability, interexaminer reliability, adequate descriptions of test procedures, and tester qualifications. The following discussion will address the adequacy of the DIAL-R in relation to these criteria:

1) The test manual needs to *define the standardization of normative sample* clearly in order to enable the test user to determine its suitability for a particular population (APA, 1974; Weiner & Hoock, 1973). The DIAL-R clearly defines the standardization sample for the original sample of 2,447 children. However, a computer was used to extract a subsample that resembles the 1980 census in relation to white and non-white ethnicity. It is unclear how the variables of sex, age, community size, and geographic regions are affected by this manipulation. The tables in the manual reflect data on the sample of 2,447, not the census-related sample.

2) For each subgroup examined during the test's standardization, an *adequate sample size* should be used (APA, 1974) with 100 or more subjects considered the lower limit (Salvia & Ysseldyke, 1981; Weiner & Hoock, 1973).

For the original sample of 2,447, the DIAL-R fulfills this requirement. However, it is unclear whether the census-related sample of 1,863 contains at least 100 or more in each age subgroup. In addition, norms tables are provided for the white and the nonwhite populations. The manual does not state how many children were in each of the age groupings for these populations.

3) Test reliability and validity are promoted through the use of *systematic item analysis* during item construction and selection (Anastasi, 1976). Quantitative methods used to study and control item difficulty, item validity, or both need to be reported in the test manual (McCauley & Swisher, 1984). The selection of items, as previously discussed, was based on both teacher input and on statistical analysis of developmental trends and item interdependence. Factor analysis of the items revealed two factors: 1) motor and concepts and 2) language (Mardell-Czudnowski & Goldenberg, 1983). The DIAL-R manual does not present data on individual items; however, sufficient analysis appears to have been conducted. In a personal communication with one author (D. Goldenberg, October 30, 1985) it was learned that revisions of items occurred prior to norming, but deletion of items occurred after norming and item analysis.

4) Measures of the *central tendency and variability* of test scores (e.g., means and standard deviations for the total raw scores) should be reported in the manual for relevant subgroups examined during the objective evaluation of the test (APA, 1974). The means and standard deviations of subtest scores and total scores are charted by three-month intervals for the sample of 2,447. However, they are not reported for other subgroups or the census-related population. Thus, differences across groups cannot be ascertained.

5) Evidence of *concurrent validity* should be reported in the test manual. The DIAL-R manual meets this requirement through the analysis of the relationship of DIAL-R to the Stanford-Binet. These results have previously been discussed in the technical aspects section of this review.

6) Evidence of *predictive validity* (APA, 1974), which empirically demonstrates that the test can be used to predict later performance on another valid criterion, should also be reported in the test manual. The DIAL-R manual refers to a predictive, longitudinal study conducted with the original DIAL in 1974 (N = 249). Multiple correlations with test criterion measures ranged from .45 to .73 with the DIAL subtest scores. As previously noted, the authors state that they feel predictive studies are unethical and illegal. However, there are means of conducting predictive validity studies (admittedly quite difficult) that are ethical, and future predictive studies are needed on the DIAL-R with respect to all of the sets of norms.

7) An estimate of *test-retest reliability* for relevant subgroups, revealing a correlation coefficient of .90 or better (Salvia & Ysseldyke, 1981) that is statistically significant at or beyond the .05 level (Anastasi, 1976), should be supplied in the test manual (APA, 1974). A study was conducted (N = 65) over a period of 3-175 days, with correlations reported at .76 (Motor), .90 (Concepts), .77 (Language), and .87 for the total DIAL-R (Mardell-Czudnowski & Goldenberg, 1983). The time between testing varied substantially, and these results seem reasonable in light of the time span involved. The significance level is not reported. It appears that the 32-item norming battery, rather than the existing 24-item DIAL-R, was used in test-retest. This difference could affect the results, with a shorter test resulting in a lower reliability.

8) Empirical evidence of *interexaminer reliability,* which reports a correlation coefficient of .80 or better (Salvia & Ysseldyke, 1981) and is statistically significant at or beyond the .05 level (Anastasi, 1976), should be given in the test manual (APA, 1974); the DIAL-R manual reports no such studies of this nature. An interrater reliability with the DIAL was conducted, yielding acceptable reliability coefficients (.81-.99); however, additional interrater reliability studies need to be done with the DIAL-R.

9) Test *administration procedures* need to be described in sufficient detail to enable the users to duplicate the administration and scoring procedures used during test standardization (APA, 1974). The DIAL-R manual is clearly written and easy to follow. Interpretation of scores is not difficult, with cutoff scores for subareas and total scores provided in charts. The revised materials are also of better quality than the previous DIAL.

10) In regard to *tester qualifications,* the manual provides a list of responsibilities for the coordinator, operators, and volunteers, but necessary qualifications are not described. This should be included, as anyone conducting testing of children should have training in specific aspects of psychometrics, test administration, test interpretation, and ethical consideration in testing.

Several other aspects of the DIAL-R that need further examination relate to the norming sample. Mardell-Czudnowski and Goldenberg used the computer to extract a 73% white and a 27% nonwhite sample. The latter category combined blacks, Native Americans, Alaskan natives, Asians, and Pacific Islanders. It is questionable whether all of these ethnic groups display similar enough characteristics to form a norming sample that appropriately represents each subgroup. Mardell-Czudnowski (1985) found that Eastern children performed significantly higher in the Motor area and lower in the Concepts area. Mardell-Czudnowski concludes that the interaction among independent child variables needs to be examined when developing norms for subgroups. Goldenberg and Mardell-Czudnowski have developed the DIAL-Log, a computer program that provides a means of establishing local norms on DIAL-R and gives interim activities to work on at specific developmental levels. Further research is needed to substantiate the validity of the subgroup norms for various populations.

Another potential problem is the inclusion of handicapped children in the norming sample. The authors of the DIAL-R state that no children were deliberately excluded from the norming sample because of known handicapping conditions. They even note that "young children whose parents suspect a problem are more likely to participate in a community's screening program than a child whose parents believe (s)he is developing normally" (Mardell-Czudnowski & Goldenberg, 1983, p. 70). The potential inclusion of a higher number of handicapped or delayed children in the norming sample may serve to lower the mean score for an "average" or "OK" rating. This might result in underidentification of "potential problems" and overidentification of "potentially advanced." Future research needs to verify the accuracy of the cutoff scores.

Another consideration in the norming sample is the geographic distribution of ethnic minorities across the four geographic areas and eight sites. The manual delineates the distribution of age groups across geographic areas but not ethnic groups. If the minority representation is not proportionally distributed or comes primarily from two cities, the minority sample may not be representative of the entire country. It is not possible to determine the ethnic distribution from the manual.

The use of a cutoff for the behavioral observations is helpful; however, the recommended cutoff point for a child of 5-0 or older is one behavior out of a potential 24, and for a child of 4-0 to 4-11 years, the cutoff is two out of 24. Given the subjective nature of the scoring of the behavioral observations, the cutoffs for these two age ranges seem low. More research is needed in regard to the predictive ability of these cutoff recommendations.

References

American Psychological Association. (1974). *Standards for educational and psychological tests.* Washington, DC: Author.

Anastasi, A. (1976). *Psychological testing* (4th ed.). New York: MacMillan.

Mardell-Czudnowski, C. (1985). *Screening kindergartners in an international school.* Unpublished manuscript, Northern Illinois University, Department of Learning Development and Special Education, DeKalb.

Mardell, C., & Goldenberg, D. (1975). *DIAL (Developmental Indicators for the Assessment of Learning) manual.* Edison, NJ: Childcraft Education Corporation.

Mardell-Czudnowski, C., & Goldenberg, D. (1983). *DIAL-R (Developmental Indicators for the Assessment of Learning) manual.* Edison, NJ: Childcraft Education Corporation.

Mardell-Czudnowski, C., & Goldenberg, D. (1984). Revision and restandardization of a preschool screening test: DIAL becomes DIAL-R. *Journal of the Division for Early Childhood, 8*(2), 149-156.

McCauley, R., & Swisher, L. (1984). Psychometric review of language and articulation tests for preschool children. *Journal of Speech and Hearing Disorders, 49,* 34-41.

Salvia, J., & Ysseldyke, J. (1981). *Assessment in special and remedial education* (2nd ed.). Boston: Houghton Mifflin.

Weiner, P., & Hoock, W. (1973). The standardization of tests: Criteria and criticisms. *Journal of Speech and Hearing Research, 16,* 616-676.

Wright, B. D., & Stone, M. H. (1979). *Best test design.* Chicago: Mesa Press.

Merith Cosden, Ph.D.
Special Education Program, Graduate School of Education, University of California—Santa Barbara, Santa Barbara, California.

DEVELOPMENTAL TEST OF VISUAL-MOTOR INTEGRATION

Keith E. Berry and Norman A. Buktenica. Cleveland, Ohio: Modern Curriculum Press, Inc.

Introduction

The Developmental Test of Visual-Motor Integration (VMI) is an assessment tool that evaluates the ability of children and adults to copy geometric forms which are presented sequentially in order of their developmental difficulty. The VMI is considered to be one of the more structured of the form-copying tests (i.e., the form to be copied and area in which it is to be copied are clearly demarcated). The VMI also differs from other form-copying tests in that it was designed with a developmental scale for assessing competence on the forms. Similar to other form-reproduction tests, the VMI purports to measure perceptual motor skills hypothesized to play a role in academic and cognitive performance.

The VMI was created by K.E. Beery and N.A. Buktenica in 1967. It was designed for the early identification of children with learning and behavioral disorders. This test was based on the premise that geometric-form reproduction was related to academic achievement. In particular, the test was designed to distinguish the kinds of problems that would manifest themselves in children considered to have "learning disabilities" (i.e., difficulties in reading, writing, and mathematics as a function of poor perceptual skills or ability to organize and motorically copy information).

The VMI follows a long line of figure reproduction tests, of which the most frequently cited is the Bender-Gestalt (Bender, 1938). The Bender shares with other form-reproduction tests the goal of assessing neurological damage, and perceptual-motor integration and development. Whereas Koppitz has developed children's developmental norms for the Bender (Koppitz, 1975), the nine Bender designs allow the measurement of a developmental range from the ages of five to nine years only. The 24 VMI items, on the other hand, were specifically designed to provide developmental evaluations of perceptual-motor copying skills for children from preschool through elementray school while retaining validity for use with adults.

The 24 VMI items were reduced from an original pool of 72 geometric designs. Items were selected on the basis of their fit into a chronological-age scale and whether or not the developmental-age norms ascertained for each item could be cross-validated across samples.

The initial 1964 standardization sample consisted of 1,039 students ranging in age from three to 14 years. These students were used to develop the criteria necessary for passing each form. Although the format, test designs, and sequence of test designs remained constant, the test was renormed in 1981 based on a sample of 3,090 children, with more consideration paid to stratification on the basis of ethnicity, income, residence, and sex. This restandardization found no significant sex differences in performance; the revised scale, therefore, does not differentiate raw scores by sex. In addition, age equivalents, which in the original sample ranged from 2-10 through 15-11, were reduced to 2-11 through 14-6. Further data on the restandardization sample are presented in the new manual (Beery, 1982), which provides raw score conversions into standard scores and percentiles.

The VMI is presented in booklet format. Two different booklets are available: one containing the first 15 forms that is used with children between the ages of two-eight years, and one with the full 24 forms that is used with all subjects aged two years and older. In each booklet, each page contains three designs presented in order of sequential difficulty. A clearly outlined space in which to copy the form is provided under each design.

The examiner may administer the test individually or in groups. In either case, the instructions are brief. The individual or individuals copy the designs in the order that they are presented until the examiner tells them to stop. In the group testing examiners have no further participation in the testing process; in the individual testing the examiner needs to watch the child copy the designs in order to assess when three sequential misses have occurred at which time the examiner ends the procedure. Test scores are recorded on the booklet, using the written descriptions and pictorial examples in the manual as guides as to whether or not a design had been passed.

The test was designed for most effective use with children in preschool and early elementary school (Beery, 1982). The manual contains age equivalents for raw scores ranging from 2-11 to 14-6, with more detailed standard score and percentile information for children aged 4-14. The author notes that for practical purposes the norms provided on the 13- and 14-year-olds can also be utilized for older age groups.

In addition to the booklets and manual, the author provides a monograph (Beery, 1967) in which there are further historical information and some early data on the VMI. The author also provides remediation worksheets that students can use to enhance their skills on the task.

Practical Applications/Uses

The VMI is used to assess childrens' or adults' perceptual motor skills by obtaining measures of their ability to copy designs in a structured format (i.e., within given boundaries on a page). Using an objective scoring system, the test can be used to determine a child's developmental level with regard to this perceptual motor skill; it can also be used to determine whether or not adults have fully developed their perceptual motor skills in this area. Children thought to have neurological impairments, "learning disabilities," specific problems in perceptual motor functioning that manifest themselves in reading or writing problems, problems in differentiating right and left, or general clumsiness, would be candidates for the test. In addition, children who have problems with copying and organizing copying task, such as the Bender Gestalt, in addition to the VMI. A comparison of performance levels on these tasks might help to differentiate a problem in perceiving and copying designs (a skill ostensibly measured on each of these tests) from problems in spatial organization (a skill needed on the Bender in order to place all of the designs on the page or pages provided). A comparison of these perceptual motor tests is provided in the technical aspects section of this review.

Although the VMI can be used with children aged two years to adult, it was primarily designed for preschool and early-elementary-school students (Beery, 1982). Even though some studies have found no effects of race on performance on the VMI (e.g., Schooler & Anderson, 1979), others question this finding (Martin, Sewell, & Manni, 1977). Beery (1982) notes, however, that although some studies report statistically significant race differences, these differences are actually very small, accounting for a small proportion of the total test variance.

The VMI can be administered both individually and in groups. Two studies have examined the effects of each type of procedure on test scores; in neither case were differences in student scores found as a function of test administration format, nor were differences found in the utility of the scores obtained under each procedure for predicting cognitive effects (Curtis, Michael, & Michael, 1979; Pryzwansky, 1977).

Test procedures are clearly described in the manual, with separate instructions provided for group and individual administration. Some differences are noted for the two administration formats. For example, during group administration children are asked to attempt all forms, but during individually administered tests children may stop after three consecutive failures. On the average, the test can be administered in 15-20 minutes.

Beery (1982) indicates that the VMI can be administered and scored by classrooms teachers who are familiar with the test instructions and procedures as explained in the manual. There is some controversy raised in the literature, however, as to the reliability of scores obtained by personnel with this minimal level of training. Pryzwansky (1977) found an interrater reliability correlation of .73 between relatively untrained teachers and externs with more testing experience. This correlation went up to .98 after further training for the teachers. In a subsequent study, Lepkin and Pryzwansky (1983) found that teachers and externs trained briefly to use either the scoring system in the manual or a revised scoring system developed by the researchers had similarly high interrater reliabilities ranging from .96 to .98. Although this finding suggests that short-term training may be effective, the authors note that the correlations may have been artifically high across groups because of the small number of protocols (eight) and the homogeneity in student responses on these protocols. Snyder, Snyder, & Massong (1981), found little difference between the interrater reliability of untrained scorers and expert scorers in terms of raw scores, with correlations ranging from .92 to .98. When they examined the translation of these raw scores to age equivalent scores, however, they found a drop in interrater reliability to .89 and .95. Futher, they noted perfect agreement on only 20% of the 39 protocols, less than one-year discrepancy on 23% of the protocols, more than one-year discrepancy on 33% of the protocols, and a discrepancy of two years or more on 23% of the tests. In sum, these studies indicate that brief training on the scoring system as presented in the manual may be necessary in order to bring interrater reliability levels into an acceptable range.

Each of the 24 forms are scored as "pass" or "fail" on the basis of their match to the criteria described in both visual and written form in the manual. A raw score is determined by summing the number of forms passed up to three consecutive failures. The manual further specifies that in ambiguous situations the design should be marked "pass" because inexperienced scorers are often too stringent in their criteria. This rule at least provides some additional standardization for the scoring procedures. Once a raw score is obtained, it can be converted to an age equivalent, percentile, and standard score through using the tables in the manual.

Test scores can be interpreted in terms of the relationship of the individual's score to the provided test norms. In young children, low scores reflect developmental delays in the perceptual-motor skills measured by this test; in adult subjects a low score reflects a lack of perceptual-motor-skill development, which should have been achieved by adulthood. As described in the next section, of this review, however, the specific relationship of the perceptual-motor skills measured by the VMI to academic reading, writing, and math skills has yet to be clarified.

Technical Aspects

A number of studies have assessed the reliability of the VMI. The manual reports interrater reliabilities ranging from .58 to .99 across studies, with a median reliability correlation of .93. As previously noted, some training on the use of the manual's scoring system is necessary in order to bring reliabilities to the .90 level. Ryckman and Rentfrow (1971) found test-retest reliabilities ranging from .62 to .84 for a one-week interval, whereas other studies, summarized in the manual, found reliability coefficients over a two-week period ranging from .59 for an institutionalized sample of children to .92 for a normal sample of students. Ryckman and Rentfrow (1971) report split-half reliabilities of .74, and the manual cites unpublished data on split-half reliabilities ranging from .66 to .93, with a median of .79.

Studies on the validity of the VMI have been conceptualized in several ways. A number of studies have focused on the relationship of VMI scores to scores on number of studies have focused on the relationship of VMI scoreds to scores on the Bender-Gestalt, the other major test used to measure perceptual-motor skills. Although these studies provide information as to the similarity of the two tests, as a rule, they do not address the relationship of the perceptual-motor skills measured by either of these tests to other cognitive or academic performance measures.

The VMI and Bender share certain basic similarities, i.e., both purport to measure visual-motor skills or coordination by requiring subjects to copy a series of geometric designs. There are also a number of distinctions between the task demands of the two tests. For example, the VMI is more structured than the Bender in that it provides designated boundaries within which to copy each design. The VMI also has more designs than the Bender and allows students to stop after three consecutive failures. The major question addressed in the following studies is whether these tests are redundant (i.e., measure the same perceptual-motor skills) or whether they are similar but measure somewhat different capabilities.

Early studies on the VMI and Bender found no significant differences between these tests. Krauft and Krauft (1972), for example, found no statistically significant differences in age-equivalent scores obtained on the VMI and Bender by mentally retarded students. These investigators, as well as others (Liemohn & Knapczyk, 1974; Liemohn & Wagner, 1975) found significant correlations ranging from .65 to .79 between raw scores, as well as age-equivalent scores for mentally retarded students on these tests.

Brown (1977), however, found a somewhat lower, but still statistically significant, correlation of .43 between VMI and Bender scores for normal students. She also notes a small but statistically significant difference between mean scores on the two tests for her subjects. Other researchers have since found what they consider to be significant discrepancies between test scores on these instruments for normal students even when the correlation between the two instruments was significant. Porter and Binder (1981), for example, report a correlation of .62 ($p < .05$) for age-equivalent scores on these tests with normal subjects aged six-nine years. They note, however, that this correlation only accounts for 38% of the total variance in the test scores and that the correlations are significant only at certain age levels within the sample. Similarly, Lehman and Breen (1982) report a significant .71 correlation between the two tests for 25 regular education students, but add that further analysis indicates that the test correlations are significant only for the first- and second-graders in their sample and not for students in kindergarten or third grade. Further, they found that the Bender Gestalt age-equivalent scores were higher than the VMI scores at every grade level.

Although the literature reflects a trend for correlations between VMI and Bender scores to be somewhat higher for learning disabled subjects than for normal subjects, substantive differences have also been noted between scores on the VMI and Bender for various handicapped students. Using mean standard scores, investigators found significant differences on these tests for 93 learning disabled students, with subjects, overall, scoring higher on the VMI (DeMers, Wright, & Dappen, 1981). Although significant correlations of .44 to .65 across ages are noted for these tests, this results in an explained variance of only 20-43%. Further, using raw scores, Skeen, Strong, and Book (1982) report significant correlations of .72 between the Bender and VMI. In addition to noting that this correlation, although significant, only accounts for 52% of the shared variance, the authors examined individual differences in test-score differences for their 30 learning-disabled subjects. They found that on the two tests, 53% of their subjects had age-equivalent scores that varied from each other by less than one year; 30% of subjects had scores that varied across tests by one-two years; and 17% of the subjects had scores that varied by more than two years.

These studies have been replicated using the new norms and scoring system of the revised VMI. As in earlier studies, Breen (1982) found a significant correlation between the revised VMI and the Bender (.73) for 32 emotionally disturbed students, yet also notes that for 11 of his subjects age-equivalent scores varied across tests by 18 months or more. He does not specify any trend to the directionality of these differences. Similarly, Armstrong and Knopf (1982) found a significant correlation of .74 between test scores for 40 learning-disabled students and a significant, but somewhat lower, correlation of .36 for 40 normal students. An overall mean difference of nine months was obtained between the revised VMI and Bender scores, which also proved to be statistically significant. Finally, all three test forms (Bender, VMI, and the revised VMI) were compared in a study of 111 normal elementary-school students (Siewert & Breen, 1983). Significant, similar correlations were found between VMI and Bender scores and between the revised VMI and Bender scores (.724 and .705, respectively). There were significant differences between both VMI revised VMI age scores (82 to 84 months) and Bender age-equivalent scores (93 months).

In sum, the shared characteristics of the two tests of perceptual-motor functioning are apparent in the significant correlations between test scores for normal and learning-disabled subjects across most studies. The somewhat lower test scores found for normal subjects may be a function of these subjects reaching the lower developmental age ceiling of 11 years on the Bender while continuing to be challenged developmentally by the higher ceiling of 15 years on the VMI. Overall, no pattern has emerged with regard to which test produces higher scores: Some studies suggest that the VMI results in higher age-equivalent scores for subjects and some indicate that subjects score higher on the Bender. Although even the group statistics performed on these tests indicate that there is a considerable proportion of unaccounted variance across the two tests, it is the sizable individual discrepancies in test scores that most clearly reflect the differences in skills measured by the two tests. These discrepancies suggest the need to define the differences in task requirements of the two tests more clearly; it also suggests that the two tests are not redundant and that both may be utilized at times to obtain more knowledge about a student's perceptual-motor skills.

The use of the VMI alone or in a battery of tests to predict school performance has been achieved with mixed results. Fletcher and Satz (1982), for example, found that a screen battery, consisting of the Peabody Picture Vocabulary Test, VMI, Alphabet Recitation Test, and Recognition-Discrimination Test, and administered to 195 students in kindergarten, was a significant predictor of achievement on the Metropolitan Achievement Test when these children reached sixth grade. Similarly, Reynolds, Wright, and Wilkinson (1980) found that the VMI, administered to 151 children in kindergarten, was a significant predictor of SRA scores over the next two years, with an overall correlation of .53. Further, in the largest reported study (Friedman, Fuerth, & Forsythe, 1980) 1,251 students who had been administered a test battery at five years of age were evaluated by their teachers with regard to school performance at age nine. The VMI was found to be a significant predictor of teacher-appraised school performance, but the false positive rate was also high at 62% (i.e., 62% of the students identified by the VMI as having perceptual-motor problems at age five did not appear to have school problems by age nine). For 600 of these children who had been administered a second VMI and teacher rating at age seven, the repeated VMI at age seven was a significant predictor of performance at age nine. Although teacher ratings were the best predictors, the combined VMI—teacher rating at age seven increased the accuracy of prediction for the success or failure of students at age nine to 89%.

Not all studies, however, have found a positive relationship between scores on the VMI and measures of school performance. Flynn and Flynn (1978), for example, found that VMI scores in kindergarten did not predict performance on the California Achievement Test for 81 second-grade students. These mixed findings have led other researchers to look at the relationship of the VMI to more specific academic tasks.

In a relatively early study in this area (Hartlage & Lucas, 1976), significant correlations were found between the VMI, Bender, and Wide Range Achievement Test (WRAT) for both black and white students. This suggested that performance on the VMI was related to general school achievement. Other investigators, however, have found that the VMI is more highly correlated with the Wechsler Intelligence Scale for Children (WISC), an IQ test, than with the WRAT or other achievement measures (e.g., Richardson, DiBenedetto, Christ, & Press, 1980; Wright & DeMers, 1982). In the Richardson et al., study (1980) the VMI did not significantly correlate with any of a variety of reading measures for 77 poor readers once IQ was controlled. Similarly, Wright and DeMers (1982) found that the VMI was more highly correlated with the WISC than with the WRAT; once the effects of the WISC were partialled out, the only other significant correlation was between the VMI and the Spelling subtest of the WRAT at .20. This is somewhat discrepant from Klein's (1978) findings, however, as she reports the highest achievement correlations between the VMI and the mathematical portions of the Screening Test of Academic Readiness and the Scholastic Aptitude Test. Thus, although performance on the VMI appears to have some relationship to overall intellectual functioning and academic achievement, its use as a predicator of specific academic tasks remains to be clarified.

Critique

The Developmental Test of Visual-Motor Integration is an easily administered and scored test of perceptual-motor skills involved in figure reproduction. The test was designed to be used as a developmental measure of children's perceptual skills; this feature, in conjunction with its relatively high reliability ratings, sets the VMI apart from other figure-reproduction tests and enhances its utility in relation to these other tests. However, its value as an assessment device rests primarily on the empirical relationship between form reproduction and other academic/cognitive tasks. Although there is some suggestion in the literature that the VMI is related to other global measures of achievement and cognitive functioning, the impact of this skill on reading, writing, or mathematics has yet to be specified. Further research on the validity of this test with regard to specific academic functions is needed in order to fully assess its utility.

References

Armstrong, B. B., & Knopf, K. F. (1982). Comparison of the Bender-Gestalt and Revised Developmental Test of Visual-Motor Integration. *Perceptual and Motor Skills, 55,* 164-166.

Beery, K. E. (1967). *Visual-motor integration.* Cleveland: Modern Curriculum Press.

Beery, K. E. (1982). *Revised administration, scoring, and teaching manual for the Developmental Test of Visual-Motor Integration.* Cleveland: Modern Curriculum Press.

Bender, L. A. (1938). *A visual motor gestalt test and its clinical uses* (Research Monograph No. 3). New York: American Orthopsychiatric Association.

Breen, M. J. (1982). Comparison of educationally handicapped students' scores on the Revised Developmental Test of Visual-Motor Integration and Bender-Gestalt. *Perceptual and Motor Skills, 54,* 1227-1230.

Brown, M. J. (1977). Comparison of the Developmental Test of Visual Motor Integration and the Bender-Gestalt test. *Perceptual and Motor Skills, 40,* 981-982.

Curtis, C. J., Michael, J. J., & Michael, W. B. (1979). The predictive validity of the Developmental Test of Visual-Motor Integration under group and individual modes of administration relative to academic performance measures of second-grade pupils without identifiable major learning disabilities. *Educational and Psychological Measurement, 39,* 401-410.

DeMers, S. T., Wright, D., & Dappen, L. (1981). Comparison of scores on two visual-motor tests for children referred for learning or adjustment difficulties. *Perceptual and Motor Skills, 53,* 863-867.

Fletcher, J. M., & Satz, P. (1982). Kindergarten prediction of reading achievement: A seven-year longitudinal follow-up. *Educational and Psychological Measurement, 42,* 681-685.

Flynn, T. M., & Flynn, L. A. (1978). Evaluation of the predictive ability of five screening measures administered during kindergarten. *Journal of Experimental Education, 46,*65-70.

Friedman, R., Fuerth, J. H., & Forsythe, A. B. (1980). A brief screening battery for predicting school achievement at ages seven and nine years. *Psychology in the Schools, 17,* 340-346.

Fulkerson, S. C., & Freeman, W. M. (1980). Perceptual-motor deficiency in autistic children. *Perceptual and Motor Skills, 50,* 331-336.

Hartlage, L. C., & Lucas, T. L. (1976). Differential correlates of Bender-Gestalt and Beery Visual Motor Integration test for back and white children. *Perceptual and Motor Skills, 43,* 1039-1042.

Klein, A. E. (1978). The validity of the Beery Test of Visual-Motor Integration in predicting achievement in kindergarten, first, and second grades. *Educational and Psychological Measurement, 38,* 457-461.

Koppitz, E. M. (1975). *The Bender-Gestalt Test for Young Children, Vol. 2.* New York: Grune & Stratton.

Krauft, V. R., & Krauft, C. C. (1972). Structured vs. unstructured visual-motor tests for educable retarded children. *Perceptual and Motor Skills, 34,* 691-694.

Lehman, J., & Breen, M. J. (1982). A comparative analysis of the Bender-Gestalt and Beery/Buktenica Tests of visual-motor integration as a function of grade level for regular education students. *Psychology in the Schools, 19,* 52-54.

Lepkin, S. R., & Pryzwansky, W. (1983). Interrater reliability of the original and revised scoring system for the Development Test of Visual-Motor Integration. *Psychology in the Schools, 20,* 284-288.

Liemohn, W., & Knapczyk, D. R. (1974). Factor analysis of gross fine motor ability in developmentally disabled children. *Research Quarterly, 14,* 424-431.

Liemohn, W., & Wagner, P. (1975). Motor and perceptual determinants of performance on the Bender-Gestalt and Beery developmental scale by retarded males. *Perceptual and Motor Skills, 40,* 524-526.

Martin, R., Sewell, T., & Manni, J. L. (1977). Effects of race and social class on preschool performance on the Developmental Test of Visual-Motor Integration. *Psychology in the Schools, 14,* 466-470.

Porter, G. L., & Binder, D. M. (1981). A pilot study of visual-motor developmental inter-test reliability: the Beery Developmental Test of Visual-Motor Integration and the Bender Visual-Motor Gestalt Test. *Journal of Learning Disabilities, 14,* 124-127.

Pryzwansky, W. B. (1977). The use of the Developmental Test of Visual-Motor Integration as a group screening instrument. *Psychology in the Schools, 14,* 419-422.

Reynolds, C. Y., Wright D., & Wilkenson, W. A. (1980). Incremental validity of the Test for Auditory Comprehension of Language and the Developmental Test of Visual-Motor Integration. *Educational and Psychological Measurement, 40,* 503-507.

Richardson, E., DiBenedetto B., Christ, A., & Press, M. (1980). Relationship of auditory and visual skills to reading retardation. *Journal of Learning Disabilities, 13,* 77-82.

Ryckman, D. B., & Rentfrow, R. K. (1971). The Beery Developmental Test of Visual-Motor Integration: An investigation of reliability. *Journal of Learning Disabilities, 4,* 333-334.

Schooler, D. L., & Anderson, R. L. (1979). Race differences on the Developmental Test of Visual Motor Integration, the Slosson Intelligence Test, and the ABC Inventory. *Psychology in the Schools, 16,* 453-456.

Siewert, J. C., & Breen M. (1983). The revised Test of Visual-Motor Integration: Its relation to the Test of Visual-Motor Integration and Bender Visual-Motor Gestalt Test for regular education students. *Psychology in the Schools, 20,* 304-306.

Skeen, J., Strong, V. N., & Book, R. M. (1982). Comparison of learning disabled children's performance on Bender Visual-Motor Gestalt Test and Beery's Developmental Test of Visual-Motor Integration. *Perceptual and Motor Skills, 55,* 1257-1258.

Snyder, P. P., Snyder, R. T., & Massong, S. F. (1981). The Visual-Motor Integration Test: High interjudge reliability, high potential for diagnostic error. *Psychology in the Schools, 18,* 55-59.

Wright, D., & DeMers, S. T. (1982). Comparison of the relationship between two measures of visual-motor coordination and academic achievement. *Psychology in the Schools, 19,* 473-477.

Katherine P. Snider, Ph.D.
School Psychologist, Midland Public Schools, Midland, Michigan.
Joseph L. Snider, Ed.D.
Professor of Education, Saginaw Valley State College, University Center, Michigan.

DIAGNOSTIC READING SCALES: REVISED 1981 EDITION

George D. Spache. Monterey, California: CTB/McGraw-Hill.

Introduction

The Diagnostic Reading Scales: Revised 1981 Edition (DRS-81) is a series of individually administered tests designed to evaluate oral reading, silent reading, and auditory comprehension. The stated purpose of the DRS-81 is to identify reading strengths and weaknesses of students in elementary grades, as well as impaired readers in upper grades who are reading at an elementary level.

The DRS was originally developed by Dr. George D. Spache. Spache has had experience as an elementary school teacher, school psychologist, college professor, and head of the Reading Laboratory and Clinic at the University of Florida. He has been professionally connected with the International Reading Association, American Psychological Association, American Academy of Optometry, American Board of Examiners in Professional Psychology, National Council of Teachers of English, and the American Educational Research Association. He has authored over 100 articles, plus yearbooks for educational organizations and books on reading.

The original standardization of the DRS took eight years and was based on 2,081 students from rural and urban schools in four states. The 1972 revision added two phonics tests and made some changes in the examiner's manual. A study of 361 students from 24 schools in three states collected data on consistency of DRS scores and relationship with reading scores on the California Achievement Tests, 1970 Edition.

The 1981 revision (DRS-81) reassigned grade levels to reading selections, made minor changes in wording to remove sexism, and added 12 expanded and revised subtests of word analysis and phonics skills. The examiner's manual was again revised and reorganized. Some examples of substitutions often found in Black or Hispanic dialect are provided. A series of questions and answers in the manual covers most questions an examiner might encounter in presenting the test. Available with the test kit is a cassette that presents a model administration of the DRS-81 with examples of student performances.

The DRS-81 is made up of three word-recognition lists, two sets (eleven each) of reading selections, and 12 subtests of word analysis and phonics.

The word-recognition lists are graduated in difficulty. The first list includes 50 words intended for use with students up through first grade. The second list of 40 words is appropriate to the second and third grades. The third list of 40 words is directed to students in Grades Four and Five. These serve as a pretest, indicating the appropriate level of testing in the reading selections.

The reading selections are identified for initial testing and retesting. Content is drawn from a range of science, history, and literature similar to the content of classroom reading. Lower levels are narrative in style; upper levels may be either expository or descriptive.

The instructional level is based on the oral reading of paragraphs within the guidelines of a maximum number of reading errors and the correct responses to a minimum number of comprehension questions. At the failure level, the student is asked to read further selections silently. Comprehension is again checked, and the highest level within the guidelines is the instructional level. The potential level is based on the student's ability to answer comprehension questions when succeeding paragraphs are read aloud by the examiner.

Comprehension questions for each selection are administered orally. Most of the questions test recall of facts, but a few require conclusions, inferences, or interpretations of feelings and actions.

The word-analysis and phonics subtests are intended as supplements for use up through the fourth grade. It is not necessary to present all of the subtests in order to diagnose the difficulties. The 12 subtests are described as follows:

> *Initial consonants:* reading a list of 22 real and nonsense words beginning with a single consonant.
> *Final consonants:* reading a list of 15 real and nonsense words, all of which start with *te* and end in a single consonant.
> *Consonant digraphs:* reading a list of 16 real and nonsense words containing the digraph in initial and final positions.
> *Consonant blends:* reading a list of 27 real and nonsense words containing blends in initial and final positions.
> *Initial consonant substitution:* substituting the initial sound in a reading list of ten words.
> *Initial consonant sounds recognized auditorily:* identifying initial letters in 23 words read by the examiner.
> *Auditory discrimination:* identifying which of 33 pairs of words are identical in sound and which pairs differ by only a single element.
> *Short and long vowel sounds:* reading 16 pairs of words with the correct long or short vowel sound.
> *Vowels with "r":* reading a list of eight real and nonsense words containing a vowel followed by *r* in initial, medial, and final positions.
> *Vowel diphthongs and digraphs:* reading a list of 30 real and nonsense words containing common vowel diphthongs and digraphs.
> *Common syllables or phonograms:* reading a list of 34 clusters of letters that occur frequently in words.
> *Blending:* reading a list of ten nonsense words that have been divided into phonograms by blending the elements into single words.

Materials needed for testing include the examiner's manual, examiner's record book, student's reading book, stopwatch or clock, and pencils. Checklists of word analysis techniques and reading ability are filled out by the examiner immediately following testing. A summary record sheet includes reading levels, general observations, and recommendations.

The booklet containing the materials to be read by the student is easy to manipulate and follow. It is probable that a plastic coating would prevent finger smudges or pencil marks that might interfere with subsequent use of the book.

Practical Applications/Uses

The DRS-81 measures three reading levels for each student in addition to providing raw scores for the word analysis and phonics subtests.

The standards for determining oral reading errors are not the same as those used in the Informal Reading Inventories. These differences should be noted by anyone comparing results from these measures.

The instructional level of oral reading and comprehension is that level acceptable for group instruction and appropriate to the level of basal tests used in the classroom.

The independent reading level measures silent reading comprehension. This represents the highest level of material the student should be given for independent, silent supplemental, or recreational reading.

The potential level measures auditory comprehension and suggests the reading level that may be expected after classroom or remedial instruction.

Raw scores for the word-analysis and phonics subtests can be compared to averages found for students participating in the DRS study for 1981. Those averages are not norms or standardized scores. Identifying the error type or pattern is of greater practical use than arriving at a grade-level norm.

The time and individual nature of testing would generally preclude use of the DRS-81 by classroom teachers. Reading specialists, teacher consultants, and school psychologists could use this instrument to evaluate a student's instructional level and to identify specific reading errors. Such a diagnosis forms the basis for a program of remediation. This applies to the student in general education who may need remediation, as well as to the special education student for whom an individualized education plan (IEP) must be developed. Used as a screening instrument, determination of the instructional reading level might identify students who are capable of using more difficult materials in accelerated programs. Certain word-analysis and phonics subtests are suggested for the diagnosis of ability to relate sounds to symbols. This extends the application of the DRS-81 to encoding (spelling) as well as decoding (reading). This test is suitable for use in public or private schools and in educational clinic settings.

Applicability is based on reading functioning, not student placement level, at grade levels one through seven. Therefore, the average student in Grade Four who makes some reading errors, as well as the disabled reader in Grade Ten, could be served by this test. All responses are oral, and so results are not confounded by deficits in other domains, with the exception of students who are deficient in listening comprehension.

Some caveats are given on a few of the work-analysis and phonics subtests for specific groups. This does not present a diagnostic problem as all subtests need not be given.

No special training in the DRS-81 is required for its administration, although examiners should be familiar with individual testing procedures in general and with reading diagnosis in particular. Examiners should also be familiar with non-standard English that may be spoken by the students because dialect deviations are not considered reading errors.

Instructions to the examiner are clearly stated, but practice is needed to mark errors as the student is reading.

The word lists are presented first so that the appropriate level of reading selection may be chosen. The word lists are not necessary, however, for determining the three reading levels. The order of the word-analysis and phonics subtests is not significant, and the examiner may choose to omit any that are not needed for an individual diagnosis of reading ability. Presentation of the entire battery should be possible in less than 60 minutes, according to the manual. Timing of student performance is recorded only in determining the independent level of reading.

Scoring is accomplished as the test is presented and is the portion of administration that will require practice to note and mark quickly the five error patterns of omissions, additions, substitutions, repetitions, and reversals. Instructions are adequate, and examples are given for both reading errors and comprehension questions. The record book gives adequate space for scoring notations and examiner comments, but the examiner must be familiar with the scoring techniques presented in the manual.

Determination of instructional level is based on criteria related to the number of oral reading errors and the number of correct answers to comprehension questions. The criterion for the independent and potential levels is correctly answering a minimum number of comprehension questions.

Judgment of the examiner is applied in determining the critical error level of the word-analysis and phonics subtests. Although a table of averages is given, it is not meant to be used as a standard for performance. For the experienced reading teacher or diagnostician, such interpretation will be easy and meaningful in determining an instructional program. Persons inexperienced in reading diagnoses can, with practice, administer, score, and report the results of the DRS-81.

Technical Aspects

Basic validity of the DRS-81 was found in the studies of the 1963 and 1972 editions (Spache, 1982). The word lists were selected from Durrell's (1940) work. Relative difficulty was determined through trials of at least 100 students per level. The correlation of word-list scores with instructional level indicated the most probable test entry level. The coefficients of correlation (.78, .65, .69) were sufficient for this purpose.

Earlier validity studies (e.g., Eller & Attea, 1967; Spache, 1982) compared performance to parallel selections from the Durrell Analysis of Reading Difficulty and the Gray Oral Reading Tests. Teacher judgment of students' reading abilities were weighted heavily.

Comparisons of the DRS with Durrell Analysis of Reading Difficulty showed substantial correlations (.897 to .99), indicating that the same skills were being measured. The oral instructional levels of the Analytic Reading Inventory and the DRS correlation coefficients ranged from .917 to .991. Some subtests differed in definition, and thus correlations tended to be low. The correlation coefficients of the oral independent levels on the Analytic Reading Inventory and the DRS ranged from .587 to .861 (Layton, 1979). Use of the potential reading level to predict reading level after instruction gave some indication of reading gains that might be expected. These gains were not entirely independent of the student's ability, however.

The major revision involved in DRS-81 was the change in difficulty level assigned to each reading selection.

Current reading levels for Grades 1-3 were analyzed by the revised Spache readability formula. Selections for Grades 4-7 were analyzed by the Powers, Sumner, and Kearl (1958) recalculation of the Dale-Chall readability formula (Dale & Chall, 1948).

A study of 534 students, Grades 1-8, in 32 states provided the data for this change. A reduced sample of 290 from this pool eliminated the over-weighting at the high-scoring end. At each instructional level the students' mean grade level in school, mean grade level of assigned reading books, mean teacher estimate of student reading level, and mean reading grade equivalents from other standardized tests were used in conjunction with the readability formulas to designate the reading level of each selection.

Reliability for the DRS-81 was determined through an alternate forms procedure. Students in the 1980 study were tested two to eight weeks apart. Initially, half received Set "R," and half received Set "S." The combined Pearson product-moment correlation coefficient of instructional level scores, Grades 1-8, was .89, which indicated good alternate-form reliability. The Kuder-Richardson Formula 20 (K-R 20) was used to estimate the reliability of the word-analysis and phonics subtests. The combined Grade 1-2 K-R 20 coefficient was .87. Test-retest correlation for these grades was .75. Although test-retest may be considered a conservative estimate of reliability, it becomes misleading when some tests yield most scores at the top of the range. Five of the 12 word-analysis and phonics subtests fit that category and so correlations were low. Data were not presented above Grade Two on these subtests because most students above this level tend to "top out." Standard errors of measurement (SE_M) were reported for each subtest. Means and standard deviation (SD) for each subtest were reported for Grades 1-4.

Critique

The DRS-81 appears to be a useful instrument for assessing reading skills and diagnosing specific reading errors. The greatest utility will be with students who are encountering difficulties in the classroom with reading materials, either in early reading instruction or the content areas of the later grades.

The word tests and reading selections provide information relative to sight vocabulary, oral fluency, and understanding. The supplementary subtests define the analytic and phonetic sources of error in a student's reading. Knowledge of these errors permits building specific prescriptions in remedial reading programs for either general or special education students.

Administration, scoring, and interpretation are not complicated but do require familiarity with reading instruction and specific practice with the DRS-81.

The DRS has been used since 1963. This is the second revision. It has been favorably reviewed for its "potential in diagnosing a wide variety of reading skills" (Stafford, 1978). The phonics tests are cited for content validity and usefulness "for designating instructional strategies" (Schreiner, 1978). Standardization data and later studies (e.g., Layton, 1979; Eller & Attea, 1967; Spache, 1982) have indicated that the DRS is a valid measure of reading skills and that reliability is adequate. The lowering of the grade-level assignments for the reading selections speaks to the criticism that the DRS was not reflecting difficulty levels of recently published classroom materials.

References

This list includes text citations as well as suggested additional reading.

Barnitz, J. (1980). Black English and other dialects: Socio-linguistic implications for reading obstruction. *The Reading Teacher, 33*, 779-785.

Burke, C. (1973). Preparing elementary teachers to teach reading. In K. S. Goodman (Ed.), *Miscue analysis* (pp. 15-29). Urbana, IL: ERIC Clearing House on Reading and Communication Skills.

Dale, E., & Chall, J. (1948). *A formula for predicting readability.* Columbus, OH: Bureau of Educational Research, Ohio State University.

Durrell, D. (1940). *Improvement of basic reading ability.* Yonkers, NY: Harcourt Brace Jovanovich, Inc.

Eller, W., & Attea, M. (1967). Three diagnostic reading tests: Some comparisons. *Vistas in Reading: IRA Proceedings, 1*(2), 562-566.

Goodman, K. (1965). A linguistic study of cues and miscues in reading. *Elementary English, 42*, 639-643.

Layton, J. R. (1979). *An analysis of three tests: Durrell Analysis of Reading Difficulty, Diagnostic Reading Scales, and the Analytic Reading Inventory.* Springfield, MO: Southwest Missouri State University.

Powers, R., Summer, W., & Kearl, B. (1958). A recalculation of four adult readability formulas. *Journal of Educational Psychology, 49*, 99-105.

Schreiner, R. L. (1978). Review of Diagnostic Reading Scales. In O. K. Buros (Ed.), *The eighth mental measurements yearbook* (pp. 1242-1243). Highland Park, NJ: The Gryphon Press.

Spache, G. D. (1940). Characteristic errors of good and poor spellers. *Journal of Educational Research, 34*, 182-189.

Spache, G. D. (1953). A new readability formula for primary grade reading materials. *Elementary School Journal, 53*, 410-413.

Spache, G. D. (1978). *Good reading for poor readers.* Champaign, IL: Garrard Publishing.

Spache, G. D. (1981). *Diagnostic Reading Scales: Revised 1981 Edition.* Monterey, CA: CTB/McGraw-Hill.

Spache, G. D. (1982). *Diagnostic Reading Scales: Technical report.* Monterey, CA: CTB/McGraw-Hill.

Spache, G. D., & Spache, E. (1977). *Reading in the elementary school* (4th ed.). Boston: Allyn & Bacon, Inc.

Stafford, J. (1978). Reading test review: Reflections on the Diagnostic Reading Scales. In O. K. Buros (Ed.), *The eighth mental measurements yearbook* (pp. 1243-1244). Highland Park, NJ: The Gryphon Press. (Reprinted from *Reading World*, 1974, *14*(1), 5-8)

Young, W. (1936). Relations of reading comprehension and retention. *Journal of Experimental Education*, *5*, 30-39.

Howard W. Stoker, Ph.D.
Professor and Head, Section on Instructional Development and Evaluation, Department of Education, University of Tennessee, Memphis, Tennessee.

DIAGNOSTIC SKILLS BATTERY

O.F. Anderhalter and Scholastic Testing Service Staff and Consultants. Bensenville, Illinois: Scholastic Testing Service, Inc.

Introduction

The Diagnostic Skills Battery (DSB) is based on a selection of so-called "terminal" objectives. Some 30-40 objectives for each skill area—Reading, Mathematics, and Language Arts—are measured. Four levels are published: 12 (Grades 1, 2, and beginning Grade 3), 34 (Grades 3, 4, and beginning Grade 5), 56 (Grades 5, 6, and beginning Grade 9), and 78 (Grades 7, 8, and beginning Grade 9). Equivalent, parallel forms are provided with each level. Both objective-related and normative reporting, which, according to the publisher's catalog, ". . . make the DSB particularly useful when valid pre- and post-test comparisons are called for" (Scholastic Testing Service, Inc., 1984), are available.

The DSB was developed by Dr. O. F. Anderhalter, St. Louis University, and Scholastic Testing Service (STS) staff and consultants. To appreciate the DSB, one must have some knowledge of two other STS batteries, the Educational Development Series (EDSeries; Anderhalter et al., 1984; see this volume for a review) and the Analysis of Skills (ASK), which the DSB has replaced.

The ASK, designed to provide in-depth coverage in Reading, Mathematics, and Language Arts, provided for a detailed examination of the students' strengths and weaknesses in the skill area selected. Because the ASK tests were objective-referenced and diagnostic in nature, normative data would be of little value. Steffe (1978) was critical of the ASK:Mathematics test items, labeling their quality as "quite variable." Both the length and difficulty of the tests led him to state that the ASK:Mathematics "is not recommended for use in schools" (p. 387).

The ASK:Reading Test, reviewed in the same volume by John T. Guthrie and P. David Pearson, fared better than the math test. Guthrie (1978, p. 1231) states that the objectives are ". . . clearly stated and the items representative of the defined skills." Although Pearson (1978) labeled the ASK:Reading manual "deficient," he states that the test is assuredly a viable alternative among the numerous systems available for fine-grained analysis of reading skills in group testing situations" (p. 1234).

If one were to establish a continuum, a comprehensive, norm-referenced test (EDSeries) would be on one end, an objective-referenced battery (ASK) would be on the other end, and the DSB would be somewhere near the middle. According to the DSB general manual, the battery was developed to provide the best possible combination of norm-referenced and criterion- or objective-referenced approaches to testing. However, in this reviewer's opinion, how one decides on a good/better/best combination of norm- and objective-referenced tests is open to question. Despite the fact that the early 1970s (when the DSB was developed) was a period during which the norm-referenced/criterion-referenced test debates claimed the attention of many measurement specialists at professional meetings, it is this reviewer's belief that many questions about differences between the two types of tests were left unanswered, although some questions can be answered in simple, operational terms. For example, *How can one tell the difference between a norm-referenced and an objective-referenced test?* Norms tables *must* exist for a norm-referenced test, with (one hopes) *every* published test based on objectives. Because the DSB provides both objectives and norms, it must represent both approaches to testing. *How many items must one have to measure an objective?* The number of items will vary, depending on the objective, but the *minimum* is one. The DSB provides two items for each objective, which is either above the minimum or twice the minimum depending on how one views the counting scale. *How does one estimate the reliability of scores from an objective-referenced test?* For some scores, the methods are the same as for norm-referenced tests; for others, there are no good estimates. The DSB items are keyed to the DSB master content outline. The general manual (p. 27) recommends that potential users compare objectives and items, which would allow them to determine whether the items were content-valid for their particular situation. In this reviewer's judgment, such actions are of prime importance in the decisions related to test selection. Results of the comparisons are much more meaningful than a correlation coefficient showing the relationship between total battery scores on two different, but similar, batteries.

In summary, the authors and publishers of the DSB seem to have addressed many of the norm- and criterion-referenced questions without doing so directly. Obviously, they judged that a need existed for a test with the characteristics represented by the DSB. They did so at a time when members of the profession could not agree on the need for objective-referenced tests. The fact that the test still exists would appear to justify the authors' judgment, but one must wonder whether a ten-year-old test is still useful and whether the time for a revision is at hand. That issue can be resolved through the use of the master content outline (MCO). Are the objectives in the MCO still viable for the potential user? Are there objectives that have become part of the curriculum or objectives that are no longer considered? These questions can only be answered at the user level. It is clear, however, that a revision of the general manual is due, if not overdue. Several references that appear refer to follow-up studies, such as analyses "now being conducted." The manual carries a 1977 copyright date, and one cannot help but wonder why the results of the follow-up studies are not reported.

The DSB looks much the same as most standardized tests purporting to measure achievement in reading, mathematics, and language arts. Level 12, designed for Grade 1, Grade 2, and beginning Grade 3 students, is designed as a scannable booklet. Levels 34, 56, and 78 use separate answer sheets. Two forms are available for each level.

Type styles are pleasing to the eye. Booklets for different levels are color coded.

For example, Level 56 has a green cover with all inside print in green. Answer sheets are color coded to match the booklets. This would facilitate combined testing of several grades (directions for Mathematics and Language Arts are the same for Levels 34, 56, and 78).

As is the case with most published tests today, there is a full range of "output" one can obtain, such as alphabetical lists, group summaries, pressure-sensitive labels, and performance profiles, as parts of scoring packages, and individual skill analyses, rank-order lists, additional norms, and computer data tapes are available at extra cost. The number of available scores is large enough to satisfy the most avid data-oriented test director. Five normative scores for each total and part score are provided. In addition, part scores are broken into 36 clusters of objectives, and performance is reported for each objective (i.e., performance on the two items designed to measure the objective). A 15-page booklet related to the use of the DSB results is provided to users. However, the majority of the text simply explains how to read the various reports, and recommendations on the use of the results are at a minimum.

The best description of the DSB, its parts, and subparts is contained in the 15-page MCO, which lists every objective, the number of the objective in the DSB, and an identification of the two items that are designed to measure the objective. For example, adding two or more whole numbers, with four- or five-digit addends, is Computation Skill Objective 8 for Levels 12 and 34 and Objective 1 for Levels 56 and 78. The objective, not measured in Level 12, is measured by items 9 and 23 in Level 34, items 2 and 16 in Level 56, and items 2 and 16 in Level 78. The MCO would serve well those who wish to consider the relevance of the test for their curricula.

Practical Applications/Uses

As noted above, the DSB provides multiple-score reports. If the DSB is to be adopted, careful consideration should be given to the individual skills analysis and the performance profile. The individual skills analysis lists the students in a group and their performance on each objective (+ , P, or –). A classroom teacher could use this report to find which students have mastered specific objectives (assuming, of course, that answering two items correctly signals mastery). Thus, the individual skills analysis provides for pupil diagnosis and could provide direction for the instructional program.

The performance profile provides both normative- and objective-referenced scores for each student. Local stanines, national grade scores, and national percentiles are provided, and space is available for at least one other score. This is the type of score report that frequently goes to parents and almost as frequently leads to problems in the interpretation of scores. This reviewer believes that when testing students, users are obligated to provide understandable results to them or to their parents. A copy of the MCO, together with the individual skills analysis, appears to be a better combination for teacher-parent conferences.

The DSB is designed for in-school use with students in Grades 1-8. Chapter I schools may find the tests appropriate for functional-level testing. If the tests are used with students for whom they were not designed (e.g., Level 34 administered to students in Grade 6), the norms may have no utility. However, the individual skills analysis *would* have utility in that it would help identify the objectives that the students have not mastered.

Administrative procedures, as described in the teacher's manual of directions, are fairly standard. Time limits are clearly defined, with a total of about three hours required. A minimum of two sessions is recommended, with three being recommended for the lower levels. Materials needed for the administration are clearly identified. The directions for the administration of the Reading Test for Levels 34 differ from those for Levels 56 and 78. Directions for the Mathematics and Language Arts Tests are the same for Levels 34, 56, and 78. Directions for Level 12, which is a self-contained booklet, differ from those for the higher levels. The directions are such that one could assume that any classroom teacher could administer the test with no problems, but, having observed numerous classroom teachers administer tests, this reviewer knows this assumption to be false.

As noted above, many scores can be produced. One would hesitate to undertake the hand scoring of anything other than Level 12. The distribution of items/objective would make objective scores difficult to derive without a computer and accompanying software. Hence, one must make a decision regarding the scores that are desired. As with all programs of this type, one major concern is the length of time between test administration and score reporting. If the DSB is to be used in the pre-post testing mode, the results from the pretest must be obtained so that diagnoses can be made, instructional programs altered, and instructional time before posttest maximized. If the DSB is to be used in a normative mode, then the time it takes to obtain results is not as important.

Of the scores that can be obtained, the STS grade score is of particular interest. The manual presents an understandable general discussion of norms (pp. 41-46), as well as a discussion of percentiles, stanines, and grade-equivalent scores. According to the manual, "the STS Grade Score was developed in an attempt to utilize the strong points inherent in percentile-rank and grade-equivalent norms, while minimizing the inherent limitations of such scores. The STS does not satisfy all desirable characteristics completely, but it is designed as an optimal system."

It appears that the STS grade score is simply a normalized standard-score scale. As such, it has no more or less value than other similar scales. The uses of such scales abound, as do the misuses. People have ascribed magical powers to an IQ of 115 for many years. In reality, the IQ is probably a normalized standard-score scale, depending on which test one is using. One *must* remember that regardless of what the score looks like, it is based on the number of items answered correctly on the test.

The manual (p. 44) states that "beginning fourth-grade pupils are compared with other beginning fourth-grade pupils"—apparently in the context of norm development. Because the standardization was conducted in the *spring* of 1976, additional data must have been used in the norms development.

The STS grade score is, then, a modification of the normalized T-Score, having a mean of zero and a standard deviation of 1.0. The normalization process appears to have been done for each grade. Comparison over grades should not be advocated without the collection of data related to the vertical equating of the test levels and forms. One would hope to find such data in a revision of the manual.

Finally, although the manual makes no mention of normal curve equivalent

(NCE) scores, the STS catalog indicates that such scores are available. Although the manual is dated, score options appear to cover all needs.

Technical Aspects

The description of the standardization studies, conducted in the spring of 1976, implies that the total sample of students is fairly representative for *all levels and all forms.* Almost 10,000 students in 554 classes in 43 schools representing 15 school districts participated in the standardization administration. If one assumed that students in all eight grades participated in about equal numbers, then one could conclude that about 70 classes per grade were involved. Because one-half of the students received different forms, one estimates that about 1,000 students completed either Form A or Form B of some level.

The 1,000 figure is, of course, an overestimate. Tables in the manual show that the median Reading score for Level 12, Form A, is based on 369 students in Grade 1 and 403 students in Grade 2. Reading medians for Level 56, Form B, are based on 768 students in Grade 5 and 759 students in Grade 6. The STS catalog reports Level 56 as appropriate for Grades 5, 6, and beginning Grade 7, but no information is provided as to whether students in Grade 7 took Level 56 in the standardization administration. No information is provided as to the geographic distribution of students for any of the levels or forms.

The manual indicates that the fall 1976 standardization and follow-up studies used similar sampling plans as were used for the spring 1976 administration. Results of these studies do not appear in the manual. This, if nothing else, would argue for the publication of a revised manual.

The manual includes the basic statistics pertinent to the several tests. Mean raw scores, standard deviations, reliabilities K-R 21s, and standard errors of measurement are presented. Intercorrelations among scores within levels for each form also appear. The data are largely what one would expect in a test battery of this type. Subtest intercorrelations are generally highest within a test and lower for subtests across tests. Reliabilities are generally lower for Level 12 and, in most cases, lower for Grade 1 than for Grade 2. Means are generally lower for the lower grade represented by a level. It is always a comfort when the data agree with the model that underlies the computations.

Forms A and B, at each level, are said to be "equivalent." Operationally, that means that the same objectives are measured in each form, each with two items. This should produce equivalence in scores, as measured by means, variances, and intercorrelations among the tests. Evidence of this type of score equivalence is somewhat lacking. Although some means and variances are almost the same, others differ noticeably. For example, for Level 56, fifth-grade students, the Form A and B total Reading means differ by almost 5 raw score points, and variances differ by 35 points. For Grade 5, Form A, the intercorrelation between Word Study and Study Skills is .59; for Form B, the comparable value is .45. Such data imply that raw scores for the forms are probably not equivalent. The manual recognizes this problem and recommends the use of norms, rather than raw scores, in pretest to posttest comparisons. It further recommends the administration of the same form in cases where the pre-post time span is "sufficient." For the lower grades, an early September to May time span should be sufficient.

Critique

The Diagnostic Skills Battery appears to serve the basic purposes for which it was designed and to serve them well. The DSB can be used in a diagnostic skills assessment mode in the areas of reading, mathematics, and language arts. The existence of two forms for each level would facilitate the use of the tests in a pre-post testing situation, given the cautions noted in the technical aspects section of this review. If the objectives measured by the tests and presented in the master content outline are those one wants to measure, and if one accepts the idea that answering two items correctly will indicate mastery for the objective, the DSB appears to provide a satisfactory instrument. One can, of course, argue over the inclusion/exclusion of objectives, but that is true for any test.

When used in the norm-referenced mode, the DSB provides usable information based on a large enough number of items so that one can depend on the scores as representing the student's performance with reference to some group. As noted, the definition of the reference groups could be improved. Percentiles, stanines, NCEs, STS grade scores, and local norms can be used. In short, this author would not hesitate to recommend the DSB for consideration and possible adoption to schools and/or districts, the goals and purposes of which appear to match those outlined in the manual.

References

Anderhalter, O. F., & STS Staff and Consultants. (1976). *Diagnostic Skills Battery.* Bensenville, IL: Scholastic Testing Service, Inc.

Guthrie, J. T. (1978). Review of Analysis of Skills: Reading. In O. K. Buros (Ed.), *The eighth mental measurements yearbook* (pp. 1231-1233). Highland Park, NJ: The Gryphon Press.

Pearson, P. D. (1978). Review of Analysis of Skills: Reading. In O. K. Buros (Ed.), *The eighth mental measurements yearbook* (pp. 1233-1234). Highland Park, NJ: The Gryphon Press.

Scholastic Testing Service, Inc. (1984). *1984/1985 catalog of tests and services.* Bensenville, IL: Author.

Steffe, L. P. (1978). Review of the Analysis of Skills: Mathematics. In O. K. Buros (Ed.), *The eighth mental measurements yearbook* (pp. 385-387). Highland Park, NJ: The Gryphon Press.

Carolyn M. Callahan, Ph.D.
Associate Professor of Education, Curry School of Education, University of Virginia, Charlottesville, Virginia.

EBY ELEMENTARY IDENTIFICATION INSTRUMENT

Judy W. Eby. East Aurora, New York: Slosson Educational Publications, Inc.

Introduction

The Eby Elementary Identification Instrument (EEII), a procedural guide for the selection of academically gifted students, incorporates the use of several existing instruments, a recording matrix, and two original rating scales. These procedures were designed to identify students in Grades K-8 who would satisfy the definition of giftedness based on "a combination and interaction of above average ability, task commitment and creativity." (Renzulli, 1978, p. 182) The EEII is not, in fact, an instrument according to the traditional use of that term in the field of measurement.

The author of the EEII, Judy W. Eby, is a resource teacher with the Barrington, Illinois public schools. She is also an adjunct professor with the National College of Education, Evanston, Illinois.

No specific information concerning the test's background (e.g., rationale or developmental history) is provided in the materials included with the test. Presumably the instrument was an attempt to systematize identification of the gifted according to the "three-ring definition" of giftedness (above average ability, task commitment, and creativity). This is the first published version of the instrument and no datum relative to revisions from earlier versions is given. Two earlier publications by Eby (1983, 1984a) describe aspects of the EEII and its development as a function of an attempt by a school division to codify its identification process to include indicators of general intellectual ability, creativity, and task commitment.

The first discussion of the EEII is in the 1983 article and the materials illustrated in that article are copyrighted 1982 by the author. There are no substantial differences between the materials presented in the article and the published instrument. The only reference made to the developmental process of the EEII is that concerning the Teacher Recommendation Form, which, according to the article, was developed on the basis of input from classroom teachers.

In addition to an 11-page manual, the packet of materials includes 50 General Selection Matrices, 50 Teacher Recommendation Forms, and 50 Unit Selection Matrices, each of which are single-sheet, color coded forms. The General Selection Matrix is a recording form that calls for the entry of the following data: achievement test composite score or general intelligence test score, grade point average, Group Inventory for Finding Creative Talent(GIFT) or Group Inventory for Finding Interests (GIFFI) test score, and teacher's recommendation score. The teacher recommendation score is taken from the Teacher Recommendation Form, which is a four-point rating scale divided into three subscales (Ability, Task Commitment, and Creativity) of five items each. The Unit Selection Matrix, a four-point rating scale used to rate student performance on an assigned pretask, includes two five-item subscales: Task Commitment and Creativity. Scores from each of these sources are then entered into the matrix and then assigned weights according to a five-point scale. For example, an achievement-test score that is greater than the 98th percentile is weighted 5, an achievement-test score between the 94th and 98th percentiles is weighted 4, and an achievement-test score between the 90th and 93rd percentiles is weighted 3. The weights from the four sources of data are added together to yield a total score ranging from 20 to 0.

Practical Applications/Uses

The EEII is designed for use with students in Grades K-8. It is recommended that a General Selection Matrix should be completed for any child who meets one or more of the following criteria: 1) receives a composite score at or above the 85th percentile on a standardized achievement test given by the school district; 2) receives a grade-point average of 4.0 or above or achieves honor-roll status; or 3) is recommended for gifted programming by a classroom teacher, parent, or self.

The use of the General Selection Matrix is recommended whenever a student meets the initial nomination criteria. Scores are weighted on the matrix. If a student has a weighted score of nine or more from the achievement test, grade point average, and teacher's recommendation, then it is recommended that the Slosson Intelligence Test and GIFT and GIFFI be administered. The manual states that "the administrator has the flexibility to determine the eligibility cutoff score. A mid-point score of 12 points may be used which will result in a program made of very highly qualified students" (p. 4).

The Unit Selection Matrix is completed for students who indicate an interest in a specific unit to be taught and submit a pretask project for evaluation, accordingly. The manual suggests that any student in the school may be given the option of completing a pretask, regardless of standing on the General Selection Matrix and that these students should be given the option of participation if performance on the tasks warrants affording that opportunity.

According to Eby (1984b) the EEII was designed to "provide gifted program administrators with an easily administered, objective and comprehensive selection process for an elementary school district that wishes to select students for gifted programming on the basis of performance and behavior" (p. 3). The variables to be assessed are general intellectual ability, creativity, and task commitment.

As the EEII currently stands, it is limited in utility to those students who can reasonably be expected to complete a standardized group achievement test, a general group intelligence test (the Slosson is recommended), and the GIFT or GIFFI. This would preclude its use for identifying physically handicapped, learning disabled, blind, or even disadvantaged gifted students.

The only practical use of this instrument would be in public or private schools as part of the process of identifying intellectually gifted students. It could be used by counselors, administrators, or committees which have been assigned the responsibility of screening for and identifying gifted students. Because of its highly specific definition of giftedness, it should be used only in those settings where that definition reflects the prevailing philosophy of the school division. Because no norms or criteria are designated, it cannot be used on an individual basis or in private practice settings. Finally, it could not be used to identify students with specific academic abilities, talent in the fine and performing arts, or outstanding leadership abilities. There have been no other uses of this instrument reported in the literature or described in the manual. Further, it is unlikely that the EEII has utility outside of educational settings.

The role of the examiner using this instrument varies according to who and when the instrument is used. Quite obviously the intelligence test, the achievement test, and the GIFT or GIFFI must be administered according to the requirements of those instruments. The Teacher Recommendation Form is completed by a teacher who is familiar with the nominated student's work. The manual does not specify who should complete the Unit Selection Matrix, although earlier publications imply that this matrix should be completed by administrators or teachers in the gifted program.

The matrices and Teacher Recommendation Form are completed by teachers or administrators and have no specific conditions for administration (e.g., setting, timing). No directions are given for training teachers on the use of the Teacher Recommendation Form and the directions given for the pretask assignment given for the Unit Selection Matrix are limited to the following (Eby, 1984b, p. 8):

> For example, if a research project on the Brain [*sic*] is planned, a pre-test or pre-task is announced to all eligible students. In this example, the pre-task might consist of a drawing of the brain with appropriate labeling. A due date for this pre-task is also announced. On the due date, these drawings are evaluated using the Unit Selection Matrix.

The time required to complete the General Selection Matrix would be minimal once all tests and tasks had been administered.

Scoring the EEII consists of entering and tabulating scores and completing the Teacher Recommendatin Form and the Unit Selection Matrix. However, no specific directions are given for scoring either this form or matrix. The individual who would use these forms could have difficulty because terms are not clearly defined and no criteria are given for ratings beyond a four-point scale, labeled from "Highly Superior" to "Below Average."

The interpretation of the EEII scores is vague. The author suggests that students who attain a total of 12 or more on the General Selection Matrix would constitute a very able or gifted group, but also suggests that the school division may set percentage, number, or other criteria in selection. The manual also sets a criteria for selection using the Unit Selection Matrix, but does not present that criteria as an absolute. The manual also suggests taht "the completed matrix is used as the basis for communicating to the students and their parents whether the child has earned a place in the unit of study or not. This communication helps the child to understand specifically what he needs to improve in order to qualify for future units" (p. 8).

It is difficult to judge the level of sophistication and training required to adequately and properly interpret this instrument. On the one hand it appears simple; on the other hand, close examination reveals that the EEII would actually require considerable understanding of the needs, characteristics, and performance of gifted children to adequately implement its use.

Technical Aspects

The author provides no evidence of the reliability and validity of the EEII. The reliability of the Slosson Intelligence Test, the GIFT, GIFFI, and the many standardized achievement tests that might be used are not of concern here. At the time of this review, the Teacher Recommendation Form, the Unit Selection Matrix, and the General Selection Matrix had not been examined for evidence of either reliability and validity.

Critique

The Eby Early Identification Instrument fails to provide an adequate system for the identification of gifted and talented students for a number of reasons. First, the general guidelines offered for nomination and collection of screening data offer nothing new to the process except a form for entry and that is even more limited in both options and recommended instruments than are a number of other identification matrices that have existed for a number of years. The strong recommendation that the Slosson be administered to all students who meet the initial criteria represents an extremely limited approach to identification.

Secondly, the individual rating scales, which were developed for use in this process, are offered with no evidence of reliability or validity. In fact, it is probable that one would have difficulty establishing either the reliability or validity of the scales. In terms of reliability, they are both limited in the number of items on each of the subscales, which purport to measure such complex concepts as creativity and task commitment. The lack of direction to teachers and the vagueness of task, time limits, descriptors used on the rating scale would probably contribute to unreliability. It is also unclear how one would guard against rater bias and generosity and halo factors.

The notion of a structured pretask that directs students to complete a standard task does not, in fact, even have face validity if one carefully considers Renzulli's definition of task commitment and his curricular notions. The selection of a specific task and specific product violates his notion that students will demonstrate task commitment when the choice of task and the mode of expression are of their own choosing. Several examples of the importance of this option are given in Renzulli's work (1979). In addition, the use of grades as one of the major variables in the General Selection Matrix gives "school learning" a very heavy weight in the matrix. Because Renzulli clearly states that giftedness is *not* school learning, that variable should not be given such heavy weight in a matrix that is purportedly based on his definition of giftedness.

The use of a matrix for the identification of gifted students is certainly efficient and widely used. However, one must seriously consider whether we have done justice to considering student needs when we translate their performance (e.g., on achievement tests, in classrooms) into five-point scales, add those scores, and then declare students "gifted" or "not gifted."

The translation of the scores into five-point scales is itself questionable. The percentile scores on achievement tests are not themselves interval and yet are translated into a one-to-five-point scale as if they were. No theoretical rationale or empirical evidence is given for the translation of any of the scores into the assigned weights. On what basis can one say that a teacher recommendation total of 55-60 is a 5? Suppose that teacher *never* gives a recommendation over 50? That is, there is considerable danger of applying cutoffs and criteria that appear arbitrary and certainly are not justified by the data presented in the manual.

In the absence of evidence of reliability, validity, and any justified criteria or directions for establishing individual school norms or validity for use within a given school, use of the EEII is not recommended for the screening and identification of gifted students.

References

Eby, J. W. (1983). Gifted behavior: A nonelitist approach. *Educational Leadership, 40,* 30-36.

Eby, J. W. (1984a). Developing gifted behavior. *Educational Leadership, 41,* 35-43.

Eby, J. W. (1984b). *Eby Elementary Identification Instrument.* East Aurora, NY: Slosson Educational Publications.

Renzulli, J. S. (1978). What makes giftedness: Reexamining a definition. *Phi Delta Kappan, 60*(3), 180-184.

Renzulli, J. S. (1979). *A guidebook for developing individualized educational programs for gifted and talented students.* Mansfield Center, CT: Creative Learning Press.

Allan L. LaVoie, Ph.D.
Professor of Psychology, Davis & Elkins College, Elkins, West Virginia.

EDINBURGH PICTURE TEST

Godfrey Thomson Unit for Educational Research, University of Edinburgh. London, England: Hodder & Stoughton.

Introduction

The Edinburgh Picture Test (EPT) represents a significant revision of the Moray House Picture Intelligence Test (Mellone, 1944; for reviews of the first edition see Keir, 1953, and Pringle, 1953; for a description of the second edition see Buros, 1965, p. 751). As with its predecessors, the EPT has as its primary purpose the screening of seven-year-olds in the United Kingdom. Although it contains five scales (e.g., analogies and sequences), these scales contribute to the total score rather than being used independently. The total scores are standardized as Reasoning Quotients (RQ), with a mean of 100 and standard deviation of 15. Low RQs result in referral for intensive individual testing to classify the student's mental disability.

Practical Applications/Uses

The EPT has been designed for use in groups of up to 30 children. Two proctors are recommended to insure that instructions have been understood and that no child gets off the track. Each scale consists of ten scored items and two practice items. The group works on one scale at a time beginning with extensive, clearly written instructions that are read by one of the proctors. There are up to six minutes allowed for each scale, a rather generous interval. In trial use this reviewer has found that no one took longer than the suggested maximum time. Total testing time in trial use was about 45 minutes, although the manual (Godfrey Thomson Unit for Educational Research, 1985) suggests an hour.

Norms for total scores have been based on about 11,000 British school children ranging in age from six years, six months to eight years, three months. The only criticism of the norm table concerns the likelihood that someone will confuse RQ with IQ. Otherwise it is easy to read, the resulting scores are easily understood, and the norm sample is adequate. The manual indicates that the scale scores could be used to build a student's reasoning profile, but no norms are given for the scale scores. Further, no screening cutoff scores have been reported.

Technical Aspects

According to the manual, reliability for the norm sample approached .91. The standard error of measurement, used to calculate the confidence interval around raw scores, was approximately five points; that is comparable to the precision of a well-developed group intelligence scale. Clearly, the reliability reaches acceptable limits for group work.

The developers should have demonstrated that the EPT can effectively screen for intellectual handicaps, that is, can detect a very high proportion of the intellectually handicapped, and the efficiency of various cutting scores should have been reported. Instead, the manual reports that the items of the EPT consistently fell into the same five scales through cluster analysis, that the items correlated highly with the total scores, and that the items were selected to be moderately difficult. In other words, we do not know about the validity of the test as a screening instrument. It could be assumed that validity would be the same as for the Moray House Picture Intelligence Test 1 and 2, but the changes (many new items, the elimination of strict time limits, the elimination of four scales, and the revision of many items) seem too great to justify that assumption. In short, is would be better to think of the EPT as a newly developed test.

Critique

The EPT was to have eliminated items liable to sex or culture bias, but some of the items are line drawings of a baby buggy, a ceramic toast rack, a gas ring, and a pencil being sharpened with a hobby knife. American children will have trouble with these items. Some of the other items are ambiguous even to adults.

In summary, the test has as many virtues as it has drawbacks. The virtues include the table of standard score equivalents. But despite these equivalents, it seems unlikely that the EPT will be useful in American schools. The items contain ambiguities and culturally specific information, and some of the problems are not typical of what American children would expect on a test. In this reviewer's experience, children raised in this country score lower than would be expected from a knowledge of their IQ scores. For screening in American classrooms this reviewer suggests using a test such as the Short Form Test of Academic Aptitude (Sullivan, Clark, & Tiegs, 1970) or the Columbia Mental Maturity Scale (Burgemeister, Blum, & Lorge, 1972; for a review see Brown, 1985). However, in the United Kingdom the EPT will undoubtedly continue to hold its respected position as a classic screening test used in conjunction with achievement tests as students make the transition from infant to junior schools.

References

Brown, S. W. (1985). Review of Columbia Mental Maturity Scale. In D. J. Keyser & R. C. Sweetland (Eds.), *Test Critiques* (Vol. II, pp. 182-190). Kansas City, MO: Test Corporation of America.

Burgemeister, B. B., Blum, L. H., & Lorge, I. (1972). *Columbia Mental Maturity Scale.* Cleveland: The Psychological Corporation.

Buros, O. K. (Ed.). (1965). *The sixth mental measurements yearbook.* Highland Park, NJ: The Gryphon Press.

Godfrey Thomson Unit for Educational Research. (1985). *Edinburgh Picture Test manual of instructions.* London: Hodder & Stoughton.

Keir, G. (1953). Review of the Moray House Picture Intelligence Test 1. In O. K. Buros (Ed.),

The fourth mental measurements yearbook (pp. 409-410). Highland Park, NJ: The Gryphon Press.

Mellone, M. A. (1944). *Moray House Picture Intelligence Test 1.* London: University of London Press.

Pringle, M. L. K. (1953). Review of the Moray House Picture Intelligence Test 1. In O. K. Buros (Ed.), *The fourth mental measurements yearbook* (pp. 410-411). Highland Park, NJ: The Gryphon Press.

Sullivan, E. T., Clark, W. W., & Tiegs, E. W. (1970). *Short Form Test of Academic Aptitude.* Monterey, CA: CTB/McGraw-Hill.

Arlene I. Rattan, Ph.D.
Research Fellow in Psychology, Ball State University, Muncie, Indiana.

Raymond S. Dean, Ph.D.
Associate Professor of Psychology-Educational Psychology, Director of Doctoral Programs, Ball State University, Muncie, Indiana.

EDUCATION APPERCEPTION TEST

Jack M. Thompson and Robert A. Sones. Los Angeles, California: Western Psychological Services.

Introduction

The Education Apperception Test (EAT) is an individually administered, projective measure designed to assess preschool- and elementary-school-aged children's perception of school and related activities. The test contains 18 items that were designed to elicit responses in the following four areas: reaction authority, reaction toward learning, peer relationships, and home attitude toward school. school.

The EAT was developed by school psychologists, Jack M. Thompson and Robert A. Sones (1973), for use with young children in an educational setting. Using a psychoanalytic rationale similar to the Thematic Apperception Test (TAT), it was believed that the EAT could elicit valuable information in understanding a child's perception toward school. Remediation strategies could then be developed for those children experiencing emotional difficulties in school.

Information concerning the development of the EAT is scant. Indeed, the reader is often left to make assumptions concerning the procedures used in its development. In general, an unspecified number of black and white photographs were taken of middle-school-aged children in a variety of school and school-related settings. The primary focus of these photographs were children in individual or group settings. Seven of these cards, however, portray teachers and parents involved in various settings. The photographs were mounted on cardboard plates and suggested for use by school psychologists as an adjunct measure with children referred for psychological evaluation.

The selection of photographs included in the EAT was based on ratings by school psychologists on a five-point scale. Those items that received low ratings were eliminated and replaced by others. Unfortunately,the authors provide no information to indicate what constituted a "low rating" or on what basis these judgments were made. The criteria used for inclusion of content for an item involved whether it contained 1) figures that elementary-school children could readily identify, 2) a realistic but ambiguous situation, 3) appropriate content, and 4) simulated stories as opposed to descriptions.

The selection of stimuli by school psychologists was a two-stage process. Initially, six school psychologists used a preliminary set of pictures with 120 children referred for a variety of undefined problems. In the second rating period, five school psychologists and one clinical psychologist used a revised set of items in their evaluation of school children. Unfortunately, no information is provided to indicate the number of pictures or children used in these rating periods. All of the items in this revised set were included in the final stimuli. Following this try-out, all 18 plates were deemed useful by the authors for school psychologists working with elementary-school children. This assumption seems to have been based entirely upon clinical judgment, rather than on an empirical basis. Moreover, no information regarding any further norming or standardization procedures is presented in the manual.

Since the introduction of the EAT in 1973, no revisions have been reported by the publishers. In addition, no research has been conducted with the EAT to examine the content validity or other psychometric characteristics of the instrument. Based on these factors the EAT fails to satisfy the minimum requirements for educational and psychological tests as recommended by the American Psychological Association (1974).

The materials for the EAT consist of a manual and eighteen 4½"x6½" black and white photographs mounted on 6"x7" cardboard plates. There are a total of eight cards that are appropriate for each gender, with two included for use with boys and girls. The photographs portray children in the classroom, on the playground, and in the home with school material present. Details in the photographs, such as clothing, hairstyles, and classroom materials, are dated and may be seen as somewhat comical or unrealistic by contemporary standards. The content of the photographs reflect a white, middle-class society without individuals from other racial groups. The extent to which these photographs portray typical school problems is questionable, and the manual reports no systematic attempt to survey problems typically dealt with by psychologists in school settings. Parallel items depicting similar scenes were prepared for males and females; however, little data are offered to convince the user that these pictures are indeed parallel.

Each of the 18 picture cards is coded on the reverse side with letters and numbers. The numbers appear to be arbitrary because the authors argue that the card order is based on the examiner's experience and does not necessitate a particular sequence. The letters are more useful, however, as they indicate the apparent gender of the subject for that card—that is, whether the item is appropriate for boys (B), girls (G), or both (BG).

Each EAT card corresponds to one of four areas in which the test was designed to evoke responses. Cards 3B, 3G, 7B, 7G, and 9BG are thought to correspond to "reaction toward authority" whereas cards 1B, 1G, 2B, 2G, 10B and 10G are believed to assess the "child's reaction toward learning." The authors note that it may not be necessary or appropriate to administer all of the cards to each child because specific cards are thought to correspond to a particular area of concern, such as "reaction to learning" or "peer relations." Based on clinical judgment, the examiner may choose to administer a limited number of cards, depending on the purpose for testing.

Practical Applications/Uses

The EAT is somewhat unique as a projective instrument because few apperceptive tests that deal exclusively with the child in an educational setting are available. This uniqueness, however, may limit the utility of the EAT to psychologists and counselors interested in gaining information regarding a child's behavior in school. Many advocates of the use of projective measures suggest that they may add to the incremental validity in forming diagnostic impressions of the child (Knoff, 1983), but it has also been argued convincingly that such presumptive validity is merely an illusory correlation (Peterson & Batsche, 1983).

Although the EAT was developed for children of preschool and elementary-school age, the authors suggest its use with adolescents. Specifically, Thompson and Sones (1973, p. 1) argue that the EAT "has been found to be useful with adolescents." They support this claim with two case studies (one of a 14-year-old subject and one of a 17-year-old subject), but, other than case studies, the manual provides no empirical support for the notion that the EAT should be appropriate for use with adolescents. The EAT may also be inappropriate for use with children at extreme ends of the age range. Children at the lower end (5-6 years) of the EAT age range may be too immature to adequately describe their preceptions, whereas those at the upper end (10-11 years) may find the test comical due to the dated nature of the stimulus content.

The manual provides little information regarding administration time; however, based on experience with similar projective instruments, administration of the EAT would require approximately 30 minutes. As in any testing situation, rapport must be established with the subject at the beginning of the session. The authors suggest that whenever possible the EAT should be presented as a game rather than as a test. It is recommended that the examiner sit next to the child and present one card at a time. All cards but the one being presented are laid face down by the examiner in order of presentation. Instructions are unstandardized, which is typical of projective measures. The child is asked to tell a story about the picture and describe what is happening, what the child in the picture is thinking and feeling, and what will happen next. During the administration the examiner records the child's behavioral reactions and verbal responses as completely and as accurately as possible for later interpretations. In addition to the child's verbal and nonverbal responses, examiners are urged to be aware of their own behavior during the testing session. This is true because the examiner's behavior is thought to affect the subject's responses.

Because the EAT utilizes an "eclectic scoring system" instead of a quantitative one that is used with other measures, such as the TAT and Children's Apperception Test (CAT), the scoring procedures and interpretative analyses of the latter may be inappropriate for use with the EAT. Interpretation of the EAT is highly subjective with little information provided in the manual to serve as a guide. The authors (Thompson & Sones, 1973, p. 3) suggest that experienced school psychologists have "probably developed their own method of analysis through experience with the TAT and/or CAT." As an interpretation guide, a summary of one method of analysis is provided in the manual. The summary includes a listing of seven topics or areas of interest that include the main theme, the main character, attitudes toward other figures, identification, nature of anxieties and conflict about the educational process, reaction toward the learning situation, and outcome of stories. In addition, several short questions are suggested for consideration in interpreting the child's story.

The manual offers little information concerning the validity of inferences that might be drawn from stories elicited from the EAT. Therefore, caution must be taken in any clinical inferences based on the measure. When interpreting children's stories, the clinician must consider effects, such as pretesting conditions, the atmosphere created by the testing situation, the stimulus cards themselves, and the notion of projection of repressed and/or unconscious ideas. Rather than using a projective method, it may be more appropriate to simply ask the child about school. Additionally, a child's age, gender, mental ability, social background, and verbal skills need to be considered because they may effect the length and complexity of the stories (Koppitz, 1982).

Until more is known about the effect created by the above variables one must demonstrate caution in making inferences from the stories to the child's behavior. Without research to support the construction, administration, scoring, and interpretation of the EAT, making any diagnostic statement becomes a projective endeavor for the interpreter.

Technical Aspects

Caution should be observed in the use of the EAT because it fails to meet any reasonable psychometric standards (e.g., American Psychological Association, 1974). Indeed, no information is provided in the manual regarding the reliability of the EAT. With the lack of structure in the administration, scoring, and interpretation, one would have to expect difficulties in ruling out a substantial error component. The EAT is purported to have both content and construct validity. Validity refers to an instrument's ability to allow predictions of an individual's overt behavior in real situations outside of the testing session. In light of the fact that there are problems in reliability with this measure, as with other projective tests, one must question the validity without some idea of the error variance.

Apparently, the EAT's validity is based on the assumption that underlies the TAT and other projective-type tests; that when presented with unstructured stimuli subjects will project their conscious and unconscious feelings. Although the content of the EAT is thought to be representative of the behavior of interest, this instrument is designed to provide information more about the child's perception of the school. Thus, more than content validity would be required for the validation of the EAT.

Support for construct validity appears to be based solely on a rational basis. Indeed, use of the instrument by the authors and selected colleagues is the only basis for their conclusion that the EAT is a valuable instrument. This approach is less than what is called for in establishing construct validity (Lanyon & Goodstein, 1982).

Given the paucity of psychometric evidence favoring the use of the EAT, investigations that examine elements of its reliability would seem a necessary first step. Little published data have been reported for the user to consider. Because the EAT is purported to provide information of some utility regarding the child's perception of school and the learning situation, the lack of stable and meaningful information make the use of the EAT highly suspect. In addition, the manual provides no discussion of the methods of scoring for story length or number, no idea of the examiner's influence, and little guidance in scoring and interpretation. The cumulative effect of the absence of this information reduces the clinical utility of this instrument in such a way that one may have difficulty justifying its use with school-aged children.

Critique

In summary, the EAT appears to be of limited use. Major flaws in the test include unknown norming procedures, a lack of standardized administration and scoring procedures, and unknown reliability and validity. It has been suggested that a test should be administered only if it contributes specific information that cannot be obtained more efficiently by other means (Koppitz, 1982). Given the lack of evidence for the author's claim that the EAT provides valuable information and guidelines for remediation, in these reviewers' opinion, the time used for the administration of the EAT could be spent better using a more direct approach to the collection of children's perceptions (e.g., a structured interview). Overall, there appears little evidence to warrant the use of the Education Apperception Test.

References

American Psychological Association. (1974). *Standards for educational and psychological tests.* Washington, DC: Author.

Knoff, H. M. (1983). Justifying projective/personality assessment in school psychology: A response to Batsche and Peterson. *School Psychology Review, 12* (4,) 446-451.

Koppitz, E. M. (1982). Personality assessment in the schools. In C. R. Reynolds & T. B. Gutkin (Eds.), *The handbook of school psychology* (pp. 273-296). New York: John Wiley & Sons.

Lanyon, R. I., & Goodstein, L. D. (1982). *Personality assessment.* (2nd ed.). New York: John Wiley & Sons.

Peterson, D. W., & Batsche, G. M. (1983). School psychology and projective assessment: A growing incompatibility. *School Psychology Review, 12,* (4), 440-445.

Thompson, J. M. & Sones, R. A. (1973). *Education Apperception Test.* Los Angeles: Western Psychological Services.

Ellyn Arwood, Ed.D.
Associate Professor of Speech and Hearing Sciences, Speech-Language and Hearing Clinic, Texas Tech University, Lubbock, Texas.

EDUCATIONAL DEVELOPMENT SERIES

O. F. Anderhalter, R. H. Bauernfeind, Mary E. Greig, George Mallinson, Jacqueline Mallinson, Joseph F. Papenfuss, and Neil Vail. Bensenville, Illinois: Scholastic Testing Service, Inc.

Introduction

The 1984 revised edition of the Educational Development Series (EDSeries) is a battery of tests measuring students' ability (nonverbal and verbal cognitive skills), achievement (reading, science, language arts, mathematics, reference skills, and social studies), and career and school interests. The comprehensive battery consists of eleven parts designed to measure students' interests in school as compared with their rate of educational development, which can then be compared to students in their school or with national norms. The complete EDSeries consists of Career Interests and School Plans (Grades 4-12); School Interests (Grades 2-12); Non-Verbal and Verbal Skills (Grades K-12); Reference Skills (Grades 1-12); Reading, Language Arts, and Mathematics (Grades K-12); and Science and Social Studies (Grades 1-12).

The EDSeries was developed by O. F. Anderhalter, St. Louis University; R. H. Bauernfeind, Northern Illinois University; Mary E. Greig, Chicago Public Schools; George and Jacqueline Mallinson, Western Michigan University; and Joseph F. Papenfuss and Neil Vail, Racine Public Schools; it is published by Scholastic Testing Service, Inc. (STS). The EDSeries was originally developed in 1963, and the 1984 edition presents the following major changes:

1) The 1963 battery was for children in Grades 2-12, whereas the 1984 battery extends coverage to include kindergarten and first grades. Kindergarten testing includes cognitive ability and achievement for reading, language arts, and mathematics; first grade includes the kindergarten areas, plus reference skills, science, and social studies.

2) Test booklets for kindergarten and first and second grades are available for machine scoring, whereas the previous edition made only single-sheet scoring possible.

3) Because the previous EDSeries had some problems in assessing children across numerous levels while retaining accuracy and normative comparisons, the revised 1984 EDSeries edition has increased the number of levels (10-18). The content of levels 10-14 are aimed at Grades K-4, with levels 15-18 having two forms (A and B) for grade pairs (5-6, 7-8, 9-10, and 11-12). Form B is considered to be somewhat more difficult than Form A and can be used for the higher grade of each pair.

4) A Reference Skills Test and two-part scores for the Basic Skills tests at the upper grades were added. Reading yields a vocabulary and a comprehension score; Language Arts yields a language score and a writing mechanics score; and

Mathematics provides a concepts/reasoning score, as well as a computation score. Because some of the tests now provide two scores, which also increases the number of test items, the length of the Basic Skills tests is also increased. In addition, the former English Test, which included language arts items, is now called "Language Arts" (grammar, spelling, and language structure).

The development of the EDSeries followed a typical standardization procedure in which content was manipulated to meet rigorous validity checks and items were analyzed to meet reliability requirements. STS used contingency tables to develop what they call "blue prints" for each test so that items and skills could be compared. For example, in order to measure how well a student could recognize facts in social studies, the "blue print" contingency table placed the Recognition of Facts skill on one dimension and the content areas of social studies on another. Because the resulting number was greater than the final number of test items to be used, when item analyses (conventional and point-biserial correlations) were performed items that did not meet statistical requirements were eliminated and only those items that fit the statistical specifications for a given test were included.

Standardization of the battery was quite complete. The national norms for the 1984 tests were developed during the 1982-83 school year. Test records of more than 250,000 schools were assigned to grade by region and to spring or fall norms. Over 140,000 students were tested in October-November; 53,000 students were tested in the spring; and 65,000 students, chosen by appropriate demographic data (geographic region, school system, sex, and "related variables"), were targeted for spring testing. The total number for Grades K-12 of the 65,000 students was chosen according to relative frequencies by grade in the total population. All schools participating in the standardization were required to test all grades to provide adequate control of socioeconomic variables across grades. The distribution of these students was made according to 1980 census figures. For example, if 26% of the population were in the north central region, then 26% of the sample would be from that geographic region for each grade level. The total number of spring students tested was 59,882, with 51% being boys, 49% being girls, 90.1% in public schools, and 9.9% in private or parochial schools.

The only provision made for considering race or ethnic backgrounds was done by asking administrators, with the "guesstimate" of racial mix being 85% white, 13% black, and 2% other. It was suggested that 4% of the students may have been bilingual and 2% handicapped, although those categorized as having "speech handicaps" were not included.

A similar procedure was used for the fall norms with 41,693 total cases. These 1981-1982 norms were compared to the 1975 norms using the STS grade score (GS), a normalized standard score with a national equal to grade placement having no more than a 1.0 standard deviation at all grade levels. According to the technical report (Scholastic Testing Service, 1985a), on the Basic Skills tests of Reading, Language Arts, and Mathematics there were "no noteworthy differences" between the 1975 and current norms for Grades 2-8. For the secondary grades the GS in 1982 was identical in Language Arts to the 1975 norms, and although the norms were slightly lower in Reading and Mathematics in 1982, they were not significantly different.

The Rasch one-parameter model was used in all aspects of developing the EDSeries in order to develop an STS expanded standard score scale. This *consis-*

tency in model yields excellent design and analysis for standardization. The Rasch one-parameter model allows for horizontal equating of scores so that the average standard score for each test is at the same point. This "ingrade" equating of items provides a look at the average ability within a grade compared to others of the same grade. Forty-six items from all tests were used to equate across levels (vertical equating). As the technical report (p. 7) states, "Because of the large number of students at each grade level (N = 1,000) and because of the large number of common items used at each equating level, the established raw-score-to-standard-score relationships should exhibit very high stability for many years to come."

The STS expanded standard score is the primary measure of students within and across grades compared to the norms. However, several other measures, including percentile-rank scores developed to match test difficulty with student ability for Forms A and B in a given grade, may be reported. Changes in ability between the fall norms and spring norms were accounted for by examining the fit (.2) of the fall with the fit (.8) of the spring. STS reports a fit in every instance so that not more than the remaining .4 or 25% change would occur between spring (April) and fall (October).

STS also provides normal curve equivalents (NCEs), which take the scores and conform them to a normal bell-shaped curve so that NCEs can be compared to a national percentile rank.

For the EDSeries program most schools receive student scores reported as local stanines as well as scores expressed as national stanines. The stanine is a 1-9 system that places 5 in the center of the bell curve (4-6 is average or 76-40th percentile) so that stanines of 9 to 7 represent a high rating (99-77th percentile) and stanines of 3 to 1 represent low ratings (23-1st percentile). Most standardized batteries use stanines because of their simplicity in reporting the results.

STS provides information about grade levels as either STS grade scores or grade equivalents (GEs). STS grade scores use the percentile added to a standard deviation level. For example, a child who is at the 85th percentile and in the fifth grade has an STS grade score of 5 plus the z score of +1.0 (from a table), or 6. The GEs show performance in terms of grade placement. The STS expanded standard score scale provides the median basis for GEs.

Subskill performance ratings equating 5 to, at, or above the 90th percentile, 4 to 67-89th percentiles, 3 to 34-66th percentiles, 2 to 11-33rd percentiles, and 1 at or below the 10th percentile are also available for the subskills within tests (e.g., vocabulary is a subskill of the Reading Test).

One of the most interesting measures reported by the EDSeries is the Cognitive Skills Quotient (CSQ). This quotient is the product of chronological ages compared to the mean of students' performances at the same age. The CSQ may be as low as 65 or as high as 149 for children from five years, seven months to 18 years, one month. STS does not report this as an equivalent to IQ, and users should not do so either. The CSQ is more a function of achievement than ability, but so are many commercial IQ measures.

The best *productive* measure on the EDSeries comes from the STS Expected Performance Indicator, which compares the Cognitive Skills scores to a given achievement test. Several of these measures are actually numerical ways of looking at children's class performance compared to their achievement rate, which may or may not reflect their actual learning rate. The assumption here is that achievement and rate of learning are comparable, and for most children that assumption is a given. However, children with learning differences will show poor performance with good CSQ or perhaps good performance on the achievement test with poor class performance coupled by inadequate social skills. Many of the verbal items will identify these children as poor performers, but without necessary qualitative data available through additional clinical testing these children's actual problems will not be assessed.

Instructions for administration of the EDSeries are presented in manuals (usually 20 pages) for each level so that administration is standardized. Each manual emphasizes that "directions should be followed carefully." The examiner is told in advance what materials should be available and the tests' time constraints so that there is adequate preparation before testing. The manuals address classroom prerequisites, direction familiarity, testing irregularities, how to announce the testing to students, how to handle guessing, and how to instruct students on completing the forms. *Exact* instructions are written for a practice session as well as for administration of *all parts* of the testing battery. Administration of the EDSeries is well-covered in these manuals; therefore, there is no reason for the test results not to be part of a *standardized* battery.

The EDSeries consists of 11 parts, which the technical report describes as follows:

Career Interest (Grades 4-12): Students make two most liked choices from 18 career areas covering all major occupations: personal service, sports, mining, factories, farming, military service, government service, shop, transportation, construction, stores, offices, sales, business, fine arts, communications, social services, and sciences. It is useful in planning for a school's curriculum based on area career interests or for counseling an examinee about career choices in terms of national and local opportunities matched to interests and abilities. The predictive value of a student choosing a career in fourth grade having high reliability with a chosen college major is realistically not expected by STS for this test, which is more for counseling students regarding interests.

School Plans (Grades 4-12): Students select the plan they expect to follow from six plans: 1) quit school and go to work as soon as possible, 2) finish high school before going to work, 3) finish high school before going to a trade school, 4) finish high school and then go for two years of community junior college, 5) finish high school and go for a four-year college diploma, and 6) four years of college plus more college training. Data are cross-referenced with Basic Skills for each student so that those students who rank higher than the 75th percentile on Basic Skills and do not plan for college, as well as those who rank lower than the 25th percentile on Basic Skills and do plan for college, are "flagged." A group analysis is also provided so that school or community trends may be checked by grade.

School Interests (Grades 4-12): Determines curriculum for students by grades or classes. A nine-point rating scale (semantic differential) is used (e.g., 9 = "like"; 1 = "dislike") for eight subjects: music, art, mathematics, science, social studies, English, foreign language, and vocations. The odd-number of points on the scale allows for midpoints to be easily selected so that 1) median ratings can be reported, 2) there are more points than number of subjects, 3) students can give each subject a different number if they desire, and 4) the nine points allow adequate differentiation on a single-digit scale. STS reports a "high degree" of reliability for one-week and one-month retests. Results can be used to compare an individual's performance on subjects of interest with achievement, future plans, and current school-curriculum practices.

Non-Verbal Skills (Grades K-12): Used to calculate a cognitive quotient score similar to an IQ. Assesses basic reasoning skills, using more visual perceptual types of skills than symbolic concept types. Because STS had made an attempt to consider students' cultural or educational backgrounds, this test uses "culture-fair figures," figures, geometric shapes, or designs presented in a row of five. Students select the one shape out of five that is different. For example, if four shapes each have a line dividing the shape into two *equal* parts and one has a line dividing the shape into two *unequal* parts, the latter is the correct answer. There are 40 items for Grades K-3 and 50 for Grades 4-12. According to the technical report (p. 4), the instructions can be given in any language or dialect, and this part has been "consistently useful" with Spanish, French, Vietnamese, and Laotian backgrounds, as well as with English-speaking students from various "geographic-ethnic dialects." It is used to identify students who show good nonverbal performances while scoring low in other verbal conceptual areas of Reading, Language Arts, and Mathematics. Because it does not use any reading or mathematical skills, there is little verbal contamination except by concept or symbol development. For example, a student who can symbolically identify the shapes and has had symbolic development of the concept "half" may respond quicker and with more accuracy. Although STS does not directly address this type of verbal contamination in this part, STS does recognize research that shows that students with discrepant performances can be helped to improve educational performance. Scores correlate in the 30s, 40s, and 50s with the other educational development scores on the battery, suggesting that it is measuring something different than many other nonverbal measures and might help the educator gain insight into a child's total profile.

Verbal Skills (Grades K-12): Assesses students' ability to manipulate concepts. For the kindergarten and first-grade levels, the teacher says a word and the student marks the representative picture. On the higher levels, synonyms are marked (e.g., "price" matched to cost, purpose, wealth, bargain, or dollars). There are 30 items for Kindergarten, 40 for Grades 1-3, and 50 for all higher levels. National reliability coefficients within-grade groups are reported to be in the 90s, and scores correlate in the .50s, .60s, and .70s with the other general educational development measures. Thus, these items are related to learned concepts found in educational curricula, and performance could be influenced by educational background.

Reference Skills (Grades 1-12): Assesses students' ability to follow directions; read graphs, maps, charts; and interpret library references, government forms, and newspaper materials. STS reports the reliability for national within-grade groups to be around .90. The results from this subtest can be used to adjust group curriculum and identify students who can work independently at the library or who need extra help to work on independent projects.

Reading (Grades K-12): Assesses knowledge of the alphabet at kindergarten level; analyses of words and simple story comprehension at higher levels; and analyses of complex material, such as political speeches, at the 12th-grade level. There are 40 items for Kindergarten and Grade 1, 50 for Grades 2 and 3, and 80 for all higher levels. Although timed, this is not a "power" test in that most students have ample time to complete the tasks. Test items include a variety of different kinds of reading material and a gradual increase in vocabulary difficulty. Results should correspond with a student's academic reading performance. Therefore, any discrepancy between classroom achievement of reading material and this part could be used to identify more closely children who could do better in class or who need additional language development for better reading.

Language Arts (Grades K-12): Covers written communication skills that might also be used in speaking. Although this part appears to deal with only the written form, many of the items are questions using "natural punctuation." For example, in the sentence stem, "Get down from that window________," the correct choice ("right now?" or "right now," or "right now." or "right now!") would probably depend on how the sentence is spoken. Subtests usually correlate in the .60s, .70s, or .80s with other educational measures of speaking and writing. Students who do well should also be doing well in reading and achieving well in content areas. Results could suggest a need for changes in curriculum or possible remedial help for a particular child. There are 30 items for Kindergarten, 40 for Grade 1, 50 for Grade 2, 60 for Grade 3, and 80 for all higher levels. Items begin with students selecting a picture that best fits a stated sentence and continue with those of spelling, punctuation, capitalization, and grammar arranged in difficulty from constructing to analyzing and organizing sentences.

Mathematics (Grades K-12): A "functional skills" or operations test beginning with counting, moving to computation, and finishing with complex equations and word problems. There are 40 items for Kindergarten, 70 for Grades 1-3, and 80 for all higher levels. This part presents "real-life" word problems, with computation operations at all levels above second grade (Level 12). Results should correspond to students' achievement in mathematics and provide information on how individuals or groups of children compare to the national norms.

Science (Grades 1-12): Measures development in biological, physical, and earth sciences and assesses knowledge of scientific facts represented by drawings, then that of scientific principles presented in written form, and finally application, analysis, and comprehension of scientific knowledge. Items use a number of visual displays similar to those found in lab manuals. There are 40 items for Grades 1-3 and 60 for all higher levels. Scores usually correlate in the .50s, .60s, and .70s with other biological, physical, and earth-science development measures. Results should provide the educator with information about how a student should be performing in science now and possibly in the future. Students who do well in this content test might be encouraged to consider more science education, whereas students who do poorly might be counseled about career choices. Likewise, group scores might give a school feedback about its adequacy in teaching science knowledge.

Social Studies (Grades 1-12): Divided into history, geography, sociology, anthropology, economics, and political science; begins with pictorial representations at the kindergarten level and proceeds onto facts and principles in written form, then problems calling for application, analysis, and comprehension of knowledge. Many items have visual materials for interpretation (e.g., political cartoons, maps, and charts). STS reports correlations in the .50s, .60s, and .70s for these scores with other social studies measures. Results can identify weak or strong students and areas of strength or weakness for social studies curricula in schools.

STS can report the EDSeries results in many ways, depending on how many of the tests have been administered. Tests are arranged into four battery formats: Complete Battery, Core Achievement Battery (excludes Non-Verbal, and Verbal Skills), Basic Skills Battery (excludes Non-Verbal, Verbal, and Reference Skills; Science; and Social Studies), and a Cognitive and Basic Skills Battery (excludes Reference Skills, Science, and Social Studies). Reports for any of these batteries include standard scores, local stanines, and national norms, plus a 21-page interpretive manual (Scholastic Testing Service, 1984). These reports (three copies) are alphabetical lists of students with each student's age, school plans, career interests, and performance data. Each student's data are also provided on a pressure-sensitive label to be put on the student's records. Three copies of group summary reports are provided so that the schools and individual classes can be compared to each other and to national norms. List reports may be provided by grade within each school or by class within each grade in school. STS also offers several other types of data reports and/or profiles. All tests are machine scored by STS, with results being returned in about ten days. A 243-page norms manual (Scholastic Testing Service, 1985b) is also available.

Practical Applications/Uses

There are several ways in which the EDSeries may be appropriately used: 1) following achievement compared to ability over time for a given student or groups of students, 2) comparing students' achievement performances to local and/or national students' performances, 3) counseling students for appropriate career choices, 4) counseling college-bound students in deciding the level of courses for basic skills, 5) deciding on administrative curriculum changes based on students' performances compared to national levels.

The EDSeries Battery appears to be *most* useful for group testing or for measuring children's performance over several years of measuring. Even though results are provided for each child compared to national figures, the most reliable interpretation of a given child's performance comes from comparing the child's performance to that of the local or school group and *then* the group to the national levels. In this way, the examiner could be sure that the child's performance fit the local expectations before deciding on how the child's interests, achievements, or abilities fit into long-term (nonlocal) expectations. For example, if John Brown scored below average in Basic Skills, then the examiner might concentrate on John Brown's lack of skills although he was at the top of his class. Without local or school results, the examiner would not know that John is doing well compared to his peers and that emphasis needs to be put on the school's curricula, not on John. However, the examiner could have obtained information on John's interests compared to achievement level for career planning by the single examination. Even though single administrations yield this sort of information, the battery could provide its best set of data when given as a battery to a group over several grades so that individual children may present a more reliable (consistent over time) performance.

In addition to establishing a variety of ways to present data (e.g., standard scores, stanines, percentile levels, raw scores, normal curve equivalents, grade scores, Cognitive Skill Quotients), STS had also opened a number of ways to use the data to help individual children and groups of children receive the best assistance educationally for achievement in basic skills and for counseling based on performance and interest. This battery could be an invaluable tool for junior-high and high-school counselors if all data were used. For example, a student's interests and abilities or achievement levels may not match these results, thus providing a counselor with much data on how to help the adolescent make career options. The EDSeries interpretive manual provides the user with explanations on how the counselor might use some of the data.

School administrators should be using a battery like the EDSeries to interpret how their children are progressing compared to national norms so weaknesses and strengths in curricula at various grade levels can be identified. The data provided from the EDSeries administration would give school administrators an excellent battery from which to judge their school's performance by groups or by schools. School administrators would best benefit from the group results, whereas school counselors could use the individual's results for counseling of career choices or for dealing with possible individual academic problems. Classroom educators would be interested in the EDSeries for checking both individual and group performances. Because the battery yields a Cognitive Skills Quotient, which can be compared to achievement levels, the educator can identify children who are achieving well at the present time or those who are not achieving as well as they should. By identifying these children, the teacher could attempt to resolve discrepancies in achievement compared to ability so as to avoid individual frustration or failure in the academic setting due to learning differences.

Data can be reported by school and/or by individual performance. Specific patterns showing discrepancies with children's performance are marked so that these children can be readily identified by educators or counselors. Although most of these patterns revolve around interest-ability-achievement discrepancies, it should be noted that there are other ways educators can use the data, such as going through each child's results comparing the results to class performances. A well-developed battery such as the EDSeries can provide a wealth of information to counselors, administrators, and educators if these persons are trained in test-result interpretation. Underinterpretation can be as useless as overinterpretation if the examiner is not trained. STS can provide these persons with numerous references for maximum use of the data.

Technical Aspects

The 105-page technical report, compiled by the research division of Scholastic Testing Service, Inc. under the direction of O. F. Anderhalter, consists of 12 chapters that include information on the content of the series; national norms; the STS Expanded Standard Score Scale; development of other derived measures; reliability and other internal characteristics of the tests; validity studies in elementary, intermediate, and high-school grades; and concurrent validity. Eighty-seven tables report percentile norms, NCEs, ranks, grade scores, K-R 20 reliabilities for each level, intercorrelations for samples of norms, schools at each level, correlations between STS scores and Stanford Achievement Scores, ITBS Scores, ITED Scores, teacher grades, grade point averages, SCAT scores, PSAT-NMSQT scores, SAT scores, and CAT scores—to name a few. This report is a thorough explanation of how the EDSeries was developed and prepared using stringent statistical analyses. The reader can find validity and reliability measures calculated for about any question, with values ranging from extremely low to extremely high depending on the question asked. It should be noted that correlational data are only important if all of the questions are asked, which is why STS so carefully reports as much data as possible so that the reader is able to apply the data to individual situations in which grades, type of school, and number of tests administered across grades may differ from year to year.

To determine whether or not the tests could be readministered to students without test effects or other variable effects on performance, STS drew a sample of 1,000 students at each of the 13 grade levels (K-12) and obtained Kuder-Richardson formula 20 reliability coefficients. The K-R 20 reliabilities for STS Cognitive Skills and Basic Skills are greater than .90 for levels 10 A through 18 B. Individual K-R 20 values were also reported for each of the tests with greater than .90 for virtually all tests at all levels or grades. STS also checked for difficulty of test items across grade levels, noting an increased difficulty with medians such that improvement can be detected. It also accounted for ceiling effects by checking to see that not more than 1% of students ranked above the 99th percentile. Only one test did not have a protected ceiling: the Language Arts (level 10A) had slightly more than 1% scoring at the maximum level, suggesting that this one test at this level may not differentiate among the top few students. STS also checked for "chance" or "floor effects" and found that not more than 4% of the students were correct by chance.

Exact Standard Errors of Measurement (SE_m) have been calculated for all levels and all tests, with the SE_m being highly consistent. Score intercorrelations for samples of norm schools are also available. Correlational data of the EDSeries parts with specific commercial tests are also available for additional information regarding content validity. STS has done an excellent statistical job of developing the EDSeries to assess students' interests, abilities, and achievement, *as well* as their interrelationships.

Critique

One of the most refreshing features of the EDSeries is the actual test items. The items are presented in a variety of unique ways, including the use of many visual aids. The content of the complete battery also hints at the need to consider a student not only in terms of abilities and achievements, but also in terms of interests. STS obviously recognizes that excellent ability cannot always compensate for a lack of interest, nor can super interest make up for lack of ability. Appropriate counseling and preparation of youth for fulfilling careers is probably the most important function of secondary education. Society, as well as the individual, can benefit from assisting students in using abilities to their maximum for career fulfillment.

References

Anderhalter, O. F., Bauernfeind, R. H., Greig, M. E., Mallinson, G., Mallinson, J., Papenfuss, J. F., & Vail, N. (1984). *Educational Development Series* (rev. ed.). Bensenville, IL: Scholastic Testing Service, Inc.

Scholastic Testing Service, Inc. (1984). *Educational Development Series: Interpretive manual*. Bensenville, IL: Author.

Scholastic Testing Service, Inc. (1985a). *Educational Development Series: Technical report*. Bensenville, IL: Author.

Scholastic Testing Service, Inc. (1985b). *Educational Development Series: Norms manual*. Bensenville, IL: Author.

Randall Parker, Ph.D.

Professor, Department of Special Education, University of Texas at Austin, Austin, Texas.

EMOTIONS PROFILE INDEX

Robert Plutchik and Henry Kellerman. Los Angeles, California: Western Psychological Services.

Introduction

The Emotions Profile Index (EPI), a personality test that is based on a theory of emotion developed by Plutchik (1955, 1960, 1962, 1965), measures eight basic emotional dimensions related to personality traits. The EPI, coauthored by Robert Plutchik and Henry Kellerman (1974), appears to have resulted directly from Kellerman's (1964) doctoral dissertation. Plutchik obtained his Ph.D. in experimental psychology in 1962 from Columbia University. Kellerman obtained a Ph.D. in clinical psychology in 1964 from Yeshiva University. Both authors, particularly Plutchik, have published extensive research on the relationship of emotions to personality development, treatment of emotional disorders, and personality measurement.

The EPI was published in 1974, and although the manual (Plutchik & Kellerman, 1974) was reprinted in 1983, the test has not been updated or revised as of the writing of this review. The EPI consists of a three-page test booklet and a one-page profile sheet. The first page of the test booklet contains blanks for identifying information regarding the client (e.g., name, age, sex) and test instructions. The second page has a list of definitions of the 12 terms used in the test items. The second and third pages contain the 62 test items.

In addition to spaces for recording client identifying data, the profile sheet contains a grid on which raw scores and percentiles are recorded. On the bottom half of the profile sheet is displayed a series of ten concentric circles. The innermost circle represents the 10th percentile, the next represents the 20th, and so on, with the outermost circle representing the 100th percentile. Eight lines running through the center of the circles divide the circles into eight wedges of equal size. Each wedge represents one of the eight basic dimensions of emotion: trustful, dyscontrolled, timid, depressed, distrustful, controlled, aggressive, and gregarious. Wedges opposite one another on the circular profile represent opposite emotional orientations.

According to the manual (p. 1), the test "may be given to subjects of any age beginning with early adolescence." However, because norms are provided for 500 males and 500 females of college age and older, conservative use of the EPI would limit its administration to similar individuals.

Practical Applications/Uses

The EPI is particularly useful in research situations where the researcher is interested in obtaining an assessment of subjects' self-reported emotions, related personality traits, and potential conflicts in emotional expression and social relationships. Because the EPI was developed within a research context, its use in emotion and personality research is unquestionably its "strongest suit." The brevity of administration (approximately 10-15 minutes) and ease of scoring make it well-suited to situations where emotions must be measured repeatedly. Furthermore, its forced-choice format reduces the likelihood that response biases will play a major role in the scores.

The authors (Plutchik & Kellerman, 1974), however, indicate that the EPI was designed primarily for clinical applications and also recommend it for use in counseling high-school and college students, particularly in instances when emotional conflicts arise. According to the authors, the EPI may be a useful supplement to a vocational guidance battery. Although specifics are not suggested, the authors state that the test provides personality information that is related to job performance and job success.

Finally, the EPI is recommended for classroom use. The test may be administered in classes dealing with the nature of emotions and the relationship of emotions to personality structure. Scoring and interpretation of the test may lead to fruitful discussions of the nature of emotions and their influence on personality.

The EPI is an untimed, paper-and-pencil test that may be administered to either individuals or groups. After the examinees furnish the identifying data requested on the test booklet, they are told to read the instructions on the first page of the booklet and to review the definitions of the 12 adjectives that make up the items. The 62 items represent all paired comparisons of the 12 adjectives, excluding four pairs which were omitted because they measured the same personality categories; the 62 items pair adjectives that reflect different dimensions of emotion.

The examinees are instructed to circle one adjective in each pair (e.g., adventurous or impulsive; affectionate or cautious). In the test booklet each adjective pair is followed by a nine-column grid containing small cirlces in one to three of the nine columns. For each adjective of the pair the examinee selects as being more descriptive, the small circle(s) following the selected adjectives is (are) marked with a check. The sum of the checks in each of the nine columns comprises the raw scores for the nine scales. The manual suggests that if one or two items are not answered by the examinee, the scorer should flip a coin to randomly choose one of the pair of adjectives as the answer. If more than two items are not answered, the test results are probably invalid.

Once the raw scores are calculated, the percentile equivalents are determined from the appropriate table of norms. The percentiles for the eight emotion dimensions are then plotted on a circular profile grid. The ninth score, Bias, is not plotted on the grid because it is a validity scale rather than an emotion scale.

Interpretation of the EPI focuses on the circular profile grid on which the percentiles for the eight emotion dimensions are displayed. The interpretation proceeds first by inspecting the percentiles for the eight emotion dimensions, noting which scales have high scores (above the 60th percentile) and which have low scores (below the 40th percentile). The manual presents brief interpretive descriptions (one to five sentences in length) for high- and low-scoring individuals on each of the eight dimensions. In addition, the manual presents interpretations for six common pairs of high and/or low scores (e.g., High Gregarious + High Timid; High Trustful + Low Timid).

Finally, it is pointed out that if two opposite emotions (i.e., opposite one another on the circular profile) both have above average scores, a strong conflict is indicated on that bipolar dimension. The four bipolar dimensions are Timid vs. Aggressive, Trustful vs. Distrustful, Controlled vs. Dyscontrolled, and Gregarious vs. Depressed. High scores on the ninth scale, Bias, indicate that examinees tend to describe themselves in a socially desirable way; low scores suggest the opposite tendency.

Technical Aspects

Among the technical characteristics of psychological tests, reliability and validity are the most important. The EPI test manual presents two reliability studies. Test-retest reliability was obtained for a group of 60 females, 40 of whom were mental hospital patients and 20 of whom were normals. The test-retest coefficients for the nine EPI scales with a three-day interval between the first and second testing "were all over + .90" (Plutchik & Kellerman, 1974, p. 5). The exact test-retest coefficients are not reported.

The second reliability study reported split-half reliability coefficients for a sample of 50 college freshmen. These coefficients ranged from .61 for the Distrustful Scale to a .90 for the Gregarious Scale, with a median of .78.

More extensive reliability information should be reported, particularly because the authors recommend the EPI for use in clinical assessment, counseling, and vocational guidance with individual clients. Thorough reliability data are especially important because reliability coefficients indicate how much error variance the scales contain. Error variance, as measured by the standard error of measurement, allows professionals to estimate how precise each score is and enables them to tell clients how much each score is apt to vary by chance.

Although a dozen validity studies are summarized in the EPI manual, the brief summaries, of usually one to two sentences, are difficult to evaluate. Generally speaking, however, EPI scales appear to have low to moderate positive correlations with similar scales and low to moderate negative correlations with dissimilar scales. These scales include the Minnesota Multiphasic Personality Inventory (MMPI), the Edwards Personal Preference Schedule (EPPS), the Gough Adjective Check List (ACL), the Barrett Impulsivity Scale, and the Clyde Mood Scale. The EPI also appears to be able to differentiate among a variety of groups, mostly various hospitalized psychiatric patient groups.

Although the validity data are somewhat more extensive than the reliability data, the validity studies reported in the manual are too limited in extent and detail, and too focused on psychiatric patients (as are the reliability studies). Moreover, the studies are more than a decade old.

Critique

The EPI is an instrument with promise, particularly in the research arena. It requires only 10-15 minutes of testing time and is readily scored. The EPI reveals constructs that few other tests measure and appears to be effective in research requiring repeated measures of emotions over time.

However, according to the highly critical review of the EPI by Douglas N. Jackson (1978), the "negative features are almost too numerous to list easily" (p. 787); he summarized his comments by stating that the EPI is "psychometrically unsound, based on poor domain sampling, with misleading statistics on reliability and inadequate validity data, and unsubstantiated claims" (p. 788).

Although Jackson's review might be regarded as overly severe, the lack of detail presented in the EPI manual regarding the technical aspects of the test suggests that much more work needs to be done before one can use the test confidently in applied situations. Furthermore, the test is overdue for a revision. The manual should also be updated, revised, and lengthened; the present manual is only 11 double-column pages in length, including references and tables. It is this reviewer's opinion that the EPI may be employed in research on emotions when other, more thoroughly developed instruments are not available. However, the test should not be used in clinical situations where the results may influence treatment decisions.

References

Jackson, D. (1978). Review of the Emotions Profile Index. In O. K. Buros (Ed.), *The eighth mental measurements yearbook* (pp. 786-788). Highland Park, NJ: The Gryphon Press.

Kellerman, H. (1964). *The development of a forced-choice personality index and its relation to degree of maladjustment.* Unpublished doctoral disseration, New York University, New York.

Plutchik, R. (1955). Some problems for a theory of emotions. *Psychosomatic Medicine, 17,* 306-310.

Plutchik, R. (1960). The multifactor analytic theory of emotion. *Journal of Psychology, 50,* 153-171.

Plutchik, R. (1962). *The emotions: Facts, theories, and a new model.* New York: Random House.

Plutchik, R. (1965). What is an emotion? *Journal of Psychology, 61, 295-303.*

Plutchik, R., & Kellerman, H. (1974). *Emotions Profile Index manual.* Los Angeles: Western Psychological Services.

Joseph L. Snider, Ed.D.
Professor of Education, Saginaw Valley State College, University Center, Michigan.

Katherine P. Snider, Ph.D.
School Psychologist, Midland Public Schools, Midland, Michigan.

EXPRESSIVE ONE-WORD PICTURE VOCABULARY TEST: UPPER EXTENSION

Morrison F. Gardner. Novato, California: Academic Therapy Publications.

Introduction

The Expressive One-Word Picture Vocabulary Test: Upper Extension (EOWPVT-UE) measures the ability to identify a single object or group of objects on the basis of a single concept. It indicates expressive language functioning that is below age level but does not identify the factor(s) that may be responsible.

The original EOWPVT was published in 1979 for use with children aged 2-0 to 11-11. The Upper Extension was developed for the older age group of 12-0 to 15-11, for whom there are few tests of expressive vocabulary.

The EOWPVT, EOWPVT-UE, and a companion test of receptive vocabulary (ROWPVT) were developed by Morrison F. Gardner, Ed.D., who is a psychologist with Children's Hospital of San Francisco. Gardner (1983) states his belief that a test of acquired vocabulary can estimate what children have learned from their environment and formal education.

Test materials include individual test forms, an examiner's manual, and a booklet of test plates. The test requires about 10-15 minutes to administer and about five minutes to score.

The Upper Extension is made up of 70 pictures arranged in order according to difficulty. The picture may show a single concrete object or collection of objects designed to elicit a one-word identifying response. After two examples, the examiner begins testing at the point designated for that child's chronological age. As each plate is exposed, the child is asked to respond with the word that best describes each picture. All responses are recorded on the test form. In group administration instructions are the same, but children must write their responses instead of speaking them. A basal level of eight consecutive correct responses and a ceiling level of six consecutive incorrect responses limit testing to a critical range. This provision cannot be applied easily in group administration, although it must still be applied in scoring.

Practical Applications/Uses

The stated purpose of this instrument is to "obtain a basal estimate of a child's verbal intelligence" (Gardner, 1983, p. 8). The vocabulary of children reflects their ability to process in language what they have learned through auditory and visual perception. According to the author (Gardner, 1983), information can be ascertained relative to speech defects, possible learning disorders, a bilingual child's fluency in English, auditory processing, and auditory-vocal association ability.

The test can be administered to Spanish-speaking children as well as to English-speaking children. It can be administered to groups if writing skills of each student are sufficiently developed.

The Upper Extension might appropriately be used by psychologists and teachers in bilingual, speech and language, and possibly some special education programs. Comparisons of expressive and receptive vocabulary levels may suggest oral expressive difficulties. Such a measure of expressive vocabulary may be used in determining the bilingual child's readiness for instruction in English-speaking education programs and curricula.

The norms given in terms of deviation IQs do not extend more than three standard deviations from the mean; therefore, this test could be used with educable mentally impaired children but would not provide differentiation among those in the trainable or severely mentally impaired groups (IQ below 55). At the other end of the scale it would not differentiate among the highest ability levels.

The Upper Extension will generally be administered individually. It can be given to small groups if the students have sufficient spelling and handwriting skills to put the desired word on paper. No special skills are required to administer or score this test. This is not a timed test but can usually be given in less than 15 minutes. The usual testing provisos relative to environment, student preparation, and rapport are given in the manual. Examiners should have experience with individual testing procedures. When administering the test in Spanish, the examiner must be fluent in the Spanish language and mindful of geographic linguistic variations.

Technical Aspects

The initial bank of items for the Upper Extension was provided by teachers, students, and other professionals in psychology and education. This group of 110 items was administered to 188 children, and responses were inspected for ambiguity and analyzed for sex bias and difficulty level. Seventy items were selected for the final form, which was administered to 465 students of ages ranging from 12-0 to 15-11. These students resided in the San Francisco Bay Area and were enrolled in public, private, and parochial schools (Gardner, 1983).

Content validity of the Upper Extension was determined by selecting symbols, objects, and concepts within the range of experiences of most twelve-year-olds as suggested by the above contributors.

Criterion-related validity was based on correlations of raw scores from the Upper Extension with raw scores from the Peabody Picture Vocabulary Test-Revised (PPVT-R; Dunn & Dunn, 1981) and with raw scores from the Vocabulary subtest of the Wechsler Intelligence Scale for Children-Revised (WISC-R; Wechsler, 1974).

Correlations of the Upper Extension with the PPVT-R at each of four age levels ranged from .69 to .80. Correlations with the WISC-R Vocabulary ranged from .74 to .84. The slightly higher correlations for the WISC-R might reasonably be expected because these both require verbal expression (Gardner, 1983).

The reliability of the Upper Extension was determined by the split-half method. The resulting coefficients of correlation ranged from .89 to .94. The standard error of measurement for each of the four age groups (12-0 to 12-11, 13-0 to 13-11, 14-0 to 14-11, and 15-0 to 15-11) provided confidence levels for both raw scores and the deviation IQs. The SE_Ms for raw scores ranged from 2.73 to 4.03 (Gardner, 1983).

Critique

The EOWPVT-UE is one measure of expressive vocabulary. Caution is suggested in making inferences beyond that (e.g., IQ, learning disabilities) without supporting data. A picture measure of expressive vocabulary does not have the latitude or sampling range that is available in the receptive vocabulary measures or words definition lists. In this test, however, the response must originate within the child, and no test-taking "strategies" can be employed in arriving at an answer.

Only about ten of the 70 pictures appear to deal with abstract or descriptive concepts. Most show concrete objects or specific and familiar symbols.

The standardization sample for this instrument was drawn from a limited geographical area. Users must determine the extent to which the results can be generalized to their own students.

Mental ages are given but are only estimates based on correlations of raw scores with the PPVT-R.

The EOWPVT: Upper Extension appears to provide information relative to a child's level of expressive vocabulary. The range of uses for this test may not be so great or so definitive and generalized as envisioned by the author, but this instrument does deserve a place in the repertoire of language-assessment tests.

References

Dunn, L., & Dunn, L. (1981). *Peabody Picture Vocabulary Test-Revised: Manual and Form 1.* Circle Pines, MN: American Guidance Service.

Gardner, M. (1979). *Expressive One-Word Picture Vocabulary Test: Manual.* Novato, CA: Academic Therapy Publications.

Gardner, M. (1983). *Expressive One-Word Picture Vocabulary Test-Upper Extension: Manual.* Novato, CA: Academic Therapy Publications.

Wechsler, D. (1974). *Wechsler Intelligence Scale for Children-Revised: Manual and form.* Cleveland, OH: The Psychological Corporation.

Mary Mira, Ph.D.
Associate Professor of Pediatrics (Psychology), Children's Rehabilitation Unit, University of Kansas Medical Center.

S. Joseph Weaver, Ph.D.
Associate Professor of Pediatrics (Psychology), Children's Rehabilitation Unit, University of Kansas Medical Center.

FAMILY RELATIONS TEST: CHILDREN'S VERSION

Eva Bene and James Anthony. Windsor, England: NFER-Nelson Publishing Company Ltd.

Introduction

The children's version of the Family Relations Test (FRT:C) is an individually administered test of a child's feelings toward family members and his or her perception of their reciprocal feelings. It is a structured, objectively scored measure utilizing an innovative doll play format.

Eva Bene and James Anthony are a psychologist and psychiatrist, respectively, who were affiliated with the Institute of Psychiatry at the University of London when they developed the FRT:C in the mid-1950s. They perceived a need for a test "that would indicate objectively, reliably, and rapidly the direction and intensity of a child's feelings toward the various members of his family, and, of no less importance, his estimate of their reciprocal regard for him" (Anthony & Bene, 1957, p. 541). They emphasized the need for such a test by stating, "In child guidance clinics, an objective assessment is made of the young patient's cognitive abilities and . . . the nature of his 'projected' emotions. With regard to family feeling, however, clinicians on the whole appear curiously satisfied with simple, subjective 'hunches', based often on scanty information from unreliable sources" (Anthony & Bene, 1957, p. 541).

Although the test initially lacked the usual normative, reliability and validity studies, its face validity and attractiveness to children and examiners alike aroused interest. Researchers at George Peabody College of Vanderbilt University (Frankel, 1965; Kauffman, Weaver, & Weaver, 1972) and the University of Calgary (Frost, 1969; Frost & Lockwood, 1973) supplied some limited reliability and normative data on selected samples of normal and clinic children. Gradually individual researchers found the test useful, and it began to be applied in an increasing variety of settings.

The test was revised slightly by its authors in 1978 (Bene & Anthony, 1978). The revisions were confined to some minor changes in the wording for three items in the older children's version and two items in the younger children's version to encompass cross-cultural differences because the test was being widely used in North America.

Some other variations of the test have been devised. Kauffman, Weaver, and Weaver (1971, 1972) altered the scoring by assigning a weight of "2" to all of the "strong" responses. Frankel (1965) developed a group paper-and-pencil version, which included only 35 Outgoing items and substituted 14 Sibling Preference items for the original 18 Parental Overprotection-Overindulgence items. Roche (1970) experimented with three alternate forms of administration, namely, 1) normal administration technique; 2) multiple card technique in which the child is given four copies of each item card, thus allowing that item to be dropped into four boxes; and 3) a paired-comparison technique in which the family figures were presented two at a time, forcing a choice. Only the paired-comparison technique produced an effect manifest by greater emphasis being assigned to the mother figure. Kauffman and Ball (1973) argued for revising the test to eliminate the multiple assignment of items and to revise some items that were seldom discriminative; Bene (1973) argued against those changes.

Several studies have reported use of versions developed for Israeli children (Jaffe, 1977; Rich & Rothchild, 1979). Jaffe (1977) felt that the format of the test allowed its use with children from diverse ethnic backgrounds. Bibliographic sources indicate that it has been translated for use in several European countries.

The FRT:C consists of 21 line drawings on cardboard of individuals of both sexes and all age ranges from infancy through elderly. Each of these ambiguously drawn figures is attached to a cardboard box, approximately three inches square with a slotted opening in the top. The child is helped to select from this array the figures that represent the members of the family, including self. The family composition is determined by the child; extended family members or others living in the household may be included. One drawing, a back view of a figure called "Mr. Nobody," is selected by the examiner.

The test items are individually printed on small cards. There are 47 items for children aged 3-7 years and 99 items for children aged 7-15 years. Each item is read to or by the child and placed into the box of the family member to whom it is attributed. An item may be assigned to more than one family member or, if it fits no one, may be posted to Mr. Nobody.

The statements on the cards refer to feelings characterizing the child's perceived relationships with family members. The major group of items can be schematically distributed as follows:

POSITIVE OUTGOING	POSITIVE INCOMING
NEGATIVE OUTGOING	NEGATIVE INCOMING

In the section describing scoring (below) it will be seen that plotting the scores according to such a grid is a preliminary step in the interpretation of the child's responses.

The younger children's items assess the child's attitudes in the following areas:

1) Positive feelings toward others.
2) Positive feelings the child perceives as coming from others.
3) Negative feelings toward others.
4) Negative feelings seen as coming from others.
5) Feelings of dependence on others. (Items in this category are not included in the 2 x 2 scoring grid).

The older children's items are categorized as follows:

1) Positive attitudes toward others. These are further categorized as milder attitudes of friendliness and stronger expressions of affection. A mild outgoing item would be similar to "This person is nice to be around"; a stronger outgoing item would be similar to "I wish this person would hold me close."

2) Positive feelings perceived as coming from others, classified again as either mild, such as "This person smiles at me," or strong, such as "This person likes to hold me close."

3) Negative feelings toward others, both mild, related to unfriendliness and disapproval, such as "This person sometimes is cranky," and strong, such as "Sometimes I'd like to kick this person."

4) Incoming negative feelings both mild and strong. An example of the former would be something like "This person may not always like what I do," and of the latter would be "This person beats up on me."

5) Items reflecting the child's perception of which family members are recipients of maternal or paternal overindulgence ("This is the person in the family father [or mother] spoils too much").

6) Items of perceived maternal overprotection ("Mother worries that this person . . . might catch cold").

Items in the last two categories, although used in the interpretation of the child's responses, are not plotted on the schematic 2 x 2 grid.

Ostensibly, the examiners's role is to assist the child in selecting the figures, reading the items, and insuring that each item card is inserted in the box the child designates. Yet, clinical skill is required at each step to assure that no significant family member is ignored in figure selection, to prevent an exuberant child from selecting too many peripheral figures, and to modify or stop the testing when the child's reactions suggest that it would be better to do so.

Although the FRT:C is described as useful for children as young as age three, it is best used for those whose language comprehension skills are at least at the second-grade or eight-year level. The test is of questionable value for many children beyond the mid-teen years. Although children easily understand the procedure of the test, some of the language is archaic (e.g., "This person . . . nags sometimes"), making it difficult for younger children to understand.

After the child has placed all of the items the examiner removes them from the boxes and records the assignment of each on the scoring booklet. The booklet provides a two-way grid listing items by category along the side with columns for each family member across the top. Scoring is easy because the item number is printed on the face of each card. To obtain a test profile the examiner merely sums the number of items in each category (e.g., positive incoming, positive outgoing) for each family member.

When the boxes are not in use they may be collapsed, folded flat, and stored in the shoe-box-sized, cardboard container. A test case designed for carrying the material would be preferable to the box supplied with the test.

There are several positive features of the test format. The use of boxes into which the child posts the response is interesting for children and may reduce some of the emotionally threatening reactions to some of the test items. The fact that this test is scored by tallying responses results in greater reliability of scoring than one often finds in measures of emotional issues. Another positive aspect of the test is that the child has the opportunity to express as many positive as bad or negative feelings, allowing a balanced picture of the child's feelings in this domain.

Practical Applications/Uses

The FRT:C is useful to the psychologist in clinical practice for several reasons. First, it offers information about the child's view. Most psycholgists, whether espousing a psychodynamic, behavioral, or humanistic approach, acknowledge the primacy of family relationships and the child's thoughts concerning them. Yet is is seldom that a systematic, reliable or objective measure is made of this important dimension. The FRT:C, as a measure of the child's view is a valuable complement to an assessment battery.

A second reason for its use is its inclusiveness. The test may reveal an otherwise overlooked, important family member whose identity might not have been disclosed by a questionnaire or a parent interview. Divorced parents may not perceive the continued centrality of the separated parent to the child's view of the family; deceased parents, siblings, or other relations may also occupy an important role for the child. Many times these "other" family members are only revealed after extensive work with a child. The clinician in private practice may welcome an instrument that is used easily in the office and provides such a broad view of the child's life.

Another practical value of the FRT:C is its ease of administration. A psychologist can confidently turn the administration task over to a trained psychological assistant with resulting savings to both client and professional. Another value of the test is that the questions cover a broad range of ways in which family members interact, thus allowing for maximal expression of the child's feelings.

The issue of what kind of professionals should use the test is not a simple one. On the one hand, it is useful to school psychologists and counselors operating within the schools because it provides valuable information about family issues that are often difficult for such professionals to examine directly. This positive feature is offset by two negative factors. One is that, because the test delves into highly personal and emotionally laden issues of family interactions, it reveals information that some people feel does not properly come under the purview of the school system. Some states and school districts strongly discourage the exploration of private family issues. A second concern about the use of the test in other than mental health settings or private clinicians' offices is that the nature of the items could trigger anxiety in the child about sensitive family relations. These considerations lead these reviewers to suggest that the FRT:C not be used in school settings unless appropriate clinical supervision is available and unless the psychologist is aware that school district policy supports the use of such an instrument.

The FRT:C measures objectively and in standardized fashion the child's emotional family relationships. At the simplest level, it measures the positive and negative feelings that the child has toward various family members and what the child believes to be the feelings the members have toward him or her. At another level, the interpretation of the pattern of responses may provide information about the relative importance of the different family members, the child's self critical attitude, ambivalence toward family members, sibling rivalry, and the consistency of the child's expressed feelings with his or her actual behavior (Bene & Anthony, 1978; Philipp & Orr, 1978).

The original use of the FRT:C was in the initial diagnostic assessment of children seen in a child guidance clinic setting. The child's responses brought to light information about often unsuspected dimensions of the child's interests and helped to "localize a disturbing influence in the home" (Anthony & Bene, 1957, p. 547). The author's of the test present a multidimensional interpretation strategy, basic to which is the notion that the child's psychic reality may be more relevant to the development of symptomatology than the objective information generally obtained from a case history.

The FRT:C has been used in a range of settings. It has been applied in settings where variations from typical family life exist, for example, in kibbutz systems (Regev, Beit-Hallahmi, & Sharabany, 1980) and institutional settings for dependent children (Jaffe, 1977). Its use to discriminate among various clinical groups of children has been upheld by a number of studies. Differences from normal children in perceptions of interfamily feelings have been reported for emotionally disturbed children (Kauffman, 1969; Philipp & Orr, 1978; Schmid, 1974); among clinic, delinquent and nonreading groups (Frost, 1969); in chronic misbehaviors (Rich & Rothchild, 1979), and institutionalized emotionally disturbed and school disordered boys (Kauffman, 1971). The FRT:C has been used with abused children to evaluate their view of the family (Geddis, Turner, & Eardlet, 1977). It has also been used to study male children with sex-role developmental disorders (Rekers et al., 1983). It has been used to study differences in perceptions of family relations of children with chronic conditions, such as cardiac defects (Howe, 1972), leukemia (Spinetta & Maloney, 1978), and stuttering (Moore & Nystul, 1979). In these clinical/research applications the FRT:C has documented differences between groups—differences that have lent themselves to logical clinical interpretation.

Other applications include its use to assess effects of birth order on perceived family relations (Laitman, 1975) and to determine the relationship of perceived family relations to health and social characteristics of the family (Linton et al., 1961).

Several studies have investigated parents' ability to predict their children's responses to the FRT:C (Kauffman, Hallahan, & Ball, 1975; McNight-Taylor, 1974; Schmid, 1974). In certain family configurations parents were able to predict their children's feelings about family affective interchanges, although one study

(Kauffman, Hallahan, & Ball, 1975) found significant discrepancies between children's and parents' responses. The reviewers do not feel that this second-order use of the FRT:C has yet been validated with sufficient rigor for such clinical use.

The FRT has had its primary application in settings serving children with emotional/behavioral disorders. As such, it has been used primarily by psychologists. In light of the normative limitations discussed below it seems appropriate that its use should be restricted to those whose clinical training and experience would lead them to use its results judiciously. It is most appropriately used in mental health clinics, pediatric hospital and clinic settings, psychiatric facilities, and social agencies that employ clinical psychologists.

If the FRT:C were to be restandardized and if more extensive norms were available it could have the potential for providing clinicians with significant and important information about how children view their family relationships. As a needed standardized instrument it could provide objective information in areas where we have previously not had such data, such as in child custody and preadoptive determinations.

The FRT:C is most useful for children with vocabulary levels of at least second grade. Although the younger children's form may be used below that level, the interpretation of responses of those below age four should be done with caution (Geddis, Turner, & Eardlet, 1977). After the age of about 15 years, children tend to respond indiscriminately to the items with Mr. Nobody, reducing the discriminate ability of the test.

The FRT:C has been used experimentally with a range of subjects: emotionally disturbed youth (Frost, 1969; Kauffman, 1971; Philipp & Orr, 1978; Schmid, 1974; Swanson, 1969), disabled learners (Kauffman, Weaver & Weaver, 1972), low income black children (McNight-Taylor, 1974), urban slum children (Linton et al., 1961), abused children (Geddes, Turner, & Eardlet, 1977), and dependent or deprived children (Jaffe, 1977; Williams, 1961).

Inspection and experience with the text suggest that it can be used with children with limited vision. Although it has not been validated as such, it deserves study as a possible test for hearing-impaired children administered by manual communication. The test does not require motor proficiency so it could be used with children with motor deficits.

The FRT:C should be administered in a setting appropriate for psychological assessment of children, such as a quiet room with minimal distractions. There should be a testing table, chairs, and a second table or shelf on which the complete set of 21 figures can be displayed at the beginning of the session. The professional responsible for the administration and interpretation of the test must be qualified by education, training, and where applicable, licensure to conduct psychological assessment. In the United States and Canada only psychologists are considered so qualified, except psychiatrists who have obtained specialized education and training in psychological measurement. A psychological assistant or associate could administer the test if the psychologist responsible has verified their competence to do so. The FRT:C, therefore, may be administered and scored by other professionals, such as teachers, social workers, or clerical assistants, as long as the psychologist has ascertained their competence.

The test administration consists of two phases. First, the examiner questions the child about who the members of the child's family are. When this is established the examiner asks the child to select from all of the figures arrayed those that best represent these family members. When this is done the examiner selects the Mr. Nobody figure, adding it to the family group. The remaining figures are put aside. The child is told that he or she will be given a series of cards with statements on them which the child is to read and place in the box of the figure that the statement best fits. If the statement fits no one, the child is to assign the item to Mr. Nobody. If the statement fits more than one person, it can be attributed to several members, in which case the card is to be handed to the examiner. The second phase consists of placing the individual item cards that the child selects into the family figure boxes.

The instructions for administration in the manual are adequate and clear. There are examples of ways that the examiner can respond to questions that children might raise. Several problems may arise in the administration of the test. One is the issue of including absent, deceased, or "new" parent figures or relatives. The manual suggests including new parent figures in the family composition.

Another problem may arise if older children have reading difficulties because the manual suggests allowing children to read the items themselves. The reading difficulty level of the items is not reported. The reviewers suggest that if there is a doubt, the examiner should ask the child to read some sample items to be sure that the child understands the content before proceeding. If there is any doubt about the child's reading competence, the examiner should read the items from the cards. The examiner must not, however, explain the items to the child.

Another problem may arise in giving the child instructions for handling a message that fits several people. The child has been instructed to hand the card to the examiner who notes its multiple assignment. If too much emphasis is placed on this point, some children may invalidate the test by assigning an excessive number of items to all family members. On the other hand, if the child does not understand that multiple assignments are allowed, feelings toward one family member may not be expressed. The best way of handling this instruction is to present it in a matter-of-fact manner without undue emphasis.

The FRT:C is easily administered by a competent and reasonably sensitive individual who studies the manual and practices the test. It is necessary to establish a degree of rapport before starting because a child who is fearful, angry, or significantly uncooperative may give responses that are meaningless. Because one purpose of the test is to dramatize the family situation, the examiner should not be too obtrusive, fostering the child's emotional interaction with the family figures, not with the examiner. Young children enter into emotional play with the figures quite well and may even react to them as in doll play, vocalizing for and to them, moving them around in actions, and occasionally hitting or shoving them. For these reasons, some examiners prefer to sit to one side of the child rather than directly across the table in the child's direct line of sight. Because some children will reveal important feelings directly through their dramatization with the family figures, the examiner has an additional opportunity to make note of significant behavior on the part of the child as the child acts out the relationships between the figures or elaborates on the feelings expressed by the item. The examiner should also be alert to evidence of defense reactions against the item content. The test administration requires about 30 minutes on the average, with a range between 20-45 minutes.

The ease and objectivity of scoring is a major strength of the FRT:C. All that is necessary is for the items to be taken out of the family figure boxes and the numbers of the items checked on the scoring sheet. Although the manual encourages the examiner to allow the child to assist, it is generally easier and quicker to do it alone. Examiners would be wise to keep the already scored items next to their respective boxes until all of the boxes have been emptied and the score sheet checked to make sure that every item number has a mark. The numbers of the items given multiple assignment, which the examiner has noted during administration, are added to the scoring sheet. The tabulation of the score takes only five minutes. Machine and computer scoring are not available.

Once all of the scores have been tabulated, clinicians may find it helpful to follow a conventional way of presenting the results graphically. Kauffman, Weaver, and Weaver (1972) modified a graphing method suggested in the test manual.

Figure 1.
Facsimile of a schematic representation of FRT responses.

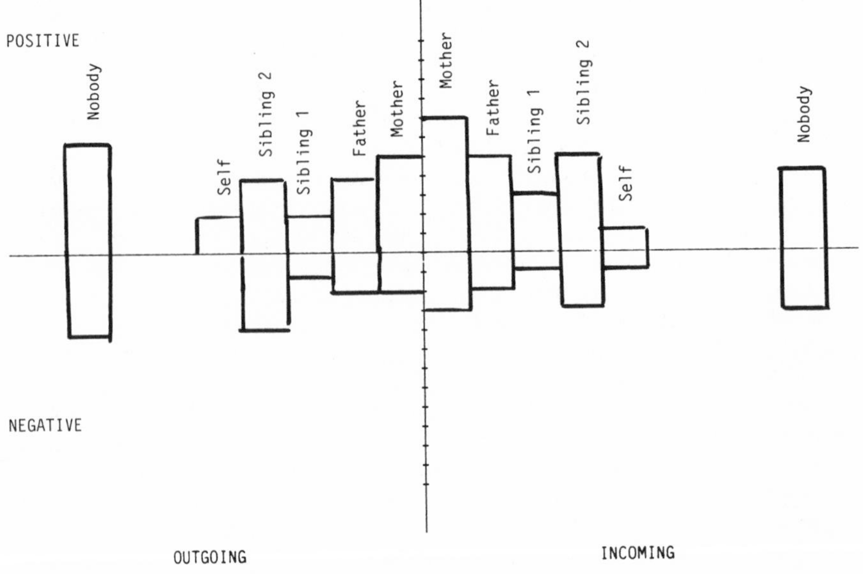

The examiner constructs a simple graph such as that in Figure 1 with horizontal lines separating positive and negative feelings and a vertical line separating incoming and outgoing feelings. Equal intervals are marked off along the vertical line to represent frequency of responses. The responses for each family member are then drawn as a bar graph with positive feelings above the horizontal line and negative feelings below it. Outgoing items are placed to the left and incoming items to the right of the vertical/middle line. It is useful to arrange the family members in the order depicted in Figure 1, with Mother next to the central vertical line, followed by Father, then Siblings, and Self at the end. Mr. Nobody's responses are depicted somewhat apart from family members at the extremes. Clinicians and researchers alike have found it useful to depict the family relationships in this fashion. Deviant response patterns can be noted at a glance, and testing results communicated easily, making the graph worth the extra effort.

Interpretation of the test is based on objective scores that are the sum of the child's responses in each category for each family member. Interpretation is facilitated if the examiner constructs a diagram of the distribution of the child's responses in the four quadrants as discussed above. The interpretation is considerably influenced by the examiner's clinical skills, including 1) knowledge of how children of different ages respond to testing in general, 2) familiarity with the limited normative material and the broad interpretive guidelines provided in the manual, 3) experience with the FRT:C across a broad age and diagnostic range, and 4) the examiner's basic clinical acumen.

The authors of the test suggest that the examiner consider the following in evaluating and interpreting the child's pattern of responses:

1) The distribution of total responses to each family member. The manual provides information about expected distribution of responses, but no numerical data is given.

2) Characterization of the interaction that the child perceives self as having with each family member, noting if there is an overemphasis on positive or negative feelings or evidence of ambivalence (a perceived interaction with one family member in which either positive or negative responses are not at least ⅔ as frequent as the other).

3) Reliance on denial of feelings through excessive use of Mr. Nobody. It has been shown that for males between the ages of 7-12 years there are significant age trends in the use of this figure, such that the age of the child should temper the interpretation of the child's use of this figure (Frost & Lockwood, 1973). This points out again the need for more normative information.

4) Discrepancy between a child's reported feelings toward a family member and how the child thinks that person feels toward him or her.

5) Characterization of the child's defense system. The test authors feel that these are revealed by the patterns of the child's responses. Examples used in the manual include: *Displacement* (more items given to a peripheral family member), *Idealization* (excessive positive feelings attributed to a person and negative feelings to Mr. Nobody), *Denial* (excessive use of Mr. Nobody), and *Wish fulfillment* (claiming most of the over-protective and indulgent items).

6) Although the authors suggest that it may be possible to refer to the intensity (mild/strong) of items in the interpretation, they feel that the necessary study of this has not yet been done.

The interpretation of an individual child's responses, as well as the use of the FRT:C for research purposes, is limited by the lack of solid normative information on various clinical and other groups. Factors influencing collection of normative information on various groups are the wide variation in the patterns of family configuration and the differences in the types of interactional pathology across groups (Kauffman, 1971). Nevertheless, additional normative information is vital.

The few normative studies that have been done indicate age and gender effects, which should be taken into account in interpretation (Rosen & Brigham, 1984).

Technical Aspects

Several reliability studies have been carried out on the FRT:C with encouraging results. Anthony and Bene (1957) reported odd-even correlations ranging from .68 to .90. Kauffman, Weaver, and Weaver (1972) found respectable test-retest reliability in children referred for reading problems. Correlations for total responses ranged from .77 (Father) to .88 (Nobody); for total positive responses they ranged from .71 (Sibling #1) to .87 (Mother); and for total negative responses they range from .59 (Father) to .90 (Sibling #2). All correlations excluded Self responses because clinical experience indicates that children have difficulty assigning items to Self and frequently make nonsensical assignments. Bean (1976) investigated the reliability of the FRT:C with normal and emotionally disturbed children and concluded that test-retest correlations for each of the groups were of a generally acceptable level. His figures were basically equivalent to those reported above. The relative congruence of reliability coefficients established on samples of emotionally disturbed children, children with reading problems, and normal children auger well for the extension of the FRT:C to more diverse groups.

Investigations of the validity of the FRT:C have been scattered over the years and have involved studies of diverse theoretical formulations, different and small samples, and changes in both the administration and scoring of the test. Under these circumstances few generalizations regarding the validity of the test can be made. The test's authors (Anthony & Bene, 1957) argue for its validity by providing case histories, data from siblings, and predictions based on psychiatric diagnoses, all of which provided congruent validity information.

Frost (1969) compared FRT:C results from 190 eleven-year-old children (86 boys, 104 girls) to the results of the original clinic group reported in the manual and to those of a delinquent group and a nonreader group studied earlier, and found many significant differences. Compared to all other groups, the delinquents had less positive responses to Father and more negative references to Mr. Nobody. The nonreader group dispersed its positive statements throughout the family more than the other samples, which diminished the number of responses to parents to a point significantly below the normal or clinical groups. Frost and Lockwood (1973) supported the hypothesis of inhibition in boys made by the test authors. In their sample of 217 boys aged 7-12 years, positive assignments decreased and aggressive items increased with age. Howe (1972) used a revision of the FRT:C with families of well and cardiac children. She found significant associations between reported affective relationships and sex, age, birth order, and health status. In a study of family relations as an intervening variable in the relationship of birth order and self-esteem, Laitman (1975) administered the FRT:C and the Coopersmith Self-Esteem Inventory to 89 junior-high boys and girls from two- and three- child intact families. The FRT:C data indicated that firstborns were relatively more negatively involved with siblings. A comparison of Coopersmith and FRT:C data indicated that high self-esteem was associated with low negative interaction with Father, high positive interaction with Siblings, and low negative interactions within the family, suggesting that family relations had a strong impact on self-esteem.

A study from another culture, which bears on the validity of the FRT:C, was carried out by Rich and Rothchild (1979) in a special Israeli educational setting. They compared chronically misbehaving adolescents with well-behaved classmates, using a somewhat revised FRT:C and collapsing incoming and outgoing scores. They found significant differences favoring the well-behaved group on eight of the nine tested areas. Another Israeli study indicating the value of the FRT:C in discriminating groups was that of Regev, Beit-Hallahmi, and Sharabany (1980). They compared FRT:C results for three groups: kibbutz children raised communally with peers, kibbutz children raised in families, and city children raised in traditional families. The children raised communally avoided most often the expression of positive and negative feelings toward significant family figures. The bearings of this study on the validity of the FRT:C are clouded by the fact that only 48 test items were used and a weighting system was employed. Nevertheless, striking differences in family structures were reflected in differences in test scores.

A few studies have found little or no discriminative validity for the FRT:C. Philipp and Orr (1978), studying the ability of the FRT:C to discriminate among emotionally disturbed inpatients, outpatients, and normals, found only a few significant results leading to their conclusion that "the FRT is only able to make a few quantitative differentiations between a clinical and a normal sample of boys. . ." (p. 121). Bean (1976) concludes that far fewer significant differences were found between an emotionally disturbed and normal group than would be desired for acceptable construct validity.

Critique

The FRT:C has such clinical potential that a large-scale revision is indicated. This should include the selection and development of items, as well as their field testing on large normative samples. Even as it stands in its present form, the FRT:C provides crucially important information, collected in an objective and systematic fashion on vital areas of a child's world.

Those who have studied the FRT:C have rated it highly for its innovative methodology and on the fact that it is the only standardized instrument that measures this dimension of the child's emotional world. At the same time, there is caution expressed because the test has not been subjected to rigorous study and because there is limited normative data.

"It is unique in its purpose and construction, it yields data relevant to an important but neglected area of personality research, it holds intrinsic appeal for children, and the scoring procedures are completely objective" (Kauffman, 1970, p. 18). Jensen (1959) states the following:

> The test would seem to have possibilities, considering that there are few, if any, other objective techniques which serve the functions for which it is designed . . . A good deal of clinical wisdom as well as an accumulation of experience with the FRT . . . [is] necessary for making judicious interpretations . . . It can be recommended for use by those who are primarily interested in investigating the test itself. (p. 132-133).

According to Semeonoff (1976, p. 169), "Methodologically, the technique is elegant, but since the measures it yields are at least partially ipsative it has many of the shortcomings inherent in that form of measurement." He further states that "It is clear that the Family Relations Test can yield information about the individual, and there is no reason why it could not be used as the first step in an investigation which could then be pursued along whatever lines the clinician found acceptable. (p. 170).

The Family Relations Test measures objectively in a standardized fashion a child's emotional family relations. It gives the clinician a picture of the balance of the child's feelings within the family and the child's perceptions of the family's feelings toward him or her. It is badly in need of complete revision and the development of relevant norms. Given that, these reviewers feel that it would become almost a universal instrument in child clinical assessment.

References

Anthony J., & Bene, E. (1957). A technique for the objective assessment of the child's family relationships. *Journal of Mental Science, 103,* 541-555.

Bean, B. W. (1977). An investigation of the reliability and validity of the Family Relations Test (Doctoral dissertation, University of Kansas, 1976). *Dissertation Abstracts International, 37,* 4127B.

Bene, E. (1973). Reply to Kauffman and Ball's note regarding the Family Relations Test. *Journal of Personality Assessment, 37,* 464-466.

Bene, E., & Anthony, J. (1978). *Manual for the Children's Version of the Family Relations Test — Revised.* England: NFER Publishing Co., Ltd.

Frankel, J. J. (1967). The relation of a specific family constellation and some personality characteristics of children (Doctoral dissertation, George Peabody College for Teachers, 1965). *Dissertation Abstracts International, 28,* 2620B.

Frost, B. P. (1969). The Family Relations Test: A normative study. *Journal of Projective Techniques and Personality Assessment, 34,* 409-413.

Frost, B. P., & Lockwood, B. (1973). Studies of Family Relations Test patterns: 1. Test inhibition. *Journal of Personality Assessment, 37,* 544-550.

Geddis, D. C., Turner, I. F., & Eardlet, J. (1977). Diagnostic value of a psychological test in cases of suspected child abuse. *Archives of Disease in Childhood, 52,* 708-712.

Howe, J. H. (1972). Interpersonal attitudes in families of well and cardiac children (Doctoral dissertation, Florida State University, 1972). *Dissertation Abstracts International, 33,* 2529A.

Jaffe, E. D. (1977). Perceptions of family relationships by institutionalized and noninstitutionalized dependent children. *Child Psychiatry and Human Development, 82,* 81-93.

Jensen, A. (1959). Family Relations Test: An objective technique for exploring emotional attitudes in children. In O. K. Buros (Ed.), *The fifth mental measurements yearbook* (pp. 132-133). Highland Park, NJ: The Gryphon Press.

Kauffman, J. M. (1969). Perception of family and school related variables by school adjusted, school disordered, and institutionalized emotionally disturbed preadolescent boys. (Doctoral dissertation, University of Kansas, 1969). *Dissertation Abstracts International, 31,* 562A.

Kauffman, J. M. (1970). Validity of the Family Relations Test: A review of research. *Journal of Projective Techniques and Personality Assessment, 34,* 186-189.

Kauffman, J. M. (1971). Family Relations Test responses of disturbed and normal boys: Additional comparative data. *Journal of Personality Assessment, 35,* 128-138.

Kauffman, J. M., & Ball, D. W. (1973). A note on item analysis of Family Relations Test data. *Journal of Personality Assessment, 37,* 248.

Kauffman, J. M., Hallahan, D. P., & Ball, D. W. (1975). Parents' predictions of their children's perceptions of family relations. *Journal of Personality Assessment, 39* (3), 228-235.

Kauffman, J. M., Weaver, S. J., & Weaver, A. (1971). Age and intelligence as correlates of perceived family relationships of underachievers. *Psychological Reports, 28,* 522.

Kauffman, J. M., Weaver, S. J., & Weaver, A. (1972). Family Relations Test responses of retarded readers: Reliability and comparative data. *Journal of Personality Assessment, 36,* 353-360.

Laitman, R. J. (1975). Family relations as an intervening variable in the relationship of birth order and self-esteem (Doctoral dissertation, Case Western Reserve University, 1975). *Dissertation Abstracts International, 36,* 3051B.

Linton, H., Berle, B. B., Grossi, M., & Jackson, E. (1961). Reactions of children within family groups as measured by the Bene-Anthony tests. *Journal of Mental Science, 107,* 308-328.

McNight-Taylor, M. (1975). Perception of relationships in low income black families (Doctoral dissertation, University of Virginia, 1974). *Dissertation Abstracts International, 35,* 5127A.

Moore, M., & Nystul, M. S. (1979). Parent-child attitudes and communication processes in families with stutterers and families with non-stutterers. *British Journal of Disorders of Communication,* 14(3), 173-180.

Philipp, R. L., & Orr, R. R. (1978). Family relations as perceived by emotionally disturbed and normal boys. *Journal of Personality Assessment, 42*(2), 121-127.

Regev, E., Beit-Hallahmi, B., & Sharabany, R. (1980). Affective expression in kibbutz-communal, kibbutz-familial, and city-raised children in Israel. *Child Development, 51*(1), 232-237.

Rekers, G. A., Mead, S. L., Rosen, A. C., & Brigham, (1983). Family correlates of male childhood gender disturbance. *Journal of Genetic Psychology, 142*(1), 31-42.

Rich, Y., & Rothchild, G. (1979). Personality differences between well and poorly behaved adolescents in school. *Psychological Reports, 44* (3, PT 2), 1143-1148.

Roche, D. J. (1970). The Bene-Anthony Family Relations Test: Variations of reliability of administration procedure. *Papers in Psychology, 4,* 12-15.

Rosen A. C., & Brigham, S. L. (1984). Sex differences in affective response on the Bene-Anthony test. *Journal of Personality Assessment, 48* (5), 520-524.

Schmid, R. E. (1974). Perception of family relationships by families with a disturbed child and families with normal children (Doctoral dissertation, University of Virginia, 1974). *Dissertation Abstracts International, 35,* 2091A.

Semeonoff, B. (1976). *Projective techniques.* London: John Wiley, Ltd.

Spinetta, J. J., & Maloney, L. J. (1978). The child with cancer: Patterns of communication and denial. *Journal of Consulting and Clinical Psychology, 46*(6), 1540-1541.

Swanson, B. M. (1969). Parent-child relations: A child's acceptance by others, of others, and of self.(Doctoral dissertation, University of Oklahoma, 1969). *Dissertation Abstracts International, 30,* 1890B.

Williams, J. M. (1961). Children who break down in foster homes: A psychological study of patterns of personality growth in grossly deprived children. *Journal of Child Psychology and Psychiatry, 2,* 5-20.

Kaye Theimer, Ph.D.
Psychologist, Private Practice, Santa Barbara, California.

FAMILY RELATIONSHIP INVENTORY

Ruth B. Michaelson and Harry L. Bascom. Los Angeles, California: Psychological Publications, Inc.

Introduction

The Family Relationship Inventory (FRI) is a counseling tool used to examine family interactions and relationships. It is useful for individual and group administration; as such, it is designed to clarify both interpersonal behavior and individual behavior and individual feelings. On an individual basis the FRI can facilitate understanding of personal feelings toward self (e.g., esteem, appraisal), as well as portraying the individuals' feelings toward others in the family. Further, administration to the entire family results in a "familygram" representation of the interrelationships within the family. The purpose of the "familygram" is two-fold: the FRI aids in the counseling process by helping individuals (separately or in a family unit) understand their own and other family members' feelings and in doing so facilitates therapeutic change within the family or individual.

The FRI was developed along the lines of Dr. Ruth Michaelson's Family Relationship Scale, focusing on the social distance of the family members. This concept of social distance was later broadened to include self-distancing, or the degree to which one esteems and accepts self (Nash, Morrison, & Taylor, 1982). In 1974 the FRI was published by Michaelson and Harry L. Bascom, following a further broadening of some specific areas of the instrument by Bascom. In 1982, the FRI and its manual were revised, with Louise Nash as editor, W. Lee Morrison as technical advisor, and all rights given to Psychological Publications, Inc.

No further information regarding the FRI's development is given in the manual, and no specific information as to the norm group, reasons for revisions, or the criteria used in its development are found in the literature.

The FRI is simple to administer and useful for adults of all ages and children as young as five years. It is an appropriate test for individuals or for family units. In addition to its utility and simplicity, the FRI is easy, if not fun, for those individuals taking the test.

The test consists of a manual, 50 2¼" x 3¾" item cards, tabulating forms, scoring forms, individual relationship wheels, and Familygram tables. The cards are divided into two groups, with 1-25 positively valenced and 25-50 negatively valenced. This valencing refers to the word or phrase on the cards describing a personal characteristic or behavior. The respondent is expected to elicit a response regarding self or other members of the family. The tabulating form is used by each

---

I wish to acknowledge Robert Ruh for his assistance in the process of preparation of this manuscript and thank him for his contribution to the final product.

individual taking the inventory. The scoring form is used when the family unit is being tested and gives a representation of each person's total score utilizing the results from the tabulating forms. The individual relationship wheel and Familygram are a means of providing graphic representation of the interrelationships when administering the test to more than one person or a family unit, respectively.

The examiner's participation in the test requires verbal administration and observation of the subject. The counselor reads the cards aloud to the individuals who score their own responses on the tabulating forms. Suggestions for order of administration of the cards are given in the manual as well as suggestions for administration to special populations (e.g., young children).

Practical Applications/Uses

The FRI is designed to examine family relationships, individual feelings, and interpersonal behavior within the context of the family system. It is intended to assess how individual family members perceive themselves, their parents, children, siblings, and significant others in the family. How each member functions and is affected by one another is the focus of the test design.

In actual use the process of administration has become as helpful as the test ratings themselves. The "identified patient" is focused on in the family context. Problems that have not been verbalized or otherwise been expressed can be approached more readily. The test was designed to act as an initial rapport builder and can serve that purpose effectively.

The test is recommended for use by psychologists, social workers, marriage and family counselors, youth counselors, and family life educators in mental-health clinics, private-practice settings, and child-development centers. This test can be easily administered and interpreted in a nonjudgmental manner. Due to this feature, a new application might be in the corporate or business community as part of a stress-management program to identify those psychosocial stressors related to relationships in the family unit.

For the private practitioner, if the entire family unit is not present, the perception of the family relationship can be acquired in a nonthreatening and game-like format. It is a convenient way to get a visual portrayal of the family as a system with corresponding bonds and alliances of closeness or distance. As an "ice-breaker" the practitioner can pick up many verbal and nonverbal cues. The authors emphasize process as well as the rating outcome. This instrument also gives insight into sibling relationships and parent-child interaction.

For the person in the mental-health field the FRI can serve as an instrument in a battery of tests aimed at primary prevention. It avoids the use of diagnostic labels but has specific statements that can act as an initial starting place for a therapeutic plan. Marriage counselors can build on positive feelings that couples express.

For the high-school counselor the FRI provides a framework of the family system so that the feeling of responsibility is shared by the student with the entire family. The counselor can stress the student's role in the structure of the family. It can assist the counselor to refer to a family agency or individual counselor if more intensive individual therapy is needed. The FRI is inappropriate for individuals who tend to blame parties who are not present for the assessment.

The FRI can be administered to young children five years or older if they are able to understand and give meaningful responses, as well as to adolescents and adults. It can be administered individually or to a family unit in a conjoint session. This test could be adopted easily for use with families of handicapped children, as it does not require children to be able to read as long as there is verbal comprehension. No research literature or clinical applications have been reported as to this use.

The examiner is not required to have any special certification, but it is recommended that a "professional with relevant training in the field of psychology, counseling, marriage and family, child development, educational psychology, etc." (Nash, Morrison, & Taylor, 1982) administer the test.

To administer the FRI, the examiner conveys to the family that the measure reflects 1) what each person feels about self and other members of the family and 2) a way of looking at the relationships within the family. After the examiner makes the suggested introductory remarks given in the manual, each person is given an FRI tabulating form and is asked to write his or her name in the first column and the remaining members of the family in order of age at the top of each column. The examiner then administers the 50 FRI items in the order suggested in the manual. As each item is read, respondents must decide whether it best describes themselves, other family members, or no one ("wastebasket"), and then record the corresponding number in the appropriate column on the tabulating form.

It is recommended that the FRI be administered individually to children in kindergarten and primary grades and be introduced as a game. Instead of using the FRI tabulating forms the child is asked to draw pictures of mother, father, sister, brother, and other family members on separate sheets of paper and spread them out on a table or floor. They may ask to include extended family members, such as babysitters.

There is no time limit, and the inventory is administered in an informal, relaxed, unhurried manner. It can easily be administered in 15-20 minutes using the standard procedure; this procedure is recommended for a more specific representation of the interrelationship within the family rather than the alternative methods reported in the appendix to the test manual.

The directions for administration are written in narrative form and are somewhat difficult for the reader to follow. There are suggested introductory remarks and two recommended procedures, one for older children and adults and one for younger children. The administration procedures are quite simple and the sequence can be altered in any way deemed necessary.

The examiner and subject participate in the scoring, and the procedures are clearly presented. It takes the examiner 10-20 minutes to learn how to score. Depending on the number of family members administered the test, it takes five to ten minutes to score. The scoring for multiple members of the family is more cumbersome because each set of scores has to be transferred from the tabulating form to the scoring forms.

There are four FRI scoring forms: the tabulating form, scoring form, Familygram, and individual relationship wheel. A case example of a family that assists the examiner in recording the scores is presented in the manual. To use the tabulating form, respondents mark a " + " beside items 1-25 and a "–" beside items 25-50 after each member has assigned the items on the cards to self, family members or "wastebasket." They then add the positive and negative items in each column and subtract the smaller sum from the larger sum to derive a total positive or negative score for self, family members, and "wastebasket."

To use the FRI scoring form when the FRI is administered to more than one person the family members (oldest to youngest) are listed across the top and down the left side of the form and their scores transferred under their names. After each set of ratings has been transferred from the tabulating to the scoring form, a total " + " or "−" score is derived for each respondent by adding the scores and subtracting the smaller sum from the larger sum, retaining the sign from the larger. The name and total score of the person who receives the highest overall rating are recorded in the box labeled "most esteemed." The person receiving the lowest score is placed in the box labeled "least esteemed." The names of the two individuals who rated each other highest are recorded in the box labeled "strongest relationships." The lowest combined ratings are recorded in the box labeled "poorest relationships."

To complete the individual relationship wheel, the respondent's name, self-esteem score, and total score are transferred to the center of the wheel. Each member is then assigned a spoke of the wheel, the members' names recorded in the curved box on the rim, and each of their ratings placed in the arrow-shaped box on the spoke that points to the center of the wheel.

When the FRI is administered to the entire family, the FRI Familygram involves the transfer of the individual relationship wheels to graphically depict the interrelational dynamics within the family unit. Scoring is done easily by hand and becomes time-consuming only if administered to a large family.

When counseling one family member, regardless of age, Nash, Morrison, and Taylor (1982) suggest its use as a diagnostic and counseling instrument. They also recommend the use of the Taylor-Johnson Temperament Analysis (Taylor & Morrison, 1966) in conjunction with the FRI to look at personality as well as relationships. Scoring is based on raw, rather than normative, scores.

The test is best used as one instrument in an entire test battery to give the examiner an idea of significant relationships and the respondent's role within the context of the family. Its suggested use as a measure of self-concept is highly dependent on the clinician's accurate clinical judgment and other valid diagnostic assessment. This is less of a factor when evaluating closeness or distance in the family relationships. It is probably best used in conjoint family counseling situations, marriage counseling, or child and adolescent group sessions. An advantage to selecting specific responses is to facilitate problem-solving and ways of changing behavior in therapy.

Technical Aspects

According to the manual, the FRI, since its original publication in 1974, has "gained acceptance among psychiatrists, psychologists, social workers, and marriage and family counselors throughout the United States" (Nash, Morrison, & Taylor, 1982, pp. 27). The authors note favorable results with these clinicians, which in turn is linked by the authors to the test reliability and validity through the favorable response to its applications. It is noted in the manual that the validity of an instrument is an "unending process" that is carried out by an instrument's users. The authors suggest from this information that the FRI does reveal the degree of social distance within the family, which is the purpose of the test.

The manual further points to the content validity being ensured by the procedures used in the test construction—that is, the 25 positively valenced and 25 negatively valenced phrases on the cards were derived from a pool of 100 such adjectives or phrases and were reduced to 50 items "using appropriate statistical techniques." A study at the American Institute of Family Relations reports further evidence for the construct/content validity (Nash, Morrison, & Taylor, 1982).

Criterion validity is confirmed by a correlation of .55 in a study of 19 high school students in 1974. Comparing the FRI to the Rosenberg's Self Esteem Scale, this correlation suggests that the FRI responses are related to self-esteem.

The reliability of the FRI was confirmed on a test-retest design, with the second test administered two and one-half weeks following the initial one. The results of the study (of the same 19 high-school students tested in 1974) show that there was no significant difference for either means or standard deviations (.05 confidence level with t = 2.110). The reliability coefficients for the scores on Self, Mother, Father, and Subject are .77, .82, .88, and .90, respectively. Given the correlation coefficient of .55 with an N of 9, validity and reliability based on these studies alone is not a warranted conclusion.

Critique

In establishing a thorough test for professionals, as well as laypersons, the investigator must have an adequate basis of information regarding test construction, development, and the research carried out in both its formulation and publication. Further, citation of this information by the author or editor in the test manual is crucial if the researcher wishes to further pursue points or information that may be abbreviated in the manual. This is where the FRI may have its central criticism. The information given in the manual is both vague and uncited. Where citations do exist, they are tangential information to the instrument or are not cited according to the style of the American Psychological Association. Caution regarding conclusions of the validity is evident from a sample size of 19 subjects. Further data identifying professionals or agencies who have used and gained favorable results with the FRI would be beneficial.

In regard to construct validity, the manual goes into detail concerning the administration of a study with 40 families through the American Institute of Family Relations in Los Angeles (1974, uncited). It is noted that white, black, and Hispanic families were included in this study; however, no information is given as to the cross-culture nature of the construction items.

The most obvious strength of the FRI is the attractiveness of the instrument as a counseling tool. The instrument is easy to administer and score. Also, the game-like nature of the FRI has several strong points for the counselor-client interactions. Primarily, it may serve to place the clients at ease with the counselor and the therapy situation. Much information can be brought to light through this game-like interaction and be quite useful in therapy. Moreover, the FRI may well serve as an "ice-breaker" for initial sessions. Lastly, the simplicity of the instrument and the "fun" nature of it makes it useful with young children who may otherwise be overlooked, given the dynamics of family interaction.

The FRI is a tool that must be used by the counselor on a conscientious and discretionary basis—that is, counselors must ultimately decide the appropriateness of the FRI in a given situation and the weight that they ascribe to the resultant information.

References

This list includes text citations as well as suggested additional reading.

Bogardus, E. S. (1959). *Social distance.* Yellow Springs, OH: Antioch Press.

Michaelson, R., & Bascom, H. (1974). *Family Relationship Inventory.* Los Angeles: Psychological Publications, Inc.

Nash, L., Morrison, L., & Taylor, R. M. (1982). *Family Relationship Inventory.* Los Angeles: Psychological Publications, Inc.

Nunnally, J. C. (1978). *Psychometric theory* (2nd ed.). New York: McGraw-Hill.

Robinson, J. P., & Shaver, P. R. (1969). *Measures of social psychological attitudes.* Ann Arbor: Institute for Social Research, University of Michigan.

Satir, V. (1967). *Conjoint family therapy.* Palo Alto, CA: Science and Behavior Books, Inc.

Taylor, R. M., & Morrison, L. P. (1966). *Taylor-Johnson Temperament Analysis (T-JTA).* Los Angeles: Psychological Publications, Inc.

Raymond E. Webster, Ph.D.
Assistant Professor of Psychology, East Carolina University, Greenville, North Carolina.

Theodore W. Whitley, Ph.D.
Associate Director, Division of Research, Department of Emergency Medicine, East Carolina University School of Medicine, Greenville, North Carolina.

FORER STRUCTURED SENTENCE COMPLETION TEST

Bertram R. Forer. Los Angeles, California: Western Psychological Services.

Introduction

The Forer Structured Sentence Completion Test (FSSCT) is comprised of 100 sentence stems developed to identify individuals' attitudes and views about themselves, others, and the world. Sentence stems reflect an approximately equal balance among third-person and first-person singular and plural stimulus presentations. The structure of the FSSCT involves both the specificity of the sentence stems and the evaluation system used to assess the quality of responses.

Historically, sentence completion techniques were derived from the basic word association procedure popularly associated with psychoanalytic theory and practice. In the FSSCT manual (Forer, 1982), Forer presents a brief summary of several studies that have used the sentence completion technique. A more comprehensive review can be found in Rabin and Zlotogorski (1981).

The test package currently available represents the fourth printing of the FSSCT, but there is no evidence that there have been any substantial or noteworthy changes in the test since the FSSCT was first presented by Forer in 1950 in the *Journal of Projective Techniques.*

The manual offers a concise and accurate summary of how sentence-stem responses can be analyzed using a three-pronged perspective. This perspective involves examining the structure, content, and underlying dynamics (called substrates by Forer) for each response. It is this interpretative approach that is represented in Forer's structural evaluation scheme. The idiographic philosophy underlying analysis of client responses on the FSSCT is best summarized in the following:

> While statistical evidence enables a short cut from the surface characteristics of responses to diagnosis without the intermediate inferences about underlying dynamics, there is apt to be a loss of the material which adds the full flavor of individuality to a psychological report. (Forer, 1982, p. 2)

Forer notes the potential limitations of idiographic analysis and the necessity for additional data on which to base hypotheses about personality structure and functioning. Clearly, the FSSCT is to be used as one component of a total psychological test battery that includes behavioral observation data. Forer (1982, p. 2) further cautions that the FSSCT is an "open-ended attitude test or controlled projection test rather than a test of minimally controlled associative processes."

Four forms of the FSSCT are available according to the gender and age of the client: M (adult males), W (adult women), B (adolescent boys), and G (adolescent girls). In the manual, Form W is referred to as Form F. A comparison of the forms at each age level indicates that the sentence stems are identical except for some of the pronouns and nouns used in the stems.

Practical Applications/Uses

The FSSCT is designed for use as a projective diagnostic instrument to encourage clients to express their attitudes in each of four areas deemed important to psychological and interpersonal functioning by the test author. These areas were determined on the basis of the author's clinical experience, which suggested their importance. Although two forms (B and G) are designed for adolescents and two forms are designed for adults (M and W), there is no information in the test manual describing lower age boundaries, reading levels, or intellectual levels below which the test should not be administered. A readability analysis of the items comprising the adolescent and adult forms conducted by these reviewers yielded the following grade level equivalent scores using three different reading analysis procedures:

Reading Analysis Procedure	*Adolescent Forms*	*Adult Forms*
Spache	2.2	2.8
Dale-Chall	below 5.0	5.0 to 6.0
Fry	1.0	3.0

These readability estimates describe the reading level based on word length and number of syllables. They do not account for conceptual differences among words. There are several phrases (e.g., Form M, #45) and value-laden terms (e.g., Form M, #57; Form B, #63) that may be confusing to or misinterpreted by persons functioning near or below these reading levels. In these instances, the test may need to be administered orally and individually, rather than in the manner it is typically given. The senior author's experience suggests that this test is not useful with individuals younger than about 11 years old, regardless of intellectual ability or reading level.

The FSSCT can be administered by any professional with training in test administration procedures. The critical component in using the FSSCT is the person who is interpreting and evaluating the quality sentence-stem reponses. The test is designed for either individual or group administration. Respondents write their replies directly on the form provided. It has been these reviewers' experience that the most effective use of this test occurs when the stems are read aloud to the respondent and initial response times, as well as the completions, are recorded. Response-time data provide the examiner with further behavioral information about the impact of an item on the individual. Mean reaction times can be computed, and items that deviate substantially from the mean reaction time can be more closely examined. This kind of administration requires approximately 15 to 20 minutes, depending on the client's intellectual characteristics.

Analysis and interpretation of the FSSCT should be done only by a qualified professional with advanced graduate-level training in the areas of projective testing and personality theory. Forer has developed a Checklist and Clinical Evaluation Form for both the adolescent and adult forms. These forms provide a structured evaluation scheme that the examiner can use to group individual items into one of four categories: Interpersonal Figures, Wishes, Causes of Own (feelings and behaviors), and Reactions (to other people). Each item is rated according to "attitudes toward" and "characteristics of" in the first two categories and "attitudes toward" in the last two categories. All of the terms used have specific clinical operational definitions and clear implications about the structure and organization of one's personality. Forer has attempted to define these terms operationally in the manual (pp. 4, 5). Nonetheless, without the proper training, understanding and using these terms in clinically appropriate and meaningful ways becomes obscured. Thus, the ultimate interpretation and utility of the FSSCT are based on the clinical judgment and expertise of the professional evaluating sentence-stem completion. Although Forer has attempted to organize or structure the scoring/interpretation process using the Checklist and Clinical Evaluation Forms, the importance of examiner competence in scoring and interpreting FSSCT responses is critical.

Scoring is done on an item-by-item basis and takes approximately 20 minutes once the examiner has become accustomed to Forer's rating format. Individual items are not quantified, nor are summed total scores calculated for each of the four categories for comparative purposes. No norms are available to determine a person's performance relative to others with similar characteristics. The test manual (p. 6) does imply that norms will be available in the future. The lack of a quantified norming system and norms may be seen by some as serious limitations. Still, the purpose of this test is to understand the individual and how the individual views himself or herself in relation to others. It is definitely possible to develop some kind of quantified rating system to represent performance in each category. However, translating concepts into numbers does not necessarily represent the construct one seeks to measure more accurately nor make an instrument more valid in a clinical sense. The thrust of most clinical work is on the total individual, and interest in individual-to-group normative comparisons is not always, or perhaps even often, present.

Technical Aspects

The reliability and validity of projective tests in general have been long-standing concerns to psychologists. The necessity for a systematic methodological approach toward establishing the reliability and validity of these instruments was raised as early as 1942 by Macfarlane. Yet, for many clinicians, the perceived utility of an instrument in meeting clinical purposes and goals is sufficient justification for its use, regardless of the statistical data describing its reliability and validity for groups of people. Interest in the individual frequently overrides reliance on statistical probabilities at the group level. The interested reader is referred to Macfarlane and Tuddenham (1951) for a more detailed analysis of the variables associated with the reliability and validity of projective instruments.

With this information as a framework, it should be neither alarming nor surprising that the FSSCT test manual contains no narrative information or statistical data describing the instrument's reliability or validity. The manual also does not provide norms for actuarial analysis and interpretation. A review of the literature revealed few studies specifically examining the validity of the FSSCT and only one study examining its reliability.

The FSSCT may be seen as having both content and face validity. Claims for content validity may be based on the instrument's apparently systematic examination of content in each of the four major categories used in the scoring analysis. Further, the areas within each category appear to logically and intuitively reflect many of the important topics related to the category. But, there are no data supporting the assignment of items to each category. Apparently, these items were developed a priori on the basis of the author's clinical experience and intuition about critical content areas for each category. However, Anastasi (1982, p. 135) notes that evidence of content validity is inappropriate for personality tests because of the ambiguous relationship between test responses and the domain being sampled. For example, the same item might produce identical responses from two people, but the psychological mechanisms underlying each response and their significance for each individual may be quite different. The relationship among test item, response, and underlying dynamics becomes increasingly complex and unclear as the structure of a test decreases.

Several studies suggest that the FSSCT is a relatively structured instrument for a projective technique. Studies examining the level of personality tapped by the FSSCT suggest that it "elicits materials from a range of levels but with the bulk of it being fairly close to awareness" (Hanfmann & Getzels, 1953, p. 290). Stone and Dellis (1960) used the FSSCT as part of a total test battery administered to hospitalized psychiatric patients to determine the relationship between degree of structure of the test and extent of psychopathology revealed by the client. Using blind ratings by judges, they found that the FSSCT revealed more significant ideational content than the Wechsler Adult Intelligence Scale but less than the Thematic Apperception Test (TAT), Rorschach, and Draw-A-Person Test. These findings support the observation of Hanfmann and Getzels regarding the level of personality addressed by the FSSCT.

The studies cited in the preceding paragraph are also consistent with the findings from other investigations showing that incomplete sentences are more structured stimuli than inkblots (Rabin & Zlotogorski, 1981) and that they measure personality contents rather than structure (Harrison, 1943). The kinds of information that can be derived from the FSSCT include specific feelings, attitudes, and reactions to situations and people. A more complete review and discussion of the impact of degree of structure on sentence completion tests in general can be found in Goldberg (1965).

If one accepts the findings from these four studies as sufficient empirical substantiation of the level of personality addressed by the FSSCT, then the conclusion may be drawn that the instrument possesses content validity. With the present availability of multivariate statistical techniques, it should be a relatively direct task to establish other types of validity for this test. Two specific types of data that would be particularly useful are those describing the predictive validity and construct validity of the instrument.

Only one study examining the construct validity of the FSSCT was located. This study was conducted by Carr (1956), who examined the relationship between expression of hostility, positive feelings, anxiety, and dependency as inferred by responses to the FSSCT and TAT with Rorschach responses commonly interpreted to reflect these affects. Participants were 50 male patients in a mental-health clinic ranging from 24 to 41 years of age. Intelligence estimates ranged from 84 to 147, with a mean of 111. Chi square revealed significant relationships among these constructs as measured by the three instruments.

Face validity refers to what a test appears to measure. Typically, it pertains to whether the test looks valid to examinees and to professionals administering the test, as well as to the relevance of test items to the age and gender of the person taking the test. It is an important aspect of testing that involves establishing rapport and credibility with the respondent. The four forms of the FSSCT contain items adjusted for the age and gender of the respondent. The sentence stems are constructed in a way that allows the respondent maximum flexibility in responding. The items are concrete and specifically refer to various people and interactions common to most people. These characteristics are commonly viewed as desirable qualities for sentence completion stems.

Turning to the reliability study, Karen (1961) evaluated the reliability of eight questions from the FSSCT for a group of 86 students in the areas of sex, love, and marriage. Judges rated responses on a three-point scale using operationally defined criteria. Reliability estimates, determined by the Pearson product-moment correlation procedure, were .90 and higher. Ratings in the love and marriage dimensions were more reliable than those in the sex category.

In summary, there is a paucity of research examining the reliability and validity of the FSSCT. Research on the FSSCT was conducted prior to 1961. The few studies that have been conducted provide evidence that the FSSCT has some desirable technical characteristics.

Critique

The emphasis in psychological testing on actuarial interpretation and statistical validation have created an atmosphere in which instruments lacking such information are viewed negatively. The FSSCT was typically part of a total test battery used to evaluate identified psychiatric patients with a wide range of personal and emotional characteristics. Several of the remaining studies were N-of-1 case studies designed to illustrate the application of projective test data to diagnosis and treatment (see Shneidmann, 1952a, 1952b, 1961). Sentence completion tests such as the FSSCT were developed specifically for clinical use with individuals. Evaluating their utility according to criteria established for tests designed for other purposes may be unreasonable.

The FSSCT does not have a formal quantitative scoring system to analyze or organize responses. The focus of the test seems to be describing, rather than quantifying, significant issues for the person. Checklists are available to organize individual responses more homogeneously according to the four categories presented by Forer. The sentence stems represent an adequate distribution of first-person, third-person, and situationally based test items. Ultimately, however, the usefulness of the FSSCT is highly dependent on the skill and knowledge of the clinician interpreting the responses.

Forer's descriptive emphasis is consistent with the view that a sentence-by-sentence interpretation is the most appropriate way to evaluate responses. Through content analysis of individual items, the clinician can develop an overall description of the personality (Holsopple & Miale, 1954) and generate hypotheses about critical areas in the person's present life situation. Research supporting this impressionistic perspective is weak, with interpretation once again limited by the clinician's skills (Goldberg, 1965, p. 27).

Although the FSSCT can be administered individually or to groups, it combines both speed of responding with power (i.e., the person is asked to write the first thing that comes to mind). The test should not be used by anyone who has not had formal graduate-level clinical training, nor should interpretation extend beyond describing the contents of an individual's personality and potential areas of conflict within it.

The FSSCT is one additional tool to supplement a battery of psychological tests. When compared with instruments like the Rorschach and the TAT, it is relatively nonthreatening to the respondent. The FSSCT has the potential to provide useful information to focus an interview or further testing, but its utility depends on the expertise of the clinician using it. Attempts to move away from subjective interpretations toward more objective methods of data analysis will require a great deal of research examining the factor structure, reliability, and validity (construct, predictive, and discriminant) of the instrument.

References

This list includes text citations as well as suggested additional reading.

Anastasi, A. (1982). *Psychological testing* (5th ed.). New York: Macmillan.

Carr, A. (1954). Intra-individual consistency in response to tests of varying degrees of ambiguity. *Journal of Consulting Psychology, 18,* 251-258.

Carr, A. (1956). The relation of certain Rorschach variables to expression of affect in the TAT and SCT. *Journal of Projective Techniques, 20,* 137-142.

Carr, A. (1968). Psychological testing and reporting. *Journal of Projective Techniques and Personality Assessment, 32,* 513-521.

Forer, B. (1950). A structured sentence completion test. *Journal of Projective Techniques, 14,* 15-29.

Forer, B. (1957). Research with projective techniques, some trends. *Journal of Projective Techniques, 21,* 358-361.

Forer, B. (1960). Word association and sentence completion methods. In A. Rabin & M. Haworth (Eds.), *Projective techniques with children* (pp. 210-224). New York: Grune & Stratton.

Forer, B. (1982). *The Forer Structured Sentence Completion Test manual* (4th printing). Los Angeles: Western Psychological Services.

Goldberg, P. (1965). A review of sentence completion methods in personality assessment. *Journal of Projective Techniques and Personality Assessment, 29,* 12-45.

Hanfmann, E., & Getzels, J. (1953). Studies of the sentence completion test. *Journal of Projective Techniques, 17,* 280-294.

Harrison, R. (1943). The Thematic Apperception and Rorschach method of personality investigation in clinical practice. *Journal of Psychology, 15,* 49-74.

Holsopple, J., & Miale, F. (1954). *Sentence completion.* Springfield, IL: Charles C. Thomas.

Karen, R. (1961). A method for rating sentence completion test responses. *Journal of Projective Techniques, 25,* 312-314.

Macfarlane, J., & Tuddenham, R. (1951). Problems in the validation of projective techniques. In H. Anderson & G. Anderson (Eds.), *An introduction to projective techniques* (pp. 26-54). Englewood Cliffs, NJ: Prentice-Hall, Inc.

Meyer, M. (1955). Parental figures in sentence completion tests, in TAT, and in therapeutic interviews. *Journal of Consulting Psychology, 19,* 170.

Rabin, A., & Zlotogorski, Z. (1981). Completion methods: Word Association, sentence, and story completion. In A. Rabin (Ed.), *Assessment with projective techniques: A concise introduction* (pp. 121-150). New York: Springer Publishing Company.

Shneidman, E. (1952a). The case of Jay: Psychological test and anamnestic data. *Journal of Projective Techniques, 16,* 297-345.

Schneidman, E. (1952b). The case of Jay: Interpretation and discussion. *Journal of Projective Techniques, 16,* 444-475.

Schneidman, E. (1961). The case of El: Psychological test data. *Journal of Projective Techniques, 25,* 131-154.

Stone, H., & Dellis, N. (1960). An exploratory investigation into the levels hypothesis. *Journal of Projective Techniques, 24,* 333-340.

Dennis N. Thompson, Ph.D.
Associate Professor of Educational Psychology, College of Education, Georgia State University, Atlanta, Georgia.

FOSTER MAZES

William S. Foster. Chicago, Illinois: Stoelting Company.

Introduction

The Foster Mazes were devised by William S. Foster in 1923 as a laboratory demonstration of the learning characteristics of adult subjects. Subjects completing each maze are blindfolded and must trace the maze patterns with a stylus. Scores are recorded for the time taken to complete each maze, the number of errors made, and the particular style used by the subject in terms of what might be labeled a "cautiousness-impulsiveness" continuum.

The mazes, which have a history that extends back into Greek mythology, were used during the early twentieth century more than any other device for the study of animal learning and intelligence. Mazes were adopted by Porteus (1924) as a combined measure of child intelligence and personality and by Arthur (1930) as one of the series in her Point Scale of Performance Tests.

It was during this period when psychology was making its transition from animal reflexology to applied psychology that the Foster Mazes were devised. Unlike the work of Porteus and Arthur, the Foster Mazes were not intended to be a standardized measure of general mental ability. No current literature is available on the mazes, and to date the major description of the them appears in Foster and Tinkers' text, *Experiments in Psychology,* published in 1929.

In the early twentieth century, it was frequently held in experimental psychology that reflexes are an appropriate means for studying cognition. Foster and Tinker (1929) draw on Russian and Pavlovian reflexology of the era to support the rationale for the mazes. In the introduction to their chapter on the mazes they argue that because of the loose coordination of reflexes in animals they often respond to new situations by a complex variety of random or trial-and-error movements. Adult humans, on the other hand, have a far more "plastic" nervous system that is far more susceptible than animals to the formation of learned "habits." It was the original purpose of the Foster Mazes to demonstrate the formation of these learned habits in humans.

The Foster Mazes are offered in two patterns, A and B, which are sold separately. Each is cut through its own 8½" by 11" wooden board. Blind alleys are outlined in white for easy scoring. Maze A consists of ten such blind alleys, whereas Maze B contains twelve. The publisher provides a stylus with each kit for tracing the maze. A pair of goggles for blindfolding is available from the publisher at additional cost.

Practical Applications/Uses

In administering a maze, an error is determined by any movement into a blind alley or by any movement backwards within the correct path. Because both patterns A and B include blind alleys containing several choice points, any additional turn within a blind alley is also considered an error. In addition to an error score, time taken to complete the maze is also recorded. The administration of the maze is repeated until the subject reaches three successive trials without error and the time in running one of the three trials is not greater than 15 seconds. Foster and Tinker (1929) maintain that based on test runs of 125 subjects, the average number of trials to reach the criterion is 36 trials for Maze A and 39 trials for Maze B.

In addition to time and error scores, Foster and Tinker suggest that the mazes can also be used to measure the "planning" ability, or impulsivity of the subject. The procedure for recording this score is outlined in their text.

Technical Aspects

The manual for the Mazes provides no information on reliability or validity and contains no description of norms. The manual does provide average times to complete each maze and average errors based on 58 subjects for Maze A and 65 subjects for Maze B.

Critique

The Foster Mazes were never intended to be a standardized measure of general mental ability. Individuals interested in using a measure of maze learning for personality and ability testing may wish to consider either the Porteus Mazes (1965) or the Maze subtest of the Wechsler Intelligence Scale for Children-Revised (WISC-R; Wechsler, 1974). In addition to general mental ability, both of these measures provide for the scoring of individuals on a dimension that might be called "planning ability."

The Foster Mazes have fairly limited utility. They may be considered for demonstration purposes in psychology classes or be of interest to psychologists interested in acquiring the "hardware" of early experimental psychology. Finally, they may be of interest to researchers interested in adult cognition and problem solving, but here several cautions are in order. Although the mazes are clearly at a difficulty level appropriate for adults, it is unfortunate that the subjects used to obtain averages listed in the manual are not described either in terms of age or sex. Furthermore, in terms of the averages provided, Maze B appears more difficult than Maze A, and the mazes, therefore, do not constitute a matched set. No rationale is provided for the differences in the difficulty level. Finally, the manual provides only very limited information on the mazes and contains several key errors. Individuals purchasing the mazes may wish to consult Foster and Tinker's (1929) description in their text for more detail.

References

Arthur, G. (1930). *A Point Scale of Performance Tests. Vol. I., Clinical manual.* New York: The Commonwealth Fund.

Foster, W., & Tinker, M. (1929). *Experiments in psychology (rev. ed.). New York: Henry Holt and Company.*

Porteus, S. (1924). *Guide to Porteus Maze Test* (Publication No. 25). Fineland, NJ: The Training School, Department of Research.

Porteus, S. (1965). *Porteus Maze Test: Fifty years' application*. Palo Alto, CA: Pacific Books.

Wechsler, D. (1974). *Manual for the Wechsler Intelligence Scale for Children-Revised.* Cleveland: The Psychological Corporation.

Steven A. Stahl, Ed.D.
Assistant Professor of Elementary Education and Reading, Western Illinois University, Macomb, Illinois.

GATES-MACGINITIE READING TESTS, SECOND EDITION

Walter H. MacGinitie with Joyce Kamons, Ruth L. Kowalski, Ruth K. MacGinitie, and Timothy McKay. Chicago, Illinois: The Riverside Publishing Co.

Introduction

The Gates-MacGinitie Reading Tests, Second Edition (Levels A-F) are a series of norm-referenced survey tests, suitable for the assessment of reading ability in Grades one through twelve. Each level of the test contains two subtests, vocabulary and comprehension. In addition, there is a test which may be administered at both the beginning and end of first grade (Level Basic R) as part of this series; however, the Basic R test will not be considered in this review.

The Gates-MacGinitie Reading Tests trace their ancestry back to two of the more widely used early reading survey tests, the Gates Silent Reading Test and the Gates Primary Reading Test, both published in 1926. These tests were continually revised until 1965, when Arthur Gates and Walter MacGinitie published their first edition. The second edition, completed in 1978, revised the tests' content as well as made the norms more current.

The test has six levels, Level A intended for the latter part of first grade, Level B intended for grade 2, Level C intended for Grade 3, Level D intended for Grades 4-6, Level E intended for Grades 7-9, and Level F intended for Grades 10-12. These grade levels are for reference only; there is provision for out-of-level testing with each of these levels. Levels A, B, C, and F have two alternate forms. Levels D and E have three alternate forms. Levels A, B, C, and D come with either machine-scorable or hand-scorable answer booklets. For Levels D, E, and F several different types of separate machine-scorable answer sheets are also an option. Teachers manuals are provided for each level and all technical information is in a separately available technical manual.

For all levels, the Vocabulary subtest is alloted 20 minutes of testing time and the Comprehension subtest 35 minutes. The tests are group administered, with scripted instructions and general guidelines provided in the teacher's manual. The tests are intended to be given by teachers. If the directions are followed specialized training is not necessary for test administration or scoring. Scoring templates for hand scoring are available for all forms of the test and a table of correct answers is given in the teacher's manual.

Vocabulary. For levels A and B the vocabulary subtests consist of 45 pictures, each paired with four graphically similar words. For example, for a picture of a mule, the words might be "male," "mole," "mule," and "mile."

The use of graphically contrasting distractor choices allows one to not only assess the child's general level of reading vocabulary, but also to analyze the child's use of decoding skills. A decoding skills analysis form is available for this purpose. This analysis may be used for identifying common problems in a classroom of students or in individual students.

Three cautions should be given here. First, a student may miss an item for many reasons. An item may be missed because the word is not in the student's meaning vocabulary, the student made a careless error, or the student has an inability to decode. Second, the Gates-MacGinitie is intended as a survey test. Individual decoding skills are not assessed with enough items to make a reliable diagnostic judgment. Hypotheses about a child's lack of a decoding skill should be followed up with an individually administered, reliable diagnostic phonics test. Third, the decoding analysis may not be applicable for Spanish-influenced or other bilingual students. The teacher's manual gives suggestions for follow-up with these students.

For levels C through F, the vocabulary subtests consist of 45 target words with either four or five choices. The correct answer is a synonym for the target word and the others are distractors. At these levels, the emphasis has shifted from decoding words probably known in speech to understanding the meanings of words.

Comprehension. As on the vocabulary subtests, Forms A and B use a pictorial format to measure comprehension. Here the student is presented with a "story," ranging in length from one sentence to a short paragraph, and told to indicate which of four pictures the story describes. For example, for a sentence, "Here are some numbers," the choices might be one number, several letters, several numbers, and several words.

For Levels C through F, the student is presented between 14 and 22 short paragraphs, each followed by two, three or four multiple-choice questions. The paragraphs are generally three to five sentences in length, covering varied subject matter. On each level, paragraphs are of varied difficulty. Britton and Lumpkin (1982) found the readabilities of these passages varied between forms of the same test. For example, they found readabilities of between fifth and tenth grade on Level E, intended for grades 7-9, although the majority of the readabilities were within the target grade levels. They did not, however, find that the passages necessarily increased in difficulty within each form.

Care has been taken to ensure that the subject matter content is not only varied but also reflects typical subject matter used in the target grades. The test developers have classified comprehension passages into four subject matter areas—narrative-descriptive, social sciences, natural sciences, and the arts—and provided percentages at different grade levels. Eighty-five percent of the passages are narrative-descriptive at Level A, gradually diminishing to 32.5% on Level F. The percentages of the other three categories correspondingly increase. The decrease of importance of narrative materials and increase in importance of content area materials corresponds to trends in reading over the school years. Similarly, the percentage of questions that the developers rated as "literal" decreases from approximately 90% on Level A to approximately 55% on Level F, with a corresponding increase in "inferential" questions. Literal questions are defined here as questions whose answer is explicitly stated in the passage while inferential questions ask the student to summarize, use inductive or deductive reasoning, infer the views of a character or author, or otherwise draw unstated inferences based on the reading of the passage. The change in emphasis is also consistent with current school practices.

Practical Applications/Uses

As reading survey tests, the Gates-MacGinitie Reading Tests are intended to compare the reading abilities of both individual children and groups of children with a norming population. A survey test may be used by a teacher or principal to identify children as either extermely below or above grade level and in need of further individual testing, or for consideration for Chapter I remedial reading or gifted children services. When used as group-administered tests, these tests should be used as a screening device to identify children in further need of individual testing. The results can also be used by principals, superintendents, and others to evaluate the performance of entire classes, schools, or districts in relation to the norming population. These tests may also be used in a clinical or remedial reading setting, as one measure among many different reading tests. The provisions for out-of-level testing and the extended scale norms make the Gates-MacGinitie Reading Tests especially useful in clinical settings.

For the teacher or principal, the Gates-MacGinitie gives a wide range of scores that would be useful for comparing children both within a school and to the norming population. Grade equivalent scores, or the grade level for which each raw score was the median raw score, are provided. Grade equivalent scores can be highly misleading; therefore, their use is generally not recommended (Baumann & Stevenson, 1982; International Reading Association, 1982). Percentile scores, or scores which compare a student's score with the percent of children in the norming population scoring below it, are also given. The distances between both grade equivalent and percentile rank scores are not equal and these scores shoud not be averaged (Harris & Sipay, 1985). Normal Curve Equivalent (NCE) scores, which are based on percentile ranks but converted into an equal interval scale, can be averaged and are probably the most useful in making stable comparisons among children in a way that is interpretable by laymen. Stanine scores, which divide the achievement continuum into nine segments, are somewhat broader and are useful in making rough judgments of skill level. Extended Scale Scores (ESS) are also provided. These scores provide a single continuous equal unit scale stretching between levels and over the school years, and allow for the evaluation of a child's or group's progress over long periods of time.

All of these scores can be derived easily by hand scoring and are explained clearly in the teacher's manual. With machine scoring, these scores can be supplemented with a stanine band display (indicating graphically whether there is a significant difference between vocabulary and comprehension scores), a computer-generated narrative description of each child's results, local norms, building and school system averages, etc. These scoring services are typical with tests in the Gates-MacGinitie's class. For Chapter I programs, the publisher's scoring service will also provide summaries of pretest-posttest data, including statistical comparisons.

Another useful feature of the Gates-MacGinitie is the provision for out-of-level norms. Out-of-level norms are used to evaluate children whose achievement is either very much above or below their grade placement. Multi-level tests such as the Gates-MacGinitie tend to be more accurate at the middle of their range, because at the extremes one or two answers guessed correctly or incorrectly have greater score influence. Roberts (1978) indicates that a test is most reliable when the mean raw score of a group is equal to or above one-third and less than three-fourths of the maximum. Smith, Johns, Ganschow, and Masztal (1983), for example, found that out-of-level testing produced more reliable test scores for fourth and fifth grade remedial readers, as did Smith and Johns (1984). However, Smith and Johns also found no significant differences in derived scores (NCEs, ESSs, Grade Equivalents) between out-of-level and on-level testing for fourth- and fifth-grade below average readers.

Some out-of-level norms are provided in the teacher's manual for each level. Others are provided in a separately purchased out-of-level norms booklet. In group administration, out-of-level testing is facilitated by common sample items for Levels A and B and for Levels D, E, and F, so that the same directions can be given to students in the same class using different levels.

Even with the provisions for clinical and remedial uses, tests analogous to the Gates-MacGinitie are best used for management and policy purposes, not for diagnosis. The purpose of these tests are to give a broad perspective of the reading achievement of individuals and groups in two general areas. The tests do not indicate what skills an individual knows or does not know, as a diagnostic test might. This is true even with the decoding skills analysis on Levels A and B. For this analysis, there are too few items measuring each skill area to achieve a reliable individual diagnosis. The information from this analysis, however, can be combined with information for other sources to strengthen individual diagnoses. The information from this analysis could also be used for class planning.

For other levels, MacGinitie et al. do not provide information that would allow these tests to be used for such skill analysis. For example, although the comprehension tests were developed to reflect certain percentages of literal and inferential questions at each grade level, these questions are not identified in the materials available. This means that in order to differentiate performance on these two types of questions, the teacher must classify the questions independently. These classifications may or may not be reliable. If this type of differentiation is important, it is recommended that a test which breaks questions down this way be given instead.

It is possible to determine whether students differ substantially in their vocabulary and comprehension abilities. It is recommended that a difference of at least two stanines represents an important difference. On most forms, however, the correlations between vocabulary and comprehension are high: only a few are below .80. Therefore, it is likely that few children will show meaningful differences between these two abilities. Duffelmeyer (1980) found 83% of the ninth graders and 73% of the twelfth graders he tested had vocabulary and comprehension scores within one stanine of each other.

The tests, then, are best suited for three purposes—communication, management, and planning. For communication of a child's achievement level, the types of information provided by the test developers seems appropriate, especially the narrative reports provided by the scoring service.

For management, the test can be used to provide rough groupings of children in a class by achievement level or screen out children who are in need of individual attention. Horowitz, Samuels, and McGue (1981), however, classified sixth-grade students as either above or below grade level readers on four measures: the Gates-MacGinitie, teacher judgment, and two experimentor-developed measures of word recognition. They found that 40% of their subjects shifted from good to poor reader categories depending on the criteria used. However, the Gates-MacGinitie showed the highest correlation with their independent measure of comprehension. Because of the error inherent in any achievement test score, it is recommended that multiple criteria be used in any classification decision.

The provision for out-of-level testing has allowed the Gates-MacGinitie to be used to determine eligibility for remedial reading in Navy training programs. Jones and Armitage (1984) found that Levels D, E, and F used out-of-grade level gave more accurate results for their recruits than two tests normed on adults. Brown and Kincaid (1982) discuss cutoff scores so that the Armed Services Vocational Aptitude Battery could be used to assign recruits to an appropriate level.

For planning, this test may be used to compare individuals and classes to national norms and thus evaluate the effectiveness of developmental and remedial instruction. For developmental programs, comparisons of mean NCE scores at different grade levels may indicate strengths or weaknesses in the instruction of different skill areas. For example, an overall weakness in vocabulary scores at sixth grade may indicate the need to improve instruction in vocabulary at that or earlier levels. For these purposes, the NCE scores are the most appropriate. Grade equivalents and percentiles, because they are not based on equal interval scales, cannot be averaged. The decoding skills analysis can also be used for curriculum planning, as discussed above, as can Extended Scale Scores which may allow a superintendent to compare the average growth in reading over a period of time with that normally expected.

These tests, however, provide only general levels in the two areas tested. Lack of skill differentiation may mask weaknesses in certain reading programs. For example, some programs may overstress answering of literal, detail-type questions. Upper-grade children in these programs may do worse in inferential-type questions, and consequently on this test, but the information provided would not allow one to diagnose the problem.

For remedial programs, the Gates-MacGinitie is especially useful for program evaluation because of the out-of-level testing provision and the Extended Scale Scores that allow pretesting on one level and posttesting on another. The ESSs are useful in tracking the progress of individual children over the course of several years in a program. They are also beneficial in evaluating the progress of children whose progress indicates that they may have reached the ceiling of the test level used as a pretest. Gains of one or two years in a clinical program are not unheard of, but large gains may push a child out of the range of the level used as a pretest.

ESSs allow the accurate evaluation of such children.

As noted previously, the scoring service also provides data analysis similar to that required by most Chapter I evaluations.

These recommendations, however, should be tempered by judgments about the test's validity for individual curricula, as discussed below.

Technical Aspects

The Gates-MacGinitie Reading Tests were normed on approximately 70,000 students in Grades 1-12 from October 1976 to May 1977. An additional 30,000 students were used in equating studies, to establish alternate form equivalence, concurrent validity, equating of levels, and equating of the second edition with the first edition. These students were drawn from public and parochial schools in a stratified random sample, with region, family income level, race, and parents' education used as sampling criteria. The sample was weighted to be representative of the school age population as of the 1972 census.

Reliability, or the degree of consistency of the results of the test, was measured three ways. Internal consistency was measured using Kuder-Richardson Formula 20. All of these coefficients were above .88 with the majority being above .90. Alternate form reliability, or the correlations between different forms, was also high, with the majority of the correlations above .90, but a few as low as .84.

The Standard Error of Measurement, a measurement of the probable error involved in a single score, was also reported in terms of Normal Curve Equivalent scores. These range from 5.2 to 9.1. A standard error of measurement of 9.1 (obtained on Level F for tenth graders) indicates that the chances are two to one that the "true" score of a student receiving an NCE of 50 would range from 41 to 59. While an NCE of 50 in October of tenth grade is equal to a grade equivalent of 10.1, an NCE of 41 is equivalent to a grade of 8.1 and an NCE of 59 is equivalent to a grade of 11.7. This is a potentially wide range, and cautions should be taken in comparing children with relatively close scores.

Although the alternate form correlations are adequate for a test such as this, correlations only mean that children who do well on one form will do well on another form and children who do poorly on one form will do poorly on another. One form may be generally easier or more difficult than another and the correlation between the two will still be high. Johns (1984) reports that this may be the case with Level E, Forms 1 and 3. He gave the comprehension subtests from these forms to 69 seventh graders and 57 eighth graders one week apart. He did not find significant differences between the performance of the seventh graders, but found Form 3 to produce significantly lower scores than Form 1 with the eighth graders on all derived scores except the grade equivalents. Britton and Lumpkin's (1982) readability analysis indicated differences between forms of the same levels which might affect difficulty. If the Gates-MacGinitie is used for group evaluation purposes, it might be worthwhile to counterbalance form use or take other precautions to ensure that different form difficulty does not produce spurious gains.

The only validity data provided in the technical manual is for concurrent validity, i.e., the correlation between performance on the Gates-MacGinitie and the Metropolitan Achievement Test (MAT). Concurrent correlations are presented between Levels D and E and corresponding subtests of the MAT. These are between 0.79 and 0.92, with the higher correlations for total test scores. These are acceptable, but it is disappointing that concurrent correlation coefficients are not presented for other levels. In a study by Hoge and Butcher (1984), the Gates-MacGinitie does appear to correlate well with teacher's judgment of pupil achievement in grades 3-8 ($R^2 = 0.72$). Correlations between the Gates-MacGinitie Levels D and E and scores on the Cognitive Abilities Test, a group-administered aptitude test, are said in the technical manual to range from 0.73 to 0.85. These are not evidence of concurrent validity since the two tests are intended to measure different abilities.

Critique

The Gates-MacGinitie Reading Tests have several features which distinguish them from other tests in their class—the out-of-level norms, the Extended Scale Scores, the Decoding Skills Analysis—as well as features common to other similar tests, such as high reliability, ease of scoring and the availability of a number of scoring options, and a well-written teacher's manual. These features make the Gates-MacGinitie especially desirable for use in remedial programs as well as suitable for use as survey tests in developmental programs.

There is very little evidence avilable about the concurrent validity of the Gates-MacGinitie, but two other types of validity, curricular and construct validity, are probably more important in evaluating tests of this type. Curricular validity is the degree to which a test is congruent with the curriculum it is intended to evaluate. For example, Jenkins and Pany (1978) found that children who would have mastered all of the first- and second-grade words in their reading series would have received vastly different scores on different tests. Similarly, gains in reading scores attributable to a district changing to a test more aligned to its curriculum are not uncommon. Whether this test is appropriate for a particular curriculum must be decided by the individual user.

Construct validity is the degree to which a test measures the construct it is intended to; in this case, reading comprehension and vocabulary. Evaluation of construct validity means evaluating how close the criterion task is to the construct the task represents. In this regard, criticisms of the Gates-MacGinitie are common to other tests in its class, but worth repeating here.

For the vocabulary subtests, there are different concerns for the primary and intermediate levels. For Levels A and B, the vocabulary subtests appear to largely measure decoding ability. In these grades, reading vocabulary involves both recognition of sight words and decoding unfamiliar or regular words. Therefore, the tests may not offer a complete coverage of word recognition skills in first and second grades. Further, these tests may mismeasure progress in classes where teachers hold a different philosophy of beginning reading.

For Levels D, E, and F, where children's meaning vocabulary rather than word recognition skills are assessed, a different problem may arise. Research in vocabulary indicates that children know different numbers of words in isolation than in context (Anderson & Freebody, 1981; Graves, 1980). The synonym match format used here measures only knowledge of definitions. While the total number of words children know in isolation and in context are probably correlated, it is possible for a child to have an extensive vocabulary of words in context but a meager knowledge of definitions. This child's score would not reflect his good functional vocabulary knowledge.

For the comprehension tests, two questions have been raised regarding the construct validity of tests such as these. One question is "How many of the questions can be answered without reading the passage?" A number of test questions have been found to be relatively passage independent, that is they can be answered without reference to the passage itself. In his review of the Gates-MacGinitie, Jongsma (1980) judged that nearly all of the questions required reading of the passage. This has been this reviewer's impression as well. Hill and Larsen (1983), who used interviews and probe tasks to analyze in detail the cognitive processes used by majority and minority children in answering questions similar to those on Level C, found that children's answers reflected a variety of cognitive and ethnocultural influences, in addition to their comprehension of the passages.

The second question about construct validity is how does the reading task used here relate to the type of reading a student does ordinarily in school or at home. The Gates-MacGinitie measures comprehension using short passages, shorter than most tests of this type in the upper grades. Using a large number of short passages, as opposed to a few longer passages, may reduce the chance that a student gets a particularly high or low score because of knowledge of one of the passage topics (Johnston, 1983). Instead, the comprehension tests require knowledge about a number of different knowledge domains. However, the short paragraph format used here may be very different from the student's ordinary reading demands. A child may do well on short paragraphs such as these, but be unable to comprehend chapter length material. A greater danger would be for a school to increase the reading of short, isolated paragraphs in preparation for the test, and neglect "real," functional reading. Because of the brevity of the passages, the Gates-MacGinitie is especially subject to this criticism.

The Gates-MacGinitie has been constructed so that nearly every student will finish the test in the alloted time. This separates the factors of power and speed, which have often been confounded in group-administered tests. However, the authors have dropped the Speed and Accuracy subtests of the first edition, not allowing a rate vs. power comparison. This may be very important, especially in the middle grades, where automaticity of word recognition may be as important for the development of comprehension skills as accuracy (Perfetti & Lesgold, 1979). At these grade levels, it is not atypical to find a number of poor readers who lack automatic word recognition skills. These children often show problems in comprehension, especially in the completion of longer assignments typical at that level, because their slow word recognition forms a "bottleneck" interfering with their ability to comprehend. The combination of the generous time limits and the short passages may allow "plodders" to score higher on the Gates-MacGinitie than they would perform in the classroom.

These concerns do not diminish the usefulness of the Gates-MacGinitie. It is a reliable instrument that does the many things it is designed to do well. It may be impossible for a single test to measure reading in a way that would approximate everyday reading skill and still provide the convenience of machine scoring and group administration. Every test of this type is a compromise between these two goals. Provided that the user is aware of its limits, the Gates-MacGinitie can be highly recommended for school and clinic use.

References

This list includes text citations as well as suggested additional reading.

Anderson, R. C., & Freebody, P. (1981). Vocabulary knowledge. In J. T. Guthrie (Ed.), *Comprehension and teaching: Research reviews* (pp. 77-117). Newark, DE: International Reading Association.

Baumann, J. F., & Stevenson, J. A. (1982). Understanding standardized reading achievement test scores. *The Reading Teacher, 35*, 648-654.

Britton, G., & Lumpkin, M. (1982). Readability of the Gates-MacGinitie Reading Tests: Cautions for test givers, test takers, and test makers. *Reading Psychology, 3*, 199-209.

Brown, C. J., & Kincaid, J. P. (1982). Use of the ASVAB for assignment of Gates-MacGinitie Reading Test levels: Focus on the trained person. (ERIC Document Reproduction Service No. ED 223 671).

Duffelmeyer, F. A. (1980). A comparison of reading test results in grades nine and twelve. *Journal of Reading, 23*, 606-608.

Graves, M. F. (1980, April). *A quantitative and qualitative study of students' vocabularies.* Paper presented at the annual meeting, American Educational Research Association, Boston, MA.

Harris, A. J., & Sipay, E. R. (1985). *How to increase reading ability* (8th ed.). New York: Longman.

Hill, C., & Larsen, E. (1983). *What reading tests call for and what children do.* (ERIC Document Reproduction Service No. ED 238 904).

Hoge, R. D., & Butcher, R. (1984). Analysis of teacher judgments of pupil achievement levels. *Journal of Educational Psychology, 76*, 777-781.

Horowitz, R., Samuels, S. J., & McGue, M. (1981). *Strategies for classifying readers: Effects on prose processing findings.* Paper presented at the annual meeting, American Educational Research Association, Los Angeles, CA. (ERIC Document Reproduction Service ED 211 948).

International Reading Association (1982). Misuse of grade equivalents. *The Reading Teacher, 35*, 464.

Jenkins, J. R., & Pany, D. (1978). Curriculum biases in reading achievement tests. *Journal of Reading Behavior, 10*, 345-357.

Johns, J. L. (1984). Equivalence of Forms 1 and 3, Form E, Gates-MacGinitie Reading Tests. *Journal of Reading, 28*, 48-51.

Johnston, P. (1983). *Reading comprehension assessment.* Newark, DE: International Reading Association.

Jones, P. L., & Armitage, B. J. (1984). *A comparison of three reading tests for determining reading grade level of Navy recruits.* Paper presented at the annual meeting, Mid-South Educational Research Association, New Orleans. (ERIC Document Reproduction Service ED 249 481).

Jongsma, E. (1980). Review of the Gates-MacGinitie Reading Tests (2nd ed.). *Journal of Reading, 23*, 340-345.

MacGinitie, W. H., Kamons, J., Kowalski, R. L., MacGinitie, R., & McKay, T. (1978). *The Gates-MacGinitie Reading Tests, Levels A-F* (2nd ed.). Chicago: The Riverside Publishing Co.

MacGinitie, W. H., Kamons, J., Kowalski, R. L., MacGinitie, R., & McKay, T. (1978). *The Gates-MacGinitie Reading Tests, Levels A-F (2nd ed.): Teacher's manual.* Chicago: The Riverside Publishing Co.

MacGinitie, W. H., Kamons, J., Kowalski, R. L., MacGinitie, R., & McKay, T. (1978). *The Gates-MacGinitie Reading Tests, Levels A-F (2nd ed.): Technical manual.* Chicago: The Riverside Publishing Co.

Perfetti, C. A., & Lesgold, A. M. (1979). Coding and comprehension in skilled reading and implications for reading instruction. In L. B. Resnick & P. A. Weaver (Eds.), *Theory and practice of early reading,* vol. 1 (pp. 57-84). Hillsdale, NJ: Erlbaum.

Roberts, S. J. (1978). *Test floor and ceiling effects. ESEA Title I evaluation and reporting system.* (ERIC Document Reproduction Service ED 185 106).

Smith, L. L., & Johns, J. L. (1984). A study of the effects of out-of-level testing with poor readers in the intermediate grades. *Reading Psychology, 5,* 139-143.

Smith, L. L., Johns, J. L., Ganschow, L., & Masztal, N. B. (1983). Using grade level vs. out-of-level reading tests with remedial students. *The Reading Teacher, 36,* 550-553.

Sposato, S. E. (1979). *A comparison of oral reading and silent reading on a standardized reading achievement test.* Unpublished master's thesis, Kean College of New Jersey, Union, NJ. (ERIC Document Reproduction Service ED 169 513).

Barbara B. Schoenfeldt, Ph.D.
Assistant Professor of Education, Sul Ross State University, Uvalde Study Center, Uvalde, Texas

GILMORE ORAL READING TEST

John V. Gilmore and Eunice C. Gilmore. Cleveland, Ohio: The Psychological Corporation.

Introduction

The Gilmore Oral Reading Test (GORT) is a short, individually administered test of oral reading for use with students in Grades 1 to 8. It has two forms (C and D) which are described as equivalent and allow for pre- and post-test evaluation, although at the end of the manual there is information that the differences in the distribution of raw scores on the two forms is a reflection of differences in difficulty between the forms. The test consists of a series of ten graded paragraphs, each of which has five comprehension questions.

The GORT is intended to provide diagnostic information in three areas: accuracy of oral reading, oral comprehension, and rate of reading. Its primary purpose is to "provide a means of analyzing the oral reading performance of individuals and groups" in grades one through eight "so that subsequent instruction in both oral and silent reading can be adjusted more appropriately to individual and groups strengths and weaknesses" (Gilmore & Gilmore, 1968, p. 2). The GORT can be analyzed by studying the particular types of oral reading errors made by each subject on the paragraphs, or by comparing the individual's performance to a normative group in terms of accuracy, comprehension, or rate in words per minute. Raw scores for both oral reading accuracy and comprehension can also be converted to grade equivalents.

The GORT was authored by Dr. John V. Gilmore and Eunice C. Gilmore. Dr. J. Gilmore is Emeritus Professor of Psychology at Boston University's School of Education, where he has been on the faculty since 1945.

The original reading paragraphs, designated Forms A and B, were "constructed according to certain specifications which, in the judgment of the authors and in light of recent research, constitute desirable characteristics of an oral reading test" (Gilmore & Gilmore, 1968, p. 22). Forms C and D were developed in 1968 in the same fashion as the original forms. Form D is a revision of material contained in Form A but with new questions. Form C is made of entirely new material. The paragraphs in each form have a family theme that continues through all levels.

The paragraphs for Forms C and D were constructed to ensure a gradation of difficulty of the paragraphs. The three variables used to produce increased difficulty levels were vocabulary, sentence structure, and interest.

The difficulty level of the vocabulary was controlled by several means. Besides increasing the paragraph length for each higher level, three controls concerning the difficulty of the vocabulary were used. To determine which words to include several graded published word lists were consulted in writing the paragraphs. Difficulty was also regulated through controlling the number of multisyllable words included per paragraph (with a gradual introduction of words with three or more syllables). Thirdly, consideration was also given to the concreteness or abstractness of the words used, with more abstract words appearing on higher levels.

The variable of sentence structure was controlled by the factors of increasing sentence length and percent of complex sentences present in each paragraph. An attempt was also made to control interest. This was done by including materials in the paragraphs that would be of interest to, and within the experiences of, pupils at the various grade levels covered by the test.

It was assumed that comprehension of the GORT paragraphs would become progressively more difficult since the material was carefully graded to be more difficult orally. Comprehension for each paragraph is assessed by five questions which relate to "some item mentioned in the paragraph" (Gilmore & Gilmore, 1968, p. 24). Most of the items require directly stated information (literal level comprehension) or very low level inferences (questions with obvious correct or best choice answers).

The GORT test materials include the reading paragraphs for both forms contained in a spiral-bound booklet, two forms of the record blanks, and a test manual which includes the directions for administering and scoring the GORT.

The record blanks are color coded to easily distinguish the two forms. Each is a 12-page booklet about 5½" x 8½" in size. On the front there is a section for recording identifying data and on the back there is a test summary section to record information as to scores on oral reading accuracy, comprehension, and rate. There is also a section to record information regarding stanine, grade equivalent, and rating, as well as a section for comments. Inside the record blank each page contains a copy of the selection, the five comprehension questions regarding the paragraph, and a section to record the number of errors made under any of eight different categories (substitutions, mispronunciations, words pronounced by the examiner, disregard of punctuation, insertions, hesitations, repetitions, and omissions).

A special edition of the GORT is available for the visually handicapped and may be obtained from the American Printing House for the Blind, 1839 Frankfort Avenue, Louisville, KY 40206.

The examiner's role is described in detail in the manual. A stopwatch is required to ensure the accuracy of the reading rate. The examiner is to establish rapport with the student, and then fill out the identifying data on the front page of the record blank. The examiner then reads a paragraph from the manual to the student to introduce the test as a group of stories that will be about one family. This paragraph also informs the subject that there will be questions asked after the oral reading.

Suggestions are given to the examiner to help decide on which level to begin testing. The first step in the examination is to establish a basal level. The basal level is that level at which the student makes no more than two oral reading errors. Neither the comprehension score nor rate is considered. Once the basal level is established the examiner continues presenting the paragraphs in numerical order until the ceiling level is reached (the student makes ten or more errors).

As the pupil reads, the examiner is to record each error on the record blank, and keep track of the amount of time required to read the paragraph. Eight different kinds of errors are to be marked on the paragraph.

Comprehension questions are asked by the examiner as soon as the pupil has finished a paragraph. The student may not refer back to the paragraph to find the answer. Only an abbreviated comprehension answer key is provided in the manual since in most cases the correct answers to the comprehension questions are clearly indicated in the paragraphs.

The GORT is appropriate for school-age children reading on, at least, the first-grade level to approximately the eighth-grade level. Since there is only one first-grade level paragraph the GORT provides little opportunity for discriminating among students reading below the first reader level.

Practical Applications/Uses

The GORT is designed to analyze the oral reading performance of students. It is reasoned that since oral reading "well taught" has certain values or benefits a "continuous analysis of oral reading performance by a well-established oral reading test is of great aid in any reading program" (Gilmore & Gilmore, 1968, p. 2). Other assumptions made by Gilmore such as "it is reasonable to assume that if one can read well orally he can read well silently" (Gilmore & Gilmore, p. 2) are quite doubtful for many students with poor English background or for those who have been taught to read with an overly strong phonics background.

While the GORT was designed to analyze oral reading errors, the manual suggests it could also be used to determine instructional level for classroom placement. The limited sample of reading on each grade level and the inadequate comprehension check, however, makes this procedure questionable. As a measure of oral reading errors, the GORT is appropriate for use in the regular classroom, remedial reading class, or in reading clinics.

The authors recommend that testing be done on an individual basis in a quiet room as free from distractions as possible and that no other persons be present. In order to mark all errors with the correct notations while the student is reading, the examiner needs to have a great deal of experience in oral reading testing. Because of this requirement the GORT would seem to have limited value for other than experienced reading teachers and clinicians.

The administration directions in the manual are quite clear. Directions are given as to where to begin and stop testing, what mistakes are considered errors, recording of the errors, and recording the time. There is also a partial key for scoring the comprehension questions. The marking symbols to be employed and the kinds of oral reading errors to be marked are fairly traditional as compared to other oral reading tests. Disregard of Punctuation, Hesitations, and Self-corrections are counted as errors on the GORT, however, even though they are not usually counted as oral errors on other oral reading tests. While reading rate is measured, the time does not influence the oral reading Accuracy Score but is instead evaluated on a separate scale.

Once the test is completed an experienced examiner should take only a few minutes to complete the scoring. All scoring must be done by hand. The first step of scoring involves computing an oral reading Accuracy Score for each paragraph. The score is 10 minus the number of errors made on each paragraph. The highest possible score for any paragraph is thus a 10. In addition, full credit is also given for each unread paragraph below the pupil's basal level. The assumption is made that the pupil would have read those paragraphs without error. The Accuracy Score for the test is the sum of all the oral reading accuracy scores (either obtained or credited).

The Comprehension Score is computed by giving one point for each of the five questions correctly answered. Additional points are also given for levels that have not been read. In the paragraph immediately below the pupil's basal level, credit is given for answering correctly one more question than in the basal or preceding paragraph and so on. Thus, if on the basal level the student had only gotten three questions correct, credit is given for four questions on the level below that, and five questions credit for each lower level. The student may also receive credit for questions not asked from paragraphs above the ceiling level. In the paragraph immediately above the ceiling level, credit is given for answering correctly one less question than was answered on the ceiling level. On each higher level credit is given for one less question on each level until the number reaches zero. The credited points above the ceiling level are based on the questionable assumption that the student would be able to understand (answer questions correctly about) paragraphs that he could not read accurately aloud. The Comprehension Score is the sum of all entries in the "number right or credited" column.

The Rate Score is computed by totaling the time required to complete each paragraph read (except the ceiling paragraph), and dividing this sum by the total number of words in all the paragraphs read (except the ceiling paragraph).

Interpretation of scores on the GORT may be either by "detailed" individual or group "analysis of oral reading ability" (Gilmore & Gilmore, 1968, p. 15), or through the use of norms that permit comparison of the subject to the normative group. All interpretations via the norms are made using the objective data; however, the testing situation does allow one to observe other behaviors that may have diagnostic value.

The analysis of individual or group performance may be used to reveal pupil and class strengths and weaknesses which can then be used to determine appropriate remediation. Some of the suggestions for this analysis made in the manual include determining which particular kinds of oral errors the student has made and whether the predominant oral errors made may have changed in relation to the difficulty level of the paragraph being read. Suggestions for analyzing the Comprehension and Rate scores include looking at the consistency of number of errors or of the rate as the subject attempted more difficult paragraphs.

The derived performance ratings from each area are also interpretable in terms of the standardization norms. The Accuracy and Comprehension performance raw scores, listed separately by form, may be classified as being on the poor, below average, average, above average, or superior level for each of the eight grade levels. These classifications may also be interpreted as stanines or percentiles. The raw scores for both Accuracy and Comprehension are also interpreted as Grade Equivalents.

The Rate raw scores are also interpretable in terms of performance rating. The lowest quarter of the raw scores for each grade level were given a rating of "slow," the middle 50% "average," and the top quarter "fast" for each of the eight grade levels.

Technical Aspects

The only validity information available for the GORT is from Form A. The present forms are considered to be quite similar, however, and Form D was based rather directly on Form A. The validity data consisted of comparisons of scores on the GORT Form A with those obtained from other established oral reading tests. Correlations with the Accuracy Scores tended to be fairly high (in the .73 to .90 range), while the Rate and Comprehension correlations tended to be much lower (most around the .45 level).

Reliability was assessed using alternate form reliability to yield a measure of the stability of the test scores. Fifty-one third-graders and 55 sixth-graders were given first Form C and then Form D two weeks later. The Accuracy score reliabilities of the third- and sixth-graders in the sample were acceptable (.94 and .84), but the comprehension and rate reliabilities fall below accepted standards (.54 to .70).

The standardization data for Forms C and D were collected in six school systems in various parts of the United States. The 4,455 normative subjects, in Grades 1 through 8, were selected to include cases from a variety of socioeconomic backgrounds. The students were tested near the end of the school year. This could be a problem when using the GORT since diagnostic testing is frequently done at the beginning of the school year.

The two forms were administered randomly within each grade and scored by fifteen examiners. Each student was also given the paragraph meaning subtest of the Stanford Achievement Test. Analysis of the students' scores on the Stanford indicated that the groups given Forms C and D were equal in reading ability. Therefore, it was concluded that the differences found between the two forms (C tends to be more difficult) were reflections of true differences in difficulty between the forms.

Critique

Reviewers (see Harris, 1972; Smith, 1972; and Stafford, 1978) have tended to offer similar criticisms of the GORT. These range from the minor problem that the middle-class nature of the stories may be more appropriate for non-disadvantaged children than for the disadvantaged to more serious questions as to some of the major assumptions used to construct the GORT.

The GORT's Comprehension Score not only has poor reliability but also poor content validity for several reasons. First, it is based on oral reading but the basic assumption of the GORT that one can test a "silent reading act (comprehension) with a test of oral skill (fluency, etc.) is extremely doubtful" (Smith, 1972, p. 1147). Second, the items used to measure it are almost entirely from one area of reading comprehension (literal level, detail questions), and thus the GORT Comprehension Score turns out to be more a measure of a student's memory of detail than of comprehension. The method used for computing the Comprehension Score is also questionable. Students are given credit for answering questions beyond the level at which oral testing is concluded based on the assumption that all students would have greater skills in comprehension then in oral accuracy.

The Rate Score also has questionable reliability and content validity. Since the rate score is not independent of accuracy or even comprehension (students reading inaccurately would also tend to be reading at a slower rate), a substantial correlation between Rate and Accuracy would be expected. But "correlations among the three scores are not given in the manual (a strange omission)" (Harris, 1972, p. 1147). Eliminating timing and the rate score, in fact, would not only simplify administration, but would cause "little loss in useful information" (Harris, 1972, p. 1147).

There are also concerns regarding the oral reading Accuracy Score of the GORT. Questions include the selection of which oral errors are counted. For instance, even if a student self-corrects an error it is still counted, despite the fact that most educators would consider such self-correction to be a positive sign indicating that the student was monitoring his oral reading for comprehension. Also, "in light of recent psycholinguistic research, it is difficult to conceive that each of these error categories could be of equal weight" (Stafford, 1975, p. 1316), but no weights are used on the GORT. As with any oral reading test, there is also the problem that "even after considerable training and practice teachers tend to record inaccurately a large percentage of the errors," but the manual fails "to describe the reliability with which the various errors can be coded" (Stafford, 1975, p. 1316).

While a user should question certain assumptions and practices of the GORT, the test does have certain attributes which make it useful. It is fairly easy and quick to administer and it has a comprehensive manual. Also, it is among the best standardized tests of accuracy in oral reading of meaningful material. The GORT also has value as an oral reading sample that can be analyzed using nonstandardized evaluations. For instance, an analysis of the types of oral errors made by the student could allow the teacher to concentrate on instruction of the student's points of greatest interest. In addition, if the student were to have oral reading errors that change the meaning of the text, it may be an indication that the student is not reading for meaning. Another advantage is that the GORT provides two fairly equivalent forms which may be useful for research purposes or, as previously stated, for pre- and post-testing.

Those who use the GORT, however, need to keep its limitations in mind. The reliabilities and validities of the Comprehension and Rate Scores are questionable and these scores have little value. Since it is difficult to code in all the correct markings on oral reading tests a lot of practice is required for examiners before one can feel comfortable that the score obtained is correct. Also, because the Accuracy Score is based on more types of errors than are typically counted on other standardized or informal oral reading tests, the obtained score may be lower then expected. For this reason, and since the comprehension measure on the GORT is questionable, it would be inadvisable to use a GORT score for classroom reading material placement.

References

Gilmore. J. V., & Gilmore, E. C. (1968). *The Gilmore Oral Reading Test manual.* New York: Harcourt Brace Jovanovich, Inc.

Harris, A. J. (1972). Review of Gilmore Oral Reading Test. In O. K. Buros (Ed.), *The seventh mental measurements yearbook* (pp. 1146-1147). Highland Park, NJ: The Gryphon Press.

Smith, K. J. (1972). Review of Gilmore Oral Reading Test. In O. K. Buros (Ed.), *The seventh mental measurements yearbook* (pp. 1147-1148). Highland Park, NJ: The Gryphon Press.

Stafford, J. (1978). Review of Gilmore Oral Reading Test. In O. K. Buros (Ed.), *The eighth mental measurements yearbook* (pp. 1315-1316). Highland Park, NJ: The Gryphon Press.

Cindy P. Loser, Ph.D., CCC-A
Assistant Professor of Speech, Speech and Hearing Clinic, Butler University, Indianapolis, Indiana.

GOLDMAN-FRISTOE-WOODCOCK AUDITORY SKILLS TEST BATTERY

Ronald Goldman, Madalyne Fristoe, and Richard W. Woodcock. Circle Pines, Minnesota: American Guidance Service.

Introduction

The Goldman-Fristoe-Woodcock Auditory Skills Test Battery (G-F-W Battery) by Ronald Goldman, Madalyne Fristoe, and Richard Woodcock was published by the American Guidance Service, Inc., in 1976. The text expands on the Goldman-Fristoe-Woodcock Test of Auditory Discrimination (Goldman, Fristoe, & Woodcock, 1970), a test designed to make brief measures of auditory discrimination and attention. The G-F-W Battery increased the number of auditory skills measured from two to twelve. The areas measured include selective attention, discrimination, memory for content, memory for sequence, sound recognition, sound mimicry, sound analysis, sound-symbol association, reading of symbols, spelling of sounds, recognition memory and sound blending. According to the technical manual (Woodcock, 1976), which provides normative data for subjects aged 3-80 years, "the intent of the G-F-W Battery is to identify children or adults who are deficient in auditory skills and to describe these deficiencies" (p. 1). The G-F-W Battery was designed for use by special educators, reading specialists, school psychologists, and speech and hearing clinicians.

Ronald Goldman, Ph.D., and Madalyne Fristoe, Ph.D., hold Certificates of Clinical Competence in Speech-Language Pathology from the American Speech, Language and Hearing Association. Dr. Goldman has been honored as a Fellow of the American Speech, Language and Hearing Association in recognition of distinction in one of three areas: 1) original contributions to the field; 2) distinguished educational, professional, or administrative activity; and/or 3) outstanding service to the association. Dr. Fristoe is Associate Professor of Speech Pathology at Purdue University. Richard Woodcock, Ed.D., is the director of Measurement/Learning/Consultants.

The authors developed the G-F-W Battery to measure auditory perception. Auditory perception is the cluster of abilities found on a continuum between auditory acuity and auditory comprehension, two auditory functions for which extensive, well-established tests are available. According to Woodcock (1976, p. 5), six criteria were used to develop the G-F-W Battery:

1. The battery should assess a broad spectrum of skills, ranging from simple auditory attention and discrimination to the complex association of sounds with symbols in written language.

2. The tests should be designed primarily for clinical use, to provide fine discriminations among subjects whose performance is deficient for their ages.
3. The battery should provide detailed diagnostic information in at least two areas of auditory skills: speech-sound discrimination and knowledge of grapheme-to-phoneme correspondence.
4. The tests should be designed to minimize the effects of irrelevant subject characteristics.
5. The procedures for test administration should be easy to learn.
6. The test procedures and materials should be designed to maximize the likelihood of correct, standardized presentation.

The development of the battery involved preparing a set of specifications for the whole battery and each individual test, developing an item pool for each test, conducting an item analysis, and selecting the final test content. For tests dependent on pictures, an early study was conducted to rule out any proposed word-picture association that might be too difficult.

The normative population for 11 out of the 12 tests included 5,773 subjects, aged 3-80 years, from California, Florida, Maine, and Minnesota, with the majority from Minnesota. The normative sampling was reported in three age groupings: 3-8 years (comprising 35.5% of the sample), 9-18 years (comprising 47.5% of the sample), and 19-80 years (comprising 17% of the sample). According to the technical manual (p. 19), "normative data was concentrated in the age range of three to twelve years because the most rapid development of auditory skills takes place during that time." The percentages by race of the normative subjects were reported as 88.6% white, 7.2% black, and 4.2% other. The normative data for the twelfth test, Reading of Symbols, was based on data gathered for norming the Word Attack Test of the Woodcock Reading Mastery Tests (Woodcock, 1973), which involved 4,790 subjects aged 3-18 years. Age equivalent scores and percentile rank norms for 40 age intervals were calculated for each test. Standard scores and stanine scores were also determined.

The twelve tests comprising the battery are divided into four clusters representing increasing cognitive complexity: Auditory Selective Attention Test, Diagnostic Auditory Discrimination Test, Auditory Memory Tests, and Sound-Symbol Tests. Easel-Kits are used, with the examiner side containing easy-to-understand instructions for administering the test, and the subject side containing the stimulus/response material.

Five of the twelve tests (Selective Attention, Discrimination, Memory for Content, Memory for Sequence, and Sound Recognition) utilize pictures requiring a pointing response from the subject. Training sessions introduce these tests to minimize vocabulary differences among subjects and to teach the word-picture associations used in the tests.

Five tests (Sound Mimicry, Sound Analysis, Sound-Symbol Association, Reading of Symbols, Spelling of Sounds) utilize nonsense words to prevent confounding effects from subject's familiarity with the words. The final two tests (Recognition Memory and Sound Blending) use familiar words as test stimuli.

Pre-recorded cassette tapes are provided for presentation of all auditory stimuli. Use of earphones is recommended but not required.

Well-designed, color-coded answer forms are provided. The forms are easy to use, requiring the test administrator to indicate correct or incorrect responses for each stimulus. A raw score is determined for each test; percentile rank and age-equivalent, standard, and stanine scores are easily found in tables provided in the test manuals.

Tests can be administered and interpreted separately or as a complete battery. A battery profile is provided to summarize all 12 tests, as well as additional relevant tests from other sources. The profile provides space for recording age-equivalent scores and percentile ranks. Summary areas for the Sound Confusion Inventory (SCI) and Reading Error Inventory (REI) are also provided. SCI results provide information on discrimination error patterns, whereas REI results provide information on significant reading error patterns. Additional space on the profile allows for the recording of recommendations for further testing and remediation in the four cluster areas.

Practical Applications/Uses

The G-F-W Battery is designed to identify children and adults with auditory deficiencies and describe those deficiencies. It is appropriate for use by speech/language pathologists, reading specialists, special educators, and school psychologists in a variety of settings, including clinics, schools, industry, and research facilities. Although the G-F-W Battery is intended for use with a wide age range (3-80 years), the battery appears to be most useful with children aged 3-12 years because the normative sample is more substantial in this age range. However, preschool children may show signs of fatigue if the entire battery is administered. Further, according to the authors of the battery, older children and adults receive nearly perfect scores on some of the tests of basic auditory skills.

The 12 tests and the abilities that they measure are described as follows:

The Auditory Selective Attention Test measures the ability to focus on an auditory signal while ignoring distracting background noise of varying intensity and type (fan-like noise, cafeteria noise, and voice).

The Diagnostic Auditory Discrimination Test measures the ability to discriminate between speech sounds.

Three auditory memory tests evaluate a person's short-term retention of auditory stimuli: *Recognition Memory* measures the ability to recognize whether an auditory element has occurred in the recent past; *Memory for Content* measures the ability to recognize a "set" of auditory events occurring in the recent past; and *Memory for Sequence* evaluates the ability to remember a "sequence" of auditory events in the recent past.

Seven sound-symbol tests measure abilities underlying the development of oral and written language skills: *Sound Memory* measures the ability to imitate syllables; *Sound Recognition* measures the ability to recognize a familiar word when presented with the isolated, sequenced phonemes of the word; *Sound Analysis* measures the ability to identify phonemes in nonsense syllables; *Sound Blending* measures the ability to synthesize isolated sounds into familiar words; *Sound-Symbol Association* measures the ability to learn new auditory-visual associations; *Reading of Symbols* measures the ability to make grapheme-to-phoneme translations; and *Spelling of Sounds* measures the ability to make phoneme-to-grapheme translations.

The technical manual extensively documents the relationship between auditory perceptual skills and articulation, reading, and school learning.

The G-F-W Battery requires individualized administration is a well-lighted, quiet room with a flat working surface and two chairs. Background room noise must be at a minimum. The battery can be administered with minimal preparation or training. Each test contains a clear, concise manual with diagrams explaining equipment, test materials, set-up, and procedures. The Easel-Kits provide easy-to-follow, step-by-step instructions during administration. Because tape cassettes are provided for all auditory test stimuli and live-voice presentation is not recommended, altering test sequence is difficult. Administration of the entire battery is time-consuming, taking three hours or more, although any of the 12 tests can be administered separately.

Each of the tests is easily scored by placing ''1'' in the appropriate space on the response form for a correct response or ''0'' (zero) for an incorrect response. After a raw score (the number of correct responses) is determined, tables in the test manuals provide information to determine the percentile rank, age equivalent, standard score, or stanine score, based on the raw score. Further, each manual provides performance curves representing the 25th, 50th, and 75th percentiles across the age range of the sample, graphically depicting the growth and then gradual decline of performance on each test with increasing age. However, the authors caution that performance curves are based on cross-sectional, not longitudinal data, making generalizations of expected performance across an individual's lifespan inappropriate. Overall interpretation of results is easily accomplished.

Two inventories can be determined using the Reading Symbols Test and the Diagnostic Auditory Discrimination Test. These inventories, Reading Error Inventory (REI) and Sound Confusion Inventory (SCI), require additional scoring time, but provide additional diagnostic interpretations. The REI allows the examiner to see the type and consistency of errors made by a subject during grapheme-to-phoneme translations, and facilitates remedial planning. The SCI allows the examiner to determine if a subject's discrimination errors are 1) generalized, 2) associated with certain target-sound clusters, or 3) associated with certain target-lure combinations. Again, this information may help in determining remediation strategies.

Technical Aspects

To evaluate the validity of the G-F-W Battery, it is appropriate to examine content, construct, and concurrent validity. Content validity was effectively demonstrated in the technical manual by tables summarizing the major similarities and differences among the tests of the G-F-W Battery and other tests not in the battery.

Construct validity was demonstrated in three ways. First, intercorrelations among the 12 tests for three age ranges were reported in correlation matrices. If two tests were measuring different traits, their correlations would be much lower than either of the tests correlated with itself. In general, the correlations supported the conclusion that the 12 tests measured different auditory preception skills, particularly for the 3-8 and 9-18 age ranges. For the 19 and older age range, correlations between tests in at least two instances (Memory for Content correlated with Memory for Sequence and Recognition Memory correlated with Sound Recognition) were nearly as high or higher than the correlation obtained when each test was correlated with itself. This suggests that for adults some of the tests may be overlapping in the traits they seek to measure.

Construct validity was also evaluated by correlating subject age with the auditory skills of each of the 12 tests. Because auditory skills are developmental in nature, direct relationships between the maturity of the skill (age) and test scores should be evident. The technical manual reports moderately high positive correlations (median r = .59) for the 3-8 age range, low positive correlations (median r = .30) for the 9-18 age range, and moderately high but negative correlations (median r = –.60) in the 19-80 age range, suggesting a decline in auditory skills following maturity.

Finally, construct validity was evaluated by administering the tests to two clinical sample groups, one with mild speech or learning difficulties and one with severe learning difficulties. Analysis of variance was used to compare the two sample groups to normals. According to the technical manual (p. 29), in all cases mean scores for the clinical groups were lower than for normals. However, in the case of the mildly involved group, some differences were not significant. Although one of the criteria in developing this battery was to provide fine discriminations among subjects at lower developmental levels, this was not effectively demonstrated by the authors.

No attempt at demonstrating concurrent validity was made by the authors. Concurrent validity examines whether a new test correlates well with other measures of the same variable. At the time of this review, concurrent validity has not been addressed. Condon (1984) examined two of the tests of the G-F-W Battery (Auditory Discrimination in Noise and Memory for Sequence) as screening devices for initial identification of central auditory function in 20 normal children ages seven to ten years. Correlations between these tests and an established test for central auditory function, the Staggered Spondaic Word Test, were obtained. Correlations were generally low to moderate (–.03 to .79), suggesting that the predictive value of the two tests from the G-F-W Battery as screening instruments for central auditory function was limited at best.

Two types of reliability should be addressed in test standardization, split-half or internal consistency and test-retest. The technical manual reports split-half reliability coefficients for each test over three age ranges. Coefficients ranged from .78 to .97 for ages 3-8, from .46 to .96 for ages 9-18, and from .73 to .97 for ages 19-80. Over 50% of the reliability coefficients were below .90, suggesting that internal consistency is lower than what is desirable for tests of this nature.

Test-retest reliability was not examined by the authors—a serious drawback to the standardization of the G-F-W Battery. Baran and Gengal (1984) examined the test-retest reliability of three of the G-F-W Battery subtests (Diagnostic Auditory Discrimination Test, Selective Attention Test, and Auditory Memory Tests). Subjects included 20 children ranging in age from five years, seven months to eleven years, ten months. The study reports that for the Auditory Selective Attention

Test small changes in raw scores from test to retest resulted, in some instances, in large changes in percentile rank. The Diagnostic Auditory Discrimination Test suffered from the same problem. The Auditory Memory Tests demonstrated only moderate test-retest correlations (.56 to .77). The study concludes that because test-retest reliability is questionable, a low performance on one of these subtests should require a readministration of the test before a clinical judgment is made. No test-retest reliability studies are available on the Sound-Symbol Tests of the G-F-W Battery. Further examination of the entire battery's test-retest reliability is warranted.

Critique

This reviewer agrees with previous reviewers (Butler, 1978; Oakland, 1978) that the G-F-W Battery assesses a wide spectrum of auditory perceptual skills useful in the diagnoses of subjects suspected of having speech, language, and learning difficulties. Katherine Butler states that the G-F-W Battery "deserves serious consideration by those interested in the measurement of auditory processing skills." But Thomas Oakland cautions that "in using norm-referenced measures, the development and initiation of intervention programs for individual persons based on results from one battery is risky." This author agrees and suggests that the G-F-W Battery be used in conjunction with other tests of auditory processing skills before appropriate intervention strategies are selected.

Although the Easel-Kits make for ease of administration, and instructions and scoring procedures are concise and clear, portability of the entire battery is difficult because necessary test materials are bulky (five Easel-Kits, two sets of earphones, and a tape player). Further, time constraints in the clinical setting may make the entire battery difficult to complete in one session because administration is time-consuming (three hours or more). Preschool children would be particularly prone to fatigue. Caution should also be used when setting the loudness level of the prerecorded tapes. The authors suggest setting the tape player at a "comfortably loud" level, but this level will vary from child to child and from examiner to child. An audiometric screening of the child's hearing before administering the battery would allow the examiner to adjust the loudness accordingly. The examiner should also be aware that significant background noise in the testing vicinity could confound results.

The G-F-W Battery appears to be most useful for children aged 3-12 years because the gathering of normative data was concentrated in this age range and older children tend to receive near-perfect scores on some of the tests. The battery is useful, particularly in identifying children with severe auditory perceptual deficits. Fine discriminations between lower functioning subjects (mild to severe) is questionable.

Test-retest reliability of the 12 tests in the G-F-W Battery remains at issue. The authors failed to establish test-retest reliability during standardization, and a recent study (Baran & Gengal, 1984) suggests that the test-retest reliability is questionable for several of the subtests. Small changes in raw scores translate into large changes in percentile rank in some instances. Therefore, a low test score warrants a readministration of that test before making a clinical judgment.

As long as the above cautions are noted in administration and interpretation of results, the G-F-W Battery can be a useful diagnostic tool for professionals interested in assessing auditory perceptual skills.

References

This list includes text citations as well as suggested additional reading.

Baran, J. A., & Gengal, R. W. (1984). Test-retest reliability of three G-F-W subtests. *Language, Speech and Hearing Services in the Schools, 15,* 199-204.

Burk, K. W. (1979). Review of The Goldman-Fristoe-Woodcock Sound-Symbol Tests. In F. L. Darley (Ed.), *Evaluation of appraisal techniques in speech and language pathology* (pp. 154-156). Reading, MA: Addison-Wesley Publishing Company.

Butler, K. G. (1978). Review of The Goldman-Fristoe-Woodcock Auditory Skills Test Battery. In O. K. Buros (Ed.), *The eighth mental measurements yearbook* (pp. 1457-1458). Highland Park, NJ: The Gryphon Press.

Condon, M. (1984). Performance of normal-hearing children on the SSW Test, G-F-W Noise subtest, and the G-F-W Memory for Sequence subtest. *Language, Speech and Hearing Services in the Schools, 15,* 192-198.

Goldman, R., Fristoe, M., & Woodcock, R. (1970). *Goldman-Fristoe-Woodcock Test of Auditory Discrimination.* Circle Pines, MN: American Guidance Service, Inc.

Kent, L. R. (1979). Review of The Goldman-Fristoe-Woodcock Auditory Memory Tests. In F. L. Darley (Ed.), *Evaluation of appraisal techniques in speech and language pathology* (pp. 150-153). Reading, MA: Addison-Wesley Publishing Company.

Lasky, E. Z., & Katz, J. (Ed.). (1983). *Central auditory processing disorders.* Baltimore, MD: University Park Press.

Leach, E. A. (1979). Review of the Goldman-Fristoe-Woodcock Auditory Selective Attention Test. In F. L. Darley (Ed.), *Evaluation of appraisal techniques in speech and language pathology* (pp. 148-149). Reading, MA: Addison-Wesley Publishing Company.

Oakland, T. (1978). Review of The Goldman-Fristoe-Woodcock Auditory Skills Test Battery. In O. K. Buros (Ed.), *The eighth mental measurements yearbook* (pp. 1458-1460). Highland Park, NJ: The Gryphon Press.

Woodcock, R. W. (1973). *Woodcock Reading Mastery Tests.* Circle Pines, MN: American Guidance Service, Inc.

Woodcock, R. W. (1976). *Technical manual for the Goldman-Fristoe-Woodcock Auditory Skills Test Battery.* Circle Pines, MN: American Guidance Service, Inc.

Vetter, D. K. (1979). Review of The Goldman-Fristoe-Woodcock Test of Auditory Discrimination. In F. L. Darley (Ed.), *Evaluation of appraisal techniques in speech and language pathology* (pp. 157-161). Reading, MA: Addison-Wesley Publishing Company.

Roger D. Carlson, Ph.D.
Associate Professor of Psychology, Lebanon Valley College, Annville, Pennsylvania.

HARDING W87 TEST

Christopher P. Harding. Queensland, Australia: Harding Tests.

Introduction

The Harding W87 Test (Harding, 1977) measures abilities at a high level of achievement. The object of the test is to integrate thinking, creative, and informational abilities through the measurement of convergent, divergent, and condivergent thinking processes in order to yield a single unified score called the Ability Quotient (AQ). It is suitable for individuals with Ability Quotients of 140 to 173.

The Harding W87 Test is one of several tests developed by one of a group of individuals who are interested in the psychological measurement of human ability at very high levels. Mensa admits members who distinguish themselves by performing better on standardized tests of intelligence than 98% of the population. Intertel also makes use of standardized tests in order to admit those who perform better than 99% of the population. The Harding W87 Test was developed in concert with the formation of the International Society for Philosophical Enquiry (ISPE) and is used by that society in order to admit individuals who perform superiorly to 99.9% of the population. As such, it is one of several instruments that have been specifically developed in order to make fine discriminations between people *within* the top 2% of the population.

The development of the W87 (the name refers to its language bias and to the length of an early form) must be understood within the context of the purposes of admitting individuals to the ISPE, as well as within the context of a whole "family" of other tests being developed by Harding and others. The test's author, Christopher P. Harding, is an English-born Australian who founded ISPE. He is a member of Mensa; Intertel; Triple Nine Society; Prometheus Society; and the elite one-in-one-million, Mega Society, as well as having been listed as among the highest to have scored on an IQ test (McWhirter, 1982, 1983, 1984). Harding developed the Skyscraper Test (Harding, 1973) in order to select the most able people by means of an extremely high level test of ability and add a new dimension to society. The W87 was developed by him to replace the Skyscraper Test, which was also used as an instrument for admitting individuals to the ISPE.

The W87, obtained from a tryout pool of over 1,000 questions, had 87 items in its earlier form and 64 items at the point at which it achieved listing in reference books (34 general reasoning and 30 analogies). It currently has 45 items (22 general reasoning and 23 analogies) in the form used by ISPE, which now has sole use of W87.

This two-page ISPE version of the W87 is a paper-and-pencil test with two sets of items. Set I contains letter and number series, missing letter items, rearrangement of letters to form words, word synonyms, antonyms, rhyming and connecting words, and a mathematical equation. Items are of both multiple- and free-choice formats. Set II contains exclusively word analogy items in a multiple-choice (ten) format.

Practical Applications/Uses

The ISPE, unlike other sister societies for the highly gifted, uses two tests for admission. The W87 (like the earlier Harding Skyscraper Test) is used in conjunction with the Vocabulary Test, Forms A, B, or BC (Harding, 1975), which test for a high level of linguistic aptitude through analogies. According to Davis (1980, p. 11), Forms A and B were originally developed as screening tests to eliminate candidates who were not qualified to take the Skyscraper Test; the second opinion of the Vocabulary Test thus "confirmed I.Q. or A.Q. test scores, screened out less literate applicants, and assured high intellectual ability in entrants."

In a personal communication (August 13, 1985) Harding writes:

> These tests are all *POWER* tests and the information content is in reality quite low to those obtaining very high performances in this test and others of similar ilk. It only appears otherwise to more normal people. Analysis of the test items shows that failure with an item is due to a failure to grasp the underlying ideas involved in the question. We have always asked subjects to state their reasoning in working the questions. This has been a long standing practice that has stopped us from becoming distanced from what we are trying to measure, i.e., the quality of thought!

The developer of the W87 has assumed a linguistic and informational common denominator that is prerequisite for individuals taking the W87 as evidenced by superior performance on the Vocabulary Tests, allowing for the attribution of variance between individuals to be due to problem-solving skills alone. Further, it seems to be assumed that those who do not display such high linguistic ability yield scores on the W87 that probably *are* attributable to linguistic and informational variance. Thus, in order not to contaminate the interpretation of performance on the W87 with linguistic and informational variation, the effects of language and informational background are partialed out in effect by the linguistic and informational prescreening of a selected sample of W87 examinees with assumed homogeneity of linguistic facility and informational background. This is one reason for apologies not being made for the sample used for validation of the W87, which was composed exclusively of members of high IQ societies that draw their membership from individuals who have obtained certified scores on intelligence tests within the top 2% of the general population as their minimum standard for admission.

The test is self-administered on an unsupervised basis. There is no time limit, although it is usually completed in three hours, and instructions recommend that one attempt every item, preferably in a single three-hour session. Test forms, on which one writes the answers and is required to sign a certification that no "o-utside" aids, etc. were used, are sent to ISPE for scoring. The score report contains a statement explaining that the reported "P-Score" (takes the form of $1/n$) represents the approximate incidence within the general population, which corresponds to the reported selection index "Q" (mean = 100, *s* = 23.33), which is similar to Cattell scale IQ. The range of IQ detected by the ISPE version of the W87 is about 130 to 165.

Technical Aspects

According to Harding (personal communication, August 13, 1985), validity of the 64-item W87 was established by soliciting Mensans to volunteer to take the test on an unsupervised basis during a single sitting. Results yielded a sample of more than 500 members of Mensa, Intertel, Triple Nine Society, ISPE, Four Sigma, and the 501 Society. Respondents were asked on what test their selection to Mensa was based and to give the score. Using these data, the W87 was shown to correlate .84 with the Harding Skyscraper Test, .79 with Scholastic Aptitude Test results, .75 with the Miller Analogies Test, .68 with the Verbal Form of the Cattell Test, and .45 with the California Test of Mental Maturity. Harding also cites the newsletters of the ISPE and the Mega Society in reporting correlations between the W87 and the Bloom Analogies Test, the Langdon Adult Intelligence Test, and the Hoeflin Intelligence Test (also tests designed to measure very high levels of ability), using 1,825 test pairs, which range from .85 to .92 between the instruments. Obvious falsification of previous score reports where volunteers are used in test construction/validation is estimated by Harding to occur in only 0.5% cases. Harding does not report any studies of reliability.

There are obvious problems in the methods that have been used in order to make the reported data comparable with data obtained for other tests of intelligence and ability. None of the data presented on the W87 is readily available in a test manual published by the author because no manual exists. None of these data is reported in a professionally edited journal wherein peers, who are formally trained in psychometrics, evaluate the scientific standing of the studies published, and wherein test authors, usually members of professional associations, are bound by ethical codes to adhere to the highest standards of accuracy in the conduct and reporting of validation studies. Understandably, because Harding does not appear to be a professional psychometrician and thus does not have ready access to samples of subjects on whom he can conduct controlled studies, he has resorted to methods that have many intrinsic problems. These problems include obtaining data through unstandardized, uncontrolled, unsupervised self-administration with no time constraints or standardized conditions of testing. There is no way to assure that "aids" have not been used. Certified copies of transcripts or letters of licensed psychologists for the reporting of test scores are not required in order to validate test score reports. In short, there is no way to assure the accuracy or truth of either the conditions under which the W87 was taken or the score reports allegedly attained on other instruments used for conducting construct validity studies. In his instructions for the Mega Test, a sister to the W87, Hoeflin (1983, p. 8) states: "So that no one will gain an unfair advantage by cheating, everyone is permitted and encouraged to use reference aids." Such instructions only serve to assure the inclusion of a myriad of variables contributing to the contamination of any validity studies that might be performed. Recently, vos Savant (1985), another member of many high IQ societies and advocate of unsupervised testing, acknowledges the poor validity of tests that are self-administered, but typical of the bastardized meanings that are given to standard psychometric terms by amateur psychometrists. Vos Savant naively writes:

> Even though this type of test is taken in the privacy of your home, it is still considered 'group-administered' because many individuals are being tested in the same way that they would be if they were all sitting in a room together. You simply can't see each other because you're all taking it at different times and in different places. The end result is the same, however: there is no individual attention. (p. 59)

If Harding wishes to share or borrow professionally developed standards for validity through the use of correlational methods, then it seems that he must also adhere to rigor in the collection of data to be put into the formulas. Correlations themselves and derived inferences about the construct validity of the W87 because the *reported* performances on it correlate with the *reported* performances on other tests of intelligence and ability have no meaning if the data used are not comparable to those used by other publishers on psychological and educational tests.

The ways in which the ISPE derives the "P-Score" and the "Q-Score" also remain mysterious. Because there do not exist normative studies of the general population in performance on the W87, it is presumed that the "P" associated with a performance on the W87 (the incidence in the general population, $1/n$) is obtained by first knowing a score that the person has obtained on an established test of intelligence (thus, the interest of these test developers in knowing performances on other tests of intelligence) and finding the normative data associated with that score. This is despite the fact that the examinees may have obtained that score at a very different point in their life and that IQs can fluctuate significantly during the life span. (Harding requests no data on *when* the score was obtained.) The percentile associated with the reported performance on the established test is assumed to be the percentile ranking associated with the derived score on the W87. Thus, apparently, score reports have not been developed from norms of the W87 itself, but rather from norms of numerous other tests that have been reported by the examinees.

There are reasons for test standards as they have evolved, not the least of which is to have a common language (e.g., so that all of us know what "construct validity" is and how it is ordinarily derived). Instead of adhering to rigorous standards, Harding attempts to establish the credibility of his work by intellectual elitism and ad hominem argument forms. An interesting example is with respect to item selection and retention. Harding (personal communication, August 13, 1985) writes, "Items that we were unable to defend by logic as well as by item analysis were discarded. Since such defence has occurred *by people whose IQ/AQ has shown repeated measurement in the 160-200 range, something much in our interest, we are confident of the validity of the test as a measure of both high IQ and AQ* [emphasis added]." In addition, he states that "the answers and data have been available to those best able to fault our procedures should such complaint be valid." These answers and data are not available to the academic/professional psychometric community through the publication of a manual or the inclusion of the data in professional journals. Harding apparently desperately seeks acceptance as evidenced by citations of his

Skyscraper Test in *The Eighth Mental Measurements Yearbook* (Buros, 1978) and a reference to a possible brief mention of the W87 in Mitchell's (1985) *The Ninth Mental Measurements Yearbook* (C. P. Harding, personal communication, August 13, 1985). Interestingly, Buros (1978) simply *lists* Harding's Skyscraper Test, and yet reference is made to that listing by vos Savant (1985, p. 34) as follows: "Chrisopher P. Harding of Queensland, Australia, *listed in Buros' Mental Measurements Yearbook for his work in psychometrics* [italics added] . . ."

In referring to psychologists who might criticize his psychometric procedures, Harding (personal communication, August 13, 1985) replies, "I'm afraid though to most of these psychologists there has grown up a world that is to them quite unreal. The view across the 'mental classes' is regretfully as hazy as perceptions across the social classes and I don't expect to convince them of anything! Ah well!" Harding would do well to heed the criticism of Professor Max Hamilton (1963/1965, p. 1462) who, when writing about Eysenck's (1962) popular book for unsupervised self-testing of intelligence (a book that shares many of the types of items used by Harding), remarks, "The best that can be said for these tests is that they are a bad joke. Anybody with a little sophistication in the design of tests can discover any number of items to which perfectly legitimate alternative answers can be found. It may well be that these tests will survive in the literature chiefly as awful examples of how not to devise intelligence tests." Recently, Morris (1984) points out how that point is surely the case with respect to sequence-completion-type items.

Harding's hope to measure convergent, divergent, and "condivergent" thinking through the use of his instrument also strikes this reviewer as naive. Harding has presented no studies of construct validity showing that the scores on his tests correlate to other measures of divergent thinking (e.g., Torrance, 1974; Christensen et al., 1960) nor does he define what is meant by his novel term, "condivergent" thought. Presumably he is referring to the fact that the individual must overcome functional fixity of one's own thinking and thus *diverge* in one's thought before being able to *converge* on the "right" answer. Such a notion fails to really denote what psychometrists trying to measure creativity have been attempting to do, nor does it even begin to address the criterion problem with measures of creativity; however, it does serve to lead the reader into believing that the W87 measures *more* than only intelligence.

Critique

The W87 was developed to split mathematical hairs within the highest percentages of the normal distribution. The author has apparently lost sight of the notion of the standard error of a test score—particularly the scores reported by his participants in "validity" studies. This is a serious oversight when the concept of intelligence, and particularly single IQ-score reporting, is being seriously questioned and viewed as poor practice (*especially,* when done without adequate professional explanation) and when studies of intelligence have shown considerable modifiability and fluctuation in scores over time. "Intelligence," as a technical concept used by psychometricians for the prediction of school success, is a term that was never intended to be used in the absolutistic and elitist ways in which Harding uses it. Spearman's (1927) *g* concept, which Harding is attempting to measure, is a cousin of unitary theories of intelligence. It is only a theoretical point of view and thus is not and cannot be true or false. Many alternatives have been proposed (see Thurstone, 1938; Guilford, 1957). Cyril Burt, also a British psychometrist educated in the tradition of Spearman and whose own research data and conclusions about intelligence have been seriously questioned, initiated the founding of the Mensa Society on the premise that it would be interesting to have people of high intelligence form a panel. People were admitted to Mensa when they presented evidence of attaining a score on a *standardized* test of intelligence that had been shown to be valid at the top 2% of the general population. The W87 contributes to an unfortunate but probably well-deserved skepticism on the part of the general public in the United States about the efficacy and, most importantly, the *validity* of mental testing. Harding contributes to this by arrogant psychometric judgmentalism that leads to a kind of self-assumed convergent elitism by encumbering the general population with arbitrarily selected items, and answers given within an arbitrary context (certainly not providing real options for creativity). At the same time, the ubiquitous human quest for overcoming self-doubt and assuredness and achieving self-validation lures one into the lair of psychometric social climbing or at least score leap-frogging. Even if the W87 were a psychometrically valid instrument, psychometric validity would not mean self-validity. Arbitrary items and binary units of measure encapsulating human performance and summated into a score on an assumed equal interval, ratio scale only serves to linearize and judge one's existence and not let humanity and human performance stand. One really needs to ask: What is the purpose of the W87? In what contexts was it developed or to be used? Its purpose is to select individuals for membership into an elite society that presumably has to do with self-glorification and socializing among the self-glorified. Used for these purposes and understanding its arbitrary nature and the meaning of success on it being convergent with a group's particular system of thought, it may have value. In terms of contributing anything psychometrically valid to understanding *any* segment of the general population, this reviewer has doubts.

On the positive side, the items are cleverly devised and challenging in terms of attempting to understand the author's psycho-logic. Such tests beg for good rigorous validity studies to be done; unfortunately, none have been.

References

Buros, O. K. (1978). *The eighth mental measurements yearbook.* Highland Park, NJ: The Gryphon Press.

Christensen, P. R., Guilford, J. P., Merrifield, R. P., & Wilson, R. C. (1960). *Alternate uses.* Orange, CA: Sheridan Psychological Services.

Davis, R. J. (1980). *The history of the International Society for Philosophical Enquiry from December 1974 through May 1980.* Belmont, MA: International Society for International Enquiry.

Eysenck, H. J. (1962). *Know your own I.Q.* New York: Penguin.

Guilford, J. P. (1957). *A revised structure of the intellect* (Rep. No. 19). Los Angeles: The Psychology Laboratory, University of Southern California.

Hamilton, M. (1965). [Review of *Know your own I.Q.* by H. J. Eysenck]. In O. K. Buros (Ed.), *The sixth mental measurements yearbook.* Highland Park, NJ: The Gryphon Press. (Reprinted from *British Journal of Psychiatry,* 1963, *109,* 835)

Harding, C. P. (1973). *Skyscraper Test*. Queensland, Australia: Harding Tests.
Harding, C. P. (1975). *Vocabulary Test, Forms A, B, and BC*. Queensland, Australia: Harding Tests.
Harding, C. P. (1977). *W87 Test*. Queensland, Australia: Harding Tests.
Hoeflin, R. K. (1983). The Mega Test. *Vidya, 42*, 7-13.
McWhirter, R. (1982). *Guinness book of world records*. New York: Sterling.
McWhirter, R. (1983). *Guinness book of world records*. New York: Sterling.
McWhirter, R. (1984). *Guinness book of world records*. New York: Sterling.
Mitchell, J. V., Jr. (Ed.). (1985). *The ninth mental measurements yearbook*. Lincoln, NE: The Buros Institute of Mental Measurements.
Morris, F. (1984). One sequence problems in I.Q. tests. *Vidya, 56*, 16-17.
Spearman, C. E. (1927). *The abilities of man: Their nature and measurement*. New York: Macmillan.
Thurstone, L. L. (1938). Primary mental abilities. *Psychometric Monographs, 1*.
Torrance, E. P. (1974). *Torrance Tests of Creature Thinking*. Columbus, OH: Personnel.
vos Savant, M. M. (1985). *Omni I.Q. quiz contest*. New York: McGraw-Hill.

Joan Gallini, Ph.D.
Associate Professor of Educational Psychology, University of South Carolina, Columbia, South Carolina.

HEALY PICTORIAL COMPLETION TEST

William Healy. Chicago, Illinois: Stoelting Company.

Introduction

The Healy Pictorial Completion Test II (PCT II) is an individually administered test of mental ability and intelligence for individuals aged five years and over. It is a subtest of the Arthur Point Scale of Performance Tests, Revised Form II (Arthur, 1947). The PCT II is oriented to measure the specific ability of apperception, a component considered essential to "any fair attempt to measure intelligence" (Healy, 1964, p. 189). With the PCT II, apperceptive ability is measured according to the subject's capability to make connections between different portions of a series of picture sets. Eleven brightly colored 5" x 3½" pictures, each of which has a missing part, are arranged on two boards in a particular sequence depicting a story of a day in the life of a schoolboy. The first picture from the series presents a simple idea to serve for demonstration purposes. The next ten are the test pictures, with ideas from one picture carrying over to the subsequent pictures. The examinee is asked to choose from 60 squares the one square that will complete the meaning of each picture. By definition, the task involves apperceptive ability in that the examinee is required to perceive gaps in patterns by identifying their connections with the appropriate parts of the given picture set. In addition, because the task's focus is on visually presented materials, visual organization plays an important role in successful performance (Rapaport, 1945). Its pictorial and nonlanguage content helps to eliminate possible bias in test performance due to language deficiencies.

The range in levels of complexity makes it useful in assessing mental ability in populations having either normal mental functioning or mental impairments. The test has been of particular interest to clinical psychologists because it appears to vary more than any other performance test with the emotionally impaired.

William Healy was employed with the Judge Baker Foundation in Boston when he developed the first version of a pictorial completion test (Healy, 1914). Healy has been recognized as a notable clinical psychologist who has made constructive contributions to enlarging the field of intelligence and mental testing for such reformatory institutions as juvenile court clinics. His work demonstrates the practical utility of the services of clinical psychology in a variety of contexts.

The wide use and considerable attention given to the test in the literature (e.g., Pinter & Anderson, 1917) stimulated Healy to make significant improvements in the test, resulting in the PCT II in 1917. It was first exhibited at the December, 1917 meeting of the American Psychological Association. Shortly afterward, it was adopted along with a battery of other mental performance tests by the U.S. War Department for testing army personnel. The picture-based tests were to provide opportunity for those with language handicaps to demonstrate their ability.

Unlike the original version, Pictorial Completion Test I (see Arthur, 1943), the PCT II incorporates a pictorial narrative series of eleven pictures, with elements for interpretation carried over from one picture to another. The task evoked by the use of pictures is analogous to the language-based task requiring a subject to understand a passage by carrying over its significant elements from a sentence or paragraph to later passages.

Healy developed the test in response to the need unsatisfied by the language completion tests of Ebbinghaus and others (e.g., Trabue, 1916). In 1897 Ebbinghaus developed the completion test or "cloze" method, requiring examinees to fill in missing words interspersed throughout a passage. Healy (1914) contended that such a language-based test was limited for three major reasons: 1) there are vast differences in individual opportunities for acquiring a command of the English language, with unusual words and those with "special shades of meaning" especially increasing the difficulty of interpretation for those with language deficiencies and giving individuals with good training in the languages an advantage; 2) language ability is a specialized ability, sometimes demonstrating lower correlations with other intelligence tests, thus vitiating support for the cloze tests as indicative of apperceptive ability; and 3) because intelligence tests measuring apperception require a fair number of complex situations and considerable time for reading, an extraneous variable of "memory span" for ideas confounds the intended measurement of apperceptive ability.

Thus, Healy purported that a completion test employing pictures rather than language could overcome the confounding factors of language ability and reading requirements and result in a more valid measure of apperceptive ability. Furthermore, the advantages of using pictures instead of words would provide opportunity for presenting a plethora of "ideational detail at a glance," which would otherwise require pages of text to adequately cover (Healy, 1964, p. 2).

A revised form to the original 1917 test was later developed for study. The revisions focused primarily on modern dress and current pictorial environment. Test-retest reliabilities were determined for comparison between the old and revised forms (Schwerin & Fitzwater, 1954). In one random sample, 50 school-aged children (mean age of 11.5 years) were tested twice with the original form, another 50 were tested twice with the revised form, and a third group (N = 50) was tested with the original and revised forms. A time interval of three weeks was used between the testings for each group. In addition, school grades (i.e., GPA) of the sample were used as a validating criterion for both tests. No significant differences were found in the reliabilities between the two tests. However, validity for the revised form was significantly higher ($p < .01$) than that of the original tests. The results support the replacement of the original form by the revised. The only changes made to the PCT II test were the elimination of the time limits originally set by Healy and the use of nonverbal instructions. Aside from these modifications, all materials and methods proposed by Healy remained the same when the PCT became a component of the Arthur Point Scale, a battery of mental, nonverbal tests.

Practical Applications/Uses

The PCT II (as part of the Arthur Point Performance Scale II) is intended as a clinical instrument for adequate use by trained clinicians in psychology and psychiatric clinics. However, its use can be applied to other settings, such as a school or learning clinic. If used in such settings, procedures are simplistic enough to allow for the test to be administered by teachers or school counselors who are properly trained in the procedural rules.

The test is appropriate for populations aged five years and older, representing a wide range of mental abilities and emotionally disturbed levels. In addition, given its nonlanguage-based content, the test is appropriate for the hearing impaired, subjects with language deficiencies, and non-English-speaking subjects. The test is not appropriate for individuals whose cultural backgrounds differ significantly from the culture of the average urban student.

Because the test is intended for application to a broad spectrum of individuals, the series of incomplete pictures range from simple elements capable of being readily rationalized by immature minds to features of much greater difficulty requiring more complex reasoning skills. However, there can be content validity problems concerning the appropriateness of some pictures with populations from other countries, as well as a lack of sufficient empirical evidence to corroborate the PCT II's construct validity, thus warranting the need for investigations of both test validity and reliability.

As part of the Arthur Point Performance Scale II, the Healy PCT is to be presented last. Administration procedures are fairly simple, and the manual (Healy, 1964) is clear in describing the role of the examiner, with one particular exception: when the Healy PCT II became a component of the Arthur Scale, the use of nonverbal instructions was incorporated. The manual lacks clarity on the importance of this and to what extent verbal communication can take place.

Of particular importance in the administration of the test is that the 60 pieces for selection by the examinee be presented in the predetermined order as indicated in the box of the test. Although the test is not timed, it is advisable that a stopwatch be used to record the amount of time spent on the test. The manual does not make this recommendation, nor does it give an approximate time for completing the test.

Test administration must be implemented according to rule by an individual properly trained in the procedures. The examiner's role is to describe the sequence of the pictures by pointing to pictures in the sequence they occur and to indicate the aperture that is to be completed by selecting one of the 60 pieces containing a picture appropriate to the meaning of the story. The examiner signals the examinee when to move ahead, then records all responses on a score form. Instructions are primarily nonverbal, with minimum verbal instructions permitted for the hearing, English-speaking subjects.

From each of the pictures a one-inch-square piece is cut out; to complete the picture, the examinee selects a square from the accompanying small pieces or blocks. Each square is numbered on the back for scoring purposes. Only one of the pieces accurately represents the object needed to precisely complete the idea of the given picture. Although several of the squares are designed to make logical sense if the examinee takes only part of the idea suggested by the given picture into account, most of the 60 pieces are inconsistent with the story line portrayed in the illustration.

The scoring procedures are simple. Each of the 60 blocks has an identification number on the back that specifies the predetermined order that the blocks are to be presented to the examinee. A table of values developed by Healy (1964, p. 8) specifies the points assigned for the correct block chosen for each of the ten pictures. Each piece given no value in the table for a given picture is assigned –5, indicating an extremely irrational choice. Blocks that provide a plausible, but incorrect, solution are awarded some point value (1–18 points). The point values vary with respect to the difficulty of the picture and the reasonableness of the chosen block for the picture.

The score sheet, which provides a simple method for the examinee to record responses during the testing, consists of three columns: 1) the picture number (1–10); 2) the number of the block (1–60, found on the back of the block) inserted by the examinee in the respective picture; and 3) the point value assigned to the block for the given picture, according to the set of tables available in the manual. The ten-point values assigned to the respective pieces selected by the examinee are summed to obtain the total raw score. The raw score is converted into a point value obtained from a set of available tables (Arthur, 1947, p. 30). The point values earned by the ten blocks selected are then summed to obtain the total point score, which in turn is converted into years and months of mental age, using the same set of tables. The scoring procedures are simple to follow and provide an objective interpretation of test results in terms of mental age. However, a limitation of the tables lies in the lack of norms for discrete categories beyond the age of 15.5 years.

As indicated in the test manual, the test's composition was designed to provide for little or no equivocation in the interpretation of an examinee's response. That is, the ideas presented in the pictures are "so clear that they present scant room for equivocal issues." Consequently, incorrect responses are viewed as "directly perceptual and inferential in character, involving faulty observation or faulty reasoning concerning objects and phenomena universally known and among the most plainly observable in the illustrations" (Healy, 1964, pp. 14–15). This statement, however, should be cautiously interpreted, given the lack of empirical evidence of the test validity.

Technical Aspects

American norms for the PCT II were originally established by Healy for ages 6–16 years inclusive (Healy, 1921) and confirmed by Arthur (1947). However, the literature points to the lack of adequate standardization of the PCT II (e.g., Watson, 1951), and, consequently, related research on the test is encouraged.

A limited number of validity and reliability studies of the PCT II are reported. Unfortunately, this reviewer was unable to locate any current documents.

At the time of its inception, the PCT II received favorable comment from various users (e.g., see Pinter & Anderson, 1917). A major feature of interest, especially to clinical psychologists, has been its ability to measure varying degrees of emotional maladjustment. Although the test has been useful in assessing intelligence for a variety of populations, at the same time questions about its construct validity have been raised in the literature. As reported in a study by Schwerin and Fitzwater (1954, p. 248), "although reliability and validity were not adequately established, the PCT is among the most widely used performance tests today as a component of the Arthur Point Scale." Low correlations (about .4 to .5) with the Binet test of intelligence have implications for its measurement of a specific component of general intelligence, such as the apperceptive abilities intended in its design. However, low discrepancies in the Binet and the Healy mental ages are demonstrated (Vernon, 1937, p. 120), with the Healy IQs being about 15 points lower than the Binet. Such findings are suggestive of the test presenting a specific kind of difficulty to abnormal populations, but are too inconclusive regarding what the test is really measuring.

Several of the early studies focused on the concurrent validity of the PCT II, using the Stanford-Binet test as a measure of general intelligence (Johnson & Schriefer, 1922; Werner, 1940; Worthington, 1926; Vernon, 1937). For one sample in the Worthington study, a correlation of .41 was obtained between the Binet and the PCT II. The sample consisted of 141 subjects with mental ages ranging from 3-13 years and characterized by various mental defects or behavioral difficulties. A later study reported a correlation of .42 based on 50 subjects with similar characteristics. The findings generally support those of the Johnson and Schriefer study.

For the most part the reported investigations resulted in low but positive correlations between the PCT II and the Binet thus suggesting that the PCT might be measuring another, more specific dimension of the "g-intelligence" construct. Such a hypothesis is viable, given that the test was designed to measure the specific dimension, apperceptive ability; however, the lack of empirical evidence to substantiate the measurement of this trait underlying the intelligence construct impedes one from drawing any conclusions.

The Arthur Point Scale, of which the PCT II is a subtest, consists of a battery of nonverbal performance tests intended to supplement the Stanford-Binet. PCT correlations with the Binet, however, are among the lowest of the subtests, yet considered significant enough to justify its use among adolescents and adults (Vernon, 1937, p. 35). The test appears to provide a measurement of mental abilities along a wide continuum (the mentally competent and mentally disabled individuals and those with varying degrees of emotional impairments). The relatively low to moderate correlations with the Binet are suggestive of the test representing a more specific component of ability, perhaps an apperceptive component (though questionable), as intended by the test's designer. The nature of the test provides face validity to its overall intent of measurement. That is, the test items are visual, nonlanguage, and ideational, requiring examinees to express their comprehension and perceptions of the story by completing each of the eleven pictures with one of 60 illustrated pieces. At the same time, however, the exclusive use of imagery raises the question about its measurement of apperceptive ability.

A study by Schwerin and Fitzwater (1954) is among the few reporting reliability characteristics of the PCT II. The study focuses on a comparison between the reliability indices of the original PCT II and a revised form (revisions made to modernize the pictures).

A random sample of 150 school children with a mean age of 11.6 was selected from Lima, Ohio, public and parochial schools. Fifty subjects were randomly assigned one of three groups: the first group was tested twice with the original test, the second group was tested twice with the revised test, and a third group was tested with both the original and the revised forms to obtain test-retest reliabilities. A time interval of three weeks was used between the testings for all groups. Public school grade-point averages were used as the criterion for determining test validity. Results showed reliabilities of .78 and .89 for the original and the revised tests, respectively. A *t*-test demonstrated no significant differences ($p > .01$). However, validity of the revised form ($r = .73$) was significantly higher ($p < .01$) than the original form ($r = .41$). Thus, the study justified the replacement of the original form by the revised, up-dated version of the test.

A more detailed study of item responses was conducted by Dorcus (1926). The five-year study constituted a sample of 102 subjects, ranging from ages 6-18 years. The study provides norms that can be compared with the Healy (1964) norms. Data were analyzed in terms of chronological age, number of retests, type of responses to each item, and the time taken to complete each test. Results demonstrated very little differences in the average completion times for the different age groups on the first test. Successive retests over the five years, however, resulted in a reduction in the average time for all groups, probably due in part to practice effects. Observations of an increase in the selection of correct responses accompanied by an increase chronological age reflect a growth in the subjects' abilities to perceive relations within the particular design and between successive pictures.

In summary, early studies demonstrate an acceptable reliability of the PCT II; yet, there is inadequate evidence to support the validity of the test as measuring a specific intelligence dimension, such as apperceptive skills. Nevertheless, the test is applicable to a variety of populations and age groups and appears to provide an assessment of some underlying dimension(s) of intelligence. Such positive features justify the recommendation for conducting investigations of the psychometric characteristics of the test, using latent trait models and other sophisticated current methodologies.

The PCT II was designed to measure a specific ability underlying the "general intelligence" construct. Healy (1964, p. 7) identified that specific ability as apperception, asserting that apperceptive abilities represent the following:

> . . . capacity for putting two-and-two-together in the realm of thought, the ability to turn things over in the mind, to rationalize about perceptual material with what may be drawn on from the ideational and other memory stores of the minds, [and that such ability is of] the very essence of intelligence and of very great importance in civilization. This, if anything, may be spoken of as a higher mental power.

Despite such claims of the test's design, the early literature states that "least of all the common performance tests do we know what it [PCT] measures" (Vernon, 1937, p. 120). This suggested construct validity problem with the PCT II can partly be attributed to the ambiguity in the definition of what "apperceptive ability" means and how it is reflected in performance on the PCT II. But more importantly, there is a lack of sufficient empirical evidence of what the test is measuring.

In efforts to at least hypothesize what the PCT may be measuring, it would be useful to investigate the test within the context of the more recent developments in information-processing research. The related theories of intelligence are directed to specify the "processes" by which intelligence performance is generated (Sternberg, 1985). On the surface (i.e., from a face validity perspective), then, one might consider what mental processes are involved in selecting the one appropriate piece out of 60 that completes each of the PCT II's eleven pictures. The hypotheses should then be tested in empirical investigations of the PCT II's construct validity.

Let us consider one of the test items in terms of the mental processes that might be inferred from different choices of the 60 pieces to complete the picture. For example, in one picture a boy is walking to school, carrying a bookstrap with a green and yellow book; however, it appears that something has fallen from the bookstrap. The aperture to be completed by the examinee is below the bookstrap. The examinee who reasons correctly will utilize information presented in the previous picture to determine what fell from the bookstrap. In picture one, the boy is eating breakfast and his bookstrap with a red, yellow, and green book is on the table. Thus, the choice of the red book reflects the examinee's ability to utilize the relevant information from a prior source (picture one) and apply that information to a new context (picture two) to propose a solution. Such learning is characteristic of problem solving, a higher order of processing (Gagné, 1977; Voss, 1983, in press).

Two other plausible choices are either the piece with the blue book or the piece with the red and yellow book. However, such choices reflect that examinees are operating at a lower level of reasoning. Examinees are probably inferring from the picture that something fell from the bookstrap, which is quite obvious just by looking at the picture; however, they are failing to utilize information obtained from the previous picture in solving the problem. Other responses, such as the footprint are also reasonable, but suggest perceptions made only at the "single picture" level. Almost any other choice except the red book is indicative of the examinees' failure to capture the essence of the picture itself or that examinees are simply guessing.

One might describe the processes involved in solving the PCT II items, such as picture two, in terms of three components and processes used in most knowledge acquisition (see Sternberg, 1985, p. 107):

1) *Selective encoding:* Recognizing what information among all the pieces of information is relevant for one's purpose (Schank, 1980). This process is somewhat basic to any learning. In picture two selective encoding is represented, for example, when examinees associate that the missing piece is related to something missing from the boy's bookstrap.

2) *Selecting combinations:* Combining selectively encoded information to form an integrated whole (Mayer & Greeno, 1972). With respect to picture two, examinees try to test their hypotheses against the 60 possible pieces from which they can make a selection to complete the picture.

3) *Selective comparison:* Relating newly acquired information to prior information. This higher level of processing is reflected in the examinees' selection of the red book, which implies the utilization of related prior information to solve the problem.

The analyses of the test in this research domain offer support to the PCT II's usefulness as a measure of some underlying dimension of intelligence. It offers support to such claims that the test measures "thinking or reasoning ability rather than the learning ability that consists of memorizing material" (Arthur, 1947, p. 24). In other words, the test appears to have the potential for measuring higher-order learning, such as intellectual skills, as opposed to the lower level or "verbal information" associated with recall of memorized facts (Gagné, 1977). Furthermore, there is a hierarchy in the levels of higher-order learning that seems to be tapped by the test, thus making it possible to assess subject performance at varying levels of mental functioning. As stated by Healy (1964, p. 14), the test has been developed to include "simpler elements capable of being readily rationalized by very immature minds and at the same time embodying features of much greater difficulty, up to those relationships which require close thought by competent reasoners." For this reason the PCT II has been used to assess different levels of ability and emotional impairments.

Some points need to be made regarding the appropriateness of the test for different populations. For instance, although the nonlanguage-based context of the test is appealing in that it does indeed offer possible validity for special populations, such as the hearing impaired and those with language deficiencies, its application to subjects from other countries must be made with caution. No test of intelligence is totally "culture-free" just because it is nonlanguage-based because all tests require some degree of acculturation for their successful completion (Sternberg, 1985, p. 77). For example, in the PCT II, some pictures in the scene (e.g., an American flag) may not be appropriate to subjects from other countries. Appropriate changes may be needed. In addition, there is some question regarding the appropriateness of the test for all age levels from a content validity point of view. The subject matter of the test, a day in the life of a schoolboy, may be of little relevance to adults.

There is also a need to modernize several of the illustrations and to eliminate stereotyped images. For example, the scene of the mother sitting in the chair sewing can convey a biased image of the role of women, especially given that the examinee is exposed to a limited set of illustrations on the test.

Critique

In summary, the PCT II manifests some positive features and has potential as a measure of intelligence. Thus, it can be useful to test hypotheses regarding the specific dimensions of intelligence that it is measuring. Early research supports some claims to its validity and reliability, but at the same time suggests inadequate empirical reports on the test itself. The existing literature supports a recommendation that investigations of some of the unresolved issues discussed above, particulary that of validity, be conducted to provide updated information to the potential user of the Healy Pictorial Completion Test II.

References

This list includes text citations as well as suggested additional reading.

Arthur, G. (1943). *A Point Scale of Performance Tests: Clinical manual* (Vol. 1). Chicago: Stoelting Company.

Arthur, G. (1947). *A Point Scale of Performance Tests, Revised Form II: Manual for administering and scoring the tests.* Chicago: Stoelting Company.

Bijou, S. W. (1942). An experimental analysis of Arthur performance quotients. *Journal of Counseling Psychology, 6,* 247-251.

Bilger, R. C. (1958). Limitations of the use of intelligence scales to estimate the mental ages of children. *Volta Review,* 321-325.

Dorcus, M. D. (1928). Analysis of specific responses of children in the Healy Pictorial Completion Test II. *Journal of Genetic Psychology, 35,* 574-586.

Gagné, R. (1977). *The conditions of learning.* New York: Holt, Rinehart and Winston, Inc.

Guilford, J. P. (1980). Components versus factors. *Behavioral and Brain Sciences, 3,* 591-592.

Hanfmann, E. (1939). A qualitative analysis of the Healy Pictorial Completion Test II. *American Journal of Orthopsychiatry, 9,* 325-330.

Harrower, M. (Ed.). (1950). *Recent advances in diagnostic psychological testing.* Springfield, IL: Charles C. Thomas.

Healy, W. (1914). A pictorial completion test. *Psychological Review, 21,* 189-203.

Healy, W. (1921). Pictorial Completion Test II. *Journal of Applied Psychology, 5,* 225-239.

Healy, W. (1964). *Pictorial Completion Test II.* Chicago: Stoelting Company.

Horn, J. L. (1979). Trends in the measurement of intelligence. In R. J. Sternberg & D. K. Detterman (Ed.), *Human intelligence: Perspectives on its theory and measurement.* Norwood, NJ: Ablex.

Johnson, B., & Schriefer, L. (1922). A comparison of mental age scores obtained by performance tests and the Stanford Revision of the Binet-Simon Scale. *Journal of Educational Psychology, 13,* 408-417.

Mayer, R., & Greeno, J. (1972). Structural differences between learning outcomes produced by different instructional methods. *Journal of Educational Psychology, 63,* 165-173.

Myklebust, H., Bannoche, M., & Killen, J. (1971). Learning disabilities and cognitive processes. In H. R. Myklebust (Ed.), *Progress in learning disabilities* (Vol. 2, pp. 213-251). New York: Grune & Stratton, Inc.

Perry, D. (1922). Interpretations of the reactions of the feeble-minded on the Healy Pictorial Completion Test II—social implications. *Journal of Delinquency, 7,* 75-85.

Pinter, R., & Anderson, M. (1917). *The Picture Completion Test.* Baltimore: Warwick and York.

Pinter, R., & Patterson, D. G. (1917). *A scale of performance tests.* New York: Appleton and Company.

Rapaport, D. (1945). *Diagnostic psychological testing* (Vol. I). Chicago: Waverly Press, Inc.

Sarason, S. B., & Sarason, E. K. (1946). The discriminatory value of a test pattern in the high grade familial defective. *Journal of Clinical Psychology, 38*(2), 39-49.

Schank, R. (1980). How much intelligence is there in artificial intelligence? *Intelligence, 4,* 1-14.

Schwerin, E., & Fitzwater, M. (1954). Comparative reliability and validity of the Healy Completion Test II and a revised form. *Journal of Clinical Psychology, 10,* 248-251.

Skaggs, E. B. (1920). A comparison of results obtained by the Terman-Binet Tests and the Healy Completion Test. *Journal of Educational Psychology, 11,* 418-420.

Spearman, C. (1923). *The nature of intelligence and the principles of cognition.* London: MacMillan.

Sternberg, R. J. (1983). Components of human intelligence. *Cognition, 15,* 1-48.

Sternberg, R. J. (1984). Higher-order reasoning in post-formal-operational thought. In M. Commons & C. Armon (Eds.), *Beyond formal operations: Late adolescent and adult cognitive development.* New York: Praeger.

Trabue, M. R. (1916). Completion-test language scales. *Teacher Collection of Contributions in Education, 77,* 1-118.

Vernon, P. E. (1937). A study of the norms and validity of certain mental tests at a child guidance clinic: Part II. *British Journal of Educational Psychology, 7,* 115-137.

Voss, J. F. (in press). Problem solving and the educational process. In R. Glaser & A. Lesgold (Eds.), *Handbook of psychology and education*. Hillsdale, NJ: Lawrence Erlbaum Associates.

Voss, J. F., Green, T. R., Post, T. A., & Penner, B. C. (1983). Problem solving skills in the social sciences. In G. Bowers (Ed.), *The psychology of learning and motivation: Advances in research and theory* (Vol. 17). New York: Academic Press.

Watson, R. I. (1951). *The clinical method in psychology.* New York: Harper's.

Wechsler, D. (1941). *The measurement of adult intelligence.* Baltimore, MD: Williams and Wilkins.

Werner, H. (1940). A comparative study of a small group of clinical tests. *Journal of Applied Psychology, 23,* 231-236.

Worthington, M. R. (1926). A study of some commonly used performance tests. *Journal of Applied Psychology, 10,* 216-227.

Yoakum, C. (1920). *Army mental tests.* New York: Holt and Company.

Robert J. Drummond, Ph.D.
Program Director, Counselor Education, University of North Florida, Jacksonville, Florida.

INFERRED SELF-CONCEPT SCALE

E.L. McDaniel. Los Angeles, California: Western Psychological Services.

Introduction

The Inferred Self-Concept Scale (ISCS) is a behavioral rating scale for use by teachers, counselors, psychologists, and researchers to assess the self-concept of children in Grades 1-6. The scale's author, E.L. McDaniel (1973), states that the scale has two principal uses: individual evaluation and research. Using a five-point scale, respondents rate students on 30 items (statements) that describe various behaviors.

The basic assumption behind the construction of the test was that self-concept can be inferred from behavior. According to the author (McDaniel, 1973), the instrument provides a simple method for appraising the self-concept of individuals from different classes and cultures because the subjects are not penalized due to differences in verbal ability and/or test experience. McDaniel maintains that the ISCS should be particularly useful for assessing the self-concepts of children from lower socioeconomic or culturally different groups. The test was initially developed because she saw a need for an instrument that would be appropriate to use with these particular groups.

The original pool of items was developed from traits and behaviors identified in the literature as dimensions of the self-concept. A list of 100 items was developed and presented to eight judges. The items that received 75% consensus by the judges were initially selected for the scale. Seven of these items were eliminated by the author because they were repetitious. The final revision consisted of 30 items. McDaniel completed the normative data on the test in 1965.

The ISCS is printed on the back and front of one sheet. There are boxes for the rater to include information on the child, such as name, date of birth, school, ethnic group, age, and sex; examiner; and date. There are also boxes that the researcher or counselor can use to record supplemental information such as IQ, achievement data, and birth order. The directions and eight items are listed on the first page, and 22 items are listed on the second page. Boxes are at the bottom of the second page to count the response values in each column and then compute for the total score.

Practical Applications/Uses

The ISCS is a rating form that could be used by counselors, teachers, or researchers to assess a student's self-concept, an important construct to be considered in the school environment. Knowing students' self-concept is helpful to teachers in developing effective strategies to use with students, and the ISCS could be a helpful tool in aiding counselors and teachers to identify behaviors that could be modified. For instance, if self-report inventories are used, teachers' or counselors' perceptions could be compared with those of students. The ISCS can also be used in research studies.

The normative data on the test were developed from a sample of students in first through sixth grades. The author claims that the test is easy to administer but should be administered by teachers, counselors, or other educated observers. Raters circle one of the five numbers (indicating "never" to "always") at the right of each statement (e.g., Gives up easily; Stops activity when it takes effort), according to their perceptions of the students' behaviors.

The directions for scoring are discussed in the manual. Eight items are worded in a reverse direction from the other items in order to avoid response set. There is limited information to guide users in the interpretation of the results. McDaniel (1973) states that inferred self-concept scores range from a low of 30, representing a socially undesirable or negative concept, to a high of 150, representing a socially desirable or positive concept of self. Means for the beginning and end of the school year ratings by teachers of Grades 1-6 are presented, but no standard deviations are given and no norms are presented by grade or age. Without normative data, the test would be difficult for examiners to interpret.

Technical Aspects

McDaniel (1973, p. 5) presents some reliability data on the ISCS. She correlated the relationship between counselors and teachers ratings of the same students. The correlations ranged from −.55 to .94 for 180 students, with the median falling in the .31 to .40 range. Correlations for each item between teacher and counselor ratings ranged from a low of .07 on "Plays with smaller or younger children" to .58 on "Seems to have a 'chip' on his shoulder." The median coefficient was .32. Split-half reliability coefficients were .86 for a group of counselors and .85 for teachers. Alpha coefficients were reported to be .92 for counselors and .91 for teachers.

McDaniel (1967) presents correlations of the scale with grade, age, family size, intelligence, and achievement variables. There are significant but low positive correlations with student achievement and intelligence. Factor analysis indicates that there are two factors: one reflecting the individual's maturity in interpersonal relationships and a second reflecting self-attitude. No correlations are given between the ISCS and widely used self-report inventories such as the Piers-Harris or the Coopersmith.

The ISCS has limited validity information, questionable reliability evidence, and insufficient information for users to interpret the results. The concept of inferred self-concept has been used in a few recent studies (Marsh, 1984; Friesen & Der, 1978) and as a criterion to validate other instruments (Hughes & Leatherman, 1982).

Critique

Sundberg (1978), in reviewing the Inferred Self-Concept Scale, concludes that the idea of the scale as an attempt to get at the self-concept of students, especially those from low socioeconomic and minority groups, has merit, but that more evidence is needed on the reliability and validity of the test. One of the major problems he cites is the lack of information on how to interpret the scores. If used, he states that the ISCS should not be treated as a test but as one source of data in the context of more information about the child. In addition, he questions whether the reversing of the eight items to control response set accomplishes its purpose and whether the items are behaviorally stated.

This reviewer has worked with the ISCS and finds that teachers and counselors are willing to use the scale if they have only a few students to rate, but blocking and refusing if they are requested to rate many students. They also prefer all simple behavioral statements that would require low inference to interpret and that they could just check if present. The reliability of the rating would then be higher. Another disadvantage of this scale is the insufficient guidance given to users concerning the meaning of scores. Additionally, teachers and counselors recognize that the instrument is dated by the sex-biased language used in the test.

In the manual the author states that the instrument is experimental but has research value. Although McDaniel's idea of measuring the self-concept of special populations has merit, the test has not been one that has been reported in the professional literature as being widely used. Some possible reasons—both practical and technical—for this have already been noted in this review. Much research and theory development has been done on the self-concept construct since the instrument was published. Unless the test is revised to meet the criticisms identified by some of the reviewers (e.g., Sundberg, 1978) and developed to meet the current standards for educational and psychological tests, it will have little value to users even as a research tool.

References

Friesen, J. D., & Der, D. (1978). *A program of consultation, training and counselling of children with learning and behavioral problems and their parents and teachers* (Report No. 78:48). Vancouver, British Columbia: Educational Research Institute of British Columbia. (ERIC Document Reproduction Service No. ED 169 467)

Hughes, H. M., & Leatherman, M. K. (1982, August). *Refinement of the Maryland Preschool Self-Concept Scale.* Paper presented at the annual meeting of the American Psychological Association, Washington, DC.

Marsh, H. W. (1984). Relations among dimensions of self-attribution, dimensions of self-concept, and academic achievements. *Journal of Educational Psychology, 76,* 1291-1308.

McDaniel, E. L. (1967). *Final report on head start evaluation and research—1966-67 to the Institute for Educational Development. Section VIII. Relationships between self-concept and specific variables in a low-income culturally different population* (Report No. IED-66-1). Austin: The University of Texas Child Development Evaluation and Research Center.

McDaniel, E. L. (1973). *Inferred Self-Concept Scale.* Los Angeles: Western Psychological Services.

Sundberg, N. D. (1978). Review of the Inferred Self-Concept Scale. In O. K. Buros (Ed.), *The eighth mental measurements yearbook* (pp. 861-862). Highland Park, NJ: The Gryphon Press.

Larry A. Pace, Ph.D.
Manager, Organizational Effectiveness, Reprographic Manufacturing Operations, Xerox Corporation, Webster, New York.

INVENTORY OF INDIVIDUALLY PERCEIVED GROUP COHESIVENESS

David L. Johnson. Chicago, Illinois: Stoelting Company.

Introduction

The Inventory of Individually Perceived Group Cohesiveness (IIPGC) is a self-report measure of an individual's perceptions of intragroup cooperation, expectational control, and task communication. These three factors are summed to provide a nominal group cohesiveness score. The IIPGC is untimed but, according to the manual (Johnson, 1979), typically takes no longer than 12 to 15 minutes.

The author of the IIPGC is David L. Johnson, Ph.D., a social psychologist, research sociologist, and consultant. The IIPGC was developed in order to provide a more objective, limited measure of cohesiveness than does the sociometric concept of interpersonal attraction.

The IIPGC was apparently developed prior to 1974 (Johnson & Ridener, 1974), although few specifics of the development process are given in the author's technical report (Johnson, 1977) and manual. The normative populations listed run the gamut from preschool to graduate school, from groups of two to 30 people, and from hospitals to business settings.

The IIPGC is a one-page, 20-item, self-report, self-administered inventory. Each of the items stresses a different aspect of group cohesiveness (e.g., interactions, teamwork, cooperation). On the back of the inventory are spaces for recording the three scale scores for feedback and tracking purposes. The inventory is quite straightforward. Each item is rated on a five-point scale from 0 (no emphasis in the group) to 4 (a great deal of emphasis in the group).

Practical Applications/Uses

The IIPGC has been used in a wide variety of settings to study group cohesiveness as a composite of three variable social processes: cooperation, expectational control, and task communication (or task influence).

An advantage of the IIPGC is that its format lends itself to use in the field before, during, and after group meetings. Subjects from elementary-school age and up should have no difficulty understanding the items in the inventory.

Applications could include research on 1) the relationships between the scales of the IIPGC and variables such as group performance and member satisfaction, 2) optimum conditions for group cohesiveness, and 3) variables that affect group cohesiveness.

No special expertise is required of the examiner, although much of the research cited in the manual and a previous technical report (Johnson, 1977) also included observations by trained group observers.

Technical Aspects

The reliability of the IIPGC is defended largely on the basis of stability of IIPGC scores across two points in time. The author refers to five studies in which no significant differences in variable means were noted between the first presession and the fourth postsession measures for each of five diverse groups. No reference is made to correlational estimates of the degree of stability of the IIPGC. One reference to internal consistency is found in the manual, a K-R 20 coefficient of .90 (N = 23). It is not explained whether this estimate refers to one or a composite of the three scales in the IIPGC. No mention is made of scale intercorrelations.

Validity evidence is presented in the form of two studies (Johnson, 1977). In one study overall IIPGC scores were found to be positively related to self-disclosure. Another study was performed in which more cohesive groups were found to exhibit more cooperative, helpful, and friendly behavior on a prisoner's dilemma task.

Critique

The IIPGC suffers from an unusual malady. Are the scale scores and the overall cohesiveness scores predictors or criteria, independent or dependent variables? Because cohesiveness can be hypothesized and has, in fact, been shown to affect and be affected by many intrapersonal, interpersonal, institutional, and cultural variables, the answer to the above question probably depends on the situation. Cohesiveness, therefore, could more accurately be described as an *intervening* variable.

This, however, poses a dilemma for the IIPGC's author. Because he chose to define cohesiveness as a composite of variable processes, stability measures are irrelevant. Unfortunately, the bulk of the evidence for the inventory's reliability comes from stability measures. Similarly, the validity of any instrument should be estimated, calculated, or judged from its ability to measure what it is intended to measure. Yet, no hard evidence is offered that the scales indeed correlate significantly with independent measures of expectational control, cooperation, perceived task influence, or group cohesiveness. In addition, because these factors are assumed to vary with the situation and the ongoing group process, it would seem impossible to find stable measures of them with which to correlate IIPGC scores.

A fruitful endeavor for those who desire to use measures of cohesiveness would be the development of models of the theoretical relationships among cohesiveness and various group input and output variables. These models could then be used to develop hypotheses concerning differences between groups on any number of variables. Coupled with this research should be a thorough examination of the internal consistency of the IIPGC scale scores and their interrelationships, as well as construct validation of the intervening variable, group cohesiveness.

At this time, because of the inconclusive nature of the data on which this inventory is founded and its meaning is interpreted, the IIPGC must be considered experimental in nature.

In general, cohesiveness is one of the most frequently studied (Festinger, 1951; cited in Worchel & Cooper, 1983) and least understood variables in group behavior. As the IIPGC's author correctly points out, cohesiveness is easily confused with attraction or affiliation (Johnson, 1979). Thus, the direction taken by the IIPGC in limiting and objectifying the construct is laudable. It is to be hoped that subsequent research will continue in this vein.

References

Festinger, L. (1951). Informal communication in small groups. In H. Geretzkow (Ed.), *Groups, leadership and men: Research in human relations.* Pittsburgh: Carnegie Press.

Johnson, D. L. (1977). *Summary of field studies and uses of the Inventory of Individually Perceived Group Cohesiveness* (Tech. Rep. No. 2). Albuquerque: Institute of Human Resources.

Johnson, D. L. (1979). *Inventory of Individually Perceived Group Cohesiveness instruction manual.* Chicago: Stoelting Company.

Johnson, D. L., & Ridener, L. (1974). Self-disclosure, participation, and perceived cohesiveness in small group interaction. *Psychological Reports, 35,* 65-66.

Worchel, S., & Cooper, J. (1983). *Understanding social psychology* (3rd ed.). Homewood, IL: Dorsey Press.

Barbara A. Hutson, Ed.D.
Professor of Education, Northern Virginia Graduate Center, Virginia Polytechnic Institute and State University, Falls Church, Virginia.

KAUFMAN DEVELOPMENTAL SCALE

Harvey Kaufman. Chicago, Illinois: Stoelting Company.

Introduction

The Kaufman Developmental Scale (KDS) is described by its author as an instrument designed to serve both assessment and programming needs for normal children and for mildly to severely retarded persons of all ages. The scale provides an overall Developmental Quotient and quotients in each of six areas of functioning: Gross Motor, Fine Motor, Receptive, Expressive, Personal Behavior, and Interpersonal Behavior. These scores can be plotted on a Progress Graph, used to predict expected and actual gain over several months, and on a Developmental Profile, which makes visible the differences in scores across various domains. There are attractive features but also serious problems that prevent the KDS from attaining some of its goals.

In 1971 an experimental Habilitation and Evaluation Schedule was developed by Harvey Kaufman, E. Connors, and B. J. Halverson to assess the developmentally impaired. They adopted items from psychological research, including intelligence tests. "Once items were selected, weights were assigned so that each item provided necessary input to the total developmental quotient to create a highly significant relationship to tested intelligence" (Kaufman, 1974, p. 3). This form was tested both on a mixed sample of 58 individuals ranging academically from preschool through Grade 4 and in intelligence from severely retarded to very superior, and on a group of 12 retarded persons (mean IQ 45) ranging in age roughly from 10 to 30. For the mixed group, sample sizes at some ages were as low as two or three, and it is not clear whether the proportions of retarded individuals in this sample were evenly distributed across ages. For the sample of retarded subjects, there were in most instances only two or three subjects for each five-year age span.

The manual does not indicate that results from these initial samples were used to select items or check their placement, or to evaluate whether the developmental levels assigned to various subscales matched those found in the sample on other measures of those domains. Means for the overall Developmental Quotient and for Developmental Quotients on each subscale, as well as correlations of these quotients with IQ, were reported for the two initial samples and for a number of other samples that are not clearly described.

The test given to the later samples was apparently unrevised except for the name; it was published by Kaufman in 1974 as the Kaufman Developmental Scale. Most of the samples were small, with the exception of a mixed sample (N = 135) that ranged in age from 9 months to 10 years and in IQ from 15 to 145. There was some imbalance, with more than twice as many males as females, and with nearly 40% identified as retarded. No information is provided about whether the ability levels in the sample differed appreciably from age group to age group. Scattered statistics are also provided for other small samples. In the largest sample of mentally retarded subjects, ages birth to four years, however, there was only one subject in the 0-12 months group, and there were two or three times as many males as females in the one-year-old and two-year-old groups. Because the mixed groups for whom test results were reported contained a larger than normal percentage of retarded and possibly other special groups, they adequately represent neither a normal population nor a clinical one. Suggested age equivalents, though, do not seem to be based upon empirical study of any of these groups.

There was in effect no norm group for the KDS. The developers selected items they expected to correlate with intelligence tests and weighted them to maximize this relationship, on the basis of either informal experience or an unreported study. Although overall means and correlations with various IQ tests are reported, no information is reported and perhaps none was obtained about the actual difficulty of various items and levels within the scales.

No revisions or adaptations of the scale for handicapped or non-English-speaking individuals are reported. On the lowest levels of the Gross Motor subscale, however, some allowances are made in scoring items for subjects using body braces. The KDS can be adapted to a wide range of individuals, if one is willing to forego developmental quotients. Dr. Kaufman does not suggest omitting subtests, but does state that for a handicapped person the examiner should not compute an overall score, because averaging in the deficit area would be a misrepresentation. A group or institution might modify administration of the KDS and norm it within a particular handicapped group, but before beginning that effort should assess carefully whether the items reflect their learning objectives and program.

The test kit consists of a manual, a booklet of Evaluation Cards to be used in administering the scale, record blanks, and objects such as cubes, jump rope, pegboard, cups, and candy (some for a task, some for reinforcement). All the items are packed in a handsome, sturdy, lockable briefcase, with neat compartments for the paper items, though once unwrapped the other items tend to rattle around. Items such as the felt pieces of a clown face could be lost rather easily, and others, such as the paper puzzles, the cards for sequencing, and the paper clock, are likely to become soiled. To avoid problems, the user may want to mount these items on heavier cardboard and to laminate or spray them. Apart from these considerations, the materials are suitable and attractive.

The small KDS manual provides tables of statistics as well as brief guides to administration, scoring, and prescriptions. Also included are a few completed profiles to illustrate scoring, interpretation, and use of the KDS to guide educational prescriptions. The manual could be clearer in its presentation of statistics, more detailed in its description of administration and scoring, and better organized. It would be useful, for example, to have the various types of information presented in a sequential pattern that matches the examiner's sequence of activities: administer items, score items, calculate quotients, plot results, derive prescriptions.

In administering the KDS the examiner stays busy. For most items he or she observes a behavior ("Does the individual use body language such as clapping, waving goodbye expressively and spontaneously?"), elicits a skill verbally ("Sing a song for me") or sets out materials, such as a puzzle, for a task. The examiner need not score all items on the run, but must score enough to determine basal and ceiling during the test session. He or she marks each item as correct, incorrect, or partially correct. After testing is complete, the examiner totals the number of months' credit for each item, a cumbersome process. The examiner is directed to plot the results on the Progress Graph and the Developmental Profile and to derive from these a list of prescribed activities in each area.

Most of the items are familiar from other tests or observation scales for young or retarded subjects. The majority are directly observed as the examinee undertakes simple tasks, but some may be obtained by interviewing the child's parent or caretaker. The manual recommends the use of the KDS for normal children from birth to age ten and for retarded individuals of all ages. Items on most subscales range in rated difficulty from infancy to later adolescence/adulthood. For reasons discussed more fully in the following sections, though, the scale is not likely to be useful with normal school-aged children.

The record blanks allow marking of all items, organized as a matrix of the 6 subscales by 9 developmental levels, infancy to late adolescence/adulthood. This makes it easy to see an individual's areas of high and low scores. The record blank also provides a Progress Graph.

Practical Applications/Uses

The Kaufman Developmental Scale was intended to be used to assess an examinee's general level of functioning and levels of functioning in six domains, and to guide the development of prescriptions for instruction. The norming and validation procedures compromise the former objective, and the procedures for identifying objectives and generating items weaken the latter one. The most frequent use of this test seems to be in clinical settings, especially mental health facilities and residential facilities for the retarded.

Although the test manual recommends the KDS for use with normal children up to age 10 and retarded individuals of any age or ability level, the items beyond the 4 to 6-year-old level seem too gross to be informative about normal children. For example, one of the five items on the 6 to 8-year level of Inter-personal Behavior is "Addition and Subtraction," and the items at the 8 to 12-year level are third-grade reading (word calling), multiplication (one item), fourth-grade reading, and division. That provides little guidance for educational programming during this two-year span. Another problem with items at the upper levels is their sparseness; on the next to last level, for instance, there are no items for the Gross Motor, Fine Motor, Receptive, or Expressive areas, only one item for Personal Behavior, and three for Inter-personal Behavior. Sparseness is less of a problem at most earlier levels, except for Inter-personal Behavior, for which only one item is provided on each of the first three levels. In general, the KDS as a whole is best used with those whose mental levels are not above the 4 to 6-year level and not below the 1-year level.

With today's heroic medical procedures, increasing numbers of children are saved, with some deficits. At the same time, the public schools extend services to a wider range of students, so that the populations served in clinical settings include a greater proportion of multiply handicapped individuals. Some cannot perform or cannot demonstrate their cognitive ability through tasks in their areas of disability; given this, it is important to use measures with subscales that each have well-established validity and can thus be used independently.

Validation of the KDS was based on overall score, not the individual scales. Although the KDS makes no provision for using the scales separately, the examiner may sometimes need to do so. The primary consideration is the fairness of a particular subscale for a given individual. In some cases the problems are obvious. A visually disabled child, for example, should not be penalized on Fine Motor tasks because she cannot see the examiner's demonstrations, and a motor-handicapped individual functioning at a high level cognitively should not be asked to struggle with Gross Motor items such as walking backward heel to toe, with failure on any item affecting his overall developmental quotient. If the subject's disability is moderate, the examiner might choose to administer at least some items on the scale if the items themselves are of interest, but should not attempt to compute developmental age on that scale. If the disability is great, it is best not to administer the affected scale even though an overall Developmental Quotient cannot then be computed.

In other cases there are more subtle problems, hidden within scales whose names suggest no problems. For example, a visually disabled individual is not necessarily handicapped in receptive language. The receptive modality scale of the KDS, though, is a melange of items, some of which are inappropriate for the visually disabled. For instance, for an item at the 8 to 12-year level of RM the examiner shows moderately complex line drawings for 5 seconds, then asks the examinee to draw the design from memory. Other items on this subscale ask for completion of a thin paper puzzle (difficult also for the motor-handicapped), identification of missing details in pictures, and picture sequences. Failure on such items would lower scores on Receptive, when in fact the examinee had no problems in receptive language, as might be inferred from the score, but was doubly penalized for blindness. There are subtle problems for persons with hearing or motor disabilities on other scales. Failure on a single item can prevent one from receiving credit for a given level of development, because "a basal will be established with successful accomplishment of an entire developmental stage [within a subscale]" (Kaufman, 1974, p. 17).

The problem is not in reporting successes and failures but in interpreting them appropriately in light of the handicap and in drawing up prescriptions that fit the individual. An examiner can use the Kaufman Developmental Scale for assessing persons with a wide range of handicapping conditions, as a description of current functioning on a variety of tasks, but only if he or she 1) exercises judgment about whether a given item or scale should even be administered to that person and then 2) uses the information descriptively rather than normatively.

The KDS can be administered in any reasonably quiet setting with suitable table and chairs. Testing should not be done in the sight of other examinees who may be tested on this measure. The KDS is an individual test, not suitable for use in groups or in a paper-and-pencil form.

Actual test administration is reasonably simple, well within the ability of teachers, paraprofessionals, secretaries, or proctors. Yet, because interpretation should be guided by observation, it would be inadvisable to assign administration of this test to anyone (including psychologists) without thorough training in the nature and assessment of intelligence, learning, and development and in the effects of handicapping conditions on test performance. This is especially true when the test is used to make major decisions (e.g., institutionalization or placement in programs that offer more hope for mainstreaming or more support for an individual's needs) affecting the pattern of an individual's life.

The only major problem in KDS administration is that the item names are not listed on the record blank, so one must keep out both the record blank and the manual (in which the item name, brief description of task, and criteria are listed). A few items can be assessed by asking a parent or caretaker (or at later ages, the examinee) about some behavior, but in most cases the examiner sets up a simple task to elicit a behavior and then notes results on the record blank.

No time limits are given, and the KDS is described as a power test. Though not specifically suggested in the manual, an examiner might vary the order of administration of various scales or even give them on different days not too far apart, though it would be best not to alter the order of items within scales. Users are advised to apply standardized individual testing procedures, though these are not defined. Where cultural bias or regional differences might negatively affect results, the examiner is invited to substitute appropriate alternatives such as a TV commercial in place of a nursery rhyme.

Scoring of individual items is easy enough because criteria for most items are unambiguous. Items are marked as "–" for failure, " + " for clear pass, and "1/2" for half credit (half of the assigned months' growth). Items for which half credit is allowable are marked on the record blank with an asterisk. Within each subscale or modality, items are laid out sequentially by levels, making it easy to see whether an individual has passed all items at a given level on a subscale.

Translating item scores into scores for a subscale as a whole is more of a chore. The examiner looks on the record blank to find how many months of growth each item on that level of that scale is worth. If the performance was scored as half credit and if half credit is allowable for that item, the number of months for that item is divided by two, and the item credits for this level are totalled and then added to the credits earned on previous levels to yield a Developmental Age. In general, a basal is established when an individual demonstrates or is expected to demonstrate mastery of all items on a given level, and a ceiling is established when all items on a level are failed or the examiner expects them to be failed. Except for establishment of basal and ceiling, developmental level seems not to be used, as all scoring is based on credits for individual items.

To derive a Developmental Quotient, the Developmental Age is divided by the Chronological Age for subjects up to age 10, beyond which a conversion table is used. This table provides a Developmental Quotient higher than the ratio division procedure. For example, an individual with a Developmental Age of 6-0 at age 12 is credited with a Developmental Quotient of 60 rather than the 50 that would be derived by dividing by chronological age. (Neither the rationale nor the statistical procedures are described.) The procedure is repeated for each subscale to yield a

Developmental Quotient for each subscale. The six subscale quotients are averaged to obtain the overall Developmental Quotient.

Machine scoring for the Kaufman Developmental Scale is not available, although much of the cumbersome and error-inducing burden of translating item scores into scores for the subscales could thus be eased.

Interpretation is based on objective scores, though it must be tempered by clinical judgment. In fact, given the problems in those objective scores, perhaps they should be leavened by large doses of clinical and educational judgment. Many aspects of item scoring are mechanical and could in some instances be turned over to paraprofessionals, but this is seldom advisable because interpretation of the scores should be guided by intimate knowledge of *how* the examinee performed. Only the summing and plotting of item weights assigned by the psychologist should be entrusted to others, and interpretation of the scores should not be delegated by the psychologist. If the test were divested of the quasi-intelligence test features of developmental quotient, profile, and prediction chart, teachers and others could administer and score test performance as a criterion- or objective-referenced test.

Kaufman (1974) states that "All items assessed are samples of the type of items that can be taught" (p. 1); he encourages the examiner-programmer to develop a program based on deficit areas as well as those behaviors expected to develop in the near future. He suggests that while a detailed program might be furnished to a professional, the developmental prescription given to a parent should contain only a few items at any one time in order to avoid overload and unrealistic expectations.

Technical Aspects

The *Standards for Educational and Psychological Tests* (American Educational Research Association, American Psychological Association, and National Council on Measurement in Education, 1974) suggest three types of reliability for any assessment: comparability of forms, stability over time, and internal consistency.

Information about internal consistency was provided for the normal intelligence subjects (37) and the retarded subjects (21) in the initial sample of 58, and for another sample of 59 retarded subjects (within the mixed sample of 135) ranging in age from birth to four years, with a mean chronological age of 2.8. The procedure used for assessing reliability was described as an odd-even sampling corrected with the Spearman-Brown prophecy formula. For the Developmental Age these estimates were .98 and .99. In most cases, the estimates for subscales were .96 or better, though the coefficients for Expressive in the normal group and for Interpersonal Behavior in the retarded groups were noticeably lower. The Spearman-Brown reliability procedure, however, tests only whether the odd items in a scale are approximately as difficult as the even items.

The scale as a whole and most of the subscales are reliable in the limited sense of internal consistency, but no evidence is presented for test-retest reliability (the stability of scores over time). This is a serious limitation in an instrument to be used for measuring progress. As there is only one form of the scale (a limitation in a test designed to be used repeatedly), alternate-form reliability could not be computed. The suggested use of the same form at retest intervals of six months or less can inflate scores as examinees or caretakers are sensitized to specific items, but this is likely to be less of a problem among lower-functioning individuals.

The *Standards for Educational and Psychological Tests* list four kinds of validity: *concurrent* (the degree to which standing on one measure is related to performance on some other measure at roughly the same time); *predictive* (the extent to which we can predict future score on some measure by knowledge of current functioning on this measure); *content* (the adequacy of the test items in representing an area of behavior); and *construct* (the network of relationships of the test with its parts or with other measures).

Information about the concurrent validity of the KDS is presented in the form of correlations between overall Developmental Quotient and quotients on each of the subscales with scores on any of a variety of individual intelligence tests. This was reported for the initial mixed sample of 58, the mixed sample of 135, and a subsample of 59 retarded children drawn from the sample of 135. Correlations between overall DQ and IQ ranged from .94 to .96. This and the similarity of means indicate a substantial overlap between these measures, not surprising as the KDS items were chosen and weighted in terms of their expected relationship with IQ scores. Concurrent validity is established for the total score; for the subscales, however, evidence is somewhat weaker—correlations with IQ range from .79 down to .40, which indicates that only 16% of the combined variance is accounted for by the overlap of that subtest with IQ. No evidence is presented for concurrent validity in terms of relationship to individuals' success in a curriculum.

There is no mention in the text of any procedure for testing predictive validity, yet near the end of the manual appears a Predictive Table, to be used in determining if the overall growth is commensurate with expectation. No information is given about how the table was derived—it seemed at first that it might have been based on regressions computed for one or more of the samples. Closer inspection of the table, however, suggests that it was not a statistical analysis but simply an arrangement of mental age/IQ equivalents. For example, for Borderline/Mild, defined as a DQ of 64 to 84, a low estimate of Developmental Age at the chronological age of 10 years is 6.40 and a high estimate is 8.4. This would not constitute a test of predictive validity. Yet, given the correlations with IQ, it is likely that over large or wide-ranging groups overall Developmental Quotient at one time would predict reasonably well scores on the KDS or on another intelligence test over at least a short period. There is no way of telling how accurate that prediction would be for individuals.

The correlations between overall DQ and IQ may or may not be evidence for construct validity, depending on the definition of what this test is measuring and the use to be made of the information. Kaufman (1974) states that the KDS is not an intelligence test, yet his validation procedures are closer to those for intelligence tests than for achievement tests. For an intelligence test, 1) correlations between the KDS and IQ tests should be high and their overall means should be similar, and 2) subtests should have moderate correlations with overall test score but only modest correlations with one another. The first condition is met, the second is not, and the test fails in other ways to meet the standards of careful preparation expected of a modern test of intelligence.

Ideally, a curriculum test should have a relatively high correlation with IQ, but not too high, because that would indicate that the scale was just another less-than-optimal IQ test. To be useful as separate scores, the subscales should have moderately high correlations with the total KDS quotient but relatively low correlations with one another, as higher correlations would indicate that the subscales were all measuring the same thing rather than independent areas of functioning. Further, the subscales should have moderately high correlations with external measures of the same domain, and lower correlations with tests measuring other domains. For example, the KDS receptive modality subscale should correlate rather highly with a test such as the Peabody Picture Vocabulary Test, but less so with a test of fine-motor skill or personal behavior.

In fact, the subscales have moderate correlations with the full KDS (differing across samples) and inconveniently high correlations between subscales in the later (younger) samples, suggesting that at least for younger subjects the various subscales are measuring roughly the same area of functioning rather than six independent areas. (It's puzzling that in the last two samples subscales are more highly correlated with one another than with the overall score.) No information is offered about relations of subscale quotients to other measures of the same domains.

To be useful in assessing an individual's level of functioning, a test should have a small standard error of measurement (estimate of the degree to which scores for that individual are likely to deviate from his/her theoretically true score). This issue is especially important if the test is to be used to measure change in individuals, as the estimate of change includes any error on both the pre- and the post-test. The Kaufman Developmental Scale has a small enough standard error of measurement for the overall DQ, but there are problems on some subscales. For example, in the normal subjects the standard error was 4.9 and 4.8 for Expressive and Personal Behavior, respectively. The examiner could thus be reasonably sure that the true score for an individual with a Developmental Quotient of 90 on these scales was somewhere between 85 and 95, and quite sure that the individual's true level was between 80 and 100. The professional must judge whether that degree of precision is adequate.

Reflecting the same problem at the group level are the very high standard deviations in some samples. For example, in one sample the mean for Receptive was 86, but the standard deviation was 42.5, indicating wide variability within the sample. In fact, the smallest standard deviation for a subtest on this sample was 33.

To be useful in guiding educational prescriptions, a test should be based on analysis of the kinds of learning that are required to survive or thrive in a given environment and that can be taught. Although no comprehensive curriculum analysis was described, the Kaufman Developmental Scale reflects an implicit curriculum—a curriculum on how to take intelligence tests. This includes some topics often covered in preschool learning centers. Although it is possible to teach tasks like those on the KDS, an individual's scores on a test of general developmental level are typically used as *estimates* of overall functioning; these estimates may be inflated and thus less useful if the items are directly taught. If, on the other hand, the KDS is used descriptively as a criterion-referenced test, without use of the quotients and so on, it is quite appropriate to try to teach individual items. The major concern then becomes whether the test contains the right items and whether those items tap effectively the targeted areas of learning. From this perspective, most KDS items on the lower levels are not bad, but items assessing educational progress are too gross and too sparse to be helpful, and the nature of items tapped on some scales varies markedly across levels.

Critique

There are two potential uses for an instrument like the Kaufman Developmental Scale: as a replacement for an individual intelligence test and as a guide to developing instructional plans. When a well-constructed test yields approximately the same score as a well-established individual intelligence test, but at an appreciable savings in time or in expertise required for administration, as with the Slosson Intelligence Test (Slosson, 1961-81) or The Quick Test (Ammons & Ammons, 1958-62), it may be useful as a substitute in at least some situations. Although the total KDS Developmental Quotient is highly correlated with scores on individual IQ tests and the means are similar, the KDS could not be recommended as a substitute for an intelligence test because of its casual validation, apparent lack of any formal procedure for selecting or validating items or levels, lack of norms, and lack of information on critical aspects of reliability and validity. The quotients and graphs give an appearance of precision. Anastasi has pointed out, though, that "the availability of scores from clinical instruments does not assure accuracy of interpretation; it may create only an illusion of objectivity and quantification" (1985, p. xxv). The manual states that the instrument should not be used as a clinical diagnostic assessment of intelligence, yet at other places this use seems implied, and the fact that the score is reported as a quotient may tempt some to use it as a intelligence test, an invitation to litigation.

A more reasonable use of the KDS is to guide educational programming for individuals, yet even for this purpose it has limitations. The individual items do not seem to have been chosen to reflect the behavioral objectives of a learning program, and there is no direct information about when various items and developmental levels are actually mastered by children; the age levels were apparently assigned based on the developers' expectations. If used without the statistical overkill, the items themselves may be useful as a criterion-referenced test for describing attainments in a rough sequence and for predicting informally the kinds of growth that are likely to occur and should be encouraged over the next few months.

Comparison of relative growth across areas in a profile is only meaningful if the areas are presented in comparable units of measurement, which is usually made possible by computing scaled scores. Yet on the KDS, which does not use scaled scores, the means on various scales differed by as much as 40 points, making comparison across scales hazardous. As Eichorn (1978, p. 309) pointed out, "the 'profile' obtained is probably not valid." It is best not even to plot the various subscales on the Profile Chart, as the dramatic visual differences may tempt one to make illegitimate inferences about an individual's relative strengths and weaknesses.

Clinicians should be even more cautious about using the Progress Chart to lay out precise expectations for growth. The uncertainties about how predictions were derived combine with the uneven distribution of number and difficulties of items within scales to bring into question the usefulness of the prediction table and Progress Chart.

The major problem with the Kaufman Developmental Scale is that its developers tried to create a test that would do everything—assess overall mental functioning, social maturity, language, academic success, and so on. But the KDS is not as effective a measure of social maturity as the Vineland (Doll, 1984), and not as effective a measure of language as the Peabody (Dunn, 1981). It is not as well tailored for a special population as the Leiter International Performance Scale (Leiter & Arthur, 1936-55) or the Columbia Mental Maturity Scale (Burgemeister, Blum, & Lorge, 1954-72), and not as well calibrated for measuring growth at lower mental ages as tests like the Bayley Scales of Infant Development (Bayley, 1969-84). The KDS measures neither overall mental functioning as well as many well-constructed IQ tests nor academic achievement as well as many achievement tests, such as the Metropolitan (Balow, Farr, Hogan, & Prescott, 1978).

The Kaufman Developmental Scale could be modified to be more useful. It would be more credible as a measure of overall mental functioning if more systematic procedures were used for selecting and placing items, and if the test were normed on a large, carefully designed norm group, reflecting either the population as a whole or a specified clinical group. Subscale scores could be used speparately if these were normed as well, and validated against trusted measures of each domain.

Increasing the usefulness of the KDS as a source of prescriptions for learning would require starting over with an analysis of "What should learners know to succeed in this environment?", using that analysis as a basis for item specifications, and then norming the test on a sample like those for whom it is to be used or, if it is to be used as a criterion-referenced test, assessing typical age of mastery and setting cutoffs.

These are obviously major changes, but without such changes, the KDS is a seriously limited instrument.

References

American Educational Research Association, American Psychological Association, & National Council on Measurement in Education. (1974). *Standards for educational and psychological tests.* Washington, DC: American Psychological Association.

Ammons, R. B., & Ammons, C. H. (1958-62). *The Quick Test.* Missoula, MT: Psychological Test Specialists.

Anastasi, A. (1985). Mental measurements: Some emerging trends. In J. V. Mitchell, Jr. (Ed.), *The ninth mental measurements yearbook* (pp. xxiii-xxix). Lincoln, NE: Buros Institute of Mental Measurements.

Balow, I. H., Farr, R., Hogan, T. P., & Prescott, G. A. (1978). *Metropolitan Achievement Tests* (5th ed.). New York: The Psychological Corporation.

Bayley, N. (1969-84). *Bayley Scales of Infant Development.* New York: The Psychological Corporation.

Burgemeister, B. B., Blum, L. H., & Lorge, I. (1954-72). *Columbia Mental Maturity Scale* (3rd ed.). New York: The Psychological Corporation.

Doll, E. A. (1965). *Vineland Social Adaptivity Scale.* Circle Pines, MN: American Guidance Service.

Dunn, L. M. (1981). *Peabody Picture Vocabulary Test-Revised.* Circle Pines, MN: American Guidance Service.

Eichorn, D. H. (1978). Review of the Kaufman Developmental Scale. In O. K. Buros (Ed.), *The eighth mental measurements yearbook* (pp. 308-309). Highland Park, NJ: The Gryphon Press.

Kaufman, H. (1974). *Kaufman Developmental Scale.* Chicago: Stoelting Co.

Leiter, R. G., & Arthur, G. (1936-55). *Leiter International Performance Scale.* Chicago: Stoelting Co.

Slosson, R. L. (1961-81). *Slosson Intelligence Test.* East Aurora, NY: Slosson Educational Publications.

Ferris O. Henson, Ph.D.
Associate Professor of Special Education, Alabama A & M University, Huntsville, Alabama.

Leatha M. Bennett, Ph.D.
Director of Special Services, University of Alabama in Huntsville, Huntsville, Alabama.

KAUFMAN TEST OF EDUCATIONAL ACHIEVEMENT

Alan S. Kaufman and Nadeen L. Kaufman. Circle Pines, Minnesota: American Guidance Service.

Introduction

The Kaufman Test of Educational Achievement (K-TEA; Kaufman & Kaufman, 1985c) was designed to measure school achievement of children enrolled in Grades 1-12. The data obtained from the K-TEA is normalized by age (six years, 0 months to 18 years, 11 months) or by grade level. It consists of two overlapping forms: Comprehensive and Brief. The Brief Form globally samples the areas of reading, mathematics, and spelling, whereas the Comprehensive Form measures more specific skills in the areas of reading decoding and comprehension, mathematics applications and computation, and spelling. Norm-referenced measures are included in both forms. The Comprehensive Form also provides criterion-referenced assessment data to analyze the students' errors in each subtest content area. Additionally, all standard scores in both forms are set at a mean of 100, with a standard deviation of 15, to allow for comparisons between the K-TEA and previously obtained standard IQ scores.

The K-TEA (1985) was authored by Alan S. Kaufman, Ph.D. and Nadeen L. Kaufman, Ed.D. Alan Kaufman is currently Professor and University Research Fellow at the University of Alabama and is affiliated with the California School of Professional Psychology in San Diego, California. Additionally, he is a Fellow of the American Psychological Association. Nadeen Kaufman is currently Adjunct Associate Professor of Education, School Psychology, and Special Education at the University of Alabama. She is certified as a teacher and a school psychologist. They have previously authored other children's scales, including the Kaufman Assessment Battery for Children (K-ABC; Kaufman & Kaufman, 1983).

According to the K-TEA Comprehensive Form manual (Kaufman & Kaufman, 1985b), the development of the battery required four years and proceeded through several stages. The first stage included the development of the subtests' outline, which included the writing of items for each subtest. The authors were assisted by the staff of the publisher, American Guidance Service, and curriculum specialists. Most of the items were written specifically for the K-TEA, whereas some were taken directly from the Kaufman Assessment Battery for Children. The final stages included a series of national administrations of the Comprehensive Form of the K-TEA. The final version of the K-TEA was shortened by 20%, based on the data collected during the standardization process.

Both forms of the K-TEA consist of a kit that includes the user's manual, a self-supporting easel containing the items of the various subtests, an answer booklet containing a score profile on which to record the child's responses, and a parental reporting form. The K-TEA Comprehensive Form consists of 280 items and five subtests: Mathematics/Applications, Reading/Decoding, Spelling, Reading/Comprehension, and Mathematics/Computation. It is noted in the Comprehensive Form manual that the items in this form are totally different from those on the Brief Form, which consists of 144 items and three subtests: Mathematics, Reading, and Spelling. The test manuals for both forms provide guidelines as to which form of the K-TEA is appropriate. For screening purposes the Brief Form should be given. It is recommended by the test authors that the Brief Form be used for testing unless there is a specific rationale for using the Comprehensive Form. For detailed assessment and data yielding student strengths and weaknesses, the Comprehensive Form is recommended. Both forms can be used as pre-post measures, and the test authors suggest that if the Brief Form is used for screening, the Comprehensive Form should become a choice for in-depth assessment.

The Comprehensive Form subtests are described as follows (Kaufman & Kaufman, 1985b):

Mathematics/Applications (60 items): Measures the child's concepts in a wide variety of arithmetic concepts and the application of these concepts, along with reasoning skills, to real-life situations. The student must attend to visual stimuli presented from the easel; items are presented orally by the examiner.

Reading/Decoding (60 items): Measures the child's skill in the areas of letter recognition and word pronunciation, both phonetic and nonphonetic.

Spelling (50 items): Assesses spelling with the child spelling (in writing) words that are verbally presented and used in a sentence. The words increase in level of difficulty, and a child who is not capable of writing the words can spell them orally.

Reading/Comprehension (50 items): Measures literal and inferential comprehension. Two different types of items are used. The easiest and most difficult items include the examiner giving a set of commands to the child and the child responding either gesturally or orally. The remainder of the items include paragraphs for the student to read. Two questions follow each paragraph and the student must respond orally to the questions.

Mathematics/Computation (60 items): Assesses written computation skills. Uses a pencil-and-paper format in which the student is required to do the four basic operations, as well as more complex computations such as algebra.

The Brief Form subtests are described as follows (Kaufman & Kaufman, 1985a):

Mathematics (52 items): Assesses basic math skills, as well as applications to life-like situations and numerical reasoning. Computational items are written and are the easiest. More difficult items include concepts and applications and are presented orally with accompanying visual stimuli.

Reading (52 items): Assesses decoding of printed words and reading comprehension. Beginning items include presenting a list of words with increasing difficulty, and the student must correctly identify and pronounce each of the letters or words. The items related to comprehension include reading a printed statement and responding to it with oral answers or other gestural responding as dictated by the statement.

Spelling (40 items): Assesses spelling ability using a list of increasingly difficult words, which are read and used in a sentence. The student must write the correct spelling of the words. If the student is unable to write sufficiently well, he may spell the words orally.

Practical Applications/Uses

According to Kaufman and Kaufman (1985b), the K-TEA was designed to 1) be used as a single measure in a multifaceted comprehensive educational, psychological, or neurological evaluation of a student; 2) assess a student's strengths and weaknesses in the areas of reading, math, and spelling in order to design an appropriate educational program; 3) assist in group-program planning by providing norm-referenced scores to facilitate educational placement of a student; 4) be used for educational research purposes requiring achievement data; and 5) be used as a measure in evaluating a child for special education placement decisions.

Features of the two forms of the K-TEA are given in the test manuals. The authors of the test maintain that these features are useful for educational testing purposes (Kaufman & Kaufman, 1985b). One characteristic is the wide range of both forms of the K-TEA. It is appropriate to assess educational achievement continually from the child's entry into the primary grades through Grade 12. Another feature is that two separate but highly correlated forms of the K-TEA exist. This feature allows for the administration of alternate forms for pre- and post-measures needed for research purposes, as well as on-going testing of the same child in an applied setting. The test authors also utilized the Rasch-Wright latent-trait model, along with conventional item-analysis procedures to attempt to insure an item-gradient reflective of children's on-going development. The purpose of this was to control for characteristics of potentially unique population samples that could affect the item development and normalization. Another feature mentioned in the test manuals is the utilization of Angoff's method for detecting bias against the variables of sex and race (i.e., male vs. female; black vs. white). Any item that showed significant and consistent bias was eliminated.

Other valuable characteristics of the K-TEA include age and grade norms. Age norms range from six years, 0 months to 18 years, 11 months. Grade norms range from 1 to 12. Either norms can be used, depending on examiner preference or the data required. Age-referenced norms can be utilized when comparing the child's performance with IQ scores on tests such as the WISC-R, the K-ABC, or the Stanford-Binet, which yield age-based norms. Age-based norms are also valuable for classifying children as learning disabled, as PL 94-142 requires such categorization. Grade-based norms are valuable for comparing students within the same classroom or school when one is interested in performance level without regard to age.

Generally speaking, professionals in the field of psychology and special or general education, including educational diagnosticians and psychometrists, are qualified to administer the K-TEA. The Comprehensive Form manual includes utilizing social workers and others in the field of social services, but it is these reviewers' opinion that professionals in the field of social services are not typically trained in educational assessment. It is mentioned also in the manual that paraprofessionals may be specifically trained to administer the K-TEA, but only if no qualified psychological or educational personnel is available to do the testing. Again, it should be emphasized that if paraprofessionals or professionals in the field of social services are to be utilized for administration of the K-TEA, sufficient training in the area of standardized procedures should be undertaken. This training should include following specific directions, not rewarding correct responses but responding in general, establishing rapport with the child, and other skills associated with the administration of standardized, individual performance-based tests.

If a qualified examiner in either psychology or education is not available and paraprofessionals are to be trained, it is recommended that the training be given in a "formal" in-service format by qualified professionals in the field of standardized testing. Additionally, the K-TEA authors recommend that a minimum of two administrations and evaluation of test protocols of the Comprehensive Form by the trainee be observed for accuracy by the professional. Interpretation of the results requires more training than administration and scoring. Thorough knowledge is needed in the areas of error of measurement, nature and uses of various derived scores, application of statistical procedures necessary for determination of a student's strengths and weaknesses, and deriving educational implications of the student's performance. Kaufman and Kaufmann (1985a) suggest graduate training in special education and/or psychology as the primary source of such knowledge.

In addition to the above, any qualified examiner must study the K-TEA manual, as well as the easel and other materials, and become well aware of the specifics of both the Comprehensive and Brief Forms. The test authors note that skills in giving other tests are not a substitute for familiarity with the K-TEA.

The administration of the K-TEA is relatively straightforward. It is similar to other performance-based assessment instruments. In other words, the testing materials and instructions to the examiner are contained within the easel. The results of the child's responses are recorded on a separate response form. The K-TEA manuals provide specific instructions for administering the test. The Comprehensive Form can be administered in an average time period of 60-75 minutes, whereas the Brief Form requires about 30 minutes to administer. However, both forms require less time for students in the first or second grade. A table for average test times by grade level is available in the manuals.

The authors suggest that the examiners become familiar with the test to the point that it becomes "second nature." If examiners become thoroughly familiar with the test, then they can spend more time establishing and maintaining a sensitive, valid, and enjoyable relationship with examinees. The test authors stress the importance of establishing and maintaining rapport with the child throughout the testing process. To accomplish this, they suggest that examiners use the child's name, introduce themselves to the child, use language that is at an appropriate level, focus on the child's interests and hobbies, and use any other technique that enhances the climate for a relaxed administration. Examples are also provided for testing anxious or insecure students. The examiner is further admonished to convey a positive attitude about the test situation (i.e., developing a substantive relationship with examinees and showing regard for their needs and feelings). The test authors elaborate on this point, and it should be heeded by the examiner.

Because the K-TEA is not a group-administered test, students' test-taking behavior can be readily observed. The examiner should attend closely to the examinee's behaviors in an unobtrusive manner. Such behaviors might include motivational behaviors, visual-motor coordination, smiles, frowns, signals of stress, attitude toward the testing situation, and other actions or gestures that may be useful in assessing the child. These types of clinical observations provide data that make the time involved in such singular administrations worthwhile. If a child needs to be reinforced for responding in a manner beyond the normal verbal praise that might be given in such an assessment, it should be noted by the examiner and considered when interpreting the results. Throughout both test manuals, the authors continually emphasize the importance of following the precise directions for administration and scoring so that the examiner can adhere to standardized procedures.

The authors particularly note the importance of three areas to be attended to during the administration. The first concerns following directions. The test authors state that any deviation from the outlined procedures violates traditional norms in administering standardized tests and as a result could invalidate the results. For example, the authors specifically state that paraphrasing, simplifying, or modifying instructions are not allowed when administering the Mathematics/Applications and Spelling subtests. The examiner is not allowed to spell any words in any subtest or pronounce any words for the examinee during Reading Comprehension. The second area emphasizes the giving of feedback to the examinee. At no time should the examiner give reinforcement to the child regarding the correctness of responses. The examiner is cautioned to be aware of both nonverbal and verbal cues. The third area elaborates on objective scoring. Objectivity in scoring is as important as following the administration procedures, and the rules for acceptable responses are to be strictly followed. Deviation from the specified procedures could affect the results in ways that are representative of variables other than those being tested.

Scoring is recorded on an answer booklet, which is a convenient manner of keeping the separate subtest data intact. The instructions are precisely written, and the examiner needs only to follow the test authors' directions to score the responses of the student accurately. Once the responses are recorded, only one transfer is made to the score profile. No partial points are given for any item because items are either correct or incorrect.

Technical Aspects

The standardization of the K-TEA was conducted in 25 cities within 15 states. The sample populations, stratified by grade, were representative with regard to geographic region, sex, socioeconomic status, and educational levels of the parents.

Five types of norms were developed for the K-TEA: normalized standard scores with a mean of 100 and a standard deviation of 15, percentile ranks and stanines, normal curve equivalents, age equivalents, and grade equivalents. The procedures used to develop these norms are described in the Comprehensive Form manual (pp. 173-181).

A thorough analysis of reliability is presented in the Comprehensive Form manual as split-half reliability coefficients, which are presented in tabular formats for each subtest at each age and grade level. The tables represent the mean coefficients from both the fall and spring standardizations. The test authors explain why the traditional odd-versus-even correlations were not used, the prime rationale concerning the nature of the testing procedure, which establishes ceilings and, hence, the lack of opportunity to utilize each item with each child on each subtest. The overall reliability coefficients ranged from .87 to .95 for all ages.

Internal consistency was measured using Guilford's (1954) formula, and the results showed strong reliability in this area. Test-retest reliability was rated across 172 students, distributed equally among the twelve grades. The time interval ranged from 1 to 35 days. In most cases the results showed a .90 or better test-retest coefficient. Practice effects were also examined from this data and were found to be from two to three standard score points higher on the subsequent testing for all subtests with the exception of Mathematics/Computation, which showed no gains in the mean performance for Grades One to Six.

Because there are two forms of the K-TEA (Brief and Comprehensive), reliability between the two was examined. The overall results showed interform reliability coefficients to be in the low .90s, with a range from .87 to .96 for the different grade levels and .90 to .97 for the separate age groups. The Comprehensive Form Mathematics Composite and the Brief Form Mathematics subtest were the lowest of the group, with a mean coefficient of .84 by grade level and .85 by age level and with ranges from .76 to .92 by grade and .79 to .90 by age. Interform reliability coefficients in the areas of reading were higher (in the .90s) for younger children and fell into the upper .70s for older children. The test authors attribute this to the nature of the items for reading in younger children, which differed from that of older children. Overall, these reviewers found the reliability information presented by the test authors to be quite comprehensive.

The Comprehensive Form manual also presents data concerning standard errors in measurement. The values generally span three to four points on either side of the obtained score, with the smallest bands of error occurring in Reading/Decoding and the largest in the two mathematics subtests of the Comprehensive Form.

Validity for the K-TEA proceeded through the stages corresponding to Anastasi's (1982, 1984) multistage approach to validation. The first stage involved a rationale for the subtests to be developed and the establishment of content validity. Curriculum consultants were used for this stage, and the process was conducted for each subtest. The initial pool of items for children from 6.0-12.6 years of age were taken directly from the K-ABC (1983) achievement subtests in Arithmetic, Reading/Decoding, and Reading/Understanding. Some of the items were adapted, and many new items were written for the entire six- to 18-year range. Consultants, the test authors, and American Guidance Service staff members participated in this writing process. The Comprehensive Form manual (pp. 196-200) describes the rationale and process for each of the subtests.

The second stage of validation involved an empirical analysis of the items developed in stage one. This was accomplished by administering the K-TEA to large numbers of students in a series of what the test authors label "national tryouts." These administrations occurred in the fall of 1981, spring of 1982, and winter of 1983. Based on the analysis of each of these tryouts, the items were then used as the source of both forms of the K-TEA.

In the spring of 1983 final standardization occurred for the Comprehensive Form, which was then reduced by 20% in length. As mentioned previously, Angoff's techniques for analyzing bias with regard to sex and race were utilized, and in most cases those items reflecting such biases were eliminated. It should be noted that in some instances some biased items were maintained because 1) they had excellent psychometric properties and were considered important both for reliability purposes and for maintaining appropriate concentrations of items at different difficulty levels and 2) they were approximately counterbalanced so that the overall test did not favor whites or blacks, males or females (Kaufman & Kaufman, 1985b).

The third stage included internal and external analyses of concurrent and content validity. Some of the analyses evaluated internal properties, whereas others were concerned with correlating the subtests of the Comprehensive Form with existing measures of achievement. The results and descriptions of the internal properties of the subtests and composites are presented in the Comprehensive Form manual. Internal consistency coefficients ranged from .77 to .85 by grade level and from .82 to .88 by age group. Only one correlation in either the grade level or age group dropped below .70. These properties include age differentiation and internal consistency, or homogeneity among subtest scores and composite scores.

Finally, data that correlate performance on both forms of the K-TEA with other achievement tests are presented. The other tests included the Wide Range Achievement Test, the Peabody Individual Achievement Test (PIAT), the Metropolitan Achievement Test, the Stanford Achievement Test, and the K-ABC. The test authors present data to support relatively strong correlations on most of these measures (e.g., K-ABC ranged from .83 to .88; PIAT ranged from .75 to .86).

Critique

Other reviews of the K-TEA were not available at the time of this review. This is probably due to the recent publication date of the K-TEA, which was early 1985. The K-TEA appears to be an excellent tool for assessing school achievement of children in Grades 1-12. It should be particularly useful as an educational diagnostic instrument for determining a child's need of special education services and for developing an IEP.

The K-TEA is useful in a variety of settings. Advantages include well-written manuals and an easy-to-use easel format containing all of the test items and instructions for administering the test. The test authors spent extensive time constructing the K-TEA and methodically approached its development in an empirical manner. The necessary precautions for controlling for reliability and construct and content validity were well heeded. Extensive norming data, such as that of age ranges, racial composition, and sex, are provided. These reviewers were impressed with the detailed information presented in both manuals, but particularly in the Comprehensive Form manual.

Administration and scoring of the test is straightforward, but a trained professional is needed to analyze and interpret the results. Raw scores must be converted to derived scores, which are uniform throughout all subtests, age levels, and grade levels. The K-TEA manuals provide specific guidelines for making the score conversions.

Overall, the K-TEA appears to be an excellent assessment instrument for evaluating school achievement in most elementary- and secondary-school environments, including special education. It is highly recommended by these reviewers who hope that the field of educational assessment will be advanced by its availability.

References

Anastasi, A. (1982). *Psychological testing.* New York: Macmillan.

Anastasi, A. (1984). The K-ABC in historical and contemporary perspective. *Journal of Special Education, 18,* 357-366.

Guilford, J. P. (1954). *Psychometric methods* (2nd ed.). New York: McGraw-Hill.

Kaufman, A. S., & Kaufman, N. L. (1983). *The Kaufman Assessment Battery for Children.* Circle Pines, MN: American Guidance Service.

Kaufman, A. S., & Kaufman, N. L. (1985a). *Kaufman Test of Educational Achievement Brief Form manual.* Circle Pines, MN: American Guidance Service.

Kaufman, A. S., & Kaufman, N. L. (1985b). *Kaufman Test of Educational Achievement Comprehensive Form manual.* Circle Pines, MN: American Guidance Service.

Kaufman, A. S., & Kaufman, N. L. (1985c). *Kaufman Test of Educational Achievement.* Circle Pines, MN: American Guidance Service.

Danielle R. Zinna, Ph.D.
Assistant Professor of Education, Department of Education and Counseling, Trinity College, Washington, D.C.

LINDAMOOD AUDITORY CONCEPTUALIZATION TEST

Charles H. Lindamood and Patricia C. Lindamood. Allen, Texas: DLM Teaching Resources.

Introduction

The Lindamood Auditory Conceptualization (LAC) Test is an individually administered measure designed to assess two associated skills. First, the measure examines the individual's ability to discriminate one speech sound or phoneme from another, as these phonemes are presented in isolation. More significant is the measure's focus on an individual's skill in segmenting a spoken word (in this case, a pseudo word) into its constituent phonemic units. For these tasks, the examinee must demonstrate an ability to identify the number and order of phonemes within a spoken syllable by arranging a sequence of colored blocks to represent the sound sequence.

The development of a measure to systematically examine such specific skills resulted from the experiences of the test authors, Charles and Patricia Lindamood, in the teaching and remediation of language skills. These experiences led to the development and publication of *The A.D.D. Program* (Lindamood & Lindamood, 1975), a program that is considered very successful in providing the groundwork for literacy training and remediation in language and reading. Throughout these experiences, the Lindamoods were impressed by a unique skill that they observed to be poorly developed in students needing remediation. It appeared that these students were unaware that the spoken word was composed of smaller phonemic units and that, by monitoring articulatory movements, sounds and sequences of sounds within words were more readily identified.

Currently, Charles Lindamood is Professor Emeritus at California State Polytechnic College. He has completed graduate work in speech pathology, psychology, remedial education, and linguistics. Patricia Lindamood holds a Master of Science degree with specialization in speech pathology and audiology from the University of Oregon. Both are codirectors of the Lindamood Language and Literacy Center, a clinical, research, and training facility in San Luis Obispo, California.

The LAC Test was normed on 660 students in Kindergarten through Grade 12 at the Monterey Peninsula United Schools, Monterey, California. Although data on the proportion of the normative sample in various ethnic and economic categories are not reported, the manual (Lindamood & Lindamood, 1979) does indicate that the school district from which the sample was selected includes a variety of ethnic, economic, and social groups.

In order to utilize a random selection procedure that would provide an equal number of males and females who were high and low achievers at each grade level, a fairly complicated selection procedure was employed. Each of 15 regular classrooms at each grade level, K-6, was divided into four groups based on sex and school performance (male-high, male-low, female-high, and female-low). Four students (one from each group) were randomly selected from each classroom. In this manner, 60 students were selected at each grade level.

A similar procedure was used to determine the sample for Grades 7-12. Each grade was divided by sex and performance, and ten students were randomly selected from each group for a total of 40 students per grade level. Additional samples were utilized to determine reliability, and research has been conducted with larger groups of first-graders, third-graders, and college students to determine the predictive validity of the LAC Test.

Although the LAC Test has been revised from a previous version, the revisions have not been substantive. The examiner's manual has been expanded and includes information regarding the item analysis and a good review of the educational implications of poor performance on this measure. Since the 1971 edition, examiner directions and commentary have been developed for Spanish-speaking individuals. Separate norms are not available for the Spanish population, but the authors indicate that their experience suggests that performance deficiencies are not attributable to native language issues.

Test materials are well-packaged in a bookshelf-sized box. A 72-page examiner's manual provides a general test overview, which includes a discussion of the test rationale and instructions for preparing to test, test administration, scoring, and intepretation. An audiocassette tape, included as a supplement to the manual, demonstrates how to pronounce various test patterns and guides the examiner through selected portions of the test. Two equivalent forms (A and B), which include different but equivalent test patterns, are provided, thus allowing retesting in a pre- posttest situation. The test forms also serve as a recording form for student responses. A detailed examiner's cue sheet, with commentary presented in both English and Spanish, and a set of 24 wooden blocks (four blocks in each of six colors) to be utilized during evaluation are included.

The LAC Test is composed of two distinct subtests or categories, and a precheck that must be administered prior to testing. For the precheck, the examiner guides the subject through a review of the concepts of same/different, first/last, left-to-right order, and number concepts to four. Items missed on the precheck are presented a second time, with the examiner engaging the subject in a dialogue to clarify the error. Sample dialogue is included in the manual.

Following completion of the precheck, items in the actual test portion of the test are presented. The authors note that testing is continued even if concepts evaluated by the precheck are not adequately demonstrated. For items in Category 1A, the subject must discriminate between isolated sounds presented by the examiner by identifying the number of sounds presented and indicating whether the sounds are the same or different. For this task, the subject must place the appropriate number of blocks in a row, utilizing different colors for different sounds and the same color for like sounds. A similar procedure is utilized for Category 1B; however, the authors indicate that the patterns presented are somewhat more difficult.

A procedure for handling errors made on the subtest is well-explained in the manual. In Category 2, pseudo words are pronounced by the examiner, and the subject must create and then alter block sequences to represent sound changes. For example, if the syllable /ib/ were presented, the subject would be expected to select two different colored blocks. For the following syllables, /tib/ and /tab/, the subject would be expected to add a third color block in the initial position when presented with /tib/ and subsequently change the block in the medial position when presented with /tab/. Although this task is difficult, the examiner does complete a full demonstration sequence. Should errors occur during test administration, an alternate item sequence is provided.

Practical Applications/Uses

As previously indicated, the LAC Test is designed to assess auditory perception, as defined in terms of the discrimination of one speech sound from another, and conceptualization of speech sounds, as indicated by skill in identifying the number and order of sounds within a spoken word. This test is quite often categorized as a speech and language measure and is most frequently administered by a speech and language clinician. However, it may be appropriately utilized in the assessment of individuals who have been referred to a special education or reading teacher due to poor reading skills, and as an instrument administered in an early identification or first-grade screening program. The authors report that this measure can be administered to an individual of any age or functional level who understands the concepts of same/different, number to four, and left-to-right sequencing.

The LAC Test is designed as an individually administered measure and demands quite a bit of involvement on the part of the examiner. Individuals likely to utilize this measure include speech and language clinicians, reading and special education teachers, school psychologists, and researchers interested in precursors to and correlates of reading and spelling acquisition. The administration of the test is carefully detailed in the manual and on the audiotape. The examiner's cue sheet and the test recording form provide all of the commentary and conversation for the examiner. It is important to note that there are some errors on the audiotape that refer the listener to the wrong page in the examiner's manual. This problem is easily reconciled by searching the page headings, rather than page numbers, in the examiner's manual. The actual testing time, not including precheck time, ranges from ten to 20 minutes.

The scoring of this instrument is completed quickly by hand. The recording sheet includes the stimulus pattern for each item, followed by spaces in which to record the subjects response and response accuracy. Because different categories are weighted differently, once the total number correct is determined for each category, that number is converted. The recommended minimum converted scores for individuals in Grades K-6 and Grade 7 through adult are included on the recording sheet.

Although the instrument has been standardized and does provide the examiner with a concrete cutoff point for different aged individuals, it is through observation of the individual's performance on the segmenting task in Category 2 that the most valuable information is obtained. Both Appendix B and Appendix C in the manual provide explanations of various patterns of performance on this measure as viewed in light of skills in reading and spelling. Also in Appendix C, a case study format is utilized in which remedial procedures are outlined and outcome described.

Technical Aspects

Alternate-form reliability was determined by pre-/posttesting of a sample of 52 students (four at each grade level, K-12) from the Lucia Mar Unified School District, Pismo Beach, California. The manual reports a reliability coefficient of .96 between Form A and Form B of the LAC Test. Although the test authors report that reliability and stability are considered high, several factors must be considered in interpreting the reliability coefficient as reported. As indicated in the manual, the interval between alternate-form administrations was not less than four weeks. Although it is generally accepted that the shorter the interval between administrations, the higher the estimated reliability, it would be informative if the authors reported the interval range and, thus, included the maximum time between alternate-form administrations. Secondly, reliability indexes are not reported for each grade, nor are these data presented in tabular form. Of particular concern, therefore, is the authors' combining of Kindergarten through Grade 12 data for calculating reliability. Such a practice may be producing a spuriously high alternate-form correlation.

Predictive validity was investigated by computing the correlation of the LAC Test total score with the combined Reading and Spelling scores from the Wide Range Achievement Test (WRAT; Jastak & Jastak, 1978). For these analyses, the LAC Test and the WRAT Reading and Spelling subtests were individually administered to 660 students in Grades K-12 in the Monterey Peninsula Unified Schools, Monterey, California. Correlations with the WRAT combined Reading and Spelling scores ranged from .66 to .81 at different levels. Stepwise linear regression was run based on the total LAC Test as the primary predictor, with the subtests allowed to make residual contributions. The total LAC Test was able to account for at least 55% of the variance in the combined Reading and Spelling WRAT scores at each grade level.

Correlations between the LAC Test subtests (i.e., categories) and WRAT performance indicate that at the kindergarten level, sound discrimination is the major contributor to predictive validity. For Grades 1-3, both Category 1 and Category 2 performance is related to performance on the WRAT. By Grade 4, however, only Category 2 scores are strongly related to WRAT performance.

Critique

The Lindamood Auditory Conceptualization Test provides an examiner with a standardized means of examining a significant and often misunderstood correlate of reading and spelling disability. In the reading research literature, it has been well-documented that phonemic awareness, the skill actually measured by the LAC Test, is predictive of success among children in learning to read (Blachman, 1983; Bradley & Bryant, 1983; Liberman, 1973; Lundberg, Olofsson, & Wall, 1980; Mann & Liberman, 1984). A study conducted with adult illiterates has provided evidence that this awareness is not merely developmental but is enhanced by reading experience and instruction (Liberman, Liberman, Mattingly, & Shankweiler, 1980; Morais, Cary, Alegria, & Bertelson, 1979).

In addition to the relationship of phonemic awareness to reading acquisition, the relationship between the development of spelling skills and phonemic awareness has been recently examined. Results of a study conducted with kindergartners identified performance in a phoneme analysis test patterned after Lundberg et al. (1980) as the best predictor of spelling performance as indicated by representation of phonemes on an invented spelling task (Liberman, Rubin, Duques, & Carlisle, in press).

The Lindamood Auditory Conceptualization Test has been available to educational practitioners since 1971. Few individuals outside of the field of speech and language have utilized the measure, however. The LAC Test provides a means of early identification of reading and spelling problems, and with current emphasis on basic literacy, the test may become more widely utilized. Although normative data are provided, the test can be effectively used to provide teachers with an informal measure of phonemic awareness and possibly allow them to identify students at risk of reading failure.

References

This list includes text citations as well as suggested additional reading.

Blachman, B. (1983). Are we assessing the linguistic factors critical in early reading? *Annals of Dyslexia, 33,* 919-1009.

Bradley, L., & Bryant, P. E. (1983). Categorizing sounds and learning to read—a causal connection. *Nature, 301,* 419-421.

Fox, B., & Routh, D. K. (1980). Phonetic analysis and severe reading disability in children. *Journal of Psycholinguistic Research, 9,* 115-119.

Goldstein, D. M. (1976). Cognitive-linguistic functioning and learning to read in preschoolers. *Journal of Educational Psychology, 68,* 680-688.

Helfgott, J. (1976). Phoneme segmenting and blending skills of kindergarten children: Implications for beginning reading instruction. *Contemporary Educational Psychology, 1,* 157-169.

Jastak, J. F., & Jastak, S. (1978). *Wide Range Achievement Test.* Wilmington, DE: Jastak Associates, Inc.

Liberman, I. Y. (1973). Segmentation of the spoken word and reading acquisition. *Bulletin of the Orton Society, 23,* 65-77.

Liberman, I. Y., Rubin, H., Duques, S. L., & Carlisle, J. (in press). Linguistic skills and spelling proficiency in kindergarteners and adult poor spellers. In J. Kavanagh & D. Gray (Eds.), *Dyslexia: Biology and behavior.* Parkton, MD: York Press, Inc.

Lindamood, C. H., & Lindamood, P. C. (1975). *The A.D.D. Program: Auditory discrimination in depth.* Hingham, MA: Teaching Resources.

Lindamood, C. H., & Lindamood, P. C. (1979). *Lindamood Auditory Conceptualization Test manual.* Allen, TX: DLM Teaching Resources.

Lundberg, I., Olofsson, A., & Wall, S. (1980). Reading and spelling in the first school years, predicted from phonemic awareness in kindergarten. *Scandinavian Journal of Psychology, 21,* 159-173.

Mann, V. A., & Liberman, I. Y. (1984). Phonological awareness and verbal short-term memory: Can they presage early reading problems. *Journal of Learning Disabilities, 17,* 592-599.

Morais, J., Cary, L., Alegria, J., & Bertelson, P. (1979). Does awareness of speech as a sequence of phonemes arise spontaneously? *Cognition, 7*, 323-331.

Rosner, J. (1975). *Helping children overcome learning difficulties.* New York: Walker.

Michael D. Franzen, Ph.D.
Director of Neuropsychology, West Virginia University Medical Center, and Assistant Professor of Behavioral Medicine and Psychiatry, West Virginia University School of Medicine, Morgantown, West Virginia.

LURIA-NEBRASKA NEUROPSYCHOLOGICAL BATTERY, FORM II

Charles J. Golden, Thomas A. Hammeke, and Arnold D. Purisch. Los Angeles, California: Western Psychological Services.

Introduction

The Luria-Nebraska Neuropsychological Battery (LNNB), Form II is an attempt to provide both an alternate form to Form I and some improvements over the original form. The second test is organized in the same way as the first, with the exceptoin of an additional scale, C12 (Intermediate Memory). In response to criticism regarding the content validity of the scales, the names have been removed and replaced with numbers, C1 through C11 for the clinical scales, S1 through S5 for the supplementary scales, L1 through L8 for the localization scales, and numbers for the factor scales. The LNNB is suggested for use with subjects over the age of fifteen years. Because of its reliance on verbal instructions, the LNNB may have limited utility in assessing subjects with receptive language impairments. Revised administration instructions, which allow for alternate response modalities, extend the utility of the instrument for subjects with expressive language impairments.

Consistent with the aims of the LNNB, Form I, Form II combines features of Alexandr Luria's theories of brain function with a standardized approach to assessment. Therefore, many of the comments made with regard to Form I in an earlier review (Franzen, 1985) would also apply here and will not be repeated in great depth. Lurian theory specifies that observable behavior is the result of multiple areas of the brain working in cooperation. No single task can be strictly localized. It is by comparing performance on multiple items that differ in small aspects of stimulus characteristics or task demands that the evaluator can make statements regarding a dysfunctional process. For the sake of psychometric convenience, items on the LNNB are grouped into scales that share a central set of functions. For example, all items from the first scale require mainly motor operations for their successful completion. These item scores are then summed and transformed to provide T-Score measurements of the function that underlies the respective scales.

The stimulus materials for Form II are similar to those of Form I. The visual stimuli have been bound into a single booklet arranged in the chronological order required for administration, an improvement over the separately bound portions of Form I. Additionally, the stimulus print has been enlarged so as not to penalize subjects with poor vision for peripheral impairment reasons. The audiotape stimulus for the C2 (Rhythm) Scale is identical to the audiotape for Form I.

In some instances, entirely new stimuli have been devised for Form II, using the same rationale as was used in devising the original items. For example, the CB (Reading) Scale shares no items across the two forms, nor does the C11 (Intellectual Processes) Scale. As mentioned above, the C12 (Intermediate Memory) Scale was a new development in Form I. In other instances, items were retained across the two forms, as in the case of the C2 (Rhythm) Scale, where 92% of the items originally appeared in Form I.

Form II is divided into 12 scales, which are similar to the original scales in Form I. In each of the scales the items are arranged from simple to more complex procedures. The Form II scales are described as follows:

C1 (Motor Functions): Measures basic and complex motor skills. Motor ability is measured in timed and untimed procedures sampling from the hands, arms, face, and mouth. Some items require coordinated movements across both sides of the body, whereas other items require isolated movements. Motor activity is assessed both from imitation and verbal instructions.

C2 (Rhythm): Measures the accurate perception and production of pitch and rhythm relationships. The first few items require the subject to determine whether the pitches and rhythmic patterns heard are the same or different, whereas later items require the subject to reproduce rhythms and pitches heard and to produce rhythms and melodies from verbal description.

C3 (Tactile Functions): Measures ability in different kinesthetic and tactile skill areas. It includes measures of location by tactile sensation, discrimination of pressure and pain, determination of movement, two-point discrimination, and stereognosis.

C4 (Visual Functions): Measures object recognition with different degrees of clarity and identification of overlapping objects, items similar to Raven's Progressive Matrices, a block rotation task, and other visual skills.

C5 (Receptive Speech): Measures auditory discrimination of phonemes and words either by repetition or dictation, the ability of the subject to follow auditory instructions, the comprehension of verbal spatial relations, and the comprehension of complex and inverted grammatical structure.

C6 (Expressive Speech): Assesses the ability of the subject to repeat phonemes, words, phrases, and sentences. In some of the items, the stimuli are presented in an auditory modality, and in some the stimuli are presented in a written modality. Confrontation-naming tasks are also included in this scale. Additionally, the production of spontaneous speech is evaluated as is the production of overlearned speech.

C7 (Writing): Measures the ability to state the number of letters in given words, to spell words, to copy words and letters from written stimuli and from memory, and to produce spontaneous writing on a given topic. As mentioned above, this scale has been decomposed into Motor Writing and Spelling subscales.

C8 (Reading): Measures the ability to read letters, morphemes, and words from written stimuli and to identify words when they are spelled auditorily. The subject is also asked to read sentences and a short paragraph.

C9 (Arithmetic): Assesses number recognition and the ability of the subject to write numbers from dictation. Simple and complex arithmetic operations are also assessed. Finally, the subject is asked to perform serial subtractions.

C10 (Memory): Assesses immediate memory and memory after a slight delay. Pictorial and verbal memory, as well as one instance of rhythmic memory, are assessed. Memory is assessed in a meaningful context, and unrelated objects are used as stimuli. However, this scale should not be construed as a comprehensive memory assessment, but rather as a screen for memory problems.

C11 (Intellectual Processes): Measures thematic understanding of pictures, the identification of humorous aspects of a picture, simple word definitions, proverb understanding, abstraction abilities, the comprehension of analogies, and verbal arithmetic.

C12 (Intermediate-Term Memory): Measures the ability to recall aspects of items that were given previously in the test. As such it can be construed as a test of incidental memory, as well as of a test of delayed memory with interference.

Practical Applications/Uses

Because of the great similarity between the two forms of the LNNB, information regarding administration and scoring can probably be assumed to be equivalent. Research regarding the amount of training necessary to achieve reliable scoring indicates that approximately 40 hours of training will produce adequate administration by a B.A.-level technician. The tests are administered from test protocols that contain the administration instructions and basic scoring criteria. More detailed scoring instructions are contained in the manual. In addition, a patient response booklet contains space for the written and drawn responses of the subject and the printed stimuli for the C4 Scale. In both forms, scores are represented in the form of standardized T-Scores, with a mean of 50 and a standard deviation of ten points. A critical level is computed with a regression formula using the age and level of education of the subject as predictors.

Western Psychological Services has published a microcomputer scoring program for the LNNB. Thus far the program is available only for IBM personal computers. The program is copyrighted and an internal disk counter keeps track of each time the program is run. When the purchased number of runs is completed, the portion of the program that provides the score is deleted. Also available is a mail-in computer scoring service. Both of these scoring systems calculate the scale scores for basic clinical and supplementary scales and provide information regarding the ipsative comparison of scale scores of the same individual. A sample report is contained in the manual. Although computer scoring may save clerical time, the mail-in service may actually increase the latency between test and report.

The publisher also publishes a new manual to accompany Form II (Golden, Purisch, & Hammeke, 1985). Actually, it is a combined manual for both forms, and at 323 pages, plus various appendices, it is a substantial addition to the original manual. The new manual includes information regarding new derived scales, such as the Impairment and Elevation Scales. These scales contain items that are drawn from across the various scales, the patterns of which provide information regarding the acuteness of an injury and the probability of behavioral compensation following injury. There is also a power and a speed scale composed of items that were theoretically hypothesized to be related to those constructs. T-Score conversions are available for the Impairment and Elevation Scales, based on a normative sample of approximately 800 cases. T-Score conversions for the Speed and Power Scales are based on a normative sample of 45 medical patients. Initial empirical studies (Sawicki & Golden, 1984) suggest that a relatively higher Profile Elevation Scale (over the Impairment Scale) is related to recency of injury and the probability of compensation and that a relatively higher Speed Scale (over the Power Scale) is related to a posterior focus for the injury. More research is needed before these rules can be strongly recommended for clinical use.

Other changes in the manual include decomposing the C7 (Writing) Scale into the Spelling and Motor Writing subscales. Although users of the LNNB were probably already making that distinction in formulating an interpretation of results, this change helps insure that process. A major change involves the development of a set of qualitative categories that can be scored independently of the quantitative scores. These categories can be summed and the frequency counts compared to the frequency of occurrence in a normative sample (N = 48). Because of the limited size of the normative sample, interpretation of the qualitative information is best conducted with reference to neuropsychological theory. However, the qualitative categories serve a useful function by helping assessors to systematize their observations. In order to make the qualitative scores more useful, one would need a larger normative sample and a comparison sample of impaired subjects.

Expanded administration instructions in the new manual provide guides for administering the LNNB to individuals with peripheral sensory losses. The manual also contains a set of 25 cases written by James A. Moses. These are helpful and can serve as a beginning step in learning some aspects of interpretation. There are also discussions of illustrative profiles for different localizations. Although these features can be an aid in learning interpretation, they should not be used as a substitute for supervised learning experiences.

Because of the heterogeneity of the scale composition, interpretation of the LNNB must not be limited to scale interpretation, although that is a necessary first step. Full interpretation must also take into account scores on the empirically derived localization scales, the factor-analytic scales, comparisons of items across scales, and a consideration of the qualitative aspects of the subject's performance. Interpretation is best left to individuals who have received specialized training in neuropsychological assessment and who are familiar with Lurian theory.

The appendices to the manual contain information regarding the factor structure of Form I, item difficulty indices, and information regarding mean performances for each item. Similar information regarding Form II is needed.

Technical Aspects

Form II was developed and standardized on a sample of 73 subjects who were given both forms of the test. There were no significant differences in raw scores for any of the scales. Scale scores for Form II were then derived by regressing the raw scores for Form II against the raw scores for Form I and applying the linear solution to T-Score transformations for Form II. Form II was then administered to a sample of 125 normal subjects, 140 subjects with central nervous system dysfunction, and 34 schizophrenic subjects. A MANOVA conducted on the data resulted in significant differentiation among the groups. Subsequently, Form II was administered to 100 normal subjects and 100 neurologically impaired subjects. Use of the clinical rules stated in the manual resulted in classification accuracy rates equivalent to that of Form I. Although these studies help us to evaluate the validity of Form II, much of the research originally conducted on Form I now needs to be conducted on Form II. Also needed is a separate normative sample for the derivation of T-Scores for Form II. Although the above mentioned research indicates that Form I and II appear to be equivalent, a separate normative sample will help insure the accuracy of estimates of the precision of scores obtained from the use of Form II.

Critique

Overall, Form II of the LNNB shows promise as a clinical neuropsychological assessment instrument. Initial research supports its equivalency with Form I. There are approximately 150 published studies using the LNNB Form I. Not all of this research needs to be replicated with Form II, but the basic reliability and validity studies are in need of replication.

References

Franzen, M. D. (1985). Review of the Luria-Nebraska Neuropsychological Battery, Form I. In D. J. Keyser & R. C. Sweetland (Eds.), *Test Critiques* (Vol. III, pp. 402-414). Kansas City, MO: Test Corporation of America.

Golden, C. J., Purisch, A. D., & Hammeke, T. A. (1985). *Luria-Nebraska Neuropsychological Battery: Forms I and II.* Los Angeles: Western Psychological Services.

Sawicki, R. F., & Golden, C. J. (1984). The Profile Elevation Scale and the Impairment Scale: Two new summary scales for the Luria-Nebraska Neuropsychological Battery. *International Journal of Neuroscience, 23,* 81-90.

Mark Stone, Ed.D., ABPP

Professor of Psychology, Forest Institute of Professional Psychology, Des Plaines, Illinois.

MAUDSLEY PERSONALITY INVENTORY

H. J. Eysenck. San Diego, California: Educational and Industrial Testing Service.

Introduction

The Maudsley Personality Inventory (MPI) attempts to measure two variables identified as extraversion-introversion and neuroticism-stability. The MPI was developed by H. J. Eysenck, and the American edition utilizes a manual prepared by Robert Knapp (1962). The MPI does not provide for the comprehensive measurement of personality in such a way as the MMPI, 16PF, CPI, or other current personality inventories. Instead, the MPI measures only two traits defended as independent and uncorrelated. Eysenck argues that these two relatively independent factors account for most of the variance in the personality domain. He also argues that the subdivision of any personality inventory into more scales produces subscales that are almost always highly intercorrelated, and when all of these scales are analyzed only two or three major factors account for most of the variance. Hence, Eysenck's position is that the MPI provides a straightforward measure of the two most important factors of personality: extraversion-introversion (E) and neuroticism-stability (N).

High E scores on the MPI are indicative of extraversion and as such are purported to identify outgoing, impulsive, and uninhibited persons interested in social and group activities. A low-scoring individual on Scale E tends to be quiet, retiring, introspective, and reserved. High N scores are indicative of emotionally overresponsive persons with neurotic tendencies. Low E scores suggest a stable personality structure.

The MPI consists of a manual, test sheet, and two overlay stencils for hand scoring. The test itself is contained on a single sheet of paper, with directions and identification information on the face side and the 48 items of the MPI on the reverse side. The MPI was designed using 24 items for each of the two major variables.

Potential MPI users should know that the Eysenck Personality Inventory (EPI; Eysenck & Eysenck, 1963) is a further development of the MPI and should be investigated as an alternate instrument.

Practical Applications/Uses

The MPI is appropriate for use with adolescents and adults. The items are simply and clearly written. Because the statements are straightforward, examinees should have little difficulty understanding the intent of the questions. For illiterate individuals or the visually handicapped, the items could be read aloud and the responses recorded. Hence, the MPI is generally suitable for all subjects aged 15 years and above. It is appropriate in clinical diagnosis, educational and vocational counseling, and various experimental applications.

The relatively small amount of time required to administer the test allows this instrument to be added easily to any test battery; it usually takes an individual approximately 10-15 minutes to complete the 48 items. The instructions are clear, but the examiner should be assured that they are fully understood by the examinee.

The test is scored using two hand stencils: one for the Extraversion Scale and the other for the Neuroticism Scale. Scoring weights of one or two are indicated on the stencils, making it particularly important that the scoring be done with clerical accuracy. Having scored the MPI with these stencils, this reviewer recommends that the publisher find a better way to assure that the scoring stencils are properly aligned on the answer sheet. This would prevent the accidental movement of the scoring stencil on the answer sheet and allow the examiner to determine if the answer sheet and the stencil are always aligned.

Raw scores are determined from the count of the weighted values given on the stencil. These scores are recorded in the appropriate space provided on the test form. One norms table, based on slightly more than 1,000 college students, provides centiles and stanines for a college-aged population. The means and standard deviations for a wide variety of subsamples are given in the manual.

Interpretation of the MPI is straightforward, using the normative data for the two scales; however, examiners are then dependent on their clinical expertise in order to make further diagnostic interpretations. The ease with which this test can be administered and scored may allow wider usage and subsequent misinterpretation by untrained persons, but this possible misuse and misapplication are inherent dangers of any instrument, not just the MPI. Aside from the general introduction to the two scales comprising the MPI, the manual gives little information to help an untrained examiner. Use of the MPI presupposes a high level of expertise with respect to measurement, psychopathology, and clinical diagnosis.

Technical Aspects

Eysenck (1963) argues for the primacy of factorial validity and supports his contention with studies that support his position for the two major personality variables. Concurrent validity is demonstrated by moderately high correlations of the MPI with a variety of other personality scales, including the Taylor Manifest Anxiety Scale, A.S. Reaction Scale, and Cattell's CPS Scale. Correlations between these scales and the MPI were all significant at the .01 level, with a shared variance of more than 50% across all of these studies. Moderate concurrent validity is supported by these studies.

Reliability is demonstrated by split-half and Kuder-Richardson coefficients ranging from .75 to .85 for the Extraversion Scale and between .85 and .90 for the Neuroticism Scale. Retest reliabilities for the scales (N = 100) ranged from .81 through .83. Additional studies of test-retest reliability indicated similarly high coefficients. Moderate reliability is demonstrated in these studies.

Critique

The MPI was reviewed thoroughly in *The Sixth Mental Measurements Yearbook* (e.g., Jensen, 1965; Lingoes, 1965; Stephenson, 1965; Vernon, 1965). The reviews included such statements as "a brief and highly reliable measure of two relatively independent broad factors of personality—neuroticism and extraversion" (Jensen, 1965), "the MPI is excellently produced" (Stephenson, 1965), "of some use in educational guidance and personality counseling" (Vernon, 1965), and "a quickly obtained index of two important personality trends" (Stephenson, 1965). These commendations should not be interpreted as complete endorsement; however, they do indicate some of the reviewers' positive comments.

In summary, this reviewer recommends the use of the MPI by trained psychologists when it is appropriate to gather information on the variables of extraversion-introversion and neuroticism-stability. This personality inventory is not comprehensive and should not in any way be considered similar to the MMPI, CPI, and other multivariable personality inventories. However, when psychologists and other professionals need to measure these two variables, they should give close attention to the MPI as an efficient and valid tool.

References

This list includes text citations as well as suggested additional reading.

Bendig, A. W. (1960). Item factor analyses of the scales of the Maudsley Personality Inventory. *Journal of Psychological Studies, 11,* 104-107.

Eysenck, H. J., & Eysenck, S. B. G. (1963). *Manual for the Eysenck Personality Inventory.* San Diego: Educational and Industrial Testing Service.

Eysenck, H. J., & Eysenck, S. B. G. (1968). *Junior Eysenck Personality Inventory.* San Diego: Educational and Industrial Testing Service.

Furneaux, W. D., & Gibson, H. B. (1961). The Maudsley Personality Inventory as a predictor of susceptibility to hypnosis. *International Journal of Clinical and Experimental Hypnosis, 9,* 3.

Furneaux, W. D., & Gibson, H. B. (1966). *New Junior Maudsley Inventory.* San Diego: Educational and Industrial Testing Service.

Jensen, A. R. (1958). The Maudsley Personality Inventory. *Acta Psychologica, 14,* 314, 325.

Jensen, A. R. (1965). Review of the Maudsley Personality Inventory. In O. K. Buros (Ed.), *The sixth mental measurements yearbook* (pp. 288-301). Highland Park, NJ: The Gryphon Press.

Knapp, R. (1962). *Maudsley Personality Inventory Manual.* San Diego: Educational and Industrial Testing Service.

Lingoes, J. C. (1965). Review of the Maudsley Personality Inventory. In O. K. Buros (Ed.), *The sixth mental measurements yearbook* (pp. 291-302). Highland Park, NJ: The Gryphon Press.

Stephenson, W. (1965). Review of the Maudsley Personality Inventory. In O. K. Buros (Ed.), *The sixth mental measurements yearbook* (pp. 292-293). Highland Park, NJ: The Gryphon Press.

Vernon, P. E. (1965). Review of the Maudsley Personality Inventory. In O. K. Buros (Ed.), *The sixth mental measurements yearbook* (pp. 293-294). Highland Park, NJ: The Gryphon Press.

Gene Schwarting, Ph.D.
Project Director, Preschool Handicapped Program, Omaha Public Schools, Omaha, Nebraska.

MAXFIELD-BUCHHOLZ SOCIAL MATURITY SCALE FOR BLIND PRESCHOOL CHILDREN

Kathryn E. Maxfield and Sandra Buchholz. New York, New York: American Foundation for the Blind.

Introduction

The Maxfield-Buchholz Social Maturity Scale for Blind Preschool Children, developed by Kathryn E. Maxfield and Sandra Buchholz (1959), is an adaptation of the Vineland Social Maturity Scale (Doll, 1965; first published in 1935). It is designed to provide an inventory of social competence for young blind children by comparing their skills with other blind children within the age range of birth to six years. Administration of the instrument results in a social age, as well as a social quotient.

Work on the scale was begun in 1936 at the Arthur Sunshine Home and Nursery School for the Blind, as a need was noted for an instrument that could measure the social development of young blind children. The Vineland Social Maturity Scale had recently been published, and two investigators involved in that project, B. Elizabeth McKay and Katherine Bradway, conducted studies with the Vineland using blind preschool children. Both studies indicated that the Vineland held promise for use with this special population and a grant to collect data enabled Kathryn Maxfield and Harriett Fjeld to proceed to develop an adaptation, with an article being published in 1942.

Following World War II, Samuel P. Hayes collected and analyzed data on the Maxfield-Fjeld Scale, with a guide for use of the instrument being published in 1953 by Maxfield and Eunice Kenyon. As the instrument grew in popularity, however, it became evident that the Maxfield-Fjeld adaptation of the Vineland was flawed, requiring deletion and addition of some scale items, as well as rewording or relocation of others. As a result, the instrument was extensively revised and restandardized by Maxfield and Buchholz and published in 1957.

The Maxfield-Buchholz Scale consists of a 45-page manual (Maxfield & Buchholz, 1957) and a seven-page score sheet, which contains 95 items sequentially arranged into six age categories of one year each. These items could be categorized within the skill areas of general, dressing, eating, communication, locomotion, socialization, and occupation, although scoring is done by years of social development rather than by area.

Practical Applications/Uses

The Scale was designed as a measure of social maturity for blind preschool children and should be useful for psychologists, teachers, and specialists who work with young, visually impaired children. Results of the measure may be used to compare social development with cognitive or motor development, as a measure of adaptive behavior in an evaluation, to measure progress, or to determine educational objectives.

There are no specific requirements as to the training of the examiner, but it is noted that experience with psychological testing and diagnostic interviewing would increase effectiveness. Throughout the interview process the questioning is to be done in a nonthreatening, conversational manner. The presence of the child is not required, but may be useful to the examiner for observational purposes. It is necessary to elicit information as to whether the item is routinely performed by the child without undue urging in order to score the items for full credit or partial credit. Both the wording of the items, as well as the scoring criteria, require the use of professional judgment. The order of administration of items may vary, as will the amount of time required.

Administration follows the format of the Vineland, with the examiner interviewing the parent or another person familiar with the child, who need not be present. The examiner is encouraged to establish rapport and put the interviewee at ease prior to administration. Items are not to be given as direct questions, but rather as part of an ongoing conversation regarding the development of the child, using probing when necessary to elicit specifics as to the rating given the child on the skills indicated.

Scoring also parallels the Vineland procedure, with items scored as "+" (pass), "+F" (formerly performed the task but now does not due to restraints or lack of opportunity), "+NO" (has never performed due to lack of opportunity), "±" (a transitional or emergent skill), or "−" (has not gained the skill). Items scored as "+" or "+F" receive full credit; "+NO" receives full credit if within the range of continuous plus scores, half credit if the last in a series of plus scores, and no credit if within the range of continuous minus scores; items scored as "±" receive half credit. The number of items per age level varies among 10, 15, and 20, so the credit value assigned to individual items varies from .1 to .07 to .05. The decimal social age values of the six age levels are added and, when divided by the child's chronological age expressed in years as a decimal, result in a social quotient.

Technical Aspects

The normative group used in the standardization consisted of 398 children, most of whom came from the north and mid-atlantic states and were categorized as legally blind. These were enrolled in six agencies serving such children aged five months to five years, eleven months. Where the cause of blindness was established, it was found that 60% of the cases were diagnosed as retrolental fibroplasia. No information is available as to the children's race, sex, socioeconomic status, cognitive development, or other test results. Likewise, data concerning the validity or reliability of the scale are not provided; rather, the authors refer to the construction of the instrument as a type of validation.

Critique

The instrument is unique in the field in terms of the population for whom it is intended. Obviously, the selection of the Maxfield-Buchholz Scale restricts comparisons to a blind/visually impaired norm group as opposed to a normal population, which offers both advantages and disadvantages. In addition, the norm group is not necessarily typical of young, visually handicapped children today, due to the large number diagnosed as having retrolental fibroplasia, which is no longer as prevalent as it was in the 1950s. Neither validity nor reliability are reported, so whether the instrument measures what it purports to measure or whether this measurement is consistent cannot be established empirically. Certainly, some indication of comparative validity using another measure of adaptive behavior/social development would provide a greater amount of security with the instrument.

Another area of concern is the minimal direction provided to the examiner. Familiarity with administration and scoring of the original Vineland Scale is almost a requirement, and even then precision is extremely limited. The authors correctly warn that the Social Quotient (SQ) be interpreted cautiously due to the false impression of precision it presents. In addition, because the SQ is based on a direct relationship between chronological and social ages rather than on standard deviation units, as is true of most major IQ tests in use today, cautious interpretation of difference scores is required.

In conclusion, the Maxfield-Buchholz Scale serves a unique need in the field because it was developed for a particular population. The scale could be a useful tool for psychologists, educators, and others dealing with visually impaired children as long as there is a certain degree of skill in interviewing techniques and test administration. Disadvantages include the age of the instrument (copyrighted in 1957), imprecise scoring procedures, a lack of validity and reliability data, and the applicability of the norm group.

References

This list contains text citations as well as suggested additional reading.

Bradway, K. P. (1937). Social competence of exceptional children: The deaf, the blind, and the crippled. *Journal of Exceptional Children, 4,* 1-69.

Diebold, M., Curtis, W., & DuBose, R. (1978). Developmental scales versus observational measures for deaf-blind children. *Exceptional Children, 44,* 275-280.

Doll, E. A. (1947). *The Vineland Social Maturity Scale: Manual of directions.* Washington, DC: Educational Test Bureau.

Doll, E. A. (1965). *Vineland Social Maturity Scale.* Circle Pines, MN: American Guidance Service.

Hayes, S. P. (1952). The status of measurement of the preschool blind child. In S. P. Hayes

(Ed.), *First regional conference in mental measurements of the blind* (pp. 27-30). Watertown, MA: Perkins School for the Blind.

Katoff, L., & Reuter, J. (1980). Review of developmental screening tests for infants. *Journal of Clinical Child Psychology, 9,* 30-34.

Maxfield, K. E., & Buchholz, S. (1957). *Maxfield-Buchholz Social Maturity Scale for Blind Preschool Children: A Guide to its use.* New York: American Foundation for the Blind.

Maxfield, K. E., & Fjeld, H. A. (1942). Social maturity of visually handicapped preschool children. *Child Development, 13,* 1-27.

Maxfield, K. E., & Kenyon, E. L. (1953). *A guide to the use of the Maxfield-Fjeld tentative adaptation of the Vineland Social Maturity Scale for use with visually handicapped preschool children.* New York: American Foundation for the Blind.

Timothy Z. Keith, Ph.D.
Associate Professor of School Psychology, University of Iowa, Iowa City, Iowa.

McCARTHY SCALES OF CHILDREN'S ABILITIES

Dorothea McCarthy. Cleveland, Ohio: The Psychological Corporation.

Introduction

The McCarthy Scales of Children's Abilities (McCarthy) is designed to assess a variety of intellectual and motor abilities for children aged 2½ to 8½ years. The McCarthy takes about an hour for administration by a trained psychologist and seems to provide an enjoyable and valid method for assessing young children's abilities.

The McCarthy was authored by the late Dorothea McCarthy and published by The Psychological Corporation in 1972; it was designed to measure children's cognitive (McCarthy avoided the term *intelligence*) and motor abilities. The McCarthy consists of 18 short mental and motor tests grouped into five scales: Verbal, Perceptual-Performance, Quantitative, Memory, and Motor. The first three are nonoverlapping and are further combined into the General Cognitive Index (GCI), a measure of overall cognitive functioning that is similar to an overall IQ.

The tests are grouped in a variety of combinations, with several appearing on two of the five scales, which are described as follows:

Verbal: Consists of five measures of verbal expression and verbal concept formation, including Pictorial Memory that asks the child to recall a series of pictures named by the examiner; Word Knowledge consisting of two parts: receptive language and picture vocabulary (part one) and defining words (part two); Verbal Memory requiring the child to repeat a series of words or sentences (part one) and retell a story after the examiner has told it (part two); Verbal Fluency in which the child names objects in a category within a time limit; and Opposite Analogies where the child completes sentences with an appropriate opposite word.

Perceptual-Performance: Consists of seven measures of perceptual and spatial abilities and nonverbal reasoning including Block Building in which the child copies formations of blocks; Puzzle Solving requiring the child to put together a series of simple, colorful puzzles; Tapping Sequence in which the child copies a series of notes on a toy xylophone; Right-Left Orientation given only to children above five years who are asked to differentiate right and left on oneself and on a picture of a boy; Draw-A-Design asking the child to copy a series of geometric designs; Draw-A-Child where the child draws a picture of a child who is the same sex as self; and Conceptual Grouping, a logical classification task on which the child sorts brightly colored blocks on the basis of size (large and small), shape (circle and square), and color (three colors).

Quantitative: Consists of three measures of facility with numbers, basic pre-arithmetic concepts, and arithmetic reasoning, including Number Questions requiring the child to solve oral arithmetic problems; Numerical Memory in which the child recalls simple digits, including digits forward (part one) and digits reversed (part two); and Counting and Sorting requiring the child to count blocks and sort them into equal groups, and display knowledge of such concepts as "each" and ordinal numbers.

Memory: Consists of four measures of short-term auditory and visual memory from the first three scales (Pictorial Memory, Tapping Sequence, Verbal Memory, and Numerical Memory).

Motor: Consists of five measures of fine and gross motor coordination, including two tasks from the Perceptual-Performance Scale (Draw-A-Design and Draw-A-Child), plus Leg Coordination requiring the child to perform gross motor tasks such as walking a straight line, standing on one foot, and skipping; Arm Coordination requiring the child to bounce a ball (part one), catch a bean bag (part two), and throw the bean bag at a target (part three); and Imitative Action requiring the child to copy a series of the examiner's movements, such as twiddling thumbs and looking through a tube.

The standardization of the McCarthy, which was carried out from October 1970 through September 1971, was excellent. It consisted of a nationally representative sample of children aged 2½-8½ years, with approximately 50 girls and 50 boys included at each of ten age levels (every six months between 2½ and 5½ years and every year from 5½ to 8½ years). It was stratified based on age, sex, color, geographic region, and father's occupational status in accordance with 1970 census estimates and informally stratified as to rural versus urban residence. Although the sample was composed of primarily "normal" children and excluded institutionalized and other severely handicapped children, it did include those with suspected or presumably mild handicaps. The final standardization sample included several extra cases for a total of 1,032 children.

The McCarthy test materials are all attractive and functional. And, unlike many tests for children this age, the McCarthy materials are interesting enough, when used by a skilled examiner, to retain the interest of all but the most distractable children. The manual (McCarthy, 1972) is well organized and generally complete, although frequent users would be advised to supplement the manual with Kaufman and Kaufman's (1977) excellent text on the test's development and use. Although the record forms, which have ample space for notes and observations, are easy to use, they do require considerable transferring of scores and clerical accuracy. However, the main drawbacks of the kit are the carrying case, which is made of the usual flimsy material, and the high cost of the kit.

Practical Applications/Uses

The McCarthy provides a general measure of cognitive development for young children. As such, its most frequent use will probably be with children suspected of having problems in learning, behavior, or development. The McCarthy should also be considered for inclusion in any standard psychological assessment battery for children in this age group, and, thus, could replace the Wechsler Preschool and Primary Scale of Intelligence (WPPSI), the Wechsler Intelligence Scale for Children-Revised (WISC-R), or the Stanford-Binet Intelligence Scale: Form L-M. (For reviews of these instruments see Elbert & Holden, 1985; Vernon, 1984; and Holden, 1984, respectively.) The McCarthy is most appropriate for clinical, counseling, and school psychologists in educational or clinical settings. As with most individually administered intelligence tests, the McCarthy requires training and practice by qualified examiners—generally psychologists—in order to be administered and interpreted properly. With practice, the McCarthy's administration is smooth and natural and takes an experienced examiner approximatly 45-60 minutes to complete. By way of comparison, the McCarthy is probably slightly more difficult to learn than the WISC-R or the Kaufman Assessment Battery for Children (K-ABC; for a review see Merz, 1984), but somewhat easier than the Stanford-Binet.

The directions for scoring individual tests are generally clear and straightforward. A few of the tests (e.g., Word Knowledge and the drawing tests) are subjective and somewhat more difficult to score, but again the directions in the manual are fairly complete and easy to follow. However, the process of converting from raw scores to derived scores is considerably more difficult. Raw scores, some weighted by a factor of two or one-half, are transferred to the back of the record form and are added together in various combinations into the five scales, then transferred to the front of the record form, where the Verbal, Perceptual-Performance, and Quantitative Scales are further summed into the raw General Cognitive Index (GCI) score. Tables are then used to convert these raw scores into standard scores, with the resulting GCI having a mean of 100 and a standard deviawhile the standard scores of the other scales have means of 50 and standard deviations of 10. The standard scores may then be plotted on a profile on the front of the cover sheet as a means of visual comparison of strengths and weaknesses. Obviously, such score conversion is somewhat cumbersome, and the juggling required can easily cause mistakes. This review highly recommends double and triple checking the scoring.

Although somewhat involved, scoring the McCarthy is not difficult with training and practice. What is more unfortunate is that there is no method provided to prorate spoiled or invalid tests, a not-uncommon occurrence when working with children at this age level. In this reviewer's experience, for example, the Right-Left Orientation Test often gives unsatisfying results because children who have no understanding of the concepts of right and left occasionally score better by random guessing than those who are just beginning to develop an understanding of the concepts and answer consistently, but incorrectly. (Indeed, Right-Left Orientation is probably the weakest of all the McCarthy tests and if the McCarthy is ever revised, the publishers should consider discarding this test.)

Fortunately, instructions for prorating, along with tips on administration and scoring, are provided by Kaufman and Kaufman (1977). Anyone who regularly uses the McCarthy should have access to this book, which is also invaluable for interpretation of the test results. Although the manual's discussion of the tests and scales is helpful in interpretation, the book aids immensely in this task by presenting a logical system for comparing scores on scales and individual tests and by presenting a number of alternative methods of interpreting the resulting combinations of scores. As with any such intelligence test, it is in the interpretation that training and supervised practice are most important.

Technical Aspects

Evidence to support the reliability and validity of the McCarthy is presented in the manual. In addition, there has been considerable research performed with the McCarthy in the 13 years following its initial publication; much of this research is reviewed carefully in Kaufman (1982). Considering the volume of research that has been performed on the McCarthy Scales, this brief review will draw heavily from these two existing sources (Kaufman, 1982; McCarthy, 1972; for a review of early research on the McCarthy see Kaufman & Kaufman, 1977), and will not discuss studies in detail.

The McCarthy GCI seems to provide a reliable measure of overall intellectual ability: internal consistency estimates are generally reported in the .90s and stability estimates in the .80s over a variety of test-retest intervals. There is also evidence to support the reliability of the other McCarthy scales, with stability and internal consistency estimates (when applicable) generally in the .70s to .80s.

The McCarthy GCI seems to correlate with Weschler and Binet IQs as well as these measures correlate with each other (.70s-.80s), thus supporting the validity of the GCI. Similarly, with correlations of .55-.68, the GCI correlates substantially with the newer K-ABC Mental Processing Composite (Kaufman & Kaufman, 1983). The McCarthy GCI and other scales also correlate substantially with measures of achievement, an important criterion for a measure of intelligence. Although the coefficients vary considerably, research suggests that the GCI correlates significantly with a variety of measures of achievement when administered concurrently (.27-.84, with most in the .5 to .75 range) or when the achievement tests are administered later (.48-.76), and further that the GCI correlates about as highly with achievement measures as do other tests of intelligence (Kaufman, 1982).

There is mixed support for the construct validity of the various McCarthy scales in factor analyses of both normal (e.g., Kaufman, 1975) and exceptional (Keith & Bolen, 1980; Naglieri, Kaufman, & Harrison, 1981) children. Such analyses have offered strong support for the General Cognitive Index as a measure of overall functioning. In addition, factor analyses have offered support for the Verbal, Perceptual-Performance, and Motor Scales of the McCarthy, with memory factors appearing less often and quantitative factors appearing rarely. For example, in their analysis of referred children, Keith and Bolen (1980) found no quantitative factor, but did find that the quantitative tests were among the best measures of the general cognitive factor found.

There are some problematic aspects of the McCarthy, however. There are few items to assess social comprehension, judgment, or abstract reasoning, and especially verbal abstract reasoning (Kaufman & Kaufman, 1977). The ceiling on most tests is inadequate to assess school-aged gifted children, although most scales seem to work well with low achieving school-aged children, the type of child most frequently referred for psychoeducational assessment. Finally, there is evidence that the McCarthy yields slightly lower scores for learning disabled (LD) children than does the WISC-R, although this difference appears to be nowhere near as large as was initially reported. For example, Kaufman (1982) estimates a GCI/ Weschler Full Scale difference of about six points with LD children, as compared to three points for normal children. However, the differences may be larger with retarded children, with the McCarthy producing substantially lower scores. (For more information about such studies, including a critique of the earlier studies, see Kaufman, 1982.)

Critique

The McCarthy Scales of Children's Abilities is a well-developed, extremely well-standardized test of ability for children ages 2½ to 8½ years. Its weaknesses include a paucity of items to assess social comprehension, judgment, and verbal abstract reasoning; an inadequate ceiling for gifted children above about six years and normal children above about seven years; and the possible underestimation by the GCI of WISC-R or Binet IQs for exceptional children. However, the McCarthy's strengths seem to outweigh its weaknesses. It has excellent norms and standardization. It assesses a variety of cognitive and motor skills and provides a diagnostically useful profile of scores; with the addition of Kaufman and Kaufman's (1977) book, the McCarthy is a flexible assessment device and can be interpreted from a variety of perspectives. Finally, the test is attractive and, perhaps most importantly, children find it interesting, a characteristic lacking in most other tests for this age group. Thus, although not appropriate for older normal or gifted children, the McCarthy should probably be considered the test of choice for preschool children and for children up to about age eight who are referred for learning problems.

References

Elbert, J. C., & Holden, E. W. (1985). Review of the Wechsler Preschool and Primary Scale of Intelligence. In D. J. Keyser & R. C. Sweetland (Eds.), *Test critiques* (Vol. III, pp. 697-709). Kansas City, MO: Test Corporation of America.

Holden, R. H. (1984). Review of the Stanford-Binet Intelligence Scale: Form L-M. In D. J. Keyser & R. C. Sweetland (Eds.), *Test critiques* (Vol. I, pp. 603-607). Kansas City, MO: Test Corporation of America.

Kaufman, A. S. (1975). Factor structure of the McCarthy Scales at five age levels between 2½ and 8½. *Educational and Psychological Measurement, 35,* 641-656.

Kaufman, A. S. (1982). An integrated review of almost a decade of research on the McCarthy Scales. In T. R. Kratochwill (Ed.), *Advances in school psychology* (Vol. 2, pp. 119-169). Hillsdale, NJ: Erlbaum.

Kaufman, A. S., & Kaufman, N. L. (1977). *Clinical evaluation of young children with the McCarthy Scales.* New York: Grune & Stratton.

Kaufman, A. S., & Kaufman, N. L. (1983). *K-ABC: Kaufman Assessment Battery for Children: Interpretive manual.* Circle Pines, MN: American Guidance Service.

Keith, T. Z., & Bolen, L. M. (1980). Factor structure of the McCarthy Scales for children experiencing problems in school. *Psychology in the Schools, 17,* 320-326.

Merz, W. R., Sr. (1984). Review of the Kaufman Assessment Battery for Children. In D. J.

Keyser & R. C. Sweetland (Eds.), *Test critiques* (Vol. I, pp. 393-405). Kansas City, MO: Test Corporation of America.

McCarthy, D. (1972). *Manual for the McCarthy Scales of Children's Abilities.* New York: The Psychological Corporation.

Naglieri, J. A., Kaufman, A. S., & Harrison, P. L. (1981). Factor structure of the McCarthy Scales for school-age children with low GCIs. *Journal of School Psychology, 19,* 226-232.

Vernon, P. A. (1984). Review of the Wechsler Intelligence Scale for Children-Revised. In D. J. Keyser & R. C. Sweetland (Eds.), *Test critiques* (Vol. I, pp. 740-749). Kansas City, MO: Test Corporation of America.

E. Wayne Holden, Ph.D.
Postdoctoral Fellow, Pediatric Psychology, Department of Psychiatry and Behavioral Sciences, University of Oklahoma Health Sciences Center, Oklahoma City, Oklahoma.

C. Eugene Walker, Ph.D.
Professor, Pediatric Psychology, Department of Psychiatry and Behavioral Sciences, University of Oklahoma Health Sciences Center, Oklahoma City, Oklahoma.

MICHIGAN SCREENING PROFILE OF PARENTING

Ray E. Helfer, James K. Hoffmeister, and Carol Schneider. Boulder, Colorado: Test Analysis and Development Corporation.

Introduction

The Michigan Screening Profile of Parenting (MSPP) (Helfer, Hoffmeister, & Schneider, 1978) is a self-report questionnaire designed to identify individuals who are at risk for displaying unusual child-rearing practices. The MSPP was constructed as a relatively brief screening instrument based on the contention that parents' self-report is a significant predictor of actual parenting practices. Items measure perceptions of childhood experiences, expectancies about children's behavior, and beliefs about current interactions with family and friends. Additional information is obtained about family demographic characteristics, children's current behavior, and a number of life stressors. The MSPP yields four summary scores, which are purportedly related to parenting potential.

The MSPP was developed by Ray E. Helfer, M.D., James K. Hoffmeister, Ph.D., Carol Schneider, Ph.D., and their colleagues over a twelve-year span (1966-1978). All three authors were involved in scholarly work in the area of child abuse and neglect during the period of test development. Helfer has made the most noteworthy contributions to the child abuse and neglect literature, coauthoring several texts with C. Henry Kempe (e.g., *Helping the Battered Child and His Family* [1972]; *Child Abuse and Neglect: The Family and Community* [1976]). Helfer continues to work actively in the area of child abuse and neglect as a faculty member at Michigan State University. Hoffmeister is a psychometrician who devised the statistical technique of convergence analysis (Hoffmeister, 1975), which is utilized in scoring MSPP responses. He is currently with the Test Analysis and Development Corporation, which markets the MSPP. Schneider is currently engaged in the private practice of psychology in Boulder, Colorado.

The MSPP emerged from the authors' interests in preventing child abuse and neglect. Their orientation to prevention was initially introduced into the literature by Kempe and Helfer (1972). Their original intent was to construct a brief self-report questionnaire that could be used to screen parents or prospective parents during critical developmental periods and to screen within groups of parents considered to be at risk by other criteria (Helfer, 1976). By identifying individuals at risk early, they sought to provide preventive intervention and subsequently reduce the incidence of violence and neglect perpetrated against children.

Based on the contention that perceptions of childhood experiences and perceptions of current interactions with children and adults are significant predictors of risk for abuse or neglect, a 108-item questionnaire entitled "Survey on Bringing Up Children" was initially constructed. Four stable factors were identified through cluster analysis, and the total number of items was reduced to 74 in initial research examining the responses of abusive mothers and controls (Schneider, Helfer, & Pollock, 1972). A subsequent study conducted with 500 mothers revealed similar responses for known abusers and for mothers at risk for dysfunctional parenting. Based on these results, the authors concluded that the questionnaire might be better suited for screening mother-child interaction problems than for specific orientation towards the early identification of individuals at risk for abuse and neglect (Schneider, Hoffmeister, & Helfer, 1976). Eight cluster scores were generated in this study, but only four identified dysfunctional parenting at clinically useful rates. Convergence analyses were used to examine the internal consistency of responses within these four clusters of items. Extreme variability of scores across items was considered to be indicative of inconsistency and was labeled nonconvergence. A large percentage of high risk mothers displayed nonconvergence responses on three of the four clusters. When nonconvergence and magnitude of score were taken into account, false positive rates were lowered to clinically acceptable levels. Subsequently, the questionnaire was shortened and renamed the Michigan Screening Profile of Parenting.

Between 1975 and 1978, field studies were conducted at several sites across the country to examine the validity of the MSPP as a screening instrument. These data are summarized in an extensive research report (Helfer, Schneider, & Hoffmeister, 1978). In that report, five scores were recommended as summary measures of MSPP responses. The scores were labeled as Emotional Needs Met, Relationship With Parents (i.e., the relationship of the child's parents with their own parents), Coping, Expectations of Children, and Dealing With Others. Norms for all five cluster scores based on the responses of 1,800 parents were compiled, and cutting scores were developed to classify individual respondents. Only the most sensitive cluster score, Emotional Needs Met, was deemed clinically useful in identifying mothers at risk for displaying unusual child-rearing practices.

A manual (Helfer, Hoffmeister, & Schneider, 1978) for the research and clinical use of the MSPP was made available shortly after publication of the previously described research report. In this manual, a four-cluster-score solution was adhered to, based on a cluster analysis of over 2,400 test protocols (including all data available at the time from normative and clinical populations). The Dealing with Others Scale was eliminated as a summary measure in this manual. The authors continued to advocate the use of only the Emotional Needs Met cluster score in identifying at-risk parents.

In its current form, the MSPP consists of 74 items. Contact with the examiner is minimal because both the individual test items and the instructions are printed on the two-page answer sheet. The MSPP is intended for completion by parents and prospective parents.

The answer sheet is divided into four sections. Section A is composed of 17 items encompassing family demographic characteristics and current life stressors. Response parameters for each item are displayed on the answer sheet. The 30 items in section B evaluate the respondent's perceptions of childhood experiences and current interactions with family or friends. Section C, which is completed only if the respondents have a child, consists of 18 items that provide information about the respondent's child and the respondent's interactions with that child. Section D, which is completed only if respondents do not have a child, consists of nine items that evaluate prospective parents' expectancies of how they will interact with their child. Items in sections B through D are answered on a seven-point, Likert-type rating scale ranging from "strongly agree" to "strongly disagree."

It should be noted that the four cluster scores are generated from responses to items included in section B. No summary scores are available for items in sections A, C, or D. A brief description of each of the four summary scores is given as follows:

Emotional Needs Met: High scores or nonconvergence identify individuals at risk for displaying unusual child-rearing practices. Includes responses to eight items that reflect a pattern of relationship between self and others that is thought to be learned during the early developmental years. Negative perceptions or nonconvergence indicate that the respondent is currently unable to experience support in interpersonal relationships and may have been reared in a punitive environment. Positive perceptions are indicative of a nurturant atmosphere during rearing and the ability to experience support in interpersonal relationships.

Relationship With Parents: Based on responses to three questions that tap emotions experienced in current interactions with parents, especially mothers. Positive perceptions suggest a close relationship with parents, whereas negative perceptions indicate strained relationships with parents.

Expectations of Children: Based on responses to three items that evaluate perceptions of how children should behave and how sensitive children should be to their parents. Low scores or positive perceptions indicate realistic expectations, whereas high scores or negative perceptions indicate unrealistic expectations.

Coping: Based on three items that tap the individual's emotional responses to crisis situations. Positive perceptions reflect coping strengths, whereas negative perceptions reflect coping difficulties.

For a small additional fee, respondents' scores on each of the four factors are listed and classified as positive, middle, or negative perceptions on an individual report form provided by the publisher. When nonconvergence occurs, scores for an individual factor are not computed.

Practical Applications/Uses

The MSPP is used to identify individuals who could benefit from further assessment of their parenting skills and possible intervention. Programs designed for early detection in at-risk populations appear to be good settings for MSPP administration. The MSPP may be particularly useful in educational or other settings where individuals are participating in programs not directly connected with the mental-health delivery system. Scores could be used to identify and refer parents or prospective parents for further evaluation. The test should only be used to identify individuals who are in need of further assessment, however, and should be limited to female populations, due to the paucity of data available on males (Helfer, Schneider, & Hoffmeister, 1978). The MSPP was not constructed as—nor does it purport to be—a diagnostic instrument yielding all the information necessary for treatment planning. It possesses limited utility in settings where dysfunctional parenting has already been identified and questions regarding possible intervention strategies are being addressed.

This latter point needs to be reiterated because the MSPP cluster scores, on a conceptual level, appear to provide information useful to treatment planning. It is unfortunate that Expectations of Children (e.g., Friedman, Sandler, Hernandez, & Wolfe, 1981) and Coping (e.g., Magrab, 1984) have been recommended as indicators for diagnosing specific deficiencies in parenting skills in abusive populations. This has occurred despite limited research on the validity of individual cluster scores, with the exception of Emotional Needs Met (Gaines, Sandgrund, Green, & Power, 1978; Helfer, Schneider, & Hoffmeister, 1978) and controversy regarding the overall factor structure of the MSPP (Gaines et al., 1978; Spinetta, 1978). Clinical applications should be limited to screening for potential problems in parenting, utilizing only the Emotional Needs Met criterion, until further research is conducted on the diagnostic utility of the other factor scores.

The MSPP's self-report format and administration time of 20 to 30 minutes make it readily applicable to group administration. The reading level required to comprehend individual items accurately has not been determined empirically, but the instructions and items are clearly worded, and ease of administration with all populations studied during test development was reported (Helfer, Schneider, & Hoffmeister, 1978). Although one should consider intellectual level and reading ability in individual cases, the MSPP appears to be generally applicable to lower SES and less well-educated populations where deficits in parenting skills are often prevalent.

As opposed to administration, scoring presents significant difficulties for the examiner. The computerized scoring system, available through Test Analysis and Development Corporation, requires mailing protocols to the publisher and a significant fee for each protocol. The individual items comprising the four clusters are listed in the manual, but a specific scoring key or method for determining the convergence/nonconvergence of scores is not provided. Unless one is willing to tolerate an interval between test administration and test interpretation (with an accompanying fee), it is not possible to obtain the cluster scores as advocated by the authors. At best, scoring based on material in the manual would eliminate the contributions of the convergence/nonconvergence dimension, which are critical to the clinical sensitivity of the test. Other scoring systems are available, but have not been investigated extensively (Gaines et al., 1978; Spinetta, 1978).

Another noteworthy problem in scoring is the absence of summary scores for items in sections A, C, and D. These items are not utilized in computer scoring, and no empirical data that is relevant to their interpretation have been published. Furthermore, the manual does not provide any information about responses to individual items in these sections. Although the relevance of items in evaluating demographic information is apparent, interpretation of the remaining items is currently unclear.

Cutting points are provided in the manual for interpreting individual cluster scores that meet the convergence criterion. Ranges are specified for negative, neither negative nor positive, and positive perceptions. Interpretation is an objective process that relies on quantitative analysis of cluster scores. Sample report forms from Test Analysis and Development Corporation, which include narrative interpretations, are provided in the manual to assist the examiner. Some attention is given to interpreting cluster scores other than Emotional Needs Met, although, as noted previously, the validity of such interpretations is suspect. Consideration should be given, however, to false positive biases reported in lower socioeconomic, non-Caucasian populations (Helfer, Schneider, & Hoffmeister, 1978) and self-report distortion, which may occur in adjudicated populations (Spinetta, Elliott, Hennessey, Knapp, Sheposh, Sparta, & Spriegle, 1982) during interpretation of the Emotional Needs Met score.

Technical Aspects

The MSPP's four summary scores were derived from a cluster analysis of over 2,400 test protocols collected from a number of different urban and rural geographic locations across the United States. Each item loaded above .50 on the dimension that it was assigned to. The large number of subjects and wide range of demographic characteristics included in this sample significantly enhance the validity of the results. Furthermore, empirical support for generalizability was reported in the MSPP research report, and a similar four-cluster-score solution was found in independent analyses of MSPP protocols collected in two foreign countries (Helfer, Schneider, & Hoffmeister, 1978).

These results, however, have been challenged by factor-analytic investigations of the MSPP. Gaines and associates (1978) report a three-factor solution derived from 240 subjects. Individual factors were labeled 1) relationship with parents—feelings about one's childhood, 2) self concept—adequacy, and 3) perfectionism—denial of problems. Spinetta (1978) identifies a six-factor solution based on 100 test protocols. Spinetta's factors were labeled 1) relationship to parents, 2) tendency to become upset/angry, 3) tendency to be lonely/isolated, 4) high expectations of children, 5) inability to separate one's feelings from those of the child, and 6) fear of external threat or control. Moreover, convergence analyses were not used to examine factor scores, and individual items comprising factor scores were not reported in these investigations. The limited number of subjects employed and the absence of independent confirmation of factorial solutions in other populations limits the applicability of these results. Due to these limitations, it is difficult to compare results obtained with different factor scores and to compare results obtained with factor scores to results obtained with cluster scores. However, data bearing on MSPP reliability and validity and utilizing both factor analytically derived scores and cluster scores have been accumulated (Gaines et al., 1978; Helfer, Schneider, & Hoffmeister, 1978; Spinetta et al., 1982).

Despite its importance in test construction, minimal attention has been devoted to evaluating reliability. Percentage agreement across positive, middle, negative, and nonconvergent scoring categories for an unspecified interval is reported in the manual as a test-retest reliability estimate. Emotional Needs Met (85%) was the most stable dimension, with Relationship With Parents (69%), Expectations of Children (62%), and Coping (65%) significantly less stable. Correlations between cluster scores or factor scores have been reported as indices of internal consistency. Moderately significant positive relationships (.26 to .43) between Emotional Needs Met and Relationship With Parents and between Emotional Needs Met and Coping were found (Gaines et al., 1978; Helfer, Hoffmeister, & Schneider, 1978). Negligible correlations, however, are reported between the factors identified by Gaines and associates (1978). These results suggest that summary scores are relatively independent and that the MSPP is measuring a set of divergent, rather than convergent, dimensions.

Substantial support for the discriminant and concurrent validity of the Emotional Needs Met cluster score is presented by the authors. Sensitivity rates between 78 and 90% and specificity rates between 80 and 83% are reported when negative perceptions and nonconvergence were used to identify dysfunctional parents in data collected during test development (Helfer, Schneider, & Hoffmeister, 1978). In addition, high risk scores on Emotional Needs Met were significantly related to independent self reports on a specially constructed questionnaire of poor nurturing as a child, negative perceptions of infants as measured by the Carey Infant Temperament Scale, and life stress as reported by the parents. Furthermore, substantial agreement is reported between the classification of abusive parents by the Emotional Needs Met cluster score and classification by the Altemeir Interview, which is designed to identify abusive parents. Relatively poor agreement, however, was found in the accurate classification of nonabusive controls by these methods.

It should be noted that socioeconomic and racial biases were found in the data collected during test development (Helfer, Schneider, & Hoffmeister, 1978). Parents identified as dysfunctional by independent criteria and their Emotional Needs Met score were typically poor, non-Caucasian mothers, whereas those who did not meet these criteria were typically Caucasian and middle-class or above. The authors report additional support for these biases in normative populations. Relatively high rates of negative perceptions and nonconvergence were present in lower SES, non-Caucasian subjects who had not been classified independently as dysfunctional. These measurement biases have not been clarified in subsequent research.

Other results relevant to the evaluation of MSPP validity, however, have been reported. The Emotional Needs Met and Coping cluster scores entered as significant variables in a discriminant function that classified abusive, neglectful, and control mothers (Gaines et al., 1978). Although these results support discriminant validity, they are complicated by the fact that two of the three factors identified by Gaines and associates were also significant variables in the discriminant function, but in the suppressor direction. The Emotional Needs Met, Coping, and

Relationship With Parents cluster scores were correlated significantly with an abuse proneness score from the Upstate Child Rearing Questionnaire in the same investigation. A significant correlation was also reported between Relationship With Parents and Total Life Stress. Spinetta (1978) found significant differences on all six of his factor scores between controls and abusers, controls' and abusers' spouses, as well as controls and neglectors. Moreover, significant differences between self-referred and adjudicated mothers participating in a treatment program for child abuse and neglect were reported, with the self-referred mothers reporting themselves as more dysfunctional (Spinetta et al., 1982).

Three major points addressing the technical aspects of the MSPP can be summarized from the literature. First, cluster scores rather than scores derived from factor-analytic investigations should be used as summary measures. Substantially more data are available on the reliability and validity of the former, as opposed to the latter, approaches. Second, only the Emotional Needs Met cluster score has adequate reliability and validity as a screening measure. Questionable reliability and inconclusive validity data are reported for the other cluster scores. Third, all technical aspects of the MSPP, especially reliability, are in need of further extensive evaluation.

Critique

It is apparent that numerous problems with the MSPP currently limit its applications, especially in clinical settings. Scoring difficulties, limited information on reliability and validity, and the small number of test items used in screening for dysfunctional parenting are the major obstacles to recommendations for widespread use. It would seem imprudent clinically to administer all 74 MSPP items when only eight items have an adequate psychometric foundation for identifying individuals at risk for displaying unusual parenting practices. The authors are aware of the current limitations of the MSPP and have recommended against its clinical use until further extensive research is conducted (J. K. Hoffmeister, personal communication, November, 1985). Until the above issues are resolved, it would appear that other self-report instruments that have been developed to screen for and diagnose dysfunctional parenting (e.g., Parenting Stress Index, Child Abuse Potential Inventory) have greater clinical applicability than the MSPP. Researchers, however, may find that the MSPP offers unique measurement characteristics, such as the evaluation of inconsistency of self-report, that could ultimately prove to be efficacious in the refinement of strategies for the early detection of dysfunctional parenting. In combination with other measures, MSPP variables may prove to be important in the early identification of abuse-prone parents and the continuing evolution of multivariate models of the abuse phenomenon.

References

Friedman, R. M., Sandler, J., Hernandez, M., & Wolfe, D. A. (1981). Child abuse. In E. J. Mash & L. G. Terdal (Eds.), *Behavioral assessment of childhood disorders* (pp. 221-258). New York: Guilford Press.

Gaines, R., Sandgrund, A., Green, A. H., & Power, E. (1978). Etiological factors in child maltreatment: A multivariate study of abusing, neglecting, and control mothers. *Journal of Abnormal Psychology, 87*, 531-540.

Helfer, R. E. (1976). Basic issues concerning prediction. In R. E. Helfer & C. H. Kempe (Eds.), *Child abuse and neglect: The family and community* (pp. 363-375). Cambridge, MA: Ballinger Publishing.

Helfer, R. E., Hoffmeister, J. K., & Schneider, C. J. (1978). *A manual for use of the Michigan Screening Profile of Parenting*. Boulder, CO: Test Analysis and Development Corporation.

Helfer, R. E., & Kempe, C. H. (Eds.). (1976). *Child abuse and neglect: The family and community*. Cambridge, MA: Ballinger Publishing.

Helfer, R. E., Schneider, C. J., & Hoffmeister, J. K. (1978). *Report on research using the Michigan Screening Profile of Parenting (MSPP): A twelve year study to develop and test a predictive questionnaire* (Prepared as partial fulfillment of Grant 90-C-423 provided by the Office of Child Development, Health, Education, and Welfare Dept.). Washington, DC: U.S. Government Printing Office.

Hoffmeister, J. K. (1975). *Convergence analysis: A clinical approach to quantitative data*. Boulder, CO: Test Analysis and Development Corporation.

Kempe, C. H., & Helfer, R. E. (Eds.). (1972). *Helping the battered child and his family*. Philadelphia: J. B. Lippincott.

Magrab, P. R. (1984). Child abuse. In P. R. Magrab (Ed.), *Psychological and behavioral assessment: Impact on pediatric care* (pp. 337-363). New York: Plenum.

Schneider, C. J., Helfer, R. E., & Pollock, C. (1972). The predictive questionnaire: Preliminary report. In C. H. Kempe & R. E. Helfer (Eds.), *Helping the battered child and his family* (pp. 271-282). Philadelphia: J. B. Lippincott.

Schneider, C. J., Hoffmeister, J. K., & Helfer, R. E. (1976). A predictive questionnaire for potential problems in mother-child interaction. In R. E. Helfer & C. H. Kempe (Eds.), *Child abuse and neglect: The family and community* (pp. 393-407). Cambridge, MA: J. B. Lippincott.

Spinetta, J. J. (1978). Parental personality factors in child abuse. *Journal of Consulting and Clinical Psychology, 46*, 1409-1414.

Spinetta, J. J., Elliott, E. S., Hennessey, J. S., Knapp, V. S., Sheposh, J. P., Sparta, S. N., & Spriegle, R. P. (1982). The pediatric psychologist's role in catastrophic illness: Research and clinical issues. In J. N. Tuma (Ed.), *Handbook for the practice of pediatric psychology* (pp. 165-227). New York: Wiley.

Norman W. Mulgrave, Ph.D.
Professor of Educational Psychology, University of Pittsburgh, Pittsburgh, Pennsylvania.

MILL HILL VOCABULARY SCALE: 1982 EDITION

J. C. Raven. London, England: H. K. Lewis and Company Ltd.

Introduction

The Mill-Hill Vocabulary Scale: 1982 Revision, (MHV) consists of 88 words that are divided into two parallel series of 44 words each (Sets A and B). This vocabulary scale is available in three forms: the Definitions Form in which the subject is asked to define all 88 words; the Synonym Selection Form that contains both sets of words in a modified multiple-choice format in which a person is asked to underline the synonym for the target word from a group of six alternative words; and the combined Definitions and Synonym Selection Form in which persons are asked to write the meaning of each word in one set and select a synonym from a group of six alternative words in the other set. There is also a Junior Form on which the eleven most difficult words are omitted, and a Senior Form on which the ten easiest words are eliminated, resulting in four forms of the test under the definition and synonyms selection procedure. For Form 1 (Junior and Senior), Set A is in the definitions format and Set B is in the synonym selection format, whereas for Form 2 (Junior and Senior), Set A is in the synonym selection format and Set B is in the definition format.

Another form of the test, The Crichton Vocabulary Scale (CVS), consists of the first 40 words of the MVH and another set of 40 words that have been matched for difficulty with the first 40 words in the MHV. This scale is used to provide a wider dispersion of scores for children and "defectives." In addition, a Short Form of the MHV consists of every fifth word in Sets A and B from the original MVH, making each correct definition worth five points. When using the Short Form, which is recommended when the goal is the study of the thought processes and language usages of the respondent, the respondent is asked to define each word in detail and use it in a sentence.

The MHV is to be used together with the Raven Progressive Matrices (RPM) and is primarily a measurement of "reproduction . . . or . . . acquired information" (Raven, Court, & Raven, 1978, p. 12). The RPM is a nonverbal test of intellectual functioning, whereas the MHV is a complementary verbal measure.

Raven, Court, and Raven (1982) assert that using two separate tests in place of a single test of general intelligence makes it possible to distinguish clearly between a person's capacity for rational judgment (RPM) and that person's present ability to recall verbal information (MHV). They further state that "in this way, it is possible to assess the degree to which present recall of verbal information agrees with present capacity for intellectual activity, and to infer the significance of discrepancies between them" (p. 5).

The first edition of the MHV, which appeared in 1938, was developed by J. C. Raven, the author of the Progressive Matrices. Both the RPM and the MHV had their beginnings in Spearman's (1927) *Investigations into the Nature of Intelligence*. J. C. Raven, a student of Spearman's, designed the RPM to be a measure of education; the MHV was designed as a measure of reproduction.

The MHV was developed by taking 500 words, selected at regular intervals, from *The Concise Oxford Dictionary*. Fifty words at a time were given to children aged 5-14 and were then arranged in approximate order of difficulty. It was found, however, that there were too many easy words and so a further sample of 150 words was taken from *Roget's Thesaurus*. In order to accomplish this, two persons were each asked to read down pages that had been previously selected until they came to a word they thought an intelligent adult might know but would have difficulty defining. From these 650 words, 112 words, which had synonyms of about the same order of difficulty, were chosen on the basis of their apparent suitability for an experimental scale. The remaining words were used as distractors in the synonym selection format of the test. Further investigation revealed that certain words had vague colloquial uses and other words were widely known but poorly understood, hence they were removed from the scale. After further investigation 88 words were finally retained and arranged in ascending order of difficulty and divided into two exactly parallel sets of 44 words. Correlations between the scales ranged from between .90 to .95 (Raven et al., 1982).

The original standardization in 1943-44 was carried out on children aged 4-14 years who were attending school in Colchester Essex, Great Britain, with 823 children tested individually and 1,419 tested on a group basis. The standardization indicated that there was an annual increment of about three words per year.

The standardization of the group test for adult males was conducted during 1946 and 1947 among engineers, postal workers, and male employees of a photographic company.

Studies carried out in Great Britain, Ireland, Australia, and other English-speaking countries over the years revealed that the difficulty of some of the words had changed, and in 1976 the MHV was revised and the words in both Sets A and B reordered according to difficulty level.

As a result of a 1979 standardization study of 3,500 children who formed a representative sample of British children aged 6-16 years, the MHV was again revised in 1981. As in other studies, the younger and less able children were tested orally; the older and more able children were tested in groups. Again, on the basis of the results obtained in that study, the order of the words in the scale was revised because of changes in difficulty level, and one answer on the Synonym Selection format changed. There is some evidence that the vocabulary test is useful in most English-speaking countries. Although norms have not been developed for North America and the MHV has not been widely used there, normative studies are being carried out in the United States at the time of this review.

All of the forms of the MHV are printed on 8″x10″ white paper in black ink. The first page contains identification and demographic information, the two inside pages contain Set A and Set B of the appropriate MHV form, and the last page contains a scoring sheet for the appropriate form. The Definitions Form of the test, designed for respondents up to the age of 11 years, has the 44 items from Set A and the 44 items from Set B, followed by dashed lines on which the definition is to be written by the examiner. There are six of these lines to the inch, so that the examiner must write small in order that the definition can fit between the lines. According to the manual (Raven, Court, & Raven, 1982), the Definitions Form is the form with the greatest utility because individuals are asked to explain the meanings of the words in each set and their replies are noted on a record form by the examiner.

The instructions for this form of the test are not exact. The child may be asked "You know what a ________ is?"; "What is it?"; "Tell me what a ________ is."; "What is a ________ like?"; or "So, what is a ________?" The goal of the questioning is to encourage the person to give a definition of the word. If a definition is not forthcoming, the examiner can say "How do you use the word ________?" After the individual has used the word, the examiner must ask, "So what does ________ mean?" It is only the answer to the latter question that is scored. If the test is being administered to adults, usually a statement such as "Tell me the meaning of the ________" is adequate. If necessary, however, adults may be told that an exact definition is not required and that all that is needed is to know that they understand the word.

When the Definitions Form is being administered to individuals under 11 years of age, they are asked the meaning of each word in Set A until all the words they seem able to explain without undue pressure have been attempted. After this decision, which is left up to the examiner, is made, Set B is attempted and the child is asked each word until six consecutive words are missed. The administrator should then return to the first set attempted to see if the child can explain the meanings of any more words in that set.

The instructions are slightly different for adults. They are given every fifth word initially until they find it difficult to explain the meaning of a word. The administrator then asks each word in turn until six consecutive words are clearly missed. The administrator then returns to the first word incorrectly explained and asks the meaning of each word in turn from this point toward the beginning of the scale until the administrator is satisfied that all the rest of the words can be explained.

The Combined Definitions and Synonym Selection Forms are divided into the Junior version, suitable for children aged 11-14 and a Senior version for individuals over 14 years. In the Synonym Selection Form the word to be defined is printed in boldface uppercase letters and the six words are printed in two columns of three beneath the word. The instructions are simply to underline the word that means the same as the word in heavy type above the group of six words. The directions in the test booklet are straightforward. A machine-scorable version is available only for the Synonym Selection format (both Junior and Senior Forms). According to the manual (p. 6) this form is "most suitable when an accurate estimate of the person's attainments is not necessary" and "there is a fund of qualitative information and more accurate scoring when the definitions form of the test is used."

The Short Form of the MHV is intended to be used in clinical situations where the interest is in individuals' language usage, as well as their knowledge.

The Crichton Vocabulary Scale has been designed for use with persons of impaired intelligence, as well as for children under 11 years of age. It was designed to provide a wider dispersion of scores for children and the mentally retarded. This test must be individually administered, but the instructions for this test are the same as for the Definitions Form of the MHV.

Practical Applications/Uses

The recommended use of the MHV is to "record a person's present recall of acquired information and ability for verbal communication" (Raven et al., 1982, p. 4). It is to be used in conjunction with the RPM, which measures a person's capacity for rational judgment, so that both verbal and nonverbal measures of intelligence are at hand. According to the manual (p. 5) "in this way it is possible to assess the degree to which the present recall of verbal information agrees with the present capacity for intellectual activity, and to infer the significance of discrepancy between them."

The MHV has been widely used in English-speaking countries outside North America. In conjunction with the RPM, it has been widely used in personality and psychiatric studies to control for intelligence and screening and in studies comparing characteristics of various psychiatric diagnoses among other uses. It seems to be a quick measure of intelligence if the goal of the measurement is to place people in rather gross categories. For example, the norms give the raw scores for various age groups on the 5th, 10th, 25th, 50th, 75th, 90th, and 95th percentiles. On the other hand, this limited range of norms prevents overinterpretation of slight differences in scores.

Because the Mill Hill Vocabulary test correlates in the .80s and .90s with the Wechsler Adult Intelligence Scale Vocabulary, the full scale Stanford-Binet IQ, and the Terman-Merrill IQ and correlates with the Terman-Merrill Vocabulary Test, there would seem little need to use the MHV in the United States unless it was in conjunction with the use of the RPM.

The test is useful for subjects ranging in age from approximately four and one-half years to geriatric populations. There are forms of the MHV appropriate for each age group and with the Crichton Vocabulary Scale it may be used to evaluate the verbal competence of mentally retarded and other mentally handicapped individuals. The Definitions format where the subject is questioned orally could be used with the visually handicapped. Its written format may also be useful for literate hearing-impaired persons.

Prior to 11 years of age, the test is individually administered orally with the administrator writing the responses of the person taking the test. After age 11 the test can be given in groups. It can, for example, be given in a classroom and, according to the authors, a nonprofessional may be trained to give the examination. The MHV instructions, although somewhat vague, seem to be adequate, and with some training and supervision an individual should be able to learn to give this test in a short period of time. The test takes about 30 minutes to complete, but most persons will finish the test in less time.

Instructions for scoring are clearly presented in the manual for the 1982 revision of the MHV; however, under the title "Criteria for Marking Responses," the following statement is made ". . . it is impossible to give exact principles according to which an explanation of a word's meaning can be said to be strictly 'right' or 'wrong'. A dictionary can, of course, be consulted in cases of ambiguity" (Raven et al., 1982, p. 24). It should not, however, be difficult to make a key for these forms of the test, and once an individual has scored 10 or 20 of these tests scoring should be easy and fast. The score is simply the number correct in Set A and Set B. There is machine scoring for the Synonym Selection Form in which both Set A and Set B are offered in the synonym selection mode.

For interpretation it is recommended that individuals be placed in one of five categories according to their percentile rank. Examinees receive a grade of I (verbally superior) if their score lies at or above the 95th percentile; II (definitely above average in verbal ability) if the score lies at or above the 75th percentile, and II+ if the score lies at or above the 90th percentile; III (verbally average) if the score lies between the 25th and 75th percentiles, III+ if the score is greater than the 50th percentile, III– if the score is less than the 50th percentile; IV (definitely below average in verbal ability) if the score lies at or below the 25th percentile, IV– if the score lies at or below the 10th percentile; and V (verbally defective) if the score lies at or below the 5th percentile. Interpretation based on the score is straightforward; however, one must consider the difference between the two halves of the test because the score on the Synonym Selection is usually higher than it is on Definitions. There is a table in the manual of the difference normally expected for any total score. If there is agreement between a person's score on the two halves of the test, then the results can be accepted as consistent. Hypotheses concerning large differences between the two halves (e.g., ability to read, but poor ability or inability to spell and/or formulate thoughts in coherent language) are offered in the manual.

Technical Aspects

MHV reliability is adequate. Test-retest reliability with a one-month interval on adults and school children shows reliabilities ranging from .87 to .98 (Raven, 1948; Foulds & Raven, 1948). Reliability has been checked for a variety of different groups in one study by Eysenck (1945), who reports a test-retest reliability of .95 with a six-week interval on 100 male senile patients. In another study of 1,947 children aged 5-14 years, Forms A and B were administered together and correlated .87 for boys and .83 for girls (Dunsdon & Fraser-Roberts, 1955).

In terms of validity, there are a number of studies that report high correlations between the MHV and the WISC vocabulary, the Terman-Merrill Vocabulary Test, the Terman-Merrill Mental Age, and the Stanford-Binet IQ. In the Dunsdon and Fraser-Roberts (1955) study of 1,947 children the correlations between the MHV Forms A and B, with the WISC vocabulary and the Terman-Merrill Vocabulary Test range from .78 to .87. Foulds and Raven (1948) found a correlation of .93 between the MHV and the Terman-Merrill Mental Age.

Critique

The most comprehensive compilation of references for Raven's Progressive Matrices and the Mill Hill Vocabulary Scale is the fifth edition of the *Researchers' Bibliography*, revised and updated (Court, 1980), and the supplement (Court, 1982).

This lists in excess of 1,500 studies reporting the reliability, validity, and usefulness of the RPM and MHV in research studies and surveys. This is an international bibliography and includes research articles from a large part of the Western world.

There is no question that the Mill Hill Vocabulary Scale is a reliable and valid measure of verbal intelligence. It correlates highly with other tests that are verbally loaded and reliable. The question of its usefulness in North America is an open one because there are a number of vocabulary tests that are normed on the American population, with some of which the MHV is highly correlated. Currently, William Summers, a school psychologist recruited by John Raven, is developing norms for the United States population. There is some evidence RPM norms developed in England are suitable for use in other English-speaking countries, such as British Columbia, New Zealand, Australia, Ireland, and Scotland, and there is some indication that British norms may be used appropriately in the United States. The MHV finds its usefulness in conjunction with the RPM. There are some school psychologists who believe that the RPM and the MHV can be used to obtain qualitative information on the nature and source of cognitive processing deficits and thought disorders. However, if it were not for its usefulness with the RPM, the MHV would be considered simply another vocabulary scale measuring verbal intelligence.

References

Court, J. H. (1980). *Researchers' bibliography for Raven's Progressive Matrices and Mill Hill Vocabulary Scales.* Bedford Park, South Australia: Flinders University.

Court, J. H. (1982). *Researchers' bibliography for Raven's Progressive Matrices and Mill Hill Vocabulary Scales: 1982 Supplement.* Bedford Park, South Australia: Flinders University.

Dunsdon, M. I., & Fraser-Roberts, J. A. (1955). A study of the performance of 2,000 children on four vocabulary tests: Grown curves and sex differences. *British Journal of Statistical Psychology, 8,* 3-15.

Eysenck, M. D. (1945). An exploratory study of mental organization in senility. *Journal of Neurology, Neurosurgery, and Psychiatry, 8,* Nos. I & II.

Foulds, G. A., & Raven, J. C. (1948). Normal changes in the mental abilities of adults as age advances. *Journal of Mental Science, 94,* 133-142.

Raven, J. C. (1948). The comparative assessment of intellectual ability. *British Journal of Psychology, 39,* 12-19.

Raven, J. C., Court, J. H., & Raven, J. (1978). *Manual for Raven's Progressive Matrices and Vocabulary Scales: Section 2.* London: H. K. Lewis.

Raven, J. C., Court, J. H., & Raven, J. (1982). *Manual for Raven's Progressive Matrices and Vocabulary Scales: Section 5A.* London: H. K. Lewis.

Spearman, C. E. (1927). *The nature of intelligence and the principles of cognition.* London: McMillan.

Kurt F. Geisinger, Ph.D.
Associate Professor of Psychology and Chairperson, Psychology Department, Fordham University, Bronx, New York.

MILLER ANALOGIES TEST

W.S. Miller. Cleveland, Ohio: The Psychological Corporation.

Introduction

The Miller Analogies Test (MAT) is an objectively scored, group administered test of mental ability. The test is composed of 100 multiple-choice analogy items, arranged in order of increasing difficulty. The publisher defines the test as a "high-level mental ability test which requires the solution of a series of intellectual problems stated in the form of analogies, mostly verbal" (The Psychological Corporation, 1984, p. 9). Each analogy item has four parts, arranged in two apparent pairs. Three of the four component parts are given: one apparently complete pair and another that has one member identified and requires the examinee to select the counterpart from four options. Hence, the examinee's goal is to determine the relationship that exists in the first pair of components and then select from among the four competing options the one that causes the relationship in this pair to parallel the former pair. The following examples are provided in a useful examinee-preparation brochure (The Psychological Corporation, 1984).

A:B::C:?

a. A
b. B
c. C
d. D.

The above question might be imagined as "A is to B as C is to what?" The correct answer, of course, is found in option *d*, the letter *D*. The following is a more realistic question:

Light:Dark::Pleasure:?

a. Fun
b. Peace
c. Pain
d. Night.

The correct answer in this instance is *c* because pain is the opposite of pleasure, just as light is the opposite of dark. In both of these examples, the fourth component of the analogy is left blank and the examinee is called on to solve the analogy problem by selecting the option that, when placed in this spot, completes the analogy. Any of the four parts of a MAT item can be missing. In fact, the test form

---

This reviewer would like to thank Ms. Janet F. Carlson and Ms. Carol DeVictoria of the Fordham University Psychology Department for their help in the preparation of this review.

provided by the Psychological Corporation to this reviewer contained 24 items where the first word was missing, 26 where the second was missing, 25 where the third was missing, and 25 where the fourth was missing—the number of each type is clearly almost identical.

The subject matter contained in the test items is varied and, according to the publisher, comes from many academic disciplines, such as literature, the social sciences, chemistry, biology, physics, mathematics, and general information. Possession of both a good vocabulary and a wealth of general information is a necessary precondition to successful performance on the test. However, it is the ability to recognize verbal relationships rather than the possession of knowledge per se that leads to a high score on this test. Sternberg (1974) has identified seven classification systems used to describe the relationships found in the MAT items: similarity/contrast, description, class, completion, part/whole, equality/negation, and nonsemantic. Recent forms of the MAT have not included nonsemantic items.

An examinee is given 50 minutes to complete the MAT's 100-items. Thus, examinees have only 30 seconds to respond to the average question. Although these time constraints appear extremely limited under the common rule—one item per minute—evidence indicates that the test is largely a power test with scores earned without time limits correlating well over .95 with the scores by the same examinees under timed limits. Probably the short length (e.g., few words) of the analogy items in contrast to other multiple-choice items explains the lack of a significant speededness effect on test scores.

The MAT is administered at more than 450 testing centers overseas, in Canada, and in 49 states in the United States. (Due to "Open Testing" legislation mandating the release of tests administered in New York, the MAT has not been administered there since 1979.) The majority of these testing centers are counseling centers, psychology departments, and other offices at colleges and universities throughout North America. The tests are administered under the auspices of knowledgeable, trained examiners, who are instructed *not* to administer the examination to large groups—a rarity for an objective, self-administered test of this type. Instead, examiners are given the instruction to administer the test individually or in small groups so that they are better able to control testing circumstances and test security. Such procedures are extremely advantageous with regard to the test standardization (Geisinger, 1984). The starting and finishing instructions are given orally, so an examiner must be able to communicate effectively. More problematic are the statements that instruct examiners to 1) allow time for all of the examinees to read the instructions and 2) answer appropriate questions. Making determinations such as these may well tax some examiners, especially clerical personnel and graduate assistants with minimal training.

An examinee's score is simply the number of correct answers out of 100 that the individual answers (frequently called the raw score). There is no correction for guessing; therefore, examinees should be instructed to use option-elimination strategies where appropriate and random guessing for all questions that they cannot answer based on knowledge.

The four-page test booklets are reusable. Machine scorable answer sheets are used so that examinations may be scored with optical-scanning equipment or by hand; they may be scored locally at the testing center or mailed to The Psychological Corporation. As is the case with many hand-scoring templates, examiners who score the examination by hand must be certain to check if an examinee has marked more than one response to a single question.

There are seven MAT forms, which were disseminated at different times: J(1952), K(1959), L(1963), M(1969), R(1950; formerly H), S(1974), and T(1980). Before individuals take the MAT they must complete two survey-like information cards that 1) inform the examiner if they have taken a form of the MAT recently and 2) provide various demographic information. Because a score on the same form within 12 months is invalidated, candidates who choose to take the MAT a second time within a year are administered a different form. Scores that are over five-years-old are not reported. When there are multiple scores taken within two years of the score report all are reported, but if more than one score is on record and each was earned two to five years earlier, only the most recent is reported. Three score reportings are included with the price of the test and others may be obtained from the publisher for a nominal fee.

Although the test manual describes test administration for handicapped examinees, scores from such procedures should be interpreted with extreme caution. Two kinds of handicaps are discussed in the manual, visual impairments and those physical handicaps that make the marking of an answer sheet difficult or impossible. For all handicapped examinees, the test is administered in an untimed fashion. For the visually handicapped, braille and large-print versions are available. Where appropriate, one can also use a reader rather than the printed test booklet. For both the visually and physically handicapped, one can use oral responses in lieu of marking the answer sheet directly. There does not appear to be either a braille or a large-print answer sheet. No research has been performed concerning the effects of the changes in test administration for handicapped subjects, and one must seriously question the usefulness of such testing.

Practical Applications/Uses

The MAT is used primarily in the selection of students, during their college senior year, for advanced (graduate and professional) education. It was originally developed about 40 years ago by W. S. Miller of the University of Minnesota to help in the selection of graduate students at that institution. Its popularity in that setting led to its dissemination to other universities for the same purpose prior to its publication by The Psychological Corporation. Of the seven forms, Form R is used primarily for retest purposes; Forms J and R, marketed as the Advanced Personnel Test, are used for selecting high-level employees (e.g., management) in industry.

The norms tables provided in the test manual (Psychological Corporation, 1981) yield information pertaining to the MAT's users (i.e., those who make graduate-admission decisions), the majority of whom are in psychology and education departments. There are several reasons for this unusual pattern. First, psychologists and educators, as relatively informed test users, are more apt to be aware of the test and its advantages. Second, Miller was a professor of education. Third, the test received substantial acclaim when it was found in early longitudinal research (Kelly & Fiske, 1951) to predict which trainees in clinical psychology would complete their studies and earn their doctoral degrees. Psychologists in the 1950s and 1960s were also the most apt to be impressed with the administration procedures and security of this test.

The test differs from its chief competitor, the Graduate Record Examination (GRE), in various ways. One of the main advantages of the MAT is its ceiling. A rather difficult test, it appears to be able to make distinctions among highly capable examinees. Another advantage is that the MAT may be administered to meet an individual's schedule; the time of administration is determined at a time of mutual convenience to the examinee and the testing center.

The booklet given to MAT examinees informing them about the test includes 100 practice analogies—a plus. The score reporting of the MAT, as described in the above section, is also excellent. A disadvantage relates to its cost; each administration site is permitted to set its own fees, and variations in cost may adversely affect some examinees, such as those who are only near one testing center.

The MAT may well have a place in making admission decisions for graduate and professional schools or for hiring workers, but good testing practice must be employed. For example, it must be recognized that scores from this test are only one index of performance; they must be evaluated professionally within the limits of the test's validity (The Psychological Corporation, 1981, p. 2).

Technical Aspects

Test Development and Item Selection: All of the MAT's seven forms were constructed according to the same procedure and new forms will apparently be built similarly. In each case, a pool of 300-400 analogy items were written, compiled, and divided into groups of 15-20 items. These minitests are then administered experimentally to examinees taking a current form of the MAT. Items are then selected according to three criteria: 1) they must have a high positive point-biserial correlation with the total MAT score with which it has been experimentally paired, 2) they must appear to be of appropriate levels of difficulty, and 3) they must sample subject matter in a manner consistent with previous forms of the test. Items are arranged within the test in order of their difficulty.

Each new test form is equated to its preceding form in the following manner. Both forms are given in counterbalanced order to several hundred college seniors and graduate students. The MAT manual reports that if "means, standard deviations, and raw score equivalents of selected percentiles . . . are judged to be sufficiently similar, the two forms are considered equivalent" (The Psychological Corporation, 1981, p. 21). The lack of explicit specificity on the criteria of test equating is problematic to this reviewer. Although The Psychological Corporation does issue test reports for each newly issued test form, one would like to see the criteria employed in equating in the manual, especially when the manual makes the claim that "the various forms . . . are equivalent for practical purposes" and that "all norms tables . . . may be entered directly with J, K, L, S, T, or R raw scores" (p. 7).

Norms: The manual provides separate norms for educational and industrial purposes. The educational norms are subdivided into applicant and enrolled student pools. These norm groups are, of course, further divided by field of study.

From the applicant pool, The Psychological Corporation has sampled between

1,600 and 2,000 examinees, typically college seniors applying to senior graduate school, for each year of test administration since 1974. Those who have taken the test previously or whose proposed major was left off of the MAT information card are eliminated from consideration and replaced with data from another examinee. The samples are stratified by year of test administration and proposed graduate program/major. Graduate programs represented include psychology (clinical, unspecified, and total), education (general, administration, elementary, special, guidance and counseling, reading and language, and total), natural sciences, social sciences, humanities, social work, and nursing and business (1981-1985 only), with the largest groups being psychology and education. There were 3,952 examinees in the psychology norm group for the years 1974-1980 and 3,167 from 1981-85. There were 5,465 examinees in the education norm group for the years 1974-1980 and 3,212 from 1981-85. The size of the subdivided groups in education and psychology may be said to range from minimally acceptable to acceptable, from 159 for reading and language and 244 for elementary education to 757 for general education. Similarly, the norms for 1981-1985 for the other groups range in number from 270 for natural sciences to 693 for social work. Further accentuating these small numbers is the smorgasbord effect of combining the various disciplines composing the natural sciences, social sciences, humanities, and business. The usefulness of these conglomerate norms must be questioned. Finally, it should be noted that *no* differentiation is made for whether the students are applying for master's or doctoral programs. The basic norms table, Table 1 in the manual, provides data from 1974-1980, broken into 15 subject-matter areas or combinations of areas, with the following statistical information provided: number of examinees (in the area); mean; standard deviation; and raw score at the 99th, 97th, 95th, 90th, 85th, 80th, 75th, 70th, 65th, 60th, 55th, 50th, 45th, 40th, 35th, 30th, 25th, 20th, 15th, 10th, 5th, 3rd, and 1st percentiles. Mayberry and Williams (1985) essentially provide a 1985 update of this norms table.

Normative data for enrolled students are provided in an appendix of the manual but they are extremely dated. The data presented include the score at the 90th, 75th, 50th, 25th, and 10th percentiles for each of twelve disciplines, which are largely similar to those listed above except for the addition of rehabilitation counseling, theology, engineering, medicine, and psychoanalytic training. For each of the twelve disciplines, the number of examination scores involved in the norm data, the mean and the standard deviation are provided. This reviewer could not find updates of these data. It should also be noted that the norm groups for some of the disciplines (e.g., rehabilitation counseling) include both doctoral and master's students with no differentiation.

Appended to the MAT manual is a table of industrial normative information, but there is no organization to the kinds of jobs that are represented. Instead, The Psychological Corporation has reviewed various studies performed in industry and listed the means, standard deviations, and number of employees in each of approximately 16 companies. In some companies, stratifications for as many as seven education levels or job classifications are given. A sampling of these jobs include college graduate employees of a large meat packing corporation, engineers and scientists in an atomic power laboratory, and top-level supervisors of a large multicompany in a humanities training program for executives.

Test Reliability: Numerous reliability studies, the results of which are provided in the manual, have been performed on MAT data. Thirteen split-half reliability analyses over all forms of the test indicate the range of reliability coefficients to be from .92 to .95. These studies, which averaged over 250 subjects, used the Spearman-Brown method of estimating the reliability coefficient—not a preferred method.

Eight studies cited in the manual employed the alternate-forms method (seven different pairings of test forms were utilized) and found reliability coefficients from .85 to .91. These studies counterbalanced the presentation of test forms, which, given a fairly large practice effect on the test, would indicate the coefficients to be underestimates.

Two studies are reported in the manual as estimating the test-retest reliability of the MAT. In the first study, a large sample was split into two samples (for unknown reason), with the second administration coming eight months after the first. The test-retest reliability coefficients were .82 and .89 for the two samples. It might be noted that the average gain in test score on the second testing was approximately seven points over the first testing. The second study employed a sample of approximately 500 examinees and a six-month time interval between testings and found a test-retest reliability coefficient of .75. The practice effect may also have an impact in reducing these three estimates of test reliability; however, the effect would be indeterminate.

The standard error of measurement for the MAT depends on the type of generalization a test user would be interested in making. The manual is deceptive in that it only provides the standard error of measurement for the odd-even, split-half reliability analyses; although there may be reasons for this (e.g., the standard deviations of the two tests are not identical in the alternate forms and test-retest analyses), because the split-half estimates of reliability are the highest the manual is misleading. The standard errors calculated based on these split-half analyses range from 3.7 to 4.5. This reviewer calculated standard errors of measurement for the alternate-form data. These values range from about 5.00 to 6.25. It is not possible to calculate the standard error for the test-retest analyses because no standard deviations are provided in the manual. Using a *guesstimate* standard deviation for the raw test scores of 16.5, one finds the standard error of measurement to range from 5.5 to 8.25 points over a period of approximately six months. These values are quite large and could impact decision making.

Test Validity: The MAT has relied continually on three arguments to justify its use in selecting students: 1) common sense/face validity, 2) predictive validity with criteria, and 3) correlations with other tests of mental ability.

There are three traditional conceptualizations of test validity: content, predictive, and construct. The MAT makes little, if any, claims regarding content validity. Whereas the manual claims that the analogy items come from literature, social sciences, chemistry, biology, physics, mathematics, and general information, it also states that "the examinee is not required to be a specialist in any of these areas," an applicant for graduate school or for a high-level industrial position will have been exposed to much if not all, of the precise information needed," and "the test items requrie the recognition of relationships rather than the display of enormous erudition" (p. 5). Hence, the manual reports that the test measures so-called mental ability rather than specific (e.g., course-related) knowledge. Content validity may be claimed for a test that samples relevant abilities systematically, but the manual makes no claims that the test content samples any model of abilities in a well-delineated manner. The content of the MAT has been previously described as a "hodgepodge of subject matter which reflects no clear philosophy of graduate education" (Guilford, 1953, p. 407; Willingham, 1965, p. 749).

The lack of explicit content validity is not critical in that the manual justifies the test's usefulness through a great deal of evidence of predictive validity. It provides reports of 1) 12 correlational studies where the MAT predicts success in graduate or professional school, 2) studies that contrast the average MAT scores of two groups, and 3) studies in which industrial criteria are predicted. The manual, however, provides only two validity studies performed in industrial settings: one predicting success in a management-training program with moderate accuracy ($r = .38$) and the other predicting employee success in five types of jobs at a large oil company (e.g., marketing personnel, refining personnel), with validity coefficients ranging from .21 to .36.

Many of the 12 correlational predictive validity studies subdivide students into graduate programs (e.g., psychology or education), and, therefore, a total of 41 correlations are presented. These studies also employ a variety of criteria: graduate grade-point average, first-year grade-point average in professional school, and preliminary examinations. All of these criterion indices typically suffer from serious problems that inhibit their usefulness (Willingham, 1974): restriction of range, unreliability, and ambiguity of meaning. In addition, the manual might be faulted in that it provides a "bewildering array of correlations [which] is . . . difficult to comprehend" (Humphreys, 1965, p. 747). Although a majority of the correlations presented are statistically significant (at least those based on samples of at least 30 subjects), the magnitude of the correlations is not impressive, a conclusion shared by Sternberg (1974). Thus, this reviewer felt the necessity to summarize the correlations with an average correlation by averaging all of these correlations, regardless of educational criterion employed. The technique for averaging these correlations was the weighted root mean squared method, where each correlation was weighted in terms of the number of subjects involved in that particular study. The average correlation that was found was .26, not impressive evidence of predictability. It should be further noted that there is no explanation of how or where The Psychological Corporation learned of the studies it reports. To be sure, some are listed as personal communication. Humphreys (1965) considered this method of collecting and reporting the results of studies "deplorable, though commonplace" (p. 747). He continues by stating that the accumulation of evidence through a sampling of publications and voluntary submission to The Psychological Corporation is an incredibly biased method. Thus, whereas the criteria used probably reduce the correlations found in the validation studies (due to restriction of range, unreliability, etc.), the procedures employed for sampling studies most assuredly overestimate the population values of the validity coefficients. The size of these effects is simply indeterminate.

The MAT is certainly most likely to be used in conjunction with grades from undergraduate training, other test scores, interview information, and related pertinent data in making admission decisions. Yet there is no evidence provided in the manual that relates to the incremental validity—the value of adding the MAT to these other data. With an average correlation of approximately .26, as cited above, it appears unlikely that the MAT would have incremental validity in all instances, or even the typical situation. Nevertheless, Humphreys (1965) is less pessimistic in reporting that "It is probably safe to conclude that this test will make a contribution toward the prediction of academic success in most situations" (p. 472). This reviewer does not see evidence for this claim, and in one study (Kirnan & Geisinger, 1981), it was certainly not true. In that study, although the MAT predicted performance on a master's comprehensive examination in psychology with a highly significant validity coefficient of .34, it did not improve the prediction of comprehensive performance when scores from the verbal portion of the GRE were available. Programs that employ the MAT in order to improve on the predictability already present in other admission materials would be well-advised to check the incremental benefits of the test.

The MAT manual also provides average test scores from six studies that contrasted varying groups. The studies cited portray from two to four groups and differ with respect to the amount of information provided. All list means and numbers for each of the groups. Four provide standard deviations, and only shows a *t*-test value indicating the significance of the contrasted groups. These studies provide some comparative information for the following contrasts: accepted vs. rejected applicants to graduate programs, doctoral vs. master's students, students who attain the Ph.D. vs. those who do not, graduate students for whom English is the primary language vs. those for whom it is secondary, graduate students in various fields, M.A. vs. M.Ed. vs. M.S. students, and recipients of fellowships vs. finalists vs. other applicants. In general, mean differences are present in the expected directions. Clearly, however, in some of these cases, the MAT scores might have caused or influenced the decisions in the first place (e.g., when comparing accepted vs. rejected students); such evidence certainly would not be conclusive of test validation.

Construct validation may be evaluated and inferred, at least in part, from all the evidence presented above. Further evidence regarding construct validity may be learned from the 86 correlations with numerous tests provided in the manual. These correlations can be used in two ways. First, they provide evidence of both convergent and discriminant validity. Second, they help an informed user to determine when the MAT is apt to be useful with regard to incremental validity. The greatest number of correlations (10) are found with the GRE; the median correlations for the verbal and quantitative portions are .71 and .48, respectively. There are four correlations with the GRE Advanced Psychology Test, with a median correlation of .36. Single-sample correlations with the Advanced Education, Physics, and Chemistry Tests of the GRE are .61, .55, and .51, respectively. Two studies report correlations with the WAIS tests; median correlations are .60, .56, and .41 for Full Scale, Verbal, and Performance IQs, respectively. A considerable number of correlations cited in the manual are not reviewed here. A sampling of the correlation coefficients with the MAT, which are presented in the manual, might include the Medical College Admissions Test, the Scholastic Aptitude Test, the National Teacher Examinatins, the Terman Concept Mastery Test, the Raven Progressive Matrices, the Watson-Glaser Critical Thinking Appraisal, the Space

Relations Test of the Differential Aptitude Tests, the Army General Classification Tests, the Guilford-Zimmerman Aptitude Survey, and various personality tests.

An on-balance review of these correlations might indicate that the MAT is a test of reasoning ability, most specifically of verbal reasoning. It is frequently paired with a test of quantitative reasoning, most typically the Doppelt Mathematical Reasoning Test, also published by The Psychological Corporation. Schrader (1965) also recommends using it with a reading test, a suggestion that seems to have merit. The MAT is probably not correlated with values or personality constructs.

Critique

Evaluative comments regarding the MAT have been interspersed throughout this review. An overall evaluation of the MAT may be divided into three sections: the problems with the test itself; the problems with test score interpretation, which is partially a problem of the test manual; and the strengths of the test.

Problems with the Miller Analogies Test: Three concerns are raised in this section. These concerns relate to 1) the contents of the test, 2) the validity of the test, and 3) the trainability of test performance. As has been previously stated, the analogy items on the test do not intentionally represent any specific disciplines or areas of knowledge in a careful and systematic manner. No philosophy of education or of knowledge is reflected in the test contents. Indeed, the items are largely selected so that the test is internally consistent and has a high ceiling. Finally, although the analogy paradigm seems an effective way of measuring verbal reasoning, it has drawbacks. Willingham (1974) faults educational tests as "forcing attention on fairly limited aspects of competency" (p. 598). With its sole reliance on analogy items the MAT is even more guilty of this problem than are many tests.

Regarding its validity, the MAT correlates about as highly with criteria of graduate-school performance as any other test that is frequently used. It correlates so highly with the GRE-V that employing the two in combination would rarely be needed. Because the GRE is used more frequently, one might suggest that the MAT is simply not required for general use in making graduate-admission decisions. The test is most likely to aid in the prediction of a criterion when the other predictor tests assess quantitative reasoning, reading, performance IQ, or an affective variable.

The largest problem, which has been only alluded to thus far, relates to the strong possibility that successful performance on the MAT may be radically improved in short-term test-preparation sessions. Sternberg (1974) makes this claim, and the evidence indicating that an examinee who takes two forms of the test in close temporal proximity benefits in a meaningful way suggests that performance on the MAT may be taught. No such findings are discussed in either the manual or the literature, at least to this reviewer's knowledge. Yet, the suggestion of trainability is particularly negative because those examinees who can afford the coaching will benefit, whereas the poor will be further disadvantaged.

Problems with score interpretation and with the manual: There are numerous minor revisions in the manual that are requested. The inclusion of certain information would simply make a test user's judgments more valid. For example, it would be beneficial if the manual included the criteria used in test-form equating and a summary of the validation evidence that was acquired prior to 1970. (The manual contains only research since 1970.) Schrader (1965) calls for the printing of standard errors of the correlations coefficients that are presented in the manual; because many of the correlation coefficients are based on small sample sizes, interpretation would be improved with this information. Greater detail in describing the norm group would also aid the test user. Lastly, if the manual would simply tell readers how the authors learned of the various validity studies that are presented, the readers could judge for themselves the extent to which the sampling of studies is not representative.

The biggest problem with the manual may be a distressing lack of necessary research regarding the differential performance and resultant potential adverse effects of using this test with ethnic and cultural minorities. The manual simply does not deal with the issue. The only evidence that one might infer regarding such use of the test that comes from the manual relates to a single contrasted pair of means presented in the validity section. As mentioned previously, the manual reports a study where graduate students with English as a primary language performed substantially better than those with English as a second language. In psychology, social work, and education the means were 56.3 and 33.3, respectively, and in counselor education the means were 48.5 and 27.0, respectively. Furthermore, the sample sizes were substantial. These findings are not desirable, especially if one imagines that the English-as-a-second-language group was largely Hispanic. The findings are even more distressing if one assumes that the English-as-a-second-language students took the *Test of English as a Foreign Language* and other standard admissions tests (as are required by most graduate schools) because these students probably show high academic abilities with well-developed reasoning skills as well. Clearly, The Psychological Corporation would be well-advised to research these issues. As mentioned previously, research is also needed to demonstrate the validity of scores for handicapped examinees.

Strengths of the Miller Analogies Test: Regardless of the test, manual, and research flaws cited above, the present reviewer concurs with most of the preceding reviews in that the MAT is well-constructed and difficult enough to have plenty of room for differentiating highly capable students. The latter strength is reflected in its high reliability, even when evaluated in populations with a highly restricted range of ability. It is a relatively brief test, but is not speeded. It is readily available, yet highly secure. It is easily scored. Its predictive validity needs to be evaluated in settings which it is used, but this requirement only makes it like virtually all other published psychological tests. As a relatively short test of verbal reasoning, the MAT has earned a unique place for itself in the history of psychological testing and is likely to maintain its respected position as a screening test that provides useful information for making graduate-admission decisions.

References

Geisinger, K. F. (1984). Test standardization. In R. C. Corsini (Ed.), *Wiley encyclopedia of psychology* (pp. 414). New York: Wiley.

Guilford, J. P. (1953). Miller Analogies Test. In O. K. Buros (Ed.), *The fourth mental measurements yearbook* (pp. 406-407). Highland Park, NJ: The Gryphon Press.

Hovland, C. I. (1953). Miller Analogies Test. In O. K. Buros (Ed.), *The fourth mental measurements yearbook* (pp. 407-408). Highland Park, NJ: The Gryphon Press.

Humphreys, L. G. (1965). Miller Analogies Test. In O. K. Buros (Ed.), *The sixth mental measurements yearbook* (pp. 747-748). Highland Park, NJ: The Gryphon Press.

Kelly, E. L., & Fiske, D. W. (1951). *The prediction of performance in clinical psychology.* Ann Arbor, MI: University of Michigan Press.

Kirnan, J. P., & Geisinger, K. F. (1981). The prediction of graduate school success in psychology. *Educational and Psychological Measurement, 41,* 815-820.

Mayberry, P. W., & Williams, M. E. (1985). *Miller Analogies Test: A report on Miller Analogies Test scores of applicants to graduate school, 1981-85.* Cleveland: The Psychological Corporation.

Psychological Corporation, The. (1981). *Miller Analogies Test manual: 1981 revision.* Cleveland: Author.

Psychological Corporation, The. (1984). *Information bulletin: Bulletin of information and list of testing centers with 100 practice items for the MAT.* Cleveland: Author.

Schrader, W. B. (1965). Miller Analogies Test. In O. K. Buros (Ed.), *The sixth mental measurements yearbook* (pp. 748-749). Highland Park, NJ: The Gryphon Press.

Sternberg, R. J. (1974). *How to prepare for the Miller Analogies Test.* Woodbury, NY: Barron's Educational Series, Inc.

Willingham, W. W. (1965). Miller Analogies Test. In O. K. Buros (Ed.), *The sixth mental measurements yearbook* (pp. 748-749). Highland Park, NJ: The Gryphon Press.

Willingham, W. W. (1974). Predicting success in graduate education. *Science, 183,* 273-278.

Frank J. Dyer, Ph.D.
Psychologist in Private Practice, Montclair, New Jersey.

MILLON ADOLESCENT PERSONALITY INVENTORY

Theodore Millon, Catherine J. Green, and Robert B. Meagher, Jr. Minneapolis, Minnesota: NCS Professional Assessment Services.

Introduction

The Millon Adolescent Personality Inventory (MAPI) is an objective personality measure of the true-false type that assesses a number of personality dimensions, expressed concerns, and behavioral correlates in adolescents aged 13 to 18 years. The inventory comprises eight scales measuring personality styles based on Millon's (1969, 1981) theory of personality types; eight scales designed to tap subjects' expressed concerns, such as peer security and acceptance of sexual maturation; and four scales assessing subjects' actual behavior. The MAPI yields normative scores that are adjusted for personality-trait-prevalence data on each of the personality style, expressed concern, and behavioral correlate scales. A narrative report interprets scores on each of the three sets of scales, identifies noteworthy responses to individual items, lists applicable DSM-III diagnoses (which differ somewhat in their criteria from the theoretical framework of the MAPI), and discusses therapeutic implications for use in treatment planning. A briefer guidance interpretive report that omits the DSM-III diagnoses and discussion of the more "clinical" issues is also available.

The authors of the MAPI are Drs. Theodore Millon, Catherine J. Green, and Robert B. Meagher, Jr. Millon, the primary author, is currently a professor and director of doctoral clinical training at the University of Miami. Millon, who received a Ph.D. in personality psychology from the University of Connecticut, is well-known as a researcher and author in the areas of clinical psychology and behavioral medicine. He is the creator of the Millon Clinical Multiaxial Inventory (MCMI; see McCabe, 1984 for a review), an adult clinical measure of personality intended as an alternative to the Minnesota Multiphasic Personality Inventory (MMPI), and primary author of the Millon Behavioral Health Inventory (MBHI; see Davis, 1985 for a review). Green, coauthor of the MBHI, as well as the MAPI, is currently an associate professor and director of the Psychological Services Center at the University of Miami and is on the editorial board of several major journals. Meagher, also a coauthor of the MAPI and MBHI, is a staff psychologist at the Veterans Administration Outpatient Center in Los Angeles where he directs the behavioral stress clinic and pain treatment programs. Both Green and Meagher are coeditors of the *Handbook of Clinical Health Psychology.*

Just as the MCMI was intended to supplant older clinical adult instruments with a diagnostic measure grounded in a consistent theory of personality and developed according to psychometrically rigorous procedures, the MAPI was devised to fulfill the same need in clinical work with adolescents. As the test manual notes (Millon, Green, & Meagher, 1982), other commonly used personality measures, the application of which has been extended to adolescent populations, miss the mark owing to the adult language in which test items are couched and lack of focus on specifically adolescent concerns. Thus, from its inception, the MAPI was designed to serve as *the* clinical diagnostic inventory for adolescents.

The eight personality-style variables are derived from Millon's (1969, 1981) theory of personality, which categorizes styles of personality functioning according to a 4X2 matrix. The first dimension of this matrix describes subjects' characteristic attitude toward primary sources of reinforcement. The model posits detached types who experience few rewards or satisfactions, dependent types who are preoccupied with how others feel about them, independent types whose satisfactions are gauged in terms of their own values and desires, and ambivalent types who are in conflict over conforming to others' demands or following their own opposing desires. The second dimension of the matrix describes subjects' basic pattern of instrumental or coping behavior as either active or passive. According to the manual, the eight resulting personality styles are described as follows:

Introversive: Passive-detached—has minimal emotional needs, and is emotionally isolated from gratifications and dangers of interpersonal relationships;

Inhibited: Active-detached—withdraws socially, mistrusts others, and fears rejection;

Cooperative: Passive-dependent—seeks relationships in which others provide security and support, has little initiative or autonomy, and is clinging;

Sociable: Active-dependent—has strong needs for attention and approval from any source, and is superficial, capricious, and manipulating;

Confident: Passive-independent—has air of self-assurance and high self-esteem, is exploitive, and takes others for granted;

Forceful: Active-independent—strives for control and power, expresses anger, and is suspicious and hostile;

Respectful: Passive-ambivalent—possesses a mixture of subservience and anger, fears social disapproval, and superficially conforms despite oppositional feelings;

Sensitive: Active-ambivalent—is emotionally labile and conflicted, and alternates between explosive anger and contrition.

It will be noted that these scales represent theory-derived styles rather than unidimensional traits that would result from factor-analytic methods. Millon's theory posits the 4X2 matrix as the most meaningful and practical categorization of behavioral styles, and the MAPI personality style scales reflect this directly.

The eight areas of expressed concern are Self-Concept (development of identity); Personal Esteem (self-acceptance and positive valuation), Body Comfort (acceptance of one's own physical appearance and body image), Sexual Acceptance (adjustment to sexual maturation and impulses), Peer Security (concern with peer acceptance and its effect on self-esteem), Social Tolerance (interpersonal sensitivity and respect for others), Family Rapport, and Academic Confidence.

The four behavioral areas that are assessed through empirically derived scales rather than direct self-reported concerns are Impulse Control, Social Conformity, Scholastic Achievement, and Attendance Consistency. High base rate (BR) scores on these scales (i.e., scores that reflect the prevalance data for personality traits as identified by counselor's ratings) indicate that the subject has responded to certain groups of items in a manner characteristic of students with poor impulse control, inability to conform to rules and norms, poor academic achievement, or school attendance problems.

In addition to being guided by Millon's theory of personality, the development of the MAPI was influenced by the published observations of leading psychometricians and psychometric clinicians from the late 1950s to the early 1970s as to how an objective measure of personality should be constructed. Many of the technical publications that influenced the MAPI and its adult predecessor, the MCMI, were reactions to retrospective criticisms of the test development procedures employed in the construction of the MMPI. The MAPI was developed according to a three-stage model comprising theoretical-substantive, internal structural, and external-criterion phases. The theoretical-substantive stage involves the derivation of test items from an explicit theoretical framework, which in the case of the MAPI is the senior author's theory of personality. A similar set of test items, geared for adults, was created for the MCMI, thus the first stage of the construction of the MAPI was partially a replication of this earlier work. The second phase of the MAPI's developmental model, labeled internal-structural, involves specifications as to the degree of purity of the instrument's individual scales and the character of their expected relationships. The criteria employed for retention of individual MAPI scale items at this stage were maximization of scale homogeneity, appropriate overlap with other theoretically congruent scales within the instrument, and satisfactory endorsement frequency and stability over time. A factorial model of test construction, despite its endorsement by many leading psychometric theorists, was deliberately avoided. The rationale for this choice was that the theoretical model on which the MAPI is based does not assume scale independence, which factorial approaches are assumed by the MAPI authors to require (Millon et al. 1982, p. 44). The third stage, external-criterion validation, involved correlations of MAPI items with a variety of external criteria including "normal" vs. "problem" clinical status and counselors' clinical judgments. The manual also presents a series of correlations of MAPI scale scores with scales of other widely used personality instruments, although it is noted that this type of validity evidence is inferior to studies of the test's relationship to nontest ("real world") criteria.

The test was normed on groups of "clinical" and "nonclinical" subjects ranging in age from 13 to 19 years. The normal group consisted of 1,071 males and 1,086 females enrolled in public and parochial schools in a number of cities in various parts of the United States. The clinical group consisted of 430 adolescents, of whom 325 were outpatients and 105 were inpatients. The sample was 84% white, 11% black, 3% Hispanic, 1% Oriental, and 1% other. The standardization sample roughly matched the Hollinghead-Redlich estimated percentages for socioeconomic status groups within the general population. Based on the results of a separate validation study using the sample of 430 "clinical" cases raw scores on the MAPI were transformed into base rate scores. The authors state in the manual that such transformed scores are more meaningful and have greater practical utility than standard scores because of differential base rates among personality types and clinical syndromes. This is a sophisticated refinement that should improve the diagnostic accuracy, or "hit rate," of the instrument.

Owing to the recency of the MAPI's development (1982), no revisions have become necessary. There are no special forms at the time of this review, although the authors recommend ongoing research to develop new clinical scales from the existing items.

Practical Applications/Uses

The MAPI is completely self-administering. The answer document consists of two attached 8½" by 11" sheets. The cover sheet contains directions for filling in the name grids and marking answers. Responses are made by blackening in circles directly on the answer document using a soft pencil. Responses are either read by optical scanning equipment when the answer sheet is mailed in for processing or are transmitted directly to the scoring center at NCS Professional Assessment Services by means of terminal hookup procedures. The use of code numbers is suggested as a means of maintaining subject anonymity. Hand scoring the protocols is not recommended by the authors, and the manual notes that there are no scoring templates currently available. No special skills are required of the examiner beyond adherence to the normally accepted procedures for examining subjects with a self-administering instrument, including provision of an adequate work space, minimization of distraction, and brief orientation of the subject with emphasis on following the printed directions on the test form.

The MAPI manual states that the test was designed for use by school counselors, guidance personnel, and other mental-health service professionals in understanding a wide range of psychological attributes of adolescents. It is of interest that no specific mention is made of the group of practitioners who would conceivably represent a major segment of MAPI's user population, namely school psychologists. The MAPI, with its eight personality-style dimensions, eight expressed concern scales, and four behavioral-correlate measures, provides exactly the sort of information that school psychologists require to formulate a realistic picture of students' adjustment given the time constraints of a typical school consultation setting. The MAPI is also a useful instrument for the clinical psychologist in an agency setting as a briefer alternative to the MMPI. The issue of length is especially important where adolescent subjects are concerned, as those with mild attentional problems are likely to be easily fatigued by the MMPI's more than 500 items, as opposed to a total of 150 items on the MAPI. Clinical psychologists or other practitioners concerned with purely diagnostic issues may find the MAPI clinical narrative report's section on parallel DSM-III diagnoses helpful as a supplement to their own diagnostic impressions.

Among the uses recommended in the MAPI manual are two that are cause for concern. The clinical, or pathologically oriented, nature of the MAPI clinical interpretive report may mislead guidance personnel who have not had extensive training in psychometrics and psychopathology. Guidance counselors and other school personnel who do not provide direct clinical services to students will find the briefer guidance interpretive report more informative and of greater applicability to counseling issues. School guidance personnel should also be cautious about inferring the presence of psychopathological conditions from the BR scores for personality styles and expressed concerns listed in the manual. The guidance interpretive report deliberately omits diagnostic information. The second use of the MAPI that is highly questionable is as a routine testing procedure on entrance into school, as recommended in the manual (p. 2). Because of the highly personal information contained in both the clinical and guidance reports (e.g., discussions of how subjects cope with their sexual impulses), the routine administration of the MAPI to students other than those referred to special services would appear to be decidedly inadvisable. It is to be borne in mind that parents and students have considerable access to student records as a result of recent legislation. Routine gathering of information on students' sexual adjustment difficulties may easily be construed as a gratuitous invasion of privacy. On the other hand, school psychologists who are seeking to gain parental acceptance of an individual educational plan that includes therapy or special class recommendations in connection with sexual issues will find the results of an objective self-report measure easier to present than inferences based on imagery or themes contained in projective test responses. The ipse dixit argument can be very compelling in situations where the child-study team attempts to form an alliance with parents to address their child's emotional problems.

Technical Aspects

The validity of a psychological test refers to the degree to which it measures that which it purports to measure. The research establishing the validity of the MAPI was conducted as an integral part of the development of the test, primarily through statistical correlation of subjects' responses to individual test items with objective criteria of psychological adjustment. The first of these criteria was membership in a group rated positive (i.e., pathologically high) for one of the 20 scales of the instrument versus nonmembership in the target trait group. Subjects for this validity study were all classified as emotionally disturbed or "problem" students. Allocation to particular trait groups was made on the basis of ratings by the subjects' counselors or therapists of their standing on each of the 20 traits. Thus, the empirical keying of MAPI items was not simply guided by a "normal-clinical" distinction, but by discriminating those within a group of exclusively "clinical" subjects who scored high and low on each of the measured variables. The second criterion employed statistical correlation of each of the 150 test items with total scores on each of the 20 scales, subsequent to completion of the initial scale-construction stage. Those test items that displayed a moderate correlation (usually .30 or higher) with any scale other than a theoretically incompatible one were added to that scale. This criterion differs from the preceding one in that it is an internal or within-test measure because one segment of the test (item) is correlated with another segment (scale).

Further validity research was undertaken subsequent to the completion of the final form of the MAPI. Although the authors of the MAPI state that correlations of the scales of one personality measure with those of another is a less significant gauge of its validity than research employing real-world behavioral criteria, an extensive table of such correlations is presented in the manual as supplementary evidence of the instrument's validity. In general, the 20 individual scales of the MAPI display moderate correlations in the expected direction with relevant scales of the California Psychological Inventory, 16 PF, and the Edwards Personal Preference Schedule.

Factorial validity is a term employed by factor analytically oriented psychometricians that describes the validity of a test as a measure of some set of factorically pure constructs, or underlying traits. Research on the factorial validity of a test may take the form of a factor analysis of the *items* of one particular test to examine their intercorrelational patterns of clustering into scales. It may also involve factor-analytic studies of the intercorrelations of *scales* of several different measures to determine whether a particular test's scales represent pure measures of the various factors disclosed in the multitest study. A classic example of strict adherence to these methods is the development and validation of the Gordon Personal Profile-Inventory (Gordon, 1978). Their relevance to practical test interpretation issues is discussed in the interpretive guide to this instrument (Dyer, 1984). The MAPI manual presents a factor-analytic study based on the administration of the test to 569 males and 569 females from a number of high schools and mental-health settings. There is some question as to the appropriateness of the method employed in this factor analysis, as the procedures were designed to yield uncorrelated factors (varimax rotation). The test manual emphasizes in several of its sections that the personality scales of the MAPI are correlated, both because of the nature of their theoretical basis and because many test items are keyed on more than one scale. The authors' rationale for employing a factor-analytic method that extracts uncorrelated, or orthogonal, factors is not stated in their presentation of the research.

This questionable analysis produced four orthogonal factors that accounted for greater than 75% of the variance. The first factor, which accounted for nearly half of the variance (specific percentages are not listed), appears to be defined by the Inhibited Scale and by the Peer Security Scale, with loadings of .895 and .888, respectively. It is interpreted as measuring an anxious fearfulness, dissatisfaction regarding self, and perceived problems with peer relationships. The second factor, accounting for approximately 25% of the variance, is defined by the Scholastic Achievement and Academic Confidence Scales, with loadings of .899 and .862, respectively. Scales relating to impulse control and conformity also have high loadings in this factor. Factor 3 is defined by the Forceful Scale and measures subjects' tendencies toward a tough, vigilant stance and acting out. Factor 4 is defined by the Introversive Scale, which has a negative loading of .955. It is felt that alternate factor-analytic procedures devised to yield nonorthogonal factors would have produced a set of factors that more closely approximates the actual personality style scales of the instrument.

Test reliability, or the extent to which a psychometric instrument is precise in its measurement, is evaluated in terms of stability over time (test-retest reliability) and internal consistency (split-half reliability, coefficient alpha, K-R 20). Two test-retest studies employing samples of 105 and 59 produced stability coefficients generally within the acceptable range. The results were artificially depressed to some unknown extent by three characteristics of the subject population. The subjects were from the "clinical" segment of the standardization population and, therefore, presumably more inconsistent in their responding than normals would be, and all were adolescents, a group generally viewed as more variable in behavior than adults. The third contaminating factor resides in the fact that all subjects were engaged in an active program of counseling that produced changes in their psychological functioning between the test and retest (a period of 5 months for the first group and one year for the second). An analysis of the internal consistency of all 20 MAPI scales, employing the Kuder-Richardson Formula 20 reliability statistic, produced a median reliability coefficient of .74, with a range from .67 to .84. The findings are within the acceptable range for scales of this type.

The psychometric structure of the MAPI presents something of a paradox because, while being overly abundant, it is also lacking in certain classes of measured "dimensions." It overly abounds "dimensionally" in that its scales, which are conceptually a product of trait-type psychology, attempt to measure types without first elaborating a set of factorially distinct traits. The resulting personality type scales do not conform to the classical psychometric requirement, restated in contemporary latent-trait theory, that individual scales should attempt to measure one underlying and unidimensional trait. Each *type* scale, formulated psychometrically as though it were a *trait* scale, is actually multidimensional, reflecting the complexity of the eight underlying personality types in Millon's theory. For example, a high scorer on the Cooperative Scale, which typifies the passive-dependent pattern, is described in the test manual as being soft-hearted, sentimental, and kindly, as well as nonassertive, dependent, and avoiding leadership roles. This reviewer's clinical observation of test-behavior relationships indicates that a typically soft-hearted and kindly adolescent who is also fairly independent and who assumes leadership roles frequently can achieve a high score on the Cooperative Scale by endorsing the keyed items that tap kindheartedness and sentimentality while endorsing the keyed leadership and independence items in the direction opposite to that scored for the Cooperative Scale.

As discussed above, the published research on the MAPI also contains too few dimensions from a factor-analytic point of view. Although the orthogonal factor solution employed in the manual's factor analysis of the instrument disclosed only four factors, other procedures utilizing alternative means of extracting factors as well as rotating the axes, might have produced more realistic results. On the other hand, the author's practice of adding any items with a .30 correlation or better to a particular scale in their inspection of the whopping 150X20 correlation matrix may have confounded the separate scales beyond redemption. A factor analysis of the *items* would be informative. Interestingly, the authors seem to equate factor analysis with orthogonal rotation methods, as evidenced by their statement in the manual (p. 44) that ". . . the structure of the MAPI, as with the MCMI, is best constructed in accord with a model that stresses internal scale consistency, *but does not require the scale independence that characterizes factorial approaches* [italics added]."

Actually, most trait-type psychologies posit correlated personality factors or traits because the notion of a personality type is based on the clustering of sets of traits within discriminable groups of individuals. This is the logic underlying the development of older personality instruments such as the 16 PF and Gordon Personal Profile-Inventory, which, however, lack a fully elaborated theory of personality as a developmental framework. It should be pointed out that the MAPI authors are well aware of the tradeoffs between subscribing to an empirically determined, factorial approach to designing a personality instrument and basing their test construction methods on a coherent theoretical model that may not conform to any known empirically derived set of personality factors. They have deliberately chosen the latter course with an appreciation of the psychometric ramifications in mind.

Critique

On the practical side, it is felt that users of the MAPI, especially those who specify the clinical rather than the guidance interpretive report, will find the narrative too negative and pathologically oriented for most typical cases seen in schools and guidance clinics. For 13- and 14-year-old subjects the language is too adult, as for example the following statements taken from MAPI clinical interpretive reports on younger subjects received by this reviewer: "To avoid humiliation or social disparagement, she assumes the public role of being overly respectful, even ingratiating and self-righteous, with both peers and persons in authority"; "When others become irritated or alienated she is likely to react initially with contempt and flimsily substantiated rationalizations"; and "Guilt and self-condemnation are likely to become prominent features and she may impose punitive judgments upon herself as a form of symbolic expiation." It is also somewhat disconcerting that very little attention is paid to the positive aspects of subjects' adjustment in the personality style segment of the narrative report, which is typically a litany of psychopathology. This problem receives brief mention in the manual in its discussion of the limitations of automated reports (Millon et al. 1982, p. 29). However, the expressed concerns and behavioral correlates sections do contain positive language. It would be helpful for school psychologists writing individualized educational plans to extract some positive statements about students' adjustment by achieving a familiarity with the personality scale descriptions given in the manual and formulating their own interpretations.

In spite of these shortcomings, the Millon Adolescent Personality Inventory represents a major advance in assessment technology for adolescents. It has the advantages of combining a personality-style measure with a personal-problems checklist in a single instrument that employs test items written in language to which adolescents can relate and that addresses issues of specific concern to this peculiarly stressful transitional period of development. Its empirical validation of individual test items as an integral facet of the test construction process and use of base rate scores that take into account the prevalence rates of measured characteristics at different age levels are sophisticated refinements that enhance the utility of this instrument as part of the school psychologist's or clinician's battery.

References

This list includes text citations as well as suggested additional reading.

Davis, D. D. (1985). Review of Millon Behavioral Health Inventory. In D. J. Keyser & R. C. Sweetland (Eds.), *Test Critiques* (Vol. III, pp. 454-460). Kansas City, MO: Test Corporation of America.

Dyer, F. J. (1984). *Gordon Personal Profile-Inventory: an interpretive guide.* Cleveland: The Psychological Corporation.

Gordon, L. V. (1978). *Gordon Personal Profile-Inventory manual* Cleveland: The Psychological Corporation.

Green, C. J., Meagher, R. B., Jr., Zuskar, D. M., & Melamed, A. R. (n.d.). *Adolescent Psychological Inventory (MMAI): An effective tool in the counseling setting.* Unpublished manuscript.

McCabe, S. P. (1984). A review of Millon Clinical Multiaxial Inventory. In D. J. Keyser & R. C. Sweetland (Eds.), *Test Critiques* (Vol. I, pp. 455-465). Kansas City, MO: Test Corporation of America.

Millon, T. (1969). *Modern psychopathology.* Philadelphia: Saunders.

Millon, T. (1981). *Disorders of personality: DSM-III—Axis II.* New York: Wiley Interscience.

Millon, T., Green, C. J., & Meagher, R. B., Jr. (1982). *Millon Adolescent Personality Inventory manual.* Minneapolis: Interpretive Scoring Systems.

Plotkin, L. S. (1982). *A study of inpatient and normal adolescent personality and patterns of behavior using the Millon Adolescent Personality Inventory* (Second-year Research Project). Unpublished manuscript, University of Miami, Coral Gables, FL.

Zuskar, D. M., Green, C. J., & Meagher, R. B., Jr. (1977, March). *The uses of an adolescent psychological inventory in the classroom.* Paper presented at the American Personnel and Guidance Association Convention, Dallas.

Brian Bolton, Ph.D.

Professor, Research and Training Center in Vocational Rehabilitation, University of Arkansas, Fayetteville, Arkansas.

MINNESOTA SATISFACTORINESS SCALES

Work Adjustment Project. Minneapolis, Minnesota: Vocational Psychology Research, University of Minnesota.

Introduction

The Minnesota Satisfactoriness Scales (MSS) is an observer rating instrument that summarizes an employee's level of job performance as judged by the employer. Thus, by definition "satisfactoriness" refers to the adequacy of the employee's vocational adjustment when viewed from the perspective of the employer. Use of the MSS presumes a work environment composed of a series of tasks that must be performed and a set of rules that must be followed. The employee's behavior within this environment is the basis for the evaluation of satisfactoriness.

The MSS was constructed in conjunction with the formulation and development of a theory of vocational adjustment, which was initiated in 1957 at the University of Minnesota. The theory, the Minnesota Theory of Work Adjustment (MTWA), has been fully described in a book by Dawis and Lofquist (1984) and is summarized in a recent chapter by Dawis (in press). The principal developers of the MTWA, Rene V. Dawis, Lloyd H. Lofquist, and David J. Weiss, are Professors of Psychology at the University of Minnesota. They have authored more than 100 monographs, journal articles, and research reports concerned with various aspects of the MTWA.

Briefly, the MTWA postulates that an employee's work satisfactoriness is a function of the correspondence between the individual's occupationally relevant abilities and the ability requirements of the job in which the individual is employed. In an analogous fashion, the employee's job satisfaction is postulated to be a function of the correspondence between the individual's vocational needs (similar to work values) and the need reinforcers available from the job. The ultimate criterion of the MTWA, the individual's vocational adjustment, which is operationalized as job tenure, is hypothesized to be a function of the employee's levels of satisfactoriness and satisfaction.

The MSS consists of 28 items that can be completed by an employee's supervisor in about five minutes. It is scored on four statistically derived factors (subscales), in addition to a total score for general satisfactoriness. The employee is rated by the respondent on the first 27 items using a three-point scale that compares the employee to coworkers (3 = better than, 2 = about the same as, and 1 = not as good as). The final item requires a judgment of overall competence that allocates the employee to a quartile category (e.g., "in the top 1/4," "in the top half, but not among the top 1/4").

The four MSS subscales, with illustrative items (paraphrased or abbreviated) are as follows:

Performance: Concerns how well employees handle their work, reflecting characteristics such as promotability, competence, adaptability, and quality and quantity of work output (e.g., transfer to higher level job, give pay raise, accept job responsibility).

Conformance: Concerns employees' willingness to accept job limitations and their cooperation with supervisors and coworkers (e.g., respect authority of supervisors, work as a team member, follow work rules).

Personal Adjustment: Concerns aspects of employees' mental health and personal problems that may interfere with job performance (e.g., become easily upset, seem bothered by problems, seem to tire quickly).

Dependability: Concerns employees' lack of motivation, consistency, and attentiveness that imply disciplinary problems and poor work habits (e.g., absent from work, require disciplinary action).

Practical Application/Uses

The MSS is applicable in a variety of employment counseling situations and has been used in several research investigations in vocational rehabilitation and industrial settings. At the most fundamental level the MSS can be used as a diagnostic instrument with employees who are experiencing adjustment difficulties on the job. Each of the first 27 items addresses a specific work behavior that entails an independent judgment of above average, average, or below average relative to other workers in the organization.

Systematically identifying the employee's work deficiencies (behaviors rated below average) is a good beginning point for job counseling. This strategy can be elaborated by asking employees to rate their work performance using the MSS and comparing the self-ratings with supervisors' evaluations. The result of such an examination would be a list of specific work behaviors that require remedial action.

In addition to examining the employee's specific behavioral deficits, scores can be calculated in each of the four areas of job satisfactoriness subsumed by the MSS subscales (i.e., Performance, Conformance, Personal Adjustment, and Dependability). Subscale scores can be calculated by using the simple hand key given in the manual (Gibson, Weiss, Dawis, & Lofquist, 1970, p. 3) or the computer scoring service provided by the publisher, Vocational Psychology Research.

Raw scores for each of the four subscales and general satisfactoriness can be converted to percentile equivalents using normative tables for four occupational groups described in the *Dictionary of Occupational Titles* (DOT; U. S. Department of Labor, 1965) and a workers-in-general group that is representative of the entire U. S. labor force. The four occupational groups are professional, technical, and managerial; clerical and sales; service; and machine trades and bench work. Separate norms for males and females in clerical and sales occupations are provided.

The process of scoring and interpreting MSS results is illustrated in the manual (pp. 5-14) with two cases of hypothetical workers. An especially commendable feature of the MSS scoring procedure is the recommendation that scores be reported as percentile bands rather than point estimates. Standard errors of measurement for each of the five scales are given in the normative tables. To assist the user in identifying the correct norm group, extensive descriptive data for each of the normative samples are provided in the manual (pp. 38-49).

In addition to employment counseling applications in vocational rehabilitation and industrial settings, the MSS has been used to evaluate the adequacy of job placement programs. In particular, it provides an independent criterion measure for the evaluation of training programs designed to prepare individuals for employment in the competitive labor market. For such purposes, the MSS enables program designers to diagnose the strengths and weaknesses of the training program and to appropriately modify the training curriculum. The MSS has also been used in various research studies of occupational adjustment, some examples of which are given in the next section.

Technical Aspects

The development of the MSS began with a thorough review of the pertinent literature by Scott, Dawis, England, and Lofquist (1960). Their review suggests several types of information that the employer might use to evaluate employee satisfactoriness, such as quality and quantity of work, job suitability, promotability, recommendations for pay raises, absences, lateness, accidents, and disciplinary action.

The first edition of an instrument for measuring employee satisfactoriness (Carlson, Dawis, England, & Lofquist, 1963) was composed of three forms—the Supervisor Evaluation Form, the Personnel Records Questionnaire, and the Alternation Ranking Form—that provided data on ten indicators of satisfactoriness, including the characteristics identified in the earlier literature review. Factor analyses of the ten indicators for several subject samples (i.e., white-collar and blue-collar handicapped and nonhandicapped workers) consistently produced two factors: job performance and conformance to rules.

Weiss, Dawis, England, and Lofquist (1966) report the development of a revised satisfactoriness questionnaire designed to "overcome some technical problems which limited efficiency and accuracy of measurement" (p. 5) of the first satisfactoriness instrument. The specific goals of the revised MSS were to improve reliability and to increase the number of dimensions of satisfactoriness measured while retaining brevity and ease of administration. Using a sample of 1,750 men in six occupational groups, Weiss et al. (1966) constructed a 29-item inventory that measured three factors—performance, conformance, and personal adjustment—with scale reliabilities in the .80s.

The third and current edition of the MSS described in the manual improved the previous edition by deleting one redundant item, extracting a fourth factor termed *dependability,* revising the scoring weights, and expanding the normative groups. The developmental sample of 2,373 employees represented the full range of U. S. occupations (e.g., engineers, salespersons, clerks, nurses, typists, machinists, and janitors).

Because the factor analysis that generated the four MSS subscales used an orthogonal rotation, and because items were assigned only to the factor with which they correlated highest, the four subscales are only moderately intercorrelated. The median intercorrelation among the four subscales of .58, with a range from .52 to .65, indicates that the subscales are sufficiently independent to support the separation of the four components of satisfactoriness, and at the same time justifies the summation of all 28 items into a total score representing general satisfactoriness.

Internal consistency reliabilities for the four subscales and general satisfactoriness, calculated for the normative sample of workers-in-general (N = 1,000), were .90 for Performance, .85 for Conformance, .74 for Personal Adjustment, .85 for Dependability, and .94 for General Satisfactoriness. Test-retest stability coefficients with a two-year interval between administrations for a broadly representative sample of 725 workers were .59, .50, .49, .45, and .59, respectively, suggesting that satisfactoriness is a reasonably stable characteristic of workers. Additional data suggest that the MSS is a valid measure of satisfactoriness: satisfactory workers are less likely to leave their jobs than unsatisfactory workers, employee age is meaningfully related to MSS scores, and rated satisfactoriness is virtually independent of measured job satisfaction.

Because the MTWA was developed as a theory of vocational adjustment for persons with disabilities, it is not surprising that several research studies using the MSS have focused on this population. In an early follow-up study of former vocational rehabilitation (VR) clients, Tinsley, Warnken, Weiss, Dawis, and Lofquist (1969) compared 239 handicapped employees with 523 of their coworkers. The former VR clients were rated only slightly lower on the MSS than were their coworkers. As part of an intensive follow-up investigation of 38 former VR clients, Bolton and Roessler (1985) asked supervisors to complete the MSS for the study subjects. As in the Tinsley et al. (1969) follow-up, the 38 employees with handicaps were judged only slightly lower on the average than the MSS workers-in-general normative sample.

Bates, Parker, and McCoy (1970) used the MSS in an investigation of three hypotheses derived from Holland's theory of vocational choice with a sample of former VR clients. The research hypotheses were not confirmed. In a study designed to predict the work adjustment of a sample of 25 mentally retarded clients at a rehabilitation center, Hollender (1974) found that clients who were subsequently competitively employed had been rated higher on the MSS by their work adjustment supervisors.

Three studies illustrate the use of the MSS as a research instrument in organizational psychology. Seiler and Lacey (1973) adapted the MTWA to investigate the utilization of professional engineers in a manufacturing setting. The MSS measured job competence. The authors conclude that the MTWA is an effective model for assessing the level of professional utilization in manufacturing organizations. The MSS was used to measure job performance in a study of the relationships between job satisfaction and job performance by Wanous (1974). Results suggest that while job performance determines intrinsic satisfaction, extrinsic satisfaction causally influences job performance. In an investigation of manager-subordinate interactions by Pulakos and Wexley (1983), 171 managers each rated one subordinate on the MSS. Managers who perceived themselves to be more similar attitudinally to their subordinates judged them to be more satisfactory employees.

Critique

The MSS is a carefully developed and extensively refined questionnaire for measuring the job satisfactoriness of employees. It is a brief, reliable, multidimensional instrument with adequate normative data to facilitate interpretation of scores. For counseling purposes, the items provide specific behavioral indicators, and the four subscale scores measure intermediate-level performance criteria with good reliability. The general satisfactoriness score can be regarded as an overall index of job suitability from the perspective of the employer. The manual is a good reference source for counseling practitioners in vocational rehabilitation and industrial settings. Because the norms are 20-years-old, users of the MSS should probably limit normative interpretations to the workers-in-general group. A carefully designed study to establish new norms would greatly enhance the utility of the MSS in counseling and research applications.

References

Bates, G. L., Parker, H. J., & McCoy, J. F. (1970). Vocational rehabilitants' personality and work adjustment: A test of Holland's theory of vocational choice. *Psychological Reports, 26,* 511-516.

Bolton, B., & Roessler, R. (1985). After the interview: How employers rate handicapped employees. *Personnel, 62*(7), 38-41.

Carlson, R. E., Dawis, R. V., England, G. W., & Lofquist, L. H. (1963). *The measurement of employee satisfactoriness* (Minnesota Studies in Vocational Rehabilitation: 14). Minneapolis: University of Minnesota, Vocational Psychology Research.

Dawis, R. V. (in press). The Minnesota Theory of Work Adjustment. In B. Bolton (Ed.), *Handbook of measurement and evaluation in rehabilitation* (2nd ed.). Baltimore, MD: Paul Brookes.

Dawis, R. V., & Lofquist, L. H. (1984). *A psychological theory of work adjustment.* Minneapolis: University of Minnesota Press.

Gibson, D. L., Weiss, D. J., Dawis, R. V., & Lofquist, L. H. (1970). *Manual for the Minnesota Satisfactoriness Scales* (Minnesota Studies in Vocational Rehabilitation: 27). Minneapolis: University of Minnesota, Vocational Psychology Research.

Hollender, J. W. (1974). Prediction of work adjustment for adolescent male educable retardates. *Journal of Counseling Psychology, 21,* 164-165.

Pulakos, E. D., & Wexley, K. N. (1983). The relationship among perceptual similarity, sex, and performance ratings in manager-subordinate dyads. *Academy of Management Journal, 26,* 129-139.

Scott, T. B., Dawis, R. V., England, G. W., & Lofquist, L. H. (1960). *A definition of work adjustment* (Minnesota Studies in Vocational Rehabilitation: 21). Minneapolis: University of Minnesota, Vocational Psychology Research.

Seiler, D. A., & Lacey, D. W. (1973). Adapting the work adjustment theory for assessing technical-professional utilization. *Journal of Vocational Behavior, 3,* 443-451.

Tinsley, H. E. A., Warnken, R. G., Weiss, D. J., Dawis, R. V., & Lofquist, L. H. (1969). *A follow-up survey of former clients of the Minnesota Division of Vocational Rehabilitation.* (Minnesota Studies in Vocational Rehabilitation: 26). Minneapolis: University of Minnesota, Vocational Psychology Research.

U. S. Department of Labor. (1965). *Dictionary of occupational titles.* Washington, DC: U. S. Government Printing Office.

Wanous, J. P. (1974). A causal correlational analysis of the job satisfaction and performance relationship. *Journal of Applied Psychology, 59,* 139-144.

Weiss, D. J., Dawis, R. V., England, G. E., & Lofquist, L. H. (1966). *Instrumentation for the theory of work adjustment* (Minnesota Studies in Vocational Rehabilitation: 21). Minneapolis: University of Minnesota, Vocational Psychology Research.

Thomas W. Low, Ph.D.
Assistant Professor of Psychology, Sangamon State University, Springfield, Illinois.

MOTHER-CHILD RELATIONSHIP EVALUATION

Robert M. Roth. Los Angeles, California: Western Psychological Services.

Introduction

The Mother-Child Relationship Evaluation (MCRE) is a self-report personality instrument utilizing Likert-type scales in the assessment of maternal attitudes relevant to the mother-child relationship. The inventory yields four attitude scores (Acceptance, Overprotection, Overindulgence, and Rejection) based on maternal responses to 48 statements sampling child-rearing attitudes. Percentile ranks are provided for each attitude. The objective inventory is intended for use in research on parent-child relationships and clinically, as a diagnostic aid to facilitate treatment of mothers and children.

The evaluation was developed in the 1950s by Robert M. Roth as part of his doctoral studies in counseling psychology at the University of Texas. Dr. Roth was interested in maternal attitudes that might be related to positive outcomes in the rehabilitation training of students with cerebral palsy. Dr. Roth employed concepts for the instrument proposed by Symonds (1949) and Fitz-Simmons (1940) in delineating the mother-child relationship. The original instrument was published in 1961 and was based on the author's study of 80 middle class mothers between the ages of 25 and 35 living in the same community. Originally, four variables presumed to be operating in the mother-child relationship were cited: Acceptance, Overprotection, Overindulgence, and Rejection. According to the instrument's theory, the last three attitudes actually represented different types or forms of maternal rejection. A fifth variable, derived from scores on the first four attitude scales and intended to assess the extent to which a mother's attitude is dominated by consistency or confusion, was also present in the initial version of the test.

Criticisms of this assessment by Bell (1965) cited the lack of operational definitions for the variables. What appears in the 1980 version of the instrument are definitions of the maternal attitudes followed by theoretically-associated parental attitudes and behaviors, parental psychodynamics, and the child's anticipated responses (Roth, 1980). In the 1980 version the fifth scale indicating the extent to which a mother's attitude is based on confusion is mentioned only briefly. This reviewer is not aware of any alternate versions developed for this test.

The test consists of a four page record booklet with space for basic demographic data at the top of the first page. The child-rearing attitude statements are numbered from 1 to 48 and mothers rate their agreement with each statement on a five-point scale from "Strongly Agree" to "Strongly Disagree." The final page of the record form is a profile sheet allowing the plotting of percentiles (and T scores) for the four variables based on Roth's original study of 80 mothers (Roth, 1980). This profile indicates "cut off" percentiles of above 75 as high and below 25 as low on each of the variables.

Practical Applications/Uses

This test, with its focus on maternal attitudes of acceptance, overprotection, overindulgence, and rejection, can be used as a diagnostic tool by psychologists and workers in the child-care field. The author cautions that the test is not a refined clinical instrument and is best used in an exploratory, tentative fashion (Roth, 1980). A problem with using the measure in a clinical setting is that only four variables are provided yielding a very narrow range of diagnostic information. Indeed, since the variables of overprotection, overindulgence, and rejection are all conceptualized as forms of maternal rejection, the assessment would seem to essentially yield information on only the two attitudes of acceptance and rejection.

The inventory also has a use in psychological research on maternal attitudes and has been employed in this capacity (Krauthamer, 1979). It would be appropriate for literate subjects of at least near-average intelligence. The test can be easily used without any special training beyond an understanding of basic descriptive statistics.

A strong point of the MCRE is its ease of administration with individuals and groups. The directions for the instrument are brief but adequate. In using the measure in a counseling context this reviewer has found 15 to 20 minutes usually sufficient for subjects to complete the inventory. As a self-report measure, its inclusion in a battery can save professional time. Scoring is easily accomplished by totaling point values assigned to responses circled in columns designated by the first letter or letters of the variable measured. This process can be completed (with practice) in approximately five minutes.

Criticism of the MCRE has focused on the lack of information concerning interpretation of test results and the absence of details regarding the norm group upon which the assessment is based (Bell, 1965). The manual offers only three short case studies as illustrations of test interpretations, and little information is available on the empirical correlates of various percentile scores. The standard errors of measurement for the scales are reported to be large but are not specifically cited. Some brief suggestions are made concerning profile pattern interpretation (e.g., when Acceptance is high and Rejection is low) but the source of these interpretations is not clear. Therefore, single scale interpretations would reasonably seem to be the most useful approach in accordance with the theory of the instrument. Because of the lack of information concerning correlates of percentile scores, interpretation of an individual case is problematic and would have to be approached in a tentative fashion. In this reviewer's use of the MCRE involving a few cases, single scale results have generally been consistent with other case data and have also provided useful clinical hypotheses for further exploration. Clearly, as the manual specifies, the 1980 version of the test is not a well-substantiated instrument and its clinical use remains open to question.

Technical Aspects

The manual reports reliability data based on Roth's study of 80 middle class mothers. Split-half reliabilities are cited between the first and second half of the test which range from .41 for Overprotection to .57 for Acceptance. These reliabilities are extremely modest and as Harris (1965) noted are not adequate for a clinical instrument. A research study investigating use of this inventory with mothers of handicapped children (Jillings, Adamson, & Russell, 1976) indicated eight items which did not correlate with their respective scales suggesting that further scale refinement of the instrument is needed. It appears that further reliability studies are needed to develop the instrument as a diagnostic tool.

Few validity studies of the MCRE have been completed to date. In using the MCRE, Jillings, Adamson, and Russell (1976) found a similar pattern of scale intercorrelations as reported by Roth but using a different normative sample. Figures cited in their study lend support to the notions that overprotection, overindulgence, and rejection are all related forms of material rejection and are distinct from acceptance as measured by this instrument.

Although the number of studies using the MCRE has not been very large; in general, results have been supportive of the construct validity of the instrument. Maternal attitudes of rejection have been found to be associated with alcoholic mothers (Krauthamer, 1979), with mothers with a learning disabled child (Wetter, 1972), and with mothers of nonachieving high school males (Hilliard & Roth, 1969). Acceptance as measured by the MCRE has been found to be higher for non-alcoholic mothers (Krauthamer, 1979) and mothers of achieving high school males (Hilliard & Roth, 1969).

Additionally, mothers with a first-born learning disabled child were found to score higher on the Overprotection scale of the MCRE than mothers of a second-born learning disabled child (Epstein, Berg-Cross, & Berg-Cross, 1980). Similarly, parents of a learning disabled child scored higher on Overprotection and Overindulgence scales when compared with parents not having a learning disabled child (Wetter, 1972). The results cited above are outcomes that would be predicted by the theory of the instrument and are congruent with the construct validity of the scales.

Critique

The 1980 version of the MCRE remains relatively untested from a reliability standpoint and lacks the kind of empirical validation that would allow it to be used with confidence in the clinical context. Additionally, the test is rather narrowly-conceived and does not yield the range of data needed of a diagnostic instrument competing for time and space in a clinical test battery. Its primary use would appear to continue to be experimental. A personal conversation with Western Psychological Services indicates that a multifaceted and better-standardized replacement for the MCRE examining parent-child relations is in the process of development. Despite its limitations, however, the MCRE has the advantages of ease of administration and scoring and a sound theoretical basis. Another reviewer has noted it also has the advantage of being non-threatening (Harris,

1965). Finally, it has generally been supported from a construct validity standpoint by the limited number of reported studies where it has been employed. Used carefully and tentatively, this reviewer believes it has a limited application in clinical work with mothers and children experiencing difficulties.

References

Bell, J. E. (1965). The Mother-Child Relationship Evaluation. In O. K. Buros (Ed.), *The sixth mental measurements yearbook* (pp. 319-320). Highland Park, NJ: The Gryphon Press.

Epstein, J., Berg-Cross, G., & Berg-Cross, L. (1980). Maternal expectations and birth order in families with learning disabled and normal children. *Journal of Learning Disabilities, 13*(5), 45-52.

Fitz-Simmons, M. (1940). *Some parent-child relationships.* New York: Bureau of Publications, Teachers College, Columbia University.

Harris, D. B. (1965). The Mother-Child Relationship Evaluation. In O. K. Buros (Ed.), *The sixth mental measurements yearbook* (p. 320). Highland Park, NJ: The Gryphon Press.

Hilliard, T. & Roth, R. M. (1969). Maternal attitudes and the nonachievement syndrome. *Personnel and Guidance Journal, 47,* 424-428.

Jillings, C. R., & Adamson, C. A., & Russell, T. (1976). An application of Roth's Mother-Child Relationship Evaluation to some mothers of handicapped children. *Psychological Reports, 38,* 807-810.

Krauthamer, C. (1979). Maternal Attitudes of Alcoholic and Nonalcoholic upper middle class women. *The International Journal of Addictions, 14*(5), 639-644.

Roth, R. M. (1980). *The Mother-Child Relationship Evaluation Manual.* Los Angeles: Western Psychological Services.

Symonds, P. M. (1949). *Dynamics of parent-child relationships.* New York: Bureau of Publications, Teachers College, Columbia University.

Wetter, J. (1972). Parent attitudes toward learning disability. *Exceptional Children, 38,* 490-491.

Raymond H. Holden, Ed.D.
Professor of Psychology, Rhode Island College, Providence, Rhode Island.

MULLEN SCALES OF EARLY LEARNING

Eileen M. Mullen. Cranston, Rhode Island: T.O.T.A.L. Child, Inc.

Introduction

The Mullen Scales of Early Learning (MSEL) is a developmental test that assesses a young child's learning abilities and patterns. It has a strong theoretical base in neuropsychological development and information processing. The test is designed to measure a broad set of developmental processes utilizing a unique intrasensory and intersensory learning model that analyzes both visual and language skills at receptive and expressive levels. The MSEL is intended for evaluating toddlers and preschool children aged 15 to 68 months. It is individually administered and can be completed in 35 to 45 minutes. It is designed for use by early childhood educators, clinical psychologists, special educators, early intervention program specialists, and professionals in Head Start programs, day-care centers, and nursery schools. The test is divided into four major scales of visual and language learning and mental capacity: Visual Receptive Organization (VRO), which assesses visual discrimination, sequencing, organization, and memory; Visual Expressive Organization (VEO), which assesses unilateral and bilateral hand skills such as folding, cutting, and writing; Language Receptive Organization (LRO), which assesses language comprehension, verbal/spatial awareness, and short- and long-term memory; and Language Expressive Organization (LEO), which assesses verbal ability. The designation of specific scales to assess separate learning functions has potentially important diagnostic value. It provides quantitative information on receptive and expressive performance in visual and language modalities and qualitative information on organizational skills.

Eileen M. Mullen, Ed.D., the author of this test, is a developmental psychologist who has been in the field of education for more than 30 years. For the past 12 years she has been director of the diagnostic program and supervisor of psychological services at Meeting Street School, an internationally known educational and treatment center for multihandicapped children and adolescents. Mullen has been a diagnostician for special needs children whose handicaps range from mild learning disability to cerebral palsy, and she has lectured extensively throughout the country in the areas of child development and differential diagnosis.

Over 30 years of clinical experience testing young children with delays in learning or mental retardation resulted in the author's decision to develop a test that would examine modality performance and differentiate uneven learning patterns. Analysis of the learning problems of approximately 1,600 children indicated that visual and language learning are discrete but influence one another considerably.

For example, it was noted that children aged three to five years who had significant delay in visual-spatial organization and sequencing often had associated delay in verbal concepts and sequencing. The test manual (Mullen, 1984) quotes Satz, Taylor, Friel, and Fletcher (1978): "Preschool children who are delayed in perceptual motor performance will be delayed in learning to reaa. Although many of these children will eventually learn the early skills if given enough time, they will lag in conceptual linguistic skills and require extra time to acquire them, if they ever do" (p. 2). Preliminary findings with the MSEL suggest that early evaluation of toddler and preschool children can provide quidelines for intervention that may assist in reducing gaps in learning and lead to a more even distribution of prereadiness and readiness skills.

The manual (Mullen, 1984) and test materials come neatly packaged in a sturdy carrying case measuring 41" x 30" x 4". The test materials themselves are colorful toys that are attractive to young children and made mainly of plastic for ease of cleaning. In addition, there is a separate plastic booklet for picture cards (much like the Stanford-Binet picture cards) and a smaller booklet for picture vocabulary and copy forms. An individual four-page record form is used for each child, with the front page providing space for a summary of items passed at various age levels, a total age score for each of the four scales, and conversion to T-Scores (from tables in the manual). The two inner pages of the form provide room for scoring (" + " or "–") individual items, four items for each six-month period on each scale. The format is an age scale, as on the Stanford-Binet, with the requirement that both a basal age and ceiling be obtained. The range in mental age is from one year, six months to five years, six months. Although it might appear cumbersome to have to administer 16 items for every six-month period (four items each on each of the four scales), several test items are scorable over a range of ages in one administration. For example, picture vocabulary (LEO) can be scored at five different age levels; comparative concepts (LRO) can be scored at four different age levels; and copying tasks (VEO) can easily be grouped together to obtain a ceiling (over eight different age levels).

Practical Applications/Uses

This unique test can be very valuable in assessing developmental skills in specific neurosensory and expressive areas of children who may be suspect for learning disability or who have evidence of maturational or developmental delay in one or more areas. With proliferation of Head Start programs, young children of various ethnic backgrounds can be evaluated to determine relative effects of either cultural, sensory, or socioeconomic deprivation. With such data available, more specific academic planning can be accomplished to enhance prereadiness or readiness skills.

The manual suggests that although it is vital to maintain standardized conditions for administration of test items, it is also important to "provide a positive climate and appropriate reinforcement" by creating an atmosphere of acceptance that recognizes a child's individual learning style, pace, and temperament; letting the children know that it is acceptable if they do not know an answer, and determining "what is reinforcing to the child and provide appropriate reinforcement." For example, the manual states that "a child who is tactilely oriented often enjoys touch (a pat on the hand or head); an auditory learner usually enjoys verbal support (praise); and a visual learner will look for positive facial cues (a frequent smile, nod of the head) which indicate approval" (Mullen, 1984, p. 19). The manual admonishes the examiner to encourage the child but not to give extra hints about test questions. Usually, one should avoid excessive verbal directions or small talk and control the pace of the testing to accommodate the child's tempo. If a child is fidgety, clumsy, or distractible, the physical space between the examiner and the child should be decreased, and the examiner should demonstrate an upright and attentive position.

Looking at pictures or reproducing block models are good starting points for the test administration and give the examiner an opportunity for informal observation of a child's learning approach, willingness to verbalize, and postural adjustment. If a child is easily vocal, picture vocabulary is a good place to begin testing. Naturally, the examiner should have a thorough knowledge of all of the subtest items before beginning actual testing. The subtests are numbered and arranged to facilitate assessment of learning competencies and weaknesses, but a strict sequential order need not be followed.

Scoring is easily completed with a " + " or "–" notation next to each item, and scoring directions, as well as directions for administering each subtest, are clearly indicated in the manual. No machine or computer scoring is available at the time of this review.

Technical Aspects

The MSEL was standardized on a stratified sample of 866 children, ranging in age from 15 to 68 months and divided into nine age groups (at half-year intervals). The standardization sample was stratified by age, sex, race, parental occupation, and urban/rural residence (see Table 1).

Table 1

MSEL Standardization Sample Characteristics

A. By sex	*% Male*	*% Female*
Total (N = 866)	48.8	51.2
New England (12,349,493)	48.0	52.0
B. By race	*% White*	*% Non-white*
Total (N = 866)	93.5	6.4
New England	93.8	6.2
C. By urban/rural residence	*% Urban*	*% Rural*
Total (N = 866)	89.5	10.5
Rhode Island (1980 census)	87.1	12.9

There were 100 children tested at each age level, with the exception of ages one year, six months and five years, six months where the Ns were 64 and 93, respectively. The concordance of the test sample with Rhode Island and New England census data is quite impressive (see Table 1).

Test-retest reliability was assessed by administering the MSEL scales twice to 65 children. The average time between administrations was two weeks. The sample was divided into three age groups: ages 15 to 27 months (N = 18), ages 28 to 40 months (N = 16), and ages 41 to 66 months (N = 31). Test-retest reliability ranged from .83 to .98 for all age groups and reflects excellent stability over a short time period. Interscorer reliability was assessed by pairing evaluators, with one person administering the test, another observing, and each person scoring the test independently. The sample (N = 24) ranged from 17 to 44 months. Interscorer reliability was .99, indicating that the directions for administration and scoring are extremely detailed and clear. Concurrent validity was assessed by administering the MSEL language scales (LRO and LEO) and the Preschool Language Scale (Zimmerman, Steiner, & Evatt, 1969) to 66 children in the normative sample. The sample was divided into three age groups: 15 to 19 months (N = 22), 20 to 27 months (N = 20), and 28 to 58 months (N = 24). The coefficients of correlation ranged from .77 to .98 (Mullen, 1984, p. 18) and represent excellent concurrent validity. This confirms the strength of the test when compared with another measure of receptive and expressive language ability.

Critique

The MSEL has two functions: 1) it serves as a diagnostic indicator of readiness for learning in visual, auditory, and language areas, and 2) it is a vehicle for determining potential modalities to stimulate sensory and motor development. One should start by appreciating the theoretical rationale that is the basis for the development of this scale. Receptive and expressive aspects of behavior, both visual and auditory, have long been considered in practical learning situations in the classroom and preschool settings by clinical psychologists and special education, nursery, and early-elementary-school teachers. However, to this reviewer's knowledge, no previous test has been fashioned for toddlers and preschool children with these considerations in mind. In a practical manner, the test materials are quite intriguing and appropriate for young children, and the test manual is both suitably detailed and clear and enjoyable to read. Throughout the manual there is an attitude of complete acceptance and understanding of individual children with specific problems who do not understand why they cannot perform as acceptably as others their own age. This is a tribute to Mullen's thoughtful knowledge and empathy as a clinician. Appropriate research probes have been conducted to insure adequate reliability and validity, and the standardization sample of 866 children is clearly congruent with sex, race, and residential status of the New England population (see Table 1). The MSEL has not been reviewed previously. Although this reviewer suggests the usual recommendations that further studies should assess the usefulness of this scale on various populations, Mullen is to be commended on accomplishing what may be a milestone in appropriate diagnostic and remedial assessment of the early potentially learning disabled child.

References

This list includes text citations as well as suggested additional reading.

Ayres, A. J. (1972). *Sensory integration and learning disorders.* Los Angeles: Western Psychological Services.

Beery, K. E., & Buktenica, N. A. (1967). *Developmental Test of Visual-Motor Integration.* Chicago: Follett.

Belmont, I., Birch, H., & Karp, E. (1963). The disordering of intersensory and intrasensory integration by brain disease. *Journal of Neurosurgery and Mental Diseases, 141,* 410-418.

Chalfant, J., & Flathouse, V. (1971). Auditory and visual learning. In H. Myklebust (Ed.), *Progress in learning disabilities* (Vol. II, pp. 252-292). New York: Grune & Stratton.

Gaddes, W. H. (1980). *Learning disabilities and brain dysfunction.* New York: Springer-Verlag.

Luria, A. R. (1966). *Higher cortical functions in man.* New York: Basic Books.

Mullen, E. M. (1984). *Mullen Scales of Early Learning manual.* Providence, RI: T.O.T.A.L. Child, Inc.

Piaget, J. (1952). *The origins of intelligence in children.* New York: International Universities Press.

Satz, P., Taylor, H. G., Friel, J., & Fletcher, J. M. (1978). Some developmental and predictive precursors of reading disabilities: A six year follow-up. In A. L. Benton & D. Pearl (Eds.), *The psychophysiology of thinking.* New York: Academic Press.

Zimmerman, I. L., Steiner, V. G., & Evatt, R. L. (1969). *Preschool Language Scale.* Columbus, OH: Charles E. Merrill Publishing Company.

Donald I. Templer, Ph.D.
Professor of Psychology, California School of Professional Psychology, Fresno, California.

MULTIPLE AFFECT ADJECTIVE CHECK LIST—REVISED

Marvin Zuckerman and Bernard Lubin. San Diego, California: Educational and Industrial Testing Service.

Introduction

The Multiple Affect Adjective Check List—Revised (MAACL-R) is a self-report instrument with scales of Anxiety, Depression, Hostility, Positive Affect, and Sensation Seeking. Each item, which subjects indicate as applying to them, is based on adjectives concerning one of these five dimensions.

The MAACL-R reflects three stages of development over a quarter of a century, with the first, the Affect Adjective Check List (Zuckerman, 1960), constructed as a measure of anxiety. Using it as a model, Depression and Anxiety Scales were added to expand the instrument to the Multiple Affect Adjective Check List (MAACL; Zuckerman & Lubin, 1965). Although the MAACL has been widely used and cited in the last two decades, it had psychometric weaknesses that were fortunately recognized by its authors. The three scales correlated too highly with each other to infer that the separate scales have good discriminant validity. In general, the correlations among the three scales were of about the same magnitude as the reliability of the individual scales. Additionally, the correlations with measures of response set, especially social desirability, were higher than desirable. The MAACL-R development was intended to overcome these limitations, and its mission was a success.

In the development of the MAACL-R, the 132-item MAACL was administered to several groups of normal subjects and factor analyzed. The items retained for the five scales were those that consistently loaded .30 or higher on associated factors: Anxiety, Depression, Hostility, Positive Affect, and Sensation Seeking (Zuckerman, Lubin, & Rinck, 1983; Zuckerman & Lubin, 1985).

In addition to the scores on the five scales, one may add the Anxiety, Depression, and Hostility scores to obtain a Dysphoria score. One may also add the Positive Affect and Sensation Seeking scores.

The authors, Martin Zuckerman and Bernard Lubin, are both Professors of Psychology, Diplomates in clinical psychology, and Fellows of the American Psychological Association. Both have substantial scholarly contributions in personality assessment and theory, as well as in other areas of psychology.

The MAACL-R consists of 132 adjectives that are alphabetically arranged in three columns on one side of a single sheet of paper. There are two forms: the State Form, requiring subjects to answer each item according to how they feel today, and the Trait Form, requiring them to answer according to how they generally feel. The items consist of commonly used adjectives.

The MAACL-R is untimed and requires approximately five minutes to complete. The examiner's task is to read the test instructions to the subjects, but clarification is permitted if the subject has questions. All words are at or below the eighth-grade level, but the manual cautions that an eighth-grade education does not necessarily imply an eighth-grade reading level.

The scale scores can be obtained by adding the number of adjectives on the five scales. The exception to this rule is that for Sensation Seeking four items are scored positively if they are not endorsed. The MAACL-R answers can be machine scored by Educational and Industrial Testing Service or may be locally scored by prior agreement with this testing service. Because the MAACL-R contains all 132 items of its predecessor rather than the 70 items needed to score the revised instrument, one has the option of using the three MAACL scales in addition to or instead of the MAACL-R.

Practical Applications/Uses

The MAACL-R appears to be quite useful for research involving affect and/or subjective state. This reviewer has been especially impressed by the sensitivity to change over time of the MAACL. In one study (Velebar & Templer, 1984) there were significant increases in anxiety, depression, and hostility one hour after double blind administration of the MAACL. There is no reason to believe that the revised form will prove less sensitive to change over time. In fact, the MAACL-R reflects anxiety increase over time prior to a classroom examination (Zuckerman, Lubin, & Rinck, 1983).

In this reviewer's opinion, the MAACL-R Depression Scale is often more suitable for a normal population than the standard scales of depression because most depression scales tap the classical elements of the *depressive syndrome* such as sleep difficulty, weight loss, and decreased libido, whereas the MAACL assesses *mood*. Nevertheless, research (e.g., Zuckerman, Lubin, & Rinck, 1983; Zuckerman & Lubin, 1985) has indicated that the MAACL-R can discriminate patients with various psychiatric diagnoses in the predictable direction.

The revised instrument now contains indices of both positive and negative affect and in that respect has a common element with the Affects Balance Scale (Derogatis, 1975). That instrument contains an "Affect Balance Index," which is essentially a ratio of positive to negative affect. A suggested additional score was called "total affective change" (Templer, 1985), which is essentially a sum of positive and negative affect scores and conceptualized as bearing some resemblance to the sum of color responses on the Rorschach and to the sum of the Depression Scale and Hypomania Scales T-scores of the MMPI. This reviewer is here suggesting a comparable index for the MAACL-R resulting from the summation of the Anxiety, Depression, Hostility, Positive Affect, and Sensation Seeking T-scores. Perhaps a label such as "composite affective experience" would be appropriate.

Technical Aspects

The internal consistency is good with both the state and trait forms of the MAACL-R. The stability over time of the trait form is, generally speaking, rather good. The test-retest coefficients for the state form are considerably lower. However, the lower state stability coefficients probably reflect sensitivity to changes over time rather than greater measurement error with the form. Response set does not appear to be a problem with the MAACL-R. Reasonable normative information is provided.

The construct validity of the MAACL-R is both broadly based and impressive. The MAACL-R scales correlate in the predicted direction with other measures, including the MMPI, the Profile of Mood States (McNair, Torr, & Droppelman, 1971), self-ratings, peer ratings, observer ratings, psychiatric diagnoses, self-reported health and self-reported social activities and symptoms. Furthermore, the pattern of correlations support the differential validity of the individual MAACL-R scales. For example, the highest positive correlations of the MMPI Depression Scale tend to be with the MAACL-R Depression and Dysphoria (Anxiety + Depression + Hostility) Scales. The highest negative correlations are with the MAACL-R Positive Affect and the sum of Positive Affect and Sensation Seeking.

Critique

The MAACL-R is an instrument that is brief and easy to administer, contains both state and trait measures, assesses five dimensions of affect, and is sensitive to change over time. It has good reliability, relative independence of response set, and commendable construct validity. It has a wide range of research applications with normal and abnormal populations, perhaps especially in assessing change in affect over time.

The MAACL-R is definitely superior to the MAACL as a psychometric instrument. Some persons may prefer the older instrument because of the greater accumulation of usage and literature by which it is buttressed. Furthermore, the correlations between the old and new Anxiety, Depression, and Hostility Scales are acknowledged as low to moderate in the manual, which prudently cautions that "users of the new scales must be wary about assuming that past results with the old scales will apply to the new scales bearing the same names" (Zuckerman & Lubin, 1985, p. 10). On the other hand, because all 132 items are answered with both the MAACL and MAACL-R, the user can choose to use one or both.

References

Derogatis, L. R. (1975). *Affects Balance Scale*. Towson, MD: Clinical Psychometric Research.

McNair, D. M., Lorr, M., & Droppelman, L. F. (1971). *Profile of Mood States: Manual*. San Diego: Educational and Industrial Testing Service.

Templer, D. I. (1985). Review of Affects Balance Scale. In D. J. Keyser & R. C. Sweetland (Eds.), *Test critiques* (Vol. 2, pp. 32-34). Kansas City, MO: Test Corporation of America.

Veleber, D. M., & Templer, D. I. (1984). Effects of caffeine on anxiety and depression. *Journal of Abnormal Psychology, 93*(1), 120-122.

Zuckerman, M. (1960). The development of an affect adjective check list for the measurement of anxiety. *Journal of Consulting Psychology, 24*, 457-462.

Zuckerman, M., & Lubin, B. (1965). *Manual for the Multiple Affect Adjective Check List*. San Diego: Educational and Industrial Testing Service.

Zuckerman, M., Lubin, B., & Rinck, C. M. (1983). Construction of new scales for the Multiple Affect Adjective Check List. *Journal of Behavioral Assessment, 5*, 119-129.

Zuckerman, M., & Lubin, B. (1985). *Manual for the Multiple Affect Adjective Check List-Revised*. San Diego: Educational and Industrial Testing Service.

Donna E. Alvermann, Ph.D.
Associate Professor of Reading Education, University of Georgia, Athens, Georgia.

THE NELSON READING SKILLS TEST

Gerald Hanna, Leo M. Schell, and Robert Schreiner. Chicago, Illinois: The Riverside Publishing Company.

Introduction

The Nelson Reading Skills Test (RST) is a group-administered reading survey test that measures not only word meaning and reading comprehension but also provides a limited amount of diagnostic information about an examinee's reading rate and knowledge of word parts. The RST is designed to help educators make effective instructional decisions, assess students' progress through a program of study, and make initial within-class assignment of students to groups. The RST consists of two forms, forms 3 and 4, each of which includes three levels of tests appropriate for use with Grades 3-9.

Historically, The Nelson Reading Skills Test dates back to 1931, when it was first published under the name of The Nelson Silent Reading Test. Three decades later a revised edition appeared, this time under the name of The Nelson Reading Test. According to Robinson (1965), the 1962 edition showed a marked improvement in the paragraph comprehension section and the vocabulary section, which contained the best items from the original forms. The present 1977 edition reflects an attempt to improve the diagnostic nature of the instrument. Scores are now available on two optional subtests, namely Word Parts and Reading Rate. All of the content in the 1977 RST is new. Another change in the current edition is the inclusion of three overlapping levels, which provide for individualizing out-of-level testing. Also, the norms for both spring and fall testings are new.

In its present form, the RST retains the name of Nelson (after the late M.J. Nelson), although it is actually authored by a three-person team from the disciplines of educational measurement and reading. Gerald Hanna and Leo M. Schell are Professors of Education at Kansas State University, and Robert Schreiner is Professor of Education at the University of Minnesota. All three individuals have experience in public school teaching. In addition, each brings to the author team a particular area of expertise, e.g., test construction, reading comprehension, and diagnosis and remediation of reading problems.

Each form of the Nelson Reading Skills Test consists of a 24-page, reusable, multilevel booklet. Level A tests are appropriate for use with students in the third grade and the first half of fourth grade. Level B tests are for the second half of fourth grade through Grade 6. Level C tests are for Grades 7 through 9. Two subtests, Word Meaning and Reading Comprehension, are found at all levels. The subtest called Word Parts (i.e., Sound-Symbol Correspondence, Root Words, and

Syllabication) is found only at Level A; the Reading Rate subtest is only at Levels B and C. The length of the Word Meaning test varies from 22 items at Level A to 29 items at Level C. Likewise, there is a variation in the number of Reading Comprehension items, ranging from 31 at Level A to 41 at Level C. The Word Parts subtest consists of 15 Sound-Symbol Correspondence items, 19 Root Word items, and 15 Syllabication items. For Reading Rate, there are five items at each of Levels B and C.

The Word Meaning subtest appears as the first section in all three levels of the RST and measures a student's ability to identify the meanings of common words drawn from the humanities, social studies, and science. The stimulus words occur in one of three contexts: 1) in a multiple-choice test in which the stimulus word is presented in isolation followed by four alternative answers; 2) in a multiple-choice test with four alternatives but within the context of a phrase (e.g., *satisfied* customer); or 3) in the context of a paragraph (e.g., paragraphs that appear in the Reading Comprehension subtest).

The second section of the RST at each level is the Reading Comprehension subtest. This subtest, which is a measure of silent reading, consists of passages whose content is also drawn from the humanities, social studies, and science. The passages increase in length and complexity as one advances in the levels. Both narratives (e.g., storylike pieces) and expository writing (e.g., informational articles) are represented, with an emphasis on the latter. Several multiple-choice questions, consisting of a stem and four alternative answers, follow each passage. These questions tap a variety of responses, ranging from merely recognizing the correct answer as stated in the passage to drawing inferences in identifying cause and effect relationships.

In the optional Sound-Symbol Correspondence subtest, students are required to select the correct phonetic respelling (from among three alternative choices) of common stimulus words. In Root Words, students are asked to identify the base or root word of a stimulus word from among the three words or word parts listed. In Syllabication, students choose the correct syllabic division of a stimulus word, again from among three choices. Finally, in Reading Rate, which is a test to determine how quickly one can silently read with comprehension, students are required to read passages of about 600 words on content similar to the kind they would encounter in their school textbooks. After reading for one minute, students mark their answer sheets to indicate how much they read and then answer five comprehension questions following the passage.

Other RST materials include a detailed teacher's manual (Hanna, Schell, & Schreiner, 1977c), an equally detailed technical manual (Hanna, Schell, & Schreiner, 1978), and two Self-Marking Answer Sheets, one for Level A and one for Levels B and C. Machine scoring of the RST is available also, in which case the answer sheet to be used is an MRC Answer Sheet.

Practical Application/Uses

As a group-administered survey test, the Nelson Reading Skills Test will be of value primarily to school districts that typically use a fall and spring (pre/post) assessment instrument or for screening purposes. For instance, RST scores could be used to identify students needing remedial instruction, in either Chapter I classes or in district-supported remedial reading classes. An individual's standing on the RST could be compared to his or her standing on an academic aptitude test. Such a comparison could provide clues as to whether an individual is performing at or near the level in reading that would be expected considering his or her school aptitude functioning level. A significantly lower score on the Reading Comprehension test than on a verbal aptitude test may point to a need for remedial instruction in reading comprehension—an idea at least worthy of exploration. In comparing RST and academic aptitude scores, one point to bear in mind is that an individual's aptitude score may be depressed not because of low ability but rather because of the reading demands made by a group-administered academic aptitude test. In this instance, remedial instruction might be dismissed as a possibility when in fact it should be considered.

Another probable use of the RST is in decision-making concerning the placement of students within classes. According to the teacher's manual of the RST, "the most suitable score for general placement purposes is Total Reading" (p. 21). The RST's authors properly caution potential users to consider any assignment of a student to a reading group as tentative at best and the need for evaluation in light of other pertinent information about the student.

Potential users must also keep in mind that the RST is first and foremost a survey test. Although it was designed to provide a limited amount of diagnostic information, by and large a survey test is designed to sample knowledge or proficiency in an area, not analyze strengths and weaknesses in individuals (cf. Harris & Hodges, 1981). Nonetheless, the classroom teacher could recommend additional testing by the remedial reading teacher or school psychologist of any skill weaknesses tentatively identified by the RST. The teacher's manual contains several illustrations of diagnostic inferences that classroom teachers might draw based on a comparison of subtest scores. There are also a limited number of instructional suggestions offered to accompany each of the subtests. For example, if a student is judged weak in word meaning, the authors of the RST provide suggestions such as, "Try to provide a direct experience for students before presenting new words. . ." (p. 25) or "Present lessons about prefixes, suffixes, synonyms and antonyms" (p. 26).

The RST's teacher's manual contains standardized and clearly written directions for test administration. A two-color scheme is used to highlight what the teacher is to say to the students. Practice is provided in helping students fill out the answer sheets, including how to change an answer. Each subtest is timed. For all levels, a total of 33 minutes is given to Word Meaning and Reading Comprehension. If the Word Parts test in Level A is given, the examiner must plan on an additional 25 minutes. The Reading Rate test in Levels B and C takes three minutes to administer.

If the answer sheets are to be hand scored, the teacher tears off a perforated strip at the top of the answer sheet and discards the carbon paper that was the means for transferring student answers to the scoring page. Each mark that appears in a correct answer position on the scoring page is counted as correct. Raw scores are recorded for each subtest and for Total Reading and then transferred to the Class Record Sheet. Tables provided in the teacher's manual permit the examiner to convert raw scores into grade equivalents, percentile ranks, percentile bands, stanines, and normal curve equivalents. Verbal descriptors, which are also provided, correspond to the performance levels obtained on the World Parts and Reading Rate subtests. The directions for scoring are clearly presented and are simple and quick to follow.

Scores on the RST are interpreted after converting raw scores to derived scores, based on a national reference group. The test's authors strongly advise users not to attempt to interpret a student's performance on any group of questions that is less than a full subtest in length. For example, performance on literal level questions should not be compared with performance on inferential or higher level questions. Classroom teachers, including those having little or no experience in test interpretation, should be able to use the suggestions in the teacher's manual with relative ease.

Technical Aspects

The technical manual for the RST consists of 20 pages and includes information that was deemed inappropriate for inclusion in the teacher's manual. Technical aspects of testing, such as the equating and scaling of the two forms of the test, the intercorrelations of scores, spring and fall standardization samples, and a detailed treatment of reliability and validity factors, are included in the technical manual for users who have specialized needs and interests. For the typical user, however, the teacher's manual contains all of the necessary technical data.

The development and standardization of The Nelson Reading Skills Test spanned a four-year period of time. The standardization sample included about 3,800 students per grade and involved 57 school districts across five geographic regions and various community socioeconomic characteristics. In an attempt to avoid unintentional bias or unfairness toward any minority group, the RST's authors obtained input from several representative groups. They also eliminated sex-role bias in language and provided normal curve equivalent scores for Title I (Chaper I) use.

The split-halves method was used to obtain estimates of reliability, which were then adjusted for full length using the Spearman-Brown formula. Reliability coefficients ranged from .81 to .93 for the Word Meaning and Reading Comprehension subtests. For the Word Parts subtests, coefficients ranged between .77 and .90, and for Total Reading from .91 to .94.

Validity issues were dealt with in a variety of ways. The passages were developed to reflect the background of experiences and interests of children and adolescents in Grades 3 through 9. A diversity of writing styles ensured that students were exposed to both expository and narrative text. Care was also taken to make the content of the Reading Comprehension and Rate passages unfamiliar or novel to most students. The American Heritage *Word Frequency Book* (1971) was used in developing both the stimulus words and the alternative answers on the Word Meaning subtest. Other attempts to develop a test that would withstand the normal threats to its validity included studying item difficulty and checking for readability beyond the mere arithmetical calculations of grade equivalent indices.

Critique

The Nelson Reading Skills Test is clearly a product of careful development and standardization procedures. The documentation is complete, straightforward, and easy to read and use. Like other survey tests that contain only multiple-choice items, the RST samples but a subset of the cognitive processes associated with reading. Potential users will need to weigh the pros and cons of basing diagnostic decisions (however cautiously) on what can be determined from scores on a group-administered test that requires a student only to recognize, not produce, the correct answer. On the other hand, if the RST is used primarily as it was intended—to assess student progress in specified reading tasks over a period of time—then there is no doubt that it is a well-constructed and reliable instrument.

The teacher's manual contains a wealth of background information. One of the many positive features of that manual is the description of the various derived scores on pages 18-20. The tables and charts are clearly labeled and easy to interpret, as is the text of the manual as a whole. The authors do not go beyond the capabilities of the test; for instance, they discussed in the teacher's manual the feasibility of dividing the subtests into more scoring units but then provided reliability reasons for why this was not a feasible approach. Finally, the teacher's manual reflects a concern for educating the novice test user. Copious illustrations and examples serve the functional purpose of making difficult testing concepts more readily comprehended.

References

This list includes text citations as well as suggested additional reading.

Carroll, J. B., Davies, P., & Richman, B. (1971). *Word frequency book.* New York: American Heritage.

Crowell, D. C., Au, K., & Blake, K. M. (1983). Comprehension questions: Differences among standardized tests. *Journal of Reading, 26,* 314-319.

Drahozal, E. C., & Hanner, G. S. (1978). Reading comprehension subscores: Pretty bottles for ordinary wine. *Journal of Reading, 21,* 416-420.

Guthrie, J. T. (1981). Research: Invalidity of reading tests. *Journals of Reading, 25,* 300-302.

Hanna, G., Schell, L. M., & Schreiner, R. (1977a). *The Nelson Reading Skills Test, Levels A, B, and C* (Form 3). Boston: Houghton Mifflin.

Hanna, G., Schell, L. M., & Schreiner, R. (1977b). *The Nelson Reading Skills Test, Levels A, B, and C* (Form 4). Boston: Houghton Mifflin.

Hanna, G., Schell, L. M., & Schreiner, R. (1977c). *The Nelson Reading Skills Test, Levels A, B, and C* (Forms 3 and 4). Boston: Houghton Mifflin.

Hanna, G., Schell, L. M., & Schreiner, R. (1978). *The Nelson Reading Skills Test, Levels A, B, and C* (Forms 3 and 4). Boston: Houghton Mifflin.

Harris, T. L., & Hodges, R. E. (Eds.). (1981). *A dictionary of reading and related terms.* Newark, DE: International Reading Association.

Johnston, P. (1983). *Reading comprehension assessment: A cognitive basis.* Newark, DE: International Reading Association.

Robinson, H. A. (1965). Review of The Nelson Reading Test, revised edition. In O.K. Buros (Ed.), *The sixth mental measurements yearbook* (p. 802). Highland Park, NJ: The Gryphon Press.

Schreiner, R. L., Hieronymus, A. N., & Forsyth, R. A. (1969). Differential measurement of reading abilities at the elementary school level. *Reading Research Quarterly, 5,* 84-99.

Barbara D. Stoodt, Ph.D.
Professor of Education, School of Education, University of North Carolina at Greensboro, Greensboro, North Carolina.

THE NEW SUCHER-ALLRED READING PLACEMENT INVENTORY

Floyd Sucher and Ruel A. Allred. Oklahoma City, Oklahoma: The Economy Company.

Introduction

The New Sucher-Allred Reading Placement Inventory is a nonstandardized, individualized test designed to evaluate reading achievement through a Word-Recognition Test and an Oral Reading Test. In this inventory, students are asked to read increasingly difficult word lists and graded reading passages and to answer questions about each passage. This inventory helps classroom teachers place students at appropriate reading levels in a relatively short period of time. With careful administration, a teacher can identify the level at which the student 1) can read independently, 2) can benefit from instruction, and 3) becomes frustrated.

The authors of this test are Floyd Sucher, Ed.D., and Ruel A. Allred, Ed.D. Sucher is Professor of Education at Alaska Pacific University and an Adjunct Professor at Brigham Young University. He is also principal of an elementary school in Alaska and has held teaching and administrative positions in elementary schools, high schools, and universities. He is a coauthor of the Keys to Reading Program, published by The Economy Company. Allred is Professor of Education and coordinator of graduate elementary education at Brigham Young University. He has served as a consultant for reading and spelling in several states; has taught at the elementary level; and has served as teacher, principal, and curriculum writer for the Brigham Young University Laboratory School. Sucher and Allred coauthored The Keys to Reading Competency Skills Test, a group reading inventory.

The authors developed this instrument as a screening test to help classroom teachers identify students' reading levels. In order to select the vocabulary for the word-recognition component of the test, the authors compared the vocabulary listed in popular basal readers and in word-frequency lists to determine the words frequently used and their approximate grade level placement. After proper nouns were excluded, words were selected for each grade level. The authors conducted a study to identify the words that were the best predictors at each grade level. These words form the basis for the Word-Recognition Test, which is comprised of 12 word lists ranging in difficulty from primer through ninth-grade reading level.

The selections for the Oral Reading Test were chosen on the basis of interest and readability. They were carefully screened, and the readability was calculated for each. In calculating the readability of the primary-grade selections, the Spache formula was used, whereas the Dale-Chall formula was used for calculating the readability of the fourth- through ninth-grade selections. These selections were excerpted from a variety of sources, including *Reader's Digest, This Week* and *Parade* magazines, and four Economy Company publications: *Phonetic Keys to Reading, Keys to Independence in Reading, Keys to Reading,* and *Keys to Good Language.*

This test has undergone one revision, at which time some of the reading selections were updated and a second form of the test was written. The second form (Form B) facilitates pre- and post-testing of students. Normative data are not provided for this instrument.

Materials for administration of the Sucher-Allred Inventory include the teacher's manual (Sucher & Allred, 1981) and the student test booklet. In addition, a tape recorder is useful for taping students' oral reading. The teacher's manual is self-instructional and was designed to prepare teachers to screen students for reading placement. The manual is divided into an introduction and six sections that 1) describe nine steps for the test administrator to follow in screening and properly placing students for reading, 2) describe the nature of reading levels, 3) discuss the materials and procedures for gross screening, 4) explain how to administer the New Sucher-Allred Reading Placement Inventory, 5) present a review test for the individual who is preparing to administer this inventory, and 6) contain a class record for the inventory. In addition, the manual includes test plates of the word lists and reading passages for both Form A and Form B of the inventory.

The test administrator uses the student test booklet to record word-recognition errors and comprehension errors and to compute reading levels. Therefore, the words in the Word-Recognition Test, the reading selections, the comprehension questions, and possible answers are printed in this form. After a student reads the words and responds to the questions, the teacher records the number of word-recognition errors in the blanks following each passage. The teacher then identifies the student's reading level or listening capacity by checking the number of the student's errors in the summary section, which follows each reading selection. The teacher also categorizes word-recognition errors and comprehension errors on the summary of errors section. Word-recognition errors are classified in six categories: mispronunciation, nonpronunciation, omission, insertion, substitution, and regression. Comprehension errors are classified by the type of question to which students are responding when they make an error. These question types include main idea, facts, sequence, inference, and critical thinking.

Practical Applications/Uses

The New Sucher-Allred Reading Placement Inventory was designed for classroom teachers to use in identifying the appropriate level of reading materials for pupils whose anticipated reading levels fall between the primer level and ninth-grade level. In addition, this inventory can be used to evaluate students' progress in reading and to identify individuals requiring further diagnosis.

This inventory is inappropriate for diagnosing reading difficulties because it is a nonstandardized, informal inventory that assesses only oral reading skills. The test is further limited by the description of the categorizing system for pronunciation errors, which would be difficult for inexperienced teachers to apply.

This individually administered inventory is most appropriately administered in a quiet location such as a conference room. It can be administered by a classroom teacher, a guidance counselor, or a reading teacher.

The Sucher-Allred Inventory is relatively easy to administer. Generally, the test manual provides straightforward, easy-to-follow instructions. However, the procedures for conducting the Gross Screening are vague. This could present significant problems to a test administrator because the gross screening is used as a basis for determining the proper starting point for administering the inventory.

The scoring pattern for this test is clearly explained and is relatively easy for an experienced examiner to comprehend. The Word-Recognition Test is scored by tabulating the number of errors on each word list. The examiner also counts the word-recognition errors occurring during oral reading of the passages. The authors provide examples of each type of word recognition error for the test administrator. Nevertheless, classifying and coding word-recognition errors present the greatest problem to inexperienced examiners. Teachers need considerable practice to develop these skills.

In addition to identifing the word-recognition errors occurring in the Oral Reading Test, the examiner asks the student questions about the passage. The student may not refer to the passage in order to answer the questions. The number of incorrect responses for the five questions is totaled and recorded in the scoring box in the student record booklet.

Each portion of this inventory is accompanied by scoring criteria that aid interpretation. Further assistance is provided in the summary of errors section where the student's responses are summarized and categorized. However, the administrator must use professional judgment when classifying word-recognition errors and when evaluating the answers to questions. Interpreting the test and selecting appropriate reading materials require greater sophistication on the part of the examiner than administering and scoring the inventory.

Technical Aspects

Technical data are not available for this nonstandardized inventory.

Critique

The New Sucher-Allred Reading Placement Inventory is a well-organized instrument with an excellent self-instructional manual. Teachers find this instrument useful for identifying the proper level of reading materials for students. The reading content of the oral reading passages is similar to that of basal readers used in the majority of elementary school classrooms.

The criteria for identifying the independent, instructional, and frustration levels of reading in this inventory are lower than the traditional criteria developed by Betts. In fact, the authors do not reveal the source or basis for the criteria they use. Although the Betts criteria are questioned by some authorities in the field of reading (Stafford, 1975; Johns, 1972), they are commonly used for informal inventories. A more important aspect of this problem is the fact that this inventory overestimates students' reading level, relying almost entirely on analysis of oral reading as a basis for identifying it. Thus, it creates a very narrow perspective on the complex process of reading. Silent reading is a significant aspect of the total reading process, and because it becomes more and more important as students move through the grades, this instrument is inappropriate for students above the primary grades.

Construction of this inventory is suspect in several areas. For example, the authors are vague regarding the selection of words for the Word-Recognition Test and the field testing of these words. They are also vague about the selection and validation of reading passages for the Oral Reading Test. A number of these passages are dated, which suggests that a greater proportion of the content should have been updated in the second edition of the instrument. Form B was a welcome addition to this inventory, but the authors do not reveal any data regarding the equivalence of the two forms. Therefore, users cannot assume that the two forms are equivalent.

Construction of the questions used to evaluate comprehension is problematic because some of the questions do not represent the thinking level indicated by the inventory. For example, the inference questions are opinion questions. The main idea question in each set of questions asks the student to think of a good name for the story. The critical reading questions address students' experiences rather than their reasoning skills. Knowledge of sequence is assessed by asking students to identify the event that followed a stated one. Some of the questions can be answered with a yes or no response, thus failing to produce diagnostic information (Johnson, 1978; Johns, 1972).

Gross screening is a concept that appears to be unique to this instrument. Many inventories suggest that teachers use the score on the Word-Recognition Test as an indication of the appropriate place to begin administration of the Oral Reading Test. The authors of The New Sucher-Allred Inventory recommend gross screening as a means of identifying an appropriate starting point. However, the teacher must select the materials and use rather vague guidelines to perform gross screening when administering the inventory. Such a process requires considerable experience and expertise from the teacher. In fact, a teacher who is capable of administering a gross-screening procedure would find it unnecessary to use the inventory.

Administration of the Sucher-Allred begins one grade level below the student's anticipated reading level. Beginning at a level this high will frustrate disabled readers, which often causes students to give up trying, thus prohibiting the accumulation of needed diagnostic information. The procedures for administering this test could be strengthened by recommending that the Oral Reading Test begin two levels below the independent level identified on the Word-Recognition Test. In addition, the manual should instruct test administrators to stop testing when the student exhibits symptoms of frustration.

The scoring procedure for this inventory could be altered to make it more valuable. As it stands, examiners do not write students' actual responses to the word-recognition items; they simply indicate whether the item is correct or incorrect. Analysis of actual responses could provide valuable diagnostic information to teachers. Likewise, responses to the reading-comprehension questions are simply marked correct or incorrect, thus losing another source of diagnostic data. Scoring the inventory in this manner leads to quantitative rather than qualitative analysis.

Experienced teachers can adapt the New Sucher-Allred Reading Placement

Inventory by revising the questions and evaluating the students' answers carefully. In addition, they will wish to record all of the students' word-recognition errors in order to evaluate the quality of students' miscues. Making such revisions would increase the usefulness of the inventory for placing pupils at their proper reading levels. However, it seems more appropriate to call this instrument an inventory rather than a test because no reliability and validity data are available for it.

References

This list includes text citations as well as suggested additional reading.

Daines, D., & Mason, L. (1972). A comparison of placement tests and readability graphs. *Journal of Reading, 25*(9), 597-603.

Johns, J. (1972). Sucher-Allred Reading Placement in Reading. *Reading World, 12*(1), 72-74.

Johnson, M. (1978). Review of the Sucher-Allred Reading Placement Inventory. In O. K. Buros (Ed.), *The eighth mental measurements yearbook* (pp. 1225-1226). Highland Park, NJ: The Gryphon Press.

Stafford, J. (1975). Reading test review: The Sucher-Allred Reading Placement Inventory. *Reading World, 14*(4), 269-271.

Sucher, F., & Allred, R. (1981). *The New Sucher-Allred Reading Placement Inventory teacher's manual.* Oklahoma City: The Economy Company.

Wardrop, J. (1978). Review of the Sucher-Allred Reading Placement Inventory. In O. K. Buros (Ed.), *The eighth mental measurements yearbook* (pp. 1226-1227). Highland Park, NJ: The Gryphon Press.

Harold Takooshian, Ph.D.

Assistant Professor of Psychology, Social Science Division, Fordham University, New York, New York.

NON-VERBAL REASONING

Raymond J. Corsini. Park Ridge, Illinois: London House Press.

Introduction

The manual for this test introduces it succinctly: ''The Non-Verbal Reasoning test measures a person's capacity to think logically through the medium of pictorial problems'' (Human Resources Center, 1985, p. 1). More specifically, the Non-Verbal Reasoning (NVR) offers itself as a nonverbal group test of intelligence to be used in selecting adult male job applicants for unskilled or semiskilled industrial positions, including applicants with limited literacy or testing experience. It should be used in conjunction with other ability tests.

Non-Verbal Reasoning was introduced in 1957 as an improved revision of the now nonexistent Picture Test, developed in 1942. In 1957, NVR was one of the few nonverbal group tests of intelligence on the market, along with Cattell's Culture-Fair Test of ''g'' and a few others. NVR was introduced with three self-described aims: that the items be ''unthreatening'' to job applicants, ''minimally affected by cultural factors,'' and have high ''face validity for those using it'' (Human Resources Center, 1985, p. 7). These aims in 1957 were prescient of later trends within applied psychology of increased sensitivity to minority groups and test subjects' needs. The 1957 NVR was developed by Raymond J. Corsini, early in the career of this prolific researcher-clinician and editor of the four-volume *Encyclopedia of Psychology* (1984). It should be noted that Corsini's involvement seems limited to developing the test itself because the 1957 test manual was authored by its publisher (Human Resources Center) and the 1985 reprint of this manual is by its current publisher (London House Press). Corsini did not seem to author the manuals or use the test subsequently for his own published research.

The seven-page NVR test booklet contains 44 items of the same type. Each item is a set of five simple, horizontal-line drawings depicting faces, objects, geometric figures, and sundry other familiar things. The subject must put a slash through the one of four drawings on the right that goes best with the drawing at the extreme left.

Unlike most widely used ability tests, there is only one NVR. There is no alternate form, nor has it been translated into other languages during the past three decades. The same 44 items introduced in 1957 are still used today.

Practical Applications/Uses

NVR is easy to administer and score. The instructions and practice items take no more than three minutes to read aloud and adequately set the stage for even the most inexperienced examinee. The test is untimed and typically takes examinees 10-20 minutes to complete the 44 items. The test seems skillfully designed so that the items become progressively more difficult; few subjects miss the nine items on the first page while they are becoming accustomed to the instrument. The manual gives a mean raw score of 33.9 on the 44-item test. With the printed template inserted in the manual, hand-scoring can be effortlessly and accurately completed in less than 30 seconds per test.

The test's content and format seem well-suited to the challenge of assessing industrial workers with little test experience. Still, this reviewer has found a few slight difficulties in NVR's usage, of which users should be aware. First, the instructions could be clearer on one point. They ask the applicant to pick the one out of four drawings that ''goes best with'' the fifth drawing. Thus, some subjects look for the direct opposite rather than the match, leading to wrong answers based on an ambiguous instruction. For example, on one difficult item involving faces, subjects often choose the face that looks most different from the others, because it is the only one that is bald, bespectacled, and shown in profile. Nowhere in the printed instructions does it specify that the subject should mark the ''most similar drawing,'' so examiners should specify this orally in their instructions.

Second, about five of the items are perceptually unclear. For example, one drawing pictures an upside-down clock, but the numbers are so tiny that some subjects cannot see them. Another item pictures a person handling a small object, which not all subjects correctly discern to be a jack-in-the-box even though this is an essential element in determining the correct answer. In fact, each stimulus in NVR is about 27 millimeters square, about twice as large and discernible as in comparable tests, such as Cattell's Culture-Fair Test of Intelligence or the SRA Pictorial Reasoning Test (see Takooshian, 1984). Nonetheless, this occasional ocular difficulty poses a problem for some examinees that is unrelated to their intelligence.

Third, the answers are debatable for at least six of the 44 items. Ideally, the answer to an item should ''click'' once the subject sees it or hears the explanation, but a number of NVR items have correct answers that seem arbitrary or unclear even after they are scored. (Perhaps the publisher should add one page to the manual, briefly noting a reason for each item's solution).

Fourth, even tests with no time limit must come to an end. Though this reviewer has found that all subjects finish the items within 20 minutes, some are tempted to stare endlessly at their more doubtful answers until given a welcome external nudge. Test users would be wise to tell subjects that they should complete and submit the test after 20 minutes.

Finally, the conversion of the raw score to a percentile is clumsy. The manual requires the raw score to be translated into a standard score using one table, and then this standard score to be converted into a percentile using a second table. The standard score table is provided in order that the examiner can combine the NVR score with the results of other tests. There is no reason why the manual could not use the second table to convert raw scores directly into percentiles without the standard scoring, resulting in examiners choosing which of the two methods they prefer.

Technical Aspects

Lewis Terman was one of the first to use a standardized ability test to aid in hiring for industry when, in 1917, he found that his Stanford-Binet predicted job performance for California police officers. Since then, ability tests have proven invaluable in business decision making (Ghiselli, 1966).

London House has developed a reputation for supplying psychological tests to suit the needs of business. This shows in the manual of the NVR test, which is clearly aimed towards personnel officers in industry who may have limited knowledge of psychometrics, yet who seek a simple and useful test for their decision making. The remarkable simplicity of the NVR manual has both its positive and negative facets.

On the positive side, the 16-page manual provides the novice examiner with a concise, lucid mini-course in psychometrics. It defines and distinguishes three types of reliability and two types of validity, norms, and standard scores. It tells the examiner that a percentile "states the percentage of individuals in the normative population which is surpassed by the subject. For example, a percentile of 75 means that the subject's raw score is 'equal to or higher than' the scores achieved by 75 percent of other persons tested" (Human Resources Center, 1985, p. 4). Even the most inexperienced business user will have little trouble using and understanding this test.

Yet a more seasoned psychologist will be sorely disappointed with this manual. It provides very little data. The 1957 test manual indeed was developed before the appearance of the American Psychological Association's (APA) 1966 test standards, which enunciated minimum reliability and validity information for published tests. However, the 1985 reprinting of the NVR manual falls far short of virtually every element of the current APA (1985) test standards for norms, reliability, and validity.

The normative group for the NVR is unclear. The 1985 manual provides a mean raw score (33.9), standard deviation (6.1), and percentiles for a large group of 4,862 industrial personnel tested before July of 1972. However, we have virtually no data on who these people are. Some 2,543 of them are members of one of nine groups: hourly (151), managers (192), supervisors (102), professional (281), technical (59), district sales managers (148), industrial sales (1,430), federal government supervisors (63), and accountants (117). We know nothing about these workers' education, age, years of experience, or other factors relevant to their test performance. Moreover, we know nothing about the other 2,319 uncategorized workers who have become part of the percentile table. (At different points in the manual the number given is 4,682 or 4,862, indicating a typo or two.)

The manual defines three methods of gauging a test's reliability, yet presents NVR data for only one of these, internal consistency. It offers several estimates of this, including a K-R/20/ of .83 for a total of 371 workers tested in 1957 on the 44-item test. This is certainly a respectable internal consistency, even considering that the test is composed of highly homogeneous items. Of course, the K-R/20/ reliability will vary with the degree of variability within the sample. The manual offers no alternate form reliability because there is only one version of NVR. Oddly, the manual does not offer any test-retest reliability for the NVR, even though this is relatively easy to check in industrial samples where the same subjects can often be located for retesting two or three years later. Though the NVR is probably as reliable as other nonverbal ability tests, its manual's efforts to establish this as a fact seem incomplete.

The validity data on NVR are far less complete. There are almost none. At one point, we are told that 124 office workers tested in 1957 had a higher mean score (38.1) than 247 blue-collar workers and foremen (31.8). So what? Why should we assume that a salesperson is at a "higher occupational level" and, thus, more intelligent than a foreman? The critical question is whether this test correlates with some behavioral measure of performance in doing one's job; this is what employers want to measure, and the NVR makes no attempt at all to provide this sort of correlation. The only correlation in the manual regarding validity is between NVR and the Verbal Reasoning Test, another industrial test from London House, introduced by Corsini and Richard Renck in 1958. The two tests correlate +.61 for 137 workers tested in 1957. Though this correlation is high, it remains unimpressive for several reasons: 1) A high correlation with one other test does not make an instrument valid. Where are correlations with a few more established measures? 2) The Verbal Reasoning Test has its own dubious aura. Reviewers have concluded it has "no demonstrated validity of any kind" (Kennedy, 1965b, p. 786; see also Ryans, 1965b). In fact, to establish its validity, the Verbal Reasoning Test's manual cites the same +.61 correlation with NVR! *Caveat psychologicus.*

Judging by current standards, the 1957 NVR test and its manual have other limitations as well.

It is not clear that the NVR is culture-free, or even culture-fair. "Since it is relatively culture-free and is not influenced by facility in language, it is fair to people who have not had much formal education . . . " (Human Resources Center, 1985, p. 1). Assertion is not evidence. With hindsight, psychologists today recognize that nonverbal tests are not automatically free of bias (Anastasi, 1982, pp. 341-352) and that at best they are "culture-reduced" (Cronbach, 1984, pp. 321-334). By 1985 standards, the manual should use discriminant validity procedures or known-groups method to show that the test does not correlate with cultural factors and that the mean scores and correlations for different groups are the same. Instead, for some reason, London House decided in 1985 to reprint the 1957 manual rather than thoroughly revising it.

The items on the test may also be anachronistic after almost three decades. The stimuli are not as out-moded as those of some other early tests (such as the figures in the Thematic Apperception Test). However, as a matter of principle, items should be rechecked and, if necessary, revised periodically, particularly if they purport to impact the careers of individual workers.

It seems clear that the normative sample needs expansion as well. Women work too. Though the test was intentionally limited to male job-seekers in 1957, this seems an embarrassing limitation by modern standards.

The use of such a homogeneous nonverbal test as NVR to predict a complex criterion-like job performance is inherently limited. As Anastasi notes, "a single homogeneous test is obviously not an adequate predictor of a highly heterogeneous criterion" (1982, p. 115). The 1985 manual (p. 1) seems to recognize this implicitly: "Since low scores on a verbal test may be contaminated by non-intelligence factors (e.g., years of education, familiarity with verbal activity, etc.), a non-verbal test serves as a check on these other factors when the results of the two types of tests are compared." The manual strongly suggests that NVR not be used alone, but as one in a battery of measures predicting job applicants' performance. It also recommends NVR for employees in lower levels of industry because those at advanced occupational levels (e.g., "professionals") average 38.5, too close to the test's ceiling of 44 points.

Perhaps more than any other drawback, NVR is limited by its lack of independent validation. It is common for an appealing test like NVR to be widely used in research within a few years on the market, but there are hardly any published studies at all using NVR (Baehr, Furcon, & Froemel, 1969; Laurent, 1968). Corsini himself does not seem to have used it in published research. Whatever studies have been done seem to be in-house, as-yet-unpublished studies known by the publisher. This contrasts sharply with several other nonverbal ability tests. The Cattell Culture-Fair Tests of Intelligence have been reported in at least 175 published studies since 1933; over 500 published studies used the Goodenough-Harris Drawing Test since 1926; over 900 publications involved Raven's Progressive Matrices since 1938.

Any psychometrist who scrutinizes NVR must reach the same conclusion, that this test needs a "systematic effort to obtain and make available more extensive data. No one possessing even moderate sophistication in behavioral measurement would use this instrument in its present form" (Ryans, 1965a, p. 752; see also Kennedy, 1965a). London House seems quite aware of this problem, and one of its senior psychologists has described plans for change to this reviewer. To the extent NVR was not assertively marketed before London House assumed ownership of it in 1982, its use by outside clients was limited. Even now, the frequent in-house users apply NVR only as one of a four-test battery in their consultations with industry (Baehr, 1983). Specifically, NVR is used with three other brief ability tests as part of its elaborate System for Testing and Evaluation of Potential (S.T.E.P.) program for organizational development. There are tentative plans to publish a monograph in 1986 or 1987 to finally present what scientific data there are on NVR and its battery of companion London House tests. This reviewer hopes that the publisher will also encourage outside clients who have used the test to publish their findings independently. After a quarter of a century, there should be more data to be published.

Meanwhile, those in personnel testing who seek a short ability test to help select job applicants from diverse backgrounds should keep their eyes wide open. NVR is not necessarily a poor test as much as it is a very, very unproven one. A number of other industrial tests can be found in *Tests* (Sweetland & Keyser, 1983) or elsewhere. These include the Flanagan Aptitude Classification Tests, Flanagan Industrial Tests, SRA Nonverbal Form, Beta-II, the Purdue Non-language Personnel Test, Raven's Standard Progressive Matrices and Advanced Progressive Matrices, Cattell's Culture-Fair Intelligence Tests, and the D-48 or D-70 Dominoes Tests. Those who choose NVR will find it easy to use, but requiring much faith in its accuracy of measurement and some skill in developing local organizational norms for the test.

Critique

The Non-Verbal Reasoning test debuted in 1957 as one of the few nonverbal group intelligence measures for industrial selection. The 44-item test takes only 10-20 minutes, and the nontechnical 16-page manual is suitable for even novice examiners. Alas, the test and manual have remained unchanged through 1985, and the lack of evidence on its reliability and validity has become increasingly apparent over the past quarter-century. There is virtually no clear evidence that the test correlates with any criterion of industrial behavior or is culture-fair. Those who choose NVR as an ancillary in their personnel selection program should be prepared to develop local norms and validity data to compensate for this gap in the published materials.

References

American Psychological Association. (1966). *Standards for educational and psychological tests and manuals.* Washington, DC: Author.

American Psychological Association. (1985). *Standards for educational and psychological tests* (rev. ed.). Washington, DC: Author.

Anastasi, A. (1982). *Psychological testing* (5th ed.). New York: Macmillan.

Baehr, M. E. (1983). *Research report #2: Evaluation of potential for successful performance in higher-level positions.* Unpublished manuscript, London House, Park Ridge, IL.

Baehr, M. E., Furcon, J. E., & Froemel, E. C. (1969). *Psychological assessment of patrolman qualifications in relation to field performance.* Washington, DC: U.S. Government Printing Office.

Corsini, R. J. (Ed.). (1984). *The encyclopedia of psychology.* New York: Wiley.

Corsini, R. J., & Renck, R. (1958). *Verbal reasoning.* Park Ridge, IL: London House Press.

Cronbach, L. J. (1984). *Essentials of psychological testing* (4th ed.). New York: Harper & Row.

Ghiselli, E. (1966). *The validity of occupational aptitude tests.* New York: Wiley.

Human Resources Center. (1985). *Non-Verbal Reasoning: Interpretation and research manual.* Park Ridge, IL: London House Press.

Kennedy, J. E. (1965a). Non-Verbal Reasoning Test. In O. K. Buros (Ed.), *The sixth mental measurements yearbook* (pp. 751-752). Highland Park, NJ: The Gryphon Press.

Kennedy, J. E. (1965b). Verbal Reasoning. In O. K. Buros (Ed.), *The sixth mental measurements yearbook* (pp. 785-786). Highland Park, NJ: The Gryphon Press.

Laurent, H. (1968). Research on the identification of management potential. In J. A. Myers, Jr. (Ed.), *Predicting managerial success* (pp. 1-34). Ann Arbor: Foundation for Research on Human Behavior.

Ryans, D. G. (1965a). Non-Verbal Reasoning Test. In O. K. Buros (Ed.), *The sixth mental measurements yearbook* (pp. 752-753). Highland Park, NJ: The Gryphon Press.

Ryans, D. G. (1965b). Verbal Reasoning. In O. K. Buros (Ed.), *The sixth mental measurements yearbook* (pp. 786-787). Highland Park, NJ: The Gryphon Press.

Sweetland, R. C., & Keyser, D. J. (1983). *Tests.* Kansas City, MO: Test Corporation of America.

Takooshian, H. (1984). SRA Pictorial Reasoning Test. In D. J. Keyser & R. C. Sweetland (Eds.), *Test critiques* (Vol. III). Kansas City, MO: Test Corporation of America.

Grant Aram Killian, Ph.D.
Assistant Professor of Psychology, Nova University, Fort Lauderdale, Florida.

Brian Mathew Campbell, Ph.D.
Assistant Professor of Psychology, Nova University, Fort Lauderdale, Florida.

OBJECT RELATIONS TECHNIQUE

Herbert Phillipson. Windsor, England: NFER-Nelson Publishing Company Ltd.

Introduction

The Object Relations Technique (ORT), advanced by Phillipson (1953, 1973), is a projective test developed in the era of other apperception tests such as Murray's (1943) popular Thematic Apperception Test (TAT). However, the ORT departs from the standard apperception tests in that test stimuli are more highly ambiguous than those found in any of its "look-alikes." In fact, the stimulus cards of the ORT approach the level of ambiguity and abstraction found in Rorschach cards.

The ORT is based on the object relations (O-R) theory of Klein (1948) and Fairbain (1952). The O-R theory assumes that the pattern of adult relationships is an outgrowth of early childhood relations ("objects") with whom the infant is dependent for the satisfaction of biological and psychological needs. These early object relationships are considered to be of utmost importance to the developing child, so much so that it is thought that all aspects of adult perception and thought will bear traces of one's early object relations. The theory goes on to suggest that there are two types of overlapping object relations systems within each person. The first of these—a mature, rational, adaptive system of object relationships—is thought to develop as a result of a long period of repeated socially validated experiences. The second object relations system—a primitive, irrational, and inadequately adaptive system—is based on early childhood experiences wherein relationships are established by means of repressed unconscious fantasies that serve as a means of gratification. It is believed that the way in which each individual reconciles these two internal systems determines the person's idiosyncratic behavior and reaction towards people and things.

Following this line of reasoning, it is suggested that when the balance of the object relations systems is tipped such that the immature object system dominates, the unconscious object fantasies will find direct expression in the adult relationship and result in an impaired and restricted interpersonal style. To state it in another way, Klein (1948) and Fairbain (1952) hypothesize that the unconscious object relations will superimpose primitive patterns on the socially validated ways of conducting mature interactions. The degree to which the immature object system overthrows and/or intrudes on the mature sytem is thought to be determined by the extent to which the environmental setting matches the unconscious relationships in terms of 1) the dynamics of the relationship, 2) the immediate stimulus, 3) the objects present in the physical setting, and 4) the emotional climate. When constructing the stimulus cards for the ORT, Phillipson (1953) attempted to incorporate these four components of the theoretical model in order to provide a means of assessing the nature and balance of object relations exhibited by the individual client.

The ORT consists of three series (A, B, C) of four cards each and a blank card, making a total of 13 cards. Each of the three series contains a situation depicting one person (cards A1, B1, C1), a situation depicting two persons (cards A2, B2, C2), a situation depicting three persons (cards A3, B3, C3), and situations depicting groups of people (cards AG, BG, CG). When developing the pictures, an attempt was made to have all figures drawn so as to be ambiguous with respect to age, sex, movement, expression, attitude, and dress. In addition, each series of cards differs with respect to the amount of detail contained in the pictures, the physical setting portrayed, and the emotional climate portrayed. For example, the pictures in series A contain the most detail and are intended to be the least ambiguous. When considered as a whole, the various feature components and stimulus gradations inherent in the 12 picture cards, together with the obvious highly ambiguous blank card, are intended to "pull for" information beyond the simple object relations paradigm. It is obvious that the ORT cards have been constructed in order to yield stories containing issues and conflicts that might have relevance when interpreted from a more general psychoanalytic orientation—issues such as oedipal conflicts and transference issues.

Series A consists of human figures drawn in silhouette. The medium in which the figures were drawn appears to have been charcoal, and the figures are lightly shaded and misty in quality. In series A, no identifiable details are provided with regard to the physical setting "surrounding" the figures. Thus, the subject is given considerable latitude in interpreting the environmental context. Series B also contains silhouetted figures, drawn as black-and-white pencil sketches. However, in contrast to series A, series B contains definite details of the physical setting. Therefore, there is much less latitude for the subject with regard to interpreting the environmental context. The pictures in series C are even more enhanced and detailed than either series A or B. The human figure silhouettes are darkly shaded, and there are additional details with regard to the setting in which the figures occur. These settings are more realistic than those occurring in either series A or series B. However, the most notable distinctive feature of series C is the addition of color to the stimulus cards. Although most of each picture in series C consists of a darkly shaded black-and-white pencil sketch, color has been added to selected portions of each card. Phillipson (1973) suggests that the reason he added color to the pictures in series C was to evoke "feelings" and "emotional responses." However, the only research study to date that has focused on the issue of color (Gleed, 1974) fails to shed light on the significance of this particular feature. Moreover, it is by no means clear as to how the element of color is to be interpreted within the context of the object-relations theory (Meyer, 1958/1970).

The Object Relations Technique requires few materials and minimal space; any quiet setting with adequate illumination where the subject can be comfortably seated with sufficient room to look at the 9" x 11½" cards would be considered adequate. Although the test manual (Phillipson, 1973; also available on microfiche) contains a section entitled "Methods of Administration," the section focuses mainly on describing techniques for developing adequate rapport between the subject and examiner and provides very little detailed information with regard to the precise methods and procedures for administering the test. For example, there is no mention of whether the examiner or the examinee should record the subject's responses.

The administration of the ORT involves three phases. During the first phase, the testing phase, subjects are presented with each of the stimulus cards and asked to make up a story about the picture they have just been given. The actual instructions from the test manual (p. 10), which are similar to those contained in the TAT, are as follows:

> I am going to show you some pictures. Will you look at each one as I give it and try to imagine what it could be. As you bring it to life in your imagination, make up a brief story about it. First of all you should say how you imagine this situation came about—this you can do in one or two sentences. Then you can imagine what is going on in the situation and tell me about it more fully. Finally imagine how it turns out, or what happens in the end—this final part you can do again in just a sentence or so. The story is to be done in three parts; the beginning [*sic*] the middle bit which you do more fully, and the ending. I suggest we do the first one as a sample, then you can ask me about it afterwards, and I will tell you whether it is all right.

After completing the first story, the subject is prompted to give a past, present, and future to the story and to elaborate on any section of it that the examiner feels is inadequately covered. Unfortunately, examples or descriptions of what constitutes inadequate coverage are not provided in the manual. It simply states that the examiner might want to ask the subject more about what is going on in the story or about the people placed in the story. After this initial probing, the manual recommends that, generally, the examiner should take the stories as given by the subject, but suggests that if subjects find the story-making task particularly difficult, "it is permitted to prompt them with non-directive questions (using what they have already given as a lead) in order to get more information about the three parts required" (p. 10).

Phase II of the ORT consists of the inquiry. After the entire administration is completed, the manual recommends that the examiner conduct a brief (no more than ten minutes) inquiry on only those stories where the subject appeared uncertain or where verbalizations were unclear.

The final phase of the ORT consists of "testing of limits." The manual describes several different techniques that can be employed by the examiner during this phase in order to elicit additional information that might be of importance when interpreting object relations. First, when examiners regard subjects' perception of a stimulus card to be unusual in some way, it is permissible to request another story about the picture or ask the subjects if they can see the picture in another way. Second, if examiners become aware of possible conflict areas as manifested in the content of any story, they can request more details about the people in the story. Third, if examiners feel that subjects omitted or avoided important elements of the pictures, they should point out the omissions to the subjects and generate discussion about what they have left out. Fourth, examiners can ask subjects to select which of the stimulus cards they liked best and liked least and to provide reasons for their choice of a certain picture. Finally, examiners can request alternative stories to the ones subjects first provided in order to assess the extent to which the subjects' feelings have changed toward the examiner following the initial testing phase.

Overall, the procedures for administering the ORT are at best vague and at worst incomplete and imprecise. For example, given the lack of precision associated with the testing of limits phases, it is difficult to see how any two examiners would elicit the same type of data from a subject. These limitations are further compounded when one considers the way in which the test data from the ORT are interpreted.

The interpretation of the ORT is based solely on the qualitative analysis of the subject's stories (Phillipson, 1973). There are no quantifiable raw scores or derived scores, and it is therefore impossible to compare a subject's performance with that of other persons of the subject's own age. Psychoanalytic interpretations are launched from information gleaned from four main areas: 1) perception (e.g., what it is that is seen), 2) apperception (e.g., what themes occur), 3) the object-relation content (e.g., the kinds of people seen, how or to what extent they are differentiated, how they interact) and 4) the story structure (e.g., does it meet the task, is it balanced, is there conflict, is it logical, is it emotional, are problems worked through, is resolution achieved). In order to evaluate the overall personality, Phillipson (1973) suggests that it is essential to follow some basic psychoanalytic rules: 1) examiners should realize that the people portrayed in a subject's stories do not represent the subject's actual parents; 2) the people chosen in the stories are important individuals in the subject's past and/or present; 3) part of the subject's internal experience is unconscious and anxiety laden but is currently masked by the subject's defenses; 4) the unconscious object relations will include images of whole objects (e.g., parents), as well as parts of objects (e.g., breast or penis), and the relationship between the two; and 5) the situations portrayed in a story may represent unconscious parts of the self that are experienced as external to the self.

Practical Applications/Uses

At the present time, the practical applications of the ORT are largely open to question. Only a handful of studies have addressed its use as a diagnostic or therapeutic tool, and it is difficult to assess its practical value to the clinician.

To begin with, the target population of the test is unclear. Phillipson (1973, p. 22) suggests that "extensive experience has conferred the suitability and usefulness of the techniques for subjects of 14 years and upwards"; however, because of the total absence of standardization data for the test, there is no way to evaluate this clinical judgment or to ascertain other data (e.g., whether the test is more suitable for men or women, whether there is a minimal intellectual level required).

Some limited research has been advanced to suggest that the ORT might be useful as a screening device for predicting which clients will be more apt to participate verbally in therapy (Aston, 1970) and which clients will tend to stay in group therapy for a longer period of time (Aston, 1971); however, the use of the ORT as a screening device would appear to be problematic, given practical limitations with regard to the length of time that seems to be necessary to administer the test.

Although Phillipson (1973) suggests that the entire ORT procedure can be completed in 90 minutes, it would appear that the total time required by the clinician from start to finish would be considerably longer, especially if one takes into account what might prove to be a rather lengthy interpretive process. Westby (1970) regards the test-time issue to be a critical limitation of the ORT, which he considers to be either a likely routine examination method for teaching hospitals and clinics that are generously staffed or a luxury research instrument that could lead to a more economical technique. According to Westby (p. 251), "if, in addition to administration, four or five hours are spent in scoring and interpretation, the test is too expensive in time for the average clinical psychologist."

No indication is given in the manual as to whether it is possible to administer a short or abbreviated form of the test. Interestingly, it would appear that only one modification of the test has been forthcoming since the ORT was first published. This modification consisted of an experimental children's version (CORT) of the ORT that was first reported by Wilkinson (1975). Unfortunately, the initial investigation of the CORT was based solely on two clinical case studies, and it does not appear that this modification has generated any subsequent research attention or clinical interest.

Phillipson (1973) claims that the ORT is a valuable tool in industrial selection; however, he fails to report any data on the 3,000 candidates he presumably tested on the ORT. When using the test for this purpose, Phillipson recommends that the clinician use only six or eight cards, but his rationale for selecting the six cards is far from clear, and he fails to provide any justification on standard statistical grounds (e.g., reliability data). He simply suggests that the cards should be chosen so that some dynamic match occurs between the ORT cards and the human relations situation the candidate is seeking. He states that "in this way O-R issues inherent in the selection situation and the projected work situation will tend to be highlighted" (Phillipson, 1973, p. 21). At present, the value of the ORT in personnel selection is questionable. Kutash (1957/1970, p. 1134) states that "unfortunately, the data presented while highly interesting and pertinent for the clinical worker does [*sic*] not bear on the possibilities in the fields of personnel selection and guidance." According to Nevis (1957/1970, p. 1134) "the Object Relations Technique as it now stands will probably be of little value in personnel assessment work."

Another possible practical application of the ORT is its utilization as an adjunct to the therapy process itself. Phillipson (1973) suggests that the technique can facilitate associations that will enhance increasingly deeper levels of insight into how a patient relates to others. Until appropriate research is conducted on this topic, the reader will have to decide whether or not to take him at his word. Furthermore, it could be argued that the functions that Phillipson describes (i.e., deeper levels of insight into how a patient relates to others) could be adequately served by already existing tests such as the TAT. Although at least one author has argued that the ORT is unique and has no rivals in the testing marketplace (Hetherington, 1956/1970), other authors (e.g., Beech, 1970; Meyer, 1958/1970) question the advantage of the ORT over other existing tests. Beech (1970) states that the ORT may be at a disadvantage due to its comparatively brief history as well as its fundamental similarity to other currently available projective techniques. According to Meyer (1958/1970, p. 1133), the ORT has "little creativeness," is "a slightly modified combination of already existing techniques," and has not yet demonstrated the advantage of its "ambiguity over existing stimuli."

Finally, it should be noted that the process of developing meaningful interpretations and insights from the ORT stories appears to be a difficult and complex undertaking that relies heavily on an in-depth knowledge of psychoanalysis. This is a major limitation of the test in that years of specialized training and experience in psychoanalysis are not readily available to all test users, and such skills are certainly not attained by simply reading the test manual. Although this practical limitation is not addressed in the manual, others have been quick to point it out. For example, Beech (1970, p. 475) states that, based on published records of patients' ORT responses, "only persons with a specialized knowledge of psychoanalytic theory and a particular kind of experience would be in a position to duplicate the interpretations offered" and the ORT's usefulness could depend on both the examiner's limitations and limitations of psychoanalytic theory. In Meyer's (1958/1970, p. 1133) opinion, the application of Phillipson's psychoanalytic knowledge, rather than the technique itself, provides the rich information and, "with minor reservations, his approach can be used with other stimuli . . . a warning that there is no magic in the stimulus alone and it will provide rich results only if the examiner can bring a wealth of background to it."

Technical Aspects

The ORT fails to meet even minimally acceptable standards of reliability, validity, and normative breadth (American Psychological Association, 1985). The present manual contains only one clinical case study, and no information at all is presented regarding reliability (test-retest, alternate-form, and internal consistency), validity (content, criterion-related, or construct), or a standardization sample. Phillipson (1973) makes an unconvincing attempt to excuse these major limitations by stating:

> It is almost an impossible task to provide comprehensive and precise data on the stimulus values within projective material . . . normative data is [*sic*] built up largely from the experience of the psychologist with the Technique. After extensive experience the psychologist accumulates a knowledge of the wide variety of response [*sic*] such tests provide, and within the context of such experience can evaluate them in terms of their unusualness and their fit with the stimulus. Moreover with his extensive experience in looking at the material and examining responses in detachment, i.e. [*sic*] when not involved so fully as the patient, the psychologist learns to set aside his own subjective impressions and can thereby judge the unusual or reasonableness of a response in terms of its match with the stimulus properties. (p. 10)

Phillipson's own words suggest the demise of the ORT. Because the normative data are "built up largely from the experience of the psychologist," then the 17 years of normative data within Phillipson die with him.

Given today's standards for psychological tests and measures, one would go so far as to propose a moratorium on the ORT. The test is not acceptable by any objective scientific standards, and its use at this stage of development may constitute a violation of ethical principles and possibly leave the user open to criticism and perhaps litigation.

Critique

The problem with most projective tests is always the same—they allow the interpreter to project as much as the patient (Killian, 1985a). Tests are essentially rulers for the purpose of measurement, but not all rulers are created with equal accuracy and durability. A tape ruler made of an elastic cord that can be stretched when readings are taken will yield different measurements depending on how far one stretches the cord. Not all people will pull the cord the same way. On the other hand, if a tape ruler were made of metal, no matter how one chose to pull the ruler, the measurements would not change due to one's strengths or weaknesses; therefore, external measurements of the world and other people will be less apt to be influenced by the subjective "pull" of the examiner. A ruler (the ORT in our analogy) that allows for a variety of interpretations at the hands of different users may perhaps be a more accurate measure of the user's personality than the subject's.

Another analogy is also appropriate. Projective tests such as the ORT are basically tools—tools that have been developed to cut through surface defenses to uncover unresolved conflicts. However, all tools are not created equal, and neither are the users of such tools. By way of analogy, a knife in the hands of a surgeon can be a scalpel to cut through surface skin for exploratory surgery, but the same knife in the hands of a butcher remains only a knife for slicing meat. The skill is not in the tool but in the hands of the user. If, however, the tool is a cleaver, whether the user is a surgeon or butcher, the tool is still a cleaver and can only be used for chopping. Studies such as those by Wildman and Wildman (1975) clearly show that instruments like the TAT and the ORT have poor validity and perform at chance levels for predicting pathology. Additionally, when these tools are combined with more reliable and valid tests such as the MMPI, they reduce the accuracy and predictive power of the better instrument.

Whether projective tests can be more likened to an elastic ruler or a knife in the hands of a butcher or surgeon, three things are clear. First, the accuracy of projective tests, more than objective tests, varies with the skill and experience of the user (e.g., the surgeon vs. the butcher). Second, projective tests tend to allow the interpreter to project as much as the patient (e.g., the elastic ruler vs. the metal ruler). Third, based on the present review, it seems that the psychometric properties of the ORT fall short of today's standards, and the test seems to lack the required focused relevance for the practicing clinician or experimental psychopathologist. Psychological studies should be directed at valid assessment techniques that can reliably differentiate processes and functions that may be clearly implicated in various disorders (Killian et al., 1984). The use of unreliable techniques that are recommended only by their availability, familiarity, or novelty should be abandoned (Killian, 1985a). Instead, reliable and valid tests that provide information about processes and functions in various disorders should be developed and used (Killian, 1985b). Tests that lack the standards set forth by the American Psychological Association (1985) should not be employed by licensed psychologists because of the potential legal risks to the test user. According to the American Psychological Association standards (1985), the entire responsibility of test use and interpretation lies solely on the practitioner, not the developer or publisher.

Thirty years ago, Hetherington (1956/1970) maintained that the ORT would be used widely by clinical psychologists, regardless of their familiarity with object-relations theory, because the ORT "undoubtedly produces projective material the value of which is by no means dependent on psychoanalytic interpretation" (p. 1131). Hetherington assumed that this technique would become popular because of his clinical judgment. The time has come when empirical data must outweigh clinical judgment, and one can no longer be content with unreliable and incomplete studies, or else we shall sound like Keir (1956/1970) who stated 30 years ago that one should be "content with what information we have on this technique" (p. 1131). Thirty years have come and gone, and still not content we echo Beech's (1970) remarks:

> In summary it might be said that the ORT is a projective technique with a largely unknown development, without information respecting its reliability, and not having any very acceptable evidence concerning its validity. The claims made for the technique have yet to be substantiated and users of projective techniques may well feel that the ORT has no obvious advantages over the available alternatives. (p. 234)

References

This list includes text citations as well as suggested additional reading.

American Psychological Association. (1981). Ethical principles of psychologists. *American Psychologist, 36*(6), 633-638.

American Psychological Association. (1985). *Standards for educational and psychological testing.* Washington, DC: Author.

Aston, J. P. (1970). Predicting verbal participation in group therapy. *British Journal of Psychiatry, 116*(530), 45-50.

Aston, J. P. (1971). Predicting participation length in group therapy. *British Journal of Psychiatry, 119*(548), 57-58.

Beech, H. (1970). Objects Relations Technique. In O. K. Buros (Ed.), *Personality tests and reviews* (pp. 475-476). Highland Park, NJ: The Gryphon Press.

Bellak, L. (1951). *A guide to the interpretation of the Thematic Apperception Test (revised).* Cleveland: The Psychological Corporation.

Fairbain, W. R. (1952). *Psychoanalytic studies of personality.* London: Tavistock Publications.

Gleed, E. A. (1974). Some psychological mechanisms in agoraphobia. *British Journal of Projective Psychology and Personality Study, 19*(2), 27-33.

Hetherington, R. (1970) Object Relations Technique. In O. K. Buros (Ed.), *Personality tests and reviews* (pp. 1131-1132). Highland Park, NJ: The Gryphon Press. (Reprinted from *British Journal of Medical Psychology,* 1956, *29,* 173-174)

Keir, G. (1970). Object Relations Technique. In O. K. Buros (Ed.), *Personality tests and reviews* (pp. 1131). Highland Park, NJ: The Gryphon Press. (Reprinted from *British Journal of Educational Psychology,* 1956, *26,* 231-232)

Killian, G. A. (1985a). Review of the House-Tree-Person. In D. J. Keyser & R. C. Sweetland (Eds.), *Test critiques* (Vol. I, pp. 338-353). Kansas City, MO: Test Corporation of America.

Killian, G. A. (1985b). Review of the Stroop Color and Word Test. In D. J. Keyser & R. C.

Sweetland (Eds.), *Test critiques* (Vol. II, pp. 751-758). Kansas City, MO: Test Corporation of America.

Killian, G. A., Holzman, P. S., Davis, J. M., & Gibbons, R. (1984). Effects of psychotropic medication on selected cognitive and perceptual measures. *Journal of Abnormal Psychology, 93*(1), 58-70.

Klein, M. (1948). *Contributions to psychoanalysis.* London: Hogarth Press.

Kutash, S. B. (1970). Object Relations Technique. In O. K. Buros (Ed.), *Personality tests and reviews* (pp. 1134). Highland Park, NJ: The Gryphon Press. (Reprinted from *Personnel & Guidance Journal,* 1957, *35,* 539-540)

Meyer, M. M. (1970). Object Relations Technique. In O. K. Buros (Ed.), *Personality tests and reviews* (pp. 1133-1134). Highland Park, NJ: The Gryphon Press. (Reprinted from *Journal of Projective Technique,* 1958, *22,* 250-252)

Murray, H. A. (1943). *The Thematic Apperception Test manual.* Cambridge: Harvard University Press.

Nevis, E. C. (1970). Object Relations Technique. In O. K. Buros (Ed.), *Personality tests and reviews* (pp. 1134). Highland Park, NJ: The Gryphon Press. (Reprinted from *Personnel Psychology,* 1957, *10,* 133-135)

Phillipson, H. (1953). A modification of the Thematic Apperception Technique based on the psychoanalytic theory of unconscious relations. *Bulletin of the British Psychoanalytic Society, 19,* 28.

Phillipson, H. (1973). *A short introduction to the Object Relations Technique: A projective method for the study of interpersonal relations.* Windsor, England: NFER-Nelson Publishing Company Ltd.

Sells, S. B. (1970). Object Relations Technique. In O. K. Buros (Ed.), *Personality tests and reviews* (pp. 1132). Highland Park, NJ: The Gryphon Press. (Reprinted from *Educational and Psychological Measures,* 1957, *17,* 160-162)

Semeonoff, B. (1970). Object Relations Technique. In O. K. Buros (Ed.), *Personality tests and reviews* (pp. 1132). Highland Park, NJ: The Gryphon Press. (Reprinted from *British Journal of Psychology,* 1956, *47,* 73)

Shneidman, E. S. (1970). The Michigan Picture Test. In O. K. Buros (Ed.), *Personality tests and reviews* (pp. 250). Highland Park, NJ: The Gryphon Press. (Reprinted from *Journal of Projective Technique,* 1955, *19,* 192-193)

Westby, G. (1970). Object Relations Technique. In O. K. Buros (Ed.), *Personality tests and reviews* (pp. 251-252). Highland Park, NJ: The Gryphon Press.

Wildman, R. W., & Wildman, R. W., II. (1975). An investigation into the comparative validity of several diagnostic tests and test batteries. *Journal of Clinical Psychology, 31,* 455-458.

Wilkinson, N. W. (1975). Spontaneous and defensive movement in the children's O.R.T. development of the self. *British Journal of Projective Psychology and Personality Study, 29*(1), 15-27.

John O. Crites, Ph.D.
Professor of Counseling Psychology, School of Education, Northwestern University, Evanston, Illinois.

OHIO VOCATIONAL INTEREST SURVEY: SECOND EDITION

The Psychological Corporation. Cleveland, Ohio: The Psychological Corporation.

Introduction

The Ohio Vocational Interest Survey: Second Edition (OVIS II), a paper-and-pencil inventory of vocational interests, is an extensive 1981 revision of OVIS (D'Costa, Winefordner, Odgers, & Koons, 1970). In addition, an OVIS II Microcomputer Version (OVIS II/Micro) became available in 1984. Both OVIS II and OVIS II/Micro are published by The Psychological Corporation as measures of job-activity preferences for 23 job clusters cross-coded to cognate classifications by Data-People-Things as outlined in the *Dictionary of Occupational Titles* (DOT; U.S. Dept. of Labor, Bureau of Employment, 1977). The survey consists of 253 items (job-activity statements) and 23 interest scales, each of which contains 11 items that are answered along a five-point Likert-type scale, according to respondents' likes or dislikes (1 = Dislike very much, 2 = Dislike, 3 = Neutral, 4 = Like, and 5 = Like very much). Raw scores, which range from 11 to 55, are transformed to percentile ranks and stanines for age, grade, sex, and local and/or national norm groups, and a scale clarity index indicates whether ratings of items in a scale are consistently likes or dislikes. A variety of individual and group reports and collateral materials, such as the *Handbook for Exploring Careers* and the *Career Planner,* are also available.

The OVIS II/Micro is essentially the same as the paper-and-pencil edition, except that the survey is administered and scored using a microcomputer, specifically the Apple II, Apple II+, or Apple IIe. It can be used either for students who missed group testing or for occasional individual administration because one of its advantages is that examinees can leave the program at anytime and resume and finish it later. Other advantages are that the scoring is on location and immediate, and step-by-step instructions for using the microcomputer are included in the program.

The precursor to the OVIS was the Vocational Planning Questionnaire (VPQ) developed by John G. Odgers in 1953, when he was superintendent of the guidance services section in the Ohio Department of Education. The VPQ was not a bonafide interest inventory but rather a survey instrument designed for curriculum planning by school administrators. It served as a starting point, however, for the initial conceptual work on the OVIS, which began in 1966.

From these first theoretical formulations there emerged a cubistic model of vocational interests (D'Costa & Winefordner, 1969), the schematic framework for the construction and development of the OVIS. The purpose of the cubistic model was essentially twofold: to systematically define the domain to be measured and to link measures of the domain to the most widely used informational resource in the field of vocational counseling and guidance—the DOT. Working together as a research team, in consultation with the editorial staff of The Psychological Corporation, D'Costa, Winefordner, Odgers, and Koons (1970) introduced a three-dimensional cube, defined by the DOT tripartite classification of the components of work activity—data, people, and things. These three dimensions, in combination with three levels of involvement (High, Average, and Low), form a cube with 27 cells. For example, a cell including "automobile service mechanic" is rated as Average (data), Low (people), and High (things), indicating that this occupation largely involves working with things. Most of the occupations in the DOT can be classified into the cubes accordingly, although three cubes were not used in the construction of the original OVIS, and one has subsequently been eliminated. Moreover, some cubes are measured by more than one OVIS or OVIS II interest scale (e.g., Manual Work, Customer Services, Literary, Machine Work, and Medical).

Once the cubistic model had been articulated, a long and comprehensive program was undertaken to write items for the 24 OVIS interest scales, field test them, determine their psychometric characteristics, refine them, and then conduct standardization and normative studies. According to the OVIS manual (The Psychological Corporation, 1981), the research program for the original edition proceeded through five stages over a period of two years (1967-1969), culminating in the publication of OVIS in 1970. It was standardized and normed on a well-selected national representative sample of over 20,000 male and female students in Grades 8-12. Some gender differences were found on five scales, for which separate scoring keys were constructed, and norms were reported on all scales separately by sex. Grade norms were also reported, but interestingly enough, there did *not* appear to be developmental trends on the OVIS scales from the lower to upper grades, whereas research on other interest inventories (e.g., Strong, 1955) reveals considerable change during the high-school years. The 1970 manual (p. 31) states only that "the data gives evidence of the stability of interests with age." Why this variant finding with the OVIS was obtained is not clear.

The OVIS II revision was occasioned by the publication of the fourth edition of the DOT in 1977 and the *Guide for Occupational Exploration* (GOE; U.S. Dept. of Labor, Employment and Training Administration, 1979), both of which changed the occupational coding system for data-people-things and eliminated Volume II of the DOT. In the revision, only about one-fourth of the original items were retained, and a new standardization on 16,000 students nationwide in Grades 7-12 and 2,800 freshman and sophomore college students was conducted. Some clusters were dropped and others roughly equated, but the cubistic structure for the OVIS II interest scales (reduced from 24 to 23) was largely retained. Particular care was given to sex differences, of which there were notable instances on certain scales, as is true of most interest inventories. Although a deliberate attempt was made to reduce gender bias as much as possible, there were still differences on approximately 20% of the items, and the decision was made to report both separate and combined sex norms—or none if requested.

The standard version of the OVIS II consists of a booklet with answer sheets, which can be either hand or machine scored, the Student Report Folder, and optional summary reports for school purposes (e.g., Local Survey and Group Guidance Report). The four-page student report, listing scale names and reporting percentile ranks (PRs), stanines, and scale clarity indexes, is clear and well organized. Scales are ordered by magnitude of PRs and stanines from high to low in order that stronger interests can be easily identified. The accompanying narrative that is computer-printed on the student report form, however, seems complicated and overly abtruse. Certainly it was not meant to be used without counselor assistance. In contrast, the print-out from the OVIS II/Micro seems much better designed and more user friendly, particularly if augmented with such supplementary materials as the *Career Planner.* Administration of both OVIS II versions presents no problems, although some assistance is needed on the OVIS II/Micro in scoring it (e.g., inserting diskettes).

The *Career Planner* is intended to take the student systematically through a series of career exploration steps and interpretations of the student report but, as well-designed as it is technically, it bogs down hopelessly in overly detailed and complex explanations of concepts and worksheets. It appears to have been written for self-administration, but a student (particularly at the junior-high-school level) would need the guided assistance of a counselor or teacher. In contrast, the *Handbook for Exploring Careers* (1983), a hybrid of the old DOT Volume II and the new GOE, comes off considerably better. It provides highly usable, condensed information about occupations in the 23 OVIS II clusters and is attractive in format and layout.

Practical Applications/Uses

Although there are college norms for the OVIS II, and the publisher advocates its use with mid-career-change adults, its development and standardization are clearly keyed to Grades 7-12. For this educational span, it is well conceived and constructed and quite applicable. The manual presents case studies for individual profile interpretation, includes an entire chapter outlining a career-education program for group/classroom use, and provides materials for a career resources center. There is no question that these uses have been carefully designed and thought through, although no mention is made that they have been field-tested. The only caveat is that the OVIS II program must be administered and delivered by individuals who are thoroughly trained in career guidance and occupationology. Despite the obvious effort made to write interpretative materials that are "self administering," they are lengthy, sometimes abstruse and complex, and require lengthy reading with long periods of concentration. What the fatigue factor is in completing the profile interpretation and worksheets is not reported, but it must be considerable. Use of the OVIS II for descriptive and exploratory purposes should also be underscored. Its content and, to a lesser extent, construct validity support these uses, but there is little or no evidence for its predictive validity.

Because the conceptual framework for the inventory is directly linked to the DOT occupational structure and the GOE workgroups, there is no reason for excluding its appropriateness for adults, *except* that there are no norms for gainfully employed workers. Therefore, until these norms are available applicability should be restricted to high-school and college students.

Technical Aspects

The careful conceptual development of the OVIS II gives it considerable face validity, and the process of item writing and editing provides content validity, based on reviewers' expert opinion, which is unusual for interest measures. There are some nagging questions, however, that still need to be addressed. Foremost among these is why some cells in the cubistic model are *empty*. For the content and ultimately the construct validity of OVIS II to be coherent and compelling, an explanation for these lacunae is needed. Another, somewhat related, concern is the question of evidence for the assumption that the 1970 manual (p. 4) makes: that "the 11 job activities comprising each scale adequately represent all the jobs in the cluster of worker—trait groups defining the scale." Conspicuous by its absence, although evidently available for the standardization, are data on the factorial composition of the scales. Finally, there are *no* criterion-related validities reported. The only remotely relevant statement in the 1970 manual (p. 32) appears to be contradictory: that the "use of the results [from the OVIS] in predicting future behavior is not considered to be as important as their immediate use in career orientation and vocational exploration. The validity and reliability of the instrument should be assessed in terms of how well it helps students, parents, and counselors to develop realistic plans for the *future* [italics added]." But the latter is exactly what criterion-related validity does.

In contrast to the dearth of validity data on the OVIS and OVIS II, the results on its reliability are quite respectable. With a four-week interval on samples of males and females in Grades 8-10 (N = 564 and 348, respectively), the median stability coefficients for the 23 revised scales varied from .76 to .82, with a slight tendency to be higher for females. Findings are also reported on scale intercorrelations for OVIS II high-school and college samples, based on the national standardization, with medians ranging from .316 to .608, but with marked sex- and educational-level differences. Thus, the scales appear to be measuring different interests reliably, yet they are sufficiently interrelated to provide evidence for the cubistic model of interest organization.

For a 25% sample of the standardization group, Cronbach alpha coefficients were calculated to estimate scale internal consistencies, all of which were greater than .83, the median *r*s being between .88 and .90. Not only do the scales appear to be homogeneous by this criterion, they more than adequately meet other criteria for 1) own scale and 2) other scale correlations. In general, the OVIS II interest scales are highly stable and internally consistent.

Critique

OVIS (1970) was reviewed in *The Seventh Mental Measurements Yearbook*, but much of these reviews (Frantz, 1972; Rothney, 1972) dealt with limitations of the inventory that were subsequently rectified in the 1983 edition. Some comments, however, are still relevant and echo the criticisms of this review. Frantz (p. 1442) concludes, for example, that "no concurrent, or predictive or any kind of criterion-related validity information is offered." Rothney (p. 1444) reiterates this criticism and adds:

> The authors do not discuss such matters as transparency of the items, deliberate or unintentional faking, arbitrary assignment of numbers to responses, elaboration of the obvious, superficiality of items, vocabulary difficulties, variability in moods and sets, forcing of choices when there is no genuine choice, and many other criticisms of the inventory approach that have appeared in the literature.

These are criticisms that Rothney makes of most interest inventories; however, as long as there are no criterion-related validity data on the OVIS or OVIS II, to show that "it works," these criticisms have to be taken into account.

There is no question that the OVIS and OVIS II have been carefully constructed and developed. The cubistic model provided an explicit conceptual schema for scale construction, as well as a "built-in" linkage with the world-of-work through the DOT and GOE occupational structure. The standardization and norm base are more than adequate for high-school students and are also applicable, although to a lesser extent, to college students. The content and construct validity of OVIS II are articulate and compelling, although a much more extensive nomonological network of relationships with other variables for the latter is needed. If it were available, the criterion-related validity of OVIS II would be greatly augmented because little, if any, data on it are reported in the current manual.

If there are shortcomings to OVIS II, they are in its criterion-related (both concurrent and predictive) validity and its appropriateness for use with adults. There are no adult norms reported to support its proposed use with mid-career-change adults or, for that matter, other decisional problems, although there is no reason why OVIS II could not be used with adults, given such norms. In this reviewer's opinion, probably the most extreme and undocumented claim made in the advertising for the OVIS II is touting it as "America's most popular interest survey." What of the Strong-Campbell Interest Inventory (SCII) and Holland's Self-Directed Search (SDS)? They are much more extensively used with adults and younger age groups than the OVIS II. Finally, caution should be exercised in interpreting OVIS II to make clear that it assesses *interests*, not *aptitudes*. Because the worker characteristics sections of the *Handbook for Exploring Careers* indicate which aptitude patterns are required for specific work groups, there may be a tendency to infer aptitude qualifications where they have not been measured. In summary, the OVIS II is a well-constructed and conceptualized inventory of job activity preferences that are explicitly related to the occupational structure. It should be highly useful with high-school and college students in their career planning and cognate educational choices.

References

D'Costa, A. G. (1968). *The differentiation of high school students in vocational education areas by the Ohio Vocational Interest Survey.* Unpublished doctoral dissertation, Ohio University, Athens.

D'Costa, A. G., & Winefordner, D. W. (1969). A cubistic model of vocational interests. *Vocational Guidance Quarterly, 17,* 242-249.

D'Costa, A. G., Winefordner, D. W., Odgers, J. G., & Koons, P. B., Jr. (1970). *Ohio Vocational Interest Survey.* Cleveland: The Psychological Corporation.

Frantz, T. T. (1972). Review of the Ohio Vocational Interest Survey. In O. K. Buros (Ed.), *The seventh mental measurements yearbook* (pp. 1441-1442). Highland Park, NJ: The Gryphon Press.

Psychological Corporation, The. (1981). *Ohio Vocational Interest Survey: Second Edition manual.* Cleveland: Author.

Rothney, J. W. M. (1972). Review of the Ohio Vocational Interest Survey. In O. K. Buros (Ed.), *The seventh mental measurements yearbook* (pp. 1443-1444). Highland Park, NJ: The Gryphon Press.

Strong, E. K., Jr. (1955). *Vocational interests after 18 years after college.* Minneapolis: University of Minnesota Press.

U.S. Department of Labor, Bureau of Employment Security. (1977). *Dictionary of occupational titles* (4th ed.). Washington, DC: U.S. Government Printing Office.

U.S. Department of Labor, Employment and Training Administration. (1979). *Guide for occupational exploration.* Washington, DC: U.S. Government Printing Office.

Russell H. Lord, Ed.D.
Associate Professor, School of Education, Eastern Montana College, Billings, Montana.

ORGANIC INTEGRITY TEST

H. C. Tien. East Lansing, Michigan: Psychodiagnostic Test Company.

Introduction

The Organic Integrity Test (OIT) is intended by its developer, H. C. Tien, as an objective neuropsychiatric screening test to assess cerebral dysfunction. Tien (1965) asserts that the OIT can serve "as a quick and efficient diagnostic aid to assess central nervous system deficit, as a loss of pattern recognition" (p. 20). According to the author it was designed as a means of measuring "organic brain deficit due to any brain disease" in settings where it "can be readily applied for mass screening in psychiatric clinics, schools, hospitals, or as a routine neuropsychiatric test in the office of a general practitioner." Tien claims that the OIT "measures form perception as an indication of organicity as unrelated to intelligence" for adults, and that, in children, an "OIT value outside the normal range indicates either a developmental lag, organicity, psychosis, or definite mental retardation" (p. 13). The author also claims that the OIT can "be useful as a screening test to detect early reading disability" (p. 18).

In this attempt to assess cerebral dysfunction due to any brain pathology, the OIT presents color-form stimuli similar to other sorting tests which attempt to assess cognitive functioning through nonverbal concept formation and categorization tasks. Other tests similar to the OIT include the Color Form Sorting Test (sometimes called Weigl's Test), The Object Classification Test, the Object Sorting Test, and the Wisconsin Card Sorting Test.

H.C. Tien, M.D., designed the OIT at Ypsilanti State Hospital, Michigan, in 1959. The first paper which presented the OIT to the field was submitted by the author as his master's thesis in neurology at the University of Michigan Medical School. The author's stated purpose was the construction of a simple, objective, color-form perception for detecting brain damage or schizophrenia.

Apparently, the OIT was modeled closely after an unpublished test designed by Casagrandie as part of his anthropological studies. It was developed intact rather than through item analysis of a data pool and subsequent normative procedures. At this point in time, no revisions of the test, its underlying assumptions, or its claims, have been made. No mention is made of alternative forms of the OIT being available for uses with certain special populations.

Distributed throughout the four reprinted articles and three appendices that constitute the OIT manual, there are several "standardization" tables, "tabulations . . . of the Four Diagnostic Groups," "diagnostic" and "differential diagnosis" charts, and, in Appendix B, *The OIT Diagnostic Chart (Adults & Children)—(Interpolated)* gives *OIT Scores at Various Age Levels.* It is unclear if some or all of these are to be considered the "norms" for OIT scores. Also unclear is the identity of the specific group(s) from which the diagnostic OIT scores in Appendix B were derived. Since age categories extend to kindergarten age, it seems that the Appendix B scores were derived from more data than the 220 subjects reported in the original 1959 OIT paper (which constitutes the first component in the manual).

The original normative sample contained 220 subjects who were selected from 400 people tested because they fit into one of the following groups: 1) normal, N = 70; 2) nonorganic nonpsychotic, N = 33; 3) organic, N = 52; or 4) psychotic, N = 65. The manual states that the normal group consisted primarily of student nurses and attendants in the state hospital (with "a few volunteers"); the nonorganic nonpsychotic group included patients in "a state hospital outpatient clinic" and "many were inmates from a state prison"; the organic group was entirely hospitalized mental patients (given the OIT "randomly" with individual diagnoses checked later); and the psychotic group contained only patients designated as "schizophrenic reaction, paranoid type."

The OIT consists of just 10 sets of three illustrations each; each set consists of one free single and a "united double." All pictures are incomplete, with various parts omitted to make accurate identification of any picture less certain. The clarity of each picture is further confused by the staples and, apparently, Scotch® tape used to hold them in place while they were photographed. In each set, the paired pictures are of different colors, while the free single is similar to one of the pair in color and purportedly similar to the other of the pair in its form. As an example, similar but not identical to pictures included on the OIT, a free single that depicts a portion of a green sweater might have to be matched with one of a pair that contains one picture which is a portion of a green necktie and its "united double" which is a corner breast pocket on a blue sportcoat. In each of the 10 sets, examinees are asked: "Which two *pictures* are alike?" or requested to "tell me which two pictures are *alike*." The 10 sets are presented serially, from set A through set J, and total time for administration and scoring takes approximately five minutes. Set B is considered a "bluff-set" since the free single is identical to one of the united doubles in both form and color (in fact, they are the very same picture), and both are complete rather than partial pictures.

The examiner is not to explore any of the subject's responses nor make any evaluative or influential statements during administration of the OIT, but is to simply repeat the instructions patiently and firmly, deflecting any probing questions asked by the subject. Tien claims that the OIT is equally useful with all subjects aged five or older, and states that, while data are not available for children younger than five, the OIT "process probably is demonstrable as early as the third year of the child's life" (p. 16). Despite a statistically significant negative correlation ($r = -.37$, N = 220, $p < .001$) between age and OIT score reported from his initial study (clearly indicating that younger subjects showed OIT scores higher than predicted by chance), Tien claims that "age alone certainly is not responsible for the high level of significance obtained" (p. 11). The significance to which he refers is the difference in OIT scores between 1) the normal and organic groups and 2) the normal and psychotic groups ($p < .01$). He does not report the statistical significance of the correlation observed.

Scoring sheets or record forms are apparently unnecessary for proper use of the

OIT, since they are not a part of the test materials. Raw scores are the number of form responses given by the examinee, and a list of the pairings which constitute form responses is provided on p. 6 of the first article in the manual. Raw scores are "not very revealing" and must be transformed to "set-values" "in order to give a more meaningful score to the test." The set-values are proportional values, "based on the frequency of occurrence in normal population," and the "OIT value is the sum of the set-values." This means that OIT scores are based on the frequency with which the 70 subjects in Tien's original normal subject group paired the free single with the united double picture on the basis of some classification scheme or category other than color. Thus, the highest possible OIT score is 100, and an individual who misses the bluff-set (since B and B-2 are identical) "is defined . . . as having zero gestalt perceptual ability."

OIT scores do not produce a profile of strengths and weaknesses, but yield only one global number representing the examinee's placement with respect to the "unitary concept" that Tien claims the OIT measures. Tien claims that low OIT scores are "an expression of a general neuro-physiologic deficit," which he labels "chromaphilia" (p. 33). His claims rest on several assumptions (that will be addressed later in this review) about both the OIT as a specific test instrument and human perception in general.

Practical Applications/Uses

As stated earlier, Tien originally intended the OIT as a screening instrument for use by psychiatrists and neurologists as a diagnostic aid in the assessment of organic brain dysfunction independent of the examinee's intelligence or the underlying physiological cause of the dysfunction. Subsequent to the original claims, Tien recommended the OIT as a screening device to detect early reading disability, as an objective indicator of developmental lag of form perception, for mass screening in schools, and even as part of "a pilot program of early detection and inoculation against reading disabilities as vaccines are given to prevent polio" (p. 31). Though mention is made of using the OIT as part of a battery, Tien seems to emphasize OIT use as a single, diagnostic instrument to serve as a screen in settings ranging from the neurologist's office to the normal classroom.

Used by a trained neuropsychologist, the OIT would seem a likely candidate for "warming up" an examinee who will subsequently be thoroughly evaluated across the many dimensions involved in neuropsychological functioning. As such, the OIT presents a seemingly innocuous task, without right or wrong answers, that would be unlikely to evoke much test reactivity on the part of the examinee. Such tests often serve very well as "icebreakers" between the examiner and examinee.

Use of the OIT by individuals untrained in neuropsychological assessment, who would have only the author's claims to guide their conclusions and judgments, seems most inappropriate. Many of the claims are far too speculative because they are based upon assumptions that are neither openly declared nor empirically supported and go beyond the neuropsychological sophistication that can reasonably be expected of personnel in many "mass screening" situations (such as in the schools Tien mentions).

The OIT seems to hold potential as a research instrument, but this research potential seems far greater than its proclaimed power to diagnose any cerebral dysfunction, no matter what the cause of the deficits.

A well-defined, specific population of subjects for whom the OIT would be expected to prove valuable is difficult to identify. To make a basic distinction between unimpaired and grossly impaired examinees, the OIT would seem feasible, but in such cases, the individual's general psychological functioning is likely to be so severely disturbed that differences on the OIT might well be artifacts of a more basic underlying dimension—general functioning, not circumscribed organic deficits. As stated by noted neuropsychologist Ralph M. Reitan, "almost any psychological test can separate such groups" (1972, p. 283). However, the large and often speculative claims of the author that the OIT accurately detects organic dysfunction independent of cause and unrelated to age or intelligence are not justified in view of neuropsychological research.

Administration and scoring of the OIT are quite simple, but, while the exact qualifications that examiners must possess are never mentioned, it seems prudent that only individuals trained in neuropsychological assessment use the OIT as a diagnostic screening instrument. Administration of the OIT demands no special environmental conditions other than a place for examiner and examinee to face each other in a comfortable setting without interruptions. Interpretation is made by use of the diagnostic charts or other tables provided in the manual, and is to be objective rather than subjective or clinically determined. This apparent ease of interpretation for something as intricately complex as neuropsychological functioning seems to be misleading.

Technical Aspects

The OIT manual is actually four articles authored by Dr. Tien between 1960 and 1966, supplemented by appendices providing instructions, scores in a diagnostic chart, and a very brief presentation of the author's theory of pattern recognition. Articles by others who have obtained results contradicting the large claims made by Tien (Snelbecker, Sherman, & Schwab, 1968; Watts & Haerer, 1970) are not listed in the manual and the immense wealth of information related to neuropsychology obtained during the last 19 years is also omitted. Such obvious omissions raise serious questions about current use of the OIT within the context of Tien's original claims and assumptions.

Until a test has been conclusively shown to obtain consistent results (i.e., results relatively free from test-produced error) it does not demonstrate reliability. And, reliability, which must be firmly established mathematically prior to the establishment of any meaningful type of validity, is nowhere discussed in Tien's original presentations of the OIT. Such an omission did not, however, give rise to cautious guesses about the OIT's validity. Instead, validity claims were unusually sweeping in both breadth and depth.

In the third article comprising the manual, Tien refers to a study in which Astrom "found the OIT test-retest reliability coefficient to be 0.775 on a small series" (p. 20). There is no further explanation of this crucial technical foundation upon which any claims of validity must ultimately depend. In fact, were a reliability coefficient of .775 applied to the standard deviations reported by Tien, and the standard error of measure computed, several of his reported groups (and ages) would have unusually large standard errors of measure. Such results indicate that examinees' scores contain a relatively large amount of variability due to unpredictable, "error" factors. This imposes serious reservations concerning any possible interpretations, and occurs because the standard error of measure enables an examiner to set limits on either side of an obtained score within which one can be reasonably sure that the examinee's score actually falls. Obviously, as that "margin" gets larger, the confidence one should place in the test results must decrease.

Additionally, Tien (1968) recommends repeated uses of the OIT with the same examinee, even claiming that the OIT can serve "as a daily mental status indicator" (p. 875). Given the paucity of information regarding the OIT's reliability and the lack of empirical verification of OIT consistency and variability under controlled circumstances for purposes of establishing its reliability, such claims are inappropriate. If the test is highly reliable (i.e., it yields consistent results from administration to administration) then it seems that daily use would at least raise some interesting questions and problems.

Were the reliability of the OIT firmly established at an impressively high level (say, $r = .90$ or greater), its validity for the purposes claimed by Tien would still be suspect. Tien repeatedly makes speculative claims for the OIT, without providing the necessary empirical support. He based both the test and his claims for it upon assumptions about human neuropsychology that are inconsistent with preexisting as well as more contemporary data, and fails to cite and deal with data that challenge his assumptions and claims.

In the literature available when Tien was developing the OIT as a sorting/categorizing test similar to work by Goldstein, Weigl, and others, there were reports by McFie and Percy (1952) and Parker (1957) showing no significant differences between normals and organically impaired examinees on such tests. Sorting tests are thought to "demonstrate how the patient thinks and handles certain kinds of abstraction problems" (Lezak, 1976, p. 398). Research since then (DeRenzi, Pieczuro, Savoiardo, & Vignolo, 1966) has continued to support the view expressed by Lezak (1976, p. 398) that, "on scored sorting tests, few significant differences show up between the mean scores obtained by groups of brain injured patients and normal control patients." More recent summaries by other experts continue to express the very same conclusion, making it seem more and more certain (Golden, 1981).

The following assumptions are made by Tien: 1) color domination over form in perceptual tasks where both cues are equally available accurately indicates "cortical damage" and cerebral dysfunction; 2) brain dysfunction is sufficiently homogeneous that OIT scores fall no matter what the underlying cause or area of involvement; 3) OIT instructions sufficiently cue the examinee to use a categorization scheme favoring form over color; and 4) paranoid schizophrenia is an organic brain syndrome evidencing signs similar to, if not indistinguishable from, other organic, physiological dysfunctions.

Turning to the first assumption, a couple of issues seem paramount. "Color is the most immediate visual sensation" (Thompson, 1985, p. 196), and is a categorization scheme imposed by us on our world since "color does not exist in the world; it exists only in the eye of the beholder" (Thompson, 1985, p. 196). Our ability to convert reflected wavelengths of light into colors that allow us to differentiate (and sort) objects, represents an absolutely crucial adaptation with tremendous evolutionary importance. When color is equally available as a perceptual cue, it seems reasonable to expect it to be used unless one is explicitly directed to avoid it, if possible. In fact, on the Rorschach cards to which Tien refers occasionally, where color and form are both available, Lezak (1976, p. 290) states that "the number of form responses that also take into account color is likely to be one per record for brain damaged patients, whereas normal subjects typically produce more than one FC response."

Related to problems regarding color perception is Tien's total reliance on "gestalt perceptual ability" to indicate "the intact central nervous system" (1965, p. 5). This appears to be founded, perhaps indirectly, upon some misconceptions or, at least, misapplications of gestalt psychology. "Gestalt" most closely refers to form or configuration in the sense that the whole is different from the sum of its parts. It stands as a view of perception that is opposed to perception of entities as separate, independent components to be collected or summed—it does not stand in similar opposition to color perception (Gilinsky, 1984). Additionally, it seems that Tien is close to, if not actually taking, the dated view known as the "principle of isomorphism" that was prevalent among gestalt psychologists years ago, but has been left behind as "modern psychology attempts to analyze perception from quite different standpoints" (Luria, 1973, p. 229). That principle incorrectly postulated structures in the brain which were the basis of sensation and perception by virtue of being absolutely identical with the primary stimuli being received. That is *not* the manner in which human perceptual processes operate. Our perceptions only reflect the actual, physical, and visual events "out there" as we manipulate them for interpretation and meaning (Ludel, 1978). There is no inherent superiority of form present, not in Tien's or any other ambiguous pictures which could predictably produce "correct form" sorting by individuals having intact cerebral functioning while anyone with any brain dysfunction relied upon color categories.

Tien's second assumption, the homogeneity of brain damage, has been without empirical support for many years, beginning at least with Broca's reports in the 1860s, and continuing to the present (Beaumont, 1983; Kolb & Whishaw, 1980; Thompson, 1967). Test performance by individuals with organic brain deficits has not produced the kind of homogeneity that is an absolute prerequisite if any one simple sorting task is to accurately assess "cortical damage due to any brain disease" as Tien claims. Instead, empirical results show the opposite, an incredible variability exists when brain function is assessed through behavioral/psychometric means (Beaumont, 1983; Golden, Hammeke, Purisch, Berg, Moses, Newlin, Wilkening, & Puente, 1982; Haynes & Sells, 1963).

The third assumption made by Tien is implicit and deals with both OIT instructions and form as a unitary, unambiguous dimension inherent in the OIT pictures. As is clear in the instructions, the examinee is at no time cued to exclude color, prefer categories other than color, nor to use the unclear form/function dimension rather than the more visibly clear dimension of color present in all sets of the pictures. In fact, the "bluff-set" may lead the examinee to guess that color is to be used since the pictures to be matched are identical not just in form and function, but also in every detail and shade of color. The manual asserts that "the OIT elicits form responses from the subjects only" (p. 5), but the directions in no way support such a claim.

Related to the color dimension of this assumption is the "form" of the ambiguous object. What Tien refers to only as a unitary dimension of "form" seems to include several other dimensions commonly used by individuals as we sort, classify, and categorize our perceptual worlds in order to make sense of that world. How do "function," "set," "movement," "purpose," "familiarity," and untold other schemes that influence our recognition and interpretation processes influence OIT scores? To what extent does the ambiguous instructional cue to tell the examiner "which two pictures are alike" make it possible that the examinee will employ some or all of the other schemes available and not rely upon "form" as in "gestalt perceptual ability"? Such possibilities, generated by both "personal, common sense" and the research literature in psychology, are completely ignored in the OIT manual and its cited research studies.

The final assumption is that paranoid schizophrenia "is an organic brain syndrome." While the "differential diagnosis of schizophrenia from brain damage continues to be a controversial issue in clinical neuropsychology" (Golden, 1981, p. 150), that issue revolves around differential diagnoses, *not* the equivalency of schizophrenia and brain damage. Some schizophrenics are brain damaged, to be sure, but others are definitely not (Golden, 1981). The arguments dealing with the relationship between laterality and brain dysfunction and functional psychiatric states is, as yet, unresolved, with no model or theory having sufficient support to preclude others (Beaumont, 1983), but this by no means supports Tien's claims. In fact, the gap known to exist between organic brain disease and psychiatric disorder is such that Bloom, Lazerson, and Hofstadter (1985, p. 247) probably address Tien's claim as sympathetically as possible when they state that "many psychiatrists . . . believe that the diagnosis of a psychiatric condition should be based on more than simply the exclusion of organic illness." Not only are schizophrenia and organic brain deficits different entities, but they are so different that many clinicians have taken the exclusion of organic dysfunction to indicate the presence of the former in a patient with presenting problems.

In addition to the failure to support his assumptions and provide the prerequisite technical data, Tien repeatedly made a serious methodological error. Only once did the data he claimed as empirical validation for the OIT present data for subjects whose brain damage was supported by anything approximating certainty of independent diagnosis. More often, no specific neurological diagnostic information (established with certainty independent of the author) is even presented. Without considerable corroboration of that type, any claims as to the validity of the OIT are, at best, speculative.

Critique

The OIT is an interesting instrument for one to use in researching certain, limited aspects of neuropsychology as these specific sorting tasks might be indicative of previously unexplored relationships between them and newly emerging areas of understanding in neuropsychology. Its erroneous underlying assumptions, insufficient technical data, and inadequate empirical base, combined with the author's highly speculative (but nonetheless emphatic) and unsupported claims, make the OIT inappropriate for its recommended use as a screening instrument. In fact, Lezak's (1976, p. 398) conclusion upon reviewing the lack of empirical documentation for sorting tests (among which the OIT was specifically listed) seems very appropriate here: "This does not invalidate sorting tests except for screening purposes." Such tests, then, are invalid for just the purpose most emphasized by Tien for the OIT.

It is of considerable concern to this reviewer that Tien has not updated his claims in response to the tremendous amount of new information that has been reported in the last several years. Instead, he states his claims as if they are universally unchallenged and accepted throughout the field of neuropsychology—when, in fact, many have been repudiated effectively. Given the tremendous advances in clinical neuropsychology, it is disconcerting that unsubstantiated assumptions and claims which are 15-20 years old should still be presented as unassailable. In this reviewer's opinion, the OIT should not be viewed as a viable diagnostic or screening instrument for detecting organic brain dysfunction, although a trained neuropsychologist might find it useful as a "warm-up or icebreaker" instrument.

References

This list includes text citations as well as suggested additional reading.

Beaumont, J. G. (1983). *Introduction to neuropsychology.* New York: The Guilford Press.

Bloom, F. E., Lazerson, A., & Hofstadter, L. (1985). *Brain, mind, and behavior.* New York: W. H. Freeman and Co.

DeRenzi, E., Pieczuro, A., Savoiardo, M., & Vignolo, L. A. (1966). The influence of aphasia and of the hemisphere side of the cerebral lesion on abstract thinking. *Cortex, 2,* 399.

Dimond, S. J., & Beaumont, J. G. (Eds.). (1974). *Hemisphere function in the human brain.* London: Elek Science.

Filskov, S. B., & Boll, T. J. (Eds.). (1981). *Handbook of clinical neuropsychology.* New York: Wiley-Interscience.

Gaddes, W. H. (1980). *Learning disabilities and brain function: A neuropsychological approach.* New York: Springer-Verlag.

Gilinsky, A. S. (1984). *Mind and brain: Principles of neuropsychology.* New York: Praeger Publications.

Golden, C. J. (1979). *Clinical interpretation of objective psychological tests.* New York: Grune & Stratton.

Golden, C. J. (1981). *Diagnosis and rehabilitation in clinical neuropsychology* (2nd ed.). Springfield, IL: Charles C. Thomas.

Golden, C. J., Hammeke, T. A., Purisch, A. D., Berg, R. A., Moses, J. A., Jr., Newlin, D. B., Wilkening, G. N., & Puente, A. E. (1982). *Item interpretation of the Luria-Nebraska Neuropsychological Battery.* Lincoln, NE: University of Nebraska Press.

Haynes, J. R., & Sells, S. B. (1963). Assessment of organic brain damage by psychological tests. *Psychological Bulletin, 60,* 316-325.

Kolb, B., & Whishaw, I. Q. (1980). *Fundamentals of human neuropsychology.* San Francisco, CA: W. H. Freeman and Co.

Lezak, M. D. (1976). *Neuropsychological assessment.* New York: Oxford University Press.

Ludel, J. (1978). *Introduction to sensory processes.* San Francisco, CA: W. H. Freeman and Co.
Luria, A. R. (1973). *The working brain.* New York: Basic Books.
Luria, A. R. (1980). *Higher cortical functions in man* (2nd ed.). New York: Basic Books.
McFie, J., & Percy, M. F. (1952). Intellectual impairment with localized cerebral lesions. *Brain, 75,* 292.
McFie, J. (1975). *Assessment of organic intellectual impairment.* London: Academic Press.
Parker, J. W. (1957). The validity of some current tests for organicity. *Journal of Consulting Psychology, 21,* 425.
Reitan, R. M. (1972). Organic Integrity Test. In O. K. Buros (Ed.), *The seventh mental measurements yearbook* (pp. 282-283). Highland Park, NJ: The Gryphon Press.
Russell, E. W., Neuringer, C., & Goldstein, G. (1970). *Assessment of brain damage: A neuropsychological key approach.* New York: John Wiley.
Snelbecker, G. E., Sherman, L. J., & Schwab, E. L., Jr. (1968). Validation of the Organic Integrity Test. *Perceptual and Motor Skills, 27,* 427-430.
Thompson, R. F. (1967). *Foundations of physiological psychology.* New York: Harper & Row.
Thompson, R. F. (1985). *The brain: An introduction to neuroscience.* New York: W. H. Freeman and Co.
Tien, H. C. (1965). *Tien's OIT Organic Integrity Test.* East Lansing, MI: Psychodiagnostic Test Company.
Tien, H. C. (1968). Organic Integrity Test (OIT) as an empirical guide in the treatment of schizophrenia. *The British Journal of Psychiatry, 114*(512), 871-875.
Watts, C. C., & Haerer, A. F. (1970). The Organic Integrity Test evaluated. *Journal of Clinical Psychology, 26*(1), 77.

Thomas S. Serwatka, Ph.D.
Director, Special Education, and Associate Professor, College of Education and Human Services, University of North Florida, Jacksonville, Florida.

PICTURE SPONDEE THRESHOLD TEST

Paul Waryas and Gail Gudmundsen. Allen, Texas: DLM Teaching Resources.

Introduction

The Picture Spondee Threshold Test (PSTT) is a form of speech reception threshold (SRT) test designed for use with populations who are difficult to test. SRT tests are used to determine what is the lowest decible or loudness level at which individuals can hear 50% of the words presented to them from a list of spondees (i.e., two-syllable words with equal accent on both syllables). In particular, the PSTT was designed to be used with populations that have difficulty using standard SRT test procedures. These populations include young children; persons with specific speech impairments; persons who are diagnosed as being developmentally delayed, mentally retarded, aphasic, or cerebral palsied; persons who use dialects that are difficult to understand; persons who have had a laryngectomy; and specific groups of geriatric persons. The alternate procedure used in the PSTT to accommodate the needs of individuals from these populations is that of having the respondent point to a picture representing the spondee as opposed to orally repeating the spondee back to the examiner.

The PSTT was developed in order to offer clinicians a standard set of pictures and spondees to use in following the above described procedure when giving a SRT test. The procedure itself has been suggested in the literature for a number of years (Martin, 1978), but until the development of the PSTT, clinicians had to find their own pictures and select which of the available spondee lists to use if they chose to implement this procedure.

The authors of the PSTT, Paul A. Waryas and Gail I. Gudmundsen, have both practical and research experience in the area of audiological assessment for difficult-to-test populations. Waryas serves on the faculty at the University of Houston. He has been a research associate at the University of Kansas and has been on the faculty at the University of Mississippi. Gudmundsen is an audiologist in private practice and an adjunct faculty member at both Northern Illinois and Rush Universities. She also serves as an external practicum supervisor at Northwestern University.

The PSTT kit contains two identical sets of clearly drawn picture cards. Each card represents one of the 25 spondees selected for use in the test. One set of cards is used as a source for the correct picture; the other set is used as a source for the foils used in each test item. The 25 spondees selected for use were taken from three of the most commonly used lists of spondees. The words were selected based on their ease of transfer to visual form and their low vocabulary level.

The test kit also contains an administration manual for the test (Waryas & Gudmundsen, 1983). The manual is written in a format that is easily understood by professionals in the field of audiology. It gives information on administration and scoring of the test. In the center of the manual there is a reproducible data sheet for recording and scoring clients' responses.

It is suggested in the manual that two persons are needed to administer the test. The audiologist actually presents the words while a second person sits in the sound booth with the client and arranges the pictures for each test item.

Practical Applications/Uses

The PSTT is designed to be used by audiologists when testing individuals who have difficulty in giving oral responses for any of a number of reasons. As with all SRT tests, the PSTT is meant to be used as an individually administered test. Administration of the test requires an audiometer, equipped for live-voice presentation, and the use of a sound booth. According to the authors (Waryas & Gudmundsen, 1983), the second person does not have to be professionally trained and can be a parent or aid.

The first step in administering the PSTT is determining which of the 25 words the client knows receptively. To make this determination, the client is presented with each of the 25 words at a decibel level sufficient to guarantee that the client will clearly hear it. Words or spondees that the client is able to identify during this pretest are then used in the actual test situation.

In administering the PSTT an ascending presentation of the words is suggested by the authors. When using this type of presentation, spondees are initially presented at a decibel level well below the client's threshold. The audiologist then continues to present each set of spondees at increasingly louder decibel levels until the client is able to identify correctly at least two out of four of the spondees at a given decibel level. After a recheck, this decibel reading becomes the client's speech reception threshold level.

During the administration the person sitting in the booth with the client is responsible for correctly arranging the response picture cards and the three foil picture cards for each test item. A copy of the data sheet is given to this person as a guide.

The actual scoring of the data sheet is a process that is ongoing during the test administration. Using this form should pose no difficulty for a trained audiologist.

The more difficult part of administering the test rests with the person in the booth. Quickly organizing and arranging the pictures in the format suggested in the manual and on the data sheet and doing so without giving subtle indicators as to which picture is the correct picture may require skills more sophisticated than the manual suggests. The use of members of the client's family for this role ought to be discouraged because of tendencies to give the client clues as to which is the correct response in unintentional ways.

The authors give no indication as to the estimated time needed to administer this test. However, 20-30 minutes is probably a reasonable estimate.

Technical Aspects

Although face validity of the PSTT appears strong, no data are given on construct or concurrent validity. Likewise, no data are given on the reliability or internal consistency of the test. Studies on the use of this test with the various populations for which it has been designed would be helpful to the audiologist in determining whether to use the test or not. Studies comparing the administration of the test using an ascending method of presentation as opposed to the often recommended descending method (Northern & Downs, 1974; Newby & Popelka, 1985) would be helpful also.

Critique

The PSTT provides audiologists with an alternative to spending time finding their own pictures and selecting their own word lists when testing individuals who are difficult to test using standard procedures. Although audiologists may appreciate having this alternative, they might well appreciate two changes in the test format. First, by limiting the words to the 25 low-vocabulary-level spondees selected, the resulting pictures have taken on a child-like appearance. This child-like appearance makes these pictures less than ideal for use with adult populations. A second list of spondees and corresponding pictures could solve this problem.

The second change in format that would improve the test would make it easier to administer. If picture cards that had the correct response and the three foils on the same card were developed, this would make the job of the second person considerably easier. It would also limit the possibility of nonverbally cuing the client on which is the correct response. This would increase the number of cards necessary to include in the kit, but it seems worth the cost and effort.

For audiologists who prefer a descending method of presentation, the test is easily adaptable. It would cause an audiologist no difficulty whatsoever to use the kit in this manner.

References

Martin, F. N. (1978). Speech tests of hearing: Age one through five years. In F. N. Martin (Ed.), *Pediatric audiology* (pp. 236-264). Englewood Cliffs, NJ: Prentice-Hall.

Newby, H. A., & Popelka, G. R. (1985). *Audiology* (5th ed.). Englewood Cliffs, NJ: Prentice-Hall.

Northern, J. J., & Downs, M. P. (1974). *Hearing in children.* Baltimore: Williams & Wilkins.

Waryas, P., & Gudmundsen, G. (1983). *Picture Spondee Threshold Test.* Allen, TX: DLM Teaching Resources.

David G. Ward, Ph.D.

Assistant Professor of Psychology, Fordham University, Bronx, New York.

POLYFACTORIAL STUDY OF PERSONALITY

Ronald H. Stark. Larchmont, New York: Martin M. Bruce, Ph.D., Publishers.

Introduction

The Polyfactorial Study of Personality (PFSP; Stark, 1959) is an objective personality inventory designed to assess ideational disturbance and provide information similar to what might be obtained using projective tests. The 300 items in true-false format yield a profile of 11 scales: Hypochondriasis (physical complaints), Sexual Identification (homosexuality), Anxiety, Social Distance (introversion and withdrawal), Sociopathy (antisocial thought), Depression, Compulsivity (rigid thinking), Repression (emotional instability), Paranoia (excessive sensitivity and suspiciousness), Schizophrenia (bizarre and distant thinking), and Hyperaffectivity (manic symptoms). Norms are provided.

Ronald H. Stark is the author of the PFSP, which was designed in part to improve on other objective personality instruments, such as the Minnesota Multiphasic Personality Inventory (MMPI). The specific problems of the MMPI are described in the examiner's manual as excessive length, unclear items, inappropriateness for normal subjects, and insensitivity to various degrees of ideational disturbance. In addition, it states that "its rationale is purely statistical and empirical, but disregards clinical considerations" (Stark, 1959, p. 2).

In constructing the PFSP, 400 items were selected from existing paper-and-pencil personality inventories, then modified. Items were selected based on 1) "purity of factor-analytic relationship with other items in the same nosological category" and 2) "degree of correlation with the criteria and absence of correlation with items in the same category" (Stark, 1959, pp. 2-3). In addition, 300 new items were created, and the selected items were administered to new samples, followed by more item analysis. The final criterion was the factor purity of the item. The criteria included the Rorschach, the House-Tree-Person Test (H-T-P), the clinical scales of the MMPI, and diagnoses based on interviews. Based on their "diagnostic efficiency" and tested against independent diagnoses, 86 "validated" Rorschach indices and 24 "validated" H-T-P indices served as criteria. Correlations between each item and each criterion were computed, as were multiple correlations for each criterion, in which all Rorschach criteria were given double weight. These correlations were used in the factor analyses for item selection.

Discriminant function analysis was used in assigning weights for erasures, marks, and omissions of items when scoring. According to the manual, using analysis of multiple classification variance and Tukey's test for comparing individual means, there were no significant differences between males and females, except on the Sexual Identification Scale. When reverse scoring was used for females, there were no significant sex differences.

Populations employed in developing the PFSP included hospitalized patients, prison inmates, outpatients in therapy, and normals. The 224 hospitalized patients included 47 manic depressives, depressed type; 23 manic depressives, manic type; 83 paranoid schizophrenics; and 71 functional psychotics, unclassified. The range of hospitalization was six months to nine years, with a mean of 3.1 years. About one third of the patients were female. There were 555 prison inmates, all male: 86 convicted for public homosexual acts; 144 convicted of misdemeanors involving violence; 172 convicted of felonies involving violence; and 153 drug addicts. Almost all the prisoners were repeat offenders.

The 302 outpatients consisted of 22 neurotics, primarily hypochondriacal; 65 unclassified neurotics, primarily hysterical; 28 with a diagnosis of neurotic depression; 36 nonneurotic psychopaths, sociopathics, and character disorders; 72 compulsives, obsessives, and obsessive-compulsive neurotics; 38 borderline psychotics; and 41 unclassified ambulatory psychotics, prepsychotics, and psychotics. The outpatients were in psychotherapy at either a Veterans Administration Hospital, a public agency, or one of two private agencies. All were in therapy less than six months, with a mean of 4.1 months, and approximately one-fourth were female. The 2,576 normals consisted of 216 white-collar and midmanagement employees, half of whom were male, and 2,360 applicants for white-collar and middle-management positions of unspecified sex.

The test itself consists of a seven-page booklet containing 300 items in true-false format, similar to those in the MMPI. Responses are recorded on a one-page answer sheet. Intended for adults, the PFSP is self-administering and is easily completed in about 45 minutes. The 11 scale scores may be plotted in standard score form for a visual representation of the profile. The normative data are based on a sample of 2,560 adults, half male, half female. The same norms are used for both sexes, with the exception of the Sexual Identification Scale, which is reversed for females.

Practical Applications/Uses

The PFSP was primarily designed to assess ideational disturbances and give diagnostic information such as might be provided by the Rorschach and other projective tests. The PFSP might be considered for use in hospitals, prisons, outpatient clinics, and counseling and personnel settings by psychiatrists, psychologists, and personnel specialists. The PFSP appears to be designed for a wide range of adult subjects from normals to the seriously disturbed. Presumably, the test could be adapted for the blind, to whom the test could be read.

The PFSP was primarily designed as a group test; individual administration is possible, though not encouraged. Administration and scoring may be done by a clerical person. Subjects are told to read the instructions on the front of the booklet, write their names and other identifying information, and answer every item, preferably using a ballpoint pen, which allows easier scoring of erasures and other marks. The administrator is encouraged to ensure that the first few answers are marked properly and to supervise testing. The directions seem clear for the administrator and for the examinee.

For scoring, there are 11 templates, one for each scale. According to Stark (1959), the raw score is the algebraic sum of all weights (one = all visible marks; two = each erasure, answer change, and omission for each scale). The raw scores are converted to standard scores using the table of norms, and standard scores are plotted on the profile. Scoring by hand should not take long, although the answer sheet needs to be scanned visually to detect any erasures, answer changes, and omissions. Such findings increase scoring time, especially in assigning weights. Because the answers are recorded on an IBM sheet, computer scoring could be possible but does not appear to be available.

The manual recommends that interpretation of PFSP scores and content be made only by a psychologist, psychiatrist, or personnel specialist trained in personality dynamics, such as in Rorschach interpretation, and that no one scale score should be regarded as providing a sole basis for differential diagnosis. Certain scale combinations are suggested as representing particular diagnostic categories. For example, high Sexual Identification and Hyperaffectivity scores may indicate acting out of homosexual impulses. The degree of sophistication and training needed to interpret the PFSP properly appears to be considerably high.

Technical Aspects

The validity of the PFSP may be addressed in the following manner. The face validity of the items appears similar to that of the MMPI and other such instruments in terms of assessing the kinds of personality aspects that the scales purport to measure.

The validity statistics reported in the manual are based on a sample of 2,000 people, half of whom were institutionalized in either a psychiatric hospital or a prison. Although this sample is quite large, further description of the sample would be helpful because it is not clear if this sample was part of the sample used in constructing the PFSP. The author (Stark, 1959) reports that the content validity of the PFSP is demonstrated by the pattern of scale intercorrelations between 1) PFSP scales, 2) the PFSP and corresponding MMPI scales, and 3) the PFSP and the Association Adjustment Inventory (AAI). Such relationships may be more properly used to evaluate the convergent and discriminant validity of the scales rather than their content validity.

Within the PFSP, there are significant positive correlations between Anxiety and Hypochondriasis, Compulsivity, and Repression; between Paranoia and Hypochondriasis, compulsivity, and Schizophrenia; and between Depression and Social Distance and Schizophrenia. There are significant negative correlations between Sociopathy and Anxiety, Compulsivity, and Social Distance, and between Depression and Hyperaffectivity. A similar pattern of scale intercorrelations is shown between the PFSP and the MMPI; the range of corresponding scale correlations is from .23 to .81. Correlations between the PFSP and the AAI, both of which were standardized on the same sample, range from .59 to .84 for corresponding scales.

Criterion-related validity statistics are not provided in the manual, though the manual states that 86 validated Rorschach indices and 24 validated H-T-P indices were the criteria.

The reliability of the PFSP was assessed using a test-retest interval of one week on a sample of 400 male prison inmates (age range: 17 to 22 years). The reliability coefficients range from .699 for Anxiety to .927 for Schizophrenia, with a median of .841. The manual states that "a prison population appeared to be a compromise between a normal population and an institutionalized psychotic population" (Stark, 1959, p. 7). Without further information about the characteristics of the prison sample, it is difficult to evaluate its adequacy. Further, it is not known to what extent, if any, reliabilities differ for normals, institutionalized psychotics, or other diagnostic groups.

Critique

In evaluating the Polyfactorial Study of Personality, it is difficult to improve on the incisive reviews provided by Cohen (1965), Peterson (1965), and Bordin (1960, 1965). For example, Cohen (1965, p. 350) states that although compared to the MMPI, the PFSP is shorter and has more clearly and simply worded items, "it is difficult, at this stage of development, to see how the PFSP represents an effective improvement over its major competitor." Further, in explaining the validity of the PFSP scales in terms of their intercorrelations, Cohen notes that there is considerable item overlap between the correlated scales. For example, the correlation between Hypochondriasis and Anxiety is $r = .42$, which is not surprising because the two scales share 25 items in common.

More fundamentally, Cohen notes that the manual does not specify the relationships between PFSP scales and the projective test scores and diagnostic criteria used in constructing the test. That the PFSP and MMPI scales are correlated in expected patterns follows because items were modified from the MMPI, and the MMPI was a criterion measure. Cohen also notes that the PFSP does not correct for test-taking attitudes (e.g., defensiveness) as do the MMPI and other personality inventories. Finally, the numerous spelling errors in the manual may lead one to question other information, such as in tables.

Peterson (1965) questions the methods of test construction, namely the unspecified populations used in item preselection and the ability to have items that have pure factor-analytic relationships, yet are uncorrelated with other items in the same scale. Peterson notes that the "validated" Rorschach and H-T-P indices were not specifically stated to be cross-validated. In general, there is lack of specification of the means of scale validation. The test was constructed using 1,081 subjects in 15 clinical groups and 2,576 "normal" white-collar employees and job applicants, but it is not clear how many or which ones were used to develop which scales, nor is it specified whether all subjects took all tests (Peterson, 1965, p. 351).

Peterson notes that the particular factor analytic procedures, such as the extraction method, determination of number of factors, and rotation procedures (if any), are not specified. The voluminous tables and other validational statistics that might help answer these important questions do not appear to have been published elsewhere. The correlations between the PFSP and the AAI follow because both are self-report measures standardized on the same sample; Peterson notes that such evidence does not indicate a common factor of "ideational disturbance" without further validation. The validity of the PFSP for predicting other criteria, such as job success, is unknown.

In summarizing his review, Peterson states: "Indeed it is difficult to see what purpose the test can serve that is not already served better by an existing instrument" (p. 351). Such tests as the MMPI, the California Personality Inventory, the factor analytic instruments such as Cattell's Sixteen Personality Factor Questionnaire, and the Rorschach are well-researched and may provide desired information. Peterson concludes that the PFSP may be of research use, though the catalog and manual do not present it in this light.

Bordin (1965, p. 352) concludes his brief review: "Why was this test issued after so little developmental analysis?"

Other questions concern the lack of a definition of "ideational disturbance." It is not specified if the normative sample (2,560 adults, half of whom are male) is the same as the "normal" sample used in test construction, a sample that is of unspecified racial and ethnic composition and of questionable representativeness. Although the intended goal of the PFSP may be valuable, the lack of clear validation and the ambiguous means of construction make it of limited current use. A review of the psychological literature found no published reports of its application or employment. To quote from the author: "The history of paper and pencil personality tests covers scores of instruments, but few of them are based on thorough statistical procedures" (Stark, 1959, p. 2). In this reviewer's opinion, this statement applies to the PFSP as it is currently designed.

References

Bordin, E. S. (1960). Review of the Polyfactorial Study of Personality. *Journal of Consulting and Clinical Psychology, 24,* 100.

Bordin, E. S. (1965). Review of the Polyfactorial Study of Personality. In O. K. Buros (Ed.), *The sixth mental measurements yearbook* (p. 352). Highland Park, NJ: The Gryphon Press.

Cohen, B. D. (1965). Review of the Polyfactorial Study of Personality. In O. K. Buros (Ed.), *The sixth mental measurements yearbook* (pp. 349-350). Highland Park, NJ: The Gryphon Press.

Peterson, D. R. (1965). Review of the Polyfactorial Study of Personality. In O. K. Buros (Ed.), *The sixth mental measurements yearbook* (pp. 350-352). Highland Park, NJ: The Gryphon Press.

Stark, R. H. (1959). *Polyfactorial Study of Personality.* Larchmont, NJ: Martin M. Bruce, Ph.D., Publishers.

Harold R. Miller, Ph.D.
Clinical Psychologist, Hamilton Psychiatric Hospital, and Associate Professor of Psychiatry (Psychology), McMaster University, Hamilton, Ontario, Canada.

PSYCHIATRIC DIAGNOSTIC INTERVIEW

Ekkehard Othmer, Elizabeth C. Penick, and Barbara J. Powell. Los Angeles, California: Western Psychological Services.

Introduction

The purpose of the Psychiatric Diagnostic Interview (PDI) is "to determine whether an individual is suffering from, or has ever suffered from, an established psychiatric disorder" (Othmer, Penick, & Powell, 1981, p. 1). The PDI is a structured interview that provides information relevant to the operationalized criteria used to define the presence of a variety of disorders. The criteria are modifications of those of Feighner et al. (1972).

In addition, the authors wanted an instrument that would provide longitudinal data regarding a person's psychiatric history, could be easily administered by lay personnel, and possessed adequate reliability and validity. After reviewing the various diagnostic procedures that were available, the authors concluded that none met these requirements. Consequently, in 1973, they began an eight-year effort to develop their own, drawing heavily on their experience with criterion-based diagnosis from Washington University. The PDI is the culmination of their efforts and identifies 12 basic disorders and syndromes: organic brain syndrome, alcoholism, drug dependency, mania, depression, schizophrenia, antisocial personality, hysteria/somatization/briquet syndrome, anorexia nervosa, obsessive-compulsive neurosis, phobic neurosis, and panic attack syndrome. In addition, it reviews three derived syndromes (polydrug abuse, schizoaffective disorder, and manic-depressive disorder) and three optional syndromes (mental retardation, homosexuality, and transsexualism).

A disorder, or syndrome, is defined as present if a series of criteria specific to it are met, and absent if they are not. Syndromes are independent of one another; a person may meet the criteria for a variety of different syndromes simultaneously. The three derived syndromes are obtained from combinations of the 12 basic syndromes, and the three optional syndromes are administered at the examiner's discretion. A final PDI category, Undiagnosed Psychiatric Disorder, classifies established psychiatric problems that are not otherwise identified by the PDI.

Each of the 12 basic and three optional syndrome are reviewed independently by asking a series of questions that are divided into four sections. The number of questions vary greatly from syndrome to syndrome but, for the most part, lend themselves to "yes/no" answers. *Cardinal* questions are asked first; these refer to critical events or symptoms that must always be present to define the presence of a particular syndrome. If these cardinal criteria are not met, the interviewer abandons the remaining questions for that particular syndrome and proceeds to the cardinal questions of the next syndrome. However, if these criteria are met, the interviewer proceeds to the next set of questions that deal with the *social significance* of the symptoms identified in the cardinal section. (However, the organic brain syndrome section has no social significance questions.) These questions provide information about the degree to which the symptoms interfered with or disrupted the respondent's life. If the symptoms have not been disruptive (i.e., if the social significance criteria are not met), the interviewer stops reviewing that syndrome and proceeds to the next. *Auxiliary* questions are asked if the social significance criteria have been met. They review the problems that have been identified in considerable detail by asking about additional symptoms or situations that are usually a part of the complete syndrome. A respondent must have experienced a variety of these to meet criteria for the auxiliary section. A syndrome is not positively identified unless the criteria for each of the cardinal, social significance, and auxiliary sections have been met. Once the presence of a syndrome has been established, *time profile* questions define a syndrome's date of onset, its duration, and whether or not it is currently active.

Questions for the PDI are conveniently organized by syndrome in a reusable spiral-bound booklet. The interviewer records the respondent's answers in a separate recording booklet. In most cases, the interviewer simply blackens the appropriate circle in the recording booklet when the response to a question is "yes"; verbatim or summarized responses to the interview questions are not needed. Each syndrome is self-scoring; separate scoring materials are not required. The recording booklet also contains test materials used in assessing the organic brain syndrome (geometric forms to be reproduced by the respondent and a figure identification task); a time profile chart, which visually presents the onset and durations of all syndromes that have been identified for a respondent; and a face sheet for recording basic demographic information, the respondent's chief complaints and symptoms, a summary of the respondent's treatment history, and the differential diagnosis obtained from the PDI. Some of this information is obtained in an initial discussion with the patient when the interviewer is developing rapport and assessing whether the respondent is capable of completing the formal interview. The remaining information is recorded at the conclusion of the interview.

Practical Applications/Uses

The PDI is designed to identify psychiatric syndromes in an adult psychiatric population. It is of interest to anyone who wants to use a structured, criterion-based diagnostic procedure to do this. The authors suggest a variety of clinical, research, and educational applications, including screening patients to establish the presence or absence of psychiatric difficulties, defining research groups, and teaching students to identify and distinguish major psychiatric disorders and their distinctive features.

The lower age limit for the PDI is 18 years; therefore, it should not be used with adolescents younger than this or with children. It has no upper age limit, making it appropriate for use throughout the adult life span. Respondents who are cooperative, able to concentrate, and capable of sitting through a sometimes lengthy interview are suitable for the PDI, whereas those who are confused, agitated, uncooperative, or unable to understand the questions will be unable to complete it. The PDI is available only in English.

The PDI is administered in an individual interview, the length of which varies considerably depending on the number of syndromes that must be reviewed completely and the loquaciousness of the respondent. Those with no or only one syndrome present can often complete the PDI in as little as 15 minutes, whereas multisyndrome respondents may take an hour or more. Professional training is not required to administer the PDI, although training and supervised experience with the interview is. The manual's basic instructions are clear, although the addition of verbatim examples of the proper scoring of difficult or vague responses would be helpful. If necessary, the interviewer is instructed to ask for examples and clarifications until enough information is obtained to score a response confidently. Questions may also be reworded, provided the essential element of the question is retained. This provides the interviewer with flexibility and may make the interview more comfortable for the respondent. However, it may increase the subjectivity of the interview and subtly alter the intent of a particular question, thereby changing the meaning of the data that are obtained. Familiarity with each syndrome and its questions will help avoid this. A skillful and creative interviewer is apt to obtain more data from a vague or tangential patient than is one who sticks closely to the PDI's established format.

Because each syndrome is reviewed independently of the others and there are no exclusionary criteria, one respondent may meet the criteria for several different syndromes. However, this becomes a problem if a single differential diagnosis is desired. To deal with the multisyndrome respondent, the authors have developed a hierarchical system of differential diagnosis based on the premise that some syndromes take precedence over others. Three general considerations were used to order the 12 basic and three derived syndromes into a diagnostic hierarchy: the ability of one syndrome to mimic another, the degree of personal distress caused by the syndrome, and the extent to which one's life is disrupted by the syndrome. In most cases, the placement of a syndrome in the hierarchy is obvious, although some are placed arbitrarily based on the authors' clinical judgment and experience.

The four syndromes that are highest in the hierarchical system (organic brain syndrome, polydrug abuse, alcoholism, and drug dependency, respectively) are considered masking disorders. Because these syndromes can mimic the symptomatology of a variety of other disorders, the authors maintain that no other differential diagnosis can be made confidently if a masking syndrome is present. Consequently, a masking syndrome takes diagnostic precedence over any other syndrome below it. The remaining syndromes, in order of hierarchical priority, are schizoaffective disorder, manic-depressive disorder, mania, depression, schizophrenia, antisocial personality, hysteria/somatization/briquet syndrome, anorexia nervosa, obsessive-compulsive neurosis, phobic neurosis, and panic attack syndrome. If no masking syndrome is present, then the syndrome highest in the hierarchy becomes the differential diagnosis, regardless of the number of additional syndromes that have been identified. The optional syndromes of mental retardation, homosexuality, and transsexualism are not included in the differential diagnostic hierarchy.

Two diagnoses are available from the PDI: a current diagnosis and a lifetime diagnosis. The current diagnosis is defined as the syndrome highest in the differential diagnostic hierarchy that occurred in the two years immediately preceding the PDI interview, whereas the lifetime diagnosis is that syndrome highest in the diagnostic hierarchy that occurred at any time during the respondent's lifetime. The syndrome identified as the lifetime diagnosis must have preceded a masking syndrome by at least two years or continued for at least two years following the termination of a masking syndrome; otherwise the masking syndrome becomes the lifetime diagnosis. That is, a masking syndrome that is the lifetime diagnosis will have occurred within two years of the onset or cessation of another syndrome, thereby taking precedence over it in the diagnostic hierarchy.

It is important to note that users of the PDI are not restricted to the use of this hierarchical system to arrive at a differential diagnosis. Because all of the syndromes for which a respondent has met criteria are listed in the recording booklet, these data can be used in a variety of ways. However, normative data regarding current or lifetime diagnoses will not be applicable unless the hierarchical system has been followed.

The syndromes defined by the PDI are not strictly compatible with those disorders defined by the DSM-III (American Psychiatric Association, 1980). The PDI is most comparable to the descriptive diagnostic criteria of Feighner et al. (1972). The authors do provide information on the closest DSM-III equivalents to PDI syndromes and indicate that those respondents who meet PDI criteria for a syndrome usually meet the DSM-III criteria as well. Because the PDI criteria are frequently more stringent than the DSM-III criteria, the opposite is not necessarily the case. The publisher (R. A. Zachary, personal communication, August 29, 1985) indicates that a revision of the PDI is currently in progress and will, among other things, "conform more closely to existing DSM-III criteria." This should increase the attractiveness and relevance of the PDI in situations where DSM-III diagnoses are desired.

Technical Aspects

After the decision was made to develop an instrument that would identify the syndromes recognized by Feighner et al. (1972), items were rationally and intuitively developed from a variety of data sources, including symptom checklists, other existing interviews, and clinical descriptions of various syndromes. Psychiatric patients then reviewed these preliminary items to eliminate those that were irrelevant to the patients' personal experiences, were ambiguous or vague, and could not be confirmed through actual behavioral examples. Patients were also asked to suggest ways of rewording or otherwise improving the items.

The authors provide no information regarding how many items were originally considered for each syndrome or how many were eliminated at each of these steps. They indicate that at least 20 patients were used to verify items for those syndromes frequently seen in clinical settings, although they specify neither the specific syndromes nor the number of verification subjects used for each. For less common syndromes, such as anorexia nervosa or transsexualism, at least two "pure" representatives of the syndromes were used to verify the items, although the authors do not specify how these representatives were selected. It is not clear how the authors decided what items to include in the cardinal section of each syndrome; presumably this was done on a rational basis. Most items that are specific to standards from Feighner et al.'s (1972) criteria appear in the auxiliary sections.

The following reliability and validity studies were conducted by the authors during the PDI's developmental years. Unfortunately, they used a preliminary version of the PDI. After these studies were completed, 32 items were added to increase compatability between PDI syndromes and their DSM-III counterparts; these are listed in the manual. The additional items did not change the scoring criteria except in drug dependency where the criteria became more stringent. The authors indicate that the additional items resulted in no diagnostic changes in 98% of the cases used in the reliability and validity studies and suggest that the two versions of the PDI are highly comparable. Nonetheless, the current version has not been investigated, and the data reported in the manual refer to a somewhat different interview schedule. The following studies are summarized with these qualifications in mind.

According to Othmer et al. (1981), interrater reliability of the preliminary PDI was examined by asking six mental-health professionals who had modest previous experience with the PDI to independently score videotaped PDI interviews with four different psychiatric patients. The raters showed perfect agreement in scoring syndromes as present or absent and in determining both the current and lifetime diagnoses for each patient. Approximately three months later, four of the six original raters again viewed two of these interviews, which were randomly selected, to determine intrarater reliability. There were no scoring differences from the first to the second interviews. All of the PDI items were administered to each of the respondents in these interviews; the interviewers did not have the opportunity of abandoning a syndrome and proceeding to the next when criteria were not met.

In an examination of test-retest reliability, 38 psychiatric patients were given the PDI on two separate occasions by different interviewers who had no knowledge of previous PDI results. The test-retest intervals were quite variable, ranging from 11 days to three months, although they averaged six weeks. A nonsignificant reduction in the mean number of syndromes identified from the first to the second administration (2.3 to 2.1 syndromes) and a correlation of .75 between the total number of syndromes identified on each administration were found. Cohen's kappa (Cohen, 1960) was used to assess the stability of current and lifetime diagnoses across both testings. This statistic provides an index of degree of agreement after allowing for the base rates in each category and controlling for agreements due to chance. Kappas of .93 for current diagnosis and .85 lifetime diagnosis were obtained. However, no patients met criteria for either current or lifetime diagnosis of hysteria, anorexia nervosa, obsessive-compulsive neurosis, phobic neurosis, panic attack syndrome, mental retardation, homosexuality, or transsexualism. In addition, the drug dependency and polydrug abuse syndromes and the mania, depression, manic-depressive disorder, and schizoaffective disorder syndromes were combined because relatively few patients met the diagnostic criteria for each separate syndrome. Recomputing kappa without these combinations results in .72 for current diagnosis and .67 for lifetime diagnosis.

When the PDI was administered to two samples of 59 and 67 psychiatric inpatients, respectively, drawn from the same general population, the authors found a highly similar pattern of current and lifetime diagnoses emerged; rank-order correlations of .99 between the two samples were obtained for both current and lifetime diagnoses. Again, however, these results are attenuated by highly variable numbers in the various diagnostic categories. In the first sample, alcoholism, schizoaffective disorder, mania, and depression account for 68% of the current diagnoses, whereas alcoholism, manic-depressive disorder, and schizoaffective disorder account for the same percentage of lifetime diagnoses. Similar results are seen in the second sample, with the same four syndromes accounting for 65% of the current diagnoses and the same three syndromes accounting for 61% of the lifetime diagnoses.

Validity of the PDI has been assessed in a variety of ways. First, it appears to be sensitive to the extent of psychiatric disturbance. The PDI identified a mean of 2.51 syndromes in a group of 71 psychiatric inpatients, a mean of 1.85 syndromes in a group of 61 presumably less disturbed psychiatric outpatients, and a mean of .26 syndromes in a group of 70 medical patients with no known psychiatric history. Roughly equal numbers of males and females comprised the three groups.

A psychiatrist, familiar with Feighner et al.'s (1972) criteria, made both current and lifetime diagnoses after reviewing the medical charts of a group of 67 discharged male patients, who had been given the PDI while in an inpatient psychiatric unit. The psychiatrist had no knowledge of the PDI results. Perfect agreement between the rater and the PDI was found in 67.2% of the cases for current diagnosis and 64.2% of the cases for lifetime diagnosis. When partial agreements were considered, which were defined as diagnostic discrepancies that are "generally considered of relatively minor clinical significance" (Othmer et al., 1981, p. 60), the percents agreement rose to 82.1% and 77.6%, respectively. When the psychiatrist was given the opportunity to revise the diagnosis after personally examining those patients for whom no or partial agreement between the PDI and chart review diagnosis was found, the agreement between the PDI and psychiatric diagnosis increased considerably.

In another study (Othmer et al., 1981), relatively pure diagnostic groups were stringently defined to serve as criterion groups for the syndromes of alcoholism, drug dependency, manic-depressive disorder and mania, depression, schizophrenia, antisocial personality, mental retardation, and homosexuality. The remaining syndromes were not included due to their rarity in the settings from which the groups were drawn. Group size ranged from 13 for mental retardation to 31 for drug dependency, with a mean group size of 21. Although only 50% of the antisocial personality group met the PDI's criteria for the antisocial personality syndrome, from 94.7 to 100% of the remaining groups met PDI criteria for their respective syndromes. Current and lifetime diagnoses were not examined, although inspection of the tabular material in the manual suggests that the hierarchical differential diagnosis, as opposed to simply identifying a syndrome as present, would show less agreement with the criterion groups.

The manual reports that the PDI also shows good agreement with an early version of the National Institute of Mental Health's Diagnostic Interview Schedule (DIS; Helzer et al., 1977). Counting matches between current or lifetime diagnosis from the PDI and any DIS diagnosis resulted in percents agreement that ranged from 80% for depression to 100% for organic brain syndrome, homosexuality, and transsexualism. Unfortunately, only 86 patients were studied, and no information is given about the number of patients in each diagnostic category, although it is likely that relatively few patients comprised some of the less frequent syndromes. (Weller et al., 1985, provide similar data using the current version of the PDI and a more recent version of the DIS.)

At first glance, the PDI's reliability and validity results are impressive. However, they are attenuated by several factors. First, as previously mentioned, they were developed on a preliminary version of the PDI and should be confirmed using the current version. Next, many of the studies used relatively small samples. The authors comment that this was done deliberately because the purpose of the PDI is to provide diagnostic information on individuals. However, this begs the point, as the small samples and the restricted range of diagnoses available in the pool of potential subjects resulted in the exclusion of more than half of the diagnostic possibilities in some of the validity studies. Further, percents of agreement may be artificially inflated due to the small number of subjects in some of the diagnostic groups. Finally, in most cases, the majority of the psychiatric patients used in the various studies came from the Veterans Administration Medical Center in Lexington, Kentucky. Tapping additional sources for potential subjects may make a wider variety of diagnostic groups available for study and thus extend the generality of the PDI.

Critique

The PDI is attractive in situations where a reasonably objective, inexpensive screening device for identifying the presence of psychiatric disorders is needed. The efficiency of its step-wise administration format and its ease of administration and scoring are attractive features, and it is generally well-received by respondents. Its manual is well-written and includes a good summary of many issues in psychiatric diagnosis. Unfortunately, the PDI is virtually unmentioned in the published literature, even though it has been available for several years. (Exceptions are Powell et al., 1982, and Weller et al., 1985.) Although this tells nothing about how frequently the PDI is used in clinical practice, it does suggest that it has not been accepted as a viable research tool.

The PDI and other similar instruments will be used to the extent that they provide reliable, accurate information that cannot be obtained in any other way or at least cannot be obtained as easily or efficiently. Essentially, the PDI is a self-report instrument and is subject to the strengths and weaknesses of this source of data. To use the PDI, one assumes that respondents have provided accurate information about themselves. Respondents whose lack of accuracy is suspected in advance should not be assessed with the PDI. Some respondents may exaggerate their symptomatology and even provide reasonable examples when questioned, whereas others may deny certain questions because they actually believe that these questions do not apply to them. In the first case, the PDI will identify syndromes that may not actually be present (false positives), whereas in the second, the PDI may miss syndromes that are present (false negatives). In some situations the cost of these errors may be considerable. It becomes particularly important if the PDI is the sole selection criteria for a research study or if it is used for diagnostic screening of newly hospitalized patients, for example. It is hoped that further research will explore the sensitivity (the ability to identify positive instances) and specificity (the ability to identify negative instances) of the PDI in syndrome identification. Although the authors state that the PDI must be evaluated in the context of other information about a respondent, it seems that many advantages of the PDI are lost if additional resources are needed to develop this.

As noted above, the reliability and validity studies of the PDI done by the authors should be elaborated by other investigators using the current version of the interview, larger samples, and a wider range of diagnostic possibilities. In particular, the PDI needs additional confirmation of its ability to reliably identify independently defined members of "gold standard" criterion groups. The PDI's ability to identify many syndromes was not studied because adequate criterion groups could not be developed from the available pool of subjects. However, if a syndrome is important enough to be included in the PDI, then a criterion group should be established for it. If it is still not possible to develop an adequate criterion group from an expanded pool of potential subjects, then it is questionable whether that syndrome should continue to form a part of the PDI.

As noted, the PDI is a promising instrument for objectively determining the presence of selected psychiatric disorders. It needs to be refined along the lines noted above and would profit from empirical demonstration by independent investigators that it is more accurate or efficient than rival techniques. The publisher (R. A. Zachary, personal communication, August 29, 1985) indicates that a revised version of the PDI is currently being developed, which will include four additional clinical syndromes (bulimia, post-traumatic stress disorder, generalized anxiety, and adjustment disorder), eliminate two of the current optional ones (homosexuality and transsexualism), and be more compatible to the DSM-III. It is hoped that the re-revisions will attend to some of the above difficulties as well. As it stands, the PDI is a potentially useful addition to the existing armamentarium of structured diagnostic interviews, although it should be used cautiously and in conjunction with other sources of information for most purposes at the present time.

References

American Psychiatric Association. (1980). *Diagnostic and statistical manual of mental disorders* (3rd ed.). Washington, DC: Author.

Cohen, J. A. (1960). A coefficient of agreement for nominal scales. *Educational and Psychological Measurement, 20,* 37-46.

Feighner, J. P., Robins, E., Guze, S. B., Woodruff, R. A., Winokur, G., & Munoz, R. (1972). Diagnostic criteria for use in psychiatric research. *Archives of General Psychiatry, 26,* 57-63.

Helzer, J. E., Clayton, P. J., Pambakian, R., Reich, T., Woodruff, R. A., & Reveley, M. A. (1977). Reliability of psychiatric diagnosis: II. The test-retest reliability of diagnostic classification. *Archives of General Psychiatry, 34,* 136-141.

Othmer, E., Penick, E. C., & Powell, B. J. (1981). *Psychiatric Diagnostic Interview (PDI).* Los Angeles: Western Psychological Services.

Powell, B. J., Penick, E. C., Othmer, E., Bingham, S. F., & Rice, A. S. (1982). Prevalence of additional psychiatric syndromes among male alcoholics. *Journal of Clinical Psychiatry, 43,* 404-407.

Weller, R. A., Penick, E. C., Powell, B. J., Othmer, E., Rice, A. S., & Kent, T. A. (1985). Agreement between two structured psychiatric diagnostic interviews: DIS and the PDI. *Comprehensive Psychiatry, 26,* 157-163.

David L. Streiner, Ph.D.
Professor of Psychiatry, Chief Psychologist, McMaster University, Hamilton, Ontario.

PSYCHOLOGICAL SCREENING INVENTORY

Richard I. Lanyon. Port Huron, Michigan: Research Psychologists Press, Inc.

Introduction

The Psychological Screening Inventory (PSI) is a 130-item, true-false, self-report questionnaire designed as a screening device "to be used in detecting persons who might profitably receive more intensive attention" (Lanyon, 1978, p. 3). It is not intended to be a diagnostic instrument but to detect people over the age of 16 who should be referred for more extensive examination or therapy. The PSI can be administered either individually or in a group setting. Although the author recommends not mailing the test out to respondents, he states that "it is reasonable and often practical to have reliable respondents take it away and mail it back" (p. 4).

The author of the PSI, Dr. Richard I. Lanyon, is Professor of Psychology at Arizona State University. The development of this test, which began in 1964, was influenced by two major issues: to answer specific questions that would be raised by a variety of mental-health workers and to assess specific areas that have the greatest predictive value. To attain the first goal, the objective of this test should assist nondoctoral-level mental-health workers in deciding whether a person should be referred for further examination by a psychologist or psychiatrist; it is not designed to help the worker make a differential diagnosis. In regard to the second objective, Lanyon (1978) maintains that the most powerful constructs in psychology are the dimensions of anxiety (also called neuroticism, perceived maladjustment, and discomfort) and extraversion (expression or undercontrol).

Two of the five scales on the PSI—Discomfort (Di) and Expression (Ex)—measure these two dimensions. The other scales are Alienation (Al), Social Nonconformity (Sn), and Defensiveness (De). Because of earlier objections that the De Scale could not adequately differentiate a "faking bad" set from random responding (e.g., Butcher, 1971), a sixth scale, Infrequency or Random Response (Ra), was added. However, it is not scored on the profile sheet, and only incomplete norms are given for it. The PSI scale names were deliberately chosen to be nontechnical and to underplay the implication of pathology in order to avoid possible misinterpretation or misuse "by individuals with insufficient understanding of its purpose" (Lanyon, 1978, p. 3). The five primary scales are transformed to T-Scores, with a mean of 50 and a standard deviation of 10. The conversion from raw scores to T-Scores can be done by either looking up the values in a table in the manual or by plotting the scores directly onto a profile sheet. Separate norms exist for males and females.

The items were chosen to satisfy six criteria. First, objectionable items, covering such areas as sex, religion, eliminative functions, and family relationships, were avoided. Second, the statements were short and capable of being understood by a person with a grade-school-level education. Third, the items had face validity (incorrectly referred to as "content validity" in the manual). Fourth, wording was used to minimize the effects of social desirability. Fifth, each scale would have an equivalent number of items answered in the true and false directions in order to minimize any acquiesence response bias. Last, the five scales were to have non-overlapping items, eliminating a major objection to other personality tests. Because of an error during the construction of the test, one item is, in fact, shared by two scales. The final 130 items are printed on two sides of an 8½" x 11" sheet of paper. Subjects indicate their responses by filling in one of two circles next to each item, thus eliminating the need for separate question booklets and answer sheets. Versions of the PSI exist in Spanish, Polish, Japanese, Danish, and Hebrew; it is not indicated whether a tape-recorded version also exists. It is recommended that the examiner read the short instructions to the subjects as they read the printed ones at the top of the sheet, and then ask if there are any questions. The first item is not scored on any scale and can be used by the examiner to indicate how the items should be answered. It is suggested that if five or more answers are omitted, the subject be asked to fill additional items in until a maximum of four are left out.

The initial item pool consisted of 220 statements. This was administered to a normal construction group, consisting of 100 males and 100 females. No attempt was made to draw a random sample of people; rather, Lanyon and his students approached individuals in shopping centers, post offices, and railway stations in New Jersey, trying to balance the number of city, suburban, and rural addresses. About 600 inventories were given out (we do not know how many people were asked and refused), of which 300 were subsequently returned. The final 200 inventories were selected to be representative of the age distribution of the United States in 1966, and to closely match the mean educational level of the country. Four comparison groups were used: two from state psychiatric hospitals (71 and 69 patients, respectively), 50 male and 50 female prisoners, and 100 college undergraduates, equally divided between males and females.

The psychiatric groups were used in developing the Alienation Scale. For each item, a chi-square was calculated contrasting the normal construction group's responses with those of the first psychiatric group. The second group was used "because the pattern of chi-square validity coefficients generated by this analysis was somewhat different than what had been anticipated on the basis of the items initially written for this scale" (Lanyon, 1978, p. 15). Of the 25 items finally selected, 14 discriminated both psychiatric groups from the normal construction group, and the 11 remaining items were added later and used only with the second patient group. The questions in this scale relate to sensory distortions, naive or defensive denial of normal expressive behavior, a lack of understanding of what is going on in the environment, and a lack of a sense of personal responsibility for one's destiny. The scale is designed to indicate the respondent's similarity to hospitalized psychiatric patients, with a high score pointing to the need for formal examination.

For the Social Nonconformity Scale, a similar item analysis was used, comparing the normal construction group with the prisoners. This procedure resulted in a 25-item scale, indicating the respondents' similarity to people who have been jailed for antisocial behavior.

The 20-item Defensiveness Scale was derived by asking the group of college students to first "fake good" on the PSI and, two to four weeks later, to "fake bad." Items that differentiated between the normal administration and the two faking sets were chosen. High scores indicate that subjects were attempting to portray themselves in a favorable light, whereas low scores reflect an abnormal degree of readiness to admit to undesirable characteristics. In both content and intent, it appears similar to the K Scale on the Minnesota Multiphasic Personality Inventory (MMPI).

The Discomfort and Expression Scales each have 30 items. These were chosen purely on the basis of internal consistency (presumably with the normal construction group), and not because they discriminate among criterion groups. The former scale is intended to reflect susceptibility to anxiety and decompensation under stress, a lack of enjoyment of life, and the perceived presence of many psychological difficulties. Low scorers see themselves as satisfied, adaptable, resourceful, and flexible. High scorers on the Expression Scale are sociable, extraverted, undercontrolled, unreliable, and impulsive; whereas those who have low scores are introverted, overcontrolled, indecisive, reliable, and thorough.

The norms were based on the original normal construction group, plus 400 males and 400 females from three new locations in the United States: Iowa, Denver, and Los Angeles. They were recruited in similar locales and in a comparable way as the normal construction group, and were not meant to be representative of the United States, merely "diverse."

Practical Applications/Uses

The PSI is designed to be used in a wide variety of settings, such as community clinics and referral agencies, student counseling offices, courts, and reformatories. The major limitation on the people for whom the test is appropriate is that it should be used only "where deliberate response distortion is not a significant concern" (Lanyon, 1978, p. 3). On tests like the MMPI or the Millon Clinical Multiaxial Inventory (MCMI), correction factors are added to or subtracted from various scales to attempt to compensate for defensiveness or a too-ready admission of pathology. The PSI's De Scale is not used in this way; it simply assesses the degree and direction of the defensiveness.

The PSI is a "Level B" test, meaning that the user should have some technical knowledge of test construction and use and at least a passing familiarity with statistics, individual differences, and psychopathology. For unsupervised use, the minimum qualification would be a master's degree in a mental-health-related field. The PSI is also intended to be used by people with less training who are working under the supervision of a qualified psychologist. The manual does not recommend using the PSI in business and personnel situations unless the interpretation is supervised by a qualified psychologist. These recommendations are in keeping with the intended use of the test as a "flag" for more sophisticated interviewing or testing.

Administration and scoring of the PSI are fairly straightforward. Having the subjects put their responses alongside each item eliminates potential sources of error because subjects cannot omit an entire column or begin on the wrong side of the answer sheet. The test can be completed in about 15 minutes. The ten scoring templates are sturdily constructed and easy to use. It takes, at the most, five minutes to score the PSI and plot the results on the profile sheet. It is quite feasible for a nurse, clerk, or secretary to administer and score this instrument.

Scores on the PSI do not appear to be influenced by geographic location or intelligence, but people with a "low" education tend to score high. Between the ages of 16 and 60, the mean PSI scores on the different scales vary by no more than five or six points. Kantor, Walker, and Hays (1976) found mean score deviations of more than eight points on scales Al and De in subjects between 13 and 16 years of age, reinforcing the contention that the PSI should be used only with extreme caution with younger respondents. It is assumed that race does not play a major role, but this is still untested.

The first step in profile interpretation is to ensure that no more than five items have been omitted. If Scale De is over 70, it is recommended that the test be readministered and the subject urged to be more open. Conversely, if the scaled score is below 30, the subject should be asked "to be less completely frank" (Lanyon, 1978, p. 6).

Interpretation of the test requires considerably more experience than scoring. The manual provides a brief description of each scale, with characteristics of high scorers. For the De and Ex scales some descriptors of low scorers are also provided. A few rules have been derived for discriminating among groups by looking at two scales at a time. However, almost no research has been done regarding two-point or three-point codes, analogous to the "cookbooks" that exist for the MMPI.

For the most part, scales are interpreted if they deviate more than one standard deviation from the mean; this is a considerably looser criterion than is used with many similar tests where scores less than two standard deviations from the mean are considered normal. This naturally would result in significantly more profiles being called abnormal.

The specific purpose of the PSI is to enable a mental health worker "to make predictions and decisions that represent an improvement from an overall economic point of view over the predictions that would be made without using the test" (p. 6). This is always difficult to do, as the positive predictive value of a test is extremely dependent on the base rate of the disorder in the population. In a way that can only be highly commended, the manual explicitly makes this point and instructs the user how to choose a cutting point that will maximize the proportion of correct predictions, based on the prevalence among the user's clientele. Unfortunately, it is questionable how many clinicians have the needed information or will go through the time and effort necessary to establish local cut-points.

Technical Aspects

Based on a sample of 100 college students, the internal consistencies of the five scales ranged from a low of .51 (De) to .85 (Di). After ten days, the test-retest reliability ranged from .73 (Al) to .89 (Sn); after one month, both Al and De correlated .66, whereas the reliability for Sn surprisingly rose to .95 (Lanyon, 1978). No reliability studies appear to have been done with patients or the general population. The correlations among the scales are quite variable and dependent on the nature of the respondents; even normal groups differ from each other. In almost every case Scale Di showed a high negative correlation with De (median of −0.47), although it was only −.06 for a group of 75 female prisoners. The median correlation between Al and Di for males was .40 and .29 for females. However, the range of correlations across samples was from −.06 to .66. Looking at the median correlations, it appears that, in general, De is negatively correlated with Sn and Di, whereas Al is positively correlated with Di. Weaker correlations exist between Sn and Di (.24), Sn and Ex (.21), and Di and Ex (−.23).

Many studies have correlated the PSI scores with other personality instruments, such as the MMPI, California Psychological Inventory (CPI), the Eysenck Personality Inventory (EPI), and the Maudsley Personality Inventory (MPI). In general, the PSI appears to have good construct validity. The Alienation Scale correlates with MMPI Scales F, Sc, Pa and, to a lesser degree, with Pt Scales, which tap varying degrees of pathology. Social Nonconformity correlates with Pd on the MMPI and a separate scale of sensation seeking and has a strong negative correlation with the Marlowe-Crowne Social Desirability Scale (SDS). The Discomfort Scale correlates well with various indices of anxiety, such as the MMPI's Pt Scale and the MPI's Neuroticism Scale, whereas the Extraversion Scale has a strong negative correlation with Si and a strong, positive relationship with the MPI and EPI Extraversion Scale. As would be expected, the Defensiveness Scale is closely associated with the MMPI's L and K Scales, although the strength of the association varies considerably from one sample to another.

Several factor analyses of the PSI were reviewed by Vieweg and Hedlund (1984). Two factors, Extraversion/Introversion and Neuroticism/Emotional Adjustment, appeared in all five of the analyses. Another factor, Serious/Major Psychopathology, was not found in a sample of college students but was present in the other four analyses. A Social Maladjustment factor was present in three of the five studies.

As mentioned previously, the major purpose of this test is to predict which respondents should be referred for further assessment. Unfortunately, few studies have addressed this issue. Bruch (1977) conducted one of the few studies that used the PSI predictively, differentiating college students who later did or did not attend a student counseling service. Although statistically significant differences were found on all scales except Ex in no case did the groups differ by more than 1.75 points, nor did the counseled group's scores deviate from 50 by more than three points. Further, no attempt was made to assess the accuracy of predicting which individuals would seek help, as opposed to looking only at group means. A number of articles have shown that the scales can discriminate, for example, between delinquents and normals (Broskowski, Silverman, & Hinkel, 1971; McGurk & Bolton, 1981); and between normals and psychiatric patients (Overall, 1974). Although this is necessary to establish validity, it does not address the issue of predictive power. This difference was best expressed by Golding (1978):

> The PSI is not designed to differentiate psychiatric patients who are already hospitalized from normals who are not; it is designed to differentiate cur-

rently non hospitalized normals who may in the future require hospitalization from non hospitalized normals who will not. Data bearing on the former issue (as detailed in the manual) speak to the latter issue only under the counter-factual assumption that non hospitalized normals who may require hospitalization are just like hospitalized patients. Common sense and empirical data alike do not support this assumption. (p. 1022)

Critique

The PSI occupies a unique niche in the realm of objective personality testing. Unlike the MMPI and MCMI, it is not a diagnostic instrument. On the other hand, unlike the CPI and 16 PF, it is to be used with groups where psychopathology or sociopathy are expected. In this light, what can we say about the test?

On the positive side, obviously much work has gone into the development of this instrument. Although the normative samples leave something to be desired in terms of representativeness (Butcher, 1971, p. 417, refers to the "casual method of collecting the normal group"), later validation studies have used samples from different geographic and ethnic backgrounds. The test is easy to administer and score, and versions exist in numerous foreign languages. Further, this is one of the few tests that attempts to use Bayes' Theorem to minimize the false positive and false negative rates in classifying respondents.

On the negative side, though, are two important issues. First, the definitive validity studies regarding the predictive power of the test have yet to be done. We are still awaiting published reports whether the use of the PSI will indeed be cost-effective in terms of yielding more information about the need for further assessment than would otherwise be available. The other major criticism is the susceptibility of the test to various faking sets. The manual states that it should be used "where deliberate response distortion is not a significant concern" (p. 3). However, the two major groups for whom it is intended—persons with psychopathology or sociopathy—are those most prone to exaggerate or deny the presence of significant problems. Boor (1973), for example, found that the SDS correlated –.57 with Sn, –.38 with Di, and .58 with Ex in a group of patients making initial contact with a mental-health clinic. He concluded that "the susceptibility of these scores to social desirability bias substantially diminishes the values of PSI as a clinical assessment instrument" (p. 239). Similar correlations and conclusions were reached by Orpen (1971) in a group of students.

In his *Mental Measurements Yearbook* review, Golding (1978) concludes that "The PSI appears to be an interesting research instrument, but its use as a psychiatric screening device in normal applications should be approached cautiously. . . . To be fair, it has not yet been examined in this light and it may yet be shown to be useful" (p. 1022). A slightly more positive conclusion was reached by Vieweg and Hedlund (1984). They state that the test "has reasonably well-demonstrated potential usefulness, especially with regard to the screening of college undergraduates in counseling settings, young reformatory and prison inmates, and perhaps psychiatric outpatients. Additional research is needed to extend its recognized (valid) use with other group [*sic*] and settings" (p. 1392). Although this test was first introduced 15 years ago, these conclusions still appear valid; it is an interesting concept in test development, filling a specific need in the community. However, its potential utility still remains to be proven.

References

Boor, M. (1973). Social desirability bias on the Psychological Screening Inventory in a clinical population. *Journal of Clinical Psychology, 29,* 238-239.

Broskowski, A., Silverman, R., & Hinkel, H. (1971). Actuarial assessment of criminality in women. *Criminology, 9,* 166-184.

Bruch, M. A. (1977). Psychological Screening Inventory as a predictor of college student adjustment. *Journal of Consulting and Clinical Psychology, 45,* 237-244.

Butcher, J. N. (1971). Review of the Psychological Screening Inventory. *Professional Psychology, 2,* 416-418.

Golding, S. L. (1978). The Psychological Screening Inventory. In O. K. Buros (Ed.), *The eighth mental measurements yearbook* (pp. 1019-1022). Highland Park, NJ: The Gryphon Press.

Kantor, J. E., Walker, C. E., & Hays, L. (1976). A study of the usefulness of Lanyon's Psychological Screening Inventory with adolescents. *Journal of Consulting and Clinical Psychology, 44,* 313-316.

Lanyon, R. I. (1978). *Psychological Screening Inventory manual* (2nd ed.). Port Huron, MI: Research Psychologists Press, Inc.

McGurk, B. J., & Bolton, N. (1981). A comparison of the Eysenck Personality Questionnaire and the Psychological Screening Inventory in a delinquent sample and a comparison group. *Journal of Clinical Psychology, 37,* 874-879.

Orpen, C. (1971). Susceptibility to faking of the Psychological Screening Inventory. *Journal of Clinical Psychology, 27,* 463-465.

Overall, J. E. (1974). Validity of the Psychological Screening Inventory for psychiatric screening. *Journal of Consulting and Clinical Psychology, 42,* 717-719.

Vieweg, B. W., & Hedlund, J. L. (1984). Psychological Screening Inventory: A comprehensive review. *Journal of Clinical Psychology, 40,* 1382-1393.

Dennis N. Thompson, Ph.D.
Associate Professor of Educational Psychology, College of Education, Georgia State University, Atlanta, Georgia.

QUICK WORD TEST

Edgar F. Borgatta and Raymond J. Corsini. Itasca, Illinois: F. E. Peacock Publishers, Inc.

Introduction

The Quick Word Test (QWT) is designed to provide a time-saving, easily applied, and reliable measure of general mental ability often measured by much longer and more complicated tests.

The QWT is available in three levels that are appropriate for testing elementary school students through college-educated adults. The Elementary Level was normed for children in fourth through sixth grades (Borgatta & Corsini, 1967a). Adult versions were designed to measure verbal ability in the general and high-school populations (Level I), and college and professional populations (Level II). In addition, a supplement for Level I provides norm tables for junior-high-school students (Borgatta & Corsini, 1967b). Tests at all three levels are published with parallel forms. The Elementary Level and Level II each have two versions that were matched for difficulty, whereas Level I has four.

All tests consist entirely of vocabulary items. Items are in multiple-choice format and consist of a stem word of five letters followed by four four-letter alternatives. The examinee's task is to choose the correct synonym. According to the authors, the foils provided were specifically designed to suggest plausible associations with the stem. There are 50 items on the Elementary Level and 100 items on each of the more advanced levels.

The QWT is essentially self-administering. A brief set of instructions directs the respondent to choose a word that means the same as the first. A sample item is provided. The QWT is a power test, and for most individuals administration time ranges between ten and 20 minutes.

All three levels of the QWT utilize a spiraling omnibus format. Throughout the tests, items are presented in blocks with five items per block. Within each block items range from easy to difficult. The manuals (Borgatta & Corsini, 1964, 1967a, 1967b) provide data that indicate that blocks are adequately matched with each other for difficulty level. The authors of the QWT state that because the first five items on the tests have a difficulty level equal to the last five items, the interest level of the examinee is maintained, and the progressive discouragement found with some other formats is lessened.

Practical Applications/Uses

The QWT is a group test that does not require special training to administer or score. A few instructions are provided on the answer sheet, and the test format is straightforward enough for persons taking the test to understand readily. Although the QWT is generally hand scored, the test is presented on IBM test sheets and may also be machine scored.

Borgatta and Corsini (1964) state that the QWT was based on a consensus among psychometrists and psychologists that a measure of vocabulary provides the best single indicator of general mental ability. Borgatta and Corsini (1960) justify this statement in an early study by reporting that the QWT (Level I, Form AM) correlates .85 with the Verbal Scale of the WAIS and .84 with total WAIS IQ. These data also support the authors' contention that the QWT can be used as an initial screening as part of a larger test battery or when the efficiency of time, effort, or money is the main consideration.

There are many possible uses for the QWT. Borgatta and Corsini (1964) suggest that the QWT might be used in school settings where an attempt is being made to identify exceptional pupils for whom more lengthy and time-consuming testing might be justified. Secondly, the authors argue that because the QWT is composed of blocks of items that are matched for difficulty, a percentage score can be recorded for a part of the test. This feature seems particularly useful in clinical and institutional settings where the anxiety, fatigue, or disinterest of the examinee may contaminate results obtained with longer and more time-consuming measures. Thirdly, Grotelueschen and McQuarrie (1970) argue that the QWT is especially useful as a screening device in adult education programs, allowing for a more homogeneous grouping of individuals. Finally, most of the recent published research on the QWT (e.g., Cavannaugh, 1983) have used the QWT to match groups of subjects on verbal ability.

There are, of course, some limitations to the use of the QWT. Most particularly, because the QWT is highly correlated with other measures of verbal intelligence, careful consideration should be given before using it with individuals who have limited facility with the English language.

Technical Aspects

The manuals are clear and present detailed information on the tests, as well as tables and explanations that allow examiners to translate easily raw scores into percentiles and stanines. According to the manuals (Borgatta & Corsini, 1964, 1967a) split-half reliabilities range from .90 to .93 for the various levels and forms of the tests. Alternate-forms reliability coefficients are in the range of .90 among the four forms available for Level I and the two versions available for the Elementary Level. Numerous correlations between the QWT and other established measures of mental ability are presented. Examples include a .80 correlation with the Otis Quick Scoring Test of Mental Ability and a .84 correlation with the Lorge-Thorndike Intelligence Test Level 5 (Verbal). Data are also presented on the standard error of measurement of the test and for equating the QWT with other tests of general ability. Construct validity is further discussed in terms of an item discrimination index and ratings regarding the internal consistency of the test.

Although the QWT correlates significantly with measures of verbal intelligence, there is evidence in the literature that the QWT may also include a reasoning or a problem-solving component. On this point, the manuals state that the tests are designed so that for some items the examinee's immediate response may be to consider the stimulus word as a noun, whereas the correct option may be expressed as a verb. In noting this format, Sax and Oda (1965) argue that the change in set function may be contributing to the high correlations between the QWT and omnibus measures of mental ability. Similarly, Westbrook and Sellers (1967) report that the QWT correlates significantly ($r = .44$) with the total score of the Watson-Glaser Critical Thinking Appraisal, a test of general problem solving.

Critique

As stated earlier, one of the more frequent uses for the Quick Word Test reported in the literature in recent years is for research purposes for the identification, screening, and matching of subjects. In particular, several researchers have commented on the advantages offered by the QWT over longer measures for gerontological research. This was commented on recently by Cavanaugh (1983) who found that the difficulty level and range of items on the QWT (Level I) were particularly appropriate for use with older subjects. Some years ago Grotelueschen and Knox (1967) stated that because the test is a power test and does not rely on motor responses or cause fatigue, it is highly appropriate for adult education settings. More recently, Thompson, Holzman, and Doll (1985) state that because the test has a spiraling omnibus format, small portions of the test can be used for rapid selection of subjects in gerontological research where fatigue is a major consideration. In short, because the QWT was first published in its present format in 1964, it remains a viable test that continues to have new uses. It appears that it has lived up to its claim of being the economical, easily applied, and reliable measure of verbal ability that it was originally intended to be.

References

Borgatta, E., & Corsini, R. (1960). The Quick Word Test (QWT) and the WAIS. *Psychological Reports, 6,* 201.

Borgatta, E., & Corsini, R. (1964). *Quick Word Test manual.* New York: Harcourt, Brace, and World.

Borgatta, E., & Corsini, R. (1967a). *Quick Word Test, elementary level manual.* New York: Harcourt, Brace, and World.

Borgatta, E., & Corsini, R. (1967b). *Quick Word Test supplementary report.* New York: Harcourt, Brace, and World.

Cavanaugh, J. (1983). Comprehension and retention of television programs by 20 and 60 year olds. *Journal of Gerontology, 38,* 190-196.

Grotelueschen, A., & Knox, A. (1967). Analysis of the Quick Word Test as an estimate of adult mental ability. *Journal of Educational Measurement, 4,* 169-177.

Grotelueschen, A., & McQuarrie, D. (1970). Cross validation of the Quick Word Test as an estimator of adult mental ability. *Adult Education Journal, 21,* 14-19.

Sax, G., & Oda., E. A. (1965). Review of Quick Word Test. *Journal of Educational Measurement, 2,* 257-258.

Thompson, D., Holzman, T., & Doll, L. (1985). *The use of advance organizers with adult prose learning* (Final Grant Report). Washington, DC: National Institute on Aging.

Westbrook, B., & Sellers, J. (1967). Critical thinking, intelligence, and vocabulary. *Educational and Psychological Measurement, 27,* 443-446.

Jeffrey Gorrell, Ph.D.

Associate Professor of Educational Psychology, Southeastern Louisiana University, Hammond, Louisiana.

RING AND PEG TESTS OF BEHAVIOR DEVELOPMENT

Katharine M. Banham. Murfreesboro, Tennessee: Psychometric Affiliates.

Introduction

The Ring and Peg Tests of Behavior Development by Katharine M. Banham provide relatively brief measures of the ambulative, manipulative, communicative, social-adaptive, and emotive behavior of children from birth to six years. Described by the test author as being more comprehensive than standard intelligence tests, the Ring and Peg Tests are intended to reveal levels of intelligence and of adaptive capacity, including such factors as cooperation, independence, interest, drive, and purposefulness of young children.

Banham, Associate Professor, Emeritus, at Duke University is a developmental psychologist who was at Duke University during and following the time that she developed these scales. Her avowed purpose was to provide psychologists attached to child-welfare agencies with a convenient and easily administered intelligence test for developing a child's profile in the five areas of concern listed above. Banham's tests were published at a time when the predictive value of developmental scales was a controversial question. As an early entry in the field of developmental scales, the Ring and Peg Tests have historic value as well as a practical value to contemporary researchers.

Early development of the tests relied on selecting items found in the Stanford-Binet, Kuhlmann-Binet, Gesell Schedules, Vineland, and other infant and preschool scales and arranging these items according to difficulty and ascending age of the children. In addition, the author indicates that her professional experiences in testing several hundred infants formed the basis for a few of the items, but it is not clear what those items are and what formal criteria were used for adopting them.

Validation of the tests was performed from 1958 to 1960 on a total of 95 children ranging in age from about eight months to five years. The first form of the tests reported scores on an age scale; the 1975 revision converted the tests to a point scale in order to represent the child's development in each of the five areas more precisely. There are no forms available for special populations, such as visually impaired or non-English-speaking.

The Ring and Peg Tests of Behavior Development consist of five subtests, each of which contain subsections of performances for three major age ranges. There are

52 items for each subtest, beginning with items that represent a behavior range of 1/2 month and ending with items that represent a behavior age of 72 months. Alternate items are listed to allow for the possibility that testing circumstances may not allow for administration of all of the primary items.

Because there is quite a large range of behavior differences between infants and six-year-old children, each subtest necessarily involves different test items from the beginning to the end. The following gives brief indications of the ranges of each of the five subtests.

Ambulative: Tests for development of sitting, walking, balance, throwing, and catching, depending on the child's age range.

Manipulative: Tests for visual tracking of an object, grasping, imitation of actions, manipulation of objects (rings, pegs, and peg holes), drawing, tying (shoelaces), and paper folding.

Communicative: Tests for attention to sounds in the environment, vocalization, linguistic development (holophrases, telegraphic speech, word recognition), rhythm, memory, and comprehension.

Social-adaptive: Tests for social observation, smiling, behavioral imitation, following instructions, and seeking or giving advanced information.

Emotive: Tests for responsiveness to people and objects, interest in the environment, following orders, emotional interaction, and participation.

The particular manipulative items provided with the tests are a set of three pegs, which can be inserted into a base, and a set of yellow and blue plastic rings of increasing size, which can be placed over the pegs or handled in other ways. For some of the test items, other common objects, such as an eraser, small ball, writing paper, pencil, and black and white shoe laces, are required.

The answer form records basic information about the child (e.g., name, birthdate) and the point scores and behavior age equivalents for each of the five subtests. A summary chart provides a simple profile of the point score of the highest item credited in each subtest and the concomitant behavior age, along with an average for the whole scale. The final developmental quotient is derived by dividing the child's age into the child's average behavior age and multiplying that number by 100.

Practical Applications/Uses

The Ring and Peg Tests are most useful in settings where one desires a convenient estimate of behavioral functioning of preschool children. Because it has not been validated in any extensive fashion, the instrument is more appropriate for research purposes and experimental settings than for formal assessment. Used in conjunction with other developmental scales, such as the Bayley Scales of Infant Development and the Uzgiris-Hunt Ordinal Scales of Psychological Development, the Ring and Peg Tests may be used to extend the observation of infant and preschool behavioral development. Because of the limited range of observations, however, the tests may not provide enough information for practitioners who need full-range scores.

The tests are designed to assess the child's overall functioning, not just the child's cognitive abilities. Social workers, psychologists, and educators may find the separate subtests useful for gaining initial data regarding their clients. The first three subtests are relatively independent of each other, but subtests four and five overlap. It is not clear from the instructions, however, whether any particular subtest can be used independently without sacrificing the larger value of the instrument.

Subjects for whom these tests are appropriate are children from one month to six years of age. There is no apparent restriction according to socioeconomic status, race, sex, or ethnic background. It is presumed that the child functions within the range of normal hearing and speech and is without physical disabilities.

The tests can be administered in any comfortable setting. Emphasis is placed on the child's feeling relaxed enough to interact fully with the examiner. No special training is necessary for administering the tests, but full familiarity with the instructions and some practice in making smooth transitions from item to item is essential.

The examiner arranges for a comfortable and nonthreatening environment and begins testing the child at a level just below the child's age and progresses through the items within each subtest until the child cannot perform the required actions. For children under two or three years, a parent may be present during the administration in order to help put the child at ease. The parent does not participate in the examination unless specifically requested by the examiner. Interestingly, the manual suggests that parental statements regarding the child's performance of the requisite behaviors can be accepted in lieu of actual performance at the test site if the parents are judged to be reliable reporters of their child's performances.

It is not necessary to follow each subtest in the order presented nor all at the same time, as long as all items eventually are covered during the assessment. Rearrangement of the order of test items may be performed according to the examiner's judgment. The examiner is encouraged to keep the testing periods brief, so as to avoid reaching unreliable levels of fatigue or resistance.

Instructions to the examiner are minimal. Apparently, it is assumed that there is a certain degree of testing sophistication already present. Those unaccustomed to administering developmental tests may prefer some further explanation regarding the range of behavior expected of children at these ages and might profit from further explanation of the theoretical foundations for such tests. Additionally, the extensive use of abbreviations for examiner, child, etc., create some confusion for the reader of the manual.

Scoring procedures are simple and take little time. There is no need for machine scoring or for professional consultation in scoring. The manual clearly indicates the numerical values for each performance (1, 2, or 6 points, depending on the section of the test) and the equivalence of these points in behavior age. The examiner records the highest test item passed, multiplies by the point value for that section, and subtracts the points for any lower test items failed. Behavior age in months is calculated by dividing this score by two. The simplicity of the relationship between point scores and behavior age is an advantage of using this test.

Interpretation of the scores is based on the objective numbers collected. The examiner is unlikely to need any training in interpretation of the scores, but sensitivity in the observations that lead to the scores is necessary, particularly in determining whether the child has adequately satisfied the requirements of a particular item.

Technical Aspects

Little has been done to validate this instrument. Although it has been available since 1958, the only validation studies are the few that were performed from 1958 to 1960. These studies, cited in the test manual, have been performed on small groups of children. Mean ages for each study were 8.1 months; three years, 11 months; and five years, two months. Comparisons have been made with the Cattell Infant Intelligence Scale, yielding a rank difference correlation between the two scales of .81 (for infants) and .73 (for preschool children), and with the Stanford-Binet Intelligence Scale, Form L, yielding a rank difference correlation of .89 (for five-year-olds). Reliability of the tests, determined by using the split-half method (odd- and even-numbered items), has been computed to range from .96 to .98.

Unfortunately, the validation studies have been performed on a limited number of subjects with measured IQs averaging 50 and 91 on the Cattell Scale and 59 on the Stanford-Binet. This limited range of subjects provides little or no information about the applicability of the tests to normal populations. However, because the tests are intended as behavior tests, rather than formal intelligence tests, the examiner may be more interested in particular performances than in an ultimate score.

The Ring and Peg Tests were reviewed in *The Seventh Mental Measurements Yearbook* (Hunt, 1972; Werner, 1972). These reviewers cite certain advantages of the tests and suggest that they have potential for increasing our understanding of behavior development, but point out the lack of standardization and validity studies on the tests, a condition that still pertains in the mid-80s.

Critique

The Ring and Peg Tests are interesting and potentially valuable behavioral measures but need to be validated and standardized more fully before they can be used as reliable substitutes for other existing intelligence measures or behavioral scales. Although the tests appear to have been neglected as research instruments for the last 25 years, they offer the researcher or clinician alternative procedures for assessing behavior development that deserve further consideration. Until more extensive validation of the tests is performed, however, the Ring and Peg Tests are likely to be more interesting historically than clinically.

References

Banham, K. M. (1975). *Manual for The Ring and Peg Tests of Behavior Development: Point scale for ages birth to six years.* Munster, IN: Psychometric Affiliates.

Hunt, J. V. (1972). Ring and Peg Tests of Behavior Development. In O. K. Buros (Ed.), *The seventh mental measurements yearbook* (pp. 762-763). Highland Park, NJ: The Gryphon Press.

Werner, E. E. (1972). Ring and Peg Tests of Behavior Development. In O. K. Buros (Ed.), *The seventh mental measurements yearbook* (pp. 763-764). Highland Park, NJ: The Gryphon Press.

Howard Lerner, Ph.D.
Professor of Psychology, University of Michigan, School of Medicine, Ann Arbor, Michigan.

Paul M. Lerner, Ed.D.
Faculty of Medicine, University of Toronto, Toronto, Canada.

RORSCHACH INKBLOT TEST

Hermann Rorschach. Bern, Switzerland: Hans Huber. U.S. Distributor—Grune & Stratton, Inc.

Introduction

The past decade has witnessed a significant resurgence of the use of the Rorschach Inkblot Test for the study and understanding of people, a virtual revival of what Millon (1984) has referred to as its "rich heritage of the 1940's and 1950's." In the previous decade, the 1960s, both personality assessment and personality theory had fallen into disrepute, and hit hardest were the projective techniques, including the Rorschach, and psychoanalytic theory. The veritable explosion of new treatment modalities onto the psychotherapeutic marketplace, many of which stressed brevity and cost efficiency, together with the expanding roles being filled by psychologists seemed to render traditional personality assessment obsolete, if not anachronistic. Anti-test attitudes were rampant and have been well recorded in the testing literature (Holt, 1967, 1968; Shevrin & Schectman, 1973; Millon, 1984). Humanistic psychologists reviewed assessment as exploitive, as robbing clients of their individuality and dignity; those with a social perspective equated assessing with labeling and argued that the diagnostic process itself was dehumanizing and antitherapeutic; and those psychologists in academia insisted that statistically derived predictions were superior to clinically based ones.

With respect to the Rorschach the drought is over. Catapulting renewed interest in the Rorschach has been the empirical work of John Exner and his colleagues (Exner, 1974, 1978; Viglione & Exner, 1983) together with major shifts in psychoanalytic theory. With regard to the latter, the relatively recent integration of modern object relations theory, a broadened psychodynamic developmental theory, and a systematic psychology of the self into the mainstream of traditional psychoanalytic theory is now providing the conceptual basis for a more comprehensive, fruitful, and systematic Rorschach theory.

The purpose of this critique is to examine and summarize the current status of the Rorschach, beginning with a review of the contributions of Hermann Rorschach, the originator of the test. This will be followed by a discussion of the most significant issue permeating contemporary Rorschach theory and practice—conceptual versus empirical approach. One major conceptual approach, that based on psychoanalytic theory, will then be outlined. Included in the outline will be a review of the contributions of David Rapaport, together with a discussion of the impact of Rorschach research and clinical use on conceptual shifts in psychoanalytic theory, and concluding with future directions these reviewers believe that work with and on the Rorschach will take.

Contributions of Hermann Rorschach: According to Rickers-Ovsiankina (1977), "grasping the inner workings of man was a life-long concern of Rorschach's" (p. x). It was toward this broad goal that he directed his experiments with inkblots. Employing inkblots (i.e., using forms obtained through chance by folding over a piece of paper into the center of which ink had been dropped) to explore an aspect of personality did not begin with Rorschach. In 1857, Kerner (note Pichot, 1984) reported on his experiments with inkblots, and at the turn of the century Binet used chance inkblots to assess imaginative capacities in children.

Rorschach went beyond these early researchers. He not only standardized an inkblot procedure, but was also able to synthesize the procedure with Jung's work on the Word Association Test and Bleuler's notions regarding personality assessment. Jung published his research with the Word Association Test between 1906-1909 under the general title "Diagnostic Association Studies." Basic to his research were the important insights that any one particular act (i.e., handwriting, choice of clothing, etc.) could represent the whole person and that one could explore personality by systematically studying an individual's reactions to a stimulus. Bleuler had made similar observations, noting that such reactions could be taken as "an index of all mental activity so that it is only necessary to decipher them in order to know the entire man" (Pichot, 1984, p. 595).

When responses to inkblots had been used to assess imagination, emphasis was placed on the content of the responses. By contrast, Rorschach stressed not the content, but rather the formal properties of the response, and, as such, this enabled him to conceptualize the test as one of perception and not of imagination. He was then able to demonstrate that peculiarities in perception were dependent upon the nature of the underlying personality structure, including pathological deviations. In other words, by noting the intimate relationship between perceptual reactions and other psychological functions, Rorschach was able to conceptually place his technique in the middle of the assessment of total personality functioning.

Rorschach codified his theoretical understandings of the inkblot procedure by developing categories for analyzing responses—the determinants. Later Rorschach workers (Rickers-Ovsiankina, 1977; Pichot, 1984) consider this to be his most important contribution.

Contemporary Issues: As Weiner (1977) points out, historically clinicians and researchers have struggled with issues of Rorschach validity. Out of this struggle, according to Weiner (1977), three types of opinions have emerged concerning the psychometric status of the Rorschach. One extreme opinion claims that the Rorschach, despite thousands of research studies and a voluminous clinical and theoretical literature, has failed to demonstrate its validity according to strict psychometric standards. According to this point of view, the Rorschach should be discarded as an assessment procedure. A second, more clinical opinion holds that the Rorschach is not a test at all and therefore should not be judged by psychometric criteria. This point of view holds that the Rorschach is a special type of clinical interaction based upon the skills and sensitivities of the examiner rather than the psychometric characteristics of the instrument. In keeping with this point of view, psychometric studies of validity are inappropriate to the nature of the instrument and statistical studies have no bearing on its clinical utility. Weiner (1977) represents a third, more integrated point of view: ". . . some psychologists have been determined to maintain their scientist's respect for objective data without sacrificing the richness and utility of the Rorschach in which they had come to believe as clinicians. This determination has engendered thoughtful criticism of previous validity studies and proposals for new approaches to Rorschach validation that combine sophisticated research design with adequate attention to the nuances of clinical practice" (p. 576).

Evolving out of the debate concerning the validity of the Rorschach, two major approaches to using and evaluating the instrument have recently emerged: the empirical sign or psychometric approach and the conceptual approach. While these somewhat divergent approaches to the Rorschach are not mutually exclusive, issues pertaining to either a more psychometric or conceptual approach to the Rorschach underlie much of the research and clinical studies found in the contemporary literature. The evaluation of each approach will be outlined with a view toward uncovering those major issues at the forefront of Rorschach inquiry today.

Practical Applications/Uses

The empirical sign or psychometric approach to the Rorschach began with Hermann Rorschach (1921/1942) as he compared previously selected diagnostic groups and found that certain "signs" or scores occurred more frequently in some groups than in others. While this approach has spanned the Rorschach's history and has cut across theoretical orientations to the instrument, through a number of major books and publications, Exner and his colleagues (Exner, 1974, 1978; Exner, Weiner, & Schuyler, 1979) have become the most thorough, instrumental, and contemporary representatives of the Rorschach's psychometric or sign approach. What these authors term the Comprehensive System, an integration of five major Rorschach systems, synthesizes, according to psychometric criteria, the most reliable and useful indices from other systems. Supplementing the Comprehensive System are selected variables, scores, and ratios that demonstrate high interscorer reliability and correlate with other psychological variables. Much of the research conducted by Exner and his colleagues involves further delineation of the constructs associated with these variables and collection of vital normative data on the Rorschach.

According to Viglione and Exner (1983), studies based on the Comprehensive System are united by understanding the Rorschach as primarily a "problem-solving" task that activates relatively consistent styles of coping behavior. According to these authors: "The data gleaned from the subject's responses, or solutions, provide a glimpse of how the individual works with the world, how he responds to ambiguity and challenge. These data are quantified in the various scores and more indirectly expressed in the words and other behaviors that are observed. The impressive temporal consistency of the various Rorschach scores, as derived from test-retest studies (Exner, 1978; Exner, Armbruster, & Viglione, 1978), suggests that these solutions to the Rorschach problem are representative of one's relatively stable, idiographic style of coping with the world" (p. 14). The problem-solving orientation to the Rorschach, and with it an emphasis on habits and decision operations, stands in marked contrast to the instrument seen in terms of a "projective process" and wedded to a theory of personality independent of the test itself.

The foundation for Rorschach interpretation based upon the Comprehensive System is what Exner (1978) terms the "4-square," which incorporates the basic scores and ratios thought to be characteristic of one's problem-solving style. The four indices of the 4-square are 1) Erlebnistypus (EB, the ratio of human movement to weighted color responses); 2) Experience Actual (EA, the sum of human movement and weighted color responses); 3) Experience Base (eb, the ratio of non-human movement to shading and gray-black responses); and 4) Experience Potential (ep, the sum of non-human movement, shading, and gray-black responses). According to Exner and his colleagues, these four variables taken as a whole incorporate the fundamental information about the psychological habits and capacities of an individual and represent the crucial interpretative departure from previous Rorschach systems. The four variables comprising the 4-square are thought to be symmetrical, that is, two ratios (EB, eb) with a corresponding sum (EA, ep). In keeping with Rorschach's (1921) original formulations, EB generates information on individuals' tendencies toward ideational or affective coping responses to stress. By combining both sides of the EB to form the sum EA, an index is formed to represent the "amount" of organized resources available for coping (Beck, 1960). Based on the formulations of Klopfer, Ainsworth, Klopfer, and Holt (1965) that non-human movement and some shading and gray-black responses correspond to psychological activity outside of deliberate control, Exner extended Klopfer's ratio to incorporate all shading and gray-black responses and formed the "eb." Following Beck (1960), Exner added the two sides of the "eb" to produce "ep," which is thought to reflect the degree of psychological activity not readily accessible to deliberate control and frequently experienced as stimulation acting or impinging upon the individual.

Much of Exner's research based on the Comprehensive System has involved studies delving into the stimulus-input of the ten cards and the emergence of relatively consistent response styles (Exner, 1980). These studies conducted on adult populations demonstrate that many variables included in the Comprehensive System, especially the 4-square, are reliable and temporally consistent.

Most validation studies for the Comprehensive System have revolved around the 4-square interrelationships (Viglione & Exner, 1983). Research conducted by Exner and his colleagues involving temporal consistency data indicate that the EA:ep ratio stabilizes through development and achieves permanence by adulthood (Exner, Armbruster, & Viglione, 1978). Normative data indicate that EA increases relative to ep as children mature and that more normal subjects than patients have EA greater than ep. Collectively these findings demonstrate that the EA:ep relationship represents a stable, personality characteristic indicating the relative "amount" of psychological activity organized and available for "coping purposes" as opposed to more immature experiences that impinge on the person. Treatment studies reveal increases in EA, both alone and in relationship to ep, among patients who improved in psychotherapy (Exner, 1978). For subjects beginning treatment with ep greater than EA, a reversal has been demonstrated in most cases; that is, EA becomes greater than ep in retest records when intervention continues for more than a brief period of time (Exner, 1978). Exner (1978) suggests that treatment either facilitates the organization of psychological resources or relieves stress. According to Exner the occurrence of ep is not always disruptive or pathological, but rather, ep activity in moderate amounts stimulates underlying motivational processes.

While much of the Comprehensive System research has involved reliability, temporal consistency, and correlational studies of normal adult populations, Exner and his colleagues have recently initiated studies involving the usefulness of the Rorschach in differential diagnosis, particularly unraveling the relationship between borderline, schizotypal, and schizophrenic patients. In general, the findings of these studies (Exner, 1978; Viglione & Exner, 1983), particularly involving the borderline patient's emotional immaturity, excessive self-centeredness, need for closeness, intense anger, and chaotic interpersonal world, are consistent with other Rorschach studies (Spear, 1980; Lerner, Sugarman, & Gaughran, 1981; Lerner & Lerner, 1982; Lerner & St. Peter, 1984) based upon a more conceptual approach to the instrument and utilizing scales representing composite variables derived from contemporary psychoanalytic theory.

The contributions of Exner and his coworkers represent the most recent advances in a psychometric or empirical "sign" approach to the Rorschach. Based upon major advances in computer science, data processing, and data analysis, the contribution of these researchers revolve around the psychometric features of the Rorschach and the nature of the instrument itself. As such, these contributions address directly previous psychometric critiques of the Rorschach as nonreliable and not suitable for research. In addition, Exner's careful accumulation of normative data fills an important gap in the vast Rorschach literature which contributes to our understanding of development, the Rorschach response process, and an important baseline for further research in differential diagnostic issues.

In marked contrast to the psychometric or sign approach to the Rorschach, the "conceptual" approach to using and evaluating the Rorschach evolved from the recognition that the fundamental purpose of the instrument is to assess personality processes (Weiner, 1977). According to Weiner (1977): "In the conceptual approach personality processes provide a bridge between Rorschach data and whatever condition is to be evaluated or behavior to be predicted. Viewed in this frame of reference, the Rorschach successfully identifies the presence of some condition or predicts some aspect of behavior only when the instrument accurately measures personality variables that in turn account in substantial part for the condition or the behavior" (p. 595). In contrast to the sign approach, the conceptual approach addresses issues of "construct" as opposed to "criterion-related" validity. Criterion-related validity, according to Weiner (1977), consists of the extent to which Rorschach scores correlate with some concurrent condition of the subject or a predicted aspect of behavior. On the other hand, construct validity addresses the extent to which a theoretical formulation can account for relationships between selected aspects of a Rorschach protocol and some condition or behavior. While these two forms of validity are not mutually exclusive, positive outcomes in construct validity studies of personality measures validate both the theoretical formulations concerning the personality variables studied and the tests used for assessing these variables. Personality theory, from a conceptual approach to the Rorschach, is seen as an essential guide for appropriate clinical and research applications of the instrument.

While the relationship between a conceptual approach to the Rorschach and psychoanalytic theory has a long history of mutual benefit, the most contemporary proponents of this point of view are reflected in the work of Blatt, Mayman, the Lerners, and Sugarman. Rorschach assessment from a conceptual vantage point in general and a psychoanalytic perspective in particular is markedly different from more traditional psychometric testing. Effective utilization of the Rorschach within a conceptual framework does not divorce the instrument from its clinical foundation and as Blatt (1975) notes, research requires that judgments reflect the distinctions made in clinical practice. According to Blatt: ". . . many studies have simply failed to find support for some of the most fundamental Rorschach assumptions because researchers used test scores in an undifferentiated way without understanding the basic assumptions and interpretive rationale for the procedure. Many studies have simply failed to integrate into their research methodology the finer distinctions made by experienced clinicians in interpreting a Rorschach" (p. 329). From a conceptual perspective it is important that the Rorschach as a research instrument not be used in a mechanical way; that is, the same distinctions, qualifications, and integrations made in the clinical application should carry over to research.

A conceptual utilization of the Rorschach, in contrast to the psychometric testing, maintains both a foundation in clinical application and a coherent theory of personality. As Mayman (1964, p. 53) noted, "In testing a patient for clinical purposes, we are not simply measuring: we observe a person in action, try to reconstruct how he went about dealing with the tasks we set for him, and then try to make clinical sense of this behavior" (p. 2). In pioneering this approach, Rapaport foresaw how test administration, scoring, and interpretation were inextricably interwoven. He demanded that the test administrator be thoroughly familiar with the mechanics of each test and that the examiner feel free to engage him- or herself with the subject rather than the test. Thus an integral part of the verbatim Rorschach protocol includes the examiner's own comments and the patient's spontaneous remarks.

Psychometric and clinical testing differ significantly in regard to the role and value accorded the examiner. In psychometric testing the test administrator is seen as a source of bias and error variance, hence this role is standardized and minimized as much as possible. In contrast, in clinical testing the examiner's role is maximized as his or her skill, judgment, and intuitive sensitivity are not only valued, but are regarded as the most sensitive and perceptive clinical tools available. The scope of interpersonal interactions which arise in the patient-examiner relationship are neither avoided or acted upon; rather, they are carefully observed and used as an essential aid in bringing informed meaning and understanding to the subject's behavior and attitudes.

The psychologist using the Rorschach in a clinical manner, as Schlesinger (1973) and Sugarman (1985) note, have several sources of information available. First, he or she has the subject's behavior in the standardized testing situation, the ways in which the subject interacts with the examiner, and the nature of changes in the testing relationship over time. Second, the examiner has the content of the subject's test responses, including the subject's idiosyncratic awareness of and reaction to his or her own performance. As previously noted, the examiner's own subjective reactions, stemming from what Mayman (1976) terms an "emphatic-intuitive" immersion into the testing relationship and test responses, are regarded as an important source of data that can be utilized in a disciplined and psychometrically reliable and valid way. Recently, Sugarman (1981) has applied contemporary psychoanalytic notions of countertransference derived from psychotherapy to the psychological testing situation. A final source of information the examiner can draw upon is the form aspects of the subject's test responses, including test scores and their interrelationships. As Schlesinger (1973) observes, the examiner's task is to become attuned to these various sources of data and to integrate them in a coherent and meaningful way. Each source of information must be given its due and be seen as having its own consistency and relationship with other levels of observation. The art and science of psychological testing, according to Schlesinger (1973), consists of a sensitive and informed shifting of attention from one source of data to another and careful drawing and checking of inferences throughout the course of testing and interpreting.

Along with a solid clinical foundation, the other cornerstone of Rorschach utilization from a conceptual point of view rests upon the grounding of test administration, scoring, and interpretation within a comprehensive theory of personality. Sugarman (1985) has outlined four major functions served by a comprehensive theory of personality. First, a comprehensive theory of personality serves an organizing function. An implicit theory of personality both in clinical practice and in research aids the Rorschach examiner in comprehending and organizing data that are complex, often exceedingly rich, as well as inconsistent. Second, a comprehensive personality theory goes beyond organization to integration of seemingly unrelated pieces of data. Third, a comprehensive understanding of personality theory can guide the well-trained and disciplined diagnostic clinician or researcher in filling in data gaps in an informed manner. Constriction as well as marked fluctuations in functioning on the Rorschach challenge the examiner to understand theoretical relationships on the one hand as one way of explaining the data, but caution the examiner, on the other hand, not to allow theoretical bias to distort clinical test data or results. Fourth, a theory of personality facilitates prediction. As Blatt (1975) notes, it is crucial that the examiner take into account the complex social matrix when attempting to predict on the basis of psychological variables alone; that is, in predicting, it is important that the behavior mediated is generated by the personality variables tapped by the instrument.

The contemporary trend within the conceptual approach to the Rorschach is to reduce the welter of isolated but overlapping variables and ratios based on traditional scoring categories into what Blatt and Berman (1984) term "molar variables" that integrate various Rorschach scores in a way that is psychometrically reliable and that measure central dimensions of personality. According to these authors, this conceptual approach assesses dimensions of personality independent of the test itself; that is, "These more composite variables (e.g., thought organization, quality of object representation, thought disorder, defense) are not a replacement for the traditional scoring of a Rorschach protocol, but rather offer a higher order of organization of the data. This higher order of organization is based on conceptual models and personality theories that provide a framework, external to the Rorschach itself, for integrating various aspects of responses to the Rorschach stimuli" (p. 236).

Contributions of Rapaport: Whereas Rorschach did not wed his procedure to a specific theory of personality, Rapaport did. The marriage forced by Rapaport between the Rorschach and psychoanalysis was a perfect one of technique and theory. Rapaport fashioned the relationship out of a test rationale and a specific perspective as to how the test was to be used.

Rapaport based his theoretical rationale for psychological tests, in general, and the Rorschach, in particular, on the construct "thought processes." Accordingly, the exploration of projective tests and the exploration of thought processes were considered synonymous. He conceived of thinking and its organization as the mediating process connecting behavior with its psychodynamic underpinnings on the one hand to test performance and test responses on the other. It was from this organization of thought including subprocesses such as concept formation, anticipation, memory, judgment, attention, and concentration that Rapaport derived inferences to other facets of personality functioning. This conceptualization of the predictive power of thought processes is especially well-stated by Schafer (1954): "A person's distinctive style of thinking is indicative of ingrained features of his character makeup. Character is here understood as the person's enduring modes of bringing into harmony internal demands and the press of external events, in other words, it refers to relatively constant adjustment efforts in the face of problem situations. The modes of achieving this harmony are understood to consist essentially of reliance on particular mechanisms of defense and related responsiveness to stimulation associated with these defenses" (p. 17).

Rapaport envisioned the relationship between tests and theory as a two-way street. In one direction he saw how theory could provide the clinical examiner with a bedrock of conceptualizations that would allow for test inferences with remarkable depth and range. In discussing this aspect of Rapaport's work, Mayman (1976) states: "Rorschach inferences were transposed to a wholly new level of comprehension as Rapaport made a place for them in his psychoanalytic ego psychology and elevated psychological test findings from mundane, descriptive, pragmatically useful statements to a level of interpretation that achieved an incredible heuristic sweep" (p. 200). In the other direction, Rapaport also saw how the tests themselves provided a means for operationalizing concepts that were hazy, elusive, and highly abstract; how this would then permit the testing of key psychoanalytic formulations; and then, in time, how this could add to the overall evolving scope of psychoanalytic theory.

The pioneering work begun by Rapaport has been continued by others, such as Schafer, Schlesinger, Holt, Blatt, Mayman, Lerner, Sugarman, and Spear. Parallel with the evolving scope of psychoanalytic theory, both clinicians and researchers have sought to translate more recent psychoanalytic observations and formulations into empirical, test-related concepts and then, like Rapaport, employ these as tools for evaluating hypotheses generated from the theory.

Psychoanalysis has never been a static body of knowledge. Consequently, it is not a closed, tightly knit, well-integrated, totally coherent personality theory.

Rather, it is a loose-fitting composite of several complementary, internally consistent submodels, each of which furnishes concepts and formulations for observing and understanding a crucial dimension of personality development and functioning. The following section will briefly review each of these models followed by a discussion of Rorschach endeavors that are reflective of and rooted in that specific conceptual base.

Shifts in Psychoanalytic Theory—Drive Theory: In his earliest stages of theory construction, Freud was primarily interested in identifying the basic instincts. Despite changes in his theory of instincts over time, his latest writings finally settled upon two instincts: libido and aggression. Drive theory, then, refers to the instincts and their vicissitudes and changes they undergo throughout the course of development. While predating Rapaport's work, this aspect or model of psychoanalytic theory that is rooted in drive theory represents a significant contribution to the Rorschach literature.

Robert Holt (1968) developed a Rorschach scoring system for the "primary process" and "secondary process" concepts. Freud, in 1900, had first distinguished primary process thinking from secondary process thinking in his work *The Interpretation of Dreams*. Primary process, a term coined to indicate a developmentally earlier form of thinking, is organized around drive discharge and involves the formal properties of a disregard for logic and reality. As described by Lerner and Lewandowski (1975), "In primary process, ideas are fluid, they lose their identity through fusion and fragmentation, reflectiveness is abandoned and thoughts are combined in seemingly arbitrary ways. Secondary process, in contrast, is under ego control and operates in accordance with the reality principle; it is goal directed, logical, and uses delay of impulses, detours and experimental action until appropriate avenues of gratification have been realized" (p. 182).

Holt's system calls for the scoring of four sets of variables: content indices of primary process, formal indices of primary process, control and defense, and overall ratings. The part of the system most firmly grounded in drive theory, the content indices, involve ideational drive representations. A distinction is drawn between responses reflecting drives with libidinal aims and those with aggressive aims. The libidinal category is further subdivided into sections corresponding to the stages of psychosexual development. The aggression category is subdivided as well; however, these subcategories are based on whether it is the subject (aggressor), the object (victim), or the result (aftermath) that is emphasized in the destructive action. The formal indices reflect formal aspects of the response processes. Herein, categories were developed to assess the perceptual organization of the response, the thinking underlying the response, and the language used to communicate the response. The specific categories roughly parallel characteristics in thinking outlined by Freud (condensation, displacement, symbolism, etc.) and further refined by Rapaport (peculiar verbalizations, confabulations, etc.). The control and defense scores are attempts to measure the way in which the primary process material is regulated and the relative successfulness of those attempts. Two scoring aspects are included, one involving the identification of the specific defensive operation and the other involving a judgment as to whether the operation improves or further disrupts the response. The control and defense categories include remoteness, context, reflection, postponing strategies, sequence, and overtness.

The final section, overall ratings, involves summary ratings of form level, creativity, demand for defense, and effectiveness of defense. Several summary scores are also involved, including percentage of primary process, mean defense demand, mean defense effectiveness, and adaptive regression. Research involving the scoring system has primarily made use of these summary scores.

Holt's scoring system has generated an impressive amount and array of personality research. Studies involving the scoring system have included the following: 1) attempts to relate the drive and control measures to behaviors and characteristics conceptually related to primary process thinking, 2) the use of specific scores as criterion measures in studying the effects on thinking of experimentally induced or clinical conditions, and 3) attempts to find differences in the expression of and control of primary process thinking among groups differentiated on the basis of another variable such as diagnosis or level of conscience development.

Various investigators attempted to relate categories in Holt's manual to specific cognitive and perceptual variables that, on a theoretical basis, are linked to primary process forms of thinking. The variables studied include the thinking of individuals who have undergone unusual religious experiences (Allison, 1967; Maupin, 1965), the capacity to deal with cognitive complexity (Blatt et al., 1969; Von Holt et al., 1960), creativity (Cohen, 1960; Gray, 1979; Pine, 1962; Pine & Holt, 1960; Rogolsky, 1968), the capacity to tolerate unrealistic experiences (Feinstein, 1967), conjunctive empathy (Bachrach, 1968), and tolerance for perceptual deprivation (Goldberger, 1961; Wright & Abbey, 1968; Wright & Zubek, 1969). Overall, the results of these various studies indicated that several summary scores from the manual are related to a host of conceptually based cognitive and perceptual variables. Specifically, the adaptive regression summary score was found to relate to the capacity to tolerate and adaptively deal with situations in which reality contact is temporarily suspended (Zen meditation, conversion experiences, perceptual isolation). These studies further demonstrated that subjects who have the capacity to modulate drive expressions and integrate logical and illogical thoughts into acceptable Rorschach responses are better able to tolerate unrealistic experiences, are more empathic in treatment relationships, and are more effective in handling a variety of cognitive tasks (Lerner & Lewandowski, 1975). No clear-cut relationship has been found between manual scores and creativity. The inconsistency in findings that has been reported seems to be due to the sample used, the measure of creativity employed, and the specific manual score studied.

A second group of studies employed specific Holt scores to evaluate the effects on thinking of particular experimental and clinical conditions. The conditions investigated included subliminally presented aggressive stimuli (Silverman, 1965, 1966; Silverman & Candell, 1970; Silverman & Goldberger, 1966; Silverman & Spiro, 1967), drugs (Saretsky, 1966), and myxedema psychosis (Greenberg et al., 1969). From these studies the following results were reported: 1) disturbed thinking, defined by increases in the formal indices section of the manual, increased following presentation at a subliminal level of aggressive stimuli; 2) following the use of chlorpomazine there was an increase in the mean defense effectiveness score and this increase was related to an independent measure of clinical improvement; and 3) in a patient treated for myxedema psychosis, predicted changes were noted in the mean defense demand score, the mean defense effectiveness score, and three formal scores.

A third group of studies were designed to determine differences in the expression and control of primary process manifestations among groups differentiated on the basis of other variables. In these studies it was found that groups distinguished on the basis of varied factors such as diagnosis (Silverman, 1965), subdiagnosis (Zimet & Fine, 1965), and conscience development (Benfari & Calogeras, 1968) differed in the extent and quality of primary process manifestations and these differences were in the predicted directions.

Taken collectively, the above studies lend consistent and convincing support to the notion of Holt's scoring system as a valid measure of primary process thinking. As such, Holt, in keeping with a tradition begun by Rapaport, has made operational a concept (primary and secondary process thinking) basic to psychoanalytic theory and thus has provided a most valuable tool for investigating the hypothesis generated by this aspect of Freud's theorizing.

Shifts in Psychoanalytic Theory—The Structural Model: From his early concern with drive identification, Freud's interest shifted to an emphasis on studying and understanding those processes which controlled and regulated the drives and their vicissitudes. With this shift he began to outline the characteristics, synthesis, and functions of the ego with particular emphasis on the defensive function. This change in theoretical emphasis ushered in the structural model and eventuated in Freud's formulations regarding the tripartite (ego, superego, id) structure of the personality. Although Holt's system for assessing primary process manifestations (especially the section on control and defense) is theoretically rooted in this model as well as drive theory, Schafer's (1954) work on the defensive aspect of Rorschach responses best characterizes the contribution of the structural model to Rorschach theory and usage.

Based upon the pattern of formal scores, the content of the response, the nature of the patient-examiner relationship, and the attitude the patient takes toward his or her responses, Schafer outlined seven general and 36 specific types of expressions of defense and/or defended against as they might appear on the Rorschach. Also included are provisions for determining the overall success or failure of the defensive operation. The categories and expressions of defense, together with the indications of success or failure, are applied to the specific mechanisms of repression, projection, denial, regression, reaction formation, isolation, and undoing. For each defense Schafer elaborated the theoretical underpinnings, outlined expected Rorschach manifestations, and provided clinical examples.

To illustrate the above points, Schafer's treatment of the defense of repression will be presented. Based upon Fenichel (1945), Schafer defines repression as "unconsciously purposeful forgetting or not becoming aware of internal impulses or external events which, as a rule, represent possible temptations or punishments for, or mere allusions to, objectionable, instinctual demands" (p. 193). Implicit in this definition, as Schafer points out, is the aim of blocking the unacceptable impulses and their derivatives, as well as the formulation that the repressed continues to exist outside of awareness. Because repression prevents part of the personality from growing and developing, a prolonged emphasis on repression often results in marked ego restriction and various expressions of immaturity. Therefore, in a repressed individual one expects to find impulsiveness, unreflectiveness, naïvete, diffuse affects, emotional lability, superficiality, and a tendency to relate to others in a childlike way.

From these behavioral characteristics commonly associated with a strong reliance on repression, Schafer then devised Rorschach indices reflective of these traits. For example, to indicate the relative paucity of ideas and narrowness of ideation, he suggested that the test record should reveal a comparatively low number of total responses and human movement responses as well as a limited range of content categories. Long reaction times and card rejections, he further noted, were to be expected. For Schafer, formal aspects of the test record related to affect and anxiety were likely to be prominent. He anticipated a protocol with a conspicuous number of responses involving color and shading and suggested that the extent to which form entered into color and shading responses reflected the way in which the individual experienced and expressed affects. Turning from formal scores to the patient's attitude toward the examination process, Schafer suggested that one would anticipate an attitude characterized by self-centeredness, defensive vagueness, childish naïvete, and impenetrable unreflectiveness. Finally, Schafer depicted an interpersonal relationship in which the examiner was looked to for reassurance as well as permission.

In the above example, we have attempted to illustrate Schafer's methodology; how, with each defense, he began with the psychoanalytic definition of that defense, inferred from the defensive operation likely behavioral and attitudinal correlates, and then from the scores, content, and testing relationship identified Rorschach indices reflective of those correlates.

Schafer's application of the concept of defense to the Rorschach has become an indispensable part of the clinical armamentarium of the psychoanalytically-oriented examiner. Concurrently, Schaefer's work has generated considerable research which, in turn, has broadened and refined the theory surrounding the concept of defense.

Contemporary Psychoanalytic View of the Rorschach: The conceptual approach to the Rorschach and psychoanalytic theory are at present in a state of evolution. New orientations in psychoanalytic theory involving the emergence and elaboration of object relations theory, self psychology, and developmental psychoanalysis have converged into a phenomenological point of view and a developmental structural perspective that intersects with both more traditional formulations and other disciplines including cognitive, developmental, and social psychological theories. While traditional psychoanalytic propositions are being questioned and core concepts such as thought processes, defenses, and the impact of formative interpersonal relationships on psychological structure formation are being reconceptualized, these new developments in turn are being transformed and operationalized into a more phenomenological Rorschach test theory.

From a historical perspective, Mayman (1963) was one of the earliest Rorschach investigators to delve into more experiential and clinically relevant dimensions of personality. As Blatt and Lerner (1983a) note, he consistently stressed the need to develop a theory of psychoanalysis based on what he termed a "middle level language" as part of the "complex multileveled theory" of psychoanalysis and to distinguish among what he saw as three coordinated sets of concepts or languages. First, according to Mayman (1963, 1976), there is the language used by the therapist in transaction with the patient during the treatment hour, a language more akin to poetry than science. Outside the consultation room the clinician utilizes a "middle language" of "empirical constructs" that helps formulate clinical generalizations about an individual. A third, more abstract language consists of "systematic" or "hypothetical constructs," a system of impersonal concepts using more objective, distant, third-person terms that constitutes psychoanalytic metapsychology. Mayman argues that these three levels of abstraction should not be confused with each other but rather need to be coordinated with constant reference back to the original primary data base, the clinical material. In the remainder of this section we will discuss several of these theoretical advancements and then present research endeavors and clinical test material that reflect innovative ways of utilizing the Rorschach from a conceptual point of view.

Psychology of the Self: In a series of major publications, Kohut (1971, 1977) has laid the conceptual groundwork for a systematic psychoanalytic psychology of the self. Tolpin and Kohut (1978), in a paper with major diagnostic implications, drew important distinctions between more classical neurotic pathology and pathology of the self. Unlike the former, which is presumed to originate in later childhood and at a time when there is self-other differentiation, full structural development (id, ego, superego), and oedipal passions, self-pathology begins in earlier childhood and at a point when the psychic structures are still in formation. Because of the absence of a cohesive sense of self, in self-pathology symptoms occur when the insecurely established self is threatened by dangers of psychological disintegration, fragmentation, and devitalization. Further, in treatment, unlike the neurotic patient who develops a transference neurosis in which the therapist is experienced as a new edition of parents, patients with self-pathology develop therapeutic relationships in which the therapist is used to correct or carry out a function that is ordinarily, with optimal development, carried out intrapsychiatrically.

Based on these formulations, Paul Lerner (1979, 1981, in press), in a series of papers, has attempted to describe the test behavior and pattern of Rorschach responses of a selected subgroup of outpatients with self-pathology who, on the basis of their test performance, exhibit an identifiable self-system and mode of interpersonal relationships, definable style of thinking, and characteristic manner of experiencing affects. According to Lerner, these patients enter testing under a cloak of extreme vigilance with a readiness to be distrustful. They are described as hyperalert, highly sensitive, and extremely vulnerable. Accompanying the sensitivity is a style of compliance and accommodation. Similar to chameleons, they sensitively attune to the nuances, expectations, and anticipations of others and mold themselves and their behavior accordingly. They present what Winnicott (1960) has referred to as a "false self." They swiftly scrutinize all aspects of the examiner during the test situation, including his or her tone of voice, attire, and office furnishings. Consequently, the examiner experiences him- or herself as being viewed under a microscope and as a result may feel inhibited or as if "walking on egg shells," carefully selecting words and unconsciously fearing damage to the subject's self-esteem.

Lerner (1979) has identified a Rorschach determinant which is especially sensitive to hypervigilance and heightened sensitivity; that is, the (c) response. This score is applied to responses which are delineated and determined by variations in shading. Because the perception of variations in shading on the Rorschach are subtle, to generate a (c) response one must scrutinize the blot extremely carefully, sensitively attune to finely differentiated nuances, and feel one's way into something that is not blatantly apparent. To accomplish this, according to Schactel (1966), requires perceptual sensitivity in addition to a searching, articulating, and penetrating activity.

The tendency toward compliance becomes manifested in Rorschach imagery or content. Lifeless figures whose actions and intentions are controlled externally, such as puppets, mannequins, and robots often populate the examinees' protocols. Further, quasi-human figures distanced in time or space such as ghosts, clowns, snowmen, skeletons, and masks convey their sense of lacking substance and illusory feelings.

Lerner further describes this group of patients in terms of a specific cognitive style characterized by concreteness, passivity, and egocentricity. These individuals often exhibit a nearsighted clarity accompanied by a blatant loss of backdrop or perspective; that is, they lack reasonable objectivity and detachment. Accordingly, life events are not critically examined or placed in logical context, but rather are experienced in terms of their most obvious and immediately personal qualities. As Lerner puts it, "The present dominates and the significance of the past and of the future vanishes" (p. 25). While the (c) response vividly reflects impairments in maintaining perspective, the arbitrary and incompatible blending of color with content, as seen in the FC arbitrary score (e.g., blue monkeys, pink wolverines), and the offering of responses in which spatial or temporal relationships in the blot are concretely taken as real relationships (fabulized combinations) capture the loss of distance from the cards together with the relinquishment of a more objective, critical, and self-imposed evaluative attitude.

According to Lerner, these patients described by Kohut and his colleagues also experience distinctive and identifiable affects. Specifically, they are subject to lowered self-esteem, disintegration anxiety, and depletion depression. Disintegration anxiety, a term used by Kohut (1977), refers to a type of primal anxiety or agitated depression prompted by threats to self-cohesion and fears revolving around fragmentation and a loss of aliveness. The depressive affect involves unbearable feelings of deadness and nonexistence and a self-perception of emptiness, weakness, and helplessness. Recently, Wilson (in press) has linked these Rorschach determinants to Blatt's (1974) formulations concerning anaclitic depression, a type of pre-oedipal depression characterized by helplessness, hopelessness, and a future quest for need gratification.

Developmental Theory: A second recent advance within psychoanalysis has been the elaboration of an empirically based, dynamic, developmental theory. Mahler, Pine, and Bergman (1975) have observed the steps in the separation-individuation process, beginning with the earliest signs of the infant's differentiation or hatching from a symbiotic fusion with the mother, proceeding through the period of the infant's absorption in his or her own autonomous functioning to the near exclusion of the mother, continuing through the all-important period of rapprochement in which the infant, precisely because of his or her more clearly perceived state of separateness from the mother, is prompted to redirect attention back to the mother, and concluding with a feeling of a primitive sense of self, of individual identity, and of constancy of the object.

Based upon these formulations, Kwawer (1980) developed a Rorschach scale designed to assess early object relations, particularly self-other differentiation, in patients with severe character pathology. He first identified, theoretically and clinically, very early stages of levels of relatedness in the developmental emergence of selfhood through differentiation from a primary mothering figure and then constructed Rorschach content scores to assess these stages. An initial stage, termed "narcissistic mirroring," includes responses in which mirrors or reflections play a prominent role. Percepts such as "two men mirroring each other, two little mimes" or "somebody grabbing hold of himself in a mirror" would be included under this heading. These responses are understood as reflecting a state of self-absorption in which the other is experienced solely as an extension of the self and used for the exclusive purpose of mirroring or enhancing the self. A second stage, referred to as "symbiotic merging," consists of responses which indicate a powerful push toward merger, fusion, and reuniting. "Siamese twins joined at the stomach and they have but one hand" and "a butterfly that flew into a wall and seems to be at one with wall" are illustrative responses included in this category. A third stage of interpersonal differentiation is found in responses conveying "separation and division" content. The Rorschach imagery is reminiscent of the biological metaphor of cell division: "These two things appear to have been once connected but broke apart . . . it's as if on the inside there was some continuity between the two." An analogous process is suggested by the following response: "It's an animal dividing going from one to two . . . it almost looks like it's breaking away into two separate objects." The fourth and final stage, according to Kwawer (1980), termed "metamorphosis and transformation," is reflective of the experience of a very early and rudimentary sense of self. Here incipient selfhood is manifested in themes of one-celled organisms, fetuses, and embryos. An example of this type of response is "Two ants dressed up in men's clothes . . . it seems like their bodies are transformed into human bodies, but their heads remained ants. They were acting like human beings."

Technical Aspects

Modern Object Relations Theory: Psychoanalytic theorists and researchers are increasingly aware of the complex interactions among early formative interpersonal relationships; the level and quality of internal psychological structures including thought processes and defensive organization; the internal representational world; and the nature of ongoing interpersonal relations and the ways they are internalized and become part of the personality. This comparatively recent perspective has provided the conceptual foundation for several innovative Rorschach studies.

One major thrust is seen in the varied attempts to assess the construct "object representation." Defined broadly, object representation refers to the conscious and unconscious mental schemata, including cognitive, affective, and experiential components of objects encountered in reality (Blatt & Lerner, 1983a, 1983b). Beginning as vague, diffuse, variable sensorimotor experiences of pleasure and unpleasure, they gradually expand and develop into differentiated, consistent, relatively realistic representations of the self and the object world. Earlier forms of representation are based more on action sequences associated with need gratification, intermediate forms are based on specific perceptual features, and higher forms are more symbolic and conceptual. Whereas these schemata evolve from and are intertwined with the developmental internalization of object relations and ego functions (Mahler et al., 1975), the developing representations provide a new organization for experiencing object relations.

Two primary research groups have contributed to the systematic study of the object representation construct by means of the Rorschach and other projective techniques through experimental procedures. These two research groups represent different but not mutually exclusive approaches to the study of object representations. Mayman and his colleagues at the University of Michigan have focused on the thematic dimension of object representations and using a variety of projective procedures (e.g., early memories, manifest dreams, written autobiographies), including the Rorschach, have studied the relationship between this construct and the severity of psychopathology, character structure, quality of object relations, and capacity to benefit from psychotherapy. Blatt and his colleagues at Yale University, by contrast, have emphasized the structural dimension of object representations. While this group has also developed independent projective measures and scales (e.g., parental descriptions, Thematic Apperception Test scales), they have studied the developmental level of object representations across a wide spectrum of normal and clinical populations. Although the contributions of both groups are conceptually rooted in an integration of ego psychology and object relations theory, Blatt and his colleagues have integrated the developmental cognitive theories of Piaget and Werner into their Rorschach scales and formulations.

Based on the theoretical contributions of Jacobson and Erickson, Mayman (1967, 1968) conceptualized object representation as templates or internalized images of the self and of others around which the phenomenological world is structured and into which the ongoing experience of others is assimilated. Methodologically, he contended that the manifest content of dreams, early memories, and Rorschach content was more than simply a screen that both expressed and concealed deeper and more significant levels of unconscious meanings. He argued that manifest content in its own right could reflect levels of ego functioning, the capacity for object relations, and the nature of interpersonal strivings. According to Mayman (1967): "When a person is asked to spend an hour immersing himself in a field of impressions where amorphousness prevails and where strange or even alien forms may appear, he will set in motion a reparative process, the aim of which is to replace formlessness with reminders of the palpably real world. He primes himself to recall, recapture, reconstitute his world as he knows it, with people, animals, and things which fit most naturally into the ingrained expectations around which he has learned to structure his phenomenal world. A person's most readily accessible object representations called up under such unstructured conditions tell much about his inner world of objects and about the quality of relationships with these inner objects toward which he is predisposed" (p. 17).

Equipped with these notions, together with a commitment to a clinical empathic-intuitive approach to the analysis of projective test data, in an early study Mayman (1967) operationalized selected Rorschach responses, particularly the human response, as expressions or facets of object representations. Building on the clinical observation that the human content of good psychiatric residents featured "warmth, openness, and a sense of contact" and those of poor residents expressed "cynicism . . . bitterness . . . fearfulness or alienation from the people they described" (p. 21), Mayman developed a technique of distilling Rorschach protocols into clusters of object representational responses independent of reference to traditional scoring categories in order to test the validity of inferences made from object representational aggregates of Rorschach responses. Mayman compared independent ratings of these responses using the Luborsky Health-Sickness Scale with similar ratings by clinicians based on clinical interviews, and found an impression correlation ($r = .86$) between the two measures for a group of patients.

Mayman's seminal contributions to the Rorschach have spawned a number of object representation scales and a host of construct validational studies conducted by his students that have further refined the concept (Urist, 1973) and have extended the thematic analysis of object representations to manifest dreams (Krohn, 1972), autobiographical data (Urist, 1973), and the capacity to benefit from insight-oriented psychotherapy (Hatcher and Krohn, 1980). The various scales designed to unearth object representational levels as specific points on a developmental continuum have been correlated with each other (Urist, 1973) and have been applied and correlated across data bases including manifest dreams, the Rorschach, early memories, and health-sickness ratings (Krohn & Mayman, 1974). These studies reflect Mayman's focal interest in thematic content, his distinct and gifted clinical approach to projective data that capitalizes on the empathic-intuitive skills of trained clinicians, and his abiding interest in variables relevant to psychoanalytic theory and treatment.

Using a scale designed by Mayman and Ryan (1972) to evaluate object representational content dimensions in early memories, Ryan (1973) found a positive relationship in neurotic patients between levels of object representation and the capacity to enter into an elementary psychotherapeutic relationship. Drawing upon Mayman and Ryan's scale, Krohn (1972), through a pilot study, developed the Object Representation Scale for Dreams. Designed to tap the degrees of wholeness, differentiation, consistency, and overall intactness of object representations with an impressionistic survey of dreams, Krohn's scale was example-anchored and intended for use by "intuitive, trained clinicians" in an empathic manner. With a view toward establishing the reliability and construct validity of the object representation concept as an empirically, researchable dimension of personality, Krohn (1972) and Krohn and Mayman (1974) applied the dream scale across a range of projective media including written manifest dream reports, early memories, and Rorschach protocols that they then demonstrated to be related to therapist-supervisor ratings of patients'overt object relations and Luborsky's health-sickness dimension. The authors report a number of important findings. Strong, statistically significant correlations were found between object representations assessed on the Rorschach, early memories, and dreams; and high correlations emerged between projective object representation scores and criterion ratings of psychopathology and level of object representation. Analyzing the data through partial correlations, the dream and early memory scores emerged as the best predictors to therapist-supervisor ratings of patients' object relations while the Rorschach ratings correlated most significantly with more global health-sickness scores. Krohn (1972) found that patients' Rorschach ratings were consistently lower; that is, less intact than scores based on either manifest dreams or early memories. "The fundamental conclusion to be drawn from this study," according to Krohn and Mayman (1974), "is that level of object representation appears to be a salient, consistent, researchable personality dimension that expresses itself through a relatively diverse set of psychological avenues ranging from a realm as private as dream life to one as interpersonal as psychotherapy. Moreover, it is not a redundant construct synonymous with level of psychopathology or severity of symptomatology" (p. 464).

Consonant with the methodological thrusts of Mayman and integrating the theoretical contributions of Kernberg and Kohut, Urist (1973), in a sophisticated construct validational study, examined the multidimensional qualitative aspects of the object representational concept by correlating several Rorschach scale ratings of 40 adult inpatients covering a broad range of psychopathology with independent ratings of written autobiographies. The specific scales designed by Urist were gauged to reflect the developmental ordering of stages in the unfolding of object relations along a number of overlapping dimensions including mutuality of autonomy, body integrity, aliveness, fusion, thought disorder, richness and complexity, and differentiation and individuation. The focus of the measures, particularly the Mutuality of Autonomy Scale, is on the developmental progression of separation-individuation from symbiosis to object constancy. Urist reports significantly high correlations among the various measures of object relations which reflect an impressive consistency among internal self and object representations across a wide range of sampled behavior. In terms of the ability of the Rorschach to tap qualitative aspects of the representational world, Urist observed, ". . . the individual's internal world of mental representations is indeed mapped into his percepts on the Rorschach" (p. 113).

In keeping with his initial hypothesis and bolstered by factor analytic techniques, Urist demonstrated that object relations are not unidimensional areas of ego functioning. A factor analysis discerned an important distinction between two related but separate structural underpinnings of object representation; that is, an integrity factor related to issues of self-other differentiation, stability, and consistency (an index of secondary narcissism), and a boundary factor related to developmental gradations in fusion-merger tendencies and thought disorder associated with the ability to maintain a cognitive-perceptual sense of boundary between self and other and between one object and another (an index of primary narcissism).

Utilizing the same data, but highlighting the Mutuality of Autonomy Scale, Urist (1977), in a further construct validational study, correlated Rorschach ratings with independent measures of the same dimension applied to the written autobiographies and behavioral ratings of ward staff. Obtaining several Rorschach scores in order to sample the range as well as the average and "best subjective overall rating," Urist reported a consistency across all variables and range of measures that point to an enduring consistency in patients' representations of relationships, and he demonstrated that the Rorschach can be utilized effectively to systematically assess aspects of mutuality of autonomy within patients' experience of self and others.

The contributions of Mayman and his colleagues at the University of Michigan, summarized by Blatt and Lerner (1983a), ". . . reflect a focal interest in thematic content—allowing the data to speak for themselves, a steadfast clinical focus which is experience-near, and which is comprehended through empathic-intuitive skills while at the same time achieving psychometrically respectable levels of validity, and finally, an abiding commitment to investigating reactive variables directly relevant to psychoanalytic theory and the treatment process" (p. 210).

A second major approach to the study and systematic assessment of object representations is represented in the work of Blatt and his colleagues. In contrast to the University of Michigan group, which stressed thematic analysis and a more clinical-intuitive methodology, the group at Yale, employing more experimental methodologies, has focused upon the structural dimension of the object representation construct.

Conceptualizing the establishment of ego boundaries between self and nonself and between fantasy and reality (inside and outside) as the initial and most fundamental stages in the development of object representations, several studies (Blatt & Ritzler, 1974; Brenneis, 1971) have involved an assessment of boundary disturbances in psychotic and borderline patients. Using three of Rapaport's classic indices of thought disorder (contamination, confabulation, fabulized combination) as measures of varying level of severity of boundary disturbances, Blatt and Ritzler (1974) found such indices to be related to a variety of ego functions (capacity for reality testing, quality of interpersonal relations, nature of object representations) in a mixed schizophrenic and borderline sample. The authors also found that poorly articulated boundaries occurred most frequently in more disturbed, chronic patients who had impoverished object relations, impaired ego functions, and a lifelong pattern of isolation and estrangement. Using the manifest content of dreams, Brenneis (1971) reported significantly more boundary disturbances in a group of schizophrenic patients as compared with other psychiatric patients having a diagnosis indicating less severe psychopathology. Johnson (1980) provided empirical support for Blatt and Ritzler's contention that patients with more articulated boundaries are more actively involved in interpersonal relations. And, more recently, Lerner, Sugarman, and Barbour (1985) have expanded the scope of research in this area by finding that independently diagnosed borderline patients can be distinguished from both schizophrenics and neurotics on the basis of boundary disturbance. These authors found support for Blatt's findings that schizophrenia involves a deficit in maintaining the distinction between self and others. In drawing developmental distinctions between groups, Lerner et al. (1985) found that borderline patients experience difficulty maintaining the inner-outer boundary as assessed through the confabulation response; that is, these patients experience difficulty discriminating between an external object and their own internal affective reaction to that object.

Building on their initial investigation of boundary disturbances, Blatt, Brenneis, Schimek, and Glick (1976) developed a highly comprehensive and sophisticated Rorschach manual for assessing object representations. Based upon the developmental theory of Werner (1948) and ego psychoanalytic theory, the system calls for the scoring of human responses in terms of the developmental principles of differentiation, articulation, and integration. Within each of these areas, categories were established along a continuum based on developmental levels. Differentiation refers to the type of figure perceived, whether the figure is quasi-human detail, human detail, quasi-human, or a full human figure. For articulation, responses are scored on the basis of the number and types of attributes ascribed to the figure. Integration of the response is scored in three ways: the degree of internality of the action, the degree of integration of the object and its action, and the integration of the interaction with another object. Responses are also second along a content dimension of benevolence-malevolence.

In an early study (Blatt et al., 1976) this particular scoring system was applied to the Rorschach protocols of normal subjects on four separate occasions over a 20-year period. In this longitudinal study of normal development the authors found a marked increase, over time, in the number of accurately perceived, well-articulated, full human figures involved in appropriate, integrated, positive, and meaningful interaction. In a second study, the records of the normal subjects obtained at age 17 were compared with the Rorschachs of a hospitalized sample of disturbed adolescents and young adults. In comparison with the normals, patients gave human figures that were significantly more inaccurately perceived, distorted, and seen as inert or engaged in unmotivated, incongruent, nonspecific, and malevolent activity. The combined studies' results lent strong support to the construct validity of the concept object representation and the manual devised to assess it.

This construct validity study had particular relevance for understanding psychopathology (Blatt et al., 1976). These researchers found that while the Rorschach responses of hospitalized schizophrenic and borderline patients were at lower developmental levels, these responses were primarily accurately perceived in terms of form level. Paradoxically, patients were found to have a significantly greater number of responses at higher developmental levels than normals on inaccurately perceived Rorschach responses; that is, hospitalized patients had a significantly greater number of developmentally more advanced responses—responses that were undistorted, intact, well articulated, integrated, and benevolent. These findings, according to Blatt and his colleagues, indicate that patients, as compared with normals, function at lower developmental levels when in contact with conventional reality but that hospitalized patients function at higher developmental levels than normals when they give idiosyncratic interpretations of reality. These findings have been replicated by Ritzler, Zambianco, Harder, and Kaskey (1980) who found this pattern to be more apparent in schizophrenic than non-schizophrenic psychotic patients.

Recently Lerner and St. Peter (1984) applied the Concept of the Object Scale (Blatt et al., 1976) to the Rorschach protocols of independently diagnosed outpatient neurotic and borderline subjects as well as hospitalized borderline and schizophrenic patients. Analyzing the results separately for perceptually accurate and inaccurate responses, Lerner and St. Peter found, consistent with previous studies, that schizophrenic patients produced significantly fewer accurate responses and portrayed realistic human figures at lower developmental levels than the other three groups. This impairment in the representation of objects serves as a distinguishing factor between schizophrenic and borderline patients and is consistent with previous clinical and research reports. Unexpectedly, however, the inpatient borderline sample functioned at the highest developmental level of differentiation, articulation, and integration for inaccurate responses and, in general, produced more inaccurate responses in these categories than the other three groups. The results, particularly in regard to the hospitalized borderline group, highlight the content dimension of object representation as being a particularly discriminating variable. The inpatient borderline subjects produced the most human responses with malevolent content and were the only group to offer inaccurately perceived malevolent responses. Whereas only 25% of all other subjects offered malevolent human responses, the inpatient borderline sample attributed malevolency to 42% of their human responses and to 94% of their quasi-human characters. These findings clearly illustrate the enormous difficulty these patients experience in managing aggression within the interpersonal relationships.

In order to assess the clinical utility of the Concept of the Object Scale, Blatt and Lerner (1983b) applied the instrument to the Rorschach records of several patients, each of whom was independently selected as a prototypic example of a specific clinical disorder. These authors not only found a unique quality of object representation for each of the clinical entities, but their findings, based on Rorschach data, were remarkably congruent with clinical expectations. In a nonparanoid schizophrenic patient the object representations were found to be inaccurately perceived and at lower developmental levels of differentiation. The representations were inappropriately articulated and seen as either inert or involved in unmotivated action. Little interaction was seen between figures and the content was basically barren. With a narcissistic-borderline patient, the object representations were found to progressively deteriorate either over time or with stress. Initially, the representations were accurate, well differentiated, and appropriately articulated; however, this gave way to representations that were inaccurately perceived, inappropriately articulated, and seen as part rather than whole figures. An infantile character with an anaclitic depression (Blatt, 1974) represented objects accurately but with little articulation. Interaction was perceived between figures, but this usually involved an active-passive transaction in which one figure was seen as vulnerable and in a depriving, rejecting, undependable relationship. In an acutely suicidal patient with an introjective depression (Blatt, 1974), the author found an alternation between representations at higher developmental levels and others at lower developmental levels. The latter representations featured activities between objects that were destructive and with malevolent intent. The representations of a delinquent adolescent were well differentiated, limitedly articulated, and characterized by activity that lacked purpose and direction. Finally, a patient diagnosed as hysteric provided representations that were clearly differentiated and highly articulated, although the articulation was primarily in terms of external physical details. The interactions ascribed between figures was mutual and reciprocal but, nonetheless, childlike.

Whereas several of the above studies involved individual cases, Spear (1980) investigated differences among diagnostic groups on the Object Representation Scale. Using a summary score, he found significantly greater impairment in representing objects in a schizophrenic group as compared with two groups of borderline patients.

Finally, other investigators have related parts of Blatt et al.'s scoring manual to psychological variables conceptually linked to object representation. Johnson (1980) reported significant correlations between the degree of articulation of the representation and more advanced developmental levels of interaction and an independent measure of field independence. He also found a significant correlation between scale measures of the integration of the object with its action and the portrayal of congruent interactions in a role-playing task. Fibel (1979), in a sample of seriously disturbed adolescent and young adult hospitalized patients, found a significantly positive relationship between scale scores and independent clinical assessments of quality of interpersonal relations.

In summary, in an earlier article Blatt (1974) made a substantial contribution to the theoretical literature on the construct object representation. In particular, he explained the relationship between level of object representation and the nature and severity of depression. Out of this theoretical groundwork, bolstered by the integration of theories of cognitive developmental psychology with psychoanalytic theory, has come a psychometrically refined scoring manual for the systematic assessment of object representation. Studies involving the development of object representations in normal subjects, differences in object representations among different individual patients representing varied clinical disorders, and investigations regarding the relationship between object representations and other theoretically linked variables have all contributed to the construct validity of the scoring manual.

A second innovation, emerging from the integration of object relations theory with more classical psychoanalytic theory, has been an attempt to investigate the more primitive defenses of the borderline patient. Kernberg (1975) has identified two overall levels of defensive organization associated with pre-oedipal and oedipal pathology. At the lower level, splitting is the core defense with a concomitant impairment of the ego's synthetic function. In addition, splitting is abetted through the related defenses of primitive idealization, primitive devaluation, denial, and projective identification. At a more advanced level, repression replaces splitting as the major defense and is accompanied by the related defensive operations of intellectualization, rationalization, undoing, and higher forms of projection.

Based upon these theoretical conceptualizations of defense advanced by Kernberg (1975) and the clinical test work of Mayman (1967), Pruitt and Spilka (1964), Holt (1968), and Peebles (1975), Lerner and Lerner (1980) devised a Rorschach scoring manual designed to evaluate the specific defensive operations presumed to characterize this developmentally lower level of defensive functioning.

This scoring manual is divided into sections on the basis of the specific defenses of splitting, devaluation, idealization, projective identification, and denial. Within each section the defense is defined, Rorschach indices of the defense are presented and clinical illustrations are offered. The sections on devaluation, idealization, and denial call for an identification of these defenses as well as a ranking of the defense on a continuum of high versus low order. In keeping with Kernberg's notion that these defense organize (as well as reflect) the internalized object world, and with the empirical relationship found between human responses on the Rorschach and quality of object relating (Blatt & Lerner, 1983b), the system involves a systematic appraisal of the human figure response. In assessing the human percept, attention is paid to the precise figure seen, the way in which the figure is described, and the action ascribed to the figure.

To evaluate the construct validity of the manual the authors (Lerner & Lerner, 1980) conducted two separate studies. In one study Rorschach records of borderline patients were compared with those of neurotic patients, while in the second study the protocols of borderline and schizophrenic patients were compared with respect to manifestations of primitive defenses.

In the first study (Lerner & Lerner, 1980), 30 Rorschachs, 15 from borderline patients and 15 from neurotic patients, were selected from private files and scored using the proposed system. Independently-obtained mental status examinations and social-developmental histories were also available on each patient. Because the testing was initially done for research purposes, it was not used in the formulating of a diagnosis. As each of the patients subsequently entered either psychotherapy or psychoanalysis, the initial diagnosis was confirmed in discussions with the patient's therapist or analyst. The patients were matched as groups on the variables of age, sex, and socioeconomic status. The Rorschach records obtained from the two groups did not differ significantly with regard to the number of total responses.

For purposes of reliability, all Rorschachs were coded, scored independently by two raters, and then the ratings were correlated. The resultant correlations were as follows: .76 for splitting, .96 for projective identification, and .58 to 1.00 for the continuum variables.

A review of the findings indicated that borderline patients used scale indices of lower level devaluation, splitting, and projective identification significantly more often than did the neurotic patients. Strikingly, measures of splitting and projective identification appeared exclusively in the borderline groups. By contrast, indices of high level devaluation and high level denial were found significantly more frequently among the neurotic patients. The authors further found that the use of excessive depreciation and idealization by the neurotics was typically mitigated through forms of higher level denial. Such was not the case with these borderlines. Their expressions of blatant devaluation and idealization were not mitigated, controlled, or regulated.

In the second study (Lerner, Sugarman, & Gaughran, 1981), which involved a comparison of borderline and schizophrenic patients, Rorschach protocols were selected from the records of a population of psychiatric inpatients hospitalized at a university teaching hospital. Patients selected for the study were between 16 and 26 years and showed no evidence of organic impairment. The schizophrenic sample, consisting of 19 patients, was selected using the Research Diagnostic Criteria (Spitzer et al., 1975). The borderline sample, which consisted of 21 patients, was selected in accordance with criteria set out in DSM-III.

Obtained reliability results, also involving interrater agreement, were comparable to those reported in the 1980 study. In this study the borderline patients were found to use test indices of primitive devaluation, primitive idealization, lower level denial, splitting, and projective identification significantly more often than the schizophrenic patients. As in the first study, scores for projective identification occurred exclusively in the borderline group.

Both studies' combined findings lend convincing support to Kernberg's (1975) contention regarding the unique and discernible defensive constellation of borderline patients as well as to the reliability and construct validity of the scoring manual developed to assess these defenses. Empirically, the scoring manual was found to be effective in distinguishing among diagnostic groups on the basis of an evaluation of defensive organization. Conceptually, implicit in the scale's development was the notion that representational capacities and each of the defensive functions are inextricably related. Because of this, the authors (Lerner & Lerner, 1982) elaborated upon their findings and advanced a developmental-structural model of defense, conceptualized within an object representational framework. More specifically, they suggested that "as development proceeds and a representational capacity is achieved, defenses take on an increasingly organizing function and protect the cohesion and integrity of poorly differentiated self and object representations. At higher developmental levels featured by enhanced affective cognitive differentiation and corresponding representational capacity, more encapsulated defenses, limited in scope and related to specific drive affective derivatives, function to protect a well structuralized ego from anxiety stemming from conflict between intrapsychic structures composed of more fully established and specific self and object representations" (pp. 35-36).

Cooper (1981, 1982) and his colleagues (Arnow & Cooper, 1984) have developed a comprehensive and sophisticated Rorschach defense scale based on a careful examination of a broad range of content, including the patient-examiner relationship, and geared toward drawing distinctions between levels of defense reflective of developmental arrest (Stolorow & Lachmann, 1980) and structural conflict. Cooper offers definitions of borderline defenses and specific scoring criteria and examples for the Rorschach assessment of splitting, devaluation, primitive idealization, omnipotence, and projective identification.

Future Directions: Recently, there has been a growing interest in the study of people by means of the Rorschach. This critique has reviewed the two major approaches to the Rorschach, the psychometric and the conceptual, and has outlined, from an historical perspective, advances in the psychoanalytic basis of Rorschach investigations. From a relatively narrow but solid clinical foundation established by Rapaport and articulated by Schafer and Holt, recent advances in the psychoanalytic understanding of primitive mental states including borderline, narcissistic, and psychotic disturbances have dramatically expanded this base by providing new formulations for significant and innovative clinical and research efforts. Examples of these developments include the investigation of core contemporary psychoanalytic variables including boundary disturbance, object representation, and defensive organization. Collectively, these endeavors have operaionalized newer, more phenomenological concepts based on a conceptual model of personality and, in turn, have proved methodologies and Rorschach scales for systematically assessing and evaluating the reliability, validity, and clinical utility of constructs generated by this expanded body of knowledge. One may expect this trend toward approaching research with higher-order variables, based on a model of personality independent of the test itself, to continue.

Blatt and his colleagues (Blatt et al., 1985) have recently presented a major study of opiate addictions based, in part, on the Rorschach. These investigators used a combination of structural and content variables that has been the focus of extensive validation and research, as well as being clinically relevant to opiate addiction. These variables were based on conventional scores, ratios, and content categories. These researchers further used well-established, reliable, and extensively validated Rorschach scales to capture significant dimensions of personality organization such as thought disorder, developmental level of object representation, and primary-secondary process thinking. By controlling for response productivity and using factor analytic statistical techniques, they developed seven composite variables that significantly distinguished a sample of opiate addicts from a control group. With regard to a conceptual approach integrated with traditional Rorschach scoring, Blatt and Berman (1984) state: ". . . these new approaches to the Rorschach based on personality theories seem to provide ways of more effectively managing what is often experienced as a confusing and overwhelming array of isolated scores and of making the Rorschach more useful for the systematic investigation of a wide range of clinical phenomena" (p. 238).

Critique

Psychoanalytic theory and the conceptual approach to the Rorschach is and has been in a constant state of evaluation. As noted previously, from an early concern with an identification of the instincts and their vicissitudes to an emphasis on studying the ego, interest has now shifted to a systematic exploration of the early mother-child relationship and its impact on the development of the self and the quality of later interpersonal relationships. Each shift in theory has provided new and stimulating conceptualizations that have served to broaden the theoretical basis for the Rorschach's clinical and research application.

There has been a resurgence of interest in projective tests, in general, and the Rorschach, in particular. C. Piotrowski (1984), in an article entitled "The Status of Projective Techniques: Or, 'Wishing Won't Make it Go Away' ", analyzed the predicted decline in usefulness of projective techniques from a number of perspectives: the academic, APA's Division of Clinical Psychology members, internship centers, the applied setting, and private practitioners. On the basis of an extensive review of empirical surveys and position studies completed in the past two decades, Piotrowski found tremendous support for the utility of projective techniques in all settings with the exception of the academic. Noting that the role and function of the clinical psychologist continues to change and that the role of psychometric assessment increasingly is being passed onto technicians, the popularity and clinical acceptance of the Rorschach should, in the opinion of these reviewers, remain high and continue to grow.

References

The following selected references may be regarded as the most significant of the vast Rorschach literature reviewed in this chapter. The Society of Personality Assessment's annual convention and the *Journal of Personality Assessment* serve as the major contemporary forums for Rorschach research as well as for the discussion of issues raised in this review. Text citations follow.

Allison, J., Blatt, S., & Zimet, C. (1968). *The interpretation of psychological tests.* New York: Harper & Row.

Blatt, S., Brenneis, C., Schimek, J., & Glick, M. (1976). Normal development and psychopathological impairment of the concept of the object on the Rorschach. *Journal of Abnormal Psychology, 85,* 364-373.

Exner, J. (1974). *The Rorschach: A comprehensive system* (Vol. 1). New York: John Wiley & Sons.

Exner, J. (1976). *The Rorschach: A comprehensive system, current research and advanced interpretation* (Vol. 2). New York: John Wiley & Sons.

Holt, R. (Ed.). (1968). *Diagnostic psychological testing* (rev. ed.). New York: International Universities Press.

Kwawer, J., Lerner, H., Lerner, P., & Sugarman, A. (Eds.). (1980). *Borderline phenomena and the Rorschach test.* New York: International Universities Press.

Lerner, H., & Lerner, P. (Eds.). (in press). *Primitive mental states and the Rorschach.* New York: International Universities Press.

Rapaport, D., Gill, M., & Schafer, R. (1945-1946). *Diagnostic psychological testing* (Vols. 1 & 2). Chicago: Year Book Publishers.

Schachtel, E. (1966). *Experiential foundations of Rorschach's test.* New York: Basic Books.

Schafer, R. (1954). *Psychoanalytic interpretation in Rorschach testing.* New York: Grune & Stratton.

Weiner, I. (1977). Approaches to Rorschach validation. In M.A. Rickers-Ovsiankina (Ed.), *Rorschach psychology.* Huntington, NY: R. E. Krieger.

Allison, J. (1967). Adaptive regression and intense religious experiences. *Journal of Nervous and Mental Disorders, 145,* 452-463.

Arnow, D. & Cooper, S. (1984). The borderline patient's regression on the Rorschach test. *Bulletin of the Menninger Clinic, 48*(1), 25-37.

Bachrach, H. (1968). Adaptive regression, empathy and psychotherapy: Theory and research study. *Psychotherapy, 5,* 203-209.

Beck, S. (1960). *The Rorschach experiment: Ventures in blind diagnosis.* New York: Grune & Stratton.

Benfari, R., & Calogeras, R. (1968). Levels of cognition and conscience typologics. *Journal of Projective Techniques and Personality Assessment, 32,* 466-474.

Blatt, S. J. (1974). Levels of object representation in anaclitic and introjective depression. *Psychoanalytic Study of the Child, 29,* 107-157.

Blatt, S. J. (1975). The validity of projective techniques and their research and clinical contribution. *Journal of Personality Assessment, 39,* 327-343.

Blatt, S., Allison, J., & Feinstein, A. (1969). The capacity to cope with cognitive complexity. *Journal of Personality, 37,* 269-288.

Blatt, S., Brenneis, B., Schimek, J. G., & Glick, M. (1976). Normal development and psychopathological impairment of the concept of the object on the Rorschach. *Journal of Abnormal Psychology, 85,* 364-373.

Blatt, S., Rounsaville, B., Eyre, S., & Wilber, C. (1984). The psychodynamics of opiate addiction. *The Journal of Personality Assessment, 42,* 474-482.

Blatt, S., & Berman, W. (1984). A methodology for the use of the Rorschach in clinical research. *Journal of Personality Assessment, 48*(3), 226-239.

Blatt, S., & Lerner, H. (1983a). Investigations in the psychoanalytic theory of object relations and object representations. *Empirical Studies of Psychoanalytic Theory, 1,* 189-249.

Blatt, S. J., & Lerner, H. (1983b). The psychological assessment of object representation. *Jour-*

nal of Personality Assessment, 47, 77-92.

Blatt, S. J., & Ritzler, B. A. (1974). Thought disorder and boundary disturbances in psychosis. *Journal of Consulting Clinical Psychology, 42,* 370-381.

Brenneis, C. B. (1971). Features of the manifest dream in schizophrenia. *Journal of Nervous and Mental Disorder, 153,* 81-91.

Cohen, I. (1960). *An investigation of the relationship between adaptive regression, dogmatism and creativity using the Rorschach and dogmatism scale.* Unpublished doctoral dissertation, Michigan State University, East Lansing.

Cooper, S. (1981). *An object relations view of the borderline defenses: A Rorschach analysis.* Unpublished manuscript.

Cooper, S. (1982, March). *Restage versus defense process and the borderline personality: A Rorschach analysis.* Paper presented to the mid-winter meeting of the Division of Psychoanalysis of the American Psychological Association, Puerto Rico.

Exner, J. (1974). *The Rorschach: A comprehensive system* (Vol. I). New York: John Wiley & Sons.

Exner, J. (1978). *The Rorschach: A comprehensive system, current research and advanced interpretation* (Vol. II). New York: John Wiley & Sons.

Exner, J., Armbruster, G., & Vigilione, D. (1978). The temporal stability of some Rorschach features. *Journal of Personality Assessment, 42,* 474-482.

Exner, J., Weiner, I., & Schuyler, W. (1979). *A Rorschach workbook for the comprehensive system.* Bayville, NY: Rorschach Workshops.

Feinstein, A. (1967). Personality correlates for unrealistic experiences. *Journal of Consultative Psychology, 31,* 387-395.

Fenichel, D. (1945). *Psychoanalytic theory of neurosis.* New York: Norton.

Fibel, B. (1979). *Toward a developmental model of depression: Object representation and object loss in adolescent and adult psychiatric patients.* Unpublished doctoral dissertation, University of Massachusetts, Amherst.

Goldberger, L. (1961). Reactions to perceptual isolation and Rorschach manifestations of the primary process. *Journal of Projective Techniques, 25,* 287-302.

Gray, J. (1969). The effect of productivity on primary process and creativity. *Journal of Projective Techniques and Personality Assessment, 33,* 213-218.

Greenberg, N., Ramsay, M., Rakoff, V., & Weiss, A. (1969). Primary process thinking in myxoedema psychosis: A case study. *Canada Journal of Behavioral Science, 1,* 60-67.

Hatcher, R., & Krohn, A. (1980). Level of object representation and capacity for intense psychotherapy in neurotics and borderlines. In J. Kwawer, H. Lerner, & A. Sugarman (Eds.), *Borderline phenomena and the Rorschach test.* New York: International Universities Press.

Holt, R. (1967). Diagnostic testing: Present situation and future prospects. *Journal of Nervous and Mental Disorder, 144,* 444-465.

Holt, R. (1968). *Manual for scoring primary process manifestations in Rorschach responses.* Unpublished manuscript, New York University, Research Center for Mental Health.

Johnson, D. (1980). *Cognitive organization in paranoid and nonparanoid schizophrenia.* Unpublished doctoral dissertation, Yale University, New Haven.

Kernberg, O. (1975). *Borderline conditions and pathological narcissism.* New York: Jason Aronson.

Klopfer, B., Ainsworth, M.D., Klopfer, G., & Holt, R. (1954). *Developments in the Rorschach technique: Vol. I. Techniques and theory.* New York: World Book.

Kohut, H. (1971). *The analysis of the self.* New York: International Universities Press.

Kohut, H. (1977). *The restoration of the self.* New York: International Universities Press.

Krohn, A., & Mayman, M. (1974). Object representations in dreams and projective tests: A construct validational study. *Bulletin of the Menninger Clinic, 38,* 445-466.

Krohn, A. (1972). *Levels of object representations in the manifest dreams and projective tests.* Unpublished doctoral dissertation, University of Michigan, Ann Arbor.

Kwawer, J. (1980). Primitive interpersonal modes, borderline phenomena, and the Rorschach test. In J. Kwawer, H. Lerner, P. Lerner, & A. Sugarman (Eds.), *Borderline phenomena and the Rorschach test* (pp. 89-106). New York: International Universities Press.

Lerner, H., & Lerner, P. (1982). A comparative study of defensive structure in neurotic, borderline, and schizophrenic patients. *Psychoanalysis and Contemporary Thought, 1,* 77-115.

Lerner, H., Sugarman, A., & Barbour, C. (1985). Patterns of ego boundary disturbance in neurotic, borderline, and schizophrenic patients. *Psychoanalytic Psychology, 2,* 47-66.

Lerner, H., Sugarman, A., & Gaughran, J. (1981). *Borderline and schizophrenic patients: A comparative study of defensive structure.* Unpublished manuscript.

Lerner, P. (1979). Treatment implications of the (c) response in the Rorschach records of patients with severe character pathology. *Ontario Psychologist, 11,* 20-22.

Lerner, P. (1981). Cognitive aspects of the (c) response in the Rorschach records of patients with severe character pathology. Paper presented to the Internal Rorschach Congress, Washington, DC.

Lerner, P. (in press). Rorschach indices of the false self concept. In H. Lerner & P. Lerner (Eds.), *Primitive mental states and the Rorschach.* New York: International Universities Press.

Lerner, P., & Lerner, H. (1980). Rorschach assessment of primitive defenses in borderline personality structure. In J. Kwawer, H. Lerner, P. Lerner, & A. Sugarman (Eds.), *Borderline phenomena and the Rorschach Test.* New York: International Universities Press.

Lerner, P., & Lewandowski, A. (1975). The measurement of primary process manifestations: A review. In P. Lerner (Ed.), *Handbook of Rorschach scales* (pp. 181-214). New York: International Universities Press.

Lerner, H., & St. Peter, S. (1984). Patterns of object relations in neurotic, borderline, and schizophrenic patients. *Psychiatry: The Study of Interpersonal Process, 47,* 77-92.

Levy, M., & Fox, H. (1975). Psychological testing is alive and well. *Professional Psychology, 6,* 420-424.

Mahler, M., Pine, F., & Bergman, A. (1975). *The psychological birth of the human infant: Symbiosis and individuation.* New York: Basic Books.

Maupin, E. (1965). Individual differences in response to a Zen meditation exercise. *Journal of Consultation and Psychology, 29,* 139-145.

Mayman, M., & Ryan, E. (1972). *Level and quality of object relationships: A scale applicable to overt behavior and to projective test data.* Unpublished manuscript, University of Michigan.

Mayman, M. (1963). Psychoanalytic study of the self-organization with psychological tests. In B. T. Wigdor (Ed.), *Recent advances in the study of behavior change: Proceedings of the academic assembly on clinical psychology.* Montreal: McGill University Press.

Mayman, M. (1964). *Some general propositions implicit in the clinical application of psychological tests.* Unpublished manuscript, Menninger Foundation, Topeka, KS.

Mayman, M. (1967). Object representations and object relationships in Rorschach responses. *Journal of Projective Techniques and Personality Assessment, 31,* 17-24.

Mayman, M. (1968). Early memories and character structure. *Journal of Projective Techniques and Personality Assessment, 32,* 303-316.

Mayman, M. (1976). Psychoanalytic theory in retrospect and prospect. *Bulletin of the Menninger Clinic, 40,* 199-210.

Millon, T. (1984). On the renaissance of personality assessment and personality theory. *Journal of Personality Assessment, 48,* 450-466.

Peebles, R. (1975). Rorschach as self-system in the telophasic theory of personality development. In P. Lerner (Ed.), *Handbook of Rorschach scales* (pp. 71-136). New York: International Universities Press.

Pichot, P. (1984). Centenary of the birth of Hermann Rorschach. *Journal of Personality Assessment, 48,* 591-596.

Pine, F., & Holt, R. (1960). Creativity and primary process: A study of adaptive regression. *Journal of Abnormal and Social Psychology, 61,* 370-379.

Pine, F. (1962). Creativity and primary process: Sample variations. *Journal of Nervous and Mental Disorder, 134,* 506-511.

Piotrowski, C. (1984). The status of projective techniques: Or, "Wishing won't make it go away." *Journal of Clinical Psychology, 40,* 1495-1502.

Pruitt, W., & Spilka, B. (1964). Rorschach empathy—object relationship scale. *Journal of Projective Techniques and Personality Assessment, 8,* 331-336.

Rickers-Ovsiankina, M. (1977). *Rorschach psychology* (2nd ed.). Huntington, NY: Robert E. Krieger.

Ritzler, B., Zambianco, D., Harder, D., & Kaskey, M. (1980). Psychotic patterns of the concept of the object on the Rorschach test. *Journal of Abnormal Psychology, 89,* 46-55.

Rogolsky, M. (1968). Artistic creativity and adaptive regression in third grade children. *Journal of Projective Techniques and Personality Assessment, 32,* 53-62.

Rorschach, H. (1942). *Psychodiagnostics.* Bern: (Hans Huber).

Ryan, E. R. (1973). *The capacity of the patient to enter an elementary therapeutic relationship in the initial psychotherapy interview.* Unpublished doctoral dissertation, University of Michigan, Ann Arbor.

Saretsky, T. (1966). Effects of chlorpromazine on primary process thought manifestations. *Journal of Abnormal Psychology, 71,* 247-252.

Schactel, E. (1966). *Experiential foundations of Rorschach test.* New York: Basic Books.

Schafer, R. (1954). *Psychoanalytic interpretation in Rorschach testing.* Boston: Grune & Stratton.

Schlesinger, H. (1973). Interaction of dynamic and reality factors in the diagnostic testing interview. *Bulletin of the Menninger Clinic, 37,* 495-518.

Shevrin, H., & Shechtman, F. (1973). The diagnostic process in psychiatric evaluation. *Bulletin of the Menninger Clinic, 37,* 451-494.

Silverman, L., & Candell, P. (1970). On the relationship between aggressive activation, symbiotic merging, intactness of body boundaries and manifest pathology in schizophrenia. *Journal of Nervous and Mental Disorders, 150,* 387-399.

Silverman, L., & Goldberger, A. (1966). A further study of the effects of subliminal aggressive stimulation on thinking. *Journal of Nervous and Mental Disorders, 143,* 463-472.

Silverman, L., & Spiro, R. (1967). Further investigation of the effects of subliminal aggressive stimulation on the ego functioning of schizophrenics. *Journal of Consulting Psychology, 31,* 226-232.

Silverman, L. (1965). Regression in the service of the ego. *Journal of Projective Techniques and Personality Assessment, 29,* 232-244.

Silverman, L. (1966). A technique for the study of psychodynamic relationships: The effects of subliminally presented aggressive stimuli on the production of pathological thinking in a schizophrenic population. *Journal of Consulting Psychology, 30,* 103-111.

Spear, W. (1980). The psychological assessment of structural and thematic object representations in borderline and schizophrenic patients. In J. Kwawer, H. Lerner, P. Lerner, & A. Sugarman (Eds.), *Borderline phenomena and the Rorschach* (pp. 321-342). New York: International Universities Press.

Spitzer, R., Endicott, J., & Robbins, E. (1975). Research diagnostic criteria. *Psychopharmacological Bulletin, 11,* 22-24.

Stolorow, R., & Lachmann, F. (1980). *Psychoanalysis of developmental arrest.* New York: International Universities Press.

Sugarman, A. (1981). The diagnostic use of countertransference reactions in psychological testing. *Bulletin of the Menninger Clinic, 45,* 473-490.

Sugarman, A. (1985). The nature of clinical assessment. Unpublished manuscript.

Tolpin, M., & Kohut, H. (1978). The disorders of the self: The psychopathology of the first years of life. In G. Pollock & S. Greenspan (Eds.), *Psychoanalysis of the life cycle* (NIMH Publication). Washington, DC: U. S. Government Printing Office.

Urist, J. (1973). *The Rorschach test as a multidimensional measure of object relations.* Unpublished doctoral dissertation, University of Michigan, Ann Arbor.

Urist, J. (1977). The Rorschach test and the assessment of object relations. *Journal of Personality Assessment, 41,* 3-9.

Von Holt, H., Sengstake, C., Sonoda, B., & Draper, W. (1960). Orality, image fusion and concept formation. *Journal of Projective Techniques, 24,* 194-198.

Viglione, D., & Exner, J. (1983). Current research in the comprehensive Rorschach systems. In J. Butcher & C. Spielberger (Eds.), *Advances in personality assessment* (Vol. 1). Hillsdale, NJ: Lawrence Erlbaum.

Weiner, I. (1977). Approaches to Rorschach validation. In M. A. Rickers-Ovsiankina (Ed.), *Rorschach psychology.* Huntington, NY: Robert E. Krieger.

Werner, H. (1948). *Comparable psychology of mental development.* New York: International Universities Press.

Wilson, A. (in press). Depression in primitive mental states. In H. Lerner & P. Lerner (Eds.), *Primitive mental states and the Rorschach.* New York: International Universities Press.

Winnicott, D. (1960). Ego distortion in terms of true and false self. In D. Winnicott (Ed.), *The maturational processes and the facilitating environment.* London: Hogarth Press.

Wright, N., & Abbey, D. (1965). Perceptual deprivation tolerance and adequacy of defense. *Perceptual and Motor Skills, 20,* 35-38.

Wright, N., & Zubek. J. (1969). Relationship between perceptual deprivation tolerance and adequacy of defenses as measured by the Rorschach. *Journal of Abnormal Social Psychology, 74,* 615-617.

Zimet, C., & Fine, H. (1965). Primary and secondary process thinking in two types of schizophrenia. *Journal of Projective Techniques and Personality Assessment, 29,* 93-99.

Marcia D. Horne, Ed.D.
Associate Professor of Education and Special Education Area Chair, University of Oklahoma, Norman, Oklahoma.

ROSWELL-CHALL AUDITORY BLENDING TEST

Florence G. Roswell and Jeanne S. Chall. La Jolla, California: Essay Press.

Introduction

The Roswell-Chall Auditory Blending Test (ABT) samples the ability to fuse separately presented sounds into words. Although the stimuli are received auditorily, the blending is done mentally. After the examiner presents the parts of a word orally, pausing briefly between the parts, the examinee's task is to fuse the constituent parts into a word and pronounce it. No visual stimuli are involved.

Blending occurs mentally in both auditory blending and visual blending, but the two differ in their task demands. Whereas the sounds are provided by the examiner in auditory blending tests (the stimuli are auditory), in visual blending the pupils must first determine, for themselves, the sounds represented by the letters (the stimuli are visual).

The ABT was developed by Drs. Florence G. Roswell and Jeanne S. Chall while they were on the faculty of the City University of New York. Apparently it was constructed to be used in ''a longitudinal study of factors which make for success in beginning reading,'' and grew out of the authors' observation that ''children with severe reading disabilities also had extreme difficulty in learning phonics, particularly in blending and synthesizing sounds" (Chall, Roswell, & Blumenthal, 1963, p. 113).

Both Roswell and Chall, particularly the latter, have contributed widely to the literature on reading ability and disability. Roswell's most recent major work was on the third edition of *Reading Disability: A Human Approach to Learning* (1977). Chall's voluminous list of publications includes the original classic and the revision of *Learning to Read: The Great Debate* (Chall, 1967, 1983a) and *Stages of Reading Development* (Chall, 1983b). They are also the authors of the Roswell-Chall Diagnostic Reading Test of Word Analysis Skills (1978). There is only one form of the ABT, which has not been revised since its publication in 1963.

Three sample items and three ten-item parts constitute the test. None of the sample items are exactly like the stimuli in Part I, which requires the ability to blend a consonant sound and a vowel sound, such as */ă/* + */m/* = *am* or */f/* + */ū/* = *few*. The recording form, which indicates the stimuli, presents the printed forms of the words (e.g., *s-o*) rather than their spoken forms (e.g., */s/* - */ō/*). This should not present any problems for administration or interpretation because the stimuli are common real words, and this format allows for dialectal variations. Seven items are comprised of an initial single consonant sound and a final vowel sound (five long vowels, one digraph, one diphthong); three begin with a short vowel sound and end with a single consonant sound. Each item in Part II consists of an initial consonant sound (seven single consonants, two blends, and one digraph) and a vowel-consonant phonogram (e.g., *im, ule*) or a vowel digraph (*ay*), which are presented as a unit (e.g., /ĭm/, /ūl/, /ā/). All ten items in Part III contain three phonemes, such as /s/ + /i/ + /p/ = *sip*. Eight are comprised of a single consonant-short vowel-single consonant sound; one contains a single consonant-short vowel-consonant blend; and one consists of a single consonant-long vowel-consonant blend sound. The mean raw scores, which appear in Chall, Roswell, and Blumenthal (1963) but not in the ABT manual (Roswell & Chall, 1963), indicate that the three parts were of increasing difficulty at each level tested (Grade 1, Grades 2 and 3, Grade 4).

Practical Applications/Uses

The ABT is intended for use with children in first through fourth grades and, according to the manual (p. 1), for "older children with reading difficulties who are still deficient in word recognition and analysis skills." It yields one "score" whether or not the child displayed adequate auditory blending.

As its title indicates, the ABT was designed to measure the ability to mentally blend orally presented sounds into whole words. Apparently the test authors believed that auditory blending is an important ability in the acquisition of phonics (decoding) skills. The manual seems to suggest that the ABT could be used to determine who is ready for phonics instruction or to determine why phonics may not have been effective.

The test might be used by classroom teachers, but its use by them is apt to be limited because the ABT must be administered individually. It is more apt to be given by reading specialists or psychologists who want to determine the extent to which weak auditory blending ability might be contributing to a child's problem in learning to decode printed words.

Data regarding raw scores, reliability, and validity were based on the performance of lower to lower-middle class black children from New York City, who had average intelligence. The sample began with 62 first-graders, but was reduced to 40 by the second grade. More limited data are also presented for 25 disabled readers in Grades 3-5 who had "average to high intelligence with a median age of 10-5" (Chall, Roswell, & Blumenthal, 1963, p. 114). No other description of the subsample is provided. Users of the ABT should be aware of this very limited sample, especially when comparing the performance of those whom they test against the ABT criteria for determining auditory blending adequacy.

The ABT is administered individually, and preferably in a quiet setting. It is an easy test to give and interpret; no special training is required. However, the examiner should practice pronouncing the stimuli and learn to present them as distortion free as possible. The examiner's ability to enunciate clearly and to eliminate extraneous sounds is likely to influence test results. For example, it is probably easier to blend /h/-/a/-/t/ than /huh/-/ah/-/tuh/ into a recognizable word. Regional and cultural dialects, especially those involving vowel sounds, should be considered in the administration and interpretation of the ABT. Marked differences between the examiner's pronunciation and the rendition to which the child is used to hearing could influence test performance. Somewhat similarly, the examiner should accept children's responses that are in accord with their dialects but which may differ from that of the examiner's pronunciation. Use of a well-rehearsed tape would provide consistency of stimuli in the ABT's administration.

Directions for administering the ABT are clear, as are instructions for the examinee. The three sample items are given first to make sure that the child understands the task. According to the manual (p. 2), if the task is not understood, the examiner must "stop and illustrate how the separate sounds may be blended together to form a word."

All 30 test items are presented unless the child demonstrates difficulty in performing the task. An exact guideline as to when testing should be terminated in such cases is not provided, but the manual states (p. 2) that "it is advisable to omit Part III if the pupil shows a considerable amount of failure in Parts I and II."

According to the manual (p. 2), the separate sounds in each word are to be presented "at the rate of about one-half second for each sound." Although this direction could be interpreted as meaning that each sound is presented for ½ second, it probably means that there should be a ½-second pause between the sounds. (This procedure is used on all other auditory blending tests.)

The manual also states (p. 2) that a test item may be repeated "only if the pupil's attention wandered or you are fairly sure that he did not hear the word the first time." How an examiner chooses to interpret this guideline may influence test results. Certainly the examiner should record items repeated for the pupil and take such information into consideration when interpreting test performance. Inability or unwillingness to attend to the task at hand may be adversely influencing the child's learning.

On the line next to each test item, the examiner is to record a plus for a correct answer (the term "acceptable" rather than "correct" would be more proper), a minus for an incorrect response, and a zero for an item that the child does not attempt. In the latter case, the manual does not provide a guideline as to how long a child should be given to respond to an item. Items that are not presented are to be crossed out. It might be of diagnostic value and may aid interpretation if the unacceptable responses (including partial responses) were recorded phonetically.

The answer sheet also contains spaces for recording the number of correct responses for each part; the total raw score, whether blending is or is not adequate; and comments.

Scoring the ABT is simple. One point is given for each correct (acceptable) response, regardless of the part on which it occurs. The number of pluses are tallied to obtain a total raw score, which is used to determine the adequacy of the pupil's auditory blending. According to Table 1 in the manual, adequate auditory blending is indicated by a total raw score of at least 7 for first-graders, 11 for second-graders, 15 for third-graders, 19 for fourth-graders, and 26 for those in Grade 5 and above.

The manual does not indicate how these cutoff scores were derived; however, they appear to be based on the mean raw scores reported in Chall, Roswell, and Blumenthal's (1963) article. The mean total raw score obtained by the 62 first-graders was 7.61 (although it was 8.59 for the 40 first-graders on whom complete data were obtained), and the cutoff score indicated in the manual is 7. The mean for 40 second- and third-graders (some of whom were tested at the end of second grade, others at the beginning of third grade) was 13.69. Because the cutoff scores for Grades 2 and 3 are 11 and 15, respectively, one might assume that an arbitrary decision was made to subtract and to add two points from and to 13. If so, these criteria are open to serious question. The mean for 40 fourth-graders was apparently rounded off from 18.76 to 19. This inferred procedure would account for the consistent increase of four points from one grade level to the next (e.g., 7, 11, 15, 19). Although the means are not presented in either the manual or the Chall, Roswell, and Blumenthal (1963) article, it might be assumed that the cutoff score for pupils beyond the fourth grade was based on the performance of 25 disabled readers from Grades 3-5, the majority of whom were in the fourth grade. A justification for the use of these means as a basis for deciding whether auditory blending ability is inferior or adequate is not offered by the authors. This is a serious omission because test performance is interpreted in light of these criteria.

The ABT is hand scored, but because the bulk of the scoring occurs during the test administration, it should take only a few minutes to finish the scoring. After the test is administered, the examiner needs only to count up the pluses for each part, add them together (which may be unnecessary), consult Table 1 in the manual, and place a check in the appropriate box (Adequate Blending or Inadequate Blending).

If one accepts the basis on which the means were determined and does not question the use of these means as a criterion for adequate auditory blending ability, the ABT can be interpreted quite easily. Either the child does or does not have adequate auditory blending ability. According to the manual (p. 3):

> In general, when a pupil scores within the adequate range for his grade, he should not experience undue difficulty in learning phonics. Where the pupil scores within the inferior range for his grade, and the qualitative evaluation confirms weakness in auditory blending, he will probably experience difficulty in learning phonics.

Presumably this qualitative analysis involves determining the possible reasons for inadequate test performance for which the manual (p. 3) suggests two possible causes. The first deals with unsuccessful functioning on the test due to unfamiliarity with sounds because the child was never exposed to phonics instruction or to exercises in auditory discrimination of sounds. When the ABT was constructed over 20 years ago such a possibility was more probable, especially for first-graders, because of the nature of the phonics instruction provided in the basal reader programs and the frequent delay of phonics instruction until the end of first grade. Although phonics are taught earlier and much more intensely today, there is still the unanswered question as to how well, or even if, blending is taught in most of today's reading programs, which are not strongly oriented toward teaching reading skills.

The second reason that the manual gives for inadequate test performance refers to the difficulty in blending due to developmental factors—the ability to analyze and synthesize component parts of words which appear to be related to neurophysiological development, a function of maturation. If such be the cause, what is one to do? Wait for maturation to occur, or can a pupil profit from direct instruction in how to blend?

There is some evidence that auditory blending problems also may reflect a poor memory for individual sounds when more than four sounds must be blended (Moore, Kagan, Sahl, & Grant, 1982). This is not a likely possibility on the ABT because the pupil needs to blend only three component sounds at most for any test item.

Interestingly, the manual (p. 3) recommends that teachers give phonics instructions to those children who do poorly on the ABT because it is difficult to determine whether lack of aptitude in blending is due to slow maturation or insufficient instruction and recommends "that such instruction might begin with developing auditory discrimination followed by teaching a few symbol-sound associations, and proceeding to increasingly more difficult blending tasks." It further suggests that for children who still display inadequate blending skills after a reasonable amount of instruction, phonics instruction be postponed and an alternative method of teaching word recognition be employed. Such advice is sound because there is little sense in teaching a child to analyze words into their component parts and teaching symbol-sound associations *if* the child truly cannot blend sounds into words.

If one questions not only the generalizability of data gathered from a small number of subjects whose racial and geographic composition was very restricted, but also the use of their mean scores as a criterion, the interpretation of the ABT becomes difficult, if not impossible. Even if the use of mean scores for such a purpose were defensible, one should ask how well the mean raw scores obtained by 40 to 62 lower to lower-middle class, black, New York City children over 20 years ago compares to what one could reasonably expect of the various segments of today's school populations.

Even though the reported reliability quotients (which are detailed in the technical aspects section of this review) are high, one must question the faith that can be placed in the indicated cutoff scores. Data indicate a great deal of variability in test performance (Chall, Roswell, & Blumenthal, 1963). For example, the standard deviation for first-graders' mean total score (7.61) was 5.51. Apparently the vast majority of the scores ranged from approximately 2.0 to 13.0.

Test users cannot be certain as to how accurately the criterion scores really indicate whether or not a child's auditory blending ability is adequate. There is no evidence, for instance, as to how much difficulty, if any, a first-grader who scored below 7 on the ABT would have in even the one aspect of decoding (i.e., blending) which the ABT samples. It is also quite possible for first-graders to respond correctly only to seven items of Part II, but have extreme difficulty in a decoding program that required them to blend three or more phonemes rather than an initial consonant sound with a phonogram as required on Part II.

Technical Aspects

Split-half (odd-even) reliability coefficients, corrected for attenuation, are reported to range from .86 to .93 for the total test score. These were based on the performance of 40 to 62 children in Grades 1-4. A reliability coefficient of .94 was derived from the test scores of 25 disabled readers who were in Grades 3-5. Uncorrected reliability coefficients ranged from .77 to .89 (Chall, Roswell, & Blumenthal,

1963). Test-retest reliability is not indicated, and because the ABT is individually administered, one wonders why standard errors of measurement were not supplied.

Test validity is based on correlations between ABT total scores and scores on the Pintner-Cunningham IQ Test (.03-.54), the Gray Oral Reading Test (.45-.59), the Roswell-Chall Diagnostic Reading Test of Word Analysis Skills (.46-.66), and the Metropolitan Reading Test (.26-.51). Such correlations indicate a moderate relationship, at best. More importantly, these correlations do not answer the basic question: *Valid for what?* Correlations between the ABT and such broad measures of reading as the Gray and the Metropolitan may only suggest that those who tend to score high (or low) on the ABT also tend to score high (or low) on measures of oral and silent reading. The exact nature of the relationship is unknown.

Research findings regarding the exact nature of the relationship between auditory blending and reading ability are equivocal. The correlation between the two factors ranged from .19 to .67 in the 21 studies reviewed by Whaley and Kibby (1979). Richardson, DiBenedetto, Christ, and Press (1980) found that Illinois Test of Psycholinguistic Abilities (ITPA) auditory blending scores were significantly related to reading achievement, even when IQ was partialled out; Kavale (1981) did not. But little is known regarding the cause-effect relationship because the data are almost exclusively correlational. Data derived from the ABT do little to clarify the cause-effect issue.

Critique

The ABT probably measures auditory blending ability as it is commonly defined, but the ABT lacks adequate validity and reliability for its proposed purpose. Its biggest drawback is the cutoff criteria, which apparently were based on the mean scores obtained by a small, very restricted sample over 20 years ago. Use of the ABT to determine whether or not a child has adequate auditory blending ability discrimination is not recommended by this reviewer. However, it might be used to help determine why a child might be having difficulty with one aspect of decoding, the skills of which, according to Harris and Sipay (1985), involve visual analysis, symbol-sound associations, and blending. Additionally, it might be used to obtain some information regarding the viability of a particular blending approach for a pupil.

References

Chall, J. S. (1967). *Learning to read: The great debate: An inquiry into the science, art, and ideology of old and new methods of teaching children to read 1910-1965.* New York: McGraw-Hill.

Chall, J. S. (1983a). *Learning to read: The great debate* (rev. ed.). New York: McGraw-Hill.

Chall, J. S. (1983b). *Stages of reading development.* New York: McGraw-Hill.

Chall, J., Roswell, F. G., & Blumenthal, S. H. (1963). Auditory blending ability: A factor in success in beginning reading. *The Reading Teacher, 17,* 113-118.

Harris, A. J., & Sipay, E. R. (1985). *How to increase reading ability: A guide to developmental and remedial methods* (8th ed.). New York: Longman.

Kavale, K. (1981). The relationship between auditory perceptual skills and reading ability: A meta-analysis. *Journal of Learning Disabilities, 9,* 539-546.

Moore, M. J., Kagan, J., Sahl, M., & Grant, S. (1982). Cognitive profiles in reading disability. *Genetic Psychology Monographs, 105,* 41-93.

Richardson, E., DiBenedetto, B., Christ, A., & Press, M. (1980). Relationship of auditory and visual skills to reading retardation. *Journal of Learning Disabilities, 13,* 77-82.

Roswell, F. G., & Natchez, G. (1977). *Reading disability: A human approach to learning* (3rd ed.). New York: Basic Books.

Roswell, F. G., & Chall, J. S. (1963). *Roswell-Chall Auditory Blending Test manual of instructions.* La Jolla, CA: Essay Press.

Roswell, F. G., & Chall, J. S. (1978). *Roswell-Chall Diagnostic Reading Test of Word Analysis Skills.* La Jolla, CA: Essay Press.

Whaley, W. J., & Kibby, M. W. (1979). Word synthesis and beginning reading achievement. *Journal of Educational Research, 73,* 132-138.

Arthur B. Sweney, Ph.D.
Professor of Management, Wichita State University, and President of Test Systems International, Ltd., Wichita, Kansas.

ROTHWELL-MILLER INTEREST BLANK

J. W. Rothwell and K. M. Miller. Hawthorn, Victoria, Australia: The Australian Council for Educational Research Limited.

Introduction

The Rothwell-Miller Interest Blank is an extension of the Rothwell Interest Blank, which was prepared in 1947 to provide an instrument that would be economical of both time and money and meet the perceived needs for vocational counseling and orientation among secondary-school pupils. It was recognized at that time, and to a larger extent later, that it would have additional applications to adults in other settings who need a quick assessment of their vocational interests.

With the help of Dr. Kenneth Miller, a highly recognized educational and industrial psychologist in the British Commonwealth, the test was expanded from nine to 12 scales and modified to fit a wider range of respondents. In 1958 the Australian edition of the Rothwell-Miller Interest Blank was published, and ten years later the English and UK adaptation was made available for general distribution.

This later, 1968 edition is comprised of two separate matched forms (one for males; one for females) containing nine sections. Respondents are asked to rank twelve occupations, each of which represents one of the twelve occupational families or scales being measured. Items for these scales are staggered in each presentation to disguise the nature of the scales being measured and to prevent a position bias from developing. A simple grid at the bottom of the test sheet provides the test scorer a system for reordering the items for direct scoring.

The simplicity of administration and scoring has given this test a boost in usage in settings that might find the Strong-Campbell Interest Inventory (Campbell, 1977) or the Kuder Preference Record (Kuder, 1956) unnecessarily complex or burdensome. This directness of approach and its face validity make it less of a psychological test than a direct system for cataloging the respondents' conscious attitudes toward vocations of which they are presumably familiar. This may ultimately serve as both its strength and its weakness, but should, in either case, well qualify its use as the first step in any inquiry into vocational attitudes.

The scales currently being measured by the Rothwell-Miller Interest Blank are Outdoor, Mechanical, Computational, Scientific, Persuasive, Aesthetic, Literary, Musical, Social Service, Clerical, Practical, and Medical. No rationale is provided for this particular sampling of the vocational universe, but on inspection it would seem to have been influenced strongly by the Kuder Preference Record Vocational

Form. Although no mention is made of factor analysis, the low correlations among scales would indicate that scales could form reasonably orthogonal factors.

Practical Applications/Uses

The authors of this test have provided the user with a wide variety of norms, as well as case studies involving a number of different settings. These should increase the applicability of this instrument. The research has been conducted primarily in educational settings, which might govern its primary area of application but should not automatically limit its usage.

The reading difficulty of some occupational titles would limit its application at lower age levels. Most of the titles are recognizable by North Americans so that its use in the United States or Canada requires only minor changes. The directions are simple enough for it to be used with lower intelligence samples, particularly when the special administration instructions, in which the individuals are guided step-by-step in comparing alternatives, are used.

The major limitation to its use is the face validity of its format and the prior information that respondents must have concerning the occupation involved. Respondents are expected to know what rewards are gained from each of the occupations sampled in order to make meaningful choices. The absence of this level of understanding may be the precise reason that the respondent does not possess a clear career direction in the first place. This is the reason that this reviewer sees it as a ''first step'' instrument that needs further supplementation at some later time with more disguised tests such as the Strong Campbell Vocational Interest Blank or the Vocational Interest Measure (Sweney & Cattell, 1978).

Technical Aspects

The internal consistency reliabilities reported for the various scales were calculated using corrected split-half correlations, presumably based on fairly small samples. The sizes were not designated for the Australian samples, which were identified in the manual (Miller, 1958) as ''two of the student groups.'' The English samples were drawn from a technical grammar school and includes two groups of boys (N = 89 and 73) and two groups of girls (N = 93 and 96). The reliabilities reported (.76 to .95) indicated a fairly high saturation of usable variance. The most potent scales for boys seem to be Computational, Musical, Practical, and Mechanical. For girls the greatest discrimination would be obtained on the Computational, Scientific, Musical, Clerical, and Medical Scales. The weakest scale for all groups was the Outdoor. The range of consistencies extended from .56 in one girls' group on Persuasive to .91 in a boys' group on Computational and Musical.

By necessity, the split-half reliabilities would have to be calculated on small but unequal halves of four against five items. These splits would be highly sensitive to the chance composition of each part. There is no report of any effort by the authors to make other trial splits to provide a range of split-half correlations or whether this method was used, and only the highest corrected correlations were reported.

These problems could have been avoided if Cronbach's alpha had been used to measure the quality.

Unfortunately, the stability coefficients calculated on the Australian samples are reported as ranges for the test as a whole rather than for each articulated scale, even though two different time periods have been reported. Females did seem to have less stable vocational patterns than the males, based on the medians and lower ends of the ranges, but this might be an artifact of the larger sizes of the women's groups.

The stability coefficents for the English samples of 170 boys and 190 girls and two samples of 102 and 77 engineering apprentices were each reported by scale. There were no indications that these correlations were corrected for attenuation due to the lack of homogeneity of the scale itself on the populations being measured. This makes it difficult to interpret whether the coefficients reflect lack of stability or merely lack of homogeneity. In some cases the stability coefficients were dangerously close to the homogeneities calculated on other samples indicating ''perfect" stability or some other anomaly. With these facts in mind, the coefficients can be considered high enough to confirm that vocational interest measured in this manner is a highly stable attribute.

A comment is in order on the authors' use, to conclude stability, of changes in median scores over time for their two samples of teachers. The use of the medians makes it impossible to apply normal parametric inferential tests of significance, even though the small samples would preclude them anyway. If means had been used on self-ipsatized scales such as these, one would expect the changes down over time to be exactly matched by the changes up. This was not even closely approximated in either sample and would indicate that some of the distributions for the various scales are highly skewed, a fact that is not directly disclosed by any of the statistics provided in the manual.

The discussion on validity reflects some lack of uniformity in the use of terms, but this may reflect the date of publication more than real confusion by the authors. Their ''construct validity'' would correspond to ''concurrent validity'' as identified by Cronbach and Gleser (1957). Rothwell and Miller rather appropriately used the Kuder Preference Record and the Allport, Vernon, and Lindzey Study of Values (1960) for this purpose and found reasonably high agreements between their scales and the two other instruments where comparisons were possible. Because corrections for attenuation, due to lack of homogeneity of the scales involved, were not calculated, it is difficult to estimate what the "true score" relationships would actually have been. One would have to assume that the actual homogeneities are higher than the lower bounds obtained from the "split half" computations or such validities would not be possible. This is particularly true because there is a restricted range for many of the scales for the relatively homogeneous samples that have been selected. Disregarding the true similarity between correponding scales, one would expect lower agreements on scales associated with the selection variables. In the reported validities this principle seemed to be true with female teachers and, to a somewhat lesser degree with the male, psychology and education students. These general trends suggest that the authors should have calculated their validities on the total sample or else have corrected these correlations for restricted range. In either case, the reported validities would be conservative rather than liberal estimates of the true values.

The tendency for the authors to report the ranks of the average ranks rather than using normed scores makes it difficult to assess the validity for scales in their criterion-related validities. This may have been necessitated by the absence of general population norms. Without these norms, scores cannot be calculated or compared. Thus raw scores for the scales are compared in ways that give the illusion that the scores are meaningfully comparable, which, of course, they are not.

Because the term *mean* in the manual's tables is not identified as the means of summed ranks or the mean percentiles, the reader is apt to assume the latter when it is actually the former. This is particularly misleading when using ranks because opposite conclusions would be made depending on the assumed meaning. Much of this confusion could have been avoided had standard scores of some form been used.

The thoroughness with which the authors have examined their data is highly commendable, but, in most cases, the results should have been summarized rather than expanded into unnecessary tabular form in the manual. This is particularly true of the endless tables of ''norms'' for almost every conceivable kind of subsample. In spite of .067 being the highest reported correlation of any scale with age, there were still separate norm tables made for separate age groups within this age range.

Incidentally, these norm tables do not assume normality because they are constructed from medians and quartiles rather than the reported means and standard deviations. The amount of direction of skewedness can be deduced from the distance the 50th percentile deviates from the means for the particular scale and sample being considered. This meticulous attention to detail is typical of the thoroughness and precision with which these authors have documented their work.

Some of these awkward tables suggest that the authors recognized some of the assumptions that their kind of data violated and were unnecessarily hesitant to handle them in some of the more rigorous ways that were possible. In some cases normality was assumed and Pearson product-moment correlations were calculated. In other cases with equally large samples, only medians were reported, and the reader was left to draw his own conclusions.

Critique

The manual for this instrument documents the operation of this test and its strengths and weaknesses well. It is simple in form and makes no assumptions, except that respondents understand the rewards offered by the vocations being ranked. The internal consistency and stability measures of the scales are sufficiently high to indicate that they are measuring saturated and stable attitudes. The face validity of the test makes it difficult to imagine its providing any subtle attitudes or interests because the outcomes are directly related to the consciously controlled inputs. The Rothwell-Miller Interest Blank is seen as a screening instrument for individuals who wish to systematize their stereotypic attitudes about vocations. Unless they were coached ahead of time, these might reflect little or no real vocational information and, therefore, measure only presumed interest.

References

Allport, G. W., Vernon, P. E., & Lindzey, G. (1960). *Study of values.* New York: Houghton-Mifflin.

Campbell, D. P. (1977). *Strong-Campbell Interest Inventory.* Palo Alto, CA: Stanford University Press.

Cronbach, L. J. (1951). Coefficient alpha and the internal structure of tests. *Psychometrika, 16,* 297-334.

Cronbach, L. J., & Gleser, G. C. (1957). *Psychological tests and personnel decisions.* Urbana: University of Illinois Press.

Guilford, J. P. (1954). *Psychometric methods.* New York: McGraw-Hill.

Johnson, H. G. (1950). Test reliability and correction of attenuation. *Psychometrika, 15,* 115-119.

Kuder, S. F. (1956). *Kuder Preference Record Vocational Form.* Chicago: Science Research Associates.

Miller, K. M. (1958). *Manual for the Rothwell Interest Blank* (Miller Revisions). Melbourne: Australian Council for Educational Research.

Miller, K. M. (1960). The measurement of vocational interest by a stereotype ranking method. *Journal of Applied Psychology, 44,* 169-171.

Rothwell, J. W., & Miller, K. M. (1968). *Rothwell-Miller Interest Blank.* Melbourne: Australian Council for Educational Research.

Schmidt, F. L., & Hunter, J. E. (1973). Development of a general solution to the problem of validity generalization. *Journal of Applied Psychology, 62,* 529-540.

Sweney, A. B., & Cattell, R. B. (1978). *Vocational Interest Measure.* Champaign, IL: Institute for Personality and Ability Testing.

Jerry B. Hutton, Ph.D.

Professor of Special Education, East Texas State University, Commerce, Texas.

SCHOOL BEHAVIOR CHECKLIST

Lovick C. Miller. Los Angeles, California: Western Psychological Services.

Introduction

The School Behavior Checklist (SBC) is a behavior rating scale designed for teachers to record observations of student behavior in the school setting. The instrument may be used as one component in a general assessment of child psychopathology or in research. Professional mental-health workers knowledgeable in child psychopathology may interpret the results of the SBC ratings. There are two forms of the SBC: Form A1 for children four through six years and Form A2 for children seven through 13 years.

Form A1 consists of 104 items, each of which is scored "true" or "false" by the teacher to indicate if the item describes the behavior of the target student. The nine scales and the number of items in each (some items counting on more than one scale) are as follows: Low Need Achievement (LNA), 26 items; Aggression (AGG), 36 items; Anxiety (ANX), 18 items; Cognitive Deficit (CD), 18 items; Hostile Isolation (HI), 7 items; Extraversion (EXT), 12 items; Normal Irritability (NI), 14 items for males, 11 for females; School Disturbance (SD), 18 items; and Total Disability (TD), 88 items.

The form for older students, Form A2, is composed of 96 items, with the teacher using the same procedures as with Form A1. There are seven scales in Form A2, with six scales in common with A1. Two of the A1 scales (NI and SD) are dropped in A2. The CD Scale in A1 is replaced in A2 by Academic Disability (AD). Other changes involve 28 items instead of 26 on the LNA Scale and a few items in the various scales rewritten to make them more age-appropriate. The AD Scale has eight items instead of the 18 on the SD Scale of Form A1, and TD on Form A2 consists of 95 items.

The original SBC items were taken from the Pittsburgh Adjustment Survey Scales (Ross, Lacey, & Parton, 1965), with other items taken from the Louisville Behavior Checklist (Miller, 1967, 1968), a behavior rating scale for parents. The Form A1 CD Scale contains some items taken from the Minnesota Child Development Inventory (Ireton & Thwing, 1972). The cross-validation and normative study of the SBC was published by Miller in 1972, and the SBC was published by Western Psychological Services in 1977. Miller (1972) computed a factor analysis on 2,627 boys and 2,746 girls, using a principal-components factor analysis with unity in the main diagonals, and identified the six factors presently found in both Form A1 and Form A2. The factor structure was similar for boys and girls.

The norms for the SBC are reported by Miller (1977) to have been drawn from the city of Louisville and Jefferson County, Kentucky. The 295 boys and 299 girls in the Form A1 sample were analyzed to determine demographic characteristics. Blacks and six-year-olds were overrepresented in the sample, and Miller (1977) noted that the sample of preschool children can probably be considered representative of urban children. It was further indicated that males, younger children, lower-income children, and children of less educated mothers were rated as having more deviant behavior than others in the sample. Children whose parents were married, widowed, or remarried were rated more favorably than those whose parents were divorced, separated, or unmarried.

The norms for A2 were established on 2,627 boys and 2,746 girls from city, county, parochial, and private schools in Jefferson County and Louisville, Kentucky. Within the sample, 3,919 children had received an intelligence test at school, and the sample had a mean IQ of 103.01 (SD = 14.83). In the A2 sample, approximately 49% were boys, 19% were black, 61% were protestant, and 82% were attending county or city schools as opposed to 17% in parochial schools. The age and grade distributions were fairly regular. Miller (1977) notes that the higher the child's intellectual functioning is, the more favorable the behavior will be. Less favorable ratings in the sample were attributed to children with lower income, males, and blacks.

The SBC consists of two separate checklist forms, answer sheets, and a manual. Scoring templates can be obtained to facilitate hand scoring. Raw scores can be converted to standard scores by referring to a table in the manual. The standard scores have a mean of 50 and a standard deviation of 10, and appropriate percentiles can be determined. Standard scores may be plotted on the answer sheet or profile form.

Practical Applications/Uses

Miller (1977) indicates that the SBC is designed for clinicians to use as a part of their assessment battery in diagnosing child psychopathology. The SBC can assist the clinician by giving scores based on teacher ratings of the target student's behavior in the school setting. This type of information is valuable to the clinician because it expands the view of the student's behavior in various settings as reported by a variety of people. Not highlighted by the author, but also important, is the need to obtain behavior ratings from more than one teacher because student behavior may vary considerably from one school setting to another and may be perceived differently from one classroom to another.

The SBC ratings are relatively easy for the teacher to record because only a true or false decision is involved. However, the teacher may complain that the behavior is "sometimes true" or "sometimes false." The author tries to assist the teacher by indicating on the directions that "If you are in doubt, blacken the answer that is most characteristic of the child." The author states in the manual that the SBC can usually be completed in eight to ten minutes. It may take longer, however, with some teachers requiring 15 to 20 minutes when they are unsure of the presence or absence of several stated behaviors.

The SBC is appropriate for school counselors who receive referrals of problem students from teachers. The counselor may use the SBC information to set priorities for waiting lists, to identify possible areas for further assessment and intervention, and to assess classroom behavior prior to the initiation of counseling. The SBC postcounseling scores can assist in providing the counselor with information regarding the effect of the counseling on classroom behavior. Likewise, school psychologists may find the SBC helpful as a screening instrument in the assessment of emotional disturbance.

The SBC may be useful in research. Studies published recently have compared the SBC with direct observation of problem behavior (Cosper & Erickson, 1984; Kuveke, 1983), with self-concept (Zimet & Farley, 1984), and with sociometric status (French & Waas, 1985).

Technical Aspects

The item selection of the SBC involved the inclusion of items from various other scales. Items appear to be neither too specific nor too broad, and most are stated to maximize the possibility that the behavior has been observed rather than inferred. Some items (e.g., "self-confident," "stubborn") are more ambiguous than others, of course, and may require more inference than description.

A major weakness of the SBC is the geographically limited standardization sample. A norm-referenced measure should be normed on a national sample, and the SBC sampled children only from Jefferson County and Louisville, Kentucky. A more than ample number of children were included in the sample, however. The author acknowledges the limitation of his sample but reasons that the norms probably approximate an urban population.

The response scaling is simple but dichotomous (True/False). As noted by Edelbrock (1983), a dichotomous scaling is inadequate because only two possible points result in the possibility of missing important quantitative and qualitative differences. Most behaviors are present in some degree, not just present or absent.

Reliability is reported by Miller (1977) in terms of internal consistency and test-retest reliability. The internal consistency or content sampling reliability is good for both the A1 and A2 forms. For Form A1, The TD Scale had a split-half reliability of .95 for Form A1 and .93 for Form A2. The split-half reliability was lowest on both forms on the HI Scale, with coefficients of .58 on Form A1 and .44 on Form A2. The low internal consistency on HI may be attributed to the number of items on that particular scale (seven items).

Test-retest reliability for the SBC Form A2 is good. Ninety-one students were rated with a six-week test-retest interval and the resulting coefficient on the TD Scale was .89. Other test-retest coefficients ranged from .40 on the HI Scale to .89 on LNA. Although coefficients are not given in the manual, it was noted that Webb (1973) compared the SBC scores of 110 boys and girls rated by different teachers in different settings with an 18-month interval between ratings. Correlations between ratings were significant for all scales but lower than those with a six-week interval. Some of the findings have implications for predictive validity. Because a major potential use of behavior rating scales includes the comparison of ratings across settings and raters (teachers), it would be helpful if more information concerning interrater reliability were reported in the manual.

Miller (1977) reports that content validity of the SBC may be lacking because items sampling extreme deviance were not included. However, the items were developed using various sources, and independently developed measures have similar items to the SBC, with the items describing mildly and moderately deviant behavior. Criterion-related validity is demonstrated in a study reported in the manual comparing phobic, learning disabled, aggressive, and "normal' students. A multiple *F* test and multiple discriminant analysis showed the SBC to discriminate between the four samples of students. More recently, researchers report significant relationships between the SBC and staff ratings of behavior in a psychiatric intensive care unit (Kazdin, Matson, & Esveldt-Dawson, 1984). In addition, Camp (1976) reports significant correlations (LNA, .36; AGG, .52; HI, .13; EXT, .35; TD, .45) between the SBC and the Boehm Test of Basic Concepts, and Ardi (1978) reports that the SBC discriminates between brain-injured and emotionally disturbed children. Construct validity also appears good for the SBC. Findings indicate that aggressive behavior at home predicts total deviant behavior at school (Bloch, 1971), and there is a low positive relationship between home and school behavior in both age groups (Miller, Hampe, Barrett, & Noble, 1971). Further, the factor-analytic studies of the SBC support the construct validity of the SBC (Cosper & Erickson, 1984; Miller, 1972).

Critique

The SBC is an established behavior rating scale designed specifically for clinicians to use by having teachers rate the behavior of individual students in their classrooms. The items are well-written and allow the teacher to describe whether or not a certain behavior has been observed. The dichotomous scaling limits the SBC, with only the presence or absence of each of the behaviors noted by the teacher on a True/False-choice option. The validity of the SBC is perhaps its strongest feature, with considerable research going into its development and several studies being conducted more recently showing relationships between the SBC and other criteria.

A major limitation of the SBC is its lack of a national sample for its normative group. Although the author analyzed the normative sample more than most behavior rating scales are studied and attempted to show how the sample compares in its various demographic characteristics, the sampling is limited to one state and may not even be representative of students in that particular area.

The length of the SBC will appear reasonable to most clinicians because many rating scales and self-report measures have more items. However, the 104 (Form A1) to 96 (Form A2) items may appear to be quite lengthy to teachers who are already overburdened by paperwork. The clinician utilizing the SBC as a part of the diagnostic procedures will need to make sure that the teacher who is asked to complete the SBC is aware of the importance of taking enough time to give due consideration to each of the items. Additionally, the length of the SBC may deter clinicians from having all of the child's teachers complete a separate rating on the child. This would be unfortunate because some of the most important comparisons involve an analysis of the child's behavior in multiple settings. In that regard, it would be helpful if the SBC manual reported more information regarding interrater reliability.

Clinicians who use the SBC may also wish to consider the Louisville Behavior Checklist (Miller, 1977; for a review see Trapp, 1985). Parents are apt to describe the behavior of their child at home in a different manner from teachers at school (Hampe, 1975), and the Louisville Behavior Checklist may be used to collect parent observations. However, users of the SBC need to be aware that the SBC may not adequately represent the national population of children between four and 13 years of age.

References

Ardi, D. B. (1978). The relationship of functional academic achievement to the clinical categories of brain injury and emotional disturbance. *Dissertation Abstracts International, 39*(2-A), 806.

Bloch, J. B. (1971). *Agreement between parents' and teachers' ratings of childhood emotional adjustment.* Unpublished master's thesis, University of Louisville, Louisville, Kentucky.

Camp, B. W. (1976). Stability of behavior ratings. *Perceptual and Motor Skills, 43,* 1065-1066.

Cosper, M. R., & Erickson, M. T. (1984). Relationships among observed classroom behavior and three types of teacher ratings. *Behavioral Disorders, 9,* 189-195.

Edelbrock, C. (1983). Problems and issues in using rating scales to assess child personality and psychopathology. *School Psychology Review, 12,* 293-299.

French, D. C., & Waas, G. A. (1985). Behavior problems of peer-neglected and peer-rejected elementary-age children: Parent and teacher perspectives. *Child Development, 56,* 246-252.

Hampe, E. (1975). Parents' and teachers' perceptions of personality characteristics of children selected for classes for the learning disabled. *Psychological Reports, 37,* 183-189.

Ireton, H. R., & Thwing, E. J. (1972). *Manual for Minnesota Child Development Inventory.* Minneapolis: Interpretive Scoring Systems.

Kazdin, A. E., Matson, J. L., & Esveldt-Dawson, K. (1984). The relationship of role-playing assessment of children's social skills to multiple measures of social competence. *Behaviour Research and Therapy, 22,* 129-139.

Kuveke, S. H. (1983). School behaviors of educable mentally retarded children. *Education and Training of the Mentally Retarded, 18,* 134-137.

Miller, L. C. (1967). Louisville Behavior Checklist for males, 6-12 years of age. *Psychological Reports, 21,* 885-896.

Miller, L. C. (1968). *Standardization of Modified Pittsburgh Adjustment Survey Scales* (Report for the United States Department of Health, Education, and Welfare, Project #7-0-011). Louisville: Child Psychiatry Research Center, University of Louisville.

Miller, L. C. (1972). School Behavior Check List: An inventory of deviant behavior for elementary school children. *Journal of Consulting and Clinical Psychology, 38,* 134-144.

Miller, L. C. (1977a). *Louisville Behavior Checklist.* Los Angeles: Western Psychological Services.

Miller, L. C. (1977b). *School Behavior Checklist.* Los Angeles: Western Psychological Services.

Miller, L. C., Hampe, E., Barrett, C. L., & Noble, H. (1971). Children's deviant behavior within the general population. *Journal of Consulting and Clinical Psychology, 37,* 16-22.

Ross, A. O., Lacey, H. M., & Parton, D. A. (1965). The development of a behavior checklist for boys. *Child Development, 36,* 1013-1027.

Trapp, E. P. (1985). Review of the Louisville Behavior Checklist. In D. J. Keyser & R. C. Sweetland (Eds.), *Test Critiques* (Vol. II, pp. 430-435). Kansas City, MO: Test Corporation of America.

Webb, J. S. (1973). *A comparison of teacher ratings of classroom behavior on the School Behavior Check List.* Unpublished master's thesis, University of Louisville, Louisville, Kentucky.

Zimet, S. G., & Farley, G. K. (1984). The self-concepts of children entering day psychiatric treatment. *Child Psychiatry and Human Development, 15,* 142-150.

Ellis D. Evans, Ph.D.

Professor of Educational Psychology, College of Education, University of Washington, Seattle, Washington.

SCHOOL READINESS SURVEY

F. L. Jordan and James Massey. Palo Alto, California: Consulting Psychologists Press, Inc.

Introduction

The School Readiness Survey (SRS) is a brief and untimed measure of children's general readiness for Kindergarten that is designed primarily for use by parents concerned with appraising their own child's development. Accompanying the SRS are suggestions to parents for facilitating their child's development in selected skill areas by way of constructive play at home. Thus, administration of the SRS purports to assist parents in better understanding their child's capabilities and developmental needs prior to or during the kindergarten year of school. Simultaneously, results of the SRS may, in combination with other readiness criteria, serve an initial screening function for educators concerned with children's group placement and enrichment.

The SRS was developed in collaboration between two California public school system personnel members: F. L. Jordan, an elementary classroom teacher and administrator, and James Massey, a school psychologist. Origins of the SRS are traced to discussions initiated in 1965 by the authors (Jordan & Massey, 1975b) concerning problems of decision making about school entry for children whose developmental maturity may be questionable. The authors preferred to take a preventative approach to the risks of early failure by children ill-prepared for school. Eventually, and with economic criteria in mind, the authors chose to involve children's parents in an assessment and readiness-building strategy. The basic objective was to formulate a comprehensive, yet uncomplicated, parent-administered measure of general school readiness.

This objective required attention to specifics of the readiness domain that, over the course of a year or so, were defined according to teacher opinion and existing kindergarten evaluation forms used for determining children's early school progress. These readiness skill or attribute definitions were then matched against items contained in a variety of existing readiness scales, tests, and surveys. Items were categorized, then discriminated on the basis of administrative ease. A trial version of the SRS was created and distributed to 100 parents for administration to their children. Subsequently, by way of an unspecified process, certain alterations culminated in an edited version of the instrument. One thousand copies of this final, edited version were then distributed to parents who were registering their youngsters for Kindergarten in May prior to the regular September school entry. These families represented 18 schools serving an economically diverse population in Cupertino, California, Union School District. Standardization was completed on 842 children from these 18 schools, and the published version of the SRS first appeared in 1967. This modest developmental process was sufficient to convince the authors, first, that parents could be fairly objective in assessing their children's abilities and, second, that their procedure was potentially useful in managing the school readiness problem.

For reasons unspecified in the technical manual (Jordan & Massey, 1975b), the SRS was restandardized in 1975, using a population of 383 preschool children enrolled in 20 different schools in Santa Clara and San Mateo counties (California). The current published form is apparently identical in content to the original version. Moreover, like its predecessor, this second edition is published in English only.

Content of the SRS is organized into seven segments of items that purport to measure early school-related skills (Jordan & Massey, 1975a). Items are presented in booklet form with instructions for administration and scoring for each section. The measure is designed for individual administration by a parent to the kindergarten-aged child, although a teacher or other competent adult could serve this function. Items were selected by a criterion that most children will respond accurately to 70-75% of the total 93 items. Accordingly, Jordan and Massey (1975b) suggest that a child who scores "substantially below" this criterion level is a likely candidate for "special assistance or additional time for growth" prior to school entry. The seven subtests are described as follows:

Number of Concepts (7 items): focuses on counting skills;

Form Discrimination (11 items): measures visual discrimination between geometric forms or familiar objects (e.g., printed capital letter reversals) by requiring child to choose which of five figures is not like the others;

Color Naming (7 items): measures ability to name different colors printed in the test booklet;

Symbol Matching (16 items): requires line drawing from an array of objects in one vertical column to identical objects in a second, adjacent column;

Speaking Vocabulary (20 items): requires naming common objects and animals that are pictorially represented in boxes pointed to in succession by the examiner;

Listening Vocabulary (12 items): requires discrimination (by marking) of still further common objects from among a variety of objects or actions in a picture-stimulus array; and

General Information (20 items): requires free recall of past experience and the completion of simple analogies.

These seven subscales are supplemented by a 25-item checklist for general readiness in a yes/no format to be completed by the parent. This checklist is not scored and, thus, does not figure directly in the survey's principal mission. Rather, the checklist results are intended to provide additional information of potential usefulness to parents who are concerned about developmental characteristics possibly related to early school success. For the seven core subscales, a scoring guide, from which separate and collective scale scores can be determined, and general guidelines for interpretation are provided. Score levels are differentiated in magnitude to indicate one of three main diagnostic summaries: "ready for school," "borderline readiness," or "needs to develop."

Practical Applications/Uses

The SRS can be envisioned as a reasonably objective tool to facilitate involvement of parents with educators in assessing prekindergarten, school-related behavior and possibly as a rough guide for preparing a child for school entry. Jordan and Massey (1975b) state that such involvement can reduce, if not eliminate, parent resentment or resistance occasionally noted in response to teachers' or school psychologists' appraisals of children. In addition, the authors maintain that parent assessment can facilitate better home/school cooperation and save "hundreds of hours" of professional time for educators involved in diagnostic placement decisions about children. According to the authors, anxious parents involved with SRS assessment can be reassured about their child's status, thereby reducing pressures on the child and school personnel.

These arguments, however appealing, are not supported by research evidence and, thus, must be considered only as working hypotheses. Clearly the principal stated use of the SRS is to supply data to parents about their children's readiness. If the authors' ideal prescription is taken to heart, assessment should take place several months prior to school entry—around spring registration time for fall kindergarten entry, if not before. Jordan and Massey (1975b) recommend that, whenever possible, school personnel should provide parents with an orientation to the SRS prior to its use. Trained teachers could manage the assessment process as well. At best, SRS results can provide preliminary, but somewhat limited, clues for thinking about a child's repertoire of readiness skills. Children whose performance is reliably low should be taken to a more comprehensive stage of diagnostic assessment by trained personnel.

It is imperative to note that the SRS was designed for use with normally functioning four-to-six-year-old preschool children anticipating regular kindergarten entry. The SRS has no accommodation for handicapped children or children whose native language is not English. Jordan and Massey (1975b) maintain, however, that the measure can be used "profitably" in conjunction with compensatory education projects. Regardless, the SRS should be administered individually by the parent or teacher in a distraction-free setting. Administration procedures are straightforward and comparatively simple. All instructions are built into the SRS booklet on pages opposite from those on which the children record their responses with a pencil. With the SRS booklet placed flat on a table or desk between the administrator and the child, instruction and scoring can take place successively throughout the first six subtests. Subtest seven (General Information) calls solely for a child's verbal responses to questions, the correctness of which can be noted and scored immediately. Instructions for administration are clear. Few problems appear to complicate the use of this measure short of parental illiteracy or lack of motivation for the child to participate. Nothing in the technical manual indicates that subtests must be administered in their prescribed order. Hence, flexibility in administration could be exercised as needed. Conceivably, this flexibility could be extended to administer different portions at different times throughout a day or week, but standard procedure calls for administration at one sitting. Although no range of completion time is stated in the manual, the SRS should require approximately 30 minutes under ideal conditions. During administration, praise and encouragement, but not prompting and cuing, are permissible.

Because scoring is done during administration from recordings made directly on the test booklet, scoring time is not an issue with the SRS. All items carry a one-point value and are summed separately by subtest and collectively as a total score. No special training is required for this purpose. The test booklet contains a simple guide to scoring in appropriately qualified terms for interpretive ease. One possible threat to scoring objectively is that parents tend to score too liberally if they think their child knows an answer or has indicated an understanding at some time other than the test period. Jordan and Massey (1975b) report that parents show a tendency to score their children from two to five points higher, on the average, as compared to trained administrators, although this finding could reflect a rapport factor as well. Given the gross nature of this assessment, such a point differential seems to have little practical significance.

As indicated earlier, point totals are translated into three categories to summarize status: "ready for school," "borderline readiness," or "needs to develop." Perhaps the most critical issue about scoring is what action should be taken, if any, about a child who "needs to develop." Jordan and Massey (1975b) indicate that parent-guided educational activities are warranted in such a case. Their implicit assumption is that children unready for school in May can be boosted by September. Otherwise, children may be candidates for deferred entry to school. Feasibility of this option can be challenged on many grounds, including public law. Thus, educators are compelled to search for better defensible and purposive follow-up assessment to arrange for schooling for children whose SRS performance is deficient.

Technical Aspects

This issue about appropriate action is highlighted by a full consideration of the technical qualities of the SRS. Reliability data in the technical manual are limited to two stability coefficients derived from a June-October test-retest with two small groups of children. The first group (N = 32) was tested by teachers trained in administration. The second group (N = 20) was tested by their parents, then retested by teachers. Coefficients obtained were .79 and .64 for the two groups, respectively. The authors point out that both coefficients are significant well beyond the .01 level of confidence. Average gain per child across testing periods was five points.

These stability coefficients are moderately high, given the sample sizes and the time-interval lapse between administrations. But it would be informative to determine reliability both from a larger group with a shorter (two-four weeks) retest period and from calculations for coefficient of internal consistency. The latter would seem simple enough to obtain from data on the two standardizations of this survey. The issue is of considerable importance in light of potential decisions about children on the basis of their SRS scores. This is because such a large proportion of variance in measurement stability is unaccounted for by the test-retest method. Complicating the SRS reliability issue is the absence of subscale reliability coefficients, information about standard error of measurement, and interscorer agreement data.

The case for validity of the SRS data is based on one study (Jordan & Massey, 1975b) of 383 preschool children from 20 California elementary schools. This group fully represents the restandardization population from which descriptive statistics to assist score interpretation have also been calculated. Validation procedures involved initial administration of the SRS by parents to children either unsupervised in the home setting or under supervision of personnel in the school setting. Either way, testing took place during the May before September kindergarten entry. Thereafter, in May of the kindergarten year, teachers rated these children's overall school progress on a five-point scale from lowest to highest achievement. Teacher's ratings were then correlated (Pearson formula) with total and subscale SRS scores to yield an estimate of predictive validity for the SRS. A correlation of .62 was obtained for the total scale and the teacher rating criterion. As would be expected, subscale correlations were lower, ranging from a high of .52 (Number Concepts) to a low of .36 (Listening Vocabulary).

Interpretation of these validity coefficients is impeded by lack of information about reliability of the criterion variable (i.e., the global teachers' ratings). No further objective, independent criteria figure with validation procedure (e.g., relationship of SRS scores to standardized achievement performance; other readiness measures; or measures of intellectual, affective, or personal-social behavior). This lack applies both to short-(out of kindergarten) and long-term conditions (primary-grade educational progress or indices such as retention-in-grade or special-class placement). As for the validation population, standardization-group children are not claimed to be representative of the U.S. population as a whole: minority-group children composed less than 5% of the total group, and, according to the technical manual, parental education level averaged "well above" national norms. If attention to cultural bias problems was given during the development of the SRS, it is not made explicit in the technical manual.

Norms for the SRS are based on the method of cumulative percentage, that is, total scores are associated in three-point intervals with the cumulative percentage of children (by sex) achieving successive levels of SRS performance. These norms appear in table form, as do means and standard deviation (again by sex) for each of the seven subscale and the total scale scores. Score distributions by subscale and sex and subscale intercorrelations are also presented in tabular form.

Inspection of the norm tables indicates that where score differentials occur, they tend to favor females slightly, especially at the lower end of the total scale. Yet, overall, sex differences appear insignificant. Age level was discounted for norming because of variation in age criteria for school entry across various states. But a minimal entering age of four years, nine months (as of September 1 of the kindergarten year) is the basis for existing norms. Potential users are advised that these norms are limited to percentages and comparisons by sex of children. Age or percentile norms are not provided. Cumulative percentage norms reveal that, based on SRS performance, over 8% of males and 5% of females in the standardization group were at high risk for school readiness ("need to develop"). Accepting the authors' apparently arbitrary cutoff score of 79, nearly one-third of all children were classified as "borderline" or below. This constitutes a sizable group for ''special assistance'' and/or ''additional time for growth'' before school entry if SRS performance is taken as an accurate index for developmental status.

Critique

Development of the SRS is consistent with a long-standing educationally significant concern for preventing early school failure and individualizing learning programs for children whose preschool status places them at risk for normal educational progress. Problems of economically and technically sound assessment and diagnosis associated with this concern are widely acknowledged throughout the early childhood education literature (Barnes, 1982; Evans, 1974; Goodwin & Driscoll, 1980). It is no secret that the search for acceptable readiness assessments has been seriously hampered by insufficient attention to technical qualities, a point aptly illustrated by the SRS—that is, shortcomings in reliability and, especially, validity for the SRS call for the exercise of extreme caution about use of this instrument other than for familiarizing parents with a narrow range of general ideas about children's development of school readiness.

To be sure, the idea of parental involvement in cooperative assessment and informal teaching to benefit children has merit. Use of the SRS by parents may provide a useful, albeit limited, way to parental enlightenment and sensitization to certain aspects of their children's conceptual development. Low performances, to the extent that they are reliable, could serve as signposts for further screening and diagnosis as the authors suggest. But even high performances, although potentially gratifying for parents and educators, could mask social or motivational problems that may interfere with learning and, thus, are no guarantee of school success. Longitudinal validity studies are therefore in order. Apparently, no such studies are available for public inspection even after two decades of SRS existence. Nor are data available about the effects on parents, children, and parent-child interactions among those who engage the SRS process. Thus, despite a restandardization to show that children tend generally to score higher on the SRS than did similar children in the 1960s, little seems to have been learned and placed in the public domain about the practice and theory of the SRS.

Reservations and limitations of the SRS are shared among previous reviewers of this instrument. Egelund (1970), for example, expresses concern about the lack of statistical justification for item selection and subscale development. Noting the limited technical data for reliability and validity, Egelund judges the SRS to present the early stages of experimental development in scale construction. He also warns about its value for making individual decisions about a child's school readiness. Bennett (1967) concurs in this assessment by pointing to a weak assumption of validity for the SRS.

Several years later, a thoroughgoing evaluation of the SRS was performed at the UCLA Center for the Study of Evaluation (Hoepfner, Stern, & Nunmedal, 1971). Four evaluative criteria—validity, reliability, administrative usability, and examinee appropriateness—were applied according to a standard, systematic numerical rating system developed at the center. These numerical ratings translated to ''poor'' ratings for technical qualities of the SRS and ''fair'' ratings for the consideration of practicality and suitability for child respondents. It should be noted that most measures of the preschool and kindergarten children received similar ratings. This underscores the general problem of quality for early childhood readiness assessment noted above.

More recently, Downing (1978) reviewed the restandardized version of the SRS again to emphasize technical problems, notably deficiencies in predictive and concurrent validity and a lack of a rationale for the 70% cutoff score to denote readiness lack. Like Egelund (1967), Downing (1978) also questions the authors' assumption about efficacy of their suggestions to parents for enhancing children's school readiness. These suggestions, or practice exercises, are addressed especially to parents of low-readiness children as a follow-up to assessment. Perhaps most telling, however, is Downing's criticism of the implicit concept of school readiness on which the SRS seems based: that readiness is a constellation of largely cognitive skills that, if mastered, will enable the child more successfully to adapt or fit into a prescribed and relatively static kindergarten curriculum. Policies of adaptive education based on attention to a wide range of individual differences seem more applicable to current educational practice.

Granting that the SRS is only remotely, if at all, couched in a sound theoretical rationale, its limitations in validation constitute the central issue for practitioners. It is incumbent on the developers to provide a much more rigorous and thorough empirical foundation for this instrument before its use should be considered anything more than experimental. Users could perform their own validity studies in local contexts, a practice that has much to recommend it even if the authors were to provide additional validation data. Because the principal purpose of the SRS is to involve parents in evaluating and preparing their children for school, efficacy studies directly germane to this purpose are sorely needed as well. These would include studies of the impact of SRS on parental perceptions and interactions with their children and any change in children's readiness status subsequent to the parental evaluation process. Until such studies appear, testimonials and guesswork must prevail.

To conclude, the School Readiness Survey, in concept, is inherently appealing to educators concerned with parental involvement and gross screening for readiness risk. Yet, as measured against accepted standards for test development, this instrument carries little authority. That it is not exceptional in this regard is perhaps less of a problem for developers than for undemanding publishers and users of such measures. The SRS may, in fact, be stronger than its supporting evidence would indicate. Sadly, the rich opportunities to disclose any strength across two standardizations and two decades of use have seemingly been lost.

References

Barnes, K. E. (1982). *Preschool screening: The measurement and prediction of children at risk.* Springfield, IL: Charles C. Thomas.

Bennett, D. E. (1967). School Readiness Survey (Review). *Journal of Reading, 11,* 148.

Downing, J. (1978). Review of the School Readiness Survey, second edition. In O. K. Buros (Ed.), *The eighth mental measurements yearbook* (pp. 1347-1348). Highland Park, NJ: The Gryphon Press.

Egelund, B. (1970). School Readiness Survey (Review). *Journal of Educational Measurement, 7,* 58-59.

Evans, E. D. (1974). Measurement practices in early childhood education. In R. W. Colvin & E. M. Zaffiro (Eds.), *Preschool education* (pp. 283-341). New York: Springer Publishing Company.

Goodwin, W. L., & Driscoll, L. A. (1980). *Handbook for measurement and evaluation in early education.* San Francisco: Jossey-Bass Publishers.

Hoepfner, R., Stern, C., & Nunmedal, S. G. (1971). *CSE-ECRC Preschool/Kindergarten test evaluations.* Los Angeles: Center for the Study of Evaluation, Graduate School of Education, University of California at Los Angeles.

Jordan, F. L., & Massey, J. (1975a). *School Readiness Survey* (2nd ed). Palo Alto, CA: Consulting Psychologists Press, Inc.

Jordan, F. L., & Massey, J. (1975b). *Professional manual, School Readiness Survey.* Palo Alto, CA: Consulting Psychologists Press, Inc.

Gary R. Galluzzo, Ph.D.
Associate Professor, Department of Teacher Education, College of Education and Behavioral Science, Western Kentucky University, Bowling Green, Kentucky.

SCHOOL SOCIAL SKILLS RATING SCALE

Laura Brown, Donald Black, and John Downs. East Aurora, New York: Slosson Educational Publications, Inc.

Introduction

The School Social Skills Rating Scale (S³RS) is designed for school personnel (e.g., teachers, counselors, and principals) who want to identify selected social behaviors/skills that students may be lacking. The basic premise that undergirds the S³RS is that a strong sense of social and emotional well-being is a necessary condition for success in life. In the school setting, this means that successful performance in the academic arena hinges on the social and emotional self-assurance that is possessed and displayed by the student. This premise also implies that poor academic performance can be explained by a student having underdeveloped social and emotional skills. The S³RS was developed with the specific purpose of providing teachers, counselors, and principals with a usable and easily interpreted instrument that directly assesses and describes, in behavioral terms, a student's propensity toward the mastery of prosocial behavior in four areas: Adult Relations, Peer Relations, School Rules, and Classroom Behaviors.

A second and related purpose for this instrument is to provide school personnel with specific profiles for each student with whom the test is used. This profile describes both the areas of strength (i.e., those social skills that students have already mastered) as well as those that they have yet to achieve. From each profile, a plan of action can be derived that seeks to reinforce positively those prosocial behaviors that are developed, while seeking to develop those in which the student is lacking. The potential user of the S³RS should be cautioned, however, that the authors of this scale make it quite clear that there are no prescriptions for remediation included in the instrument. The most appropriate use of the S³RS is for the description of student behavior. What can be taught as a result of diagnosis with the S³RS can be derived from the data generated by the scale, but issues of curriculum and instruction are left to the discretion of the user.

The S³RS draws on the notion that social skills are taught and learned both inside and outside the classroom. The rationale of the authors is based on the efforts of those who have worked toward developing environments in which teaching prosocial skills was a focus in the development of a healthy child/student. Two such examples are the works of Phillips et al. (1974) in the development of the Teaching-Family Model and the work of Coughlin and his associates (1983) who studied and described the goals, objectives, and instruction of Boys Town, the well-known home for disruptive boys. Both of these programs emphasize academic instruction but also include instruction toward nurturing and encouraging social and emotional growth.

The 40 school-related social skills that comprise the S³RS can be traced to five previously developed student behavior assessment instruments: 1) the Behavior Rating Profile (Brown & Hammill, 1978), 2) the Structured Learning Skill Checklist (Goldstein, Sprafkin, Gershaw, & Klein, 1980), 3) the Social Behavior Assessment (Stephens, 1980), 4) the Student Referral Scale (Hoeltke & Toker, 1981), and 5) the Behavior Evaluation Scale (McCarney, Leigh, & Cornbleet, 1983). The items that comprise each of these five instruments formed an item pool of 342 typical student behaviors. The purpose for aggregating the items from each of the five aforementioned instruments was to identify a set of behaviors that are typically seen in the behavior of students. Stating the behaviors as positive or prosocial makes the S³RS different from the other instruments, not all of which state or describe student behavior in positive terms; each item of the S³RS is specifically described in behavioral terms. For example, the skill "Attends to listening activities" includes the following descriptors that should be displayed: 1) Remains awake, 2) Looks at the person presenting, 3) Quietly listens to presentation, 4) Maintains a pleasant facial expression, and 5) Sits straight. The user of the S³RS rates the student on this behavior by using these five descriptors as behavioral referents.

The items that comprise the S³RS were then categorized into the four areas of interaction (Adult Relations, Peer Relations, School Rules, and Classroom Behaviors). Some of the items overlapped into two of these areas (e.g., Adult Relations and Peer Relations), and the instrument contained 44 behaviors. A careful analysis of the items, conducted by the authors, eliminated two of the items and reduced the scale to 42. The first round of field tests was then conducted using 73 middle-school and high-school teachers in both residential settings and typical school settings across academic areas. As is consistent with the authors' intentions, each of the 73 teachers rated six to ten students in the fall of the academic year, with a retest conducted with the same students and the same teachers in the spring. The teachers then responded to a questionnaire designed to give the authors feedback about the S³RS as to the appropriateness of the items. This field test led to the deletion of two more items, thereby reducing the total number of items on the scale to its present 40.

The S³RS package includes copies of the instrument and a manual for administration (Brown, Black, & Downs, 1985), which describes the development of the S³RS. The manual is a comprehensive and descriptive, 21-page booklet that includes the references relevant and necessary for fully understanding the background literature on the identification of student prosocial behaviors. It is essential that the user be familiar with the manual and the 40 items prior to rating a student.

The four-page instrument is neatly printed and easily read. The cover page asks the rater for the name of the student who is being assessed, and other data can be included in the "Information" section (e.g., student's age, school, birthdate, and class or grade, and the name of the rater). The remainder of the cover page provides directions for the rater as to the appropriate use of the S³RS.

The ensuing three pages include the 40 items, with page two containing the 12 items in Adult Relations, page three containing the 16 items in Peer Relations, and the fourth page containing the six prosocial behaviors that characterize School

Rules and the six items that comprise Classroom Behaviors. To the left of each of the 40 behaviors is a series of six boxes that represent the following six-point Likert-type scale, which describes the frequency at which the student under study displays the behavior (1 = No opportunity to observe the behavior, 2 = Never uses the skill, 3 = Rarely uses the skill, 4 = Occasionally uses the skill and/or uses it at incorrect times, 5 = Often uses the skill under appropriate conditions, and 6 = Always uses the skill under appropriate conditions).

Raters mark the box on the rating scale to represent their judgment regarding the frequency at which the student demonstrates each behavior. There is no separate answer sheet. One instrument is used for each student who is rated. Ratings of 2, 3, or 4 on each behavior fall into a shaded area that indicates that the student is deficient in that behavior. These are then transcribed to the upper right-hand corner of the page. According to the directions, all ratings must be based on the rater's actual observation of each behavior in the school setting within the past month.

Practical Applications/Uses

The S^{3}RS is designed to assist school personnel in identifying the deficiencies students may have in interacting in the school setting. It purports to measure school-related social skills by describing the 40 prosocial behaviors and asking the extent to which a student possesses each one. The scale is appropriate for students in Grades K-12 in school and residential settings. According to the authors, it is also appropriate for special education students. In sum, the S^{3}RS is intended to be used with school-aged children in school settings for the purpose of describing the extent to which they possess generally accepted prosocial behaviors.

It is also appropriate for counselors in school and residential settings who seek to identify the social behaviors in which certain students are deficient for the purpose of developing a counseling strategy. In addition, social workers and educational psychologists in community mental-health centers would also find the S^{3}RS as a reference of prosocial behaviors that can be stressed with individual students or taught as part of a curriculum. Remedial programs that seek to enhance a student's competence in interacting with the society-in-school or society-at-large would find the S^{3}RS a useful tool for diagnosis and prescription. To some degree, even "typically average" students would be deficient in one skill or another, and an informal reinforcement schedule could be designed for them.

The S^{3}RS is typically administered after the first month of school in the fall and again in the spring of the academic year. The purpose for using this procedure is that a curriculum for the development and enhancement of social skills can be incorporated into instruction during the school year. It is administered, or more precisely, it is completed, by the classroom teacher. One instrument is used for each student for each administration. The rater observes the student for a one-month period, then rates the extent to which the student demonstrates each skill on the scale in his or her daily behavior. No particular training other than a thorough familiarity with the scale and manual is required to rate students. The manual states that each completion of the scale should take approximately ten minutes, and that no more than two or three ratings should be completed at one time so that the rater does not confuse the skills of one student with those of another.

Scoring the S³RS is relatively simple in that the completed scale immediately reveals those skills in which the student is competent, as well as deficient. The rater can then decide which skills are the most essential for the student to develop and what strategies for change are most efficient. Interpretation of the data is as simple as scoring the scale. Raters select those skills that they want to develop or enhance in the student's repertoire of prosocial skills.

Technical Aspects

Two types of validity were assessed in the development of the S³RS: content and criterion-related. Content validity, or the degree to which a sample of test items represents the content that the test is designed to measure, was assessed through the creation of an item pool of the other current social skills rating scales. Additionally, content validity was measured by reviews of the related literature conducted by the authors, whose backgrounds as school personnel are germane to the content of the rating scale, and through the results of the questionnaire to which teachers responded in the field tests. In the field test, 70% of the teachers who used the S³RS were satisfied with the 42-item draft of the S³RS. However, two items were deleted from this penultimate draft because of the comments offered by the remaining 30% of the teachers who suggested revisions.

It is becoming more acceptable to group together concurrrent and predictive validity because each relates to the degree to which a test measures an individual's behavior on some other variable or criterion. As with both concurent and predictive validity, criterion-related validity is reported in terms of a test's correlation with another measure, that is, whether or not the S³RS correlates with another measure of prosocial behaviors as they would be observed in school. Brown, Black, and Downs (1983) claim to have uncovered no other measures of school social skills that express student behavior in prosocial terms that would serve as a criterion measure:

> In terms of validity, the prospective user of the S³ Rating Scale should ask, "Is this instrument valid for the purposes to which I wish to put it?" If that purpose is to determine with which of these 40 school related social skills is a student or group of students competent or deficient, then the S³ Rating Scale is a valid instrument. (p. 7)

It would be easy to criticize the validity of the S³RS because of the validity studies conducted thus far. However, it is premature to give a negative evaluation of the S³RS because of the validity studies. This type of instrument, which seeks to define in behavioral terms different characteristics about people, can be found throughout the fields of psychology and education. Using normative standards to derive an assessment of the validity studies, the S³RS falls into the category of acceptability for such a new instrument. That is, thus far in the development of this instrument, content validity is acceptable, and no claims are made regarding the criterion-related validity of the S³RS.

Reliability is defined as internal consistency or stability measured over time. Two methods for estimating reliability were employed: test-retest and interrater. Test-retest reliability was established by correlating the level of agreement on two ratings with the S³RS. The ratings were conducted between ten and 21 days with elementary and middle-school teachers in a residential elementary and middle-school setting (N = 23), a residential high-school setting (N = 26), with regular middle-school teachers (N = 30), and with special-education teachers in a regular middle-school setting (N = 30). A descriptive approach to calculating the correlation coefficient was used, with the calculation based on the percentage of agreement on each item between the test and the retest. The coefficients were then calculated by dividing the number of agreements by the total number of agreements and disagreements. The coefficients for each of the four subscales with each of the four samples ranged from .78 to .97. On the total S³RS (i.e., all four areas combined) the coefficients ranged from .81 to .93. The S³RS shows stability and consistency over time when using this method of calculating test-retest reliability.

Interrater reliability was established by correlating the level of agreement between the ratings conducted by independent observers. As with test-retest reliability, interrater reliability was computed by dividing the number of agreements by the total number of agreements and disagreements. Three settings were used in the interrater reliability study: 1) elementary and middle school in a residential setting (N = 28), 2) a middle-school special-education setting (N = 30), and 3) a middle school in a regular setting (N = 30). The correlation coefficients for each of the four subscales in each of the three settings ranged from .65 to .91. The lowest correlations were in the special-education middle setting on the Classroom Behaviors subscale (.65), followed by the special-education middle-school setting on the Adult Relations subscale (.68). The remainder of the coefficients are above .70. On the total S³RS (i.e., all four areas combined) the coefficients ranged from .70 to .78.

Critique

In a very general way, the S³RS is a "user-friendly" student observation instrument that provides a description of a student's behavior in reasonably reliable terms. The expression "user-friendly" is used in this context to connote that the S³RS is easily used. It appears to be appropriate for teachers in both residential and regular school settings. In the manual and on the instrument the authors use language typically used by teachers when discussing the behavior of students. The behaviors are aptly described and are easily observed in students. School personnel who believe that instruction for social and emotional growth is a portion of the curriculum will find that the S³RS was designed with them in mind. It seems to be helpful in describing student behavior, with the goal being the development of a curriculum that seeks to change behavior toward that of prosocial.

As a research-based instrument, the S³RS may show some areas for concern. The S³RS is a new instrument that has yet to withstand the tests of empirical research. The validity and reliability studies were appropriately conducted and yielded evidence that supports the scale. For example, for the user who needs more supportive literature of an empirical nature regarding the S³RS, it is premature. There are no studies of the factor structures that lie within the S³RS. Acceptable levels of reliability and validity reported by the authors must suffice. However, a greater question emerges. It is much wiser, in this reviewer's opinion, for the potential user to ask the question of validity: "Is this instrument appropriate for my purpose?" It is essential when selecting any instrument that the user is certain that it is consistent with the intended outcomes. In the absence of solid empirical support for the S^3RS, the validity that this scale presents is left to the subjective judgment of the potential user.

A final comment on the S^3RS relates to its potential as a research instrument. This reviewer has a difficult time envisioning large-scale studies of adequate sample size that seek generalization using the S^3RS. This instrument seems best suited for school personnel who want to conduct isolated case studies of individual students who need some structured learning experiences designed to promote social growth. For example, teachers may identify, in a general way, that one or two of their students exhibit socially immature behavior. The S^3RS is a valid instrument for diagnosing and describing with some degree of specificity in which behaviors a student is most deficient. Although the S^3RS provides no prescription, it does provide numerous characteristics of prosocial behaviors, which can be taught through a structured reinforcement system. As opposed to a large-scale use of the S^3RS, it is less likely that all students observed will need reinforcement toward producing the same set of prosocial behaviors. In sum, the S^3RS is best used with individual students who require some form of intervention; however, group use is not precluded. It is possible that after diagnosis, groups of students who need instruction in the same social behaviors can be formed.

This concern should not dissuade the potential user from considering the S^3RS as a measurement tool for studies larger than a case study. The S^3RS describes student behavior in terms that teachers understand and seems capable of guiding teachers to make decisions about interventions. For such intervention activities, the user will need to develop a program to guide the student toward social growth. The pathways for intervention are not as clearly marked in the S^3RS materials. Again, the authors do not claim to offer prescriptions for change. The most appropriate use of the S^3RS will rest with users' subjective judgments that it meets their needs in describing student prosocial behavior.

References

This list includes text citations as well as suggested additional reading.

Brown, L., Black, D., & Downs, J. (1983). *School Social Skills Rating Scale manual:* East Aurora, NY: Slosson Educational Publications, Inc.

Brown, L. L., & Hammill, D. D. (1978). *Behavior Rating Profile: An ecological approach to behavioral assessment.* Austin, TX: PRO-ED.

Cartledge, G., & Milburn, J. F. (1978). The case of teaching social skills in the classroom: A review. *Review of Educational Research, 1,* 133-156.

Coughlin, D. D., Maloney, D. M., Baron, R. L., Dahir, J., Daly, D. L., Daly, P. B., Fixsen, D. L., Phillips, E. L., & Thomas, D. L. (1983). Implementing the community-bases Teaching-Family Model at Boys Town. In W. P. Christian, G. T. Hanna, & T. J. Glahon (Eds.), *Programming effective human services: Strategies for institutional change and client transition* (pp. 27-51). New York: Plenum Press.

Goldstein, A. P., Sprafkin, R. P., Gershaw, N. J., & Klein, P. (1980). *Skillstreaming the adolescent.* Champaign, IL: Research Press Company.

Goldstein, A. P., & Stein, N. (1976). *Prescriptive psychotherapies.* Elmsford, NY: Pergamon Press, Inc.

Hoeltke, G. M., & Toker, M. L. (1981). *Student Referral Scale.* Kearney, NE: Educational Systems Associates, Inc.

McCarney, S. B., Leigh, J. E., & Cornbleet, J. A. (1983). *The Behavior Evaluation Scale.* Columbia, MO: Educational Services.

Phillips, E. L. (1968). Achievement place: Token reinforcement procedures in a home-style rehabilitation setting for "pre-delinquent" boys. *Journal of Applied Behavior Analysis, 1,* 213-223.

Phillips, E. L., Phillips, E. A., Fixsen, D. L., & Wolf, M. M. (1974). *The teaching-family handbook* (rev. ed.). Lawrence, KS: University of Kansas Printing Service.

Stephens, T. M. (1978). *Social skills in the classroom.* Columbus, OH: Cedars Press, Inc.

Stephens, T. M. (1980). *Social Behavior Assessment* (rev. ed). Columbus, OH: Cedars Press, Inc.

James J. Ryan, Ph.D.
Professor of Psychology, University of Wisconsin-La Crosse, La Crosse, Wisconsin.

SCOTT MENTAL ALERTNESS TEST

The Scott Company. Chicago, Illinois: Stoelting Company.

Introduction

The Scott Mental Alertness Test is an early paper-and-pencil group test intended to measure one aspect of intellectual ability, the ability to "size up a situation quickly, to see its relation to other situations and to arrive at a sound judgment as to the best solution" (Scott & Clothier, 1923, p. 227). It consists of six brief (between one and four minutes) subtests, each of which requires either a choice response or a single constructed response. The separate scores on each subtest are summed to obtain a single raw score. It was intended for the selection of clerical and office personnel.

The test, originally titled The Scott Company Mental Alertness Test, was developed by the Scott company. The company, which has been identified as the first industrial psychology consulting firm, was founded by Walter Dill Scott, one of the pioneers and earliest practitioners of industrial psychology. He was also among the team of psychologists who developed tests for the military during World War I. The Scott Test was first published in 1923 and neither it nor its 1½-page manual have ever been revised. The most detailed information about the test is provided in the classic text, *Personnel Management* (Scott & Clothier, 1923), and in the book's second edition (Scott, Clothier, & Mathewson, 1931). The test is reproduced in full in these texts. According to Scott and Clothier (1923), the Scott Company, rather than Scott himself, was the author of this test (although Scott did author two other tests).

The nature of the test and the general rationale underlying its construction, according to the test's manual (Scott Company, 1923, p. 1), involves "arithmetical reasoning, quickness of thinking, quickness and accuracy of judgment, clearness of perception, degree of comprehension and ability to follow specific instructions." Time limits were made short enough that the most alert person could not make a perfect score and easy enough that the less mentally alert could make an appreciable one. The test was designed to be as free as possible from formal schooling influences, including the exclusion of difficult and unusual words, and to avoid statements or problems that necessitate knowledge "of an unusual or strange nature."

It appears that the test authors, like others of their time (e.g., Bills, 1923; Freeman, 1921) viewed "mental alertness" as synonymous with intelligence and respective measures thereof. Scott and Clothier (1923) imply without any further qualification that this test was an extension or variation of the tests developed for the Army during World War I, presumably general intelligence tests such as the Army Alpha. However, in the second edition, Scott, Clothier, and Mathewson

(1931, p. 215) refer to mental alertness tests and intelligence tests separately and make the somewhat ambiguous distinction that the most general intelligence tests can measure is the ability to solve problems that demand accuracy in relation to speed for their solutions, a characteristic that the authors term *mental alertness* (the ability to size up a problem and make a quick and accurate solution) or *mental nimbleness* (a factor of human intelligence). In addition to measuring mental alertness, they maintain that "intelligence tests" also measure other qualities, such as vocabulary, memory, learning, and reasoning. What the authors seem to be implying is that mental alertness is the principal quality or attribute underlying performance on intelligence tests.

The Scott Mental Alertness Test consists of six subtests, each of which is contained on a single page; responses are made directly on the page. The subtests are described as follows:

> *Subtest A* (4 minutes): Consists of 17 brief arithmetic word problems. Requires constructed response.
> *Subtest B* (1 minute): Consists of 25 common adjectives for which the opposites are selected from four alternatives.
> *Subtest C* (1½ minutes): Consists of 25 verbal analogies from which the answer is selected from four alternatives.
> *Subtest D* (2 minutes): Consists of 14 items, each of which contains a solid stack of blocks represented in a single three-dimensional perspective that are to be counted (including those not visible in the lower, back rows). Requires written numerical response.
> *Subtest E* (2½ minutes): Consists of a 20-letter rearrangement or anagrams that spell common animal names. Requires written response.
> *Subtest F* (3 minutes): Consists of 12 items requiring the determination of the number of coins (e.g., pennies, nickels, dimes, quarters) necessary to attain a given total when the total number of coins is specified (e.g., What 3 coins = 85 cents?).

None of the items in any of the subtests appear to be difficult for most adults and are not likely to be beyond the ability of the average ten-year-old if sufficient time were allowed or beyond the reading vocabulary of the average seven-year-old. Given the time limits and the stated intent of the test, it is predominantly a test of the speed with which the various kinds of tasks can be carried out.

The administration instructions for the examiner are quite brief, indicating the need to recognize the possible anxiety and/or low motivation of some examinees and including suggestions to elicit examinee cooperation and effort. For each subtest, the instructions also give the time allotted and scoring scheme (one point for each correct response for all subtests except A, which receives one-half point). The examiner is given no other instructions on test procedure.

The general pretest instructions for examinees are printed on the front of the test booklet. They indicate the number of subtests, that the directions for each are at the top of the test page, and that the examinee should not turn to a new page until told to do so. These directions further state that a good score does not require finishing each test, that the average person completes only about half of each subtest in the allotted time, and that performance is not necessarily dependent on education.

It is with respect to these test procedures that there is a serious flaw in the construction of the test. The brief time allotted for each subtest *includes* that required to read and comprehend the directions and examples in addition to that allowed to perform the test tasks. For rather obvious reasons, it has been generally recognized for some time (Myers, 1960), and a test construction practice for much longer, that it is necessary to exclude the test directions from the time allocated for the test tasks themselves. This is especially critical for highly speeded tests such as this one. This deficiency is probably attributable to the lack of sophistication of test developers in the 1920s and/or a failure to distinguish between the ability to perform a task and that needed to comprehend the nature of the task.

It appears that it is this procedural flaw that most clearly dates the test, along with the construct of mental alertness as a quality that was presumed to be adequately assessed by test tasks that predominantly involve speed. In contrast, the specific content of the test items themselves is not dated in any way that would probably affect the performance of an examinee today. The only indications of its date of publication are the values of various items in the arithmetic problems, such as those concerning costs (e.g., board costing $4 per week, weekly wages of $21, and railroad fare costing three cents per mile), transportation speed (e.g., driving six miles per hour), or some spelling (e.g., aeroplane). In contrast, all of the words in the analogies and opposites subtests and the names of animals in the anagrams subtest are still common today, which clearly reflects the attempt on the authors' part to minimize difficulty level and/or the differential influence of education in order to mainly assess speed of performance. Although some of these tasks are structurally similar to those found in many contemporary intelligence tests, it should be emphasized that the difficulty level is such that only a speed factor is apt to be reflected in performance for a large proportion of the adult population, as well as those much younger.

Practical Applications/Uses

Scott and Clothier (1923) recommended that the test be used primarily to select office personnel (typists, secretaries, file clerks, messenger boys, and bookkeepers), but, at the same time, indicated that secretarial positions require a higher level of mental alertness than typists. They also viewed mental alertness as differing from clerical aptitude, for which they recommended a different test. In addition, they recommended it as a method of assessing vocational abilities, which could be used in vocational counseling. However, one could not recommend that this test be used for that purpose today (or even in the past) due to—if nothing else—the procedural flaw that would result in the test scores reflecting factors logically unrelated to those that the tasks are measuring.

Because of the test's brief administration time and relatively low cost ($.37/copy), one possible use for it might be as a demonstration test in an introductory psychological testing and measurements course. In addition to exposing students to a variety of test tasks (some, of more historical interest), the test might serve—with some modification of the administration procedure such as separating the instructions from the test task timing—to demonstrate why this separation is a standard practice or to show the spuriously high internal consistency reliabilities obtained on speeded tests. Under these conditions, it could also be used to obtain class data to determine intercorrelations among subtest scores and possibly other test characteristics.

There are a variety of other research questions concerning speed vs. power or depth of processing for which these test tasks might provide appropriate stimulus materials for assessing speed. Whether these test tasks would be any better for such purposes than those of current tests that emphasize speed (e.g., clerical aptitude tests) or that might be quite readily devised is difficult to say.

Technical Aspects

The technical limitations and implications of the procedures requiring subjects to read and comprehend directions within the testing time, which is also reflected in the test score, would seem to be quite evident. Clearly, reading speed, familiarity with test tasks of each type, and reading through the instructions rapidly are all likely to be factors that vary among examinees and are independent of task performance speed, but would affect total test performance. It would seem then that examinee differences in the time required to read and comprehend the subtest tasks would contribute a major source of unintended variance to overall performance differences and one that is not logically defensible as such. It is probable, especially at an earlier time when this test was initially being used, that the time needed to process the directions would have a strong relationship with educational level and its correlate general test familiarity or test sophistication. With or without this limitation, this test appears to be a clear example of a "pure speed" test as defined by Nunnally (1978), which is a test on which if given sufficient time, all examinees would get all of the items correct.

The test manual mentions nothing concerning reliability evidence. The only validity evidence in the manual is a brief description of a concurrent validity study on 30 employees, on whom ordered category ratings were compared with their rank-order on the test. It is stated only that these rankings ". . . showed an amazing agreement." However, in the texts by Scott and Clothier (1923) and Scott et al. (1931), there are tables showing the results of several concurrent and predictive validity studies carried out by the Scott Company using this test. From these tables rough estimates of the linear correlations between the test scores and performance ratings could be computed. These ranged from .56 (N = 102) to .85 (N = 40). However, given the probable range in educational level among those in these samples, which is likely to correspond quite highly with familiarity with objective tests or other types of tests, it is most likely that these relations are reflecting family differences in general test sophistication as well as task familiarity, along with reading speed and/or self-confidence with respect to such tasks. The only norms provided in the manual are average scores for an unknown number of stenographers, bookkeepers, and clerks of both sexes and office boys. No other characterization of these groups is provided, although even if it were, it would be clearly out of date.

Critique

Apparently there have been no prior reviews of the Scott Mental Alertness Test, which might be why this test may have the dubious distinction of being the oldest unrevised psychological test on the market today.

The overriding and fatal deficiency of this test—inclusion of the test directions within the timing interval for the test tasks—has been clearly emphasized above. This is a flaw that in itself should preclude any meaningful empirical evaluation and, consequently, any use of this test for the usual professional assessment purposes.

Although it may be a moot point, there appears to be little evidence over the years, especially as reflected in available tests, that the qualities this test was intended to measure can, in fact, be assessed by tasks that simply involve speed of processing. In any event, there appears to be a number of other tests on the market with adequate technical characteristics that can serve the purposes for which this test was apparently designed. One only hopes that the statement in the test publisher's recent catalog (Stoelting Company, 1982, p. 18) that the test ''is still widely used'' is and has been for some time a highly overstated promotional claim that is about the same age as the test.

References

Bills, M. A. (1923). Relations of mental alertness test scores to positions and permanency in company. *Journal of Applied Psychology, 7,* 154-156.

Freeman, F. N. (1921). Intelligence and its measurement. *Journal of Educational Psychology, 12,* 133-136.

Myers, C. T. (1960). Symposium: The effects of time limits on test scores (introduction). *Educational and Psychological Measurement, 20,* 221-222.

Nunnally, J. C. (1978). *Psychometric theory* (2nd ed.). New York: McGraw-Hill.

Scott, W. D., & Clothier, R. C. (1923). *Personnel management,* New York: A. W. Shaw.

Scott, W. D., Clothier, R. C., & Mathewson, S. B. (1931). *Personnel management* (2nd ed.). New York: McGraw-Hill.

Scott Company. (1923). *The Scott Company Mental Alertness Test examiner's manual.* Chicago: Stoelting Company.

Scott Company. (1923). *The Scott Mental Alertness Test.* Chicago: Stoelting Company.

Stoelting Company. (1982). *Testing materials.* Chicago: Author.

Evelyn J. Sowell, Ed.D.
Professor of Education, University of Texas at Tyler, Tyler, Texas.

SEQUENTIAL ASSESSMENT OF MATHEMATICS INVENTORIES: STANDARDIZED INVENTORY

Fredricka K. Reisman. Columbus, Ohio: Charles E. Merrill Publishing Company.

Introduction

Sequential Assessment of Mathematics Inventories: Standardized Inventory (SAMI) is a test designed to measure mathematics achievement of students in kindergarten through eighth grade. Eight subtests are included: Mathematical Language, Ordinality, Number/Notation, Computation, Measurement, Geometric Concepts, Mathematical Applications, and Word Problems. Although intended primarily for students with difficulties in mathematics, this test can also be administered to students achieving at the normal level. This is an individually administered test.

The SAMI was developed by Fredricka K. Reisman, chair, Department of Instructional Design and Evaluation, Drexel University. The test grew out of the author's interest in diagnostic teaching in mathematics and developed over a period of six years. Reisman is also the author of two books on this topic, *A Guide to the Diagnostic Teaching of Arithmetic,* third edition (1982), and, with S. H. Kauffman, *Teaching Mathemetics to Children with Special Needs* (1980).

Test items for the SAMI were developed and used in three tryouts with students. When the test was completed, it was standardized using a representative sample of over 1,450 students. Care was taken to ensure that racial/ethnic backgrounds were adequately sampled along with geographic regions, sex of students, and grade levels.

In the SAMI, students must provide their own answers to questions that are presented in pictures or symbols by pointing, telling, or writing. The SAMI includes four components: the test, a student response booklet, a record form, and an examiner's manual (Reisman & Hutchinson, 1985). Each of the 243 test items, printed in black and maroon on white paper, is presented on a separate page of a spiral-bound book (approximately 7″ x 10″) that forms an easel. No student, however, is expected to answer all items. Two sections of the test, Mathematical Language (9 items) and Ordinality (8 items), are administered to students in Grades K-3 only, and Mathematical Applications (19 items) is given to students in Grades 4-8 only. The remaining subtests, Number/Notation (62 items), Computation (77

This reviewer wishes to thank Mark A. Lewis for his helpful comments on an earlier draft of this review.

items), Measurement (29 items), Geometric Concepts (21 items), and Word Problems (18 items), are given to all students. Start points in Number/Notation and Computation vary according to the grade levels of examinees, with older students beginning at more advanced questions.

In giving the test, the examiner reads all worded material to the student. If students can read, they are asked to read with the examiner. The examinee must interpret all numbers and pictured information. Written responses are recorded by the examinee in the student response booklet. Regardless of response mode, the examiner follows the keyed answers in the record form and marks the student's response correct (+), incorrect (–), or no response (0). Whenever the examinee misses or fails to respond to three consecutive questions, the examiner discontinues questions in that subtest.

The spiral-bound examiner's manual is easy to use. In addition to the administration and scoring procedures, the manual provides detailed information on background and design information, item development, technical characteristics, and norm-referenced interpretations. The manual also lists objectives on which the SAMI was based and contains norms tables for interpreting scores.

Practical Applications/Uses

Educational diagnosticians, school psychologists, and teachers (especially those in special education) will find the SAMI useful in assessing student performance in mathematics. The SAMI would also be helpful to people who are learning how to measure student performance (e.g., graduate students or inservice teachers in mathematics clinics).

Intended uses of the SAMI include 1) comparing the student's current level of performance to normative data on age-level or grade-level peers, 2) analyzing the mathematics content in which the student shows strengths or weaknesses, and 3) analyzing the mathematical processes in which the student shows strengths or weaknesses. The developer points out that whereas the SAMI uses one or two items to measure the instructional objectives sampled over the K-8 curriculum, "a thorough analysis of the student's strengths and weaknesses should be based on giving the student many more items over those few objectives that appear to be most important in the curriculum at his or her current instructional level" (Reisman & Hutchinson, 1985, p. 52).

This test can be used with students in kindergarten through eighth grade and with students above Grade 8 who do not demonstrate an understanding of content taught in K-8 mathematics curricula. At this time there is only an English version of the SAMI.

This test is administered individually by the examiner who must attend to both the test questions and the student's responses. Potential examiners include specially trained individuals, such as educational diagnosticians, counselors, and school psychologists. In addition, classroom teachers could administer the test, provided they understood the need for and followed directions for start and stop points in the question sequences. Most classroom teachers would probably benefit from learning to administer, score, and interpret the SAMI under the supervision of a knowledgeable individual.

Test administration and scoring procedures are clearly stated. The test is not timed, with the exception that if the examinee hesitates more than ten seconds on an item, the examiner repeats the directions. The test may take between 20-60 minutes to administer, depending on how many questions the examinee answers. To reduce the time required by older students, they begin at different start points on the Number/Notation and Computation subtests.

According to the manual, only the answer listed as a "Correct Response" is acceptable. There is a minor difficulty with this instruction, especially in the measurement section where examinees are asked to calculate perimeter, area, or volume. When children perform the calculation correctly, some say the number but not the measure (e.g., centimeters or square miles). According to the scoring rules, these answers are not correct. There are no provisions in the directions for probes by the examiner on these questions, altthough probes are included in a different subtest.

Directions for computing raw score totals and establishing confidence intervals are clearly stated in the manual. Scores from the SAMI can be interpreted using within- or across-grade norms as either percentile ranks or standard scores. Although the manual details the information on interpretation, background in understanding norm-referenced testing would be helpful. There are also clear directions on making curriculum-based interpretations.

Using the norms tables on pages 61-77 of the manual poses a minor inconvenience. Columns containing norms for Geometric Concepts and Measurement are in reverse order of their placement in the sequence of subtests. Test interpreters, therefore, must use extra care to be sure that they use the correct norms.

Technical Aspects

Since the SAMI was developed in 1985, the only data available concerning its validity and reliability were those collected by the developer and reported in the manual. Three forms of validity (content, construct, and criterion-related) and two forms of reliability (test-retest and internal consistency) are discussed.

The SAMI was designed to measure mathematics instructional objectives in eight subsets of content, knowledge, or skills that span kindergarten through eighth grade. Each test item measures a specific objective, a procedure that ensures a high degree of content validity.

Construct validity for the SAMI was studied by examining the intercorrelations among subtests given to the standardization groups Grades K-3 and 4-8. The Number/Notation subtest was correlated with each of the other subtests, as was the Computation subtest. For grades 4-8 the coefficients ranged from .49 to .68, and for grades K-3, from .26 to .74. Most correlations are moderate at best, with the lowest correlations between Geometric Concepts and Computation (.26) and Geometric Concepts and Number/Notation (.31) for K-3. (Note: There is an error in the heading for Table 3.14 on page 31 of the manual. It should read "Intercorrelations for the SAMI Subtests. N = 176 in Grades 4-8.")

Criterion-related validity was estimated through correlations between SAMI subtest scores and other measures of mathematics achievement given to the same students. Number/Notation and Computation subtest scores were positively correlated (coefficients = .73 and .46, respectively) with the Metropolitan Readiness Quantitative Test (Nurss & McGauvran, 1976) for kindergarten students. These same subtests were also positively correlated with the California Achievement Tests (CTB/McGraw-Hill, 1977, 1978) in mathemetics for students in Grades 1-7. Coefficients ranged from .50 to .82. However, these estimates of correlation were based on a small number of cases (average N = 21 in Kindergarten, N = 24 in Grades 1-7) and the type of correlation (Pearson *r*, biserial, etc.) is not mentioned. Moreover, stanines were used from the Metropolitan test and grade equivalents from the California Achievement Tests, but raw scores from the SAMI were used. The meaning of these coefficients is ambiguous, given the small number of cases and the absence of the type of correlation.

Reliability of SAMI scores was studies by test-retest data from students at Grades 3, 5, and 8 who were given the SAMI two times, six weeks apart. Scores from the two administrations correlated positively on all subtests in all grades and ranged from a low of .43 on Word Problems to a high of .89 on Mathematical Language in Grade 3. There seems to be no particular pattern to the correlation coefficients. Again, however, these correlations were calculated with scores from 25, 28, and 32 students only. A larger sample for the test-retest study would inspire more confidence in the stability of the SAMI scores.

Number/Notation and Computation subtests were examined for internal consistency. K-R 20 coefficients were computed for each subtest at each grade level, then grouped K-3, 4-6, 7-8. All K-R 20 coefficients were high, ranging from .72 (Kindergarten Computation) to .97 (Grade 8 Computation). All coefficients for the groups were in the low to mid .90s, suggesting that items are rather homogeneous. These coefficients seem high, given that this test is intended to provide analysis of student strengths and weaknesses in content and mathematical processes.

Critique

The SAMI was developed as a measure of student performance in mathematics. Because it is administered individually, this test is expected to give better information than a group test about the performance levels of students with difficulties in mathematics. Because few items measure each objective, however, analyzing student strengths and weaknesses in content or process is problematic.

The SAMI is an attractively packaged test that can be administered, scored, and interpreted easily by most counselors, school psychologists, and other personnel with training in testing. Classroom teachers could also use this test, provided they worked with a knowledgeable supervisor.

That the SAMI has adequate content validity is evident, but criterion-related validity and test-retest reliability are questionable. The number of students ($N < 30$) involved in both of these studies was too small, and additional evidence is needed.

References

CTB/McGraw-Hill. (1978). *California Achievement Tests, Forms C and D.* Monterey, CA: Author.

Nurss, J. R., & McGauvran, M. E. (1976). *Metropolitan Readiness Tests.* Cleveland: The Psychological Corporation.

Reisman, F. K. (1982). *A guide to the diagnostic teaching of arithmetic* (3rd ed.). Columbus, OH: Charles E. Merrill Publishing Company.

Reisman, F. K. (1985). *Sequential Assessment of Mathematics Inventories: Standardized Inventory.* Columbus, OH: Charles E. Merrill Publishing Company.

Reisman, F. K., & Hutchinson, T. A. (1985). *Sequential Assessment of Mathematics Inventories: Standardized Inventory, examiner's manual.* Columbus, OH: Charles E. Merrill Publishing Company.

Reisman, F. K., & Kauffman, S. H. (1980). *Teaching mathematics to children with special needs.* Columbus, OH: Charles E. Merrill Publishing Company.

Brent Edward Wholeben, Ph.D.

Senior Graduate Faculty and Associate Professor, Department of Educational Leadership and Counseling, University of Texas at El Paso, El Paso, Texas.

SIXTEEN PERSONALITY FACTOR QUESTIONNAIRE

Raymond B. Cattell and IPAT Staff. Champaign, Illinois: Institute for Personality and Ability Testing, Inc.

Introduction

The Sixteen Personality Factor Questionnaire (16PF) is an objective test of 16 multidimensional personality attributes arranged in omnibus form. In general, it provides normed references to each of these attributes (the primary scales). Four additional factor scores, second-order scales (Cattell, Eber, & Tatsuoka, 1970), are also computable—based on linear combinations of the 16 primary scales. Conceptualized and initially developed by Raymond B. Cattell in 1949 as a broad, multipurpose measure of the "source traits" of individual personality, the 16PF is appropriate for a wide range of multifaceted populations. It provides a global representation of an individual's coping style, the person's reactive stance to an ever-fluid and transactional environment, and that individual's ability to perceive accurately certain specific environmental requisites for personal behavior. Unlike such instrumentation as the Minnesota Multiphasic Personality Inventory (MMPI), the 16PF attempts to measure personality attributes and behavioral styles of a more "normal" rather than a "pathological" population, although a more clinical use of the 16PF may be appropriate (Karson & O'Dell, 1976).

The 16PF assesses a total of 16 indices, or attributes, of the human personality, attempting to convey a map of the individual's "personality sphere" as originally intended by Cattell. Based on the subject's reaction to certain situations, namely, individual interpretations based on certain questions, a profile of that subject's personality is constructed based on each of the following sixteen factors:

Warmth (Factor A): detached, critical, cool, impersonal vs. outgoing, participating, interested in people, easygoing;

Intelligence (Factor B): concrete-thinking vs. abstract thinking, bright;

Emotional Stability (Factor C): emotionally less stable, easily upset, changeable vs. mature, faces reality, calm, patient;

Dominance (Factor E): mild, accommodating, easily led, conforming vs. aggressive, authoritative, competitive, stubborn;

Impulsivity (Factor F): prudent, serious, taciturn vs. impulsively lively, enthusiastic, heedless;

Conformity (Factor G): disregards rules, feels few obligations vs. persevering, proper, moralistic, rule-bound;

Boldness (Factor H): restrained, threat-sensitive, timid vs. socially bold, uninhibited, spontaneous;

Sensitivity (Factor I): self-reliant, realistic, no-nonsense vs. intuitive, unrealistic, sensitive;

Suspiciousness (Factor L): adaptable, free of jealousy, easy to get along with vs. opinionated, hard to fool, skeptical, questioning;

Imagination (Factor M): careful, conventional, regulated by external realities vs. careless of practical matters, unconventional, absent-minded;

Shrewdness (Factor N): natural, genuine, unpretentious vs. calculating, socially alert, insightful;

Insecurity (Factor O): self-assured, confident, secure, self-satisfied vs. self-reproaching, worrying, troubled;

Radicalism (Factor Q_1): respecting established ideas, tolerant of traditional difficulties vs. liberal, analytical, likes innovation;

Self-sufficiency (Factor Q_2): a joiner and sound follower vs. prefers own decisions, resourceful;

Self-discipline (Factor Q_3): careless of protocol, follows own urges vs. socially precise, following self-image, compulsive; and

Tension (Factor Q_4): tranquil, torpid, unfrustrated vs. frustrated, driven, restless, overwrought.

(Aiken, 1976; Cattell, Eber, & Tatsuoka, 1970; Karson & O'Dell, 1976; Krug, 1981; Lanyon & Goodstein, 1982).

The four second-stratum measures of the subject's personality are constructed based on factor loadings from each of the 16 profile aspects of human behavior. These second-order aggregates are identified and described as follows:

Extraversion (Factor Q_I): introversion vs. extraversion; principally accounted for by the four primary factors of warmth (high A), impulsivity (high F), boldness (high H), and group dependence (low Q_2);

Anxiety (Factor Q_{II}): low anxiety vs. high anxiety; principally accounted for by the six primary factors of emotional instability (low C), threat sensitivity (low H), suspiciousness (high L), guilt (high O), low integration (low Q_3), and tension (high Q_4);

Tough Poise (Factor Q_{III}): sensitivity, emotionalism, vs. tough poise; principally accounted for by the three primary factors of detachment (low A), tough-mindedness (low I), and practicality (low M); and

Independence (Factor Q_{IV}): dependence vs. independence; principally accounted for by the three primary factors of dominance (high E), rebelliousness (high Q_1), and self-sufficiency (high Q_2).

(Aiken, 1976; Cattell, Eber, & Tatsuoka, 1970; Institute for Personality and Ability Testing, Inc., 1970, 1972, 1979, 1985b; Karson & O'Dell, 1976; Krug 1981).

The 16PF is constructed in five forms requiring an administration time of 30-60 minutes, depending on the form. Separate forms vary in readability requirements from a seventh-grade level for Forms A and B to a third-grade level for Form E. The target population for administration is high-school senior through adult. The test is objective, forced-option, and composed of 6-13 items per each of the surveyed 16 personality attributes. Most items are declarative elicitors requiring the subject to give only a short, reactive response to a generally described situation or milieu. The test is usually untimed and, due to its ease of hand scoring, can often be interpreted for the subject immediately after the administration.

In the early 1940s, Cattell's consuming interest in the concept of the "personality sphere" (the global specification of all personality factors or traits that can be measured directly and then subsequently analyzed to understand better the phenomenon of human behavior and interpersonal coping) led him to build on the earlier work of Allport and Odbert (1936). Allport and Odbert identified 17,954 "trait names" relative to human behavior, reduced them to a list of 4,504, and called them "real traits." Cattell further reduced this list to 171 terms by simply eliminating synonyms; through a cluster analysis of peer ratings he identified several clusters that he named "surface traits." Using the then-revolutionary technique of factor analysis, Cattell eventually identified a total of 20 distinct factors that he called "source traits." The result was the composition of the 16 primary personality factors measured in the 16PF instrument originally published in 1949 (Lanyon & Goodstein, 1982).

Subsequent editions of the 16PF, including the construction of seemingly parallel forms (possibly better referred to as extended, repeated measurement forms), were published in 1956-57, 1961-62, and 1967-69. A total of five forms now exist: Forms A, B, C, D, and E. Recently (1985), Form E has been renormed for highly diverse populations, including prison inmates, culturally disadvantaged, physical rehabilitation clients, and limited schizophrenic patients. The norms and interpretive data for the use of the remaining forms (A-D) are based on updated validity and reliability studies conducted in 1970 (Forms A-B) and 1972 (Forms C-D). Normative data comparisons are based on the demographic characteristics of gender and age for senior high school, college, and more general populations, but age corrections can be applied when widely age-ranging populations are being compared.

The 16PF has been translated, or structurally adapted, into over 50 languages in Europe, South America, Africa, and Asia. Most of these translations were initiated by the actual user of the test. Over the past several years, a series of structured analyses have been conducted concerning the effect of the "administration language" on the resulting measurements of individual personality by the instrument (see Cattell, Schroder, & Wagner, 1969; Kapoor, 1965; Nowakowska, 1970; Rodriguez, 1981). Normative comparison tables for culturally disadvantaged populations based on the administration of Form E in the United States (Institute for Personality and Ability Testing, Inc., 1985b) may eventually assist a resolution of this concern for the probability of uncontrolled bias in results based on the language of administration. However, Form E is administered in English, albeit at a reduced literacy competency of a third-grade reading level.

Each of the five forms of the 16PF contain a collection of declarative elicitors that require the subject to respond to a specific situation by choosing from among three forced-choice options in Forms A, B, C, and D or from among two forced-choice options in Form E. Because the number of items differ by form (187 items in each of Forms A and B; 105 items in each of Forms C and D; 128 items in Form E), the administration times are relationally affected; approximately one hour is required for Forms A, B, and E, whereas 30-45 minutes may be sufficient for Forms C and D.

According to the Institute for Personality and Ability Testing, Inc. (1970, 1972, 1985b), reading grade levels are 7.5 for Forms A and B, 6.5 for Forms C and D, and 3.3 for Form E. However, Forms C and D may replace A and B whenever administration time must be limited due to other constraints (Cattell, Eber, & Tatsuoka, 1970).

Items used in the 16PF may be of ordinal or nominal form. For example, in Forms A, B, C, and D (as given in the "examples" section of Form A, 1967-68 Edition R) an ordinal form item would state: "People say I'm impatient," with options being a) true, b) uncertain, and c) false, whereas a nominal-form item would state: "Adult is to child as cat is to —," with the options being a) kitten, b) dog, and c) baby. In Form E (as given in the "examples" section of Form E, 1967 Edition) subjects would respond to an ordinal-form item such as "Do you like to play" with either "jokes on people" or "do you not like to do that," whereas on a nominal-form item they would indicate their preference by marking either "Would you rather play baseball" or "go fishing."

Subjects respond by checking the item number of their appropriate response on an accompanying answer sheet. Scoring templates, wherein specific choices from among the available options are tallied for producing summative, raw weights, promote a relatively time-efficient and accurate scoring framework for each individual instrument. The raw weights are then converted to sten scores, half-interval standard score equivalents, based on appropriate normative tables supplied with the instrument. These sten scores are subsequently depicted graphically on a subject profile sheet for each of the 16 primary personality factors suggested by the subject's responses.

Second-order factor scores (Extraversion, Anxiety, Tough Poise, and Independence) are easily extracted from the individual primary scale results by the use of a hand-calculating worksheet. Sten scores for the second-order factors are entered on the individual profile sheet but are not graphically depicted. In the event that repeated measurements are indicated (e.g., administering both Forms A and B on separate occasions), aggregated measures and combinatorial sten scores can be computed and entered on the profile sheet for subsequent comparison.

Practical Applications/Uses

The attributes of human personality are three-fold: 1) what of a given situation one is able to perceive, 2) how one perceives the situation and subsequently interprets it, and 3) what one does in response to that situation based on this interpretation. The approach of the 16PF to personality assessment—the predictable reactive interpretation of a subject based on the variable indices of individual personality—is an evaluation of the subject's projective view of "self" rather than a reactive view toward the intentions of "others."

The 16PF is described as appropriate for ages 16 and above. The items in the various forms are representative of situations that middle-school children and adults encounter daily in our modern, complex, and sophisticated world. In addition, although considerable research still needs to be accomplished, the 16PF may provide a vehicle for better understanding the dynamics of personality development, change, and influence throughout the various maturational benchmarks of the adolescent child.

Aside from a purely clerical function, the administrator or examiner is simply a convenor, and distributor of materials. For some populations, the administrator may wish to read aloud the simple, one-page instructions prior to the beginning of testing. However, most subjects will read the instructional page privately and commence testing at their volition. Although the administrator's manual for the 16PF (Institute for Personality and Ability Testing, Inc., 1979, p. 14) suggests that approximately every ten minutes the administrator remark to respondents: "Most people are now doing question —," this reviewer does not advise doing so. Subjects may begin to view their performances as substandard (e.g., in the case of a particular subject being slower in terms of response time than others) and thus elicit a personological response that would uncontrollably influence subsequent responses to the items in the instrument.

According to Lanyon and Goodstein (1982), the quantity of references for the 16PF is second only to the MMPI. Of the over 2,000 research citations that exist today concerning the formal application of the 16PF as a personality assessment instrument (e.g., Buros, 1978; Institute for Personality and Ability Testing, Inc., 1977, 1979, 1985a; Mitchell, 1985), the major thrust of application has recently been in terms of career guidance, vocational exploration, and occupational testing. Of the seven machine (computer) generated reports that are based entirely on the 16PF, three are linked directly to career, vocational, and/or occupational assessment: 16PF Narrative Scoring Report, Personal Career Development Profile, and Law Enforcement Assessment and Development Report. As a more direct example, for nearly ten years (1971-80) participants in the National Institute of Education's research and development effort to rehabilitate the hard-core unemployed in Montana, Idaho, Wyoming, Nebraska, and North and South Dakota (Mountain-Plains Education and Economic Development Program, Inc.; later, Family Training Center, Inc. in Glasgow, Montana) were evaluated by the 16PF to better understand the personological dynamics of this disadvantaged population. Unfortunately, few, if any, of these data records were formally analyzed in aggregate or subsequently disseminated in published form.

The 16PF has provided information in a multitude of settings, from the study of personality and motivational factors related to potential aviation accidents among U.S. Naval Academy graduates to the study of personality differences between U.S. Olympic national and nonnational swimmers (Institute for Personality and Ability Testing, Inc., 1985a). Research professionals interested in personality relationships to such areas as cancer treatment, cross-cultural acclimation, teachers of the emotionally disturbed, juvenile delinquency, religion, child abuse, imminent death anxiety, air traffic control, nutrition behavior, controlled substance abuse, long-term effects of concentration camp internment, attitudes towards variable physiological functioning, the screening of seminarians for the priesthood, and child adoption have selected the 16PF as their instrument for the study of personality (see Buros, 1978; Institute for Personality and Ability Testing, Inc., 1977, 1979, 1985a; Mitchell, 1985).

As mentioned in a previous section of this review, the changing mores and standards of an increasingly complex society have provided an opportunity to utilize the 16PF on many diverse populations. Moreover, the demands for leadership and excellence in all occupations, education, and formal training identify our needs to understand better human personality and the reactive behavior associated with it.

The 16PF identifies ages 16 years through adulthood as the primary targets for personality assessment by this instrument. For widely ranging population comparisons in terms of age, score corrections for age are available.

The current norms for Forms A, B, C, and D were constructed for high-school juniors and seniors, college students, and a general nation-wide population of age and income levels commensurate with then current U.S. Bureau of Census figures. These original norms have been updated to reflect the dramatic societal changes since the late 1960s. For example, Form E, which has recently (1985) entered its second edition, provides newly composed norms for culturally disadvantaged, rehabilitation, and prison inmate populations that have attempted to assist better normative interpretations based on present societal attitudes and perceptions toward human behavior.

As with most tests, skillful modification of recommended administration procedures make the 16PF useful for special populations. For example, the publisher has made available video cassettes for substituting a visual testing in American sign language for the Form A version. With caution, the test could also be administered verbally to special populations for whom reading and/or writing are precluded (e.g., the learning disabled and/or multiple handicapped). Although not available at this time, a braille reader or Kurzweil text-character interpreter could also facilitate individual administration with visually handicapped populations without sacrificing validity or reliability of the subject's responses.

The 16PF can also be utilized to complement other measures typically associated with more generally psychopathological populations, although this might be contested by Butcher (1985). Experience on the part of this reviewer demonstrates that this test can add to the information gained through such administrations as the MMPI to cross-reference other results, as well as validate the responses of the more "nonnormal" clientele populations.

The administration of the 16PF is straightforward and simple, requiring little or no training on the part of the examiner. Subjects respond individually and directly to each item in the test booklet by marking the appropriate blank on the answer form. With the possible exception of the examiner reading aloud the brief directions that appear on the front page of the test booklet, there is no interaction between examiners and examinees. For this reason, the examiner could be a secretary or other untrained staff person; in the case of some examinees, it is plausible that individuals could enter the examination room, begin the test at their volition, and return the completed test to a predesignated area. In such open exit situations, an examiner may not be necessary at all.

The 16PF may be administered individually or in a large group setting. With some preparation and training, an examiner could administer the test orally to a large group, with participants recording their individual responses on separate answer forms. This could be particularly helpful for English-language-deficit populations for which even the Form E (third-grade reading level) might be precluded.

The administrator's manual (Institute for Personality and Ability Testing, Inc.,

1979) is equally straightforward and simple to follow. Step-by-step instructions are presented (pp. 14-15) for direct use by the examiner. Combined with the directions printed on the front cover of the test booklet for the examinee to read during test preparation, little confusion or ambiguity typically results. As mentioned in a previous section of this review, the recommendation by the test developers that the examiner report general progress to the examinee group as a whole is not recommended by this reviewer. The manual also provides information regarding the various profile scales of the 16PF, including a listing of relevant validity and reliability coefficients and directions for hand-scoring and interpreting final results.

Generally, the time required for adequate administration of the 16PF, assuming the particular form and associated reading level have been properly selected, is approximately 60 minutes for Forms A, B, and E. For Forms C and D, 30-45 minutes have usually been found to be sufficient for adequate completion of all items. Because the test measures underlying facets of human personality and the intrinsic motivations associated with personal behavior, it is essential that the administration and testing environment not introduce extraneous stimulants that will bias the response behavior of the subject.

Scoring of the 16PF may be accomplished by hand or optical scanning device. Scoring templates (overlays) are available for hand-scoring. In addition, computer scoring, including computer-generated interpretations for the gestalt of the subject's responses, is also available from the publisher. With the exception of Form E, a subject's raw score for each of the 16 primary factors is obtained through a weighted procedure where particular responses count as "1" summatively toward the final raw score, whereas others count as "2." Form E counts all appropriate responses as a "1" towards the unweighted sum. These weighted or unweighted sums are then compared to the desired normative score tables in the particular tabular supplement (Institute for Personality and Ability Testing, Inc., 1970, 1972, 1985b) where a particular sten score is identified based on the magnitudinal range of the response and the individual normative demographics of the respondent. This sten score is entered on the profile form and subsequently depicted graphically for ease of interpretation.

A separate worksheet is available for calculating by hand each of the four second-order (higher-order) scales. This involves transforming each of the various 16 sten scores as weighted factor loadings of standardized variables in a regression equation for each of the second-stratum scales. The arithmetic result is the interpretable sten score for the particular second-order scale. Simple integer multiplication, addition, and subtraction are required. However, the worksheet is such that the procedure is straightforward and uncomplicated.

Scoring requirements in terms of time depend specifically on the scorer. With a little practice, total scoring for one test can be accomplished easily within ten minutes. This time estimate includes conversion of raw measures to sten scores and entering them graphically on the interpretive profile. Additional scoring requirements are associated with determining individual validity measures for "probable faking" by the subject, which is discussed in the technical aspects section of this review.

Interpretation of the 16PF may be surmised through study of the individual profile sheet or through the use of one of the many computer-generated interpretive reports available from the publisher. Of course, interpretation in each of these situations should be construed differently.

As with all standardized tests concerned with the assessment of human personality, the terminology of interpretation provides an inherent bias that is often uncontrollable. For example, when considering the term *impulsivity,* which describes a scale for the extent to which a subject is prudent or serious as opposed to enthusiastic, many individuals think of the adjective "impulsive" as representing a negative condition of the human spirit. Yet, if one were to use the juxtaposed descriptors "prudent vs. enthusiastic," it might be difficult to determine which represented the more "preferred" state or condition. The use of terminology to describe various personological substates that might be interpreted incorrectly because of their colloquial usage has always been a major difficulty associated with personality assessment. This is not, by any means, a select criticism of the 16PF, for all tests are susceptible to this charge; however, the 16PF seems to be easy enough to understand that an untrained observer might draw erroneous conclusions based on a misinterpretation of the terminology used.

The computer-generated interpretive reports, the 16PF Narrative Scoring Report, 16PF Single-Page Report, Personal Career Development Profile, Marriage Counseling Report, Karson Clinical Report, Law Enforcement Assessment and Development Report, and Human Resource Development Report provide easy-to-read summative narrative based on individual subject responses to the 16PF. For the professional untrained in test interpretation, such reports can be very helpful as they consolidate the technical record of each subject into readable summaries based on sten-score ranges. On the other hand, such machine-scoring opportunities can also provide the environment for generalized misuse and abuse and once again restate the need for only "qualified professionals" to have access to such data.

One of the strengths of the 16PF is its ease of usage for structuring the interpretive interview with the client or subject. The profile sheet is easy to read and quickly understood (cautiously, of course, as mentioned above) in the presence of the trained professional. Discussing the profile with the client will often illuminate future points or issues for further discussion, especially if the test were administered in preparation for upcoming counseling or therapy sessions with the client.

Technical Aspects

The various technical reports available from the publisher (Cattell, Eber, & Tatsuoka, 1970; Institute for Personality and Ability Testing, Inc., 1970, 1972, 1979, 1985b) divide their validity assessment efforts into direct and indirect construct (or concept) comparisons. Similarly, reliability assessments are test-retest analyses for what the authors call "dependability and stability." In addition, equivalence coefficients between separate forms have also been evaluated.

Direct construct validity is reported in the form of multiple correlation coefficients, representing the degree of relationship between each of those items that "load" the particular personality factor (the particular primary factor of the 16PF) and the magnitude of the factor itself. Forms A and B are reported to have the greatest total direct validity where each form has seven scales with validity coefficients of at least .70 magnitude. At the same time, Form A has the lowest direct validity coefficients across all four forms, with .35, .41, and .44 correlational magnitudes for Intelligence, Shrewdness, and Imagination, respectively. For Form E, direct construct validity coefficients fall below a .70 magnitude in six areas: Warmth (.66), Conformity (.65), Suspiciousness (.66), Imagination (.41), Shrewdness (.21), Radicalism (.59), and Self-discipline (.67). These coefficients for Form E were derived from a sample of 914 male convicts.

Indirect construct validities for Forms A, B, C, and D are also reported in the form of multiple correlation coefficients, representing the degree of relationship between each primary scale magnitude and the total remaining primary scale magnitudes in the 16PF. The authors refer to this form of investigation as relating each specific factor with all other factors, namely, comparing all of what is "A" with all of what is determined as "not-A." As might be anticipated, correlational coefficients fall below a .80 magnitude in only two instances: .63 for Shrewdness and .74 for Imagination. No indirect validities are reported for Form E.

Dependability coefficients, reliability coefficients calculated by test-retest with short intervals (single or multiple day) between administrations, demonstrate relatively acceptable coefficients, with only sporadic instances of a scale falling below a .70 magnitude. For stability coefficients, test-retest administrations conducted over long intervals (several weeks), magnitudes are expectedly reduced. These results are available for Forms A and B only. For Form E, only stability coefficients are reported, and only the Sensitivity Scale lies above a .80 magnitude. The sample in this exercise was limited to 32 male and female rehabilitation clients, with a test-retest, median interval of six years, four months.

Equivalence coefficients, intercorrelations between primary factor scales generated from different test forms, are generally low. Few equivalence coefficients are greater than .50 magnitude when Forms A and B are compared. Fewer coefficients of .50 or more magnitude exist for Forms C and D. However, when combined administrations of A and C are compared with similar administrations of B and D, correlational magnitudes increase dramatically where 12 of the 16 scales display equivalence coefficients greater than .50 magnitude. When Form E results are compared with combined Forms C and D administrations, equivalence magnitudes generally fall within the .50 to .69 magnitudinal range.

Unfortunately, most of the validity and reliability analyses for all forms except Form E are based on data collected almost 15-20 years ago and are representative of populations who might have viewed their behavioral responses and, therefore, their personality in a different light than might be representative of today's societal mores. In addition, much of the data was collected by second parties not under the direct, standardized control of the publisher.

Internal respondent validity is also discernible for only Form A administrations using a publisher-supplied validity (appropriate response verification) key for determining "faking good" and "faking bad" potential when the subject may wish to appear more normal or less normal, respectively. Based on this supplementary analysis, a correction for distortion is calculable (see Krug, 1978). In addition, a similar analysis is available through the computing of the "motivational distortion scale" for Forms C-D (Institute for Personality and Ability Testing, Inc., 1972).

Critique

The 16PF provides an inventory of personal "source traits" that relate to individual perception, human behavior, and reactive (coping) potential. The test has a wide variety of uses ranging from career guidance to precounseling (intake) assessment. Originally developed for individuals aged 16 years or older, the primary factor scales, which are calculated from subject responses, provide a useful tool for better understanding personological differences between subjects and, furthermore, might provide a highly valid technique for explaining the underlying dynamics of cultural norms and ethnicity-based mores.

The 16PF is best used in individual personality assessment as a means of comparing individual and group mean differences. Its use as an instrument for determining actual trait-specific personality factors (that a subject definitively portrays one behavioral aspect as opposed to another) has been in dispute since the test's original publication (Anastasi, 1976; Bloxom, 1978; Bolton, 1978; Butcher, 1985; Lanyon & Goodstein, 1982; Mossholder, 1985; Walsh, 1978; Zuckerman, 1985). These concerns range from mild remonstrations regarding the use of the test for certain purposes to harsh criticism concerning the use of the instrument for any purpose whatsoever.

The low validity and reliability coefficients for the various testing forms do little to instill consistent faith in the instrument. It is somewhat disconcerting that more research and validation studies have not been initiated by the developer to enhance the utility of the test. However, criticisms regarding potential misuse of the instrument often overshadow the real value of the test in other areas.

Much of the criticism of the 16PF could be dispelled through an updated standardization of the test and its various forms. This would include, of course, a regeneration of norms to identify the dynamics of current societal populations better. An equally strict analysis of validity and reliability coefficients, based on clearly identifiable subpopulations, would serve to enhance the correlational magnitudes that presently exist as marginal. Much of the validity and reliability coefficients formally reported for the test are based on second-party studies not under the direct control of the developer. Although combined administrations of different forms of the test may improve overall validity and reliability measures considerably, the significant increase in terms of administration time and the transient-situational aspects of personality itself may preclude such an option.

These criticisms notwithstanding, the 16PF is a valuable means for identifying differential behavioral attributes in individuals and groups. The type of items and their wording, the situational relevancy described by these items, and the simplicity of response offer a potentially high value for this test in behavioral research and attitudinal exploration with diverse populations. The renewed emphasis on cross-cultural research in multiethnic populations also holds significant promise for the future application of this instrument.

References

Aiken, L. R. (1976). *Psychological testing and assessment* (2nd ed.). Boston: Allyn and Bacon.

Allport, G. W., & Odbert, H. S. (1936). Trait names: A psycho-lexical study. *Psychological Monographs, 47* (Whole No. 211).

Anastasi, A. (1976). *Psychological testing* (4th ed.). New York: Macmillan.

Bloxom, B. M. (1978). Review of the Sixteen Personality Factor Questionnaire. In O. K. Buros (Ed.), *The eighth mental measurements yearbook* (pp. 1077-1078). Highland Park, NJ: The Gryphon Press.

Bolton, B. F. (1978). Review of the Sixteen Personality Factor Questionnaire. In O. K. Buros (Ed.), *The eighth mental measurements yearbook* (pp. 1078-1080). Highland Park, NJ: The Gryphon Press.

Butcher, J. N. (1985). Review of the Sixteen Personality Factor Questionnaire. In J. V. Mitchell, Jr. (Ed.), *The ninth mental measurements yearbook* (Vol. I). Lincoln, NE: Buros Institute of Mental Measurements. (BRS Document Reproduction Service No. AN 0910-679)

Cattell, R. B., Eber, H. W., & Tatsuoka, M. M. (1970). *Handbook for the Sixteen Personality Factor Questionnaire (16PF).* Champaign, IL: Institute for Personality and Ability Testing, Inc.

Cattell, R. B., Schroder, G., & Wagner, A. (1969). Verification of the structure of the 16PF Questionnaire in German. *Psychol. Forsch., 32,* 369-386.

Institute for Personality and Ability Testing, Inc. (1970). *Tabular supplement no. 1 to the 16PF handbook: Norms for the 16PF, Forms A and B (1967-68 edition).* Champaign, IL: Author.

Institute for Personality and Ability Testing, Inc. (1972). *Tabular supplement no. 2 to the 16PF handbook: Norms for the 1969 edition of Forms C and D.* Champaign, IL: Author.

Institute for Personality and Ability Testing, Inc. (1977). *16PF research bibliography 1971-1976.* Champaign, IL: Author.

Institute for Personality and Ability Testing, Inc. (1979). *Administrator's manual for the 16PF* (2nd ed.). Champaign, IL: Author.

Institute for Personality and Ability Testing, Inc. (1985a). [Compilation of research citations of 16PF use]. Unpublished raw data.

Institute for Personality and Ability Testing, Inc. (1985b). *Manual for Form E of the 16PF* (2nd ed.). Champaign, IL: Author.

Kapoor, S. D. (1965). Cross-validation of the Hindi version of the 16PF test (VKKJ). *Indian Journal of Psychology, 40*(3), 115-120.

Karson, S., & O'Dell, J. W. (1976). *Guide to the clinical use of the 16PF.* Champaign, IL: Institute for Personality and Ability Testing, Inc.

Krug, S. E. (1978). Further evidence on 16PF distortion scales. *Journal of Personality Assessment, 42*(5), 513-518.

Krug, S. E. (1981). *Interpreting 16PF profile patterns.* Champaign, IL: Institute for Personality and Ability Testing, Inc.

Lanyon, R. I., & Goodstein, L. D. (1982). *Personality assessment* (2nd ed.). New York: John Wiley & Sons.

Mitchell, J. V., Jr. (Ed.). (1985). *The ninth mental measurements yearbook.* Lincoln, NE: Buros Institute of Mental Measurements.

Mossholder, K. M. (1985). Review of the Personal Career Development Profile. In J. V. Mitchell, Jr. (Ed.), *The ninth mental measurements yearbook* (Vol. I). Lincoln, NE: Buros Institute of Mental Measurements. (BRS Document Reproduction Service No. AN 915-2082)

Nowakowska, (1970). Polish adaptation of the Sixteen Personality Factor Questionnaire (16PF) of R. B. Cattell. *Educational Psychology, 13*(4), 478-500.

Rodriguez, F. N. (1981). Normas Argentinas del test 16 PF para sujetos de 17 y 20 anos. *Acta Psiquiatrica y Psicologica de America Latina, 27*(3), 219-226.

Walsh, J. A. (1978). Review of the Sixteen Personality Factor Questionnaire. In O. K. Buros (Ed.), *The eighth mental measurements yearbook* (pp. 1081-1083). Highland Park, NJ: The Gryphon Press.

Zuckerman, M. (1985). Review of the Sixteen Personality Factor Questionnaire. In J. V. Mitchell, Jr. (Ed).), *The ninth mental measurements yearbook* (Vol. I). Lincoln, NE: Buros Institute of Mental Measurements. (BRS Document Reproduction Service No. AN 0910-679)

R. E. (Ed) Stone, Jr., Ph.D.
Associate Professor, Department of Otolaryngology—Head and Neck Surgery, Indiana School of Medicine, Indianapolis, Indiana.

SKLAR APHASIA SCALE: REVISED 1983

Maurice Sklar. Los Angeles, California: Western Psychological Services.

Introduction

Conventionally, aphasia is viewed as a generic diagnostic label identifying the existence of a disorder that results from cortical and/or subcortical brain damage affecting one or more previously acquired language-related processes. These may include the reader's or the listener's *decoding* of the written or printed (visual) symbols and the audible symbols that are used by an informant. Language processes also include the encoding, and to some extent the transmittal, of written (graphic) and audible (oral) symbols employed by a person to convey thoughts.

The diagnosis of aphasia is usually made by a physician based on observed or reported changes in language performance and on medical and neurological evidence of damage to the cerebral structures. Often, specification of which language processes are involved and the degree of involvement is assessed by a speech-language pathologist singularly or in cooperation with a neuropsychologist. This is done by requesting the individual with known or suspected damage to perform certain tasks and noting the person's responses for accuracy and quality. In order to detect similarities and differences within an individual over time or across patient groups the tasks would be, by necessity, the same. Even if the tasks were not identical, they would be similar, and the consistency in their administration would have to have the same characteristic.

Multiple tasks used to observe how a patient uses a given language process are generally presented together before tasks of another nature are presented. These collections of tasks constitute subtests of the testing process and may be thought of as a battery of tests. Over the past 30 years a large number of these formal test batteries have been devised, standardized, and utilized widely. One of these is the Sklar Aphasia Scale (SAS), first published in 1966, revised in 1973, and again revised in 1983.

The test author, Maurice Sklar, has a long established history as a speech-language pathologist. He received his Bachelor of Science degree from City College of New York in 1935, and his Master of Science degree in 1950 and Doctor of Philosophy degree in 1957 from the University of Southern California. He then assumed the position of chairman of the speech pathology program at the Wadsworth Hospital Veterans Administration Center in Los Angeles and in 1961 also become Assistant Professor of Speech Pathology at the University of California at Los Angeles. He is a member of the American Speech-Language and Hearing Association and holds the Certificates of Clinical Competency in both speech and audiology. Additionally, he holds certification in clinical psychology. Now, even in retirement, he remains on staff at Student Health Services at UCLA and is a consultant at Santa Monica and St. Johns Hospitals in Los Angeles.

Following his original training as a musician he entered the army and received training in radar and related fields. After the service he worked in radio and then as an instructor in radio where he was introduced to postwar aphasics during their rehabilitation. This sparked an interest in the aphasics' communication problems, which he studied at the master's and doctoral levels. Inception of the SAS began in the late 1950s (then labeled "Aphasia Evaluation Summary"), with its initial overview presented in 1959 by Sklar (Sklar, 1959). In 1963 standardization data and validation studies were reported (Sklar, 1963), and in 1966 the test battery was published by Western Psychological Services. The revision in 1973 included minor changes in the format and increased the response categories to the current five. The 1983-version manual (Sklar, 1983) indicates that 1) some changes were made in the format; 2) some pictures of objects were added in order to eliminate the necessity of using actual objects during administration; 3) the preliminary interview, which was given increased structure, was incorporated into the protocol booklet; 4) interpretive levels were recalculated based on information provided from new normative data.

In its current form, the SAS is a medium-length test, divided into a preliminary interview and 100 test items. The preliminary interview provides a tentative evaluation of the predominant aphasic characteristics and may be used to help alleviate patient anxiety surrounding the test situation. The 100 items examine the patient's remaining language competence and performance by sampling behaviors involving four areas of linguistic processes: Auditory Decoding, Visual Decoding, Oral Encoding, and Graphic Encoding, which are described as follows:

Auditory Decoding (25 items): involves presenting verbal stimuli and requires gestural (motor) responses. The test items allegedly sample auditory comprehension (recognition of body parts), orientation (person, place, and time), awareness of environment (recognition of the names of items in the room), identification of common objects, and memory span.

Visual Decoding (25 items): samples visual symbol comprehension by sampling the recognition and analysis of different types of graphic symbols (simple letters and words), word-picture association (labeling), sentence completion tasks involving various parts of speech, arithmetic, and silent reading/recent memory.

Oral Encoding (25 items): assesses the oral speech process through the patients' sharing of vital information, repeating, naming, answering questions about a story read to them (recent memory), and picture description tasks.

Graphic Encoding (25 items): requires the patients to write identification information (name, date, etc.), copy words, label common objects, write to dictation, and write descriptions of events in a picture.

SAS materials consist of a manual, stimulus cards, and a protocol booklet. The first page of the protocol booklet is for recording patient information and summarization of patient performance. Page two allows for noting patient responses during the preliminary interview and the remaining two pages present a well-organized array of the test items of the four subtests and provides for convenient scoring of responses. Common objects, not provided with the test, may be gathered by the clinician for use as stimuli in lieu of the pictures provided.

Practical Applications/Uses

The SAS appears to be suitable for teenage and adult patients whose pre-ictus reading and intellectual development approximates that of a person with a fourth-grade education. As distributed, the test is only appropriate for administration to those familiar with the English language. Ethnic or geographic (urban/rural) background and experience of the examinee probably would not be significant.

Examiners using the SAS should have a general knowledge of speech and language disorders and be acquainted with general principles and limitations of test interpretation. During the test the examiner's role is that of presenting the stimuli and recording responses. The test booklet presents verbatim script, which can be used. Because even moderate deviations from the script probably would not be significant, administration appears relatively simple. The booklet advises the examiner that some subtests might not be appropriately administered. For example, test items requiring visual acuity might be deferred until the patient's glasses were available.

The SAS is economical in terms of administration time (approximately 45 minutes), and probably portions of the test could be given on subsequent sessions without sacrificing test performance. Repeated administration of the test would jeopardize obtaining valid results due to learning on only a few items.

Evaluation of the patients' performance during the preliminary interview is made in terms of the examiner's subjective impressions of impairment (mild, moderate, or severe) of spontaneous speech in regard to fluent speech reflecting paraphasia and to nonfluent-effortful speech, anomia, apraxia, and dysarthria. Auditory comprehension is noted in terms of the same degrees of difficulty in tasks requiring pointing to common objects in the room and recognizing functions of objects. The same three degrees of difficulty associated with the patients' reading comprehension (recall of facts related through silent reading) are also noted, as well as difficulty in writing (subjects write their name and address and a simple sentence).

Scoring of patient responses to the 100 items is based on a subjective nominal scale containing five points. Each point of the scale is anchored by descriptors: "0" = correct, "1" = delayed, "2" = assisted, "3" = distorted and "4" = incorrect. In addition, space is provided on the test form to make brief notations concerning interesting behaviors of the patient. By treating the numerals that identify the type of response a patient emits as if they represented arithmetic value and summing the scores obtained for each of the 25 responses within a subtest, the examiner derives four "impairment scores" (i.e., one score for each subtest). Presumably, an overall estimate of total impairment is derived by adding the impairment scores and dividing by four.

The patient's language behavior and emotional behavior are checked off on the protocol booklet, which provides one-word descriptions of each. Additionally, the impairment profile may be completed by plotting the summed scores for each subtest and the total impairment score on a graph. Interpretation of the degree of impairment in the four tested areas and the overall impairment, according to placement of the scores of the graph, is guided by shaded areas of the profile indicating minimal-mild, moderate, and severe impairment.

Technical Aspects

Validity with which the SAS differentiates between aphasics and nonaphasics is acceptable, and the work of Cohen, Engel, Kelter, List, & Strohner (1977) supports this conclusion. Seventy-three aphasic patients and 86 nonaphasic patients (schizophrenics, brain-damaged patients without aphasia, and normals) constituted the sample on which it was determined that at least two independent judges using a German-translated version of SAS could differentiate between aphasic and nonaphasic subjects with a 98% agreement between judges. Additionally, a Friedman analysis of variance by ranks showed that the subtests had different levels of difficulty for the two groups. Statistically significant differences for the groups were found also by chi square—fluent aphasics, chi-square = 16.63, and nonfluent, chi-square = 17.57, df = 3, $p < .001$. Wilcoxen matched pairs signed-rank test showed that nonfluent aphasics made more errors on Oral Encoding and Graphic Encoding than on Auditory Decoding and Visual Decoding ($p < .01$). Fluent aphasics made more errors on Visual Decoding, Oral Encoding, and Graphic Encoding than on Auditory Decoding. None of the differences, however, could distinguish between the fluent and nonfluent aphasics. Likewise, no differences between the nonaphasic groups of subjects were significant.

When patient performance on this test was compared to that of other earlier aphasia tests (Sklar, 1963), the scores on the SAS were found to correlate well with the Eisenson (1954), the Halstead-Wepman (1949), and the Schuell (1955) tests of aphasia. Correlations of the SAS with the Token Test (De Renzi & Vignolo, 1962) were .75 for fluent aphasics and .85 for nonfluent aphasics (Cohen et al., 1977). As further validation of the test instrument, Sklar (1963) reported significant correlation (Kendall's tau .70, $p = .02$) between test results of 12 patients with later autopsy findings of amount and location of anatomical deterioration of the cerebral cortex.

The German translation of the SAS, developed by Cohen et al. (1977), also provided information of interrater reliability and ability of the test to discriminate between aphasics and other types of patients who might have compromised linguistic skills. Assuming that differences in clinician's subjective assignment of numerals to describe patient behavior is the greatest source of test reliability, and because interrater reliability is small, it is fair to assume test-retest reliability of this instrument.

Critique

The SAS's basic value is that of providing an overall index of severity of involvement. It seems to lend itself readily to careful translation into other languages of the Western world without undue influence on interpretation of the results, and clinicians serving acute care facilities would appreciate the structured way in which the this scale allows them to view their patients. However, the SAS does not contribute much information that would be useful in establishing a differential diagnosis of a particular type of aphasia. Additionally, the information that the test elicits from the patient may not be useful in determining specific treatment plans that should be implemented.

The advocated scoring system of the SAS is simple and straightforward and requires only a minimum of mathematical skill. Scoring of the test, however, is one of its major theoretical shortcomings because it is based on treating nominal data as if they were ratio scaled. However, such reservation about the SAS may not have clinical importance and precedence is set for ignoring such concerns by subsequent tests, such as the Porch Index of Communicative Ability (Porch, 1967). While the Sklar Aphasia Scale has not been widely used, it remains, as Benson (1979) concurs, a major testing tool in speech rehabilitation centers.

References

Benson, D. F. (1979). *Aphasia, alexia and agraphia.* New York: Churchill Livingstone.

Cohen, R., Engel, D., Kelter, S., List, G., & Strohner, H. (1977). Validity of the Sklar Aphasia Scale. *Journal of Speech and Hearing Research, 20,* 146-154.

De Renzie, E., & Vignolo, L. A. (1962). The Token Test: A sensitive test to detect receptive disturbances in aphasics. *Brain, 85,* 665-678.

Eisenson, J. (1954). *Examining for Aphasia.* (rev. ed.). New York: The Psychological Corporation.

Halstead, W. C., & Wepman, J. M. (1949). The Halstead-Wepman Aphasia Screening Test. *Journal of Speech and Hearing Disorders, 14,* 9-15.

Porch, B. E. (1967). *Porch Index of Communicative Ability.* Palo Alto, CA: Consulting Psychologists Press, Inc.

Schuell, H. (1955). Diagnosis and prognosis in aphasia. *AMA Archives of Neurology and Psychiatry, 74,* 308-315.

Sklar, M. (1959, Spring). Aphasia Evaluation Summary. *Western Speech,* 89.

Sklar, M., (1963). Relation of psychological and language test scores and autopsy findings in aphasia. *Journal of Speech and Hearing Research, 6,* 84-90.

Sklar, M. (1983). *Sklar Aphasia Scale: Revised 1983 manual.* Los Angeles: Western Psychological Services.

Judith Margolis, Ph.D.

Professor of Special Education, California State University, Los Angeles, and Adjunct Professor of Education, University of California, Los Angeles, Los Angeles, California.

SLINGERLAND SCREENING TESTS FOR IDENTIFYING CHILDREN WITH SPECIFIC LANGUAGE DISABILITY

Beth H. Slingerland. Cambridge, Massachusetts: Educators Publishing Service, Inc.

Introduction

The Screening Tests for Identifying Children with Specific Language Disability are commonly referred to as the Slingerland Screening Tests (SST) or just "The Slingerland" in deference to its author, Beth H. Slingerland. According to Slingerland, the purpose of the test is to identify school children who are either evidencing specific language disabilities or showing the potential to develop a language disability. Slingerland defines a Specific Language Disability (SLD) as a severe disability in learning to read, write, spell, and, sometimes, in using oral language. She uses the terms SLD and dyslexia interchangeably.

According to Slingerland, SLD children have no diagnosed neurological impairment, emotional disturbance, or general mental retardation. They do have weaknesses in auditory, visual, kinesthetic functions, or in integration between sensory channels. The purpose for administering the screening tests is to identify those individuals who need a specific multisensory educational approach in school. According to the author, this educational approach is not only for the purpose of remediation, but also to prevent learning problems from occurring in children who show weaknesses on this test (Slingerland, 1970).

Slingerland, a proponent of a multisensory approach to teaching children with specific language disabilities, was a student of Anna Gillingham and Bessie Stillman, pioneers in the field of dyslexia, who based their methods on the theory of Samuel Orton. Slingerland refers to her approach as a classroom adaptation of the Orton-Gillingham method. It is based on teaching reading, writing, spelling, and concept building through the interrelationship of auditory, visual, and kinesthetic channels.

In 1960, Slingerland began training teachers to use her method. The screening tests are an outgrowth of teaching others to use her training program. The SST for children in Grades 1 through 4 were originally published in 1962, then updated and revised in 1964 and 1970. In the preface to the 1970 edition of the teachers manual, Slingerland states that the revisions resulted from information obtained from teachers, other educators, and results of research projects that used the SST. In 1974, Form D for children in Grades 5 and 6 was published.

The SST are available at four grade levels. Form A (first grade and beginning of second grade), Form B (Grade 2 and the beginning of third grade), Form C (third and fourth grades), and Form D (fifth and sixth grades). Subtests were designed to test the same abilities across grade levels and differ primarily in difficulty of the vocabulary used. Administration and scoring is consistent across forms. Forms A, B, and C share a common teachers manual. Form D comes with its own manual. The technical manual (Fulmer, 1980) is available from the publisher at no charge.

All forms are organized into nine subtests, each of which measures a specific perceptual ability or integration of abilities across grade levels. Subtests 1 and 2, requiring copying (first from a wall chart and then from a page), test for accuracy in letter formation, reversals, insertions, inversions, and transformations; Subtest 3 tests recall of visually presented words, letters, numbers, and symbols; Subtest 4 requires matching to sample; Subtest 5 requires reproducing visually prescribed words, letters, numbers, and symbols; Subtest 6 requires writing the letters, numbers, and phrases the child hears from orally presented stimuli; Subtest 7 tests the ability to identify initial and final sounds in words; Subtest 8 requires circling numbers and words that have been dictated; and Subtest 9 (essentially motor-free and administered individually to those children who show some difficulty on Subtests 6, 7, and 8) tests auditory memory. Although the first eight subtests are generally group administered, they may also be given on an individual basis.

Detailed directions for administering and scoring the SST are provided in the teachers manual. Each student is provided with a test booklet in which all work is done. Other materials required for administering the test are a duplicate pair of wall charts for the student to copy (Subtest 1); a set of 14 cards containing words, letters, and numbers (Subtest 3); and a set of 15 cards containing a combination of words, phrases, groups of letters, numbers, and geometric forms (Subtest 5). Administration time is calculated at approximately one hour; however, because this is not a timed test, the teachers manual suggests that no child be rushed into finishing, provided the amount of time needed is not excessive. With the exception of Subtests 1 and 2, there is a built-in delay of several seconds before the child responds in order to introduce a memory component. Administration should be done in two or three sessions in order to prevent fatigue.

Practical Applications/Uses

The Slingerland Screening Tests were designed to identify children with SLD or dyslexics, children who are normal except for having severe and persistent problems in learning to read, write, and spell. Little is known about the cause of this disability, although some medical doctors and educators, including Slingerland, propose a neurological dysfunction. To this reviewer's knowledge there is no neurological test that can identify these children with any degree of accuracy beyond the finding that some of these children do poorly on perceptual tests. This leads to the assumption by some professionals that perceptual problems are the basis for the language disability. Slingerland (1979) states that perceptual-motor development is at the very core of language development and higher cognitive abilities, which explains why the SST are presented as perceptual tests measuring auditory, visual, and kinesthetic abilities. The SST subtests were designed to assess the interrelationship between these abilities, with each subtest examining a different combination of abilities. Unlike other perceptual tests in common use, this test does not measure perception in the abstract. To the credit of the author, she used tasks that are part of the everyday classroom routine. Subtests require children to demonstrate the ability to copy materials from the board and a page, match to visual and orally presented samples, write from memory, and identify initial and final sounds of words.

The SST are used to sort and separate children into groups of "normal," "SLD," and "unready." According to the teachers manual, normal children can continue in regular classes with regular curriculum, unready children are immature and need to be watched, and those in the SLD category need a special multisensory educational approach whether or not they are failing in school at the time of testing. In order not to identify children whose poor performance on the SST is the result of lack of educational opportunity, socioeconomic conditions, or bilingualism, Slingerland suggests that local norms be developed. The fact that national norms are not available limits the usefulness of the test to those school districts that have adopted the Slingerland method on a large scale and taken the time and effort to establish norms. Although clinicians in other settings might wish to observe some child performing the school-like tasks that make up the SST, doing so might not be the wisest use of time because the absence of derived scores affords no basis for comparison with either other children or other test data.

The Slingerland tests are economical to use. As screening measures, they were developed to be group administered in the classroom by the regular teacher. They are individually scored, and this may also be done by classroom teachers provided they have been trained in the Slingerland procedures. Remediation, when indicated, may occur either in the classroom or in a special class. Special summer workshops are available to train teachers in interpreting test results and providing a multisensory program for identified children. Slingerland stresses the need for support from school administrators to provide the climate and facilities for the program. Administrative support is particularly important in light of the three or more years of special training that are recommended for those children found to be specific language disabled.

Directions for administering the SST are easy to understand and follow. Procedures for scoring, evaluating answers, and comparing performance on tests are also presented in the teachers manual. These, however, are quite complex and require a good deal of individual judgment, even though examples of acceptable, acceptable but poor, and not acceptable work are included. Raters are required to mark the test booklets with a variety of symbols and enter information onto protocol sheets under points and types of errors. Error categories that are scored are RIT (reversals, inversions, and transportations), SO (substitutions and omissions), and INC (incomplete answers). In addition, poor formations (PF), faulty spatial organization (SPO), and self-corrections (SC) are noted. Errors and self-corrections are scored, but correct answers are not, resulting in a negative score with higher scores indicating poorer performance.

In addition to the complexity of the scoring system and the many decisions on the correctness of an item that the scorer must make, another factor that is apt to cause concern for clinicians is the floating "break-off" score (that score above which one is categorized as SLD). According to Slingerland (1978, p. 9), "Errors of less than 10, or at the most, 15, are usually not too significant unless the child is known to be bright. Then, approximately 10, or even no more than 8 errors, can indicate the possibility of disability that may be masked. . . ." Slingerland then goes on to state that information on classroom achievement; intelligence; family patterns of disability in reading, writing, and spelling; and socioeconomic background must all enter the decision of whether or not this child is SLD. After taking all of the other variables into consideration, the floating cutoff score, and the degree of clinical judgment allowed, one wonders how accurate the tests alone are in identifying children with SLD. According to this reviewer, the real strength of the SST lies in the fact that they are wonderful measures of many skills children need and use in the classroom every day. Too often, teachers focus on the academic part of a task, losing sight of the importance of assessing the child's ability to keep his or her place, to attend to the task at hand, and to use listening skills and strategies for remembering. The SST can provide the classroom teacher with important information in these areas.

Technical Aspects

Several estimates of reliability for the SST have been reported. The SST technical manual provides information on internal consistency, test-retest reliability, and interscorer reliability for a sample of 804 children from six school districts. Other reported reliability data by Burns and Burns (1977) include internal consistency for a local sample of 208 children. Both studies also provide information on standard error of measurement for their samples.

Internal consistency refers to the extent that items within a test or subtest measure the same construct. Two methods in common use for arriving at this statistic are split-half and coefficient alpha. Burns and Burns (1977) used the split-half procedure and arrived at coefficients of reliability ranging from .86 for Form A to .96 for Form B. Fulmer (1980) computed coefficient alpha statistics for visual composites, auditory composites, and total scores for all four forms of the test. Alpha coefficients ranged from .88 to .92 for visual composites, .88 to .94 for auditory composites, and .93 to .96 for total scores. Results from both the Burns and Burns and the Fulmer studies thus indicate that the items within the tests are measuring the same ability or abilities.

Test-retest reliability is often referred to as stability reliability because it represents the extent one might expect a score to vary from one administration of the test to another. Fulmer (1980) reports test-retest information for both total SST scores and for individual subtests for each form. Total test reliability coefficients ranged from a low of .71 for Form A to a high of .85 for Form C. There is not general agreement on how high a test-retest coefficient must be before the test is considered reliable. Salvia and Ysseldyke (1985) suggest .90; however, Sattler (1982) states that for a test of special abilities, .80 or higher is generally acceptable. Therefore, except for Form A, SST total test scores can be considered reliable. An examination of the reliability coefficients for individual subtests, however, shows that most do not even approximate acceptable standards for reliability. Of the 33 coefficients reported, only five exceeded .59 and only two, Auditory Recall on Forms B and C, exceeded the recommended .7 for subtest reliability. A particularly surprising finding was that the lowest reported reliability coefficients were found for Form D, administered to the oldest group of children.

Two points should be made in regard to subtest reliability. The first is that many of the subtest means and standard deviations showed a constriction of range, which would tend to underestimate the reliability of the subtest while also limiting the generalizability of results. The second point is not as easily explained. Reliability coefficients for Form D ranged from .02 for Auditory Association to .45 for Auditory Recall, with eight of the nine subtests showing coefficients under .40. Unstable performance is sometimes seen with very young children who on first administration of a test do not understand the demands of the task. When one finds this type of erratic performance on a test administered to fifth- and sixth-graders of normal and superior intelligence, one can only conclude that the test is not a reliable measure at this level, even though the total test reliability coefficient is .80.

Information concerning interrater reliability is particularly important in situations requiring a judgment on the part of the scorer. These ranged from .69 for Form A to .91 for Form C (Fulmer, 1980). Although one would expect .9 for all forms of the test, the real concern is not in the numbers but in the lack of stability of placement decisions. Fulmer reports that between 71% and 87% of the children were placed in the same category (normal, SLD, or unready) following a second administration and scoring of the SST as they had been placed following the first administration. In effect, what this tells us is that between 13% and 29% of the children were placed in different categories by different scorers. The number of children who changed categories from nonhandicapped to handicapped and vice versa is too high for comfort. Although Fulmer explains this by stating that many factors other than performance on the SST enter the placement decision, these are not specified in the manual to a degree that allows for accuracy across examiners and raises the question of the precision of the test in identifying children with SLD.

Basically, there are two types of questions concerning validity: 1) How faithfully do the scores represent the domain or construct the test purports to measure and 2) how useful is the test as an indicator or predictor of another behavior? For the SST both types of validity should be ascertained. Slingerland states that SST subtests can measure distinct areas of perceptual strength and weakness. To determine if the SST are valid tests for this purpose the first set of validity questions must focus on the tests themselves as measures of these abilities.

In the SST manual, Slingerland specifies the perceptual abilities that each subtest measures. To determine the number and kinds of abilities that are actually being measured, Fulmer (1980) performed a factor analysis for all four forms of the SST by subtest. Results published in the technical manual show Form A had a one-factor solution, with all subtests having loadings of .48 or higher on this factor, whereas Forms B and C had a two-factor solution involving general perceptual processing (with no distinction between visual and auditory) and kinesthetic-motor functions (as expressed in far-point and near-point copying). Form D showed a three-factor solution, with an emphasis on ability to respond to auditory stimuli, ability to respond to visual stimuli, and kinesthetic-motor functioning. It is apparent from these results that separate perceptual abilities are not being measured.

Dinero, Donah, and Larson's (1979) results support the finding that the subtests are not measuring separate perceptual functions. These investigators identified a group of first-grade children by means of their poor performance on the SST. Another group of children who had done well on the SST were used as a control group. Significant differences between performance on all subtests for the two groups were determined. The authors performed a discriminant-functions analysis to determine the relative contribution of each SST subtest toward the prediction of the child as a member of the SLD group. They found that Subtest 1 and Subtest 7 together accounted for 38.32% of the total 45.43% difference between the SLD and non-SLD groups when all eight subtests were taken into account. Results of the studies by Fulmer, Dinero, Donah, and Larson suggest that the various subtests are not measuring separate perceptual abilities or combination of abilities. In addition, Fulmer's results indicate that whatever it is that the tests are measuring is not the same across forms.

In regard to the ability of the SST in indicating and predicting severe language disabilities as Slingerland suggested, a review of information found in the technical manual and the few empirical studies that have been published raise some concern about the predictive ability of the SST with children of normal to superior intelligence. There is some evidence, however, that whatever the SST is measuring may be important for reading, writing, and spelling.

The SST lack predictive validity for normal to superior IQ children according to a study by Meade, Nelson, and Clark (1981). These investigators compared the SST performance of children enrolled in special education classes for the learning disabled and educable mentally retarded with the performance of children in regular classes. They found a consistent relationship between IQ and SST scores and, therefore, included IQ as a covariate in their analyses. When IQ was taken into consideration, learning disabled children did not consistently make more errors than those in regular classes; however, still taking IQ into account, mentally retarded children did make significantly more errors on the SST than either the learning disabled or the regular class children. According to the authors this finding suggests SST performance is not independent of intelligence.

There is also some evidence that the SST not only tend to overpredict disability status, but that these predictions are not stable. Fulmer (1980) reports the results of a study undertaken to provide reliability and validity data for all four forms of the SST. The population of children used in the study were tested with the SST and assigned categories of normal, SLD, and unready in accordance with procedures specified in the manual. Between 28% (Form A) and 48% (Form D) of the children were categorized SLD. These figures are a concern when one considers that the incidence of SLD in the population has been estimated at between 3.5% and 6% (Yule & Rutter, 1976). An additional concern is the lack of stability of the assigned categories. When these same children were retested 30 days later it was found that between 13% and 29% were reclassified into other categories. Although the lack of stability of category assignment is a reflection on the reliability of the test, it also casts doubt on the predictive ability of the SST.

The technical manual also includes criterion-related validity information (referring to the relationship between test scores and some criterion, usually other test scores or some behavior) concerning the SST. The criterion measure may either be administered at approximately the same time as the test being validated, in which case the results are reported as concurrent validity, or at some future prespecified time, in which case the results may be reported as predictive. The distinction between these two kinds of criterion-related validity is important; whereas concurrent validity provides information on the congruence between a test and a criterion measure, predictive validity provides information on the ability of a test to predict another behavior.

The criterion-related validity information presented by Fulmer (1980) includes results of two studies correlating SST scores with achievement test scores. In a study by Oliphant (1969), first-grade children were tested on the SST, Form A, and scores were correlated with Stanford Achievement Test scores. Moderate correlations, ranging from −.57 to −.65, were achieved. In a more extensive study, Fulmer correlated SST total scores for all four forms with the California Test of Basic Skills (CTBS) Total Reading, Total Language, and Spelling subtests. Correlation coefficients ranged from moderate (−.57) to high (−.86). The negative correlations are a result of errors on the SST being correlated with correct responses on the achievement measure. Fulmer interprets results from both of these studies to support the predictive validity of the SST. Actually, these are concurrent validity data. To have presented predictive validity, Fulmer would have had to demonstrate significant differences in achievement test scores between those children scoring above "break-off" and those scoring below "break-off" on the SST at some previous time. The concurrent relationship noted between SST and achievement test scores is large enough, however, to require some explanation. The relationship can be interpreted in the following way: Because the two tests are not testing the same domain, another factor or factors common to performance on both measures is responsible for the observed relationship. Meade, Nelson, and Clark (1981) found a "strong relationship between intelligence and SST subtest errors, and intelligence and SST categories of errors," concluding that "perhaps the SST are an indirect and uneconomical measure of intelligence" (p. 266). Because a high correlation between IQ and achievement test performance is well-documented, IQ might be that common factor. Fulmer (1980) tends to disagree. She reports correlations of the same or greater magnitude between the SST and IQ as those reported by Meade et al.; however, she interprets these as only moderate correlations "indicating that the trait that is being measured is not strongly related to intelligence" (Fulmer, 1980, p. 13). Whether one prefers to call it moderate or strong, there is a relationship between IQ and SST performance that needs to be clarified.

Additionally, another type of validity question appropriate for the SST is in regard to two assumptions underlying the tests and training program: 1) that there is a direct relationship between perceptual-motor development and language development and 2) that matching teaching methods to a child's perceptual strengths and weaknesses will result in better school performance. Although both of these assumptions are intrinsically appealing and have been accepted by many in education, at the time of this review, research evidence to support these beliefs has been disappointing. Users, therefore, should be aware that there is some concern regarding the theoretical model Slingerland has chosen as the basis for her tests.

In summary, both reliability and validity of the SST appear questionable. The reported coefficients of correlation for total SST test-retest are on the low side but might be considered adequate for a screening measure were it not for the fact that the reliability of the subtests is so poor. The question that must be asked is: Can one accept the reliability of the total score when the subtests that make up the total score are not reliable? Interscorer reliability is also far from what one would usually expect and accept. As for validity, results from both a factor-analytic study and a discriminant-functions analysis indicate that the various subtests are not measuring the perceptual functions they were designed to measure. In addition, studies designed to test the construct validity of the SST report that the test lacks construct validity. As for criterion-related concurrent validity, a moderate correlation between SST scores and achievement test scores exists but has yet to be explained satisfactorily.

Critique

Individuals who are normal in every respect yet appear to be unable to learn to read, write, or spell with any degree of proficiency have been a concern of physicians, educators, and psychologists for at least the past hundred years. The SST were designed to identify these children before too much time has passed and provide them with an alternative to traditional education. At the time the SST were designed, perceptual testing and modality training were the accepted procedures for identifying and educating these children. The SST are representative of many such tests. Unlike the other perceptual tests developed and used during that period, the SST have not been subjected to the same rigorous examination as the others. This may be partly due to the fact that as unnormed screening tests they lack derived scores, making it difficult to compare SST performance with performance on other measures. That the SST were not scrutinized during the frenzied overuse of perceptual testing and training in the 1970s is both to our advantage and disadvantage. It is an advantage because had the SST been lumped into the category of perceptual tests, we would have thrown the SST baby out with the bath water. Although Slingerland states that she has developed a perceptual test, the data in the technical manual accompanying the SST show that she has not done so. What she has done is develop a good informal measure of many of the requisite skills on which reading, writing, and spelling are based. This reviewer is not arguing that perceptual and language skills are not involved in performing the tasks but merely stating that the test does not measure either perception or language directly. What it does do is clue the teacher to what students can and cannot do, which way they can handle information more easily, and if they need help with listening skills or in developing strategies for remembering.

The major disadvantage that has resulted from lack of national norms is that we really do not know much about what the test is actually testing. The few published studies that are available are, of necessity, biased. They were done in school districts opting to use the SST on a large scale and willing to develop norms. This seriously limits the generalizability of results from these studies. Additional research is needed to explain the strong relationship between IQ and SST performance and the moderately high correlation between SST performance and achievement test results.

The current movement for excellence in education will undoubtedly cause a renewed interest in the SST as a measure for early identification of children who might need special help. It is important that those planning to use the SST keep in mind that they are gross screening measures and were never designed to identify children for placement in special education programs. They are not normed tests, and their reliability and validity are questionable. This is not meant as a condemnation of the SST, but rather a suggestion that users be aware of the many limitations of the measures and use the test with these facts in mind.

References

This list includes text citations as well as suggested additional reading.

Burns, W. J., & Burns, K. A. (1977). The Slingerland Screening Tests: Local norms. *Journal of Learning Disabilities, 10,* 450-454.

Dinero, T. E., Donah, C. H., & Larson, G. L. (1979). The Slingerland Screening Tests for Identifying Children with Specific Language Disability: Screening for learning disabilities in first grade. *Perceptual and Motor Skills, 49,* 971-978.

Editor's Interview. (1978). Doing it our way: Putting the children first. A conversation with Beth H. Slingerland. *Journal of Learning Disabilities, 11,* 263-273.

Fulmer, S., & Fulmer, K. (1983). The Slingerland Screening Tests. *Journal of Learning Disabilities, 16,* 591-595.

Fulmer, S. P. (1980). *Pre-reading screening procedures and Slingerland Screening Tests for Identifying Children with Specific Language Disability: Technical manual.* Cambridge, MA: Educators Publishing Service.

Meade, L. S., Nelson, R. O., & Clark, R. P. (1981). Concurrent and construct validity of the Slingerland Screening Tests for Children with Specific Language Disability. *Journal of Learning Disabilities, 19,* 264-299.

Meyers, M. J. (1983). Information processing and the Slingerland Screening Tests. *Journal of Learning Disabilities, 16,* 150-153.

Oliphant, G. (1969). *A study of factors involved in early identification of specific language disability.* Unpublished doctoral dissertation, United States International University, San Diego.

Proger, B. (1971). Test review no. 7: Screening test for identifying children with specific language disability. *Journal of Special Education, 5,* 293-299.

Salvia, J. G., & Ysseldyke, J. E. (1985). *Assessment in special and remedial education* (3rd ed.). Boston: Houghton Mifflin.

Sattler, J. M. (1982). Assessment of children's intelligence and special abilities (2nd ed.). Boston: Allyn & Bacon.

Slingerland, B. H. (1970). *Teachers manual to accompany Slingerland Screening Tests for Identifying Children with Specific Language Disability.* Cambridge, MA: Educators Publishing Service.

Slingerland, B. H. (1978). *Why wait for a criterion of failure.* Cambridge, MA: Educators Publishing Service.

Slingerland, B. H. (1982). Specific language-not learning-disability children. *Australian Journal of Remedial Education, 14,* 30-40.

Yule, W. (1973). Differential prognosis of reading backwardness and specific reading retardation. *British Journal of Educational Psychology, 43,* 244-248.

Yule, W., & Rutter. (1976). Epidemiology and social implications of specific reading retardation. In R. M. Knights & D. J. Bakkers (Eds.), *The neuropsychology of learning disorders.* Baltimore: University Park Press.

Stanley H. Cohen, Ph.D.

Professor of Psychology, West Virginia University, Morgantown, West Virginia.

M. Judith Cohen, Ph.D.

Learning Disabilities Specialist, Monongalia County Schools, Morgantown, West Virginia.

SLOSSON DRAWING COORDINATION TEST

Richard L. Slosson. East Aurora, New York: Slosson Educational Publications, Inc.

Introduction

The Slosson Drawing Coordination Test (SDCT) is a screening instrument designed to identify individuals who have various forms of brain dysfunction or perceptual disorders involving eye-hand coordination. Children with learning difficulties in school can be identified, diagnosed, and placed in an appropriate school curriculum. Adults with brain damage can also be identified, diagnosed, and referred for vocational rehabilitation. The author (Slosson, 1980) maintains that if an abnormal amount of distortion is noted on the SDCT results, then further evaluation should be conducted.

The test consists of a single sheet of paper with 12 geometric figures, each of which is to be copied three times by the subject. Although a pencil is used by adults and children over five years of age, younger children may use a crayon. This test is intended for all ages from one year to adult, but the age of the subject determines how many items are attempted. The examiner reads the directions to the subject and records and interprets the results. Answer sheets have six designs on each side and three boxes underneath each design where examinees record their responses.

According to Slosson (1980) the SDCT is intended to be used by professionals as a screening instrument to help identify brain damage and aid in diagnosing visual-perceptual or motor coordination problems. These professionals include educators, psychologists, and vocational rehabilitators. This test is generally appropriate for use with those individuals experiencing learning difficulties.

Practical Applications/Uses

The SDCT can be administered either to a group or individual. The test is not difficult to administer, and no special training is necessary, although some interpretation of the results is required in scoring. The manual (Slosson, 1980) clearly lists specific directions for administration, and what the examiner is to say to the examinee is written on the score form. Administration and scoring requires approximately 10-15 minutes per protocol.

Instructions for scoring are also clearly presented. Many examples of correct and incorrect responses are shown in the manual, plus written directions stating what must be counted as a correct response. After each drawing is scored "plus" or "minus" by comparison with the original figure, the examiner counts the total number of "minus" drawings to obtain the raw score and obtains the accuracy score (a percentage) from a chart that gives the percentage figure for the appropriate age according to the number of errors. According to Slosson (1980) "an Accuracy Score below 85% indicates sufficient drawing distortion as to warrant further evaluation to determine the cause and extent of the difficulty." This test is scored only by hand. Neither machine nor computer scoring is available.

Although interpretation is based on internal clinical judgment, the directions for interpreting the results are explicit.

Technical Aspects

Given the time that has elapsed since the 1962 publication of the SDCT, very few reliability and validity studies have been conducted on the test, and none of those reported has been either extensive or systematic. These studies (Alcorn & Nicholson, 1972; Rogers & Richmond, 1975) have used convenience samples such as individuals referred for evaluation by vocational rehabilitation centers, initially screened for exceptionality, or enrolled in sheltered workshop programs. The original normative sample in the establishment of the test consisted of 200 individuals ranging in age from four to 52 years. The children in this group were heterogeneous with respect to racial origin and urban/rural residence, but had no diagnosed exceptionality. In contrast, the adults were mostly referrals for evaluation from vocational rehabilitation units. All individuals resided in New York State. Test-retest administration of the instrument (during the same interview session) yielded a reliability coefficient of 0.96. Reliability is not reported on any homogeneous subgroup for which diagnosis is usually intended. Validity per se was not established by the author through statistical analysis but rather through qualitative analysis of normative performance based on individuals (the number not reported) "known to be brain damaged, epileptic, suffering from cerebral palsy, birth injury or accident [who] have been tested and their drawings observed" (Slosson, 1980). Accuracy scores below 85% appear to have successfully identified these individuals.

In a study with 191 mentally retarded adolescents, Alcorn and Nicholson (1972) report moderate, but statistically significant, correlations ($p < .01$) between the SDCT and the Benton Visual Relation Test ($r = .546$), the Raven Progressive Matrices ($r = .430$), and Wechsler Performance IQ ($r = .436$). Using the 85% cutoff score, only 8% of the sample above this score showed perceptual difficulties on the Benton test. In contrast to these results, a study of 54 sheltered workshop clients, 13 to 52 years of age, found a high degree of misclassification (Rogers & Richmond, 1975). Although the SDCT identified 29 subjects as possibly brain damaged, the Bender Gestalt assigned 17 subjects into this category, and clinical judgments by two psychologists classified only 13 subjects as brain damaged.

Critique

The SDCT is designed to help identify brain damage and to screen individuals with visual-perceptual or motor coordination problems. It is not intended as a definitive diagnostic instrument (Slosson Educational Publications 1984 Catalog). The instrument is simple to administer and easy to score. Although these features enhance its usefulness in clinical diagnosis, the test itself needs to be adequately validated. Both the construction and materials of the test reflect a high degree of face validity. However, the few empirical studies of the SDCT have not consistently demonstrated any functional validity with respect to the test's objectives.

The SDCT had adequate development to recommend its use as part of an initial screening battery for identifying individuals with possible perceptual or motor coordination deficits. However, it should be followed up by the administration of additional diagnostic tests.

References

Alcorn, C. E., & Nicholson, C. L. (1972). Validity of the Slosson Drawing Coordination Test with adolescents of below-average ability. *Perceptual and Motor Skills, 34,* 261-262.

Rogers, G. W., Jr., & Richmond, B. O. (1975). *Results on the Slosson Drawing Coordination Test with Appalachian sheltered workshop clients.* (ERIC Document Reproduction Service No. ED 115053)

Slosson, R. L. (1980). *Slosson Drawing Coordination Test manual.* East Aurora, NY: Slosson Educational Publications, Inc.

Slosson Educational Publications. (1984). *1984 Catalog.* East Aurora, NY: Author.

Stanley H. Cohen, Ph.D.
Professor of Psychology, West Virginia University, Morgantown, West Virginia.

M. Judith Cohen, Ph.D.
Learning Disabilities Specialist, Monongalia County Schools, Morgantown, West Virginia.

SLOSSON ORAL READING TEST

Richard L. Slosson. East Aurora, New York: Slosson Educational Publications, Inc.

Introduction

The Slosson Oral Reading Test (SORT) is given individually and is based on the ability to pronounce words at different levels of difficulty. The SORT is composed of ten lists of 20 words each. The first list is reported to be at the primer reading level. Succeeding lists correspond to grade levels one through eight, with the last one at a high-school level. According to the front page of SORT (Slosson, 1963), words on the SORT "have been taken from standardized school readers and the Reading Level obtained from testing represents median or standardized school achievement."

The only materials needed to administer the test are two identical word lists: one for the student to read and one on which the administrator marks responses. The examiner decides which list the child uses to start (i.e., the list on which the child can be expected to pronounce all 20 words correctly). The examiner then determines which words are pronounced correctly and subsequently makes the decision to terminate the test. The examiner keeps score on a test form separate from the one the child is reading. A check mark is placed after each error, and a plus sign is placed after each correct word. The number of correct words is entered at the bottom of each list. The accompanying table for converting the raw score into a reading level (grade equivalent) is simple to use.

Practical Applications/Uses

The SORT is useful to anyone (e.g., psychologist, educator, speech pathologist) who desires to know the reading level of a particular student. It takes approximately three to five minutes to give and to score, so it is time efficient. The author states that because of its high reliability it can be used frequently to monitor a student's progress in reading.

This test is designed to give a quick measure of reading ability. It is given individually and can be administered in any setting that is quiet and relatively free from distractions. It is appropriate for use with children who can read from primer to high-school level.

Anyone who knows the correct pronunciation of the 200 words on the word lists (e.g., teachers, psychologists, parents) can administer this test. The examiner allows the child to read from one sheet while score is kept on another. If the child misses any word on the first list, the examiner goes back to an easier list where all 20 words are pronounced correctly. Once the "starting list" is found, the child reads through all the lists until a list is encountered where the child is unable to pronounce any of the 20 words correctly (the stopping point). The child should not (unless the child stutters) spend more than five seconds on a word.

There is no manual for this test. Clearly written directions on the back of the word list sheet make the SORT easy to administer. Because instructions for scoring are clearly presented, it takes the examiner only a few minutes to learn how to score this test. A minute or two is all that is required to score it. The examiner keeps score by putting a check mark after each error or a plus sign after each correct word. The number of correct words is entered at the bottom of each list. A word is counted as an error if it is either mispronounced, omitted, or takes more than five seconds to pronounce. The word is also counted as incorrect if the child gives more than one pronunciation for it, even though one of them may have been correct. The total number of words correct equals the raw score. The reading level or grade equivalent is obtained by looking up the value of this raw score on a table on the score sheet or by taking half of the raw score.

Interpretation is based directly on objective scores. There is a minimal level of difficulty in interpreting the test results, which requires no training. An analysis of the types of errors made by the examinee may prove helpful to the examiner in determining areas of weakness.

Technical Aspects

Slosson (1963) reports a test-retest (one-week interval) reliability coefficient of 0.99. In the same sample of 108 children enrolled in Grades 1-12, he found a validity coefficient of 0.96 based on the correlation between SORT scores and comparable scores obtained on Gray's Standardized Oral Reading Paragraphs. No further information is presented on the demographic characteristics of this normative population. Also, reliability and validity values *within* age groups are not reported. Because the test is often given to individuals with a restricted age range, this information must be considered as essential if the score is to be clinically adequate.

Several studies have assessed the validity of the SORT for diagnosing reading level through its correlations with other standardized reading mastery (comprehension, recognition) or reading readiness tests. Using samples of 62 children (Memory, Powell, & Callaway, 1980) and, later, 194 children (Powell, Moore, & Callaway, 1981) in Grades 1-10, reported correlations between the SORT and the Woodcock Word Comprehension Test ranged from .437 to .733, with higher correlations with the Woodcock Word Identification Test (WWI) reported. However, the reading graded score from the WWI are "on the average up to one year lower than the grade equivalent scores obtained on . . . the SORT" (Powell et al., 1981, p. 52). A similar finding was noted by Jenkins and Pany (1978) not only for the SORT, but for the Wide Range Achievement Test (WRAT). This inaccuracy or bias actually arises from the lack of correspondence between word lists in these tests and those in basal reading series.

In another concurrent validation study, Tramill, Tramill, Thornthwaite, and Anderson (1981) administered the SORT along with the reading subtests of the WRAT, the Peabody Individual Achievement Test-Reading Comprehension (PIAT-RC), and the entire WISC-R. Their sample consisted of 122 male and female academically low-functioning students ranging in age from six to 16 years. The SORT exhibited differential validity with the reading measures in that it yielded an r = .63 ($p < .001$) with the PIAT but had a statistically nonsignificant correlation (r = .26) with the WRAT. Low correlations were also reported between the SORT and the WISC-R subtests. According to Tramill et al. (1981, p. 152), "the SORT appears to measure a different dimension of reading achievement . . . normative studies [need to] be conducted if the SORT is to continue to be used in educational evaluations and research."

Another important application of reading measures, including the SORT, is their use in assessing improvement in outcome following a remediation program or intervention. In a study of peer tutoring of third-graders by seventh-grade tutors, the third-graders scored significantly higher on the SORT than either placebo or control groups (King, 1982). Ayres (1972) compared groups of school children identified as having learning disorders that classified them as "generalized dysfunction" or "auditory-language." The remedial program was targeted at the latter individuals and consisted of sensory integration activities. Pre- to post-testing on the SORT and other evaluation measures showed intended gains with the specific learning-disabled sample but not the generalized dysfunction sample. Finally, a five-week summer-reading-program intervention to prevent reading regression was implemented by Cornelius and Semmel (1982). Fifteen learning-disabled students in Grades 3 to 8 participated. All of the enrollees were at least two or more years below grade level in reading. A group of 30 control subjects were matched to the experimental group on the basis of school attended, reading level, IQ, age, and sex. In each of two reading program sessions, experimental participants exhibited statistically significant mean grade-equivalent gain scores on the SORT—approximately one-half grade. A corresponding decline in reading level was found in control participants who did not receive the program.

Critique

The SORT is an oral reading proficiency test that is easy to administer and simple to score. Although the instrument only requires the examinee to *pronounce* lists of words taken from standardized school readers, scores on the SORT have shown adequate correlations with many well-known, comprehensive reading tests. Unlike these other instruments, the SORT does not yield a reading comprehension score or indicate specific areas of reading disability. Also, grade equivalent or reading level is the only available standard score. Apparently, the grade-equivalent score on the SORT in comparison with other reading tests tends to overestimate reading level.

Thus, the SORT adequately measures global reading level and can be used easily by a variety of professionals in the school setting. It provides a reliable and valid assessment of reading grade equivalent for many purposes, including placement and remediation. The SORT is also a sensitive measure of outcome, following program interventions designed to change individual reading skills.

References

Ayres, A. J. (1972). Improving academic scores through sensory integration. *Journal of Learning Disabilities, 5,* 338-343.

Cornelius, P. L., & Semmel, M. I. (1982). Effects of summer instruction on reading achievement regression of learning disabled students. *Journal of Learning Disabilities, 15,* 409-413.

Jenkins, J. R., & Pany, D. (1978). Standardized achievement tests: How useful for special education? *Exceptional Children, 44,* 448-453.

King, R. T. (1982). Learning from a PAL. *Reading Teacher, 35,* 682-685.

Memory, D., Powell, G., & Callaway, B. (1980). A study of the assessment characteristics of the "Woodcock Reading Mastery Tests." *Reading Improvement, 17,* 48-52.

Powell, G., Moore, D., & Callaway, B. (1981). A concurrent validity study of the Woodcock Word Comprehension Test. *Psychology in the Schools, 18,* 24-27.

Slosson, R. L. (1963). *Slosson Oral Reading Test (SORT).* East Aurora, NY: Slosson Educational Publications, Inc.

Tramill, J. L., Tramill, J. K., Thornthwaite, R., & Anderson, F. (1981). Investigations into the relationships of the WRAT, the PIAT, the SORT, and the WISC-R in low functioning referrals. *Psychology in the Schools, 18,* 149-153.

Barbara D. Stoodt, Ph.D.

Professor of Education, School of Education, University of North Carolina at Greensboro, Greensboro, North Carolina.

SPADAFORE DIAGNOSTIC READING TEST

Gerald J. Spadafore. Novato, California: Academic Therapy Publications.

Introduction

The Spadafore Diagnostic Reading Test (SDRT) is a criterion-referenced reading inventory designed to assess the decoding skills and comprehension skills of individuals reading at the primer through twelfth-grade levels. Students are asked to read increasingly difficult word lists and graded reading passages. The graded word lists and reading passages comprising this test are representative of the reading tasks students perform at each grade level. This instrument identifies the individual's independent, instructional, and frustration reading levels based on the traditional criteria developed by Betts (1957). The SDRT contains four subtests, which are described as follows:

Word Recognition: Consists of 260 words, with 20 words at each of 13 grade levels from primer through twelfth grade. Assesses the student's ability to recognize individual words.

Oral Reading and Comprehension: Consists of 13 short reading passages that start at the primer level and continue at one per grade level through the twelfth grade. Each passage is followed by a series of comprehension questions.

Silent Reading Comprehension: Consists of 13 short reading passages beginning with the primer level and continuing through the twelfth grade. A series of comprehension questions accompanies each selection.

Listening Comprehension: Consists of 13 short reading selections that span the primer level through the twelfth grade level. Each selection is accompanied by a series of comprehension questions that are read aloud by the examiner.

Gerald J. Spadafore, Ed.D., the author of this test, is a professor in the Department of Counselor Education and Special Education, as well as director of the school psychology program at Idaho State University at Pocatello. He is the Idaho delegate for the National Association of School Psychologists, and past president for the Idaho School Psychology Association and the Idaho Council for Exceptional Children. Spadafore's professional experiences include guidance counseling, social studies teacher, special education teacher, and school psychologist.

The author's goal in writing the SDRT was to prepare an instrument for assessing a wide spectrum of reading and comprehension skills over the full range of reading ability. In addition, the author sought to create a flexible format for evaluating current grade level of reading performance or in-depth diagnosis of reading skills. The author considers this design particularly suitable for use with older students who are reading well below their expected reading level and for individuals who are learning disabled (Spadafore, 1983).

In designing the Word Recognition subtest, the author selected 20 words for each grade level. At the early grade levels, frequency of occurrence was the criterion for selecting words. In contrast, the words selected for the upper-grade level word lists included words that appear infrequently because these words enable students to demonstrate advanced word-attack skills.

The Word Recognition subtest was field tested to ascertain the relative degree of word difficulty for the words selected. In the field test, the Word Recognition subtest was administered to 15 first-grade students, 15 fifth-grade students, and 15 ninth-grade students because these grade levels represent a wide range of reading performance. The words were then ordered from the least to the most difficult within each grade-level list. Words that failed to discriminate between grade levels were eliminated, and additional words were inserted and field tested in order to maintain a list of 20 words for each grade level.

The reading passages and comprehension questions in the SDRT parallel reading and diagnostic materials representing expected reading performance for each grade level. After developing and refining the selections, the author used the Minnesota Interactive Readability Approximation Program (MNIRAP), a computerized program, to evaluate their readability. The sequencing of these reading passages is based on field testing with 50 elementary, 25 intermediate (junior high), and 35 secondary students.

Materials needed for the SDRT's administration include the test plates that the examinee reads, a test booklet for recording the examinee's responses, a test manual to guide test administration, a pencil for recording responses, and a stopwatch or watch with a second hand for monitoring the time limits of the Silent Reading Comprehension subtest. In addition, a tape recorder is recommended for recording students' oral reading.

The test plates are printed on sturdy white paper and are bound with plastic in a booklet. The examiner's record booklet contains word lists and passages, comprehension questions, scoring criteria for each list and passage, and charts for summarizing test data. The test manual includes directions for administration and scoring, suggestions for interpretation and remediation, profile interpretation, information regarding reading literacy levels and vocational choices, case studies, and development and technical data.

All of the subject's responses are written on the test booklet as the SDRT is administered. The word lists, reading selections, and accompanying questions are printed in the scoring profile to aid test administration. The criteria for identifying reading levels are printed after each word list and each reading passage. In addition, blanks for categorizing mispronounced words are printed after each oral reading selection. The scoring profile includes a cover page for summarizing the test data and for determining the literacy classification of the student, which may be professional, technical, vocational, or functional. The final page of the scoring profile is reserved for interpreting the test data and making recommendations.

Practical Applications/Uses

Elementary and secondary teachers, vocational counselors, and reading teachers can use this test to assess the reading skills of students whose anticipated reading levels fall between the primer and twelfth-grade level. Additionally, they can use it to identify the appropriate reading level for these students. This inventory can also be used to identify students requiring further diagnosis. Many of the SDRT reading passages are concise expository selections, making it useful for testing older students who are reading below their expected level. The nature of the inventory content also makes it appealing for evaluating students in adult literacy programs. In addition, counselors can use the literacy-level data in the testing profile when advising students.

This inventory is inappropriate for diagnosis of reading difficulties unless the administrator possesses considerable training and experience in reading disability. The manual does not include sufficient information regarding classification of oral reading errors for the novice. In addition, test interpretation would present considerable difficulty to the unsophisticated administrator.

This is an individually administered test that is most appropriately administered in a conference room or similar private setting. The test can be administered by a classroom teacher, psychologist, guidance counselor, or reading teacher.

The test manual provides straightforward, easy-to-follow instructions. Suggestions are included for altering the sequence of the test to address different objectives and different types of students. The test is relatively easy to administer. Students' responses can be tape recorded for later analysis. The test can be administered and scored in 30 to 60 minutes, depending on the examiner's objectives.

Administration of the SDRT requires that the examiner identify whether the objective of the examination is grade-level administration or performance-level administration. This objective alters the level of passages presented to the student. For example, an examiner who needs information about the grade-level performance of a third-grade student would administer only the third-grade-level materials in each subtest. When examining a disabled reader the examiner uses performance-level guidelines, which suggest beginning one grade level below the student's expected reading level and continuing until the student reaches frustration level.

While administering the Word Recognition subtest the examiner writes a "plus" if the student correctly pronounces a word and a "minus" if the student pronounces a word incorrectly. The examiner records the errors as the student is identifying the words. After the student reads each list of words, the examiner computes the independent, instructional, or frustration level by entering the number of errors in the spaces provided.

During the Oral Reading and Comprehension subtest the student reads aloud and the examiner categorizes pronunciation errors in the following six categories: reversals, insertions, mispronunciations, omissions, substitutions, and repetitions. The administrator then reads the comprehension questions and notes whether the student's responses are correct or incorrect. After the student completes each selection, the examiner can compute the frustration level, instructional level, or independent level by comparing the student's responses with the criteria printed after the selection.

When administering the Silent Reading Comprehension subtest the examiner uses a stopwatch to monitor the time limits for reading each passage. After the student reads a passage, the examiner reads the related questions that the student is to answer without referring to the passage. The examiner records any incorrect answers and identifies the student's level of functioning by comparing the number of errors with the printed criteria following the selection.

In the Listening Comprehension subtest, the examiner reads a passage to the student from the test booklet. Then the examiner asks a series of comprehension questions. After determining the number of incorrect answers, the examiner checks the appropriate comprehension level in the test booklet.

Scoring this test is relatively easy for the professional examiner. After one practice administration of the test a professional user is well prepared to score the instrument. The scoring criteria, which are provided after each word list and reading selection, make the test easy to score. Categorizing the student's pronunciation errors presents the greatest problem in scoring this instrument. This test is scored as the student progresses through it; therefore, completing the test profile requires very little time. Test data can be recorded on the summary page in approximately five minutes. However, interpretation of the test data is problematic for inexperienced test users.

The Word Recognition subtest of the SDRT is scored by writing a plus after each word that is identified correctly and a minus after each word that is identified incorrectly. Following each grade-level list of 20 words, the examiner writes the number of errors and identifies the functional level. For example, an individual who makes zero-one errors on the grade-three list is reading at the independent level, an individual who makes two-three errors on the fifth-grade list is classified at the instructional level, and an individual who makes four or more errors on the grade-seven list is reading at the frustration level.

Each of the comprehension subtests is scored in the same manner. Following each passage in these subtests, labeled blanks are provided for recording decoding errors, comprehension errors, pronunciation errors, and positional errors. Accompanying the blanks for recording decoding errors and comprehension errors are criteria for ascertaining the student's level of functioning. At the grade-two level an individual who makes from two-five errors in decoding is classified at the instructional level, whereas an individual who makes two or more comprehension errors is functioning at the frustration level.

Pronunciation errors are classified as to type, and blanks are provided for recording these errors following each passage. The blank beneath the appropriate error classification is checked, thus providing the examiner with a means of analyzing oral reading errors. The same system is used for identifying positional errors in word pronunciation. Machine scoring and computer scoring are not available for this test because mechanized scoring is not appropriate for oral reading tests.

Each portion of the test is accompanied by scoring criteria, and the summary page of the record booklet enhances the objectivity of the instrument. However, an examiner must use clinical judgment in evaluating the student's pronunciation of words, oral reading, and responses to comprehension questions. The interpretation of each subtest on the evaluation summary page relies on the professional preparation and the experience of the examiner. Although the explanatory material provided in the test manual is helpful, it cannot compensate for professional training and experience. Using this test to identify an appropriate reading level does not require a high level of sophistication, but individuals who have an undergraduate degree with a minimum of two courses in reading can use it more effectively. Greater sophistication on the part of the examiner would be required if this instrument were used for diagnostic purposes.

Technical Aspects

Test-retest reliability was used to analyze the reliability of the SDRT with the retesting completed two weeks after the initial test administration. The test-retest correlations range from .95 to .99 and indicate that the relative performance of the students tested did not change significantly over time (Spadafore, 1983).

Due to the degree of subjectivity involved in conducting an error analysis of oral reading, interrater reliability was computed. In this procedure, a taped reading sample was presented to a group of raters, each of whom had completed a brief training session on how to conduct an error analysis. The author states that "generally, there is sufficient agreement among the raters to indicate that the procedure outlined for conducting error analysis is effective in identifying areas of remedial concern" (Spadafore, 1983, p. 59).

Concurrent validity of the SDRT was examined by comparing subtest performance with other tests that measure similar abilities. The Word Recognition subtest was compared to grade-equivalent scores from the Reading subtest of the Wide Range Achievement Test (WRAT). This comparison yielded a correlation of .95, indicating that the two subtests measure similar abilities (Spadafore, 1983).

Validity of the comprehension subtests was examined by administering each subtest concurrently with the Passage Comprehension subtest of the Woodcock Reading Mastery Tests (WRMT). These correlations range from .81 to .86 and lend support to the validity of these subtests as measures of reading comprehension. An additional analysis of the validity of the SDRT was conducted by administering the full test to matched pairs of learning disabled and non-learning-disabled students. The results of this analysis indicate that the SDRT was effective in differentiating the learning disabled from non-learning-disabled students (Spadafore, 1983).

The population for the test-retest reliability of the Word Recognition subtest included 30 students from first through ninth grade, whereas 15 students from first through ninth grade were administered the comprehension subtests (Spadafore, 1983). The basis for selecting these subjects was not reported. The author also does not state his reasons for including 30 students when computing the reliability of the Word Recognition subtest when only 15 students completed the comprehension subtests. The limited number of subjects involved in the reliability analysis leaves the data open to question.

Interrater reliability studies were completed with ten raters, with only one rater disagreeing substantially with the overall group (Spadafore, 1983). Again, the author fails to describe his subjects, and neither the educational and experiential backgrounds of the raters nor the basis of their inclusion in the study are described.

Validity of the Word Recognition subtest was computed on the basis of 20 students from Grades 1 to 6 whose scores on the SDRT were compared with their reading scores on the WRAT (Merwin, 1972). Twenty students seem to be a small number on which to base validity. In addition, the author does not indicate the basis for subtest selection. He also fails to state the number of subjects tested at each grade level, creating the possibility that no students were tested at some grade levels.

Validity of the comprehension subtests was examined by concurrent administration of the SDRT and the WRMT to 20 students in Grades 2 to 10. This is a small population and the author's failure to identify the subject selection process and to describe the population leaves the prospective user with little information. No information is provided regarding the number of subjects tested at each grade level, which again creates the possibility that no subjects were tested at some grade levels.

Finally, 16 matched pairs of learning disabled students and non-learning-disabled students were administered the SDRT. This population is not described beyond the labels of "learning disabled" and "non-learning-disabled." Thus, there is no way of knowing whether the non-learning-disabled students were gifted, average, or below average. Also, learning disabled students may vary considerably because they may also be gifted, average, or below average.

Reliability refers to a test's capacity to yield consistent information. A reliable test is one that can be depended on time and time again to measure what it is expected to measure. Reliability coefficients are stated positive in value (+1.00), with a value close to 1.00 indicating high reliability and a value close to 0.00 indicating low reliability. Reliability coefficients of .80 and above are common and desirable for norm-referenced tests (Pyrczak, 1979). Reliability of the SDRT was analyzed in two ways, a test-retest approach and interrater reliability (Spadafore, 1983). Both of these statistical approaches to reliability are appropriate means of analyzing the reliability of a test, and the coefficients of correlation are appropriately high. However, acceptance of these data must be modified by the fact that the populations used for both the test-retest and the interrater reliability were not adequately described.

Validity refers to the usefulness of a test for a given purpose. A diagnostic reading test is designed to help an examiner identify strengths and weaknesses in reading skill. Thus, a diagnostic reading test is valid to the degree that it aids in achieving these goals. Tests may have construct validity, which is the extent to which scores yielded by the test are meaningful in relation to a given concept, such as reading or reading disability. Content validity refers to the appropriateness of the content and skills covered by the instrument. Criterion-related validity refers to test quality that is evaluated in terms of the extent to which scores correlate with independent measures of the trait being examined. The degree of criterion-related validity is expressed with a correlation coefficient, a statistic with a range from –1.00 to +1.00. In practice, validity coefficients are stated in positive values, with a coefficient close to 1.00 indicating high validity and a coefficient close to 0 indicating low validity. Validity coefficients higher than .75 are rare (Pyrczak, 1979). Concurrent validity is a type of criterion-related validity that is obtained by administering two tests at about the same time. Because concurrent validity is related to criterion validity, the validity coefficients are stated in the same manner.

The concurrent validity of the SDRT was computed by comparing reading subtest performance on the WRAT with performance on the SDRT's Word Recognition subtest. The validity coefficient on this measure was .95 (Spadafore, 1983), which is exceptionally high; however, the value of this coefficient must be considered in relation to the validity of the WRAT. The WRAT is not considered a valid diagnostic reading test or a valid reading achievement test by many reading authorities (e.g., Merwin, 1972).

Concurrent validity for the comprehension subtests was analyzed by administering SDRT subtests concurrently with the WRMT. This analysis yielded validity coefficients of .81 to .86 (Spadafore, 1983), which are quite high. Again, we must consider that this coefficient of validity depends on the validity of the instrument administered concurrently, and measurement authorities do not wholeheartedly endorse the WRMT (e.g., Dwyer, 1978).

The author fails to include any information regarding the correlation between equivalent passages. This is of critical concern, because the instrument is based on the assumption that the reading passages in the three comprehension subtests are of equal difficulty. However, this assumption is not supported by data, thus prospective users cannot be certain that the selections are equivalent.

Critique

The SDRT manual is well organized and has an attractive format. Determining general levels of reading ability is probably the most appropriate use for the SDRT, but it can be used to identify students who need additional diagnosis. However, it is not a diagnostic instrument; only examiners who have extensive diagnostic background can obtain diagnostic information with the SDRT.

After reading the manual carefully, this reviewer found the test easy to use. The data provided regarding the reading level required by various occupations are interesting and potentially useful to guidance counselors. Although the case studies included in the manual are also interesting, the recommendations given are general. Major deficits in the manual include lack of information regarding adult reading problems, reading as related to learning disabilities, and analysis of oral reading errors.

The student record booklet is well designed, and test data can be conveniently summarized in the scoring profile on the front page. Inclusion of the criteria for ranking the student at frustration level, instructional level, or independent level with each word list and reading passage is efficient and effective. The evaluation summary is a useful page for the experienced diagnostician.

When scoring the Word Recognition subtest, the examiner writes a plus or minus rather than the word pronounced by the student, thus eliminating an additional source of diagnostic data. Furthermore, research in miscue analysis suggests a need for qualitative analysis of errors instead of mere quantitative analysis.

Many of the words on the upper levels of the Word Recognition subtest are quite unusual. The author included these words to assess students' decoding abilities; however, the words are so unusual and difficult as to discourage disabled readers. When students fail to complete the test, teachers are unable to obtain needed information.

The reading selections are short, which is a strength of the instrument because disabled readers tend to be frustrated by lengthy selections. Another strength of the reading passages is the high proportion of expository content reflecting the nature of reading content at higher grade levels. On the whole, the selections are well constructed to encourage student thinking, which is difficult to accomplish in short passages. However, in order to achieve this, the author has sacrificed language flow, resulting in choppy syntax in some passages. In addition, many of the questions accompanying the reading passages are awkwardly phrased, making them difficult for students to answer. When these questions were rephrased, students were able to answer them correctly; however, the test manual directs administrators to ask the questions exactly as they are stated in the directions, which raises the possibility that an answer could be counted as an error because the student did not understand the question.

The SDRT lacks the validity and reliability that are valued in standardized testing instruments. This is unfortunate because the author attended to the technical aspects of validity and reliability but failed either to control these factors carefully or to apprise potential users of the data. Thus, validity and reliability of the SDRT become significant stumbling blocks to using the test. At present, this instrument would be most useful to teachers and counselors who are guiding secondary students and adults to vocations that are appropriate to their literacy levels. The SDRT is useful under these circumstances because other instruments are not available to meet this need.

References

Betts, E. (1957). *Foundations of reading instruction.* New York: American Book Company.

Dwyer, C. (1978). Woodcock Reading Mastery Tests. In O. K. Buros (Ed.), *The eighth mental measurements yearbook* (pp. 1303-1311). Highland Park, NJ: The Gryphon Press.

Merwin, J. (1972). Wide Range Achievement Test, Revised Edition. In O. K. Buros (Ed.), *The seventh mental measurements yearbook* (pp. 66-68). Highland Park, NJ: The Gryphon Press.

Phelps, S. (1985). Test review: Spadafore Diagnostic Reading Test. *Journal of Reading, 28*(4), 328-330.

Pyrczak, F. (1979). Definitions of measurement terms. In R. Schreiner (Ed.), *Reading tests and teachers: A practical guide.* Newark, DE: International Reading Association.

Spadafore, G. (1983). *Spadafore Diagnostic Reading Test manual.* Novato, CA: Academic Therapy Publications.

William E. Jaynes, Ph.D.

Professor of Psychology, Oklahoma State University, Stillwater, Oklahoma.

SRA NONVERBAL FORM

Robert N. McMurry and Joseph E. King. Chicago, Illinois: Science Research Associates, Inc.

Introduction

The SRA Nonverbal Form (NVF) is mostly a measure of general aspects of intellectual ability. The more specific nature of the traits it reflects depends on one's theoretical point of view. From the standpoint of Vernon's (1965) hierarchical theory, it primarily measures the most general form of intellectual ability and to a lesser extent a subgeneral spatial ability trait. In the theoretical framework provided by Cattell (1963), it is mostly a measure of a subgeneral fluid ability trait and to a lesser degree general intellectual ability. According to Sternberg (1982), tests of this type are one of three kinds of measures of inductive reasoning.

The items in the NVF are entirely pictorial. Each item presents five drawings of either common objects or simple geometric figures. Examinees are to select the one object or figure that differs the most from the other four. Items of this kind, involving detection of differences and similarities in sets of common stimuli, are categorized by Sternberg (1982) as inductive reasoning items of the classification type rather than those of the series and analogy types.

Buros (1949) indicates that the NVF was developed by McMurry and Johnson in 1946-1947. In 1973, the examiner's manual was revised by King and McMurry who are listed as the authors of the current version. No further information is available concerning the development of this test.

The NVF is intended for children in Grades 9-12 and adults. Its difficulty level is supposed to make it appropriate for examinees who have 12 or fewer years of education.

The NVF test booklet is composed of a cover sheet, containing instructions and sample items, and three sheets fastened together at the left and right edges. The middle sheet is carbon paper. Sixty items are presented on the front and back of the three sheets.

The examiner's participation in the testing process is minimal. The instructions on the cover sheet are to be read aloud by the examiner while the examinees read silently. The examiner's only other major function is to give the examinees the exact time prescribed for the test.

Forty of the NVF items each involve five realistic drawings of common objects. Each of the other 20 items present five simple geometric figures, which constitute every third item throughout the test. Examinees answer by marking a small box in the lower left-hand corner of the one picture out of five that differs the most from the others. These marks are transferred by the carbon paper to a scoring grid on the inside of the third sheet. Because this grid is designed to yield only one score, no profile is provided.

Practical Applications/Uses

As a relatively quick measure of the general and spatial/fluid aspects of intellectual ability, the NVF may be useful in a wide variety of settings. The examiner's manual indicates that the test is intended for selection and placement of applicants for entry-level jobs in business and industry. Recent research (McCormick & Ilgen, 1985; Pearlman, Schmidt, & Hunter, 1980; Schmidt, Hunter, & Caplan, 1981; Schmidt, Hunter, & Pearlman, 1981) suggests that the general facets of intellectual ability are important in nearly all jobs except perhaps those at the very lowest level of complexity. Those outside of business and industry may also find the NVF to be of practical value when they want a brief measure of the general and spatial/fluid aspects of intellectual ability. This test, however, is inappropriate for assessment of verbal:educational or crystallized intellectual ability.

The NVF was designed for use in business and industry. It has also been employed in clinical, correctional, rehabilitative, health, school, and research settings, and in education of the deaf (Buswell, 1951; Eber, Cochrane, & Branca, 1954; Holden, Mendelson, & DeVault, 1966; King & McMurry, 1973; Levy, 1966, 1968; Levy & Moore, 1966; Odell, 1971; Phillips & Berg, 1967; Stratton, 1968).

Industrial, clinical, and counseling psychologists, when interested in the most general and spatial/fluid aspects of intellectual ability, are likely to find the NVF particularly useful. School counselors; educators; and school, educational, and developmental psychologists may also find uses for it, but mostly as a supplement to tests of verbal:educational or crystallized intellectual ability.

The NVF could be more widely applied as a measure of general and spatial/fluid intellectual ability. It could also be further developed as a measure of intellectual ability for use in non-English-speaking countries and other settings where inductive reasoning skill based on visual communication might be more interesting than verbal ability.

Although the NVF purports to be appropriate for a wide range of subjects differing in age, linguistic culture, and handicaps, it is presumably especially appropriate for those who have difficulty reading or understanding the English language and/or those with 12 or fewer years of education. It is highly inappropriate for those who are visually impaired or distractible. Likewise, it is not well-suited to subjects who lack the motor coordination to place marks in small boxes quickly and accurately. However, development of instructions in other languages would make it suitable for other linguistic cultures, and development of nonverbal or minimally verbal instructions would make it more appropriate for those who are more handicapped in verbal or crystallized ability.

Because the NVF is a group test that is relatively easy to administer, personnel clerks or comparable technicians can readily be trained to serve as examiners. The examiner's manual gives clear and brief instructions for administration. During the presentation of the instructions, questions from examinees are to be answered by rereading appropriate parts of the printed instructions. Because the test items are numbered from 1 to 60, with 30 on the front and 30 on the back of the three sheets, examiners have no discretion concerning the sequence in which the items are encountered.

Because the NVF is a short speeded test, exact timing of the testing period is extremely important. Examinees are to be given precisely ten minutes to work on it. This may demand the use of a mechanical or electronic timer, which is more dependable than a sweep second hand on an ordinary watch.

The instructions for scoring are presented clearly in the examiner's manual. Personnel clerks or other technicians should be able to learn how to score this test in ten minutes or less by reading the two short paragraphs of instructions given. However, one possible source of confusion exists: The instructions to the examinees printed on the cover sheet specify that a circle is to be drawn around the outside of the small box previously marked in order to change an answer. The administration and scoring instructions in the manual indicate that marks are to be circled within the response boxes, and marks circled in this way are not to be counted.

Five minutes or less is an adequate amount of time to score one copy of this test. Scoring is accomplished by tearing off the perforated left and right edges of all sheets and discarding all but the sheet with the scoring grid. On this sheet, the scorer starts at an arrow and follows a chain of squares, counting only those containing marks that have not been circled. All scoring is by hand, and no inherent problems, such as fragile templates, are present. The nearly self-administering and almost self-scoring nature of the NVF are two of its particularly appealing features.

Interpretation of the NVF is based entirely on one objective score that is converted to a percentile rank. The percentile ranks are easy to interpret, and appropriate interpretation is adequately indicated by the examiner's manual. The relation of differences in percentile ranks to differences in raw scores, also discussed in the manual, is moderately difficult to understand, with the most probable source of confusion being the paragraph concerning the use of the standard error of measurement. This statistic is unfortunately called the "standard error of estimate." A numerical value based on reliability estimates is given for it. This is applied to a score without specifying whether the score is a raw score or a percentile rank, but the latter is implied. Because the standard error of measurement applies directly to raw scores rather than percentile ranks, this paragraph may lead to reporting of inappropriate ranges for percentile ranks.

For hiring in business and industry, a low level of examiner sophistication and training is sufficient for adequate and proper interpretation of this test. For interpretation concerning assessment of intellectual ability, however, a moderately high level of sophistication and training, such as a master's degree in measurement, is required.

Technical Aspects

The examiner's manual reports four criterion validity studies, all of which seem to be of a concurrent nature. Criteria in these studies are ratings of employees by supervisors in three studies, together with "production reports of percentage of efficiency (speed)" in one of these, and ninth-grade student grade averages in the fourth study. The employees in the three studies are life-insurance claim adjusters, office personnel, and food-service route salesmen, making these groups perhaps somewhat inappropriate. Two split-half odd-even reliability studies are also summarized briefly. One of these is based on ninth-grade students and the other on sixth-grade students. All six of these studies involve convenience samples. Sample sizes are small (i.e., 39-53 for the three employee validity studies and 82 for the ninth-grade academic achievement validity study).

The only reliability studies discussed in the manual are two with school children. These samples are moderate (506 ninth-graders and 272 sixth-graders), and reliability estimates are at best only marginally satisfactory (.62 and .69, respectively). Further doubt concerning reliability stems from the failure to indicate whether or not these estimates involve corrections based on the Spearman Brown prophecy formula.

The validity study results are reported only in the form of *t* tests in one study and *F* ratios in two other studies. Failure to translate these results into correlations makes it difficult to determine the strength of the association between the NVF scores as a predictor and the criteria. The *t* tests and *F* ratios for the three rating criteria are statistically significant at the .05 level, but the *t* test for the production report criterion is not. A correlation of .56, significant at the .01 level, is reported in the fourth validity study concerning ninth-grade scholastic achievement. The brief summaries of three of the validity studies also provide the overall sample means and standard deviations. These results may be of interest from the normative standpoint, but none of these samples are included in the norm group.

The norm group is composed of 2,492 employees from ten firms in widely dispersed geographic locations and highly varied lines of work. The number of employees per firm ranges from 40 to 1,217, and no information is given concerning the specific details of the sampling procedures.

Critique

Although all of the NVF items have the same format, the items based on realistic drawings of common objects and those involving simple geometric figures probably measure different mixtures of intellectual ability traits. Vernon (1965, pp. 71-72) states: "In general, no test can claim to measure nothing but g (and error variance). The type of material used for expressing intellectual ability, whether verbal or nonverbal, always imposes some group factor, though it may be fairly small if the material is unfamiliar. . . ." Research findings concerning the kinds of intellectual ability reflected in the common object items are not readily available. The geometric figure items have been called figure classification items (Thurstone, 1938), and research has indicated that they measure spatial ability in addition to general intellectual ability (Cattell, 1963; Eysenck, 1939; Thurstone, 1938).

According to Cattell's theory (1963), the NVF is an indicator of fluid intellectual ability rather than crystallized intellectual ability. In this context, fluid ability is an inherited and unlearned "ability to adapt to a new problem or situation" (Buss & Poley, 1976, p. 52), whereas crystallized ability depends primarily on previous learning. Research findings (Horn, 1970; Horn & Cattell, 1966) show that fluid ability increases until age 18-20 and then declines. The same findings reveal that crystallized ability increases rapidly until adolescence and then gradually through adulthood and into old age. These findings are confirmed by research (Stratton, 1968) that shows that mean IQ scores derived from the NVF are lower than mean full scale IQ scores from the WAIS in the age range from 35 to 54.

Eight studies reported in the examiner's manual and eight articles in the scientific research literature deal mostly with the relation of the NVF to other tests. The highest correlations of the NVF scores are with Revised Beta Examination scores, $r = .66$ (Levy, 1968); Wechsler performance scores, median $r = .72$ (Holden et al., 1966; King & McMurry, 1973; Levy, 1968); SRA Verbal Form quantitative scores, median $r = .60$ (King & McMurry, 1973); and SRA High School Placement Test reasoning and arithmetic scores, $r = .59$ and .41, respectively (King & McMurry, 1973). NVF scores correlate less with Otis Self-Administering Test of Mental Ability scores, median $r = .38$ (Levy, 1968); SRA Verbal Form linguistic scores, median $r = .56$ (King & McMurry, 1973); SRA High School Placement Test reading and language arts scores, $r = .24$ and .35, respectively (King & McMurry, 1973); Wechsler verbal scores, median $r = .65$ (King & McMurry, 1973; Levy, 1968; Holden et al., 1966); Peabody Picture Vocabulary Test scores, $r = .49$ (Odell, 1971); education, $r = .48$ (Holden et al., 1966); SRA Pictorial Reasoning Test scores, median $r = .47$ (King & McMurry, 1973); and Raven Progressive Matrices scores, $r = .17$ (King & McMurry, 1973). The low correlations with the SRA Pictorial Reasoning Test and the Raven Progressive Matrices are puzzling. The rest of the correlations suggest that the NVF does indeed measure both a general intellectual ability trait and a subgeneral spatial/fluid ability trait, but it does not entail a subgeneral verbal/crystallized ability trait.

One study in the examiners manual and seven articles in the research literature explore the use of the NVF to estimate Wechsler full scale IQs. Four of these are based on the same data (King & McMurry, 1973; Levy, 1966, 1968; Levy & Moore, 1966). Three of the studies involving different samples (Eber et al., 1954; Holden et al., 1966; Stratton, 1968) found the mean NVF estimates to be too low, and the other two studies based on different data (Levy, 1968; Phillips & Berg, 1967) discovered that the mean NVF estimates were too high. One study (Stratton, 1968) indicates that the NVF tends to overestimate high and underestimate low WAIS full scale IQs. The same study shows that the NVF overestimates WAIS full scale IQs in the age range of 18-24 and underestimates in the age range of 35-54.

One study concerned NVF estimates of Peabody Picture Vocabulary Test IQs (Odell, 1971), and another compared Wechsler and NVF scores in black and white samples (King & McMurry, 1973). The mean NVF estimate of the mean Peabody Picture Vocabulary Test IQ was found to be too low. Both the mean Wechsler full scale IQ score and the mean NVF raw score were lower for blacks than whites, but the two NVF means differed by less standard deviation units than the two Wechsler means.

Further examination of correlations of the NVF with comparable tests would be of interest. In this regard, NVF scores should be correlated with scores from the Culture Fair Series: Scale 3, which has a figure classification subtest, a figure series subtest, and a matrices subtest. NVF scores should also be correlated with scores from other nonverbal reasoning tests such as the Employee Aptitude Survey Test #6-Numerical Reasoning and the Non-Verbal Reasoning test.

Additional research should also be done concerning standard scores from the NVF and verbal/crystallized ability tests in groups with special difficulties. In particular, groups with difficulty in reading and understanding English and with deficiencies in formal education or both should be studied. Despite the theoretical expectation that such groups will have higher standard scores in spatial/fluid than in verbal/crystallized ability, previous research (Loehlin, Lindzey, & Spuhler, 1975) leaves this matter in doubt.

The examiner's manual should be improved in six ways: First, the portion of the section on interpretation of norms concerning the standard error of measurement should be rewritten to correctly label this concept and apply it to raw scores rather than percentile ranks. Second, the section on components of the norm group should give more information about the sampling procedure involved in developing the norm group. Third, the two sections on administration and scoring should be revised. The administration instructions should indicate that in changing a response a circle is to be drawn outside the previously marked response box, and the scoring instructions should say that circled marks should not be counted without specifying the location of the circles relative to the scoring grid boxes. Fourth, the discussion of the Wechsler and NVF mean scores for black and white samples in the section on fairness should not say the NVF means are "significantly closer" to each other than the Wechsler means. Fifth, the validity studies should be done with more appropriate groups and reported in greater detail, especially by giving correlations, as well as the results of tests of statistical significance. Sixth, reliability studies should be done with more appropriate groups of subjects, and more complete information should be supplied concerning the computation of the reliability estimates.

Because of its low reliability, uncertain validity, and possible adverse impact in comparison to verbal/crystallized ability tests, the NVF is not recommended for entry-level jobs or other individual decision-making concerning those deficient in education and/or comprehension of Engligh. It is recommended for experimental use and further development by psychologists who want to measure the most general and spatial/fluid aspects of intelligence.

References

Buros, O. K. (Ed.). (1949). *The third mental measurements yearbook.* Highland Park, NJ: The Gryphon Press.

Buss, A. R., & Poley, W. (1976). *Individual differences: Traits and factors.* New York: Gardner Press.

Buswell, G. T. (1951). The relationship between the rate of thinking and rate of reading. *School Review, 59,* 339-346.

Cattell, R. B. (1963). The theory of fluid and crystallized intelligence: A critical experiment. *Journal of Educational Psychology, 54,* 1-22.

Eber, H. W., Cochrane, C. M., & Branca, A. A. (1954). Brief intellectual assessment of patients with behavioral disorders. *Journal of Consulting Psychology, 18,* 396.

Eysenck, H. J. (1939). [Review of *Primary mental abilities*]. *British Journal of Educational Psychology, 9,* 270-275.

Holden, R. H., Mendelson, M. A., & DeVault, S. (1966). Relationship of the WAIS to the SRA Non-Verbal Test scores. *Psychological Reports, 19,* 987-990.

Horn, J. L. (1970). Organization of data on life-span development of human abilities. In L. R.

Goulet & P. B. Baltes (Eds.), *Life-span developmental psychology: Research and theory* (pp. 423-466). New York: Academic Press.

Horn, J. L., & Cattell, R. B. (1966). Age differences in primary mental ability factors. *Journal of Gerontology, 21,* 210-220.

King, J. E., & McMurry, R. N. (1973). *SRA Nonverbal Form.* Chicago: Science Research Associates.

Levy, R. H. (1966). The gauging of academic achievement among "court-labelled" delinquent boys. *Journal of Correctional Education, 18,* 14-17.

Levy, R. H. (1968). Group administered intelligence tests which appropriately reflect the magnitude of mental retardation among wards of the Illinois Youth Commission. *Journal of Correctional Education, 20,* 7-10.

Levy, R. H., & Moore, W. F. (1966). Cross-sectional psychometric evaluation of court-labelled delinquent boys. *Journal of Correctional Education, 18,* 7-9.

Loehlin, J. C., Lindzey, G., & Spuhler, J. N. (1975). *Race differences in intelligence.* San Francisco: Freeman.

McCormick, E. J., & Ilgen, D. R. (1985). *Industrial and organizational psychology* (8th ed.). Englewood Cliffs, NJ: Prentice-Hall.

Odell, L. M. (1971). Maternal intellectual functioning. *Johns Hopkins Medical Journal, 128,* 362-368.

Pearlman, K., Schmidt, F. L., & Hunter, J. E. (1980). Validity generalization results for tests used to predict job proficiency and training success in clerical occupations. *Journal of Applied Psychology, 65,* 373-406.

Phillips, R. M., & Berg, T. O. (1967). Use of the SRA Verbal and Non-Verbal Forms at Gallaudet College. *Journal of Rehabilitation of the Deaf, 1,* 59-62.

Schmidt, F. L., Hunter, J. E., & Caplan, J. R. (1981). Validity generalization results for two job groups in the petroleum industry. *Journal of Applied Psychology, 66,* 261-273.

Schmidt, F. L., Hunter, J. E., & Pearlman, K. (1981). Task differences as moderators of aptitude test validity in selection: A red herring. *Journal of Applied Psychology, 66,* 166-185.

Sternberg, R. J. (1982). Reasoning, problem solving, and intelligence. In R. J. Sternberg (Ed.), *Handbook of human intelligence* (pp. 225-307). Cambridge: Cambridge University Press.

Stratton, A. J. (1968). Validity of the SRA Non-Verbal Form for adults. *Psychological Reports, 22,* 163-167.

Thurstone, L. L. (1938). *Primary mental abilities.* Chicago: University of Chicago Press.

Vernon, P. E. (1965). *The structure of human abilities.* New York: Wiley & Sons. (Original work published 1950)

Arthur B. Sweney, Ph.D.

Professor of Management, Wichita State University, and President of Test Systems International, Ltd., Wichita, Kansas.

SRA VERBAL FORM

L. L. Thurstone and Thelma Gwinn Thurstone. Chicago, Illinois: Science Research Associates, Inc.

Introduction

Many educators were surprised when L. L. Thurstone revolutionized the concepts of cognitive competencies with his use of oblique rotated factor analysis to study "primary mental abilities." His psychometric laboratory at the University of Chicago became the focus for education and research into the basic methodologies needed for adequate test construction and usage. Out of this ambience, the SRA Verbal Form (Thurstone & Thurstone, 1973), as well as its sister instruments, was developed.

The "surprise" with this instrument is that the quantitative reasoning and linguistic elements are both loaded on the same verbal primary mental ability factor. Until Thurstone published his research, these qualities were seen as polar opposites. Girls were expected to have better vocabularies, and boys to have better math skills. This sexual bias was but one of many justifications for seeing these opposites as difficult processes. Since the first publication of this test in 1947, the recognition of mathematics as a language has become increasingly clear, and this association is less surprising to modern educators even though curriculum development has not made the successful integration, which can be carried out cognitively by the individual.

Each of the test's two forms (A and B) consists of 84 short items to be completed within a time limit of 15 minutes. The items are arranged in repetitive blocks of seven items: two vocabulary recognition, one narrative math, two vocabulary recall, and two number series. In this way the Quantitative Scale includes 36 items and the Linguistic Scale includes 48.

This spiral construction does not seem to get progressively more difficult and, hence, does not qualify as a spiral omnibus test as defined by Aiken (1979). This homogeneity of difficulty simplifies the interpretation of scores because difficulty and speed are not confounded by each other. Because the spacing of various types of items are uniform, unequal time rates or the various skills involved could only be discovered if items were skipped in some consistent patterns.

The test can be group administered and requires few instructions beyond those available on the front of the booklet. Trial exercises make it possible for the respondent to learn the format for the items and develop some skill and interest in solving them. A pleasant environment free from distractions is highly desirable to allow the respondents to maximize their performances. The time limit of 15 minutes should be emphasized in the instructions.

Because reading ability is part of the content being measured, one would not disqualify its use at marginal levels if that is one of the skills that one wishes to measure. Although the items are difficult enough to challenge adults, the manual (Campbell, 1973) reports studies on subjects as low as the ninth grade that yielded meaningful results. Educational norms are provided for groups as young as 12 years of age, and the median number of items correctly completed by this group is appreciable.

The responses are recorded directly on the test booklet, making rapid scoring into the two constituent scales possible. The scores are then converted into percentiles for both quantitative and linguistic ability, and the sum of the two raw scores are converted into a verbal percentile. Thus, these highly related scores are made available for use in five minutes or less of scoring time.

Practical Applications/Uses

The handbook emphasizes the SRA Verbal Form's usefulness in both educational and industrial settings. Although the publishers caution about interpreting the Quantitative and Linguistic Scales separately, crude patterns can be observed that would signal areas for more intense investigation by a diagnostician. The scales are simple and straightforward, and the scores are directly interpretable.

One of the advantages of this test is its ease of administration and scoring. With relative ease one can obtain a valid measure of verbal ability from a group-administered instrument. It does not require the numerous short-time intervals needed for the Wechsler or Binet individual intelligence scales or even the Cattells' group-administered Culture Fair Series.

The use of intelligence scales in educational settings can be a delicate problem, but almost all communities find the measurement of verbal ability a natural and less threatening activity. This test could be a meaningful standard against which to measure situationally influenced achievement tests either on an individual or group basis. The current concern about the quality of our educational system as it now stands could be investigated by comparing an aptitude measure of this kind against performance measured on achievement tests. Adequate national norms are available in the handbook to make rough comparisons possible.

This test is particularly useful for industrial applications where long periods of time taken away from work in order to take tests would be costly. The relationship between this kind of ability and positive performance on many jobs is reported in the test manual but is well documented in the professional literature as well (Tiffin & Lawshe, 1943; Ghiselli, 1963; Bahn, 1979). The higher a position is in an organization, the more it requires verbal ability. Many personnel placement agencies would favor this test to the Wonderlic if its availability were better known.

Mean scores and ranges are available for various occupational groups, making it possible to match candidates to the jobs toward which they aspire. Although this form of mental ability would not be the only consideration, it might represent a limitation when the mismatching becomes too great. Tests of this kind have been found to sample a different region in variable space than the interest and personality tests normally used for career counseling and, thus, they can be incorporated very profitably into batteries of tests assembled for this purpose.

Technical Aspects

This instrument was developed out of a very sophisticated program of research and, hence, may have fewer technical defects than many others purported to serve similar purposes. In spite of this, however, the discriminating user should be aware of some of the inherent characteristics that might influence its usability or the interpretation of the obtained results. These fall into the normal categories of reliability and validity, but may also disclose some other concerns as well.

The reliabilities reported for this instrument in its handbook concentrate primarily on the equivalency of Form A to Form B and on the internal consistency resulting from the correspondence between the quantitative and linguistic subsections of each form. These direct correlations range from .72 through .80 without the upward correction that would result from the Spearman-Brown formula. Each subscale is related to the total score, of which it is part, with correlations ranging between .89 and .96. From these figures it becomes clear why the authors of the manual caution the user from trying to interpret the quantitative or linguistic sections as diagnostically meaningful.

The failure of the manual's authors to report internal consistencies based on matched rather than mismatched split halves or by Cronbach's alpha is, on first inspection, somewhat surprising. They may have recognized that timed tests overstate the item validities for those items in the later part of the tests because of the difference in completion amount of those involved. This would introduce some difficulty in calculating homogeneity coefficients, but it would also artificially inflate the correlations reported between the Linguistic and Quantitative Scales because the number of items completed for one scale would directly affect the number of items completed for the other. For this reason one might suspect that the separate variances associated with the abilities themselves are confounded by the common variance associated with speed, resulting in a spuriously high correlation between the two interlocking parts of the test. One can only hope that the true lower bound of the homogeneity is sufficiently high to make the speed contamination minimal. It would have been much better to design a means of studying homogeneity that would take these problems into account. Several strategies seem to be possible. One would be to gather data on untimed administrations, recognizing that this would constitute a different test than the timed version. Another would be to examine a section of the test which everyone in the sample completed, and expand that coefficent to correspond to the total test. This would assume that the later items were equivalent in form and difficulty to those analyzed earlier, which on superficial inspection seems to be true.

The determination of true homogeneity is extremely important for interpretation reasons. Four different subscales actually make up the total score. Thus, planned heterogeneity must be operating to some degree unless one assumes congruent dynamics for all four types of items, which, on the surface, seems highly unlikely. If the only binding principle between items is speediness, then the user should know this. This reviewer suspects that there are other real sources of homogeneity, but they are not disclosed by the data given, nor would they yield correlations nearly as high as the pragmatic equivalencies reported.

Without homogeneity measures it is impossible to correct for attenuation due to lack of internal consistency. This limits users' ability to estimate the amount of true-score variance associated with their results. Stability coefficients have not been reported, although these, too, would have to be corrected for attenuation to separate the real degradation with time from the lack of saturation of the measures being compared. These considerations alert the user to the possibility that the reason the instrument works as well as it does may have more to do with the timing constraint than the actual content of the items themselves.

The levels of reported predictive validity coefficients seem to reflect a direct proportionality to the amount of ability needed to directly influence outcomes in the activity area from which the sample has been gathered. Thus, the correlations of the scale with performance is higher for chemical operators (.33) than for truck drivers (.04). Because the sizes of these two samples are nearly the same, a direct comparison is possible. It is important to the interpretation of these various reported "validity" figures that the differences in sample size is critical to the absolute level of the correlation, making many other comparisons dangerous. It is sufficient to conclude, however, that many correlations were found significant between the test results and unspecified measures of job performance for various occupational groups.

The author of the manual is sensitive to the restriction-of-range problems that are generated by post hoc testing designs. They seem to imply that the validity coefficients would have been higher had the predictor scale range not been reduced by the rejection from the job of individuals who would have contributed lower scores and, hence, greater variance to the sample had they been left in. A superficial inspection of validity coefficients with standard deviations shows that the group with the second lowest range (10.2) yielded the highest validity (.33), whereas the group with highest range (15.0) yielded the fifth lowest validity (.09). This seems to show the opposite effect from that claimed by the authors.

The test purports to be racially fair based on similarities between validity coefficients for the scale calculated on black and white samples. This method of comparison hides the fact that correlations are not sensitive to absolute values. The same correlations could have been obtained if all of the black population had scores below the cutting level and all of the whites had scores above, as long as those relatively higher on the scale were also relatively higher on the performance ratings. This separate example technique does not allow the two groups to actually be compared, even though this is implied by the manual's narrative. If separate cutting scores were applied to the two groups, then these computations would have some meaning, but newer court decisions on reverse discrimination would make this practice undefensible.

On the other hand, there is nothing reported in the manual or handbook that indicates that the test is racially biased. Although vocabulary is very much an artifact of culture, there is evidence that, with mass media and mass education, the critical discrimination is along the educational and active cultural assimilation continua rather than racial ones, and this seems to be the direction that this instrument has taken. The critical study would compare the scale racial samples with members who had been matched across samples for years of education and socioeconomic status to determine whether significant variances were associated with the racial variable itself. Unfortunately, it has become part of public policy not to conduct such studies for fear of negative side effects on affirmative action and other programs directed toward rectifying the historically caused imbalances in opportunities for different ethnic components in our culture.

All age groups reported in the handbook show positive correlations between this scale and job performance. It is interesting that the highest relationship (.46) was found in the oldest group, 42 years and older. In another study on electric-plant workers the newly hired sample displayed a negative correlation between the scale and job performance. These data might indicate that the abilities (or acquisitions) measured by this scale become more useful either with age or with the higher position given to older persons in organizations. This reviewer would tend to favor the latter interpretation.

Another interesting speculation focuses on the action of the speediness variable on job performance. Because older persons generally tend to be penalized by speed tests, in business there may be a larger deviation in the number of items completed correctly at this age group, reflecting variance in the level of maintained alertness. This condition itself may reflect level in the organization or the amount of real responsibility these individuals fulfill. Whichever hypothesis is supported, the construct validity of the test is not diminished but rather enhanced at this older level where the user might otherwise be hesitant to employ a timed test.

The question of whether this is an ability or achievement measure is not addressed by the handbook, nor need it be questioned for other than pragmatic reasons. The high correlations (.14 to .63) between the test and grades and grade-point averages would suggest a high achievement component. This seems to be borne out by the patterning of grades by courses. Typing, shop, and algebra show the lowest relationships (.14, .25, and .25, respectively), whereas science (.47) and English (.56) show the highest. In view of the work done by Cattell (1963), Horn (1982), and others (e.g., Knapp, 1960; MacArthur, 1963) on fluid and crystallized intelligence, one could assume that this test falls squarely in the crystallized area and that caution should be used concerning the labeling of scores as reflecting native ability.

These characteristics would make it important to include in the same battery with this scale other measures that tap the fluid intelligence area such as the SRA Nonverbal Form (McMurry & King, 1947) or the Culture Fair Series, Scales 2 and 3 (Cattell & Cattell, 1973). The relatively high correlations (.56 to .76) reported between the SRA Verbal and Nonverbal Forms still leave sufficient independent variance to make their coimplementation worthwhile. Comparisons of results of the SRA Verbal and Nonverbal Forms would be a valuable addition to the handbook in order to highlight the basic difference between these two methods for measuring mental ability.

By using such items as "mental ability" and "proficiency" the authors have avoided identifying "intelligence" as the primary nature of the test. The high validities (.74 to .82) between this instrument and self-proclaimed intelligence scales justifies considering the Verbal Form as a measure of some kind of intelligence. There are probably two reasons this claim has not been made. One is Thurstone's desire to redirect thinking away from Spearman's concept of *g* or general intelligence and to substitute the concept of empirically related but conceptually independent primary mental abilities. The other reason may be less overt: to provide the test to a wider user group than certified psychologists. By using nonprofessional nomenclature the test can be legitimately used by personnel agencies, school counselors, and research organizations, all of which may not be staffed with professional psychologists who can administer the more demanding and sophisticated individually administered intelligence scales.

Critique

The SRA Verbal Form demonstrates the technical characteristics sought in a measure to be used in the industrial and educational areas. The inappropriately reported reliabilities do not in any respect detract from the strong validities obtained. A test of this kind should be interpreted carefully because the true nature of what it is measuring may require many years of active research to discover. Its use as an untimed instrument should be explored because the speediness variable may serve as a theoretical confoundment even if it can be justified on pragmatic and operational grounds.

References

This list includes text citations as well as suggested additional reading.

Aiken, L. R. (1979). *Psychological testing and assessment* (3rd ed.). Boston: Allyn and Bacon.

Bahn, C. (1979). Can intelligence tests predict executive competence? *Personnel, 56*(4), 58.

Campbell, B. (1973). *SRA Verbal examiner's manual.* Chicago: Science Research Associates, Inc.

Cattell, R. B. (1941). Some theoretical issues in adult intelligence testing. *Psychological Bulletin, 38,* 592.

Cattell, R. B. (1963). Theory of fluid and crystalized intelligence: A critical experiment. *Journal of Educational Psychology, 54,* 1-22.

Cattell, R. B. & Cattell, A. K. S. (1973). *Handbook for the Culture Fair Intelligence Test.* Champaign, IL: Institute for Personality and Ability Testing, Inc.

Ghiselli, E. E. (1963). The validity of management traits in relation to occupational levels. *Personnel Psychology, 16,* 109-113.

Horn, J. L. (1982). The theory of fluid and crystalized intelligence in relation to concepts of cognitive psychology and aging in adulthood. In F. I. M. Craik & S. E. Trehub (Eds.), *Aging and cognitive processes* (237-278). Boston: Plenum.

Horn, J. L., & Cattell, R. B. (1967). Age differences in fluid and crystalized intelligence. *Acta Psychologia, 26,* 107-129.

Horst, P. (1951). Estimating total test reliability from parts of unequal length. *Educational and Psychological Measurement, 11,* 368-371.

Jensen, A. R. (1982). Reaction time and psychometric *g*. In H. J. Eysenck (Ed.), *A model for intelligence* (pp. 93-132). New York: Springer-Verlag.

Knapp, R. R. (1960). The effects of time limits on intelligence test performance in Mexican and American subjects. *Journal of Educational Psychology, 51,* 14-20.

MacArthur, R. S., & Elley, W. B. (1963). The reduction of socioeconomic bias in intelligence testing. *British Journal of Educational Psychology, 33,* 107-119.

McMurry, R. N., & King, I. E. (1947). *SRA Nonverbal Form.* Chicago: Science Research Associates, Inc.

Sweney, A. B., & Cattell, R. B. (1978). *Vocational Interest Measure.* Champaign, IL: Institute for Personality and Ability Testing, Inc.

Thurstone, L. L. (1935). *Vectors of mind.* Chicago: University of Chicago Press.

Thurstone, L. L., & Thurstone, T. G. (1973). *SRA Verbal Form.* Chicago: Science Research Associates, Inc.

Tiffin, J., & Lawshe, C. H., Jr. (1943). The Adaptability Test: A 15-minute mental alertness test for use in personnel allocation. *Journal of Applied Psychology, 27,* 483-493.

Rebecca Bardwell, Ph.D.
Associate Professor of Educational Psychology, School of Education, Marquette University, Milwaukee, Wisconsin.

SUICIDE PROBABILITY SCALE

John G. Cull and Wayne S. Gill. Los Angeles, California: Western Psychological Services.

Introduction

The Suicide Probability Scale (SPS) is a self-report measure that assesses the risk of suicide in adults and adolescents aged 14 years and older. Subjects are asked to rate the frequency with which they experience 36 thoughts, feelings, and behaviors on a four-point Likert scale that ranges from "None or little of the time" to "Most or all of the time." The test can be scored to reveal an overall suicide risk score on four subscales: Hopelessness, Suicide Ideation, Negative Self-Evaluation, and Hostility.

The development of the SPS, which was published in 1982, came about as a result of the authors', John G. Cull and Wayne S. Gill's, clinical experiences and a felt need for an empirically validated measure for predicting suicide behaviors. The scale is based on the assumption that seriously suicidal individuals will experience a generalized sense of isolation, hopelessness, anxiety, depression, and suicide ideation, and report feelings and behaviors related to these experiences. It is further assumed that item responses that differentiate between people who attempt suicide and those who do not will be relevant for predicting future suicide behavior. As a theoretical base for their instrument, the authors used the work of Shneidman (1966) and Weisman (1971). In their work Shneidman and Weisman portray the act of suicide as impulsive, although they maintain that the predisposition to commit suicide or engage in life-threatening behaviors is long-standing and characterological. Thus, the SPS purports to measure both the trait and state dimensions of suicide risk.

Based on their own clinical experience and the state-trait theories of suicide, the authors generated a list of over 200 items that they thought would be helpful in assessing suicide potential. They administered these items to individuals who had attempted suicide in order to assess the discriminative power of each item to differentiate between those who have attempted suicide and those who have not. Because the SPS is designed to predict a suicide attempt, this is an important distinction to make because the authors have identified a population of persons who have attempted suicide. They have not, for obvious reasons, identified those who have been successful at suicide. Therefore, in order for the SPS's results to be of value one must accept the assumption that there is a similarity between those who attempt suicide and those who actually succeed.

Following the assessment of the discriminative power of the items, the items with the highest discriminative power were submitted to a panel of clinical judges who rated their clarity and appropriateness. From the original group of 200 items, 36 were retained. The authors (Cull & Gill, 1982) report that retention of the final 36 items was based on the following criteria: 1) relation to at least one theoretical explanation for suicide; 2) clinical importance judged on the basis of interviews with suicidal clients and retrospective analyses of suicidal notes; 3) easy conversion into a feeling or action statement; 4) equal relevance and comprehension by clients irrespective of sex, age, or ethnic background; and 5) unique, nonoverlapping contribution to the predictive validity of the scale.

The instrument was standardized on a sample of 562 adolescents and adults (220 males and 342 females) from the San Antonio, Texas area. From the sample, those who responded that they had a previous psychiatric history or had made a serious suicide attempt were excluded from the sample. This sample of "normals" was compared to two criterion groups: a psychiatric inpatient group consisting of 260 individuals (87 males and 173 females) and a group of 336 individuals (100 males and 236 females) who had attempted suicide (i.e., had made a potentially lethal attempt, such as a serious drug overdose, a deep slashing of the wrist, or a self-inflicted gunshot wound to the head). All of the second group were tested individually within 48 hours of their attempted suicide.

Thus, the total sample was composed of individuals aged 19 years and older, of various ethnic backgrounds (Hispanic—43.8%; black and other minorities—13.2%; and white—43.1%), of educational backgrounds that included those with some high school through college graduates, and persons who were single (40.5%), married (36.4%), divorced (14.7%), separated (6.1%), and widowed (2.2%).

Following the development of the instrument, the authors researched whether weighting the response options would increase the utility of the instrument. In doing so they compared five methods of weighting, using a double cross-validation design. The weights were determined on a sample of even-numbered subjects and cross-validated on a sample of odd-numbered subjects, or derived on a sample of odd-numbered subjects and cross-validated on a sample of even-numbered subjects. Six types of analyses were conducted: 1) analyses of variance for each weighted score across the three criterion groups in the cross-validation sample, 2) calculation of coefficient alpha for each weighted score, 3) classification accuracy of using a cutoff score to discriminate between criterion groups using each weighted total score, 4) inspection of the intercorrelations between the various weighted scores, 5) a study of alternate forms reliability for each weighting method applied to the standard scale and an experimental alternative form, and 6) relationship of each weighted score to the profile scales of the MMPI in order to examine concurrent validity.

The SPS is a single page, 36-item rating form. The 36 items include statements that one might use to describe one's feelings and behaviors. Subjects are instructed to rate each item on a four-point Likert scale (None or a little of the time, Some of the time, Good part of the time, and Most or all of the time), according to how often the statement is true for them.

The rating form has two layers with carbon paper between them. The top layer is intended for the client and the bottom layer for the psychometrician. The top layer asks for demographic and identifying information on the client, the client's self-report of major stresses of the last two years, and responses to the 36 items. The bottom layer includes the responses to the 36 questions, spaces to rate the nature, date, and severity of the reported stressors and record previous suicide attempts, and a checklist of the indicators for major depressive episodes from DSM-III.

The SPS is an efficient, quick, and inexpensive test to use. The testing time is somewhat dependent on the respondent, but usually the entire scale can be administered, scored, and interpreted in less than 20 minutes. Part of the efficiency of the scale is due to the two-copy rating form; a key is imbedded in the administrator's part to facilitate scoring.

Because of the self-report nature of the instrument and its susceptibility to distortions, the authors recommend that it *not* be used as the sole method for assessing suicide risk when the individual is suicidal.

Of the four subscales on the SPS, the most helpful is Suicide Ideation, which reflects the extent to which a person reports thoughts or behaviors associated with suicide. These range from a specific mention of plans to more ambiguous items that have been linked to persons who are suicidal. This subscale can give the clinician a sense of how frequently the respondent has suicidal thoughts, some of the reasons for the suicide ideation, and a sense of the extent to which the subject has actually been planning suicide. A high score on this scale should, without a doubt, be followed up by careful clinical interviews. However, low scores must be interpreted with caution because they can represent an attempt to deny or disguise the suicide ideation.

The other three subscales, Hopelessness, Negative Self-Evaluation, and Hostility, help the clinician to understand some of the underlying dimensions of the suicide risk. The development of these subscales stems from the theoretical framework that finds suicide to be a multidimensional phenomenon (Bedrosian & Beck, 1979; Farberow, 1980). The Hopelessness subscale assesses individuals' dissatisfaction with life and their sense of despair about the future. The Negative Self-Evaluation subscale is an assessment of the extent to which individuals feel close to the persons around them and the extent to which it is felt that others feel close to the individuals. All of the items on this subscale are worded in the positive direction and scored in the reverse direction. The Hostility subscale reflects an individual's feelings of hostility, isolation, and impulsivity.

Practical Applications/Uses

The major application of this test is in clinical settings where the clinician suspects that a person may be at risk for suicide. Some suggested settings where this instrument might be used are psychiatric outpatient clinics, inpatient units, prisons, juvenile detention centers, crisis clinics, hospital emergency rooms, geriatric facilities, hospital wards, private offices, suicide prevention centers, and drop-in clinics. It might also be used to monitor an at-risk individual who is being seen on an outpatient basis or as part of followup care for a person who has attempted suicide. It might also be used as an aid in developing a treatment program for someone suspected of being at risk for suicide or someone who has attempted suicide. The subscales are particularly helpful in assessing the individual's particular relationship to suicide and addressing those areas directly. Although the instrument is relatively easy to administer, it should be stressed that its administration—and particularly its interpretation—should be either conducted or directly supervised by a professional with advanced clinical training and experience.

Additionally, the SPS can be used for research. By assessing the particular subscales researchers might become more aware of the underlying dimensions of suicide and better understand procedures for alleviating its stress. Likewise, the effectiveness of a new suicide prevention program could be evaluated in reference to its effect on the reduction of one's overall risk for suicide and assessing its effects on the individual dimensions of suicide risk.

Although the authors do not suggest its use in school counseling, the SPS might be valuable in this area. With the serious outbreaks of suicide within high schools today, a school counselor could administer the instrument to a large number of students in a school and, thus, use it as a preliminary measure to identify students who might be at risk.

The test was developed to be used with adolescents aged 14 years and older and adults. The standardization sample included different ethnic groups, suggesting it is appropriate for different ethnicities. The authors do not discuss any special forms of the test developed for the handicapped, such as a braille form. Because misunderstood terms can be discussed, it might be possible to read the test to someone who is unable to read it. Due to the fact that the response would be made directly to the examiner, this method could reduce the examinee's willingness to respond candidly, but by recording the questions the person could respond in private. None of these alternate methods of administering the instrument have been researched and, thus, one would have to interpret the results with caution. Nevertheless, in the case of suspected suicide any additional clue to the risk can be of help.

The instrument can be administered in an individual setting or in a group setting. However, it should be combined with a private individual interview, including a skilled clinical assessment of the client's history and mental status, when there is any hint that the person is at risk for suicide. The actual administration of the test is a relatively straightforward process because the test is primarily self-administered. Thus, it can be easily administered by a trained paraprofessional or psychiatric technician. However, the ultimate responsibility for its use, administration, and interpretation should be under the direction of a professional with clinical training who should also be reponsible for the clinical interview that coincides with this instrument.

The examiner should determine that the demographic data are correctly recorded at the top, go through several statements with the respondent to assure that the respondent understands the instructions, and leave the respondent to answer the questions alone. Because the test is designed for adolescents and adults it is unlikely that there will be many questions, but if an individual does not understand a statement or a word in a statement, the examiner should explain it in a neutral manner. It is important that the examiner develop and maintain rapport with the test respondent so as to minimize the chance of intentional distortion of the responses, particularly a denial of suicide ideation.

It is recommended that the administrator have the respondent fill out the demographic information and respond to the 36 items before asking for information about the life stressors and suicide ideation. This is done so the respondent is less sensitized to suicide and suicide attempts; less suspicious that the scale is, in fact, assessing suicide risk; and more apt to respond candidly.

The scoring is relatively simple. To score the SPS, the administrator merely separates the two forms of the test and removes the examiner's version. The item weights are given for each item on this form, and the scorer merely counts the numbers of the boxes that the respondent has marked, then converts the raw score to a T-Score, using a table in the back of the test manual (Cull & Gill, 1982).

Machine scoring is not available, though for clinical purposes the scoring is so rapid that computer scoring would not be an advantage. If one were using the instrument for research purposes where large numbers of subjects were being assessed, a computer command could be written easily as a part of the analysis to sum the item responses.

The interpretation of the test results is the most sensitive part of this test. Clinicians should use their own judgment, utilizing the test results only as a guide. This instrument is primarily helpful for the client who has been reluctant to suggest any suicide ideation face-to-face, yet responds at risk on the instrument. When assessing a situation as serious as suicide risk it is preferable to err on the side of suspecting suicide when it is not a risk than to overlook the possibility of suicide when it is a risk.

Technical Aspects

The internal consistency and the split-half reliabilities were assessed using a sample of 1,158 cases (562 normals, 260 psychiatric inpatients, and 336 individuals who attempted suicide). The internal consistency was found to range from .62 to .89 for the individual subscales and to be .93 for the total instrument. The split-half reliability ranged from .58 to .88 for the subscales and was .93 for the total instrument. In each case the Negative Self-Evaluation subscale had the lowest reliability and the Suicide Ideation subscale had the highest reliability (Cull & Gill, 1982).

Test-retest reliability was assessed on two different occasions (Cull & Gill, 1982). The first included a sample of 80 relatively homogeneous individuals who were not suicidal. The time between the initial test and the retest was three weeks, and the reliability was .92. A second assessment of test-retest reliability included a sample of 478 heterogeneous subjects. There was an interval of ten days between the two testings, and the reliability was found to be .94.

Validity was assessed in three different ways (Cull & Gill, 1982): content validity by using item analysis, criterion validity by comparing the responses of the individuals who had attempted suicide with those who had not, and construct validity by comparing the scores on this instrument with scores on other measures of suicide risk.

The assessment of content validity included several steps. The first included qualitatively comparing the individual items on the subscales with the theroretical rationale that had been used to initially develop the measure. Secondly, content relevance and concurrent validity were assessed by correlating the SPS items with an experimental scale on the MMPI designed to assess suicide risk. The subjects were 51 clinical patients (15 males and 36 females), most of whom had attempted suicide. The subjects' scores on the SPS were compared with their scores on the MMPI experimental scale. Correlations ranged from –.19 to .54, with 15 items correlating higher than .30 ($p > .05$).

Of perhaps greater importance with a scale such as this is the ability of the scale to differentiate between those who are at risk and those who are not. The criterion validity was assessed by first obtaining point-biserial correlations between the items and membership in one of the groups, and thus assessing how well each item discriminated between those who had attempted suicide and those who had not. These correlations ranged from a low of .06 to a high of .65, with all relationships being significant except the low item with the .06 correlation. Comparing the subscale scores across three groups (i.e., normals, psychiatric patients, and those who had attempted suicide) found all the differences to be significant at the $p < .001$ level (Zachary, Roid, Cull, & Gill, 1982).

When comparing the SPS with individual clinical subscales of the MMPI, the pattern of correlations was consistent with clinical descriptions of suicidal individuals and with previous research on the use of the MMPI for suicide evaluation. The various subscales on the SPS correlated positively with the Depression, Psychopathic Deviate, Paranoia, and Schizophrenia Scales on the MMPI (Zachary, Roid, Cull, & Gill, 1983). Additionally, because combined scores on the MMPI are often used and the 2-7-8 scale combination (i.e., high scores on the Depression, Psychasthenia, and Schizophrenia Scales), has been found to be an indication of suicidal tendencies (Deurie & Farberow, 1967; Lachar, 1974; Leonard, 1977; Simon & Gilberstadt, 1979), Cull and Gill (1982) compared subjects with this MMPI profile with those who did not have this profile on their SPS scores. They were found to differ at the $p < .001$ level, suggesting the construct validity of this scale.

Critique

The SPS is a brief measure of suicide risk containing four subscales (Hopelessness, Suicide Ideation, Negative Self-Evaluation, and Hostility). It requires only about 20 minutes to administer and score and serves as a valuable addition to a clinical interview when assessing suicide risk. Because it is a self-report questionnaire and answered in private, there is a chance that individuals might be more honest in their responses than they would be in a face-to-face interview. It should be cautioned, however, that this instrument should be used only as an additional aid in assessing the possibility of suicide and that the results should be compared with the clinical interpretation of a trained professional. In no way should the results of this test stand alone as an assessment of suicidal potential. One should also remember that when assessing the risks of suicide and attempting to identify someone who might be at risk it is better to err in the direction of the predicting suicide risk when it is not present and treating it as such, than it is to fail to recognize the risk when it is, in fact, present.

References

Bedrosian, R. C., & Beck, A. T. (1979). Cognitive aspects of suicidal behavior. *Suicide and life-threatening Behavior, 9,* 87-96.

Cull, J. G., & Gill, W. S. (1982). *Suicide Probability Scale.* Los Angeles: Western Psychological Services.

Deurie, A. G., & Faberow, N. L. (1967). Multivariate profile analysis of MMPIs of suicidal and nonsuicidal neuropsychiatric patients. *Journal of Projective Techniques and Personality Assessment, 31,* 81-84.

Farberow, N. L. (1980). *The many faces of suicide: Indirect, self-destructive behavior.* New York: McGraw-Hill.

Lachar, D. (1974). *The MMPI: Clinical assessment and automated interpretation.* Los Angeles: Western Psychological Services.

Leonard, C. V. (1977). The MMPI as a suicide predictor. *Journal of Consulting and Clinical Psychology, 45,* 376-377.

Shneidman, E. S. (1966). Orientations toward death. *International Journal of Psychiatry, 2,* 167-174.

Simon, W. & Gilberstaadt, H. (1958). Analysis of the personality structure of 26 actual suicides. *Journal of Nervous and Mental Diseases, 127,* 555-557.

Weisman, A. D. (1971). Is suicide a disease? *Life-threatening Behavior, 1,* 219-231.

Zachary, R. A., Roid, G. H., Cull, J. G., & Gill, W. S. (1982, August). *Validation of the Suicide Probability Scale.* Paper presented at the annual meeting of the American Psychological Association, Washington, D.C.

Zachary, R. A., Roid, G. H., Cull, J. G., & Gill, W. S. (1983). *Relationship between a brief suicide-risk scale and the MMPI.* Paper presented at the meeting of the Western Psychological Association, San Francisco.

Gene Schwarting, Ph.D.

Project Director, Preschool Handicapped Program, Omaha Public Schools, Omaha, Nebraska.

SYMBOLIC PLAY TEST: EXPERIMENTAL EDITION

Marianne Lowe and Anthony Costello. Windsor, England: NFER-Nelson Publishing Company Ltd.

Introduction

The Symbolic Play Test: Experimental Edition is designed to evaluate the language potential of children aged one-three years who have not as yet developed skills in this area. Its design was to serve as a diagnostic tool while remaining completely independent of both receptive and expressive language. The evaluation depends on the child's interaction with miniature toys and purports to measure nonverbal symbolic thinking.

The authors of the instrument are Marianne Lowe, Department of Psychological Medicine at the Hospital for Sick Children, and Anthony Costello, Medical Research Council Unit on Environmental Factors in Mental and Physical Illnesses—both apparently in England. Biographical information and the qualifications of the authors are not provided, and the only background information on the instrument itself is that it is based on a developmental study (Lowe, 1975) of representational play in infants.

The authors emphasize that the instrument is experimental and should be viewed as a pilot project, with further evaluation and investigation to be conducted. The standardization sample consisted of 241 tests conducted on 137 children with an age range of 12-36 months. The tests were evenly divided as to sex and age level of the children who were enrolled in welfare centers and day nurseries in London. Children known to be physically or mentally handicapped were excluded, with those remaining (number unknown) being randomly assigned to the standardization group. The socioeconomic status of the parents appears to be reasonably distributed, and the sample includes a small number of non-English-speaking parents. Information as to race is not presented, and it is assumed that all children are from an urban environment.

Practical Applications/Uses

Qualifications of examiners are not noted in the manual; however, a background in testing young children and skill in observation would appear appropriate. Because a major purpose of the instrument is to evaluate nonverbal functioning and make comparisons with language development, speech therapists would appear to be the most likely consumers, with psychologists and teachers of young, language-delayed children also being possibilities. The instrument, designed for use with children aged 12-36 months, must be administered individually. Testing time is estimated at 10-15 minutes, and the setting requires a table and chair for the child. Due to the need to manipulate materials, the test may not be appropriate for the physically handicapped.

Directions for administration are very limited, but appear to be adequate for the instrument's purposes. The instrument is administered by presenting the child with specific groupings of miniature toys from the test kit and observing the child's play with these toys. A "warm-up" period is encouraged to develop rapport, and the toys are presented in four preestablished arrangements with no verbal directions. The examiner then evaluates the interactions by 24 preset criteria, interceding only to draw attention to neglected toys. There are no time limits, with situations being ended when the play becomes repetitive or the child indicates boredom. The examiner records the passing or failing of specific play interactions, which vary from five to eight for the various situations. The scoring criteria mainly involve the appropriate uses of the toys (e.g., placing a toy person in a car as opposed to under it). The total number of passes can then be converted into an age score and into standard deviation units by means of tables.

Scoring directions require familiarity with the item criteria, as well as some skill in observation and recording of behavior. It is unclear as to whether "–" scores indicate failure and what to do if a " + " score follows on the same item. The record form is simple and well executed, with space available for observations to be recorded.

Technical Aspects

Test items for each of the four situations form a sequence as to the level of difficulty and have been arranged into Guttman scales. Split-half reliability has been determined for seven age groups and varies from .52 to .92, with the entire scale having a reliability of .81. Test-retest reliabilities for intervals of three, six, nine, and 12 months vary from .71 to .81 (Lowe & Costello, 1976). Standard errors of measurement vary from one to two scale points, depending on chronological age. Validation studies involve the correlation of the *Symbolic Play Test* with the *Reynell Developmental Language Scales* (Reynell, 1969) and with McCarthy's measure of sentence length (McCarthy, 1954). These correlations vary considerably according to chronological age and are highest for the 21-30 month range, with the overall relationships being .28 and .31, respectively. The predictive value of the instrument rests on higher correlations obtained between the three measures with 3-12 month time intervals, which range from .40 to .70 (Lowe & Costello, 1976).

As previously noted, the population involved is from London, raising questions as to the applicability of the norms to children in the United States, particularly those from rural or suburban areas. Likewise, the small size of the norm group must be considered a detriment. Reliability, although less than what is usually considered acceptable, is comparable to that of other instruments designed for very young children. Of greater concern are the very low concurrent validity data and the predictive validity, which, although somewhat higher, is based on another instrument normed in England.

Critique

The Symbolic Play Test is hampered by its standardization sample and to a somewhat lesser extent by the reliability and validity data reported. The test kit itself is well-constructed, with the toys appearing to be appropriate; however, due to their small size, care must be taken that young children do not put them in their mouths. The forms themselves are well-designed, although the scoring system is somewhat vague and requires judgment on the part of the examiner.

This instrument is presented as experimental and should be viewed in that context (even though it is published and available for use to the public). The development of more appropriate norms should be strongly encouraged, and the present norms should be used cautiously. The manual indicates applicability for children raised in non-English-speaking homes, but data are not available to support this position. If these caveats are kept in mind, the Symbolic Play Test could be a useful additional tool for those evaluating the language potential of young children.

References

This list includes text citations as well as suggested additional reading.

Elder, J. L., & Pederson, D. R. (1978). Preschool children's use of objects in symbolic play. *Child Development, 49*, 500-504.

Lowe, M. (1975). Trends in the development of representational play in infants from one to three years—an observational study. *Journal of Child Psychology and Psychiatry, 16*, 33-47.

Lowe, M., & Costello, A. (1976). *Manual for the Symbolic Play Test*. Windsor, England: NFER-Nelson Publishing Company Ltd.

McCarthy, D. (1954). Language development in children. In L. Carmichael (Ed.), *Manual of child psychology* (pp. 492-630). New York: Wiley & Sons.

Reynell, J. (1969). *Manual for the Reynell Developmental Language Scales*. Windsor, England: NFER-Nelson Publishing Company Ltd.

Russell, C., & Russnaik, R. N. (1981). Language and symbolic play in infancy: Independent or related abilities. *Canadian Journal of Behavior Science, 13*, 95-104.

Terrell, B. Y., Schwartz, R. G., Prelock, P. A., & Messick, C. K. (1984). Symbolic play in normal and language-impaired children. *Journal of Speech and Hearing Research, 27*, 424-429.

Udwin, O., & Yule, W. (1982). Validation data on Lowe and Costello's Symbolic Play Test. *Child Care, Health, and Development, 8*, 361-366.

Ungerer, J. A., Zelazo, P. R., Kearsley, R. B., & O'Leary, K. (1981). Developmental changes in the representation of objects in symbolic play from 18 to 34 months of age. *Child Development, 52*, 186-195.

Watson, M. W., & Jaackowitz, E. R. (1984). Agents and recipient objects in the development of early symbolic play. *Child Development, 55*, 1091-1097.

Thomas L. Layton, Ph.D.
Professor of Speech and Hearing Sciences, University of North Carolina, Chapel Hill, North Carolina.

TEST OF LANGUAGE DEVELOPMENT

Donald D. Hammill and Phyllis L. Newcomer. Austin, Texas: PRO-ED.

Introduction

The rationale for the Test of Language Development as reported by the authors (Newcomer & Hammill, 1982; Hammill & Newcomer, 1982) serves four purposes: 1) to identify children who are significantly below their peers in language, 2) to determine children's specific strengths and weaknesses, 3) to document children's language progress as a consequence of special intervention programs, and 4) to serve as a measurement device in research involving language behavior.

The test is available in two editions: Primary (TOLD-P) and Intermediate (TOLD-I). Although they have the same rationale and theoretical model, they contain different subtests, are standardized for different populations, and were designed for different age groups. The TOLD-P contains seven subtests and is intended for use with children aged four years, 0 months to eight years, 11 months, whereas the TOLD-I contains five subtests and is intended for children aged eight years, six months to 12 years, 11 months.

The seven TOLD-P subtests are described as follows:

Picture Vocabulary (25 items): Measures understanding (reception) of single-word meanings (semantics). From a set of four pictures, the child points to the one that best represents the meaning of the stimulus item. For example, if the stimulus item is the word "dome," the child selects from a picture of a castle, a door, a ranch-style house, and a domed capitol building. Approximate time is ten minutes.

Oral Vocabulary (20 items): Measures ability to define (express) common single words (semantics), such as bird, sugar, season, and month. Approximate time is eight minutes.

Grammatic Understanding (25 items): Measures the understanding (reception) of sentences. Although semantics are involved, this subtest places more emphasis on the syntax of the sentence. The child points to the most appropriate picture from a set of three. For example, if the stimuli indicate that a bicycle has been stolen, the child must choose from a picture of someone about to steal the bicycle, someone stealing the bicycle, and the bicycle missing or already stolen. Approximate time is eight minutes.

Sentence Imitation (30 items): Measures ability to produce (express) sentences by imitation, assuming that children produce/imitate sentences that are already part of their linguistic system better than they produce/imitate unfamiliar ones. The examiner says the sentence, and the child repeats it. Approximate time is ten minutes.

Grammatic Completion (30 items): Measures ability to understand (comprehend) common English morphological forms, such as plurals, progressive tense (-ing), past tense (-ed), comparative (-er), possessives, and irregular past. The examiner reads simple sentences and/or part of a sentence (e.g., "I have a mouse. She has a mouse. We have two ________ ."), and the child completes the necessary item (i.e., mice). No pictures are included, which prevents giving the child any additional visual cues. Approximate time is ten minutes.

Word Discrimination (20 items): Measures ability to hear or judge two-word pairs that differ in minimal sound contrasts (e.g., pig-big, sat-sad, conical-comical). No pictures are used. The examiner presents the contrasting pair of words, and the child must judge whether they are the same or different. Approximate time is ten minutes.

Word Articulation (20 items): Measures ability to produce (express) speech sounds (phonemes) that are elicited from stimulus pictures and sentences. For example, the child is presented with a sentence stating that "big kids ride a ________ ." and a picture of a bike. No differentiation is presented for which error sounds are being elicited per test item. Approximate time is five minutes.

The five TOLD-I subtests are described as follows:

Sentence Combining (25 items): Measures the ability to expressively formulate compound sentences from two simple sentences. The examiner produces two or more simple sentences (e.g., "I found a nickel. I found a dime."), and the child is required to combine them into one compound or complex sentence (i.e., "I found a nickel and a dime."). Approximate time is eight minutes.

Characteristics (50 items): Measures higher-order understanding (reception) of words and relationships. Requires child to determine the validity or truth of simple statements spoken by the examiner. Each statement contains a noun and verb phrase with key content words. To succeed, the child must understand the key content words and the relationship between them. For example, the child must listen and decide whether sentences such as "All horses are fast." or "All tunes are melodies." are true or false. The child does not have to correct any false sentences. Approximate time is 12 minutes.

Word Ordering (25 items): Measures expressive syntactic abilities. Requires the child to reorder a series of random words (e.g., "party, fun, was, the") into a complete, correct sentence. The random words range in length from three to seven items. Approximate time is seven minutes.

Generals (25 items): Measures expressive ability for word relationships. Requires child to tell how three words spoken by the examiner are alike (e.g., hot, cold, warm = temperature). Approximate time is 12 minutes.

Grammatic Comprehension (40 items): Measures ability to judge whether a sentence is grammatical or agrammatical. Contains ten grammatically correct and 30 agrammatical sentences (e.g., "You was here yesterday."). The child is not asked to correct the agrammatical sentences, but to identify the spoken sentence as incorrect. Approximate time is 12 minutes.

A two-dimensional model (see Table 1) underlies the TOLD and was validated empirically by the authors. One dimension of the model includes the linguistic areas being tested (i.e., semantics, syntax, and phonology), whereas the other

Table 1

	Linguistic Systems*	
	Listening (Reception)	*Speaking (Expression)*
Semantics	P-Picture Vocabulary I- Characteristics	P-Oral Vocabulary I- Generals
Syntax	P-Grammatical Understanding I- Grammatic Comprehension	P-Sentence Imitation P-Grammatical Completion I- Sentence Combining I- Word Ordering
Phonology	P-Word Discrimination	P-Word Articulation

*Two-dimensional model of language structure used to generate the TOLD subtests.

includes processing areas (i.e., listening and speaking). Although language activities may include both listening and speaking, the authors (Newcomer & Hammill, 1982; Hammill & Newcomer, 1982) suggest that each of the subtests are primarily one or the other.

Newcomer and Hammill (1982) state that they selected the subtests for the TOLD-P on the basis of practical considerations and experimental investigations of the model. However, no reasons are provided for the selection of the five subtests on the TOLD-I.

Subject selection was sufficiently and adequately handled in both tests. The authors took great care to ensure that they selected a broad sample of children who reflected a "normal" population. Subjects were selected from all regions of the United States and controlled for sex differences, residence, race, geographic area, and occupation of parents. The TOLD-P was standardized on 1,836 children, with 198 subjects being represented at the smallest age level (i.e., four years), whereas the TOLD-I was standardized on 871 children, with 166 being the least number per age level.

Practical Applications/Uses

According to the authors (Hammill & Newcomer, 1982; Newcomer & Hammill, 1982), both TOLD tests are designed for use by teachers, counselors, psychologists, language therapists, or other professionals who have had experience administering standardized tests. Examiners should initially practice administering the test no fewer than three times. The tests are designed for individual administration in a quiet environment free from extraneous distractions.

The tests are normed nationally, but the authors suggest that local norms be established for comparative purposes. Both tests are easy to administer and are straightforward in their scoring.

Both the TOLD-P and TOLD-I yield five different types of scores: raw scores, language ages, percentiles, standard scores (set at 10 with standard deviation of 3), and quotients for composite scores. The language ages are obtained from the raw scores across age levels; percentiles represent the distribution that a raw score will fall on a scale up to 100; and composite quotients are scores computed on various combinations of subtests—these scores have a mean of 100 and a standard deviation of 15. The composite quotients include a spoken language quotient (a general index that is a pooling of the five principal subtests), listening quotient, speaking quotient, semantics quotient, and syntax quotient. These composites help to identify specific areas of language deficit.

The authors (Hammill & Newcomer, 1982; Newcomer & Hammill, 1982) offer four cautions regarding interpreting the TOLD: 1) test results should be regarded as hypotheses for further investigation and not definitive information; 2) the tests do not provide a suitable basis for planning instructional programs; 3) the test norms do not indicate why a student's performance is high or low; and 4) poor performance may be due to a variety of reasons and should not necessarily serve as the basis for a disability label.

Case examples for interpreting test scores are provided in both manuals. This is quite helpful, but many more examples are needed before one can feel qualified as an interpreter. It would be helpful if the manual included an appendix containing additional case studies describing various language profiles.

Technical Aspects

Reliability scores were reported in three areas for both the TOLD-P and TOLD-I. The first was internal consistency. On the TOLD-P, two studies (Newcomer & Hammill, 1982; Wong & Roadhouse, 1978) report split-half procedures with Spearman-Brown correction formulas to measure internal consistency. The resulting coefficients were greater than .80 for all subtests except Picture Vocabulary, where coefficients ranged between .61 and .72. Similarly, low coefficients were obtained for two subtests, Oral Vocabulary and Grammatic Understanding, at the five- and eight-year-old groups. For the TOLD-I only one study (Hammill & Newcomer, 1982) reports internal consistency, using a coefficient alpha (N = 200); all of the coefficients were greater than .80. Therefore, the data for both of the TOLD tests suggest good internal reliability.

The second measure of reliability was testing for stability (Hammill & Newcomer, 1982). For the TOLD-P, 21 children were tested twice over a period of five days; on the TOLD-I, 30 children were tested after one week. In both cases, Pearson product-moment coefficients were computed on the raw scores, with coefficients being above the .80 level for all measures. Thus, both TOLD tests are stable instruments.

The third measure of reliability was standard error of measurement. This was reported for both editions (Hammill & Newcomer, 1982; Newcomer & Hammill, 1982). The standard errors were quite small and stable across age levels. However, the authors caution against the internal consistency of the Picture Vocabulary and Grammatic Understanding subtests and the Listening composite on the TOLD-P because of their low reliability scores.

Three measures of validity were reported for both tests: content, criterion-related, and construct. For content validity, the authors (Newcomer & Hammill, 1982) solicited a group of professionals to rate the various subtests along two dimensions of language: 1) semantics or syntax and 2) listening or speaking. The authors found that the two dimensions existed according to how the authors had predicted them in their model. This, they state, provides support for the content validity of their tests.

For criterion-related validity, the authors (Hammill & Newcomer, 1982; Newcomer & Hammill, 1982) compared the two TOLD tests to existing criterion measures. This procedure was done adequately for the TOLD-P because several criterion measures, such as the Peabody Picture Vocabulary Test, Weschler Intelligence Scale for Children-Vocabulary, Northwestern Syntax Screening Test, Detroit Test of Learning Aptitude, Illinois Test of Psycholinguistic Abilities, and Templin-Darley Tests of Articulation, were available for the authors to use. However, it was less adequately done for the TOLD-I because the authors used only their own test, Test of Adolescent Language (TOAL; Hammill, Brown, Larsen, & Wiederholt, 1980). In this instance, the model and test construction for both instruments were similar, leaving one to question the choice of the TOAL as a criterion measure. Furthermore, the TOAL has been published for only two years, which makes it questionable as a well-established test. The resulting correlation coefficients between the TOLD-I and the TOAL were adequate, but the data would have been stronger if the authors had chosen another instrument to validate their tests.

There were more serious problems between the TOLD-P and its criterion measures. Although it should be pointed out that most of the correlations were found to be statistically significant, several of the coefficients were quite low, making one question whether those subtests were measuring similar traits to those reported in the criterion measures. For example, the Grammatic Understanding subtest had a correlation coefficient of .13 at the four-year-old level and .47 at the eight-year-old level when compared to the Northwestern Syntax Screening Test's Reception subtest. In a similar way, the Picture Vocabulary subtest had only a .54 correlation with the Peabody Picture Vocabulary Test at the four-year-old level and .68 correlation at the eight-year-old level. In addition, the Grammatic Completion subtest had a .55 and .49 correlation at the four- and five-year-old levels, respectively, when compared to the Illinois Test of Psycholinguistic Abilities Grammatic Closure subtest (Newcomer & Hammill, 1982).

These subtests, Picture Vocabulary and Grammatic Understanding, as noted earlier, were the ones about which the authors had expressed concern during internal reliability. Having used these subtests clinically, this reviewer questions what they are actually measuring. Both use pictures from which the subject must choose the most appropriate one. The problem is that the graphics are not clear, contain a lot of clutter, and have such poor selections for foils that it makes it difficult to determine whether the child is being asked to demonstrate ability to discriminate visually or to measure proficiency in vocabulary/language comprehension. Because of this, this reviewer deletes these two subtests when administering the TOLD-P and replaces them with the criterion instruments used by the authors in their validation.

The last measure of validity was construct validity. This was demonstrated by reporting increases in mean raw scores across the ages for both tests, with the resulting scores improving progressively as the children became older. Intercorrelations were also computed for construct validity; the results yielded moderate correlations (i.e., in the .40s and .50s), suggesting an interrelatedness to both instruments, but one that is not too related, and also suggesting that each subtest is measuring the same trait. The last measure of construct validity compared both instruments to criterion measures of intelligence and school achievement. The TOLD-P correlated positively and significantly with the Slosson Intelligence Test for Children (Gray, 1978) at or above the .42 level (with most pairwise correlations being above the .70 level) and with the Wechsler Intelligence Scale for Children (Wong & Roadhouse, 1978) at the .56 level for Performance, at the .74 level for Verbal, and at the .70 level for the Full Scale. The TOLD-I was not correlated with any measure of intelligence.

The TOLD-P was also correlated with tests of reading, writing, readiness, and achievement in a series of studies (Boyles & Hammill, 1977; Edmiaston, 1980; Gray, 1978; Magee & Newcomer, 1978; Reid, Hresko, & Hammill, 1981; Wong & Roadhouse, 1978). In all cases, the results were highly significant and of such magnitude (range .42-.68) to support construct validity. The TOLD-I was compared only to seven subtests on the TOAL that related exclusively to reading and writing (i.e., Reading Vocabulary, Reading/Grammar, Writing/Vocabulary, Writing/Grammar, Reading, Writing, and Written Language). Of the correlations, approximately half were significant and above the .35 level, the median being .35. Hammill and Newcomer (1982) maintain that these findings support construct validity of the TOLD-I.

Critique

The authors (Hammill & Newcomer, 1982; Newcomer & Hammill, 1982) provide several cautionary notes regarding the use of their instrument with local norms. These cautions are quite helpful for test users and provide several suggestions for interpreting scores, accounting for situational and student variables, testing the limits, and sharing results. These suggestions should be read before administering the tests. All in all, the authors have an excellent test battery with the exception of the two subtests on the TOLD-P (Picture Vocabulary and Grammatic Understanding). As it is now, these two subtests make it difficult to recommend the entire test as a diagnostic instrument. The TOLD-I is the newer of the two instruments and has not undergone sufficient clinical use to make a thorough and precise judgment of its strengths and weaknesses. Additional validity measures are needed with TOLD-I because the current data are limited to comparisons with a single test, the TOAL.

References

Boyles, C., & Hammill, D. (1977). *Relationship of spoken language abilities to reading comprehension.* Unpublished manuscript, PRO-ED, Austin, Texas.

Edmiaston, R. (1980). *An investigation of the interrelationship of selected aspects of oral and written language.* Unpublished doctoral dissertation, University of Texas at Austin.

Gray, R. (1978). *The relationship of oral language proficiency in five- and six-year-old preschoolers to readiness for school success.* Unpublished doctoral dissertation, University of Texas at Austin.

Hammill, D., Brown, V., Larsen, S., & Wiederholt, J. (1980). *Test of Adolescent Language.* Austin, TX: PRO-ED.

Hammill, D., & Newcomer, P. (1982). *Test of Language Development-Intermediate.* Austin, TX: PRO-ED.

Magee, P., & Newcomer, P. (1978). The relationship between oral language skills and academic achievement of learning disabled children. *Learning Disabilities Quarterly, 1,* 63-67.

Newcomer, P., & Hammill, D. (1982). *Test of Language Development-Primary.* Austin, TX: PRO-ED.

Reid, D., Hresko, W., & Hammill, D. (1981). *The Test of Early Reading Ability.* Austin, TX: PRO-ED.

Wong, B., & Roadhouse, A. (1978). The Test of Language Development (TOLD): A validation study. *Learning Disabilities Quarterly, 1,* 48-61.

John C. Houtz, Ph.D.
Professor of Educational Psychology, Division of Psychological and Educational Services, Graduate School of Education, Fordham University, New York, New York.

THINKING CREATIVELY WITH SOUNDS AND WORDS

E. Paul Torrance, Joe Khatena, and Bert F. Cunnington. Bensenville, Illinois: Scholastic Testing Service, Inc.

Introduction

Thinking Creatively with Sounds and Words (TCSW) is based on theory and research that has been developing over approximately the past 40 years. There have been numerous contributors to the field, but E. Paul Torrance is probably the one individual most associated with the study of creativity, having devoted a lifetime's work to the field. Torrance's efforts have been directed at identifying and understanding the creative potential of the "average person." Torrance's views are well-documented (e.g., Torrance, 1963, 1965, 1979; Torrance & Myers, 1970) and are worth an attempt at summary here.

There are some educators and researchers who are disdainful of the study of creativity, claiming it to be too ethereal a phenomenon, too mysterious or fragile to be subjected to attempts at measurement and manipulation. Torrance believes this is not the case—if we do not try to learn as much as we can about encouraging individuals' creative potential, we may doom our society to decay and eventual extinction. Very few of us can be the type of creative genius like an Einstein or a Mozart, but each of us can become individually more creative, better at solving problems, and more effective in our daily lives.

Torrance believes that the environment plays a critical role in creative thinking. Social forces often stifle creative expression of new ideas, new possibilities. Although change can be threatening to others, it can also be encouraged, cultivated, and rewarded. The environment can just as easily reinforce creative behavior as it can inhibit it. Torrance believes that creativity is a natural life process; if it can be encouraged in the home, in the school, in the society at large, even the so-called "average person" can become more creative, with potentially great benefits to the individual and the culture. He states that, particularly in the schools, teachers can make use of a wide variety of methods and techniques to stimulate creative thinking.

This reviewer wishes to thank Professors Joe Khatena and E. Paul Torrance for their support and assistance in the preparation of this review. These gentlemen certainly practice what they preach about encouraging creative thinking. This reviewer must also thank Mr. Alan Frankel for his help (and creativity) during the work on this review.

The publication of the Torrance Tests of Creative Thinking (TTCT) in 1966 and 1974 marked an important milestone in this field. There now existed a systematic means for assessment of creative potential, which Torrance defines as the "process of becoming sensitive to problems, deficiencies, gaps in knowledge, missing elements, disharmonies, identifying the deficiencies, searching for solutions, making guesses, formulating hypotheses, testing these hypotheses, modifying and retesting them, then communicating the results" (Torrance, 1974, p. 6). The TTCT are based on several important creativity principles, as is the TCSW. Foremost among them is the generation by subjects of a large number of imaginative responses to each stimulus. This ability, termed *ideational fluency* or *divergent production,* is rooted in the theory that if the individual is encouraged to continue responding, the more common, unoriginal responses will be exhibited first and the more unusual, creative responses will come out later.

The TCSW and the TTCT are scored according to the criterion of originality of ideas. This concept is defined by statistical infrequency. If a large number of subjects respond with the same idea to a particular sound or word on the TCSW, then that idea is not regarded as original. On the other hand, if an individual's response is relatively unique among all responses to a particular stimulus, that response is awarded points for originality—the rarer the idea, the more points. Other scoring of the TTCT and TCSW depends on the principle of "creative strength." This quality of an idea comes from the degree of detail or elaboration incorporated into the idea or the variety and flexibility of different elements combined into a coherent wholeness to form the idea.

The TCSW was developed to complement the TTCT, originally titled "How Imaginative Are You?" (E. P. Torrance, personal communication, November 3, 1985). Torrance and Joe Khatena maintain that imagination imagery is a critical aspect of creative thinking (Khatena, 1978, 1982, 1984, in press). Interestingly, the concept of imagery has had a rather checkered history in psychology (Eysenck, 1984), having been both in and out of favor more than once as an appropriate and fruitful topic. With the resurgence of cognitive psychology in the past 25 years, however, imagery has again been considered worthy of study. A book by Miller, Galanter, and Pribram (1960) put the "image" squarely back in the center of modern theories of human problem solving. Later works by cognitive psychologists (see Neisser, 1967, 1976) detailed imagery abilities and phenomena in reliable and revealing fashion.

Now, imagery has been shown to be an important educational variable (Khatena, 1984), affecting how much and how well individuals can learn, remember, and solve problems. Imagination imagery is also a major dimension wherein the individual can combine feelings, emotions, values, attitudes, and other affective elements with the cognitive components of thinking. The mysteries and memories of the unconscious mind may not be well-understood, but psychological theories of creativity have long regarded the vast unconscious as an important, if not the only, source of creation. Imagery may be a "window" to the unconscious (Gowan, 1975).

The TCSW consists of two separate tests: Sounds and Images (SI), developed by E. Paul Torrance and Bert F. Cunnington, and Onomatopaeia and Images (OI), developed by Joe Khatena. Both instruments attempt to measure creativity (originality of responses) by providing individuals with stimuli (sound effects or words) to which they respond by describing what mental "image" or association is created by the stimuli. The individual's responses are scored according to the relative infrequency of the responses in the general population and by a general criterion described by Torrance as "creative strength."

In SI, several familiar and abstract sounds are presented (e.g., the sound of thunder or surf or audio-generator sweep sounds). The sounds are presented several times, each time followed by a pause, during which individuals write down what the sound makes them think about or feel. In OI, common words that have "sound qualities" (onomatopaeic effects such as "boom," "crackle," and "fizzy") are used. As with SI, the stimuli are presented several times to force individuals to generate more and more original responses.

The introductions ("warm-up"), directions, stimulus sounds and words, and pauses are all recorded on a 12", 33 1/3rd r.p.m., long-playing record album. There are two albums (Level I for Grades 3-12 and Level II for adults), each of which has two records (Forms A and B). There is a directions manual and scoring guide (Torrance, 1973b) for each form, as well as a special response booklet for subjects. The norms-technical manual (Torrance, 1973c) contains data for both SI and OI.

Practical Applications/Uses

Level I is intended for subjects between the ages of 8 and 20 years (Grades 3-12) and Level II is intended for older subjects (above high school age). Norms for these age ranges are provided in the norms-technical manual. However, flexibility in application to younger ages for each form (A and B) may be appropriate, depending on the backgrounds and abilities of the subjects to be tested.

The directions manuals clearly state that the SI and OI are to be considered separate tests. No combined score is computed. It is recommended that the two parts of the TCSW be administered at different test sessions. The general instructions recorded for both tests and both forms of each test are similar. They stress creative thinking, and words such as creativity, magic, mystery, music, imagination, images, feelings, excitement, and interesting are used to help subjects understand and warm-up to the task. The recorded scripts for the younger subjects are simpler in some parts but not briefer. The pauses for responses are 15 seconds for adults and 30 seconds for younger subjects. The directions interspersed between the repetitions of the stimuli remind subjects where to write their responses in the answer booklet and encourage them to think of more imaginative, unusual, and original ideas that are different from their previous responses.

There are four different sounds, repeated three times, for each of the two alternate forms of SI, younger version. There are five onomatopaeic words, each repeated four times, for each of the two alternate forms of OI, younger version. In the adult forms, the only difference is that there are ten stimulus words in OI. The sound effects are the same for the younger and adult versions of SI. The five onomatopaeic words on the younger forms of OI are five of the ten words on the adult forms. Both younger and adult forms take approximately 35 to 40 minutes to administer for each separate test (SI and OI).

The directions for both the younger and adult versions of TCSW encourage some degree of flexibility in test administration. Consistent with creativity theory, examiners who wish to assess creative potential in their subjects should make it clear that creative, original, unusual responses are desired. Sufficient "warm-up" time and activities should be provided. The testing situation should be com. rtable, pleasant, and nonthreatening. References by the examiner to "tests" and "grades" should be avoided.

The TCSW may be administered in small to moderately large (approximately 30-40 subjects) groups or individually, as needed. Subjects who cannot write can respond verbally (or in sign) during individualized testing while the examiner (or perhaps appropriate recording equipment) records the responses. All of these issues are clearly presented in the directions manuals.

Scoring of both SI and OI is based on the statistical infrequency of subjects' responses. Each and every idea generated gets a point-value assigned to it. The values range from zero to four: zero is given for irrelevant responses and responses to the particular stimuli that occur 5% or more of the time in the norm population; one point is assigned for responses of 4.99% to 3% frequency; two points are assigned for responses of 2.99% to 2% frequency; three points are assigned for 1.99% to 1%; and four points are assigned for responses that occur less than 1% of the time or that exhibit "creative strength."

What constitutes "creative strength" is difficult to determine. The scoring guides provide a few examples for SI and OI stimuli of what the authors consider responses with creative strength. However, the concept of creative strength is not explained well. To have a good understanding, one needs a thorough background in Torrance's works and the concepts of flexibility and elaboration, as well as statistical infrequency or originality. Ideas with creative strength are not only rare but possess these other qualities.

After a response to each repetition of each stimulus (sounds or words) is assigned a point value, total scores are generated, one for SI and one for OI, by summing all the values in each test. As stated previously, there is no grand total score combining the SI and OI responses.

Technical Aspects

Technical data for the SI and OI are reported separately in the norms-technical manual, although the data are quite similar. The publication date of the TCSW is 1973, and there have been no revisions or updates formally published since then, although one is anticipated in 1986 (J. Khatena, personal communications, Oct. 31, 1985). In 1973, the authors (Torrance, Khatena, & Cunnington, 1973c) reported interjudge, alternate form, and split-half reliabilities in the high .80s and .90s. Test-retest reliabilities over a one-week period were also as high, but over a three-month interval the correlations were much lower. These data were obtained from a variety of samples, children to adult, but the ethnic and social-status backgrounds of the subjects did not vary much. For the most part, the subjects were white and middle-class.

For validity, correlations to several other measures of creative thinking or creative potential are reported in the norms-technical manual. These measures include the Runner Studies of Attitude Patterns, Raven's Progressive Matrices, the

Remote Associates Test, the TTCT, and a variety of creativity self-report checklists and biographical inventories. Generally, correlations of .30s to .50s were obtained between the TCSW and other measures of creativity or creative potential. Lower correlations were obtained between the TCSW and measures of intelligence. Again, the samples providing the data were the same or similar to those for reliability—few minorities or individuals from different socioeconomic levels were involved.

The norm groups for children and adult forms of the TCSW consist of a little over 1,300 individuals from West Virginia, Ohio, Georgia, New Jersey, North and South Carolina, Florida, and New York (a small group from Fordham University). The majority of the subjects were white and middle-class. There was one highly gifted group of individuals aged 12, 13, and 14 years included for comparison. Norms are given for grade levels and for males and females.

Since the 1973 publication of the TCSW, both Torrance and Khatena have continued their research and writing. A number of studies that add more construct validity data to the TCSW have appeared since 1973. These are extensively reviewed in Khatena's publications, *Educational Psychology of the Gifted* (1982), *Imagery and Creative Imagination* (1984), and in a chapter in S. G. Isaken's (Ed.) *Frontiers of Creativity Research: Beyond the Basics* (in press). Numerous topics have been investigated, including the longitudinal development of imagery ability, relationships of various personality characteristics to imagery ability, gender and cultural differences in imagery production, and the effects of training exercises and programs on imagery.

These various studies added much construct validity data, but what have generally been lacking are data related to predictive validity. No predictive validity data were reported in 1973, but Torrance (1982) reports one longitudinal study of third- through sixth-graders in 1961, followed with a questionnaire in 1980. Significant correlations were obtained between SI scores and indicators of young adult creative achievements (CAs). The criteria for CA included a number of publicly recognized creative achievements, quality of CA as rated by several judges, creativeness of future career image, and a number of creative styles of life achievements. Scoring for the SI included originality and a number of other procedures, such as strangeness of images, fantasy images, unusual sensory images, colorfulness of images, and synthesis into coherent whole images.

Khatena also varied the scoring procedures for OI, categorizing the types of analogies used by subjects in their image responses (Khatena, 1982). As expected, direct analogies were most common, with personal, fantasy, and symbolic analogies being used to a much lesser degree. According to Khatena (1982), this type of finding exemplifies how poorly developed our average imaginative abilities are. What great potential there may be if only we would attend to the encouragement of these creative abilities through research and training programs.

Critique

The TCSW is clearly labeled "research edition" and prominently described in the first few pages of the manuals as suitable for research purposes only. Neither the SI nor the OI has been established with sufficient background work for assessment of individual creativity, although the authors do communicate the expectation that the TCSW can be a useful device if used as part of a larger, carefully planned program to develop creative thinking and imagination. The TCSW should be used as an aid to evaluate such programs but not as the sole criterion.

The strengths of the TCSW are its consistency of purpose and design and its simplicity. The TCSW is intended to assess creative imagination potential and be an aural complement to the verbal TTCT. The TTCT and the TCSW are backed by a substantial degree of theory (albeit from a wide variety of individuals, philosophies, and approaches) and research into the creative process. The TCSW makes use of well-established creativity principles in its format and administration and is probably an interesting experience (for a test) for its subjects.

Unfortunately, the technical evidence for the TCSW is not as extensive as for the TTCT. The 1973 norms are inadequate for today's needs. In a way, the expansion of the general awareness for attention to gifted and creative children in the past ten years has made the TCSW seem even more limited. New programs have been created for the disadvantaged gifted, the handicapped gifted, special talent gifted individuals, gifted children with learning and behavior problems, gifted children from minority ethnic and cultural backgrounds, and life-long learning programs, to name just a few. Unfortunately, these types of individuals and groups are not part of the normative samples.

As with other creativity measures, including the TTCT, predictive validity research is needed. As mentioned earlier, only one such study was discovered for the TCSW and that was for the SI only. An obvious recommendation, then, is for more researchers to begin such studies. For the "believers" in the field of creativity, as well as for the benefit of all of us, validity data should be the number one priority.

Finally, Khatena (personal communication, Oct. 31, 1985) and Torrance (personal communication, November 3, 1985) both indicate that continued work is being done to update the norms and publish new scoring procedures. Khatena expects that in 1986 Scholastic Testing Service will have available new TCSW test booklets, manuals, and a cassette version of the recorded sounds and words to replace the phonograph records. These new materials should greatly increase the ease and flexibility of use of the TCSW. This reviewer hopes that one important issue addressed in the new materials will be the concept of "creative strength." Creative strength as a major criterion for awarding the most points during scoring remains poorly described in the current manuals. Only a person well-versed in the creativity literature would feel comfortable identifying creative strength in a response.

In conclusion, the TCSW remains a research instrument, but the field of creative thinking and imagination research remains an exciting and productive one for those individuals such as Torrance and Khatena who are active in and committed to it. The TCSW can be positively and generally recommended for further research and development activities.

References

This list includes text citations as well as suggested additional reading.

Arietti, S. (1976). *Creativity: The magic synthesis.* New York: Basic Books.

Clark, P. M. (1978). Review of Thinking Creatively with Sounds and Words, Research Edition. In O. K. Buros (Ed.), *The eighth mental measurements yearbook* (pp. 376-378). Highland Park, NJ: The Gryphon Press.

Eysenck, M. W. (1984). *A handbook of cognitive psychology.* Hillsdale, NJ: Lawrence Erlbaum.

Gowan, J. C. (1975). *Trance, art, and creativity.* (Available from the author, 9030 Darby Ave., Northridge, CA 91324)

Guilford, J. P. (1967). *The nature of human intelligence.* New York: McGraw-Hill.

Guilford, J. P. (1977). *Way beyond the IQ: Guide to improving intelligence and creativity.* Buffalo, NY: Creative Education Foundation.

Khatena, J. (1978). *The creatively gifted child: Suggestions for parents and teachers.* New York: Vantage Press.

Khatena, J. (1981). *Creative imagination imagery actionbook.* Starkville, MS: Allan Associates.

Khatena, J. (1982). *Educational psychology of the gifted.* New York: Wiley & Sons.

Khatena, J. (1984). *Imagery and creative imagination.* Buffalo, NY: Creative Education Foundation.

Khatena, J. (in press). Research potential of imagery and creative imagination. In S. G. Isaken (Ed.), *Frontiers of creativity research: Beyond the basics.* Buffalo, NY: Creative Education Foundation.

Miller, G. A., Galanter, E., & Pribram, K. (1960). *Plans and the structure of behavior.* New York: Holt, Rinehart, & Winston.

Neisser, U. (1967). *Cognitive psychology.* New York: Appleton-Century-Crofts.

Neisser, U. (1976). *Cognition and reality: Principles and implications of cognitive psychology.* San Francisco: W. H. Freeman.

Smith, M. L. (1978). Review of Thinking Creatively with Sounds and Words, Research Edition. In O. K. Buros (Ed.), *The eighth mental measurements yearbook* (pp. 378-379). Highland Park, NJ: The Gryphon Press.

Torrance, E. P. (1963). *Education and creative potential.* Minneapolis: University of Minnesota Press.

Torrance, E. P. (1965). *Rewarding creative behavior: Experiments in classroom creativity.* Englewood Cliffs, NJ: Prentice-Hall.

Torrance, E. P. (1974). *The Torrance Tests of Creative Thinking.* Lexington, MA: Personnel Press.

Torrance, E. P. (1979). *The search for satori and creativity.* Buffalo, NY: Creative Education Foundation.

Torrance, E. P. (1982). 'Sounds and images' productions of elementary school pupils as predictors of the creative achievements of young adults. *Creative Child and Adult Quarterly, 7*(1), 8-14.

Torrance, E. P. (1985). *Cumulative bibliography: Thinking Creatively with Sounds and Words.* Athens, GA: Georgia Studies of Creative Behavior.

Torrance, E. P., Khatena, J., Cunnington, B. F. (1973a). *Thinking Creatively with Sounds and Words.* Bensenville, IL: Scholastic Testing Service, Inc.

Torrance, E. P., Khatena, J., & Cunnington, B. F. (1973b). *Thinking Creatively with Sounds and Words: Directions manual and scoring guide.* Bensenville, IL: Scholastic Testing Service, Inc.

Torrance, E. P., Khatena, J., & Cunnington, B. F. (1973c). *Thinking Creatively with Sounds and Words: Norms-technical manual.* Bensenville, IL: Scholastic Testing Service, Inc.

Torrance, E. P., & Myers, R. E. (1970). *Creative learning and teaching.* New York: Dodd, Mead, and Company.

James E. Organist, Ph.D.
Adjunct Assistant Professor, Department of Rehabilitation, College of Education, University of Arizona, Tucson, Arizona.

WIDE RANGE INTEREST-OPINION TEST

Joseph F. Jastak and Sarah Jastak. Wilmington, Delaware: Jastak Associates, Inc.

Introduction

Joseph F. and Sarah R. Jastak are the authors of the Wide Range Interest-Opinion Test (WRIOT), which is published by Jastak Associates, Inc., formerly Guidance Associates of Delaware, Inc. The WRIOT was copyrighted in 1972, and a revised edition of the manual was published in 1979.

At the time of this review, one form of the WRIOT is available and is described as being appropriate for children (Grades K-12) and adults. The test consists of a 154-page picture booklet and an answer sheet. It can be administered individually or in groups of up to 30-40 examinees. The estimated time for individual administration is 40 minutes, with group administration requiring approximately 50-60 minutes. the WRIOT can be either hand scored with stencils or computer scored by the publisher.

The WRIOT was designed to measure work interests. It is reading-free, consists of 450 pictures arranged in 150 combinations of three, and measures subjects' strengths on 18 interest and eight attitude clusters. The WRIOT can also be administered using a 35mm film strip. The work activities portrayed in the pictures are designed to cover as many areas and levels of human activity as possible. The pictures consist of line drawings of individuals performing certain work activities within a specific context, but some leisure-type activities are also included. The work activities portrayed in the pictures are purported to be representative of those listed in the *Dictionary of Occupational Titles* (DOT; U.S. Department of Labor, 1977). The WRIOT manual also includes a list of specific DOT job titles for each of the 18 vocational interests clusters.

It appears that the authors' major rationale for developing a pictorial format for assessing interests relates to perceived limitations inherent in verbal approaches. For example, they assert that WRIOT pictures evoke direct identification with the portrayed activities that are presumed to be relatively independent of language-related lexigraphic and semantic distortions. Presumably, examinee responses are more personalized and less subject to influences from external factors, including expectations of parents, teachers, relatives, and friends. The theoretical basis articulated by the Jastaks for the pictorial approach used in the WRIOT is not clearly developed. Little empirical evidence is cited supporting the value of such an approach to the measurement of interests. In all fairness to the Jastaks, the use of pictorial approaches in the measurement of career interests is a relatively new development. Much research is needed before definite conclusions regarding the validity of such approaches can be reached.

Practical Applications/Uses

Due to the broad range of work and leisure activities portrayed in the pictures, the WRIOT is regarded as appropriate for all age groups and socioeconomic levels, as well as with lower functioning and/or individuals with disabilities (e.g., persons with deficits in intellectual ability, learning disabled, deaf or hearing impaired, and emotionally disturbed).

The WRIOT test booklet and manual (Jastak & Jastak, 1979) are relatively well-designed to enhance understanding. The instructions presented in the manual are straightforward, with a vocabulary level that is of average difficulty. One potential problem has to do with the examinee's capability of retaining all of the directions throughout the testing session. For example, the manual directs the examiner to provide instructions to the examinee that include nine separate elements. Given lower functioning examinees, who may have receptive language difficulties or memory problems, or who may be experiencing situationally based anxiety, these instructions may be excessive when verbalized in one presentation. Some of the pictures are also ambiguous, requiring the examiner to provide further explanation. This could prove problematic during group administration or if the examinee were unsupervised when taking the inventory.

With respect to administration of the WRIOT, examinees are asked to indicate which one of the three activities they like least and which one they like best. Responses are recorded on the answer sheet by the examinee or the examiner if necessary. Males and females are given the same pictures, but the results are analyzed differently as a function of examinee sex.

Hand scoring is done with a set of 24 stencils. The directions provided for scoring are generally adequate with the following exceptions: Instructions for scoring are not specific enough with respect to lining up the stencils carefully on the answer sheet, resulting in easily made scoring errors; 2) scoring instructions for the final category (i.e., Interest Spread) are located in a different place in the manual; and 3) instructions for the Interest Spread category are somewhat general and vague.

The WRIOT provides a client profile that includes scores on 18 occupational cluster descriptions and eight work attitude categories. Raw scores are converted to T-Scores using the appropriate norm tables from the manual. The T-Scores are then identified on the profile as falling into seven descriptive categories ranging from "Very Low" to "Very High".

Technical Aspects

The face validity of the WRIOT for both males and females is good. The items reflect a range of work activities that are familiar to most examinees. The fact that the format is nonverbal is motivating for individuals who have reading difficulties or a conditioned aversion to standard psychometric approaches.

The section of the WRIOT manual devoted to reliability contains a rather lengthy discussion where the authors basically assert that reliability measures are neither as accurate nor as important as they are made out to be. The rationale for their arguments is not very persuasive. After rejecting the importance of reliability data, the authors go on to report split-half reliability coefficients for 25 subtest areas ranging from .82 to .95, demonstrating that the scales are homogeneous. The sample utilized for the reliability study included 150 males and 150 females. Although it is not totally clear in the manual, this group was apparently comprised of adults.

The only information presented in the manual with respect to validity involves a study comparing the WRIOT and Geist Picture Interest Inventory (Geist, 1964). For a sample size of 100 (55 males and 45 females), correlations presented ranges from –.03 to .61. Very little descriptive information listing reference characteristics of the sample utilized in the concurrent validity study is provided. As was the case with reliability, the authors embark on a rather unconvincing generalized discussion devoted to discounting most validity concepts and how difficult it is to determine the statistical validity of a test. With respect to the WRIOT, it is asserted by the authors that correlational methods cannot attest to the clinical adequacy of the instrument. Basically, they argue that the instrument must be validated on a daily basis by clinicians who utilize it.

Original (i.e., 1972) norms for the WRIOT included tenth- and eleventh-grade high-school students and adults. Separate norms were available for males and females. The original standardization group consisted of 1,289 males and 1,077 females.

The 1979 revised manual presents more extensive normative data, including seven separate age range norm tables for males and females. The breakdown of age ranges is 5-7, 8-11, 12-15, 16-19, 20-24, 25-34, and 35 and older. The number sampled in each age category ranges from 100 to 3,134, and the total sampling for all age ranges is 9,184. Conversions from cluster raw scores to T-Scores are provided. The manual also reports data on three homogeneous subgroups, including prison inmates (N = 100), priesthood applicants (N = 63), and vocational students (N = 32).

Critique

The WRIOT has a number of attributes that make it a useful instrument in assessing interests for the purposes of vocational exploration and career planning. Its nonverbal format, straightforward administration approach, and the ease and convenience of hand scoring are definite strengths. The WRIOT items also cover a representative sample of work and human activities, making it appealing to a variety of examinees and clients. It is particularly appropriate for adult rehabilitation populations, including individuals with intellectual limitations and learning disabilities, and persons who are prelingually deaf.

It seems that many users are drawn to the rather obvious attributes mentioned above and overlook serious deficiencies that compromise the utility of the WRIOT. A majority of deficits involves a lack of supporting technical data. For example, the authors articulate a rather lengthy, but unconvincing, argument aimed at rejecting the need for statistical evidence attesting to the reliability and validity of the instrument. They then provide statistical data from single reliability and validity studies.

Based on reported reliability coefficients, the WRIOT scales are of high internal consistency. Unfortunately, no specific reference data other than sex are presented on the sample used in the reliability study. Presumably, the population was made up of adults. The user is left at a disadvantage when attempting to determine how consistent the WRIOT might be with various examinee and client subgroups (e.g., different age groups, persons with disabilities, and racial/ethnic minorities). Because the inventory is viewed as especially appropriate for rehabilitation populations, one wonders why specific reliability data are not available on such aforementioned subgroups.

Problems similar to those mentioned above hold with respect to validity. The single study comparing WRIOT and Geist Picture Inventory scores produced a list of modest correlation coefficients that is not very revealing. Additionally, no reference data on characteristics of the sample utilized other than sex are provided. In their discussion, the authors tend to discount the value of the coefficients and assert that the instrument will need to be validated daily by those who use it.

A major criticism advanced by Zytowski (1978) in his critique of the WRIOT relates to a lack of adequate norms. To a large extent, the 1979 restandardization addressed this criticism, as more comprehensive norms comprised of seven age groups are available and published in the revised manual (1979). The user is in the position of not having specific reference characteristics of the normative groups other than age and sex. The authors purport that no attempt was made to obtain a representative national sampling but claim that groups were in no way restricted to selected economic, intellectual, or racial populations. Without descriptive data, it is difficult to determine the applicability of the norms with respect to a variety of examinee or client characteristics, including socioeconomic level, disability, minority/ethnic status, and geographical location. The authors do indicate that a majority of the norm group had been examined with a variety of intelligence or personality measures. Unfortunately, none of this data is provided in the manual.

References

Geist, H. (1964). *Geist Picture Interest Inventory: Men and Woman.* Los Angeles: Western Psychological Services.

Jastak, J. F., & Jastak, S. R. (1979). *Wide Range Interest-Opinion Test manual.* Wilmington, DE: Jastak Associates, Inc.

United States Department of Labor. (1977) *Dictionary of occupational titles.* Washington, DC: U.S. Government Printing Office.

Zytowski, D. T. (1978). Review of Wide Range Interest-Opinion Test. In O. K. Buros (Ed.), *The eighth mental measurements yearbook* (pp. 1641-1643). Highland Park, NJ: The Gryphon Press.

Antonio E. Puente, Ph.D.
Assistant Professor of Psychology, University of North Carolina at Wilmington, Wilmington, North Carolina.

WISCONSIN CARD SORTING TEST

David A. Grant and Esta A. Berg. Odessa, Florida: Psychological Assessment Resources, Inc.

Introduction

The Wisconsin Card Sorting Test (WCST) is a test of abstract abilities and "shift set" used for both normal and brain-damaged individuals. The test focuses on learning strategies for color, form, and number sorting.

The WCST was developed originally to assess complex cognitive strategies in normals. Unfortunately, numerous versions of the test have been and are currently available, and as a consequence standardization and normative information has been relatively difficult to obtain. Each laboratory or clinic has developed specific administration methods aided with local norms.

According to Heaton (1981), variations have existed according to 1) response cards and deck sizes; 2) order of cards within decks; 3) use of a card-sorting tray; and 4) criteria for shifting sorting strategies, number and order of sorting, categories, and critieria for test completion. In addition, Heaton reports numerous variations for scoring the WCST, including 1) overall measures of success, 2) measures of perseverative tendencies, and 3) measures of nonperseverative sources of error. Individuals responsible for the early WCST versions include E. A. Berg, David A. Grant, Brenda Milner, Ralph Tarter, and Hans Teuber. Of these, Berg (1948) is credited with the first version of the WCST, which she based on Harry Harlow's Wisconsin General Test Apparatus (Harlow, 1959). Harlow used the apparatus to examine learning set problems, as well as reversible shifts in learning strategies. This apparatus has since been adopted to test memory and visual perception abilities in both monkeys and humans.

The current version of the WCST is authored by David A. Grant and Esta A. Berg. The new manual is authored by Robert K. Heaton of the University of Colorado. A standardization sample of 208 inpatients with brain disorders and 150 normal controls were used with the latest version. Approximately half of the brain-damaged group had focal frontal lesions, whereas the other half had nonfrontal lesions. The controls were paid volunteers with no central nervous system dysfunction. The use of specific test protocols with substantial normative information clearly provides the most significant psychometric advancement of the test to date.

No other forms of the tests are currently available from the publisher. However, versions of this test can be relatively easily adapted to sensory-impaired (including hearing-impaired) populations. All that is needed for this test to be adapted for use with other populations is a translation of verbal instructions. Although cross-cultural norms would assist in the adaptation of the WCST to other cultures, its relative culture-free nature makes such norms useful but not necessary.

The test is comprised of response cards and a scoring and recording form. There are 128 cards divided into two identical decks of 64 cards each. Each card has one to four figures (plus sign, star, circle, or triangle) in one of four colors: red, green, yellow, or blue. On the back of each card is a number that identifies the standard order in which the stimuli should be presented. According to the test manual (p. 19), "no two response cards in succession have the same color, form or number." In addition to the two decks of response cards, four stimulus cards are also provided. A one-page scoring and recording form allows the examiner to record demographic and response data. The response portion is subdivided into seven columns containing space for recording 128 responses. Each item on the response form is labeled C (color), F (form), N (number), and O (other). The materials are housed in a sturdy 8¾" x 11¼" cardboard box.

This test is designed to be administered to adults. Furthermore, there is a strong indication that age is related to WCST scores. Strong positive correlations were found by Heaton (1981) between age and total errors, perseverative error, percentage of perseverative errors, and perseverative responses for both normal and brain-damaged subjects. Statistically significant negative correlations were observed between age and categories achieved and percentage of conceptual level responses. Presumably in anticipation of these findings, Grant and Berg (1948) provided simplistic instructions for the administration of the WCST to children. It is important, nevertheless, to note that the mean normative age for normals in the Heaton sample was 35.9 and for brain-damaged individuals 42.1; thus, adequate norms for children are not yet available. The test is designed so that a variety of difficulties are presented to the subject; however, education and full scale IQ are generally negatively correlated with the WCST measures. Therefore, the achievement of basic sorts or categories may be difficult for low-functioning individuals.

Practical Applications/Uses

The WCST is an instrument widely applicable to the study of conceptual ability, or "learning to learn." One would expect the test to be of use in a wide variety of settings, including private practice, mental-health centers, hospitals, and educational settings. Although there are no restrictions to its use, it is probably most applicable to the understanding of cognitive issues in individuals suspected of brain dysfunctions. Numerous mental-health professionals may find the WCST of use, but it has been developed for those with neuropsychological interest, especially those focusing on frontal-lobe dysfunction. The WCST could be used in the diagnosis of dysfunction due to neural complication in general, as well as in following progress in rehabilitation efforts. One application that warrants more attention is the use of the WCST to assess cognitive dysfunction in schizophrenics where it perhaps could be used to provide not only diagnostic data, but prognostic data. Of added interest with this population is the use of the WCST to determine changes of cognitive abilities due to neuroleptic drug treatment. In addition, the use of the WCST with the learning-disabled populations should also be explored because the specific ability of this test to measure "learning to learn" provides a useful tool for assessing learning disabilities.

According to Heaton (1981), the WCST was developed to assess cognitive abilities in general and abstraction and learning strategies in particular. Six specific variables purport to measure these factors: correct (total number of correct responses), errors (total number of errors), perseverative responses (responses that are perseverative), nonperseverative errors (incorrect responses that are not perseverative), perseverative errors (incorrect responses that are perseverative), and categories (from 0 to 6 categories, two each for color, form, and number).

The test should be administered individually in a quiet room or office. It is not intended for group application or for situations where distractions occur. As indicated earlier, a psychologist, especially a neuropsychologist, is best suited for the administration of the test. However, a well-trained technician could probably suffice, especially in research settings.

Although the WCST can be used easily with a variety of clinical populations, especially those with cognitive deficits, it does require that the patient have adequate vision and upper extremity control. Thus, the test may pose difficulty for the elderly or for those with skeletal, muscular, joint, or connective-tissue disease. Its application to blind populations, at least in the current state, appears impractical.

The administration of the WCST is composed of two basic steps. First, patients are instructed to take the top card from one of the decks and match it to one of the four stimulus cards placed in front of them. The examiner then responds affirmatively or negatively, depending on whether or not a correct sort is achieved. After the patient completes ten consecutive sorts, the scoring criterion shifts from color to form, then to number. The test terminates when either six complete sets of sorts have been completed or when the 128 cards have been sorted by the patient. Although the test is not timed, the examiner must maintain a steady and moderate sorting procedure. This requires the examiner to score the patient's responses (which requires some practice) simultaneously. In most instances, the test administration should take no more than one hour. Length of administration, of course, depends on the patient's response rate.

The recording of the subject's responses takes practice and requires keen attention. The scoring of the responses can be accomplished more leisurely, but requires a significant understanding of variables scored. If examiners were using the test for the first time, it would be useful for them to refine scoring procedures by scoring approximately ten records that have already been scored. The first few records whould then be scored carefully. Once the procedure is understood, scoring should take no more than a few minutes. A well-practiced test administrator can accelerate the scoring process by keeping tally of sorts while coding the subject's individual responses.

WCST scoring is accomplished in several stages. First, the total number of responses and errors are recorded. Next, the perseverative responses and errors are counted. The operational definition of perseverative is "one that would have been correct in the previous stage" (Heaton, 1981, p.22). Two exceptions exist: 1) a correct consecutive response within a sorting category and 2) three unambiguous, incorrect consecutive sorts relative to either a correct or a previously incorrect sort. The final score reflects the total number of sorts completed. Several "experimental" scores are described by Heaton (1981), including percent of perseverative errors, trials to complete first category, percentage of conceptual level responses, failure to maintain set, and "learning to learn." Of these, the last score may have the greatest application over a wide variety of populations due to assessment of the efficiency of learning strategies. At the current time there are no machine-scoring systems available; therefore, the test must be scored by hand.

Interpretation is largely based on the objective scores of the basic measures outlined earlier. Of these, perseverative scores are most useful when using cutoff scores. Several limitations of interpretation including faking positive and faking negative, are addressed by the manual. Clinical judgment should supplement the objective information, although strict objective interpretation of the WCST using numerical data is possible. As indicated earlier, coding and scoring are by far the most complicated aspects of this test. As with most neuropsychological tests, however, the more training the examiner has, the more sophisticated the interpretation will be. This is especially true when ancillary information (e.g., neurological findings) are to be integrated with test results.

Technical Aspects

According to Heaton (1981), a total of 358 patients were included in the normative studies, with 208 patients having cerebral lesion and 150 being normal controls. The brain-damaged group was divided into two groups: 94 subjects with diffuse damage and 114 with focal lesions. These two groups were further divided into frontal lobe (N = 43), nonfrontal lobe (N = 35), and frontal and nonfrontal area (N = 36). The types of lesion ranged from tumors to infectious diseases (e.g., meningitis). The mean age for all brain-damaged subjects was 42.1 years, and the mean educational level was 12.7. Normal paid volunteers were carefully screened to avoid the inclusion of neurological disorders. These individuals had a mean age of 35.9 years and a mean educational level of 13.9. Participants were administered a variety of psychological tests by trained technicians of the neuropsychology laboratory at the University of Colorado Health Sciences Center. The psychological tests included the Wechsler Adult Intelligence Scale and the Halstead-Reitan Battery.

Means and standard deviations were provided for each demographic and full scale IQ, the Halstead-Reitan Impairment Index, and ten separate WCST variables. These variables included categories achieved, total errors, perseverative errors, percentages of perseverative errors, nonperseverative errors, perseverative responses, trials to first category, percentage of conceptual level responses, "learning to learn," and failures to maintain set. Additionally, mean percent error scores were presented for each category for brain-damaged and normal groups. Finally, correlations were computed between the previously outlined WCST variables, demographic variables, and neuropsychological variables. Age and educational variations were provided according to key WCST measures. Cutoff scores were provided with correct classification in the 70% plus range. False positive and false negative classifications were carefully considered.

No test-retest, alternate form, split-half, or other forms of reliability were presented. Of course, the actual WCST protocol presents split-half and related reliabilities from being computed. Also, practice effects and retest issues were not presented. However, considering the procedures used by Heaton (1981), content validity appears well established. Criterion-related validity is well established due to rigorous subject selection and comparison to summary neuropsychological measures. Construct validity is addressed in a general fashion by the correlation of the WCST measures to Wechsler and Halstead-Reitan scores. Overall, reliability measures are not presented. Despite the fact that internal consistency may be difficult to assess, comparison over time and a comparable alternate form (beyond short forms of the WCST) may be an area that could be addressed in the future. Of course, Heaton's (1981) standardized version of the WCST will go a long way in allowing these issues to be adequately addressed.

Critique

Although it is important to note that the WCST does not replace the Halstead Category Test, there is strong evidence that the WCST is an excellent addition to any library of tests. As Robinson, Heaton, Lehman, and Stilson (1980, p. 614) state, the WCST is not only a "fairly good screening test for brain damage, it is probably the most efficient test for assessment of perseverative function."

The WCST is an excellent test of abstraction and "learning to learn." Although it has gained popularity in neuropsychological circles, the overall use is still quite restricted. The use of this test in answering cognitive questions and predicting efficacy of rehabilitation programs (especially those requiring retraining of function) is needed. The application of this test to other populations (e.g., schizophrenics) also seems warranted. Finally, the use of the WCST in nonneuropsychological settings, most notably educational environments, appears promising. Although information on reliability is limited, there is strong support for the validity of the WCST. The standardized version of the WCST should go far in popularizing the test in both research and clinical settings.

References

This list contains text citations as well as suggested additional reading.

Beaumont, J. G. (1981). A Pascal program to administer the Wisconsin Card Sorting Test. *Current Psychological Reviews, 38*, 113-115.

Berg, E. A. (1948). A simple objective test for measuring flexibility in thinking. *Journal of Abnormal Psychology, 39*, 15-22.

Drew, E. A. (1976). The effect of type and area of brain lesions on Wisconsin Card Sorting Test performance. *Cortex, 10*, 159-170.

Grant, D. A., & Berg, E. A. (1948). A behavioral analysis of degree of reinforcement and ease of shifting to new responses in a Weigl-type card sorting problem. *Journal of Experimental Psychology, 38*, 404-411.

Grant, D. A., & Berg, E. A. (1981). *Wisconsin Card Sorting Test.* Odessa, FL: Psychological Assessment Resources, Inc.

Harlow, H. F. (1959). The development of learning in the rhesus monkey. *American Scientist, 47*, 459-479.

Heaton, R. K. (1981). *Wisconsin Card Sorting Test manual.* Odessa, FL: Psychological Assessment Resources, Inc.

King, M. C., & Snow, W. G. (1981). Problem-solving tasks performance in brain-damaged subjects. *Journal of Clinical Psychology, 37*, 400-404.

Jones, B., Parsons, O. A., & Tarter, R. E. (1972). Cognitive deficits in chronic alcoholics. *Toxicomanies, 5*, 335-343.

Milner, B. (1963). Effects of different brain lesions on card sorting. *Archives of Neurology, 9*, 90-100.

Nelson, H. E. (1976). A modified card sorting test sensitive to frontal lobe defects. *Cortex, 12*, 313-324.

Pendleton, M. G., & Heaton, R. K. (1982). A comparison of the Wisconsin Card Sorting Test and the Category Test. *Journal of Clinical Psychology, 38*, 392-396.

Robinson, A. L., Heaton, R. K., Lehman, R. A., & Stilson, D. W. (1980). The utility of the Wisconsin Card Sorting Test in detecting and localizing frontal lobe lesions. *Journal of Consulting and Clinical Psychology, 48*, 605-614.

Tarter, R. E. (1973). An analysis of cognitive deficits in chronic alcoholics. *Journal of Nervous and Mental Disease, 157*, 138-147.

Tarter, R. E., & Parsons, O. A. (1971). Conceptual shifting in chronic alcoholics. *Journal of Abnormal Psychology, 77*, 71-75.

Paul C. Hager, Ph.D.
Associate Dean for Academic Affairs, Berea College, Berea, Kentucky

---

WOODCOCK-JOHNSON PSYCHO-EDUCATIONAL BATTERY

Richard W. Woodcock and Mary Bonner Johnson. Allen, Texas: DLM Teaching Resources.

Introduction

The Woodcock-Johnson Psycho-Educational Battery (WJPEB) is a comprehensive, individually administered set of standardized tests designed to measure the concepts of cognitive ability, scholastic aptitude, academic achievement, scholastic/nonscholastic interests, and independent functioning. It is intended for both handicapped and nonhandicapped populations from infancy through age 60 years and over. For the most part, the WJPEB is norm-referenced rather than criterion-referenced. Woodcock states that the major uses of the battery include ". . . individual assessment, selection and placement, individual program planning, guidance, appraising gains or growth, program evaluation, and research" (1978, p. 4). The battery consists of four parts: Tests of Cognitive Ability (I), Tests of Achievement (II), Tests of Interest Level (III), and Scales of Independent Behavior (IV).

The WJPEB scales were developed by a team of specialists, with Richard W. Woodcock as senior author. The first three parts were developed by Woodcock and Mary Bonner Johnson. Woodcock received his Ed.D. in psycho-education and statistics from the University of Oregon. He served as Professor of Special Education, senior researcher and acting director of the Institute on Mental Retardation, and director of the Research Group on Sensori-Motor Disorders and Adaptive Behavior at George Peabody College of Vanderbilt University. Since 1972, Woodcock has been director of Measurement/Learning/Consultants. Johnson is assistant director of Measurement/Learning/Consultants.

Part IV (Scales of Independent Behavior) was developed by Woodcock and three other authors: R. H. Bruininks, R. F. Weatherman, and B. K. Hill. Bruininks, who received his Ph.D. in special education from Peabody/Vanderbilt, is presently chair of the educational psychology department and a professor at the University of Minnesota. He has served as director of the Developmental Disability Planning Office, Minnesota State Planning Agency. R. F. Weatherman, who holds an Ed.D. in special education from Michigan State University, is currently Professor of Educational Psychology at the University of Minnesota and principal investigator for the Minnesota Severely Handicapped Delivery System Project. B. K. Hill, who received his M.A. and is a doctoral student in educational psychology at the University of Minnesota, has worked in a number of professional organizations concerned with the handicapped.

The WJPEB was developed to meet the need for a comprehensive, wide-age range set of measures that would be useful in a variety of settings. According to Woodcock (1978), the broad criteria serving as guides to the instrument's development included a broad set of measures that could provide a comprehensive psycho-educational evaluation from preschool through adult levels; high technical quality with APA standards followed at all times; packaged materials for ease of administration by persons with minimal psychometric experience; subtests and clusters designed to be administered separately if a comprehensive assessment is not required; and reporting procedures designed so that individual scores would be presented with due regard to commonly accepted score precision (i.e., in terms of SE_m and percentile bands).

Data for Parts I-III were gathered from 4,732 subjects from 49 communities selected from 18 states in 1976 and 1977. Subjects aged 6-17 years (N = 3,577) were chosen from 42 communities. Preschoolers (N = 555) and adults aged 18-65+ years (N = 600) were selected from seven additional communities. The norms for all three parts are based on the same sample of subjects, allowing for direct comparison of groups or individuals across all parts of the battery. The standardization sample for Part IV is based on a different sample of 1,700 subjects from over 40 communities tested in the early 1980s. The communities and settings for all four parts were selected so as to approximate the rural/urban, race and sex composition, regional representation, and socioeconomic characteristics of the 1970 census data as closely as possible. Although the samples for Parts I-III did not include severely handicapped subjects unless they were "mainstreamed," Part IV norms incorporated extensive samples of handicapped subjects, including the moderately-severely handicapped (Woodcock, 1978; Bruininks, Woodcock, Weatherman, & Hill, 1984).

After battery objectives were determined, specifications were developed to meet these objectives. Pools of items for each subtest were developed and preliminary forms were prepared and administered. The first preliminary form was administered to a few subjects at all levels. From the data gathered, a calibration-norm battery was prepared and administered to 1,000 subjects chosen from the norm samples. As a result of an extensive data analysis, some items and two subtests were dropped because they contributed little or nothing to the battery's discriminating power. Additional items were added to eight subtests, primarily at the lower and upper ranges. Validity studies with normal and clinical samples were also carried out at this stage. Additional redundant items were dropped after another 2,000 subjects were tested and data reanalyzed using the Rasch model. Because the Rasch procedure 1) allows the researcher to identify items that do not fit the test model and need to be discarded or revised and 2) specifies the probability that subjects will correctly answer an item based on their abilities, item difficulty and subject ability are measured on the same scale, permitting the development of equal-interval scales of test items. In general, 5-10% of the items were dropped in the final version (Hessler, 1984). The final correlation, multiple-regression, factor, and other analyses were carried out on the total sample of over 4,000 subjects, with a similar procedure followed for Part IV. At the time of this review, there have been no revisions of the battery, except for the addition of Part IV in 1984 and the development of a Spanish form (Woodcock-Johnson Spanish Educational Bateria) for Parts I and II covering ages 6-18 years.

The complete battery, consisting of three flip-page easel books designed to stand on the table during administration, is individually administered in its entirety or as single tests or clusters to meet specific appraisal needs. Each book contains the items for each subtest and instructions for administration. Separate manuals provide instructions for scoring, administrator training materials, and the tables necessary for score interpretation. The parts may be purchased separately except for II-III, which are printed together. A prerecorded cassette tape for Part I (Cognitive Ability), recommended for standardized administration of the three subtests for which exact pronunciation and presentation is required, may be used as a pronunciation guide and training aid. Only three subtests (Visual Matching, Calculation, and Dictation) require written responses from the subject, although the subject may use a type of scratch paper for Applied Problems if desired. Some subtests contain sample items to be used as teaching devices to introduce controlled-learning tasks. Both timed and untimed formats are used, with the untimed predominating. The use of basal and ceiling levels makes it possible to match the difficulty level of subtests to the individual being tested.

A response booklet is provided for each of the four test parts in which the administrator records responses, summarizes results, and interprets test performance. Technical manuals are purchased separately. Examiners must furnish pencils, watch or clock (stopwatch preferred), and a cassette player with good reproduction. Microcomputer scoring is available.

Parts I-II are suitable for subjects aged 3-65 years and beyond; Part III is most suitable for Grade 5-65 + years; and Part IV may be administered from infancy-29 years (and older, in certain cases).

The four parts of the battery, which consist of a total of 41 subtests and a variety of clusters or scales, are described as follows:

Part I. Tests of Cognitive Ability (see Table I): Consists of 12 subtests and 11 scales covering three areas that provide a general measure of cognitive ability (Area I), measure cognitive structures necessary to academic functioning (Area II), and provide an estimate of examinees' "expected" achievement in the four most common areas of academic achievement (Area III). The differences observed between "expected" achievement as measured by the scales in Part I and "actual" achievement as measured by the achievement tests in Part II may be significant in diagnosing a student's learning difficulties (Hessler, 1984).

In Area I, the *Full Scale* (primarily verbal) is intended to cover the full range of functions from the lower to the higher mental processes (Woodcock, 1978); the *Preschool Scale* (primarily verbal) is most appropriate for preschool aged children but provides norms through the adult level (Woodcock, 1978) and can be used as an alternative to the Full Scale when a brief verbal ability assessment is needed (Hessler, 1984); the *Brief Scale,* requiring approximately 15 minutes to administer and score, correlates highest with the Full Scale cluster score (Woodcock, 1978) and provides a fast screening assessment of vocabulary and quantitative skills.

In Area II, the four cluster scales were derived statistically through factor, cluster, and multiple-regression analyses, with *Verbal Ability* measuring concrete vocabulary comprehension and expression and minimizing nonverbal abstract reasoning by using the Analysis-Synthesis score as a suppressor variable (deriving the cluster score by adding the two vocabulary scores and subtracting the

Table 1

Part I. Tests of Cognitive Ability

Areas	*Cluster Scales*	*Picture Vocabulary*	*Spatial Relations*	*Memory for Sentences*	*Visual-Auditory Learning*	*Blending*	*Quantitative Concepts*	*Visual Matching*	*Antonyms-Synonyms*	*Analysis-Synthesis*	*Numbers Reversed*	*Concept Formation*	*Analogies*
I. Broad Cognitive Abilities	Full	X	X	X	X	X	X	X	X	X	X	X	X
	Preschool	X	X	X	X	X	X						
	Brief						X		X				
II. Cognitive Factors	Verbal Ability	X							X	X			
	Reasoning Ability								X	X		X	X
	Perceptual Speed		X					X					
	Memory			X							X		
III. Scholastic Aptitude	Reading Aptitude				X	X			X				X
	Mathematics Aptitude							X	X	X		X	
	Written Language						X	X	X		X		
	Knowledge Aptitude			X			X		X				X

Analysis-Synthesis score); *Reasoning Ability* measuring the ability to carry out problem-solving strategies, nonverbal abstract reasoning, and utilization of instruction and decreasing the effects of verbal ability by employing Antonyms-Synonyms as a suppressor; *Perceptual Speed* measuring visual-perceptual fluency and accuracy and problem-solving strategies; and *Memory* measuring short-term auditory memory and the ability to manipulate or reorganize information and understand and follow directions (Woodcock, 1978).

In Area III, *Reading Aptitude* assesses verbal processing and how well examinees are expected to read rather than how well they actually read; *Mathematics Aptitude* is a composite of visual-perceptual and verbal/nonverbal abstract reasoning processes with visual and nonverbal predominating (Hessler, 1984); *Written Language* measures visual perceptual, verbal, and mathematical processing abilities and provides an expectation of the examinee's ability to understand (process) written language; and *Knowledge Aptitude* emphasizes verbal processing and assesses mathematical and verbal processing abilities necessary to learn in the sciences, social studies, and humanities.

All of the 12 subtests, most of which are untimed, begin with easier or less complex items and progress through the more difficult or complex ones. Unless noted otherwise in the following descriptions, responses to items are oral, and the starting point for each subtest is determined by the basal-level five consecutive correct responses and the ceiling-level five consecutive incorrect responses. The subtests are described as follows (Woodcock, 1978; Hessler, 1984):

Picture Vocabulary (37 items): Measures primarily expressive vocabulary skills. Requires examinee to identify pictured objects or actions.

Spatial Relations (31 items): Measures efficient problem-solving strategies and visual-perceptual and nonverbal conceptual ability. Examinee is given three minutes to make a complete shape by selecting from a series of shapes (2 or 3 components per item). After two sample items, all examinees start with the first item. Speed is a factor in the final score, but increasing difficulty of items and scoring make this equally a power test.

Memory for Sentences (22 items): Measures short-term memory and expressive syntax abilities by testing the ability to remember and repeat a sentence. The first three items are two- or three-word phrases presented orally by the examiner; the remaining 19 are on tape and are increasingly complex. The entire subtest can be read by the examiner to young examinees or those who need interaction.

Visual-Auditory Learning (seven stories with a 26-word vocabulary and two word endings): Measures ability to associate unfamiliar visual symbols (rebuses) with familiar words, translate these sequences into meaningful phrases, and possibly differentiate poor readers from good readers. Each story is preceded by teaching the names of four new rebuses to the examinee who then begins with the first story and proceeds until all stories are completed or a preestablished cumulative number of errors occur.

Blending (25 items): Measures auditory synthesis ability by testing ability to integrate, identify, and verbalize whole words (from two syllables to those composed of several single phonemes) after hearing syllables and/or phonemes of the word sequentially. Test material can be presented by examiner or prerecorded tape, depending on the examinee's need. All examinees begin with the first item and continue until five consecutive items are missed.

Quantitative Concepts (46 items): Assesses understanding of mathematical concepts, symbols, and vocabulary, rather than the ability to use them in practice, and predicts difficulty with mathematics achievement. Examinee responds to questions about quantitative and mathematical concepts, symbols, and vocabulary. No calculations or applications are required.

Visual Matching (30 items): Measures visual-perceptual fluency and accuracy and, for normal subjects, perceptual processing. A paper-pencil test requiring the examinee to find two identical words in a row of six numbers. Although two minutes are given to complete as many items as possible, this is also a power test (Woodcock, 1978).

Antonyms-Synonyms (49 items): Measures examinee's knowledge of word meanings and assesses receptive and expressive vocabulary, word definition, and (to some degree), cognitive flexibility. Requires examinee to respond with antonyms (26 items) or synonyms (23 items), with only one-word responses acceptable. Words are presented both orally and visually.

Analysis-Synthesis (30 items): Measures ability to learn symbols and their logical manipulation, abstract reasoning, and problem-solving by assessing the ability to learn symbolic formulations, use higher-level mental processing and reasoning, and apply them to problem solving. Skills measured are those required to learn mathematics and other areas requiring symbolic learning and manipulation (e.g., physics, chemistry, logic). Inability to identify four colors (yellow, black, blue, and red) correctly results in a score of zero and examinee is not tested. Examinees who correctly identify the first item proceed until all items are answered or predetermined cutoff points are reached.

Numbers Reversed (21 items): Measures short-term memory and ability to perceptually reorganize data by assessing ability to hold a sequence of numbers in memory and reorganize that sequence. Items (organized in groups of three) are composed of three to eight random numbers, with the first six items read by the examiner and the remaining presented by the examiner or tape, depending on examinees' needs. Basal level is established when all three items in a group are answered correctly; ceiling is established when all three items in a group are missed.

Concept Formation (32 items): Measures primarily nonverbal abstract reasoning and rule-learning ability, and possibly cognitive flexibility, analytic problem-solving strategies, and the ability to profit from instruction. A nonverbal subtest requiring examinee to identify rules underlying concepts when given examples of the concept (drawings varying along four dimensions: red or yellow, large or small, round or square, single or in pairs) and to identify instances when the concept does not apply. One or more boxes containing one or more combinations of the drawings are presented to the examinee, who determines which combination is appropriate in order for the drawings to be included in the box(es). All examinees start at the beginning and continue until all items are attempted or a predetermined cutoff point is reached.

Analogies (35 items): Assesses conceptualization, comprehension, and active word expression. Requires the examinee to complete an incomplete verbal phrase with a single word. Stimulus material is visible to the examinee and read by the examiner. Nine items are quantitative in nature.

Part II. Tests of Achievement (see Table 2): Consists of ten subtests and five cluster scales, with the first four cluster scales measuring achievement in the four most common areas of instruction in school: *Reading* (measuring basic reading skills, primarily sight-word vocabulary and phonic/structural analysis, but including some literal reading comprehension [Hessler, 1984]); *Mathematics* (measuring the most common achievement areas in mathematics); *Written Language* (measuring achievement skills in conventional and linguistic components of spelling, punctuation, capitalization, and word usage); and *Knowledge* (providing an estimate of the examinee's general knowledge across the major areas of the curriculum). The fifth scale, *Preschool Achievement,* is a combination of the three easiest skills subtests from the Reading, Mathematics, and Written Language Scales. It is designed

Table 2

Part II. Tests of Achievement and Part III. Tests of Interest Level

Cluster Scales	*Subtests*
TESTS OF ACHIEVEMENT	
Reading	Letter-Word Identification Word Attack Passage Comprehension
Mathematics	Calculation Applied Problems
Written Language	Dictation Proofing
Knowledge	Science Social Studies Humanities
Preschool Achievement	Letter-Word Identification Applied Problems Dictations
TESTS OF INTEREST LEVEL	
Scholastic Interest	Reading Interest Mathematics Interest Written Language
Nonscholastic Interest	Physical Interest Social Interest

to be used at the preschool level, but adult norms make it appropriate for administration to other special populations, such as mentally retarded adults.

All of the subtests in Part II are untimed and (with the exception of the Word Attack subtest which begins with the first item and ends when five consecutive items are missed) have basal and ceiling levels established by five consecutive correct and five consecutive failed items, respectively.

The Reading Scale consists of the following three subtests:

Letter-Word Identification (50 items): Measures ability to recognize and pronounce letters and words (printed in large type in the test book) and assesses sight-letter or word vocabulary, not reading comprehension. There is no expectation that word meaning is known. The first seven items consist of single letters.

Word Attack (26 items): Measures phonic and structural-analysis concepts. Requires the examinee to read nonsense words or infrequently used English words, beginning with simple consonant-vowel-consonant trigrams and progressing to multisyllable words. All phonemes in the English language are used (Woodcock, 1978).

Passage Comprehension (26 items): Measures literal reading comprehension. Requires the examinee to identify and supply an appropriate word to complete a short passage after silently reading the passage (a form of the "cloze" procedure). More than one response is acceptable for several of the items; seven of the 26 items include illustrations.

Calculation (42 items): Measures the given calculation skills of addition, subtraction, division, and multiplication. Includes whole numbers, fractions, and decimals, with the more complex items involving the use of trigonomic, logarithmic, geometric, and calculus operations. Procedures are specified, and no application skills are required. Items are completed on a special page in the test response booklet.

Applied Problems (45 items): Measures mathematical reasoning skills. Requires the examinee to solve practical problems in mathematics by recognizing the correct procedure, identifying the relevant data (many problems contain superfluous information), and performing the calculations. Problems are presented visually or read to the examinee to minimize the effect of reading skills. Scratch paper is permitted if requested.

The Written Language Scale consists of the following two subtests:

Dictation (40 items): Measures conventional and language components of written expression, including spelling. The examinee uses a special page from the response booklet to respond in writing to a variety of spoken instructions involving letters of the alphabet, forms, spelling, punctuation, capitalization, and language usage (e.g., contractions, abbreviations, plurals).

Proofing (29 items): Assesses conventional language usage. The examinee indicates correct usage of punctuation, capitalization, spelling, or word usage after reading passages in which errors occur.

The Knowledge Scale consists of the following three subtests:

Science (39 items): Measures knowledge of the physical and biological sciences, rather than an understanding and application of scientific methods. Items (printed only on the examiner's side of the test booklet) are read aloud by the examiner. Some illustrations and formulas are used.

Social Studies (37 items): Assesses knowledge of the social sciences (e.g., government, economics, geography). Items (many of which are printed on the examinee's side of the test book) are read aloud by the examiner. Some illustrations are used.

Humanities (36 items): Measures knowledge of the visual arts, literature, and music (including genres and styles), as well as facts and the ability to read a short musical passage. Items are read aloud and many include visual stimuli (e.g., poems, illustrations, musical passages).

Part III. Tests of Interest Level (see Table 2): Consists of five subtests and two cluster scales: Scholastic Interest (assessing the examinee's levels of interest in reading, mathematics, and written language) and Nonscholastic Interest (assessing the examinee's levels of interest in physical and social activities). Although Part III is most appropriate for Grades 5 and above, norms are provided down to Grade 3.

Each subtest item consists of two activities, one of which is relevant to the area of interest being tested. Examinees read the items from the test book (or the examiner may read items aloud if examinees have difficulty with reading) and choose which of the two activities they prefer.

The Scholastic Interest Scale consists of three subtests, each of which contains 25 items: *Reading Interest* (assessing preference for participating in activities involving reading, such as preference between going to a party or to a bookstore); *Mathematics Interest* (assessing preference for activities involving the learning or application of mathematics, such as preference between attending a party or making up mathematics games); and *Written Language* (assessing preference for various forms of activities requiring written language, such as preference between reading a newspaper or writing a newspaper story).

The Nonscholastic Interest Scale consists of two subtests, each of which contains 35 items: *Physical Interest* (assessing levels of interest in individual and group physical activities, such as choosing between mountain climbing and reading a story) and *Social Interest* (assessing levels of interest in activities involving other people, such as planning a party).

Part IV. Tests of Independent Behavior (see Table 3): Consists of four cluster scales (Motor Skills, Social Interaction and Communication Skills, Personal Independence, and Community Independence Skills) containing 14 subtests formed from 226 items, plus the Broad Independence, Short Form, Early Development, and Problem Behaviors Scales.

All items (behaviors or tasks) are printed in the interviewer's and respondent's testbook. Respondents may be the individual being examined, someone who knows the person well enough to respond, or the examiner. Typically, the respondent will be another person for very young children or persons with fairly severe emotional handicaps or retardation.

The Motor Skills Cluster Scale assesses fine- and gross-motor skills and consists of two subscales, each of which contains 17 items: *Gross-Motor Skills* (sampling skills involving the large muscles from infancy, such as sitting without support, to adult behaviors, such as regular strenuous exercise) and *Fine-Motor Skills* (assessing performance on typical hand-eye coordination skills, such as picking up small objects with the hand in infancy or small-part assembly tasks for adults).

The Social Interaction and Communications Skills Cluster Scale assesses the behaviors necessary to interact and communicate effectively with others; it consists of three subscales: *Social Interaction* (assessing performance on 16 tasks involving social interaction with others from infancy, such as distinguishing friends from strangers, to adulthood, such as participation in social activities); *Language Comprehension* (assessing the level of deriving information from spoken and written language on 16 tasks ranging from recognizing one's name to the use of reference materials); and *Language Expression* (assessing the ability to express

Table 3

Part IV. Scales of Independent Behavior

	Cluster Scales	*Subscales*
Broad Independence Scale	Motor Skills	Gross-Motor Skills Fine-Motor Skills
	Social Interaction and Communication Skills	Social Interaction Language Comprehension Language Expression
	Personal Independence	Eating and Meal Preparation Toileting Dressing Personal Self-Care Domestic Skills
	Community Independence Skills	Time and Punctuality Money and Value Work Skills Home/Community Orientation
	Short Form Scale Early Development Scale	32 items from above subscales
	Problem Behaviors Scale (Eight categories)	Presence of Problems Frequency of Occurrence Severity of Problems

one's self orally, in writing, or through other devices such as language boards on 17 tasks ranging from simple "yes/no" responses to the delivery of complex reports).

The Personal Independence Cluster Scale assesses performance in areas needed to function independently primarily within the home and consists of five subscales: *Eating and Meal Preparation* (evaluating eating skills in infancy and food preparation behaviors in adults on 16 tasks); *Toileting* (evaluating bathroom and toilet and related behaviors from infancy through childhood on 14 tasks); *Dressing* (evaluating performance in dressing on 18 tasks ranging from very simple to complex, such as the selection and maintenance of clothing); *Personal Self-Care* (evaluating performance in personal self-care on 15 tasks ranging from use of toothbrush to seeking professional help in illness); and *Domestic Skills* (evaluating skills necessary for the maintenance of a functional home environment on 16 tasks ranging from returning dishes to the kitchen to selecting appropriate housing).

The Community Independence Skills Cluster Scale assesses the behaviors necessary to function in the community, primarily outside the home, and consists of four subscales: *Time and Punctuality* (evaluating time concepts on 15 tasks ranging from telling time to making and keeping appointments); *Money and Value* (evaluates skills in determining the value of items and in use of money on 17 items); *Work Skills* (evaluating work tasks through certain prevocational behaviors on 16 tasks more developmentally advanced than other subscales); and *Home/Community Orientation* (assessing the behaviors necessary to effectively get around the home, the neighborhood, and the home community on 16 tasks).

The Broad Independence Scale (consisting of all 226 items and all 14 subscales) provides an assessment of the full range of behaviors necessary to function in everyday life.

The Early Development Scale (32 items) is designed for subjects whose developmental level is below approximately two and one-half year of age and is particularly appropriate for very young children and severely or profoundly handicapped children and adults.

The Short Form Scale (32 items) is appropriate when a brief screening or evaluation of independent functioning is needed.

All tasks on the Early Development, Short Form, and Broad Independence Scales are arranged in developmental order, with the easiest tasks presented first. Basal and ceiling levels are established, and because the tasks cover a range from infancy to adulthood, interviewers select the beginning task based on their assessment of the subjects' "operating range" (Bruininks, Woodcock, Weatherman, & Hill, 1984). Each task contains the stem asking whether or not the subject does or could do tasks completely without help or supervision. Tasks are rated by respondent, according to subject's ability, on a four-point scale (0 = never or rarely; 1 = not well or ¼ of the time; 2 = fairly well or about ¾ of the time; and 3 = very well, always, or almost always).

The Problem Behaviors Scale measures three dimensions of problem behaviors: the presence, frequency of occurrence, and severity. Problem behaviors are defined as those which, if frequently exhibited, may limit personal and social adjustment (Bruininks et al., 1984). The eight major categories of problem behaviors are hurtful to self, hurtful to others, destructive to property, disruptive behavior, unusual or repetitive habits, socially offensive behavior, withdrawal behaviors, and uncooperativeness. Each category contains several examples of such behaviors. This scale has two rating scales: frequency (scored on a continuum ranging from "less than once a month" to "one or more times an hour") and severity (scored on a five-level continuum ranging from "not serious" to "extremely serious"). The respondent indicates which of those behaviors occur, how often they occur, and which are the most serious within that category.

Practical Applications/Uses

Because of the wide range of cognition, achievement, interest, and behaviors assessed and its wide age range, the WJPEB has a large number of uses—and its potential is even greater. Woodcock (1978) and Hessler (1984) recommend four general areas of usage: 1) individual assessment, including screening, identification, and diagnosis of individual strengths and weaknesses in cognitive, academic achievement, and interest areas; individual program planning for general educational instructional objectives; and the planning of short- and long-term educational and vocational goals; 2) evaluation of individual growth and program effectiveness; 3) as a valuable instrument for research into a wide range of educational, developmental, and behavioral factors, due to the range of subtests, cluster scores, and norming; and 4) as a useful instrument for psychometric training purposes, due to the individualized nature of the administration, the use of a variety of scores, and technically superior materials.

The battery lends itself to extensive applications in both educational and noneducational settings. For example, identification of individuals with special learning problems or disabilities; diagnosis of cognitive abilities, achievements, or interests; selection or placement of subjects into appropriate groupings; and individual program planning or guidance. The age range over which it is normed makes it possible to chart individual or group growth from infancy to senior adulthood. The subtests are well-designed for research purposes in a variety of settings (Woodcock, 1978). The recent addition of the Scales of Independent Behavior (Bruininks, Woodcock, Weatherman, & Hill, 1984) makes it possible to assess the ability of individuals to function successfully in a variety of social, educational, and personal settings.

Parts I-III (Cognitive Ability, Achievement, and Interest) introduce an innovation that has been sorely needed. It is the first major individualized assessment instrument to report standardized cognitive and achievement measurements on the same samples from childhood through adulthood. This avoids the uncontrolled variance inherent in separate norms groups. The Scholastic/Nonscholastic cluster for children normed on the same sample provides a much needed assessment of children's interests (Estabrook, 1983).

Woodcock (1978) recommends Parts I-III for identifying and evaluating the behaviorally- and learning-disabled, but the norms groups were small and the evidence not conclusive. Part IV, which was developed with nonhandicapped subjects and with larger and more representative retarded, behavioral, and learning-disabled groups, appears to be a valid diagnostic instrument for evaluating independent functioning. The preliminary evidence (Bruininks et al., in press) is impressive.

The ease of administration, wide age range, and broad conceptual coverage make the WJPEB useful in a great variety of settings, such as preschool-high school, special and adult education programs, private practices, higher education, research studies, and training of psychometrists.

The battery can be administered by anyone who has had a basic introduction to measurement; however, the materials providing specific training exercises for administration are recommended for all users, regardless of the level of their training. Administration time for the entire battery is approximately three hours, with Part I requiring about one hour, Part II about 50 minutes, Part III about 15 minutes, and Part IV 45-60 minutes. Certain subjects will require more time than others. Although the battery may be given in four different sessions, it is recommended that no more than two days be used to complete it. As with any test, especially if individually administered, the WJPEB must be given in a room with a minimum of distractions and ample working space.

The scoring is complex, perhaps to the point that most errors of administration may occur at this point. Raw scores for each subtest are converted to part scores, which are summed to produce cluster scores and further summed to obtain total cluster scores. After a grade score, age score, and instructional grade range are obtained from tables for each cluster score, an expected average cluster score for the age or grade group of the subject is entered. A difference score is calculated between the observed score and the expected cluster score. The percentile ranks for cluster scores are based on this difference score (with a zero difference representing the 50th percentile), entered on the summary sheet, and transferred to the profiles in terms of confidence bands based on SE measurement. Subtest profiles are prepared using raw score confidence bands. From other tables, the Relative Performance Index (RPI) is determined and entered, and the cluster difference scores are interpreted by functioning levels ranging from ''very superior'' to ''severely deficient.'' Other types of scores (e.g., deviation IQ, T-Scores, stanines) are also available from tables, but are not ordinarily entered on the profile. Although the technical manuals (Woodcock, 1978; Hessler, 1984) state that the user determines which type of score is most useful, the scorer must complete the summary sheet through difference scores for the clusters to be able to obtain percentile ranks and standard scores. Percentile ranks are given in a separate book of norms (Marston & Ysseldyke, 1984b).

The response booklet for Part I provides a profile on which the Full Scale and subtest raw scores are plotted. An academic achievement vs. aptitude profile may be used to show the measured differences between expected learning and that actually observed by the test. The percentile rank profile provides a graphic presentation of the relative levels among the broad cognitive ability, the four aptitude scales, and the four cognitive scales.

Parts II-III response booklets provide profiles based on percentile ranks for each of the five achievement and two interest scales. A profile may also be drawn depicting relative levels for each of the ten achievement subtests, the five related subtests from Part I, and the five interest subtests. An ''instructional implications'' profile provides information about the subject's actual performance relative to others of the same grade or age with a suggested instructional level in the broad areas of reading, mathematics, written language, and general knowledge.

The Part IV response booklet contains five profiles. The first is based on percentile ranks for the Broad Independence Scale and the four major independence clusters. If available, percentile ranks from related Cognitive Ability Scales may also be plotted for comparison purposes. Another percentile rank profile may be completed based on both age and cognitive abilities. The third is a profile of scores from the 14 subscales and the Full Scale. A ''training implications'' report may be prepared depicting the relative performance of the subject compared to others the same age. A fifth profile depicts by stanine the frequency and severity of problem behaviors.

A micro-computer scoring package, COMPUSCORE (Hauger, 1984), is available for both the Apple-II series and the IBM-PC. It provides convenient scoring from raw scores for each of the 27 subtests from Parts I-III. The system allows missing scores and has considerable error checking built in. Scoring the entire battery and completing the summary sheet and profile will require between one and two hours; the COMPUSCORE computer scoring should reduce the time to approximately 30 minutes. In addition, the chance for scorer errors will be greatly reduced.

Interpretation of the battery is based on a series of objective scores rather than on clinical judgment. Various criterion- and norms-related data are provided for each subtest and cluster score. A comprehensive understanding of both the content and processes measured by each task is important, especially if the examinee's scores are significantly high or low. Further, failure to fully understand the relationships between and the meanings of individual subtest scores may result in misinterpretation of cluster scores because clusters are based on combinations of the subtests. Before attempting interpretation of the battery, users should generally have completed courses in both statistics and introductory psychometrics, as well as have had considerable experience in the interpretation of standardized tests.

Technical Aspects

The technical manual (Woodcock, 1978) provides extensive information about the methodological procedures used in norming the Woodcock-Johnson, including data on reliability and validity for Parts I-III. Preliminary data available for Part IV are adequate for this review (Bruininks et al., in press).

Reliability: Reliability is an estimate of the stability of test scores. It refers to the consistency of the scores obtained by the same person over time when reexamined with the same test, or with different sets of items from the same or equivalent test, or under variable testing conditions. Test reliability indicates the extent to which individual differences in test scores are attributable to "true" differences in the characteristic being measured and the extent to which differences are due to chance, unrelated errors. The higher the correlation coefficient on a scale of –1.00 to 1.00, the closer the relationship. Generally, coefficients of .80 or higher are indicative of test stability. Split-half reliability estimates are a measure of the internal consistency of a test (i.e., the ability of the items throughout the test to consistently measure the concept). Test-retest reliability is a measure of consistent measurement over time. Woodcock (1978) and Bruininks et al. (1984) report both.

Reliability estimates for Parts I-III were obtained by the split-half method (corrected for length by the Spearman-Brown procedure) for untimed subtests and for cluster scores. Test-retest reliabilities were obtained only for the two timed subtests. Split-half (corrected by Spearman-Brown) reliability estimates are reported for both nonhandicapped and handicapped groups for Part IV (Scales of Independent Behavior). Test-retest reliabilities were also reported for two groups of elementary-school children.

Reliabilities were reported for ages 20-39, 40-64, and 65+ years and Grades 1, 3, 5, 8, and 12 for 11 of the 25 subtests in Parts I-II. In addition to the above, estimates were also obtained for ages three and four and Kindergarten for 11 more subtests. Only elementary and secondary grades were included for the Visual Matching subtest. Median subtest reliabilities for the two parts ranged from .65 to .95, with only two falling below .80. Median cluster scores ranged from .70 (Perceptual Speed) to .97 (Full Scale). Seven of the 16 cluster-score reliabilities were .90 or above. Reliabilities were reported across all 11 norms groups for the Preschool, Knowledge, and Skills clusters and for the three adult age groups and the elementary and secondary grade levels for the remaining 13.

Reliability estimates were reported for Grades 5, 8, and 12, and ages 20-39, 40-64, and 65+ years for Part III (Interest). Median subtest reliability estimates ranged from .79 (Social) to .88 (Reading and Written Language). The two Interest cluster-score reliabilities were .93 (Scholastic) and .88 (Nonscholastic).

Part IV (SIB) subscale median internal consistency estimates ranged from .69 to .86 for three levels of normal populations. The range of cluster-score estimates was .83 to .96, with a .96 for the Broad Independence cluster. Reliability estimates for four groups of handicapped persons at two age levels (moderately/severely retarded, mildly retarded, behavior-disordered, and learning-disabled in children and adolescents/adults) and for moderately retarded adults were also reported. The median subscale reliabilities ranged from .88 to .95. Median cluster reliabilities for these groups ranged from .94 (Motor Skills) to .99 (Broad Independence). However, the sizes of the handicapped samples were generally small (N = 15 to 86), which may have inflated the estimates.

Part IV test-retest reliabilities were obtained for two small nonhandicapped samples of children (ages 6-8 and 10-11 years). The scales were administered by the same examiner over a one- to four-week period. Cluster scale test-retest reliabilities ranged from .71 to .96, with 11 of the 12 estimates in the .80 and .90 range. Maladaptive index estimates ranged from .71 to .96. Subscale reliabilities were generally high with 16 of the 20 in the .80s and .90s.

In general, reliability estimates were acceptable, with especially high reliabilities being reported for cluster and Full Scale scores. One shortcoming is the lack of test-retest data for the untimed subtests and clusters for Parts I and II, especially at the younger levels where retesting is often necessary.

Validity: To be valid, a test must measure what the author claims it measures, especially when the test results will be used to make decisions that will have long-term effects on the examinee. No test is valid in and of itself. It may be appropriate for some purposes and not for others. In a battery, some tests may be more valid than others. It is the task of the test author to present evidence of validity, that is, of the usefulness of the test for the purposes to which it will be put (Anastasi, 1982). Woodcock has presented impressive amounts of validity data. The technical manual (Woodcock, 1978) presents evidence of four types of validity: construct, criterion-related (concurrent and predictive), and content.

Construct validity is not directly measurable, but is inferred from observed relationships to other measures that appear to have the same underlying theoretical construct. For example, a measure of "quantitative ability" would be expected to show a high correlation with other measures of mathematics. In addition, it would be expected to show a low relationship with measures intuitively unrelated to mathematics, such as word attack skills. Woodcock's examples present good evidences of construct validity. For example, the Quantitative Concepts subtest correlates fairly high with Calculation (.63) and Applied Problems (.68) and lower with Word Attack (.44), a reading measure. Other data for both subtests and cluster scores show moderate to high evidences of construct validity. Unfortunately, the evidence presented is for normal populations, and no separate evidence for special populations is given.

Concurrent validity is a direct measure between a test and some other known measure of the same criterion, usually another test. Concurrent studies were reported for both normal and special populations between various parts of the WJPEB and a number of well-known instruments, e.g., Stanford-Binet, WISC-R, Iowa Tests of Basic Skills (ITBS), Peabody Individual Achievement Test (PIAT), Peabody Picture Vocabulary Test (PPVT), Wide Range Achievement Test (WRAT), KeyMath Diagnostic Test, Minnesota Behavioral Scales (MDPS), and Woodcock Reading Mastery Test (WRMT). The small special populations represented the severe learning disabled (SLD), the severe learning and behavior problems (SLBP), and the trainable mental retarded (TMR) with 20, 30, and 33 subjects, respectively.

For normal groups, concurrent validity coefficients were in the moderate range. For example, the correlation between the Cognitive Ability Full Scale and the PPVT ranged from .58 (Grade Three) to .64 (Grade Five). The highest reported relationships were between the WJPEB Reading Cluster score and other reading measures (.75 to .90) than for either mathematics or written language which generally ran in the .70s and .80s.

Concurrent relationships groups fell into the moderate range for the TMR between the Preschool Cognitive Ability Scale and MDPS scales and Language Word Flow Chart (median, .69). Coefficients for the TMR sample between the Achievement clusters and the MDPS scales range between .56 and .86, with a median correlation of .71. The correlations between the achievement clusters and the PIAT, KeyMath, and WRAT Spelling are even lower for the SLD sample (.28 to .84, median of .55).

Bruininks, Woodcock, Weatherman, and Hill (in press) report concurrent validity coefficients between the Broad Cognitive Ability score of Part I and the cluster scores of Part IV for two age levels of handicapped and nonhandicapped groups. These range from high for both groups of children (high .70s and .80s) to low for nonhandicapped adults (.20s to low .40s). This pattern is replicated in the correlations reported between chronological age and the Scales of Independent Behavior, where only at the lower age levels is a significant relationship found. These findings tend to support the hypothesis of the scale's authors (Bruininks et al., 1984) that functional independence does vary with age and stage of development. On the other hand, low relationships reported between the maladaptive behavior scales and chronological age support the assumption that such behaviors are nondevelopmental in nature. Good discriminant validity for the Problem Behaviors Scale, in general, is shown by the relatively high mean scores of the behavior-disordered children and the zero scores for normal, high-ability, and learning-disabled subjects.

Content validity is the extent to which a test samples the ability under investigation. It is established by systematically examining the test content to determine whether it is a representative sample of the behavior domain to be measured (Anastasi, 1982). As with other types of validity, Woodcock (1978) provides adequate information on which to judge. The achievement, interest, and adaptive behavior domains appear to be adequately covered; intellectual or ability are somewhat less so, especially as they relate to special groups.

Predictive validity is the ability of a test to predict performance on some other measure of the same concept, usually other test scores, grades in specific classes, or overall academic performance. All of these predictions are important, especially when testing subjects in an academic setting. Unfortunately, at the time of this review only predictive studies involving performance on other tests have been reported for the WJPEB.

Woodcock (1978) reports the results of studies of the relationships between the four Part II achievement clusters (Reading, Mathematics, Written Language, and Knowledge) and three measures of academic aptitude (PPVT, WISC-R, and the WJPEB, Part I cluster scales). For normal groups, the relationships among the various measures are moderately high (primarily, .60s to .80s), with the highest relationships reported between the Part I and Part II clusters. This last finding is not unexpected because both were normed on the same groups. It should be noted that the Broad Cognitive Scale (Part I) is as good a predictor of performance on any of the achievement clusters as are corresponding aptitude cluster scores.

Prediction of achievement cluster scores from aptitude cluster scores proved more troublesome for the three special groups. Although moderately high predictive validity coefficients were reported (.63 to .86, median of .76), there was a significant discrepancy between the expected scores on the achievement clusters and those predicted, with predicted scores averaging almost 20 points below those expected. Later research has confirmed that problems may exist with using Part I with exceptional groups. McGue, Shinn, and Ysseldyke (1982) found that neither cognitive nor aptitude factor clusters appeared to be valid for assessing learning-disabled fourth-graders. Reeve, Hall, and Zakreski (1979) and Ysseldyke, Shinn, and Epps (1981) found significant discrepancies between Part I of the WJPEB and the WISC-R Full Scale for learning-disabled students.

For a behavior-disordered population (some of whom were also learning-disabled) Phelps, Rosso, and Falasco (1984) found a high concurrent validity between the Broad Cognitive score (Part I) and the WISC-R Full Scale IQ score, with only a 2.33 point average difference in means. However, an analysis of the differences between WISC-R subtests and Part I cluster scores indicated discrepancies in what was being measured—discrepancies that may call into question the applicability of Part I to this population. Other researchers have also raised questions about the use of Part I with handicapped populations (e.g., Algozzine, Ysseldyke, & Shinn, 1982; Breen, 1983; Marston, 1980; Marston & Ysseldyke, 1984a). Woodcock (1984a, 1984b) counters that the discrepancy is methodological rather than actual. However, when Thompson and Brassard (1984a) controlled for the methodological errors claimed by Woodcock, discrepancies between Part I and WISC-R still existed. Thompson and Brassard concluded that lower Part I scores for LD populations were a function of the instrument's heavy emphasis on achievement rather than systematic error in the Part I norms.

On the other hand, both Harrington (1984) and Weaver (1984) found Part I useful and "adequate" in the assessment of the achievement of mentally retarded children, and Mira (1984) found both Parts I and II useful in the assessment of hearing-impaired children. Because of the oral nature of the WJPEB's presentation, Fewell (1983) suggests that parts of both Parts I and II are useful in evaluating visually impaired preschool children. In a study of learning-disabled college students, Gregg and Hoy (1985) found no differences in performance on the WAIS-R and the Part I cluster scores.

Woodcock (1978) analyzed the relationship among the aptitude and achievement cluster scores, sex, and race. (Sex and race membership were carefully matched to 1970 census data.) The prediction of achievement cluster scores from aptitude clusters did not appear to be generally affected by either race or sex. The only exception was the finding that older boys were more likely to be inappropriately identified as having a deficit in written language skills than were older girls, for whom the opposite was true. Arffa, Rider, and Cummings (1984) found no significant differences between mean scores on the Stanford-Binet and the Preschool Cognitive Scale (Part I) for a sample of 60 black preschoolers. However, the correlation between the two tests was a modest .45, indicating that the two instruments are probably measuring different concepts. The Knowledge Scale (Part II) mean for the group was significantly lower than either the Stanford-Binet or the Preschool Cognitive scores. Both findings may suggest that the cultural loadings of the WJPEB may be biased somewhat towards white, middle-class, preschool children. Further research with culturally distinct groups is needed in this area, Arffa, Rider, and Cummings (1984) suggest.

The "mean-score" discrepancy also raises important psychometric issues with regard to the usefulness of the WJPEB with special populations (Estabrook, 1983). The purpose of this test is to evaluate and predict more accurately in order that more valid placement or treatment decisions can be made. If Part I does not predict performance on other measures accurately, especially for exceptional groups, its use may be more harmful than helpful. The sources of the mean-score discrepancies, therefore, need to be identified. Several possible sources have been suggested. Reeve et al. (1979) suggest that the problem may lie with differences in difficulty between the aptitude and achievement tests. Shinn et al. (1982) and Thompson and Brassard (1984a) believe the source to be the high achievement-oriented content of Part I when compared to other measures (WISC-R or Stanford-Binet). Higher verbal saturation of the Part I tasks may also be the culprit (Cummings & Moscato, 1984a). The resolution of the psychometric problems (both theoretical and practical) of Part I is essential if this instrument is to reach its full potential.

Critique

The Woodcock-Johnson Psycho-Educational Battery is a significant addition to the American psychometric "pantheon," even taking into consideration its shortcomings with regard to exceptional groups, cost, and difficult scoring procedures. The technical information presented in the various support publications is comprehensive and psychometrically sound. The concurrent norming of Parts I-III (and, it is hoped by this reviewer, Part IV in the near future) is an innovation long needed. The norms are generally representative of the nonhandicapped population of the United States. In short, the battery compares very favorably with other tests in use in this country and in Canada. It deserves careful consideration when setting up or adding to a comprehensive testing program.

References

This list includes text citations as well as suggested additional reading.

Algozzine, B., & Ysseldyke, J. E. (1981). An analysis of difference score reliabilities on three measures with a sample of low-achieving youngsters. *Psychology in the Schools, 18,* 133-38.

Algozzine, B., Ysseldyke, J. E., & Shinn, M. (1982). Identifying children with learning disabilities: When is a discrepancy severe? *Journal of School Psychology, 20,* 299-305.

Anastasi, A. (1982). *Psychological Testing* (5th ed.). New York: Macmillan.

Arffa, S., Rider, L. H., & Cummings, J. A. (1984). A validity study of the Woodcock-Johnson Psycho Educational Battery and the Stanford-Binet with black pre-school children. *Journal of Psychoeducational Assessment, 2,* 73-77.

Bracken, B. A., Prasse, D., & Breen, M. (1984). Concurrent validity of the Woodcock-Johnson Psycho-Educational Battery with regular and learning-disabled students. *Journal of School Psychology, 22,* 185-192.

Breen, M. J. (1983). A correlational analysis between the PPVT-R and Woodcock-Johnson Achievement cluster scores for non-referred regular education and learning disabled students. *Psychology in the Schools, 20,* 295-97.

Breen, M. J. (1984). The temporal stability of the Woodcock-Johnson Test of Cognitive Ability for elementary-aged learning disabled children. *Journal of Psychoeducational Assessment, 2,* 257-261.

Breen, M. J. (1985). The Woodcock-Johnson Tests of Cognitive Ability: A comparison of two methods of cluster scale analysis for three learning disability subtypes. *Journal of Psychoeducational Assessment, 3,* 167-174.

Bruininks, R. H., Woodcock, R. W., Weatherman, R. F., & Hill, B. K. (1984). *Scales of Independent Behavior.* Allen, TX: DLM Teaching Resources.

Bruininks, R. H., Woodcock, R. W., Weatherman, R. F., & Hill, B. K. (in press). *Development and standardization of the Scales of Independent Behavior.* Allen, TX: DLM Teaching Resources.

Cummings, J. A. (in press). Review of the Woodcock-Johnson Psycho-Educational Battery. In J. V. Mitchell, Jr. (Ed.), *The ninth mental measurements yearbook* (pp. 1759-1762). Lincoln, NE: Buros Institute of Mental Measurements.

Cummings, J. A., & Moscato, E. M. (1984a). Research on the Woodcock-Johnson Psycho-Educational Battery: Implications for practice and future investigations. *School Psychology Review, 13,* 33-40.

Cummings, J. A., & Moscato, E. M. (1984b). Reply to Thompson and Brassard. *School Psychology Review, 13,* 45-48.

Cummings, J. A., & Sanville, D. (1983). Concurrent validity of the Woodcock-Johnson tests of cognitive ability: EMR children. *Psychology in the Schools, 20,* 298-303.

Epps, S., Ysseldyke, J. E., & Algozzine, B. (1983). Impact of different definitions of learning disabilities on the number of students identified. *Journal of Psychoeducational Assessment, 1,* 341-352.

Estabrook, G. E. (1983). Test review: The Woodcock-Johnson Psycho-Educational Battery. *Journal of Psychoeducational Assessment, 1,* 315-319.

Estabrook, G. E. (1984). A canonical correlation analysis of the Wechsler Intelligence Scale for Children-Revised and the Woodcock-Johnson Tests of Cognitive Ability in a sample referred for suspected learning disabilities. *Journal of Educational Psychology, 76,* 1170-1177.

Fewell, R. R. (1983). Assessment of visual functioning. In K. D. Paget & B. A. Bracken

(Eds.), *The psychoeducational assessment of preschool children* (pp. 85-103). New York: Grune & Stratton.

Gregg, N., & Hoy, C. (1985). A comparison of the WAIS-R and the Woodcock-Johnson Tests of Cognitive Ability with learning-disabled college students. *Journal of Psychoeducational Assessment, 3,* 267-274.

Hall, R. J., Reeve, R. E., & Zakreski, R. S. (1984). Validity of the Woodcock-Johnson Test of Achievement for learning disabled students. *Journal of School Psychology, 22,* 193-200.

Harrington, R. G. (1984). Assessment of learning disabled children. In S. J. Weaver (Ed.), *Testing children: A reference guide for effective clinical and psychoeducational assessments* (pp. 85-103). Kansas City, MO: Test Corporation of America.

Hauger, J. (1984). *COMPUSCORE for the Woodcock-Johnson Psycho-Educational Battery.* Allen, TX: DLM Teaching Resources.

Hessler, G. L. (1984). *Use and interpretation of the Woodcock-Johnson Psycho-Educational Battery.* Allen, TX: DLM Teaching Resources.

Kampwirth, T. J. (1983). Problems in use of the Woodcock-Johnson suppressors. *Journal of Psychoeducational Assessment, 1,* 337-340.

Kaufman, A. S. (in press). Review of the Woodcock-Johnson Psycho-Educational Battery. In J. V. Mitchell (Ed.), *The ninth mental measurements yearbook* (pp. 1762-1765). Lincoln, NE: Buros Institute of Mental Measurements.

Marston, D. (1980). *An analysis of subtest scatter on the tests of cognitive ability from the Woodcock-Johnson Psycho-Educational Battery* (Research Rep. No. 46). Minneapolis: University of Minnesota, Institute for Research on Learning Disabilities. (ERIC Document Reproduction Service No. ED 203 591)

Marston, D., & Ysseldyke, J. E. (1984a). Concerns in interpreting subtest scatter on the tests of cognitive ability from the Woodcock-Johnson Psycho-Educational Battery. *Journal of Learning Disabilities, 17,* 510-591.

Marston, D., & Ysseldyke, J. E. (1984b). *Derived subtest scores for the Woodcock-Johnson Psycho-Educational Battery.* Allen, TX: DLM Teaching Resources.

McGrew, K. S. (1983). Comparison of the WISC-R and the Woodcock-Johnson Tests of Cognitive Ability. *Journal of School Psychology, 21,* 271-276.

McGrew, K. S. (1984a). Normative based guides for subtest profile interpretation of the Woodcock-Johnson Tests of Cognitive Ability. *Journal of Psychoeducational Assessment, 2,* 141-148.

McGrew, K. S. (1984b). An analysis of the influence of the Quantitative Concepts subtest and the Woodcock-Johnson scholastic aptitude clusters. *Journal of Psychoeducational Assessment, 2,* 325-332.

McGrew, K. S. (1985). Investigation of the verbal/nonverbal structure of the Woodcock-Johnson: Implications for subtest interpretation and comparisons with the Wechsler scales. *Journal of Psychoeducational Assessment, 3,* 65-71.

McGue, M., Shinn, M., & Ysseldyke, J. E. (1979). *Validity of the Woodcock-Johnson Psycho-Educational Battery with learning disabled students* (Research Rep. No. 15). Minneapolis: University of Minnesota, Institute for Research on Learning Disabilities. (ERIC Document Reproduction Service No. ED 185 759)

McGue, M., Shinn, M., & Ysseldyke, J. E. (1982). Use of cluster scores on the Woodcock-Johnson Psycho-Educational Battery with learning disabled students. *Learning Disability Quarterly, 5,* 274-287.

Mira, M. (1984). Psychological evaluation of hearing-impaired children. In S. J. Weaver (Ed.), *Testing children: A reference guide for effective clinical and psychoeducational assessments* (pp. 121-136). Kansas City, MO: Test Corporation of America.

Nisbet, R. (1981). *A comparison of the WISC-R and Woodcock-Johnson with a referral population.* Unpublished master's thesis, Moorhead State University, Moorhead, MN.

Pieper, E. L., & Deshler, D. D. (1980). *Analysis of cognitive abilities of adolescents learning disabled specifically in arithmetic computation* (Research Rep. No. 26). Lawrence, KS: University of Kansas, Institute for Research in Learning Disabilities. (ERIC Document Reproduction Service ED 217 638)

Phelps, L., Rosso, M., & Falasco, S. C. (1984). Correlations between the Woodcock-Johnson and WISC-R for a behavior disordered population. *Psychology in the Schools, 21,* 442-446.

Phohl, W. F., & Enright, B. E. (1981). A review of the Woodcock-Johnson Psycho-Educational Battery. *Diagnostique, 6*(2), 8-15.

Reeve, R. E., Hall, R. L., & Zakreski, R. S. (1979). The Woodcock-Johnson Tests of Cognitive Ability: Concurrent validity with the WISC-R. *Learning Disability Quarterly, 2,* 63-69.

Shinn, M. R. (1980). Review of the Woodcock-Johnson Psycho-Educational Battery. *School Psychology International, 1,* 20-22.

Shinn, M., Algozzine, B., Marston, D., & Ysseldyke, J. E. (1980). *A theoretical analysis of the performance of learning disabled students on the Woodcock-Johnson Psycho-Educational Battery* (Research Rep. No. 38). Minneapolis, MN: University of Minnesota, Institute for Research on Learning Disabilities. (ERIC Document Reproduction Service No. ED 203 612)

Shinn, M. R., Algozzine, B., Marston, D., & Ysseldyke, J. E. (1982). A theoretical analysis of learning disabled students on the Woodcock-Johnson Psycho-Educational Tests Battery. *Journal of Learning Disabilities, 15,* 221-226.

Skrtic, T. M. (1980). *Formal reasoning abilities for learning disabled adolescents: Implications for mathematics instruction* (Research Rep. No. 7). Lawrence, KS: Kansas University, Institute for Research in Learning Disabilities. (ERIC Document Reproduction Service No. ED 217 624)

Stein, W., & Brantley, J. (1981). Woodcock-Johnson Psycho-Educational Battery—Test review. *Journal of School Psychology, 19,* 184-187.

Thompson, P. L., & Brassard, M. R. (1984a). Validity of the Woodcock-Johnson Tests of Cognitive Ability: A comparison with the WISC-R in learning disabled and normal elementary students. *Journal of School Psychology, 22,* 201-208.

Thompson, P. L., & Brassard, M. R. (1984b). Cummings and Moscato soft on Woodcock-Johnson. *School Psychology Review, 13,* 41-44.

Weaver, S. J. (1984). Assessment of mentally retarded children. In S. J. Weaver (Ed.), *Testing children: A reference guide for effective clinical and psychoeducational assessments* (pp. 50-70). Kansas City, MO: Test Corporation of America.

Woodcock, R. W. (1978). *Development and standardization of the Woodcock-Johnson Psycho-Educational Battery.* Allen, TX: DLM Teaching Resources.

Woodcock, R. W. (1982, March). *Interpretation of the Rasch ability and difficulty scales for educational purposes.* Paper presented at the annual meeting of the National Council on Measurement in Education, New York, NY. (ERIC Document Reproduction Service ED 223 673)

Woodcock, R. W. (1984a). A response to some questions raised about the Woodcock-Johnson: I. The mean score discrepancy issue. *School Psychology Review, 13,* 342-354.

Woodcock, R. W. (1984b). A response to some questions raised about the Woodcock-Johnson: II. Efficacy of the aptitude clusters. *School Psychology Review, 13,* 355-362.

Woodcock, R. W., & Johnson, M. (1978). *Woodcock-Johnson Psycho-Educational Battery.* Allen, TX: DLM Teaching Resources.

Ysseldyke, J. E., Algozzine, B., & Shinn, M. R. (1981). Validity of the Woodcock-Johnson Psycho-Educational Battery for learning disabled youngsters. *Learning Disability Quarterly, 4,* 244-249.

Ysseldyke, J. E., Shinn, M., & Epps, S. (1980). *A comparison of the WISC-R and the Woodcock-Johnson Tests of Cognitive Ability* (Research Rep. No. 36). Minneapolis: University of Minnesota, Institute for Research on Learning Disabilities. (ERIC Document Reproduction Service No. ED 203 610)

Ysseldyke, J. E., Shinn, M., & Epps, S. (1981). Comparison of WISC-R and the Woodcock-Johnson Tests of Cognitive Ability. *Psychology in the Schools, 18,* 15-19.

Calvin O. Dyer, Ph.D.

Professor of Education, University of Michigan, Ann Arbor, Michigan.

WOODCOCK READING MASTERY TESTS

Richard W. Woodcock. Circle Pines, Minnesota: American Guidance Service.

Introduction

The Woodcock Reading Mastery Tests (WRMT) are designed as a precise measure for students in kindergarten through twelfth grade of skills in letter identification, word identification, work attack, word comprehension, and passage comprehension, with a summary total reading score. Two alternate forms of the test, A and B, were developed which may be used independently or administered together for increased reliability. A single set of items for each test is used for the wide range of ages for people tested. The tests are untimed and the manual indicates 30 to 45 minutes for test-taking time, but in practice the time is often longer depending upon the operating range of reading from basal to ceiling level for the reader. The tests may be administered easily from a durable easel ring binder. Interpretation of scores may be made from a variety of norms such as grade and age equivalents, percentiles, and combination of norm referenced-criterion referenced mastery level tables developed for special use with this battery of tests. In addition, separate norms are presented for males and females, and for several categories of socioeconomic status. Items were carefully developed by use of contemporary item response procedures and test standardization was performed across representative national groups. The battery is intended for practical use and administration by teachers, clinicians, and researchers interested in reading assessment.

The author, Richard W. Woodcock, Ed.D., is director of Measurement/Learning/Consultants. He has become well known for his ambitious development of reading, cognitive, and achievement test batteries developed within a new era of test publishing which uses concepts of criterion-referenced testing, item development procedures from emerging test theory, and elaborate merchandising of the final products. This battery had its inception in 1967 with the author's development of two letter and word identification tests which were then expanded both for age range and number of skills tested. The final product was designed to provide a more comprehensive set of interpretive norms and references than any other reading test available. It was intended both as a norm-referenced test to compare reading skills of test takers with other people of their own age and grade throughout the standardization group, and in addition, as a criterion-referenced test to demonstrate the degree of mastery of skill in each of the areas of reading measured for each individual. A special feature was a combined norm referenced-criterion referenced scale to show degree of mastery for each individual when compared with others in the same actual grade placement.

Standardization of the WRMT was accomplished during 1971 and 1972 on approximately 5,000 pupils from kindergarten through twelfth grade within 50 different school districts. These schools represented a stratified random sample of communities throughout the United States. The author selected items for both forms by using procedures developed by Rasch and modified by Wright as alternatives to traditional item analysis for item difficulty level and item discrimination.

Five areas of reading are assessed by the battery. The following is a brief description of each of the five tests:

Letter Identification (45 items): measures the ability to name letters printed in the English alphabet. The letters are printed in both upper- and lowercase with a variety of roman, sans serif, cursive, and specialty typeface letters. They are arranged in order of difficulty. It is expected that by the end of first grade students will be aware of most of these types of letters, and by the end of fourth grade most students should receive a nearly perfect score on this test.

Word Identification (150 items): presents words ranging in difficulty from beginning reading to average difficulty for high-achieving twelfth-grade students. The task is merely to name the word, with no assumption that the subject knows the meaning of the word or has ever seen the word before.

Word Attack (50 items): measures the ability to identify nonsense words by using skills of structure analysis and phonics. The items are presented in single syllable and then multisyllable combinations of most vowels and consonants, together with common prefixes and suffixes and samples of irregular spellings.

Word Comprehension (70 items): uses an analogy format to measure knowledge of word meanings. One example of a lower-level item is, "Bluebird is to fly as shark is to ________." The subject is to read the analogy phrase silently and then fill in the blank by saying aloud an appropriate word to complete the analogy.

Passage Comprehension (85 items): contains increasingly difficult reading content with a word missing from each passage. The subject is to read silently and then say aloud an appropriate word to show understanding. Pictures accompany the easier items composed of phrases and single sentences. The later items each are composed of two sentences reaching to college-level difficulty. They are considered to be an omnibus task of reading which includes comprehension, word attack, and word meaning skills.

Practical Applications/Uses

The WRMT are designed to be used in schools by teachers, administrators, reading specialists, school psychologists, and others who are interested in having an assessment of reading mastery for individuals or groups. The information may be used for diagnostic purposes in identifying reading problems or for grouping individuals in school according to their success potential in reading regardless of grade placement. The information may also be used for the study of group performance in evaluating curricula and reading programs for accountability. The data from the battery also provide derived scores which are objective and precise for research purposes.

Appropriate administration of the test requires careful reading of the manual and conscientious adherence to directions. Technical training in tests and measurements is not a prerequisite for administering the tests, but on the other hand the interpretation of results essentially requires an understanding of the use of derived scores and various types of norms as well as an understanding of the nature of reading.

The tests are administered easily from a durable looseleaf ring binder which is set up to form an easel. Separate easels and answer sheets are used for Forms A and B. The stimulus cards are presented one at a time to the subject at eye level while the examiner may read the directions from the opposite side of the easel. Answers are either tallied or recorded on response sheets organized for filling in the data for the rather complex set of information for interpretation. Scoring and interpretation require careful attention to the necessary sequence of steps and to the tables and figures in order to convert the raw scores to mastery scores and to refer to the various norms desired.

Time in administering the tests is determined both by the item level at which each test is begun and the range of ability in reading by the subject. A basal level is the point at which the subject passes five items consecutively and a ceiling level is the point of five successive failures of items. The Letter Identification and Word Attack tests are started at the beginning for all subjects, but for the three remaining tests the examiner may begin administration at a higher level depending upon information already available concerning the reading characteristics of the examinee. Administration time is shortened or prolonged depending upon how successfully the examiner is able to predict and initiate the test near the basal level. The range between the basal and ceiling is called by the author the operating range of reading and may be a wide or a narrow dispersion depending upon individual differences. Occasionally subjects perform with a double basal or double ceiling, in which case the information may be useful for further interpretation of the subject's reading.

Ultimate practical use of the tests is in successful score interpretation which in the case of this battery does not occur automatically without learning new specially designed references in addition to more traditional norms. Several scoring and interpretation options may be used depending upon whether minimal or more comprehensive interpretation is desired. The first phase in scoring is to record the raw scores by summing items passed for each test, then referring the raw scores to a table and recording derived scores called Mastery Scores, which are then converted to a special set of grade placement scores. An individual profile is then obtained for performance on the five tests with a summary Total Reading score. Of course, the raw scores have little meaning by themselves. The Mastery Scores were created especially by Woodcock for this battery by using procedures according to item response theory in test development. The scores, in effect, are based on a common scale across all of the five tests, comparable for any age level, and that have equal mathematic intervals between scores. Thus, for example, a ten-point increase in Master Scores represents an increase from the 75th to the 90th percentile on any test, or from the 90th to the 96th percentile, depending on the level of the scores. Nevertheless, interpretation of Mastery Scores depends upon reference to other norms for explanation. The conversion of Mastery Scores to grade norms provides a Reading Grade score together with both a lower and a higher grade score designated as Failure Reading and Easy Reading levels. The interval between the latter scores is proposed as the instructional range in reading for the individual. The Reading Grade score compares the individual with average pupils of that grade who read the given material with 90% mastery. The instructional range infers an interval between 75% and 96% mastery for the individual at the respective grades for average pupils reading the material with 90% mastery. This interval represents a lower and upper bound of reading material most suitable for instructional purposes for the individual. The manual suggests that test users may stop at this level of interpretation or continue with more comprehensive interpretive references.

An alternative interpretation provides three indices from tables using the individual's actual grade placement for comparison. The first index indicates the median mastery score for pupils at the individual's grade. The second provides a measure of degree of retardation or above average reading by an Achievement Index which is the difference between the reading mastery level of the individual from the median mastery of pupils at the grade level of the individual. The third shows the percentile of performance for the individual or the percent of pupils who received lower scores for that particular grade level.

A third phase of interpretation is optional and provides separate norm tables for females and males and also for communities with several different categories of socioeconomic status (SES). These norms are provided only for the Total Reading Score and not the separate tests. To make comparisons with the appropriate communities for SES it is necessary to collect eleven items of information for the individuals tested and make adjustments to the obtained scores.

Additional sets of norms are provided in the manual's appendix. One is for interpreting performance on each individual test according to chronological age equivalent scores as well as mental age scores. Another equates any percentile with stanines and with a standard score scale having a mean of 50 and standard deviation of 10. A final table illustrates examples of reading content for respective grade levels by showing specimen items among each of the tests at both the 50% and 90% Mastery level.

Technical Aspects

Woodcock had three important objectives in developing the WRMT: to create tests as simple as possible to administer while at the same time measuring reading with greater precision and to provide new ways of reporting test scores for more comprehensive and useful interpretations. The selection and development of an item pool through appropriate statistical analysis for each test is unquestionably an exemplary feature of this battery. Item response theory was in the formative stage when the battery was developed. The author made original contributions by applying this new theory in test item development to large scale, wide ability range, achievement testing. Item response theory involves mathematical procedures which encompass information of traditional item analysis but with greater refinement and precision and with more information about item measurement error. The theory is also known as latent trait theory and sometimes also as item characteristic curve theory. The term latent trait is a statistical construct referring to an assumed unidimensional ability measured by the test. Item characteristic curves are able to be plotted by mathematical functions and applied to empirical data from the test. The item response theory is actually broad enough to describe any of several different alternative latent trait mathematical models used to generate different item characteristic curves. In one model, for example, the curves for each separate item represent information from test data showing the increase in proportion of correct answers for each item as related to increase in total score. One parameter of each curve measures slope of the curve and infers the steeper the slope the more discriminating the item. A second parameter indicates the score value at which the items reach 50% difficulty. A third parameter, for multiple-choice items, indicates the probability of achieving a correct answer by chance. Information about error may also be calculated for each item showing measurement efficiency at different ability levels. Thus, these parameters provide critical information for accepting or rejecting items, and also for sequencing the items selected according to a scale of difficulty. Items not having similar slope, for example, may be rejected.

In addition, during the item development phase, a calibration procedure is required when many different samples of subjects are to be used and when the samples encompass a wide range of ability levels. Similar subsets of items from a large pool are administered to subjects with differing types and differing levels of ability. Item response information is matched in order to link or bridge the gap across the differing groups. With this vertical equating procedure it is assumed any subset of items thereafter may be administered to any group or individual with comparable scoring results. These features lead to the view that in the final selection of test items the item curve parameters are invariant, and, thus, the items are sample-free and measure a pure single dimension of ability, expressed in equal units of scale.

As stated previously, Woodcock used the procedures formulated by Rasch and modified by Wright (Woodcock, 1973) for preparation of WRMT items and development of the reference scales. An initial set of a large number of items were prepared for the calibration procedures. Multiple calibration tests were assembled from small sets of items from the total pool for each reading test. These tests were paired in many different combinations and administered to subgroups of pupils so that part of each pair was always given in common to more than one subgroup. The calibration phase involved pupils from Kindergarten through Grade 12, as well as special education classes for mentally retarded, in a total of 90 schools. Some 1,000 to 6,000 combinations of calibration tests were administered individually at each of the grade levels; thus, vertical equating was accomplished. Item difficulty, item discrimination, and efficiency data were obtained through the Rasch-Wright analysis procedures. After scrutiny of items for acceptability, the final item sets were arranged in order of difficulty and scales of mastery were developed.

The final development phase was to norm the scale on a representative standardization sample. The assumption of sample-free measurement characteristics together with the concept of matrix-sampling procedures were the rationale the author used in selecting a relatively small subset of items for each test to be administered to the norming sample. Five thousand pupils from Kindergarten through Grade 12 representing 50 different districts were used for the 1971 and 1972 standardization. A stratified random sample of communities in the United States was selected, with pupils being tested according to prearranged plans for random selection of three boys and three girls from each grade in a particular school. The standardization plan assured an acceptable U.S. representation and provided data for separate sex and SES norms.

Evidence for reliability of the usual types of internal consistency, stability, and equivalence is presented by Woodcock from a very limited sampling. The data were collected for 103 subjects at Grade 2.9 and 102 subjects from Grade 7.9, the students being drawn from six regular classrooms in parochial and public schools. All of the subjects were administered both test forms but with one-week intervals and counterbalanced order between forms. For internal consistency evidence, correlations were obtained between unspecified halves of the tests and adjusted by the Spearman-Brown formula for total test length. The correlations are respectably high for total reading and all of the tests except Letter Identification. Excluding the latter, the correlations range from .83 through .99 across grades, forms, and tests. Only three of the correlations are below .90. For forms A and B of Letter Identification the correlations are .79 and .86 for the lower grade and .02 and .20 for the higher grade.

The evidence for both stability and equivalence is presented simultaneously by correlating performance between alternate forms administered a week apart. For the lower grade the correlations range from .88 through .94 for four of the tests, and show .97 for Total Reading and .84 for Letter Identification. For the higher grade the correlations range from .68 through .93, and show .88 for Total Reading and .16 for Letter Identification. Except for the latter, the Word and Passage Comprehension tests show the weaker evidence.

An additional set of evidence important for demonstrating reliability in interpreting individual scores is the data for standard error of measurement. In raw scores the standard errors in general are two to three across grades, forms, and tests, and five for Total Reading. In Mastery Scores the standard errors range from three to five across grades, forms, and tests, and two for Total Reading. The manual does not provide an explanation or examples of how this standard error information may be used in interpreting obtained scores for individuals.

In summation, the evidence presented for reliabilities is very positive, but less so for the Word and Passage Comprehension tests for the higher grades. The Letter Identification data at the higher grade may be an artifact of ceiling for test scores near the fourth-grade level. The very limited sampling for data is not sufficient to represent the population intended for the tests. Unfortunately, there is no explanation of rationale for the limited sampling, such as whether it is related to sample-free characteristics of items that is hypothesized by the latent trait theory that is endorsed or whether there were just limited time and resources.

The manual devotes a very small proportion of its contents to presenting evidence that the battery of tests have sufficient content, criterion-related, and construct validity. The test development and technical data chapter is devoted primarily to the explanation of item selection and scaling. For evidence of content validity the author suggests only that the tests are acceptable since they draw from actual reading tasks of identification, word attack, and comprehension. Two additional sets of data are presented in support of predictive and construct validity, but in this reviewer's opinion, are acknowledged more properly to be additional evidence of reliability. Intercorrelations from the tests and alternate forms of the previously reported small sampling of subjects were placed in a multitrait-multimethod format to show convergence in measurement by the same test with different forms. In the second set of data the mastery scores of one test form are used to predict success on items from the alternate form administered one week later. Both sets of data show evidence that scores tend to be stable over a week's time and that the alternate forms show equivalence. There is an absence of evidence in the manual for demonstrating the relationship of WRMT scores to outside criteria of reading performance from additional tests or other reading material.

There are a number of observations made by this reviewer relating to the valid use and interpretation of the battery which bring into question the success of its objectives. These observations relate to characteristics of the separate tests, cautions about assumptions in the test development, and concerns about the understanding and utility of the given forms of interpreting scores. In reference to the separate tests, the Letter Identification test, in this reviewer's opinion, is expendable in the battery for several reasons. It involves visual discrimination skill over a restricted range of stimuli, and the range of difficulty is extended upward to fourth grade only by adding a mixture of unusual printing types as stimuli. As a prediction of readiness for reading it may provide useful information, but as a component of total reading skills it has limited focus. The low performance ceiling for the test artificially inflates grade equivalent scores and the Total Reading Score. At the higher level, just one or two additional items passed unduly raises the pupil's grade equivalent. In addition, equal weight is given to the mastery score on the test with the other tests in computing the Total Reading Score, which disproportionately emphasizes the importance of the skill within the total.

The Word Identification test, while measuring word pronunciation with variable tolerance, may also measure different skills for different readers. Some may recognize the word by sight memory, others may pronounce mainly from word attack skill, and others may be able to decode the word meaning. By presenting words in isolation the task may be criticized as being artificial and limited since there is evidence that pupils may recognize more words when presented in the context of short phrases or clues.

The Word Attack test, as a measure of the pronunciation of single nonsense words according to acceptable rules, is salient to those who stress phonics and structural analysis in reading. An emphasis on this skill for adult reading is not perceived to be as important by others.

The Word Comprehension test is only indirectly a measure of word knowledge. The analogies format requires not only sufficient vocabulary but, in addition, skill in reasoning and classification to complete each analogy. Analogies are used commonly for measuring academic aptitude. In addition the analogy format requires readers to bring forth an appropriate word as contrasted with selecting one from alternatives presented. If an item is failed there is also ambiguity about which of the words is not understood, the word to be elicited or whichever of the three stimulus words were presented.

The Passage Comprehension test is a modified cloze task that measures sentence completion with a key word redundant in meaning with immediately preceding material. While the author acknowledges that this is an omnibus test of reading involving multiple skills, it does not measure memory for details, inference-making, nor does it ask for understanding of large ideas within the material. Evidence has shown that cloze tasks do not have high performance relationships for some grade levels with other conventional reading comprehension tests, which suggests that cloze tasks measure different skills for different levels and age groups. Decoding and word attack skills are helpful as components of success on these tests, and, in addition, pictures are provided with the reading passages for more than the first quarter of items as aids to comprehension. Incidentally, the pictures may be criticized for being old-fashioned and showing sex stereotyping.

Overall, the battery includes tests of reading that are traditional, some of which would not be universally important and some of which measure multiple skills which confound interpretation. Speed and fluency of reading, syntax, and grammatical aspects are not measured. Other areas in reading of psycholinguistic interest are not measured, such as understanding and inference from large idea units with evaluation of analysis and logic. The total battery is probably best conceived as an instrument for global screening in reading difficulties. In this reviewer's opinion, as indicated by the observations and critique of individual tests, to use the battery effectively would take considerable skill by reading specialists to study each reader's performance and sort out the crucial skills measured for each person. The results may provide diagnostic information for some, but only global prediction of multiple skills for others, and with limited instructional utility.

Comments have been made about content validity for the separate tests. Evidence of criterion-related validity is lacking since no studies are reported comparing the battery with other reading tests or external criteria. The following comments most closely reflect some issues of construct validity.

Although item response theory and various latent trait models were in the formative stages in the early 1970s when this battery was developed, the theory continues to need further investigation (Lord, 1980). The following are cautions to note in the selection of items and scale development using item response theory procedures: 1) Unidimensionality is an assumption yet to be fully demonstrated by empirical data. Even though item curves fit the criteria for being unidimensional, some with higher level thresholds of difficulty may still involve more complex skills which result in measuring more than one dimension. Already cited is the confounding of a vocabulary measure with reasoning ability in the analogies presented for the Word Comprehension test. 2) The related assumption that item parameters are invariant infers a notion of "sample-free" characteristics of the items which possibly may be misunderstood. Subjects may respond differently to given items depending on their stage of learning or disparate past experiences. Thus, scale values may change for these items as they are not invariant unless there is representative sampling in the calibration phase of item selection. For score interpretation, standardization procedures for the development of norms must be appropriate and representative of the total groups for which the test is designed. 3) The item scale that is finally developed has equal unit intervals in a numerical sense, but not necessarily in a psychological sense. Comparisons of score changes among subjects or between tests may be expressed in numerical ratios but cannot be translated into such statements as "twice as much," or "half as much improvement." This feature, common to interpretations of most psychological interval scales, poses problems for the interpretation of Mastery Scores in this battery. The real measure of mastery in the WRMT is actually the raw scores which tell how many of the items in each test were mastered. The raw scores, however, are converted to a derived scale common for all five of the tests and with equal interval units along the distribution. Thus, these Mastery Scores are numerically comparable across tests and among subjects at any level of performance. Practical interpretation becomes ambiguous, however, when Mastery Scores are converted to any of the referents such as percentiles or grade equivalents. An obtained Mastery Score of 100 on each of the five tests, for example, represents Reading Grade Equivalents ranging from 1.4 to 6.9. In what sense are the scores comparable when the grade equivalents vary so? There are analogous differences for Mastery Scores at other levels and for other reference norms and thus the notion of "comparability" of these scores loses its meaning.

There are additional observations to be made about the reference norms and interpretation of scores which detract from practical use of the battery. Scoring and interpretation are not easy, and test users may have a false sense of security about what the scores and norms mean. Scoring requires careful attention to a sequence of steps of reading tables and recording numbers. The effort can be tedious and subject to error; in addition, the reference norms use familiar terms but actually represent modifications of traditional forms. The following are examples of problems for successful interpretation:

1. Standard errors of measurement are listed in the manual and are quite reasonable, but are not presented with examples or in a manner useful to examiners scoring the test for interpretation of individual scores.

2. Percentile norms for showing performance at the reader's grade level, as preferred norms, are the last set to be calculated, occurring only at the end of a long sequence of scoring steps. These percentiles may be easily confused with another set of numbers in an adjacent column which shows percent of Relative Mastery at the given grade level.

3. The grade equivalents are not derived in the usual manner. They are determined by the grade level at which average students show 90% mastery of the reading material. Average is presumed to be the median. But the "mastery" term is elusive since it does not refer to the percent of items passed in the total test, but rather to some unspecified set of reading material for each grade.

4. The number and variety of reference norms available for interpretation is a feature highlighted by the manual, but their variety will also pose a challenge to the user in learning and understanding. Relative Mastery is predicted for four different sets of norms, which are not easy to differentiate from one another without study. The first three show the grade level of reading material that is comfortable (90%), hard (75%), or easy (95%) for the individual to read. The label "Failure"

for the 75% level is unfortunate. The fourth set of norms demonstrates for the individual's own grade level how easy or how hard the reading material is in percent mastery for that grade. Again for these four norms the referent is to reading material that is unspecified but represents the grade level for which average students pass 90% of the items. The concepts to be understood are multiple and somewhat abstract. The manual does not teach examiners to understand these concepts sufficiently even though the explanations that are given provide familiar words and fluent syntax. Although strong in showing procedures for scoring against the background of various norms, the manual gives only a cursory explanation for how the norms may be used or the rationale for selecting among them for various purposes.

5. The author arouses interest in the manual for criterion-referenced testing as a means of translating a score into a statement about behavior to be expected of a person with that score. The author has less success in achieving such a goal for this battery of tests. What is achieved for the tests in interpreting the scores is today most properly called *norm-referenced* and *content-domain-referenced* statements (American Psychological Association, 1985). The norm-referenced statements for the tests come from the norm table giving percentiles for the individual's own grade placement since they contrast the person's performance with others at that grade. Domain-referenced statements come from those norm tables which show percent mastery at different grade levels since they tell how successful the individual should be in reading content which is similar to the domain of material at any specified grade level. If there were criterion-referenced interpretations that could be made from the tests they would most properly state on the basis of obtained test scores the degree of expectancy for the individual in mastering some external set of skills or material of practical significance.

In domain-referenced testing, the items are samples from the actual specified content domain. In criterion-referenced testing, predictions are made from the test to an external specified target or set of objectives as criterion. In either case, domain- or criterion-referenced testing, it is necessary for useful application of the test to have clear and explicit definitions of the characteristics and boundary of the domain or criterion objectives. This important feature is not accomplished in the manual in more than a superficial manner. As an example, the manual states that both reading ability level and difficulty of reading task are represented by the mastery score scale, and scores on the scale may predict "the subject's performance on similar tasks" (p. 37). The nature of the domain for any of these "similar tasks" is not specified, and the tasks are designated only by a grade equivalent. Even the instructional range calculated in the mastery profile is designated only by numerical indicators. The closest description of behavior typical for obtained mastery scores occurs in a final table of Reference Scales which has specimen reading tasks similar to actual test items for respective grade levels. These specimens have no more meaning beyond the display of their own item content. Applications from the test would be enhanced if attention were given to defining characteristics and boundaries of the reading domain to indicate what skills are mastered, or by statements of performance objectives for respective levels, or by providing reference lists of books or other catalogued reading material which is equivalent. Expectations of test publishers at present, and indeed obligations, are to provide information from test scores with explicit statements about content and skills mastered and even prescriptive statements useful for instructional purposes.

6. There are 15 different groups or categories as backgrounds against which test raw scores may be compared. Among these norms only the grade equivalent is the prevalent mode of showing the contrast. The two norms probably most useful are the measure of comfortable reading level and the measure of performance compared to the individual's peers. The norms that are adjusted for communities with different socioeconomic status may be less useful because of the effort required in gathering data. The separate norms for male and female are probably the least useful since they show so little difference from one another. For example, at mid-distribution the median difference is only seven percentiles, ranging from zero to eleven. There is a table of equivalents for percentiles, T-scores, and stanines which is a useful reference but is not directly related to test performance.

Critique

The Woodcock Reading Mastery Tests were an ambitious undertaking when they were first developed. They achieved the aforementioned objectives of ease in administration and precision of scores but not the objective of useful applications for instructional purposes. The use of an easel ring binder with uncluttered presentation of stimuli and easy-to-read instructions was a welcome product. Confidence by test users in precision and consistency of the scores was promoted by use of a latent trait model from psychometric item response theory in selecting items and deriving an item scale.

As we know, however, reliability features of an instrument only contribute to, but do not ensure, validity features of the instrument's use. The content domain of reading, the selection of tests, and the concepts for interpreting scores are aspects of the WRMT vulnerable to criticism. Five relatively traditional types of tests were used, but otherwise the decision of what aspects of reading to assess appeared to be atheoretical. One test is oriented more to reading readiness, another to reasoning ability confounded with vocabulary, and another to omnibus skills for readers at different stages and experiences in reading.

A highlighted objective for the tests was to provide several alternative sets of norms for more comprehensive interpretation of scores. The range of contrasts includes indices of various ability levels of present functioning to comparisons with peers, sex, and socioeconomic characteristics. Underlying the use of any of these norms and indices is the concept of relative mastery to represent both ability level and difficulty of reading. Without careful study by the test user the concept is not easy to understand in its application to the various norms for interpretation. Scoring for these multiple norms takes effort to follow the sequential steps. In addition, the sequence prevents users from being flexible in their selection or omission of administering some tests or using some norms as may be desired in individual cases. There is an overemphasis on grade equivalents with their excess of meaning and problems for interpretation.

It appears that the battery would be most useful as a global screening instrument for reading problems since the ultimate interpretations from the test are limited to score indices. The destined goal of the author for criterion-referenced testing is not reached. Explicit statements about the content domain of reading for respective levels or performance objectives for reading skills are lacking in the manual. Contributions of such statements would greatly enhance the usefulness of the battery for developing instructional programs in reading for individuals or groups.

References

American Psychological Association. (1985). *Standards for educational and psychological testing.* Washington, DC: Author.

Lord, F. M. (1980). *Application of item response theory to practical testing problems.* Hillsdale, NJ: Erlbaum.

Woodcock, R. W. (1973). *Woodcock Reading Mastery Tests—Manual.* Circle Pines, MN: American Guidance Service.

INDEX OF TEST TITLES

INDEX OF TEST PUBLISHERS

INDEX OF TEST AUTHORS/REVIEWERS

SUBJECT INDEX

PSYCHOLOGY

Child and Child Development

Intelligence and Related

Marriage and Family: Family

Marriage and Family: Premarital and Marital Relations

Neuropsychology and Related

Personality: Child

Personality: Adolescent and Adult

Personality: Multi-levels

Research

EDUCATION

Academic Subjects: English and Related—Multi-level

Academic Subjects: Foreign Language & English as a Second Language

Academic Subjects: Mathematics—Basic Math Skills

Achievement and Aptitude: Academic

Educational Development and School Readiness

Intelligence and Related

Reading: Elementary

Reading: High School and Above

Reading: Multi-level

Sensory-Motor Skills

Special Education: Gifted

Special Education: Learning Disabilities

Special Education: Mentally Handicapped

Special Education: Physically Handicapped

Special Education: Special Education

Speech, Hearing, and Visual: Auditory

Speech, Hearing, and Visual: Speech and Language

Student Evaluation and Counseling: Behavior Problems and Counseling Tools

Student Evaluation and Counseling: Student Attitudes

Student Evaluation and Counseling: Student Personality Factors

Vocational

BUSINESS AND INDUSTRY

Aptitude and Skills Screening

Clerical

Computer

Intelligence and Related

Interests

Interpersonal Skills and Attitudes

ABOUT THE EDITORS

Daniel J. Keyser, Ph.D. A graduate of the University of Kansas (1974), the University of Missouri (1965) and the University of Wisconsin (1959), Dr. Keyser has worked in drug and alcohol rehabilitation and psychiatric settings, and has taught undergraduate psychology at Rockhurst College for 15 years. He is presently employed by the Veterans Administration Hospital in Kansas City as a medical psychologist. Dr. Keyser specializes in behavioral medicine—biofeedback, pain control, stress management, terminal care support, habit management, and wellness maintenance. He also has a private clinical practice in Raytown, Missouri. Dr. Keyser co-edited *Tests* and *Tests: Supplement*, and has made significant contributions to computerized psychological testing.

Richard C. Sweetland, Ph.D. A graduate of Baylor University (1953), The University of Texas (1959), and Utah State University (1968), Dr. Sweetland completed postdoctoral training in psychoanalytically oriented clinical psychology at the Topeka State Hospital in conjunction with the training program of the Menninger Foundation in 1969. Following appointments in child psychology at the University of Kansas Medical Center and in neuropsychology at the Kansas City Veterans Administration Hospital, he entered the practice of psychotherapy in the Kansas City area. In addition to his clinical work in neuropsychology and psychoanalytic psychotherapy, Dr. Sweetland has been extensively involved in the development of computerized psychological testing. Dr. Sweetland co-edited *Tests* and *Tests: Supplement*.